THE
IMMORTALS
MICHAEL KORDA

"SENSATIONAL!"
Barbara Taylor Bradford

"MAGNIFICENT!"
Oliver Stone

"GLAMOROUS,
INTELLIGENT AND PROVOCATIVE!"
Jackie Collins

"A TRIUMPH!"
Nancy Friday

"I COULDN'T PUT IT DOWN!"
Nicholas Pileggi

"I BELIEVE EVERYONE IN THE
COUNTRY WILL WANT TO READ
<u>THE IMMORTALS</u>!"
Joseph Heller

P9-BBN-316

THE IMMORTALS

"IF YOU THOUGHT YOU KNEW ALL THERE WAS TO KNOW ABOUT JFK AND MARILYN AND RFK, THEN THINK AGAIN."

Barbara Taylor Bradford

"ENGROSSING...FASCINATING, JUICY READING... A visceral portrait of larger-than-life people."

People

"CAPTURES THE EPIC SWEEP OF EVENTS... Korda transforms the Kennedys' triumphs and subsequent tragedies into a brooding film noir, using all the techniques of a skillful popular novelist to collar his readers and maintain their attention."

New York Newsday

"TAKES US WHERE WE'VE ALWAYS WANTED TO BE: right in the heart of the sexiest and most secret love affair in American history"

Jackie Collins

THE IMMORTALS

MICHAEL KORDA

AVON BOOKS ◆ NEW YORK

The Immortals is a work of fiction based on fact. As such, it would have been impossible to write without substantial research and interviewing. The factual setting of the novel is based on numerous nonfiction sources, though the characters, whether real or imaginary names are used, are the products of my own imagination and interpretation.

Excerpt from Marilyn Monroe's "Red Diary" as quoted in *Norma Jean: My Secret Life with Marilyn Monroe* by Ted Jordan. Copyright © 1989 by Ted Jordan. Reprinted by permission of William Morrow and Company, Inc.

"Happy Birthday to You" (Mildred J. Hill, Patty S. Hill) © 1935 (Renewed 1962) SUMMY-BIRCHARD MUSIC, A Division of SUMMY-BIRCHARD, INC. All Rights Reserved. Used by permission.

AVON BOOKS
A division of
The Hearst Corporation
1350 Avenue of the Americas
New York, New York 10019

Copyright © 1992 by Success Research Corporation
Inside back cover author photograph by Sigrid Estrada
Published by arrangement with Poseidon Press, Simon and Schuster, Inc.
Library of Congress Catalog Card Number: 92-22265
ISBN: 0-380-72099-X

First Avon Books Printing: November 1993
First Avon Books International Printing: May 1993

AVON TRADEMARK REG. U.S. PAT. OFF. AND IN OTHER COUNTRIES, MARCA REGISTRADA, HECHO EN U.S.A.

Printed in the U.S.A.

RA   10   9   8   7   6   5   4   3   2   1

For MARGARET

*And in memory of
Jeanne Bernkopf*

I would like to express my indebtedness to the major published sources on which I have relied.

Patricia Bosworth:	*Montgomery Clift*
Ben Bradlee:	*Conversations with Kennedy*
Steven Brill:	*The Teamsters*
Peter Collier and David Horowitz:	*The Kennedys*
Curt Gentry:	*J. Edgar Hoover*
Fred Lawrence Guiles:	*Legend*
Ted Jordan:	*Norma Jean*
Patricia Seaton Lawford:	*The Peter Lawford Story*
Dan E. Moldea:	*The Hoffa Wars*
Kenneth P. O'Donnell and David Powers:	*Johnny, We Hardly Knew Ye*
Lena Pepitone:	*Marilyn Monroe Confidential*
Arthur M. Schlesinger, Jr.:	*A Thousand Days*
Arthur M. Schlesinger, Jr.:	*Robert Kennedy and His Times*
William V. Shannon:	*The Heir Apparent*
Sandra Shevey:	*The Marilyn Scandal*
Anthony Summers:	*Goddess*
Maurice Zolotow:	*Marilyn Monroe*

CONTENTS

"I say to you, you will face pain in your life.
It is not aimed at anyone but it will come your way."
　　　　　　—TED ROSENTHAL

"Say a prayer for Norma Jean. She's dead."
　　　　　　—JIM DOUGHERTY

"The Kennedy story is about people who broke the
rules, and were ultimately broken by them."
　　　　　　—CHRIS LAWFORD

"Big tits, big ass, big deal."
　　　　　　—MARILYN MONROE

PROLOGUE

Camelot

I T WAS ANOTHER LATE EVENING AT THE WHITE HOUSE. THEY were serving coffee and liqueurs to the accompaniment of the Marine string orchestra playing selections from *Camelot*, when the President caught my eye. A naval aide in dress blues had just given him a message.

I knew the form. The President made his apologies, whispered something to Jackie, and left. I waited a few minutes, then slipped out discreetly to join him.

The same aide was waiting for me outside the Blue Room, and asked me to follow him. To my surprise, we didn't go upstairs to the family quarters where Jack had a study. Instead, we took a roundabout route through the empty corridors to the Oval Office, where the aide knocked on the door and opened it for me.

Jack was making himself a drink—a strong one, from the color of it. He looked at me, and I nodded. He made another and handed it to me; then we sat down facing each other. He was sitting stiffly upright in his rocking chair, but he didn't rock it. His expression was remote and hard to read, even for someone who knew him as well as I did.

He had developed the face of a Roman emperor in the past few months. His jowls were heavier, the lines on his face deeper, his eyes sadder than I had ever seen them before. Power corrupts, as we are always being reminded by political commentators, but it also matures. The man before me looked as if he had been through the fires of hell—which, of course, like every president, he had.

"God, I hate *Camelot!*" He spoke wearily. "I've *begged* Jackie to tell them to play something else, but it's like talking to a goddamn brick wall. . . ."

He sipped his drink. Whatever he had on his mind, he

seemed reluctant to approach it. "I just spoke to Peter," he said finally.

"Lawford?" I raised an eyebrow. I could not imagine why a call from the President's brother-in-law required an emergency meeting.

The distaste on Jack's face was evident as he nodded. I knew how deep his contempt for Lawford ran. Lawford had introduced him years ago to his circle of Hollywood friends—Sinatra and so on—had put his Malibu beach house more or less permanently at Jack's disposal as his West Coast "love nest" and set him up with innumerable starlets—made himself, in short, the presidential pimp, for which Jack roundly despised him.

Like his father, Jack hated people who could be bought, especially those who looked after his pleasures. In some ways he had a puritan sense of morality, though only about other people.

He gave me a look that made it clear I was about to hear bad news. "She's dead," he said brusquely.

I knew instantly whom he meant. "Dead?" I repeated numbly.

"Suicide, apparently. Pills. Booze." Jack shook his head in puzzlement. No Kennedy could ever understand suicide—they were all too fiercely attached to life.

"I see. Where's Bobby?"

"On his way back to San Francisco." Jack's voice was flat. "To Ethel and his loving family," he added savagely.

I nodded. If he didn't want to give me the details, I wasn't about to ask for them.

"Will you go to California?" he asked. He knew I wouldn't want to, so he put it on the line: "As a favor to me, David," he added.

"You can count on me, Mr. President." The moment seemed to call for the formality.

"Thank you." He hesitated. "I need someone I can trust. Someone who knows his way around out there. There may be a few brushfires to put out."

"The press."

"Yes." He sipped his drink. He looked exhausted now. "The police. The coroner." He paused. "And so on."

"I have good contacts in Los Angeles," I assured him. "And first-rate people working for me."

"I want you to handle this yourself, David."

"Of course." The thought of what had happened was becoming real to me. "Poor girl," I said.

"It's a hell of a thing," he said miserably. There were tears in his eyes. He rubbed them, as if in fatigue, then turned back briskly to the business at hand. It was as much of a benediction as she was going to get from him—probably as much as anybody would ever get. He was not a man to dwell on grief, any more than his father was.

"I've got an Air Force plane waiting for you at Andrews," he said. "Can you leave right away?"

"Certainly, Mr. President," I was about to say—but then I realized that I could hardly even speak, for I had a sudden image of Marilyn standing in a doorway, and my own eyes filled with tears.

PART ONE

The Blonde
On The Phone

1

THE MOMENT JACK AND MARILYN SET EYES ON EACH OTH-
er, I knew there was going to be trouble.

They met at Charlie Feldman's house in Beverly Hills, the
summer of 1954. Jack had come out to "the Coast" (as he
liked to call it, with an ironic grin) to breathe new life into
the California Democrats with a display of Kennedy glamour—and more important, Kennedy vigor. Eisenhower had
beaten Adlai Stevenson in '52 by a landslide, and given Ike's
popularity, whoever ran against him in '56 was going to
lose again, so while Jack's ostensible mission was to rally the faithful, his *real* purpose was to drop the hint that
he'd be around to win in '60. That, and to get laid—since,
then as now, LA was to sex what Washington is to politics.

I accompanied him because my old friend Joe Kennedy had
asked me to—*asked,* not told; neither Jack nor his father was
in a position to order me around. The Old Man and I (everybody, including Jack, called Ambassador Kennedy "the Old
Man" behind his back) went back together a long way, and
shared a lot of secrets, even though I was his junior by a
generation.

We had met in Hollywood, when he was trying to beat
Mayer, Cohn, Zanuck, and the Warner brothers at their own
game, and I was trying to persuade them that there is a
difference between the art of "public relations" and hiring
a flack.

It was a lesson the studio bosses never learned, but Joe did.
The maverick Irishman, with his ties to bootleggers, his notorious affairs, and his reputation for shady dealing as a Wall
Street raider, was soon to emerge as FDR's head of the SEC,
ambassador to the Court of St. James's, would-be Democratic kingmaker, and paterfamilias of America's most photogenic

political dynasty—a transformation, I must confess, that was partly my doing.

Joe owed me for that, and recognized the fact. I owed him too, and was grateful: without his help I would have found it difficult to raise enough money on Wall Street in the grim thirties to launch what was to become the largest international public relations company in the world. Besides that—and perhaps more important—we *liked* each other. I admired his toughness and unconcealed rough edges; I think *he* admired my smoothness and gift for conciliation. He was an old bully, Joe Kennedy, but he never tried to bully me.

I suppose this is as good a time as any to introduce myself. My name is David Arthur Leman. My father spelled the family name "Lehrman," but when I started out in business on my own, I thought it a good idea to simplify it for those clients—of whom there were still a good many then—who preferred to be represented by a Leman rather than a Lehrman. Nobody, by the way, in the interests of simplicity or otherwise, has ever presumed to call me Dave. David I have always been to everyone, including my mother, my wives, and Jack Kennedy.

I was born into the kind of wealthy New York German-Jewish family that discouraged informality—and affection: the beloved only son who is at once pampered and relentlessly pushed to achieve. My father—with whom I do not think I exchanged two intimate words in our life together—was the owner of a thriving art book publishing house, in whose footsteps I never had, from earliest childhood, the slightest intention of following.

I grew up in a big, antique-filled apartment on Central Park West, progressed through New York's then excellent public school system as an overachieving honor student, and did the same at Columbia. To my father's undisguised annoyance, I went to work after graduation as a publicity man for Jed Harris, the Broadway producer, though he should not have been surprised—my mother was hopelessly stagestruck, and the fondest memory of my childhood was going to the theater with her.

With hindsight, I know what I sought in my profession was something of the theater's glamour and excitement—an escape from respectability. I can also see now that what attracted me to Joe Kennedy was that he and his family represented the polar opposite of my father—they were brawling, aggressive, unashamedly sentimental, outspoken, and fiercely attached to one another.

Besides, for somebody like myself, whose secret passion was politics, Joe was a fascinating friend and mentor. Back then, in the thirties, he was as close to FDR as anybody ever got; more than anyone it was he who had brokered FDR's nomination in 1932. He still cherished the illusion then that one day he might be not just a kingmaker but the king himself. It wasn't until 1939, when his fierce isolationism and his pro-appeasement record put him at odds with history and FDR, that Joe turned his presidential ambitions toward his eldest son.

I'm an old man now, as I write this—older than anybody has the right to be. When I look at photographs taken then, I see a different person altogether, one I hardly even recognize. Before me is a snapshot of Marilyn and myself sitting on the famous zebra-skin banquette at El Morocco, smiling for the photographer. Marilyn's smile is dazzling, the kind only a movie star can put on at the sight of a photographer's flashgun, instantly radiating on command high-voltage happiness and sex appeal, though I seem to remember she was near tears a moment before. She is wearing a white evening gown—white was her favorite color, perhaps because of its associations with virginity. The neckline plunges unvirginally to her navel, exposing her shoulders and most of her breasts, and she is holding a glass of champagne in her right hand.

The man sitting beside her with a big grin on his face is a tall, well-built fellow, broad-shouldered without any suggestion of being athletic. The face, as I look at it now, is handsome, but slightly too self-satisfied, too smug—a powerful nose; a good, strong chin; a full head of hair, worn a bit on the long side, as if cut by an English barber; a brisk military mustache.

He wears a chalk-striped suit of impeccable cut, this stranger, with a broad-striped shirt with a plain white collar and cuffs, a somber embroidered silk tie, and a white silk waistcoat with lapels and pearl buttons—clearly a personal sartorial trademark. In the lapel of his jacket is a miniature white carnation. Unmistakably, he fancies himself as a dandy.

That person has long since gone, alas. If Marilyn were alive today, I remind myself, she would be sixty-six. Jack would be seventy-five. I am over eighty myself, God help me.

Well, I've had a good life, as well as a long one, and looking back on it, my friendship with Joe—and his sons—was one of the best parts. I wouldn't have missed a minute of it, despite all the pain and the tragedy. It's taken me more than two decades to come to grips with the truth of it—and my role in what happened—but my age being what it is, it's now or never if I'm going to tell the story.

It's odd. If it hadn't been for Joe, I would have given up my business in the 1950s and moved to England and missed it all. I was rich, bored with my work, disgusted by the McCarthy era, recently remarried. I had always loved England—three of the best years of my life were spent there during the war as a public relations officer for the Air Force, with a colonel's eagles on my shoulders and a suite at Claridge's. It had always been my dream to live there. I already had my eye on a pretty little house in Wilton Mews, and was beginning to correspond with estate agents about Georgian manor houses in the country, when Joe got wind of my plans and took me to dinner at Le Pavillon to torpedo them. "Don't you do it to yourself, David!" he begged me.

"What are you talking about, Joe?" I said. "I've always wanted to live like an English gentleman."

"Horseshit. That's the point. You're *not* an English gentleman. Deep down where it counts, behind all that fucking politeness, the Limeys will hate your guts. Need I remind you I was our ambassador there? I *know* those people, David."

Joe leaned over and touched my hand, a surprisingly gentle gesture, at odds with the cold blue anger in his eyes. "Besides," he said softly, "don't jump ship when it's close to home, David. Jack's going to run, you have my word. When he does, he's going to win. I need you, David. *He* needs you. And once he's in the White House, who can say?" He shook his head. "Backstabbing old fraud that he was, I wouldn't have missed being in FDR's inner circle for any goddamn thing, David, let alone spending the rest of my life in a country where everybody talks through their noses and it rains six days out of seven."

Joe had me, of course, as he knew he would. The two things I most envied him were his relationship to FDR and his ambassadorship, badly as both had turned out for him. Besides, I knew he wasn't kidding. Jack did not seem like presidential material to me—or to anyone else except his father, so far as I knew—but if Joe said he was going to run, I was prepared to believe it. And he was right. Being an insider in a presidential race is the biggest adventure American life can offer, and we both knew I couldn't resist it.

Right there at Le Pavilion, over the rack of lamb, I knew I wasn't going to buy that mews house. I remember Joe's laughter when he realized he'd won, so loud that people looked up from their food all over the restaurant. He had laughed like that the first time I ever gave *him* a piece of advice, at a booth in the Brown Derby in Hollywood, after he asked me how he could go about changing his image—he was not thinking, even then, so much of himself as of his boys. I told him that Walter Ivy, the creator of "public relations" as a business, had been asked the same question by John D. Rockefeller, and came up with the brilliant suggestion that the old robber baron try giving away a dime to every child he met, accompanied by a little homily on the virtues of thrift—a strategy that worked so well John D. senior was practically canonized in his own lifetime. Joe Kennedy thought about it for a few moments, then leaned back, bared his big, uneven white teeth, and laughed. "The hell with it," he said. "I'm not giving *my* money away to strangers."

Lots of people liked to think of the Kennedys, father *and* sons, as if they were somehow imbued with the spirit of the old-time Irish politicians like Rose Kennedy's father, Honey Fitz, but I knew better. The old pols genuinely loved people—those who were on their side, at least. Their laughter was real and happy, but Joe's heartiest laughter was reserved for stories about other people's misfortunes. Even Jack, a far more attractive figure than his father, lacked the common touch of the born politician—he was never entirely able to hide the fact that he regarded most people as his inferiors.

I could hear Jack laughing then, in Feldman's enormous living room, with the big sliding glass doors opening out onto the pool and the obligatory collection of Impressionist paintings on the walls. Second-rate Impressionists, of course—the best ones seldom end up in the collections of Hollywood talent agents, however wealthy.

I could tell just by listening to Jack's laughter that he was no more impressed by Feldman and the Democrats assembled in his living room than I was by the paintings.

The truth was, a lot of the people in the room were old enough to still nurse bitter feelings about Joe Kennedy, who during his brief stay in Hollywood had been one of the most hated men in the history of the movie business, so not all of them were inclined to greet his son with open arms. In fact, Jack's first task here was to show that he wasn't anything like his father.

He was seated in the center of the room, stiffly upright—I could tell by the way he stretched out first one leg, then the other, that his back was giving him more pain than usual—drinking scotch, while Feldman, standing beside him, called people over one by one to introduce them to the Senator.

Feldman leaned over to say something, and Jack laughed again, even louder. Then there was a truly theatrical silence—and everybody except Jack turned toward the glass wall facing the pool. I did too, just in time to see Marilyn make her entrance.

It took Jack a moment to realize he had lost the attention of his audience—even here, among the richest and most powerful people in Hollywood, Marilyn Monroe's appearance brought an instant hush of amazement and excitement. Then he turned too, with some difficulty, to see who had eclipsed him, and rose to his feet, while Feldman abandoned his position beside the Senator to go over to the door and greet Marilyn, who looked woefully helpless and vulnerable, like a little girl who had wandered in on a grown-ups' party by mistake.

She was wearing a tight black dress of some shimmering material, which seemed to be several sizes too small for her, a white fox stole, costume jewelry earrings, and a cheap black patent-leather handbag. The whole outfit looked as if it might have been purchased from a thrift shop. Not that it mattered—Marilyn was beyond good taste, or bad. At this point in her life she was perhaps the biggest star in Hollywood: *River of No Return* had just been released, she had completed filming *There's No Business Like Show Business*, and she had been married to Joe DiMaggio for about six months.

I took the opportunity to move closer to Jack, whose expression resembled that of a man getting his first glimpse of the Grand Canyon or Mount Everest—some natural wonder of awesome proportions and reputation.

"Jesus *Christ!*" he whispered.

"Don't even *think* of it, Jack," I whispered back.

He grinned wickedly. "I don't know what you mean, David."

I ignored that. "She's the most visible woman in America," I warned him.

He nodded. "It's a challenge, certainly."

"She's married."

"So am I. So are you."

"There's a rumor she's having an affair with Charlie Feldman."

Jack looked at Feldman as if he had never seen his host before, then shook his head in puzzlement. Feldman was elderly and stout, his skin tanned to the color of crisp bacon. He wore a well-crafted hairpiece. "Why would she do that?" Jack asked. "He can't make her a star. She's *already* a star."

"Who knows what goes on in a woman's mind?"

That made sense to him. "Ah—who indeed?" he said.

Feldman had Marilyn by the elbow now, and was moving her in our direction, while she held back as if she were shy. I thought then that Marilyn was a better actress in everyday life than in front of the camera. Nothing that happened later was to change my mind.

Jack closed the distance, determined to reach Marilyn before I did, took her hand, squeezed it briefly rather than shaking it, and gave her his most dashing smile. She smiled back. "I can't *believe* you're a *senator?*" She cooed, in her tiny, breathless voice. She had a charming habit of ending every sentence as if it were a question. "I thought they were all old men?"

She hadn't removed her hand from his, and I could see that Feldman's face was a mixture of regret and dismay—he must have been wishing he'd never invited Jack here, or that he hadn't invited Marilyn. "Are you *sure* you're a senator?" she asked, giggling. "You look just like a *boy*."

She could hardly have said anything more certain to charm him. He looked her over from top to toe, appreciatively, lingering on the full wonder of all that lush, incredible beauty. "Well," he said at last, "you look just like a girl."

I knew my cue. I asked Feldman to introduce me to a couple of important California Democrats who had just arrived, giving Jack and Marilyn a few moments to talk alone.

I didn't find out what happened until the next day—though I could have guessed.

I caught up with Jack the next morning at the pool of the Bel Air Hotel. I was on my way to my LA office, in our own building on Sunset Boulevard. He was lying in the sun, wearing swimming trunks and wraparound sunglasses, and smoking a cigar. He hated to be seen smoking cigars in public, partly because he was afraid it would lose him votes among women, partly because it seemed like a middle-aged, wealthy man's habit and he wanted to appeal to the young as long as he could, but no hotel was more private than the Bel Air in those days, which was why we were staying there instead of at the Beverly Hills.

I sat down beside him, and ordered breakfast. Jack had finished his and was sipping at his coffee, with the *Los Angeles Times* in his lap. Half a dozen papers were spread around his chaise. He devoured newspapers; no story was too trivial to escape his attention if he thought it was something he could put to use. "I lost you last night," I said. "How was the rest of your evening?"

"Ah—interesting. *Very* interesting." He gave me one of those smiles that always made me wonder how anybody could vote against him. "You were right about Feldman, by the way."

I raised an eyebrow.

"She *is* fucking him."

"She told you that?"

"She's a remarkably—ah—*frank* young woman."

"I see." I tried to imagine a good reason why Marilyn Monroe would tell Jack she was having an affair with Feldman on their first date—if you could describe whatever took place between them as that—but none came to mind.

"She wanted me to know," Jack said. "She didn't think there should be any secrets between us." He smiled. "I sat next to her at dinner—"

"I saw."

Jack did not take criticism—even implied criticism—easily, even from me. "I can't be expected to work for the party *all* the time, David," he snapped, very much his father's son. "This isn't Soviet Russia. . . . Anyway, as I was saying, I sat next to her at dinner, and I happened to put my hand on her leg. A friendly pat, you know. . . ."

"I know." I did not want to add that most of the more important Democrats in Hollywood had noticed that the Senator's right hand was under the tablecloth throughout the meal, obliging him to eat with his left.

"Well, I moved it up to her thigh—she didn't object, you know, didn't even appear to notice. Then finally she turned to me and said, 'Before you go any higher, Senator, you'd better know I never wear panties, just so you're not surprised.' She said it with the most innocent expression. . . ."

"And was it true?"

"Oh, yes. Absolutely true!"

"Is she still in the hotel?"

He shook his head. "She left early this morning, before anybody else was up."

I gave a silent prayer of thanks. The staff at the Bel Air was famous for its discretion, but Marilyn was not the kind of person about whom it was easy to be discreet.

"I take it you had a good time?"

He stared out across the pool, his expression hidden by cigar smoke. "She's a lot smarter than you'd think," he said at last, which didn't really answer my question.

"Not just a dumb blonde?"

"Not a dumb blonde at all. She's going to divorce DiMaggio, you know."

That was news. "They were only just married, surely?"

Jack shrugged. He had a jaundiced but tolerant view of other people's arrangements about life, his own being designed entirely to suit him. "DiMaggio's jealous." He recited what she had told him: "He wants her to have kids and give up her career. His idea of a good time is watching a ball game on TV, or sitting around with his cronies at Toots Shor's, talking sports. The sex was great at first, but now even that's no good." He took a contented puff on his cigar. "She says she's afraid of him."

"Women always say that in California when they're thinking about divorce. That's because 'physical cruelty' is the only sure-fire grounds the courts here accept."

"It sounded to me as if she was telling the truth. Of course, you never know, with women."

"The two of you certainly seem to have had a good chat," I said, trying to disguise my envy.

Jack took off his sunglasses, and gave me a wink. "Well, she's quite a talker."

"I'm sure she has other talents."

"I would say so, David. I would *certainly* say so." He chuckled. "Do you know what she told me? When she signed her first big contract with Twentieth Century-Fox, she looked Darryl Zanuck right in the eye, gave him a sweet smile, and said, 'Well, I guess I'll never have to suck Jewish cock again, will I?' "

His robust laughter rang out across the pool, drowning out the noise of the sprinklers and the faraway hum of traffic on Sunset Boulevard.

I let him get on with what he wanted to tell me, without asking why, if Marilyn's story was true, she was sleeping with Charlie Feldman.

Jack was as entitled to his illusions as the next man, I decided.

Later that day, Jack and I sat together in the first-class cabin of American's LA/Washington flight. Jack always reserved the window seat on the right side of the first row. He needed to be in row 1 so he could stretch his legs out, because of his back, but why he had to be on the far right, I don't know. Perhaps it was just a habit, perhaps he thought it was lucky. He was a great believer in luck.

Once he was settled in, his coat and shoes off and his tie loosened, he gave the stewardesses a professional once-over. One of them attracted his attention, and he flashed her the famous Kennedy smile. I guessed that before we landed, she would receive a small gold-edged card with blue engraved script reading "United States Senate" at the top and Jack's private telephone number penciled below it in his firm, sprawling hand. Jack was like a man who always needed to know where his next meal was coming from, even when he wasn't hungry.

"All those movie people," he said, getting back to business. "What do they think of me?"

"I think they were interested."

He stared at me coldly for a moment, the living image of his old man, as if he was thinking he didn't need me to tell him what he already knew. "The truth is, they like Adlai better," I said. "He reminds them of Jimmy Stewart in *Mr. Smith Goes to Washington*. A simple, honest country boy taking on the slick big-city pols. Movie people like to see things in movie story terms."

"Governor Stevenson isn't a country boy. He isn't honest or simple either. He's a wealthy man and a god-awful snob."

"I know that, Jack. You know it. But the rest of the world doesn't. Maybe it's the photo of him with the hole in the sole of his shoe."

"What else?" he said. "I may not be the most sensitive guy in the world, but I noticed a certain, ah, *reserve*, at Feldman's."

"Well, for a start, a lot of people there remember your father. . . ."

Jack's face hardened. "I'm not interested in that crap," he snapped. Jack had had a lifetime of dealing with the fact that he was Joe Kennedy's son, but he still wasn't good at it.

"Your other problem," I went on, happy enough to change direction, "Is Joe McCarthy."

"That figures," Jack said with a sigh, and took a sip of his scotch—Ballantine, which he always asked for because his father owned the American distributorship.

Senator Joseph McCarthy's campaign against "Reds in high places" had brought him to the peak of his power. Exploiting the country's fear of the Cold War, McCarthy had made himself famous (or notorious, depending on how you felt about him) by searching out subversives and Communist sympathizers ("Comsymps," in the jargon of the day), real or imagined. Nowhere was he a more live issue than in Hollywood, where countless people had been made unemployable, and some even jailed, because of his accusations.

I happened to think (along with most "liberal" Democrats) that McCarthy was the country's major problem, as opposed to its savior, but Jack's difficulty was that most of his constituents, not to speak of his father and his brother Bobby, stood foursquare behind the senator's "crusade." Bobby was counsel to McCarthy's subcommittee, locked in fierce rivalry with Roy Cohn, an equally ambitious New York lawyer, for the senator's attention. Bobby's loyalty to McCarthy was visceral, unwavering, absolute, and his pursuit of "subversives" was as unrelentingly vicious (in my view) as his mentor's.

Jack knew I stood to his left on this issue, and I knew he was trapped, so we didn't need to discuss it in detail. "You've got to get Bobby out of there," I said. "Before it's too late."

"I know. It's not easy. He likes the limelight. And he loves a good fight."

I knew all about Bobby's love of a good fight. He had once celebrated his birthday by hitting a man over the head with a beer bottle in a Boston bar for failing to sing "Happy Birthday" when asked to, then refused to apologize. He was not a young man you wanted to cross. "Find him something else to investigate," I suggested. "The SEC, for instance. Wall Street is full of crooks."

"A lot of them are friends of Dad's. Not a great idea, David." Jack stretched, his face creasing from the sudden pain. "The problem is, I need an issue myself—one that has nothing to do with anticommunism, preferably—before I go to the convention in '56."

"It ought to be something that plays on television," I suggested. "Look what the organized crime hearings did for Kefauver."

Estes Kefauver had been a virtually unknown senator until a long list of organized-crime hoodlums taking the Fifth on television before his subcommittee made him a national hero, as well as a much talked-about vice presidential candidate for '56.

As it happened, I knew some of those heavyset men with gravelly voices who had refused to answer questions on the grounds that they might incriminate themselves, and as I thought about them, it occurred to me that there *was* one issue tailor-made for Jack—and for Bobby as well. "You might think about labor corruption," I said.

Jack raised an eyebrow.

"It's a major issue. You take the Teamsters. They're shot through with corruption. . . ."

"David," Jack said patiently. "My constituents are blue-collar. They're union members. I want the AFL-CIO on my side."

"It's the AFL-CIO that wants the Teamsters cleaned up, Jack, believe me."

"I'll think about it." He spoke without much conviction. "I'd want a guarantee in blood from George Meany that he's in favor before I made a move."

"You might get it," I said.

"That'll be the day." The stewardesses were beginning to serve dinner. Jack looked at them as they bent over with their trays, his attention diverted to more pleasant thoughts than labor unions. "Well, whatever Feldman's friends thought of me," he said, "it was worth making the trip just to meet Marilyn."

I sipped my drink, feeling that peculiar combination of relaxation and good-fellowship that accompanies a long flight. "You never *did* tell me why she's having an affair with Feldman," I said.

He chuckled. "He asked her to."

"He *asked* her?"

"They were at a party. Feldman told her he wasn't a young man anymore, and if he had a last wish, one thing he could have in the world before he died, it would be to go to bed with her."

He looked pensive. "It's not a bad line, you know. I might try it myself. Leaving out the part about being old, of course."

"And it worked?"

"It worked fine. Marilyn was really touched. She told me it seemed like such an honest thing to say. I guess she thought it wasn't such a big deal. If that was his one wish in the world, ah, why not *give* it to him? So she did."

"And then?"

"And then, I guess, she couldn't find a good way to stop without hurting his feelings."

"She's quite a girl."

The stewardess asked Jack if he wanted her to freshen his drink. She was smiling brightly, her pretty young face as close to his as she could get it by leaning over me, but Jack had turned his head to look out the window at the darkening mountains of the Southwest below, and didn't seem to notice her.

"Why, yes, she's quite a girl," I heard him say, ever so softly, and from the tone of his voice I would have said he sounded like a man who had fallen in love, if I hadn't known him so well.

2

I'M A NEW YORKER, BY BIRTH AND TEMPERAMENT, AND Washington has never been one of my favorite cities. Like Beverly Hills, it's a one-industry town where people go to bed early and where it's difficult to eat a good meal. However, I had opened up an office in Washington early on in my career, since for many of my major clients "public relations" and "lobbying" were synonymous. I never took on politicians as clients—they pay late, if at all—but I did very well in that profitable gray area where politics and big business meet.

I went there often. I went everywhere, of course, in those days—travel was part of my business. Even before jet planes made travel easier, I was constantly on the move, to California, to Europe, back again seeking clients. Having created a worldwide organization with thousands of employees, I found my job was to bring in enough business to keep them busy, and if it meant flying from New York, to LA, to Tokyo, then back to New York all in the same week, so be it. This had led to considerable strain in my first marriage, and an eventual divorce. Luckily, there had been no children to complicate things, so my first wife and I had parted on reasonably amicable terms. My second marriage, distressingly, was beginning to show signs of the same strain. My wife Maria, I noticed, no longer objected as strongly as she had at first to the amount of time I was away on business—a bad sign, in my experience.

Whenever I was in Washington, I made a point of looking up Jack Kennedy, partly because we enjoyed each other's company, partly, as Jack knew, because his father was always after me to report back on how he was doing. Over the years, as Jack and I became close friends (despite the difference in our ages), he not only came to trust my advice—it had paid off for him, after all, again and again—but also began to trust that I wouldn't tell his father anything he didn't want him to know.

We had a lot in common, Jack and I, with enough differences to keep us interested in each other. Oddly enough, Maria bore a distinct resemblance to Jackie Kennedy, long before it became fashionable to resemble her—so much so that Jack once suggested, not entirely in lest, that it would be fun to try wife swapping, just to see, as he put it, if he could "tell the difference between them in bed." Maria was a great admirer of Jack's, and I suspect she would have been less shocked by the suggestion than I was—she might not have been all that difficult to persuade, as a matter of fact.

Maria and Jackie not only looked alike, they wore the same kind of clothes, used the same decorators and hairdressers, and had many friends in common. In later years, Maria complained that "the Jackie Kennedy look" was in fact *hers*—that Jackie had simply modeled herself after Maria. This may have been true, and was no doubt all the more galling because until Jackie became a national figure in 1960, Maria was a far more famous beauty.

Since we've been divorced for decades—Maria left me, shortly after Jack's assassination, for a Brazilian multimillionaire named D'Souza—I can admit freely that I've always suspected that Maria and Jack might have had an affair at some point. He was not above sleeping with the wives of his friends. Or the friends of his wife.

Jack's second-floor Senate office was a hangover from his even wilder days as a bachelor congressman—a friendly, noisy, chaotic place, full of pretty young secretaries and the kind of Boston Irish political followers who looked like either retired boxers or Jesuit priests, with names like Mugsy, Kenny, or Red. No sign of Jackie's taste for elegance was present—the fact is, I don't think she ever visited her husband's office, which was just as well, considering what went on there.

They weren't big on ceremony either. One of Jack's Irish watchdogs—I think it was a huge ex-Boston cop named "Boom-Boom" Reardon—banged on the door of Jack's inner sanctum and hollered, "Wake up, Jack, yez got a visitor."

There was a muffled sound that might have been Jack's voice asking me to wait a moment—the doors of the Old Senate Office Building had been made of solid oak back in the days when Americans built for the ages.

It did not seem to me likely that Jack was taking a nap. I went over to the window, looked out, and was not surprised to see a young woman emerge presently from an unmarked door into the parking lot below, where the Senator's car was waiting. I thought she looked familiar as she slipped into the back seat while Mugsy O'Leary held the door open for her; then I recognized her as the stewardess who had caught Jack's eye on the flight from LA a few days ago.

There was a click as Jack turned the lock, and Boom-Boom pushed the door open for me.

"Sorry to keep you waiting, David," Jack said, yawning. "I took a nap. This weather knocks the, ah, shit out of you, doesn't it?" He was buttoning his shirt. I recognized it as a custom-made one, from Lanvin in Paris, his favorite shirtmaker. One of the things I liked best about Jack was that while he could pretend to be one of the boys, and could certainly swear a blue streak when his Irish was up, he was in fact a rather fastidious man, with refined tastes—which he did his best to hide from most of his close followers, street-fighting veterans of Boston's bare-knuckle political wars to a man.

"Are you going home?" I asked.

He nodded warily. "Jackie's expecting me," he said. "At some point. Why?"

"You might want to think about changing your shirt, that's all. There's lipstick on the collar."

He flushed, then broke into a grin. The Kennys, Mugsys, and Boom-Booms of his world were not inclined to notice such details, either because they were hardened to that kind of thing or out of some deep-rooted Catholic determination to ignore what they didn't want to know. I was never certain whether their blindness to Jack's nonstop womanizing was innocence or guile. Given the nature of the Irish, I suppose it could have been both. "That's the best advice I've gotten all day," he said. "Thank you."

"It's the *next*-to-best advice, as a matter of fact," I told him firmly. "Listen to me, please."

He was sitting behind his desk in his shirtsleeves, his shoes off and his stockinged feet on a leather ottoman. He made a steeple of his hands and stared at me with that hard edge to his expression he always had when he knew he was about to get news or advice he didn't want to hear. "Well?" he asked.

I leaned forward. "The papers are going to carry a story tomorrow that Bobby took a swing at Roy Cohn outside the committee room."

"Oh, shit."

"Bobby should know better, Jack."

"That isn't what happened," he said. "Cohn took a swing at Bobby. Bobby walked away."

"Well, that's not the way it's being reported. My guess is, Cohn leaked his version to the press first. Or maybe McCarthy, as a way of putting Bobby in his place."

"Maybe. . . ."

"Nice people, Jack. All of this, you don't need."

"I'm not going to tell Bobby what to do. He's a big boy."

This was a lofty evasion. Jack was perfectly prepared to tell Bobby what to do when it suited him, and Bobby—though he sometimes smoldered with mutinous anger—eventually obeyed. The core belief of the Kennedys wasn't Catholicism, it was primogeniture. Besides, Kennedy family loyalties went beyond politics—anybody who took a swing at Bobby might as well have taken a swing at Jack.

"It bears out what I was saying on the way back from LA, Jack. You need an issue. And Bobby needs a new set of Playmates."

"I *know* that," he said impatiently. "Why do you think I've been making speeches about getting the French out of Vietnam?"

"Nobody in this country gives two hoots about Vietnam, Jack. Outside Washington, people don't know where it is and couldn't care less whether the French are there or not. You're not going to get on TV with France and Vietnam, Jack. Now corruption in labor, that's another story. It's a pocketbook issue, a gut issue, there are villains and bad guys—bad guys, by the way, like you wouldn't believe. . . ."

"Yes, I can see that, but I still say—"

I rushed in. "I know what you said. George Meany has to sign up behind you. In blood. Well, I went to see Meany, Jack, and he gave me a message for you. He said, 'Tell Jack we're behind him one hundred percent. If he can get Dave Beck, and expose the Teamster leadership for the thugs they've become, he has our unconditional support. In blood, if you like.' That's what the man said, Jack."

Jack stared at me thoughtfully. "But not in writing, I suppose?" he asked.

"Not in writing, no. You'll have to make do with blood."

"We nail Beck and his gang to the wall for Meany and the AFL-CIO, and I get their support in '60, is that the idea?"

"That's the idea. They're scared of Beck and the Teamsters, Jack. They're giving organized labor a bad name, for one thing. For another, they're using their mob connections to grow faster than any other union."

"Why doesn't Meany do something about it, if he feels so strongly?"

"Dog don't eat dog. Labor leaders don't like attacking other labor leaders in public. Meany wants to get rid of the Beck crowd, but he'd like the United States Senate to do it for him. That's where you come in. That's where Bobby comes in. Let him take on Beck, Jack—Bobby's going to look like a hero, instead of a guy who hangs out with people like Cohn and McCarthy, persecuting file clerks who once subscribed to *The New Masses*."

Jack held up his hand. "*Stop* that!" he said firmly. "I won't have you making fun of Bobby, David. Some of those file clerks may be Communist spies. . . ."

He looked at me and sighed. This was a subject on which we were never going to see eye to eye, any more than his father and I did. On the other hand, Jack knew a lost cause when he saw one, and McCarthy was as lost as a cause could be. "How bad are things with the Teamsters?" he asked. "Really."

"Very. Corruption, sweetheart deals with mobsters, paper locals, even murder. It's a real horror story, Jack. I heard about it from a guy named Mollenhoff, who's made this something of a one-man crusade. . . ."

Jack stared out the window. Then he turned back to me. "All right," he said. "I'm willing to give it a try. Tell this fellow Mollenhoff to talk to Bobby, will you, David?"

He punched his right fist hard against the palm of his other hand, cheering up as he always did at the prospect of action. "Honest unions. That's a cause worth fighting for, isn't it?"

It would be seen that way by most people—certainly by the press. It was not, however, a cause worth *dying* for, I reminded myself, and decided to sound a note of caution. "It *could* get rough, Jack," I said. "That's the only thing."

He laughed. "They don't know what rough is until they've met Bobby," he said. "Let's have a drink." He called for Boom-Boom.

"Good enough." I congratulated myself on what seemed like a sensible change of course. I felt I'd earned my drink.

Boom-Boom shambled in, all three hundred pounds of him, a good deal of it muscle. Jack had told me that Boom-Boom had been a mounted cop until he put on too much weight, and that for years he was a fixture in Boston's Saint Patrick's Day parade, riding a white draft horse. I could believe it.

"You sure you want a drink, Jack?" the giant asked. "Shouldn't yez be gettin' home to herself?"

"When I need your marital advice, I'll ask for it," Jack said crisply, but without a trace of resentment. Boom-Boom mixed our drinks and handed them to us. I couldn't help feeling that if Jack had asked him to coldcock me with the butt of the police revolver he carried—illegally—under his jacket, Boom-Boom would have done it without any fuss. Jack's relationship to these Stone Age spear-carriers of his was feudal. He was their leader, boss, chief, and they were blindly loyal.

Boom-Boom left, slamming the door behind him. "Boom-Boom's got a point, Jack," I said.

"Don't *you* start on me too, David. That's all I hear from Bobby these days. You'd think he wanted me to run for 'Husband of the Year.' " He laughed. Jackie had never completely forgiven him for delaying the announcement of their engagement until after the *Saturday Evening Post* had run an article naming him "Bachelor of the Year."

"I'm just suggesting that you're putting too much trust in the goodwill of the press, that's all."

He gave a bark of derision. "I don't trust them an inch, David. There are simply certain kinds of stories they won't run. You know that as well as I do."

He was right, up to a point. In those innocent, pre-Watergate days, when the press still left the private lives of presidents alone, nobody had ever reported the well-known fact that Ike's wartime driver, Kay Summersby, was his mistress, or that FDR and Eleanor led separate lives. The Washington press corps knew all about Jack's womanizing, but there was very little chance they would print it. Of course, there were exceptions to this convention, and I thought I should remind him of the fact. "They won't run stories about you and any *ordinary* girl, that's true," I said. "What you have to be careful about is somebody who's so famous that her whole life is a news story. Or who just doesn't *care* about secrecy enough to bother."

He looked at me over the rim of his glass, his expression thoughtful. "Marilyn?" he asked.

"Marilyn."

There was a long silence; then he cleared his throat. "Tell me something, David," he said. "How did my father get away with having Gloria Swanson as his mistress all those years?"

It was a good question. In her time, Gloria Swanson had been as big a star as Marilyn. "To start with, he wasn't planning to run for the presidency when he and Gloria were—ah—together," I answered.

"Dad was a public figure."

The truth was, I didn't know myself how Joe had managed to get away with it. He even took Swanson and Rose to Europe on the same boat once, in adjoining staterooms, which certainly raised eyebrows. "I imagine your father got away with it mostly because he just didn't *give* a shit what people thought," I suggested. "That, and luck. And the fact that your mother is a saint."

"Well, *I* don't give a shit what people think either, David. And God knows, I'm lucky. I'm nearly forty. If I've learned one thing, it's take what you want while you can get it. You never know what's going to happen. . . ."

He had a faraway look in his eyes. Jack was no mystic, but I knew what was on his mind. Even ten years later, his brother Joe junior's death still haunted him. Joe junior had been the Kennedy heir apparent, the eldest son who was supposed to become the first Irish-Catholic president of the United States. Jack adored him, as everybody did. He had everything Jack later developed, in spades—charm, wit, dashing good looks, courage, astonishing success with women, all of it snuffed out in one bright burst of explosives when his bomber blew up over the English Channel.

I had been with the Old Man in Hyannis when they brought him the news, and I've never forgotten the look on his face. It wasn't grief—it was cold, hard, murderous rage. Joe Kennedy took everything personally; from the way he reacted to the news of his eldest son's death, I could tell that he held FDR personally responsible, as if Roosevelt had engineered America's entry into the war just to punish him. He even said as much, later that night, after he'd told Rose and had a couple of drinks. He had a telegram of condolence from FDR in his hand, which he crumpled into a ball and hurled out the window savagely. "He killed my boy, that crippled bastard!" he snarled, and went into his bedroom, slamming the door behind him.

That was part of the answer to Jack's question about how his father got away with his affair with Gloria Swanson—the part I didn't want to tell him. There were no gray areas in Joe Kennedy's soul; you were for him or against him, and that was that, and if you were against him, he would destroy you, even if it took a lifetime or cost him a fortune to do it. People were *afraid* of Joe, even FDR, and they were right to be. They weren't afraid of Jack, and I wasn't sure they ever would be.

Jack stood up. He was rail-thin. The Kennedys' most strictly guarded family secret was Jack's ill health, which Joe was determined to hide not only from the world, lest Jack be thought too sickly to be president, but more fiercely, from himself. Jack had suffered from asthma as a child, a football injury and a war wound had so damaged his back that he was in constant and acute pain—worse, the doctors feared that he might become paralyzed—and he had an adrenal deficiency that made any kind of operation dangerous.

The Kennedys had solved the problem of Jack's health by simply not talking about it, in much the same way that they denied, to themselves and to others, the very obvious fact that Jack's sister Rosemary was retarded. No matter how much Jack ate—and he was a notoriously finicky eater—he lost weight, a symptom of his adrenal disorder, which was regarded, by everyone but his family, as a fatal disease until the development of cortisone.

"Do you think going after the Teamsters will do it, David? Really?" He was clearly having second thoughts.

"So far as I can see, it's your best shot at an issue. It's red-hot, it's ready-made, and if you don't grab it fast, somebody else will. Stu Symington, maybe."

"Fuck Stu Symington. You're right."

Jack went into the bathroom to change his shirt, and I caught a glimpse of the *Daily News* on his desk. The front page was a photograph of Marilyn at Idlewild Airport—Joe DiMaggio glowering in the doorway of the plane behind her—arriving in New York to shoot *The Seven Year Itch*.

3

SHE HAD NEVER LIKED NEW YORK MUCH. IT SEEMED TO HER a mean-spirited, hard-edged, noisy city, all steam and dirt, full of ugly people pushing each other out of the way in the crowded streets. She was used to wide, empty, palm-lined streets, to friendly people, to the glitter of chrome from a million cars.

Actually, the truth was, she was a little *afraid* of New York. She didn't seem to fit in, even as a visitor. She had the wrong clothes, the wrong look, the wrong attitude. She didn't like the fancy restaurants, or the big department stores, where everybody was so rude.

She hated the hotel, too. The studio had put everyone who mattered into the St. Regis, either because they got a deal or because it was Darryl Zanuck's favorite place to stay. It was okay for Joe, she thought—Toots Shor's, where he could sit and schmooze with his cronies, was only a five-minute walk away—but she couldn't even get through the narrow, cramped lobby without causing a near riot.

In Los Angeles, people took movie stars calmly, but New Yorkers mobbed her wherever she went. Her first day at the St. Regis, she had been unable to make her way through the crowd to the street, and had to take refuge in the dark, deserted King

Cole Bar while a way was cleared for her; she had found herself suddenly alone there with the strangest man she had ever seen. He had mad, staring eyes, plastered-back dyed black hair, a waxed mustache that rose to sharp points ending at the level of his eyebrows, like tiny radio antennas at either side of his face. He wore huge rings on each finger, and by his side sat a cheetah with a jeweled collar, which he held by a gold chain. Thus she made the acquaintance of Salvador Dalí, who held her spellbound for nearly half an hour while Joe, the studio PR people, the hotel security men, and the cops tried to clear a passage for her to the front door.

She had never heard of Dalí, as it happened, but he wasn't shy about telling her that he was the greatest living painter in the world, Picasso included. With grave Spanish courtesy he told her he wanted to paint her as Venus rising from the sea, which was just about the nicest offer anybody had made to her since her arrival in New York. At first she had been afraid of the cheetah, but when she finally got up the nerve to stroke the back of its neck, it responded just like any other cat, with a deep, throaty purr.

When they came for her at last and guided her out to the canopy where Joe waited, scowling at the mob of fans, photographers, and curious passersby that now blocked Fifty-fifth Street completely, she told him about Dalí and the cheetah, but he wasn't interested, or maybe he just thought she was kidding.

"Dolly who?" he asked impatiently, pushing her into the waiting limousine so fast that she almost tripped.

Thinking about Joe gave her a headache, which wasn't improved by the fact that she had arrived in New York with cramps. Other women, most of them, seemed to cope with the problem easily enough, but like her mother she had world-class periods, so devastating and painful that she lived in fear of them. She was convinced they were part of the reason her mother had gone crazy and had to be institutionalized, which made her even more frightened that the same thing might happen to her one day.

The problem with Joe was that in her mind—in her *heart*, more important—she was already divorced from him. Yet here he was in New York, beside her as always (except when he ran off to Toots Shor's), telling her what to do and what to wear, an all-too-real, flesh-and-blood husband whom she had already dismissed from her mind—so much so that it sometimes puzzled her to wake up in the morning and find him in the bed next to her.

That was the way she was, she thought unapologetically—waiting, or going through long, slow formalities, was always intolerable to her. Years ago, when she made up her mind she no longer wanted to be married to Jim Dougherty, she had simply moved out of her in-laws' house and started dating again, as if Jim, who was still at sea somewhere in the Pacific, had ceased to exist—which, in her head, he had.

The Slugger was fading the same way, but so far she hadn't screwed up her courage to have a talk with him about it, so he had no idea—not being a particularly introspective soul—that so far as she was concerned, they were already divorced.

There were other things she hadn't told Joe—so many that her mind actually seemed to buzz with secrets, as if they were flying around inside her head. She had told him next to nothing about her plans—or rather, she had told him only what she supposed he wanted to hear.

Joe hated the "phonies" and the "movie big shots" whom he accused of exploiting her, so he wasn't unhappy that she was thinking of breaking her contract with 20th Century-Fox—particularly since he assumed, with a little help from her, that he would have her to himself for a while, playing the housewife, visiting with his family in San Francisco, perhaps even having that baby. . . .

She hadn't told him she had already agreed to form a company of her own with Milton Greene, the photographer, or that once she had jumped ship on Zanuck and Fox, she would be working harder than ever. Even in small things she had stored up a lot of trouble for herself. Joe had been incensed by the skirt-blowing scene when he read the script for *The Seven Year Itch,* not just because her panties would be exposed—though he wasn't actually too crazy about that—but because they would be exposed on location in New York City, "his town," where he had reigned as "the Yankee Clipper" for so many years.

Ordinary New Yorkers, he complained, *his* fans, would see *his* wife, in the flesh, showing her *tush* right there on Lexington

Avenue! He went on about it for days, building up a head of steaming anger that threatened to erupt at any minute, until finally she promised that the scene would be toned down, that her skirt wouldn't rise above midthigh level—except that she hadn't mentioned a word of this to Billy Wilder, the director, who was going ahead with the scene as planned.

Meanwhile, here she was, "the biggest star since Garbo," as Wilder kept telling her—although it was really Harlow she identified with—trapped in her hotel suite like an animal in a cage!

She paced restlessly, drinking champagne and occasionally spilling it on the stained and tattered old terry-cloth robe she always wore while she was being made up. Whitey Snyder, her makeup man and best friend—she had insisted on his being given a room on the same floor of the hotel—had made her up hours ago, filling her in on the weather, the news, and the latest gossip, as he always did, but there was no way she could get out of the hotel quietly.

She pulled off the robe and let it fall to the floor, and continued pacing, naked. She always left her clothes on the floor—another little habit that enraged Joe. . . .

Joe liked everything clean and tidy, but in just two days, she had already made a shambles of the elegant suite. There were piles of magazines and newspapers on the floor, her clothes spread out on every piece of furniture, makeup spilled everywhere, room service trays and ice buckets piled up faster than they could be taken away. There were so many flowers that it gave her the creeps; they reminded her of a funeral—her old boyfriend Johnny Hyde's, to be exact. She hardly even bothered to look at the cards, but one modest bouquet of roses had caught her attention, since it bore a small card with gold edges and blue engraved script that read "United States Senate," below which, in a precise hand that was not his own, was the message, "Welcome to New York! Jack."

She had called him this morning, as soon as Joe had left, and been put through immediately by a secretary who seemed to take a call from Marilyn Monroe in her stride. Jack himself had been cordial, but guarded, as if there were other people in the room. He was late for a roll call, whatever that was, he had explained, but would call her back as soon as he was able.

She had asked him when he was going to be in New York, feeling that it ought to have been *his* job to bring up the subject, not hers, but all he said was, "Very soon," crisply, as if to cut off further discussion of the subject. When she told him how difficult it was for her to leave the hotel, he said, "I'll take care of *that*" decisively; then he hung up with a quick good-bye.

Well, what did she expect, she asked herself, after one night? Sir Galahad to the rescue? Jack Kennedy was a busy man, after all, doing whatever it was that senators did, which *had* to be a lot more important than what movie people—or former sports stars—did.

The house phone rang and she picked it up. She held it to her ear and said nothing—experience had taught her that even in a first-class hotel, the crazies sometimes got through to you. It was safer to let the caller speak first. There was a pause; then the desk clerk said, "I'm sorry to disturb you, Miss Monroe, but Mr. David Leman is in the lobby and wishes to speak to you." He sounded in awe of David Leman.

The name seemed vaguely familiar, but she couldn't place it. Anyway, she didn't put much trust in names. Reporters would pretend to be anyone to reach her—on her honeymoon with Joe she had once received an emergency call from her own beloved Aunt Ana, only to find, when she got on the line, that it was a stringer for Walter Winchell, wanting a few words on what it was like to be Mrs. DiMaggio.

"Mr. Leman says he's a friend of, ah, Jack's," the desk clerk added. It came back to her then—the memory of a tall, dark-haired, exquisitely tailored man with a Clark Gable mustache and a white waistcoat, Jack's companion at Charlie Feldman's party, who seemed to know everybody in the world.

"Send him up!" she said, slipping quickly back into her robe. Then something told her that David Leman wasn't the kind of man who would appreciate a dirty old terry-cloth robe, so she went into the bedroom and exchanged it for a silk wrapper and a pair of satin mules, feeling as if she was dressed up like Joan Crawford—that *bitch*—who she assumed was probably David Leman's idea of a movie star.

She wished there were time to tidy up the suite—now that she looked at it, it was a real *mess*—but she sprayed a little of her favorite Chanel No. 5 around and hoped for the best.

She gave him her biggest, happiest smile as she opened the door for him.

Years ago, I asked my old friend Aaron Diamond, the Hollywood superagent, why he gave up representing performers in favor of bestselling novelists and as-told-to celebrity autobiographers. "I decided I wanted to sleep nights," he growled. "I got tired of all those three a.m. phone calls."

I took the same view myself, even in the days when I was a young man in Hollywood. Few egos are more fragile than those of movie stars, or more insatiably demanding.

Marilyn was no exception, the only difference being that she did nothing to hide the fragility of *her* ego—it was right there on the surface for all to see, in the puzzled, self-absorbed eyes and the hands that were constantly in motion. I found myself staring at her hands. She wrung them, she picked at her nail polish, she plucked at the edge of her silk wrapper, pulling at loose threads as if she were intent on unraveling the whole thing. She sat hunched over, as if hugging herself, apparently unaware that her hands were leading a nervous, high-energy life of their own.

She had a kind of natural sexual grace, the like of which I had never encountered before—or since. Sitting there, in an armchair at the St. Regis, I could see her breasts clearly through the thin silk of her wrapper, but I never suspected, even for a moment, that she was putting on a display for my benefit, any more than when she slipped out of her satin mules and rubbed her toes, revealing a large expanse of thigh. Later on, I was to revise this naive judgment. Marilyn, I was to discover, always knew exactly what effect she had on men, and stage-managed it carefully. Her innocence was at once real and an act.

"Would you like some champagne?" she asked, in her breathy little voice.

I said I would, even though it was still a few minutes short of noon. Apart from an astonishing profusion of flowers, there were at least half a dozen champagne coolers around the room, each containing an open bottle on ice. Apparently, Marilyn had the waiter open each bottle as soon as it was delivered, then let it sit there until it went flat. There was a bottle at her feet, leaving a damp circular stain on the rug. She filled a glass, noticed that it wasn't bubbling, and gave a charming little shrug, part surprise, part irritation. She got up, kicking the satin mules out of her way, tried a couple of bottles, and eventually found one that was fresh enough to satisfy her. She brought the glass over to me and sat down again, exposing so much leg that it was impossible not to notice she wasn't wearing any panties. Jack, I told myself, had been telling the truth.

"I hate it when the fizz goes out of it?" she said, wrinkling her nose at the rising bubbles. "When I started drinking champagne," she went on, "somebody gave me one of those gold *swizzle* sticks?" She had a habit of emphasizing unexpected words, which gave her speech a curious rhythm all its own. "You're supposed to put it in your glass and twirl it *round* to get rid of the bubbles?" She demonstrated with her forefinger. "I couldn't see the point? I mean, the bubbles are *it* for me."

It occurred to me to wonder if Marilyn was drunk, but I saw no sign of it. She seemed to treat the champagne as a prop, judging from the fact that there were three or four glasses leaving rings on the furniture, each with her lipstick on the rim, and each very nearly full.

There were millions of men who would have given their right arm, no doubt, to be sitting where I was at that moment, but the truth was that Jack's call had come at an inopportune moment. As it happened, I had an officeful of people waiting for me, having interrupted a meeting with a group of senior Ford Motor Company executives to come over here only because Marilyn had told the switchboard not to put through any calls to her. "Jack told me you have a problem," I said. "He asked me to see if I could be of any help."

She frowned. "Oh *boy*, do I ever have a problem! I can't get *out* of here!"

I nodded sympathetically. "I saw the crowd downstairs."

"It's not just the crowd. It's the reporters. They follow me everywhere. It's like a whole convoy, with convertibles for the photographers?" She looked as if she was about to cry. I'd never met anybody, not even in show business, who looked more forlorn when she was sad.

"I have a business meeting," she said. "I mean, it's with somebody whose name I don't want to see in the papers? And how come the phones don't work? I can call out, but nobody can call me?"

"You asked the operator to hold your calls. She wouldn't put me through." I wondered whom she had planned to meet. I didn't yet know about her plans to walk out on Fox, or her partnership with Milton Greene.

"Hold my *calls?* That was last night."

"Well, you have to give her the okay in the morning to put them through again," I explained.

"Is that why you came in *person?*" She bit her lip, then buried her face in her hands. "Oh, God, I'm *sorry,*" she wailed. "You had to leave home and run all the way over here. . . ."

"Look here, it's almost lunchtime. Honestly, I don't mind a bit."

"Really?" She uncovered her face.

"Absolutely."

She leaned over impulsively and gave me a quick kiss on the cheek, the kind a child might bestow on an elderly relative for a present that was slightly better than what she had expected. "You're a *dear,*" she said. "I don't know why, but I just had this *picture* of you, sitting at home having breakfast, with your wife, and a dog at your feet. . . . Are you married?"

"Yes," I said. "And we *do* have a dog. Two, as a matter of fact."

"What kind?"

"Pugs. A male and female."

"Cute! What are they named?"

"Edward and Mrs. Simpson," I said, and since there was no reaction, I added, "After the duke and duchess of Windsor, you see."

Marilyn nodded vaguely, but she didn't smile. Clearly, the duke and duchess didn't mean much to her, if anything.

Her eyes misted over. "I had a dog when I was a *little* girl," she whispered. "In Hawthorne, when I was a foster child? His name was Tippy?"

"That's nice."

She nodded. "Our next-door neighbor shot him one night, because he was barking."

I wasn't sure how to handle that. "I'm so sorry," I said finally.

It seemed to be enough. "Thank you," Marilyn whispered, taking my hand in hers and clutching it. She had surprisingly strong fingers.

We sat for what seemed like a long time facing each other, hand in hand, meditating on Tippy's death. It was not how I had expected to spend the late morning.

I cleared my throat. "Well, as to your problem," I began.

Marilyn's enormous eyes stared blankly into mine. "What problem?" she asked, her mind apparently still back in Hawthorne with Tippy.

"Getting you out of the hotel."

"Oh," she said dreamily, still kneading my hand. I noticed that she was not wearing a wedding ring, and wondered if that had any significance. "Tell me," she said, "what is it you actually *do?*"

"I own a public relations firm."

I had Marilyn's full attention now. No stars are ever completely happy with their PR. "You mean, you do, like, *publicity?*"

I shook my head. It was a common mistake. I do not do publicity, and never have done—I create an *image* for my clients, shape the way they are perceived by the press and the public. Publicity is for foot soldiers; I have always been a strategist on the grand scale. "I don't do personal publicity," I explained. "I try to 'accentuate the positive' for my clients." I laughed, but Marilyn had apparently never heard the song. "My job is to ensure that their activities are seen in the best light."

"What *kind* of clients?"

"CBS. Israel. The Las Vegas Chamber of Commerce. Ford. The Joseph P. Kennedy Foundation. . . ."

Her eyes widened. "No kidding? Jack's dad?"

I nodded.

Marilyn was all business now, Tippy forgotten. "Joe Schenck," she said, "told me he was the biggest shit who ever owned a studio."

I had forgotten that she had been Schenck's girlfriend when she was an ambitious starlet in the 20th Century-Fox talent pool. Schenck must have been in his seventies then, at the losing end of his long, bitter feud with Darryl Zanuck for control of the studio, and just released from Danbury, Connecticut, Federal Correction Institute, pardoned by Truman after serving several months of a five-year sentence for making payoffs to union racketeers in exchange for labor peace, and perjuring himself on the subject.

"Oddly enough," I said, "Joe Kennedy holds much the same opinion of Schenck."

"Joe Schenck's a tough old guy," she said with a certain amount of admiration. "I was really *scared* of him at first, you know, but he had all this *energy*—more than anybody I'd ever met, until Johnny Hyde came along. . . ." Hyde had been her agent-mentor-lover in the early years. She sipped her champagne. "You know how I met him?"

I shook my head.

"He was in his car, leaving the studio. He'd just had a meeting with Zanuck about something, and he was really *angry* about it. I was on my way to the commissary for lunch. He took one look at me, told his chauffeur to stop, opened the door, and said, 'Get inna car, goilie!' "

She had the voice down perfectly, the guttural rasping accent, New York by way of Rybinsk-on-the-Volga, a growl deepened by a lifetime of smoking cigars and screaming at people. For the first time it occurred to me that Marilyn was a pretty good actress, or at least that she *could* have been, in the right hands.

"Is Jack like his father?" she asked.

It was a question that seemed to call for an honest answer. "Not yet," I said. "He may be, though, one day."

She raised an eyebrow.

"People think Jack's a lightweight," I explained. "He's not. But he's got *grace*, you see, which Joe never had. Some people mistake that for weakness. It isn't so."

She seemed to understand. "Is he like his father with women?" she asked.

"Jack's less cynical than his father," I said, taking a deep breath. "Joe loves winning much more than he's ever loved any woman. Jack *can* fall in love with a woman. He was in love with Inga Arvad, before the war, until his father broke it up."

"Oh dear. Why?"

"Well, for one thing, the FBI thought Inga was a German spy, so Joe may have done the right thing for once. . . ."

"Is Jack in love with Jackie?"

I told her the truth. "Not yet. But I think he will be, in time."

Marilyn sat quietly for a moment, apparently contemplating the future. Then she sighed. "You won't believe this," she said, "but when it comes to men, I've never had any regrets. Even when it was bad, it was good, if you see what I mean?"

"It's a healthy attitude," I said. "Joan Crawford once said something similar to me."

Her face tightened, and I could see anger in her eyes. "*Joan Crawford!*" she spat. "Are you a friend of hers?"

"Not at all," I said carefully, conscious that I was walking a tightrope. "Joan invited me out to dinner once, to sound me out about handling Pepsi-Cola's PR, got looped on vodka, and made a grotesque pass at me, right there at Chambord, for all the world to see."

"What did you do?"

"I said no gracefully, got her home, and handed her back to her husband, Alfred Steele. By way of thanks, she spread the rumor that I'm a homosexual. Which, as it happens, I am not. I just don't like going to bed with elderly women who make a public spectacle of themselves—or who want me to cut my fees."

"We have something in common," Marilyn said quietly, then began to giggle uncontrollably.

"We do?"

"Joan made a pass at *me,* too! Right after I made *Clash by Night,* she made friends with me, and I was really impressed— I mean, I was this nobody, and here was this big star being nice to me. . . . I didn't have too many clothes then, so she was always inviting me over to her house to lend me hers, but she was about half my size, you know, so nothing fit. Then, after a couple of months, she made this pass at me, right there in her walk-in closet while I was trying to squeeze into one of her dresses. Talk about *creepy*?"

"What did *you* do?"

"I ran. I drove home without my shoes—left them in the closet with hers. Then, when I won the *Photoplay* gold medal—as the best new actress of the year, in '53—she told a reporter, 'There's nothing wrong with my tits, but I don't go around throwing them in people's faces!' " Marilyn looked grim. "She really *stuck* it to me."

"What did you do then?"

She gave an angelic smile, sweet as honey. "I told Louella Parsons how sorry I was Joan had said that about me, because having been a homeless child, I admired her so much for taking four children in, and for being such a *wonderful* mother to them."

She laughed. "*That* shut her up, and she never spoke to me again. Or about me. Actually, I thought she had pretty scrawny tits, if you want to know the truth."

I was impressed by Marilyn's counterattack, a savage knockout punch delivered with wit and style. Joan Crawford's cruelty to her children was one of those unspoken facts of Hollywood life, something insiders knew but the public didn't. "You certainly got your revenge on *her*," I said.

Marilyn shrugged. "I was pissed off? It doesn't often happen, but when it does, oh *boy,* look *out!* Did you get *your* revenge?"

I nodded. "I would say so, yes. I took Coca-Cola on as a client."

Marilyn shrieked with laughter, and gave me a kiss—the real thing this time, leaving lipstick all over my mouth.

"Oh *my!*" she cried. "I can see we're going to be *friends,* David! Now call whoever it is you have to call and get me out of here. I've got things to *do!*"

She loved Milton Greene's studio almost as much as she loved Milton. It was like a grown-up's playground, perched on the roof of the big, old-fashioned office building, with a stone colonnade all the way around it. Outside, on the flagstone terrace, there was a grape arbor, a fountain, garden furniture, so that you could almost imagine you were in Italy, while inside, the big, high-ceilinged studio was full of dark shadows, vivid backdrops and strange props—pipe racks hung with old costumes, wicker baskets full of hats, odd pieces of furniture, bric-a-brac of every description as far as the eye could see.

Whenever she saw Milton, the phrase "bright as a button" came to her mind. He looked like a soulful child, with his sad dark eyes and his round face, but that was only at first glance. She could never explain, even to herself, why she had chosen Milton, of all people, to lead her out of Hollywood or help her break the contract with Fox.

At Fox, she was always going to be their "dumb blonde"— that was the way they saw her, and that was that. Zanuck *hated* her—not just because she had refused to let him fuck

her, which he thought was his due, but because she had been
Joe Schenck's girl, and Darryl hated Joe.

Since everybody in Hollywood knew how unhappy she was
at Fox, and how much Zanuck hated her, she had been deluged with offers, many of them from people who had more
money, more experience, and more clout than Milton—which
wasn't saying much, since Milton had no money, very little
experience, and no clout at all without the use of her name.

Maybe she trusted him precisely because he *wasn't* one of
the big producers, or agents, or entertainment lawyers, who
would have tried to make her do what *they* thought she should
do, once she was free and clear of Fox. . . .

She shucked off her shoes, went into the dressing room,
slipped out of her dress and put on a robe. Milton's friend and
sidekick Joe Eula, dark, diminutive, and crackling with energy,
put his head around the door and winked at her. "Try on these,
baby doll," he said, tossing her a pair of black stockings. Joe
was as volatile as Milton was calm, and Milton was the calmest
person she had ever met, a man of so few words—and those so
softly spoken—that you had to really concentrate to hear what
he said. Milton seemed to have to think forever before saying
even the most ordinary thing, which she hoped was a sign of
intelligence, since she had more or less pledged her future to
him. She came back out and told him she was ready.

Milton shoved some papers over to her. "Do I sign these?"
she asked.

He thought about that—or something—for a long time.
"Maybe you should get a lawyer to look at them first?" he
suggested. Like her, he tended to end his sentences as if they
were questions, even when they weren't. Maybe *that* was part
of why she liked him, she thought. That and the fact that he
had burst into tears when she told him about Tippy.

"The only lawyer I've got right now is Jerry Giesler?"
she said.

"Jerry? He's a divorce lawyer."

"I know."

There was a long silence. Nobody looked gloomier than
Milton when he wanted to look gloomy, she decided. "Did
you talk to DiMaggio about our deal yet?" he asked at last.

She shook her head.

"Oy vey."

"It won't affect the deal," she said.

"Sure." His expression said it all—the knowledge that *everything* would have an effect on their deal: the weather, her periods, her love life, certainly her divorce. "You should wear paler makeup," he said, changing the subject—something he was an expert at. He waved at Joe, who came over carrying a bottle of champagne and a makeup box, put a towel around her, and got to work, occasionally glancing toward Milton, who either shrugged or nodded. "Giesler might not be the right man?" Milton suggested. "For this."

"I could get Ike Lublin? or Mickey Rudin?"

"Frank's lawyer? Yes. You could get Mickey . . ." Milton had a way of repeating what she'd said, which didn't tell her whether he was for or against whatever it was, or even if he had any opinion at all.

"So long as it's fifty-fifty," she said. "I don't care about anything else."

Milton picked up a Leica and looked at her through the finder. No matter what he was involved in, he never forgot he was a photographer first and foremost. "I don't know, Joe?" he whispered. "The hair."

"I *know*. Don't *nag*, baby! I've already *thought* about the hair." She felt Joe's fingers in her hair, pulling, shaping, undoing everything that Mr. Kenneth had wrought so carefully in the suite this morning.

"Yes," Milton said, clicking the camera a couple of times. "Yes." He repeated it quietly a few more times. Joe poured a couple of glasses of champagne, and they both stared at her.

"Try the stockings on, baby," Joe said. "You know, make a production of it." He reached overhead and adjusted some lights, then went behind her and lowered a black velvet backdrop.

Milton nodded glumly. "Not fifty-fifty," he said to her, picking up his camera.

She was leaning back in the bentwood Thonet chair, one leg pointing up at the ceiling as she pulled on a black stocking, and she froze. "What the hell are you talking about?" she asked, suddenly furious.

Milton grinned. "You get fifty-*one* percent, Marilyn," he said. "I want *you* to have control."

"Control of Monroe-Greene Productions?"

"It's going to be called Marilyn Monroe Productions. It's *your* company, Marilyn. That's what I'm trying to tell you."

She tilted her chair so far back that she almost tipped over, laughing with joy, not just at the fact that she had control of herself at last but because Milton had given it to her, because she had made the right choice when she picked him. She could hear the whir and the click of his camera, hear him whispering to himself, in his New York accent, "Bee-*you*-ti-ful!" and she already knew these were going to be the sexiest, *happiest* photographs anybody had ever taken of her.

"Pick up the phone," Joe told her. "Like one of those Vargas girls in *Esquire*."

She picked up the receiver and placed it against her ear obediently. Then, out of a spirit of mischief, she dialed the number Jack had given her. She heard the phone ring while Milton clicked his camera, and a deep voice, with an unmistakable Boston Irish accent, growled, "Senator Kennedy's office."

She asked to speak to the Senator, thinking that she could actually feel layers of Irish-Catholic disapproval for who and what she was coming over the telephone line from Washington, D.C. There was a heavy clunk as he put the receiver at his end down on the desk, and the subdued hum of conversation in the background—she thought she heard a woman's laughter—and then whoever it was shouted in a booming voice, "Jack, it's the blonde on the phone for yez."

The blonde on the phone? She felt a moment of indignation; then Jack himself came on the phone. "Did David get you out of the St. Regis?" he asked. He was whispering, so she had to strain to hear him.

"I'm out, thank you. Footloose, fancy-free, and on the town." She giggled. "Where are *you?*"

"It's been hectic here. . . ."

"Oh. I thought you told me back there in LA you'd drop everything the moment I got to New York? Well, I'm here?"

"I can get up tomorrow."

It was on the tip of her tongue to say that *this* particular "blonde on the phone" didn't wait for any man, that by tomorrow she might have found somebody else, that he needn't bother, but there was something about Jack that gave her pause. "Guess what I'm doing?" she asked, in her most sultry voice.

"Well, ah, I've no idea. . . ."

"I'm sitting on a chair, tilting it *way* back, with one leg stuck high up in the air, while I pull on a black nylon stocking and fasten it to my garter. I'm not wearing any panties either."

There was a long pause; she heard him swallow hard. "I'd like to see *that*," he said.

"Well, you'd be looking right at it if you were here, smart guy."

"Perhaps you can, ah, replay the scene for me tomorrow?"

She made a wet, kissing noise into the receiver. "Oh, I hate to repeat myself, honey," she said. "Get it while it's hot, get it while it's going, that's my advice."

"Where the hell *are* you?" There was just enough irritation in the way he asked to assure her that she had hit home, had awakened whatever small sense of proprietorship he might feel over her. She would let him think about what he was missing—it would teach him not to take her quite so easily for granted next time.

"I'm sitting here with two divine men. Drinking champagne and having a *ball*."

"You're *what?*"

"I'm having a ball with two guys." She laughed. "It's okay, honey. I'm being photographed."

He laughed uneasily. "Of course. I should have guessed that."

If it had been anybody else, she would have resented the smug tone. Once or twice when she had *really* been angry at Joe, she had called him and said loving things to him on the phone while she was in bed with another man. It had given her a sense of being in control. She pictured him at the other end of the line, watching sports on television with the sound turned down as he talked to her about how his flight had been or what the hotel was like, unaware that as they spoke, there was a man in bed beside her. . . .

"Can you meet me for dinner tomorrow?" he asked, interrupting her thoughts. "At the Carlyle?"

"Sure." It was easy to arrange. She could tell Wilder that she needed to spend the evening with Joe, and tell Joe that she needed to have dinner with Wilder to talk about her role; the chance of their meeting each other was minimal. Once Wilder started to shoot the picture, though, it would be a lot more difficult.

"I've got to run," he said, still whispering. "I'll see you tomorrow."

She blew him another kiss. "I can hardly wait." She broke the connection, and gave Milton a big grin. "Where's the Carlyle?" she asked.

He contemplated the question for a moment as if it required heavy thinking. He changed lenses, reloaded, checked his exposure, then looked up. "Madison Avenue and Seventy-sixth Street," he said. The dark eyes glistened with sharp intelligence, like the dots of two exclamation marks. "Jack Kennedy's suite is on the twentieth floor," he added softly.

For a moment she was about to lose her temper with Mr. "Bright as a Button" for being a smart-ass. Then he gave her one of his sad, little-boy smiles and she began to laugh instead, happy with the way she was going to look in the photographs, with the prospect of this new affair, with the future.

Really, she thought, crossing her fingers—she was the luckiest girl in the world!

Love always made her an optimist, every time.

She was in a hall, expensively furnished in the manner of a gentlemen's club—or what she imagined one to look like from the movies, for she had never been inside such a place in her life. The walls were decorated with old ship prints. The furniture was dark, polished mahogany and gleaming tufted leather, which reminded her of the banquettes in the Hollywood Brown Derby, where Johnny Hyde used to have a regular table for lunch.

There was a door open a crack at the far end. She went in, and found Jack Kennedy already in bed, reading the financial section of *The New York Times*. To her surprise, he was wearing glasses, which he instantly took off. There was a bottle of champagne in an ice bucket on the bedside table. He poured her a glass as she sat down beside him. "I guess I'm not going to get dinner?" she said sweetly. "I'd have ordered a club sandwich before I left if I'd known."

"Are you hungry?"

"A girl likes to get fed. I can remember when the only time

I ever got a decent meal was on a date. I used to eat enough to last me for days!"

"Actually, there's food in the living room."

She went into the living room, where a table had been prepared, picked up a shrimp cocktail and brought it back to the bedroom. She sat down again on the bed beside Jack and ate the shrimps carefully, dipping each one in the cocktail sauce by its tail, leaning forward so as not to drip anything on her dress. She offered one to Jack, but he shook his head.

There was a part of her that would have preferred to start the evening with dinner, candlelight, and conversation, but she had been around long enough to know that some men had to fuck before they could eat or talk. Jack Kennedy was obviously one of them.

She emptied her champagne glass in one gulp, then leaned over and kissed him, driving her tongue deep into his mouth.

She felt his hands behind her, tugging at the zipper of her dress, but she pushed them away. She wanted things *her* way this time! Pulling back the covers, she unfastened his robe; then, kicking off her shoes, she got up on the bed, pulled her dress up as far as it would go, and lowered herself onto him, her knees pressed against his slim waist. She held his wrists, so that all he could do was lie flat, while she controlled her own movements. It excited her, the feeling that *she* was fucking *him*, making love at her own pace, to satisfy her own needs, *using* him! All the more exciting somehow because he was naked while she was fully dressed, stockings, earrings, dress, fur stole, and all—the opposite of the days when she had to take off her clothes for men who didn't do more than unzip themselves, and sometimes insisted she do even that for them.

She heard him groan harshly, felt him throb inside her, and slowed down, holding him back. "Not yet, not yet," she told him, conscious that it was a command, not a plea—then, when she was ready, she plunged deeply down, felt him come, and let herself go, eyes closed, head back, with a cry that was like a howl of pain, and certainly audible all the way down the hall, if not to the lobby.

"*Jesus!*" he said. He sounded awestruck—as well he might be, she thought; nobody got sex like *that* every day, not even Jack Kennedy!

She stretched out her arms luxuriously. It had been even better than it was the first time, in California. She felt great—and *really* hungry now. Reluctantly she lifted herself off him. She stood up, unzipped her dress and let it fall to the floor, then went to the bathroom and slipped into one of the hotel's terry-cloth robes. She looked at herself in the full-length mirror, makeup a disaster, hair tousled, stockings wrinkled. "My God, I'm a mess!" she moaned.

Jack appeared in the doorway, wearing his silk robe, a drink in one hand, a glass of champagne for her in the other. "You don't look a mess to me," he said.

"You're sweet, but I know a mess when I see it."

"Tell me," he said. "When you closed your eyes, just before you came, what were you thinking about?"

She knew what he wanted to ask was, "*Who* were you thinking about?" which is what men always wanted to know, and women, too, if she was going to be honest about it. "I was thinking that you were the best, sugar," she said, looking him right in the eye.

The answer to the question he hadn't dared to ask would have surprised him, and a lot of other people as well. When she made love, it was, more often than not, her ex-husband, Jim Dougherty, she thought of. She had been the most virginal of brides, at sixteen appallingly innocent and uninstructed, but Jim, unimaginative as he was in most ways, took the time and trouble to arouse and awaken her on the hideaway bed in their tiny "studio" apartment in Sherman Oaks, until very shortly she couldn't get enough of him, and he nearly lost his job because he was always falling asleep at work. In the end, poor Jim was to discover that he had awakened more than he bargained for, but she was always grateful to him for the gift of her own sexuality.

"Do you do this kind of thing often?" she asked, figuring she'd earned the right to ask a few questions.

He hesitated. "I don't know about 'often.' That means different things to different people."

"Doesn't Jackie mind?"

He thought about it. "Jackie and I have, ah—an under-standing." He did not say what it was.

"You mean she *doesn't* mind?" The idea puzzled her. She would have minded like hell if Joe fucked around with other women. It was unfair, considering her own behavior, but there it was.

"I didn't say Jackie doesn't *mind*." He searched for an explanation. "You know, almost everybody who's worth a damn is a bit of a fraud. Take me: I don't always feel like a senator . . ."

"I know just what you mean, honey. I don't always feel like Marilyn Monroe."

"There you are. Well, Jackie's an exception. She's the only person I know who's *exactly* what she seems to be." He paused reflectively for a moment. "No," he went on. "That's not true. My brother Bobby's another. He's a true believer."

"In what?"

"In me."

God, what she would have given to have somebody who believed in her like that! The people who loved her most always wanted her to be somebody else—like Joe, with his dream of her becoming a housewife . . . Still, it wasn't Bobby she was interested in. "What's Jackie like?" she asked.

"Well, the two of you are quite different. . . ."

She could tell he hoped that was the end of it, but she wasn't about to let him off the hook. "How?"

"She's—ah—slimmer than you."

"I meant in bed."

There was a long, unwilling silence. She could read in Jack's face that he had gone as far as he was willing to go—farther than he had wanted to, in fact. At any moment, he was going to start resenting her because he'd answered her questions, so she gave him a kiss on the cheek, then put her arms around him and held him tightly for a few moments until he relaxed again.

Having spent most of her childhood in houses where people hardly ever touched each other, she could never have enough kissing or hugging. They sat down at the table, facing each other. She rubbed her foot against his, enjoying the touch of flesh against flesh, picked up a piece of cold chicken with her fingers and bit into it as if she hadn't eaten in days, while Jack tore small pieces off his roll. He helped himself to a slice of ham, carefully trimmed off the fat, and cut it into small pieces, all exactly the same size. She wiped the mayonnaise off her mouth. "You're a picky eater," she said. "No wonder you're so thin."

"I'm not hungry. When I am, I eat, I promise you."

"I'll bet you don't. I'm an orphanage girl, see? I never wait for the next meal because I'm never sure there's going to *be* a next meal." She made herself a sandwich and bit into it with satisfaction. "It drives them *crazy* at Fox when they see me eat," she said between mouthfuls. "They're always afraid I'll get too fat to fit into my costumes! You know how I plan to spend my old age?"

He shook his head.

"I'm going to let myself *go*. Eat whatever I want, let myself get as fat as a pig. I'm going to be big, fat, and sloppy, and not a bit ashamed of it. I've got it all worked out, see—I'm going to have a *great* old age. How about you?"

"I haven't given it much thought, to tell you the truth."

"I think about it all the time." She finished her sandwich and took a pickle off his plate—she loved to eat off other people's plates, as if what they had must always taste better than what was on her own.

"I want a big house," she said. "Somewhere on the sea, Malibu, or maybe Santa Barbara. Oh, and lots of dogs. And a cook who can make great Mexican food, enchiladas, burritos, chicken mole, stuff like that. . . . I'm going to sit in the sun and read all the books I should have read before, or maybe take up painting, or something like that. . . ."

He laughed. "I can't imagine you that way."

"I can." She held out her glass so he could refill it. "Old age," she said. She sipped her champagne, wrinkling her nose at the bubbles. She leaned forward, chin resting on her fist, looking into his eyes adoringly from close up, as if she wanted to pretend that they were an ordinary couple, at breakfast perhaps, or eating dinner at home while he filled her in on his day. "Talk to me about something else. Talk to me about what *you're* doing. Talk to me about anything but the movie business." She shuddered briefly. "Or sports."

"Most of my time lately has been spent arguing with Bobby," he said. "And my father." He looked glum. "About Senator McCarthy." He put the full spin on the word "Senator," intoning it with a respect made more pronounced by his Harvard/Boston accent.

"*Joe* McCarthy? I *hate* that guy."

He looked a little pissed off. Clearly, he didn't want to waste his time talking politics with her. She pinched his leg hard with her toes—she had always been proud of the strength of her toes—and he winced. "Don't crap out on me, Jack," she said. "I'm not Jackie. I'm not some bimbo either."

He had the grace to look embarrassed. "I never said you were."

"No, but you *thought* it."

"Okay, okay," he said, holding up his hand in surrender. "Why don't you like Senator McCarthy?"

"Do you?"

He looked thoughtful, his handsome young face suddenly dark. "Not much, frankly. I know he's a drunk, and I suspect he's a fraud. And probably a homosexual as well. You didn't answer my question."

"He hurts people. I know plenty of people in Hollywood who have had their lives destroyed by McCarthy, or his followers. . . . *Good* people, a lot of them."

"Some of them may be Communists, you know."

"Oh, 'Communist,' that's just a word, Jack. The people who've lost their jobs weren't building bombs or anything. They were acting, or writing scripts, or composing music, and now they're finished. No jobs, no money, no hope."

She could tell this wasn't the way he had thought his evening was going to be, but she didn't care. In Hollywood, the anti-Communist witch hunt was led by men like Darryl Zanuck, Harry Cohn, Jack Warner—the bosses—who were not above using it to pay off old scores. Anticommunism, in her opinion, was just another way of tightening the screws on the workers, the little people, among whom she counted herself.

"You're wrong," he said. "Communism *is* a threat. I'm not crazy about Senator McCarthy personally, but that doesn't mean a real threat to freedom doesn't exist." He didn't seem comfortable with this piece of rhetoric. She wondered if he was quoting from his father.

"My father and my brother Bobby think he's fighting the good fight. So, ah, do most of the voters in the commonwealth of Massachusetts. Bobby would follow Senator McCarthy into the fires of hell. Which he may get a chance to do, since just between the two of us, McCarthy's through. My main concern, frankly, is to get Bobby off the McCarthy ship before it, ah, goes down."

"Bobby doesn't want to abandon ship?"

"Exactly. He wants to go down with the captain. A lousy idea. I should know. When PT-109 went down, I was in the water and swimming for my life as fast as everybody else. Of course, Bobby never saw action in the war, so he has a higher regard for heroism than I do."

She was surprised. "But you *were* a hero," she protested. "I read all about it in the *Reader's Digest*."

He shrugged. "I was run over by a Jap destroyer. It was like a traffic accident between a sports car and a truck. When General MacArthur heard about it, he told the Navy to court-martial me. Then Dad got into the act, so I got a medal instead."

"You *did* save your men's lives."

"Yes. I'm not sure they *deserved* to be saved, frankly. We wouldn't have been rammed by the destroyer if they'd been on their toes. Well," he went on philosophically, "that's life, right? You get made a hero for doing something stupid; you get killed for doing something smart."

"You're not going to let Bobby go down with McCarthy, are you? Your own brother?"

Jack looked a little startled. He took family relationships seriously—they were perhaps the only thing he was serious about—but without sentimentality. "I'm going to persuade Bobby to jump ship," he said. "Counsel on the McClellan subcommittee is what I had in mind for him."

It was on the tip of her tongue to ask if the entire Senate was Irish, but she held herself back. She was curious about politics and didn't want to distract him. She nodded, and went on eating the potato salad with her fingers. "This McClellan subcommittee," she repeated dreamily, "what do they do?"

"They're, ah, going to be investigating labor unions. Hopefully, Bobby can make a name for himself there without being involved with people like Roy Cohn." The distaste on his face was evident—for a young man, she thought, he could look surprisingly patrician when he chose, and he was obviously more willing to show his contempt for Cohn than for a fellow senator.

"Gosh!" she said. "What's wrong with labor unions? Which ones is Bobby going after?"

"Does it matter?"

"It does to me. I bet you and your brother have never been in a union? I'm a Screen Actors Guild member myself. I probably know more about unions than Bobby does."

"Very likely. I'm sure he'd be happy to have you instruct him, though." He put his hand on her thigh. She noticed it was placed so that he could take a quick peek at his watch. She would have to find a way to get him to take his watch off in the future, she decided.

"I don't think SAG figures in Bobby's plans," he said. "It's the Teamsters he's after. These fellows Beck and Hoffa."

She shuddered, despite the warmth of his hand and the touch of his fingers moving up her thigh. "I know all about the Teamsters," she said.

He poured himself a demitasse. He stirred it, his eyes on her. "I know they're rough. David Leman warned me about that too. But the more Bobby tells me about them, the more I like it. I need an issue. This could be the one."

"Is David involved in this? I thought he did PR?"

"He does a lot of things. My father trusts him. So do I. He's a very bright guy, with extraordinary connections, not just here but in England. And Israel. . . ."

"David is a smart cookie," she said. "I *like* him."

He raised an eyebrow. "No kidding?" he asked, cheerful again. "How much?"

She gave a sultry look. "He's *very* sexy," she said, eyes half closed as if she were thinking about him. "I really *dig* guys with a mustache. . . ." She shivered in mock ecstasy, arms folded tightly across her breasts. "Clark Gable is my *ideal*."

"You think David looks like Clark Gable?"

"Mm."

"That's funny. Jackie's always saying the same thing. . . . I can't see it myself. Anyway, David's Jewish."

"Honey, some of the sexiest guys I've known were Jewish. Jewish is very sexy, believe me. A Jewish guy who looks like Clark Gable. . . ." She gave a little squeal of delight at the thought.

A look of frank annoyance crossed Jack's face. "I don't get the impression that Maria—*Mrs*. Leman—shares your opinion about David's sexiness."

"That's marriage for you." She giggled, then poked him in the ribs. "You're *jealous!*" she cried.

"The hell I am."

"You *are!* I'm surprised, you know? I didn't think you were the type."

"I'm not . . . well, maybe a bit . . . David and I go back a long time."

"Oh, sweetheart, don't worry. I *like* a man to be jealous."

"You *do?* What about Joe? You're always complaining about the fact that he's jealous."

"Hon-ee, he's my *husband!* A jealous *husband* is no fun at all. A jealous lover is a whole different story." She gave him a kiss. "Anyway, forget I told you David looks like Gable."

He put down the coffee cup. His hand had moved up her leg to the point where he could touch her pubic hair. He stroked it gently, while she played the game of resisting him as long as possible, pretending that she didn't feel a thing. "How late can you stay?" he asked.

"I ought to be back in my hotel by one. After that, my story for the evening wears kind of thin."

"And that matters?"

"It does to *me*," she said firmly.

His fingers were deep inside her now, stroking gently, then harder, until she was so wet that he could slip three fingers into her cunt, while his index finger slowly penetrated her asshole. She still sat there, smiling like a proper little girl at a tea party (not that she had ever been to any tea parties as a child). Then, quite suddenly, her poise deserted her, and pulling off her robe, she dropped to her knees and took him in her mouth, groaning with excitement. He drew her to her feet, and for what seemed a very long time they stood pressed close against each other, naked, their robes at their feet.

They were kissing so hard that neither of them could speak, but he broke away from her at last to take a breath and said, "In the bedroom. I can't do it standing up, not with my back."

She followed him in, let him lie down and make himself comfortable, then lay down beside him, her legs entwined with his. "God, we fit beautifully," she said. "We were made for each other." She nibbled his ear, turning over on her side so he could enter her more comfortably, her hand on his prick, guiding him in but letting him do the work this time, at his pace. "I want to spend the night with you," she whispered.

"I'll bet you look really cute when you're asleep, all curled up in bed."

"Listen," he said in a husky voice, his breath hot against her face, trying to get it right this time. "There'll be plenty of time for nights together. All the time in the world. We're going to have a long affair, you and I."

She laughed softly, settling into the rhythm of his love-making. He was holding her hard, his fingers dug deep into her flesh, and she knew he would leave bruises; she bruised easily. But the strange thing about husbands, she had long ago concluded, was that however jealous they were, they seldom noticed such things, presumably because they no longer bothered to look.

"A love affair?" she asked softly. "Is that what we're having?"

And in a voice that seemed almost surprised, as if it were the last thing he had expected to come of the evening, he said: "Why, yes, I think so."

She thought so too.

4

THE KING COLE BAR OF THE ST. REGIS WAS NEVER MY favorite place for lunch. It was as dark and claustral as Radames's tomb in *Aida,* and, on that summer Saturday afternoon, almost as empty. Marilyn had called me to ask if she could buy me lunch to thank me for having "rescued" her, though her real intention, I suspected, was to pump me about Jack. She had apparently had enough of hiding away upstairs in her suite, and somehow made the discovery that in the last booth, she was almost completely safe from prying eyes. That and the prevailing gloom were enough to protect her from her fans, or the merely curious, though she took the additional precaution of wearing sunglasses and a scarf over her hair.

Dalí was seated in solitary, eccentric splendor by the door,
if a man accompanied by a pet cheetah can be described as
"solitary," and to my surprise, Marilyn giggled as we walked
past him. "Some great painter!" she whispered to me as we sat
down. "A couple of days ago, he was telling me I was the most
beautiful woman in the world and he was going to paint me as
Venus; today he can't even tell it's *me* because I'm wearing
a scarf on my head!" She looked glum. "The cheetah didn't
recognize me either."

"Perhaps it did."

She shook her head. "No. It didn't even open its eyes."

For a moment I thought Marilyn was going to cry. Most
of her sadder stories, I was to learn, involved animals—poor
Tippy, or Mugsy, the part collie who pined away in sadness
after the breakup of Marilyn's marriage to Jim Dougherty, or
Johnny Hyde's Chihuahua, who was taken away from her after
his death, or later Hugo, who stayed with Arthur Miller after
the divorce.

"Forget about Dalí," I said. "Forget about the cat. I hear the
picture is going to be great."

Admittedly, I was trying to cheer her up, but I was also telling her the truth. *The Seven Year Itch* had been a big hit on
Broadway. Getting Wilder to direct it was a rare stroke of genius for the 20th Century-Fox management, as was casting Tom
Ewell, who had played the part on stage, as Marilyn's male
lead. After four years of mostly mediocre films and dumb-
blonde roles in Hollywood musicals, she was at last getting a
chance to do something good, and by all accounts her rushes
had been terrific so far.

"The picture? Yeah, I think it's going to be pretty good. I
mean, it's not a *total* piece of crap, like the last one."

I was about to say I had enjoyed *How to Marry a Millionaire*, but she put her index finger against my lips. "*Don't* tell
me you liked it, please, David, or I'll lose my respect for you.
Do you know what Bosley Crowther wrote about me? In *The
New York Times?*" Her eyes misted over. " 'Miss Monroe's
wriggling and squirming are embarrassing to behold.' "

I patted her hand. "The hell with him!" I said.

She shook her head. "He was right! I hated it as much as
Mr. Crowther. Maybe more. But I knew *The Seven Year Itch*
was right for me, I just *knew* it somehow. . . . Zanuck didn't

want to let me have it, and Charlie Feldman wanted me to do another musical, so when I heard Charlie was going to produce it himself, I said to myself, 'Well, this is *it*, honey, you're going to change his mind for him if it's the *last* thing you do.' "

I stared at my menu as if it required my undivided attention. Jack had wondered why Marilyn was fucking Feldman, and when he asked her, she gave him a touching story about how she felt sorry for him. I suspected that she had just told me the truth. Feldman had had it in his power to give her the part of a lifetime, and she had been determined to do anything to make sure she got it. It is a tribute to Marilyn's charm and air of innocence that I was surprised—and faintly disappointed.

Even in the dim light, she glowed. She was wearing a pale blue dress with a small matching jacket thrown over her shoulders, a single row of pearls around her neck. There was nothing sexy about her outfit—indeed, it looked as if she might have chosen it to please Joe DiMaggio, whose demand that she wear more modest clothes with high necklines and full skirts had made the news several months ago, giving rise to jokes and cartoons that must have been a good deal more embarrassing to him than seeing his wife in public in low-cut dresses with bare shoulders. Not, of course, that any of this mattered. If DiMaggio supposed that Marilyn's sexuality could be concealed by anything short of a tarpaulin, he was, I thought, an even more deluded husband than most.

While we ate, Marilyn and I chatted happily about all the people we knew in Hollywood. Of course, as a beautiful blond photographer's model and, later, a starlet, she had been taken everywhere and met everyone, long before she was famous. She had been an acting pupil of Charles Laughton's, the mistress (briefly), of John Huston, a sometime date of A&P billionaire Huntington Hartford. In her brief stint at Columbia, she was perhaps the only beautiful starlet on the lot at whom Harry Cohn *didn't* make a pass, because he discovered, by accident, that Marilyn had been raised as a Christian Scientist, the religion to which his wife Rose had converted and in which he himself had become a believer.

Between the summer of 1945, when she was discovered by an army photographer on the production line of the Radio Plane Company in Van Nuys working as a dope sprayer on target drones, to the summer of 1952, when the news that she posed nude for the famous "Golden Girl" calendar made her nationally famous, Marilyn met practically everyone who mattered in and around the movie industry. The range of her acquaintanceship was astounding, from Groucho Marx, who had given her her first real break in *Love Happy* (and pinched her ass so hard one day on the set that she screamed), to Arthur Miller, who held her toe during a soulful late-night conversation in Charlie Feldman's living room, and urged her to read Carl Sandburg's biography of Lincoln.

"I've always thought Arthur was a good playwright, but a rather dull fellow."

She chewed her lip for a moment. "Well, maybe he's a *little* bit boring, okay," she admitted reluctantly, "but he's so brilliant, and *dignified*. I could really fall for a man like that, I think. . . ."

She sounded sincere. A baseball player, a United States senator, and a distinguished playwright! I wondered what on earth attracted Marilyn to three such different men; then it occurred to me that like her, each of them was a star in his own field.

"I tried to explain to Jack why I hate Joe McCarthy," she said. "I should have mentioned that it's people like Arthur that McCarthy's talking about when he rants and raves about Communists. I told him how much I hate everything McCarthy stands for."

It was on the tip of my tongue to say that Jack stood for many of the same things, only in a smoother way, but discretion was the better part of valor. "How did Jack take that?" I asked.

"Well, he *listened*. I think he sort of agrees, in a wishy-washy kind of way, you know? It's really his brother—Bobby?—he says, who's the witch hunter of the family."

"A word of advice," I warned her gently, becoming the first of many people who would instruct Marilyn over the years on how to please the Kennedy family and handle her role as Jack's mistress-in-chief. "If you're planning on seeing more of Jack, don't call Bobby a 'witch hunter.' "

"What should I call him?"

"A 'concerned patriot' would be okay. For practical purposes, just stick to 'Bobby' without any editorializing."

"Well, okay. Jack told me he's trying to get Bobby to aim for the Teamsters instead. Big mistake, I told him."

"*Did* you?" I looked at her more closely. Despite the wide-open, innocent eyes and the glamorous face, this was no dumb blonde. Of course, I reminded myself, she had been Joe Schenck's mistress, not to speak of Johnny Hyde's and Charlie Feldman's. These were hard, successful, self-made men—*ganze machers,* to use the phrase by which they would describe themselves. Marilyn's mentors had been tough guys, and there were few subjects they were more knowledgeable about than labor racketeering.

"I know the Teamsters are tough," I said. "But Jack's a senator. I don't think there's much real risk."

"*I* do." She shivered.

As it happens, this was an example of woman's intuition to which I should have paid attention. I saw my role, unfortunately, as calming down Marilyn, not carrying her warning to Jack. "His father knows all about the Teamsters," I pointed out. "The Old Man financed a lot of the liquor business during Prohibition. And who do you think drove the trucks? Teamsters. They don't scare him a bit. Believe me, if there was any real danger, Joe would be the first to warn Jack and Bobby off. The Old Man talks tough, but he loves his kids so much it's scary."

"God, I'd *love* to be a member of a family like that!" she said sadly. There were tears in her eyes.

"No you wouldn't," I said. "Tight families aren't necessarily happy ones."

"I'd settle for an *un*happy family, David."

"Surely not?"

"Oh, honey! Christmas at the orphanage! You had to be there. Believe me, I'd have taken any family that would have me. Who wants a Christmas stocking from the city of Los Angeles?"

We sat in companionable silence for a few moments, holding hands lightly. I would have given anything to fill Jack's place, and did not entirely rule out the possibility if I played my cards right, but in the meantime, I was content to be in Marilyn's company. She had a kind of genius for making even total strangers share her moods, particularly when she talked about her unhappy childhood. The fact that much of what she said was untrue didn't matter—you still had tears welling from your eyes to match her own.

She dabbed briefly at her eyes. "I bet Jack's father would like me."

"No doubt about it," I said. "Like" was not the word!

"I wish we'd met earlier." There was a wistful expression on her face. "Jack would have been a lot better off married to me than to Jackie," she said firmly. "Of course, it could still happen. . . . Think how beautiful our children would be. . . ."

Smart as she was on the subject of the Teamsters, this was clearly an area in which she suffered from delusions. "Marilyn," I said. "Jack's Catholic."

She looked at me blankly.

"Catholics don't get divorced."

"They don't?"

"Not if they want to stay in the Church. Certainly not if they're going to run for the presidency, which Jack is."

"Oh." She looked disappointed, but not heartbroken. She was a child of the movies, for whom illusion was substance, which explains, I think, why she so often stubbed her toe on the hard edges of life.

I glanced at my watch. She was beginning to show small signs of restlessness—the nervous plucking of her fingers at the seams of her dress, the quick looks toward the door as if she were expecting someone, or hoping to get away before someone came in. "Where's your husband?" I asked.

She looked at me vaguely. "Who?"

"Your husband. Joe."

"Oh, *Joe.*" She thought for a moment. "I think he went to Yankee Stadium for some kind of award."

It came to me that there was a major ceremony honoring DiMaggio taking place even as we spoke. "I'm surprised he didn't want you there," I said.

"He did." Her expression suggested that hell could have frozen over before she'd appear beside him in Yankee Stadium. "Actually, that reminds me of something I wanted to ask you. . . ." She put her face close to mine, lips slightly parted, a look of desperate, pleading need in her eyes.

"We have a location shoot tonight," she said. "One in the morning? Outside the Trans-Lux, at Fifty-first and Lexington?"

I nodded. Everybody in New York knew this, since it had been on the front page of the *Daily News*.

"I'm supposed to be standing on a subway grating, you know? A train goes by and my skirt gets blown up?"

I had met Billy Wilder at "21" a couple of nights before and he had told me about his plans for the shot.

"The problem is," Marilyn went on, "I kind of promised Joe it wasn't going to happen."

I must have looked blank, because she gave me an irritable glance. "Well, he was upset, so I told him they had rewritten the scene so all that happens is my skirt gets blown about a little in the breeze. . . ."

"And that's *not* what's going to happen?"

She shook her head. "Billy's got a wind machine under the grating. My skirt's going to be above my shoulders when he turns it on. I'm going to be wearing a white pleated skirt and white panties. I had to give my bush a fresh platinum bleach job so it won't show through."

I sat silently for a moment, trying to picture this, then trying to put it out of my mind. "You think Joe is going to be angry then?" I asked in a strangled voice.

"Oh *boy!* Is he ever! I was counting on his not coming to see it, but now he's *insisting* on being there. . . . I guess I really screwed up this time."

"I'm not sure what I can do about it." I hoped Marilyn didn't have me in mind to play the peacemaker with DiMaggio. I didn't fancy the task of explaining that his wife had lied to him, or that he was going to be sharing his intimate knowledge of her crotch with millions of moviegoers, as well as photographers from every major daily and magazine.

"Billy promised me he'd keep the public away—that's why he's shooting at one a.m.—but I don't trust the studio PR people. They want a big media event, see, so I think they'll probably ignore Billy and let the public watch from real close. . . ."

Nothing was more certain. If I had worked for a studio, that's exactly what I would have done. I would have paid off the cops too, to move the police barriers closer to the action. What you wanted was a controlled riot, to make the headlines.

"The more people there, and the closer they are, the madder Joe will be," Marilyn said. "He's not going to be happy about his fans staring at my ass from close up."

"Not many husbands would be."

Her eyes turned cold. "Look, he has his profession, I have mine. *Fuck* what he thinks! Only I have to live with him, so what I want you to do is find a way to have the crowds keep a decent distance, okay?"

"That may not be easy."

"*Please*, David! Just do your *best*, all right? There must be *somebody* you can talk to?"

"The mayor. The police commissioner. And I shall, to both of them. But there are still going to be big crowds. I'll do what I can, I promise. I may need to spread some money to the cops, by the way. Not much, but some."

"Whatever," she said. "I've got to run. I've got to see Whitey Snyder, my makeup man."

She stood up and leaned over to give me a kiss on the lips. "Thank you, David," she said. "You're a sweetheart." She left the table, with that walk that made the modesty of her dress seem pointless.

She stopped and turned, a couple of tables away. "Whatever it costs," she called out, "send the bill to Milton Greene, at Marilyn Monroe Productions." Then she was on her way again, undulating past the row of banquettes in the complete silence that she could bring about in any public place.

It was the first time I had heard of "Marilyn Monroe Productions," or her connection to Milton Greene, and all of a sudden it occurred to me that she might have even bigger things in mind for the future than an affair with Jack Kennedy.

Because of his profession I had vaguely expected Whitey Snyder to be a homosexual, but to my surprise, he turned out to be a bulky, silver-haired, middle-aged family man, dressed in California casual clothes and wearing a massive brushed-gold ID bracelet that—he told me proudly—Marilyn had given him. He was friendly, easygoing, and ferociously protective of Marilyn—one of the first of that small group of employee-friends and loyalists who stuck up for her, and *with* her, to the very end.

And beyond, in Whitey's case. For it was poor Whitey who would go over to the mortuary the night before her funeral with a fifth of gin in his jacket pocket to see him through the ordeal of making her up to be laid out in her coffin in the pale lime-green Pucci dress she had bought for the last week in her life she was ever happy.

Whitey introduced himself to me as we were standing together near the camera, on Fifty-first Street, Marilyn having told him that I was "one of the good guys." I asked him how it was going. He shrugged. "Usually the director is ready and Marilyn ain't," he said. "This time, it's the opposite. Marilyn's ready and the director ain't. At the last minute the cops started to move the barriers back, because the crowd was too close."

The crowd still seemed to me to be pretty close, as well as huge and raucous, but I was glad to have wrought any improvement, however small. "Is it a tough picture?" I asked, conscious as I said it that I had been away from the movie business too long. It was like asking a combat infantryman if this was a tough war. All movies were hell—it was just a matter of degree.

Whitey gave me a nervous smile, showing big white teeth. "It beats *River of No Return*," he said. "We were on location way up north. It rained every day, Marilyn got a cold *and* broke a leg, and I had to do her makeup in a log cabin, while we both froze our asses off. Now *that* was a tough movie. Otto Preminger was the director, which says it all. . . ."

"Did he give you a hard time?"

"I'm a union man," Whitey said proudly. "He couldn't have given me a hard time if his life depended on it."

I wondered how much of Marilyn's knowledge about unions came from Whitey. "Tell me," I said, "no connection, but as a union man, what do you think of the Teamsters?"

Whitey looked at me a little suspiciously, wondering, I suppose, if I was some kind of fink. "They get results for their members. Nothing wrong with that, is there?"

"Nothing at all." It was a pity, I thought, that we couldn't introduce Whitey to Jack, who held the typical liberal view that labor unions were the blue-collar wing of the Democratic party.

We were standing shoulder to shoulder around the camera and the banks of lights; on three sides of us the crowds of onlookers and photographers pressed up against the police barricades and the broad, sweaty backs of the cops holding them in check. Only in New York City can you produce a crowd at one in the morning, as Wilder should have known. If *my* advice had been asked, I would have told him to shoot the scene at nine in the morning instead. New Yorkers never pay attention to anything, not even Marilyn with her skirt above her head, when they're on their way to work.

There was a stir down the street, where the stars' trailers were parked, the hum of their air conditioners almost drowned out by the roar of the big generators that powered the lights. Whitey noticed and made his way swiftly into the dark.

A moment later, Marilyn appeared in the bright pool of light in front of the camera, a figure so dazzling that to this day I can remember every detail—the white pleated skirt, the open-toe, sting-back, high-heeled white shoes, the gleaming platinum-blond hair.

She smiled at the crowd and waved timidly, as if to say, "Yes, it's me." There was a moment of silence, as if they couldn't believe their eyes; then the crowd went wild, cheering, whistling, shouting out her name, pushing and shoving against the barricades until the cops had to turn around to face them, swinging their nightsticks threateningly.

Yet the people weren't in any way hostile, you could sense that. Marilyn somehow represented their dream, the symbol of all the unattainable things that ordinary people want—sexiness, glamour, fame, money, happiness—or perhaps she was the living proof that an ordinary person could achieve all those things. Oh, sure, she was a sex symbol, but she was much *more* than that. Rita Hayworth was a sex symbol, Jean Harlow had been a sex symbol, but Marilyn was the girl-next-door who has grown up to be a star, the woman you've always wanted if you're a man, always dreamed of being if you're a woman. Marilyn's sexiness was only part of her appeal—she was, in her own way, a piece of that amorphous national yearning we call "the American Dream."

There was nothing phony about it either. Marilyn loved the crowd, the crowd loved Marilyn—symbiosis in its finest form. She pirouetted in the Klieg lights; because she was a big girl, people tended to forget how graceful she could be. She had worked hard to become a dancer, having no natural gift for it, and the fact that she had succeeded was one of the reasons why she never doubted that she could become a serious actress.

They gave her a round of applause. She blew a kiss out into the hot, sultry Manhattan night and they went wild.

Behind her in the shadows stood a few figures. I searched in vain for her husband, only to find him standing beside me, having been relegated to the area for privileged spectators. He looked angry and out of place, upset at being pushed aside. My heart did not bleed for him. After all, if he had been playing baseball, he would hardly have allowed Marilyn to stand beside him at bat during a game.

In the three years since his retirement, he had lost nothing of his athlete's build—it was easy to see why Marilyn had found him physically attractive—but he was trembling with anger at the size of the crowd. The muscles in his cheeks were working hard, as if he were chewing on his fury like a cud, his eyes flat, dark pools of anger. His muscular tension was so intense that his hands were shaking like an old man's. I moved a step farther away—if he was going to hit anyone, I didn't want it to be me.

To my surprise, I found myself standing next to a child, a boy of ten or eleven—I'm bad about children's ages, having none of my own. I couldn't help wondering what in God's name he was doing out in the street at this time of night, or how he managed to find his way into the space reserved for the privileged like DiMaggio and myself. He was a slightly built lad, his face at once innocent and intensely serious, wearing a baseball jacket with his name—"Timmy"—embroidered on the front. He carried a red notebook, and his eyes were fixed on Marilyn with an intensity that was, if anything, greater than DiMaggio's, and every bit as possessive.

Marilyn, notoriously a bundle of nerves at work, seemed relaxed, perhaps because showing her legs was a lot easier than remembering her lines. And of course, she was turned on by the crowd.

She stepped beyond the lights, turned as if she had just come out of the theater with Tom Ewell, hesitated for a second, found her mark on the first take, then burst into giggles as the breeze from the subway rose through the grating she was standing on and made her skirt billow above her knees. She pushed it down with a demure gesture. There was a chorus of whistles and cheers, fairly subdued, as if the fans had been expecting more. Beside me, DiMaggio breathed a sigh of relief.

There followed the usual interminable wait as Whitey repaired Marilyn's makeup and people talked to each other over walkie-talkies. The lights were killed, readjusted, tested, killed again, while Marilyn waited patiently. Wilder hovered over her, talking earnestly with his hands. Once or twice he acted out the movement he wanted—ending with her knees bent in a little crouch. Next to me, Timmy scribbled furiously in his notebook. I recognized in him—in juvenile form—the obsessive quality of the born "fan."

The lights came on, Marilyn and Ewell went back under the theater marquee, the clapper-boy held up his board, Wilder grinned mischievously from his seat beside the camera, and she swept through the scene again—only this time there was a gale-force wind from the grating.

She pirouetted quickly while her skirt, like a spinnaker that has been blown out of control, rose to shoulder height. She put her head back and laughed, fighting to pull the skirt down, but at the same time, sensualist that she was, obviously enjoying the rush of air on that breathlessly hot summer night.

The crowd went mad—cheers, frenzied whistling, applause. Marilyn responded to it, twirling like a ballerina, then crouching low to regain control over the skirt, just as Wilder had shown her. Caught up in the crowd's sexual excitement—and, who knows, her own as well, for she was not only at the center of it all but *creating* it—Marilyn whirled round and round in the light. Tom Ewell (who knew when he had been hopelessly upstaged) hovered beside her, bashful and admiring.

She was to repeat that shot more than thirty times that night—the last take was at 4:15 a.m.! Wilder had the wind machine cranked higher and higher, until Marilyn's skirt was lifted straight up. Whitey, it must be said, had done his work well and even in the glare of the Kliegs and the spots, you couldn't see the shadow of Marilyn's pubic triangle at all, though the cheeks of her ass were clearly defined, and from some angles—the rear particularly—she might as well have been naked.

This was the famous image that would be enlarged into a cutout figure one hundred feet high and hoisted above Loew's State Theater on Broadway, the life-sized one that Jack Kennedy would have placed on the ceiling above his hospital bed when he underwent his back operation a couple of months later, and the one that would appear over the years on T-shirts, mugs, and souvenir kitsch all over the world—probably the best-remembered photograph ever taken of Marilyn and a permanent symbol of the national libido.

At once symbol and hauntingly real, Marilyn managed to convey the notion that sex was innocent fun. Not many people can do that, and that night she put her heart and soul into it, right there in front of the camera on Lexington and Fifty-first. I couldn't take my eyes off her. The people in the crowd of spectators must have felt something similar, for gradually their rowdiness died down, as if they, too, were communicating with their most intimate fantasies. I knew at that moment that I was in love with her, and also knew it was hopeless.

By the time I turned around to look at DiMaggio's face, he was gone.

He had left before Marilyn really got into the swing of the thing, doing take after take for the camera with the abandon of a stripper.

DiMaggio missed the best takes.

I thought that was probably just as well.

It was nearly five in the morning when I finally returned home. I had told Maria that Billy Wilder had invited me to watch the shooting of his big scene with Marilyn—she had expressed no interest in accompanying me, which was just as well.

A light sleeper, she woke as I stretched out in bed, having dropped my sweat-sodden clothes on the floor. "What on earth time is it, darling?" she mumbled.

"Late." I was exhausted by the heat and the emotion, yet not at all sleepy. Without any conscious decision I put my arms around her and stroked her until she gave a small, sleepy moan, not so much of arousal, I suspect, as of surprise. Maria was a woman who liked—demanded—a certain routine to her life, even in its most intimate aspects. Sex at five in the morning was not part of the routine. I didn't care. I had seldom felt such an urgent need. My erection was so stiff that it was painful. I plunged it into her from behind with a sigh of relief.

"My goodness, David," Maria said with a certain amount of interest, "what's gotten *into* you?"

She moved farther over onto her side, to make herself more comfortable—we had been married long enough to know every curve of each other's bodies, every requirement of position, and to be bored by the knowledge. She began to moan more urgently, surrendering to her own feelings, or fantasies perhaps, of who knows whom, while in my mind, my eyes tightly closed even in the dark, I saw Marilyn's bright hair flashing in the lights as she pirouetted, her skirt flying, and imagined I felt in my hands her pale thighs and full buttocks. . . .

It was past ten when I woke to the ring of the telephone. Maria, I noticed, had picked my clothes up off the floor—a peace offering of some kind, for she did not usually bother with that kind of domestic detail. I assumed it was my secretary calling to ask where I was on a Monday morning, but a vaguely familiar voice—Whitey's, I realized—said, "You'd better get over here right away, Mr. Leman."

"What? Where?"

"The St. Regis. There's been a problem. Marilyn's asking for you."

Marilyn's suite looked as if a small tornado had struck it. A couple of chairs had been knocked over and there were shards of glass on the floor. Volume I of Carl Sandburg's *Abraham Lincoln* was propped on the windowsill, the pages open to dry, as if it had been soaked somehow. There was an emptiness to the room, the hard-to-define feeling one has when someone has moved out of a place. Without even knowing what had happened, I guessed that DiMaggio had walked out on her.

She came in from the bedroom looking so unlike the sexy, glamorous star she had been last night that it was hard to believe I was seeing the same person. Every trace of glamour was gone—even her hair had lost its dazzling, golden glow and looked drab, lifeless, bleached out. She had obviously been crying. Her face was pale and puffy, the lips swollen. I couldn't see her eyes, since she was wearing big sunglasses, with lenses that were so dark she had to feel her way into the room like a blind person. I wanted to put my arms around her, but she did not look as if she wanted to be touched, even for comforting. "I know," she said in a tiny voice. "I look like shit, don't I?"

"No you don't."

"Don't try to bullshit me, David."

"You put in a hard night's work. You should be asleep."

"I enjoyed the work. It didn't start getting hard until I came home." She was sipping what looked like iced tea. Every so often, she would pick out an ice cube and press it against her lips. I've seldom seen anybody look more miserable. "I never thanked you for getting the crowd moved back last night," she said. "Not that it did any good."

"I was standing next to Joe. He didn't look happy."

"No shit." She shook her head, then leaned over and gave me a quick peck on the cheek. "I'm sorry," she said. "It isn't your fault that Joe was pissed off." She stared into space for a moment. "It isn't mine either. I was just doing my job, just the way he did when he played ball. If he doesn't like it, the hell with him, right?"

"Right." The truth is that I wasn't entirely comfortable serving as Marilyn's version of Miss Lonelyhearts, and not only because I didn't want to make a habit of it. There are few roles more stressful than that of talking to a woman you desire about the men in her life.

"He's gone back to California, you know?" she said.

I nodded. "I guessed it was something of the sort."

"Is it going to hit the papers? That would make it worse."

"I can see that would be painful for you. . . ."

She shook her head. "I was thinking of the Slugger, David. I can take it. He's all muscle, but I'm a lot tougher than he is."

I believed her. "The story isn't out yet, that I know of. It's too soon. It would help if *you* vanished for a couple of days too. They might assume the two of you have gone off for some time together."

"That's exactly what I want," she said, something of her optimism returning. "Arthur Miller told me how beautiful Connecticut was—full of little villages and old inns. . . . Do you know any?"

"Lots."

"Could you get one of your people to reserve a double room for me somewhere? As 'Mr. and Mrs. DiMaggio'?"

"I'm sure I could, but somebody would leak that to the press right away. Wouldn't an assumed name——"

She cut me off. "No." Her tone was firm. "Just *do* it, please, David, the way I want it. As a favor to me. It's asking a lot,

I know, but I don't want to use the studio people, and my own PR girl is from LA, so she couldn't find Connecticut on a map. . . ."

"Anything you say, Marilyn, but Walter Winchell will know what inn you're at in Connecticut an hour after I make that call." I don't know why it didn't occur to me that Marilyn was establishing an alibi and hoped to send the press off in the wrong direction. I hadn't learned yet how devious she could be when she wanted something badly enough.

There was a knock on the door. Whitey Snyder stuck his head in. "It's Milton Greene, Marilyn," he said. "He says he has an appointment to see you."

"Oh God, I forgot."

I got up to go, but she grabbed me by the wrist and pulled me back. "Stay," she said. "I need all the help I can get today."

I knew Greene and his bright, pretty young wife, Amy, slightly. By now I had learned that he and Marilyn were going into business together. Plenty of people in New York knew it was happening, since Greene had been obliged to seek out financing from various people on Wall Street, including my old friend Robert Dowling, who loved dabbling in the motion picture business. He had told me something about their plans, as well as the intriguing news that Arthur Miller was taking a "personal" interest. The only people of importance who remained in complete ignorance were the executives of 20th Century-Fox, whose egos were such that they could not imagine the defection of a star in the middle of a contract renegotiation, unless to a rival studio.

Greene came in, looking like a world-weary schoolboy, and we greeted each other pleasantly enough. I had worked with him on various gala dinners or dances to raise money for the Democratic party or for Israel, and had always found him an agreeable companion. He had done a photo-essay on me for *Life* magazine with which I was surprisingly gratified. Except for the fact that he had no money and had never made a picture, Marilyn could not have placed herself in more sympathetic hands.

He looked a little nervous at my presence, and I could hardly blame him. Poor man! He was only at the beginning of the long succession of lawyers, accountants, advisers, and self-appointed protectors who would push and shove to get between him and Marilyn, and very nearly put him into bankruptcy before they were through.

He glanced around the room—Marilyn had gone off to get a fresh bottle of champagne, even in distress determined to be the perfect hostess. "Joe's not here?" he asked.

I shook my head. "He went back to California."

"Uh-oh." Milton's face turned a shade paler, his eyes darker and sadder, if that was possible. Marilyn's private life always seemed about to burst the levees and flood her professional life out of sight. Separation or divorce from DiMaggio would make it hard for her to concentrate on their new company, and turn the public's attention from Marilyn the actress to Marilyn the brokenhearted love goddess. There was even a chance that breaking up with DiMaggio might diminish her popularity.

"Did she talk to you about what we're doing?" he asked me anxiously.

"I've heard a little about it, but not from her."

"They're going to go crazy at Twentieth when they find out."

"No question. Zanuck is going to come after you with both barrels. Do you have a good lawyer?"

He shrugged as if to say that even the best lawyer in the world wasn't going to offer much protection. Greene's best bet was to hope that the studio would let Marilyn get away with it rather than risk a long legal battle with America's favorite blonde.

"If you need help . . ." I offered.

He nodded. "Oy, do I need help," he said quietly.

"This DiMaggio thing will blow over, don't you worry." I was willing to say anything, however foolish, to cheer him up.

"You think?" He looked incredulous, then sighed. "Well, it was coming, anybody could see that," he admitted. "Once she had a new man in her life, I mean."

I nodded.

"An intellectual," Greene mused. "Quite a jump from a ballplayer."

It was my turn to look incredulous. As a young man, Jack had written a book—ghosted for him by first-rate journalists whom Arthur Krock and I had selected—but nobody would have described him as "an intellectual."

"Don't get me wrong," Greene said. "I *like* him. But I think he might be a little too *serious* for Marilyn, you know?"

"Jack? Serious?"

He stared at me. "Jack? I was talking about Arthur Miller." He leaned forward and whispered. "They're having an affair, Arthur and Marilyn," he said, "which is okay. But she wants to *marry* him. I don't think that's such a hot idea, frankly."

I wondered if she had mentioned any of this to Jack. Miller was exactly the kind of self-righteous, left-wing Jewish intellectual that Jack, however discreetly, most despised.

Marilyn came in, wobbly on her bare feet, with the champagne, and handed it to Greene, who popped the cork. She had brought in three toothbrush glasses from the bathroom, and we sipped lukewarm champagne without much enthusiasm. Her face seemed to have sagged, and her eyes were unfocused. She was having a certain amount of trouble getting the glass to her mouth too. I wondered if she had been taking sedatives while she was out of the room—certainly she had the slow-motion gestures of somebody on pills.

Greene didn't appear to have noticed. "This won't take long," he said, in the soothing voice one might use with a child. "I just want to go over the points you ought to discuss with Mickey Rudin. . . ."

Marilyn blinked. "Mickey who?"

"Sinatra's lawyer. Remember? You were going to get him to look over the contracts for you, honey?"

"I *like* Frank," she said, as if one of us might be going to give her an argument.

"Me too," Greene said, taking the papers out of his briefcase.

"He's a lot more fun than Arthur."

"No doubt about that, baby."

"But Arthur's smarter."

"Maybe so. Frank's pretty smart himself." He rolled his eyes. "Marilyn honey, would you like to leave this to another day?"

"No. I want to get rid of everything. Got rid of the Slugger today." She giggled. "Got rid of Zanuck and the studio today. Start with a clean fucking slate, right, David?"

Marilyn's voice was slowing down, like a record played at the wrong speed, and her eyes were turning dull. I didn't want to get in Greene's way, but I felt somehow responsible for Marilyn. "You ought to be in bed," I said. "Milton and I are going to put you there."

"Not before I've signed these," she said, and before Greene could stop her, she took a pen, bent over the documents, found the places marked for her signature, and signed. "Whoopee!" she cried. "That does it!"

I could see that Greene was caught between conflicting emotions. He had Marilyn's signature on what was, for him, the deal of a lifetime, but being a cautious, orderly fellow in business, he knew this wasn't the way it should be done.

Greene surrendered glumly to the demands of self-interest, guiding her hand to the rest of the copies, marking with his finger the places for her to sign and initial. I had to sympathize with him—it was an opportunity not likely to be repeated, and surely beat months of negotiations.

Marilyn's eyes by now were glazed. I hoped I would never have to testify as to her condition when she signed. "We'd better get her to a doctor," I said to Greene.

She was sitting on the sofa, slumped against an arm, eyes half closed, hands on her lap. She still had on the false fingernails she had worn last night for filming, but several of them were already badly chipped. Her breathing was regular, but very slow and loud.

Greene listened to her breathing, his head bent over her chest. "No doctor," he said.

"She may need one. We don't know what she's taken. . . ."

"Look, take my word for it, David, I *know* about these things. Marilyn's taken a couple of downers, that's all, no big deal. She'll sleep this off."

His tone of voice was so calm, cool, and serious that I found myself believing him, despite my distrust of amateur diagnosticians. I certainly wasn't eager to take the risk that a doctor might remove Marilyn from the hotel in an ambulance and have her stomach pumped out in the Bellevue emergency room while several hundred reporters stood vigil outside.

"Let's get her to bed," Greene said, carefully gathering up his signed papers and putting them away.

It was easier said than done. Marilyn photographed bigger than she was—5 feet 5 1/2; 117 pounds; 37, 22, 36, statistics I remember to this day because for my fiftieth birthday she had them engraved on the lid of a silver cigarette box instead of her initials, an odd example of the way Marilyn's figure, even to her, seemed to have a greater reality than herself—but it isn't easy to pick up a woman who has passed out on a sofa behind a marble coffee table that's too heavy to move. Greene squeezed in between the sofa and the table to take her legs, while I leaned over the back of the sofa to take her shoulders.

"Heave!" he ordered, and we both heaved, eventually managing to lift Marilyn. I don't know why it didn't occur to either of us to ask Whitey Snyder to help—in Greene's case, I suspect it was a natural reluctance to let anybody near Marilyn now that she was his principal asset. In any event, we dragged her into the bedroom and put her down on the bed as gently as possible.

The room showed signs of DiMaggio's hasty departure, as well as Marilyn's habit of keeping all her possessions in torn shopping bags and bursting cardboard boxes. On the bedside table was a guidebook to Washington, D.C. I picked it up. Inside the front cover was a reservation slip for a suite at the Hay-Adams Hotel in the name of Mrs. James Dougherty—Marilyn's name in her first marriage. The suite was reserved for the weekend. I guessed that it was not Arthur Miller she was going to see.

I put the book back down on the night table. Marilyn had moved in her sleep. We had put her on her back, arms folded, but she had rolled over onto her side and curled up like a child, her head resting on her hands. Her gown had loosened, and I could see her breasts—couldn't take my eyes off them, in fact. They weren't particularly large, but they were perfectly shaped, the color of the palest pearly pink, so firm that there was not the slightest sag to them.

"Let's go," Greene said gently.

I shook my head, still overcome, my hands trembling from the touch of her skin.

I turned and followed him out of the room reluctantly. I knew now where she was going for the weekend, and why she had wanted me to make a reservation for her in Connecticut in her own name. Once the press found out, they would be combing the inns of Connecticut, not looking for her in Washington.

I caught one last look at her sleeping as I closed the bedroom door.

God, I thought to myself, but Jack was a lucky man!

Or was he? The question occurred to me the moment I arrived home to an irate telephone call from Jack's father. "What's all this about Jack and Marilyn Monroe?" he asked. "Did you know anything about it?"

I admitted that I did, as I sorted through my mail.

"You should have told me," Joe said.

"I don't think it's part of my job to keep you up to date on Jack's love life," I said.

"The hell it's not!" His voice was tight, rising in pitch with anger. "This isn't just another goddamn girl he's fucking, it's Marilyn Monroe."

"I've pointed out to Jack that there are risks involved—"

"To hell with pointing it out to *Jack!* You should have told *me!* I had to hear it from Bobby, who's worried sick over it."

I doubted that. Marilyn wasn't Jack's first movie star, even if she was the most famous, and Bobby had plenty else to worry about. Joe was just building up a case for himself, making it clear that he expected to know everything that went on in Jack's life—a task I had always refused to help him with.

"She's more sensible than people give her credit for," I said. "I'm pretty sure she wouldn't do anything to hurt Jack."

He snorted. "Movie stars are all crazy." He should know, I thought but didn't say—Gloria Swanson had led him a merry dance. His tone softened—a sure sign that he was going to ask me for a favor. "Look," he said, "I don't expect you to tell me every little thing Jack does, but keep your eye on the situation for me, will you? Jack is going to be president. He can't get mixed up in a scandal with a movie star."

"I'll do my best," I said. "I don't suppose it will last long. These things never do with Jack. Nor with Marilyn, I hear."

Joe chuckled. "Well, it can't do him any harm, so long as it isn't serious. I wouldn't mind meeting her myself."

"She says the same about you."

"Does she now? Well, well. . . ." Joe was not above making a play for Jack's girls, and sometimes he even succeeded, such was his determination to compete and win. Back in the days when his children were younger, Joe had a reputation for sleeping with the daughters of his friends and the friends of his daughters, but he didn't draw the line at the girlfriends of his sons either.

"You let me know if you think there's a problem, David," he said. "You owe me that, at least."

I acknowledged it, reluctantly.

"Christ, though, you've got to hand it to our Jack," he added—I could hear the satisfaction in his voice. "They can't say no to him, can they?"

I had never heard such parental pride from Joe, not even the day Jack won his first Senate race, defeating his rival, Henry Cabot lodge—and Joe was a sworn enemy of the Lodges and all they stood for in Boston.

I wondered if Bobby had told his father that Jack was planning to go after the Teamsters as well. I guessed not, or I would have had an earful about that, too.

5

SHE HELD HER GUIDEBOOK IN ONE HAND. WITH THE OTHER she grasped Jack Kennedy's hand, twining her fingers with his, ignoring his embarrassment at this open display of intimacy. It was the first time she'd been to Washington, and she was overwhelmed.

They were standing on the floor of the Senate, on a Sunday morning—it had taken all of Jack's senatorial clout to persuade the usher to open it up for her.

She had dressed for the occasion in a white summer dress with tiny black polka dots and a jaunty straw hat with a matching polka-dot ribbon. The dress had a tight sash around her waist in reversed polka dots, white on black. There were an awful lot of polka dots, she thought when she saw herself in a mirror, and she wondered briefly if it had been the right choice for a figure like hers. She looked at the podium and sighed. "Just think," she said. "Lincoln spoke from there."

He frowned. "Ah, I don't think he did, you know, Marilyn. The president gives the State of the Union speeches in the House—still does." He sensed her disappointment. "Webster spoke here. Clay. Calhoun. There's enough history here."

"Oh, yes." She squeezed his fingers harder, smiling to disguise the fact that it wasn't the same without Lincoln. If only she had managed to get beyond the first pages of Sandburg's book, she might not have made a fool of herself, she thought. . . .

She had to hand it to Jack! He had assumed, naturally enough, that the only sight she wanted to see in Washington was him, but once she had him on his back in her bedroom at the Hay-Adams, he surrendered gracefully enough. She was touched by his willingness to show her the sights, for until they had spent some time together, she had not realized how bad his back was, how much pain even the simplest things, like climbing the steps of the Lincoln Memorial, cost him. There was a pair of crutches in the front seat of the car; whenever they stopped to get out and look at something, his driver-bodyguard Boom-Boom offered them to Jack. Usually Jack just shook his head and limped off, his face drawn with pain, but where there were a lot of steps involved, he sometimes gave in and took them, with an expression that clearly signified fury at his own weakness.

He walked her over to his desk. She sat down, while he leaned against it, supporting his weight with his arms and shoulders. "This is where you work?" she asked.

"Most of the work is done in committee. Or by getting together over a drink. Half the business of the Senate is done in Lyndon Johnson's office after six o'clock by a pack of old farts sitting around over a bottle of bourbon, trading favors. . . ."

It was clear to her that Jack resented not being part of that. She noticed that his face had suddenly turned pale. His smile was fixed, but his knuckles were white as he pressed his hands hard against the desk. "Is it that bad?" she asked, reaching out to touch him. "The back?"

He shook his head, mouth set, as if the question irritated him. She wasn't fooled for a moment. The Slugger had his share of aches and pains after a lifetime of baseball, and even with a daily massage and hot baths there were still days when his expression was just like Jack's, and yet he wouldn't admit to her he was in pain until he was on the floor groaning, if then. Were all men stubborn and childish? she wondered.

"You ought to be lying down," she said. Then it occurred to her that the pain was really *her* fault, for making him drag himself around Washington when he was too proud to use his crutches, and she felt a stab of guilt.

He gave a crooked grin. "I *was* lying down, remember?"

They had spent the night together in her suite at the Hay-Adams. The sex between them had been as good as ever. Granted, she would have liked a little more variation, some of that muscle-stretching, high-voltage, athletic sex of the Slugger's that left her limp, but Jack was used to women pleasing *him*, which was kind of a turn-on in its own way. Besides, she couldn't help telling herself, when she slowly, carefully raised and lowered herself on his penis: I could be fucking *the next president of the United States!*

It had been disappointing, though, having at last spent a whole night with Jack, to discover that he was not any more "cuddleable" in bed than Joe. She had gone to the trouble of making sure the hotel put an extra-firm mattress and a board on the bed, but it was still too soft for Jack, who complained about it off and on all night.

She had dreamed of holding him tightly in her arms as they both slept, their limbs twined, their lips touching, of waking to see his face close to hers on the pillow. Instead, once he was finally asleep, he lay snoring gently while she tossed and turned beside him, having, at the end of their lovemaking, neglected to take her sleeping pills for fear of disturbing him by getting up.

"Is there anything else you'd like to see?" he asked.

"There is *one* thing more I'd like to see," she answered in a timid voice, like a little girl asking a grown-up for a favor—Norma Jean speaking! she thought.

"Whatever," he said, but she could tell his heart wasn't in it.

"I want to see your home."

She was delighted at the surprise on his face—dismay, really—for she had already learned that he set great store by never showing surprise. He cleared his throat. "I don't think that's such a great idea."

"I do." She pouted gracefully. "Anyway, you promised."

"I did not!"

"You said 'whatever.' That means whatever I want, doesn't it? Anyway, what's the problem? You told me that Jackie's in Hyannis Port and the servants have the day off?"

"That's true, but . . ."

"Well then." She stared at him unblinkingly. He blushed. "You're not *afraid*, are you? I mean, I came down here, didn't I? I didn't mind taking a risk."

She knew she had him now—he was the kind of man who could always be counted on to respond to a challenge.

He was glaring at her, his eyes icy; then he laughed. "Well, what are you waiting for?" he asked. "Let's go."

Boom-Boom was silent as they passed through the hot Virginia countryside, his disapproval evident in the way he drove in slow motion. Despite Jack's snapping at him to get a move on, he acted as if he were taking his driving test, braking a hundred feet before every intersection and looking in both directions with exaggerated care.

The landscape was alien to her, with its rolling, wooded hills shrouded in heat haze. She didn't like the look of it much. Woods, trees, and farmland frightened her, made her feel somehow *trapped*—she was a child of the far horizon, the Pacific Ocean or the desert, where you could see for miles and the sun burned everything clean.

"I've never seen so many farms in my life," she said.

Jack stared out the window on his side, as if the farms were new to him. There were few subjects that interested him less than farming. "Well, it's mostly gentleman farming," he said with contempt. "That's Ambassador McGee's farm." He pointed to a storybook red-brick Colonial house, set high on a hill, surrounded by huge, ancient oaks. "Texas oil and gas, then an ambassadorship, now the CIA. Has a famous herd of cattle. What are they, Boom-Boom?"

"Black Angus, boss."

"Black Angus, right. McGee paid, I think, a couple of hundred thousand dollars for a prize bull." He shook his head in wonder. "Jackie rides over there a lot, with his girls."

"She likes it here?"

"Loves it. It's the way she was brought up. Horses, hunting—all that sort of goddamned thing."

He looked out the window glumly. It was well known that his taste ran more toward the South of France than rural Virginia, but that was not the kind of signal he wanted to give the voters. For some reason, Jackie's fooling around with horses played well in the press—better, say, than sunbathing at Eden Roc, on the Cap d'Antibes—and anyway, it kept her busy and, for the most part, off his back.

"You don't like it?"

His expression turned, for an instant, sour and angry. She had clearly touched a raw nerve. "The house is too goddamned big," he snapped. "A fucking white elephant. And the commuting drives me crazy. Mornings and evenings, the rush hour traffic is unbelievable. . . . Of course, none of that makes any difference to Jackie."

"Why did you buy it, then?"

He sighed. "It's what Jackie wanted—the horses and all. And I figured we'd need a big house, for all the children!" He laughed harshly. "What an irony *that* turned out to be!"

"Jack," she said, "that isn't her fault." It was the one subject that could always arouse her sympathy for another woman. Nobody, she told herself, could have tried harder to give the Slugger the child he wanted, but she knew in the deep, private hollow of her guilt that it wasn't true.

"I didn't say it was Jackie's *fault*. It's hard for her, I know. When she had the miscarriage, the doctors told her she might never be able to have a child, ever. . . . And there's Ethel, popping kids out with Bobby, one after the other, no trouble at all. . . . That doesn't help. As you can imagine." His tone was bitter.

"I can imagine."

"It hasn't been a happy house for either of us. I can't seem to get Jackie to see that."

The car slowed. They turned up a long, twisting gravel drive, with big trees on either side, and pulled to a stop in front of a large, handsome old house—larger than she had imagined. She realized instantly that Jack was right—it was a house for a big, noisy family. Two people living here without children could only be unhappy; it must be Jackie's selfishness that made her unable to see that.

"It's so *old*," she whispered.

"It *was* the headquarters for the Army of the Potomac during the Civil War, so it's got some history. . . ."

Now that he was home, Jack took his crutches. He moved easily with them, using his powerful shoulders to swing himself up the steps to the front door.

She followed him into the big hallway as he closed the door on Boom-Boom's red, perspiring face. The house was furnished just as she had pictured it, full of antiques that had obviously been chosen by someone who knew and cared a lot about them. She knew nothing about antiques herself, but she was sure that these were the real thing.

She felt a twinge of envy, the familiar shame of coming from the wrong side of the tracks. Most of her adult life had been spent in borrowed rooms or apartments; even when she had finally forced Joe out of his family's house in San Francisco, they had rented a furnished house in Beverly Hills, near San Vicente Boulevard, with lots of bulky furniture in avocado and gold tweed and a Formica wet bar in the living room, pretty nice for North Palm Drive, but a world removed from this.

Every room seemed to have a big stone fireplace; the wide-board floors were covered in expensive Oriental rugs. Everywhere there was evidence of Jackie's pursuit—hunting prints, whips, boots, and hunt caps in the hall, foxes embroidered on cushions, ribbons hanging from beams, silver trophies. She ran her hand over the marble of the hall table. "Is this an old piece?" she asked.

He shrugged. "Eighteenth-century, I think. French. Cost a fortune. Tom Hoving—he's one of Jackie's friends in the art world—says it ought to be in the Metropolitan Museum, or the White House. Well, that's Jackie for you. She has an eye for these things."

"You must be very proud she has such good taste."

"Ah, yes." Something about the way he looked at the living room, with its exquisite pieces, arranged in perfect symmetry, seemed to suggest that he might have preferred furniture you could put your feet up on and didn't have to worry about leaving rings on with your drink.

"Satisfied?" he asked.

"Never, honey. Can we go upstairs?"

He hesitated. "Please," she asked. It was curiosity of the

meanest sort, and she despised herself for it, but once she had brought him this far, there was no point in stopping. She could not explain it to herself, this need to *see* with her own eyes how her rival—already she thought of Jackie as that—lived and dressed, where they slept, as if without that intimate knowledge there would always be a part of him that remained hidden from her.

When she was twenty-one, and passionately in love with John Carroll, the actor, she had actually persuaded him to let her move into his house, and for a time she became "best friends" with Lucille, his wife, until she asked Lucille if she wouldn't mind divorcing John so *she* could marry him—at which point Carroll reluctantly piled her belongings into his station wagon and drove her to a rented apartment on Franklin Avenue. . . .

Was it just a question of wanting to know what she was up against, she wondered, or did it go deeper than that? Was it that she wanted to find out, if she could, *why* the husband was unfaithful?

She followed Jack up the narrow, elegant stairway to the bedroom. He seemed increasingly glum. He sat down on the bed with a groan, while she busied herself in the dressing room, glancing into Jackie's closets.

Oh, how she envied those neat rows of couture clothing, none of which she could have worn, for they were all designed with the kind of skinny, flat-chested women in mind that Joe Eula liked to call "fashion freaks." She couldn't see a single dress with polka dots. She pulled out an evening gown so plain and simple and expensive that she suddenly yearned to be a fashion freak herself. The label read "Oleg Cassini." She took it out to the bedroom and held it up for Jack to see. "How do you think I'd look in this?" she asked.

He lay stretched out with his feet on the silk counterpane—he had not bothered to take his shoes off. "Put it back!" he said sharply, his eyes suddenly cold.

She hung the dress up and went back to the bedroom, kicking off her shoes and reaching behind her to undo her zipper. "Sometimes I do things that aren't very nice," she said. "There's a possibility that I'm not a nice person, you know? The jury's still out."

"Who's on the jury?"

"My therapist. The Slugger." She paused. "You, I guess."

"You get my vote."

She wasn't sure he meant it. "Even after I made you bring me here? I mean, it's an awful thing to do to another woman, isn't it? I'd go crazy if anybody did it to *me*." She leaned over and kissed him on the mouth. "It's not the first time I've done it either. I mean, it's sort of a *habit*, you know? Like shoplifting."

She unzipped his trousers, and went down on him. He gave a groan of pleasure. She looked up at him from between his knees. "Does Jackie do this for you?" she wanted to ask, but there was something in his expression that stopped her. It wasn't that he looked threatening, or that his eyes flashed a warning, or anything like that—it was, instead, a look of infinite sadness that caught her attention, a shadow image of that pessimism she had seen so often in the mirror during her own childhood.

She took him in her mouth again, and slowly, expertly made him come. Oh, she had been taught by real connoisseurs of oral sex, and it was a knowledge that gave her power over men, not to be despised.

She slid up the bed until her head was next to his on the pillow. His eyes were closed, but his expression was not that of a man who has just had one of the great blow jobs of a lifetime. "What's up, honey?" she asked gently.

"Nothing."

She knew that tone of voice, all right. It was the same as the Slugger's when what he meant was, *Shut up and mind your own business!* She reached down and gave Jack's balls a squeeze, not painfully hard but just firm enough to show him who was boss in *this* situation. "Hey," she said, "this is *me!* Remember?"

He grunted, then gave in with a sigh, like any other man forced to talk about the things he didn't want to talk about. "All right. The pain's killing me," he said quietly. "The truth is, I'm going to have to have my back operated on finally, and that scares the shit out of me."

"But honey, lots of people have back operations. . . . I mean, it's not like cancer?"

"It's as bad, in my case. They've got to take out all the crushed bone fragments, repair the disks—if they can—then put in steel pins. . . . If I don't have the operation, I'm probably going to be a cripple, certainly in pain for the rest of my life. If I do, I could end up paralyzed. Or dead. It's just my luck, but I happen to have another little problem"—he laughed bitterly—"an adrenal deficiency, which they say could make recovery, ah, impossible."

He closed his eyes, his expression stoic. "The odds stink. My doctor figures they're a lot less than fifty-fifty, and she's the goddamned *optimist!* They want to do it in two stages, but I won't let them. I'd rather get it all over with in one big operation—take my chances and the hell with it."

She wondered how many people knew—if he had even told it to Jackie. She loved him for telling *her.* She pressed close to him, squeezing him in her arms as if his life depended on keeping him next to her. "I'd *die* if anything happened to you, my darling," she said.

He started to laugh, but she smothered his laughter with kisses. "No, I *mean* it," she said. "But nothing's *going* to happen, trust me! It's going to be fine, I can *feel* it, baby. I'm never wrong."

"I believe you," he said.

"You'd *better!*"

She got on top of Jack, let her breasts rub against his face, took him inside her, used all those muscles that it took so much experience in the sack even to find, to squeeze the very last drop of pleasure out of him, then slowly, languorously fucked him in his own bed until the sadness left her.

"If *this* doesn't make your back feel better, sugar," she whispered in his ear as he came, "nothing will!"

"IT'S FOR YOU, HONEY," AMY GREENE CALLED FROM THE far end of the big, low-beamed country kitchen.

Marilyn could read the faint note of irritation in Amy's voice over the fact that she tied the phone up for hours and made hundreds of calls a day.

She smiled sweetly at Amy and took the phone. She *liked* Amy well enough, but Amy behaved as if they were sisters, casting herself in the role of Big Sister.

It wasn't clear to her why she had decided to live with Milton and Amy after she'd divorced Joe D. and walked out on Fox. It had tickled her pink to make a double declaration of independence, but once she had done it, her capacity to make decisions seemed to ebb. She hadn't wanted to stay in California, but she couldn't face the problems of finding a place to live in New York.

In times of trouble, she had always sought refuge by moving in with somebody else's family, and the Greenes had been the logical choice. Milton, she had to confess, had come through so far: he'd made arrangements with Buddy Adler for her to star as Cherie in the movie version of Bill Inge's *Bus Stop,* with Josh Logan as the director, and even more surprisingly, he was negotiating a deal for her to star with Laurence Olivier, of all people, in *The Prince and the Showgirl.* She had mixed feelings about working with Olivier, but no more mixed than her feelings about Arthur Miller.

In the past months, her friendship with Arthur had ripened into a sort of love affair, despite what was going on between her and Jack. With Arthur, she felt like a college girl whose professor has fallen in love with her—a novel feeling for her.

With a fatal passivity that she was unable to prevent, she went along with Arthur's intention to marry her as if she shared it. Events were moving so quickly they left her dizzy: first her divorce, which, while it was amicable enough—Joe, despite his pain and anger, had been the perfect gentleman—turned into an excruciating media circus like everything else in her life; then the romance with Arthur, which was proceeding at breakneck speed. She had tried to slow it down by telling him that she couldn't even *begin* to think seriously about marriage as long as he was still married, but then he walked out on his family, horrifying his friends—and her too, to tell the truth.

She picked up the phone. There was no privacy in the Greene household, but she didn't really mind. She liked the fact that the whole house revolved around *her*, a kind of instant family, surrounding her with its warmth and protection.

"Ah, am I speaking to Marilyn Monroe?" The voice startled her. It was like Jack's, with the same nasal Boston Irish quality, overlaid with long Harvard vowels, and somewhere deep in the background a certain clipped quality that was unmistakably upper-class, except that this voice was higher than Jack's, with a rapid-fire, Bugs Bunny tempo to it.

She was startled, first of all, because she had been expecting a call from Arthur, then because she thought that Jack might be playing a joke on her, and jokes always made her anxious because she seldom "got" them. Then, too, there was the small problem that she had never told Arthur about Jack, which made her nervous. Arthur had urged that they be completely frank with each other about their pasts, but the truth was, his was on the dull side, and as hers was anything but, she had edited out most of it, including Jack.

"Jack?" she asked in a whisper, since Amy was standing right next to her.

"No. This is, ah, *Robert* Kennedy. Bobby. Jack's brother."

"Oh, gosh! Jack has told me so much about you. I mean, it's almost like we've met, you know? How is Jack?"

"Well, that's, ah, why I'm calling." Bobby Kennedy's voice was cautious. She could sense endless layers of Irish-Catholic disapproval behind the stilted politeness. What was it Jack had once said? "Bobby is the best hater I know." He had said it with a politician's appreciation of a useful virtue in a brother, but it had chilled her then, and perhaps as a result, she felt chilled now. "He's in the hospital, you know," Bobby said.

"I know." Jack had entered the Hospital for Special Surgery in New York for his back operation, which was reported to have been a success. She had sent him flowers, with her initials and her telephone number in Connecticut on the card, and was more than a little pissed off that she hadn't heard back from him yet. "How is he?"

"Not too good, frankly." There was a pause. "The truth is, he might not make it." Bobby could not conceal the emotion in his voice.

"Might not *make* it? You can't mean he's going to die!"

"I'm sorry, but that's exactly what I do mean, Miss Monroe."

"Marilyn, please." She shut her eyes, remembering Jack when she had seen him last, his handsome face below hers as he lay back on the bed. There was enough Christian Science left in her to believe that putting yourself in the hands of doctors was a form of weakness and lack of faith. "Is there anything I can do?" she asked.

Bobby cleared his throat. "Well, yes, I think so. Jack's spirits are really the problem, as much as anything else. I mean, the goddamned operation was a bust, and now he's got an infection they can't cure, and a hole in his back as big as a goddamned fist." He said "goddamned" exactly the way Jack did. There was a tremor in his voice now, as if he was about to cry. "He's pretty well played out," he said. "It's the first time I've ever seen Jack without hope. . . . That's why it's so important to cheer him up."

"How am I going to cheer him up, Bobby?" It was the first time she had used his name, and it made her feel part of the family.

"Ah," Bobby said, "I've already thought of a way."

When he explained, she burst out laughing.

She hung up the telephone. "Well, Miss Goldilocks," Amy said with a knowing wink. "And how's Arthur today?"

She entered the Hospital for Special Surgery with a scarf over her hair, dark glasses, and a belted raincoat.

Bobby and Boom-Boom were waiting in the lobby, Boom-Boom for once looking glad to see her. Bobby, for all his fearsome reputation and many children (four? she wondered, or was it already five?), looked like a shy teenager in a suit with pants that were too short for him, and a button-down shirt with a collar so big it made his neck seem scrawny. When she got closer to him, she could see that he was built like a bantamweight fighter, with a wiry toughness you couldn't miss. He wasn't as handsome as Jack, or as polished, but with his pale blue eyes, his sandy hair and trademark smile, he had a star quality of his own. He shook her hand firmly. "We've got the room next to Jack's for you," he said. "Everything's there." He ushered her into the elevator. "It's great of you to do this. You're a good sport."

"Nobody ever called me *that* before!"

He blushed, looking younger than ever. "Well, I meant it as a compliment, you know."

"How is he?"

He shook his head. A veil of sadness darkened his eyes. "The same." He sighed. "Father was here earlier today, but he didn't stay. He can't bear to see Jack like this. Not sick, I mean, but *defeated*. Father doesn't believe in failure or defeat, do you see?"

"Sort of. My granny was Christian Scientist. My mom too. *They* didn't believe in illness."

"Did it work for them?"

"No," she said curtly.

They left the elevator in silence. Bobby led her down the corridor and opened a door for her. She felt frightened and trapped, and fought to conceal it from him. She hated hospitals, loathed the strange smells and the presence of sickness and death.

The empty hospital room did nothing to ease her terror. On the bed her "costume" was laid out neatly—a nurse's uniform and cap, white shoes and stockings, all in the correct size. She had given the information to Bobby's secretary, who hadn't seemed at all surprised at being sent out to buy a nurse's uniform for Marilyn Monroe: apparently the Kennedy organization was trained to produce anything. She slipped behind a cloth screen, wiggled out of her clothes, and put on the uniform. It fit perfectly. She stepped out, shook her hair loose, and pinned on the cap. "Okay?"

Bobby grinned. It made him look a lot less forbidding, even suggested he might have some portion of Jack's charm. "If this doesn't make Jack smile, he's a goner for sure. Ready?"

"Not yet." She took her makeup out of her handbag and went to the mirror. She was Marilyn Monroe, after all, and this was a performance.

"You promise Jackie isn't going to turn up while I'm in there?" she asked.

"No way."

"Let's go, then," she said.

They walked into the corridor. Boom-Boom gave a thumbs-up sign, indicating that there were no real nurses or doctors in sight. "You're on," Bobby said.

Nurse! she told herself. She knew she could play one if she put her mind to it. She rapped her knuckles against the door firmly—a nurse wouldn't have a hesitant knock; a nurse would know she *belonged* here, that *she* was in charge of things. She opened the door briskly, walked in, and suddenly gasped. "Oh my God, Jack!" she cried, stepping out of character. "What have they *done* to you?"

He didn't seem to hear. He was lying on his back in a maze of wires, pulleys, and counterweights, a cervical collar holding his head immobile. His face was so thin she could hardly recognize him. His skin, which was usually tanned, was an almost transparent white, stretched tightly over his bones. His hair was damp and matted, his cheeks deeply etched with lines of pain. Even his hands, folded over the hospital sheet on his chest, looked fragile and withered, like an old man's. Despite all the flowers, there was a smell of stale sweat and antiseptics, and the sickly sweet stench of an infected open wound.

Suddenly the joke no longer seemed funny, like a frat house prank that has somehow led to tragedy, leaving the jokers standing around looking shamefaced and guilty. She felt foolish in the face of his suffering, and helpless.

She started to cry, which wasn't in the script at all, the tears dropping onto the bosom of her starched white dress. She stood there for what felt like a long time, watching the dying man—for it was impossible for her to think of Jack as anything else. She loved him, she was sure of it, and because she loved him he would die, like everyone she loved.

She realized that Jack had opened his eyes. He stared at her as if he couldn't make sense of what he was seeing. At first his eyes seemed opaque, expressionless, dead, but very gradually they took on life again, the bright color returning. He was crying too—from pain, she thought, but then she saw they were tears of laughter: he smiled, as if it was unimaginably hard to do; the smile broadened, turned into the familiar grin, and with that, his face seemed to shed the marks of pain, defeat, and fear she had seen there. "Jesus!" he gasped through his laughter. "Whose idea was this?"

"Bobby's."

"Son of a bitch! There's hope for him yet! How did he get you in here?"

"How did *you* get into the Hay-Adams?"

"Ha!" He shook his head cautiously and winced with pain. "Well, I'm glad you're here."

He studied her carefully, still laughing silently, and winked. "You'd make a hell of a nurse, you know. You could bring Lazarus back to life, with a hard-on."

"Forget Lazarus. How about *you?*"

"It's been terrible. Still is. The goddamned doctors screwed up. The pain's bad too—worse than it was in the navy hospital, during the war, and I didn't think anything could be worse than that."

"Can't they give you anything?"

"They did. It didn't help a lot. They're not giving me much now. Father told the doctor, 'Don't give Jack too much for the pain—it's something he has to go through by himself.' " He grimaced, but she couldn't help noticing that he seemed to feel his father had been right.

"Sit down," he said, casting a glance at the chair beside his bed. "How's *your* life?"

"I'm sort of engaged."

"To?"

"Arthur Miller."

"I'd heard something about that. Congratulations are in order?"

"Maybe."

"That doesn't sound very enthusiastic."

"Oh, he's a wonderful man!" she cried out, as if she wanted to convince herself. "Really! He's such a *brain!* And so serious—*concerned,* I mean. I'm a lucky girl."

"I'm happy for you."

"Well, it's sure going to be different from being married to the Slugger, I guess."

"I would say." He closed his eyes. "If I ever get on my feet again—no thanks to the fucking doctors—let's go away someplace together. I'm going to think of that every time I get depressed here."

"Whenever, Jack. Wherever you like. Always, my darling."

"Even though you're a married lady?"

"I was a married lady before, remember?"

He smiled wearily, obviously tiring now. "Can you give me something to drink?"

She filled a glass with iced water and held the curved straw to his lips, just the way she had seen it done in the movies. He drank briefly. She put the glass back on the bed table. There was a small towel beside the Thermos; she dampened it with cold water and began to rub his brow and cheeks with it gently. He groaned quietly with satisfaction and grasped her free hand.

His breathing was soft and regular, and he was clearly falling asleep. He mumbled something in a groggy voice. She leaned close to his lips. "I love you," she thought she heard him mutter; then he was silent. She wondered if he had really said it, or she had just imagined it.

She sat there, wiping his face, her hand in his, until Bobby opened the door, worried no doubt about what had happened, and found her there in the twilight, tears streaming down her face.

"The Ambassador wants you to call him in Florida," Maria said as I entered her dressing room. She was getting ready for dinner, doing her face at her makeup table in her slip, a martini and a cigarette at her elbow. She did not turn around or look up from the mirror. That's marriage for you.

It was a shame, I thought, because she was a very beautiful woman, but we had long since reached that stage of marriage where sex seems likely to make things worse rather than better. A few years ago, I would have put my arms around her and made love to her on the dressing room floor—or at any rate felt tempted to—but I knew if I even leaned down to kiss her, she would only say, "Don't, darling, please, you'll smear my makeup and I'll have to start all over again—then we'll be late."

Of course, we were going out. I do not think I can remember

our ever spending an evening at home, unless we were entertaining. Certainly that's part of my profession—being out in the world—in addition to which Maria was, in every sense of the phrase, a *femme du monde,* for whom an evening at home was an evening wasted. Still, I couldn't help thinking one of the reasons we were out every night was so as not to be alone with each other, as well as to make sure that by the time we got home, we were too tired to do anything more than take a sleeping pill and fall into bed. . . .

"Did he say what was on his mind?" I asked.

"Jack. What else?" She wasn't annoyed. Maria adored not only Jack but also his father, who flirted with her outrageously. "He sounded upset."

I went into the living room, poured myself a martini from the iced shaker, and dialed Joe Kennedy's unlisted number in Palm Beach. He picked up on the first ring. "Where the hell have you been?" he growled.

"Creeping home from the office in rush hour traffic, Joe," I said. "What can I do for you?"

"I'm not complaining, mind you," he said. "I'd a lot rather talk to Maria than you. She's prettier and she knows more gossip."

Both of these things were true. Maria knew everything that was happening among the rich, the famous, and the notorious, and spent a good deal of time keeping Joe informed. "I can put her back on the line if you like," I said.

He laughed. "No, it's you I need, worse luck. The two of you are going to the Cassini party?"

"Yes."

"That son of a bitch sleeps with more beautiful women than Jack! And he's only a fucking dress designer!"

"That's probably one of the reasons they sleep with him, don't you think? Women will do anything for a man who can make them look good."

"I guess so. . . . Listen, have you seen all this crap about Jack? The papers are treating him as if he's *dying!*" His voice rose. *"They're writing my boy off!"*

It was true enough. The press had picked up on the seriousness of Jack's condition despite my efforts to gloss it over as a routine operation.

"I've told them it isn't true—"

"*Fuck* that! I want it *stopped,* do you hear me? What are you going to *do* about it?"

I could tell from the pitch of Joe's voice that he was about to go into one of his rages, which, while they didn't frighten me, didn't do *him* any good. "I'll think of something," I soothed. "He needs to get his teeth into something as soon as he can—a big issue, something that puts him in the public eye. . . ." I thought hard, grasping for an idea that would pacify Joe. "In the meantime, it wouldn't be a bad idea for him to write a book," I suggested.

"A book?"

Joe was silent for a moment. He had a great respect for books, though none at all for writers. He had discovered years ago that people paid attention to books, which was why he had gone to such lengths to get Jack's little book on England rewritten and published. "Having a book with his name on it will do young Jack a world of good," he had told me then, and he had been right. Even Eleanor Roosevelt, whom Joe hated—a feeling he had passed on to Jack—had praised it. "What about?" he asked suspiciously.

"Maybe something inspirational. People who have overcome great handicaps and succeeded. DeWitt Wallace would love it—the *Reader's Digest* would run it for sure."

"No cripples!" Joe barked.

"What?"

"No *physical* handicaps. Nothing about FDR and his fucking wheelchair. We don't want readers thinking that Jack's writing about cripples because *he's* a cripple, don't you see?"

I saw. As usual Joe, in his blunt way, had a point. "Courage," I said. "That's what he should be writing about. People who stood up to be counted, and changed American history by doing so." It sounded like a blurb, I realized, but that was a hazard of the profession.

"Yes. I like it, David. Find him a publisher. That fellow, what's his name, Sorensen? The speechwriter Jack likes so much? He could write the goddamn thing for Jack, now couldn't he? So long as he doesn't put a goddamn liberal twist on it."

"He'll need to write it in a hurry."

"Well, tell him to get cracking," Joe said crisply, with the confidence of a man who was used to buying writers and telling them what to do without taking any crap from them. His friend Jack Warner had once said, talking of screenwriters, "Writers are schmucks with typewriters, a dime a dozen," and Joe took the same view.

"I'll make the arrangements," I said.

"Good. No need to tell Jack yet." He sounded more relaxed now that we had a plan. "I hear Marilyn Monroe visited him in the hospital there, disguised as a nurse!" He laughed.

I hadn't heard that, and it startled me. "Jesus," I said, "that's risky."

But Joe gave a snort of contempt. The Kennedys would take any risk when it came to women, and Joe was proud of it. "Lay off, David," he said. "Let the boy have his fun."

He paused. "It can't do any harm."

7

"WELL, *MY* HAT'S OFF TO HER. SHE BROUGHT OUR JACK round sooner than all the rest of us combined."

We were sitting by the pool of the Kennedy mansion in Palm Beach—the Ambassador, Bobby, and myself—after breakfast. Bobby was wearing a baggy pair of swim trunks, his hair wet and tousled from his first ocean swim of the day. Joe was dressed for his morning golf game, in the kind of white plus fours that had been fashionable before the war, with tartan socks and a cashmere pullover. Neither Bobby nor I had wanted to join Joe in a "strategy session," as it pleased him to call his morning grouse at the world, but we weren't in a position to argue the point. Joe had brought me down here to discuss Jack's future now that he was out of the hospital.

"Marilyn certainly brought him round," Bobby agreed. "But he's still pretty bad, you've got to face it."

"I don't have to face a damned thing, Bobby. Jack's on his feet now."

"He's on crutches," Bobby said, always the realist. "So far as anybody knows, he'll *always* be on crutches."

"He's alive. He's out of the hospital. If he has to be operated on again, he'll be operated on."

"I don't know if he can take another one."

"He's my son. He can take one if he has to. He's going to recover, Bobby. I don't want to hear any more pessimistic bullshit in my house. Not from you, not from anyone. What do you think, David?"

"I thought it was a mistake to try and do it all in one operation," I said. "So did the doctors. They let Jack talk them into it, and so did you. Don't let him be his own doctor next time."

Joe chuckled indulgently. "Jack always was the one who could charm the birds off the trees. He charmed the doctors, sure—and the nurses, too." He grinned wickedly. "I guess he's charmed Marilyn Monroe, all right."

"I guess he has," I said. The more I heard about her escapade in Jack's hospital room, the more I shuddered at the public relations problem it could have caused. Bobby and I had clashed about it, but he had been unrepentant, as usual. Everything Bobby did had to be right, even if he had to twist the facts to make it so.

"I hear she's marrying this kike playwright?" Joe said. "The one who's a pinko?"

Bobby and I exchanged looks. Bobby was too much in awe of his father to confront him about things like this, which he hated. As I was the only "kike" around, I suppose it was incumbent on me to object, but I had long since accepted that kind of thing as part of the Ambassador's vocabulary—he had once referred to his old friend Cardinal Leahy of Boston, during some dispute, as "a bog-stupid, lace-curtain Mick," and to Bernie Baruch as "FDR's ambassador to the Elders of Zion."

I didn't take it personally. Joe Kennedy was simply of a generation of American men that felt no embarrassment in calling a Jew a kike, a black person a nigger, or—which said it all in Joe's case—an Irishman a Mick. I was of the generation of American Jews that took for granted Otto Kahn's dictum that "a kike is a Jewish gentleman who has just left the room," so such things did not weigh as heavily on me as they did on Bobby, who was smoldering with impotent anger in his deck chair.

I knew that the Ambassador had probably said it just to get Bobby's goat, to pay him back for his pessimism about Jack's recovery—he was like that with his children. The only exception he made was with Jack, because Jack was going to run for the presidency and therefore, in Joe's view of things, had to be kept innocent of any taint of old-fashioned bigotry, even at home. In fact, Jack *was* unbigoted, largely because he took people as they were. What mattered to Jack was beauty, talent, and wit, not race or color.

"I can't see why she'd want to marry a fellow like that," Joe went on, warming to his theme. I guessed that the notion of Miller's being a "pinko" aggravated the Old Man more than the fact that he was Jewish.

"Maybe she's in love with him," Bobby said.

"She's in love with *Jack!*" he snapped back. "Or so I've been led to believe."

We sat for a few moments in silence while Joe contemplated human frailty—his only form of soul-searching, so far as I knew—and Bobby quietly seethed. Joe glanced at his watch. "Where the hell's Jack?" he asked.

"He probably had a bad night," Bobby said.

"Christ, it's nearly nine-thirty!" The Ambassador not only believed in early rising but was so insistent on punctuality that he had electric clocks in every room in his houses synchronized centrally, so nobody would have an excuse for being late.

Bobby shook his head. He did not often rebel against his father, but when it came to Jack, he was like a ferocious but faithful watchdog. "Let him sleep," he said gently.

"You're not doing Jack any favors by being soft on him, Bobby. He's not going to get better feeling sorry for himself."

"He needs time. He's *got* time. He's got a year before he needs to be in fighting shape."

"I told you before, Bobby. 'Fifty-six isn't going to be Jack's year."

"I know that," Bobby said impatiently. "But he's going to look like an amateur if he goes to the convention without control of the Massachusetts delegation. You know what people like McCormack are calling him? 'The playboy senator,' for God's sake!"

Joe's eyes were invisible behind his old-fashioned round tortoiseshell sunglasses, but his face flushed. Congressman John McCormack was one of his enemies. "*Fuck* McCormack!" he snarled. "Who gives a shit what he says?"

"Plenty of people in Massachusetts."

"Horseshit! I know what you want to do, Bobby, and I'm not having it, do you hear me? You're trying to get Jack tied up in a fight up there in Boston with a bunch of political bums and hacks like 'Onions' Burke and Freddy Blip. For Christ's sake, can't you get it through your head he's running for president, not for alderman?"

I could see that he was dying to drag me into the argument, but I was saved by the appearance of Jack, hobbling out of the house on his crutches at last, in white shorts and an old tennis shirt, looking as thin as a Giacometti sculpture.

Jack eased himself gingerly into his chair—it had been specially made for him, with a straight wooden back and a flat seat—and stared blankly out to sea, as if it seemed so far away that he would never get there again, or swim in it.

"Did I hear the name Onions Burke taken in vain?" he asked, grinning weakly.

"I was just setting Bobby straight," the Ambassador said. He changed subjects quickly. "How's Jackie?"

Jack shrugged. "Sleeping late," he said curtly.

Jackie slept late whenever she was in Palm Beach or Hyannis, or stayed in her room "resting" in the afternoons, and it was tactfully recognized that this was her way of avoiding the rough games of the Kennedys, the fierce, competitive kidding of Jack's sisters and Ethel, the remote, chilling haughtiness of Rose Kennedy, and the Ambassador's energetic coarseness and heavy-handed inquisitions about pregnancy. Jackie, like me, wasn't afraid of the Old Man, which perhaps explains why he showed more respect for her than for anyone else around him, but she wasn't charmed by him either. She knew exactly how to handle him—hardly surprising, for in many ways he must have seemed like her own father, "Black Jack" Bouvier, except that Black Jack had a lot more charm and no gift for making money or even keeping it.

Joe made savage fun of Jackie's social pretensions, but never to her face. I think he felt that so long as she didn't make a fuss about Jack's women and produced an heir for him, Jack had made a pretty good choice in marrying her. Her discretion—in public, anyway—about Jack's affairs was beyond reproach, and not even Joe could complain that she wasn't doing her best to have a baby.

Jack gave Bobby a cold, hard, big brother's stare, indicating, I guessed, that Bobby should have kept his mouth shut. "Well," he said, "I'm not planning to get myself into a pissing match up there in Massachusetts."

"Goddamned right you're not!" Joe glanced at his watch. "I've said my piece. I guess I can watch from the sidelines while Jack takes on Onions Burke and Bobby takes on organized labor."

Bobby stared grimly at his father. "I'm not doing any such thing."

"I hear things, you know. I'm not out of touch. This fellow Mollenhoff's been filling your ears with fairy stories about the Teamsters."

"Maybe," Bobby conceded grudgingly.

"Mollenhoff's a bleeding heart. I'll tell you one thing about the Teamsters—they don't have any goddamned Reds in their union. And the Teamsters did more to get FDR reelected in '44 than the rest of the AFL and the CIO put together. He gave his Fala speech at their convention, you know. . . ."

Bobby knew and didn't care. "They're racketeers now," he snapped.

The Ambassador looked at me pleadingly. I shrugged. That the Teamsters were racketeers and worse, I knew. Beck was corrupt, vain, and pompous, ripe, I guessed, for the plucking, for his egomania and greed had long since made him careless. Hoffa was a different kind of man altogether, vicious, built like one of the Mack trucks his members drove, shrewd, gifted with a capacity for hatred that more than matched Bobby's. "Oh, the Teamsters are corrupt enough, all right," I said. "No doubt about that. I imagine people like George Meany will be happy to see them in the spotlight, whatever they say about union solidarity."

"You've thought it all out, have you?" Joe asked sarcastically.

"It's a good issue," Jack said. He sounded weary.

"Jack's going to get great mileage out of attacking Dave Beck," I went on. "Bobby too." The Ambassador gave me a look that said, *I've heard* that *before*, but I knew that at heart he didn't much care who Jack went after, so long as he went after *someone*. It was action and headlines he wanted just now—proof that Jack was alive and well. He set some store by my instincts, and a lot more by Bobby's, despite their argument about whether or not Jack should fight for control of the Massachusetts Democratic machine.

"God knows Beck's a big, fat target," Joe said, turning the idea over in his mind. "He'll fight back, though. This Hoffer fellow too."

Bobby didn't correct his father about Hoffa's name. "Let 'em," he said. "They don't know what a fight is yet."

"Mm." Joe looked sharply at Jack—a look that, from long experience, I could interpret as a warning to make sure Bobby didn't go too far. Ill as he was, Jack caught it and nodded.

Joe got up with a sigh. "So be it," he said. "On your head be it," he added, without indicating which one of us he meant. "I'm going to play golf." He walked toward the gate, where his car waited for him. "I'll probably have lunch at the club," he said. "Don't wait for me."

We sat silently for a few moments. Joe's departure always caused a kind of vacuum. "Lunch at the club," Jack said derisively. "He's got a girlfriend in Palm Beach. That's where he's going, after his game."

"Really?" I asked. "Who?" Bobby, I noticed, seemed to have gone into some kind of trance, his cheeks red with embarrassment. He idolized his father, and never cared to hear about the Ambassador's human failings.

Jack was more of a realist about such things. "She's a buxom blonde-from-the-bottle, on the right side of forty, with a nice secluded little house just past The Breakers. I believe she's, ah, separated from her husband. Good-looking lady, by the way. If she weren't fucking Dad, I wouldn't say no myself. . . . We should all be doing as well when we're sixty-seven."

He looked moody. He was housebound here at Palm Beach, with Jackie at his side most of the day. She had him to herself for once, and it was this enforced monogamy, I suspect, as much as anything, that got him started on writing his book, *Profiles in Courage*, which he worked at every day, taking the research and rough drafts done for him by Ted Sorensen and transforming them into his own prose. He turned to Bobby. "Dad's right," he said. "Beck will fight, you know."

Bobby looked mulish—a look that nobody did better. "Let him. He's scum. A bully who's sold out his own people to gangsters."

"Yes, you're right. But he's a tough nut to crack."

"I like tough nuts."

Jack smiled. He knew better than anybody how gutsy Bobby was, and what a mistake people made when they underrated him. "Well," he said after a pause, "if you're going to crack anybody's, I guess they may as well be Dave Beck's. Or Hoffa's."

Bobby rose and went into the house looking like a schoolboy, leaving the two of us together to listen to the sound of the lawn sprinklers. "What do you think, David?" Jack asked. "Just between us. I mean, you steered me onto the Teamsters in the first place."

"I warned you they were dangerous too. You don't get something for nothing."

"Spare me the wisdom, David. Exactly how dangerous *are* they?"

"I don't think they'd do anything to a United States senator, if that's what you're asking. Or his brother."

Looking back on it, I suppose I was naive, but so were we all then. It was a mistake, too, to have challenged Jack's courage. He stuck his chin out and his jaw muscles clenched automatically.

"I'm not afraid of Beck, or Hoffa, or their friends, David. Get *that* straight right away."

"I'm not suggesting you are."

"That doesn't mean I don't worry about where all this might lead. I mean, here you've got this fellow Mollenhoff giving Bobby chapter and verse on every crime the Teamsters have committed, and now Bobby's worked up a real head of steam about it. . . . Maybe it's the issue I'm looking for, but what's the bottom line? Do we go after Beck? Do we go after Hoffa? What do we do about the mob guys? I want to know where we're headed before we haul anchor."

Jack had guts, but he was no fool. Bobby was the righteous crusader—Jack merely wanted to look good in the headlines, and for that he needed a goal, something that would allow him to announce that the good guys, i.e., the Kennedy brothers, had won.

"Put Beck behind bars," I said. "Do that and you're a hero to the public, to the AFL-CIO, and to George Meany. Get your name on some serious labor reform legislation while you're at it, and you can go to the '56 convention looking like a major contender for the vice presidency."

"I don't want to be vice president, for Christ's sake."

"Fine. Then turn it down when it's offered to you. That's even better."

He stared out toward the far horizon, looking thoughtful. It was an appealing script, but I could tell he was still suspicious. "Let's say we get Beck," he said. "What about Hoffa? By all accounts he's even worse."

"If you get Beck, you can decide what to do about Hoffa later. Maybe he can be somebody else's problem. Beck's the one who's building a mansion with his union's money. He's a sitting duck for Bobby."

"Mm." Jack still did not look completely reassured. "And the mob?"

I answered him truthfully. "I don't know the answer to that one, Jack."

"Can you find out?"

"Maybe."

"Try. For me. After all, this was your bright idea in the first place. I want a sure thing, David. No loose ends, no surprises. If there's going to be a lot of trouble, we can always do something else. Hell, we've got until '60, right? I want to know *exactly* what we're getting into, okay?"

"Okay. It may not be easy."

"I'll owe you one, David."

I waved my hand. I thought of myself as Jack's friend, as well as a friend of the family. I was willing to do him a favor anytime—God knows, the Ambassador had done *me* a lot of favors in the past. One day, when Jack was president, I might ask him for something in return, but not now. I had always dreamed of being ambassador to the Court of St. James's, like Jack's father, and thought I would make a pretty good one, but now was hardly the time to bring up the subject. Besides, I was sure Jack knew about it. He had the politician's nose for knowing what other men's secret ambitions were without asking.

"Do it discreetly, David," he said. "I don't want Bobby to hear what you're doing."

I suppose it's only fair to add that Jack's request didn't come from out of the blue. The art of public relations, after all, is making people and things look better than they are—if everyone were honest and virtuous, there would be no need for the services of people like myself. Over the years, my clients had included labor union leaders, casinos in Las Vegas and Cuba, big-time entertainers, and racetracks, and it was often necessary to put "a good face," as people are so fond of saying, on rumors of mob involvement or to conceal the fact of it. The mob itself, at its highest level, was concerned with its "image," and anxious to present gangsters as men of honor, respect, and old-fashioned virtue, though they never found a way until Mario Puzo did it for them.

I quickly won the respect of the mobsters I had to deal with from time to time, mostly by keeping my mouth shut when it was necessary, never promising anything I couldn't deliver, and not fawning over them. As a result, I became acquainted in time with many of the major mob figures—among them Luciano, whom I liked; Costello, whom I didn't; Lansky, whom I saw often in Florida (he was the smartest of the lot); and Moe Dalitz in Las Vegas, a real gentleman.

I do not apologize for this. They never asked me to do anything dishonest for them, nor would I have. The dividing line between business and crime is in any case a thin one, and many of the "legitimate" figures I dealt with, or had as clients, like Howard Hughes or J. Paul Getty, seem to me, in retrospect, more corrupt than the bosses of "the Mafia."

My connections in this area were well known to Jack's father, and a source of great curiosity to Jack, who was fascinated by mobsters and ascribed to them powers that went far beyond anything they really had. Joe knew them for what they were—streetwise thugs who preyed on the weak and exploited human weakness; Jack thought they were sinister and glamorous—a mistake I had done nothing to discourage, to my shame and Jack's subsequent misfortune.

"Believe me, Jack," I said, "if there's one thing these fellows understand, it's discretion. I'll see what I can do."

"Good. Thank you, David. You're a real pal."

"One thing, though—if we get involved, they'll want something in return."

He looked at me thoughtfully. "What?"

"I don't know."

"We can't pay them money if it ever comes to that. No way."

"They won't want money. These are straight shooters, in their own way, these big-time mob guys. If they say they'll deliver, whatever it is, they will. But they'll expect the same from you."

"Sure," he said, but I could see that he hadn't really taken my warning seriously. The only person in the world about whom Jack felt any fear at all was his father. And maybe Jackie. I should have borne down harder on him at this point, but he looked so frail and tired that I didn't, and anyway, he changed the subject. It was a fatal error on my part to let him. "Jesus," he said, "but I miss the action. . . ."

"What have you been doing with yourself down here?"

"Apart from going stir-crazy? I'm working on this goddamned book—thanks a lot for *that* bright idea, David! When I've finished it, I'm going to put myself back in the doctors' hands for another fucking operation."

He closed his eyes for a moment as if to shut out the thought of going through all that pain and immobility again, and who could blame him? "Marilyn called me yesterday," he said.

"Here?"

"Luckily, Jackie was swimming."

"How is she?"

"Well, you know Marilyn. Should she marry Miller, or shouldn't she? As if I could tell her. I mean, it's probably a mistake, but then again, most marriages are, don't you think?"

I nodded. I knew his feelings on the subject.

"She wanted to come down here, to, ah, see me."

"A mistake."

"Yes. A nice thought, though. I don't think she was too disappointed when I told her it wouldn't work. She told me all about the Actors Studio, and the fellow who runs it, what's his name?"

"Lee Strasberg."

"Right. She sounded pretty cheerful, as a matter of fact. About her career, anyway. She said she could have me back on my feet again in five minutes! Told me how she'd *do* it too!" He laughed.

I had an instant, white-hot flash of sexual envy, a mental image of those lush white thighs opening for Jack.

He gave me a curious glance. "You think Marilyn's going to be a problem?"

I cleared my throat. As a matter of fact, I did think that Marilyn was almost as dangerous for Jack as Beck and Hoffa were going to be for Bobby. "You know what they say, Jack—never fuck a woman who's got more problems than you do."

For a moment I thought Jack was angry at me, but then he threw his head back and laughed, happier than I had seen him for weeks. "Oh, David," he said, gasping for breath. "They're the only kind worth fucking!"

8

SHE WAS TRYING TO CONCENTRATE ON WHAT MILTON was telling her about Larry Olivier, whom she could only think of as Sir *Laurence* Olivier, the greatest actor in the English-speaking world.

Somehow she knew, no matter how rosy a picture Milton painted, that she and Laurence Olivier were not fated to be friends. Milton had screened some of Olivier's films for her, but they merely depressed her even more, since in most of them she could hardly understand a word he said.

She liked the idea of working with Joshua Logan on *Bus Stop*, which she was going to do first, a lot better. Cherie was a role she understood, and at least Logan, whom she had met, spoke the same language and was talked of with some respect at the Studio.

"You didn't tell me Sir Olivier was going to direct the picture himself," she said.

"Not Sir Olivier," Milton corrected her for the umpteenth time. "Sir Laurence. Listen, the whole *point* is that Larry wants to direct. That's how we got him."

"I thought we got him because he needed money."

He rolled his eyes. "That too. He's directed before, lots of times."

"He hasn't directed *me*, Milton. And it's *my* money we're paying him, isn't it?"

There were beads of sweat on Milton's forehead. "Well, ours, yes," he said.

"*Mostly* mine."

He sighed. "Mostly yours, okay."

"I was just trying to make a point, see? If it's my money, I want to be told everything. And I want things to be done *my* way, not Sir Olivier's. I'm the one who's paying him, after all, and he has to understand that? Right?"

"Right."

"Milton? Are you *sure* he understands?"

"I'll make sure, Marilyn. Don't worry."

But she *did* worry. She was already beginning to resent the way Milton and Amy talked these days about Larry this and Vivien that. It was Milton's job to worry about *her* feelings, not Olivier's, still less Vivien Leigh's, just because Vivien Leigh had played the role of Elsie in *The Prince and the Showgirl* opposite Olivier on stage—the same role she would play in the picture.

"One other thing," she said, staring right in his eyes so he knew she meant business. "I talked to Paula Strasberg about putting her on the payroll."

Milton pretended to look puzzled. "Paula? Strasberg?"

"From the Actors Studio."

"Oh, Lee's wife, sure. Uh, what's she going to *do*, Marilyn?"

"She's going to be my dramatic coach, babykins."

"Uh-huh. What does that *mean*, Marilyn?"

"She goes with me to help me with my performance. Listen, Milton, this is a very big deal. Lee and Paula have never done this before, not for *anyone*, not even Marlon or Monty. I couldn't believe Paula would do it, frankly. I mean, Lee's a *genius*, and Paula's like his interpreter, or disciple, see?" She could see he wasn't enthusiastic. "Paula's a professional," she continued. "She understands me better than I understand myself. If she told me to throw myself out the window, I'd do it and know I could fly."

She stretched out her arms to show what she meant, knocking several prints of herself off the wall. The walls of his work-room were covered with pictures of her, for despite his new role as her partner and producer, Milton still photographed her all the time.

"Uh, that's great," Milton mumbled, with the nervous look of somebody trapped in a small space with a lunatic. "Have you talked all this over with Dr. Kris?"

Marianne Kris was her new analyst. She had been recom-mended by Lee and Paula Strasberg, who felt that therapy was indispensable for anybody who wanted to understand the Method—a fact that she had neglected to mention to Milton. "Marianne's very supportive," she said curtly. "She's all for the idea."

"You're really planning to take Paula to *England?*"

"You bet your ass, honey. Where I go, Paula goes." She held two fingers together.

"Larry might not like that, you know?"

"So tell Larry who's paying the bills, Milton."

He shrugged. "And if he still doesn't like it?"

"Then tell him to shove it."

There was a long silence while Milton digested this new facet of her personality. "Okay," he said, accepting his fate. "Paula's part of the deal, I guess. How much are we pay-ing her?"

She gave him a hard look. "How much are we paying for the antique furniture you charged to the company?"

He raised an eyebrow and gave her a sad smile.

"Milton, remember this: I may *look* like a dumb blonde, but I'm *not* a dumb blonde."

"Okay." He had once been a street kid from Brooklyn, smaller than all the rest and therefore obliged to be tougher. He knew all the angles, Milton did, but he also knew when he was beaten. "I'll make the arrangements with Paula," he said.

"I want it done right away, before I go back to LA. I want Paula on *Bus Stop.*" She looked him firmly in the eye. "Be generous, Milton," she said.

"*Vey iz mir.*"

"You bet." She looked at the clock and squealed—she sel-dom wore a watch because watches, however expensive, had a way of stopping dead the moment she put them on, as if there were some kind of magnetic force in her that jammed the movement. "I've got to run," she cried. "I'm going to be late."

"Late for what?"

She hesitated, on the verge of saying that she was going to meet Jack at the Carlyle. "Late for a hair appointment, in town," she said, wishing she were better at telling lies. "I've got to change. It's nearly two. Can I borrow your car?"

"Be my guest."

She laughed as she opened the door. "Milton, honey, I *am* your guest."

9

IF YOU DON'T GAMBLE, THERE'S NOT MUCH TO DO IN LAS Vegas, but I wasn't there for amusement. I was there to pump Moe Dalitz, on Jack's behalf.

Morris "Moe" Dalitz had made his mark and his money in the old Detroit "Purple Gang" during Prohibition, and had had the good sense to make a deal with the rising Sicilian mobsters instead of fighting them, unlike most of the other Jewish gangsters.

Way back then, Moe got some of his liquor from certain distilleries across the border in Canada that were owned, at arm's length, by Joe Kennedy, so when Moe moved to the warmer climate of the West Coast, about the same time that Joe took over RKO at a few pennies on the dollar, it was only natural that the two newcomers from the East would do each other a quiet favor occasionally, in which I was the go-between. Moe could intercede with Willie Bioff to ensure labor peace on the RKO lot, while Joe could make sure that his old pal William Randolph Hearst kept Moe Dalitz's name out of the papers.

In the end, Moe did better on the West Coast than Joe did and went on to become one of the founding fathers of Las

Vegas. Unlike most of his fellow mobsters, he was a rich man with money of his own to invest. He had been the only major gang leader to boldly declare to the IRS his earnings as a bootlegger during Prohibition, shrewdly calculating that if he paid taxes on the profit from his illegal business, the government wouldn't send him to prison for doing it. He built the Desert Inn and swiftly became the dean of casino owners— "Mr. Las Vegas," as the local press called him. It was Moe who made the city build sidewalks (despite the opposition of his fellow casino owners, who didn't see any reason to encourage gamblers to walk outside), Moe who built, despite ridicule, the first golf course, arguing that the casinos had to become "more than just a few guys upstairs in a hotel room playing poker."

And it was Moe who put on the first floor show and brought in the big-name stars to add glamour to the simple business of giving people an air-conditioned place in which to lose their money. In the process, he became a kind of bridge between the new breed of gangsters back in Chicago and the Midwest—men like Tony Accardo, who had inherited Al Capone's empire, or Sam Giancana, who, after much bloodletting, succeeded Accardo—and the big entertainers, bankers, and politicians without whom the business couldn't grow.

Moe was no "dese, dem, and dose" hoodlum with a pinkie ring. He was a solid, handsome man in his fifties, with brooding, sensitive eyes, sharp features like those of Dick Tracy in profile, faultless conservative tailoring, and the fingers of a concert pianist. It was said that he had once strangled a man with those fingers in the storeroom of a bar and grill in suburban Detroit, but that was many decades ago, and most of the more prominent business figures in Vegas had done such things in their time. Some were still doing them.

He was waiting for me in the center banquette of the restaurant in the Desert Inn, to which I was ushered by the maître d', whose manner was that of a cardinal presenting a distinguished visitor to the pope. He offered me a dark red, gold-tasseled dinner menu the size of the *The New York Times* as I sat down, but Moe waved it away. "The chef knows what we're having, Frankie," Moe said. He was so soft-spoken that you had to listen hard to hear what he was saying. "Are they treating you right, David?" he asked.

"Fine," I said. Las Vegas had not yet reached the peak of vulgarity for which it was to become famous, but it was still plenty lush. I had a vast suite overlooking the desert, with a marble bathroom, a bed big enough for a Roman orgy, and fruit, champagne, and flowers as far as the eye could see.

"It's comped," Moe said. "I set up a tab for you too, in case you want to play."

"You didn't have to do all that."

"*Mi casa, su casa,* as they say out here, David. Enjoy." Lying on its side in a silver wine rack on the table was a bottle of Haut-Brion '47 uncorked and breathing—a favorite of mine, as Moe knew. He had become a wine connoisseur late in life, and even managed to hire the sommelier from Le Pavillon in New York away from Henri Soulé to look after his treasures.

He poured us both a glass, sniffed the bouquet approvingly, tasted it with satisfaction, then toasted me. "Life is good, my friend," he said. "And for you?"

"Also good."

"I hear your business prospers."

"I can't complain."

He nodded gravely. Good business was a serious matter, not to be spoken of lightly. "I ordered a simple meal," he said. "I told the chef to make us a Caesar salad, T-bone steaks—the best you ever tasted, take my word—and baked potatoes."

"That sounds perfect, Moe." I meant it too. Steaks are the one thing they know how to cook in Vegas, and Moe knew his meat, having at one point acquired control of the meatcutters union in Cleveland by murdering the opposition.

We chatted, rather circumspectly, about old times while our salad was served. The steaks—as good as Moe had promised—were on the table before he got around to asking what had brought me to Las Vegas.

"I need some information," I said.

Moe's eyes suddenly seemed a lot less soulful. Still, he gave me a nod—permission to continue.

"I need to ask a few questions about the Teamsters."

"The Teamsters?" He shook his head. "What kind of questions?"

I leaned closer. "You know Joe Kennedy's boy Jack?"

"The senator?"

"Right."

He nodded, his eyes very wary now. Moe had first-rate political connections, local and national, and a number of western senators were deeply beholden to him, including, it was rumored, Lyndon Johnson. And Moe had a memory like an elephant's when it came to politics. "What does Jack Kennedy want to know about the Teamsters that his father can't tell him?" Moe asked. "Leave them alone and they might vote for him. He's a Catholic, and so are a lot of them; he's Irish, which is okay too; and he's a war hero, which they like. He's no pinko either, not like this Stevenson character. . . . Hell, the Teamsters *used* to be Democrats."

"I know," I said quickly, before he told me about FDR and Fala too. "But Bobby's going to be chief counsel for the McClellan subcommittee, and Jack's on the committee himself, and all they hear is Beck this and Hoffa that. . . . These guys seem to be surrounded by snitches—"

I caught a look of disapproval on Moe's face. "No names," he whispered.

I apologized. Every profession has its own rules, and in Moe's they mattered more than most. "What I meant to say," I went on, "is that everybody's pointing Bobby in the direction of the Teamsters. Jack's worried. Is there anything there? And how's the leadership going to react to an investigation?"

Moe grimaced. "Anything *there?* What do *you* think? Sure there's stuff there."

Moe had finished his steak. He took a last sip of the wine and called for two espressos. He looked around the room, apparently pleased to see that almost every table was filled with high rollers and the kind of leggy blondes you couldn't help looking at twice. "If Joe's boy is going after the Teamsters, he'd better have balls as big as his father's. Bigger maybe."

"I don't think that's a problem," I said. I was a little chilled. Moe was usually clean-mouthed for a gangster. If he said that Bobby was going to need big balls, he must have meant it seriously.

I felt, for the first time, that I might be plunging into deeper water than Jack had supposed. From the expression on Moe's face I could tell, with a sinking heart, that my interest in the

Teamsters wasn't going to be satisfied in an after-dinner conversation between two old friends.

The questions I asked had touched a live nerve. Now I wished I hadn't asked them, but, as we all know (and as Jack had yet to find out), you can't call back words once they are spoken. I should have flown back east on the next plane and told Jack to forget about it—warned him that he was dabbling in dangerous waters, full of man-eating sharks. If I had been with anyone but Moe Dalitz, I would have made my hasty apologies and left, but Moe was a person I really liked, and whose respect I valued, so I stayed.

On reflection decades later, I realize that I had trapped myself—and Jack. By asking questions about the Teamsters, I was stirring up the mob's interest in Jack Kennedy. Even if I had followed my instinct (or my fear) and taken the first flight out of Las Vegas I could get on, they would have come after me eventually, eager to find out what they could do for the junior senator from Massachusetts—and more important, what he could do for *them*.

"You want to know about the Teamsters, there's a guy you ought to meet," Moe said. "He's the man you want, not me."

"Where is he?"

"Here."

"Can you set it up for me?"

"Sure," he said, a little too casually. "Do you play golf?"

"Golf? A little."

"You ought to play more, David. Enjoy life, A young man like you, you shouldn't work so hard. Me, I swim, I play golf. Tennis, when it's not too hot. I wear the same size pants I did when I was twenty." He leaned across the table so close to me that I could feel the warmth of his breath on my face. "The party you should see will want to meet you on the golf course."

"Why?"

A look of mild exasperation crossed Moe's face. "Because he likes to talk to people out in the open, in the fresh air, understand? That way there aren't any hidden mikes or bugs, right?"

"How do I get in touch with him?"

Moe snapped his fingers at the maître d', who brought over two snifters of cognac and warmed them over a burner—something that seems to be part of the culture in Vegas and Miami.

Moe took a couple of Montecruz #1 Individuales from his breast pocket and passed me one.

"He'll get in touch with *you*, David," he said. "Don't worry."

The voice on the telephone was of the old-fashioned, cement mixer variety, and instructed me to be downstairs in the lobby at ten-thirty next morning, where somebody would be waiting for me.

It didn't take me more than a second to spot the "somebody" standing next to the front desk—a short, pudgy young man in a baggy summer suit, wearing dark glasses and a fedora. He was sweating, despite the fierce air-conditioning. When he turned toward me, I saw the bulge of a small revolver under his coat. That didn't mean much. More people went armed than unarmed within the Las Vegas city limits in those days. Besides, he didn't look like serious muscle—more of the gofer type, I thought. His soft handshake confirmed that impression—soft *and* damp, so unpleasantly, in fact, that it was hard to resist wiping my fingers off on my handkerchief. "Mr. Leman?" he asked in a husky voice with a New York accent. I nodded.

"You got no clubs?"

"None, I'm afraid." I had no golf clothes either. I wore a pair of gray flannel slacks, loafers, and a shirt with the sleeves rolled up and the collar unbuttoned.

We stepped outside into the blinding heat and glare. He opened the back door of a Cadillac for me, heaved himself into the driver's seat, and turned the air conditioner up to high. "It's a great climate, ain't it?" he asked.

I nodded. He had an irritating voice, whiny and high-pitched. I found the daily newspaper on the seat beside me and picked it up, to show I wasn't interested in conversation.

We drove through the desert for a few minutes, turned into a driveway, and entered Moe Dalitz's famous golf course, a triumph of man over nature. It could only be kept alive in this heat by twenty-four-hour-a-day watering—it was like building an eighteen-hole golf course in the middle of the Sahara. We parked and walked past the clubhouse and out onto the course, where a small, elderly, broad-shouldered man in leisure clothes waited, club in hand.

"Red," my driver said, "here's the guy you wanted."

I knew whom I was seeing now: Paul "Red" Dorfman, the most trusted associate of Sam Giancana and for years head of the Chicago scrap handlers union—a position Dorfman had taken over after its founder and secretary-treasurer was murdered.

Dorfman had been a featherweight champion way back in the twenties, and still carried himself in a boxer's crouch, but I remembered that he had been stripped of his title after he was accused of beating a rival union official unconscious with brass knuckles in the man's own office. The victim refused to make a complaint, of course, so it became just another of the dozens of felonies for which Dorfman had never been indicted, ranging from murder to rigging primary ballots in Cook County, Illinois.

As he swung the golf club back and forth, I couldn't help thinking that it wouldn't take much to make him aim it for my head. The famous red hair was shot with gray now, but his face had the flush of a man who wasn't by any means overjoyed to see me.

"You got no hat?" he growled. "In this sun, you gotta wear a hat." He turned to the man who had picked me up and said, "Go get him one, Jake, from the clubhouse."

He snapped his fingers at one of the caddies, standing carefully out of hearing, who handed me a club. "Play," Dorfman whispered, scanning the horizon. "If there's any FBI surveillance, you and me were playing golf, not standing around talking."

I took a few practice swings to warm up, then hit the ball about fifty yards, off course and into the desert.

Dorfman chuckled. "Try to make it look real, will you?" he said. "I shoulda bet you five bucks a stroke."

I would've liked to have him on the ski slopes with me, I thought, the son of a bitch! Or at the bridge table, except that he would probably have cheated.

"You oughta take some lessons," he said. He hit his ball straight down the fairway, while I asked myself why every mobster in Las Vegas apparently felt entitled to give me a lecture on sports and exercise. Personally, I thought I was in better shape than any of them. Certainly I have outlived them all.

"Great shot, Red!" my driver said, returning from the club-house at a trot and gasping like a gaffed fish in the surre-al heat.

"Shut the fuck up, Jake. Who asked you? Give the man the hat."

Jake handed me a white one-size-fits-all baseball-style cap with a ventilated mesh top. Embroidered in gold thread on the front of it was the logo of the Teamsters, a wagon wheel surmounted by two horse's heads. Above it was the message: "Tony Pro Invitational Golf Tournament, Las Vegas"; below it, in red capitals: "N.J. TEAMSTER JOINT COUNCIL."

I put it on gingerly as we walked. "Moe says you're ask-ing questions about the Teamsters," Dorfman said. "He says you're good people." He looked me up and down. "You don't look like no good people to me."

I ignored this, took another shot, and flubbed it.

"Putz!" Dorfman said, ever the good sport. He clapped me on the back, hard enough to make me wince. "I'm gonna *kill* you!" The word did not sound good, coming from him.

"Did Moe tell you what I wanted?"

He nodded. "Sure. Look, if the McClellan committee goes after the Teamsters, they're gonna hit pay dirt, they dig hard enough, no point denying *that*. When you're talking Team-sters, you're talking stuff that's hard to explain to civilians, you know what I mean? It's not an ordinary business. Differ-ent rules apply, you get my drift?"

I got his drift. Not every senator could be expected to understand the need for murder, extortion, racketeering, and thieving in the labor business. Most of the casinos in Vegas and half the new hotels in Miami Beach had been financed out of the Teamsters' Central States Pension Fund, brokered by Dorfman and his friends, and all the Teamsters' insurance was handled by Dorfman's stepson. Some of this was margin-ally legal, but even the part that was legal wouldn't look good once it was out in the open, and I strongly suspected that the part that was *illegal* was a bottomless abyss of horrors. "What happens if the committee starts digging hard, Mr. Dorfman?" I asked.

"Call me Red, okay?" He gave me a searching look. "A lot of guys could get mad. Dave Beck. Jimmy Hoffa." He paused. "Me."

"How mad?"

He shrugged. "Depends how far it goes, David. Listen, we're reasonable guys. We all understand how things work. If we gotta take some heat every once in a while, so be it. That comes with the territory, like the man says, am I right? Fine. A few guys get clipped maybe, a few go to the slammer, business gets fucked up for a while, the politicians get themselves reelected, life goes on. *Qué será, será.*" He looked at me. "What will be, will be," he added helpfully, in case I hadn't heard the song.

"Bobby Kennedy might not see it that way. '*Qué será, será*' is not exactly Bobby's philosophy of life."

Dorfman made a shot—another good one. He stared at me. "You want my advice, David, you tell Jack Kennedy and his little brother Bobby not to go too fucking far."

"Bobby's very tough, Red."

"Tough? Don't shit me. He's a college kid."

"Take my word for this, Red: Don't ever think of Bobby as 'a college kid.' He's tough as nails. And he's a Kennedy. He can't be bullied or bought. Neither can Jack."

"Who cares? They can be hit. If it comes to that."

I looked him square in the eye. "I doubt it."

He laughed. "Everybody can be hit, David, believe me." He said it with professional expertise. "Even a president. Hell, FDR nearly got hit in '32—only the mayor of Chicago, that scumbag Cermak, took the bullet instead. Truman almost got hit by those spics, right outside the White House, with the Secret Service all around him! You want somebody hit, my friend, whoever, there's always a way."

It seemed to me that we were getting off on the wrong foot, but I wasn't too worried. I'd heard this kind of bluster before, in the old days in Hollywood, from gangsters like Willie Bioff and Mickey Cohen who were always threatening to blow away people who annoyed them. In my experience, they only killed their own people, as a way of settling jurisdictional disputes, and by the time they settled down in LA or Vegas or Tahoe to enjoy their ill-gotten gains, they were mostly paper tigers, living off their reputation for violence.

"Nobody needs to get hurt," I said. "We're talking politics—and business."

Dorfman was gripping his clubs so hard that the knuckles on his big freckled hands were white. "Red," I went on soothingly, "listen to me, please. The Teamsters have got people leaking like sieves to the McClellan committee's investigators. Bobby can't ignore all that even if he wanted to, and Jack, who's on the committee himself, can't tell his brother to lay off, which he wouldn't do anyway, because it's not the Kennedy family tradition."

Dorfman still looked like a bull about to charge, if you can imagine a bull in tasseled golf shoes. But he was listening, particularly once he heard the word "leaking."

"Leaking like what?" he asked.

"Sieves. You know—those things you wash vegetables in."

"Yeah." Dorfman watched while I missed the ball a couple of times, but he had lost interest in my game. "Fucking stoolies." He sighed. "When I was running the scrap handlers, back in Chicago, nobody fucking leaked, believe you me. Look, if you wanna push the ball with your foot, go ahead, or we're gonna be here all fucking day."

Irritated, I took a wild swing at the ball—so wild that Dorfman jumped back—and sank it. I felt a glow of pride. If the FBI *was* filming us, J. Edgar Hoover, whom I knew and disliked, would at least see my moment of triumph. "Look, Red," I said, emboldened by my unexpected success, "all I'm trying to tell you is that there's going to be trouble—heat. Jack—Senator Kennedy—can't stop that, but he'd like to keep it within reasonable limits."

"We bend over backwards to make Bobby look good, while Jack makes like a labor statesman, that the deal?"

"Well, something like that," I said uncomfortably since it was exactly what Jack had in mind. "It's not a deal, by the way. It's more like a *suggestion*, for you to pass on to the right quarter."

He looked thoughtful. "It might work," he said. "But only if Bobby goes easy on Hoffa. And if Hoffa don't lose his temper at Bobby." He paused to choose his words. "Jimmy blows up easy, frankly. He's got a hell of a fucking temper."

I'd met Hoffa, who had reminded me of a hand grenade with the pin drawn, but I assumed, wrongly, that this was just a pose, one of those little tricks that leaders of men pick up along the way to power. I wondered too why Dorfman was more concerned with Hoffa's sensibilities than with Dave Beck's problems as the Teamsters' leader.

Dorfman moved close to me—closer than I found comfortable. "How about you offer Bobby and Jack a suggestion from *me?* We give you Beck and you leave Hoffa alone." He spoke in a whisper like sandpaper.

I couldn't believe my ears. Dorfman was offering up the president of the International Brotherhood—probably the most powerful union leader in the country—on a silver platter. I guessed that Dorfman and his Teamster pals would have no problem supplying enough documents and witnesses to send Beck to prison for life.

"Why Beck?" I asked.

Dorfman shrugged. "That's none of your goddamned business. Just tell the Kennedys, they want the fat fuck, they can have him, with enough evidence to sink a ship. But that's it, you understand? We'll throw in a few guys to make weight, but we get to choose them. Fair enough?"

It was more than fair—or would have been, if Jack were the only one concerned—but I wasn't so sure that even Jack could make Bobby swallow it. It would mean letting the Hoffa faction in the Teamsters use the McClellan committee to get rid of their own enemies while they went scot-free—exactly the kind of deal that Bobby hated.

Still, there was no question that putting Dave Beck behind bars would be a major coup. Everybody else in the labor movement, from George Meany on down, would be only too happy to see Beck in handcuffs, and grateful to Jack for doing what they didn't have the guts to do themselves.

"I'll pass it on," I said, trying not to show my excitement. "That's all I can say."

"You do that. Now let's play some golf."

I did my best, not so much because I wanted to put up a decent game against Dorfman as to get the whole damned thing over with as quickly as possible. It was brutally hot, and Dorfman's company wasn't anything I wanted to prolong now that we'd dealt with the essentials. He must have felt the same way, because he didn't offer me lunch at the club or even a drink, which was okay with me. I was so happy to get into the back of the air-conditioned Cadillac I didn't even notice I was still wearing the cap.

On the drive back to the hotel, the driver tried to be chatty. "He's quite a guy, Red, ain't he?" he said.

I nodded. The face reflected in the rearview mirror was pale, suety, and furtive; the hands on the steering wheel were fat and hairy, with stubby, uncared-for fingers.

"I learned a lot working for him."

Red Dorfman, no doubt, would have told him to "shut the fuck up," but I didn't. "I'm sure," I said curtly.

"You better believe it. He's been like a father to me, Red has."

I doubted that. Dorfman's attitude toward his driver was one of total contempt, so far as I could see.

"I got plans, you know? I'm more interested in the entertainment side of the business"—it came out "dabiznus," as if it were one word—"than the, uh, gaming side. Red's giving me a piece of action in Dallas—nightclubs, that kind of thing."

I guessed that this was probably Dorfman's way of getting rid of an employee who wasn't tough enough to be a bodyguard or serious muscle, or smart enough to handle the games. Pimping in Dallas wasn't my idea of a career advancement, but it clearly was his.

"If you're ever in Texas," he said, leaning back, "look me up, you want anything." He handed me a damp, crumpled pasteboard card that bore a drawing of a gartered woman's leg with a high-heeled pump dangling from the foot, embossed in gold against a brown ten-gallon Stetson. The words "The Golden Stripper" appeared above it in letters of twisted rope printed to look like a lariat.

I put it in my pocket and shook the sweaty hand that was offered to me across the front seat. "Jake Rubenstein, Mr. Leman," he said. "But my friends call me Jack Ruby."

10

THE BEST THING ABOUT MAKING *BUS STOP* WAS THAT IT put the prospect of working with Olivier right out of her mind. Making a movie was never a happy experience for her—*Bus Stop* was no exception—but at least it took her back to California, which, she guessed, was still "home" to her, at some level. . . .

She had been surprised and touched when Josh Logan told her he was going to give her a big party for the completion of the picture, and attributed it to her new status as a star who owned herself and made her own decisions.

Only Logan, a Broadway director, an intellectual, a New Yorker, would have had the balls to ask Bill and Edie Goetz to host the wrap party for *Bus Stop*, a picture that hadn't been made by MGM—or taken everybody's breath away by inviting Sukarno, the president of Indonesia, who happened to be in Los Angeles on his way home from Washington after a frosty meeting with Ike and John Foster Dulles that would shortly place him in the Soviet camp.

Partly because Edie Goetz was "old Hollywood," Louis B. Mayer's daughter, *everybody* came—the crème de la crème, the biggest names and powers in the industry: Sam Goldwyn, Jack Warner, Dore Schary, as well as stars who hadn't even noticed her when she was a starlet—even her idol, Clark Gable.

It was a triumphant evening—her revenge, if you wanted to look at it that way, and she did. She had reached the top. She had the whole industry at her feet, her handprints in cement outside Grauman's Chinese Theater, a bronze star on the sidewalk at Hollywood and Vine, her home on the maps the little old ladies sold to tourists taking the tour of the homes of the stars.

All the same, despite the champagne, she felt a little depressed because she didn't have a date. Loneliness gradually filled her mind, and she retreated from the noise and the press of people to the side of the room, feeling her glow fade. Her new PR girl saw her and pushed through the crowd to her side. "Tyrone Power is here," she said, full of excitement. "He's dying to say hello to you."

She had always admired Tyrone Power more than any other big star except Gable. Normally she would have dropped everything just for the chance of meeting him, but crankiness was rising in her like sap. "The hell with Tyrone Power," she said. "All those years when I was a starlet on the Fox lot and he was a big-deal star, he never tried to fuck me once."

It was the kind of thing that when it was repeated—as it would be—would take on a humorous spin and be quoted as an example of her sense of humor, but she had said it bitterly, and the PR girl, who was no fool, noticed it and looked as if she was wondering what she had gotten herself into.

Before the girl could say anything, Logan pushed his way toward them with a small brown man, In a funny cap and kind of Nehru jacket, in tow. Behind them pressed a whole mob of small brown Orientals, jabbering and hissing. The man next to Josh was clearly their leader.

She had forgotten all about Logan's distinguished foreign guest: it was simply not the kind of thing that interested her. They were face-to-face now, surrounded by the great man's entourage, his bodyguards, the Secret Service, reporters, photographers. It was clear that she was expected to do something. She flung her arms around him and gave him a kiss. "I've always wanted to meet the president of India!" she cried.

There was a sudden silence. A look of annoyance crossed the president's face, as if he suspected that he had been made the victim of some devious Western practical joke, played on him, worst of all, by a *woman*.

Logan cleared his throat nervously. "President Sukarno is the president of *Indonesia,* Marilyn," he said.

"I've never heard of it," she said. "But hi anyway, Mr. President."

There was a lot of murmuring, and all of a sudden, as if somebody had waved a magic wand, Sukarno and his people were gone. The look on his face as he turned away told her clearly enough that she had insulted him, and probably Logan as well, for now that she thought of it, he had been excited and honored by the prospect of having Sukarno as his guest and had briefed her carefully on what to say.

Feeling suddenly embarrassed and foolish, she opened a door and stepped into Bill Goetz's study—a large, dark room in the English style, with a lot of bookshelves and antique furniture—to find David Leman examining Goetz's collection of Degas bronzes.

David looked up quickly, as if he'd been caught reading Goetz's mail, and smiled. "Marilyn," he said. "I couldn't get close enough to you to say hello out there."

She gave him a kiss on the cheek. "I just insulted the president of Indonesia," she said. "I guess I've caused a diplomatic incident?"

They sat down on the sofa. He was holding a glass of champagne, which he handed to her. She took a drink and felt a little better.

"I wouldn't worry," he said. "Ike and Dulles already stepped on his corns in Washington. He'll have his people out in the streets burning American flags and stoning the windows of USIA libraries the moment he gets home."

David always had the inside scoop on everything. It was one of the things she liked about him.

"Jack met him in Washington," he went on, "and said all he wanted to know was whether Jack would give him a list of girls he could call when he got to LA."

She giggled. "I guess Jack didn't give him mine."

"I don't suppose he thinks of you as foreign aid. I hear the picture is great, by the way."

She nodded. If David was saying that, it probably reflected the opinion of the studio. He was as well connected in the movie business as he was in politics. All in all, she thought, he was a man she could be interested in, except for the fact that in her mind he was inextricably linked to Jack Kennedy. What the hell, she thought—she and Jack weren't married. She hadn't seen him in months. Anyway, Jack wasn't the kind of person you could possess exclusively any more than she was—that was one of his attractions, or at least she persuaded herself it was, for there was a tiny part of her that believed in old-fashioned, faithful love, and she wanted to believe she was capable of it with the right man, if she ever found him.

In the meantime, here was David, good-looking and clearly lusting after her—there was no mistaking *that*. She felt a sudden softening toward him, a kind of warm, liquid sensation deep inside, maybe just because she was alone and needed a man, or because in the subdued light of the library, he really did look like Gable. She leaned a little closer to him, her bosom almost hanging out of her low-cut dress, her lips parted, interested in a detached sort of way to see what would happen. "What brings *you* to the Coast, David?" she asked, a little more breathlessly than was necessary.

A furtive look crossed his face—she wondered why. "Business," he said. "I have an office here, you know."

"I know. Josh was in awe when I told him I knew you."

He laughed, but she could see he was pleased. How easy it was to flatter men, she thought, especially the smart ones. "I'm just back from Vegas," he said.

"Vegas? I didn't figure you for a gambler? I'm not, but I *like* Vegas. I went there when Frank opened at the Desert Inn. He had a table down front for his friends, and I just couldn't believe it—Liz Taylor, Cyd Charisse, Ava Gardner, and I were all at the same table. There wasn't a woman *there* Frank hadn't fucked!"

She caught the gleam in his eyes. Envy? Pain? *Go for it, David!* she said to herself, her lips only inches from his. She could tell that something was holding him back—perhaps his friendship with Jack, perhaps the fear of being discovered embracing her on the Goetzes' sofa—but that made it more of a challenge. She realized he was glancing toward the door, and it didn't take much to guess why. "Are you here by yourself?" she whispered.

He shook his head. His cheeks were red—was he blushing? "Ah, no," he stammered. "As it happens, Maria is with me."

Maria? She strained to remember who Maria was; then it came back to her. "Your wife!" she said. "She's here?"

He nodded toward the door, as if she were on the other side of it, or about to open it. "She's—ah—circulating. Maria has a lot of friends out here on the Coast."

"She was in Vegas with you?"

He shook his head again. "No, I was there strictly on business. . . . For Jack. . . ." He blushed more deeply this time, obviously regretting that he'd let it slip out. She wondered what kind of business Jack could have in Vegas. Given time, she was pretty sure she could squeeze the answer out of David, right here on the sofa.

There was a part of her that was willing to try. She had always enjoyed sex in unlikely places, the risk of discovery adding its own special excitement. She let her lips actually touch David's, very gently, almost as if by accident. She wondered if he had the guts to fuck her right now, with his wife next door circulating among her West Coast friends.

Focusing all her energy, she *challenged* him to, with an expression he could hardly mistake for anything else: *You wanted it, baby, here's your chance!* But she already guessed it wasn't going to happen—David simply wasn't the type to take that kind of risk, not even for *her*. *Fuck you!* she thought. *You had your chance!*

She pulled away slightly, still smiling at him. "I'm going to England, you know," she said, breaking the spell.

He gave a little sigh. Regret? Relief? "Yes, I know," he said. "I saw Larry Olivier in New York. He's thrilled that he's going to be working with you."

"The whole idea scares the shit out of me, frankly," she said. "England, Larry, Vivien, all that. . . ."

"You'll do fine."

"Maybe. I'm going to New York first."

"I heard. The word is, congratulations are in order for you and Arthur."

She nodded without enthusiasm. "I'm going to be there awhile, apartment hunting," she said.

"If I can be of any help . . ."

The door opened, and a lot of people came in, Pat Lawford, Josh and Nedda Logan, and a woman who looked just like Jacqueline Kennedy and whose expression made it clear that she was Maria Leman. Then she was pulled back into the party, and in a few minutes she hardly even remembered how close she had come to putting her arms around David and giving him what he wanted. . . .

WHEN JACKIE AND JACK FINALLY MOVED TO GEORGETOWN, selling Hickory Hill, their big country house in Virginia, to Bobby and Ethel—who had no problem filling it with their brood—journalists would turn it into Camelot on the Potomac, with nonstop parties of New Frontiersmen and their pretty ladies playing touch football and pushing each other into the swimming pool fully dressed, but I always found it a gloomy old place, full of rooms either too big or too small that even Jackie couldn't make cheerful. I never saw Jack at Hickory Hill when he didn't look as if he wanted to be elsewhere. Jackie too was anything but cheerful when I arrived.

I gave Jack the Tony Pro Invitational cap from Red Dorfman, which he put on with a big grin, but it didn't raise a laugh from Jackie.

He took the hat off and put it on the table as she went off to check on lunch. I added Jack Ruby's card, for a laugh. "In case you're ever in Dallas," I said.

"God forbid! I'll pass it on to Lyndon. How about a walk before lunch?"

"Can you?"

He nodded. "Not far. And you're going to carry my cane, in case I need it. But I've turned the corner. I've got a new doctor, Janet Travell, who's a miracle worker. She's given me some exercises—tough to do at first, but they make a world of difference. And I'm to keep walking, keep moving, as much as possible. I already feel like a new man."

"No pain?"

"Oh, plenty of pain, sure, but she gives me some injections for that—Novocaine, I think, straight into the muscles—and that helps."

We stepped out the French doors into the warmth of a perfect Virginia early summer's day. Jack walked slowly and with some difficulty, but it was a pleasure to see him on his feet again. We walked over to the pool. "I swim every morning too. The water has to be warmed to ninety-five degrees. Jackie complains it's like swimming in soup, but cold water just kills me. . . ."

He looked toward the horizon. "I thought it might be a good idea to get outside for this conversation," he said. "You never know."

So Jack and Red Dorfman had something in common! I wondered if Jack really thought somebody might have bugged Hickory Hill; then I thought of J. Edgar Hoover and realized that nothing was more possible. "Dorfman made me play golf in the desert sun because he was afraid of surveillance," I told him. "That's how I got the hat."

Jack nodded thoughtfully. "Then he's a smart fellow. Good. If we're going to do business with him, we don't want him behaving, ah, rashly. *Are* we going to do business?"

"Maybe, Jack. Maybe."

Jack's eyes focused on the far horizon at the rolling hills. Though he was listening to me with his full attention, he somehow managed to communicate that he was the one who would make any decisions. His illness and his two desperate operations had matured him, as a lot of people were soon to discover. "You didn't make them any promises, did you?" he asked.

"None. But they made us a serious proposition."

He nodded again. His eyes were hooded. We were walking round and round the pool at a slow pace, Jack with his hands behind his back, his face set with determination. "What do we get if we go for it?"

"Dave Beck."

He whistled. He glanced at me to see if I was joking. "Son of a bitch!" he said in awe. "They'd give him up?"

"Lock, stock, and barrel. Plus a reasonable number of his associates and all the evidence you'd need to get them sent away. Of course, there's a price."

He looked away, as if he weren't listening. "Yes?" He waited for me to tell him what it was.

"You lay off Hoffa," I said. I did not mention laying off Moe Dalitz, Red Dorfman, and their friends. If Hoffa was safe, they would be too. Besides, Jack knew exactly who the people around Hoffa were, and what would be involved if the committee accepted Beck as their sacrificial goat. There would be headlines, praise for him from labor leaders, public approval—and business as usual for Jimmy Hoffa and the mob.

If he was shocked at the prospect, it didn't show. He looked at me thoughtfully. "To be perfectly honest with you, David," he said, "even though this was your idea, I wouldn't have taken a bet you could bring it off. I must say, I'm impressed."

"If you think politicians or gangsters are tough, wait until you have to deal with the CEO of any Fortune Five Hundred company—guys like Bob McNamara, or Roger Blough, or Tom Watson. I deal with them every day."

"That's what Dad is always saying about big business."

"He knows what he's talking about."

He was silent for a moment. "Our distinguished committee chairman, Senator McClellan, will be overjoyed. He's scared shitless that he's going to step out into the limelight and come back empty-handed. If we can guarantee he gets to bring back Beck as a trophy, he's going to be one happy hunter."

"What about Bobby?"

"Ah, what about him? It's a good question. He won't be happy. For some reason, he has a hair up his ass about your Mr. Hoffa. Beck seems to me just as good a catch—maybe better in some ways—but Bobby wants to see Hoffa doing time in Lewisburg or Atlanta, sewing mailbags or whatever it is they do these days." He sighed. "Well, I'll talk to him."

"Better you than me."

Jack frowned. "I know Bobby can be a pain, David, but he's my brother. And he's a team player. Of course, the amenities are going to have to be observed. Hoffa is going to have to appear before the committee and act suitably humble. He'll have to answer some tough questions—tough enough to show we mean business. We can't have him taking the Fifth for days on end either. He has to meet us halfway."

"But the questions Hoffa's asked needn't come as a total shock to him, need they? Couldn't they be *limited*—agreed upon mutually in advance, for example?"

Jack focused on the flowers around the pool as if he were judging a garden show. "There'll be details to be worked out," he murmured distantly. "You'll be wanting to talk to Kenny or Dave about that."

I didn't like the sound of that a bit. I made a mental note to get myself out of this particular loop as soon as possible.

Jack looked across the flat, unruffled surface of the pool. Jackie was standing in one of the French windows, waving at him. He did not wave back. "Lunch," he said. "You'll pass the message on?"

I nodded. I didn't think that could do any harm.

I could tell that Jack was torn between curiosity to know how and to whom I would signal his agreement to the deal and the realization that it was something he was better off not knowing. He loved details, Jack did—nothing pleased him more than to hear about the machinations of spies, gangsters, and all the rest of the mysterious characters who lived in the shadows of public life—but he had an acute sense of when it didn't pay to ask a question.

I waited, and he said nothing.

His father would have been proud of him, I thought.

Lunch was just the three of us, and the atmosphere between Jack and Jackie was so cold and thick that you could cut it with a knife. Clearly, Jack had gone too far somewhere.

Jackie asked after Maria, who was still in California, then chattered brightly to me as the meal was served. I may as well confess that I have always liked Jackie. She is good company, attractive, gifted with superb taste and a real talent for the kind of conversation and mild flirtation that appeals to men of all ages.

I think Jack seriously underestimated just how tough she was, when he married her. His sisters and Ethel made malicious fun of her pretensions (when she had pointed out to them that her name was pronounced "Jack-*leen*," they shouted: "Rhymes with 'queen,' of course!"), but she and her sister, Lee, were made of sterner stuff. After all, they were the daughters of one of the most notorious (and charming) womanizers and drunks of his generation, while their mother, Janet, had raised social climbing to such an art that she impressed even Joe Kennedy, no mean judge of social climbers himself. The Bouvier girls had earned their degrees in the school of emotional hard knocks.

"How is Los Angeles, David?" she asked me.

I told her about Joshua Logan's party at the Goetzes', described what Maria was wearing (Jackie always wanted to know), and filled her in on what was happening in the lives of her West Coast friends. Her sister-in-law Pat had married Peter Lawford the year before, over the ferocious objections of Joe Kennedy, who said that the only thing he hated worse than one of his daughters marrying an actor was having her marry an *English* actor.

Jackie, at the beginning, got along well with Lawford, who went out of his way to amuse her, until she began to suspect that he was providing a string of Hollywood starlets for Jack, at which point she turned against him. Still, he introduced her to a lot of the more socially presentable movie people, and Jackie was no more immune to that kind of glamour than anyone else.

I told her the story about Marilyn and President Sukarno (leaving out Sukarno's request for Jack's list of the local starlets, of course), since I knew it would amuse her, and she laughed—that breathy, tinkling little laugh which the Kennedy girls found false and affected, but which always seemed to me bewitchingly sexy. "Isn't that funny, darling?" she asked Jack, who was not laughing, his mind, perhaps, on what he was going to say to Bobby.

"Nobody ever said she was a diplomat," he said grumpily.

Jackie smiled at him sweetly. "Oh, Jack darling," she said, "that's not nice! I thought you were a great admirer of hers."

She turned to me. "Jack's seen every one of Marilyn Monroe's pictures at least twice, David. He's a real fan. Next time you're in Los Angeles, you ought to get her autograph for him. He'd be *thrilled*, wouldn't you, Jack?" It occurred to me too late that Jackie had somehow found out about Jack and Marilyn. I realized that I had put my foot in it.

Jack glowered at her, his mouth set in stubborn determination not to be provoked, particularly in front of me. "That would be great," he said through clenched teeth.

"There you are, David—a little commission for you. Maybe you could even find a way of introducing Jack to her?"

I coughed uneasily. "I imagine that's possible," I said, trying to keep the tone light.

"I'll *bet* it is!" Jackie snapped savagely.

We sat in uncomfortable silence while coffee was served. Jackie was certainly entitled to her anger, I thought, but it wouldn't do her much good. She had pursued Jack hard, though everybody around him—his father, the Ambassador; his old college chum and resident court jester, Lem Billings; even Rose Kennedy and His Eminence the archbishop-cardinal of Boston—had warned her about Jack's women and the fact that he was, as they tactfully put it, "too set in his bachelor ways" to give them up. Far from being a deterrent, the warnings merely increased Jack's attraction for her, and her determination to marry him. Jackie, I suspected, was only capable of loving the kind of dangerous man her father was, not the kind of "safe" man who might love her exclusively. She once told Maria that even as a schoolgirl she had always dreamed of marrying an "experienced" man, and God knows, that was what she got, twice.

Having made her decision, she received no sympathy from Jack's family. She had a certain respect, as I said, for the Ambassador, but she hated Rose Kennedy, whom she always referred to with acid emphasis as "*Belle Mère*," and whom she often caricatured savagely and accurately, to Jack's acute discomfort.

I looked at my watch. "I must be going," I said.

"Back to New York?" Jackie asked. "How I long to get back there"—she paused tellingly—"and have some fun of my own!"

"New York, yes. Then Miami, tomorrow. I have business there."

"Los Angeles, New York, Miami—you do lead an active life, David, in all the exciting places. I'm madly envious."

"It's all business, Jackie."

She smiled. "Of *course* it is. Isn't that *always* what men say, Jack?"

I breathed a sigh of relief as the driver took me back to National Airport.

Years before, one February when the temperature in New York hadn't risen above zero for a week, I flew to Miami to get warm and, not having much else to do there, ended up purchasing, pretty much on impulse, a house in Key Biscayne.

Maria said I wouldn't use it enough to make it worthwhile, and she turned out to be right, but once I took the Miami Beach Chamber of Commerce on as a client, it seemed a good idea to keep up a residence there.

Florida, I may say now that I no longer have Miami Beach as a client, is not one of my favorite places in the world—as compared to Cap d'Antibes, for example—but there's a certain pleasure to feeling the warmth and sun on one's body or lying on one's back in the pool looking up at a clear blue sky above the palm fronds, when only two or three hours away one's fellow New Yorkers are slipping and sliding on ice.

I came out of the pool, toweling myself, to find Red Dorfman sitting in the lanai, at my breakfast table. His bodyguard—real muscle this time, unlike Jack Ruby—lurked in the background against the bougainvillea. Dorfman was dressed for the golf course. "You found your way, I see," I said to him, feigning a calm I did not feel. I had been waiting for him to call and set up a meeting.

"Big deal! You think your place is hard to find, just because you got an unlisted fucking telephone number? Don't make me laugh." He pointed in the direction of my neighbor. "Nice location too—right next to Bebe's place. I been there lotsa times, to meet Nixon."

I raised an eyebrow. I was not surprised to learn that Nixon had what later came to be called a "back channel" to the Teamsters—I merely hoped that Dorfman was a little more discreet about using Jack's name than he was about Nixon's.

"You got a nice place, David." He examined my breakfast table and nodded his approval. "You live nice."

"I try, Red, I try." I poured him a cup of coffee and put a couple of slices of fresh papaya on my plate.

"You wanna go on trying, you better have good news for me."

I ate my papaya calmly, wiped my mouth, and stared at him. "I'm the messenger, Red. If you start threatening me, you're not going to get any messages, okay?" In my experience, you can't let people like Dorfman intimidate you, even for a moment, or you lose face.

He backed down sullenly. "Okay, okay," he muttered. "Whatsa matter? You can't take a joke?"

"Was that a joke? I didn't hear you or your friend over there with the shoulder holster laughing. Maybe I missed the punch line."

"Don't be a smart-ass, David."

"Red, just so we're clear about it, the two of us, I am not a smart-ass. I'm smart. I hope you're enjoying your stay in Miami?"

He shrugged. "It's okay. I like the track, the dogs, the jai alai. I'm staying at the Deauville, where they always treat me nice."

I'll bet they do, I said to myself. The Deauville Hotel was a home away from home for gangsters—you were consorting with known felons just by sitting beside the pool or entering the bar.

Dorfman helped himself to a slice of papaya. "So what's your guy say?" he asked.

"My guy is willing to go along, in principle."

"What the fuck does 'in principle' mean?"

"Well, your guy has to show up in Washington, as we discussed, and answer questions." I caught the look on his face. "Don't worry," I said. "We'll let him have the questions in advance. He'll have plenty of time to come up with answers."

"So it's just, like, window dressing, right?"

"Exactly. Well put. Of course, he—your guy—will have to be on his best behavior."

Dorfman's face was expressionless. It crossed my mind that his control over "his guy's" good behavior might be less reliable than Moe had given me to believe in Vegas. Hoffa's temper was certainly the first thing you noticed about him, along with his white athletic socks, although the one time I did business with him, he had held it in check and we had made a very reasonable deal.

Joe Kennedy had bought the Chicago Merchandise Mart before the war as an investment for his children—then, and for all I know, still, the biggest commercial building in the world—so its profitability was a continuing concern of his. He was therefore alarmed in the early fifties when he learned that the Teamsters were trying to organize the Merchandise Mart's employees. Since I knew my way around union politics, Joe asked me to go to Detroit, from which Hoffa was running his growing midwestern empire.

Oddly enough, Hoffa then had a reputation for being a left-wing labor leader. As I was to discover, he had in fact begun his career under the influence of Eugene Debs, and as a result, many people made the mistake of assuming he was a kind of midwestern Trotsky. I hadn't been in his office five minutes before I realized this was not the case. Hoffa was an idealist gone bad. His headquarters had much the same atmosphere of corruption and violence—and many of the same kind of thugs—as a Nazi gauleiter's; I could not help thinking, during my brief visit, that many of the faces I saw there would have looked right above brown uniforms with swastika armbands.

Nevertheless, Hoffa himself turned out to be unexpectedly reasonable, and not without a certain amount of gritty charm. He made a deal on the spot, and Joe Kennedy bought himself guaranteed labor peace in Chicago. Nothing else between Hoffa and the Kennedys was to go as smoothly.

"What do you mean by 'best behavior'?" Dorfman asked, as if the concept were unfamiliar to him.

"Tell him to think of it as a parole board hearing," I suggested.

Dorfman put his head back and laughed loud enough to startle the bodyguard. "I'll tell him that," he said. "He's never done time, but he'll get the picture."

He stood up and we shook hands. "I'll be in touch with you," he told me.

"Jack may want to have somebody else look after this from now on," I said. If I had anything to say about it, he would.

He didn't let go of my hand. Instead, he squeezed it hard and shook his head, still smiling but with hard, cold eyes. "You got it wrong, David," he said. "You're our boy. Moe vouched for you to me. I vouched for you to Hoffa and to my guys in Chicago, my *padroni.*"

"I'm not sure I'm comfortable with that, Red."

He let go of my hand and gave me a big bear hug. "You got a sense of humor," he said. "I like a guy with a sense of humor. I always read that piece inna *Reader's Digest* every month—what is it, 'Laughter Is the Best Medicine'?" He laughed, as if to show he knew how. "You're in, *bubbi,* that's all there is to it. You don't wanna be found floating facedown in the pool, like the guy at the beginning of *Sunset Boulevard,* do you?"

I closed my eyes and thought about William Holden floating in Gloria Swanson's pool. "If that's the way you want it, Red," I said.

What have I done to Jack Kennedy? I wondered. Then, more realistically: What have I done to myself?

"Don't worry. It'll all work out," Dorfman said. "You'll see."

"I hope so," I said, suppressing a shiver.

"It had better!" He lingered a moment, flexing his shoulders like the boxer he had once been.

I looked him in the eye. I didn't have anything to lose, I thought. "Your ass is on the line as much as mine, Red," I said evenly.

He gave me the defiant look of a bully whose bluff has been called, but his heart wasn't in it.

I turned my attention back to my breakfast and buttered a piece of toast. By the time I'd put Cooper's Vintage Oxford marmalade on it, Dorfman and his shadow were gone, leaving behind only a faint aroma of pungent cologne, like the smell of brimstone that is said to accompany the devil.

I poured myself another cup of coffee and picked up the paper. On the front page was a photo of Marilyn arriving in London. She was smiling, but to anyone who knew her, the look in her eyes was one of stark terror. Next to her, looking distinctly uncomfortable, was Arthur Miller, holding her by the elbow as if he was afraid she might trip and fall.

They did not look to me like happy newlyweds.

12

SHE COULD HEAR AMY GREENE KNOCKING ON THE BATHroom door again. "Marilyn honey," Amy whispered, "are you okay? Everybody's waiting for you."

She *wasn't* okay. She was sitting in the toilet of the first-class cabin on Pan American's overnight flight to London, trying to pretend that none of this was happening to her—that she wasn't about to be greeted by the Oliviers on their home ground, that she wasn't committed to make a picture in which she had to play exactly the kind of dumb blonde she didn't want to be, that this wasn't—just her luck!—day one of a monumental period that left her bloated, aching, seized by cramps and unstoppable bleeding.

The thought of getting out of the airplane paralyzed her. She sat on the toilet seat in a silver-gray silk ribbed-knit dress that had been "form-fitting" when she bought it at Bendel's but in her present shape was obscenely, uncomfortably tight. She had kicked off her white, high-heeled pumps. There was a pile of damp, crumpled Kleenex on the floor; she shredded another tissue and dropped it at her feet.

The last few months had been, in Dr. Kris's words, "traumatic and stressful," leaving her with the feeling that she was reaching the crest of a roller-coaster ride, and about to plunge downward. Of course, happiness always did that to her—the moment she felt happy, she began to worry about how she'd feel when it was over. Marriage always made her happy in the beginning because it was like joining a new family. She had managed to get herself embraced by Arthur's family at first meeting—nobody could have tried harder than she did—and in his father, Isidore, a crusty, funny, outspoken Jewish patriarch, she found at once the father figure she was always searching for. She liked being a daughter, she decided, a lot more than she liked being a wife. . . .

"Marilyn!" It was Milton this time, his voice low but insistent, with an edge of panic to it. She had met Olivier in New York, and kept him waiting for over two hours. Olivier had been charming about it, on the surface, but she'd had no trouble reading the anger in his eyes—as well as a clouded look of doubt, as if he were saying to himself, Oh my God! What have I gotten myself into!

Whatever Olivier had expected, she had failed to deliver, and she knew it. Stiff, awkward, giggling nervously like a schoolgirl and hating herself for being in awe of him, she had projected about as much dazzle as a burned-out light bulb. He kept up a steady, desperate chatter about all the Hollywood friends they must have in common, while she smiled until her jaws ached. When he finally, mercifully, was ready to leave, he took her hand in his and begged her not to keep the press waiting in England. "It's different at home," he warned her. "They won't forgive you there, darling."

She had tried to talk to him about the Studio—the Method—the Strasbergs (she thought of them as a single entity, like Father—Son—Holy Ghost, Jack had joked when she tried to explain the whole thing to him), but Olivier had changed subjects with a superior smile that made it clear he didn't take the Strasbergs (or her) seriously.

Arthur wasn't any help when she talked to *him* about it. He couldn't conceal his admiration for Olivier—all she heard was Larry this and Larry that, until she began to suspect that he hoped "Larry" would perform in one of his plays one day, or that he had even discussed *writing* a play for him. . . .

Milton's worried voice interrupted her thoughts again. "Marilyn honey, do you want me to get Arthur?"

"No!" Arthur must already think she was crazy. Talking to him through a locked toilet door didn't seem a good way to improve matters between them. "Is it a mob scene out there?" she asked fearfully.

"This is England, Marilyn. Everything is under control."

"Is Mrs. Olivier there?"

"*Lady* Olivier, Marilyn. Vivien. Sure. She's waiting for you."

"What's she wearing?"

"A suit. Kind of pale mauve tweed, pleated skirt, jacket with a big open collar."

You had to hand it to Milton, she thought. How many men could describe a woman's clothes so accurately? "Glamorous?" she asked, leaning close to the door so she could whisper.

She could hear him sigh. "Sort of," he admitted. "More, like, *elegant,* but in a very English way—kind of like the Queen or Princess Margaret but better-looking, if you see what I mean."

Great! She cursed herself for having chosen a dress that rose to a high neckline in front, almost like a turtleneck sweater, showing none of what the British public wanted to see. She would be upstaged by Vivien Leigh, who had to be nearly twenty years older than she was! "Is she wearing a hat?"

There was a moment's pause. "Uh-huh. A matching hat, with a loose ribbon around it. Larry's wearing a dark suit, and he's smiling, but he doesn't look happy. Let's *go*, honey!"

A hat! She should have worn a hat! Why hadn't she realized that of *course* Vivien Leigh would be wearing a hat? She had decided to wear short white gloves to match her shoes, although she was afraid they made her hands look like Minnie Mouse's, but now she couldn't decide whether they were correct or not.

"Marilyn, Arthur's coming, and he looks really pissed off."

Whatever lay ahead, she wasn't up to another argument with Arthur, who—for all his simple, pipe-smoking calm and single-minded devotion to her—always needed to feel (and make *her* feel) he was in the right. She powdered her nose quickly, put on her goddamned, stupid white gloves, unlocked the door, and tottered out, with Milton and Amy supporting her on either side in the narrow corridor as if they were bodyguards. Arthur's tall figure was in the shadow, next to the door of the plane.

Milton gave her a desperate smile. "Arm in arm, honey," he said. "He's your *husband*. Remember? Knock 'em dead!"

"Tell Arthur not to be a stiff," she heard Amy whisper to her; then she was at the door, her arm thrust through Arthur's, and together they stepped out into the gray morning sunlight, pushed from behind by the Greenes. A roar went up—louder than anything she had heard since she entertained the troops in Korea in 1954—from a vast crowd of people only barely held in check by row after row of London bobbies. Reporters and photographers battled to get to the front of the crowd, passengers held their small children above their heads so they could see; everywhere there was pushing, shoving, and shouting. At the front of the mob, as small and neat as the figures on a wedding cake, stood the Oliviers, a nervous smile on his face, a look of fury on hers.

An airport official guided her toward them; another handed her a bouquet of flowers. Sir Laurence mumbled a greeting she couldn't hear above the noise and gave her a peck on the cheek, Lady Olivier shook her fingertips limply—she too wore gloves, though hers were long, pale mauve suede ones, as tight-fitting as a second skin—then the press broke through the barriers and swept around them like a storm. Hands plucked at her clothes and hair, flashbulbs popped in her face, questions were screamed at her. She pressed herself against Arthur's chest, while Sir Laurence and the airport security men cleared a path for her.

They plunged into the waiting Rolls-Royce like bank robbers making a getaway, Vivien Leigh sitting beside her on the back seat, Arthur and Olivier facing their wives on the jump seats. Vivien was smiling vaguely and waving to the crowd like a queen, which irritated her because the crowds had come to see *her*. Somehow she felt overshadowed by the Oliviers. She told herself that this was *her* movie, that she owned it, that she was paying Sir Laurence, but it did no good; he still looked as if *he* owned the world, sitting back elegantly in earnest conversation with Arthur—genius to genius, she thought bitterly.

She hadn't realized until she saw them together how badly dressed Arthur was in his off-the-rack seersucker jacket, baggy pants, and clodhopper shoes, in contrast to Olivier, with his florid complexion, his long hair carefully brushed in little wings above his ears, his superbly tailored double-breasted suit, his narrow, gleamingly polished shoes. He was sending about a zillion volts of English charm in Arthur's direction, while Arthur, clearly awed by his new pal "Larry," sat stiffly upright, his head grazing the roof of the car, nodding, smiling, and drinking in every word.

She and Vivien sat as far away from each other as they could, in silence, while their husbands were lost in their newfound mutual admiration society. "You played the part of Elsie on stage, didn't you?" she asked finally, hating the little-girl-being-nice-to-her-betters tone of voice.

Vivien—who had been chain-smoking ferociously ever since they left London airport—looked her in the eye for the first time. "Yes, I did," she snapped. "Larry and I did it together. It was a great success."

Vivien breathed smoke into her face and dismissed her with a grimace. "It's a shame you didn't see us—Miss Monroe." Her pronunciation was as sharp as the edge of a knife. "You would have known exactly how to play Elsie."

"I'll find my *own* way," she said, not bothering to hide her anger.

"Well, good luck to you, I'm sure."

She sat in tongue-tied rage during the rest of the trip, while Olivier, conscious at last that he had been avoiding her—or, she thought, more likely remembering that she was his meal ticket—rattled on and on about the cottage he had rented for her and Arthur. Then he stopped suddenly and peered out the window.

"The bloody press is following us," he said. "Damn! I'd hoped we'd get away from the buggers."

"Larry hates film journalists—particularly the columnists," Vivien explained. "He barred them from the studio when he was making *Henry the Fifth,* didn't you, darling? They've never forgiven it, Miss Monroe."

She herself had never felt that way about the press at all. Columnists and reporters were usually on her side back home, especially since the story was mostly Marilyn versus 20th Century-Fox, so she was cast as a kind of female David going up against Goliath.

"Paul Tandy is the one Larry hates most, Miss Monroe," Vivien said sweetly. "Isn't he, darling?" She smiled at him. "Tandy is on the *Mail,* you see. One of our most important newspapers—unfortunately for Larry. Larry got paid a lot of money to endorse a cigarette on television, and ever since then, Tandy calls him 'Sir Cork Tip' in his column." She laughed loudly. "I'm afraid Larry doesn't find it funny at all. Does *your* husband have a sense of humor, Miss Monroe?"

"Arthur? I guess so." The truth was, Arthur had no sense of humor at all about himself, nor had the Slugger, who thought of himself as a national institution, but she wasn't about to tell that to Vivien Leigh.

Vivien glanced briefly in Arthur's direction and shrugged. "How nice for you, darling," she said unbelievingly.

"Sir Cork Tip" glared balefully at his wife, but before he could say anything, they arrived at the rented house. He got out first, followed by Arthur, forgoing politeness so he could clear a path for her and Vivien through the crowd of reporters already ringing the car. She thought the two men looked like Mutt and Jeff. She could hear him pleading with them— "Marilyn's tired, give her a chance to freshen up, please, be reasonable, chaps. . . ."

Apparently, he reached some kind of understanding with them, for he turned and waved. Vivien stepped out of the car first like royalty, into a blaze of flashbulbs, a smile fixed on her face; then she followed, temporarily blinded by the flashes.

Vivien proceeded at a stately pace, and the mob parted. She wasn't sure whether it was the title that did it or simply the expression on Vivien's face, which seemed to convey that she didn't even *see* the press, that they were invisible to her, beneath her notice. Whatever it was, it worked, except for one tall, well-dressed man who blocked their way slightly. "Miss Leigh," he shouted, in one of those English upper-class voices that are so sharp they can cut glass, "how do you feel about Sir Laurence doing love scenes with Miss Monroe?"

Vivien didn't break stride. "Sir Laurence has done love scenes with *me*, Paul. I don't suppose he has anything new to learn about love scenes."

"Paul Tandy," Vivien explained as they forced their way past him. He was writing in his notebook, his face set in a quizzical smile.

She felt her face growing flushed. Vivien hadn't bothered to give *her* a chance to say something—had ensured she was going to be treated like the dumb blonde seductress and home breaker, just as she'd always been.

She rushed inside the house, where Arthur was standing in the hallway, looking out of place against the antique furniture and Oriental carpets. The "cottage" was a big country house, old, lavishly furnished, and elegant—like a movie set—with an elaborate formal garden stretching out toward the woods. "Charming view," Olivier said, "Isn't it?" He drew her into the living room. "So comfortable, don't you think?"

Beads of sweat were showing on his forehead. He seemed to her to be suggesting that a dumb American movie star like herself might not understand how valuable all these things were, or how lucky she was to be here. She didn't feel lucky about it at all. Parkside House didn't look like the kind of place where she could walk around naked, or leave her champagne glass or coffee cup on the furniture without worrying, and besides, it was costing her an arm and a leg. She smiled back at him woodenly.

"Perhaps you'd like to see the rest?" Olivier asked. "The paneling in the master bedroom is superb. . . . I expect you'll want to go and, ah, wash up?"

She nodded, suddenly too tired to speak.

Vivien led the way upstairs to the master bedroom and pointed out the bathroom. As she opened the door, desperate to get inside, Vivien placed one gloved hand gently on the door, her dark smoky-gray eyes fixed on hers like a cobra's on a mongoose, and in a low, husky whisper, the words perfectly articulated, said: "When Larry tries to fuck you, darling—as I'm sure he will—do be kind, won't you? It's been ages since he's fucked *me*, but I do remember that he needs all the help he can get, poor dear!"

With that, Vivien closed the door, leaving her alone at last.

13

THE DARK GRAY '54 FORD SEDAN WAS JUST WHERE DORFMAN had been told it would be, in the parking lot behind the Acropolis Diner, half hidden by a Dempsey Dumpster overflowing with garbage.

Dorfman got out of his car, told his driver to go get himself a cup of coffee, walked over to the Ford, carefully avoiding the rain puddles, opened the back door, and sat down. Hoffa didn't look at him, or shake hands.

Dorfman lit a cigarette, studied the back of the driver's neck, and decided it was nobody he knew. "Anybody coulda gotten inna your car, Jimmy, blown you away before you knew what fucking happened," he chided. "You oughta lock the doors, have a couple guys around, keep an eye on things. You take too many fucking risks."

Hoffa laughed, a grating sound that merely expressed his savage contempt for the world at large. He was built like a concrete mixer, and although there was no fat on him and he wasn't tall, his muscular bulk seemed to take up most of the back seat, crowding Dorfman against the door on his side. Hoffa's face was the color of raw veal, his mouth like a surgical scar; his pale eyes were expressionless.

"Anybody tries it, I'll tear the piece outa his hand, shove it up his ass, and pull the fucking trigger. How are you, Red? What have you got for me?"

Hoffa turned his head enough to get a good look at Dorfman, just in case he might be harboring any ideas about trying it himself. He knew you didn't stay alive by trusting people, not even Dorfman, who knew as much about the Teamsters as any outsider did. He had a lot of respect for Dorfman, as it happened, but it was mingled with a certain degree of contempt. Dorfman had arrived like some guinea in a brand-new metallic sky-blue Caddy, with sweeping, sculptured streaks of chrome ending in big tail fins like those of a rocketship in a cartoon—the kind of car Hoffa often gave away to people who had done him a favor, but would never dream of owning himself. Guys like Dorfman, Hoffa told himself, would rather get picked up by an FBI surveillance team than arrive in an old, beat-up car.

Hoffa bought his suits on sale at J. C. Penney, along with the short white athletic socks he always wore. Dorfman was dressed in a gray custom-tailored silk suit, a white-on-white shirt, a silver tie. Dorfman wore narrow Italian loafers and a natty hat with a band that matched the tie—he'd worked with the guineas so long he dressed like one. Some of the Teamster leaders were beginning to dress like that too, and Hoffa didn't like it.

Dorfman leaned close. Hoffa got a whiff of his cologne and frowned. He preferred the sweat of a real workingman. "We got a deal, Jimmy," Dorfman whispered, glancing at the driver.

Hoffa nodded. "Take a walk," he told the driver. "Stay close."

When the driver was gone, Dorfman told Hoffa the bare bones of the deal he had worked out with David Leman back in Key Biscayne, while Hoffa listened impassively, his eyes focused on the rain streaking the windshield.

After Dorfman had finished, Hoffa held up a meaty hand for silence and thought for a while. He had never doubted that the Kennedys would play—it was just a question of how to approach them. They were rich, and the rich were corrupt and lazy. The old man was capitalism at its greedy worst, which meant you could always deal with him, just as he had back in '52 over the Merchandise Mart thing. As for Jack, he was just a playboy, who'd make any deal to look good, and the kid brother, Bobby, was nothing more than a loudmouthed college punk. *Fuck 'em!* Hoffa simmered a little while in the warmth of his contempt for the rich. He was as firm an anti-Communist as J. Edgar Hoover, if not firmer, but the one thing you could say for the Russians was that they had cleared out all *their* rich parasites and put power in the hands of the workingmen.

The more he thought about the deal, the better he liked it. The idea of fat Dave Beck doing time in Atlanta or Lewisburg warmed his heart, but the important thing, he knew, was to give the Teamsters an in with the Democrats, just in case they won in '60. The Teamsters were the only union that regularly endorsed Republican candidates, which was okay so long as Ike was running, because Ike would always win. Nixon or Stassen or Rockefeller, or whoever it was going to be in '60, might lose, he thought, leaving the Teamsters sucking hind tit. A little insurance wouldn't hurt. Getting rid of Beck and his cronies was step number one, Hoffa reminded himself. After that, the target was George Meany.

He nodded at Dorfman. "You done good, Red."

"Thanks, Jimmy," Dorfman said in a tone that suggested he didn't need any praise from Hoffa.

A shadow of doubt crossed Hoffa's face. "But I don't like this shit about going to D.C., answering questions from Bobby. On that one, I say we tell them to fuck off, Red."

Dorfman cleared his throat. "It's part of the deal, Jimmy. Leman was a hundred percent clear on that. It's just 'window dressing,' Jimmy, to make Bobby look good, but it's gotta be. You'll get the questions in advance, with plenty of time to work out the answers with your lawyers. . . . It's no big deal, believe me, not compared to the fact they're gonna get rid of that fat putz Beck for us."

Hoffa shrugged his massive shoulders. Dorfman was right, but something still made him uneasy, some gut instinct told him it was a mistake. On the other hand, he was offering the Kennedys a terrific deal, and the old man owed him one for the Merchandise Mart, so maybe he was being too cautious. . . .

Fuck it, he told himself. I didn't get this far without taking risks! "Okay, Red," he said at last. "You tell them we'll go ahead. The questions have gotta be cleared with me and

Edward Bennett Williams, and I don't want no surprises. On your head be it."

"That's the idea, Jimmy—no surprises for either side." He hesitated. "Of course, you gotta do your bit to make it all look kosher."

"Meaning?"

"Well, you gotta show some respect for the Senate committee, Jimmy."

"Respect?"

"You know. Like it was a grand jury hearing." He had planned to say "parole hearing," as David Leman had suggested, but you could never count on Hoffa's sense of humor. "You gotta be a little bit"—he sought the right word—*"humble."*

Hoffa glared at him. "Are you telling me I gotta eat shit, right there in public, in front of the fucking TV cameras?"

"Eat shit, no, Jimmy. Just be polite, show a little respect, that kind of thing. . . ." Dorfman was sweating, sending out waves of cologne. He took off his hat—the same as Frank Sinatra's—and fanned it in front of his face. "You go there, you answer the questions, you make like the responsible labor leader the press is always saying you ain't, and act nice for the fucking senators. Is that such a big thing to ask?"

"Okay, okay," Hoffa conceded with a grimace. "It had better not go wrong, that's all I'm saying."

Dorfman held up both hands. Things could always go wrong, but this one seemed pretty foolproof to him, since both sides stood to gain. You could usually count on greed and ambition, he thought, both of which you had working here. He lit another cigarette with damp fingers, anxious to move on now that he had Hoffa's reluctant consent. "Guess who Jack Kennedy is boffing?" he said, anxious to change the subject. "Guy I know in LA, knows a guy says it's Marilyn Monroe."

"No shit? Who says?" Hoffa's voice betrayed no prurient interest because he had none. There was a deep streak of the puritan in him when it came to sex. He was never really comfortable when guys started swapping dirty stories. He didn't like sexual gossip either, unless it was something he could use as leverage against someone, in which case he listened carefully but without pleasure. Hoffa, Dorfman thought, was probably the only guy who had ever visited Vegas without getting laid.

Dorfman hummed a few bars of a song, imitating the familiar late-night, booze-and-cigarette voice of America's favorite singer. Even Hoffa, who was tone-deaf, recognized it. "Well," he said, "I guess if he's the one who said it, he oughta know."

"You bet he knows. You want me to put some guys on it? Get some pictures of Jack Kennedy and Marilyn together, maybe?"

Hoffa cracked his knuckles—a habit he had when he was thinking. "I might ask Bernie to see what he can do. If he needs any help on the West Coast, you give him what he wants, unnerstan'?"

Dorfman understood. Bernie Spindel was Hoffa's secret weapon, the best wireman in the country, a former consultant to the FBI and the CIA who had crossed over to work for Hoffa. Spindel reported only to Hoffa, and it was widely rumored that he had bugged not just the homes and offices of Hoffa's enemies but those of his Teamster colleagues as well.

Dorfman had heard countless stories about Spindel's prowess, and believed most of them: how Spindel had bugged the jury room during one of Hoffa's many trials for labor racketeering, so Hoffa knew exactly which jurors to put pressure on; how Spindel had deactivated all the bugs the FBI had placed in Hoffa's offices; how he had managed to record a conversation in a parked car between a rival of Hoffa's for the midwestern Teamster leadership and an FBI agent that resulted in the rival's subsequently being found hanging by the neck from a meat hook in the freezer of a meat-packing plant. Spindel was loyal only to Hoffa, and used only when Hoffa meant business.

Dorfman jumped at the opportunity to be of service to Spindel. "Anything Bernie wants," he said to Hoffa, maybe a couple of beats too fast, because Hoffa turned and stared at him, the pale eyes as hard as rock.

"Don't get any ideas, Red," he said. "Bernie is mine. Hands off, unnerstan'?"

Dorfman gave a grin, though his eyes reflected anger. He wasn't used to being talked to that way. "Hey, Jimmy, understood," he said. He shook hands—for a man of his strength, who liked to impress visitors to his office by cracking walnuts with his hands, Hoffa had a pretty limp handshake, by wiseguy standards anyway, but Dorfman had long since come to the conclusion that Hoffa simply didn't feel any need for the touching and feeling and firm handshakes that bound most men, criminal or otherwise.

Dorfman walked across the parking lot to his waiting car with a sense of relief—a feeling he always had when he left Hoffa. Hoffa seemed to think he was invulnerable, and Dorfman knew that was a dangerous idea for any man to have.

Hoffa not only thought he was bigger than the United States Senate—which he might turn out to be right about—but also thought he was tougher than Dorfman's people, men like Momo Giancana, who ran the Chicago mob.

Dorfman had seen the bodies of plenty of people who thought that. He got in his car and, without looking at the driver, said, "Momo's place, and step on it."

"They could hardly miss him in a metallic sky-blue '56 Cadillac Fleetwood. Top of the line. Nothing but the best for Red Dorfman!"

The Director didn't smile. His face was impassive as he sat motionless behind his big mahogany desk, hands joined on the spotless blotter in front of him, showing exactly one inch of starched white cuff at each wrist, his fingernails freshly manicured and clear-lacquered. Some thought the thin gold identification bracelet on his right wrist a little out of place for the country's top cop; others had remarked on the fact that his deputy director, close friend, and housemate, Clyde Tolson, wore an identical one, but the Director was untroubled by such innuendo.

Tolson, who was sitting at one side of the vast polished desk, exchanged a glance with him as Special Agent Kirkpatrick made his report. The Director used a '56 Cadillac Fleetwood himself, though of course, his was black.

He nodded ever so slightly to Kirkpatrick, who continued. "Surveillance from a distance established that Dorfman met with Hoffa in the parking lot of a diner. They sat in the back seat of Hoffa's car and talked for twenty-one minutes."

Hoover pursed his lips. He thought it was a criminal waste of manpower keeping watch on racketeers like Dorfman or crooked labor leaders like Hoffa. Of course people like that belonged behind bars—that went without saying—but the real enemy was godless communism; every agent engaged in the surveillance of organized crime was one man less in the more important battle to uncover Soviet spies and domestic traitors.

"Afterwards," Kirkpatrick went on, "Hoffa returned to his office, and Dorfman was driven to La Luna di Napoli restaurant, where he met with a known leader of the Chicago crime syndicate, Sam 'Momo' Giancana, over a cup of Italian coffee."

"They call it espresso," Tolson said helpfully.

Hoover stared into the middle distance, as if in touch with some deity floating invisibly at the far end of his big office. "Do we have any idea what Dorfman and Giancana were discussing?" he asked.

"No, sir. We had a bug in the restaurant at one time, but you'll remember that we had to abandon it when we moved most of our surveillance teams into the University of Chicago."

Hoover nodded. It had been done on his orders. The University of Chicago was even more undermined by Marxist agitators posing as professors than most places of higher education were. What was the point of keeping round-the-clock teams listening to Giancana and his pals fixing horse races and planning hijackings when in the University of Chicago common room, members of the faculty were actually discussing the overthrow of the United States government and the Constitution by force?

In an ideal world, he would have had the funding to do both, but since this clearly *wasn't* an ideal world—much of it being run by "liberals," even with a Republican in the White House—he had been obliged to choose, and had targeted the greater threat.

"Nothing from informants?" Hoover asked.

Tolson looked at the papers in his hand. He was wearing reading glasses. He and the Director were growing old together, like a married couple who had long since learned to live with each other's weaknesses and idiosyncrasies. "Not a lot, Director," he said—he always used Hoover's title when there was anyone else around. "Rumors that Hoffa's about to move in on Dave Beck, with mob support."

Hoover laughed. "We've heard that one before."

"I hear Bobby Kennedy's planning to subpoena Beck *and* Hoffa," Tolson said. "Probably Dorfman, too. My guess is that there's some kind of hanky-panky going on between the Kennedys and the Teamsters, maybe to make Jack and Bobby look good in the press."

Hoover sighed. Nothing was more likely, he thought glumly. He hadn't liked the idea of turning Bobby Kennedy loose on labor racketeers when he heard about it, and had told Joe Kennedy so. Bobby had fought the good fight as counsel on Senator McCarthy's committee, uncovering Communists in government, and he should have kept up the good work, in Hoover's opinion. The Ambassador had agreed, but in the end, he'd given in to his boys, as he always seemed to.

The Director had a guarded respect for Ambassador Kennedy, who had always known the score when it came to leftists, even in the days of the New Deal, when there were pinkos and fellow travelers at the very highest level of government. Kennedy had passed a lot of useful information on to the FBI then, and Hoover never forgot a favor—which was why, when young Jack became unsuitably involved in 1941 with Inga Arvad, a beautiful young Danish woman formerly married to a Hungarian flying ace, Hoover had been willing to do Jack's anxious father a favor and arranged to have her denounced as a German spy.

Hoover felt that he had thereby settled accounts with Ambassador Kennedy and owed him nothing more now than the polite respect he had for anyone who was white, wealthy, and conservative. He made no secret of the fact that he thought Bobby was ruthless and rude to his elders and betters—among them Hoover himself—and Jack merely a self-indulgent lightweight, whose personal immorality, carefully monitored by the Bureau, was bound to get him deep in hot water sooner or later. He looked forward to teaching them who was top dog in Washington, when Jack's time came, if it ever did.

Hoover prided himself on the sensitivity of his political antennae. Decades of experience had honed all his political instincts toward a single goal: his own survival as director of the FBI, whoever was president. Indeed, he had a certain contempt for presidents—and not just because he knew all their dirty little secrets. Presidents came and went every four or eight years, but he, J. Edgar Hoover, remained. Coolidge had been president when he was appointed director of the Bureau, which he then re-formed in his own image, and in all those years, no president had ever dared to challenge him. About Jack Kennedy, however, he felt a nagging doubt.

Oh, Joe Kennedy called him regularly, with honeyed words about his son Jack's confidence in him, the boy's admiration for the Director's patriotic zeal, and so on, but Hoover listened to these blandishments with a mixture of indifference and fear—and not only because he knew Ambassador Kennedy to be a smooth-tongued flatterer.

He knew very well that Jack Kennedy cracked jokes about him—jokes about the director of the Federal Bureau of Investigation!—at Washington dinner parties, with journalists present, and counted among his friends and supporters many of Hoover's severest critics. The Director was sixty years old— only five years short of federal retirement age. Like an old wolf surrounded by younger rivals, he knew instinctively that he could expect little mercy from Jack Kennedy, still less from Bobby.

He therefore watched every move of the Kennedys with unwavering attention. The Ambassador's tax returns, cocktail party gossip, Jack's affairs with women, Bobby's struggle with Roy Cohn, the machinations by which David Leman, the New York-based PR magnate, was securing good reviews for Jack's book *Profiles in Courage,* or by which the Ambassador had obtained for his long-suffering wife a papal decoration— nothing was too small to capture the Director's interest. He surveyed the future as if standing on a mountaintop, and the only danger he saw on the horizon was from Jack Kennedy.

The truth was, though he didn't want his subordinates to know it, he didn't care whether Hoffa replaced Beck or not, with or without mob support. If you removed one crook from the leadership of the Teamsters, you would merely get another in his place. He knew there was no percentage in turning his agents loose on an organization that enjoyed the support of Vice President Nixon and a large number of senators and congressmen, thanks to the Teamsters' generous campaign fund contributions.

Dorfman and Hoffa's meeting in Chicago and Dorfman's subsequent meeting with Giancana—these things interested him only because Jack and Bobby were planning to take on the Teamsters. Dirt, as he was fond of saying, attracted dirt. "Is there any hard evidence of 'hanky-panky' between the Kennedys and the Teamsters, Mr. Tolson?" he asked.

"It's mostly just gut instinct, Director," Tolson admitted. "Jack and Bobby seem very confident that they're going to put Beck away. Too confident, maybe. . . . I'll tell you what's *really* interesting. David Leman was observed playing golf in Las Vegas with Dorfman recently. We have it on film."

Hoover paused. He knew David Leman both as a powerful, wealthy big-league public relations "mogul," as *Time* magazine always called him, and as one of the few people who enjoyed, if that was the right word, the confidence of Joe Kennedy. He flicked through his mental card file on Leman (Lehrman), David A., and decided that only a personal request from Joe or Jack Kennedy would have sent Leman to play golf with Dorfman.

"I wouldn't have thought Leman was much of a golfer," he said. "Those people seldom are." He sniffed. "More interested in making money." Hoover did not consider himself an anti-Semite, but he harbored certain firmly held ideas about the races, and for decades had quietly resisted recruiting Jewish FBI special agents.

"We can play the film for you, Director. Leman got in one good shot, as a matter of fact. Probably a fluke."

"Surely, Mr. Tolson, surely." Hoover frowned. "So it's reasonable to suppose that Jack Kennedy is dealing with the Teamsters—probably the Hoffa faction—and the mob, correct?"

"Correct, Director," Tolson and Kirkpatrick said in unison.

Hoover smiled. "Well, it's not a pretty thought, is it? For a United States senator to be in cahoots with racketeers like that."

"Not pretty at all," Tolson agreed. "It would look bad if it were leaked to the press—"

Hoover held up a pudgy hand in a majestic gesture of silence. "We shouldn't even *dream* of doing that," he said. "We should let things develop while we watch and wait. We have nothing to gain by making all this public, nothing at all. Keep your eye on the ball, Mr. Kirkpatrick. Leave no stone unturned."

Hoover was in the habit of giving cryptic orders. He had once scrawled *"Watch the borders!"* on a report because the margins weren't wide enough for him to write his comments, only to discover some weeks later that hundreds of agents were patrolling the Mexican and Canadian borders looking for they knew not what threat. Mindful of this, he cleared his throat and added: "I want all the facts of this sordid transaction, in case they should be useful later on. You've done good work, Kirkpatrick. Keep it up." He looked the young agent directly in the eye, man to man—he knew how much the agents valued the little personal touches that were so much a part of good leadership. "Anything else to report?"

Kirkpatrick closed his file. "An informant in Hollywood told one of our people out there that Senator Kennedy is having an affair with Marilyn Monroe."

"I thought he was having an affair with someone else," Hoover said.

Kirkpatrick blushed. "There's a whole list of women here. . . . It's hard to keep it up to date, as a matter of fact. Our informant—he's a well-known singer—seemed to feel this affair with the Monroe woman is more serious, or I wouldn't have mentioned it."

"You did right." Hoover stared glumly at his clean desktop. Normally he enjoyed hearing the gossip his agents picked up on the sex lives of the rich, the famous, and the politically powerful, but he had always had a soft spot in his heart for Marilyn Monroe, and it saddened him to think that she was behaving like a common tramp with a womanizer like Jack Kennedy. "This kind of thing wouldn't have happened in the old days," he said. "You could count on people like Louis Mayer to keep his stars in line." He sighed. "I suppose you could see it coming a mile away. I thought *The Seven Year Itch* was a piece of prurient trash, whatever the critics said. And I hear *Bus Stop* is worse."

"You liked *How to Marry a Millionaire*, Director," Tolson said soothingly.

"That's just my point. That was decent family entertainment. First she gets talked into making decadent motion pictures, then she actually *marries* a card-carrying Communist, now she's having an extramarital affair with Jack Kennedy. . . . You can see the pattern, all right. Subversion in its most insidious form."

Hoover stood up—a rare honor—and shook Kirkpatrick's hand. He prided himself on having a good, solid handshake. He believed you could judge a man's worth by the way he shook hands, and the belief had never let him down. He had once met Alger Hiss before the war, at a reception, and Hiss had a damp, flabby handshake, so it had come as no surprise to him when Hiss was uncovered as a traitor. "Put the best men you've got on it," he ordered.

Hoover caught what he took to be a look of hesitation on the agent's face. "You may feel, Kirkpatrick," he said, "that it's beneath us to be following the personal lives of people like Miss Monroe and Senator Kennedy. That it's not as important as fighting subversion and crime. But it *is*. Information like this is vital to national security. When you see the big picture, the way I do, it all fits in. Then you understand that what Miss Monroe does isn't just her private business—oh no, not at all. It has"—he paused dramatically, as if in search of the right word—"*ramifications*. It *matters*. Everything is to come directly to me. That will be all."

Kirkpatrick nodded and left the room, closing the door quietly behind him.

"A sad business," Tolson said as Hoover regained his seat.

"Sad indeed," Hoover said, but in truth he felt a certain lightening of his heart. Sexual peccadilloes would only take him so far in insuring himself against a future with Jack Kennedy in it, but a connection between a United States senator and mobsters, fully documented—that was heavy artillery!

Of course, you could hardly count Marilyn Monroe as a sexual peccadillo, he told himself. It occurred to him with a certain glee that Jack Kennedy was exposing himself to public scandal just the way his father had with Gloria Swanson.

He clasped his hands and gave Tolson a smile. "Let's move on, Clyde," he said.

14

London is a city I've always felt I could live in happily, which is one reason why I opened a branch office there early on in my career. I always told Joe Kennedy that the only thing I envied him was his appointment as United States ambassador to the Court of St. James's. "If I had one ambition, it would be that," I once said to him, over dinner at Le Pavillon, when he was still on speaking terms with Soulé.

"Forget it, David," he had replied. "It'll cost you a pisspotful of money, and nobody back home will listen to a word you say."

All the same, over the years, the ambition had become part of my life, nor did it seem like an impossible dream, since traditionally the only qualifications for the office of American ambassador to Great Britain were to be rich and a friend of the president's. I stared at the American embassy every time I drove past it on Grosvenor Square as if it were going to be mine one day.

The last person I expected to see in the bar of the Connaught was Buddy Adler—Hollywood people usually stayed at Claridge's or the Dorchester. He waved to me and I went over and sat down.

We exchanged Hollywood gossip for a few minutes; then I asked him about Marilyn. The only news I had read about her was that she had been badly mauled by the British reporters at a disastrous press conference held in her rented house the day she arrived—a big mistake on Olivier's part, or Milton Greene's, I thought. Marilyn's charm apparently hadn't come through to the British press at all—perhaps because, despite Olivier's pleas, she kept them waiting for nearly two hours. She had lost her temper with Paul Tandy when he challenged her to name the number of her favorite Beethoven symphony, and finally flounced out of the room in tears.

That was bad, but had nothing to do with the picture. I sipped my dry martini gratefully. "How are things going on *The Prince and the Showgirl?*" I asked.

Buddy rolled his eyes. "They're in bad trouble," he said.

People said that about all of Marilyn's pictures. You always heard horror stories about her lateness, her inability to remember lines, her reliance on Paula Strasberg or Natasha Lytess, her previous coach. Her costars were always rumored to be about to walk, the director on the verge of quitting, the studio making plans to close the production down, yet somehow the pictures always got completed successfully, and so far every one of them had made money at the box office.

"No, no," he said. "I know what you're thinking, but this time it's true. They're way behind schedule. Olivier ordered Paula off the set."

That caught my attention. If Larry had been forced to order Paula Strasberg off the set, he must be at his wit's end, since it amounted to a declaration of total war against Marilyn. In any case, Buddy wasn't a man with an ax to grind about Marilyn, unlike his fellow Fox executives. He had taken on the thankless task of producing *Bus Stop* for Fox, and although practically everyone there, from Zanuck down, wanted him to fail just to teach Marilyn a lesson, he had managed to hold things together somehow and bring off a far better picture than anything she had done before—so good, in fact, that Fox was obliged to give it major promotion and back it for an Oscar nomination.

"Is Marilyn okay?" I asked him.

Buddy shook his head. "Not too good, from what I saw. The funny thing is, everybody says she comes across better in the rushes than Olivier does, and he's going crazy trying to figure out why."

He laughed and I joined in. We both knew that it didn't matter how great an actor Larry was—the camera loved Marilyn, and that was that.

"How's she getting on with Arthur?" I asked. Marilyn had married Arthur Miller only a few weeks earlier. Miller had intended it to be a small private ceremony near his home, in Roxbury, Connecticut, thus making the same mistake that Joe DiMaggio had—for nothing about Marilyn was "private," nor, at heart, whatever she said, did she really want it so. She belonged to her fans, not her husbands, and she knew it.

Poor Miller! Instead of privacy, he found over five hundred reporters and photographers encamped in front of his house in the hot July sun! When he and Marilyn came out to talk to them after the wedding to make a plea to be left alone, Maria Sherbatoff, the pretty young correspondent from *Paris-Match,* was thrown through the windshield of a car in the confusion and hysteria. On the afternoon of her wedding day, Marilyn cradled the dying girl in her arms, and as she fled back to the house, her dress soaked in blood, photographers ran after her, trampling the lawns and flowers to get a better shot.

This would have seemed to anyone like an inauspicious way to begin a marriage, and Marilyn had been understandably down when I called her the day after the wedding—though not as down as one might have imagined, for she was used to that kind of bad luck and attracted it not only for herself but for others.

Buddy heaved a sigh, which said it all. I had hoped that a couple of weeks by themselves in the English countryside might do wonders for the newly wed Millers, but judging from his face, that had not been the case. "You wouldn't know they were on their honeymoon," he said. "I'll tell you *that.*"

Before I could pump him on the subject, his date arrived, and I drank up and went upstairs to change for dinner myself.

Despite a heavy schedule of appointments, I decided to call Marilyn in the morning.

"Hello, Arthur," I said.

Miller rose from what he was doing, and we shook hands. He looked thinner and gaunter than ever, with the lugubrious air of a man who has traded one difficult marriage for another. He was sitting in the library of the big—and to my eyes, rather vulgarly overfurnished—house Larry had rented for the happy new couple, working at a card table set up in one corner of the room, as his "study," I suppose. The tabletop was strewn with Marilyn's publicity clippings, which Miller—America's greatest playwright—was busy pasting in an album. I had seldom seen a more depressing sight.

There was a beautiful color photograph of Marilyn in a frame on his table, next to an open notebook. Her face had been photographed almost without makeup, while she was lying down, her head resting against her arms, her gloriously blond hair, worn loose and long, covering part of her face, her neck, and—barely—her breasts, one rosy nipple just showing through the tendrils. Her mouth was open, smiling, her eyes half closed, her expression one of such exquisite pleasure that it was almost orgiastic. "Nice photograph of Marilyn," I said.

He nodded his head glumly. "She had it taken here, a couple of weeks ago. I liked it so much that I asked for a print."

I could see why. It was the sexiest photograph I'd ever seen of her. I made my way up the stairs and knocked on the door of Marilyn's room. "Come in," she called. Her voice was dull.

She had taken over a bedroom for her own use. It was stripped of furniture and decoration to make room for a professional hair dryer, a makeup table with a brightly lit mirror, a massage table, several pipe racks to hold her clothes and costumes, and a telephone on a long cord so she could walk around the room while she talked on it. Everywhere, there was the clutter and mess without which Marilyn was never really at home. She was sitting on the floor, leaning against a stack of cushions removed from the sofa, reading a script. Her hair was in curlers, her face washed clean of makeup; she wore a white silk blouse and tight black pants of the kind that used to be called pedal pushers. I leaned over and gave her a kiss. "Jesus, David," she said, "you don't know how good it is to see you."

I moved a pile of magazines from a chair and sat down gingerly, for it was one of those spindly antique chairs meant to be looked at rather than used.

"Be careful of the chair. There's a set of the fucking things, but we've already broken half of them. Sir Cork Tip says they're worth a fortune."

"Sir Cork Tip?"

"That's what they call Larry in one of the papers here, because he did a cigarette commercial. It suits him." She affected a prissy, superior expression and voice. " 'Let's try it *one* little time more, shall we, Marilyn darling?' "

"It's been as bad as that?"

She shivered. "Worse. The pits, David honey."

"I saw that photograph of you downstairs, the one on Arthur's table. You look happy enough in that. It's quite something."

"Yeah." She nodded and then gave me a sweet little smile.

"I fucked the guy who took it, you know. I guess that's why it's such a good picture."

It certainly explained her expression in it. I felt a sense of dismay—she and Miller had only just been married, after all.

"That sounds terrible, doesn't it, David?"

"It's none of my business, Marilyn—but yes, it doesn't sound good. Was it worth it?"

She shrugged. "Oh, David, I *know* it was a lousy thing to do, don't worry. But you can't imagine how lonely I am without Jack, or what it's like here with Old Grumpy. . . ."

"Old Grumpy?"

"That's what Paula calls Arthur." She lowered her voice. "He's got writer's block, he says. He blames me for it. On top of that, he's always taking Sir Cork Tip's side. All I hear is Larry this and Larry that, and from my own husband!"

"So you paid him back. Does he know?"

"You don't understand a thing about it, David," she said without anger—merely as a statement of fact.

"I wasn't criticizing you."

"The hell you weren't. You, by the way, are not the one who's married to Mr. Big Writer of the Century, who never wants to go anywhere, or see anyone, or have any fun."

"And who's downstairs pasting your clippings in a book?"

"I didn't ask him to. I thought he was going to write great plays, and we'd read them together and talk about them, and instead, he just sits around the house looking gloomy and telling me I'm wrong and Larry is right." She dabbed at her eyes with a Kleenex, then kneaded it into a hard ball in her fingers.

I leaned over and took her hand. "I'm sorry," I said.

"Thanks." Her hand was cold, though it was warm in the room. She sighed and shook her head. "Wrong man," she said sadly. "Wrong picture. Wrong country. How come I make so many mistakes?"

"They may not all be mistakes. You're just down today. Buddy Adler told me your rushes are terrific."

That brightened her up a bit. "No kidding? Sir Cork Tip isn't thrilled by them, but I bet that's because I'm upstaging him." She giggled.

"How's life been here otherwise?"

"What otherwise? My marriage is going to pieces, and I'm working with a guy who hates me. We're stuck in this big house and treated like freaks. We went bicycling together the first couple of days, and that was okay, but then the press started to follow us and we had to give it up. I didn't think Arthur was having much fun anyway, you know?"

I tried to imagine Marilyn and Miller bicycling through the English countryside, and failed.

I glanced around the big, untidy room. There were cardboard boxes full of her belongings all over the floor. The one nearest to me contained books. I noticed that Jack Kennedy's *Profiles in Courage* had joined Carl Sandburg's biography of Lincoln in her traveling library. "Why don't you get away from this house?" I suggested. "Take a couple of days off. Fly over to Paris for the weekend."

"Stop playing the marriage counselor, David. It doesn't suit you." She got up, poured two glasses of champagne, and gave me one. It was eleven in the morning. "Have you seen Jack?" she asked.

I could tell by the gleam of interest in her eyes how much it meant to her to be able to talk to someone about him. "He's never been better," I said.

"I miss him."

I nodded sympathetically. Since his second back operation, Jack's life had suddenly emerged from the doldrums. *Profiles in Courage* made the *New York Times* best-seller list and was already being touted, with my help, for a Pulitzer Prize. With Bobby's help—and against the Ambassador's advice—he had taken on his enemies in Massachusetts and emerged victorious from a bitter battle, with the entire state Democratic apparatus and—more important—its delegation to the national convention securely in his hands at last. He had even been picked by Dore Schary to narrate the film—*The Pursuit of Happiness*—that would open the 1956 convention, a decision that was destined to make him seem more glamorous and powerful to the delegates than poor Adlai Stevenson, the candidate himself. Dore was a friend of mine, and I had been very largely responsible for getting Jack this particular plum, despite his initial misgivings. And as if all this weren't enough, Jackie was pregnant.

I relayed all this to Marilyn briefly. "I talked to Jack a couple of days ago," I said. "He's in great shape, but walking on eggshells, if you know what I mean."

She shook her head. "I *don't* know what you mean."

"Well, Jackie's pregnancy, for one thing. You know how much that means to him. And it's been always touch and go for her. . . ."

Marilyn nodded, her expression hard to read. I hastened to move to a less emotion-filled subject. "Then there's the convention," I said. "There are a lot of people going to Chicago who think Jack would be a better choice for Stevenson's running mate than Estes Kefauver."

She brightened up and smiled. "Well, *sure* Jack would be a better choice! Does anybody disagree with that?"

"Yes. Jack. And his father, even more strongly. Adlai's going to go down in flames again, and if Jack goes down with him, everybody will say Adlai lost because Jack's a Catholic. If Jack accepts the vice presidential nomination, it's a kamikaze run—sheer political suicide."

"So what's the problem? He'll say no."

"The problem is that things could get out of hand. What we *don't* want is a last-minute Kennedy boom. Have you seen Dore's film?"

She drained her champagne glass and giggled like a naughty little girl. "I saw it," she said. "Jack screened it for me before I left for England. I'm going to tell you a secret. When he told me he was going to do it, he made it sound like it wasn't any big deal, but I could tell he was worried, so I asked Paula to coach him. Paula was so impressed she told Jack any time he wanted to give up politics, he could take up acting and join the Studio! I helped too."

It is not often that I am dumbfounded, but what Marilyn had just told me took my breath away, if only because it explained something that had puzzled me—and Dore Schary, too. Up until then, Jack's speeches were long on charm and deft historical quotation, but short on any real passion or feeling. He always won over the women in an audience instantly simply by being himself, but he came across a little shallow and younger than in fact he was. In Dore's film, Jack suddenly seemed *mature*—older, tougher, and touched by genuine passion, a startling transformation that I had attributed to his two terrible operations or perhaps his political victory in Massachusetts.

"How on *earth* did you manage to persuade him?" I asked. I had been after Jack for years to take speech lessons to improve his delivery and he had stubbornly resisted, afraid, I suspect, of losing whatever it was that worked with the voters of Massachusetts.

"I can be pretty persuasive," she said with a wink. There wasn't any doubt in my mind about that, or about the kind of persuasion that would work best with Jack.

"How did you do it?"

"Well, Paula put together a lot of film clips, so he could see what works and what doesn't. He wanted to be natural on film, but I explained to him there's no such thing. Coming across naturally on film is the hardest work of all, I told him."

"How did he take that?"

"He doesn't like being lectured, but I told him this is *my* profession—*I'm* the expert, just like some guy who knows all about banks, or Russia, or whatever. What I *really* had to get him to work on was breathing."

"Breathing?"

"Oh, honey, it's the key to everything. Jack didn't know when to stop for breath, which is the first thing an actor has to learn. He'd just talk on and on, and run out of breath just when he needed it. . . . Paula and I got some guy from CBS to bring up a lot of clips of Winston Churchill, so Jack could see that it isn't just a trick actors learn. Churchill knew how to breathe just as well as Larry Olivier, I can tell you. Well, of course that made it okay, because Jack's a real sucker for *anything* Churchill did. See, you have to take a really deep breath and hold it down here. . . ."

She demonstrated, breathing deep and patting her diaphragm. The thin fabric of her blouse stretched taut over her breasts as she did so, and I was unable to take my eyes off them. I cleared my throat—no matter how often one saw Marilyn, her figure remained an object of awe, like the best kind of art.

"Well, he owes you one," I said. "It's a new Jack. Of course, that's the problem. We're going to the convention saying, 'He's a winner, the best thing that's happened to the party since FDR made the nominating speech for Al Smith, *but for God's sake, don't give him the vice presidency!*' The last thing his father told Jack before he went off to Antibes for the summer was, 'Mind you don't let it go to your head, Jack, just keep saying no!'—as if Jack were a virgin on her way to her first dance."

She laughed. "Does Jack always do what his dad wants him to?"

"Mostly. Anyway, whatever happens, he's been busier than I've ever seen him. Bobby too."

"I wish I could be there," she said wistfully. "I've never been to a convention."

"Well, you've missed a big slice of American life."

"Anything would be more fun than this damned movie, David, believe me. Larry goes out of his way to humiliate me. He tried to fire Paula, you know?"

"I heard."

"I told him, she goes, I go! So she stayed. Then he told me he wants me to play the part just the way Vivien did! So I told him, I'm not Vivien, buster. I'm *Marilyn*! And in case you've forgotten, you're working for me."

She wiped her eyes again with a Kleenex and refilled her glass. I wondered if she was supposed to be working today. She bit her lip, then sighed. "That's when I discovered Milton had given Larry final cut! I mean, I'm paying for this movie, and I don't even get approval! I could just *kill* Milton!"

She looked as if she could, in fact, and maybe would. "He probably couldn't get Olivier any other way, Marilyn."

"I *know* that! But he should have *told* me, goddamn it, David! I can't trust anyone, that's the truth of it."

"I promise you can trust *me*," I said, I don't know why. At that moment I really believed it—it wasn't just a question of telling her what she wanted to hear.

"I know," she said, giving me a steady look that I found somewhat unnerving. I was still under the illusion that I could mediate between Marilyn and the rest of the world—a task that would have made acting as the link between Jack Kennedy and the mob an easy one!

We sat silently for a few moments. "I'm sorry the picture is such a pain," I said. "You and Larry Olivier! It sounded like a marriage made in heaven."

She laughed bitterly. "Oh, honey, if only! There's no such thing, not for me—*that* I know."

"Any chance of my visiting the set—just in case I can be of any help with Larry?"

"Sure, why not?"

"Forgive my asking, but aren't you supposed to be working today?"

She refilled her champagne glass defiantly. "I *was,*" she said. "But frankly, I was so pissed off with Larry that I called him this morning and told him I couldn't make it to the studio because I was having this monster period. Talk about *embarrassed!* I guess Vivien never said anything like that to him, huh?"

It occurred to me that she was probably right. Then again, on second thought, knowing Vivien, I wasn't so sure. In her day, she had done everything she could to embarrass Larry, and by all accounts she was still doing a pretty good job.

I decided the sooner I got to the studio and saw what was going on with my own eyes, the better.

"You picked a hell of a day to visit us! Marilyn won't come out of her bloody dressing room, dear boy! On the other hand, perhaps it's a stroke of luck. You may be able to talk to her. I give up."

Olivier was clearly unstrung, almost hysterical. He had been shooting around Marilyn—a procedure recommended to him by Logan and Cukor, both of whom had learned to ignore the schedule and shoot the scenes in which Marilyn didn't appear, whenever she was having problems.

He was partly in costume, white buckskin breeches and glossy thigh-high cavalry boots with gold spurs. With a monocle and his neck shaved, he looked like Erich von Stroheim.

I asked what happened.

"I haven't a bloody clue. Usually she's just late, doesn't know her lines, blows a few dozen takes, and spends the whole bloody day sitting in a corner while the Strasberg woman whispers to her and feeds her pills. Today she arrived in tears, God knows why. She pulled herself together and we did a couple of takes of a perfectly simple scene. Then she started to cry, flounced back to her dressing room, and slammed the door. She hasn't come out since."

"Has Milton talked to her?" I noticed he was nowhere in sight. Neither was Arthur Miller.

"She won't talk to Milton," he said. "Thinks we're in cahoots."

"I'll go see her."

He sat down and pulled his boots off with a sigh. "I'll be grateful for anything you can do to get her back to work again. I curse the day I let myself be talked into this. I must have been mad."

I know misery when I see it, and his went beyond theatrics. "I saw Buddy Adler at the Connaught," I said, to cheer him up. "He said the rushes are terrific."

He flung his head back and let out a cry. "Oh God! Of *course* they are! Take after bloody take, scores of them, and with each take she gets better while the rest of us—myself included—lose whatever we had in the beginning. On the first take, I'm good and Marilyn's hopeless—doesn't have a *clue*— and on the last one, when she's finally got it right, she's wonderful and I'm bloody *awful*. Has anybody else ever had the same experience, I wonder?"

"Just Groucho Marx, Louis Calhern, George Sanders, Paul Douglas, Robert Mitchum, and Cary Grant. This is not exactly a new complaint, Larry."

"I see. Be a good chap, go talk to her, David. Tell her it's in *her* best interest to get this film finished, not just mine. *She's* the one who's going to lose money if we fuck it up, not me. I'm just a hired hand."

I turned to go.

"David," Larry called out. "Tell her that she's doing wonderful work. Tell her I said so."

He meant it, I could tell. I made my way past the set and down a long corridor of cinder block, painted a glossy off-white, with a scuffed green linoleum floor—standard for British film studios, which have none of the flashy decor of the big Hollywood studios.

I had no difficulty finding Marilyn. At the end of the corridor, a small group of people were gathered as if they were waiting outside a hospital room for bad news. Miller sat, deep in thought perhaps, on a small, battered sofa. Milton leaned against the wall, eyes closed; his face was puffy and he looked as if he had aged years since the last time I'd seen him, in Marilyn's suite at the St. Regis.

We greeted each other warily. "I'm just going to say hello to Marilyn," I said.

"Be my guest," Milton said. He sounded exhausted. Miller said nothing.

I knocked on the door.

"Go away!" Marilyn called.

"Marilyn, it's me—David."

There was a muffled conversation on the other side, between Marilyn and Paula; then the lock clicked and I let myself in. The little group waiting outside did not seem to envy me.

The curtains were drawn, so the room was dark and stuffy, full of the kind of shabby old furniture the English like. Marilyn was sunk deep in an armchair, still in costume, while Paula, dressed as always in voluminous black, sat next to her, arms around Marilyn's shoulders as if to shield her from me.

I sat down without waiting to be asked. "Larry told me how terrific you are in the rushes," I said, trying to sound cheerful. "He told me to say that you're doing wonderful work. Those were his exact words."

Paula sniffed. "Of *course* her work is wonderful—no thanks to him. We don't need Sir Cork Tip to tell us that!"

That struck me as ungracious. "Look, perhaps the chemistry isn't right, Paula," I said rather curtly. "That happens."

Marilyn's face was hidden by the yards and yards of Paula's dress—it was odd how a woman as small as Paula could take up so much space, and odder still that although Paula had always been rather elegant, since she'd met Marilyn, she had taken to wearing a kind of black schmatte, as if she were costumed for a Greek tragedy.

Marilyn looked up and stared at me over Paula's embrace, her eyes red-rimmed and brimming with tears. I thought I had her attention. I said: "Larry can't be tougher to work with than Billy Wilder, from what you've told me, Marilyn."

Marilyn's eyes, now that I looked at them more closely, were wide open, the pupils dilated, as if she were staring right through me. There were enough pill bottles for a pharmacy on her dressing table, I noticed. She made a sad little noise, as if she had cried so much she had lost her voice. "David, tell me what you do when a person betrays you?" she asked in a hoarse whisper.

"Well, I don't know," I stammered. It was a tribute to Marilyn's power to spread guilt and a sense of failed responsibility among those around her that I thought she was accusing *me* of something, and tried to imagine what it was. I could think of nothing.

"He's disappointed in me," she sobbed.

"No, no, he just told me he *isn't,*" I said.

"Not Larry," Marilyn howled. *"Arthur!"*

I stared at her. "Arthur?" It was beginning to dawn on me why her husband was sitting outside her door in misery, and why the entourage looked like a funeral cortege in disarray. "What happened?"

"I read his notebook," she whispered.

"On his desk," Paula added helpfully.

It's always a mistake to read other people's letters, diaries, or notebooks, and all the more so when the writer is an artist—it's the marital equivalent of a child playing with a loaded gun. "The notebook on his table?" I asked. "Next to the photograph?" I remembered exactly where I had seen it.

"It was open," Marilyn said. "I was looking for my script."

I believed her. Marilyn had no great talent for lying, as it happened, least of all about things that mattered to her. I wondered how—or rather, *why*—a man as intelligent as Miller would have left his notebook where she could find it, let alone left it open. Carelessness? A Freudian slip? Or a writer's way of letting her know what he hadn't the strength to say to her?

"What did he write?" I asked.

"He thought I was some kind of an angel, but now he guesses he was wrong," Marilyn said. It was hard to understand her through her sobs and moans.

"He wrote that Olivier thinks she's 'a troublesome bitch' and 'he no longer has a decent answer to that one.' " Paula spat out the words with such venom, her face so contorted with fury and outrage, that I involuntarily moved my chair back. The veins were standing out on her forehead, and her lips were trembling.

"He compared me to his first wife," Marilyn said, snuffling.

"Wrote that he'd made the same mistake twice," Paula added, as if they were reciting in harmony.

"Oh God, I wish I were dead," Marilyn sobbed.

"Now, now, honey."

I sat there while the two women keened and wailed together, arms around each other. I had a notion that the only sensible thing to do was go outside and tell Miller to save himself a lot of agony and take the next plane back to New York, but I couldn't bring myself to do it. "Maybe it was a work in progress," I suggested wildly. "A play?"

Both women stared at me as if I were suddenly the enemy. "Of course, even if it is," I added hastily, "it's a terrible shock. Did you ask him about it?"

Marilyn shook her head.

"She isn't talking to him," Paula snapped. "Why should she?"

It was on the tip of my tongue to say because he was her husband, and that none of it was Paula Strasberg's business.

"Paula honey," Marilyn said, "I have to talk to David a moment. Could you just leave us for a couple of minutes?"

Paula shot me a look of pure hatred, but she gathered up her big handbag and made her way into the next room—of course, there was no way she would go out into the corridor and stand with Milton Greene and Arthur Miller, the traitors! My heart went out to both of them.

Marilyn wiped her eyes. "I feel like shit," she said, a little more calmly. "I look like shit, I bet."

I shook my head. "You look fine."

She tried a small smile. "Oh, David, you're a real pal. You really think those were notes for a play?"

I shrugged. "I've no idea. It's a possibility, isn't it? With a writer, the line between the real and the imaginary is sometimes hard to find. It's worth asking Arthur, if you want to stay married. If you don't, then it doesn't matter, of course. What's the name of the woman you were seeing in New York?"

"Marianne! Dr. Kris! Oh, if *only* I could talk to her, for real I mean, not on the phone. Explain what happened, ask her what to do. . . ."

"Well, why don't you? Olivier is shooting around you, anyway. Take a couple of days, fly to New York, see Dr. Kris. Take Arthur with you."

She shook her head violently, fear darkening her eyes. "I can't deal with him until I've talked to Marianne." She was beginning to recover herself, now that she had a plan to cling to and a guru to run to for wisdom. A little color had returned to her cheeks. "David," she said, grasping my hand—her fingers were ice-cold, her nails digging into my flesh—"can you get me to New York, what's it called, incognita?"

I thought about it. I knew people at the airlines who could

do that. I'd arranged it before, for reclusive clients. The best way, I decided, in Marilyn's case was to have her dress up as a stewardess returning home off duty, in a uniform and a dark wig—just another pretty girl catching up on her sleep before working her next flight. I'd need to do some fancy footwork with the immigration people at either end, but they were usually happy enough to do favors for celebrities like Marilyn if they were approached the right way.

"I can do it, yes," I said firmly. Juan Trippe, the founder of Pan American, was a neighbor and an old friend. "Give me twenty-four hours and your dress size, and have somebody bring your passport to the Connaught for me."

She flung her arms around me. "Oh, David, you're *terrific!* How about one other favor?"

I beamed happily. Marilyn, when she wanted to, could make you feel you were the cleverest, most powerful man in the world. "Name it," I said. I should have known better.

"I want to go to Chicago."

"Chicago?"

"For the convention, silly. I want to see Jack, even if he *isn't* going to get the vice presidency." She laughed. "I'll be his consolation prize!"

There were about a million reasons why this was the worst and most dangerous idea in the world, but God help me, here was Marilyn, clinging to me, her eyes close to mine, lips pressed hard on my lips, and suddenly happy again! I felt like a doctor who has just cured somebody who was mortally ill. I could perform miracles! "Why not?" I heard myself ask. Then, more cautiously: "But, what will Jack say?"

"Let's not ask him," she said.

In the end, of course, I *did* ask him, though not before it was too late to cancel Marilyn's trip home. In view of the marital crisis that was paralyzing her, Olivier and Greene were happy enough to let her go for a few days. She was certainly no good to them in the state she was in, and Miller was probably just as relieved to be rid of her as they were.

As I had predicted, getting Marilyn out of England and back into the hands of Dr. Kris was easy enough. I flew back with her, and she attracted no more attention than any other pretty stewardess in uniform deadheading home. Just to be on the safe side, I sat beside her so she wouldn't have to talk to strangers.

Marilyn had a genius for disguise, and she didn't need Paula or Lee to tell her how to play the role. Oddly enough, in her trim Pan American uniform and her dark wig, she did not radiate the sexuality that had made her famous. It wasn't that she switched it off; it simply wasn't there, an amazing act of will, or sleight of hand, or whatever it was that turned her into one more pretty girl—though not necessarily any prettier than one or two of the other first-class flight attendants, all of whom had been briefed to pay no attention to Marilyn, incidentally, since there was no way to keep the deception from the crew.

Once safely back in New York, Marilyn holed up in the half-furnished Sutton Place apartment she had bought when she first decided to move east, emerging only for her sessions with Marianne Kris—who, like all Marilyn's therapists, might as well have had only one patient. Dr. Kris and Marilyn were on the telephone to each other for hours every day, and very soon Marilyn was able to inform me that when she went back to London, Dr. Kris would accompany her.

Poor Miller, I thought. Marilyn was bringing up the heavy Freudian artillery—*his* goose was cooked! So was Olivier's, for he would now have to contend not only with Paula Strasberg telling him how to make his picture but with Dr. Kris as well.

I put off calling Jack, on the theory that once Marilyn had poured out her side of her marital problems to Dr. Kris, the good doctor, a shrewd and lively Hungarian, would surely discourage her plan. But if Dr. Kris had any objections, she kept them to herself—or perhaps Marilyn simply didn't bother to bring the matter up, as it occurred to me much too late.

I was finally obliged to call Jack, who was in Boston overseeing the political mopping up that followed his successful coup. When I reached him in his apartment on Bowdoin Street, he was undisputed leader at last of his party in Massachusetts. He sounded irritable and tired, and when he heard the subject of my call, he exploded. "Jay-zus!" he said—in Boston, Jack cultivated an Irish persona, right down to the accent, and was not even above standing on a bar counter arm in arm with Bobby to sing "Heart of My Heart" for his admirers—"What the hell do you *mean*, Marilyn is coming to the convention?"

"She'd be incognita, Jack, to use her favorite new word."

"Holy Mary, Mother of God, David! Have you gone out of your fucking mind? Incognita, my ass!"

"Look, Jack, this isn't my idea. Marilyn is doing this for you. The point I'm trying to get across is that in her present state of mind she's quite capable of flying to Chicago by herself and turning up at your hotel—"

"Christ!"

"Averell Harriman has asked me to go as an observer with the New York delegation, so I can bring Marilyn with me and keep her under control. If she goes on her own, you've got a big problem, Jack, but make no mistake about it, she's going, one way or the other."

"I've got a bigger problem than you think," he said grimly. "Jackie is coming."

"Jackie? But she's pregnant! And she never comes to this kind of thing."

"Well, she's decided to come to *this* one, David." He sighed. "It doesn't make any sense to me either. She figures that since nothing much is going to be happening for me at the convention, we'll have some time together."

"Jack, if anybody's going to tell Marilyn not to come, it's not going to be me. You have no *idea* what things were like in London—she's a basket case. The marriage is a disaster, and so is the picture, and for some reason she seems to think you're the one person who can make her feel right about herself."

"You're turning soft on me, David."

"No. There are just certain things I won't do, that's all. *You* call her and tell her not to go to Chicago. She'll take it from you. Blame it on Jackie—Marilyn's a pushover on the subject of pregnancy. Tell her about the political problems—she's a smarter lady than maybe you know. . . ."

"Don't lecture me, David." In the background I could hear Frank Sinatra singing, and a tinkle of ice cubes. It occurred to me that Jack was almost certainly not alone. There was a long pause. "All right," he said. "Do whatever you think best." He sounded more cheerful, now that he didn't have to face the task of saying no to Marilyn. "Hell, it might even be fun! A challenge anyway. Otherwise, frankly, it's going to be a hell of a dull convention for me."

"Where are you staying?" I was already thinking about the logistics.

"Jackie and I are staying with Eunice and Sarge at their apartment. I've got a suite at the Conrad Hilton, too, just for political meetings and so on, of course. . . ."

Well, of course, I thought. Jackie might be coming to the convention with Jack—her sister, Lee, had always advised her to stick close to him and give him what he wanted instead of letting him go off alone on the campaign trail into the arms of other women. But pregnant wife or not, there was always a suite, or even several, for Jack's pleasures and a staff of retainers to make sure the girlfriends didn't bump into the wife or each other. Whether this well-oiled system would work with Marilyn remained to be seen, of course. Given her extraterrestrial attitude toward time and her vagueness when it came to any plan, I wasn't optimistic.

"I'm at the Conrad Hilton too," I said. "I'll get her a suite there. It'll all be easier under one roof."

"Can you do that?" Jack asked, astonishment in his voice. Hotel rooms in Chicago had been booked months, even years, in advance for the convention.

"Trust me, I can do it." Conrad Hilton was an old friend. Like all hotel magnates, he always kept a couple of suites, just to do favors for people who mattered to him; I had no doubt that I could ask Conrad for anything I wanted and get it, no questions asked.

"Jesus!" Jack said, dropping his Irish vote-getting accent. "Talk about an embarrassment of riches! What do you think the chances are of my getting away with this?"

"Better than fifty-fifty, but not much."

"Same odds we had when PT-109 went down!" he said jubilantly.

PART TWO

Strawhead

15

There was so much energy flowing in Chicago that she hardly even noticed how hot it was. It wasn't until she and David had finally reached the hotel that she realized she was soaked in sweat, her stewardess's uniform clinging to her clammily.

It had taken nearly two hours to get in from the airport—the streets of Chicago were blocked by people waving banners and chanting, a surprising number of them wearing the green and carrying posters with Jack's picture on them.

She let David fuss around the suite for a few minutes, schmearing the help, checking the air-conditioning, opening her ritual bottle of champagne; then she pleaded a headache to get rid of him. She could tell he didn't want to leave, partly because he was falling in love with her—if he hadn't already, poor guy—partly because he saw it as his duty to hand her over to Jack like a postman delivering certified mail.

He left her with a laminated pass made out in the name of Alberta "Birdy" Welles, Town Clerk and Librarian of Milan, New York, and local Democratic heavyweight. Miss Welles had apparently tripped over her cat and broken a leg on the eve of the convention, and David had somehow secured her credentials.

He also left her with strict instructions: She was not to go anywhere without him. She was not to talk to anyone. Once she was on the floor with him, under no circumstances was she to shout, "Jack Kennedy for vice president!" or even *think* it. A lot of the New York delegates, he explained—oh, how David loved explaining!—thought Kefauver was a hick. They were committed to Mayor Robert Wagner as New York's "favorite son" candidate, but it wouldn't take a lot to stampede them into supporting Jack Kennedy. . . .

She heard a noise behind her and turned around to see Jack grinning broadly. Giving a squeal of surprise, she ran across the room to kiss him. "What's a favorite son?" she asked.

"You're looking at someone who *isn't* one. A delegation picks a favorite son so they can sit through enough ballots to get a decent price for switching their votes to a serious candidate at the last minute. It's an art form, among politicians."

"Where did you *come* from?" she asked.

"The suite next door. At the moment it's filled with politicians trying to make a mountain out of a molehill, and it smells like a cigar factory." He looked around admiringly. "Say, this is a much nicer suite than mine."

She could smell the aroma of cigars in his hair. He led her over to the bar in the corner and poured himself a drink. Then he lay down on the sofa and with a sigh put his feet up on Conrad Hilton's most expensive upholstery. There was a dish of peanuts on the coffee table in front of him. He tossed them into the air one by one and caught them in his mouth.

She sat down beside him, stroking his hair as if to assure herself that he was really there. This was what she had always dreamed of having with her husbands—a moment of quiet intimacy, however brief—but never had with any of them. "What's going on in there?" she asked, glancing toward the door that joined her suite to his.

"The fellows who don't like Estes Kefauver—big-city bosses like Mayor Daley here in Chicago, Dave Lawrence in Pennsylvania, Mike Di Salle from Ohio—they've been trying to persuade Adlai he needs me on the ticket. I've been trying to persuade *them* to lay off."

He yawned. "Dad's right. Getting the vice presidential nomination could lose me any chance at the presidential nomination in '60, maybe even in '64."

She ran her fingertips over his face gently, bending so close to him that her hair brushed against his cheeks. "Why do you want to be president?" she asked.

He didn't laugh. On the contrary, his expression was suddenly serious, even somber, as if it was something he'd asked himself many times. "It's the only thing I can do," he said quietly, none of his usual jaunty bravado in evidence for once.

"The only thing you can do?"

"Well, it's what I've been trained for—raised for, really, since Joe's death."

"Isn't it something *you* want?"

"I didn't use to. But lately it's been growing on me. When I look around me and see the assholes who want to run. . . . I mean, Jesus, there's Adlai, who can't even make his mind up about what he wants to eat for breakfast, and Lyndon Johnson, who only got where he is by kissing Sam Rayburn's ass, or Hubert Humphrey, who's just Eleanor Roosevelt's eunuch. . . . I can do better than any of *them*, that much I know. Somebody has to be president. It may as well be me."

"I wasn't challenging you, Jack. I was just curious."

"I used to wonder how I could get out of it. . . . Funny, I never told anybody that before, except Bobby."

"Not Jackie?"

"No. Jackie wants to be First Lady. She figures she's owed it by now, and maybe she's right."

"Is that the problem between you two?"

"No," he said, "that's not the problem."

Something in his voice warned her to back off.

"I always thought you were ambitious," she said jokingly. "I thought that was one of the things we really had in common, ambition."

"Oh, I'm ambitious enough, I guess. It's just that I can't think of anything less than the presidency to be ambitious *about*. It's the only job worth reaching for, you see. I mean, look at Averell Harriman—all the money in the world, ambassador to Moscow in the war, when that was a big deal, friend and adviser to FDR and Truman, governor of New York, but he never got to the White House!"

"Maybe he never wanted to."

Jack laughed. "Oh, Averell wanted it so bad he could taste it. Still does, probably. But he never fought hard enough for it, so he'll always be a footnote to history—a long footnote maybe, but that's It. It's better to go out with a blaze and rate a whole chapter."

Go out with a blaze and rate a whole chapter! That was her own life story right there, the belief that had guided her all the way to stardom. That was what made them improbably alike—they both took risks that would have stopped most people cold. Other people might doubt that Jack Kennedy could be president—he was too young, he was Catholic, his father was hated, his private life made him vulnerable—but she had the same absolute faith in his star as she did in her own.

"How much time do you have?" she asked.

He smiled. "Ten minutes. The natives are restless. A whole bunch of heavy hitters from the big cities are in there listening to Bobby tell them that they have to take Kefauver if Adlai wants him, like it or not. We're getting full marks for loyalty, but it's not the message they came to hear."

"I guess ten minutes will have to do." She pulled off her uniform jacket and blouse, tossing them to the floor, then stood up and stepped out of the skirt. It occurred to her briefly that she hadn't locked the door or put up the Do Not Disturb sign, but she didn't give a damn.

She stood for a moment, while Jack, still fully clothed and lying on the sofa, looked at her. "Jesus!" he whispered softly.

"This won't take but a minute, Senator," she said, smiling and unbuttoning his trousers. She placed her hands on either side of his head to steady herself; then, straddling him, she leaned forward and kissed him. Absurdly excited by the contrast between her nakedness and his respectable dark suit, she moved faster and faster, in control of both their bodies, pushing herself down until she could feel him deep, deep inside her.

She felt her own breath coming in quick, ragged gasps, faster and faster, until she gave a great, shuddering cry, and collapsed on top of him. It occurred to her that she was probably messing up his suit, but then she decided she didn't give a shit. "How was *that*, Senator?" she asked huskily.

"Not bad. With a little practice you could get pretty, ah, *good* at this."

She gave him a long kiss. "I wish you were mine," she said.

"Well, at the moment, I *am*."

"I don't mean right now."

"I know you don't."

She put another ice cube in his drink, brought it over to him, and poured herself a glass of champagne. "What do you think they'd all say in there," she asked, "if they knew you'd been in here fucking Marilyn Monroe?"

"They'd probably ask me to take Adlai's place on the ticket. There wouldn't be a man in the country who wouldn't vote for me if it was known."

She gave him a big, wet kiss. "That's what I think too, my darling," she said. "Maybe you ought to use it. Will I see you tonight?"

He was on his feet now, in the bathroom, already concentrating on what he had to do next. "Tonight?" he asked. "I don't know. I'll try." He did not sound as if he would try very hard. "Are you going to be on the floor for the movie?"

"David's taking me. I wouldn't miss it."

"I'll try and get word to you." He gave her an unmistakable look of warning. "For God's sake, be careful, Marilyn."

She was still naked. Well, it wasn't anything he hadn't seen before. "I'll be careful, Jack, don't worry," she said.

She tried not to resent the warning. She was not some inexperienced housewife having her first affair. She had dated Howard Hughes for several weeks way back in her fledgling starlet days, and there was nothing she hadn't learned then about secrecy and disguises, for Howard was already beginning to show the first signs of paranoid craziness and insisted on meeting her in secret rendezvous in the middle of the night, as if they were spies.

He washed his face, combed his hair with his fingers, straightened his tie, fixed his PT-109 tie clip in place. He dabbed at a few stains on his suit with a piece of Kleenex, then brushed himself off. He looked every inch the senator again.

"Knock 'em dead, tiger," she added softly as he went to the door.

He gave her a jaunty thumbs-up, and opened it. A wisp of cigar smoke drifted out. She heard a deep voice say, "Where the fuck *is* Jack? How the hell long does it take him to have a crap?"

He turned and gave her a wink. Just before the door closed behind him, she heard him reply: "Sorry about that, gentlemen, but I had a piece of business that required my, ah, *full* attention. . . ."

She put on a robe and called David on the phone. She hated eating alone—the fate, as she well knew, of every mistress of a busy man.

*   *   *

She had never seen so many people in one place except for
her visit to Korea to entertain the troops. The convention hall
was packed with people, thousands of them, waving placards,
wearing funny hats, chanting and singing, while in the background a band played "Happy Days Are Here Again," over and
over, through loudspeakers turned up so high her ears ached.
The air-conditioning was working full tilt, but no amount of
cold air could cope with the body heat of several thousand
people, and she was instantly drenched in sweat.

Holding his credentials in front of him, David pushed his
way toward the New York delegation, many of whom held
signs with Robert Wagner's name on them. None of them
looked particularly enthusiastic.

In the distance, on the flag-draped podium below giant portraits of FDR, Harry Truman, and Adlai Stevenson, somebody
was shouting into the microphone, his bellow incomprehensible above the music and the background noise. Nobody
was paying attention—people chatted, gathered in clumps to
discuss politics, greeted one another boisterously, while the
speaker, whoever he was, droned on.

She wasn't all that interested either in hearing what the
speaker had to say, but she supposed it would be polite to
listen. David was busy shaking the hands of flushed, sweating
strangers, greeting people by their first names as if *he* were
running for office, even smiling when they slapped him on the
back or gave him a bear hug. From time to time he introduced
her as Miss Welles, but in the echoing din of the hall, she never caught the name of anyone he introduced to her. Everybody
deferred to him, she noticed. Clearly, he was an important figure in the Democratic party.

Nobody paid much attention to her. She wore a dark wig, no
makeup, and a pleated linen skirt, a little on the long side, with
a modestly cut matching jacket and flat-heeled shoes. When
she looked at herself in the mirror, the word that came to her
mind was "mousy," but just to be on the safe side, she had
added a pair of horn-rimmed glasses with clear lenses, with a
cord around her neck, and a large, plain shoulder bag. Someone who was paying attention would surely notice the body
underneath the drab clothes, but certainly no one would guess
she was Marilyn Monroe—and apparently, the excitement of

politics was such that very few of the men even gave her a second glance!

. David pushed her in the direction of a tall, patrician-looking gentleman who had been complaining loudly about the sound system. At the sight of David he leaned over close, one hand cupped to his ear to hear her name above the noise. "Averell," David shouted, "this is Miss Birdy Welles. Miss Welles, Governor Harriman."

Harriman smiled, but there was a puzzled look on his face. Uh-oh, she thought, we've been here ten minutes and already we're in trouble! "Not from Milan?" Harriman asked, squinting as he tried to read the credentials pinned to her bosom. He rubbed his craggy jaw for a moment, then gave David a fishy stare. It was clear to her that he had the professional politician's memory for names and faces. "I seem to remember meeting a lady of that name in Albany," Harriman said, his accent as sharp as a knife. "A much older lady, I think. Not as attractive, to be quite frank. Not *nearly.*"

"My aunt!" she said brightly. "She had an accident, you see, so she sent me in her place."

"Isn't that a little—irregular?" the governor asked, raising an eyebrow—something he did with the skill of Cary Grant, except that with him it wasn't acting.

David's face, she noticed, was crimson, but luck was on her side, or Jack's, for at that moment the lights dimmed, the loudspeaker gave a final squawk, the crowd fell silent out of habit as the huge movie screen lit up, and Governor Harriman was pulled away by unseen hands.

There were no empty seats. In fact, there were more people standing than sitting, and most people with seats had to rise to their feet to see anything. Below the screen she could just make out a row of figures lining up on stage: she recognized Adlai Stevenson—until recently her hero; Governor Harriman, still arguing furiously, presumably about the sound system; a squat, bullet-headed man with a knowing smile whom she took to be Mayor Daley; and Mrs. Roosevelt herself, whom she, like most American children of the Depression and the war, regarded as a kind of secular saint.

She clapped and cheered and shouted for Mrs. Roosevelt. Then Jack Kennedy's voice rang crisp and clear throughout the huge hall. His face appeared in front of an American flag, looking incredibly young, handsome, and self-confident, eyes flashing, hair tousled by the wind. In a single moment, his image on the screen made everybody on the stage seem old, withered, and lifeless. Adlai Stevenson, with his rumpled suit, his bald head, and the deep pouches under his eyes, looked like a tired old hound dog, and the rest of them looked worse. She could tell that the delegates saw it too. They stared at the screen in dead silence, the way Marlon told her the audience had listened when he made his Broadway debut in *Streetcar*.

In a way, she thought, this was Jack's debut, and it was a smash hit. Nobody here really expected Stevenson to beat Ike; up to this moment, despite the noise, it had been a convention ready to acknowledge defeat before the campaign even began, prepared to cheer Adlai because he seemed like a decent man and a good loser, but conscious that he was a loser all the same. Jack, narrating the film, somehow managed to remind them that there was such a thing as a winner.

She and Paula had done well by him; he spoke firmly, paused at the right moments, radiated sincerity, looked the camera straight in the eye. As she glanced around the convention hall, she could see that women of all ages were staring at the screen as if Jack were a movie star.

It was working too, and not just with women. As Jack brought his filmed narration to a conclusion, the applause started before he had even finished, the delegates shouting, louder and louder, "Ken-nedy, *Ken-ne-dy!*" over and over again, clapping, stamping their feet, until the whole hall seemed to shake. The band took up, presumably because of its regional associations, "Yankee Doodle Dandy" and then, lest anyone forget PT-109, "Anchors Aweigh." The people on the platform looked annoyed, particularly Mrs. Roosevelt, while the chairman banged away helplessly with his gavel, trying to restore order.

All over the arena, people began to hold up pictures of Jack with the caption "Our Choice"; banners were raised with pictures of Jack and PT-109; volunteers, most of them pretty young girls, spread through the crowd passing out more banners, Kennedy balloons, even Kennedy buttons, one of which she pinned to her jacket. The noise seemed likely to go on forever, punctuated by the banging of the gavel magnified until it sounded like a Jackhammer. She grabbed David's hand. "What's *happening?*" she shouted.

He had to put his lips against her ear to make himself heard. "Jack's friends just fucked him," he said, grinning. "They're trying to stampede him into making a run. Just look at Adlai's face up there! He must be kicking himself for letting Jack narrate the movie!"

She glanced at the platform, where Stevenson was deep in what seemed to be angry conversation with Mrs. Roosevelt.

"Is that Mayor Daley up there? The bruiser who looks like an Irish cop?" She pointed at a heavyset man grinning from ear to ear, apparently having the time of his life, while Stevenson and Mrs. Roosevelt, firmly seated, glared at him disapprovingly from time to time, without effect.

David nodded. "That's him."

"Did he set this up?"

"The demonstration for Jack? I expect so. I guess Daley took care of the sound system, too. After all, Chicago is his town. I think you could safely assume that anyone with something to say that His Honor doesn't want to hear is going to have problems with the sound system."

It hadn't occurred to her that the problems with the system might not be an accident, simple bad luck. She had a lot to learn about politics, it seemed.

The demonstrations all around them went on and on, ebbing only to start again louder than ever. She had been carried away by the noise and excitement, but now she was beginning to wish it would stop. Then, quite suddenly, like an explosion, the crowd went wild.

She stood on tiptoe and saw that Jack was on the platform in person now, a shy smile on his face. He handled himself with the grace of a born actor, she thought. He did not exactly *ignore* the demonstration seething in front of him, but he managed to suggest by his detached manner that it might be for somebody else. As he leaned over to shake hands with Stevenson and Mrs. Roosevelt, his expression implied that he was as embarrassed by all the fuss on his behalf as they were.

Mrs. Roosevelt's face was a study in granite disapproval as Jack talked to her—here, at last, was a woman who was impervious to his charm! He straightened up, gave Mayor Daley and his cohorts a wink, and went over to the side of the platform to stand modestly with the party faithful, leaving the limelight to the candidate, whom the crowd was ignoring completely.

She was being pushed forward by the pro-Kennedy faction of the New York delegation, which was apparently determined to follow the Massachusetts delegates to the speaker's platform, where the television cameras would have a better view of them.

At first she found the experience exhilarating, but the thrill soon gave way to growing fear as she was swept on by the noisy crowd chanting, clapping, pushing, and shoving, carrying her along as if she were a piece of flotsam in the surf.

She lost David—couldn't even turn around to find him anymore. She was terrified of falling, or being tripped, pressed in on all sides by sweating, noisy strangers. She was used to the press of crowds, but when she was in them, there were always people on hand to whisk her away to safety if necessary.

The band was playing "When Irish Eyes Are Smiling" now, and the Massachusetts delegates were eddying against the podium, being pushed to either side by the crowds behind them. She felt someone pinch her ass hard and kicked out. She had the satisfaction of feeling her toe make sharp contact with somebody's shin and heard a man cry out in pain.

She kicked and fought her way forward, finding herself suddenly part of what seemed to be a rough conga line dancing toward the podium arm in arm. She felt her wig slip to one side; her clothes were drenched in her own sweat as she held on to the people on either side of her for dear life.

Ahead of her she saw the red-white-and-blue bunting of the platform sticking up above the crowd. Then she felt her heel break, plunging her forward. She landed against the rough, flag-draped lumber of the platform and clung to it as people bumped into her, pressing against her until she was sure she would be crushed. Her stockings were torn, one of her bra straps was broken, and she was gasping for breath. Suddenly a hand reached down from above her and grasped her wrist firmly. *"Jump!"* she heard a familiar voice shout over the noise.

She gave a leap and found a place to put her foot on the scaffolding as he pulled her by the arm; then she was clear of the crowd. From over the railing above her head, Jack was looking down at her, grinning. "Good fishing today!" he said cheerfully, hauling her up a little higher. "Nice catch."

She managed to get one hand on the railing, then swung herself over it onto the platform, tumbling into his arms. She could see the flashbulbs popping as news photographers recorded her rescue. "What's your name, honey?" a reporter shouted.

She panicked—she couldn't remember what it was supposed to be, but Jack made a show of glancing closely at her bosom to read her credentials. "Miss Birdy Welles, of Milan, New York," he called out. "What do you do, Miss Welles?"

That, she could remember. "I'm a librarian," she said.

"You sure don't *look* like a librarian," Mayor Daley growled, in what she took to be the spirit of gallantry. "If our librarians here in Chicago looked like you, I'da read more books when I was in school."

"I'm town clerk, too," she said, remembering suddenly.

"Tell the truth, you don't look like no town clerk neither."

"I'm glad to have been of service," Jack said. "It looked like a real mob scene down there. Are you okay, Miss, ah, *Welles?*" He gave her a wink.

"I broke a heel," she told him sweetly, raising her leg so he could look at her shoe—and her ankle.

"Ah, yes, I see. Well, I guess it could have been worse." He winked again. "I'll get someone to see you back to your hotel, Miss Welles, so you can change shoes." He waved off stage, and Boom-Boom appeared at a run, raising one massive eyebrow at the sight of her.

Jack was grinning from ear to ear.

"Somebody pinched my ass down there so hard I bet I'm bruised," she whispered to him.

"Nobody ever said politics wasn't a dangerous business," he whispered back. "I look forward to getting a close look at your battle scars later on."

"Promises, promises, Senator. When?"

"I can't say. Things seem to be getting out of control. . . . Order up some food—a couple of club sandwiches maybe—and I'll join you when I can."

"What about Jackie?"

"Jackie's back at the apartment, watching this on television. Let's hope she can't read lips. Let's hope *nobody* who's watching can!"

"I wish I could give you a kiss."

She said it in such a low voice that no one but Jack could

have heard her, but still, he blushed. Then she heard the unmistakable voice of Mrs. Roosevelt saying: "Birdy Welles! My Lord, I knew I heard that name before, and now it comes back to me, of course. She's a neighbor."

Mrs. Roosevelt was beginning to turn, her vision partly obscured by the press of people around Jack and by her flowered hat. For a moment Marilyn was paralyzed by the fear that she was about to have a face-to-face confrontation with Eleanor Roosevelt in front of the television cameras, but Jack took her by the arm and pushed her toward Boom-Boom, who practically tore her off the platform without letting her feet touch the ground.

"Miss Welles just left," she heard Jack say to Mrs. Roosevelt. Then she was back in the world Boom-Boom seemed to know best, that of back corridors, secret stairways, and service elevators.

It suddenly occurred to her that David must be sweating bullets at having lost her. She smiled, a little guiltily, at the thought.

She took pity on David and left a message to let him know that she was safely back in her suite. She ordered sandwiches to be brought up, a couple of bottles of Dom Perignon, and a bottle of Jack's favorite Ballantine scotch. On second thought, she called back to ask room service to put a couple of cartons of vanilla ice cream in the refrigerator, along with a bowl of chocolate fudge sauce—for Jack's sweet tooth—then settled down on the sofa in her dressing gown to read Carl Sandburg. She picked the book up each time with the best of intentions—she *wanted* to read more about Mr. Lincoln—but after three years of reading, he was still in Illinois, a country lawyer.

She put the book down and tried Harold Robbins's *79 Park Avenue* instead, which certainly moved along faster.

People often made fun of her pretensions when it came to reading, but in fact she read a lot, although without any consistent plan, as Arthur was forever tiresomely pointing out. She enjoyed reading at her own pace, and if she wanted to switch from Carl Sandburg to Harold Robbins and back again, whose business was it but her own? " 'It's just that she's not for you,' " she read. " 'She's been brought up without love and has no understanding of it.' "

She put her finger on page 23 to mark her place and closed the book. Perhaps the reason why she was such a slow reader (though that had never bothered anyone before Arthur) was that she was always finding phrases that made her stop and think. Surely that was the whole *point* of reading, she had once told Arthur, arguing back for a change, but she suspected that, like many intellectuals, he read chiefly to reinforce ideas he already had, or for new arguments to support them.

She lay back and thought about the evening. At some point she had come to the realization that Jack Kennedy was going to be the president one day. Out there on the floor of the convention, she had *felt* it in the voices of the demonstrators, seen it in the eyes of Stevenson and his supporters on the platform.

It was hard to imagine Jack as president—presidents to her were mostly old men, their faces craggy, weary, lined: Ike, Truman, FDR, and Mr. Lincoln. Jack had a kind of college boy charm, and it was easy to forget that he was not only a serious politician but a very rich man. In the movie he had narrated—to such stunning effect—he had talked about the poor, the workers, the blacks, the small farmers, ordinary people, the meat-and-potato voters who were the backbone of the Democratic party. But how much did he really *know* about people like her mother, who had earned her living processing movie film at Consolidated Film Labs before she went over the edge into madness and state care? *She* knew what it was like to be working class, it was her own, and there was some core of her in which she wasn't sure she could trust the sincerity of Jack Kennedy's commitment to the kind of people she had been raised among. Oh God! she thought. Who am I to be looking for a white knight at this stage of my life?

She was so absorbed that she didn't hear the door open at two a.m. A sixth sense told her that someone else was in the room, and she rose to find herself looking at an embarrassed Bobby Kennedy. Jack was already at the bar, pouring himself a Ballantine. David followed Bobby and closed the door behind him.

Jack took a deep drink, then came over and kissed her, running one hand down her back and leaving it there. Bobby, she noticed, looked as rumpled as if he had been standing under a shower in his suit. Only David looked cool and elegant, in a dove-gray summer-weight suit, with his trademark white vest and a flower in his buttonhole, as if the convention was a vacation for him—which, since he was a successful businessman and this was his hobby, she supposed it was.

Jack took off his jacket, dropped it on the floor, sat down on the sofa, and patted it to indicate that she should sit beside him. He stretched out, feet on the coffee table, looking so exhausted that she almost forgave him for keeping her waiting for hours.

"I'm really sorry, Marilyn," he said. "Things have been a little tense in there."

David took a brandy snifter and poured himself a large cognac. Bobby, his face an angry mask, didn't go near the bar. He leaned against the connecting door, silently massaging his face and combing the hair out of his eyes with his fingers. "You have to go, Jack, that's all there is to it," David said. "You can't cancel breakfast this late. Go and listen to what Adlai has to say—that's my advice."

"I don't need advice. I need somebody who can get things back under control."

"What happened?" she asked.

Jack sipped at his drink. He placed one hand on her thigh. She felt for a moment as if they were an old married couple; then he moved his hand a little higher, and she was reminded that they weren't. "The telephone lines have been going crazy," he said. "People calling in about the film."

David cradled his drink. He was clearly enjoying himself. "It was broadcast on national television tonight," he explained to her. "People have been calling the networks until their switchboards were tied up. And calling the delegates here to say how much they liked Jack. By the thousands."

"Old ladies mostly," Jack said with a laugh. " 'Sure and he looks like such a nice boy!' "

"They aren't *all* old ladies," David said. "But the majority of the calls were from women, yes."

"I'm not surprised," she said. She gave Jack a kiss. "You looked pretty sexy out there, Jack."

Bobby Kennedy's voice was a snarl, the voice of conscience and duty, and it made her shiver. "The question is, do you go for it or not, Jack?"

"Everybody in there thinks we've got a shot," Jack said. He didn't say what *he* thought, she noticed.

"A shot!" Bobby snapped contemptuously. "You don't want to get into this to take a goddamn *shot* at it," he said, his eyes flashing. "If you go for the vice presidency, Jack, you go to *win!*"

She caught a tone in Bobby's voice—a mixture of passion, rage, fierce determination, and reckless courage—that was like nothing she had ever heard before. His expression was stubborn, almost mulish, his eyes fixed on Jack's, challenging him. She looked at Jack, and what she saw there was just as chilling. His mouth and jaw were set as if in anger, and he suddenly seemed much older and infinitely tougher. He stared back at Bobby, and she was struck by the thought that she had never seen two colder pairs of eyes.

He's going to go for it, she thought. Then Jack took a deep swallow, his face still looking as if it were carved in granite, and said, "Tell them to start counting our delegates."

"They're already doing that. What are you going to tell Adlai at breakfast?"

Jack gave a grim smile. "To get ready for a fight."

Bobby nodded somberly—no hint of a smile.

"Who gets to tell the Ambassador?" David said.

There was a long silence while the brothers looked at each other with stony faces. Then they both turned their attention to David, who shook his head. "No," be said firmly.

She was impressed by the force with which he said it. So were Jack and Bobby, she thought. Jack did not try to persuade him. "One of us is going to have to bite the goddamn bullet," he said glumly. He closed his eyes for a moment. "It's about nine in the morning in France. He'll be having breakfast. Go call him, Bobby."

Bobby's expression was mutinous. "Why me?" he asked.

"Because you're my younger brother."

Bobby's jaw muscles clenched, but he slouched off, head down, hands in his pockets, into her bedroom—without asking her permission.

"Better him than me," David said. Jack nodded.

From the bedroom she could hear Bobby presenting his best case to his father, his voice low; then he was silent for a very long time. He stood up and paced around the room, the telephone receiver jammed between his ear and his shoulder. At one point he stopped in the doorway and held the receiver up toward them. Even from across the room she could hear the anger in Joe Kennedy's voice, rasping like an electrical storm being broadcast from the South of France.

Bobby put his hand over the mouthpiece. "Dad says we're goddamn fools."

"He could be right. Tell him we didn't want to get into this fight, but now that we're in it, we have to bet the farm."

"He says don't tell him what he already knows." Bobby held the receiver out. "He has some choice words for you."

Jack groaned, rose from the couch, took the telephone from Bobby, went into the bedroom, and closed the door. Bobby poured himself a soda. Sweat was running down his face. He rubbed his eyes—she didn't think she had ever seen anybody so haggard.

"What else did he say?" David asked.

Bobby drank his soda slowly, as if he were afraid he wouldn't be offered another for a while. "Dad says we should nail down Jim Farley right away, if we can. Joe junior did Farley a favor in the 1940 convention. He'd like you to try."

David nodded. "He's right. Your brother refused to switch his vote to FDR even when it was obvious that Farley was out of the running. There was terrific pressure on young Joe to make it unanimous for FDR, but he wouldn't budge. He didn't even like Farley all that much, but he was loyal."

"Dad thinks Farley will try to weasel out of supporting Jack. He says he's a lily-livered, ungrateful son of a bitch."

"He said the same thing in 1940, as a matter of fact. I'll give it a shot. Farley used to like me."

Bobby nodded quickly, dismissing the problem from his mind now that somebody had been assigned to deal with it. There was a kind of brisk efficiency to him that she found attractive. His gestures were emphatic but economical, his clothes not so much careless as simple and basic—wash-and-wear suits, button-down shirts, loafers, his hair long because he had no time to waste on barbers. He seemed to have no vices or luxuries, she thought, unless you counted getting Ethel pregnant once a year.

His attention suddenly fixed on her, as if he had only just noticed her presence. She felt a tiny shiver; there was so much going on in that face, or *behind* it! When he was talking to David, Bobby's face had been craggy, the lines in it harshly accentuated, the nose as sharp and cutting as an eagle's beak. As he looked at her now, his features softened, and he seemed years younger. "I'm sorry I used your bedroom," he said.

"Why? I wasn't in there or anything." He was blushing. She had thrown her clothes on the bed, she remembered, but surely the sight of a bra or a pair of stockings shouldn't embarrass a man who had so many children.

"I should have asked first."

"That's okay."

He cleared his throat. She noticed his shirt was frayed at the collar and cuffs. "The fact is, I didn't know you were here. Jack didn't tell me until he was just about to open the door. Frankly, I don't think it's such a hot idea."

"My being here?"

"It's a big risk for Jack to take. Now that he's going for the vice presidential nomination, it's a bigger one."

"It's a risk for me, too."

"Not the same kind."

There was no denying that. She didn't need Bobby to tell her that a Catholic politician with a pregnant wife who was discovered having an affair with a movie star could kiss the presidency good-bye, and probably the vice presidency as well.

She caught the gleam of accusation in his eyes, and it stiffened her backbone immediately. "He's a grown-up," she said defiantly. "He knows what he's doing."

"We're all grown-ups." He spoke sadly. "Maybe that ought to stop us from doing dumb things, but it never does. Just try to keep a low profile, okay?"

"Will he get it? The vice presidency, I mean?"

"It's going to be damned close. I don't know if he'll get the *vice* presidency, but I can guarantee you he's going to be president, because I'm going to help him get it."

Impulsively she leaned over and gave him a kiss. "I want us to be friends," she said.

She was afraid that he'd be angry, but he gave her a big smile—his smile was even bigger than Jack's. "We'll be friends," he said. "Don't worry." There was a smudge of lipstick on his cheek. She took a Kleenex and rubbed it off, feeling oddly motherly as she did so.

"Okay then." She took his hand in hers, moving his fingers until she had him in the secret handshake of her days in Van

Nuys High School, thumbs crossed, fingers interlaced. "It's a promise?"

The handshake was unfamiliar to him, but the idea of it was familiar enough, whether at Van Nuys or the more rarefied boarding schools of the East Coast that he had attended. "It's a promise," he said with a laugh, but his eyes made it very clear that he meant it. Promises, she guessed, were something Bobby took seriously.

Jack came out of the bedroom and caught David's eye. "He wants to talk to you now, David," he said. "Be prepared. He's not a happy man." He looked at her and Bobby holding hands and raised an eyebrow. "I'm glad to see the two of *you* are getting along so, ah, well together. God knows what Ethel would say."

Bobby's face flushed; he held himself back from replying. She watched with interest. It seemed to her that Bobby, tough-minded and independent as he was, would always defer to Jack—as if the relationship between them had been settled forever in childhood, during a thousand touch football games, arm-wrestling matches, and fights: Jack was older, bigger, and that was that. She searched Bobby's face for a hint of real resentment, but it wasn't there. He loved his brother fierce-ly, which, she thought, was very likely the only way he knew how to love. "Well?" he asked.

"It's a good thing I wasn't expecting a paternal blessing," Jack said with a rueful smile. "I told Dad I'd call him back after I've talked with Adlai." He winked at Bobby. "He told me not to let you drag me into a fight. 'Bobby's the goddamn hothead,' he said."

"The hell I am!"

"Listen, don't feel bad. He told *me* not to let other people do my thinking for me. It's going to be real fun taking his calls when I'm in the White House!"

Jack loosened his collar and tore off his tie. "Bobby, go next door and tell them I want to know how many votes we can count on before I have breakfast with Adlai. And no bullshit, okay? I don't want a wish list. I want to know who we can goddamn *count* on, not maybes, or should bes, or guesses."

Bobby nodded. What had to be done he would do; it was that simple. David, who had relinquished the phone at last, seemed to have found a new lease on life too. She understood, belatedly, why a man as wealthy and powerful as David Leman deferred to Jack Kennedy and gave so much of his time to his affairs. It wasn't wholly, or even primarily, friendship—David, she realized, craved the excitement, the sense of being a mover and shaker in politics. He *needed* to be an insider, to be playing, as Frank liked to put it, at the big table, one of the high rollers.

"Your father says Adlai might try to mousetrap you by floating out the name of another Catholic candidate, just to show he's not prejudiced," David said. "I think he's right."

"I guess that just *could* occur to Adlai," Jack said grimly. "That means we have to get pledges of support from Mike Di Salle and Dave Lawrence right away. Bobby, you go see them first thing in the morning, even if you have to get them out of bed. *Nail them down*, Bobby!"

He stretched, yawned, and rubbed his hands down his back, wincing in pain. "I'm going to get some rest myself. You too, David. Tomorrow's going to be a ball-breaker. How about it, Marilyn?"

Jack steered her firmly into the bedroom, leaving Bobby and David standing in the living room. He sat down on the bed wearily and pulled off his shoes. "I'm sorry," he said. "I didn't expect this."

"It's the breaks, honey." She was not as displeased as he supposed her to be. She liked action for its own sake as much as David appeared to. Maybe things would have been different with Joe, she thought, if he had still been playing instead of sitting around watching sports on TV. Maybe, too, she had underestimated the sheer tedium of a writer's life before marrying Arthur Miller.

She helped Jack off with his clothes, unfastened her dressing gown, and got into bed beside him, enjoying the feel of his beard against her lips, the taste of his sweat on her tongue. "Fuck me, my darling," she whispered in his ear, and with a sigh of contentment—the profound feeling that right now, at this very moment, she was *wanted*, deeply, passionately—she put her arms around his hard, muscular body, inhaled that lovely aroma of sweat and after-shave lotion and whatever else it was that made men smell miraculously different, and buried herself in him.

*   *   *

She slept dreamlessly, without pills for once—not from choice, she had simply forgotten to take them—her body so close to his that she couldn't tell where his began and her own left off, the bed sweetly sticky from their juices, the light in the bathroom still burning, the air conditioner roaring and changing speed like a Saturday night drag racer pulling away from a light on Ventura Boulevard, but still failing to cope with the heat and humidity of Chicago in August.

As she woke to the first light of dawn—they had forgotten to pull the blinds and curtains completely closed—she felt strangely restored. Every muscle ached pleasantly as she yawned and stretched—really, she thought, Jackie was a lucky lady, but then marriage being what it was, perhaps not.

Jack was sleeping on his back. He was built like the college athlete he had once been: long limbs, a flat, slender waist, strong shoulders, no hips. There was a mass of pale scar tissue down his spine from his wound and the three operations he had undergone. She wondered if Jackie had been expecting him home last night, or at least expecting a call. If *she* had been sitting across the city, eight months pregnant, waiting for her husband to call, she would have been mad as hell, but perhaps Jackie was made of sterner stuff, or no longer cared—and in any case, it was none of her business. It was Jack's job to worry about Jackie, not hers.

She got on her hands and knees and straddled him, her hair brushing his face, her breasts touching the matted red hair on his chest. She gave him a kiss—a butterfly kiss, as they used to call it in Van Nuys High School when the girls talked among themselves about all the subtleties of the art of kissing. She licked her lips, then touched them against his so gently that it was almost as if no more than their breaths were touching. She licked his lips softly with the tip of her tongue until he began to stir in his sleep. He opened his eyes. The lids were still half closed, the lashes—long enough that any girl would be proud of them—sticky from sleep. "Oh my God!" he muttered thickly. "What time is it?"

"Six-thirty, honey. I wanted to be the one to wake you."

"Did you now? I figured you for a late sleeper."

"I am. But it just so happens that I like kissing a guy awake."

"It beats an alarm clock any day, let me tell you."

"Doesn't it just? Can you imagine how many guys there are in the world who dream about having Marilyn Monroe wake them up like this?"

He took his watch out from under the pillow and glanced at it. There was something transparent and touching about the gesture—he was trying to calculate if he had time for a quickie.

He slipped the watch back under the pillow, put his arms around her, and pulled her down on him. "Let 'em dream," he said.

Jack came out of the bathroom in a cloud of steam, a towel wrapped around his thin hips, his hair wet and standing up. She poured him a cup of coffee—one sugar and cream, as she had learned—and a glass of orange juice, which he downed at a gulp. He padded through the suite to the connecting door, opened it, and said, "My God, it smells like the club car after an all-night poker game in here."

She heard Bobby's voice, raw with fatigue. "We figure we can count on at least two hundred sure votes on the first ballot."

"Not good enough."

"We can double that in two days if we work our butts off."

"Maybe."

"Did you get any rest?"

"I've never slept better in my life. Give me a moment to get dressed, and we'll go over the names before I go down to Adlai's suite. Then you'd better go shower and change, Bobby. It's going to be a long day. I don't want you fading out on me."

"Fuck you."

"I wish I had your gift for repartee."

"Very funny. Maybe you should look at the papers this morning, Senator. You may have to do some explaining to Jackie when she sees the front pages."

She grabbed the papers off the breakfast table before Jack could get back to the bedroom, and spread them on the bed. Nothing much caught her eye except headlines about the Kennedy boom. Jack came up behind her and peered over her shoulder, his face troubled. They both looked at the *Examiner*, but there was nothing there. She pushed it on the floor and unfolded the *Chicago Tribune*. There, on the front page, was a photograph of the "spontaneous" demonstration for Kennedy, taken at just the moment when the crowd had forced its way to the podium. In the very center of the picture, a woman was climbing up the side of the platform, legs showing right to her tush, as the Senator pulled her to safety over the flag-draped railing. He had his hands around her, and the angle of the photograph made it look almost as if they were kissing. The caption read: "Kennedy Saves a Supporter!" Below that, she was identified as "Birdy Wales, a librarian, of Milan, New York, and a lifelong Democrat."

They both stared at the photograph silently for a few moments. If you looked closely enough, she thought, you could almost make out her ass. On the other hand, her face was obscured, and the dark wig made it unlikely that anybody would guess who she was.

She giggled. "They got my name wrong." She noticed that he wasn't amused. "How bad is it?" she asked.

He rubbed his cheeks. "Well, politically speaking, it's no big deal. I pulled a pretty girl to safety. No harm in that. It might even win me a few votes, I suppose. Jackie may take a more, ah, *judgmental* view of the incident. Particularly since I didn't go home last night."

"Or phone."

"Or phone, right." A look she knew well—husband in distress—crossed his face.

"I don't see how she can make much out of this photo," she said hopefully.

"No. I think the sooner I call Jackie, the better, all the same." He gathered up his clothes. "You tell David to be careful. I don't know if it's a good idea for you to be on the convention floor at all. . . ."

She gave him a hard look. "I'm not going to stay locked up in this goddamn suite, Jack, if that's what you're thinking."

A look of anger crossed his face. "Don't give any interviews then. I mean it. There's a lot at stake."

"I'm not a dummy, Jack. I *know* that."

"Well then." He walked to the connecting door, restless to be dressed and on his way. "Wake up David," he snapped.

"He's always talking about how good he used to be at damage control, back in the old days in Hollywood. Tell him to get to it."

"Tell him yourself." She stared him down and was delighted to see him blush.

Jack stood there for a moment, his dignity sharply diminished by the fact that he was holding a small towel around his waist. He looked mildly hurt. "Well, I didn't mean it that way," he said.

"Yes you did, but I forgive you. Just don't do it again."

Having made her point, she walked over, gave him a kiss, and slipped her hands under his towel. "Just remember, lover, with me it's like baseball: three strikes and you're out. That was strike one."

She felt him stiffen. Really, she thought, it was *remarkable* how much energy he had! "Later," she said, giving him a final squeeze and a push toward the door.

He gave a reluctant glance at his watch. "I don't know when," he said.

She knew that the right thing to say was something like, "I'll be waiting," but instead, she said: "If you want me bad enough, you'll find me somehow."

He was still puzzling that one out as he opened the door and went back into his own suite, where Bobby and the Irish Mafia who had helped him win control of the Massachusetts Democratic party were waiting for him.

She went back into the bedroom, took her nail scissors, and clipped out the picture on the front page of the *Tribune*.

It was the only time, so far, that they had ever been photographed together.

For all she knew, it might be the last.

SPECIAL AGENT JACK KIRKPATRICK WAS NOT MUCH GIVEN to introspection. As far as he was concerned, his job was getting the information—it was up to somebody else to decide what to do with it, or how it fit into what the Director liked to call the big picture.

Dressed in the overalls of a hotel maintenance man and furnished with a set of blueprints of the hotel and a telephone wiring plan, he had placed a tap on each of the phones in the Kennedy suite and a mike in the baseboard of each room twenty-four hours before the convention. Kirkpatrick had learned the art of wiretapping from Bernie Spindel himself, in the days when Spindel was still operating, at least partially, on the right side of the law. Neatness and attention to detail were Spindel's watchwords. He was a master at the cosmetic concealment of his devices—no job was complete, he taught his pupils, until the paint had been perfectly retouched, every mark removed, the smallest traces of plaster dust vacuumed away. Kirkpatrick carried in his toolbox a set of camel's hair artist's brushes, tiny tubes of paint, a Swiss-made miniature vacuum cleaner, a can of English furniture polish. By the time he was through with a job, he liked to say to trainees, you could get down on your hands and knees with a magnifying glass to look for his handiwork, and never find it.

Kirkpatrick had broken into the suite to place his devices there, only to discover, from his informant behind the desk of the Conrad Hilton, that David Leman had booked the two suites next to Jack Kennedy's. A lesser man might have ignored the news—the FBI did not encourage initiative so much as blind obedience. But Spindel had taught him well: "You can never be sure where something is going to happen," he had always said, and it was true. People held business meetings in their bedrooms, or made love in their offices, or plotted murder in their cars—you never knew where the right spot was for a mike, so you tried to cover all the bases.

Kirkpatrick had thought it over for less than a minute before going back upstairs and slipping in to do a job on the adjoining suites, just in case. Luckily, all the wiring was routed into a utilities cupboard on the floor. He had used his skeleton key to open it, spent a few minutes sorting through the maze of wires, then connected his leads to the right terminals, checked them out, and marked them with a piece of tape, so he could come back and remove them later, leaving no traces.

Now he sat in a Chicago Bell Telephone Company truck outside the hotel, where three agents, changed every four hours, listened to everything being said in the three wired suites, recording it in duplicate. Normally they recorded only conversations that had a direct bearing on the subject of an investigation, but since in this case they weren't sure what they were looking for, they taped it all.

Other teams were spread out all over Chicago, and it was his job to oversee them. There was going to be an awful lot of tape to go through before this convention was over, Kirkpatrick thought. He hoped it was worth it. Each bank of recorders bore a label: the one for the Kennedy suite was marked "JFK"; David A. Leman's, "DAL"; and the big one in between them—Conrad Hilton's own, when he was in Chicago—was simply marked "?"

The agent surveilling David Leman's suite swung around in his chair for a chat—Leman was sleeping soundly, apparently. "The Director and Tolson are walking on the beach in Florida," he said. "Have you heard this one?"

Kirkpatrick shook his head. There were hundreds of stories about Hoover, and almost every FBI agent had a favorite. He himself never told Hoover stories, but he was always willing to listen. Privately, he thought that agents who told funny stories about the Director were goddamn fools—the saying "Even the walls have ears" might have been coined for the FBI.

"They keep on walking until they come to a part of the beach that's deserted. Nobody in sight. So Tolson looks right, he looks left, and he says to Hoover, 'It's all clear, Edgar. You can walk on the water now.' "

Kirkpatrick laughed. He had heard the story before, of course. He made a mental note of the agent's name—you never knew when a man's loyalty to the Director might be questioned. The agent listening in on the middle suite flipped a switch and started his recorder. He scribbled a few notes and signaled to Kirkpatrick. "Same broad as last night," he said. "We got some pretty intimate stuff on tape. Here, listen in."

Kirkpatrick took the earphones and pressed his ear against one of the rubber pads. Years of experience had reduced his prurient interest to zero. He would have traded all the groans and moans and pillow talk in the world for one good, solid indictable statement, so he could break down the door, read the perpetrator his rights, and go home to bed. He heard the soft rustle of sheets, then a familiar, breathy voice. *Can you imagine how many guys there are in the world who dream about having Marilyn Monroe wake them up like this?*

He couldn't believe his ears. You had to admire Kennedy's balls, he thought—bringing Marilyn Monroe to Chicago when his wife was across town in the Shrivers' apartment, near which a similar truck was discreetly parked. . . .

Let 'em dream, he heard Jack Kennedy say; then there were all the usual sounds of lovemaking: the wet kisses, the sighs, the soft suck of flesh opening for flesh. He had heard it all before—it didn't differ from one couple to another. A senator and a movie star didn't sound any different from a mobster and a call girl, or anyone else, come to that. He wondered if her cries were genuine or faked, but that, he decided, probably didn't matter either.

Kirkpatrick handed the earphones back.

He'd heard as much as he wanted to hear.

We were sitting in the coffee shop of the Conrad Hilton, Marilyn and I. She was reading about herself in *Life* and nibbling on a cheeseburger. There was a spot of ketchup on her chin. She picked up a french fry, dipped it in ketchup, and popped it into her mouth, managing to turn it into a sexy gesture—like everything else she did.

I had spent the morning with Jim Farley, who had proved Joe Kennedy right again by refusing to back Jack for the vice presidential nomination. Farley, I thought, was certainly going to be on the short list of people whose tax returns would be audited by the IRS the moment Jack got to the White House.

"Isn't it wonderful news about Jack being asked to make the big speech?" Marilyn asked, starry-eyed.

I didn't bother to ask how she had heard the news already—Jack was clearly keeping in touch with her if not with Jackie. "It is and it isn't," I said cautiously, unwilling to spoil her enthusiasm.

"I mean, it's great, isn't it? Stevenson asking Jack to nominate him? It's like the starring role of the whole convention!"

"The supporting role is more like it, really. Adlai's the star of this picture. But the truth is, Adlai mousetrapped Jack at breakfast. Sure, it's a big honor to be asked to make the speech nominating the candidate—it's the high point of the convention, no question about it. But—and it's a big but—it just happens to be a tradition of American politics that the person who nominates the presidential candidate isn't supposed to be a vice presidential contender."

I told her that Jack was still kicking himself—and Bobby—for having failed to foresee Adlai's move in time to spare himself an embarrassing moment, which they both attributed to Eleanor Roosevelt's meddling. Despite their later reputation for ruthlessness, at this stage of their careers Jack and Bobby were still occasionally capable of being surprised by the duplicity and cunning of older, more traditional politicians.

Marilyn's eyes were wide-open, clear blue pools of admiration for my political wisdom, or so I fancied, for nobody was better than she was at playing up to the self-importance of a man.

As it happened, her own political judgment was shrewder than mine (or Jack's, for that matter): when I told her that Jack had been persuaded to pay a courtesy call on Eleanor Roosevelt, much against his will, she rightly predicted it wouldn't do him any good. "You only had to look at Mrs. Roosevelt's face last night, when she was up there on the platform," she said. "That's a woman who doesn't forget or forgive easily. Believe me, I *know* just how she feels!"

I smiled. "It's hard to think of you and Eleanor having anything in common."

Marilyn gave me a steely stare. "She's a woman," she said. "So am I."

I turned that over in my mind. Frankly, nobody had thought of Eleanor Roosevelt as a *woman* for years—decades—not even FDR. For most of her later life she had been thought of as his ambassador to the poor and the minorities, a kind of national monument, ugly but treasured. Of course, Marilyn was right. One of the reasons Adlai got along so well with her, it occurred to me suddenly, was that in a very mild and respectful way he flirted with her—something he did rather well, since he was almost as much of a ladies' man as Jack.

Marilyn wiped her mouth daintily—every so often, traces of her genteel upbringing at the hands of foster parents shone through. She licked her lips, always a sign she was nerving herself to ask a difficult question—not necessarily difficult for her but difficult for *someone*. "David," she said, "there's one thing I don't get. Where's Jackie in all this?"

"You're already suffering from the Other Woman syndrome," I said.

"What's that?"

"An unhealthy interest in the wife."

"I was just curious. She doesn't seem to be a part of all this. How come?"

I glanced around the coffee shop, which was jammed with delegates, many of them wearing funny hats. They were packed in at the entrance like sardines, waiting for tables or a seat at the counter, men and women alike dressed in wash-and-wear, drip-dry synthetics. I couldn't imagine Jackie being any part of it. She was an unapologetic elitist, and her disdain for the sweaty, seamy side of the political process bordered on contempt. To his sisters' fury, Jack had to bargain for every public appearance Jackie made when he was campaigning, with his father or Bobby often acting as the broker.

"Well, she's pregnant," I said. "Having a baby is very important to them both. And Jackie's pretty independent—she's not exactly the kind of political wife who tags along after her husband with a smile on her face. Anyway, she's mad at Jack."

"Why?"

"They were supposed to be spending some time together here—mending fences, if you want to know the truth. Jackie assumed he'd have plenty of time on his hands and they'd spend it together—instead of which he's hardly been back to the apartment since he arrived, so she's sitting there alone watching the convention on TV and steaming, when she could have been at Hyannis Port or her mother's place at Newport."

"Mending fences?"

"There's been some kind of problem between them for months. I know it looks as if Jack can do anything he wants so far as Jackie is concerned, but there *are* certain rules, and I suspect he broke one of them."

"Such as?"

I shrugged. I had no idea what the rules might be, in fact. Keeping out of the gossip columns was certainly one of them. Not fucking friends of Jackie's was probably another, but to my knowledge, Jack had broken that one a long time ago. "I don't know," I said. "They're complicated people. It's a complicated marriage. Jack can do what he wants, but only so long as Jackie gets what *she* wants."

"Which is?"

"Prestige, respect, the right to spend a lot of Jack's money without hearing any complaints about it from him, his undivided attention when she wants it. Something like that."

"That sounds pretty cold. Does she love him?"

"Oh, she loves him, all right. And he loves her too. They're a challenge for each other. She's married a man—forgive me, Marilyn—who can't be faithful for twenty-four hours. He's married the one woman who can cut him down to size like *that*." I snapped my fingers.

"Cut him down to size?"

"When Jackie's not happy, she knows just how to drive Jack crazy." That, I thought, was putting it mildly.

"It doesn't sound like much of a marriage to me," Marilyn said. Perhaps she caught my expression, because she blushed slightly and added: "Well, I guess mine haven't been so hot either."

"Actually, I don't think it's a bad marriage, as marriages go. They're a good match for each other; they enjoy each other's company at least *some* of the time. Jack's proud of her taste, she's proud of his career, and neither of them tells the other what to do. . . . They could do a lot worse."

"But are they *happy*, do you think?"

I sighed. "No, I don't suppose so. Perhaps that doesn't matter in marriage as much as you might think."

As soon as the words were out of my mouth, I realized that I was talking about myself, but Marilyn didn't notice. "It does to *me!*" she said fiercely.

The thought of Marilyn desperately trying to extract happiness from her marriage to Miller, or DiMaggio—and perhaps never quite sure how to recognize it if she found it—saddened me immensely. It came as a relief when a bellboy pushed through the crowd to give me a message that Senator Kennedy wanted to see me upstairs urgently.

He didn't have to say there was a crisis. I could guess.

Jack was in a rage, pacing back and forth in Marilyn's suite—which he now treated like an annex to his own—his complexion a mottled red. He was eating a tuna sandwich, taking huge mouthfuls of it like a shark attacking its prey. Bobby's eyes were fixed soulfully on the sandwich, or so it seemed. She was tempted to ask why he didn't order one of his own, but it hardly seemed the right moment.

"She *sandbagged* me, the old bitch!" Jack said. "I thought we were going to meet alone, just the two of us. Instead, I come into a room full of people and she gives me a lecture on how I should have stood up to McCarthy, as if I were a fucking *schoolboy!* With Hubert Humphrey simpering away on the sofa like the teacher's pet." He glared at Bobby, who was stony-faced. "Somebody should have warned me."

"Adlai's behaved like a real prick," Bobby agreed.

"Jesus! I know *that*, Bobby!" Jack stopped pacing and stared at David. "What do *you* say, David?" he asked. He seemed not to have noticed her until this moment. He shrugged, as if to say, *I'm sorry about all this, but I can't help it*.

Now that the chips were down, David seemed to have grown in stature. It wasn't that he was older than they were by ten years or so—neither Jack nor Bobby was a respecter of age. It had more to do with the fact that he was connected in their minds with their father—and that he was a self-made success in his own high-powered world. Having caught his second wind, David had reverted to his usual cool, perfectly dressed self, a man who seemed to thrive on crises, like a Hollywood producer appearing on a set when everybody else is dropping from exhaustion, to insist on one more take. As if to reinforce the impression, he selected a cigar from an elegant crocodile case in his pocket, trimmed it with a small gold knife, and lit it calmly. "Adlai didn't happen to give you a speech, did he?" he asked between contented puffs.

Jack looked surprised. "How did you know?"

"I didn't. I guessed. I know Adlai. I know Eleanor, too. I can see her hand in this. It's just what she'd advise him to do."

"Damn that woman." Jack glumly took a few folded sheets of paper out of his pocket and handed them to David, who scanned them briefly.

"Who wrote it?" David asked, holding it with distaste, as if it were dirty.

"Arthur Schlesinger. A bleeding-heart college professor. Just right for Adlai."

David handed the speech back. "There's not a word in it you should say, Jack, in my opinion. If I were you," he said firmly, "I'd throw it away and spend the next twenty-four hours writing the speech of a lifetime."

There was a long silence. Jack frowned. Then he grinned, rolled the speech Stevenson had given him into a ball, and tossed it neatly into a wastepaper basket on the far side of the room. "Fuck him," he said. "Fuck Schlesinger. Let's do it. Bobby—get Sorensen up here on the double, and tell him to start drafting something."

He rattled off the names of people whose ideas he wanted, journalists who should be consulted, his anger and irritation giving way rapidly to ebullience.

He came over and gave her a hug and kiss, shot a string of rapid-fire instructions at Bobby, sent David off to see what the party elders were up to. Jack hadn't sought the task of making the nominating speech for Adlai Stevenson, but now that he had it, he was determined to make it a speech nobody would forget.

Once they were alone, he kicked off his shoes and made for the bedroom. "Hey!" she said. "You might at least *ask* me first!"

He turned in the doorway, pulling off his tie, an ironic smile on his face. "It's two o'clock," he said. "Though you may not know it, it's my custom to take a short nap every afternoon. When I was a very young man, in London, Winston Churchill himself told me it was the secret of his long and productive life. I figured if it worked for him, why not for me?"

"I guess." It hadn't occurred to her that a grown-up, active male might take a nap.

"Of course, there's no law against you joining me," he said.

She laughed. "Is that a fact?"

"You might even make sure I wake up—the way you did this morning."

"I'll think about it."

There was a knock on the door, and she remembered she hadn't put the Do Not Disturb sign up. "I'll be in in a moment, darling," she called. She opened the door a crack and saw a plump, balding man, with dark, furtive eyes, a nervous smile, and a thick mustache. He was wearing a white shirt with the logo of the telephone company embroidered on the front, as well as the name "Bernie," in script. He carried a toolbox, and several thick strands of wire were looped over one shoulder. His pockets bulged with what she presumed were the tools of his trade—a flashlight, a telephone handset, screwdrivers.

"Is this the suite with telephone trouble, ma'am?" He had a soft voice, with an unmistakable New York accent. She went over to the nearest telephone, picked it up, heard the dial tone, and came back.

"We haven't had any trouble," she said.

He nodded. "Well, they probably gave me the wrong room number," he said. "It happens all the time."

There was something faintly disturbing about the intensity of his look, but not enough to make her think twice. Men looked at her intently all the time, even when she was in disguise. All the same, it wasn't really the look of a man admiring her tits—it was the kind of look that would have told her "vice cop" back in the old days when she was hanging around the Ambassador Hotel with her lifeguard boyfriends. For a moment she even thought of calling down to the front desk to see if there really *was* a telephone repairman at work on the floor, but she decided she was being silly.

"I guess so," she said. "Thanks." She hung the Do Not Disturb sign on the knob, closed the door sharply, then double-locked it and fastened the security chain, though she couldn't have said why.

She decided that it was just her imagination, poured herself a glass of champagne, and went into the bedroom to join Jack.

WHEN I TOLD MARILYN THAT JACKIE WAS MAD AT JACK, I was putting it mildly. I had been over to the Shriver apartment to pay my respects and found Jackie parked mutinously in front of the television set with Jack's sister Eunice beside her. Even in a maternity dress, Jackie managed to look cool and elegant.

"Thank God *somebody* remembers I'm here," she said when I leaned over to give her a kiss. Eunice looked uncomfortable. Jack's sisters would never accept criticism of him from anyone, even Jackie.

"Jack's got his hands full," Eunice said, as if I might not have noticed what was happening at the convention.

Jackie's face was a picture of angry contempt. "How *nice* for him!" she snapped.

There was a long silence while iced tea was served by the Shrivers' maid. "Wasn't that something last night?" Eunice asked breathlessly—she had a full measure of the family's enthusiasm, and of all the Kennedy women she had always seemed to me the one who most took after her mother, a quality that would hardly endear her to Jackie.

I nodded. "The demonstration for Jack? It was incredible, yes."

Jackie gave me one of her most ambiguous looks. "And wasn't it *amusing* when Jack reached down and rescued that girl? What was her name?"

"Welles?" I said. "Something like that."

"A librarian. Isn't it *just* Jack's luck to meet the only librarian in New York State with great legs?"

"I heard she's an old friend of Eleanor Roosevelt's," Eunice said.

"Oh, *really!*" Jackie dropped the dark glasses that she wore on top of her head down over her eyes and stared at the television screen. It was a habit she shared with my wife

Maria, who had the same abrupt way of dismissing people who had overstayed their welcome or tried her patience. I finished my iced tea, made my excuses, and got up to leave.

"Did you get a chance to meet Miss Welles, David?" Jackie asked.

I shook my head. "Not at all. I only saw her from a distance."

"*What* a shame! She reminded me of someone—I'm not sure who, but it will come back to me."

She inclined her head slightly, for me to give her a good-bye kiss on the cheek, which I did. "You're a bad liar, David," she whispered.

"Perhaps so," I said. "That's why I seldom lie, you see."

She gave me a smile—Jackie and I really liked and understood each other. "You're getting a lot better at it," she said sadly. "That's what comes of hanging around with politicians. Good-bye. Give my best to Maria, please."

They were together in her suite when I returned. Marilyn was lying on the sofa wearing a robe, a towel wrapped around her hair, filing her nails while Jack, in shirtsleeves, paced up and down reading aloud from a few sheets of lined yellow legal paper. "Look at this," he said.

It was a good speech, head and shoulders above the one that Adlai had handed him. "Not bad," I said.

"Not bad isn't good enough." He took it back, went to the far side of the room, and began to declaim. He made his way through the first page—gestures, pauses, and all—while Marilyn, still working on her nails, looked at him with veiled intensity.

"You've *got* to get the breaths right, honey," she said. "If you get ahead of your breathing, you end up taking a big gasp in the wrong place or just dribbling off. . . ."

Jack had the grim look on his face that all the Kennedys got when they were determined to master something difficult or new, but more surprising to me was his willingness to take criticism from a woman.

He backed up, started again, and got it right this time—an even delivery, tremendous sincerity, long, impressive pauses at just the right moments.

"The speech still sucks," he said. I noticed there was a trail of discarded paper forming a rough oval track all around the room, and wondered how many drafts he had already gone through. He crumpled up the first page, went to the door between the two suites, opened it and tossed the paper in, aiming it high.

Through the door I caught a glimpse of some of the Kennedy team hard at work: Bobby stretched out on a sofa with a telephone receiver pressed between his ear and his shoulder; Ted Sorensen hunched over a coffee table, scribbling furiously; half a dozen old and new hands working away at index cards, or manning the many telephones that had been hastily set up in the suite. Politics has a way of destroying hotel rooms, as I had noticed over the years, and this one was no exception— it looked as if an occupying army had camped out in it, and it smelled of cigarette smoke, stale coffee, and sweat. "It's not tough enough," Jack said.

"You don't want to attack Eisenhower," Sorensen said, looking up from his labors.

Jack thought about this. He *did* want to attack Ike, for whom he had a certain degree of contempt, but he knew as well as Sorensen did that it was a dangerous thing to do, given Ike's popularity.

Marilyn looked up from her nails, a serious expression on her face, which had the paradoxical effect of making her appear much younger, almost like a schoolgirl having problems with her homework. "Arthur—my husband—always says Nixon does Ike's dirty work for him," she whispered, I suppose so Sorensen wouldn't hear her. "That way Ike can take the high road, he says."

She smiled and went back to her nails, while Jack and I stared at each other. Normally Miller's left-wing views would not have interested him, but he looked thoughtful.

"I don't *have* to attack him, goddamn it," he shouted at Sorensen. "Everybody knows he takes the high road as a candidate while Nixon takes the low road. I can say that."

"It's risky."

"Put it in," Jack snapped. There was always an edge to Jack's relationship with Ted Sorensen. Sorensen had been drafted to "help" Jack write *Profiles in Courage* and Jack was so determined to put down rumors that Sorensen had really written the Pulitzer Prize-winning book instead of him that he kept a page of the first draft in his own handwriting in his desk drawer to show to doubters. What he felt about Marilyn giving him one of his best lines, I don't know.

We chatted for a few moments, until Marilyn, who moved to her own rhythm, got up, stretched, exposing most of her bosom, and went off to bathe and dress.

Jack and I both stared at her, failing to conceal our admiration from each other; then we sat down on the sofa she had vacated. Close up, I could see how tired he was, the skin drawn tight over the bones of his face, deep circles under his eyes; he had the slightly unfocused and punch-drunk look that comes from a couple of days of high stress and only a few hours of sleep. Jack was tough—nobody was a better campaigner, not even Bobby, when his turn came—but there were limits to his endurance. He was still at the age when he could ignore the limits, but only just. "How was Jackie?" he asked.

I made a wavy motion with my hand.

He sighed. "Not too happy?"

"Not happy at all."

"I hadn't counted on this happening." He didn't make it clear whether he meant Marilyn or getting into the vice presidential race. Perhaps it didn't matter.

"It mightn't hurt to go over there. She's feeling pretty lonely."

"Yes? I guess so." He did not seem concerned.

"Jack, it's none of my business, I know, but she's angry about something too—*really* angry. I noticed it when I was at Hickory Hill for lunch last time. It was the same kind of anger I could feel today, over at the apartment—a cold, hard anger, not the kind that's about something that's only just happened. . . . Am I out of line? Or full of shit?"

"You're not full of shit, David," he said glumly, raising an eyebrow, since, as he well knew, I use words like that only when I feel there's no other way to get my point across.

"Does Jackie know about Marilyn?"

He shrugged. "Oh, probably. Not that she's in Chicago. But in general, yes."

"Is that the problem?"

"No, not really. You know Jackie and I have"—he paused, looking for the right word, or perhaps simply regretting that he had allowed the conversation to take this turn—"an *agreement?*"

I nodded. The "agreement" between Jack and Jackie was one of the deeper Kennedy mysteries, even to me. Her cool, ironic acceptance of her husband's constant—indeed, institutionalized—infidelities puzzled almost everyone, even then. Later on, when Jackie was in the White House, the stories about her wit and self-control became part of the Kennedy legend, the seamy underside of Camelot, as it were—her contemptuous dismissal of Jack's two obliging young blond staff secretaries, "Fiddle" and "Faddle," as the "White House dogs," her handing Jack a pair of black panties she had found under the pillow of their bed and telling him to see that they were returned to their owner because they weren't her size.

"So Marilyn isn't the issue?" I asked. "I thought at lunch, when Jackie brought her name up . . ."

Jack waved his hand impatiently. "It doesn't make that much difference to Jackie whether it's Marilyn or anyone else. I may have gone too far, that's all." He gave a deep sigh. "I was hoping to get a chance to talk things over with Jackie here, away from Hickory Hill," he said. "If I'd known it was going to be a three-ring circus . . ."

"Is it serious?"

"Serious enough. I'm hoping the baby will solve a lot of the problems between us. Hell, we'll see." He did not seem hopeful. If he had not been a Catholic and a politician, I would have said he sounded like a man who has already come to terms with the end of his marriage.

"I'm sorry to hear that," I said. "Surely it wouldn't hurt to go across town and see her? Having a fuss made over them is the one thing wives always want."

"Marilyn told me the same thing."

"Well, she has a lot of common sense."

"Yes." He didn't sound happy about it. "I guess there's no way to prevent Marilyn from going to the arena to hear my speech tonight, is there?"

"None that I can think of."

"Just keep her off the front page of the *Chicago Tribune* this time, David, will you?"

"I'll do my best." The truth was, I hadn't the foggiest notion how I was going to keep Marilyn—even in her librarian disguise—hidden and unnoticed.

He stood up. His eyes had the faraway expression of a man whose big roll of the dice is fast approaching. I didn't know how I would have dealt with that kind of pressure; Jack, I suspected, would deal with it by going to bed with Marilyn.

As if to confirm my guess, he made for the bedroom, taking off his tie, looking amazingly cool and calm; then he was gone, and the door closed behind him and Marilyn.

All around her the arena hummed with sound; the floor underfoot was thick with discarded paper cups, candy wrappers, trampled streamers and confetti. She didn't mind being out of the limelight for a change. Here, dumb as it was, she felt free—free from the problems of being Marilyn Monroe, free from having to worry about Arthur Miller's unhappiness, free from the threats of 20th Century-Fox, from the snide contempt of Sir Cork Tip and his fading wife, from the guilt of having to see Milton every day when they both knew their partnership was doomed. . . .

David sat beside her, clearly determined not to let her out of his sight. From time to time party bigwigs came over to pay him homage. He did not attempt to introduce her, which was okay with her, since she wasn't sure she was up to doing the Birdy Welles number again. The music blared on, competing against the drone of a voice from the platform going through some sort of procedural point.

"What this thing needs is a good director," she said.

"Another few minutes," David said, glancing at his watch.

She leaned close to him, obliged to shout into his ear to make herself heard over the din. "Is Jackie here tonight?" she asked.

David shook his head. "If Jack gets the nomination, she'll be here to stand beside him. She doesn't waste herself on small events."

"If I were married to Jack, I'd never let him out of my sight. She *really* doesn't mind that he fucks other women?"

"I suppose she *does,* at some level, yes. But she's got it under control. That's the interesting thing about Jackie, you see—she's got *everything* under control."

"You're saying she's cold."

"No. I don't think she's cold at all. I would have said that Jackie's a very passionate woman, myself. I don't think Jack would marry a woman who *wasn't* passionate—but more important, you only have to see the way she looks at him. . . . No, no, there's real fire there, believe me."

"Have you seen her since we've been here?" she asked. She was delighted to see David hesitate, like a married man whose wife has just asked after his girlfriend. David was loyal, you had to give him that.

"Yes," he said reluctantly. "I had tea with her."

Of course! *Tea with her!* What else would you have with Jackie Kennedy? "How was she?"

"Fine. She looked pretty good. Considering."

"I bet she has the *nicest* maternity clothes," she said, not even bothering to disguise the envy in her voice.

David nodded. "Well, you know what Jackie's like about clothes. Or perhaps you don't. . . . I will say that for a woman who's about to give birth, she looked very chic."

Chic! Nobody had ever described *her* as chic! "Did she mention me?" she asked.

He looked wary. "Mention you? No." He hesitated. "Not really."

"Not really? What does *that* mean?"

"She did say that Birdy Welles reminded her of someone."

"Oh God!" She felt the familiar stab of fear at being "found out." Then she reminded herself that it was Jack's problem, not hers.

"Well, it was only an impression," David said consolingly. "She couldn't help noticing you last night when Jack was hauling you out of the crowd." He stared toward the podium as if the spectacle fascinated him, though nothing much was going on there. "I think she'd been looking at the photographs in the papers very closely too. I noticed there was a magnifying glass on top of her copy of this morning's *Tribune*."

"I thought you said she didn't care?"

"She cares about *you*, apparently."

Her throat tightened. "About me? What makes you think that?"

"She mentioned you once before. When I was having lunch at Hickory Hill, oh, quite some time ago. She was furious with Jack."

"Why?"

"I don't know. She asked if I could introduce Jack to you next time he was in California. But it was the way she asked, you understand. Even *Jack* was embarrassed—which is unusual for him. It was as if she knew about something"—he paused—"something that broke whatever the rules are between them."

She felt a cold shiver. "Hickory Hill," she murmured. "That's the house in Virginia, isn't it?"

He nodded. "It's funny. It's always been *Jack* who wanted to get rid of it and move to Georgetown, and Jackie who insisted on keeping it. . . . But now it's Jackie who's after him to sell." He shrugged. "Something happened there, I don't know what, but something went wrong. . . . It's sad. Such a beautiful place."

"Yes," she said distantly, thinking back to that day in Washington with him, and the afternoon they had spent in bed together at the house, and the long line of wooded hills glowing in the late-afternoon sun when she finally rose from bed, leaving him sleeping there like a child, to slip into the dressing room and go through Jackie's drawers. . . .

"I remember the view—" she said. Then she was suddenly conscious that David was staring at her. He shook his head slowly, as if he had been stunned.

A cold chill ran through her. She had given away one of the guiltiest of her guilty secrets, and he would know now just how foolish and careless Jack had been, and perhaps guess how hard she had pushed him. She wanted David to like and respect her, and she couldn't help feeling that in one moment she had forfeited all that, which made her sad. She grabbed his hand. "Be my friend, David!" she whispered. "Please. Always. Whatever I've done? Whatever I do?"

He let out a long breath. Then, almost regretfully, like a man taking on a burden he wasn't sure he could carry, he nodded.

"Promise?" She didn't know why it mattered so much, but it did. Perhaps because she had so few friends. Husbands, lovers, lawyers, agents, business associates, doctors, and therapists—all of those, sure, but *friends?*

"I promise," he said softly, and she kissed him, tears welling up. They sat together for a few moments, hand in hand, sharing unspoken thoughts, and she was strangely comforted, as she could surely never have been by a lover.

There was a sudden hush in the arena. She had been so busy worrying about what David thought that she'd almost missed Jack's arrival. All around her she could feel a kind of tingling, electric excitement. She squeezed David's hand so tight he cried out, and leapt to her feet shouting and jumping up and down like a high school cheerleader as Jack walked onto the platform grinning and made his way slowly toward the flag-draped podium as if in a triumphal procession.

She instantly recognized "star quality" when she saw it. In an arena full of pallid, tired, sweaty people—thousands of them—he seemed like a visitor from another, more glamorous world, his skin deeply tanned, the way only movie stars and the very rich look, the big grin displaying glistening white teeth, the unruly hair proclaiming his youth, his broad athlete's shoulders hunching as he braced himself against the podium.

He made a small ceremony of getting his speech neatly placed, just as she had told him to, performing a piece of business the way an actor would, milking it for maximum suspense while the crowd cheered and chanted, *"Kennedy, Kennedy, Kennedy!"* and the band played "Anchors Aweigh" over and over again.

Jack let the celebration run its course, grinned through the release of the red-white-and-blue balloons, the waving of banners and photographs of himself. The Texas delegation made a rush for the podium, throwing novelty Stetson hats into the air while the band played "Yellow Rose of Texas." "Jack and Lyndon must be striking a deal," she heard David whisper to her. Then the Massachusetts delegation, led by a red-faced old-time Irish pol in a wide-brimmed Borsalino hat, came pushing down the aisles, cheering themselves hoarse, and the band switched to "The Bells of St. Mary's"—a choice that seemed to puzzle Jack. The noise was deafening, and seemed likely to go on forever, despite Rayburn's gavel and Stevenson's frown. Then Jack raised his arms, and as if by magic, the arena fell silent.

She shut her eyes. She knew the speech by heart—an amazing feat, she thought, for somebody who could never remember her own lines! She repeated every word to herself a beat before him, as if they were in a duet. His delivery was flawless, his pauses eloquent, the applause thunderous at just the right moments. It was not young Jack Kennedy, playboy senator, old Joe Kennedy's spoiled son, speaking but a whole new man of depth, maturity, vision, who was articulating just what everybody wanted America to be. He spoke the obligatory praise for Adlai Stevenson—after all, he was here to nominate him—but nobody could mistake the fact that this speech was for himself and for the country, not for Stevenson, who everybody knew was going to lose to Ike again in November.

Tears were running down her cheeks by the time he brought his speech to a climax. She opened her eyes and saw him turning to Adlai Stevenson, as if offering him a present. And even Adlai seemed caught up in the emotion of the moment as the crowd went wild, not for him, as he must have realized, but for young Jack Kennedy, for the future. She yearned to rush to the podium, climb up to hug him as hard as she could. . . .

Then, in the shadows at the back of the platform, she saw a small figure in a pink maternity dress edging forward, Bobby Kennedy at her side. Even in the stupendous heat, Jackie looked poised, cool, every hair in place.

Jack and Adlai exchanged stiff hugs, with the embarrassment of men who neither liked nor respected each other—and who didn't like being touched by other men. Then Jack moved quickly to take Jackie by the hand and lead her forward.

Somebody had given Jackie a bouquet of red roses, which she held across her swelling belly. If she was nervous, it didn't show. Jackie waved gracefully—like a queen, really, as if this whole convention were in *her* honor—and gazed adoringly up at Jack.

"I want to go home," she told David, crying even harder now. She put on her sunglasses.

He turned in surprise. "Jesus, Marilyn," he said. "The best is still to come! After that speech, Jack might just win it."

"I know. I want to go anyway."

"Back to the hotel?"

She shook her head. "Back to New York. Back to London. Back to work."

He took her hand in his. You couldn't fault David for insensitivity. She knew that he wanted to stay, to see his friend begin his run for the vice presidency, but he didn't hesitate.

"Let's go then, Marilyn," he said gently.

18

BERNIE SPINDEL SAT IN HOFFA'S OFFICE IN DETROIT, holding his battered, bulky old leather briefcase in his lap with both hands.

He had driven from Chicago in a car rented under an assumed name from a cut-rate company that was happy to take cash and not ask too many questions. Spindel didn't like flying. Airports were full of cops and Feds, and who knew what they were looking for, or when one of them might look up and recognize a familiar face? Besides, you had to give the airlines a name, and Spindel hated doing that. He felt safer cruising down the highways along with millions of other people, in a rusted old car with faded paint and acned chrome, which would attract no attention. He never drove above the speed limit, and always made sure all the lights were in good order before he started out, so there was no chance of being stopped by a trooper.

He stopped only once, for a quick piss—carrying his briefcase with him—a tank of gas, a cheeseburger and a Coke, arriving at the Teamster building exactly one minute ahead of schedule. Spindel was a man who believed in precision. He liked to boast to his students that they could set their watches by him, and he expected them to.

Hoffa sat behind his desk, trying to pretend he wasn't curious, his small eyes as black and dead as a shark's. Spindel didn't care. He didn't have to like Hoffa. He hadn't liked Hoover either. What he liked was the *work,* the knowledge that he was the best.

"So whatcha got?" Hoffa finally asked, cracking his knuckles so loudly that anybody but Spindel would have jumped out of his skin.

Spindel smiled. He wanted to be seduced, to hold back a little, like a broad who knows she's going to fuck the guy but still wants to be talked into it. Hoover had understood that better than Hoffa, but Spindel and Hoover had never really gotten along, and in the end, Spindel found he was more comfortable with the bad guys, and better paid, too.

"He damn near got it, Jimmy," he said. "I was almost rooting for him myself, at the end."

"Fuck you were. That fucking papa's boy with his five-hundred-dollar suits? Don't shit me, Bernie."

"Well, you know what I mean. . . . It was like a horse race. He was thirty-three and a half votes short on the second ballot, and if Tennessee and Pennsylvania hadn't switched to Kefauver on the next one . . . I never seen nothing like it, Jimmy."

"I read it in the fucking papers, Bernie. Anyway, it don't matter. Ike and Nixon are going to walk all over Stevenson."

"It'll be Kennedy in '60, you want my opinion, Jimmy."

Hoffa laughed harshly. "Over my dead body." He cracked his knuckles again. "Or his." He sat silently for a moment. "So, you got anything, or not?"

"I got." Spindel put the heavy briefcase on the big, polished desk, took out a reel-to-reel tape recorder, plugged it in, removed a reel from its unlabeled cardboard box, and threaded the tape, his fingers moving with the precision of a surgeon's. "Funny thing," he said. "When I put the taps in the phone box, in the hotel, somebody had been there before me."

Hoffa frowned. "Who?"

"FBI!" Spindel grinned. "I recognized the technique right away, see. I taught them how to do it! So I had to get back and remove my taps before he did, you know, so he didn't know mine were there too, right on top of his."

Hoffa smiled grimly. "So Hoover is building up a file on Jack too? Now *that* is interesting, Bernie. You done good. That gets you a bonus, my friend."

"You wait till you hear this, Jimmy."

Spindel pushed the button. The tape hissed, and there was a background noise that sounded like the rustling of sheets, the clink of ice cubes, perhaps the soft, liquid sound of skin moving against skin. Spindel knew his job, all right—you couldn't ever complain about the quality of his work. *This won't take but a minute, Senator,* a woman said, and even to somebody who was no movie fan, like Hoffa, Spindel knew, there was no mistaking the voice of Marilyn Monroe—that familiar high, breathless little voice, at once a little girl's and a sexy woman's, with the slight hesitation between words that was almost a stutter but not quite. Spindel could almost see her, all white and pink, with her bold mascaraed eyes and her bright straw-colored hair, just as she had been when she opened the door of her suite in the Conrad Hilton, and spoke to him. . . .

Hoffa reached across the desk and shook his hand solemnly. Then he sprang to his feet and went into a boxer's crouch, feinting and shadow-punching his way around the floor, his big shoulders working as if he were still the twenty-year-old tough guy he had once been, making his way up from the ranks of loading-dock day laborers with his fists, against men twice his size.

Spindel winced as Hoffa smacked a big fist against the palm of his other hand, with a sound so loud and sharp it might have been a gunshot. *"Bingo!"* Hoffa shouted joyfully. "Bull's-eye!"

I returned Marilyn to New York and deposited her into the care of the good Dr. Kris. Shortly afterward, she returned to England to resume work on *The Prince and the Showgirl*, taking Dr. Kris along for moral support.

I was not surprised to read in the gossip columns of the rumors of tension between Marilyn and her husband, as well as a nasty scene between her and Olivier when he tried to ban Paula Strasberg from the set again and she made him back down.

Marilyn's troubles in London were overshadowed by another item, in Drew Pearson's column—that Jack and Jackie were "estranged" and discussing separation, after the birth of a stillborn child.

I had known about the stillbirth, of course, which had taken place only a couple of weeks after the convention, though it was kept as quiet as possible. Jackie had been at her mother's, Hammersmith Farm, the Auchincloss place at Newport, so I'd called her there to commiserate. Jack was not there yet, which I found puzzling at the time, but I assumed he was hurrying back from the South of France, where he had been visiting his father and planning to take a sailing trip to unwind from the convention and prepare himself for two months of brutal nationwide campaigning for Stevenson.

A call from Joe Kennedy's secretary, asking if I could join him for dinner, was enough to put me on the alert, since I had assumed he was still enjoying himself in the luxurious villa he rented every summer at Biot, a short drive from Cap d'Antibes. I knew only a family emergency of the most monumental proportions could have brought him back to New York early, so I prepared myself for trouble.

We met at La Caravelle. Henri Soulé's Le Pavillon had been the Ambassador's favorite restaurant in New York, until the day Soulé forgot to prepare a chocolate cake for a Kennedy family celebration. Not only did Joe never go back, he even went to the trouble of financing Soulé's chef and maître d'hôtel to leave and open a rival restaurant, which was, of course, why we were dining at La Caravelle.

He was waiting for me at his usual banquette table, looking as tanned and energetic as ever. Bergson might have intended the phrase *"élan vital"* to describe Joe—"life force" was what he was all about.

We exchanged small talk while Joe waited impatiently for me to finish my drink so he could get on with the business of ordering his meal. For an Irishman, he was the least convivial of drinkers. I explained that I was a temporary summer bachelor, Maria having left for the South of France ahead of me.

He glared at the menu. "You read the news?"

"Drew Pearson's story? Yes. Is it true?"

"That slimy fucking Pearson! I'd like to break his neck for him."

I took this to be an admission that Pearson's story was correct.

"Where's Jack?" I asked.

The Ambassador sipped his drink. "He's up at Newport, with Jackie," he said tightly. "Where he belongs."

His expression was grim. I did not press him. He would tell me what he wanted me to know in his own time—or what he wanted me to do, more likely. We chatted about his "vacation" in the South of France while we ordered.

"How was your summer?" I asked. "Apart from all this."

"Apart from the fact that you and Bobby dragged Jack into a fight he couldn't win, there in Chicago—it's been dandy. Did you know they made Rose a papal countess?" He did not say who "they" were. Joe and Rose maintained what amounted to a "separate but equal" relationship with the hierarchy of the Catholic Church, hers motivated by piety and a certain degree of snobbery, his by the simple need to exert his power everywhere he could. Rose liked to spend her summers traveling from one religious shrine to another, culminating in a visit to the Vatican for an audience with His Holiness. Her pilgrimages suited both of them nicely—she was spared the direct knowledge that Joe was sleeping with his mistresses under her own roof, while he was free to do what he wanted without going to a lot of trouble to conceal it.

"A countess?" I said. "I'm impressed."

Joe grimaced. "It cost me a fortune."

"Well spent, I'd say."

He gave a small sigh of contentment, tasted his pea soup, frowned, and demanded more croutons—he believed in keeping people on their toes. "This story about Jack," he began hesitantly, between spoonfuls of soup. "How far do you think it's going to spread?"

"Is it true?" I asked again.

"Not anymore."

"What happened?"

Joe finished his soup, wiped his mouth, and glared at me. Then he took off his spectacles and wiped them. His eyes, I saw, were sunken and tired, lacking their usual flinty sparkle. "Jack came to see me at Biot. He was going off on a sailing trip with George Smathers."

I didn't need to be told what a sailing trip with Smathers would be like. Smathers and Jack had been freshmen congressmen and bachelors-around-town together. They had acquired such a reputation for fast living that the Ambassador was finally obliged to arrange for Eunice to move to Washington and take a job there so she could keep an eye on her brother. "While Jackie was at home, in the last weeks of a difficult pregnancy?" I asked, raising an eyebrow.

"There was a girl on the boat with Jack—twenty-something, blond, unbelievable figure. . . ." He chuckled. "A real beauty," he said. "I wouldn't have minded a crack at her myself." He may have caught the expression on my face, because he added rather defensively, "Hell, I thought Jack deserved a good time after Chicago."

"He'd been having a good time, so far as I know. He should have been with Jackie."

He took a sip of ice water and gave me an angry stare. I stared right back at him. That seemed to calm him down. "Jack said there'd been a lot of tension between him and Jackie," he continued. "That he needed a little time away from her. It didn't sound like such a bad idea to me."

I'll bet it didn't, I told myself. Joe had been absent at almost every moment that might have mattered in his own marriage, despite his reputation as a family man.

"When Jackie miscarried, Jack was at sea, with this girl. I radioed the news to him, but he decided to go on with the trip anyway."

"He went *on* with the trip?" Even I was surprised.

"Jack said it wasn't worth going home, since the baby was born dead," he finally said, unhappily.

I stared at my plate. "That might be thought selfish and callous," I suggested. "By some."

"Yes. Jackie's mother gave me an earful on the subject, collect on the phone from Newport to Biot. Even Bobby was . . ." He groped for the right word.

"Dismayed?"

"Yeah. Anyway, word leaked out, and Pearson heard about it. I put in an emergency radio call to Jack on the fucking yacht and told him if he didn't get back to port pronto, he could kiss his political career good-bye."

It was an unedifying story, but Jack was, above all, his father's son, and it would therefore never have occurred to him not to put his own pleasures first.

"I take it you came back to make peace?" I asked.

He nodded.

"Not an easy task, I would think."

"Not easy, no." His eyes, and the deep lines on his tanned face, made clear how hard it had been. "Not cheap either."

I could imagine. Still, there were things I didn't want to know, and that was one of them. "You were lucky the story broke in Drew Pearson's column," I said. "Even his colleagues don't trust him. If it had been Winchell, say—"

"I talked to Winchell."

"I'd talk to Jack again, if I were you." I thought hard. This kind of thing was how I made my living, after all. "What you need is a storm," I said.

"A storm?"

"A storm at sea. You radioed the yacht; they had to fight their way back against heavy seas and gales to make the nearest port. Jack was distraught, anxious, urging everybody on to put on more sail, or whatever it is they do. . . . It's got a nice resonance to it too, because it's going to remind people of PT-109. But Jack can't spread the story himself—somebody else has to make him a hero."

The Ambassador stared into the middle distance thoughtfully. How many times, over the years, had we sat together searching for some line to give the press that would present things in the rosiest possible light? "I like it," he said at last. "I like it fine."

"You need to get Jack and his pals on board fast."

"No problem there."

"How about the girls?"

"What girls?"

"The ones on the yacht."

"Their—ah—goodwill has already been secured."

A couple of pretty American girls, I guessed, were going to get a chance to travel around Europe for a while in luxury, keeping clear of the press. The Ambassador hadn't wasted any time.

"And Jackie?"

"What about her?"

"You don't want her telling people there wasn't a storm."

"She wasn't there. If Jack says there was a storm, who's to argue? The Mediterranean is funny that way. You can have great weather, a flat sea—then suddenly, out of nowhere, you get a squall. . . . A dangerous place. Every sailor knows that."

He signaled for the dessert tray, already looking happier as he caught sight of a chocolate mousse cake. He pointed at it imperiously. "It wouldn't be a bad idea to have a few pictures in *Life*, would it now? Jack and Jackie—tragedy strikes the glamorous young couple of American politics, that kind of thing."

"No, it wouldn't be a bad idea. Will she stand for it, do you think?"

Joe dug into his piece of cake with a fierce thrust of his fork. "You see if you can sell it to *Life*," he said. "I'll deal with the rest."

But in the end, the story never ran, probably because Jackie put her foot down. The legend of Jack's return to port through the raging seas to rejoin Jackie caught on well enough, however, and from time to time they even joked about it, though the subject always made Jack look a little nervous.

Early in the new year, after Jack had worked his guts out on the road for Adlai, and had the satisfaction of seeing him buried in the landslide for Ike, I would hear from Joe that Jackie was pregnant again, so the reconciliation was complete, timed perfectly for Jack's emergence as the one bright, shining hope for the Democrats as they looked ahead to 1960.

19

I DROPPED IN TO VISIT JACK IN HIS SENATE OFFICE ON one of those misleading early spring days when the grass is turning green again, crocuses are appearing and the cherry trees beginning to blossom, and winter seems over at last— the kind of day that usually precedes a cold snap or a late blizzard. He looked relaxed as we drank our coffee, from big stoneware mugs with the Senate seal on them—a gift from Jackie, he told me. Nearly six months had passed since their crisis, and they seemed to have been reconciled.

"So things are going better between you two?" I asked.

He nodded, not quite sure how much I knew. "We've decided to move to Georgetown," he said warily. "No more commuting, thank God," he added, though it was news to me that he cared. "Bobby and Ethel bought Hickory Hill."

"I guess they plan to fill it."

He laughed—a bit hollowly, I thought. "I guess they will too," he said. Then, as if eager to change the subject from Ethel's phenomenal fertility: "Jackie found a nice little house on N Street in Georgetown. A red-brick Federal."

I nodded. I knew the house. Jackie's taste, as usual, was flawless and expensive.

"Have you heard from Marilyn?" he asked me.

"She's back from England," I told him. "I hear the picture is okay—*she's* terrific, Olivier's not, which is going to surprise the critics. . . . Not that it matters at the moment. She and Miller have gone into a kind of retreat, at his house in Connecticut. She's trying to be what she calls a good wife. She bakes pies, she vacuums, she makes him coffee. She's having a baby. After all, she dragged him off to England, where he suffered from writer's block while she worked, so she feels she owes him some time to get another play under his belt. Or a screenplay."

"That's very decent of her."

"Marilyn's a very decent person."

"Do you see a lot of her?"

"A lot? No. She comes into town every once in a while to see her psychiatrist. Sometimes we have coffee, or a sandwich."

"Is she happy?"

"She puts on a pretty good show. To hear her talk, all she's ever wanted to be is a housewife. On the other hand, since she also told me she's discovered that barbiturates work faster if you prick the capsule with a pin before swallowing it, I'm not so sure. I would guess Marilyn's got a few reservations about doing Miller's laundry while he writes his play, or whatever."

"Is that true, about the capsules?"

"Probably. It's not the sort of thing she'd make up. I suspect she's pretty unhappy. I think she knows the marriage has failed—that she's just going through the motions."

He nodded glumly. It clearly wasn't a subject he wanted to pursue. "Speaking of Bobby," he said (though we hadn't been), "it looks as if he's struck pay dirt at last. He's got enough on Beck to put him away for life. Mob connections, strong-arm tactics, tax evasion, theft of union funds, you name it. Can you imagine? Beck built himself a luxurious mansion with Teamster money, then sold it back to the union at a profit and continued living in it. He used union funds to build a hundred-and-eighty-five-thousand-dollar house for his son!" He shook his head. "Some of the things going on around Beck would curl your hair, David. It's going to be a big, big story."

"With Bobby at the center?"

"With Bobby and *me* at the center, yes. My guess is, it's going to require some landmark legislation to combat these abuses, once we've got them out in the open."

Investigating Dave Beck and his cronies would make the Kennedy name familiar to voters all across the country, and a piece of major labor legislation, emerging from the hearings and bearing Jack's name, would firmly establish him as a "serious" senator, once and for all. Since I had played a role in putting together this dramatic exposé of the forces of darkness, I felt a certain satisfaction at the neat way in which the pieces were now falling into place.

Red Dorfman and I had seen each other several times in the past few months—without striking up a closer friendship, I might add. From time to time, on my business trips to the West Coast, Jack Ruby left his Dallas strip joints to hand-deliver packages of information on Dave Beck and the Teamsters to me. Ruby didn't know what was in them, of course, which galled him almost as much as having to leave "his girls" unsupervised. We usually met in dark parking lots and got our business over as quickly as possible, but not so quickly that I didn't hear from him about all the difficulties of running a string of hookers in Dallas and, with considerable pride on his part, about how good his relationship was with the cops there. I did not look upon Ruby's sweaty presence as a pleasure, but frankly, I found him less objectionable than his boss, at any rate less threatening.

Every now and then, I asked myself what I was doing with these unlikely new playmates. I can understand now that I was simply bored with my life. I already had all the money I could ever spend, my marriage held no excitement for me (or for Maria, to be fair), I had become an "elder statesman" in my own company, and it was clear, even to me, that Marilyn and I were never fated to be anything more than friends. Playing Jack Kennedy's messenger to the forces of evil gave me the kind of thrill that a love affair might have done. Looking back, a love affair would have been a better idea.

On a couple of occasions, when it was absolutely necessary, I also met with some of Hoffa's own people, in conditions of strict secrecy. Somewhat against my better judgment, I had set up a meeting between Bobby and Hoffa which was to precede the hearing—a way for each man to get a feel for the other, as well as a kind of rehearsal for Hoffa before he submitted to being questioned in public.

I was more worried about the way Bobby would behave at the hearing than I was about Hoffa—Bobby knew perfectly well that this particular horse race was fixed, but he didn't like the idea a bit, and I was afraid that he might try and win it anyway, once he was out of the starting gate. Jack, as usual, assumed things would go his way smoothly.

"When is the great event scheduled for, actually?" I asked.

"Midsummer. August of all the goddamn months! Just when I want to be on the Cape. . . . You ought to come down and watch, since you had such a lot to do with it."

Washington is not my idea of a good place to be in August, but I was tempted. I had an idea—"premonition" is perhaps too strong a word—that history was going to be made, Kennedy family history anyway.

As matters turned out, the confrontation between Jimmy Hoffa and Bobby was to take second place in the headlines to a much bigger event in most people's eyes—a new tragedy in the life of Marilyn Monroe.

"I knew something bad was going to happen, right there on the beach at Amagansett, when we saw the fish."

Marilyn and I were sitting at a back table in the Hole in the Wall Delicatessen, a tiny place on First Avenue around the corner from her apartment at 555 East Fifty-seventh Street, where she went unrecognized by Stanley, the owner; his wife behind the cash register; and the waitress. Or perhaps they were simply used to incognito celebrities, since Garbo also lived around the corner and often ate breakfast there. Marilyn's face was thin and drawn, which made her eyes look huge, like those in a Day Kean painting. Only a week or two before, she had been rushed to a hospital in New York from Amagansett, in agony. She had been diagnosed as suffering from a tubal pregnancy and operated on immediately, since she was, as the tabloids proclaimed the next day, "In mortal danger."

"The fish?"

"They were on the beach." Her eyes opened wide, as if the

scene were being reenacted on First Avenue. "See, the fisher-men pull up their nets on the beach to empty them, and the fish they can't sell, they just toss out. Sea robins? Like that?"

I nodded, though I wasn't sure exactly what a sea robin was. Marilyn bit her lip sharply. "They just lie there helpless-ly, flapping, opening their mouths and gills, until they die," she said.

She managed to invest the scene with such emotion that I was almost tempted to cry myself at the death of the sea rob-ins—Tippy all over again, I reflected.

"Arthur gave me this long, serious explanation of market forces, and how commercial fishermen make their living and so on, and all the time, I was dying, right along with the fish. So I started to pick them up, one after the other, and toss them back into the sea, even though I hate touching fish."

She shuddered. "He stood there for a while, looking grim, watching me save the fish; then he walked up beside me and started to help, and we both threw the fish back in until they were all gone. . . . I was touched, you know? Because it wasn't something he believed in, or really wanted to do. That night we made love, and I knew I was going to have his baby." She glared at me briefly. "Don't ask me how, David. Women know these things, believe me."

"I believe you."

"No you don't, but you're wrong." She took a sip of water. Outside on the street, in the muggy heat, a woman went by wearily pushing a baby carriage. Marilyn stared at her until she was out of sight, then sighed. "I knew I was going to be pregnant," she said. "I knew I wasn't going to have the baby too. The fish were like a sign, do you know what I mean?"

I didn't, because I don't believe in such things, but I nodded.

"It wasn't meant to be," she explained, in case I'd missed the point.

"It's rotten luck—"

"It hasn't got anything to do with luck!" She reached under the table and clenched my hand tightly. Her palm was wet and clammy. "I don't love him enough, you see." I must have looked puzzled, because she added: "I don't love Arthur enough to have a baby with him, so the baby died."

I felt suddenly chilled, but I couldn't think of anything help-ful to say. "It isn't your fault about the baby."

"Yes it *is*."

We sat silently, holding hands, while the waitress refilled our coffee cups. Marilyn had a scarf over her head—a cheap one, the kind you might buy at Lamston's. She wasn't wearing any makeup or her false eyelashes, and she had let her eyebrows go unplucked. Her skin was the color of mother-of-pearl, very pale, with a hint of blue, as if she were bruised. I couldn't help thinking that this was what she would have looked like if she'd remained Norma Jean.

"How's Arthur taking it?" I asked.

"He's being very sweet about it, which makes me feel even worse. He's given up his play, you know? He's writing a screenplay for me instead."

"That's nice of him."

She shrugged. "Yes. I don't know, though. From what I've read of it so far, he's made the heroine me. Or what he thinks about me."

"That might be uncomfortable. I can see that."

"Try painful."

"Is it any good?"

"That's the worst thing, David. It's the best work Arthur's done in years." She sighed. "You were right," she said. "Those notes, in England? They were for this screenplay, they weren't about me. He told me."

From the way she said it, I knew she didn't believe it. I didn't either. I guessed it was something she had to convince herself of in order to make a fresh start with the marriage. "Are you going to do it?" I asked.

"I think so," she said without enthusiasm. "Eventually. There's a part for Gable in it, as a cowboy. I've always wanted to work with Gable." She sighed again. "Anyway, I'm going to do another picture first, otherwise I'll go crazy."

"I thought you were happy being the housewife?"

She gave me an impatient look. "I'm not planning to spend the rest of my life washing dishes, David, if that's what you mean," she said sharply. "Billy Wilder's supposed to be sending me a treatment about a girl who's running away from the mob with two guys in drag. . . . Arthur thinks a comedy might be good for me."

"I thought you hated Wilder."

"I do. But he knows how to direct me, and after Sir Cork

Tip, I haven't got time for amateur directors." She seemed a little more cheerful now that she was talking about her career. "What are you doing with yourself?" she asked.

"All work, no play, basically," I said. "But I'm going to Washington tomorrow."

"I wish I could go with you."

"Well, that wouldn't be easy. I'm going down to watch Hoffa's appearance before the Senate Subcommittee. Bobby's big moment."

"Oh? I haven't been following it."

I filled her in briefly on events to date: on Dave Beck's sweaty collapse as Bobby pummeled him with questions, on the reams of testimony and evidence, much of it provided by me, that condemned Beck and his cronies.

"This whole business gives me the willies," she said.

"Hoffa? The Teamsters? It's just politics. Some people go to prison, some get reelected—that's the way the game is played."

"It's dangerous. I told Jack that."

"He knows what he's doing, Marilyn."

She shook her head irritably. "No he doesn't. Tell him to be careful, please. Real careful!"

"I will."

She did not look as if she believed me. "Tell him how much I'd love to have his baby."

I swallowed hard. "I don't think he'd appreciate that message coming from me, Marilyn."

"Maybe you're right. Tell him to call me, then."

"Okay."

"We'd have a beautiful baby, Jack and me. I can feel it, right here." She put her other hand flat against her stomach. Her nails were chipped and dirty at the edges. "I love *him* enough for the baby to be born, David, I know it." She was trying to hold back her tears now, but not very successfully. "I'd love the baby, too."

"I'm sure you would," I said.

"Jack would be the father, but he wouldn't have to *be* the father, do you see what I mean? He wouldn't have to leave Jackie, or acknowledge the baby, or anything. He'd know and I'd know, and that would be enough. I've thought it all out."

"You certainly have," I said, with as much enthusiasm as I could manage.

Washington was even hotter than New York. It was a relief to get into the committee room where the Senate Government Investigations Subcommittee, better known as the McClellan committee, after its somewhat unenthusiastic chairman, was in session. Bobby was seated at a small desk, surrounded by documents, a pair of reading glasses perched on his head. His brother sat on the dais behind him, along with the other members of the subcommittee, most of them fully occupied with the task of trying to look like serious statesmen for the media.

It was a packed house—to use the theatrical term, which was appropriate under the circumstances—for Hoffa's appearance. Hoffa was not yet the famous figure that the hearings were about to make him, but his name had come up so often in previous testimony that everybody was curious to see what he looked like.

He entered like a prizefighter surrounded by his trainers— in this case, lawyers—a small, powerful fireplug of a man, cocky and intense. He waved at Bobby, who glared back at him.

The dinner meeting between the two of them had not gone well, Jack had told me. Bobby had turned down Hoffa's invitation to arm-wrestle and, instead, asked some embarrassing questions about the paper locals in New York City, by means of which Hoffa and the mob were trying to gain control of the New York Joint Council of Teamsters.

Hoffa had left the meeting asking Bobby to tell his wife that he wasn't as bad as everyone thought he was, but Bobby told Ethel later that he thought Hoffa was worse. As for Hoffa, he came away from the dinner with the impression that Bobby was "a damn spoiled jerk."

This wasn't a happy augury, nor had matters been improved when Hoffa was shortly afterward arrested in the lobby of the Dupont Plaza Hotel by the FBI, charged with trying to bribe a witness with two thousand dollars in cash. Intermediaries had been working overtime to settle this little last-minute problem. I knew because I had seen my old friend Ike Lublin, a heavyweight lawyer in LA, who was reputed to have "mob connections," having breakfast in the Hay-Adams, and he had told me some of it—as much as he wanted me to know, no doubt.

Bobby started slowly now, guiding Hoffa through a series of cream puff questions. It was not exciting stuff, and both the press and the subcommittee members looked disappointed. Beck had been a sweaty villain, and his coconspirators a collection of earthy figures straight out of the pages of Damon Runyon, with colorful pasts that included extortion, murder, and racketeering. Hoffa, by contrast, was on his best choirboy behavior, and answered the questions in a careful, prissy style that may have been his way of making fun of Bobby. Certainly Bobby took it as such, and I could see his face turning red, his eyes that icy blue that meant trouble. He was working hard to give Hoffa an opportunity to make the brief *mea culpa* that was required of him, but Hoffa wasn't giving it to him. Hoffa's expression was richly contemptuous, as if to say that Bobby could go fuck himself.

"Some of these practices are just plain wrong, aren't they?" Bobby said at last, after what seemed like hours of futile shadowboxing.

"What do you mean by wrong?" Hoffa asked, with a sneer that he may have intended as a smile.

"Criminal," Bobby snapped. "Contrary to the best interest of your members. Does that explain it?"

"I know of no such practices," Hoffa said, frowning as if he were trying hard to think of some.

"You have made no mistakes?"

"None I can think of, Bobby."

Bobby's eyes flashed at the familiarity. "Not many men can say that, Mr. Hoffa," he said, shaking his head.

Hoffa smiled. "I can."

Bobby tried again. "Surely there's something you can remember, Mr. Hoffa, that you wish you hadn't done."

Hoffa suppressed a laugh. "I wish I'd been born a rich kid, like you, Bobby," he said, while his entourage, beefy men in polyester suits, with diamond rings on pinkies the size of German sausages, laughed and clapped. "But stuff I shouldn't have done? Zip."

He was making a mistake, of course. I could see Ike Lublin among the spectators, scribbling a note to send up to Hoffa. Jack, I noticed, was alert, as if he could sense that the whole perfectly planned scenario was about to get out of control, with God only knew what unforeseen consequences. I remembered Red Dorfman's warnings and shivered.

Bobby flipped through the papers in front of him. He had given Hoffa ample time to eat a little humble pie before the subcommittee. Now he took his time as he chose his next question. He glanced at the piece of paper he had been searching for, then looked up at Hoffa. "Do you know Joe Holtzman?" he asked.

There was a flurry of activity around Hoffa, while the lawyers on either side of him whispered in his ears. He shook his head angrily. His big jaw jutted out, his nostrils flared, his eyes were dark pools of anger—a man betrayed, I thought. "I knew Joe Holtzman."

I had no idea who Holtzman was, but it was clear it was a name Hoffa hadn't expected to hear here. "Then was he a close friend of yours?" Bobby asked.

"I knew Joe Holtzman."

"Was he a close friend of yours?"

Hoffa's face was the color of marble, rough-hewn. "Now listen here!" he shouted, his voice echoing loudly in a room where most people had to be urged to speak up. "I knew Joe Holtzman! But he wasn't any particular friend of mine."

Bobby ignored Hoffa's raised voice. Looking him right in the eye, he said, "I'll ask you again until I get a proper answer. Do you know Joe Holtzman?"

"I knew Joe Holtzman."

"Was he a close friend of yours, Mr. Hoffa?"

There was a long silence. Jimmy Hoffa had a pencil in his meaty hands, and he broke it in two with a snap that made everybody in the room start.

Ike signaled me and I slipped out of the room. "This isn't good," he said. "Your man is asking tough questions."

"*Your* man is behaving like a smart-ass. He's supposed to be contrite."

Ike sighed. "We got a problem," he said.

I thought so too, but I couldn't think of anything to be done about it. I scrawled a quick note to Jack, begging him to talk to Bobby as soon as there was a recess, gave it to a guard to pass up to him, and stepped inside again.

In my brief absence, things had apparently gone from bad

to worse. Despite the ornate trappings of the room and the presence of the television cameras, it had the feeling of a bullring, a place of combat and death—and indeed, there was something that reminded me of a bull in Hoffa's stubborn, relentless refusal to give way before Bobby's thrusts.

"We have here an expense voucher for twenty-three Minifons," Bobby was saying, his clear Boston accent cutting through the quiet room. "Mini-phones," he explained. "Small German tape recorders purchased by the Teamsters . . . for you, Mr. Hoffa. Could you tell this committee now what they were used for?"

Hoffa smiled—a shit-eating grin is how I'd describe it. "What did I do with them?" he asked. "What did I do with them?" He paused, turning to wink at his supporters. "Well, what *did* I do with them?"

"Yes. What did you do with them?" Bobby's voice was flat.

"I am trying to recall."

"You could remember that."

"When were they delivered, do you know? That must have been quite a while ago. . . ."

"You know what you did with the Minifons. And don't ask me!"

"Well, well. . . ." Hoffa feigned honest ignorance. "Let me see—what did I do with them?"

Bobby's voice was harsh now, the disgust evident on his face. "What did you do with them, Mr. Hoffa?" he repeated angrily, Hoffa's name delivered as sharp as a slap.

Hoffa looked contrite, or tried to. He was sticking to his guns out of some deep hatred for everything Bobby stood for—wealth, privilege, education, idealism—that went far beyond his self-interest, which was to make Bobby look good for the media. "Mr. Kennedy," he said, "I bought some Minifons. And there is no question about it. But I cannot recall what became of them."

Ike leaned over, from the row behind me now. "*Oy,*" he said.

"What's with the Minifons?" I whispered.

"Jimmy and his guys wore them to entrap other guys who were loyal to Beck. Stuff like that."

"That's a federal crime, isn't it?"

Ike nodded darkly. "That's why he can't answer the question."

Of *course* Hoffa couldn't answer the question. He would be incriminating himself. And he was reluctant to plead the Fifth Amendment because George Meany had now instructed all *his* people not to. Since the Kefauver hearings on organized crime, taking the Fifth had become the last refuge of gangsters, in most people's eyes sure proof of guilt.

"Yes? It must be difficult to remember with such a selective memory," Bobby said.

Jack, I could see, was reading my note. He caught my eye and shrugged, as if to say, *I will, I will, but you know Bobby. . . .*

"Well," Hoffa went on, "I will have to stand on the answers that I have made in regards to my recollection, and I cannot answer different, unless you give me some other recollection other than I have already answered."

This piece of nonsense set off a roar of laughter from Hoffa's supporters, which Senator McClellan, seeming to come to life for the first time, tried to gavel down. When the noise died, Hoffa sat smirking at Bobby, as if challenging him to do his worst.

"Mr. Hoffa, did you ever wear a Minifon yourself? In order to record a fellow Teamster?"

Hoffa cocked his head sideways. His expression was a little warier now. Bobby obviously had more information than Hoffa supposed. He had underrated Bobby's passion for doing his homework. "You say 'wear,' " Hoffa said. "What do you mean by wear?"

Bobby rolled his eyes. For over an hour he had tried to get Hoffa to make a clear reply to any question, and to offer the ritual apology that Bobby had been promised.

He brought up next the subject of two Teamster officials whom Hoffa had continued to employ and pay while they were in prison for taking kickbacks from employers. Hoffa's face registered surprise, even alarm, as Bobby concluded, "You continued paying them while they were in prison! What were you afraid of?"

There couldn't have been a question more guaranteed to make Hoffa lose his temper. Hoffa, like Bobby himself, was absolutely fearless. He had spent his life in an industry in which tire irons, guns, baseball bats, dynamite, and meat hooks were used every day against people who got out of line, and he boasted often that he had never backed down from a fight. His face turned white and he rose halfway out of his seat, as if he were going to attack Bobby, while his lawyers tried to pull him down. "I was not charged with any crime connected with them!" he shouted, the veins bulging in his forehead. " . . . I was not afraid they were going to expose me, because they have nothing to expose!"

" . . . How can you possibly explain being so solicitous of them? Unless you received some of the money yourself? Can you explain that?"

But Hoffa's rage had overcome him. He couldn't explain, or wouldn't. He shook his head. "I think I made my statement," he muttered hoarsely, his fists clenched.

Bobby was about to pursue the matter further, but Senator McClellan—prodded, I couldn't help noticing, by Jack— banged his gavel and called a recess for lunch.

I made my way toward Bobby, who was still sitting at his desk, just as Hoffa, who had broken loose from his lawyers, stormed up to him, shoulders hunched, eyes blazing. Bobby didn't move or even blink.

I was close enough to hear Hoffa's rasping voice as he stuck his face close to Bobby's and said: "You *fucked* me, you little college boy prick! You're not going to make your brother president over Hoffa's dead body!" Then, quickly, before his lawyers and the guards could drag him away: "You're dead meat, Bobby, you go on with this." His voice had dropped to a searing hiss, like steam escaping from a vent. "You and your fucking brother both.".

Bobby's expression was glacial, his lips tightly compressed. He answered in a quiet, conversational tone, without a trace of emotion: "Mr. Hoffa, I'm going to put you in prison if it's the last thing I do. And please stop calling me Bobby."

Hoffa pushed the guards and lawyers away and stood his ground, smiling at Bobby. "Hey, Bobby," he called out mockingly, "I'll promise you one thing. It's *gonna* be the last thing you do. You got Hoffa's word on that."

Ike Lublin and I had dinner together that night, both of us a little subdued. I had known Ike since he moved out to LA from

Cleveland as his mobster clients expanded their interests westward. Many of the biggest stars were his clients too, and he was respected as a dealmaker, a divorce lawyer, and, above all, the man you went to see when you were in real trouble. Ike frightened most people with his aggressive tactics, but he didn't frighten me. I happened to know that he was devoted to his wife, who had become a hopeless alcoholic after the death of their only child during a polio epidemic. There was a soft side to Ike, though he preferred to hide it.

"Bobby fucked Jimmy," he said, wolfing down his shrimp cocktail. "The deal is off."

"Come on! Hoffa didn't come through with his end, Ike. You know that."

"He delivered that putz Beck."

"He was supposed to make like a good guy for the subcommittee. Instead, he came off as a hard-ass." I'd decided it would save time to use Ike's own language.

Ike shrugged. "Why does seafood always taste better in the East?" he asked—he had ordered Maryland crab cakes for his main course.

"Maybe it's just that people back east still remember how to cook. What happens now?"

"How would I know? Ask Red. You wanna guess? Jimmy's gonna fight back. Hard. Dirty. Somebody's gonna get hurt."

"It has to be stopped."

The waiter served Ike his crab cakes, and he ate silently for a few moments; then he sighed and put his fork down. "Your salmon okay?"

I nodded.

"It can't be stopped, not unless Bobby lays off. Is he gonna lay off?"

"I'll talk to Jack, but I doubt it. Not unless Hoffa pays some respect to the subcommittee. And Bobby."

"Then it can't be stopped. Jimmy hates him now."

He ate for a while, thinking about what he'd said. "I don't mean he dislikes Bobby, unnerstan', David? He's not a reasonable man, Jimmy Hoffa, like you and me. Hear what I'm saying: *He hates Bobby!*"

"I understand."

"I don't think you do. Somebody's gotta warn Bobby that

Jimmy's *dangerous*. Somebody's gotta tell him that there are areas he can't go into, or there's gonna be real trouble."

"What areas?"

Ike finished his crab cakes and wiped his mouth. He leaned close to me in the booth, so close that I could smell his after-shave. "Stuff that involves Moe and Red, and the boys in Chicago. Stuff about the casinos and the Central States Teamsters Pension Fund. Stuff like that is very sensitive, David, very serious. People could get hurt. Where's the sense in that?"

"I understand, Ike." I did too. And I agreed.

"Personal stuff too. Listen, I *know* Jimmy, David. Money don't interest Jimmy. What the hell, you see the way he dresses! But that don't mean he's a saint. Jimmy likes to pretend he's the family man, but he's got a mistress, did you know? Some broad whose husband's in the laundry business. She's the one who introduced Jimmy to Moe in the first place. They had a kid together, Jimmy and this broad. Jimmy really cares for the kid too. . . . What I'm trying to tell you is that if Bobby gets into that side of Jimmy's life, all bets are off."

"Why are you telling me this?"

He shrugged. He took his cigar case out of his pocket, and we each lit an Upmann English Market with our brandy and coffee. Ike was picking up the check. He would charge the meal to one of his clients; still, it was a nice gesture. "I don't like trouble," he said. "I profit by it, sure, but my job is to prevent it. Preventative maintenance, David, that's the best service I can offer my clients. Jimmy Hoffa, now, I don't give a fuck about him—Bobby Kennedy sends him to Atlanta to get his ass reamed out in the showers by a lot of niggers, I'm not gonna lose any sleep, personally. But if Jimmy gets into deep trouble with the Feds, it's gonna make problems for my clients, guys like Red or Moe, maybe even Momo, God forbid. Then people start getting killed and what not, and business suffers. . . . It's not worth it, David, that's all I'm saying."

"I don't disagree."

"Of course not. You're a sensible man. Everybody knows that. I told Red and Moe that myself. I said, 'It ain't David's fault. Don't blame this on him.' "

"I'm grateful, Ike."

He nodded. "You oughta be, David," he said gravely. "I got you off the hook, frankly. If you can't get Bobby to stack off on Jimmy, just make sure he don't push too hard on Moe or Red, okay? You'd be doing me a favor." He smiled broadly. "Hell, you'd be doing *yourself* a favor."

I knew a warning when I heard one. I didn't even need to look at Ike Lublin's eyes through the wreaths of cigar smoke to take it seriously.

Jack and I had breakfast the next day in his rented house in Georgetown. There were newspapers spread out all over the dining room table. Jack had been devouring the stories about Hoffa's appearance before the subcommittee and was so pleased with himself that I almost hesitated to bring up the fact that he and Bobby had made an enemy of Hoffa.

When I did, he looked surprised. "Hoffa pissed Bobby off. He wasn't supposed to do that. *He's* the one who broke the deal."

"Well, yes, but that's not the way Hoffa sees it, Jack. The Minifon stuff—that wasn't in the script."

"Whose side are you on, anyway?"

"Yours. But you shouldn't have let it get out of control. And you've got to stop it from going farther."

Jack ate his eggs neatly. He broke his toast up into small pieces, then carefully placed a tiny fragment of toast, a piece of egg, and a piece of bacon on his fork. "David, this story is playing well. Better than what we had in mind."

He wasn't wrong. Every major newspaper and political columnist in the country, right and left, Republican and Democrat, even those who were notoriously hostile to the Kennedy family, had come out in praise of Bobby's courage in confronting Hoffa, and Jack's statesmanlike position. Hoffa came across, in editorials, cartoons, and the news stories, as a dangerous thug—Bobby might as well have been Saint George slaying the dragon.

"When you come right down to it," Jack went on, "It was a piece of good luck that Bobby and Hoffa hated each other on sight."

"Yes and no."

He raised an eyebrow, a little impatiently. From his perspective, a defiant Hoffa was a more interesting figure than an

apologetic Hoffa. The general impression the average voter—
unless he was a Teamster—would take away from the newspaper reports was that this was a fight between the Kennedys
and the forces of darkness. Jack liked the look of it all, and I
couldn't blame him. But he was dead wrong.

"You're not considering how dangerous this is, Jack," I told
him. "I had dinner with Ike Lublin last night. A lot of the mob
people who do business with Hoffa are upset, he says. They
thought Hoffa had a deal. Now they're worried. Frankly, I got
the impression from Ike that there was some talk about punishing me."

Jack laughed. "I wouldn't take that kind of thing seriously,
David."

I did not join in his laughter. Jack's feelings about danger
were not the same as mine. "I do," I said. "And I'm not the
only one who should be worrying, Jack, if Lublin is telling the
truth."

"He's probably exaggerating."

"I wouldn't bet on it."

"If you're going to go, you're going to go, David. I never
worry. And if it's going to happen, a bullet is the best way.
It's so quick you don't even know it's happened. . . ."

"I'm hoping to die of old age," I said.

Jack didn't crack a smile. "I can't imagine dying of old age,"
he said firmly.

I changed the subject. "Be that as it may, Jack, Bobby let
things get out of hand. You had a deal with Hoffa—"

Jack held up his hand. "What deal? Hoffa agreed to cooper-
ate in an investigation, as I understand it. I'm not familiar with
the details, but his attitude before the subcommittee wasn't
what I would call cooperative."

"I see." I saw, all right. Plan A, which involved Jack and
Hoffa helping each other at Dave Beck's expense, had been
shelved, due to what divorce lawyers refer to as "personality
differences." Plan B was now in effect, in which Jack made
himself a national reputation at Hoffa's expense. In the meantime, he was putting as much distance as he could between
himself and Hoffa. He was not his father's son for nothing, I
reflected. Then I thought about Red Dorfman, and his reputation for having people who displeased him hung from meat
hooks, and realized that Jack was playing with my life as well

as his own. "For Christ's *sake*, Jack," I said, my voice rising, "you're going to get us *killed!*"

He gave me a look of sheer astonishment. "Take it easy," he said.

"Take it *easy?* Do you have any idea who you're dealing with? I told you right back at the beginning of this that these are dangerous people. They're not politicians! They expect promises to be kept."

There was a look of hard, cold anger in Jack's eyes now. "I didn't make your friends any promises," he said.

That did it! I'm not normally a man who loses his temper, but Jack's ruthlessness enraged me.

"*My* friends?" I shouted. "Since when are they *my* friends, Jack? *You* asked me to get in touch with them for you. They're *your* friends now, Jack, like it or not. I made a deal with them on your behalf, and don't you forget it! I'm not going to get blown up in my car or drowned in my own swimming pool just because you can't control Bobby!"

Jack stared at me, his anger gone even though I had been shouting at him. "David," he said quietly. "Calm down."

"Calm down? When you're talking as if you had nothing to do with all this? Don't tell *me* you're not familiar with the details, Jack. Save that kind of thing for your press conferences when you get to the White House. If you live long enough to get there."

He held up his hands in mock surrender. "All right," he said with a rueful smile, "all right. Maybe you've got a point."

"You don't *really* want these guys putting a sniper on some rooftop across the street from you, do you? Because believe me, Jack, they're quite capable of it."

"I'm not afraid of that," he said, and I knew he meant it— Jack's courage was never in doubt, not even by his enemies. "On the other hand," he went on, "I guess there's no point to pissing them off any more than we have to."

I was almost as relieved that he had stopped calling the mobsters *my* friends as I was that he was seeing reason at last.

"I don't know how much I can do for Hoffa," he said. "He hung himself, right there on national television. And he threatened Bobby personally. A big mistake."

"No argument."

"I can't stop Bobby from going after him. Not after what Hoffa said to *him*."

"Just because Bobby's going after Hoffa doesn't mean he has to catch up with him, does it?" I suggested.

Jack thought this over, frowning. You never had to spell out the details with Jack. He was *born* with a mind that would have pleased Machiavelli. He chuckled. "I'd hate to think of Bobby like one of those greyhounds in the dog races, always chasing the rabbit without ever catching it."

"So would I, Jack, but it beats being killed by the mob. Does Bobby have to know?"

"No. Not yet anyway. Once I'm elected, it's another story." I noticed he did not say "if." He poured us each a cup of coffee from a silver Thermos jug. He was still in his shirt-sleeves, smelling briskly of scented soap and after-shave. "Of course, if Hoffa does something dumb again, like that bribery thing . . ."

"He says he was set up."

"Of course he'd say that. . . . Look, Hoffa's got to stay on the reservation from now on. I can't be expected to save his ass if he goes around committing major felonies in broad daylight."

"I think his associates might understand that, if it was put to them the right way."

"Can you do that for me?"

I hesitated. "I don't know if I really want to keep on doing this, Jack. It's getting a bit too dangerous for my taste."

"I know it isn't the kind of thing you like doing, David, but I can trust you. And you *do* seem to have built up a certain amount of, ah, *trust* with these fellows. . . ." It was basically the same message Dorfman had given me, more eloquently put. He looked me square in the eye. "I don't want to have to plead for your help, David, but if I have to, I will."

I sighed and gave in, as I always did. Jack had the gift of getting people to do what they didn't want to do, or think they *could* do—perhaps the most important quality for a president. Besides, I thought I could handle the problem better than anyone else—another illusion. "I'll do it," I said. "Just this once."

"Good. What do you need?"

"Well, there's a case that Hoffa has coming up in Tennessee.

I'm not up on the details, but it involves a trucking company he may have bought in his wife's name. Ike thinks it would be a good idea if the subcommittee steered clear of that and left it to the courts."

Jack nodded. "He'd like it to drag its way to trial as slowly as possible, without too much publicity, so there's plenty of time for him to get to the jurors, or the judge?"

"Something like that."

"I'll see what I can do." He did not look happy about it.

"The other thing is, Hoffa has a mistress and an illegitimate son—"

"Jesus!" Jack said, his interest always aroused by sexual gossip. "And all this time we thought he was a choirboy in that area!"

"Apparently not. Ike says to stay clear of that side of things. Hoffa's sensitive on the subject. Maybe even irrational."

"Hell, his private life's his own business, just like anyone else's. I don't see why Bobby has to go into that."

"His investigators aren't going to miss it. People talk. Ike's no dummy, and what he says is: *Don't push that button!*"

"I'll talk to Bobby." He leaned forward, his voice dropping confidentially. "Is she pretty?"

"Ike didn't say. But she was Moe Dalitz's mistress for a while, and Moe has pretty good taste."

"These guys swap mistresses?"

"Well, it's a small world, you know. The kind of people we're talking about have to be sure a girl isn't going to gossip about what she's heard."

"That makes sense." Jack was always curious to know how other more or less public figures arranged their sex lives. Up to now he'd had it easy. Nobody cared all that much about the private life of a United States senator. If he really did succeed in becoming president of the United States, his private life would be much more difficult to maintain. Between the Secret Service and the White House press corps, the president hardly has a moment when he's not being watched. President Harding was obliged to make love to his mistress in a downstairs coat closet, standing among the galoshes and umbrellas. Jack, I felt sure, would do better.

"Hoffa!" he said with a laugh. "I knew he was going to do

us some good, but if he goes on butting his head against Bobby's, the son of a bitch is going to take us all the way to the White House!"

Jack had a point, of course. Hoffa was to play the role of villain in the drama that would turn Jack and Bobby into heroes in the eyes of the public—a drama scripted, in part, by me. But Hoffa was right and royally screwed, and it was a fatal error to underestimate his rage or his capacity for revenge.

I should have known better, and should have made Jack listen, but like everyone else, I was lulled by Jack's self-confidence, as well as by the fact that we were sitting there comfortably in the seat of government, surrounded by power— the Senate, the FBI, the Justice Department, the Secret Service, all of which seemed like a mighty fortress that could hardly be threatened by the likes of one crooked, loudmouthed labor leader and his thug pals.

"Hoffa's Catholic, isn't he?" Jack asked.

"I have no idea. Why?"

"Bobby doesn't approve of Catholics having sex out of marriage." He smiled broadly. "Of course, he does make exceptions."

"Try to make sure this is one of them, Jack. For your own sake. And mine."

"Sure. Christ, I'm the last person who'd want a guy's sex life used against him politically. . . . What else?"

"Don't let Bobby go after people like Red Dorfman, or Moe Dalitz, or Sam Giancana. These guys have plenty of problems with the law as it is, so why tie your name into some kind of campaign against them? From their point of view, remember, they did you a favor."

He didn't say anything, so I continued. "You got Beck. The subcommittee got a good look at Hoffa. It's a good score— headlines, great press, a chance to write some major legislation. You don't need to bring these guys into it as well."

"One or two of them will have to appear before the subcommittee," he said cautiously. "There's no way I can stop that. It's too late."

"Okay, that's understood, but don't make them walk the plank, Jack, that's all I'm saying. No contempt citations, nobody goes to jail, okay?"

"Will they settle for that?"

"Probably. I hope so."

"I'll do my best," he said, and I could see that was all I was going to get.

Jack stretched, grimacing with pain. He used a wooden rocking chair at home instead of a regular dining chair, but sitting for any length of time still hurt him. "Do you know a Dr. Burton Wasserman in New York?" he asked.

"I know *of* him. Marilyn mentioned him."

"No kidding? I saw him last time I was there. A couple of people recommended him. Wasserman's *the* man to see for pain. He gave me an injection—B vitamins and so on—and it was like a miracle! I didn't have any pain at all for the next twenty-four hours—haven't felt so good for years!"

"Wasserman's a celebrity doctor. I know a lot of his patients. They all say he's a miracle worker. The injections work, no question about it, but the problem is, you have to keep going back to him for more. Bill Paley went to him after that skiing injury he had, and eventually he was going every day."

"Well, I don't mind going once or twice a week, if it gets rid of the pain." He grinned. "I can find plenty to do in New York, as a matter of fact."

He rose—he was moving less stiffly, I noticed—and we shook hands.

I was willing to bet that Marilyn would soon be spending more time in the city, instead of playing housewife for Arthur Miller in Connecticut.

20

IT WAS DARK IN THE BEDROOM. SHE MOVED A LITTLE CLOS-er to the man beside her and rubbed her foot against his. "You can't be ready for more," he said. "Not yet."

"I'm not. I'm pooped. Fucked out, if you want to know the truth. I just want you to hold me."

He put his arms around her and pressed her close to him.

She could feel the hair on his chest and belly against her skin, a delicate prickling sensation that she loved. She put her fingers on his penis and held it gently, loving the feel of its warmth and the slight, throbbing pulsebeat of arousal, however tired he was. She was sore, wet, sweaty, the sea-salt taste of his sperm still in her mouth—*sodden* with sex, she told herself happily.

"I was sorry to hear about the baby," he said.

There hadn't been any time to catch up when she entered the suite. He had put his arms around her and kissed her hard. She'd surrendered instantly to his impatience, tearing off her clothes as he pulled her toward the bedroom, laughing and sobbing as she fell face forward on the bed, half in her clothes, half out, while he stood behind her, driving himself deep into her with fierce, urgent thrusts. She had come twice before they even got the rest of their clothes off, turned down the bed, and slipped between the cool sheets to make love again, this time slowly, inventively, athletically.

"Your back must be better," she said now. She didn't want to talk about the baby.

"You noticed."

"I'll say! It's a change from you lying on your back with me on top."

"You didn't like that?"

"I liked it fine," she said. "I just meant I liked this better."

"We aim to please. I've been seeing that doctor everybody's talking about. Wasserman. I had one of his vitamin shots today. It's like magic. My back doesn't hurt a bit. Christ, I could go through every position in the *Kama Sutra*." He ran his hand down her back slowly, letting it come to rest on her ass, his fingers gently playing with her pubic hair.

She shivered. She could have stayed here like this forever, safe from the world. She might even be able to sleep in his arms. "Be my guest," she said. "I'm glad Dr. Wasserman performed such a miracle for you."

"David told me you went to him too."

"Mm," she murmured noncommittally.

"You don't sound enthusiastic."

"Well . . . I thought he was creepy, frankly. Did you know they call him 'Dr. Feelgood'? I mean, those injections—I don't think they're just vitamins, if you know what I mean. . . ."

"They work for me. Didn't they work for you?"

"Well, they did and they didn't. I felt good for a while, then I had these terrible downers. . . . Besides, I hate injections— they really scare me. I guess the real problem I had with Dr. Wasserman was that he wouldn't give me any prescriptions. I had to come to his office. And he used to make me undress just to give me a shot, so I decided he was just a dirty old man."

He laughed. "I'd do the same if I was a doctor."

"You're a dirty old man too."

"Not yet, but I hope to be someday. It's always been my ambition."

"It's an ambition, I guess," she said, licking the dried sweat off his chest like a cat, with long strokes of her tongue. "I always wanted one. For a while I thought 'Living well is the best revenge' might do it." She had seen that on a needlepoint pillow in Amy Greene's bedroom, and it had made instant sense to her.

"It won't do for me," Jack said. "I've always lived well."

"How about for Jackie?"

He looked thoughtful. "Yes," he said. "That might do fine for Jackie."

"How are things going now with Jackie?"

"What do you mean?"

"I read the newspapers, you know. Besides, David fills me in on all the gossip."

"He talks too much."

"He's a lot nicer to me than you are. Anyway, you may as well tell me. I'll worm it out of you sooner or later."

He sighed. "We had a breakup, it's true. After she lost the baby. Now we're back together. And Jackie's pregnant again."

"How nice," she said, unable to disguise her sadness. "What was the breakup about?"

"No one thing, you know. . . . It happens."

"*Tell* me about it. Since she's pregnant, I guess you've got things sorted out."

"Basically."

"It's a pity. Otherwise, you could have married me."

He gave a nervous laugh.

"I mean it!"

"I know you do," he said, keeping well clear of expressing any enthusiasm of his own for the idea.

"We'd be so happy," she said. "We'd have the most wonderful baby!"

She could feel him stiffen in alarm. "I was just dreaming out loud," she whispered, putting her arms around him to prevent him from getting up. "It's such a lovely dream."

He was eager to change the subject. "What are you doing next?"

"I'm going back to LA for a while, to do a picture with Billy." She reminded herself that Jack wasn't in the industry. "Wilder," she added.

He nodded vaguely.

"He directed me in *The Seven Year Itch*," she explained.

"That's great. I liked it. What's the picture going to be?"

"I've only read the outline. I'm going to play Sugar Kane, a singer and ukelele player who gets mixed up with a couple of guys who dress up as women to escape from the mob. Tony Curtis and Jack Lemmon are going to be in it with me. . . ."

"Jack Lemmon is great."

"Mm," she said. The fact was, she was terrified of working with Lemmon, who was a real pro, a "comedian's comedian," as Arthur said. Worse still was the prospect of working with Curtis, who had a reputation for being brash, tough, and highly competitive.

She longed to get back to work in Hollywood, where her stardom was uncontested, but already she was afraid of facing the camera again, of the endless takes, the pressure from the studio, the demands of the director. . . . And this time she would have to go through all that without Milton, for she had ended her partnership with him once and for all in a rage over the personal expenses she thought he had charged to *The Prince and the Showgirl*, thus breaking a friendship that had been one of the most important of her whole life. Afterward, she discovered it wasn't true, but by then it was too late.

"What's, ah, Sugar Kane like?" Jack asked, making conversation.

"A dumb blonde."

"I thought you didn't want to play dumb blondes anymore."

"I don't. But it's what I do. Like you running for president. Anyway, once I've done this picture, and maybe one more, I'm going to make the one Arthur is writing for me—

The Misfits. I play *me* in that one. That's going to be a *lot* harder."

"I would have thought it was easier."

"Oh, honey, never. Being yourself is the hardest. I'd rather play somebody else any day."

"I'm going to be out there on the West Coast a lot, later in the year."

"Mm, good," she whispered, feeling him become hard again. Her body took over, her mind drifted in neutral, she could forget about her marriage and the next picture.

But even as she moaned with pleasure, in some corner of her mind she was still wondering how she was going to manage to play Roslyn in *The Misfits,* the tormented, neurotic, unfaithful heroine Arthur had treacherously written for her. . . .

Special Agent Kirkpatrick was shown without delay into the Director's office by his motherly secretary.

Hoover was sitting behind his desk impassively, as if he were carved out of soapstone. As always, Tolson sat by his side.

"Good work, Kirkpatrick," Tolson said.

Hoover nodded agreement, his jowls wobbling slightly.

"I've got more," Kirkpatrick said, patting his briefcase. "We taped a conversation between Strawhead and Lancer a couple of nights ago, at the Carlyle Hotel in New York." As the volume of tape mounted up, Kirkpatrick had deemed it advisable to give code names to each of the major figures for security purposes, as well as to put a Top Secret classification on the whole project. He had no idea where it was going, but he knew enough about politics to smell a nasty scandal if any of this leaked out to the press.

"I know where the Carlyle Hotel is," Hoover growled, as if his familiarity with New York had been questioned.

"They say it's very nice," Tolson said.

"The Waldorf Towers is good enough for me," Hoover said. "The Kennedys keep an apartment at the Carlyle," he explained to Tolson. "The Ambassador uses it, as well as Senator Kennedy. You can imagine what for."

"Oh, I can imagine, Director," Tolson said. "It's a real shame that people like the Kennedys, with all their money, can't set a higher moral tone."

Hoover blinked, resembling for a moment a giant bullfrog. "All too often it's the rich and privileged who betray their country," he said. "Look at Alger Hiss. That's why I won't have a man from any Ivy League college in the Bureau. Hotbeds of immorality, Agent Kirkpatrick. *And* treason."

Kirkpatrick nodded. He couldn't imagine anybody from an Ivy League school like Yale or Harvard trying to join the FBI, with its miserable pay scale and slow promotion.

"It's strange," Hoover said. "You take a young man like Jack Kennedy, a war hero, wealthy, a good-looking boy. He has everything going for him, yet there's something missing, something wrong. . . ." He paused, staring at his hands, folded in front of him on the spotless, empty desk, a thick gold signet ring glittering on one pudgy finger. "I've given it a lot of thought," he went on. "His weakness is a fatal fascination with celebrities. Movie stars, gangsters, leftist authors—it doesn't matter who they are, he always falls for glamour." He let this sink in. "It's one of the reasons why he wouldn't make a good president."

As Kirkpatrick watched Clyde Tolson beam his approval, it struck him that the same could be said of Hoover, who was notoriously eager to kiss the ass of anybody famous— athletes, stars, Hollywood studio heads and columnists, particularly. But wisely, he nodded as if awestruck by Hoover's wisdom.

"You've done a splendid job, Kirkpatrick," the Director said.

"Thank you, sir. I'm sorry we slipped up on Hoffa." Kirkpatrick had been part of the team hastily assembled the previous summer to observe Hoffa passing a manila envelope full of hundred-dollar bills to a government witness. It had been a setup, of course, like most successful operations of the kind, instigated by Bobby Kennedy, who was looking for a way to trip Hoffa up. To Bobby's fury—he had promised to jump off the roof of the Capitol if Hoffa wasn't found guilty—but not to Kirkpatrick's surprise, the jury had acquitted Hoffa, who sent Bobby a parachute as a joke.

At the trial, it had seemed to him that the prosecution was less than enthusiastic, and that some of the evidence was tainted or poorly presented. He had attributed that to inefficiency in the Justice Department, but the way Hoover and

Tolson were looking at each other now made him wonder if there hadn't been a conspiracy at the very highest level of the Bureau to let Hoffa off. To humiliate the Kennedys? Very likely, he thought. Because Hoffa and the Bureau had some connection? It was possible, he decided—Hoffa, for his own purposes, might even be a secret informant. One never knew. In the FBI, only Hoover—and perhaps Tolson—had the "big picture."

"Don't worry about it," Hoover said expansively. "You did your best. No man could do more."

So far as Kirkpatrick was concerned, that clinched it. If Hoover, whose only standard for his agents was success, was willing to praise a failure, it must be because he had *intended* the case against Hoffa to fail.

"That will teach young Bobby to jump the gun," Tolson said as Hoover nodded ponderously.

Kirkpatrick cleared his throat nervously. "About the tapes, sir. I have them in my briefcase, in case you'd like to hear them."

Hoover stared into the middle distance. "I suppose I ought to, Mr. Tolson, don't you think?"

Tolson nodded.

"I don't *enjoy* listening to this kind of smut, Mr. Kirkpatrick. I have to force myself. For the good of the country."

"Yes, sir." Kirkpatrick opened his briefcase, took out the tapes, and handed them to Tolson. "I took the liberty, sir," he said, "to make a short tape of the, ah"—he hesitated for a second—"most, ah, *significant* moments." It had been on the tip of his tongue to say "*dirtiest* moments," but he was happy he'd thought better of it.

Hoover took the small reel of tape from Tolson and put it in his desk drawer. "That was a thoughtful thing to do, Mr. Kirkpatrick," he said. "It will come in very handy. The Vice President will enjoy listening to *this*, won't he, Mr. Tolson?"

"I should say so, Director," Tolson said.

"Keep it coming, Kirkpatrick," the Director said, getting up from his desk to shake hands, for the second time in Kirkpatrick's career.

Nixon! Kirkpatrick thought, beginning to see at least an outline of what was going on. He wondered if the Kennedys knew of the lineup of the forces against them, from the Teamsters and the mob to Nixon and the Bureau. He wondered if they would *care*.

Still, he wasn't paid to worry about the Kennedys, he told himself as he went back to his office.

Anybody who knew me well would have been surprised to see me enter the lobby of a motel in New Jersey, just across the George Washington Bridge, at ten in the evening.

At times like this I asked myself what a Phi Beta Kappa and graduate of Columbia University was doing dealing with people like Red Dorfman—but of course, a love of mystery and the thrill of dealing with low-life types (what the French call *nostalgie de la boue*) is a natural weakness of the educated and safe, and nowhere more than among Americans, with our fascination for gangsters. It was Maria's opinion that I was going through "a midlife crisis," and I suppose she was right, though it wasn't, perhaps, the kind of crisis she had in mind.

I had called Jack Ruby in Dallas twenty-four hours after my breakfast with Jack to tell him I needed to speak to Dorfman face-to-face, and Ruby, who usually whined and protested about everything, must have caught the tone of anxiety in my voice, because he called back almost instantly with the time and place of the meeting.

I always found it difficult to understand why Dorfman placed any trust in Ruby. He was certainly loyal to Dorfman, in the manner of some large, ugly mongrel dog, but beyond blind loyalty he had no redeeming virtues that I could see. "I'd kill for Red Dorfman," he once told me breathlessly, in the front seat of a rented car in the parking lot behind the Hollywood Brown Derby, but I figured that was just the exaggeration of a born loser who wanted people to think he was a tough guy.

The few seats in the dingy lobby of the Hideaway Motel were occupied by women who were very clearly hookers, and the people waiting to sign in at the reservations desk had the furtive look of adulterous couples nerving themselves up to pretend they were man and wife. I made my way to the elevator and, sharing it with a couple locked in passionate embrace, went up to the top floor.

I found the room number I had been given, and knocked on the door. A familiar gravelly voice said, "Come in."

Dorfman had installed himself in what must have been the

Hideaway's only suite. He was standing in the middle of the room glowering at me threateningly, a little bit like Mussolini greeting a visitor to his office at the height of his power. I refused to be intimidated, not from any special degree of courage but because I knew it would be fatal to let Dorfman know I was afraid of him. He was like one of those animals that don't become dangerous until they scent fear—wolves perhaps, or one of the more savage breeds of guard dogs. I walked over and shook his hand briskly, which disconcerted him, possibly because he had expected some kind of preliminary groveling on my part, or maybe because he wanted to be the one to offer his hand before there was any shaking.

"So what's the fucking problem?" he asked by way of a greeting.

I looked around. It was the living room of a perfectly ordinary motel suite—no special features except for enough fruit, liquor, and cocktail snacks for a hospitality suite. The door to the bedroom was ajar, and I could tell there was somebody in there—a woman, I presumed.

"It's not bugged," Dorfman said, misinterpreting my glance. "We own the joint."

"I see. Why are we meeting in New Jersey?" Dorfman was a thug, but I didn't see him as the kind of guy whose natural habitat was a cheap motel, at this stage of his career.

A look of embarrassment crossed his face. "There's a kind of"—he sought for the *mot juste*—"tradition," he tried. "You don't go into another guy's town without asking permission."

I raised an eyebrow.

"If Vito Genovese wanted to go to Chicago for some reason," he explained, taking the head of one of the five New York families as an example, "he would have to ask the permission of Momo Giancana, and vice versa. You don't go to Miami without asking for the okay from Meyer Lansky, or to Havana without getting the okay from Santo Trafficante, see? It's a question of good manners, that's all. We wanted to keep this thing secret, so we didn't get an okay from anybody in New York. That's why this place. We're on the other side of the bridge."

The "we" puzzled me, but I let it ride. Dorfman had already answered one question, and I didn't want to provoke him by asking another, even more indelicate. I took it that "good

manners" was Dorfman's way of describing a jurisdictional
dispute that was enforceable by death. One likes to imagine
(I did, anyway) that one of the advantages of being a big-time
criminal is that you can do what you please and break all the
laws, but it turns out to be untrue—they are no freer than
law-abiding citizens, and their rules are much more strictly
enforced.

Dorfman might be able to have people killed, but at least I
could cross the George Washington Bridge back into Manhattan
without asking anybody's permission. That thought cheered me
up, until it occurred to me that he could have me killed right
there and buried in some New Jersey junkyard or the Pine Bar-
rens without anyone being the wiser.

"Why don't we sit down?" I suggested. "I'll have a scotch
on the rocks." Dorfman ground his teeth together. I had the
distinct impression that he wanted to get this over with as
quickly as possible, and I therefore took a certain pleasure in
prolonging it.

"Help yourself," he said gruffly.

I made myself a drink from the well-stocked bar. Dorfman
poured himself a cup of coffee—he had the look of a man
who had once been a big drinker and had given it up—
and we sat down together on the sofa. I noticed that from
time to time he glanced at the door to the bedroom. His
expression as he did so was not so much one of longing
as of fear, as if the lady waiting for him was very impatient
indeed.

"So what's the big fucking deal that Ruby made me come
all the way out to Jersey for?"

"Ike Lublin gave me a little warning, over dinner in
Washington. He told me your people are unhappy about
what happened to Hoffa. He threatened me. He threatened
Senator Kennedy."

Dorfman blew on his coffee noisily. "He didn't threaten
nobody. He's only a fucking lawyer."

"Very well. He passed on a threat. Is that better?"

"Sure. You don't wanna go round accusing a lawyer of
making threats. A lawyer could be disbarred for doing something like that."

A lawyer could also plausibly deny almost anything he said,
I thought. "Anyway," I said, "threats *were* made."

"Hotheads," Dorfman said, shaking his head sadly. "Listen, didn't I tell you Hoffa had a short fuse, back there in Vegas? I told you."

"It's not just Hoffa we're worried about."

"I were you, I'd worry about Hoffa a lot. Jack and Bobby fucked him, the way he sees it."

"How do *you* see it, Red?"

"I don't work for Hoffa. I think he acted like an asshole, there in front of the subcommittee. So they're a bunch of schmucks, the senators, so what? There's a time when you gotta show respect, even for guys who don't deserve it, right? You piss on the cops, they break your balls. Senators too. Hoffa shoulda played nice."

"That's the view Jack takes."

"Yeah? On the other hand, Bobby's a real prick, David, you want my opinion. He provoked Hoffa, on purpose. And the bribery thing, that was a setup. Bobby had no call to do that."

"Maybe." I agreed with Dorfman, as a matter of fact. I hadn't the slightest doubt that Bobby had tried to frame Hoffa. He played by the rules of Kennedy family touch football: Anything goes so long as you get away with it. It occurred to me that Hoffa probably played by similar rules, except that the loser got killed.

"The fact is," I said, "Jack isn't any happier with the way things turned out than you are."

Dorfman laughed harshly, like a truck with a starting problem. "Who says we're unhappy?" he asked.

"I assumed from what Ike said . . ."

"Ike don't know the whole story. I got nothing against him, but he's not on the inside, you get what I mean. . . . The fact is, David, Jack and Bobby did us a favor. They got rid of Beck for us. Now we got Hoffa in his place, which is what we wanted." He smiled at me. "We didn't have to clip Beck, right? Jack and Bobby put him away for us."

"Hoffa seems to think he got a raw deal."

"Fuck him. He's president of the International. What more does he want? Between you and me, David, nobody on my side wants to see Hoffa get too big for his britches, unnerstan'? That's why Beck had to go. We don't wanna see Hoffa go to the slammer—we got a major investment in him, and anyway, he might talk—but his troubles are not necessarily our troubles, okay?"

"Okay." This was news to me. I had assumed that Hoffa and the mob were one and the same, but I was beginning to understand that while Hoffa had used the mob to get what he wanted—Dave Beck's chair in Washington—the mob intended to use Hoffa to get what *they* wanted. Neither party to this arrangement liked or trusted the other, which would have come as news to the Justice Department.

"So long as you're all happy . . ." I said.

Dorfman gave me the snarl that passed, in his range of facial expressions, for a smile. "Who says we're happy? It's time for you guys to back off Hoffa some. Enough's enough, right? We gotta live with the guy. You too."

"That may be hard to do."

"So find a way. Also, what about all these fucking subpoenas? People like Momo can't do business if they're in hiding, ducking subpoenas. It's not right."

"Their names came up in testimony. Believe me, Jack doesn't like the idea any better than you do, but they have to appear."

"They're not gonna like it."

"Tell them not to worry. Jack will make sure that nobody gets indicted. Bobby will ask them some tough questions—there's nothing we can do about that—but that's not such a big price to pay for putting Hoffa in Beck's place, is it?"

He grimaced. "You have Jack's word?"

I nodded.

Dorfman glanced at the bedroom door again. There was a faint aroma of Havana cigar emanating from the doorway. Neither Dorfman nor I was smoking. The person in the bedroom, I reflected, was surely not a woman, unless the mistresses of big-league mobsters smoked Upmanns. I guessed it was somebody higher than Dorfman in the Chicago mob, which probably meant that Giancana himself was listening to our conversation. Whoever was inside coughed once. It was a deep, guttural cough, like a lion clearing its throat. Definitely not a woman's.

Dorfman's eyes flickered back in my direction. "I guess that's okay," he said. Whether or not it was Giancana on the other side of the door, there was no doubt who was the boss here, and it wasn't Dorfman. "You tell Jack they'll testify like good citizens. These are men of respect in their world, you unnerstan'? They're not gonna shove it to the senators, the way Hoffa did. They may take the Fifth, but they'll show respect."

"Respect will be fine. I'll tell Jack. He'll be grateful."

"Yeah." Dorfman's expression said it all on the subject of gratitude from politicians.

I was rapidly coming to the conclusion that the sooner Jack moved from labor reform to the high ground of foreign policy, the better for all concerned. A man could get elected without having a domestic policy—Ike had proved that in '56. I nodded, anxious to be on my way, now that it was clear it was Hoffa who was really after our blood, not the Chicago mob.

For some reason, I was relieved.

21

THERE WAS SOMETHING ABOUT PETER LAWFORD THAT always made her nervous, an indefinable air of charm gone to seed, of hidden, secret corruption. On the surface, he was a wisecracking Englishman, but her experience in England with Olivier had made her realize that Lawford was a fake, just a kid who had been brought up English in Los Angeles to play English roles at MGM. Everything English about Lawford was phony, from his accent to the kind of clothes he wore. It was only in Hollywood, where there was no real line dividing the fake from the real, that he could pass for the Englishman he wanted people to think he was.

Lawford had no great talent as an actor, in her opinion, but he made up for it by a desperate desire to please. He sucked up to the studio heads, to bigger stars like Sinatra, to the Kennedy family, particularly Jack, and to her. Under the circumstances, it was hardly surprising that Lawford was willing to put his Malibu beach house at Jack's disposal whenever he wanted it, or that he was happy to act as Jack's beard whenever Jack was on the West Coast.

Since she had returned to Los Angeles to make *Some Like It Hot*, she'd met Jack twice at Lawford's place in Malibu—once when he came to California to make a speech, once when he appeared at a gala Democratic fund-raiser, both times without Jackie. It was easier for him to find time to get away than for her, since she was in the studio all day.

She hated the picture, now that she was actually working on it. Even with the help of Paula Strasberg, she couldn't make any sense of her role, or see any way to avoid being completely upstaged by the comic antics of Jack Lemmon and Tony Curtis in drag.

Camped out with Arthur in a bungalow at the Beverly Hills Hotel working six days a week on the picture, she found it almost impossible to escape his scrutiny. His own work on *The Misfits* was going badly—Gable, without whom it couldn't be made, seemed unable to imagine himself in the role of Gay Langland, which had been written for him—and Arthur spent his days on the set, suffering in silence while she consulted Paula instead of him. She chafed at his constant presence.

The first time, she managed to get away by pleading that she needed a day off. She and Jack spent a magical, life-restoring day in bed or lazing by the Lawford pool naked, he in the sun, she in the shade—for she remained the one California girl who didn't tan herself brown. The second time, she told her husband she had to pay a hospital visit to a friend. That too had been a magic day. Jack smoked some of Lawford's grass—there were drugs everywhere in Lawford's house, concealed in the most unlikely places, so that you took your life in your hands by putting sugar in your coffee—and she took him to the nude beach where she used to go in the old days with Jimmy Dean. She and Jack had sat there naked, unrecognized, having the time of their lives, she in a dark wig, he in nothing more than one of Peter Lawford's hats. . . .

She dozed comfortably in one of the big reclining chairs in Frank's private plane, on the way to Tahoe with Lawford. Jack had called her to say he was going to be in Palm Springs for a couple of days, and asked if she could meet him there. Palm Springs had proved to be impossible because of her schedule, but she had agreed to meet him in Tahoe instead. For

Arthur she had concocted a story about needing a rest and having been offered the use of Frank's own bungalow at the Cal-Neva Lodge, where he was scheduled to open; she knew that Arthur didn't like Sinatra and the people around him, and so would be happy to stay in LA sweet-talking Clark Gable. The fact that Peter Lawford was taking her there in Sinatra's plane added a certain degree of believability to the story, for Arthur, improbably, liked Lawford, recognizing that so far as she was concerned, he was completely harmless.

She reached over and shook Lawford's shoulder. He opened his eyes, with the deeply puzzled and unfocused look of a man waking from a drugged sleep—he had been stoned when he picked her up from the Beverly Hills Hotel in Frank's limo, had poured himself one scotch in the car and ordered another as soon as they were on the plane. "Whazza matter?" he mumbled.

"We're landing," she said. She fastened his seat belt for him.

"Good-o!" He closed his eyes. Despite years of hard living, Lawford had the bright eyes and clear skin that, as she knew, drug addicts always had until they finally went to pieces. Whatever else cocaine, heroin, and marijuana did, they gave people beautiful complexions.

The plane landed smoothly and taxied to one side of the field, where a limo was waiting with a couple of Frank's gorillas beside it, to handle the luggage and what he always liked to call "personal security." She thanked the pilot and walked down the folding steps into the warm sunshine, followed by Lawford, trailing her like a zombie.

Once they were in the limo, he poured himself a scotch from the bar, washed down a couple of pills with it, and lit a joint. The combined effect of alcohol, uppers, and grass brought him back to life again as rapidly as if a switch had been turned on, as chatty and bright as ever. When he was "up," Lawford was so chatty and bright in his brittle and bitchy English way that had she not known better, she would have thought he was a faggot. In fact, she knew, he liked girls, the younger and the more of them, the better. Group sex was his thing, he told her at every opportunity—not with poor Pat, of course—but as it happened, group sex was the one thing *she* didn't much like, since half the pleasure of sex for her was having the sole, undivided attention of a man.

"God," Lawford said. "I have to keep reminding myself I may be the president's brother-in-law one day." He shook his head, took a deep drag on his joint, and offered it to her, but she declined. "He's going to do it, you know. Joe Kennedy always gets what he wants, and what he wants most of all is the White House for Jack. Dear God, what a family!"

"You're part of it, Peter."

"Don't I know it, darling! Not the most *welcome* part of it either. The old man positively gnashes his teeth at the sight of me, and my mother-in-law can't ever seem to remember my name—or *pretends* not to be able to anyway, the old bitch. Do you know she pins reminders to herself to the front of her dress, and walks around the house with Scotch tape on her forehead to prevent wrinkles? She's a monster, darling, worse than the Ambassador, as everybody insists on calling Joe Kennedy. When Jack's sister Kathleen wanted to marry Peter Fitzwilliam—and she was madly in love with him, the real thing, you know, red-hot passion—Rose told her that if she married a divorced Protestant, she'd disown her—never see her again, ever!"

He paused for breath. "Everybody behaves as if the Kennedys were patricians! Not a bit of it. They're just a bunch of brawling bloody *Micks!* Oh, Jack has some class, I grant you, but he's the only one. At least he's a skeptic, like his father. Bobby's a religious fanatic, and the girls believe every bloody word the priests and nuns have put in their heads since they were tiny kids. I'm sorry, I don't mean to offend you, if I have. . . . You're not a Roman Catholic, are you?"

"No. I guess I'm a Christian Scientist, if anything."

"A perfectly sensible religion. At least they're not against birth control and divorce. Do you know what Rose gave me as a wedding present? A rosary, blessed by the Pope! I ask you!"

The car pulled up in front of a small white cottage, surrounded by fir trees, with a view of the lake. Jack Kennedy stood at the front door in white trousers, loafers, and a cable-stitch sweater—looking like a college boy, she thought, with a big grin on his face.

She got out, ran up the steps, and threw her arms around him. Lawford followed. "Hi, Jack," he called out. "Mission accomplished."

Jack gave a mock salute. "See you at dinner, Peter." He dismissed him without shaking his hand.

Lawford made his way unsteadily to an adjoining bungalow, stumbling badly as he tried to climb the steps. "He needs help," she said.

Jack shrugged. "He'll make it. Don't worry about him."

She felt a small chill at the coldness of his reaction. She did not like Lawford much but she felt pity for him, as well as a certain camaraderie of the spirit, for she recognized in him a lost soul, desperately looking for help but never finding it.

She pressed herself against Jack's sweater for warmth.

She woke to the sound of a voice in the next room, slipped on Jack's robe, and tiptoed to the door. She felt a little weak at the knees from so much sex after several weeks of abstinence. Her dress—a white summer frock, cut low at the neck—lay crumpled on the floor beside one of her white, high-heeled Delman pumps. Her bra, improbably, was draped over the lamp on the bed table.

"Jesus, Bobby!" she heard Jack say. "I know you have a hard-on for Hoffa, but go easy. . . . Well, yeah, but I'm not so sure we *want* him in jail, Bobby. . . . Sure he belongs there, but that's not the point. . . . I *told* you: Keep those guys' names out of it as much as you can, Talk to David about it, he'll explain. . . .

"Oh shit, who leaked *that?* Look, call Bradlee and ask him—no, fucking *beg* him, if you have to—not to run the story about Hoffa's mistress. . . .

"I *know* you're not scared, Bobby, and neither am I, but that's no reason to *ask* for a bullet in the head, is it? Right. And one thing more: Find out who it is on the staff that's leaking and cut his fucking nuts off, okay?" He caught a glimpse of her in the doorway and waved. "You have a good time too, little brother," he said, and slammed down the receiver hard.

"Problems?" she asked.

"Always."

"With Bobby?"

"With his staff. Some of them are eager beavers. They want to kick Hoffa in the balls, make an example of him, you know. . . . Bobby's a little inclined that way himself, but I'm against it personally."

"So am I. As you know."

"I know." He stood up and took the linen cover off a room service trolley, happy to change the subject. "I ordered lunch," he said. "You were out like a light, but I thought you'd probably be hungry when you woke up."

He passed her a club sandwich, and popped the cork off a bottle of champagne.

She realized she was hungry. She picked the bacon out of her sandwich and ate the rest of it in ravenous bites.

"You don't like bacon?" he asked, lifting an eyebrow at the stains on his expensive robe.

"I like it all right, but it's all salt. Salt bloats me. I've got problems enough getting into my costumes for this stinking picture as it is."

He eyed her breasts, bulging against the thin silk. "You don't look bloated to me," he said.

"You don't have to squeeze and shimmy your way into a skintight dress at the studio every day. Or put Band-Aids on your nipples so they don't show through if, God forbid, they get hard from the heat from the lights."

Jack was wearing a shirt—one of those silly-looking golf shirts with a little alligator on the chest—and Bermuda shorts, eating his sandwich in neat bites, a napkin on his lap.

She got up, unfastened the robe, removed his napkin, and sat down on his lap, holding her plate and continuing to eat. She turned her head and kissed him, plunging her tongue into his mouth, tasting him and the food at the same time.

He looked a little taken aback, not quite sure he liked it. She licked his lips clean, in tiny, catlike licks, and kissed him again.

She picked a few pieces of turkey and cheese out of his sandwich and popped them one by one into his mouth. Some of them fell on his shirt. At first he resisted mildly, but then he relaxed. She could feel him growing hard beneath her as she sat on his lap, and slowly turned around until she was facing him, opening her legs to let him enter her.

"Christ," she heard him say, his mouth still full, "I'm glad I packed a lot of clothes!"

Dressing for dinner, always a long process for her, was all the more so now, since she wasn't used to having a man around while she was doing it. She always had her own bathroom and dressing room, and at least a maid to help her, very often a makeup man and a hairdresser as well. She had finally been obliged to eject Jack from the bathroom to the small powder room. "Listen," he had said, "I'm a married man. I'm used to this kind of thing. Jackie takes hours to get ready."

"Honey, if you think Jackie takes hours, you ain't seen nothing yet," she said.

The truth was that this was at once her greatest pleasure and her greatest everyday fear. When she looked in the mirror, what she saw there, before she went to work, was Norma Jean, and it was her job to turn that plump-cheeked girl with the funny bump on the end of her pert little nose and the slightly-too-prominent chin and the naturally mousy, frizzy hair into Marilyn Monroe.

Makeup was the art she understood best. She herself had concocted the exact mixture of Vaseline and wax that she applied after putting on her lipstick, to give her lips a high gloss as well as the moist look of someone who has just been kissed. She herself had made the decision, years ago, not to cover up the mole on her left cheek but to accentuate it with an eyebrow pencil, as if it were a beauty spot.

She stood in front of the full-length mirror and turned around. She wore another simple white dress, with a pleated skirt and a neckline that bared her shoulders and much of her back. Given a choice, she always wore white. White made her feel clean.

She picked up a long white scarf to wrap around her shoulders in case the air-conditioning was too cold, walked into the living room, and did a quick pirouette for Jack's benefit.

He was lounging in an easy chair, dressed in a blue blazer, gray slacks, and a shirt and tie, talking intently on the telephone, but he looked up and grinned his approval.

"Jesus, Ben," he said on the phone, "this isn't news, it's gossip. Hoffa has a mistress. Big deal! I thought you were a serious journalist."

His tone was light and bantering, but his face betrayed real concern. "Well, then how about as a favor to me?" It was a nicely voiced plea, one gentleman to another, but the hard glint in his eyes and the grim downturn of his mouth made it clear enough that it wasn't working.

"Well, okay," he said at last, "If your answer is, 'Let the chips fall where they may,' to quote you, so be it. I guess the chips won't be falling on *your* head, will they? . . . No, I'm not being overdramatic. I think I'm being realistic. Sure, Jackie's fine. My best to Toni too. Thanks."

He slammed down the receiver with a crash. "That fucking *bastard,* with his holier-than-thou First Amendment bullshit! We're supposed to be friends, it's Toni this and Jackie that, but when I ask him for a favor, I get a lecture on the ethics of journalism, which is all a load of crap to begin with—"

She came over and gave him a kiss on the forehead to calm him down, though it didn't seem to have much effect. "Is it the Hoffa story again?"

"The guy has a mistress. She and Hoffa had a kid together. Hoffa's fond of the kid—practically adopted him. David thinks Hoffa might take it personally."

"I wouldn't be surprised. Hoffa may be thinking of the woman, you know? And the child. Is it a boy or a girl?"

"I don't remember. A boy, I think."

"It's a terrible thing to find out that you're illegitimate. I should know. Hoffa may want to spare the boy that. Why *wouldn't* Hoffa take it personally, if it hurts people he loves?"

"Hoffa's a crook, Marilyn. Don't waste tears on him."

"Even crooks have feelings, Jack." She was growing heated, she realized. "People ought to be nicer to each other," she added lamely, conscious that she had already lost the argument.

"Hoffa's not a nice man. But as it happens, I don't think a man's private life should be used against him." He gave her a rueful smile. "I mean, look at *us.* If I could stop the story, I would, but I can't. The only thing now is to hang tough, that's what I told Bobby. . . . If we apologize for the leak, we'll look guilty *and* incompetent." He sighed. "It'll probably blow over."

"And if it doesn't?"

He grinned. "Then I'll buy myself a bulletproof vest. And one for Bobby, too, I guess."

She didn't laugh—she didn't think it was funny at all. "We'd better go, if we're going to eat before we hear Frank sing," she said.

He opened the door and they strolled arm in arm toward the main building of the lodge, past other secluded rustic cabins. There was nobody in sight on the paths, which had been designed so that people could go back and forth to the lodge with the minimum chance of seeing other guests on the way. Walking arm in arm with Jack gave her a cozy domestic feeling.

As they approached the entrance to the lodge, a room service waiter appeared, pushing a trolley table. He stopped and made way for them, with a deferential bow of his head.

It was not until she was past him that it occurred to her his face was familiar. Where, she asked herself, had she seen that plump, swarthy face with the black mustache, the balding head, the tinted glasses that failed to hide a penetrating stare?

Then it dawned on her that he looked like the man she had seen in Chicago, at the door of her suite, who asked her if her telephones were working. She turned around to look at him again, but all she saw was a broad back in a white waiter's jacket, vanishing past the shrubbery that lined the winding path. The more she thought about his face, the less sure she was, and by the time they were in the lodge, where Peter Lawford was waiting for them in the bar, a young woman on either side of him, his trembling fingers clutching what was surely not his first martini of the evening, she had put the whole thing out of her mind, dismissed as a coincidence.

The table had been set for eight people, and she had assumed that Frank was planning to join them before the show, but instead, just as they were finishing their coffee, the headwaiter appeared and said that one of the owners of the lodge, a friend of Frank's, wanted to come over and say hello to his distinguished guests.

She nodded, and almost immediately, as if they had been waiting for the headwaiter's sign, there appeared a thin gentleman in his late fifties, heavily tanned, with the profile of one of the more degenerate Roman emperors, accompanied by an attractive dark-haired young woman with beautiful pale skin, wearing a pale green low-cut evening dress that matched the color of her eyes—not a great beauty perhaps, but with the unmistakable professional sexual buzz that only the highest—priced call girls know how to project.

The man, dressed in a well-cut white dinner jacket, his eyes hidden by wraparound sunglasses, gave a courtly bow, pulled out a chair for the young woman, and sat down next to Marilyn. "It's an honor to have you as a guest, Miss Monroe," he said.

He reached across the table and shook hands with Jack and Peter Lawford. "A pleasure, Senator," he said. "Any friend of Frank's is a friend of mine."

He had a low voice, warm, husky, and sexy, though there was nothing warm about his deeply lined face, with its powerful nose, prominent cheekbones, and strong jaw. His thinning hair was so black and shiny that she suspected he used Grecian Formula; he wore it combed carefully over the top of his head to hide a bald spot.

"Giancana," he said, introducing himself with an ironic smile, as if his name were a challenge. "Sam. My friends call me Momo." He placed a hairy, well-manicured hand on the young woman's bare shoulder in a gesture that was more possessive than affectionate. "This is Miss Campbell. Judy."

Miss Campbell smiled, displaying less than perfect teeth. Giancana's grasp on her shoulder had been strong enough to leave small, pale, moon-shaped indentations, which would soon turn into bruises.

Giancana's name did not ring a bell with her, but it clearly did with Jack, who was looking at his host with fascination. She couldn't help noticing that he'd taken a pretty sharp look at the Campbell woman, too.

"Are you comfortable? Is everything okay?" Giancana was busy passing himself off as a friendly innkeeper looking after his guests, but it seemed false to her. Hotel owners were invariably outgoing personalities, but Giancana's face was veiled and secretive.

She'd supposed—because it was usually the case—that this Giancana guy, whoever he was, had pushed his way to the table with his bimbo to meet *her*, but it was immediately obvious that it was Jack who interested him. Giancana asked a few perfunctory questions about what she was doing, told her which of her movies were his favorites—she had the impression, from the wooden way he recited the titles, that somebody else had selected them for him, perhaps the sultry Miss Campbell—then focused his attention on Jack, leaving her and Miss Campbell to exchange pleasantries about how much they liked Frank.

Giancana snapped his fingers the moment he sat down— a signal for the maître d' to appear with a magnum of Dom Pérignon on ice, which had obviously been kept waiting in the wings. He made a small production of clicking his glass against hers and Jack's. *"Salud!"* he croaked hoarsely—he had a real chain-smoker's voice. He did not bother to click glasses with Miss Campbell, Lawford, or Lawford's sulky girls.

"I have a great admiration for you, Senator," he said. "Even if we're on opposite sides."

"Which sides would those be, Mr. Giancana?"

"Momo, Senator, please. I meant only that I'm a Republican. No disrespect, but I like Ike."

"I thought you might be referring to other things."

Giancana smiled. He had big white teeth, like a Sicilian peasant. "Some people make the laws, some people break them," he said with disarming frankness.

Jack laughed. "That's putting it nicely, Mr. Giancana."

"I must give credit where it's due, Senator. I didn't invent that."

"Who did?"

"Al Capone, may he rest in peace. He was referring to the IRS, by the way, not himself. He felt the government had used the IRS to frame him."

"It happens. Even today." There was just a faint hint of warning in Jack's voice.

"You're frank. A man after my own heart. I'm a great admirer of your father, by the way. He too is a man of great frankness. He lets the chips fall where they may, as the saying goes."

Was it just a coincidence—surely it *must* be—that it was the exact phrase Jack had used on the phone only a couple of hours ago? Marilyn wondered. Jack didn't seem to notice; he was too busy steering the conversation away from the subject of his father.

"Ah, you *do* know, Mr. Giancana, that I'm a member of the Senate Government Investigations Subcommittee? I only mention it to spare us both a certain—embarrassment. . . ."

Giancana flashed another of his thousand-watt smiles. "Of course," he said softly, "that's understood. That has nothing to do with personal feelings, Senator. That's just politics—and business."

"What business are you in, Mr. Giancana?" she asked.

"This and that, Miss Monroe. I own a piece of this hotel. I own a piece of a lot of things. I used to be in the liquor business in a big way, like the Senator's father."

Jack frowned. He hated it when people brought up the way his father had made his fortune. "Mr. Giancana, Marilyn, is one of the leaders of the Chicago mob," he said coldly.

Giancana shook his head, smiling ruefully. "The things people say, Senator! Hoover's been bad-mouthing me for years with all this mob talk. I don't suppose he tells the truth about you either. I'm just a simple businessman, Miss Monroe. It's the same with me as it is with Frank—just because you're of Italian origins, as soon as you've made it, everybody whispers mob, *capiche?*"

"Mr. Giancana has been arrested more than seventy times, Marilyn," Jack said, his voice steely.

"And convicted twice," Giancana said with a shrug. "And both of those times were misdemeanors." He cleared his throat. "Real bullshit items." He smiled at her. "You should excuse the expression."

She nodded to indicate that it was nothing she hadn't heard before. Giancana did not exert the same kind of fascination on her as he did on Jack. She had known a good many mobsters in her time. Giancana was more courtly and presentable than most, but he was still the kind of guy who probably wouldn't hesitate to have acid thrown in a girl's face if she displeased him, which perhaps explained the nervous flicker in Miss Campbell's eyes.

"This subcommittee," Giancana said, leaning over to get closer to Jack. "I hear from a source close to you that I'm going to be called?"

Jack looked embarrassed and annoyed. "That's Bobby's decision, Mr. Giancana," he said. "But probably, yes."

"I haven't done anything to interest the United States Senate."

"I seem to remember reading something about Teamster Local three-twenty in Miami. The man who set it up worked for you, didn't he? Fellow called Yaras?"

"The name doesn't ring a bell."

"The way I read it, he was a, ah, hit man for you, back in Chicago. The FBI recorded a tape of him describing how he tortured a government informer to death with a cattle prod, a meat hook, and a blowtorch."

Giancana's smile didn't waver a bit. "I may have met this Yaras once or twice," he said. "I meet a lot of people. I don't know what a hit man is. I recall him as being in the import-export business in Havana."

"And head of Local three-twenty."

"That could be. There's no law against being a labor leader that I know of."

"No. Though I believe Mr. Yaras was arrested fourteen times, once for the murder of a Mr. Ragen, in Chicago, with an ice pick."

"Jim Ragen, rest in peace." Giancana sighed. "You've done your homework, Senator."

"To be honest, my brother Bobby did the homework. I just happen to have a good memory."

"It's a valuable asset. Forgetting is even better." Giancana let this sink in. "He's a tough guy, your brother, Senator. That's what they tell me."

"Tough enough, Mr. Giancana."

"Don't get me wrong. That's good. And it's good he's working with you. A brother, you can trust. I'm a great believer in keeping things in the family, myself. How about you, Miss Monroe?"

"I'm an orphan."

"*Madonna!* That's a shame." He placed a hand on hers before she could move it. His palm was dry—it felt the way she would have expected a snake to feel to the touch. For a small man, he had remarkable strength: he exerted enough pressure so that she couldn't move her hand out from under his. "You ever need help, Miss Monroe," he said, putting his face close to hers, "you call me. Think of me as family."

"Thank you," she said reluctantly, then wriggled her hand until he got the message and let her go.

"Senator," he said, turning his attention to Jack, his voice pitched to extreme sincerity. "It's been a real pleasure meeting you. You're doing great work for the country. I want you to know I'm on your side. Even if I do get subpoenaed. I have the greatest respect for you and your brother."

He placed his right hand briefly over his heart, as if he were pledging allegiance to the flag. "If I can help out in any way, count on me—I mean it. Information, advice, anything I can help you with—without losing honor and respect among my colleagues, of course—just let me know."

He reached into his pocket and took out a flat leather notepad and a gold pencil, scrawled a number on it, and handed the paper to Jack. "This will get me, anytime, day or night. We don't have to meet, you understand, Senator? I'll get somebody to act as a messenger, a—what's it called?— go-between, right?" His eyes flickered briefly toward Miss Campbell, then back to Jack. "Somebody we can both trust."

He put his arm around the young woman's bare shoulders. "Somebody nobody would be surprised you wanted to see anyway. That's the kind of go-between I'm thinking of."

He let his fingers rest lightly on Miss Campbell's right breast and smiled gently at her. "I'll think of somebody— you can be sure of that," he said, and gave Jack a wink, man to man.

Giancana pulled his date to her feet just as the lights began to dim and Frank stepped out onto the stage. The orchestra struck up the first bars; then Frank, as if offering a greeting in honor of somebody in the audience, began to sing, "Chi-cago, Chi-cago . . ."

She looked around and saw that Giancana and his companion had returned to their own table, where they were surrounded by large beefy men with blond-beehived wives or girlfriends. A spotlight was turned on their table, and Giancana beamed as Frank crooned his tribute to Chicago.

Giancana laughed, raising a glass to toast the famous singer, but even from a distance, the sight of him affected her like a bad omen.

She turned to look at the stage, took Jack's hand, and guided it under the table to her thigh, for comfort.

* * *

"What was *that* all about?" she asked as she was taking off her makeup, Frank's music still running through her head. He had come over to the table after the show and been at his most charming, flirting with her and trading dirty stories with Jack. Jack behaved in Sinatra's presence a little like a college freshman being interviewed for membership in a fraternity.

"Giancana, you mean?"

She nodded. It was strange, she thought, how spending the night together in a hotel produced instant domesticity. Here she was, removing her makeup in front of the bathroom mirror like any wife after a dinner party, wearing her old terry-cloth robe and her slippers, while at the sink next to her, Jack, a towel wrapped loosely around his waist, brushed his teeth with the care of somebody who had had dental hygiene drummed into him as a child. He gargled forcefully and spat.

"What did you think of him?" he asked.

"Mr. Momo? He's a gangster. Smoother than most, sure, but so what, sweetheart? Guys like him are bad news."

Jack bared his teeth and examined them closely in the mirror. He had that slightly blank expression that comes over a husband's face when his wife has just said something he doesn't agree with but isn't in the mood to argue over because he wants to get laid. Boy, did she know that expression! She tossed a wadded-up ball of Kleenex at him. "Hey, knock it off!" she said, with a smile to show she wasn't angry (though she was, a little). "We're not married, Jack."

He tried hard not to look annoyed. "Well, of course we're not. . . ."

"Then stop acting like a husband. This is a love affair, not a marriage. If you want to tell the little lady to mind her own fucking business, go home and do it to Jackie."

Just in case she had gone too far, she moved closer to him, opened her robe and let it drop to the floor. She squeezed between him and the sink, so that her ass was pressed tightly against his crotch, and carried on with washing her face.

"Okay," he said. "You're right. I'm sorry."

"Forget it," she said. She loved him too much to hold a grudge—besides, she didn't want to spoil the night ahead.

She reached over, flicked out the lights, unwound his towel, and pushed him backward into the big stall shower. She turned on the water—the hell with her hair, she would worry about that tomorrow!—and raised herself up on tiptoe to kiss him as the hot water poured onto them from every direction. He had left his gold watch on and it didn't look waterproof, but she wasn't about to stop for that. She soaped him all over, then let him soap her, laughing as the suds cascaded down until they were ankle-deep in bubbles. She opened her legs and let him wash her ass, her cunt; then, when she could tell from his expression that he couldn't wait another second, she guided him deep into her and let him lift her up, his arms under her thighs, moving her back and forth until he came, in the hot spray and mist.

They dried each other with the same towel and lay down side by side on the bed. He had poured a nightcap for himself and a glass of champagne for her to take her pills with. "Jesus," he said. "That was something."

"Mm." She hadn't come herself—as it happened, she didn't get off on fucking in the bath or shower, preferred, on the whole, to spend a lot of time alone there, dreaming happily in the warmth as if the rest of the world didn't exist. She had simply guessed it was the most unwifely gesture she could make on the spur of the moment.

"So what does Giancana want?" she asked, cuddled naked next to Jack.

"He wants to avoid being indicted. I think he was also reinforcing personally the message from the boys in Chicago. It goes something like this: Do what you have to do with Hoffa, but keep us out of it as much as possible, and please don't push him too far. In return, if you ever need any help from us, just whistle and it's yours, Senator."

"*Help?* From the Chicago mob? They're murderers!"

"Mm. Well, you never know. There are times when it might not be such a bad idea to know people who can carry out a murder. I can think of lots of people I'd love to have murdered." He laughed.

"These guys are criminals, Jack. Scum."

"Oh hell, Marilyn, let me tell you a story: One of the old-time Boston pols, when some crooks offered to make a contribution to his campaign fund, took the money and said, 'Well, Christ never turned away sinners, so who am I to turn them away?' "

"Who said that?"

"My grandfather."

She laughed, but she felt uneasy. Still, who the hell was *she*, she told herself, to preach to a third-generation politician—who was clearly on his way to the presidency? "What did you think of Miss Campbell?" she asked.

"Oh," he said, "I didn't pay much attention to her."

"Liar," she whispered. She reached over and tickled him until he was helpless, rolling back and forth on the bed and pleading with her to stop. She upended her glass and poured the rest of her champagne on his chest and belly.

"Hey, that's *cold*, goddamn it!" he shouted.

She turned out the light on the bed table and moved down under the covers to take him in her mouth. "I'll warm you up."

This one, she told herself, was for *her* pleasure, and she was going to make him do it exactly the way she liked it, and for as long as she wanted.

After all, she was a star, not some hooker like the Campbell woman!

"God," she whispered as she drew herself back up in bed to kiss him, "I could spend the rest of my life in bed with you."

I could spend the rest of my life in bed with you.

Bernie Spindel adjusted the headphones so they were more comfortable, and checked to make sure the tape was running smoothly, though that was not really necessary. He used nothing but the finest equipment—the Uher 5000, German-made, the same recorder as the networks—and always ran two units simultaneously so there was a backup in the unlikely event of a mechanical failure.

He listened to the soft, sweet sounds of lovemaking, perspiration running down his face, as he bent over the recorders he had installed in a utility closet in the main lodge.

It was ironic, he thought, that people—even intelligent people like Senator Kennedy—never managed to catch up with technology. They still believed in the sanctity of their own privacy, closed the door, pulled down the blinds, talked in whispers, before making an illegal deal, or spilling their guts out to a girlfriend, or fucking somebody else's wife—as if Spindel could be stopped by doors or drawn blinds or whispering! He used the same ceramic bugs as the CIA, marvels of electronic technology that could pick up a whisper from anywhere in a room and transmit it, crystal-clear and amplified, to recorders concealed hundreds of feet away. There wasn't a telephone in the world that was safe from him—he had even tapped the White House phones for Hoover, back in his FBI days! He had all the latest Japanese devices, things even the CIA and the NSA didn't know about yet.

The notion that privacy still existed would have made Spindel laugh had he been the laughing type, which he wasn't—for the price of eavesdropping as a profession was that his view of human nature was deeply pessimistic. Like a priest in the confessional booth, he never heard good news. His tapes recorded nothing but lies, cheating, and corruption.

Oh, Jack, JACK! Ja-aack! he heard her cry, her voice rising to a shriek, then descending to a low, animal moan. That made three times, by his count, that they had made it since she'd arrived twelve hours ago.

He tried to remember if he had ever fucked a woman three times in twelve hours, and concluded that he'd never even come close.

22

FOR ONCE, SHE WAS ARRIVING FOR WORK ON TIME, TO her own surprise—and to the utter astonishment of Billy Wilder. The moment she was in her dressing room, she took off her clothes and put on an old, cosmetic-stained silk kimono while her makeup man Whitey Snyder and the hairdresser and his assistants began the endless process of turning her into Sugar Kane.

As part of her long-term scheme of self-improvement, she had brought a copy of Thomas Paine's *The Rights of Man* with her, since Jack had mentioned it in one of his speeches, and she made her way through it doggedly, concentrating fiercely, while her hair was styled. It was even harder going than Carl

Sandburg's life of Lincoln, and she put it down gratefully while Whitey did her face. Whitey glanced at the book. *"The Rights of Man,* huh?" he asked. "What about the rights of women?"

"He hasn't mentioned any so far, Whitey, this guy Paine."

"That figures." Whitey had a blue-collar contempt for intellectuals, in which category he placed all writers, including Arthur.

He leaned down, close to her shoulder. Together they peered at her brightly lit image in the mirror as if it were a work of art in the making. Whitey shook his head. "Nobody ever had prettier skin, doll," he said. "You were born for Technicolor. I can't believe Billy is making this picture in black and white!"

"Well, you *know* why, Whitey. He showed me the tests of Jack and Tony made up as girls. Their faces looked like they'd been embalmed at Forest Lawn. It was *creepy* instead of funny. Like a horror movie, you know? So Billy had to do the picture in black and white."

"I know that, doll, but I'm thinking about *you.* What the audience cares about is how you look, not those two guys—particularly, you should excuse the expression, that snotty shithead Curtis."

Curtis had been so angered by her delays—not to mention the endless retakes in which she got better and better while he lost the edge of his performance—that he did everything he could to screw her up. When somebody asked him what it was like to play a love scene with her, he had replied, in a screening room full of Fox executives, "It was like kissing Hitler!"

Of course, she heard about it, as he intended her to, and it upset her so badly that she burst into tears on the spot. She had so desperately wanted Curtis to *like* her, just the way she had wanted Joan Crawford, and Robert Mitchum, and Larry and Vivien to like her, and instead, he had said terrible things about her, and even done savage impersonations of her at dinner parties all over town!

Thinking about it was enough to bring tears to her eyes again, or would have been had Whitey not already done her makeup. She stood up and slipped out of her robe, naked except for her bra. She had done a peroxide job on her bush a week ago—without burning herself for once, thank God!—so at least she didn't have *that* to worry about for another couple of weeks. The wardrobe people came in now, carrying the bits and pieces of her costume, which would have to be sewn together on her while she stood still.

She sighed. It wasn't easy to stand absolutely still for an hour or so, even though she knew that the slightest movement might get her pricked with a needle or a pin. Whitey cut a big circular collar out of brown wrapping paper and placed it on her shoulders to make sure the seamstresses didn't accidentally smudge her makeup. "Home stretch, doll," he said cheerfully.

Home stretch, indeed! she thought. She put on a white garter belt, slipped on her stockings, fastened them to the suspenders, taking care not to damage a fingernail, put on white high-heeled pumps, then stood still, arms outstretched. The head seamstress from Wardrobe held each piece of the dress against her body while the assistants, on their knees at either side of her, carefully sewed the dress together; she felt like one of the vestal virgins being prepared for a ceremony—a scene she remembered from some picture set in ancient Rome. Of course, the moment they started to sew, she inevitably wanted to go to the bathroom—she wondered if the vestal virgins had felt the same back then. . . .

With an effort she brought her mind back to the job at hand. The dress was finished. She turned carefully in front of the mirrors as her various helpers examined her closely, the way the designers of a new airplane might look at it before its first test flight. Even Whitey, an old hand, looked somber and serious, his brow knit in concentration, one hand rubbing his chin. Then he nodded and gave a thin smile. "Okay, doll," he said. "Showtime."

She stood—as her retinue put the finishing touches on their work—flipping over one of Whitey's newspapers, and suddenly saw a photograph of Jack and Jackie, standing arm in arm on the stoop of their new Georgetown house. "Kennedys expecting as they move into new house," the caption began. She felt suddenly sick, her head aching if she had been struck down by a migraine.

There was a muffled knock on the door, and a young man stuck his head in. "Excuse me, Miss Monroe," he said diffidently, "but Mr. Wilder wanted me to tell you he's ready—"

Without a moment's hesitation, as if she were responding to an electric shock, she turned on him and screamed, *"Fuck off!"* He blushed and shut the door.

She could feel the curtain of disapproval descend around her, even from Whitey. It was a rule of the profession: A star didn't shout at underlings who were just doing their jobs. You could tell the director, or the producer, or a fellow star to fuck off, but never, *never* the working stiffs. "Christ," she said, her head throbbing, "I'm sorry."

Everybody nodded, but their mood was mournful, like the retinue of a bullfighter who has just revealed a streak of cowardice. "I'm *really* sorry," she said, eyes wide open and humid in distress.

"It's okay, doll," Whitey said, patting her shoulder, but she knew it wasn't.

Worse still, she was ashamed of herself, even though she knew it was the shock of seeing the picture of Jack with the pregnant Jackie that did it.

At moments like this she was always tempted to go home, lock the door, and hide herself away, but she knew it was out of the question. She opened one of the dozens of bottles scattered on her dressing table, pricked a couple of capsules with a pin, and swallowed them dry so as not to smear her lipstick by taking a drink of water.

She waited to feel the hit, a kind of dull, fizzy reaction in her stomach, followed by a warmth that spread from deep in her guts to her toes and fingertips, bringing with it a kind of false peace. Before she lost the feeling—for she knew it was evanescent—she opened the door and walked out.

Wilder was sitting beside the camera, looking reproachful. "They tell me you're reading Tom Paine's *The Rights of Man*," he said—there were no secrets on a set. "That's good, but you know, the boy has his rights too."

"I know, Billy. I'm sorry."

"So." The German accent was strong—the word came out as "Zoh." He shook his head. "Respect for people who are just doing their job, that's important, yes? Respect for colleagues—say, by not being two hours late—this is important too, no?"

"Don't push it, Billy."

Wilder gave her the charming smile of a man who had once made his living, improbably, as a gigolo. "Not another word," he said. "Now let's get to work."

"Vord." "Vork." Oh, how she *hated* all that softly accented Central European bullshit, which was the lifeblood of Hollywood creativity! Half the people who mattered in the industry were German, or Austrian, or Hungarian, or something, and spoke in riddles, with accents like Bela Lugosi's.

"To repeat what you already know then," he said, speaking slowly, as to an idiot, "you knock on the door, and as you open it to come into the room, you say, 'Hi, it's Sugar.' Tony says, 'Hi, Sugar!' That's it. One take will do it, I bet. You'll see."

She had never done anything in one take in her life, and he knew it. Besides, whenever people—especially directors—told her something was simple, she immediately became suspicious. She couldn't help it—she needed to have everything explained to her exactly and in detail.

"So let's get it done, darling?" Wilder said hopefully.

But she wasn't ready. She walked across the set, past Tony Curtis, who was glowering at her, rocking back and forth on his high heels, and Jack Lemmon, who looked weary and dyspeptic, like a man who has been waiting so long for his wife that he no longer wants to see her. They didn't look like women to her—they *stood* all wrong, for one thing—and she had difficulty relating to them, as she did to all forms of transvestism.

Paula was waiting, sitting implacably, wearing the black schmatte that had so infuriated Sir Cork Tip. She sat down beside Paula. "I'm supposed to be sharing my happiness with my girlfriends," she said, as if it were a hopeless task.

Paula glared malevolently at Wilder through her dark glasses. "What does *he* know?" she asked.

"He wants me to make it light and funny. I don't see how."

"Of course you don't, poor darling," Paula murmured soothingly.

"I don't see what I'm supposed to be so fucking *happy* about either. What's my reaction when I open the door and see the two of them? Why won't he tell me?"

Paula put an arm around her shoulder, her face as close as a lover's. "Don't think about him, darling," she said. "What do you care? He doesn't understand the depths of an actor's soul. He's just a good mechanical director. And he's intimidated by working with a talent like yours."

"Yes? But how do I play the scene?"

"It's Christmas Eve. There are presents under the tree. You want to share the news with your friends." Paula stroked her hand. "You're a Popsicle, darling."

She thought about it. It made sense, if you understood Paula's language. Once, when Olivier had talked himself hoarse trying to get her to act dejected and unhappy in *The Prince and the Showgirl,* Paula had simply whispered, "You're a wet soda cracker, Marilyn," and she'd gotten it right on the next take.

"A Popsicle!" she laughed. It made sense to her, in a way that no director could. She got up and walked into the bright lights toward her mark. She stared at the bare wood of the door—unfinished on this side of the set because it wouldn't show—as if it were the door to hell. She heard the sharp clack of the clapper board, reached for the door, and opened it, momentarily blinded by the lights. "Hi, Sugar, it's me," she said, and it wasn't until she heard Wilder call out, "Cut!" and Tony Curtis sigh that she realized she'd blown it.

While they fussed over her hair and makeup to get her ready again, she tried to work out why she had screwed up over something so simple when she had been determined to get it right.

She waited for the clapper, boldly grasped the door handle, and said, "Sugar, hi, it's me."

On the next take she got it right, but she didn't say it until after she'd opened the door, which was no good.

Wilder was too smart to become abusive like Preminger, but she could see he was getting upset. There followed a dozen takes, in each of which she got the sequence slightly wrong or fluffed her line.

Finally Wilder, drained and exhausted himself, rose and came over to her, an expression of desperation in his eyes. For a moment she thought he was going to hit her, and flinched, but instead, in his gentlest voice, he said, "We'll get it right. Don't worry, Marilyn, really."

Instinctively she opened her eyes wide, becoming in real life just the dumb blonde that she hesitated to give him on screen, and replied with perfect innocence: "Worry about what?"

The look in his eyes showed her that she had made her point. He wouldn't condescend to her again.

She got the scene right on the very next take—got it so perfect that Curtis, who was tired and angry, might as well not have been in it at all! It was hers, one hundred percent, a triumph.

She was the only person who left the set that night as fresh as a daisy.

*   *   *

I had seen a rough cut of *Some Like It Hot*, and I thought it was the best thing Marilyn had ever done. It was as if she had hit her stride at last.

Whatever Marilyn thought of it, I don't believe any picture she made captured her beauty better—especially the transparent, luminous quality of her skin, or all that extravagantly luscious flesh, so soft it looked like fresh whipped cream.

As it happened, there was a reason why she looked so good—at some point during the making of *Some Like It Hot* she had become pregnant again, as she told me shortly after she returned to New York.

Since she didn't tell me that the baby was Jack's, I assumed—correctly—that it wasn't, which was something of a relief. I had visions of poor Jack dealing with *two* pregnant women in his life at the same time! Besides, I knew it had been some time since she had seen Jack, or even spoken to him. *Some Like It Hot*, like every picture she made, consumed her totally.

Marilyn and I were sitting in her apartment on Fifty-seventh Street, where I had stopped for a drink on my way home. Miller was out—he had recently taken a suite at the Chelsea Hotel, his old stomping grounds, in order to have a quiet place to work on the script of *The Misfits*.

There was nothing in the apartment to suggest it was home, to him or to Marilyn. The walls were white, the few pictures still leaning against them, stacked on the floor, the bare parquet floors scuffed and unwaxed, the windows without curtains or blinds. There was not enough furniture, and what there was might have been bought on sale at Macy's—graceless, bulky chairs and sofas, upholstered in nubbly off-white fabrics that looked worn and dusty even though they were new. Here and there was evidence of Marilyn's stardom: a professional hair dryer, stationed above a towel-draped dining chair, a chrome-and-glass manicurist's table, tangled electric cables and transformers on the floor for a photography session that had just ended.

The sequined dress Marilyn had been photographed in was draped carelessly over a chair. She was wearing a short robe now, sitting opposite me on the sofa, her bare legs tucked under her. We were drinking dry vermouth, her supply of champagne having run out for once. She glanced at the coffee table, and a look of shame crossed her face. "Gee whiz," she said, "no snacks." Marilyn had the instincts of a middle-class homemaker and avid reader of the *Ladies' Home Journal*.

She uncurled her legs and rose to her feet. I caught an opalescent flash of inner thigh and tried to hide my stare—unsuccessfully, because Marilyn laughed, that wonderful, full-throated, sexy laugh of hers.

"Dream on," she said huskily. "Are you hungry?"

I shook my head. "I had a late lunch," I said. "With Steve Smith."

Marilyn raised an eyebrow. Stephen Smith was Jack's brother-in-law, the man his father had hand-picked to look after the Kennedy fortune so his boys wouldn't have to bother. Anything to do with the Kennedy family interested Marilyn, but hunger was her first concern, so she got up and went off to the kitchen, returning a moment later with a box of Girl Scout cookies.

"How did you come by the Girl Scout cookies?" I asked, intrigued.

She laughed. "In the country. A little girl came to the door—her daddy had brought her in his car—and asked if I wanted to buy any Girl Scout cookies. She was so sweet! So I said sure, but I didn't have any change, so I gave her a fifty-dollar bill. Well, she and her daddy didn't have change of a fifty, so now I've got *cartons* of these cookies. I bet she got a badge or something for the biggest cookie order in Girl Scout history! . . . I never got to be a Girl Scout or anything like that," she added sadly. "We were too poor."

I nodded sympathetically, but perhaps not sufficiently so. "You don't believe me," she said. I told her I did.

"No you don't. But it's true. You had to buy the uniform. It didn't cost much, but my foster parents didn't have anything to spare—not for me anyway. . . ."

She set her jaw, as she often did when her childhood came to mind. She was not about to forgive anyone who had been associated with it. "Tell me about Steve Smith," she said.

"Steve? He's a tough nut—exactly the man Joe wanted at least one of his daughters to marry. Not glamorous but one hundred percent reliable. And useful. I don't think Steve could ever make a fortune himself, but he's perfect for looking after one."

"Does he know about me?"

"Probably, but he's too discreet to mention you to me."

"His wife knows."

"Jean? What makes you think so?"

"Jack told her. She'd heard about it from Pat Lawford and wanted to know if it was true, and Jack told her it was."

"He did?" I wasn't as surprised as I may have sounded. Joe Kennedy's children may have had secrets from their spouses, but seldom from each other. Jack's sisters adored him, and all of them were star-struck—even Pat, who, being married to Lawford, might have known better—so they'd be thrilled about his having an affair with Marilyn.

"Absolutely. They want me to meet his father one day."

I sighed inwardly. I guessed this was Joe's idea rather than his daughters'. "Be that as it may," I said, "I suspect that's exactly the kind of thing Jean *doesn't* talk to Steve about. He did tell me that he couldn't believe how quickly Jack had taken to fatherhood."

It was a thoughtless remark and I regretted it instantly, but to my relief, Marilyn merely smiled. "I know," she said. "All he wants to talk about when he calls me is Caroline. It's cute." She sighed. "I can hardly *wait* to be a mother so I can tell *him* about it. Just think, if I have a boy, maybe he and Jack's little girl can date one day. . . ."

"Do you want a boy?"

She nodded dreamily. "Mm. Girls have to go through such a lot of terrible things, growing up. . . . I just *feel* it's a boy too. . . . I told Jack he'd better get up here and see me *soon.* I mean, my body is doing the most *wonderful* things. . . ."

"Is Arthur happy about it?"

"Mm. I guess." She closed off this avenue of discussion firmly. "I think it's *great* Jack is such a good father, don't you?"

"Well, I don't think he's actually changing Caroline's diapers or burping her at night. But yes, I *do* think it's nice that he likes having a child, now that he and Jackie have one at last. Plenty of people don't."

"Tell me about it!" She helped herself to another cookie. "So you liked *Some Like It Hot?*"

"I think it's the best thing you've ever done. It's going to be a big hit," I said. "Count on it."

She shrugged. "Maybe. I'd rather die before I made another movie with that shit Billy, I'll tell you *that*."

"What's next?"

"The baby. Then I'm supposed to do a picture for Fox. It's about a zillionaire who falls in love with an off-Broadway actress. Older man, younger woman, you know? Jerry Wald is going to produce it. Last I heard, George Cukor's going to direct. I'm going back to California in a couple of weeks for it. . . ."

She seemed alarmingly indifferent about what sounded like yet another of 20th Century-Fox's inept attempts to showcase their most successful star. Despite Milton's efforts, Marilyn had never really succeeded in breaking away from the studio completely. Like a rebellious daughter, she was always coming home to be forgiven. "I thought you were going to do Arthur's script next," I said.

"He's still working on it. And we don't have Gable yet. Or John Huston. Anyway, I have to do another picture for Fox. It's all in the fucking contract Milton drew up for me, back in '55. Poor Milton. He should have stuck to photography."

I must have shown that I thought this was unfair, because she added quickly, "Oh, I don't mean it. I miss Milton more than anyone, really I do, but I could still wring his neck every time I think about that contract."

I didn't think the contract was Milton's fault—not entirely anyway. Over the years, Marilyn's contract with 20th Century-Fox had been amended and extended and modified and renego-tiated until it defied interpretation. It governed her life, from the number of pictures she could make to the directors the studio could offer her and even the amount of time she could spend on the East Coast. Although by now most of it had been rewritten on her behalf by countless lawyers, she was still in constant rebellion against it.

Marilyn settled herself comfortably back on the sofa, legs tucked up again, the box of cookies in her lap. "Is Jack going to be president?" she asked, her expression suddenly serious.

"I think so. Doesn't he talk to you about it?"

"Well, I think it embarrasses him to talk about it. With *me* anyway. . . ."

I could imagine that easily. Women were Jack's recreation, his way of escaping from the growing pressures of fulfilling his destiny. The last thing he would have wanted to discuss with Marilyn was the presidency.

"Things are looking good," I said. "Jack probably doesn't want to put a jinx on them by saying so, that's all."

"Oh, I'm the same way," she said. "I always say '*If* I get the part,' or whatever, never 'when.'"

"There are no sure things in politics," I said cautiously, "but Jack's doing better than anyone had hoped. Between what Jack's been doing on the Labor subcommittee and what he's been saying on the Senate Foreign Relations Committee, he's the only Democrat anybody's really talking about. Jack is beginning to *stand* for something in people's minds—a certain kind of cool, smart toughness, together with a lot of style. All he has to do is stay out of trouble and look more presidential than Lyndon Johnson or Hubert Humphrey. That shouldn't be impossible."

She giggled. "Staying out of trouble might be."

"Well, sure. But most of the press is on his side—even the reporters and columnists who don't agree with Jack *like* him. I don't think they're going to print anything about his love life."

She glanced at the watch on her wrist, frowned, and held it up to her ear to see if it was ticking. Marilyn seldom wore a watch, and even when she did, it never did much good. She simply had no sense of time, a problem that had manifested itself long before she became a star. It was entirely appropriate that, like the White Rabbit, she wore a watch that didn't work.

"What time is it?" she asked.

"A little after seven."

"Oh my gosh!" Her eyes opened wide. "I'm supposed to meet Arthur."

"What time?"

She bit her lip. "Six-thirty?"

"Where?"

"Downey's. We're going to the theater."

"You're going to have to hurry."

"Mm." She gave no sign of hurrying. Her expression suggested that the task of getting ready for the theater was beyond her. "Lena!" she shouted to her maid. "I'm late."

Lena appeared, looking flustered—Marilyn's inability to deal with time was catching, so that those who worked for her soon found themselves moving, by fits and starts, to her own uncertain rhythm. She carried a white dress on a hanger. "I'll run your bath," she said.

"Forget it. I don't have time. Besides, I like the way I smell." Marilyn glanced at the dress and shook her head, rejecting it as well as the bath.

"I'll go," I said. "I'm keeping you."

She nodded. She was on her feet now, frowning as she began to think about what she was going to wear. She had her reputation to think of: Marilyn Monroe was often late, but never a disappointment.

"Lena," she called, "get the red one, the one I wore for *Look?*" She gave me a wink. "It's cut down to here," she said, laughing, indicating a sweeping cleavage with one hand and a bare back down to her ass with the other. "What the hell, if you've got it, flaunt it, right?"

"Right." I gave her a kiss on the cheek.

"You're a real friend," she said, kissing me on the lips. I could taste her fresh, warm breath as her moist lips pressed briefly against mine, her eyes half closed as they were in the darkest and most shameful of my erotic fantasies about her. "Gotta go, honey," she whispered. Then she stopped, took both my hands in hers, and said, "I can't *wait* to be a mommy, David! I just know I'm going to be so *good* at it!"

"Of course you are," I said, but I didn't believe it. Nobody with Marilyn's problems could have been a good mother, and I suspect Marilyn—and certainly Arthur—must have known it.

As I was to learn, she turned up so late at Downey's that she never had time to eat anything, but her red dress caused a sensation, both at the restaurant and at the theater—particularly when she and Arthur went backstage after the performance to congratulate the star.

It was an evening of French songs, a one-man show by Yves Montand, who had starred in the French production of Miller's *The Crucible* in Paris, and whom Marilyn was to meet, fatefully, that night for the first time.

TIMMY HAHN SHELTERED UNDER THE AWNING OF MARILYN Monroe's building on East Fifty-seventh Street, hands deep in the pockets of his worn navy surplus pea jacket. He had skipped school again to keep his lonely vigil as the most faithful of her fans.

Timmy could hardly remember a time when he hadn't been a fan of Marilyn Monroe's. Even as a little kid, he followed her comings and goings in the press, waited for hours outside restaurants and hotels for a glimpse of her. By the time he was thirteen, he knew more about her life than any gossip columnist, and was the acknowledged leader of a small pack of youths of both sexes for whom being Marilyn Monroe fans was their whole life.

Most of these kids, in Timmy's opinion, were amateurs. He followed Marilyn's life in New York with the skill of a detective, and once managed to wave to her as she got into a cab on East Fifty-seventh Street, only to appear before she did at the door of the Actors Studio, waiting for her to arrive! When Marilyn stayed out late, he followed her faithfully, often guessing where she was going, since he knew her routines. His mother had long since given up complaining—he came and went as he pleased, sometimes spending the entire night on the street in pursuit of Marilyn, or, when he missed her, watching her old movies in all-night theaters.

By now he was something of a mascot to Marilyn. When she arrived at movie premieres or parties, she looked around for him, and if she couldn't see him in the crowd, she asked, "Where's Timmy?" and had the security guards find a place for him up front.

Through rain, snow, summer heat, and darkest night, Timmy had done his best to become Marilyn's shadow, but even he would have found it hard to explain why. Being a fan was something you couldn't explain to other people, Timmy thought. It was as if there were a bond, almost an electric current, between him and Marilyn. He knew about her unhappy childhood, and sometimes wondered if she saw in him some reflection of her own lonely years in foster homes and the orphanage. On *his* side, simply seeing her made him feel happy, that and the feeling that he was somehow serving her loyally by being there wherever she went.

It was almost like having a big sister, for he saw her not only when she was all done up, breathtakingly beautiful for some big event, but also when she was sneaking out to go shopping, her hair hidden under a scarf, without makeup or false eyelashes, wearing jeans and an old sweater. He knew which doctors she went to, the name and address of her dentist, where she shopped for groceries when she was in a domestic mood, the pharmacy where she got her prescriptions filled and bought hundreds of dollars' worth of cosmetics at a time.

He even left flowers with the doorman on her birthday, and was once rewarded with a brief note, written with what appeared to be an eyebrow pencil on a cocktail napkin monogrammed "MM," in a hand that was as unformed and childish as his own: "Dear Timmy, Thanx, you're a pal, Marilyn—P.S. Don't you ever go to school?"

The note was Timmy's greatest treasure—along with the school exercise book in which he laboriously recorded Marilyn's daily comings and goings with meticulous attention to time, place, and detail, for he thought of this as his life work.

Timmy sometimes wondered if Marilyn tried to fool him, but if that was the case, she wasn't very good at it.

It didn't take him long to find out about her visits to the Carlyle, and he was soon rewarded by the sight of Marilyn leaving the hotel disguised in a raincoat, with a scarf thrown over her hair. He did not show himself—he was adult enough to guess that she was seeing a man, and respected her privacy enough not to embarrass her by his presence, nor would he have dreamed of telling a soul. Still, he was curious to know whom she was visiting.

As a fourteen-year-old kid, he could hardly expect to get into the lobby of a hotel like the Carlyle, let alone question the desk clerk, but as luck would have it—and Timmy was a great believer in luck—he found the solution to the problem by accident, when he saw her come out of a side entrance with a man he recognized as Senator John F. Kennedy.

Politics did not interest Timmy; the fact that Marilyn was having an affair with Senator Kennedy did not impress him. He wrote it all down in his notebook, and kept as careful a log as he could of her visits to the Carlyle, but it didn't excite him the way seeing her together with another star did, like the unforgettable day when he had caught her having tea at Rumpelmayer's on Central Park South with Montgomery Clift.

He hoped she was happy. Her husband, Arthur Miller, always looked sort of grim when he was with Marilyn. Timmy, more than anything else, prayed for her happiness.

He couldn't help noticing that in recent weeks he wasn't the only person watching Marilyn. In addition to himself and the rest of the little band of loyal fans (none as loyal as *him*, of course!), there were other, more shadowy watchers, grown-ups, unsmiling men in dark suits, white shirts, and plain ties, with the highly polished, thick-soled shoes that said "cops" to Timmy (he had an uncle in the Bronx who was a detective), or even "FBI."

Night after night he stood under the streetlight, straining his eyes, and wrote it all down in his notebook in a firm schoolboy hand, while the agents watched.

He wondered why they were interested in Marilyn; then it occurred to him that perhaps it was Senator Kennedy they were interested in, not her. From time to time he said hello to them, as if they were colleagues on a stakeout, but they never said anything back, or even cracked a smile.

FBI, he concluded. Definitely.

He noted down David Leman's departure—by now he knew everybody who visited Marilyn—then settled down to wait for her to leave for dinner or the theater.

He didn't mind waiting, however long it took.

24

WHEN I GOT HOME FROM MARILYN'S I FOUND A NOTE WAIT-
ing for me—a simple, typed message, on plain paper, inviting
me to dinner the next day—from Paul Palermo.

Maria was skiing in Gstaad, where I was to join her in a few
days, and I had no plans, so I called his service and accepted.
Paul didn't frighten me; in fact, I rather liked him.

The fact that Paul even *had* a service indicates how different he was from his colleagues, most of whom still did their
business from pay phones, carrying bags of dimes. Paul was
the new breed. He owned nightclubs, restaurants, a couple of
off-Broadway theaters; he even invested in plays from time to
time, which is how I first made his acquaintance. He was also
a member of what law enforcement agencies always referred to
as "the Bonanno Crime Family," as well as, more important, a
nephew by marriage of Joseph Bonanno himself.

Bonanno was the leader of one of New York City's five
families and, as such, among the most powerful—and respected—figures in organized crime. More than this, he was a don,
a "man of honor" of the old school. Not only did he have five
hundred soldiers working for him in the streets of Brooklyn,
running numbers games, loansharking, hijacking, and carrying
out a rich and profitable trade in extortion, he was also the
respected leader of his community, a kind of lawgiver and
supreme fixer for his fellow Sicilians—and, later, the model
for Mario Puzo's "Godfather."

Although he had already moved west to semiretirement in
Tucson, leaving his son to look after the family's interests
in New York, his word was still law in most of Brooklyn,
as well as respected by his fellow dons on the Commission,
where he had until recently reigned as *capo di tutti capi*,
or "Boss of Bosses," being one of the few to give up that
honor alive.

Paul had great respect for his uncle by marriage—he would have been foolhardy not to—but he was himself a very different kind of man, at least on the surface: a graduate of Fordham who ordered his suits custom-made at Morty Sills's and had a handsomely appointed office in the Paramount Building. Once when somebody asked him if he ever carried a gun, he replied, "Sure, when I was officer of the day at Camp Pendleton." Paul had not only been a Marine, he was a member of the Knights of Columbus, the New York Veteran Police Association, and the Mayor's Task Force on Juvenile Crime.

I met him the next evening at eight, at Rao's, on 114th Street and Pleasant Avenue in East Harlem. In those days, it was still a straightforward mob restaurant. Once, just before the Fourth of July, some kids set off firecrackers in the street outside, and at the sound of the explosions everybody in the restaurant dove for cover and drew a piece. Rao's was that kind of place, and also served good, honest Sicilian food, the best in town, before celebrities like Woody Allen and Pete Hamill made it fashionable.

Palermo was waiting for me in booth 1, the nearest to the kitchen. I ordered a dry martini—the bartender at Rao's looked like an ex-prizefighter, but his skill would not have been out of place at the Ritz Bar in Paris. Paul drank wine while Annie, Vinnie Rao's wife, who helped him in the kitchen, told us what we were going to eat. There was a menu at Rao's, which never changed, but it was understood that you ate what Annie thought you should eat and what Vinnie wanted to cook, and you were better off that way. *"Bene,"* Paul said with satisfaction, as if he had chosen our meal himself. "It's good to see you, David."

I lifted my glass. Paul and I had, as they say, "a history." He usually came to me when there was trouble in store for one of my clients—a famous television comedian who ran up more debts than he could handle with a book-ie; a radio talk show host in Miami who was way behind on paying his weekly "vig" to a loan shark, despite having been held upside down by his ankles off the balcony of his penthouse suite at the Roney Plaza; a singer who had so far forgotten his roots that he turned down a request to top the bill at a Las Vegas casino. . . . In each case, Paul had gently pointed out to me, over dinner, the importance of making my clients do "the right thing," before, as he liked to put it, "things got out of hand" or "the wrong people" got involved.

Do not think that I wasn't grateful for such advice. Anything that kept my clients from being killed or jailed was all right with me. What Paul wanted in return were comparatively minor favors, mostly getting some of the bigger talent to appear in his clubs from time to time, and occasional help with PR.

We chatted about the theater while we ate our seafood salad—the best in the city, by far. It wasn't until we'd finished our veal chops with sweet and sour peppers that Palermo got down to business over the espresso and Sambuca. "You know," he said, "your friends the Kennedys might want to let up on Hoffa. It's just a friendly suggestion."

I raised an eyebrow. Hoffa's friends were in Chicago and Vegas. The New York families, so far as I knew, had other fish to fry. "Hoffa wasn't a cooperative witness," I said. "It's nobody's fault but his own. I had the impression everybody understood that."

Paul shrugged. His dark, doelike eyes were infinitely sad. "They understand. But it's a worry, you know? It was a lousy thing the papers got hold of that story about how he has a girlfriend and they have a kid together."

"I agree. So does Jack. It wasn't anybody's fault. Some hotshot young lawyer from the Justice Department leaked it. These things happen."

"Well, sure. But Hoffa's a madman on the subject, which is hard to figure because his wife knew all about the other broad anyway. She and Sylvia were friends. They all lived together for a while in one house, believe it or not—Hoffa, the wife, the mistress, and the kid. . . ." He sighed. "I should be so lucky. My wife would kill me. My mistress too, probably."

Paul shook his head. "Frankly, Hoffa is making a lot of wild threats, David. Talking about taking out a contract on Bobby Kennedy, even on the Senator." He leaned close to me across the table. I could smell the garlic on his breath. "I got a call from Tucson," he whispered, in the same tone of awe that a bishop might use to describe a call from His Holiness in Rome.

"Tucson?"

"From Mr. B." Paul always referred to the retired Boss of Bosses as Mr. B.

"I'm surprised he's interested. Isn't this a little out of his, ah, jurisdiction?"

Paul looked pained. "Just because he's in Tucson doesn't mean Mr. B. doesn't take an interest. He hears things, David. What he hears lately, he doesn't like."

He accepted a cigar and went about the business of lighting it. "Mr. B.," he went on between puffs, "thinks of himself as an elder statesman, you know what I mean? He's not going to tell the members of the Commission what to do, but he offers them his advice, the wisdom of his experience, whenever he feels there's a problem."

"And what exactly is upsetting him out there in Tucson?" I asked.

"To tell you the truth, David," he said, "we have *big* problems, which is one reason why we don't need all this Hoffa shit on top of everything else." His expression made it clear that we had come at last to the reason for this dinner. "I mean, you tell *me* how the United States government let this bearded Commie punk Castro take over in Cuba! It's like we're a second-class power! Mr. B. told me if Harry Truman was still president, this would never have happened, and he's got a point. We'd have sent in the fucking Marines. If Batista couldn't hack it, we'd have put some guy who could in his place, am I right?"

I nodded. Castro's recent seizure of power in Cuba was on everybody's mind, including Jack's, who still hoped that Castro might turn out to be a liberal reformer, sympathetic to the United States. I suspected that Mr. B. and his friends were probably correct, since they knew more about Cuba than anyone else, and had predicted just these events.

"How bad is it?" I asked.

"Bad. The casinos alone are worth billions, and they're gone, just like that." He lit a match and blew it out. "A fucking catastrophe. Ike should have dropped an A-bomb on this cocksucker Castro when he was still in the Sierra Maestra."

Paul shook his head again, presumably at the weakness of politicians and generals. The fact that Batista's fall was a financial disaster for the mob was something that nobody had as yet considered. Their investment in Havana was huge—casinos, hotels, beach resorts, prostitution, and narcotics earned them millions, far more than Las Vegas. Castro's first act had been to send them packing, even going so far as to jail Santo

Trafficante, which, so far as the mob was concerned, was the equivalent of locking up the American ambassador.

"Frankly," he went on, "the worst of the whole thing is that it makes Vegas more important than it was. Before, we had casinos in Havana and in Vegas. Now there's only Vegas— and that makes Hoffa more important." He stared at me questioningly. "Why?"

"Because construction of the Vegas casinos was financed by the Teamster pension fund?" Moe had explained this to me years ago.

He nodded approvingly. "I always said you were smart. I told Mr. B. so the other day."

I wasn't exactly pleased to have been a subject of conversation between Paul and Mr. B.

"I don't know that there's too much I can do," I said. "I'm not sure there's all that much Jack can do, come to that. Anyway, he's got to get elected first."

"Well, we know that, David. But let's say he *gets* elected, a tough policy on Cuba—*really* tough, I mean getting rid of Castro—is something that would win him a lot of friends. Powerful friends." He paused to give me a significant look. "*Grateful* friends."

"I see."

"Another thing. The people I'm talking about, they *know* Cuba—*really* know it, David, not like these fucking Ivy League amateurs in the CIA. My people can get things done over there in Cuba that nobody else can do, if somebody says the word. Nobody in this administration wants to listen to us, which is crazy. You tell the Senator that if he's gonna get tough with Castro, we're with him, all the way. He helps us, we can help him, okay?"

"I'll pass the word on, Paul."

"Good." Paul called for the check, his mission, I thought, accomplished. He leaned even closer instead. "On the Hoffa thing, all anybody asks is don't send him to the slammer. It's the one thing that really scares the shit out of him. He's afraid of getting fucked in the ass." He laughed. "We need the son of a bitch, so his worry is our worry. Besides, if he goes to the slammer, all hell is going to break loose. I mean, the Senator has to do what he has to do, sure, but tell him not to let Bobby push Hoffa too far. It's like this thing with Hoffa's mistress. I mean, how would the Senator like it if everybody knew about his girls?"

I stared at him, hoping that I looked outraged and unbelieving. "What girls?"

Paul paid the bill from a thick bankroll. "Come on, David, you know what's going on, we know what's going on. It's no big deal. What you have to remember is, *Hoffa* probably knows what's going on too. That, the Senator *should* worry about."

We stood up. Paul made his rounds, shaking hands, embracing his friends, giving a kiss on the cheek to more senior *mafiosi* of the old school. We said our lengthy good-byes to the Raos, squeezed together in the hot little kitchen, then stepped out into the street, taking a deep breath of fresh air, the salt smell of the East River bearing away the garlic odor and the cigar smoke. "Hoffa's a mad dog," Palermo said. "I've seen them before. With mad dogs, it's kill 'em or leave 'em be."

"I'll tell the Senator what you said."

Paul's car was approaching, a Cadillac with blacked-out windows. Mine was waiting across the street.

"Tell him it's what Mr. B. says, not me. Mr. B. looks at the big picture. Hoffa doesn't matter that much in the big picture. Still, something's got to be done; otherwise, someone's going to get hit in the long run."

Paul stepped into his car. "Good night, David," he called as the door closed. "Sweet dreams."

If I had expected Jack to be shocked by Palermo's offer to assassinate Fidel Castro for him, I would have been disappointed. He was too much the realist to be shocked by anything except incompetence. I could tell by the gleam in his eye that he was interested, and I instantly regretted having told him.

He was lying in bed at the Carlyle, a breakfast tray across his lap. He had come through New York at the tail end of a series of speaking engagements—since the convention, he was the one Democrat people wanted to hear from, and a whole staff of people had been engaged to schedule his appearances, as well as a new brain trust, fortified by liberal intellectuals and academics who had deserted the Stevenson camp to join him.

Relations with the eggheads, as Jack called them, were testy at first, since they had attacked him and his father bitterly during the fight for the vice presidential nomination, but the association soon paid off in the form of better, crisper speeches, numerous articles in *The New York Times* under Jack's name, and a generally enhanced intellectual atmosphere. Needless to say, the members of what Bobby called, with undisguised contempt, "the faculty club" were kept well away from the Ambassador and out of any meetings involving strategy, for fear of contaminating their innocence. There was no need for Jack's new brain trust to know that their candidate was in communication with Mafia leaders, or to hear about the deals his father was making with Democratic political bosses all over the country.

I couldn't help noticing that the sheets of Jack's bed were rumpled beyond what even the most restless sleeper could achieve, and there were lipstick stains on the pillows. There was a familiar scent of Chanel No. 5 in the room, from which I concluded that Marilyn had been there.

I helped myself to a cup of coffee from his tray while he filled me in on his plans. Bobby was coming on board to take charge of the campaign, which stood badly in need of his energy, ruthless dedication to winning, and total devotion to Jack. The Ambassador, meanwhile, was dropping—somewhat unwillingly—out of sight, on the grounds that the less the public saw of him, the better.

Jack's travels around the country, in the new family plane, *Caroline*—another useful contribution from the Ambassador—had, if nothing else, hardened his attitude toward Fidel Castro. He was beginning to discover that the opinions of the average American voter on foreign policy are diametrically opposed to those of the academics and intellectuals. Since he was determined to appeal to both groups, he had his work cut out for him.

"Your guinea friends have got the right idea about Castro," he told me. "I'll say that for them. Ike has gone weak at the knees. He's an old man—too old to be president."

"You won't be saying that when you're his age, Jack."

"Christ, I'm never going to reach his age. You say they're still worrying about Hoffa?"

"They don't like him any better than you do, but they have a major investment in him to protect. All they want is to make sure he doesn't have to go to jail."

"I can't promise that. Jail is exactly where Bobby wants him."

"You said you'd ask Bobby to stall."

He looked annoyed. I guessed Bobby hadn't been easy to win over, or that Jack hadn't even tried. "It's not in his nature to stall," Jack said. "Still, as Bobby takes over the campaign, he'll be busy. I can make sure he doesn't have the time to think about Hoffa. In the meantime, something may happen. . . . We'll see."

I thought Jack's attitude was a little too casual, as usual, on this subject. "Jack," I said, "I'm telling you: *Take this seriously*."

Something in my voice must have convinced him. "I understand," he said impatiently. "I'll take care of it, David. I promise."

Of course, looking back on it, I can see that this was the time to tell Jack I was off the case, especially since a certain shifty look in his eyes warned me that he hadn't any real intention of laying down the law to Bobby, but like Jack himself, I was suffering from presidential fever, vicariously in my case. In the big picture, the complaints of Jimmy Hoffa and the mob seemed like a minor problem, one of the countless small difficulties that could be smoothed over once Jack was in the White House.

"What else did they have to say?" he asked.

"A thinly veiled warning that they know about what Paul Palermo called your 'girls,' " I told him.

Jack threw back his head and laughed. "Jesus!" he said. "You've got to be kidding!"

I shook my head. "Paul said they knew all about them. He hinted that Hoffa may know about them too."

"Christ, *everybody* knows about them! There's hardly a journalist in New York and Washington who *doesn't* know about my private life, but you and I both know nobody's ever going to print anything."

"Well, I'm not so sure. About most of it, sure, but a story that involved Marilyn might be too juicy not to print."

"You've got Marilyn on the brain, David. Sometimes I wonder why. . . . Anyway, nobody really knows about me and Marilyn, except people who won't talk to the press, like you and Peter."

"I didn't like what Paul had to say—or rather, the way he said it, Jack. It sounded to me as if he knew a lot more than he was saying, frankly."

"Did he mention her by name?"

"No."

"There you are. How the hell would he know anything? We've been pretty goddamn discreet."

It was on the tip of my tongue to point out that bringing Marilyn to the Cal-Neva Lodge in Tahoe wasn't my idea of discretion, but I didn't. "I'll tell you what went through my mind when he was talking to me," I said. "What if somebody was bugging you?"

"Bugging?"

"Microphones. Telephone taps. That sort of thing."

He shook his head wearily. "You've been reading too many spy novels. It's not possible, anyway."

"Why?"

"Because Dad's old pal J. Edgar Hoover has somebody check that out at regular intervals—here, at home, in my Senate office—as a favor to Dad. Hoover's been taking care of that for years."

Jack, I noticed, talked about Hoover as if he were a family retainer. Knowing the old fox as I did, I didn't share that view. It was *Hoover's* listening devices I was afraid of—I had a professional sweep my office and apartment regularly—but I knew Jack had an exaggerated faith in Hoover and, of course, absolute faith in his father.

"Well, if you think there's nothing to worry about . . ." I said, unconvinced.

"Who's worried?"

"I am."

"It's not worth it, David. Worrying does no good." He stretched his arms, grimacing from the pain in his back.

"Did Marilyn talk to you about her having a baby?" I asked.

"Christ, yes! She gave me an earful on the subject! It's hard to imagine her as a mother, somehow. . . . Although she seems pretty happy about it."

"Too happy, I thought."

Jack raised an eyebrow. "After all," I went on, "having the child means affirming the marriage. And I'm not sure she *wants* the marriage. Or the father."

"He seems like a nice enough guy," Jack said with a shrug, "according to Marilyn." He chuckled. "And easygoing," he added. "For a writer."

I was not sure either of those descriptions suited Arthur Miller—though certainly they represented ideal qualities in Marilyn's husband from Jack's point of view.

"Have you ever heard of a woman who was happy with a nice enough guy as a husband? In the long run?"

He thought about this for a moment, grinning hugely. "No, I guess not," he said. "Though most of the married women I've slept with always start out by saying how much they love their husbands. Even Marilyn. Arthur is noble. Arthur is a genius. Arthur deserves a better wife than she's been. She doesn't want to hurt Arthur. She wants Arthur's happiness more than anything. Arthur would die if he knew what she was doing. All this, you understand, while she's fucking me." He sighed. "Do you suppose anybody understands women?"

"You seem to do pretty well," I said. I didn't recall hearing Marilyn say any of this to *me* about Miller. She must save it all for Jack, I thought. I glanced at my watch, anxious to leave rather than sit here listening to Jack share Marilyn's pillow talk with me.

He glanced at his own watch on the bedside table. "Christ, I've got to get going myself," he said, swinging out of bed. He slipped into his robe. "The reason I do pretty well, David"— he flashed me that famous Kennedy grin—"is that I don't even *try* to understand women. It's a waste of time, in my opinion. I leave the understanding to their husbands."

25

FROM THE MOMENT SHE WAS BACK IN CALIFORNIA AND read the script for *Let's Make Love,* she despised it. Once she was comfortably installed in her bungalow at the Beverly Hills Hotel and read it again, she despised it even more. It was typical 20th Century-Fox schlock—exactly the kind of thing that she had outgrown.

Her doubts about the script were reinforced when it became impossible to find a leading man, but Fox pushed on, determined to get a new Marilyn Monroe picture in distribution as soon as possible to capitalize on the success of *Some Like It Hot*. She had contractual approval of her leading man, but it was Arthur who finally suggested Montand.

The suggestion was an odd one, and at first nobody took it seriously, least of all her. Montand was a French singer, unknown to the average American moviegoer, although he had a certain reputation among intellectuals for his performance in *The Wages of Fear* and because he was widely known to hold left-wing views.

When she met Montand backstage in New York, she had been impressed by his compact, rough-hewn good looks and his Gallic charm, but she was more impressed by his wife, Simone Signoret, whose electrifying performance in *Room at the Top* had made her suddenly famous.

Even the presence of Mme. Montand had not prevented Montand from flirting with her, but she assumed that that was normal for a Frenchman, and attached no importance to it. Even Simone had joked about it: "Look at him!" she growled affectionately, in a low, rasping, chain-smoker's voice that managed to be sexy and tough at the same time. "He can't take his eyes off you."

The two couples became friendly in New York, often dining together after the theater, and for the first time in ages, Arthur seemed to be enjoying himself. Arthur and Yves (as she was soon calling him) shared not only a political outlook but all sorts of cultural references, as Arthur did with Simone. Simone treated Arthur with the special respect the French reserve for great writers, sometimes, only half jokingly, calling him Maître—the equivalent of calling him a genius if you were American, Simone explained to her.

The friendship with the Montands was the one bright spot in Arthur's life. She had lost the baby, and with it, any desire to try again, while he was still grimly rewriting *The Misfits* in an attempt to make Gay Langland into someone Gable could see himself playing. In some mysterious way Yves and Simone became vital to her marriage.

When it became obvious at last that none of the male stars who were acceptable to her wanted the part of the multimillionaire in *Let's Make Love*, and that she would not accept any of the studio's countersuggestions, Montand was brought up again and instantly accepted by the studio. Within twenty-four hours he was flown to Los Angeles, tested for the part, and offered more money than he had ever made before.

The truth was, as she knew perfectly well—but Yves didn't—that the studio would have accepted anyone she was willing to work with. Fox was a sinking ship. Her old nemesis Darryl Zanuck, embittered and feeble, had been driven into exile in Europe, leaving the studio in the uncertain hands of desperate, frightened men, awash in a sea of red ink. Her contract was their major asset. Her name was their only hope.

Nobody was more pleased at the news that Yves would be working with her than poor Arthur, reduced now to a minor supporting role as her husband, with nothing much to do in a town where the only thing anybody cares about is what you are doing. He arranged to have the Montands moved into bungalow 20 at the Beverly Hills Hotel, next door to them with a connecting door.

In bungalow 19, below their adjoining suites, lived Howard Hughes (who had once tried to hire her after seeing her photograph on the cover of *Laff* magazine in 1945) and his wife Jean Peters, who had played in *Niagara* with her in 1953. The idea of living in the same bungalow as Howard Hughes was fascinating to Simone, who spent many hours a day waiting in vain for a glimpse of the reclusive billionaire.

Relations with the Montands were easygoing and neighborly, as if they were sharing a summer cottage. In Hollywood, they were strangers in the world she had grown up in, happy to have her advice and companionship. She and Simone went shopping together, exchanged gossip, even cooked meals together sometimes in one of their tiny kitchenettes.

As for Yves, he stuck as close to her as a faithful dog at the studio. He had never worked in a Hollywood studio, and was acutely conscious of his own lack of status as a foreign singer whose only big movie played in "art houses." Lonely, slightly bewildered, afraid of failing now that his big break was at hand, Yves spent the time between takes in her dressing room, traveled back and forth in the same studio limousine with her, rehearsed his lines with her, asked her advice about everyone he met.

She found his presence strangely comforting. He was a good listener, unfailingly sympathetic, interested in everything she did. For the first time in years, she *enjoyed* going to the studio, and with his gentle, supportive coaxing even managed to turn up on time, or very nearly so, and remember her lines. It was, she thought, as if she were his teacher when it came to the ins and outs of Hollywood and studio politics, while he became her teacher in preparing herself for her role. Not that he was a great actor, but he approached his work with the robust calm of a competent workman, without doubts or drama, and some of his calm rubbed off on her. Of course, Paula was jealous, but for once she could live without Paula's mothering and yentalike advice. In some curious way, hating the picture, hating being back in Hollywood again, knowing her marriage to Arthur was on the skids, she was happy playing Yves's studio tour guide. . . .

When she was young, she had always wanted to be "a good girl," had but never quite succeeded. Even at twelve or thirteen, her body was so startlingly mature that nobody ever gave her the benefit of the doubt.

There was still a part of her that yearned for virtue—the good girl within, truthful, obedient, and chaste. She yearned to be true to *someone*, but being true to a man who was married, had lots of girls, and was a candidate for the Democratic presidential nomination was hard to do. She'd *told* Jack he'd better visit her soon, and he hadn't listened. Or rather, he had listened and treated it as a joke.

It wasn't anything as simple as wanting to teach Jack a lesson—she wanted him to be here, and he couldn't be, so in a spirit of resentment she told her troubles to Yves, who proved a willing if baffled listener.

Maybe it was part of Yves's charm, maybe it was because he was French, but he could listen for *hours*, fascinated by every detail, not afraid to ask the most intimate questions, quick to laugh or touch her hand in a gesture of sympathy.

It was like confessing to the world's sexiest priest—one who had made no vows of celibacy—and she felt herself offering up to him her innermost fears and secrets.

She felt bad about even the *idea* of fucking Yves, not only because of Jack but because she liked and admired Simone and thought of her as a friend. But when Simone was nominated for Best Actress by the Academy and she wasn't, she felt such rage and jealousy (which she was obliged to conceal under a nauseating mask of gracious congratulations) that she might have hopped into bed with Yves then and there out of sheer revenge. She had appeared in twenty-seven movies, in at least eleven of which she had a starring role, and had never been nominated even once, while Simone, a foreigner, had copped a nomination for Best Actress first time out, despite the fact that she was practically a Communist, according to Louella Parsons! It wasn't fair, she told herself over and over, especially since *Some Like It Hot* was the best shot she'd had at an Oscar in years.

It *still* might not have happened if Simone hadn't actually *won* the fucking Oscar, becoming, overnight, a sensation in Hollywood. For Simone's Oscar was a popular choice, proof that Hollywood could reward quality and recognize talent in a low-budget foreign movie with foreign stars; proof, too, that the dark days of the McCarthy era were over, that despite Louella Parsons, and Hedda Hopper, and Ronnie Reagan, and all the right-wing witch hunters who ran the studios, a woman who stood up for left-wing causes and was associated with the French Communist party could still win. Simone made Hollywood feel proud of itself, and it showed in the way people greeted her in the street when she went shopping, or stood up and applauded her when she entered a restaurant or the lobby of the Beverly Hills Hotel—while at the same time, nobody had a good word for *her* performance in *Let's Make Love*, which everybody in town was already dismissing as just another piece of mindless, lackluster vulgarity. . . .

She could tell that Yves wanted her, even though he liked Arthur and felt a great bond with him. Even in France, it seemed, fucking your best friend's wife was frowned upon by good guys, and Yves was a French version of a good guy.

So she and Yves managed somehow to stay on their best behavior, while she and Simone went shopping, or had their hair done together, or tried on each other's clothes, wandering back and forth from one suite to the other in their negligees (or, in Marilyn's case, undressed) as if they were all one big happy family.

If she had cried when Simone won the Oscar, she cried even harder when Jack called to cancel his LA trip for the *third* time. Oh, she understood his reason—California was in the bag, he thought, it was the East he was worried about—but she took it as a rejection, and took it harder than he knew. Still, she did her best to hold herself back.

What did it, finally, was the fact that Simone was obliged to go back to Paris to start a new picture, while Arthur, with a blindness few husbands could have matched, decided to fly to Ireland to make the final revisions on the script of *The Misfits* with John Huston, leaving her, as he put it, "in Yves's hands."

It was almost, she thought, as if Arthur *wanted* her to have an affair with Yves—or perhaps it was just that he was by now so separated from her feelings that he no longer noticed them, and therefore ignored the obvious attraction between them. Yet even when they were finally alone, she and Yves didn't go to bed together until the night they appeared at a supper party at the David Selznicks', hand in hand, causing everyone present to lift an eyebrow in surprise—except for Byron Holtzer, one of Hollywood's most famous bachelor men-about-town and toughest superlawyers, and for many reasons no friend of hers, whom she happened to overhear telling somebody that Joe Schenck was dying, had already slipped into a coma.

She felt a stabbing pain as guilt shot through her. She had known that Joe was gravely ill, but she had a thousand reasons for not going to visit him, beginning with her intense fear of death and sickness, and ending with the fact that she hadn't any desire to relive her days as Joe's mistress. All the same, Joe had been good to her—better than anyone else in those days. Once she became famous, she had neglected the old man, and was ashamed of it now.

"He *can't* be in a coma," she cried. "Someone would have told me!"

The moment the words were out of her mouth, she knew it was a mistake. Plenty of people had told her. Holtzer was a close friend of Schenck's, and a formidable opponent in court and out, who had no reason to spare her feelings. *"Bullshit!"* he growled fiercely, his powerful voice bringing the entire room to instant silence. "Save your fucking tears for somebody who doesn't know you, Marilyn."

Now that she was engaged in a contest with him, she couldn't back off. The Selznicks were Hollywood royalty—Mrs. Selznick was Jennifer Jones, David Selznick had produced *Gone With the Wind*. Almost everybody who mattered in the industry was gathered, their attention now fixed on her, Holtzer, and a puzzled Yves Montand, who didn't know who Joe Schenck was, or Holtzer for that matter.

"I've got to see Joe," she said. "Now. He needs me."

Holtzer scented blood. "*Needs* you? He's unconscious. He was naive enough to hope you'd come to say good-bye, but you didn't give a shit, did you? Now it's too late."

Even the waiters stood, trays in hand, transfixed by the scene. Her skills as an actress failed her completely. "Hold on a minute!" she stammered angrily, tears running down her cheeks, while Yves held her arm, trying to pull her away, muttering, "We have to go, *chérie,* we have to go."

She shook her arm loose and confronted Holtzer. "Joe would understand," she said.

"He understood, all right. He understood you didn't give a shit about him. It broke his fucking heart."

"If you're not going, I am," Yves said, horrified at being at the center of this storm. "I can't take this."

She hardly even heard him—or rather, she heard the words but missed their significance entirely. It wasn't until Doris Vidor and Edie Goetz had pulled her away from Holtzer, tears still streaming down her face, her hands trembling, that she realized Yves had gone, at which point, deserted and alone, knowing that everyone would surely take Holtzer's side against hers since he was one of the old guard, she pushed aside the two women and ran into the driveway screaming, "Walt for me, wait for me!"

She ran as fast as she could, stumbling on her stiletto heels, her hair coming apart, her clutch bag opening to spill keys, Kleenex, her compact, and a couple of just-in-case Tampaxes onto the Selznicks' Spanish-tiled driveway. Ahead of her she saw the taillights of Yves's rented car gleaming, but she knew she could never catch up with him. She was screaming at the top of her lungs now; then she saw the brake lights come on, and knew he had stopped, and felt her whole body inside turn liquid.

She flung open the door, grabbed him in her arms, so roughly that she tore his shirt, kissed him fiercely, driving her tongue deep into his mouth, moaning, keening in a high-pitched voice as if she were in the grips of pain too terrible to bear.

"Not here," he whispered. "Not like this." He put the car in gear, comforting her in French in a low voice.

She closed her eyes. The drive seemed endless, though it was only a few minutes from the Selznicks' to the Beverly Hills Hotel. He parked the car in the street illegally, close to the bungalow, and half carried, half dragged her inside, dropping her on the bed. Then he undressed her, slowly, carefully, as if now that he knew they were going to make love at last, he wanted to savor it fully. . . .

26

SHE HADN'T ANTICIPATED THE SIZE AND IMPACT OF THE scandal. Her affair with Jack was a secret, partly because secrecy mattered to him; partly, she had begun to realize, because the Kennedys had friends and power everywhere in the media, but Yves enjoyed no such protection. He was merely an actor and a singer, married to a movie star who had just won Best Actress—fair game for the press.

Besides, unlike Jack, Yves shrewdly sensed that the affair with her was his ticket to fame. He was intensely ambitious for Hollywood stardom. After all, Maurice Chevalier had proved years ago that a Frenchman could become a major Hollywood star, and as soon as the news about himself and Marilyn broke, people stopped asking, "Who's Yves Montand?"

As for her, she had what she had so far never had with Jack—a kind of make-believe marriage, with all the burrs and rough edges of marriage removed. Not only could she *talk* to Yves, they spent their nights together, ate together, went to work together.

She even enjoyed being told what to do by Yves, she who never did a thing her husbands wanted her to do! He played the role—which came naturally enough to him—of a European husband who puts up with no nonsense from his wife, while she played the dutiful little woman who does what he says, including turning up for work on time! She even cooked for him, in the tiny kitchen of the Miller suite, while he praised her efforts extravagantly. She felt renewed, as if she had finally succeeded in turning over a new leaf.

Her headaches stopped, her period was practically painless, she slept like a log with only a minimum maintenance dose of sleeping pills and woke up early every morning with a clear head. The only thing that made her anxious was that they never talked about the future.

Of course, not wanting to spoil things, she didn't press him—she had already guessed it wasn't something he was going to bring up himself. Yves, she knew, received letters and telephone calls daily from Simone, while Arthur, sounding tired and withdrawn over the transatlantic phone line, called her regularly, reporting on his work with Huston. At some point, she knew, he would return; at some point they would have to start work on *The Misfits;* at some point it would be necessary to discuss what had happened—but in the meantime, it was easier to forget all that in Yves's arms.

Cukor took advantage of her good mood to press on with *Let's Make Love,* with a speed never seen before on a Marilyn Monroe picture, and that made her happy too, except for the nagging thought that the sooner the picture was over, the sooner she and Yves would have to face reality.

She did not really notice how public the affair had become until it was too late. She and Yves had better things to do than read the gossip columns or the international gutter press, after all. It was as if a glass wall separated them from the rest of the world—people could see them, but nobody could reach them.

Only Cukor breached the wall to warn her gently that they were playing with fire.

She told him not to worry. She could handle it. . . .

As fate would have it, I flew to California with Arthur on his return from Ireland. I switched seats to sit next to him—I didn't want him to think I was avoiding him—but we didn't speak much. He seemed preoccupied and withdrawn, which wasn't like him really, because he was usually pretty outgoing for a serious writer.

There were a number of French film people on the airplane, traveling to Los Angeles on some deal, and I remember being embarrassed on Arthur's behalf that they were all passing around a copy of *Paris-Match* with a photograph on the cover of Marilyn and Montand kissing—clearly a passionate, private kiss captured by a hidden photographer. The French movie people talked about *"Yves et Marilyn"* all the way from New York to Los Angeles, while Arthur, hunched over in his seat, did his best to conceal his misery and, for all I knew, anger.

We talked about Ireland, about Huston, about *The Misfits,* which I thought he was clinging to fiercely. Perhaps by now he had invested so much of himself and his time in the script that he couldn't bear to let it go unmade—as if it were the only thing he could salvage from the ruins of his love for Marilyn.

At some point in the journey, after the meal, I dozed off. When I woke up, Arthur was staring out the window at the bright blue sky, his hands clenched so tightly in his lap that the knuckles showed white, his dinner tray still untouched before him. There were tears on his cheek, reflecting the harsh, stratospheric light so they shimmered and shone on his sallow skin.

Coward that I am, I closed my eyes and feigned sleep rather than confront his misery. I consoled myself that he probably wanted to be left alone.

After we arrived and I claimed my bags, I found him waiting outside with his luggage, obviously looking for a driver.

"It looks as if nobody's been sent to pick me up," he said.

I offered him a lift, and we rode together to the Beverly Hills Hotel. "It's not a town I'm fond of," he mused glumly, looking out at Sepulveda Boulevard. "It's a town for beginnings, not endings."

There didn't seem anything to say to that, so we sat in silence until we arrived beneath the hotel's famous pink porte cochere. "Good luck," I said, but he merely nodded, his mind on the coming scene.

*   *   *

I ran into Marilyn in the coffee shop the next morning. Her eyes were puffy and she looked as if she hadn't slept all night. It was as if all her glamour had gone, along with her brief happiness. "How did it go?" I asked her. "With Arthur?"

She looked at me over the rim of her coffee cup and shrugged. "Not great," she said.

"We flew in together, you know."

"He told me. He was grateful for the lift. I was supposed to order a car for him, and I forgot."

"Well, he's a gentleman. Have the two of you decided what you're going to do?"

"Stay married, I guess," she said, in a tone of utter dejection. "What are you doing here?"

"Well, the convention's going to be in Los Angeles, you know. . . ."

She looked puzzled for a moment. At this moment of her life nothing was real to her except her own problems. "Oh," she said at last, "the *convention*. Sure." Then she brightened a little. "How's Jack?"

"Good. Going twenty-four hours a day. You know Jackie's pregnant again?"

"Uh-huh." Marilyn's pupils narrowed, and she quickly changed the subject. "Is Jack going to win the nomination?" she asked, moving to safer ground.

"I think it's likely." I knocked wood on the countertop. "Have you been following things?"

"Not as closely as I'd like, frankly." That I guessed, was putting it mildly, given what had been going on between her and Montand.

I made myself comfortable and proceeded to fill her in. In the beginning of the year, I told her, Bobby had dropped the first shoe by announcing that Jack was entering the New Hampshire primary, which, as a native New Englander, he won easily. The other shoe dropped with a loud thud when the news leaked out that the Kennedy brothers had outmaneuvered their opponents by persuading the reluctant governor of Ohio to endorse Jack's candidacy, which meant Jack would be free to put all his resources into confronting Hubert Humphrey in the Wisconsin primary.

Jack had to beat Humphrey convincingly on Humphrey's own turf, and knock him out of the race early on so he could arrive in Los Angeles the favored candidate. A long, bitter struggle against Humphrey would divide the party and leave the nomination open to Symington, who had the support of Harry Truman and the older party regulars, or Johnson, who was campaigning hard in the Senate cloakroom.

Already the tide of dirty politics was washing up at Jack's feet—there were rumors that he had been secretly married before his marriage to Jackie, that his health or his religion would prevent him from being elected, that he took his orders from the Vatican. Harry Truman remarked, "It isn't the pope I'm afraid of, it's the pop"—a shaft at his old enemy Joe Kennedy. In Wisconsin, people were passing around quarters on which the bust of George Washington was altered with red nail polish to resemble Pope John XXIII, as a warning of what would happen to America if Jack Kennedy were president. The Kennedy campaign was being run, by no accident, in the spirit of the PT boat that was the campaign symbol—full speed ahead all the way because at the slightest sign of slowing down, the whole thing was likely to capsize and sink.

I explained all this to Marilyn, who sighed and said: "It's hard to imagine Jack as president, isn't it? Like Lincoln?"

It wasn't for me—though Lincoln seemed an odd choice to compare Jack to, despite Marilyn's fascination with him. "He'll still be Jack," I said. "The office doesn't change the man—it just brings out the best or the worst of what was already there."

"President John F. Kennedy," she mused in a whisper. "It's great billing."

We both laughed.

"What's *your* billing going to be, David?" she asked. "If he wins."

I shrugged. "There's nothing I want, really," I said, but the look in Marilyn's eyes clearly read: *Don't give me that crap!* so I told her the truth. "Ambassador to the Court of St. James's," I said.

She looked puzzled.

"Ambassador to Great Britain," I explained. "It's called that."

"Oh. Everything there is called something else. I couldn't understand half of what people said to me. *Englishmen!*" she said cryptically. "Oh boy!" She must have been thinking of Olivier because she crinkled her nose and asked: "Why do you want to live *there?*"

"I love England. And it would please Maria. Besides, I've always thought it was the one job I was cut out for. I'd look good in knee breeches and silk stockings, I think."

Marilyn laughed. "Well, I hope you get it if it's what you want." Her expression turned wistful. "I just wish I could find a way of helping Jack," she said.

I raised an eyebrow. So far the one rumor that *hadn't* raised its ugly head against Jack was his affair with Marilyn. If there was anything the campaign didn't need, it was Marilyn endorsing him, if that was what she had in mind, or worse yet, cheering him on in person through the primaries.

"When is Jack coming out here?" she asked. She must be conscious that others had surely taken her place in Jack's bed while she was making eyes at Montand, I thought. She had to be conscious too of the fact that Jack's star was now rising while hers was descending sharply. He was famous now, on his way to the Democratic nomination, while her affair with Yves was giving her bad press for the first time in her life, and the word about her new picture was awful.

"It may not be for a while," I said. I explained that all the big excitement was going on back east, not out here. Jack already had California pretty much sewn up, thanks to the deal Bobby and I had made with Governor Pat Brown on his behalf. In a sense, Marilyn had missed the boat—written herself out of the big story because she was busy fucking Montand while Jack was making history without her. I wanted to tell her to go back to Miller and try to save whatever she could of her marriage, warn her that there was no place for her in Jack's future—or perhaps only a place that would destroy her in the end—but to my shame, I didn't.

She took my hand and squeezed it. "Does Jack miss me at all?" she asked.

"Missing people isn't something Jack does a lot of," I said. "He lives in the present. But he talks about you a lot when the two of us are together."

She closed her eyes for a moment. The lids were pale blue, almost translucent. She seemed to me to have lost weight—

more than was good for her, I thought. "That must be tough on you," she said.

I was surprised and touched, both by her perception and by the gentle, caring way she expressed it—for she was right, of course. Jack in his hearty, man-to-man way shared many of his feelings about Marilyn with me, without ever noticing how strong—and painful—my own were, or how deep my envy ran. "It is tough," I admitted. "Sometimes."

"How are things at home?" she asked. Marilyn seldom inquired about Maria, who she seemed to feel instinctively (and correctly) was not her friend.

"Not bad," I said. It was true enough. Things between Maria and me *weren't* "bad"; they just weren't *good*.

"Poor David," Marilyn sighed. She took my hand in hers. "I want to ask a favor," she said.

"Anything."

"It's not going to make you happy."

"Is that a concern?"

She nodded. "Yes," she said. "I wish I *could* make you happy, David, I really do. But I can't. I know how you feel about me."

"And I'm wasting my time?"

"Probably. I don't know. Listen, David, the truth is, I'd only make you *un*happy. You're better off, believe me."

"Forgive me if I don't agree with you. What's the favor?"

I felt her fingers dig deep into my palm. "I want to see Jack," she said. "I have to explain what happened. Between me and Yves."

I was plunged into sudden misery by her need to explain herself to Jack, who didn't care, when I was sitting right here beside her. Still, I swallowed my pain and resentment, as I always did—which was perhaps a sign of just how much I loved Marilyn—to give her a gentle warning about Jack's position now that he was the front-runner. "You're going to have to be careful—more careful than before. It's serious now."

"I *know* it's serious, David, really I do—the White House and all. But tell him I need to talk to him."

I nodded. We sat silently in the tiny coffee shop downstairs, where, this being Beverly Hills, everybody pretended Marilyn was just an ordinary customer. For the first time since I had met her, way back in '54 at Charlie Feldman's, she seemed to me fragile. She had always been robust, fleshy, indecently healthy, a big girl straining the seams of her clothes, but this morning she seemed almost ghostlike.

She must have sensed what I thought or caught my expression, because she said, "I look like shit, I know."

"I wasn't thinking that."

"Yes you were. Christ, people are always saying I'm too fat." She laughed bitterly. "Well, they can't say that now, can they?"

"You look good to me."

"David, I'd look good to you if I was dead." She gave me a quick kiss on the cheek.

I saw her through the lobby into the waiting studio car. She walked unsteadily, leaning heavily on my arm. She looked into the car as the door was opened for her. "Yves was always in the car waiting for me," she said sadly. "This is the first time he hasn't been."

She slipped into the darkness of the limousine, with its tinted windows. She closed the door, lowered the window, stuck her head out and kissed me.

"You're a real pal, David. I hope you get to be ambassador to the Court of whatever it is." She laughed. "Toodle-oo," she said; then the window went up and the car pulled away.

Later that same day, I called Jack, who was in Oshkosh, Wisconsin, catching him in his motel room. He sounded exhausted. "California!" he croaked. "I wish to Christ I were there. It was fifteen fucking degrees below zero this morning. Dave Powers got me up at five-thirty to stand outside a meat-packing plant and shake hands with the workers."

"You sound played out."

"No shit? I'm sitting here with my hand in a bowl of warm water and antiseptic, courtesy of room service. You try taking off your glove and shaking fifteen hundred hands at fifteen below! My right hand is so bruised and scratched I can't even pick up a fork with it."

"How many votes did you pick up? As your father would ask."

"Some. It's hard to tell. People don't smile much around here—it's too cold, I guess. Jackie's out here with me, believe it or not. She's a better draw than me."

"I believe it. It sounds rough."

"Well, you know how it is. . . . One funny thing—the only one. A guy comes up to me in Ashland, where it's so cold you can't take a piss without freezing your dick off, and asks, 'Is it true you were born with a silver spoon in your mouth, that your dad's a millionaire, and you've never had to do a day's work in your life?'

"Well, it's too cold to argue, so I say, 'Yes.' So *he* holds out his hand and says, 'I'd like to shake your hand, Senator. Let me tell you—you haven't missed a fucking thing!' "

We both laughed. Telling the joke seemed to raise Jack's spirits: he was one of those very rare public men who enjoy it when the joke is on them.

"It would be great to get away to Palm Beach for a few days," he said. "Just to thaw out."

"Can you?"

"Only if I lose. Otherwise, not yet. And I'm not going to lose. How's California?"

"Brown is behind you one hundred percent. Unless you start losing primaries, of course. . . ."

"Of course." He sighed.

"I saw Marilyn this morning, Jack."

"Yes? Jesus, I wish she were here right now. She'd warm me up a lot quicker than long johns."

"That's where she'd like to be too, as a matter of fact. In Wisconsin, with you."

"How is she?"

"Going through a difficult time."

"Aren't we all?"

"She's in a bad way, Jack. I mean it."

There was a long pause, while the seriousness of my tone worked its way through his fatigue. "What happened?" he asked cautiously.

"Have you heard that she had an affair with Yves Montand? The French singer?"

"Jackie made sure I heard all about it, of course," he said.

"It hasn't done a lot for her marriage. As you can imagine."

"I can imagine," he said grimly—nobody, I thought, would know better.

"She's worried that you're angry. That you won't forgive her."

"Oh Christ, Marilyn isn't somebody who's going to sit home and do needlepoint, or cook for her husband. If you want her, you've got to take time for her, and I haven't. I guess Miller didn't either, poor guy. . . . Tell her she's forgiven. No, better yet, tell her there's nothing to forgive."

"I think she'd prefer to hear it from you."

There was another pause. "That's a little complicated," he said. "Jackie's campaigning with me. You happened to catch me while she's taking a bath, but I don't want Marilyn to start calling at all hours of the day or night. Which she will."

"So call her. She's desperate, Jack."

"I'd forgotten your sentimental side, David. It's what prevents you from being a real politician." His tone was snappish, very much his father's, and he must have realized it, because he apologized immediately. "I'm sorry," he said. "It's been a long, hard day. You'd have to be here to understand."

"I understand. And it's okay. Listen, Jack, you're going to win. That's what matters. But call her."

"Tell her I'll call her at noon tomorrow, her time, okay?" he said quickly. There was a faint noise in the background. "Here's Jackie," Jack said cheerfully. "She sends you her best, David."

"Give her mine. Tell her it's balmy here in LA. Seventy degrees."

"David says it's seventy degrees in LA, Jackie." His tone was jovial—a little too much so to sound sincere to any intelligent woman, I thought, but then Jackie was surely used to that.

I couldn't hear what she said in reply, but Jack's voice sounded strained and I wondered if she had walked in from the bathroom when he was still talking about Marilyn. "As I was saying, David," he went on, "I want a really good committee of stars out there in Hollywood." He sounded more like his old self again, as if talking about politics was all it took to revive him. "Frank can help a lot there, getting the really big names."

"I've talked to him."

"Good." Another pause. Then, with a snap of authority that once again reminded me of his father: "Just don't let him become chairman or anything like that, David. Be tactful but firm. I *like* Frank, you understand, he's a buddy, but he's got some bad friends. . . ."

"Ah, don't we all, Jack?"

He laughed—that laughter which nobody could ever resist, least of all me. "Sure, David, and you ought to have been born Irish," he said.

It was the greatest compliment he could pay. I said good night, left him to Jackie's care, and called the studio to let Marilyn know that she was forgiven.

In Wisconsin at least.

Jack's victory in Wisconsin, to his fury, was not the triumph he had hoped for. He carried six of ten congressional districts and picked up the majority of the electoral votes, in a state where Humphrey was practically regarded as a native son, but his votes had come mostly from Catholic areas, and he had lost to Humphrey in the traditionally Protestant ones. So the whole battle had to be fought all over again in West Virginia, starting the next day.

I was dragged away from my business by Jack's father to help out in what was clearly the crucial moment of the campaign. A loss in West Virginia, a rural, backwoods Protestant state, would send the signal to every politician that a Catholic couldn't carry the country in 1960 any more than Governor Alfred E. Smith had been able to carry it in 1928—a point that the Ambassador made to me forcibly and at length on the telephone from Palm Beach, where he was keeping out of sight. "Round up every big-name Protestant you can get to come out for Jack," he barked. "Who's the big man in New York?"

"The Episcopal archbishop."

"That's right. And the dean of the Harvard School of Divinity. And that fellow, what's his name, Niebuhr, and all the rest of the Protestant theologians. 'Protestants for Kennedy'—that's what we need, in a hurry."

" 'Jews for Kennedy' would be easier."

"What's the matter with you, David, for Christ's sake? Jack's already *got* the fucking Jews!"

So I got on the telephone, swept away by the atmosphere of crisis, and succeeded in persuading the eminent Protestant divines that freedom of religion was at stake in West Virginia. In his television debate with Humphrey—and more important, with the reluctant Protestant ministers of West Virginia—Jack's position as the leading Democratic candidate was guaranteed, and Humphrey was buried once and for all, along with Lyndon Johnson and Stu Symington, neither of whom had had the guts to take Jack on in the early primaries.

Yves Montand returned to France a national hero, for it was obvious to his compatriots that if Marilyn was the world's acknowledged sex goddess, her lover ought naturally to be a Frenchman.

Luckily for Marilyn, she was about to start work on *The Misfits*—luckily because working with Clark Gable would at least take her mind off the end of her affair with Montand, luckily too because it was her real chance to be a *serious* actress, and that still mattered to her.

Not so lucky was the fact that she would have to spend weeks on location in Nevada with the husband she had betrayed, and on whom she had now focused all her guilt, anger, and resentment.

27

I WAS IN KEY BISCAYNE WITH MARIA ABOUT A WEEK later, trying to get a few days' rest, when I got a call from Joe Kennedy in Palm Beach. He sounded hysterical, and for a moment I wondered if he'd had what the French call *un coup de vieux,* a sudden collapse into senility. "You've got to get her out of sight," he said. "Back to New York."

"Who?"

"Who the hell do you think? Marilyn Monroe!"

"Marilyn? What are you talking about?"

"She came down here, checked into The Breakers, and called Jack. He's over there now."

I tried to make sense of the news, and couldn't. "She didn't check into The Breakers under her own name?" I asked, praying she hadn't.

"No. But there must be plenty of people who could recognize her. There are reporters all over the goddamn place. This could destroy Jack's chances, you know that, don't you?"

He seemed to feel I was to blame, but I knew that was just the way he was—whoever he talked to first got the full blast of his wrath.

"Where's Jackie?"

"In Washington, thank God, resting. Doctor's orders. Jack just flew down here for a couple of days of sun, between stops. Is this woman *crazy?*"

There was no quick or easy answer to that question. "She's impulsive," I replied.

"Impulsive, my ass! Jack should know how to control his women. I told him so, in no uncertain terms."

It did not seem the right moment to remind Joe Kennedy that Gloria Swanson had led *him* around like a bull with a ring in his nose. Like most people, he was a lot tougher with other people's emotional problems than he was with his own.

"Well," I said, "Jack is probably the only one who can defuse the problem. He's the one Marilyn wants to see, after all."

"No. She wants to see me, too, apparently. You'd better get over here right away. We've got a full-scale crisis on our hands."

I thought so too. I made my apologies to Maria, who was dressing for lunch with her friends, at the Everglades Club, and told her I wouldn't be going with her.

"Really, David!" she said. "If one didn't know better, one would think you had a mistress."

"It was Joe Kennedy," I explained. "With a problem."

"Of course it was, darling. The D'Souzas will be heartbroken to miss you, but never mind. Be an angel and fasten these hooks for me before you go."

I stood behind her and fastened the tiny hooks and eyes that can only be found on the handiwork of major French couturiers, of whom Maria was a favorite *cliente,* because of both her money and her figure. D'Souza was a Brazilian millionaire whose hobbies were women and polo. I was not sorry to be missing his lunch. It was more Maria's kind of thing than mine.

"Is Jack here?" she asked.

I nodded.

"Tell him not to be a stranger," she said as I finished closing the last fastener. "Somebody told me he's carrying on with Marilyn Monroe? Is it true?"

"Not to my knowledge."

"It's a good thing you *don't* have a mistress, David darling. You're a rotten liar."

I found the Ambassador just where I had expected to—in his "bullpen," a fenced-off sunbathing area in which he could sit nude, wearing only a straw hat to shade his face, while he read the papers and made his calls. Joe Kennedy had a horror of pale, untanned skin, as well as something of a fetish for physical fitness, and was a firm believer in nude sunbathing as a way of warding off all sorts of ills. Nobody was allowed to intrude on his privacy, not even his own children, but he always tried to persuade young women—friends of his girls or his boys—to visit him in his hideaway by the pool, and over the years, many did. The number of upper-class young women whose early sexual experience included slathering suntan lotion on the naked body of Ambassador Joseph P. Kennedy was unknown but significant, and his boys often joked about it, albeit with a certain degree of envy.

To my dismay, Joe, Jack, and Marilyn were in animated conversation by the pool. Joe, to my relief, had his swimming trunks on. Jack, looking thin and tired, was dressed in a pair of white duck trousers and a blue tennis shirt. Marilyn was wearing a white, bare-shouldered sundress, with a scarf over her hair and dark glasses—her usual disguise. The three of them were laughing uproariously. Joe had obviously calmed down.

"Hello, David," Marilyn said cheerfully as I kissed her cheek and took a seat. "I've never seen you without a suit before. You look nice in sports clothes."

Joe was putting himself out to be charming, as he always did with beautiful women. I had interrupted him in the telling of a story about his own days as the owner of a movie studio, with which he had succeeded in reducing Marilyn to giggles. For his part, the Ambassador could hardly take his eyes off her breasts, a good part of them revealed by the low scoop neck of her dress.

"I've been telling Marilyn about the old days, David," he said.

"Oh, it's been *such* fun, Ambassador!" Marilyn cried in her most bubbly, breathless voice—the voice of Sugar Kane in *Some Like It Hot.*

"Joe, please," he corrected her, leaning forward to pat her knee.

"Joe," she said with another giggle. Jack, I noticed, looked relaxed—not at all like a man who might be on the verge of kissing the Democratic nomination good-bye because of a sex scandal with a married movie star. He had one arm resting lightly over Marilyn's shoulders, his fingers just touching the bare skin of one breast, in a manner that could only be described as proprietary. I guessed that whatever he had intended to tell her when he went to The Breakers, she had changed his mind pretty rapidly. Any thought of putting Marilyn on the next flight back to New York—or safer yet, shuttling her aboard the *Caroline*—had clearly been forgotten, even by Joe, whose sense of political reality was as strong as anyone's.

"Have we solved our public relations problem?" I inquired, a little put out.

"Jack got Marilyn out of the hotel with no trouble," Joe said. Nobody there seems to have recognized her. You might have a word with the owner, David, but they're pretty discreet over there."

Nobody would know that better than Joe, I thought. He must have had countless opportunities over the years to test the discretion of The Breakers.

"I'm just staying another day," Marilyn said. "Jack is giving me a lift back to New York on the family plane." She giggled again. "It's so nice to be with a family with its own plane." I noticed that the Ambassador's inflexible rule about not serving alcohol before sundown did not apply to Marilyn. There was a bottle of champagne in a cooler beside her, and she had a glass in her hand. I got up and poured myself a glass—Dom Pérignon, I observed; the Ambassador wasn't stinting his famous guest.

"I'll deal with The Breakers," I said to Jack. "My advice is stay clear of the pool area and the restaurants. That's where the journalists are. Put out an announcement that you have a cold and you're resting up. Once they've been told nothing's going to happen, they'll relax and go to the beach. They must have been just as cold as you were, up there in Wisconsin and West Virginia, so they'll all be glad to take a break in the sun."

Jack gave me the kind of look that means, *Why the hell aren't you working for me, since you're so smart?* and went off to give the necessary orders. I knew perfectly well that the entire press corps attached to him would shortly be stretched out on the beach or at poolside, tropical rum drinks in their hands, and that the chances of Jack and Marilyn being observed, provided she kept her hair covered, would be minimal.

Joe was preening himself under Marilyn's admiring stare. Of course, she had a knack for flirting with older men, I recalled, remembering Joe Schenck.

"I'm glad to see you looking well," I said to her. "Last time we met, you were way down in the dumps."

"Don't I know it, David honey."

"It's Jack who's cheered her up," his father said proudly. "Isn't it, dear?"

"Mm." Marilyn nodded. I couldn't see her eyes behind the dark glasses, but I would have been willing to bet that her pupils were dilated. Jack may have cheered her up, but I guessed that she'd been popping pills—uppers, I presumed—all the way from New York.

As if to confirm this, she opened her purse, took out a gaily striped capsule—there seemed to be a quantity of them rolling around loose at the bottom of the purse—and swallowed it with a gulp of champagne. "It's for my hay fever," she explained cheerfully.

"I expect it's all these goddamn flowers," Joe said indulgently. The Kennedy pool, while not grand by Hollywood standards, was surrounded by flowering shrubs, which grew a little out of control, since the Ambassador disliked the presence of gardeners when he was sitting by his pool.

"I've never been in Florida before," she said.

"You ought to come here more often." Joe gave her one of his most ferocious smiles.

"I'd love to, every once in a while."

Joe laughed. "You see, David, I'm getting old. A few years ago, she'd have said she'd love to be here every day!" He put his hand on her knee again and simply left it there, the blunt fingers, deeply tanned by the sun, dimpling her pale, soft flesh. For some reason, I found the sight nauseating, but Marilyn didn't seem to mind—or to notice. She was floating on some sparkling high, induced partly by chemicals, I had no doubt, but also by the sense of sheer adventure. She had managed to leave LA (and her husband) and get to Palm Beach on the spur of the moment.

It was as if she was playing girlish pranks in the middle of a presidential campaign, which seemed to be dangerous behavior from Jack's point of view. But Jack loved this kind of game: secret meetings, middle-of-the-night romantic assignations, always appealed to him.

Jack returned from his task looking relaxed. "No sweat," he said. "I have a cold, officially. The ladies and gentlemen of the press are on their way back to their hotels for a little well-earned R and R. Thanks, David. You've done it again. Let's go, Marilyn."

She pouted prettily—an expression that nobody ever did better or more alluringly. "I was just beginning to have fun," she said.

Whatever happened, I thought, she was going to have an ally in the Kennedy family from now on—perhaps still the most important one. "You don't waste a day like this on an old man," he said with mock gallantry.

Marilyn rose to her feet—very unsteadily—bent over, and kissed him on the forehead. "I never knew my father. I'm going to think of you as my father from now on," she said sweetly.

"Come again," he said. "And take care of Jack. He needs to rest and put some flesh on his bones."

This was a familiar message. When Jack was campaigning, he often forgot to eat, and the Ambassador had charged several of the veteran members of his son's staff—Dave Powers, Joe Gargan, and Boom-Boom Reardon, specifically—with making sure he was fed, a practice going all the way back to Jack's first congressional campaign.

Marilyn put her arms around Jack protectively, teetering slightly on her high heels. "He's in good hands," she said with a giggle, in case he missed the double entendre.

"Yes," the Ambassador said, grinning. "I can *see* that."

Marilyn came over and kissed me good-bye, blushing slightly, I was pleased to notice.

When they had left, the Ambassador and I sat silently for a few moments, while I lit a cigar.

"Jack's a lucky boy," he said at last.

"No argument. He's playing with fire, though."

"Yes."

"You're not worried anymore?"

"Of course I am. I was worried when he joined the Navy and volunteered for the goddamn PT boats, but I didn't stop him, did I? He needs to take risks, and that's all there is to it. Anyway, you came up with the solution, as usual, David, so let him have his fun."

"At the risk of losing the presidency?"

"Oh, cut the crap, David! If Jack loses—and he's not going to—it won't be because he spent an afternoon fucking Marilyn Monroe, lucky fellow. It'll be because Nixon is stronger and smarter than I personally think he is." He leaned forward, smiling—always a dangerous sign. "You know what your trouble is?" he asked.

"I know you're going to tell me."

"Don't play the smart-ass with me, David. We've known each other too long. Your trouble is, you want to fuck her, don't you? I could see it on your face a mile away—from the way you look at her."

"Well, it's not an uncommon desire. Maybe one hundred million other American men share it."

"Yeah, but the difference is, there's something *between* you and Marilyn. I can tell that from the way she looks at you, David. It's the kind of look that women give men who almost fucked them but didn't. Is that what happened?"

"Nothing happened, Joe," I said uncomfortably. "Marilyn and I are friends, that's all."

"Bullshit, David!" He lay back and closed his eyes, the sun full on his face. "You're a fool," he said in a tone that was strangely kind. "You *should* have fucked her, David, if you had the chance. There's more problems caused by *not* fucking a woman you want to fuck than by fucking one, in my experience. . . . Jack wouldn't have minded. She'd respect you more. You'd feel better about yourself. And you wouldn't be holding any bitter feelings toward Jack."

"I don't have any bitter feelings toward Jack. You're wrong about that."

He did not open his eyes. "No I'm not," he said quietly. "But I know you won't do anything about them, so I'm not worried." He paused. "All the same, keep it in mind. We're old friends, so

I can tell you this frankly: Don't ever do anything to hurt Jack just because he fucked Marilyn and you didn't. That wouldn't be fair to him, David."

"I promise you I won't."

He held out his hand to mine and we shook. His was covered in suntan lotion, and I had to wipe mine on a cocktail napkin. "That's good enough for me," he said. "Are you going to work for Jack once he's elected?" he asked after a long silence.

"I haven't given it a lot of thought."

He gave me a hard look. "Don't bullshit me, David," he said.

I was never able to hide anything from Joe—not many people could. Besides, he was clearly sounding me out. "An ambassadorship would be nice," I said casually.

He snorted. "You'll be sorry," he said. "It costs a fortune to do it in style. I should know. The goddamn government doesn't pay for anything—you have to pick up the tab for a pisspotful of freeloaders. . . . The job is all responsibility and no power. The president and the State Department call the shots. Which one do you want?"

"The Court of St. James's."

Joe's expression was inscrutable. "That's the big one," he agreed casually. "That, and Paris maybe. And of course, Moscow now, but Moscow is usually for professional diplomats. . . . Anyway, who wants to spend two or three years in Moscow?"

"Not me."

"There you are."

I wondered if that had been an attempt on Joe's part to see if I would accept a lesser embassy, and wondered too if it had been smart to let him know what I wanted. Sooner or later, I told myself, I had to make a move, and telling Joe was the same as telling Jack. Besides, Joe's feelings would have been bitterly hurt had I asked Jack for his old job without telling him first. No, I had done the right thing, I decided, and left it at that.

We sat companionably for a few minutes, the Ambassador taking the sun, I sheltered by my Panama hat.

"She phoned him here, you know," he said, breaking the silence.

"Marilyn? She called *here?*"

"How do you suppose she got the number?"

I thought about it. The Kennedy family's telephone numbers were not only unlisted and secret, for obvious reasons, but changed regularly. Nobody knew better than Joe how much trouble a telephone call could cause, particularly from a woman to a man's home. "I'd have to conclude that either she found it on Jack's desk or he gave it to her. Nobody else would."

"Mm." He opened one bright ice-blue eye and stared at me. "Do Marilyn and Jack talk a lot? Phone calls, I mean."

"A good bit. More from her. She's a compulsive late-night caller. When she can't sleep, she makes calls. Some of them to Jack, I guess."

He thought this over. "I'd hate to think that her phones might be tapped."

"The idea has occurred to me, but Jack isn't worried."

Joe looked thoughtful. "I was halfway tempted to get Hoover to have his boys check out her lines, just to make sure they're clear, but then I said to myself, why give the old bastard a piece of knowledge he doesn't have?"

"What makes you so sure he doesn't have it?"

He laughed. "You could be right. What the hell, even if he does, what's he going to do with it? Jack's girls, for Christ's sake! If the FBI's keeping a file on all of them, we should buy shares in the company that sells them filing cabinets!"

He looked at his watch and rolled over onto his stomach— his schedule for tanning was as precisely regulated as everything else in his life. "You'll stay for lunch?"

I said I would.

"You might have a word with Marilyn, though, since the two of you are such pals. Just to tell her careless lips sink ships, okay? And we'll keep Hoover out of it, shall we?"

"With pleasure," I said. The last thing we wanted was Hoover involved in Jack's love life.

"This is a big honor for you, Agent Kirkpatrick," Tolson said, showing him down the stairs. "Something to tell your children."

Kirkpatrick had no children, but decided not to correct Tolson—it *was* a great honor, undoubtedly, to be invited to the Director's home, though a bit of a disappointment, for he had expected something grander than this small, shabby house, decorated with framed photographs of J. Edgar Hoover with celebrities of every world from sports to politics.

He wondered why he was being escorted to the basement, but the mystery was cleared up when Tolson opened the door at the bottom of the stairs and ushered him into a small, dimly lit den or game room, with a small stand-up bar and four barstools at one end of the room, and a fake fireplace with a gas log at the facing end. The furniture was heavy and almost aggressively masculine: a couple of chairs made out of wine barrels, a big leather couch, a coffee table with a top taken from a green-baize gaming table.

The walls were what caught Kirkpatrick's eye, as they were surely meant to: from floor to ceiling they were covered with "cheesecake" photographs and drawings taken from magazines like *Esquire* and *Playboy*—Vargas girls, Petty girls, and Playmates of the Month exposing their breasts and buttocks or raising improbably perfect legs, ending in spike-heeled "Fuck me!" pumps, as far as the eye could see. Somebody had carefully cut them out by the hundreds, pasted them to the walls, then varnished over them.

More astounding to Kirkpatrick than the mural was the sight of the Director, standing behind the bar, while a mirror in back of him depicted a generously proportioned female nude doing something unmentionable with a swan. To one side of him was what appeared to Kirkpatrick to be the world's biggest collection of sheriff's badges, to the other a wooden board carved in folk art style with the message "Hogtown Drinking & Pistol Club—Drink all night, piss 'til dawn!" Glasses, mugs, and tankards hung in rows above Hoover's head. It was what Kirkpatrick had always imagined the bar at an Elks Club lodge might look like, though as a middle-class Catholic from Danbury, Connecticut, who had come to the FBI via Fordham Law School, he had never been in one.

"Welcome," Hoover said ponderously.

Kirkpatrick sat at the bar, uneasy in these strange domestic surroundings. There was a lever for drawing draft beer in front of him, the handle of which was a girl's legs, and coasters with *Playboy* cartoons on the polished mahogany surface of the bar. "What's your pleasure?" Hoover asked, trying hard for an expression of geniality without altogether succeeding.

Kirkpatrick was not a drinking man. "Scotch and water?" It

seemed like the simplest thing to ask for here. Hoover made the drink, then busied himself mixing two elaborate drinks for himself and Tolson, slicing fruit and sticking maraschino cherries on plastic toothpicks with surprising dexterity.

Immediately above Kirkpatrick's head was a row of boxing gloves, each signed by a World's Champion Heavyweight. Softly in the background he could hear Frank Sinatra singing. It struck him as mildly ironic that the Director enjoyed Sinatra records—Kirkpatrick had been tapping the singer's telephone lines for years at Hoover's orders, as well as Phyllis McGuire's, Peter Lawford's, and those of a whole host of other show business celebrities whose private life, politics, or organized crime connections were of interest to the FBI.

Kirkpatrick had made himself, more or less by accident, the Bureau's "show biz" expert, and even read the "trades" daily to check on the whereabouts and career moves of his targets. He had been astonished to find out how many famous names in Hollywood were under surveillance for one reason or another, and even more astonished at the number of equally famous people who had been active FBI informants for years, including well-known stars like Ronald Reagan and John Wayne, large numbers of studio executives, and producers such as Cecil B. DeMille. Agents informed on their clients, stars on their costars (and often on their spouses or ex-spouses), studio bosses on their employees, and writers on everyone.

It wasn't Kirkpatrick's idea of law enforcement, or what he had dreamed of when he joined the Bureau. He would have given a lot to get a crack at making an arrest with a tommy gun in his hands, but in the meantime, his career was soaring, so he wasn't about to complain.

"Do you follow politics?" Hoover asked.

Kirkpatrick wondered if this was a trick question.

"Keep up with *The Washington Post, The New York Times,* that sort of thing?" Tolson chimed in, before he could reply. As it happened, in his present assignment, Kirkpatrick was more likely to read the *Hollywood Reporter* or *Variety,* but he nodded cautiously—within the FBI, the *Post* and the *Times* were viewed as not very different from *Pravda.*

"Good!" Hoover said. "It's important to keep well informed."

"And to know how to read between the lines," Tolson added. "You have to separate hard news from Commie propaganda."

Hoover nodded. "Indeed. Words of wisdom, Mr. Tolson." He turned to Kirkpatrick. "Since you follow these things, it won't have escaped your attention that Senator Kennedy is the Democratic front-runner?"

"No, sir."

"It's unfortunate," Hoover said darkly, "that a brash young man of low moral habits like Senator Kennedy may end up as our president. . . . It's almost enough to make one lose faith in the democratic process."

"You think he'll win the nomination, sir?"

"No question about it," the Director said. "Kennedy will win, you mark my words. Poor Humphrey is just the kind of namby-pamby liberal do-gooder—if not an outright Marxist— who was bound to lose against Kennedy. Symington didn't put up a fight. Johnson seems to be under the mistaken impression that presidents are elected by a Senate vote." He sighed.

"And the election, sir?"

"Ah," Hoover said. "That's another story. Vice President Nixon is a bare-knuckle fighter, a formidable opponent. Of course, Nixon has his own problems, doesn't he, Mr. Tolson?"

Tolson smirked. "He certainly *does,* Director."

"To be sure, not the same *kind* of problems as Senator Kennedy's, Agent Kirkpatrick, you understand."

Kirkpatrick nodded. He hadn't thought it likely there were any sex scandals in the Director's files on the Vice President. Nixon didn't look the type, though that could be deceptive, as he well knew. . . .

Still, the thing that interested him most was that the Director was as knowledgeable about Nixon, whom Hoover liked, as he was about Kennedy, whom he *disliked.* Clearly, Nixon's phones were tapped and his home and hotel rooms routinely bugged, just like Kennedy's. He wondered whether the Bureau's microphones and wires extended into the Oval Office itself.

"Young Kennedy's success poses a dilemma for us, Kirkpatrick," Hoover went on. "Confidentially"—he glanced around the room with dark, furtive eyes—"there has been great pressure on me to make available some of the, ah, *fruits* of your labors. Senator Johnson is anxious to know whether we have compromising tapes on Senator Kennedy, and if so, what's on them. Vice President Nixon is even more anxious to know. I have to keep the best interests of the country in mind, of course. In the short run, there might be advantages to be gained from letting Nixon or Johnson hear certain sections of the tapes, even though I'm against involving the Bureau in politics. . . ." Hoover's expression was that of a martyr to patriotic duty. "But I must ask myself," he went on, "what happens if Senator Kennedy *wins* the election?"

He gave Kirkpatrick a steely glare—a warning, Kirkpatrick took it, that he was about to be initiated into the Director's darkest secrets.

"*If* Kennedy wins," Hoover went on, "your tapes will be the best way of keeping the President in line. The only way perhaps. It will be my responsibility to control the worst excesses—and impulses—of the President."

The Director's gaze focused in the middle distance, at some point beyond Kirkpatrick's Adam's apple. "One might even say that the very future and well-being of our nation may rest on these tapes, eh, Mr. Tolson?"

"And in your hands, Director."

Hoover inclined his head modestly. "So you see, Mr. Kirkpatrick, we must expand our efforts in the interests of national security. And tighten our own secrecy."

"We're already covering the Senator pretty well, sir."

"Cover his brother, Kirkpatrick. Cover Miss Monroe. She may be talking to her friends about Kennedy. He may be telling her things we should know. Spare no effort, no expense."

Kirkpatrick was enough of a bureaucrat to realize that he was being given a blank check to expand his turf. "I could use some more men," he said tentatively.

"You shall have them. Give Mr. Tolson your needs."

"And a field office of my own in LA. It isn't secure enough, working out of the Bureau field office."

"Very well."

"And better equipment. Bernie Spindel has more up-to-date stuff than we do."

Hoover frowned. "I don't want to hear that man's name again. He was disloyal to me. I can't forgive that, Kirkpatrick—not for my own sake but for the Bureau's."

"I understand, sir."

"However, you shall have what you need. Draw up a list. We'll get it from the CIA or the military, if we have to."

"Thank you, sir."

"Continue to report to myself or Mr. Tolson personally. You'll be given a cover story—put on some kind of top-secret investigation, of organized crime perhaps. You'll take care of the details, Mr. Tolson?"

"You can rely on me, Director."

Hoover smiled, displaying teeth that were so small, even, and perfect that Kirkpatrick concluded they must be false. "I know I can," he snapped.

"What happens if Senator Kennedy *doesn't* win, sir?"

"Why, then we'll just play the Nixon card," Hoover whispered.

28

SHE HATED NEVADA FROM THE DAY SHE ARRIVED.

She had been in Vegas once or twice, of course, as Frank's guest, but Reno, where she was now, had none of Las Vegas's phony, electric glamour. Reno was basically just a small town, so she could never escape from the rest of the crew—or from her husband. All the exteriors were going to be shot on the ragged, sandy wasteland around Reno—an arid, dusty, Martian land-scape, so hot she felt her brains were frying, with nothing to look at but stunted shrubs, the occasional ghost town, and the low, lumpy mountains on the horizon, which seemed to grow farther away as you drove toward them on the ruler-straight roads. It was a dead landscape, and all it reminded her of was death.

Everything conspired to depress her. Monty Clift, her old friend whom she had counted on for support, was in as bad a way as she was, apparently, and spent most of his time locked in his hotel suite with his own little entourage, while Eli Wallach, as a big-time New York actor, gravitated rather ostentatiously toward Arthur, sucking up to him, she thought, for a bigger role and better lines for himself.

Monty *could* have cheered her up if anybody could. He was witty, bitchy, unexpectedly kind, and his troubles were as bad as hers, or almost, which gave the two of them a very special kind of friendship—strong enough even to survive the fact that he was also "best friends" with Liz Taylor.

She saw him briefly in the lobby the first day, and hid her feelings at the sight of his ruined face, as she always had to do. It was painful to remember how beautiful he had been before the drunken car accident that gave him a permanent scowl. It made her nervous to look at him, since it reminded her of just how fragile beauty was, and how easy it was to lose it in a fraction of a second. There were those who believed that the accident had made Monty a better actor, but she didn't buy it, not for a moment. So far as she could tell, it had merely made him more difficult, more morose, more introspective than ever. It was as if he now wanted to hide from the world, trusting nobody but his makeup man and longtime lover.

He took her to a dark corner of the bar. His eyes seemed to stare at her angrily, but she knew it was just a result of his unfinished plastic surgery, which had made the whites of his eyes look much too large and paralyzed the left side of his face. He dabbed at his broken nose with a bandanna handkerchief—the accident had also left him with a permanent sinus condition, accompanied by massive headaches.

"You're looking good," he said. "Is it the Frenchman?"

She shook her head. "That's over. It was fun while it lasted, but he's going back to Simone." Her voice turned husky. Monty preferred to keep things bright and smart and heartless—with problems like his, he liked to say, the last thing he wanted around him was self-pity—so she fought back her tears, but of course, he noticed.

"I'm sorry," she said. "I'm still down in the dumps over him, I guess."

"I know the feeling, honey. Welcome to the club. I was once in love with a Frenchman myself. . . . This place ain't gonna help a bit, by the way. It's the dumps. '*The Misfits,* Dumps, Nevada'—that ought to be our mailing address." He laughed, an uncertain quavering laugh. "Oh, *fuck* it, Marilyn honey," he said quietly. "Happy endings are only for the god-damn movies."

"I guess."

"Oh, bullshit, Marilyn. You and I are both such suckers for happy endings." He took her hand and squeezed it in his thin, dry fingers with a kind of desperation. "My Frenchman went back to his wife too, by the way."

Monty released her hand and lit a cigarette with trembling fingers, keeping the match lit until it must have started to burn them. The accident, she knew, had left him with odd areas in which the nerves were insensitive. He was always scalding himself in the shower, or burning his lips trying to drink coffee that was too hot. He winced, and dropped the match onto the floor, grinding it out on the carpet under his heel. "Anyway, you're looking good, honey, which is more than I can say of myself. . . . No, don't contradict me, I *know* what I look like. . . . Since I assume it isn't the marriage that's making your skin bloom, does that mean that things are looking up with the Senator?"

She put her finger to her lips. "Shh!" she whispered, giggling. "I don't know what you're talking about, baby."

"This is Uncle Monty you're talking to, honey. It's the worst-kept secret in town. Even your husband must know by now."

"He does *not!* Anyway, there's nothing to know."

"God, you look pretty when you lie. Marilyn, people *know*."

"They only *think* they know."

Clift shrugged, giving her a crooked, enigmatic smile. "If you say so, honey. . . . Oh, Marilyn. You and I—Christ, we're alike. Born without armor, you know? The Kennedys, sweetheart, they're born in full armor, you can't reach *their* soft parts."

She giggled again. "I sure reached Jack's."

Despite himself, Monty laughed. She could see a ghost of his former self beneath the ruins of that angelic beauty.

He closed his eyes for a moment, his whole body trembling now, as if the effort of laughter were too much for him. He tried to light another cigarette and dropped it, his fingers twitching as if he were spastic. She picked it up and lit it for him.

"Don't *do* that!" he snapped sharply, his face contorted in what seemed for a moment like genuine rage, but he allowed her to put the cigarette to his lips anyway. He held it precariously between his thumb and forefinger in the European style, as she had come to recognize from watching Yves, though in Monty's case it was because he was afraid of dropping it and setting his pants on fire. "Oh Christ, Marilyn, I'm a fucking *mess*, aren't I?"

Watching him was like seeing her own worst fears about herself. "You're going to be okay, Monty," she said, but she didn't believe it for a second.

"The hell I am," he said. He leaned close to her. "You know what? Before I signed up for this goddamn picture, I went to the doctor. I'd been having dizzy spells, fuzzy vision, memory loss. . . . It turns out that I've got cataracts and thyroid deficiency. It's like being an old man, dear, and I'm only thirty-nine! The one thing I can't do is drink, and of course, it's the one thing I can't stop doing."

He sat for a moment without speaking, as if telling her about his condition had exhausted him. She felt an irrational fear that his condition might be catching, that it might destroy the picture, or worse yet, *her*.

"Don't, for Christ's sake, tell anyone, pussy," he whispered. "That sadistic motherfucker Huston doesn't know what kind of shape I'm in, or the studio would never have agreed to let him give me the part."

"I promise."

The truth was that Huston knew the whole story, as Arthur had told her, and had concealed it from the studio so that he could have Monty for the part of Perce Howland. He had also concealed Gable's heart condition and downplayed *her* problems.

Huston was a gambler, never happy unless the odds were against him and he was walking on the brink, and *The Misfits* was his biggest gamble so far. Still, she wasn't about to destroy Monty's illusion that he had put one over on Huston.

"Are you taking anything?" she asked.

He laughed, a harsh, croaking laughter. "Just the usual, pussy. Nembutal. Doriden. Luminal. Seconal. Phenobarbs. Vitamins. Calcium. And booze."

"Gosh!"

"Don't give *me* that innocent shit. I know what *you* take." He gave her a leer, in which she managed to read such a wealth of shared pain that she put her head close to his and kissed him softly, feeling the lifeless scar tissue against her lips. "How's the insomnia?" he asked her.

"The same as yours, I guess."

"Ain't life a bitch?"

"You must have brought quite a supply out with you?" she said, trying to make it sound casual.

"Do I take it that you're running low?"

She nodded. "The doctor I had in New York was getting to be a real pain in the ass about prescriptions, you know? So I went to another doctor, only he didn't like making the prescriptions refillable, so I had to go back and see him every time I ran out—"

"Stop, Marilyn, *please!* I know the song, every last fucking word of the lyrics. What *are* you taking, just out of curiosity?"

"About the same as you, I guess, except for booze. Uppers for the day, downers at night. Benzedrine and Nembutal, mostly."

"Do they help?"

"Life's pretty terrible with them, but I don't want to think about how it would be without them."

"What do you take at night?" he asked, as if they were a couple of cooks comparing recipes.

"Four or five Nembutals. I break them open and lick the powder right out of my hand. It's quicker that way, you know?"

He lifted one scarred eyebrow, impressed. "Does it work?"

"Sometimes. A massage helps." She was lying, of course. She had a masseur who worked on her from midnight to two in the morning, but even so, her drowsy and drugged state seldom led her into real sleep until dawn, if at all. She had slept the night through, at first, in Yves's arms, and on the rare occasions when she and Jack spent the night together, she slept like a baby, once or twice even without the help of pills. "Mostly it's shitty," she admitted quietly.

"Amen. I make long-distance telephone calls, myself. Hell, if I can't sleep, why should my friends? How are you fixed for Nembutals?"

"Okay for a while. They work better with chloral hydrate, but I couldn't get any of my doctors in New York to prescribe it."

He gave a grim smile. With trembling fingers he removed a pen from the pocket of his stained and creased linen jacket and wrote a name and telephone number on a cocktail napkin. "He's a local doctor," he said, putting the pen back in his pocket with difficulty. He had failed to retract the point, which left a bright blue ink stain on his coat. "Tell him I sent you. He's a celebrity-fucker. Play him the right way and he'll write you out a prescription for anything you want."

"Thank you," she said.

"Don't thank me, dear. It's nothing to be thankful for."

He sighed, and stood up unsteadily. One of his entourage, who had been waiting just out of hearing in the shadows of the dimly lit cocktail lounge, came forward and took him by the arm. "Beddy-bye time, Monty," he said. "Time for your nap."

Monty nodded wearily, the light going out of his eyes as if someone had turned it off. "You see how it is," he said.

She saw.

29

HISTORIANS WRITE AS IF JACK'S NOMINATION WAS A sure thing, but he didn't treat it as such, and he was right. His primary victories had given him the votes, but he knew, as we all did, that if he didn't win on the first ballot, erosion would set in and the tide might turn toward Symington or Johnson, either one of whom would have been more palatable to the old guard of the Democratic party.

Jack sent a small family army out to Los Angeles ahead of him—his father, who rented the estate of his old friend Marion Davies, Hearst's mistress; Bobby, who was at the Biltmore, along with Jack's staff; brother Teddy, who had been thrown into the fray with the responsibility of keeping the western states in line; and most of his sisters, who were spread around town. I had flown out earlier, at the Ambassador's request, to help prevent Governor Brown from backsliding. The only person missing was Jackie, whose delicate pregnancy required her to stay put at Hyannis Port, or so the story went.

Jack had sent Dave Powers out a week before everybody else with instructions to find him a secret "hideaway" in Los Angeles. On my advice, Dave rented a furnished, three-room penthouse apartment in a building owned by Jack Haley, the comedian—close to the Los Angeles Sports Arena, where the convention was being held—with a hidden entrance and a private elevator. Dave also managed to obtain a model home on display at the Sports Arena as the Kennedy "communications center"—which presented Jack with a secluded, fully furnished private hideaway at the Arena as well.

That, and the fact that he had left Jackie at home, seemed to me enough to make Jack happy, but when he arrived, he was in a foul mood, the black Irish temper having overwhelmed the Irish charm.

It was Lyndon Johnson who was responsible for Jack's anger. Johnson, it emerged, had been spreading rumors about Jack— that he was suffering from Addison's disease and wouldn't survive a term in office, that he planned to make Bobby secretary of labor (a rumor certain to cause panic among labor leaders), and, most damaging of all, that there were secrets in Jack's private life that would prevent him from being elected. Adding to Jack's anger was the fact that he had heard about all this from friendly reporters rather than from his staff.

I happened to enter his suite at the Biltmore just as he was winding up a stinging criticism of his staff, who were standing around the seated candidate with hangdog expressions, even Bobby and young Teddy, who was getting his first direct exposure to the Kennedy family business.

"You heard about what's happening?" Jack asked me. He was sitting bolt upright, an extra pillow behind his back—a sure sign that he was in pain, as was often the case after a long plane trip. All the same, he looked healthy and relaxed, in sharp contrast to Bobby, who was so thin, drawn, and exhausted that he looked every bit as terminal as Johnson claimed Jack was.

Jack sent Teddy off to work the delegates, and dismissed everybody except Bobby and me. He grimaced, then gestured for us both to sit down. "I've never liked Lyndon, and I know damned well he doesn't like *me,* but I didn't realize he *hated* me."

The relationship between the two men had always been prickly. Johnson patronized Jack, while Jack thought Johnson was a hick and a liar.

"He's an ungrateful, two-faced son of a bitch," Bobby snarled. "He told reporters you were 'just a scrawny little fellow with rickets.' He called Dad 'the man who held Chamberlain's umbrella'!"

Jack stared gloomily into space. "Yes," he said. "I heard. Actually that's a pretty good line, the one about Dad. Lyndon's got some smart people writing his stuff for him. He wouldn't have come up with that one himself. What do you think we should do, David?"

"None of it is going to hurt you much. I'd say Lyndon is just blowing smoke. . . . Except for the stuff about secrets in your private life. I don't like the sound of that."

"What does Lyndon know that everybody in the press doesn't?" Jack asked. "Anyway, he's not going to tell the world about my private life, is he?"

"We can nail *him*," Bobby said. "Dad helped him out of a financial crisis a couple of years ago. He knows stuff about Lyndon's business affairs nobody else does, even in Texas."

I glanced at Jack and shook my head. What Bobby said was true enough, but what he left out was that this help had been Johnson's payoff for giving Jack a coveted seat on the Senate Foreign Relations Committee, which had served as a perfect platform for moving him away from the narrow field of labor relations into the broader, more "presidential" uplands of foreign policy. "I think you might lose more than you'd gain," I warned.

Bobby glared at me. He was dying to be let loose at Johnson. He believed in punching back as fast and as hard as he could, never forgetting or forgiving an insult. So did Jack, as a matter of fact, but he concealed it with cool wit, and liked the world to imagine he was holding Bobby back.

"We can let the world know about Lyndon's love life," Bobby said. "I know for a fact that he's been fucking one of his secretaries for years. He's so cheap he doesn't even rent a hotel room. They do it on his desk in the Senate."

Jack smiled. "You know the first thing Lyndon said to me when I took my seat in the Senate? He said, 'I hear you're a man who likes pussy too.' " He laughed, while Bobby continued to scowl. "I can't see we'd gain anything by passing the word around that Lyndon likes pussy. He'd probably pick up a few votes, that's all. Why are you looking so glum, David?"

"I'm just wondering if somebody out there could be feeding Johnson information. Something more specific."

"Like what?"

"Well, you and Marilyn, for example."

"Who would do that?"

"The FBI? Hoffa?"

"You've got Marilyn on the brain, David, I've told you that before."

"Hoover would never do that," Bobby said. "And Lyndon wouldn't have the guts to get involved with Hoffa."

"I don't trust Hoover," I said to Jack. "And I don't trust Johnson either. I think you should be careful."

"Careful about what?"

"About being seen with Marilyn."

"Don't worry about it, David. I'm here to work, not to play," Jack said, but I noticed a gleam in his eye.

"So we let Lyndon get away with it?" Bobby asked.

Jack looked thoughtful. "Any ideas, David?"

"Spread the rumor that he hasn't recovered from his heart attack yet," I suggested. "It will make him mad as hell, but it's not too far below the belt. And Lyndon's no fool. He'll take it as a warning that if he doesn't knock it off, you'll follow it up with really bad stuff. All you have to do is show him you're ready to fight back. He's a coward and a bully. He'll back off."

"Sounds like good advice to me," Jack said, visibly relaxing. He turned to Bobby. "Do it," he ordered. "Not yourself. Get somebody else to do it, somebody who isn't connected to us."

He was learning fast, I told myself. So was Bobby. He nodded, and went off without a word of protest, and by the end of the day the rumor about Johnson's heart condition was all over town. That evening Jack even called Lyndon to commiserate with him and say how shocked he was to hear about such an irresponsible rumor. Lyndon got the message, of course, and no more was heard about Jack's secret love life, or his ill health.

All the same, I was nervous, and a call from Marilyn to my Sunset Boulevard office the next morning made me even more so. She had talked her way out of Reno, it appeared, so as not to miss the convention.

"I'm so excited," she said. She was bubbling with nervous energy just—on the edge of hysteria, I thought. "Did you hear that Lyndon Johnson had a heart attack?"

"I don't think so. . . ."

"It's all over town. Good, is what I say! He's a big, ugly, mean-minded, white-trash Texan, and I hate that kind of man."

Of course, she was right about Johnson. He was just about the most mean-spirited man I ever met in politics, and I've met quite a few, and his hatred of Jack was pure envy.

"How's *The Misfits* going?" I asked.

"Awful. Maybe I can do the picture and get divorced at the same time." She laughed uneasily. Reno's reputation as a divorce mill was such that most people only went there for that purpose—ironically, Roslyn, the character she was playing in *The Misfits*, was waiting out her divorce in Reno.

"Are things that bad, Marilyn?"

"Oh, honey. Don't ask."

"Jack's here," I said. "He arrived yesterday."

She giggled. "I know." Her voice dropped to a conspiratorial level. "Listen, honey," she said. "That's one of the reasons I called. I'm supposed to be at Jack's this morning—he called me last night—and I lost the address."

"He's at the Biltmore. Suite nine-three-three-three."

"Not that," she said irritably. "The *other* place."

"The one on North Rossmore? Jack Haley's place?"

"Right!"

"Five twenty-two is the number," I said. "The apartment right above William Gargan—"

"The guy who plays the detective on TV? Thanks a million, lover," she cried. "I've gotta run."

As it happened, I had an appointment with Jack for that afternoon, to report on my luncheon meeting with Sinatra and Lawford, who were orchestrating the appearance of the "Stars for Kennedy" both at the convention and, hopefully, at the Los Angeles Coliseum for his acceptance speech—a meeting at which the question of whether Marilyn was "under control" was raised several times.

When I turned up at the hideaway on North Rossmore Avenue, Jack himself opened the door for me, wearing a dressing gown. He was grinning, but the grin had a sharp edge to it. "If I'm elected," he said, "I'm going to nominate you for CIA director."

I stared at him, not getting the joke. "I was hoping for something better."

"No. CIA would be perfect for a guy who can keep a secret the way you can."

"What secret?" I asked. Clearly, I had slipped up on something, though I was relieved to see that he wasn't so much angry as determined to enjoy a joke at my expense.

"Marilyn's asleep in the bedroom, believe it or not. It was really great of you to give her my address here—particularly since you were the one who told me yesterday I should be careful about seeing her! You're not working for Lyndon by any chance, are you, David?"

I stared at him, blushing. "She said she'd spoken to you."

"Yes. And that she lost the address. That didn't sound a little implausible to a man of your great worldly experience?"

Now that I realized what Marilyn had done, of course it sounded wildly improbable. Marilyn was always threatening to join Jack on the campaign trail whenever we talked, and as a rule I didn't take her seriously. I recognized, with a certain degree of guilt, that I had underestimated her again. "Well, all I can say is that she sounded to me as if she was telling the truth. . . ."

"David, if Marilyn told you black was white, you'd believe her."

It was true, which made it worse. "I could wring her neck," I said.

He laughed. "Yes, I guess so, but I don't suppose you *will*. You'll forgive her." He poured us both coffee from a silver Thermos. The apartment was nicely furnished and comfortable, though there were cables all over the floor for the extra telephones that had been installed, including a direct "red phone" linking the apartment to the Kennedy "communications shack" at the Arena.

"I'm really sorry, Jack," I said.

"No harm done. Actually, I was relieved. I was thinking about what you said, you know. . . . Should I call her, should I not? And all of a sudden the doorbell rang, and there she was, carrying a bottle of champagne, at eleven in the morning. She's sleeping like a baby now."

"You're a lucky man."

"Yes," he said simply.

A door opened and Marilyn appeared, dressed only in one of Jack's shirts. "I heard noises?" she said. "I didn't know where

I was." Even from across the room I could see that her pupils were alarmingly small, tiny black pinpoints. She thought for a moment—a long moment—then said in a tiny voice: "Where am I?"

She was holding a glass of champagne in one hand and a lot of brightly colored capsules in the other. She tossed the capsules into her mouth, knocked back some champagne, and smiled, a little vaguely, I thought. "Hi, David," she said. She walked across the room as if the floor were a tightrope requiring her full concentration, and gave me a kiss. Her skin smelled as sweet and fresh as a baby's, and she gave off the warmth of someone who has been sound asleep, despite the icy air-conditioning in the apartment. She leaned against me, her face close to mine. "I'm really sorry for what I did to you," she said. Tears welled up in her eyes. "It was a shitty thing to do to a friend."

Jack was right, of course. I forgave her instantly—I couldn't help it. Kicking a cocker spaniel would have been easier.

"You're my *best* friend, David." She put both arms around my neck, giving me an ample view of her bosom. "I mean it."

"I know." There was even a certain amount of truth to it, I reflected sadly.

"I *would* have told you the truth, but I thought you might not give me Jack's address."

"I probably wouldn't have."

"So you see? I was right!" She sounded satisfied with her logic. She turned to Jack. "Did I fall asleep, or didn't I?"

"You did."

"Oh, baby, I haven't slept like that in so long. . . . I have to have some more champagne, honey."

Jack looked at his watch. "I'm not sure that's such a smart idea," he said.

Her jawline hardened, and all of a sudden she didn't look soft and helpless anymore. "I said I want some more fucking champagne, Jack," she snapped.

Jack stared at her for a moment, his face flushed; then—wisely, I thought—he decided to treat it as a joke. "You've got Irish blood in you," he said, and taking the glass, he went into the tiny kitchen and filled it for her.

She gave him a hug, then a long, sexy kiss. "Oh, lover," she moaned, "I'm sorry. I'm always cranky before my period. I didn't mean to shout at you, of all people." She went over to the sofa, rummaged through her handbag, picked out another capsule and washed it down with champagne.

"Are you sure that's wise?" I asked. "Taking all those pills on top of alcohol?"

"Oh, David, they're just for my allergies. And vitamins. Anyway, champagne isn't *alcohol?* It's, like, wine?"

Jack was grinning—having a good time. He *enjoyed* this kind of scene—it was his way of relaxing from the pressures that were building up ten minutes away in the Sports Arena, where his ambition—or his father's—was being fulfilled at last.

A telephone rang, then another. Jack picked up the nearest one and said, "I was taking a nap." He listened intently, his face turning somber. "You tell that son of a bitch his fucking *delegates* are for me. I got the biggest write-in vote in the history of Pennsylvania, and my name wasn't even on the ballot. . . . No, come to think of it, I'll tell him myself! I worked my ass off for years for this nomination, and I'm not going to have the goddamn governor of Pennsylvania fuck it up."

He banged down the telephone and picked up the other, dismissing us both with a wave of the hand. Clearly he had no more time for Marilyn, and more important things on his mind than Stars for Kennedy.

I have to say for Marilyn that when it was *absolutely* necessary, she could get herself pulled together in record time, no doubt from having spent so much of her early life in other people's bedrooms. Whatever she was taking, it apparently gave her instant energy, but at some cost. She walked unsteadily and managed to bump into several pieces of furniture on her short trip across the living room.

"Good-bye, lover," she said, giving Jack a kiss that left a smudge of lipstick on his cheek, which I hoped he would notice before he sat down to deal with Governor Lawrence of Pennsylvania.

"Do you have a car?" he asked.

"I came in my own," she said. She searched through her purse, held up a set of car keys, and dropped them on the floor.

Jack and I exchanged glances. The same thought crossed our minds simultaneously—Marilyn was in no condition to drive—and it also occurred to me that her car would be recognized by any reporter who was familiar with Hollywood. She still drove the same Cadillac convertible she had received as a gift before her marriage to DiMaggio. To those in the know, she might as well have left a sign outside 522 North Rossmore Avenue reading "Marilyn Monroe is visiting here."

"I'll drive you home," I said.

Jack nodded. "Good idea!"

Marilyn didn't object. She didn't seem to be able to pick her car keys up off the floor, so I did. I put my arm in hers and walked her to the door, leaving Jack to get on with his nomination.

Marilyn's car was parked at an angle in front of a fire hydrant, with a parking ticket on the windshield. I put her in the front seat and walked over to my car, to tell the driver to meet me at the Beverly Hills Hotel.

As I slipped behind the steering wheel, I glanced over at her. She was sitting back gracefully, one arm resting on the top of her door, the other stretched across the top of the white leather seat so that her fingers just touched the back of my neck. Her skirt had risen, and I could see a considerable portion of thigh, bisected by a lacy white garter strap. I was about to live out the most deep-seated fantasy of every American male—driving a convertible, top down, on a sunny day in Southern California, with the most beautiful blonde in the world beside me, her head back, her eyes half closed, her lips parted as if ready for a kiss.

Marilyn stroked the back of my neck as I drove, and turned the radio on—Sinatra, singing "Our Love Is Here to Stay." Marilyn sang softly along with Sinatra, as if it were a duet. She had a good voice, with a kind of breathy, sexy delivery that made men, myself included, dream. "Oh *God*, I love Frank!" she moaned. "He is so sexy."

"Mm."

"Don't be jealous, lover."

I sighed. "It would be nice to hear that *I'm* sexy for a change."

She moved closer and gave me a kiss. My eyes were on the road, but I felt her lips, wet and astonishingly warm, almost hot, on my cheek. "You're sexy," she whispered. "There. And I'm sorry for what I did, really."

She ran her hand down the front of my trousers, stroking my crotch gently with her fingertips, eyes closed, as if she were thinking about something else. She giggled. "This is *fun*," she said. "Let's go to Malibu."

I was due at the Ambassador's in a few minutes, and had appointments stacked up one after the other until late in the evening. Still, I asked myself, could I live with myself for the rest of my life if I turned down what was clearly—if I played my cards even halfway right—the opportunity to sleep with Marilyn? I knew that if I went to Malibu with Marilyn, I would end up betraying Jack—and Maria, of course—and I didn't care. I made a U-turn, and speeded up.

"We don't have swimsuits," I said.

"Mm. We'll go to the nude beach, lover. Then we'll drink some margaritas. I *love* margaritas. Then maybe we'll go dancing. . . ."

"Anything you say."

"You're a different person when you're having fun, David, you know?" She giggled again. "Maybe you should slow down, though," she said. "You just went through a stop sign."

"No I didn't."

"Believe me, sugar."

I caught a sudden flash of red lights in the rearview mirror, then heard the siren. A black-and-white police car appeared.

"Oh, shit," I said. "Better get the registration and insurance out of the glove compartment."

Marilyn looked blank. "Registration? Insurance?"

My heart sank. I pulled over, straightened my tie, and wondered whether a twenty-dollar bill slipped into my license would help matters. I thought not—the LAPD had a reputation for honesty, combined with storm trooper hostility toward traffic offenders. Then it occurred to me that my New York State driver's license was at home—I had a chauffeur in LA, so I never bothered carrying it.

The policeman was everything I had expected—tall, lean, wearing silver reflecting sunglasses, and as remote as a Martian. I explained my predicament and handed him my business card, which he held as if it were contaminated.

"Is it your car, sir?"

"No," I said, "it's this lady's." Marilyn had been staring straight ahead, still humming along with Sinatra.

"Honey," I said gently, "would you just hand me over the papers for the car?"

She opened the glove compartment, releasing an incredible avalanche of junk: stockings, an old bra, pill bottles—not to speak of loose pills—Tampax, makeup, used and unused Kleenex. Marilyn sifted through the debris deliberately, and shook her head. There were no papers for the car.

The policeman's eyes were on the pills—not a good sign. "Let me get this straight," he said to me. "You went through a stop sign. It isn't your car. You don't have a driver's license. There's no registration or proof of insurance."

"That's about the size of it. Look, I understand this is a serious matter, officer, but I have an office here, you can check up on who I am. Chief Parker knows me. I'm involved with the Democratic convention at the moment, and if there's any way of dealing with this quickly . . ." I took a shot at what mattered: "And privately," I suggested. "With the minimum of fuss and publicity."

There was no reaction. "I'm a Republican myself," he said. "Is this your car, miss?"

Marilyn stopped humming for a moment and nodded. "Yes," she whispered, her voice barely audible. "I think so."

"You *think* so?"

"I mean yes, it is. It was given to me. I don't know if it came with any papers, though?"

The policeman shook his head and took out his notebook. "If I could just explain . . ." I began, but he cut me off.

"Listen," he said, "*you,* my friend, are looking at some jail time." He turned to Marilyn, who still hadn't looked in his direction. "What's your name, miss?"

There was a long silence. "Marilyn Monroe," she said in a tiny voice.

The policeman wrote it down, then stared at it. "Don't you screw around with me, lady!" he snapped angrily, losing his cool for the first time. Then, as if she had been waiting for the moment, Marilyn took off her sunglasses and turned to face him, smiling sweetly.

"But I'm *not* screwing around, officer," she said, in that inimitable voice. "Honest."

"*Jesus!*" he said, awe in his voice. "You weren't kidding."

"I'm sorry I don't have the papers for the car," she said. "My husband probably kept them."

"Mr. Miller?" Like any Los Angeles cop, this one was well read on the home life of the stars.

"No. The husband before. Mr. DiMaggio."

"He was my hero when I was a kid."

She looked wistful. "Mine too," she said.

The officer took off his sunglasses. Without them he looked less frightening—just another third-generation California Okie from Bakersfield. "You mean you've been driving this car for what—four or five years?—without a registration slip?"

"I guess so."

"May I make a suggestion?" I interrupted, thinking quickly. "My lawyer is Ike Lublin. Couldn't he come down to head-quarters and sort all this out for us?"

The name had a visible impact on the police officer. Ike was one of the best-known attorneys in Los Angeles. Although he often defended major organized-crime figures, he kept on the good side of the cops, giving generously to police char-ities and appearing at police banquets, where he always took a whole table.

"You still have to come downtown," he said to me. "You were driving. You committed a moving violation. Miss Monroe too."

"Call me Marilyn," she said. "What Mr. Leman is trying to say is that I'd be really *embarrassed* if there was a story about this in the papers. My husband would be just *furious* with me. And the studio would be upset too." Her eyes teared up on cue. She picked up a Kleenex from the floor and dabbed at them prettily.

His Adam's apple bobbed. "Yes ma'am." He took off his hat and rubbed his head for a moment. "I tell you what I *can* do," he said. "You follow me. I'll take you into the police garage. You can call Mr. Lublin from there. That way police reporters won't even know you're there."

I could tell it was the best deal we were going to get, so we took it. We followed the black-and-white cruiser at a steady thirty-five miles an hour, while Marilyn, obeying my orders for once, dumped every pill bottle and pill out into the street.

Good as his word, our policeman whispered quickly to his sergeant—the names Marilyn Monroe and Ike Lublin did the trick—and we were placed in a small office next door to the holding pens in the basement, inhaling the smell of rank sweat, urine, and stale tobacco. Some of Marilyn's good spirits evaporated; she was brooding over the fact that I had made her throw away her pills. "Now is when I *need* them," she complained.

"No. If you think the cops will buy the allergy line, you're wrong. They may be your fans, but they live to bust people like you. Look what happened to Robert Mitchum."

She giggled. "The marijuana arrest? That was practically before I was *born*! I played opposite him in *River of No Return*. He wanted to fuck me, but he was so nasty about it I said no."

Marilyn's stories of her love life could be divided into two separate categories: people you were surprised to learn she'd fucked, and people you were surprised to learn she'd *refused* to fuck. It didn't seem the time or place to hear about it, however.

She was sitting behind a green metal desk, shielded by her dark glasses, her skin pale under the bright overhead fluorescent lights. "I hate this place," she said.

"Nobody likes police stations," I said soothingly, holding her hand. From the other side of the door came the zoolike noises of the holding cells: screams of anger, the sounds of vomiting, the noise of toilets being flushed, the crash and clank of locks and steel doors, a long, mournful, keening wail from some tormented soul.

She shivered. "It's the lights," she said. "It reminds me of the morgue."

"Come on, Marilyn. You've never been in a morgue."

"No. But I dream about it sometimes. And the lights in the dream are always like this."

"You dream about visiting the morgue?"

She shook her head. "I dream about lying there."

I recognized the signs that the effect of Marilyn's pills was wearing off. "Would coffee help?" I asked.

She shrugged. I went out, found a coffee machine, and returned with a couple of cups. Marilyn seemed to have cheered up a bit, perhaps because she had discovered one of her "allergy" pills wedged in a corner of her handbag—I noticed her palming it as she drank her coffee.

"How long are we going to be here?" she asked.

"Not much longer." Her hand was trembling. "We were about to have a great afternoon," I said to her gently. I don't think I have ever felt such a sense of loss, defeat, and failure—certainly I would feel nothing like it again until Marilyn's death, then Jack's, and Bobby's—and for a moment I was close to tears.

"Poor David," was all she said, for at that moment the door opened and Ike Lublin bustled in. He was smoking a big cigar, as was the sergeant, who came in behind him. It was clear from their expressions that the fix was in.

Within minutes, Marilyn had been smuggled into the back seat of Ike's limo and whisked off to the Beverly Hills Hotel, while Ike paid a fine for failure to register and insure a vehicle, plus over one thousand dollars in unpaid parking tickets dating back to 1954. I pleaded guilty to a moving violation and was fined fifty dollars.

Marilyn's part in the incident never surfaced, a tribute to Ike's influence in the LAPD, but my own involvement, in a much modified version, leaked rapidly outward and upward, so that when I finally got to see Jack early the next morning, his attitude was admiring.

"I never thought of you as a wild man," he said. "I guess I'd better not make you my CIA director after all."

"I don't know what you're talking about."

He laughed. "When I heard about it, I said, 'That sounds more like my little brother Teddy than my old friend David.' I couldn't believe my ears when somebody told me you'd been arrested for drunken driving. And a hooker in the car with you! It's a whole new side to your character, David. Is it a permanent change, do you think, or just a mid-life crisis?"

"It's all nonsense, Jack. A wild rumor."

"Sure." He grinned. His respect for me had obviously increased, which was ironic, I told myself with some satisfaction, considering how close I had come to fucking his girl.

I spread my papers out on the coffee table, and he began to concentrate on them. Then, all of a sudden, Jack looked up at me and grinned hugely. "Just tell me this," he said. "Was she worth what she cost?"

30

S<small>HE</small> WAS WATCHING THE CONVENTION ON TELEVISION when Jack's call came. She had hoped to watch the nominating speeches and the roll call with him, but the two days before the presidential nominations on July 13 had turned out to be unexpectedly confusing and difficult. She had seen Jack only twice, briefly—both times for a "quickie" in the hideaway on North Rossmore, with the phones ringing in the next room, and a couple of his aides waiting impatiently in the living room to take him to another state caucus or a visit to some divided delegation.

"I think we've got it," he said to her on the phone. She knocked on wood. *He* might not be superstitious, but she was. "We picked up four votes from South Dakota that had been pledged to Humphrey this morning, and thirteen and a half from Colorado. New Jersey is still a big problem. That prick Governor Meyner is still holding his delegation to vote for him as a favorite son on the first ballot, the bastard. Christ, are we going to get *that* son of a bitch when we get to Washington!"

"Where are you, lover?" she asked.

"At Marion Davies's house, with my father and mother. I'm going to have dinner here with them, then go back to the apartment and watch the balloting."

On television, Sam Rayburn was nominating Lyndon Johnson, while the Texas delegation, in white Stetsons, demonstrated. They did not look particularly excited to her. "Can I come over later?" she asked.

His voice was cautious. "The apartment isn't safe anymore. When I left, I had to climb down the fire escape at the back of the building and over a fence. It's surrounded by press and TV, and tonight will be worse. Besides, it's going to be two in the morning before I get to bed. . . ."

"Lover," she whispered, "say the word and I'll be there to help you celebrate. Even if it's at *four* in the morning. I don't care."

She could feel his resolution weakening. "I'll send a car for you," he said briskly. "There'll be someone in the garden with a flashlight to get you over the fence and up the fire escape steps. It may be one-thirty, two a.m., I can't be sure, so you'll have to stick close to the phone."

She made a soft kissing sound. "I'll be waiting. However long it takes. I'm going to give you a *presidential* kiss, sweetheart. It's a promise."

She heard voices in the background, one of them the Ambassador's. "I've got to go," Jack said. "We're going to eat."

"I'm not going to eat a thing until I get there, sugar. I'm saving my appetite for you." She giggled.

"Thank you for your—ah—support," he said: clearly, his parents were in the same room now. "I'll—ah—hold you to that promise."

"Knock 'em dead, tiger!" she said; then he hung up.

She put the receiver down, dialed room service, and ordered a fresh bottle of Dom Pérignon and a hamburger. She picked up her address book and got on with the tedious business of replacing the pills she had thrown away—she could *kill* David, she thought, for making her do it.

Keeping herself in pills took up a lot of her time. She got prescriptions from her New York internist, from Dr. Kris, and from her gynecologist in New York, but these were never enough, and the three doctors often talked to each other to make sure she wasn't getting too much medication, or the wrong kind. Luckily, she had a gynecologist and an internist in Los Angeles, too, who would write out prescriptions, but they still weren't enough to supply her needs, so although she was no hypochondriac, she went from specialist to specialist for more or less imaginary ailments ranging from back pains to allergies, and always finished by complaining of sleeplessness, or low energy, or the need to diet for a part. Very few doctors would refuse to write her out a prescription as she left the office, and if she was lucky, they sometimes made them refillable. By now nobody, not even Dr. Kris, had any idea of her total intake of barbiturates.

On the screen, Eugene McCarthy was nominating Stevenson. He had the delegates in tears as he cried out: "Do not reject this man who has made us all proud to be Democrats! Do not leave this prophet without honor in his own party!"

She cried herself, between bites of hamburger—she liked Eugene McCarthy, whom she had met in New York a couple of times, and Stevenson was the man she admired most after Clark Gable.

McCarthy's speech was followed by a tumultuous demonstration that seemed to go on forever, which would have made her worry about Jack's chances, except that he had warned her this was exactly what was going to happen. "Adlai has everything except the votes," he had said contemptuously.

The TV camera caught a fuss in the stands and zoomed in on Mrs. Kennedy, Jack's mother, taking her seat. Jack's father, she knew, was watching from the Marion Davies house because it had been decided at a tense family conference that his appearance at the Arena might frighten the delegates. It amused her that she and the Ambassador had something in common—they were both kept out of sight!

The chairman of the convention banged his gavel and called on Alabama, which cast twenty votes for Johnson and only three and a half for Jack. She cursed the southerners, racists and bigots one and all, and big, ugly Lyndon Johnson, with his mean eyes and Texas swagger.

She had sat through countless Academy Award ceremonies, but she had never felt such tension before as she wrote down the delegates for Jack in a long column, under the number 761—the votes he needed to win.

She lost track of the time, until the roll call finally reached Wyoming, with Jack still eleven votes short. Then she caught sight of his brother Teddy in the middle of the Wyoming delegation, a big, toothy grin on a face that was a coarser, plumper version of Jack's own, and she knew Jack had won, even before she heard all of Wyoming's fifteen votes go to Kennedy. . . .

At a quarter to, a car picked her up. Boom-Boom Reardon, looming hugely in the front seat, was driving. He gave her a doubtful look as she got in. "You ain't gonna be climbing over a backyard fence in that, I'm thinking," he said in his surly way, which she had learned not to take personally.

"*What* fence? I thought I had to climb a fire escape. I can do that!" She had dressed to please Jack, not for climbing obstacles. "Isn't it great about Jack?"

"Sure. But I never doubted it."

It was true, she reflected—none of the people around Jack ever seemed to doubt that he would get exactly what he wanted every time, whether it was her or the presidency. "How is he?" she asked.

"Pretty good. We had a little party for him at the apartment—sang 'When Irish Eyes Are Smiling,' while the Senator drank a beer."

"That must have been nice." She wished she had been there—wished that *she* had people around her who were devoted and loyal like Jack's. "I guess you'll be going to the White House with him if he wins."

"He'll win." She had forgotten that nobody around Jack ever said "*if* he wins."

She scrunched up in the back of the car as they passed the army of press and TV people in front of the house—even her own appearances in public produced nothing to equal *this*, she thought. They pulled to a stop in a dark alley, where two policemen and a couple of men in dark suits waited. There *was* a fence, she was dismayed to see as one of the cops turned on his flashlight, and there was no way she could imagine climbing over it in her tight dress.

"I'll never make it," she whispered—for everybody was glancing nervously toward the end of the alley, as if the TV news crews might appear at any moment.

"You can't stand around here too long," one of the security men said nervously. "You should have worn blue jeans."

"Save your advice on clothes for your wife," she snapped at him.

There was a moment of silence; then the cops exchanged glances. One of them nodded, climbed over the fence, and dropped down the other side. The first one bent over and held out his hands to form a step. She took off her shoes, tossed them over the fence, and with a giggle placed her foot in the cop's hands. She grabbed the top of the fence as he straightened up, then closed her eyes and took a blind leap over it, landing in the arms of the other cop, who swung her to the ground just in time, for the activity in the alleyway had attracted the attention of a few reporters, who had drifted down to see what was going on.

She picked up her shoes and with the policeman's help reached the bottom rung of the fire escape—he had to pick her up until she was sitting on his shoulders, shoes dangling from her hand. "Thanks," she whispered. "My ex-husband's an LAPD cop."

"I know," he said. "Jim Dougherty. I'll tell him we met."

"Don't tell him you had your head between my legs, will you?"

He laughed. "Anytime, lady. My pleasure."

Then she was on her own, climbing the steps in the dark in her stocking feet, being careful not to look down, until she reached an open window, from which Jack Kennedy, Democratic nominee for president of the United States, leaned out, a broad grin on his face.

Hoffa glared at the television screen in his office as if he could stare it into submission. Kennedy was squinting uncomfortably. The setting sun was in his eyes as he made his acceptance speech in the Los Angeles Coliseum—a rare piece of bad planning.

In Detroit, it was already late in the evening, and Hoffa had delayed taking his visitor to dinner to hear the speech. "What is all this 'new frontier' shit?" he asked petulantly.

Paul Palermo shrugged. He admired Kennedy's sense of style, which he associated with his own, and thought Hoffa was a slob with his white athletic socks and his greased-back hair, furrowed like a plowed field by the tracks of his comb.

"It's like Roosevelt's New Deal," Palermo said. "It's a good slogan. It sounds important, but it doesn't mean anything."

"Fuck him. Nixon's gonna win, you'll see. My money's on him."

Palermo reflected that this was true, literally as well as figuratively, for Hoffa was already strong-arming every Teamster local into making a contribution to Nixon's campaign fund. But Palermo wasn't so sure that Nixon would win. There was a whole world out there Hoffa knew nothing about, people one generation removed from union membership, who had college degrees, lived in the suburbs, never got their hands dirty, and aspired to some vision of glamour and style that Jack—and just as important, Jackie—now represented.

The more Palermo thought about it, the more certain he was that Kennedy was going to win. The fact that Kennedy had had the balls to defy the party elders by choosing Johnson for the vice presidential slot merely confirmed his opinion.

It wasn't really Palermo's job to tell Hoffa he was backing the wrong horse, but there *were* things he was supposed to make Hoffa understand, and he wasn't finding it easy. He stared at Kennedy on the screen, impressed by his grace and vigor. He listened to his acceptance speech with admiration marred only by Hoffa's interruptions, which he did his best to ignore.

Every so often, the TV camera panned to the audience for a reaction shot. Sitting among them were a lot of recognizable Hollywood celebrities, whom the camera lingered on—another smart move of the Kennedys, Palermo thought. He saw Frank Sinatra, Peter Lawford, Sammy Davis, Jr., Shelley Winters, Angle Dickinson, even Marilyn Monroe, staring transfixed toward the podium, tears rolling down her cheeks, hands clenched to her bosom like a Madonna, as Kennedy reached the climax of his speech. If *that* didn't win Kennedy votes, Palermo thought, nothing would!

"Ain't that Marilyn Monroe?" Hoffa asked, leaning forward for a closer look at the screen.

Palermo nodded. He had a drink, but he wanted his dinner. He knew food didn't interest Hoffa, who often skipped meals, or ate from a vending machine.

Hoffa lowered his voice conspiratorially. "She's been fucking him, every night, during the convention. Did you know that?"

Palermo knew, and it only increased his admiration for Kennedy. He stared at the screen. There was no point in letting Hoffa find out what he knew and what he didn't.

"I got it all on tape," Hoffa said. "I even got a photo of her climbing the fire escape to his bedroom. Guy took it with infrared film and a telephoto lens, clear as day. What do you think of that?"

Palermo pretended to be impressed. The more he heard of Jack Kennedy, the less he believed blackmail would work with him. Mr. B., who had been informed of Bernie Spindel's efforts on behalf of Hoffa, had not been impressed either. "So Kennedy sleeps with movie stars?" Mr. B. had said, in the safety of the Tucson basement, for the FBI not only had microphones in the rest of the house but filmed the old man night and day through the windows with high-speed telephoto cameras so that lip-readers could transcribe his conversations. "So what? Let him sleep with who he wants if he gets rid of Castro and we get our casinos back." That was Mr. B.'s view of it, and it made good sense to Palermo.

"All that's fine, Jimmy," he said to Hoffa, "the tapes, the photo, and all that, but if he's elected . . ."

Hoffa stared malevolently at the figure on the screen. "It'll never happen."

" 'If,' I said—"

"If it does, which it won't, he and his brother are dead men, they don't lay off the Teamsters. I can tell you *that* right now."

"That kind of talk is a mistake, Jimmy. If he wins, we want him to help us get our action back in Havana."

Hoffa shrugged. The vast audience in the Los Angeles Coliseum was going wild. Kennedy stood there, in front of what looked like an endless sea of people applauding, shouting, pressing forward toward the rostrum—so many people, so much enthusiasm, that even Kennedy himself seemed overwhelmed. "Fuck Havana," Hoffa growled. "I got no interest there."

The camera caught Marilyn Monroe jumping up and down in the crowd like a cheerleader, an embarrassed David Leman by her side. The image flashed on the screen so quickly that Palermo wasn't sure he'd actually seen it. "I thought we were on the same side, Jimmy," he said mildly.

"We are."

"Then our troubles are your troubles. We worry about Havana, *you* worry about Havana, right?"

Hoffa glowered at him. "You guys got Vegas—thanks to me. What do you want Havana for?"

"Vegas is way out west, Jimmy. It's a long flight. Havana is ninety miles from Key West. Half an hour by plane from Miami, three hours from New York. Do you want me to draw you a map?"

"Don't get fucking smart with me. I get the picture."

Palermo smiled with his perfect teeth, though at the back of his mind was the hope that he'd be around to watch Hoffa getting whacked when it finally happened—as he was pretty sure it would, eventually.

Palermo hated rudeness and despised Hoffa, but Mr. B.'s instructions had been crystal-clear, as always. Promise Hoffa anything, he had said. As long as the East Coast families were cut off from the lucrative Cuban gambling revenues that had made them rich, they had to go begging hat in hand to the Chicago mob for a piece of the action in Las Vegas, and that meant building more casinos, and building more casinos meant borrowing more money from the Teamster Central States Pension Fund, which meant, of course, that Hoffa was in the catbird seat.

It was really very simple—though nobody in law enforcement seemed able to grasp the dynamics of the thing: The families couldn't borrow money from banks, or float an underwriting on Wall Street, or build casinos with hundreds of millions of dollars in used bills of small denominations! Convicted felons couldn't be directors or company officials, or sign for loans, or issue stock. So they needed a front and a source of unlimited, no-questions-asked loans, and Hoffa could provide both, in return for which they supported his control over the union.

So far as Palermo was concerned, the sooner the New Jersey legislature legalized casino gambling, the better. Once Atlantic City was off and running, the East Coast families could dispense with Hoffa and take their long-awaited revenge against Momo Giancana and the Chicago mob. Unless, of course, Castro was to fall, in which case all these good things would happen sooner.

Palermo thought about the possibility pleasurably—he pictured Hoffa in the back seat of a car, a garrote around his thick neck, the beady little eyes popping as he struggled for breath, the thin-lipped mouth open like that of a gaffed fish. . . . He dismissed the image. For the moment, Hoffa was needed.

He made a small, placating gesture with his hands. "I know you get the picture, Jimmy. You're a smart guy. That's just what I'm saying."

"Try telling me something I don't know. Like why I'm up to my ass in subpoenas while your guys are sitting pretty."

Palermo knew there was some truth to Hoffa's complaint, though much of it was Hoffa's own fault. He was a loudmouth, so he drew a lot of heat down on himself. "Jimmy," he said soothingly, "if it's the grand jury thing in Tennessee you're talking about, what can I tell you? . . . Grand jury tampering is a no-no, you know that."

"It's done alla time, Chrissake."

"Sure, but not getting *caught!*"

"I'll beat the fucking rap, no thanks to your guys. If they think they can hang Jimmy Hoffa out to dry, they're wrong."

"They don't think that, Jimmy. They have great respect for you."

"I don't give a shit about their respect. When I'm in trouble, I want their help. You tell your guys, I go down, *they* go down. I want someone whacked, they *whack* him, whoever the fuck he is, even if it's J. Edgar Hoover. That was the deal."

"They understand that." They did too, and it scared the shit out of them, even Mr. B., who felt that Giancana himself should have been whacked for giving his word to Hoffa on behalf of the Commission. Now, of course, they were stuck with it—as men of honor, it could hardly be otherwise.

"They *better* understand." Hoffa glanced at his watch. "Let's go eat," he said.

He got up, walked over to the television, and snapped the set off, turning the knob so hard with his blunt fingers that he broke it off. He tossed it across the room into the wastepaper basket beside his desk. "Fuck Jack Kennedy," he growled. "Him and his brother both. They want to get tough with Jimmy Hoffa, I'll show them what tough is."

He opened the door—there were no bodyguards outside, as if Hoffa wanted to prove that he wasn't afraid of anything.

That was typical of Hoffa, Palermo thought, and stupid. A man should know when to be afraid. A man who didn't feel fear was dangerous to himself—and other people.

31

No sooner was she back in Reno from the conven-tion than *The Misfits* turned into a kind of freak show.

People came from both coasts to visit the production, mostly to see for themselves whether it was true that her marriage was breaking up, but also to catch a glimpse of Monty Clift in action. If that wasn't enough to inspire curiosity, there was Gable, struggling to keep his temper in a company of peo-ple he tended to regard as undisciplined upstarts. Journalists and photographers were everywhere—it was the most photo-graphed picture she had ever been in—as well as people like Frank Sinatra, Clifford Odets, Marietta Tree, David Leman, and Aaron Diamond, all of them drawn by the rumor that something very special was happening here.

The tone of the production was set at the very beginning, when a group photograph was taken of herself, Gable, Monty, Eli Wallach, Huston, and her husband, all of them posing together to mark the first day of shooting. She was seated in the center foreground on a broken old swivel chair, sweating in the hundred-degree heat, wearing the revealing white dress with big red cherries (a joke nobody but Monty recognized) that she herself had chosen for Roslyn, with everybody else gathered around her. Both Gable and Wallach were pissed off, when they saw it, at being pushed to the side of the photograph, though she couldn't see what they had to complain about—poor Monty, perched beside her on the desk chair with just the corner of his ass, looked so wizened and scrunched over that he might have been a dwarf.

There were many unspoken realities hovering around the company of *The Misfits* in Reno that summer. One of them was that she and Arthur were sleeping in separate bedrooms and scarcely speaking, kept together only by mutual recrimina-tions and the need to get this picture in the can. Another was that

Gable, for all his rugged appearance of manly strength, was ailing—the slightest effort turned his face ashen gray beneath the outdoorsman's tan, and when he thought nobody was looking, he popped nitroglycerin tablets, for angina.

And Huston hated Monty. Like most successful directors, Huston enjoyed playing God, and because he was so cunning, he made a dangerous game of it. He let Gable know that he didn't think he still had the guts to do his own stunts; he taunted Monty, as well as playing him off against Eli Wallach; he treated her with barely concealed contempt, as if she were a basket case.

Of course, it didn't help a bit that her character, Roslyn, was so unmistakably her husband's idea of *her*—flirtatious, destructive, impulsive, a nervous bundle of nameless, unidentifiable fears and anxieties, a basket case, in fact.

Arthur knew her as only a husband could, and knew just how to angle the blade for a thrust to the heart! Roslyn was one of those beautiful women whose only real talent is for attracting men, and whose ego is so weak that she can only survive by proving over and over again that she can seduce them, even when she doesn't want them. . . . The worst of it was, he had hit the bull's-eye—Roslyn *was* her. She didn't need to agonize over what Roslyn would do in this scene or that scene, she only had to be herself.

For her, any picture was a battlefield, but never before had she been gripped by such fierce and conflicting emotions— rage against Arthur, with whom she was obliged to share a suite, if not a bed; fear of Huston, who was like some kind of devilish magician, able to see directly into her soul and torture her with what he found there; her hopeless schoolgirl infatuation for Gable, her ideal man; and a terrible, sinking feeling of companionship with Monty, whose troubles seemed to echo, if not to dwarf, her own.

As the weeks went by, Monty got more and more remote, almost glassy-eyed, hanging by his fingernails to what remained of his sanity, while Huston continued to make savage fun of him. Her spirits went down with Monty's, as if she were in free-fall. . . .

All around her—except for Gable himself—hatred flourished: Eli Wallach and her husband rewrote the script to

turn her into a hooker and make Eli the hero instead of
Gable; Huston, like Olivier before him, tried to get rid of
Paula Strasberg. . . . Finally she went over the edge, took so
many pills that she couldn't focus her eyes, let alone say her
lines, and had to be sent back to Los Angeles and placed in
the hands of a new psychiatrist, Dr. Ralph Greenson.

She really didn't have a choice. So far as the studio was
concerned, it was that or close down the picture, and she had
too much at stake to let it be closed down. Dr. Greenson,
whom she liked immediately, put her into a nursing home,
where her dependence on Nembutal was gradually reduced
to a more tolerable level, and persuaded the studio to put the
production on hold.

Unlike Dr. Kris, Dr. Greenson was part of the industry, one
of those "reliable," "realistic" doctors whom producers called
whenever a star had a serious problem that threatened the shooting schedule. Like an army surgeon's, Greenson's job was to
patch up the wounded and get them back into the trenches as
soon as possible. Within ten days he had her back in Reno
again, ready for work.

She staggered through it, sustained now by Greenson, by
Dr. Kris—long-distance daily from New York—and by Paula.
She was determined to make it to the end, when to nobody's
surprise, she would bring the marriage to an end as well.

At the beginning of November, she played her final scene,
on the Paramount lot, with Gable, sitting in the front seat of
Gay Langland's old car. Gable leaned close to her, in the artificial moonlight, and said, "Just head for that big star straight
on. The highway's under it. Take us right home."

He did it in one take, professional to the end. The next day
Arthur moved out of the bungalow at the Beverly Hills Hotel
where she and Yves had so recently carried on their affair, and
she watched alone as John F. Kennedy was elected president
of the United States.

PART THREE

Lancer

32

JACK LISTENED TO THE RETURNS AT HYANNIS PORT surrounded by his family. He and Jackie were the only ones who looked relaxed. His sisters and his sister-in-law Ethel had the nervous look of women who had been slaving for days to prepare a big party and, now that the night was upon them, weren't sure it was going to be a success. The Ambassador, Bobby, and Teddy spent the evening on the phone, dealing with the most important men on election night: the county sheriffs who guard the ballot boxes—and can make them disappear.

I had been invited, just in case there was any high-level problem with the press or the networks, but since there wasn't, I spent the evening penciling electoral votes on a list prepared by Ethel on the back of a piece of shirt cardboard, while Maria, much to Jackie's annoyance, flirted mildly with Jack.

Jack watched television off and on all evening without saying much, except when he saw Nixon, his family beside him, as he walked past his supporters to his hotel. "The guy has no class at all," he said then. "Maybe it's just as well I'm going to be president instead of him."

About midnight, Bobby, who had been intently engaged for what seemed like hours in a conversation with Mayor Daley of Chicago about the ballot boxes in Cook County, came over and stared at my list, grim with tension. "It's close," he said, "but I think we're winning. Why doesn't that son of a bitch Nixon concede?"

Jack shook his head at Bobby. "Why should he?" he said. "I wouldn't."

He finished his bottle of beer and stood up. "I'm going to bed," he said, and left the room. He slept, as he told us later, "like a baby," and didn't discover he was the next president of the United States until he woke up in the morning.

The atmosphere the next day was curiously muted. The only person who was unabashedly elated was the Ambassador, who was already drawing up his own "enemies list" of people who had not shared his vision or had opposed it over the years.

Jackie, I thought, seemed guardedly pleased, as if Jack had finally done something she approved of, but Jack himself was, if anything, a little withdrawn. I suspect that as the Secret Service took up their posts around what was soon to be called "the Kennedy compound," the reality was finally sinking in—he was the President-elect. Perhaps he was a little awed by it all, despite himself. "What do we do now?" I had heard him ask Bobby when they saw each other before breakfast.

Since for once Bobby didn't have a ready answer, Jack went for a walk along the beach, and seemed to have recovered some of his good spirits by the time his usual breakfast was served—two eggs fried in butter, three rashers of bacon, and toast.

"I still can't believe it's over," he said to me.

"Oh, it's over, all right. You should see the telegrams. Hundreds of them already, Mr. President." It was the first time I called him that. I supposed it would get easier with time.

He grinned. "That's music to my ears!" He leaned back in his chair and lit a cigar—a sure sign he was in a good mood. Jackie and the rest of the family had come down to breakfast, so we were no longer alone. "Have you looked through them?" he asked me.

"A few." I pointed to the floor. I had brought them in a wastepaper basket that was already overflowing. Before the end of the day a full secretarial staff would arrive to take care of such things. I picked one out at random. "Congratulations from Cardinal Spellman," I said. "He's praying for you."

Jack laughed. "He supported Nixon, but he's praying for me? He should pray for Nixon."

I picked up another. "Governor Meyner. He says New Jersey is part of the New Frontier."

"He's right at the top of Dad's enemies list. Mine too, if I had one."

I had leafed through dozens of telegrams from celebrities, politicians, big businessmen, ordinary citizens, world leaders, when one caught my eye. "DEAR MR. PRESIDENT," it read, "ALL

THE STARS ARE TWINKLING AT YOUR VICTORY, BUT THIS LIT-
TLE STAR IS SHINING JUST FOR YOU. CONGRATULATIONS AND
LOVE, MARILYN."

I must have held the telegram in my hand long enough to
make everybody curious, for Jackie asked, "Who's that one
from?"

I gulped. "Some nuns at a parochial school in Los Angeles,"
I extemporized wildly. Jack grabbed the telegram out of my
hand before I could stop him.

"Oh, how sweet! Read what it says, Jack," Jackie said.

Jack glared at me for having put him on the spot. He frown-
ed, as if he found it hard to read without his glasses, then said:
"Dear Mr. President: All the faculty and children of Immacu-
late Conception are rooting for you, and praying for you and
Mrs. Kennedy. Sisters Roseanna, Mary Beth, Dolores, and
Gilda."

He folded the paper up and slipped it in his pocket. "I'll
have to answer this one personally," he said solemnly.

"Sister *Gilda?*" Ethel asked.

"That's Los Angeles for you," Jack said lightly. He stood
up and stretched. "Come with me," he said to me.

We stepped outside and walked down the beach. A brisk
breeze was blowing off the sea. The President-elect was
dressed in chinos, a sweater, and Top-Siders, while I was
shivering in gray flannels, a blazer, and city shoes. On the
dunes, silhouetted against the gray sky, we could see Secret
Service agents slipping into place as we progressed along the
beach.

"I'm not going to find it easy to get used to them," Jack
said.

"They come with the territory. Besides, you may find them
useful eventually. They caddy for Ike."

He shook his head. "I don't intend to give up my freedom
just because I'm the president."

I knew that for Jack "freedom" meant women. If anything, I
thought, the Secret Service would be helpful—no government
agents were more susceptible to presidential glamour, or more
eager to be seduced. Jack would have them eating out of his
hand before the inauguration. They would do everything short
of pimp for him.

"They've given me my code name," he said. " 'Lancer.'

Everyone and everything gets a code name, apparently. Bobby is 'Legend.' The White House is 'Castle.' In case you're wondering, you're 'Blazer.' "

"Blazer?"

"I guess they were struck by the way you dress."

I wondered if the Secret Service had a list of code names for Jack's girls as well. Later I was to discover that Marilyn's was "Strawhead"; someone there had a sense of humor.

We trudged on. "How is Marilyn?" he asked. For nearly four months he had been campaigning night and day. There had been no time for him to stay in touch with Marilyn and her troubles.

"From what I hear, the picture was a nightmare. Pills, problems, stress. . . . Huston had to interrupt shooting so she could go back to Los Angeles and spend a week or so in some kind of psychiatric nursing home. . . . The marriage is over, you know. Kaput."

I didn't tell him that adding to Marilyn's woes was the fact that Clark Gable had suffered a heart attack on Election Day, only twenty-four hours after playing the final scene of *The Misfits* with Marilyn.

"I'd better have a word with her," he said thoughtfully, "about that telegram. She's a great girl, but she's sometimes a little too—ah—enthusiastic." He glanced at me. "We don't want her trying to reach me at home all the time, do we?"

I thought the "we" was a nice touch, but I merely nodded. I wasn't about to volunteer for the task of telling Marilyn to be more careful, nor, as it turned out, was Jack willing to do it himself. The Secret Service, ever obliging, solved the problem by giving her a special number to call at the White House so there was no risk of her getting through to the private quarters upstairs, where Jackie might pick up the phone.

Much as he might have liked to talk about Marilyn, as president-elect he had other things on his mind. "Do you want a job in the administration?" he asked suddenly.

"Well, I've been giving it some thought. . . ."

He did not look particularly pleased or receptive. It occurred to me, to my dismay, that he might have been hoping I would say no. "What did you have in mind?" he asked briskly.

"Well, I was hoping—"

Before I could finish, he interrupted me. "USIA?" he suggested. "That's a possibility, I guess. I'd like to see the agency upgraded. Hell, part of our problem with the Third World is that we don't get our story out to them. We've got more to offer them than the Russians, but you'd never know it."

"I don't see myself handing out copies of *The Federalist* to the natives, Jack, if that's what you're thinking," I said to him rather stiffly. He knew damned well I wasn't interested in becoming a Washington bureaucrat, and that director of the United States Information Agency was a dogsbody job, carrying with it no access to the president and endless aggravation from right-wing congressmen who wanted copies of *Huckleberry Finn* or *The Grapes of Wrath* removed from USIA libraries all over the world.

"You can do better than that," I snapped, not bothering to hide my anger a bit.

He flushed. "Like what?"

I was pretty sure his father had passed on my desire for the London embassy to Jack. There were few secrets between the two of them where politics was concerned. "I had in mind London, frankly."

"Ambassador to the Court of St. James's?" he asked, shaking his head. We walked on in silence for a few hundred feet while he thought about it—or pretended to. "I don't know, David," he said at last. "I'm not sure the London embassy is, ah, right for you. . . ."

He was tactful enough not to say that *I* wasn't right for *it,* but all the same, I was furious. I had earned the right to ask for what I wanted, and *get* it, I thought. "I think I'd do a good job," I said sharply. "And I think I've earned it."

"I guess. I mean, sure, David, no question about *that.* . . . Let me think about it, okay?"

"Certainly." I wasn't about to plead my case further with Jack. I had too much pride for that.

Still, I was deeply hurt by his ingratitude, and angered, of course—but worst of all, I felt *foolish.* Luckily, I had shared my ambition with nobody except Joe and Marilyn—thank God I had never discussed it with Maria!—but I felt cheated, as if Jack had closed me out of his inner circle, while at the same time I despised myself for still wanting to be there.

He must have caught my expression, because he put his hand on my shoulder and said, "I'm going to need you close by me, David. Closer than London. You know how much I value your advice."

"Thank you."

"And help. I wouldn't have won the nomination without you, I know that." He could see I wasn't warming to this flattery. "I'll think about the ambassadorship, David. I really will. We'll talk about it soon."

We walked on for a while, but the mood between us was broken. Jack, I told myself, would probably end up offering me the ambassadorship after consulting with his father, and I would almost surely end up accepting it, but it wouldn't be the same as if it had been offered with enthusiasm when I asked for it, and we both knew it.

He noticed I was shivering in my blazer. "You're cold," he said. "Let's walk back." He sighed as we turned around, the wind at our backs now. "This whole business of jobs is a real pain in the ass," he went on, drawing me into it, no doubt to smooth my ruffled feathers. "I've already had three calls recommending Adlai for secretary of state. . . . Over my dead body!"

Reluctantly, I *was* drawn back into Jack's plans in the role of adviser, which was clearly where he wanted me. "What about Bobby?" I asked.

"What *about* Bobby? I'd love to have *him* at State, and he'd be damned good there, but it's out of the question. I've been thinking of putting him in Defense, but the fallout would be bad from that, too. . . ."

"What does *he* want?"

"Bobby? He doesn't know. One day he wants a major Cabinet post, the next he wants to leave Washington and teach. . . . What would you think if I made him attorney general?"

I whistled, impressed despite my anger. "Talk about controversial! With his reputation for being ruthless. . . ."

He laughed. "Bobby's no more ruthless than I am. He's just shy, that's all, but it comes across on camera as ruthlessness. It's an idea, though, isn't it? Attorney general? It would make a lot of people sit up and take notice."

"J. Edgar Hoover would be one of them."

"Ah?" A veiled expression crossed his face—that of a man

about to reveal a secret. "To tell you the truth, David, I've been thinking it might be time for Hoover to go."

We were back at the house—thank God! My fingernails were purple with cold. "Are you sure that's such a good idea?" I asked.

Jack looked at me, and for the first time it struck home to me that he *was* really the president-elect. His eyes had a determination I hadn't seen there before, his mouth was set with the firmness of granite. "Yes," he snapped, "I'm completely sure."

He opened the door, and I could feel the warmth of an open fire beckoning me, and hear the Kennedy women's boisterous laughter.

"It's time for a change," he said.

She awoke, confused and aching, in a strange room, lying naked on the cold floor. The last thing she remembered was shouting, "You can't do this, I'm Marilyn Monroe!" as the door was slammed and locked.

The room was small, furnished with a simple hospital cot, the legs bolted to the floor, and an equally immovable bedside table. The window was opaque, covered with wire mesh so you couldn't throw yourself out of it or break the glass. The tiny bathroom had no door, and the mirror was made of some kind of unbreakable plastic, firmly screwed to the tiled wall. It was a cell, really, if you wanted to face facts, which she didn't.

She lay there thinking about the events that had brought her here to Payne Whitney. Her collapse had begun with her return to New York after the completion of *The Misfits*. Arthur had moved out of the apartment on East Fifty-seventh Street, leaving behind the portrait of herself that she had given him in London, which made her feel even worse.

A week later, she drove up to Roxbury to collect her belongings from what was now his house, and say a tearful good-bye to Hugo, the dog they had bought when the marriage still seemed to have a chance. She had cried all the way home in the rented car, driving with the windows down, despite the cold, because she was afraid she was suffocating.

A few days after that, she got the news of Joe Schenck's death, followed by that of Arthur's mother, of whom she had been fond. She felt death was pressing in on her—she stayed at home, surrounded by the untouched cartons she had brought back from Roxbury, trying not to think about the future.

She heard about Gable's death when a reporter called her at two in the morning for a comment, and she became hysterical with grief and sorrow, as if Gable really *had* been her father. She knew it would provoke comment if she didn't attend his funeral in California, but she didn't feel strong enough to go, afraid she would collapse in public as she had at Johnny Hyde's, so she stayed in New York, miserable and guilty. She watched the funeral on television alone in her apartment and heard many of the mourners, as they were interviewed, wonder why she hadn't even bothered to turn up.

Other events too seemed to be happening without her, as if she were receding from life. She watched Jack's inauguration on television in the VIP lounge at the Dallas airport on her way to Juárez with her lawyer, to get her divorce from Arthur.

Her isolation from the world—and its increasing hostility toward her—made her feel like a prisoner in her apartment, but she hadn't had the strength to leave. All the people she might have called upon for help were away—Jack immersed in the crucial first hundred days of his presidency, David in Europe with his wife, Paula ill herself. . . . She had nobody to turn to, and things seemed to have reached rock bottom for her—so much so that she could hardly imagine how they could get worse.

But soon they had. A reporter called her in the middle of the night again, this time for her comment on a story that Kay Gable had blamed *her* for Gable's death. It was the final blow, the one that brought her here to this bare room in New York's most prestigious psychiatric hospital, where she had allowed Dr. Kris to commit her only because it was understood that she was going to get a chance to rest and recuperate away from the press, and where, instead, she had been treated like a dangerous lunatic in an insane asylum.

She remembered now why she was naked. She had objected to being placed in a room with a peephole in the door so the attendants could spy on her, and having lost that one, fought against being put in a short hospital gown as if she were sick. She had torn it off and ripped it to shreds in a fit of anger. The attendants, tough-looking women who reminded her more of female wrestlers than nurses, had made an attempt to get her into a fresh gown, but she fought them off, kicking, biting, and scratching.

"Squat bare-ass naked as long as you like, you crazy bitch!" the senior of them said, when they finally gave up, and that was exactly what she was doing, unable to think of anything better. Screams, shouts, threats, pleas, and begging had failed. Her nightmare—the worst one of all—had come true: she was locked up like a crazy person, locked up like her mother and her grandmother too.

She *knew* this wasn't what Dr. Kris had intended, but she had no way to reach her—or anyone else, for that matter. She was learning, the hard way, what Monty had once told her: The saner you are, the harder it is to prove it.

When the door opened, she let out a scream. The man standing there was tall, thin, balding, with the face of a Jewish intellectual and horn-rimmed glasses—the spitting image of Arthur, who she had supposed it *was* for a moment, despite the white coat.

He looked puzzled. "Mrs. Miller?" he asked. "Are you okay?"

"No!" she shouted. "Of *course* I'm not! Do I *look* okay? And I'm not Mrs. Miller anymore either. I'm Marilyn Monroe."

"Yes, I know. The only thing is, you're registered as Mrs. Faith Miller, you see. To keep the press guessing, I suppose." He peered at her hesitantly. "Ah, would you like to put a gown on?"

"I would not! I want to get out of here."

"Sitting around naked isn't going to do it, I'm afraid."

"Call Dr. Kris, *please*. She'll tell you I don't belong here. It's a mistake."

"Yes? Of course, *everybody* here says it's a mistake."

He sat down on the bed and made himself comfortable. Out of the corner of his eye he caught her glancing at the door to her room. "It's not locked," he said pleasantly. "You could probably make it through the door before I caught you. But there's an attendant outside, one of the ones who tried to put a fresh gown on you; then there's a locked door at the end of the hall, and after that, a guard at the elevator. And if you got past all that, you'd just end up in the lobby stark naked, and it's full of reporters who seem to have worked out that 'Mrs. Miller' is you."

He sighed. "We'd have to put you in a straitjacket, which is no fun at all, so why bother?"

"I'm not looking my best," she said irrelevantly.

"Is that a fact? You look pretty damned good to me. Listen, you were talking about mistakes a moment ago. Tell me: Do you think it was a mistake to open the living room window and try to throw yourself out onto Fifth-seventh Street?" He asked her earnestly, as if he wanted the answer to a reasonable question.

"I didn't do that."

"It says here you did."

"I opened the window and started to climb out on the ledge."

"But you *were* planning to take a swan dive out the window? From the fourteenth floor? Otherwise, why go out on the ledge?"

She was a little surprised by his breezy informality. "I guess," she admitted.

"Why didn't you jump?"

"I looked down and saw someone I knew walking along Fifty-seventh Street. A kid named Timmy—a fan. I couldn't do it in front of him. I should have just kept my eyes shut and jumped."

"Yes, that's the way to do it, all right."

"They say your mind blanks out when you fall—you don't know a thing about it."

"Oh, I don't think so. I've had patients who jumped and survived, more or less. They all saw the ground coming up at them, and felt it when they hit. They didn't like it a bit."

He took his glasses off and polished them with the end of his tie. He had nice eyes, gentle and shrewd. "What made you do it?"

"I was tired of life. And unhappy."

"Well, aren't we all? No, what I want to know is what *specific* thing? Did you forget to buy toothpaste, for instance?"

She stared at him in astonishment, wondering if he was making fun of her. "Toothpaste? I don't get it."

"I had a patient—an attractive, wealthy lady—who came back from shopping, realized she hadn't remembered to buy toothpaste, opened the window, and jumped out onto Park Avenue. She landed on a canopy, so she survived."

He put his glasses back on and smiled at her, as if he were seeing her clearly at last. "Forgetting the toothpaste brought home the inconsequentiality of her life, her growing inability to deal with details, the fact that a trip to the drugstore or D'Agostino's had become the high point of her day. . . . Her husband had left her for a younger woman, by the way. I suppose a strict Freudian might decide that the missing tube of toothpaste was a phallic symbol—the husband's penis, you see—but I don't think it's necessary to go symbol hunting. She knew why she tried to kill herself, and so do you."

She wrapped her arms around herself as if she were cold, though it was warm in the room. "It was the stories about Gable's death that did it," she said softly.

"Forgive me, I don't follow these things closely. He died of a heart attack, didn't he—oh, several months ago or more? So why do it now?"

"Kay—his wife—said I killed him." She had not thought she could say it.

He raised an eyebrow. She tried to explain. "It was in every newspaper, in every goddamn, stinking, fucking gossip column. Kay said it was *my* fault he had a heart attack, because of the strain of dealing with my lateness and my moods."

He did not look shocked. "And do you think that was true?"

"Everybody thinks so. Millions of people think he died because of me now."

He nodded. "Possibly, but that's not what I asked. I don't care what Mrs. Gable or the great American moviegoing public think. I want to know what *you* think."

She took her time before she answered. If anybody was responsible for Gable's death, it was John Huston, who had taunted him into a totally unnecessary display of courage and strength just to get a sharper performance out of him. She *did* feel guilty, of course, for having put Gable through so much professional misery, but he had always behaved toward her like the gentleman he was.

When she heard about Kay's accusation, she had gone numb with horror. Her grief had been silent—she had simply walked to the window and stepped out onto the ledge, and if she hadn't seen Timmy Hahn down there, in his familiar windbreaker, she would have thrown herself to a silent death. Timmy, really, had saved her life—Timmy and Dr. Kris, who had come over the moment she was called. . . .

She wanted to answer the doctor's question honestly. "I *feel* guilty," she said hesitantly, "but I don't think I *am* guilty."

He gave a satisfied smile, as if she'd passed a test. "That's very good," he said. "May I call you Marilyn?"

"Sure," she said. She was beginning to like him.

"I think it's a sign of real progress, Marilyn."

"You don't think I'm nuts?"

"Everybody here is nuts. Some a little, some a lot."

"I guess so."

"The doctors most of all," he said with a laugh. He rubbed his nose between his thumb and forefinger, just like Dr. Greenson—apparently it was something all analysts did. Along with the gesture, his expression turned suddenly serious. "To answer your question properly, Marilyn, I would say you're not any more nuts than most people in here. Or outside, for that matter. You feel things too deeply, that's all."

"Then I don't belong here?"

"Who does?" He looked through her chart again. "What kind of physical shape are you in?" he asked. "Any problems?"

She found that a little puzzling. "Why?" she asked.

"Mens sana in corpore sano. A healthy mind is a healthy body. People—even doctors—separate mental problems from physical ones. That's a mistake. The mind and the body are one."

"That's what I was brought up to believe, sort of!" she cried excitedly. "We were Christian Science."

He winked at her. "Don't tell anyone I said so, Marilyn, but Mary Baker Eddy was no dummy. I'll tell you what—stand up and do a few deep knee bends."

"Knee bends?"

"I want to see what kind of shape you're in, that's all."

She got up—it was a pleasure not to be squatting on the floor like an autistic child—and did a few knee bends.

"Thank you. Now touch your toes a few times."

She was one of those lucky women who kept in pretty good shape without doing much about it, except for dancing practice, where her roles called for her to dance. She touched her toes easily without bending her knees.

"Run in place for a while."

She ran in place, stomach pulled in tight, working up a pleasant, gentle sweat, as her breasts jiggled in time to her steps.

"*Very* nice, Marilyn," he said. "No problems so far as I can see." He rose and put his ear against her chest, then placed his hand on her left breast, about where the heart was, his palm warm and slightly damp. "Good breathing, good heartbeat. Why don't you slip that gown on now, like a good girl?"

She picked up one of the gowns the nurse had tried to get on her, and sat down on the bed. "How do I get out of here? Will you call Dr. Kris?"

"Certainly. I can see no reason to keep you here at all." He gave her a bright, reassuring smile. "Good luck, Marilyn," he said, lingering in the doorway for a moment. Then he was gone and the door clicked shut behind him.

She could feel a small but growing sense of calm coming over her. Dr. Kris would soon have her out of here. She wasn't suicidal, after all—she had merely been overcome by the accumulation of bad luck: the divorce, Gable's death, then the press furor over Kay Gable's comments. . . . Anybody would break under such a load, she told herself.

She was beginning to feel hungry at last, and wished she hadn't refused to eat the last meal she'd been served. There was a knock on the door. "Come in," she called out, hoping it was lunch.

Should she apologize to the nurses? she wondered. She supposed so. They had just been doing their jobs. . . .

But it wasn't lunch. It was another doctor, a heavyset, elderly man with an impatient expression, who frowned at her over his half-moon glasses. "I see you've decided to put your gown on," he said curtly. She disliked him on sight—he had the fussy look of an unsuccessful producer.

"When do I get out of here? Have you talked to Dr. Kris yet?"

He puffed out his cheeks. He had sideburns and the florid complexion of a man with a touchy temper. "I have *not* talked to Dr. Kris, no," he said. "I have no reason to. You are in my care at the moment, not hers. As for when you get out of here, that will depend on my evaluation of your case. Judging from your behavior so far, it will not be soon."

That was not the kind of tone she was willing to accept, now that she was beginning to feel like a star again. "Fuck *you!*" she said. "Do you know who you're talking to? Marilyn Monroe, that's who."

"I'm talking to a patient suffering from clinical depression, severe neuroses, and a variety of addictions, who attempted to take her own life, *that's* who I'm talking to, young lady."

"I don't *belong* here."

He raised an eyebrow—an ineffectual gesture, she thought. Sir Cork Tip could have shown him exactly how to do it. "Why do you think that? I would say that this is exactly where you *do* belong."

"That's not what the other doctor said. Why don't you two guys get your act together?"

"What other doctor?"

"The one who was here a few minutes ago. Younger than you, better-looking, and a lot nicer. *He* said I was fine. He told me he'd have me out of here in no time too."

A look of deep suspicion had crossed his face, as if he thought she might be suffering from delusions, but now it was replaced by an unmistakable, sweaty concern, like that of a speeding driver who sees the flashing lights of a police car in his rearview mirror. "Ah, what did this doctor say his name was?"

She looked at the small nameplate pinned to his lab coat. It identified him as "Bernard Metzger, MD." She gave him a steely look—or as steely as she could manage in the circumstances. "He didn't say, Dr. Metzger, any more than you have. Is it okay if I call you Bernie?"

Metzger blushed. "Ah, certainly, of course. . . . What did he look like?"

"Tallish, thin, nice body. He looked a lot like my ex-husband. Arthur Miller," she added helpfully. "Only the doctor was younger and not as gloomy."

"Oh God!" Dr. Metzger said. His face had gone from red to an unhealthy white.

"What's the problem? He seemed okay to me—a lot more helpful than you are, Bernie. He examined me. . . ."

"*Physically?*" There was a look of horror on his face. "Not physically, surely?"

"Well, sure? He's a doctor, after all. What's wrong with that?"

Metzger sat down on the bed. "That's the problem. He's not a doctor."

"He's *not?*"

"No. He's a patient. When he gets loose, he steals a lab coat and poses as a doctor. He's supposed to be firmly locked up. Did he give you an, ah—*intimate*—examination?"

She saw a window of opportunity. If the hospital was in the wrong, she was sure the authorities would be happy to let her go rather than be exposed to the possibility of a lawsuit—or of publicity that would make them look ridiculous. "Very intimate," she said. "I thought he was a gynecologist. He had a gentle touch too."

Metzger banged his fist against his open palm. "This is terrible," he said.

She nodded. "It sure is. I'm going to have to tell Aaron Frosch, my lawyer, for a start."

"Aaron Frosch!"

"He's a *killer,* Aaron is. And that's not even *thinking* about the publicity. I mean, wait until I call a press conference. . . ."

Metzger seemed to be mumbling in a monotonous undertone. "Ruined," she heard him say.

She put a hand on his shoulder. "Bernie," she said, "I wonder if we could talk about sneaking me out of here without any publicity—not through the lobby, if you see what I mean?—to someplace quiet where I can have a phone and get some rest."

"Why, yes," Metzger said in a strangled voice. "I'm sure we could."

"Marilyn. Call me Marilyn, Bernie."

"Marilyn."

And so, two days after being locked up in Payne Whitney, she was moved to a lovely suite in the Neurological Institute at Columbia Presbyterian Hospital, without the press being any the wiser, with round-the-clock nursing by *real* nurses, not disguised female prison guards, and without bars on the windows.

She even had a telephone.

The first number she called was the White House.

33

HOOVER WASN'T USED TO BEING KEPT WAITING, NOT EVER by presidents—*especially* by presidents, he told himself.

Presidents were ordinary men, after all—he had served them for decades, since 1924, "the year before the present attorney general was born," as he had arranged for tour guides to tell visitors to the Justice Department.

He had known all about FDR's affair, not to speak of Mrs. Roosevelt's odd "friendships"—had even recorded the embarrassing and indiscreet night she had spent with Joe Lash in a New York hotel room, and played it for the bemused President. He had had the goods on the financial shenanigans of Harry Truman's Kansas City friends in the Pendergast machine. He had intercepted all the letters to Eisenhower from his former mistress, Kay Summersby, reminding the President that he had promised to leave Mamie and marry her. . . .

Oh, he had known them, all right! Known the dirty little secrets of their sex lives, the buried political skeletons, the incautious friendships at school or college with young men who had turned to the left, or become homosexuals, or both, the flirtations with Moscow or married women, or Wall Street financiers. . . .

He did not flatter himself—he was a realist. They may not have liked him, they may not have trusted him, they may not have invited him to dinner in the White House private quarters upstairs—*but none of them had ever kept him waiting!*

The new president's appointments secretary and his chief of staff stood by the door as if they were guarding it, having exhausted their small talk. He could tell by their faces how much they disliked him. Well, let them, he told himself. Had not some Roman emperor said, "Let them hate me, so long as they fear me"? He had only to look in his files to get his sweet revenge—the forgotten subscription to some leftist magazine, the girlfriend for whom an illegal abortion had to be procured, the college "discussion group" that was, in fact, a party cell. *I've got you, you insolent young puppies!* he thought, but then, to his horror, he realized it wasn't fear he saw in their eyes, it was pity.

Pity! That could only mean he was going to be asked to resign! He felt his temples throb, his throat turn dry, his hands holding the briefcase on his knees tremble.

Retirement! What would he *do?* What would become of him and Clyde, two old men living somewhere on the Florida Gold Coast, taking sedate walks on the beach, shopping for groceries together, spending their evenings going over his scrapbooks?

"The President will see you now, Director."

Blindly he rose and walked on unsteady legs into the Oval Office. The President stood up briefly, then sat down again behind his big desk, gesturing for Hoover to sit down in front of him.

This was not what he was used to. Presidents had always left their desks for him, to sit beside him on the sofa—except for FDR, who would place him in an armchair in front of the fire, then wheel himself so close their knees almost touched.

Discourtesy! he thought wildly, frightened by the speed at which his heart was pounding. He should have realized by the way the President's young lout of a brother had treated him what was in store. Bobby—he hated to even *think* of him as the attorney general—had removed the private line that linked the director of the FBI to the attorney general, so he had to go through a secretary like anybody else! Bobby had appeared in Hoover's office unannounced and in shirtsleeves, had summoned Hoover to his office and kept him standing while he played darts, occasionally missing, so they struck the paneling, a clear desecration of government property, and—worst of all—had encouraged FBI agents to report directly to him.

He cleared his throat, willing himself not to think about these insults to the dignity of his office. "You wanted to see me, Mr. President?" he asked.

The President looked like a schoolboy, he thought. It was strange—many of the new agents seemed to him so young that he had asked whether the minimum age had been changed, and was surprised to learn that it hadn't.

The President seemed nervous. "Ah, yes," he said curtly.

There was a silence. Hoover knew more about the use of power than almost anyone in Washington. From the way he had been kept waiting, the place where he had been seated, and the President's reluctance to begin the conversation, he now knew for certain what was to come. If he was lucky, the President might agree to keep him on till his seventieth birthday, but it was unlikely—these were ruthless young men, Hoover reminded himself, their father's sons.

"I was thinking about the future," the President began.

"Fraught with danger, Mr. President," Hoover said, desperate to put off the inevitable sentence he saw in the President's eyes. "The Communist conspiracy flourishes abroad—and at home, more strongly than ever. . . ."

"Maybe. That's not what I was thinking of, Edgar. I was thinking about the future of the FBI."

"So am I, Mr. President, night and day."

A look of annoyance crossed the President's handsome young face. "At every level of government, I'm committed to new ideas, young blood, change."

Hoover was drenched in sweat, but smiling grimly. "Experience is worth something too, Mr. President," he said in a strangled voice.

Any moment now, he thought, he's going to ask for my resignation, and I'll have to give it. Not even the director of the FBI could refuse a direct request from the President.

"So is change," Kennedy said with a little smile.

Damn him! Hoover thought, he's beginning to *enjoy* this! He opened the briefcase—now or never, he told himself. "I'm all for change," he said, staring right into his executioner's eyes. "Take technology, for example. Under my stewardship, the FBI has achieved a level of sophistication in surveillance techniques unmatched by any other security service in the world, including the Soviet KGB."

Kennedy raised an eyebrow, interested—and wary. "That's very gratifying, but—"

"I have here, for example, a transcript of a conversation between a known Soviet spy and a member of your administration, recorded from a distance of over one hundred yards, in Rock Creek Park. . . ." He took a piece of paper stamped "Top Secret" out of the briefcase.

The President's face hardened. "Put it back," he said harshly. "I'm not afraid of that kind of shit, real or faked. I don't believe there's an Alger Hiss in my administration, and I'm not going to have you inventing one, but if there *is*, I'll bust his ass into a federal penitentiary before you can even pick up the phone to Westbrook Pegler." He stared at Hoover, unblinking. "Nothing is forever. Not even you."

Before the President could say another word, Hoover took a second piece of paper out of his briefcase and slipped it faceup on the desk. Sweat was pouring down his face, but he willed himself not to take out his neatly pointed breast pocket handkerchief and wipe it. "I think this conversation may interest you more, sir," he said softly.

The President picked up the piece of paper with distaste and scanned it quickly, then he read the page over a second time, very slowly indeed.

"Who is, ah, Strawhead?" he asked, but Hoover could tell he was stalling for time.

"Miss Marilyn Monroe, sir," he said, savoring every syllable.

"I see." Kennedy read it again. His face was flushed. "Where did this piece of shit come from?" he asked.

"A source."

"Don't play games with me, Mr. Hoover. Have you been taping me?" The fury in his voice would have terrified most men, but Hoover merely feigned righteous indignation.

"Certainly *not*, Mr. President," he snapped. "We believe this conversation was recorded by a so-called 'surveillance expert' who works for Hoffa and a certain mob figure. . . ."

"Am I to understand that Mr. Hoffa has been bugging my apartment at the Carlyle?"

Hoover stared at him without blinking. "It appears so, yes."

"For how long? How much of this is there?"

"Quite a lot, Mr. President. It is not, ah—limited to Miss Monroe."

"I see. And you allowed this to happen?"

"By *no* means. As soon as I discovered what was happening, I sent one of our best men, Special Agent Kirkpatrick, to check on your residences. The eavesdropping devices have been removed, Mr. President. You can breathe easy. The secret is just between you and me."

"And Mr. Hoffa."

"Well, yes. But I anticipate that Hoffa can be dealt with." He coughed, covering his mouth politely with his hand. The President's expression was one of sheer, unadulterated hatred, and Hoover, sensing victory, reveled in it. "We have things on Hoffa that you wouldn't believe, Mr. President," he whispered. "An example—"

"I don't want to know," Kennedy said.

"As you please." Hoover affected an expression of injured dignity.

"Is there anything else?"

"There are, ah—photographs. . . ."

"I meant, was there any other matter you wished to discuss?" The President had control of himself again. His expression was cold, hard, remote.

Hoover had only to look at him to know that if he ever made one slip, even the smallest, slightest one, the Kennedys would have his ass—that finding a good reason to get rid of him would be priority number one for them.

He didn't care. He felt twenty years younger—better yet, as if he were back at the peak of his career, tommy gun in hand, when he had burst upon the national consciousness with the death of Dillinger.

He would *never* give them a chance to get rid of him, he told himself triumphantly.

He would outlive them both!

"So the doctor was a phony?" Jack was still laughing at her story.

"You bet!"

"And now you're out. Cured."

"Who said cured? I'm still nuts. I've got this delusion that I'm in the Carlyle Hotel and I just fucked the president of the United States. If that doesn't prove I'm crazy, what does?"

"How was he? The President?"

"Comme ci, comme ça," she said, waving one hand from side to side.

He reached over and tickled her. "Hey, knock that off!" she gasped, between fits of giggles. She took a deep breath. "Oh God," she said, "I can't *stand* being tickled."

"Mm. How about this? How does *that* feel?"

She gave a low, throaty moan. "I *like* that."

"I thought so."

"Don't stop, Mr. President."

He didn't. She lay back and let the pleasure flow through her body, erasing all the agony of the past few weeks. There was nothing like sex for taking your mind off things, she thought—unlike pills, it never failed, and there was no limit to how much you could take. . . .

She had wondered, at first, if it was going to be different being in bed with him now that he was president, and of course, it was and it wasn't. On the one hand, he was the same old Jack, but on the other, there was an undeniable kick from fucking the president of the United States. She supposed it was the same thing that men felt about fucking *her*—that because it was *Marilyn Monroe* they were fucking, it had to be special, so, in their minds, they made it so.

"Is it different?" he asked. "Now that I'm president?"

She giggled. "I like the Secret Service better than your old guys. They're better-looking."

He laughed. "They're really ballsy guys, the best in the world. I'd hate to be the guy who tries to kill *me!*"

His eyes shone—his enthusiasm for elite units was part of his romanticism. He had regaled her with stories about his discoveries in Washington. Bobby had just found out about the Green Berets; Jack was in love with the hard core of the CIA, men who used words like "Infiltration" and calmly discussed the merits of poisoned darts versus silenced pistols. The secret agents, with their long tradition, their code words, their dark glasses and advanced technology, fitted into this category of special warriors, a small private army of James Bonds at the president's beck and call.

They held hands under the tangled sheets. "What's it like, now you've got it?" she asked.

"What?"

"The White House. The presidency."

He was silent for a moment. "It's like a wonderful machine that nobody's used in years," he said. "Whatever you want done, there's somebody in government who can do it. The trick is finding him."

He stared at the ceiling. "Some of it grabs you by the nuts," he went on. "There's an Air Force guy close to me twenty-four hours a day with 'the Football'—a briefcase with all the codes for starting a nuclear war. That makes you think, at first. Then you get used to it, like hearing 'Hail to the Chief,' or going through a door first even when you're with a woman."

He moved closer to her, his long, hard body against hers. "When I went up to Hyde Park to pay my respects to Eleanor Roosevelt," he said, "I stood aside to let her go through the door first, and she said to me, 'No, no, Mr. President—*you* always go first from now on.' "

He laughed, but she could tell he had been impressed. "That really got to me somehow, coming from Eleanor. . . ."

"Where is he now?"

"Who?"

"The guy with the codes."

"Sitting in a room down the hall, next to a secure phone."

"I'll bet he wishes he were in here."

"I'll bet he *does*. Well, fuck him. I'm the commander in chief, and he's only an Air Force warrant officer, so that's the way it is. Whoever said life is fair?"

"I don't know. Not me, for sure."

"That's my girl," he said. A telephone rang beside the bed. It was red, without a dial, and for a moment she felt her stomach turn cold. By some lunatic coincidence, was this going to be the moment when Jack would actually have to call for the Air Force warrant officer down the hall?

He picked it up and listened. "This *is* a secure line," he said with some annoyance.

He straightened up with a grunt of pain, while she slipped a couple of pillows behind his back. "Leave it to me, I'll talk to Bobby," he said. "Of course he isn't going to like it, he's got a hair up his ass over these guys, but they can't do the job in Cuba if they're in prison."

He listened impatiently. "I *said* I'd talk to my brother," he snapped, his voice cold and harsh. "I don't want to hear how difficult it is to find Castro . . . I don't *care* if he never sleeps in the same place two nights running. . . . It's your job to find out where he is, understood?"

He slammed down the receiver. "Goddamn Castro!" he said. "He's all I hear about. You'd think this administration is going to succeed or fail according to whether or not we get rid of Castro."

"I sort of *like* him," she said. "He's sexy."

His annoyance turned to interest. "You know, it's funny," he mused. "Jackie says the same thing. . . . I guess he is sexy too, if the CIA is right about his love life. . . ." He shook his head. "Castro's got star quality, all right, I'll give the son of a bitch *that*. Why is it that the people on *our* side seem so dull?"

"They aren't sexy."

"It's a problem for the free world."

"The free world has you, lover. That's sexy enough."

"If you say so."

"I say so. I'd swear it in court."

"God forbid!" he said, knocking wood on the top of the night table.

"I bet you'd *like* Castro, if you met him," she said.

"You think so?"

She nodded.

"Maybe you're right," he said thoughtfully. "He's young. He's smart. He's got a younger brother who's tougher than he is. He likes pretty women and he smokes cigars." He laughed. "I ought to have made *you* secretary of state."

He shook his head. "It's not the way it's going to be, though. Maybe Ike could get away with a Communist Cuba ninety miles from Key West, but I can't. Castro has to go. It's us or him."

"My money's on you," she said, giving him a kiss.

"Good," he said.

Then, with more doubt than she had ever heard in his voice before: "I hope to Christ you're right."

34

T HE FIRST I HEARD ABOUT THE BAY OF PIGS WAS Adlai Stevenson's indignant denial in the UN that the United States was involved in the invasion of Cuba. The next was a call from Bobby, who said, "Come on down here right away. We just broke our cherry."

That was enough to tell me that poor Adlai had been hung out to dry in full view of the world by Jack and Bobby, and that we were in it, as their father was fond of saying, "up to our ass."

The Ambassador called as I was heading out the door on my way to La Guardia. "Those fucking bastards in the CIA," he growled. "I *warned* Jack I wouldn't give a day's pay for the whole lot of them. Now look what they've done to my boy!"

He was so angry that he was almost inarticulate. His voice was odd and I wondered if he had a cold; then I realized that he was crying. *"They've ruined my son's presidency,"* he howled, and his pain made me realize just how bad things must be.

If it hadn't been for the atmosphere of crisis, the whiff of defeat tarnishing Jack's presidency almost before it had begun, I would never have plunged in to help so quickly. I was still smarting over Jack's cavalier treatment of me the day after his election. Maria and I had been his guests at the inauguration, but though she was pleased to be at the center of attention, it didn't make up for his refusal to promise me the ambassadorship I coveted. Nothing, of course, could dim *her* admiration for our new president.

In the end, if Jack (and my country) needed me, I would go. Who, after all, can resist an appeal from the President of the United States? Particularly if you've known him since he was a schoolboy.

Besides, I was feeling restless and bored after my exertions in the campaigns for the nomination and the presidency. I not only missed the political action, I even missed my role as Jack's liaison with the mob—for now that he was in the White House, he had other matters on his mind, and so, it appeared, did they. Once he was elected, Jack's interest in Hoffa diminished to zero, and Bobby, who had sworn to put Hoffa in prison, found himself with more pressing matters on his hands as attorney general—civil rights being the first, containing J. Edgar Hoover the second. The war against Hoffa was relegated to the back burner, much to the relief of the boys in Chicago, and I was spared more of Jack Ruby's messages and further meetings with Red Dorfman.

I was ushered in to see the President without delay. Jack was pale, his face puffy, his eyes sunken and glazed with fatigue.

"Well, David," he said, shaking my hand, "thanks for coming down. The shit has really hit the fan this time."

"What can I do for you, Mr. President?" I asked.

"Get on the phone right away and call in your markers, David. Damage control! Talk to Harry Luce, Punch Sulzberger, Bill Paley. . . . Do what you can. If you think my talking to any of them will help, I will, but I don't want to let myself in for any high-minded lectures on foreign policy or truth-in-government. Understand?"

"You've got it," I said. His expression was tight, all emotion banished, a stone mask. I wondered what was going on behind it. One thing about Jack I knew. He did not blame others when things went wrong; he blamed himself. "How bad is it?" I asked. "Bottom line."

He let out a long sigh. He was sitting tilted back in his chair behind his desk, his feet on the gleaming surface. "They stuck it to me good," he said.

"The Cubans?"

"The CIA."

"Strangely enough, that's what your father told me this morning."

"He's right. As usual."

There was a certain bitterness in Jack's voice. Close as he was to his father, the President of the United States was no more pleased to hear "I told you so" from him than was any other son.

"How are things going on the beachhead?"

"It's a slaughterhouse."

"Are we going to go in and help them?"

"No." His voice was remote, emotionless. "I've decided against any air strikes or naval bombardment. There's no point in reinforcing failure."

"Are we going to be able to get the men off the beaches?"

He stared out at the gray sky, his mouth set in a hard line. "Probably not," he said grimly.

"I see." In other words, it was a highly public failure, accompanied by every possible evidence of bad faith, incompetence, and subterfuge. Jack's worst enemies could not have produced a more devastating—or humiliating—scenario. He had played chicken with Castro and lost. "Where's Bobby?" I asked.

Jack shook his head. "He's been a rock," he answered, speaking slowly and softly. "I've learned a lesson, David. Bobby's the only person I can trust down here."

He picked up a paper clip and twisted it until it broke in his fingers. "The rest of them aren't worth *shit*," he said. "When we took over, Bissell told us all the wonderful things the CIA could do. 'I'm your man-eating shark, Mr. President,' he told me. Some shark! A minnow is more like it! The moment the shit hit the fan, Bissell was fielding the ball to the joint Chiefs, and they were fielding it right back. The only thing they all agree on is that I'm responsible."

He swung back and forth in his chair. The Oval Office was absolutely silent, as if there were no crisis. Clearly, he had left instructions not to be disturbed.

"I thought sitting behind this desk made you powerful," he said. "You gave orders, things happened. But the president is the most vulnerable man on earth, out on a limb twenty-four hours a day, taking the blame while the bureaucracy calls the shots."

He seemed to have aged a decade since I had last seen him, only a few weeks ago. He would recover, of course— he was too young and vigorous not to—but after the Bay of Pigs disaster, I never thought of him as a young man again. He had grown into the presidency the hard way, I decided.

"By God," he said, "we're going to play hardball from now on—no more half-assed amateur operations. Maybe I'll go down in history as the president who failed to get Cuba back—though I'm not finished with Castro yet!—but I'm not going down in history as the president who lost Laos or Vietnam."

"It's an ambitious agenda." A dangerous one, too, I thought.

"I haven't even begun." He sighed and stood up stiffly. "I can't stand these meetings, but I have to go back. They're like autopsies—a bunch of doctors standing around a corpse trying to decide what went wrong. . . . Those poor bastards on the beach."

"The survivors, if there are any, may present a few problems too, Mr. President."

He nodded. "Who can blame them? We'll take care of them somehow."

"A few of them will be mad as hell."

"They won't be the only ones. Some of your old friends were backing the landings pretty heavily."

"*My* friends?"

"You know who I mean."

I knew whom he meant, and I didn't like it. "I didn't know *our* friends were involved, Mr. President."

"You didn't hear it from me. You didn't hear it at all. But the CIA had a separate plan. It was going to be a pincer attack, you see. The mob was supposed to take care of Castro just before the landing."

"Take care of?"

"Ah, neutralize."

"Neutralize?"

"*Terminate!*" he snapped impatiently. "You know what I mean."

I was appalled at the sheer stupidity of it all. "Jesus, Jack," I cried, forgetting to address him properly for the first time. "I'm the one who passed the offer on to you in the first place, but I never thought you'd *do* it. . . . It's *dumb!*"

"Well, yes. That's what everybody says, now that it's failed. . . . The mob doesn't turn out to be any more efficient than the CIA."

"I could have told you that. I *know* these people!" I glanced at him. "I should have been consulted."

I must have shown my resentment at being left out now that Jack was in the White House, because he looked embarrassed—as well he might. "It was all on a 'need-to-know' basis, David, as they say. . . ." He had picked up the jargon. "Anyway, you were better off *not* knowing, frankly." He paused. "I'm sorry," he said. "Really."

"These people have a *relationship* with me, for better or worse, let me remind you. I don't want them blaming me for something I had no knowledge of."

"I don't think you have anything to fear, David. They blame the CIA. They blame me."

I wasn't convinced. "Who communicated with them? And with whom, on their side?"

Jack's expression grew wary. "Giancana was their point man," he said. "He was the fellow the CIA dealt with."

He coughed. "A lot of people did the communicating, as a

matter of fact," he added offhandedly. "I even had a, ah, *contact* myself." There was a guilty look in his eyes.

I was amazed. "A contact with Giancana? How *could* you take that risk? You should have used someone else. You should have used *me*."

"Yes," Jack said vaguely, nodding his head. He seemed embarrassed. "Yes, that would have been a good idea. In retrospect. But it just wasn't practical in this case, David. This was a case for a close, ah, *personal* contact. . . ."

He glanced at his watch, and I took the hint and went off to see what I could do with the press. Clearly, I was needed here, and he knew it.

Despite my efforts, the stories over the next few weeks were horrendous, even in papers that were normally sympathetic to Jack. The only ray of sunshine, so far as I was concerned, was that the mob connection never came up in any of them. I breathed a sigh of relief—prematurely, as it happened, for I eventually received a telephone call from Bobby, his voice more sharp-edged and impatient than usual, to inform me, in guarded terms, that "the natives were getting restless."

The natives in question, I guessed, were Giancana's people. I told him I didn't want anything more to do with them.

"Do it, please," Bobby said when I flew down to Washington to see him at his father's urging. Bobby had learned to mistrust the phones, a situation I found ironic for the attorney general of the United States! "For Jack's sake," he added, knowing that would clinch it.

"I don't know Giancana."

"So what? You know people who do."

"Jack—ah, the President—gave me to understand there's a direct connection to him, at a much higher level."

Bobby glared at me. "Forget you ever heard that!" he barked.

He was sitting behind his huge desk in the attorney general's dark, paneled office at Justice, with his dog, a surly Newfoundland, at his feet. It was considered a badge of honor in the New Frontier to have been bitten by Brumus, but it was not one I aspired to. I stared at the dog fiercely, and he stared back.

"My goddamn brother," Bobby said softly. "If only he

could keep his pants zipped. . . ." He sighed. "Well, never mind. Whatever you heard, she's over and done with."

It was my first inkling that Jack's "contact" was a woman. I wondered how that had happened, then decided I didn't want to know.

"I still don't think going directly to Giancana was a good idea," I said. "However it was done."

"It was a lousy idea. Let's not make the same mistake twice. If you want to use a go-between, that's fine. Use your own judgment. Do whatever you have to, just so long as the message gets home."

"What message?"

"That they'd better keep their goddamn mouths shut."

"You think they won't?"

"I think they're already leaking, hoping the press will treat them like heroes. I want it stopped."

I didn't argue with Bobby—he was in no mood for an argument. Jack had made him his "prime minister" and chief hatchet man, giving him the power to wander into the most secret and sensitive parts of the government to root out those who had failed the test of toughness or, more important, loyalty to Jack. Bobby was fast becoming the second-most important man in government, and the most feared, and it showed on his face. It was Bobby who fired people who failed Jack, turned the IRS loose on Jack's opponents, found ways to send Jack's enemies to prison.

I was happy enough to leave him, in his present mood, and flew back to New York on the next plane. As luck would have it, I was no sooner home than I got a telephone call from Marilyn, who wanted to know if I could come over and have dinner with her. I had been dreaming of a hot bath and dinner on a tray in front of the television set, since Maria was out at a theater benefit, but from the sound of Marilyn's voice, she needed company badly, so I put my coat back on and walked over there.

Dinner, I saw, was to be Chinese food from take-out cartons—not at all what I had in mind. Marilyn did not look her best. Her face was puffy, her skin blotchy; her nails were badly chipped, the roots of her hair dark. Clearly, life as a divorcée did not suit her. I moved old newspapers, magazines, and record album covers off a chair so that I could sit down, while Marilyn poured champagne into two not-very-clean Baccarat flutes.

"It's just *terrible,* all this news about Cuba," she said. "Jack must be going crazy?"

"I saw Bobby today in Washington. He was very down."

"I called Jack. He sounded awful. He said if there was any truth to reincarnation, he wanted to come back as a movie producer instead of a politician, next time. 'Oh, no you don't!' I told him."

"How are *you* doing?" I asked.

"Oh, honey! You wouldn't believe! I'm practically *unemployable.*"

"You?"

"Me. I was going to do *Rain* for NBC. You know? By W. Somerset Maugham?"

Marilyn always assumed that everybody's hold on culture was as tenuous as her own. "What happened?" I asked.

"They got cold feet when they heard about my problems," she said. She drained her champagne. "That's the breaks."

I was surprised that any network would pass up a chance to have Marilyn Monroe on prime time. Her stock must have fallen very low indeed, I thought, if even the TV people refused to buy.

She cracked open a fortune cookie. " 'Tell your best friend what's on your mind,' " she read.

"Not bad advice."

"You can't beat fortune cookies. They make more sense than analysts every time."

We ate quietly for a while, to the accompaniment of a stack of Sinatra records Marilyn had put on the turntable. When we were both sated to the point of nausea, Marilyn poured us each another glass of champagne and leaned back against a pile of cushions with her eyes shut. "David," she said. "The message from the fortune cookie? I made it up. Can I ask you about a couple of things that have been worrying me?"

"Of course. It sounded a little pat, frankly."

"Listen, if I told most people about this, they'd say I was crazy, you know? I've got a friend, a kid named Timmy Hahn. He's one of my fans—he follows me wherever I go in New York. You've probably seen him."

"About sixteen years old? Windbreaker and jeans? Sad face, like a little old man?"

"That's Timmy. I think he's kind of cute myself. He's devoted to me, anyway. He'll wait for me outside on the street when I go somewhere, sometimes until one or two in the morning. I call his mother sometimes, you know, and promise to look after him, but he doesn't know that. . . ."

"That's some fan, Marilyn."

"He worships me. I'm not exaggerating. He *literally* worships me, Timmy does. I've had dogs who looked at me more objectively." She sipped her champagne. "But he's smart, you know? He doesn't make things up. Anyway, I stopped to talk to Timmy this morning, on my way to the studio, and he told me he's been burglarized? He was really upset, poor kid."

"Well, sure. His house?"

"His room."

I raised an eyebrow. I couldn't imagine what this had to do with me, or why Marilyn seemed upset by it. Or why anybody would burglarize a sixteen-year-old kid's room.

"He keeps a diary, Timmy does," she explained. "That's what was stolen."

"Why would anybody take a kid's diary?"

"Well, it's not really a *diary*. It's more, like, he writes down everywhere I go—dates, times, places, and so on. . . . ."

"Everything?"

"Everything," she said miserably, eyes downcast. "He's a pretty observant kid, Timmy. Persistent too. He doesn't miss much."

"I see." I saw, all right, and I was horrified.

"Timmy was really upset."

"Timmy isn't going to be the only one."

"He went to the police—his uncle's a cop—but they didn't take him seriously."

"No, I can understand that."

"Though Timmy said they were surprised. Apparently it was a really professional job, you know?"

It would be, of course, I thought.

"I wondered, should I tell him to call the FBI?"

It seemed to me the consequences of that might be appalling. "I don't think telling the FBI is a good idea, Marilyn," I said carefully.

"Oh?"

"What I mean is, it may not be what Jack would want you to do."

She absorbed this. "Is it going to be a big problem, for him?" she asked.

I didn't know. There was no shortage of compromising material in circulation about Jack's private life, but on the other hand, it sometimes takes only one small spark to create an explosion. Besides, rumors are one thing, written documents quite another. Anything in writing has a life—and a permanence—of its own, which, I suppose, is why Jack never wrote love letters.

"It's probably not a *big* problem," I said hopefully. "But I think Jack should be warned."

"I can tell him in Florida."

"You're going to Florida with him?"

"Not exactly. I thought I might go see Jack's father—and Jack, if he's there."

I remembered Jack *had* mentioned that he was playing with the idea of spending a couple of days in Palm Beach, "if the dates worked out." He had not said which dates—or whose— he was thinking of.

"Didn't I read you were going back to California?" I asked, annoyed with myself for sounding as if I were Marilyn's husband or father. She had no obligation—I reminded myself— to keep me informed of her movements. Still, I felt left out, even cheated.

"First I'm going down to visit my ex," she said.

DiMaggio had reentered Marilyn's life after the Payne Whitney episode, out of genuine concern for her welfare, I believe, since he was a thoroughly decent man. It is possible that he may also have had hopes of getting together with her again, which, knowing Marilyn, I suspect she may have encouraged, but he continued to feel—as he would to the end— a responsibility toward her. She was convinced that he was the one person who would always come to her rescue if she was in real trouble, and she was probably right.

"I promised I'd cheer up Jack's dad," she went on. "He's been sick, you know."

I was so startled that I swallowed down the wrong tube and started to choke. Marilyn rushed over and got behind me, pounding away at my back until I caught my breath at last. She was amazingly strong for a woman of her size. "Are you okay?" she asked.

I nodded. My surprise had been caused by the fact that Joe Kennedy's increasingly poor health was the deepest of family secrets. Even in the family it wasn't discussed—or perhaps *noticed,* for Joe's children were so used to his robust vitality and unfailing good health that they were emotionally incapable of seeing that he was becoming old and frail. The razor-sharp tongue and hair-trigger mind were still there, but he who had always been so proud of his physique was now painfully thin, almost emaciated, his heavily veined hands trembled, and he was beginning to walk with an old man's cautious shuffle. Being who he was, he refused to acknowledge this himself. As for Rose, she had schooled herself over the decades not to see anything that could cause her pain.

Jack *had* noticed, probably because Bobby, who was so much closer to the old man, pointed it out to him—and had discussed it with me cautiously, as if he was bewildered by the phenomenon. He had proclaimed at his inauguration that the torch was being passed to a new generation of Americans— an expression of his annoyance at the way Ike had lectured him as if he were a junior officer during the transition, when he was president-elect—but he was not yet prepared for the torch to be handed over to him in the Kennedy family. Nor was his father, who was busy running a one-man campaign to put Teddy into Jack's old seat in the Senate—a project that failed to stir any enthusiasm on the part of Jack and Bobby.

"Sorry about the coughing fit," I said. "I didn't realize Jack had told you that his father isn't well."

She gave a moue, intended, I guess, to show her mild annoyance at my underrating the confidence Jack placed in her. "Baby, Jack *talks* to me. He doesn't have any secrets from *me*. . . . Well, I don't mean he tells me about the missile gap or anything. But personal stuff, you know, like his family, he tells me a lot. . . . I mean, it isn't just *sex* between us, you know? Jack can unwind with me. He talks to me a lot more than any of my husbands ever did. It's funny," she went on dreamily. "It's like having a family of my own, at last. I get these nice notes from Jack's father, even from his *sisters*. The Ambassador sent me a smoked salmon the other day. I put it in the freezer."

She had picked up the family habit of referring to Jack's father as "the Ambassador," a post he had not held for twenty years. As for the salmon, this was one of the Ambassador's small acts of institutional generosity. He had an interest in some company that imported Irish smoked salmon, and was determined to prove to the world that the Irish variety was superior to that of Scotland. Jackie had even been persuaded to serve it at the White House, until the Pacific salmon smokers got wind of it and insisted on her serving American smoked salmon instead.

The idea of Marilyn settling down to a kind of cozy illicit membership in what was rapidly becoming America's First Family was strange to contemplate.

"I *like* Jack's father," she said. "He's feisty."

"You could say that, yes."

"He was really upset about this Cuba thing, though."

"He's got cause to be."

"He told me not to worry—that Jack's going to get Castro yet. 'His days are numbered,' he said."

"He told you *that?*"

"Mm."

I leaned over and took her hand. "Marilyn," I said, "do yourself a favor, please. Don't ever breathe a word of that to *anybody.*"

She giggled, and gave me a good-night kiss. She had been taking pills throughout the evening with her champagne, and while she was not yet sleepy, her words and movements were beginning to slow down, like a movie in slow motion. "Don't worry about it," she said, articulating very carefully. "My lips are sealed."

"I'm not interested in all this gossip, Edgar, nor is my brother," Bobby Kennedy said stiffly. "It's all lies. I mean, if the President and I were going to keep a bunch of call girls on tap, do you suppose we'd put them on the twelfth floor of the LaSalle Hotel and have the Secret Service close the floor off two or three times a week for us? We might as well do it in the lobby of *The Washington Post.*"

Hoover nodded majestically. "I did not take this rumor seriously, General. But I feel it incumbent upon me to pass on any rumors relating to the President or his family."

"It's a waste of time. Whoever is digging up all this nonsense ought to be working on putting the bad guys behind bars. Who was the source for this crap, anyway?"

"A chambermaid at the LaSalle Hotel."

"Oh, *great!* Is that all?"

Hoover kept smiling, sustained by his all-consuming hatred of the Attorney General. "No," he said, "it's not all."

"If it's another rumor about a paternity suit, like last week. . . . If your people can't come up with anything better than rumors, I'm going to have to start questioning the FBI's efficiency—and common sense."

Hoover placed on the Attorney General's cluttered desk, right next to an ashtray that seemed to have been made in a kindergarten crafts class, what looked like a school notebook, with a red cover and a label on which somebody had carefully lettered, in different-colored inks, the single word "MARILYN," with the dot above the *i* lovingly rendered as a heart. Below, in less ornate letters, was the name "Timmy Hahn."

"What's this?" Kennedy said.

"It's a diary. Perhaps you should look at the pages I've had paper-clipped."

There was a long silence while Bobby Kennedy turned the pages. His expression gave nothing away—he was not about to give Hoover that satisfaction. When he had finished, he put the notebook back on his desk and sighed. "Where did this come from?" he asked.

"I'm satisfied it's genuine."

"That's not what I asked."

"We obtained it," Hoover said. "To protect the President."

"I see. Did you have a search warrant?"

"It would have been incautious to bring this matter before a federal magistrate, don't you think?"

"Mm." The Attorney General was not about to excuse a felony out loud, even in his private office.

"I think it's important that this is brought to the President's attention."

"Why?"

"First of all, to urge greater caution on him. Secondly, to show him that the FBI is working night and day to protect his interests—and privacy."

Kennedy nodded glumly. "I'll make sure he hears about it."

"Good. And we'll keep up the good work, you may be sure."

"I'm sure." Kennedy did not stand up. He merely reached across the desk to shake Hoover's hand. "By the way," he asked casually, "is there a copy of this?"

Hoover stood, feet firmly planted, chin thrust out, the living image of bulldog tenacity. "Only for my files," he said. He smiled grimly. "It's safe there."

I decided that the mission Bobby had given me to pass a message on to Giancana was best carried out by having breakfast with Paul Palermo.

We met in the Oak Room at the St. Regis, across the street from my office. Paul had several more or less legitimate business interests that could explain my meeting with him, and if anybody in law enforcement happened to notice us together, the Oak Room would at least seem like an improbable place for the commission of a felony.

"We got problems," Paul said, as soon as the waiter was out of earshot.

"I know. That's why I wanted to see you. My people"— I was not about to mention the name Kennedy here—"were disappointed by what happened. Or, to be more precise, by what *didn't* happen."

"Hey, that's too bad, but it's not our fault." Paul leaned forward, his voice a whisper. "Our people did what they were supposed to. The material they were provided was defective."

I had the wit not to ask what material he meant. I simply raised an eyebrow as I ate my eggs.

"Look," Paul went on, holding his hands out to indicate that he was being honest with me, "no workman is better than his tools, right?"

I nodded, as if I knew what "tools" he was talking about.

"These guys were supposed to poison the man's cigars, right? They risked their lives to put the poison in the cigars, and what happens? Zip, that's what happens! The man lights up one cigar after another and doesn't turn a hair. That's not our fault. Then there's the stuff we're supposed to sprinkle in his fatigues that will poison him when he starts to sweat?

Our guys got some broad to do the job while he's asleep after fucking her, some German girl, which she *does;* then he gets dressed and goes out and gives a four-hour speech in the sun, sweating like a fucking pig, and *nada!* Defective materials were supplied."

I was more than a little shaken by these revelations, but I tried not to show it. "The people you're dealing with pay only for success, Paul. I don't think they're going to buy the defective materials' argument, frankly."

"They're gonna *have* to, David. My people did what they said they would. It isn't their fault it didn't work out. They took risks. They had certain expenses. They have a right to what they were promised."

"I'm not aware that promises were made."

"All right, maybe not promises, but strong hints. Instead of which, look what's happened! Momo gets held for hours by the Feds on his way to Mexico, which is very embarrassing because he's traveling with his girlfriend. Carlos Marcello—you know who he is?"

I nodded glumly.

"Carlos gets deported to Guatemala over some bullshit citizenship thing. Put on a plane, flown out of the country, and dumped in the middle of nowhere. Look, you have to understand what's at stake here. Momo went to Johnny Roselli with this Cuba thing, and Roselli went to Meyer Lansky, laid it all out for him beside the pool of the Deauville Hotel in Miami; then Lansky brought in Carlos Marcello and Santo Trafficante because they're the ones who know Cuba inside out. . . . Momo made certain promises all the way down the line, and now he's embarrassed, he's lost respect. . . . In his line of work, that's *dangerous,* David. He's got Hoffa on his back too. He's not a happy man."

"My people aren't happy either, Paul."

"Well, but they have the big guns, David, your people. My people aren't in the White House. Not yet, anyway." He laughed. "Meantime, they're mad as hell."

"The chief concern at the moment on our side is whether they will keep their mouths shut."

Paul looked pained. "David, these are stand-up guys. They won't talk. That's not the problem. The problem is, you have to do the right thing by them. They don't think the right thing was kicking Carlos Marcello out of a car in the middle of the fucking jungle in his five-hundred-dollar alligator loafers and telling him to start walking."

I could see that. I had met Marcello once, on a visit to Havana in the old days, and he hadn't struck me as a man who did much walking.

"They just want what's right," Paul emphasized, finishing his eggs and wiping his mouth fastidiously. His diamond pinkie ring gleamed, even in the subdued lighting—the one sign that he didn't belong here. "Just so there aren't any misunderstandings."

"I'll pass it on."

"Please do. I mean, it's already *been* passed on, right to the top, they tell me, by a certain lady who shall be nameless, right?"

"Right," I said, wondering who the lady was.

He laughed. "Maybe she was too busy doing something else to make the point."

"It's possible," I said, a little stiffly.

Paul rose, and we shook hands. "Always a pleasure," he said. "The next one is on me."

Bobby and I met the next day at lunchtime at Hickory Hill.

The house had none of its former elegance. Neither Bobby nor Ethel cared about that kind of thing—their houses were designed around children and dogs. There were so many of both in the house that it was impossible to speak, so Bobby took me outside, where we paced back and forth, surrounded by a pack of large dogs, some of them Bobby's, some of them visitors from neighboring estates. He was wearing a leather flying jacket with the insignia of the squadron that had presented it to him, and his hair, longer than usual, was blowing in his eyes; he had to brush it back with his hand from time to time. His eyes, I thought, were sadder and more remote than ever, as if his new role as the President's troubleshooter was exposing him to secrets he would have been happier not knowing.

I told him about my breakfast with Palermo, and he listened silently. "I don't believe they did a thing," he said when I'd finished. "I think they fed the CIA a whole pack of promises and lies, and extorted money and weapons from them for nothing.

The whole thing was a con game from the beginning, and the CIA guys were too goddamn stupid to realize they were being taken."

"It sounded convincing to me."

"Of course it did. These guys are pros. The German girl, the poisoned cigars, the powder in Castro's fatigues—that's exactly what the CIA wanted to hear."

"Did they provide the mob with all that stuff—the poisons and so on?"

"Yes. They've been developing things in their labs you wouldn't believe. Shellfish toxins that can't be detected in an autopsy, silent poison-dart guns, transmitting devices a woman can insert in her vagina. . . ." His expression was one of disgust.

He picked up a stick and threw it, sending the dogs off in noisy pursuit. "Of course, they were dying for a chance to try out all this crap, so when these fellows Marcello and Trafficante promised to use it against Castro, they fell all over each other at Langley to give them everything they asked for. . . . Money, speedboats, radio transmitters, guns, you name it. The hoods must damn near have died laughing."

"You think it was a hoax?"

"Absolutely. And now they're back, asking for pardons! Over my dead body!"

"They think Jack promised them that—or something like it."

"Well, he didn't. He didn't promise them a goddamn thing. And I keep telling you, they didn't *do* anything either, unless you count cheating the CIA out of hundreds of thousands of dollars and all sorts of weaponry nobody should have put in their hands in the first place."

"Bobby, do you know it for a fact?"

"There are no facts here. The guys at the CIA wouldn't recognize a fact if it bit them. As for the mob guys, they have never told anyone the truth in their lives."

"How about the German girl?"

"I think they put that part in to interest Jack. That was the first question he asked—was she good-looking?"

"And?"

"Of course she was. They wouldn't have produced a photo of an *ugly* blond girl, would they?"

"Speaking of girls, Palernio mentioned there's one who's

the link between Jack and Giancana. He didn't mention any names."

"It's true," Bobby said grimly.

"Wasn't that a little dangerous?"

His eyes bored hard into me—his way of warning me to get off this subject. I stared right back—I hadn't worked for the Ambassador for so many years for nothing. "Yes, it's a problem," he said through clenched teeth. "Some things have to change, I know it, but it can't be done in a hurry. Jack is Jack—he's not about to take up a life of celibacy just because he's the president. Or give up the Sinatra connection right away either, though he knows what I think about it. So forget about Giancana's girl, this Campbell woman." He sighed. "I had to deal with one the other day who turned out to be an East German agent, and get Hoover to deport her quietly. . . ."

He paused. "There are people, particularly out on the West Coast, who have been taking advantage of Jack's good nature," he said. "When the time comes, I'm going to make sure they get what they deserve."

"Bobby," I said, "are you sure you know what you're doing?"

His eyes were ice-cold as he turned to me. "Completely sure, David," he said sharply.

I was about to argue the point, when a horde of children came pouring noisily out of the house and surrounded us. Bobby, like the Pied Piper, led them off into a rough-and-tumble game of touch football.

I went back inside, said good-bye to Ethel, and told my driver to take me to National Airport.

I tried to convince myself that Bobby was right, but I didn't believe it for a moment.

35

THE FIRST THING SHE NOTICED WAS HOW MUCH THE Ambassador had aged. Quite suddenly, in the bright Florida sun, she was looking at an old man.

"I get these goddamn shooting pains in my arm," he complained. "And headaches. I don't know what the hell's the matter with me."

She got an empty feeling in the pit of her stomach. Gable had made the same complaints during the last weeks of shooting *The Misfits*. They had been the warning signals of a heart attack.

"You should see a doctor," she said.

"I don't believe they know a goddamn thing, Marilyn. I had a bad cold, that's all, and I'm at the age when you don't bounce back. Hell, I play golf every afternoon and I'm fit as a fiddle." He gave her a roguish wink, though the effort was anything but cheerful: his lined, emaciated face was made somehow more skull-like by the big, square Kennedy teeth.

"What are you going to do with yourself now?" he asked, apparently anxious to get away from the subject of his health.

"I'm going back to LA."

"Good! New York is no damned good. The Jews have taken over the media and Wall Street, and before you know it, the niggers are going to be moving downtown from Harlem and you won't be able to walk in the streets, mark my word. I liquidated all my property there, got out while the going was good. I hope you're going back to work?"

"If anybody will have me."

"They'll have you. You're a star." He talked about her career the way he talked about his boys', she thought—as if all he had to do was will them to succeed. Maybe he was right. She hoped so. The few properties 20th Century-Fox had shown her so far were awful, remakes of remakes, or second-rate song-and-dance pictures. The studio was a different place now, since the board had finally worked up the courage to throw her old nemesis Zanuck out, and nobody seemed to have the foggiest notion what use to make of her.

"Maybe," she said. "They're not in any hurry, I can tell you."

"Wait the bastards out. And don't rent when you get out there. Renting is a mug's game. Buy a nice little house for yourself. If you have any problem raising the money, tell me and I'll help you out. You've got to *own* things, Marilyn, that's what I always told Gloria. You won't be young and beautiful forever."

She nodded like a good little girl, and thanked him for his advice.

He eyed her suspiciously. "You look just like Jack when I give *him* financial advice. He nods and forgets about it. Nobody in this family would have a pot to piss in if I hadn't made a fortune for them. How does Jack strike you?"

"He's in terrific shape."

"He's coming into his own," the Ambassador said, adjusting his rakish straw hat. "This Cuba thing did him a lot of damage, but people have short memories. He's going to be the best president of the century. There's no doubt at all in my mind on that score."

"Me too." It was true, she thought. It was scary how much faith she had in Jack, she who had never really trusted any man. She would do anything in the world for him except say good-bye, and she couldn't imagine that he would ever want her to do that.

A car door slammed, and a couple of Secret Service agents stationed themselves behind the flowering hedge, at the far side of the pool. The moment they were in place, Jack appeared through the small gate into his father's private domain, grinning cheerfully. "This is the life," he said. "They don't live this way at the Kremlin, I'll bet."

"No," his father said, "but they pay attention to business, those guys. It might not be a bad idea to follow their example."

At first she hadn't understood that the insult, the jab to the ego, was the family style, that nothing personal was involved, but she had come to understand that the Kennedy family was like a pride of lions who played, and showed affection for each other, by fighting. Their claws were retracted just far enough to leave nothing worse than a scratch, and though they might draw blood, they never bit to the bone.

"If Khrushchev could see the way we live, he'd convert to capitalism," Jack said. He came over and gave her a kiss, resting his hand on her lower back, then letting it drop an inch or two lower.

The gate opened and David Leman came over. She offered him her cheek. "You're sexier in Florida than you were in New York," he said.

"Flatterer." The truth was, she *did* look better here. She was a California girl. Sunshine usually cheered her up.

"David and I have been talking strategy," Jack said. He did not elaborate on what *kind* of strategy, but she noticed that there was a trace of anger and resentment behind the relaxed, good-natured facade—enough to make her wonder what David had come all the way down to Florida to tell Jack.

"Did you boys get your business settled?" the Ambassador asked. She suppressed a giggle. Only Joe Kennedy would describe the President of the United States and David Leman as "boys."

Jack nodded. He had slipped his sunglasses on, which made his expression hard to read. He said nothing.

"Bobby's right," the Ambassador persisted. "I *know* these guys. I've dealt with them. They're just scum. You don't want to let them push you around."

"I'm not *planning* to let them push me around."

"Well then. Tell them to go to hell. Take my word for it, they'll back off like mongrel dogs, isn't that right, David?"

David's face was a study in polite confusion. Whatever was under discussion, it was clear that he didn't agree with Joe Kennedy's rosy view of it, but also clear that he wasn't anxious to get in an argument with the old man. "Probably," he said cautiously. "But it doesn't pay to squeeze them too hard, in my opinion. Give them an out. Let them save face. That's my point."

"You're soft," Joe snapped. "Soft for a bunch of fucking guineas. Let Bobby deal with them."

"Bobby's *going* to deal with them," Jack said flatly, ending the discussion. He took her by the hand. "Let's go for a, ah, *drive,* shall we?"

She went over and gave the Ambassador a big kiss on his dry skin. He clutched her with a clawlike hand and said, "God, but I wish I were twenty years younger!" His fingers dug deep into her flesh, as if her youth and vitality might keep him going for another day.

She gave David a quick kiss while Jack said good-bye to his father; then he guided her through the gate, down a small flight of stone steps, and out through a door in a thick flowering hedge into a kind of alleyway, where an ordinary gray sedan with blacked-out windows waited, with a couple of "backup" cars behind it. There were perhaps a dozen Secret Service agents standing around, who sprang into action at the sight of the President. She was half led, half pushed into the car, which moved off before the agents standing beside it had even finished slamming the doors shut. "Lancer and Strawhead on board," the agent at the wheel said into his microphone.

As they turned into the street, a white sedan pulled out ahead of them. There was another somewhere behind them. "Isn't all this kind of obvious?" she asked. "Everybody in Palm Beach must know who you are and where you're going."

Jack grinned. "Not at all. About five minutes ago, the presidential limousine pulled away from the front door of the house with flags flying and police cars in front and behind flashing their lights. The presidential press corps is off in full pursuit, and when they get to the Everglades Club—a long drive, by the way—they're going to see my old friend Lem Billings get out."

She laughed. "They'll know you gave them the slip."

"So what? It's the old cat-and-mouse game, with me as the mouse. I figure I'm entitled to my privacy. Though it took me a while to convince the Secret Service." Both agents in the front seat laughed. They obviously enjoyed playing the game as much as Jack did.

The car pulled into a driveway screened by high hedges, a garage door rose in front of them, and they stopped inside, remaining in the car until it closed behind them. One of the agents opened a door and led them up a flight of stairs into the famous hideaway she had visited before, which the Ambassador had prudently bought years ago so his pleasures wouldn't be interrupted by the presence in Palm Beach of his wife.

Jack popped open a bottle of champagne for her. She kicked off her shoes and flopped down on the big white sofa beside him.

Jack, now that he was indoors and at rest, looked more tired and disgruntled than she had thought. He let out a sigh, slipped off his loafers, and put his legs up on the sofa. She snuggled up beside him, unbuttoning his shirt. "Is the job getting to you, Mr. President?" she asked, rubbing her hands down his back.

"You could say that."

"It's what you wanted."

"It's not what I want right now."

"I'm all for everybody having what they want," she whispered, giving his ear a gentle bite.

She let him unzip the back of her dress, then lay down on top of him, listening to the faint, antiseptic hum of the air-conditioning system. At first she thought she wasn't going to get aroused, despite her feelings at the pool when he touched her, but there was something about the scene itself that suddenly got to her—the fact that he was fully dressed while she had on only her bra; the fact that they were in a secret hideaway surrounded by armed agents, their radios crackling as they patrolled the perimeter, that he was Lancer, the president of the United States, and she was Strawhead, the country's number-one blonde; the fact, above all, that this was just about the only thing in her life that still made any sense, for the moment the only thing she could still *feel*, except panic. She had never felt more intensely how much she loved him, and it excited and frightened her at the same time.

They both came rapidly, and she lay on top of him for what seemed like a long time, her lips against his, matching her breathing to his, wondering if he was asleep and wishing that the air-conditioning weren't set quite so high, for she was beginning to get goose bumps.

"That's the best thing that's happened to me today," he said.

"Me too. I'm going back to California, you know."

"I'll be coming out there. Often."

"Good, darling. I've got to get back to work. Sitting around New York on my ass isn't right for me."

"It's quite an ass." He glanced at his watch—the one she had given him, long ago. "Christ!" he said. "I've got to be going."

He swung himself to his feet—wincing in pain as he stood up—zipped up his pants, and slipped his feet into his loafers, ready to go, whereas she was still sprawled on the sofa, bare-assed, her hair like a bird's nest and her makeup a disaster area. "You'll have to give me a few minutes," she said.

"Sure," he said. She went into the nearest bathroom, which some thoughtful soul, knowing how the house was used, had filled with every possible cosmetic and perfume, and set about repairing her face. Jack came in, restless as always after sex, and sat down on the bidet. He had a bottle of soda in his hand. "Are you going to be okay in LA?" he asked.

"I guess so, lover. I've been there before. Why?"

"It's going to be tough going back. Where are you staying?"

She shrugged. "The Beverly Hills Hotel, at first. Then, I don't know. Rent some place maybe, until I can buy a house."

"If you need anything, I can call Frank or Peter."

"I'll be fine." She wasn't sure it was true. Living in New York, she had seen more of Jack than ever before—seen enough of him, in fact, to grow used to it, for, as poor Timmy Hahn's diary no doubt recorded, the President spent the night at the Carlyle Hotel more often than anybody supposed.

It wouldn't be the same—*couldn't* be—once she moved back to LA, and she was dreading that part of it. It had been five years since she left California at Milton Greene's urging, she thought for good, to start a new life in New York as a serious actress and the wife of America's most admired playwright—as somebody who was a *person*, not the ultimate Hollywood "Blond Bombshell." Now she was returning, divorced, unemployable, and still saddled with the same contract she had been trying to break when she first met Milton, a lifetime ago.

She looked at her face in the mirror, then turned, tears forming in the corners of her eyes, and cried, "Oh, Jack, I'm so fucking *scared*."

He got up, put his soda down, and embraced her, holding her tightly against him. He held her for as long as she needed to be held, then said, in a quiet, gentle, serious voice: "Don't *ever* be scared of anything."

36

Bᴜᴛ ꜰᴇᴀʀ ꜱᴇᴛ ɪɴ ʙʏ ᴛʜᴇ ᴛɪᴍᴇ ꜱʜᴇ ᴡᴀꜱ ᴏɴ ᴛʜᴇ ᴘʟᴀɴᴇ to LA.

Five years, she told herself, was a long time. In the eyes of the world she was still the reigning blonde, but her name on a picture was no longer box office magic, and the stories about her lateness and personal problems frightened directors and producers off. Maybe she could overcome that, but what she *couldn't* overcome was her sense that she was returning to the town of her birth a failure.

She felt it so strongly in her bungalow at the Beverly Hills Hotel, the same one in which she had begun her affair with Yves and ended her marriage to Arthur, that she moved out after a week to Frank Sinatra's house—he was out of town— while she looked for an apartment, only to find that her old one, at Doheny and Cynthia Streets, was vacant.

She moved in with her suitcase, hardly even bothering to unpack. She slipped into a round of regular appointments with her analyst, Dr. Ralph Greenson; her internist, Dr. Hyman Engelberg; and several other doctors she neglected to tell Greenson about.

Gradually she began once again the endless round of acquiring what she needed in the way of prescriptions, spending her days in doctors' offices and her evenings tracking down neon-lit, all-night pharmacies where she wasn't known, for, to her terror, she required ever larger quantities of pills to have the slightest effect on her system—quantities that would have set off alarm bells in the minds of Dr. Greenson and Dr. Kris.

She was soon swept up into "the Rat Pack" as a kind of camp follower, following in their hard-drinking wake, "best friends" with Frank, with Peter Lawford, Sammy Davis, Jr., and Dean Martin, picking out the girls for them, knocking back the drinks with them, sharing their dirty jokes, noisy fun, and rebellion against all the rules of stardom and the studios.

Oh, she loved them all—thought of them as "her boys": Dino, Sammy, Frankie, Peter—and they all respected her, since they were in on the secret of her relationship with "the Prez," as she now referred to Jack, but her nights were still spent wakeful and alone in her bed, in the same rented apartment from which she had set out to conquer the world.

Frank sent her a little dog to keep her company, since after a few drinks, she would always complain tearfully about poor Hugo, the dog she had left behind in Connecticut with Arthur. The dog was small, fluffy, white, a real Miami hooker's dog, and immediately became hopelessly devoted to her. She named it Mafia, as an in-joke between herself and Frank, and quickly shortened it to "Maf," though everyone pronounced it "Mof," to rhyme with "mop," which the dog sort of resembled.

She called Jack at least once a day on the private number he had given her. She didn't always reach him, but that was understandable—she didn't expect to every time. When she did, he was sometimes able to talk for only a moment, though at other times he seemed to have time to spare.

There were times when they talked for hours, and others when he took a call from her during a meeting and spoke in a hushed whisper, pretending that she was someone in the Pentagon, and even one unfortunate slipup when Jackie picked up the telephone and hung up immediately.

All the same, the calls to the Prez kept her going, and on days when she had talked to him, she slept a little better, and needed fewer pills. Sometimes when she spoke to him late at night, she would masturbate, lost in a lazy, sensual state of half dreaming, half waking, her senses glowing with the sound of his voice, the pills, and the wine.

It was not missing Jack that depressed her the most—though that was bad enough—it was the fact that the studio really had nothing to offer their biggest star. Much as she had hated Zanuck, at least he would have put her in a picture or even two pictures by now. The new management were cost-cutting, accountant types, in the process of letting the whole studio drift into bankruptcy, yet they treated *her* as if she were Typhoid Mary!

"How've you been, kiddo?" Aaron Diamond, the superagent, shouted at her one night when they ran into each other at a party at Frank's house.

"Great, Aaron," she said, leaning over to kiss his bald head as if it were a good-luck statue, a polished Buddha.

"Then how come you look like shit?"

She wasn't offended. Diamond was tough as nails, but deeply sentimental—a combination peculiar to the movie industry.

"I thought I looked pretty good, Aaron," she said.

"Nah. You can't look *bad*, kiddo, it ain't in you, but you don't look happy. How's the love life?"

"The love life is *comme ci, comme ça*." She waved her hand.

"How's the career?"

"More *comme ci* than *comme ça*, I guess."

"Those schmucks in your own studio are talking you down, you know that, don't you? They'd rather go down the toilet with *Cleopatra* than put you to work."

"They've shown me some things. . . . Nothing I've liked."

"*Bubkis*, right? They're hoping you'll turn everything down, then they can sue you for breach. Listen, I got a property, a remake of an old Irene Dunne/Cary Grant picture, *My Favorite Wife*, I think, which Dino wants to do. It's called *Something's Got to Give* now. The script is terrific—a really smart comedy, just your kind of thing. Let me talk to them."

"Mm." She was tempted by the idea of working with someone she *liked*, like Dean Martin. Dino, she felt sure, would back her against the studio, if and when there were problems. "I'll read the script, Aaron," she said. "Send it round."

"Done. First thing tomorrow." Diamond patted her bottom and vanished into the crowd as if he had never existed, but the script turned up at her apartment the next morning.

The moment she read it, she could tell it *might* work for her. It was about a woman who has been missing for seven years and comes back to find that her husband has remarried since her presumed death. The dialogue was good, with just the kind of brittle wit that appealed to her, and there were some nice comic touches she could do something with.

Everything seemed hunky-dory, at last.

Then she fell apart.

*   *   *

When I heard that Marilyn was in a hospital in New York, I rushed over there immediately. For once, she had managed to get herself admitted with a minimum of publicity, and I found her resting comfortably, though looking as thin as Audrey Hepburn.

Apparently, she had been overtaken by a series of physical disasters. First her doctors in LA had rushed her to Cedars of Lebanon for a pancreas operation; then she had flown to New York, I guess to see Jack, where she suffered a gallbladder attack and required another emergency operation.

I hadn't realized how delicate her bone structure was until I saw her in the hospital. "How are you feeling?" I asked, giving her a kiss.

"Okay. Really. The doctor was sweet. He promised to keep the incision really tiny, and he did."

"No pain?"

"Not much. The Ambassador's old friend Marion Davies was in Cedars. Dying of cancer. She called me and said, 'Us blondes seem to be falling apart.' I guess it's true."

"You don't look as if you're falling apart."

"Oh, you'd say anything to make me happy," she said, and I could tell she didn't mean it as a compliment.

"I hear the studio is in a panic."

"Fuck the studio," she said, in her sweetest little-girl voice. "I can't help it if my pancreas and my gallbladder gave out."

"It's tough luck."

She shrugged. "The worst of it was that I was on my way to see the Prez. I mean, how do you like that? Canceling a date with the President of the United States! He's been sweet, though. He sent me a sheepskin to put under my back in bed, the one he used after his back operation. It made a big difference, he said. I told him it was a pretty lucky sheep to have had Jack Kennedy sleeping on it!"

She laughed. She seemed in pretty good spirits for a woman who had just undergone serious surgery twice in less than a month.

I didn't tell her, because I didn't want to upset her, that she had been the target of a strange series of anonymous hate letters that were being sent to the heads of the major studios, threatening to reveal that she was Jack Kennedy's mistress and promising other, sinister revelations that would bring down the Kennedys and put an end to the career of "his harlot." One of the studio heads had shown me the letters, and I thought it very likely that the threat of a major scandal explained some of her own studio's reluctance to use her.

The FBI was busy investigating the source of these letters, which were specific enough to briefly unite Hoover and Bobby in a common cause, but from the sound of them, they came from some major Hollywood "Insider," somebody who hated the Kennedys and Marilyn and hoped to destroy them both. I had the sense that the shadows were somehow drawing in over Marilyn—some presentiment of disaster—and made up my mind to keep an eye on her.

I said good-bye to her, and as I was standing in the corridor, putting on my coat, I heard her make a telephone call and say, in a voice loud enough to be heard through the door, "Jack, it's me, Marilyn."

As I moved on, I couldn't help wondering how long Jack would encourage Marilyn to be a daily caller, and what she would do if he ever put a stop to it.

She flew back to Los Angeles in a daze. She had nearly succumbed under anesthesia during the second operation because she hadn't told the anesthetist what she had already taken, and even now, a few weeks later, she still felt light-headed and butter-fingered, and had trouble with such simple things as buttoning her own clothes. Physical pain, she hardly felt at all, not that it worried her all that much, but even *emotional* pain filtered through to her in a diffused and distant way, like the tinkling of a far-off piano on a quiet day.

She had seen Dr. Kris in New York, and even through the fog of medication had noticed the expression of alarm on her face, particularly when she started to tell her about all the men she had slept with during the past few months, and about her total inability to feel any kind of pleasure with them.

The only person she wanted was Jack, but since he was seldom available, she tried to console herself with an endless succession of substitutes. Anything, she told Dr. Kris, was better than spending a night alone, but Dr. Kris looked doubtful—with good reason, for the more men her patient slept with, the more depressed and worthless she felt.

Dr. Kris agreed to call Dr. Greenson in LA, to convey her unease, but Dr. Greenson let it be known that he thought his New York colleague was being something of an alarmist. He managed to calm Dr. Kris, who still felt that Marilyn was *her* patient, and to wave aside all Dr. Kris's objections to her return to Los Angeles. Dr. Greenson would look after her like a mother hen, he promised—there wasn't a thing to worry about.

She was *longing* to place herself in Dr. Greenson's hands and let him run every detail of her life (except her intake of pills). She was simply too tired to do it herself anymore, and the decisions Dr. Kris wanted her to make were exactly the ones she couldn't face. She wasn't up to making hard choices, she told herself, and Dr. Greenson was the last person who would want her to. The only thing that disturbed her on the flight back to LA was the fact that the stewardesses all seemed to be younger than she was.

She stopped off at Schwab's drugstore—where she had once hung out with all the other young hopefuls—to fill a prescription. While she was waiting, she looked through the greeting cards. She picked one that showed a mournful bunny holding a bunch of flowers, borrowed a pen from the lady at the cash register, and wrote in large capitals:

> DEAR MR. PREZ:
> ROSES ARE RED, BUT GOSH I'M BLUE,
> THIS LITTLE BUNNY'S STILL HOT FOR YOU!
> MISS YOU BADLY. LOVE,
> MARILYN

She kissed the bottom of the card, just below her name, leaving a clear imprint in lipstick of her lips, then sealed it, addressed it to Jack in the White House, and scrawled "SWAK" on the flap.

It had become a habit, sending small gifts and messages to Jack. She had sent him a pair of cashmere socks in emerald green, with a note that said they were to keep him warm when she wasn't in bed with him, and a red flannel nightshirt with a variation of the same message, as well as a gift subscription to *Playboy* and innumerable small reminders of herself of a more or less intimate nature.

It did sometimes occur to her that what had begun as an occasional joke was becoming an obsession—that perhaps at the receiving end it might not seem as funny as it did to her—but she couldn't help herself. After the breakup with Arthur, her feelings about Jack had changed. She had always loved him, but it had been the kind of love she could keep in a corner of her life—part of the background, as it were, not the foreground—the icing on the cake. Then, in some way that was beyond her control, her feelings started to intensify, as if the relationship with Jack was filling her emotional life at just the point where Jack himself was becoming more remote, leaving her, she began to fear, behind. . . .

She went home, back to the apartment on Doheny, greeted Maf, the only living creature who seemed to have missed her and to be happy she was back, then called Dr. Greenson to ask if he could see her, which, of course, he could.

Her temporary secretary had placed her mail neatly on the dining table, not that there was much of it, and her temporary housekeeper had managed to keep the place reasonably clean, despite Maf's occasional "accidents," for nobody had time to train the poor dog properly.

She glanced around the apartment, bewildered, as if it were somebody else's. She had done nothing to make a real home of it, but because she had lived here before she made her break with Fox and married Arthur, it sometimes seemed to her that her whole life since then was a hallucination, that she had never left here at all. . . .

She took off her clothes, popped open a bottle of champagne, and took some of the pills she had bought at Schwab's. Every once in a while, she caught sight of her naked body in a mirror as she wandered around the apartment, and it looked to her as if she were a ghost, except for the angry red surgical scar. She called her answering service, but there were no messages, which made her feel even more ghostlike—Hollywood's biggest, sexiest star with no messages!—but then she remembered that she had told her secretary to change the unlisted number at regular intervals, since she was getting crank calls—the people she *gave* the number to gave it to others, until it inevitably fell into the hands of crazies. . . . That meant that a lot of people couldn't reach her, and very often she couldn't even remember the number herself. . . .

She went into the bedroom. She had put a couple of Jack's election posters above the bed so that he was looking down at her, with his firm, manly, vote-gathering expression. She blew him a kiss—she was feeling light-headed from jet lag, champagne, the pills, and the fact that she hadn't eaten anything for hours—then dressed in a pair of Jax slacks and a sweater. She needed a bath, but she couldn't be bothered, so she simply made up her face and put a scarf over her hair, then took her car keys, went to the garage, and backed her Cadillac out onto Doheny.

Dr. Greenson's office had a back entrance, to allow the more famous of his patients to slip in unseen. He wasn't the kind of stickler for Freudian etiquette who insisted on his patients lying down on the couch, but basically she liked lying down during her sessions, since she was able to talk more freely that way. All her best conversations came in the form of pillow talk.

Dr. Greenson pulled the blinds closed so his tastefully furnished office was dim, and sat back in his leather swivel chair, an expression of soulful ecstasy on his handsome face, as if he were in a postcoital mood. "So how are we?" he asked.

"Okay."

"Really?"

"Well, not so hot, actually."

"The postoperative period is never easy. You had a serious operation. Two, in fact. Don't expect miracles from yourself."

"Actually, I feel okay. About the operation and all, I mean."

"And the career?"

"That's pretty depressing. I guess I'll do this picture with Dean Martin, if Fox ever gets around to scheduling it. George Cukor is supposed to direct it."

"I heard. I read the script. I think it's a good part for you. I wrote some suggestions in the margins—a few little things about dialogue and so on."

Dr. Greenson, like everybody in Hollywood, fancied himself a scriptwriter.

"I feel kind of lost," she said. "Drifting."

"From man to man?"

"That's part of it. I mean, I can't see an *end* to all this. . . . Another guy. Another movie. Another pill. What for?"

"You have to learn to enjoy life for its own sake. You need a project, a goal, apart from the picture. I've been thinking that you should be looking for a house, perhaps. . . . That's a positive step, very life-reinforcing. . . . I know a good realtor. I'll have him call you. And I have somebody who would be a terrific housekeeper too. Just the woman you need, you'll adore her. . . . And the affectional life? Any news on that front?"

She hated the phrase "affectional life," but she let it go. When Dr. Greenson meant sex, he said "affectional moment," or so she had thought until he explained that an "affectional moment" didn't have to involve sex, which came as news to her, and would have come as even more surprising news to most of the men she had known.

"Well, with the operation and all, it's been pretty dry. . . . I still have these dreams. . . ."

He leaned forward, eyes glittering. Dreams were what he wanted to hear about most of all.

"I keep dreaming that I'm going to marry Jack Kennedy," she said.

He nodded, as if that were a normal dream.

"It's not even just a *dream*."

"No?"

"I mean, it's like, in some part of my mind, I really think it's going to *happen?*"

"There's nothing *wrong* with fantasy," Dr. Greenson said. "Fantasy is the safety valve of the unconscious." He smiled, as if he had just coined a phrase that he would use again.

"Yes?" she said. Then, after a pause: "But you see, the problem is, I'm not sure it's just a fantasy. . . ."

She was sitting next to Peter Lawford at Chasen's, in her best black spaghetti-strap dress, feeling no pain, with Frank at the head of the table, and Sammy on the other side of her, and Dino, and a lot of other Rat Packers.

They had all been at a party at Frank's, where they had, she thought, behaved pretty badly—though, mercifully, she couldn't remember the details. Then they had come here because Dino said he wanted to eat, and afterward they were going on to see some show in Hollywood that Sammy said they shouldn't miss, then probably back to Frank's, for poker and more drinks, or maybe out to Peter's place at Malibu. . . .

Peter's face seemed to be going in and out of focus, which was odd, and she wondered if the pills he had given her, "to cure her blues," might have something to do with it. They'd shared a couple of joints, too, on the sly, because their host, despite his reputation for wild self-indulgence, didn't approve of that sort of thing in his home, and with all the champagne she had been drinking on an empty stomach too, she was beginning to feel as if she were floating in the air, like one of the blimps you occasionally saw patrolling the Pacific, just beyond the beach. . . .

Lawford had been throwing bread rolls at everybody except Frank, who didn't react well to that kind of thing, but he had calmed down now, or perhaps just run out of rolls, and was leaning against her, exchanging obscene insults with Sammy while she giggled between them.

"Fuck you, man," Sammy said unrancorously. "You know who you're talking to?"

"A jig," Lawford said amiably. "A blind-in-one-eye nigger who fucks white girls."

Sammy Davis, Jr., shook his head slowly and with dignity. "No, man," he said. "You are talking to a *Jew!* I converted, remember? I expect to be treated with respect as one of the Chosen People."

"Funny, but you don't *look* Jewish."

"Luckily for you, Limey motherfucker, looks ain't everything. . . . Last time I saw Jack"—he lifted his glass in a toast—"your esteemed brother-in-law the President, I told him if he wanted a new ambassador to Israel, I was ready to serve."

"What did Jack say?"

"He said he would consider it. He asked if I'd been circumcised and if it hurt."

"I'm going to marry Jack," she said firmly, in a louder voice than usual.

Lawford's eyes snapped wide open. "I beg your pardon?"

She thought he hadn't heard her above the noise. "I'M GOING TO MARRY JACK KENNEDY!" she shouted. "I'm going to be First Lady, instead of Jackie."

"Are you sure, honey?" Sammy asked. "Are you okay?"

"Of course I am. Jack asked me."

"I'm not sure it's a good idea to be saying this in public," Lawford said, fear on his face. He was part of the Kennedy family, by no means completely accepted but still acutely aware of what the limits were. Marilyn, his expression seemed to be

saying, had just exceeded them, and he looked anxious to dis-
associate himself from her.

But it was too late. Dino, or somebody else from the far
end of the table, shouted out raucously: "What did you say,
Marilyn?" and in the silence that followed she shouted back,
as if somebody else were in charge of her voice: "DRINK UP,
EVERYBODY! JACK KENNEDY IS GOING TO DIVORCE
JACKIE AND MARRY ME!"

A hush fell over the restaurant. The waiters even stopped
serving.

She heard somebody growl, "Get her the fuck out of here!"
but she didn't care.

If none of them could take a joke, that was *their* problem.

37

B̲Y THE SUMMER OF 1961, JACK'S PRESIDENCY SEEMED TO BE
sailing on an even keel, to use one of his favorite metaphors.

The Bay of Pigs fiasco had damaged him seriously, but he
recovered, mostly because his image remained youthful and
"upbeat."

Although the ambassadorship remained a sore point between
us—one that we did not discuss—Jack kept me busy with
important commissions, and made sure I had "access," the
most coveted privilege a president can offer. I performed some
tricky unofficial diplomacy for him in Israel, where I had many
close friends in government, and in Miami, among the angry
Cuban exiles. Hoffa's name, I was happy to note, had receded
from the front pages, and apparently from Jack's mind.

What I *didn't* know was that Hoffa was still on Bobby's
mind as much as ever. In his new role as Jack's "prime
minister," Bobby at last had the authority and the power to
get Hoffa—nor was Jack, with bigger problems on his mind,
about to restrain his brother, if he even knew what he was
doing.

Lulled by this false sense of security, I was taken by surprise when I received a call from Stuart Warshavsky—one of the few old-time New York labor leaders who maintained a truce, however uneasy, with the Teamsters—begging me for a meeting with the President on urgent business. I could tell from Stuart's voice that he had a serious problem—too serious to talk about over the phone—and I knew enough about labor politics to guess Jack would probably want to accommodate him.

I'd known Stuart for years, and had gone to a lot of trouble to gain his support for Jack. When his fellow New York Jewish Liberals (with a capital L) reacted in horror to Jack's choice of Lyndon Johnson as a running mate, it had been Stuart who reminded them that the alternative to Kennedy/Johnson was Nixon/Lodge.

Jack was grateful to Stuart, all the more so because New York politics was something of a mystery to him. At first he had assumed it was sufficient to promise more arms for Israel and invoke Franklin D. Roosevelt's name as often as possible. Stuart, at my urging, had been one of those who taught him otherwise.

Since Stuart had never asked for anything on this scale before, I passed his request on with a strong personal recommendation, for what that was worth. It was worth a good deal, it seemed, for word came back shortly that Stuart had been invited to a White House dinner that Maria and I were attending.

Jack had apparently concluded that the invitation would stroke Stuart's ego. As it happened, this was a misreading of his character. His father, a Menshevik, had shared a room with Trotsky, on the Lower East Side. As a Socialist, a Zionist, and a labor leader, Stuart had never owned a dinner jacket and wasn't about to buy one. He was as puzzled by the invitation as I was, but once I had obtained special dispensation for him to wear a dark suit instead of "black tie," he accepted gracefully enough.

When he presented himself to the President and the First Lady in the receiving line, Jack shook his hand warmly, introduced him to Jackie—who was staring at his rather rumpled blue suit and badly knotted tie with a certain amount of exasperation—and whispered that he hoped to have a few words with Stuart after dinner. Somebody had the good sense to seat him next to the wife of the Israeli ambassador to the United Nations, and Stuart seemed to me to be enjoying himself, despite the elegant surroundings and the fancy food. Maria was seated between Jack and Prince Radziwill, Jackie's brother-in-law, so she was even happier, since they were the two best-looking men in the room.

Jackie had introduced classical entertainment to the White House dinners (the Eisenhowers liked to get their guests out of the White House by ten o'clock at the latest), and it was Jack's habit to sneak away for a few minutes between coffee and the beginning of whatever entertainment was scheduled, sometimes with a lady who had attracted his attention, sometimes for a bit of politics.

A White House aide discreetly ushered Stuart and me to a small sitting room, and we sat down together and lit our cigars. Jack was in an expansive mood—Jackie loved entertaining and was terrific at it, and the Kennedys as a couple never seemed happier with each other than when they were on display. As the furor over the Bay of Pigs receded, Jackie was busily improving her French for their forthcoming state visit to France, and Jack was flexing his muscles for the Vienna summit meeting with Khrushchev. Both of them were beginning to enjoy being in the White House.

"It's good of you to see me, Mr. President," Stuart said.

"You carried the ball when I picked Lyndon as a running mate, Stuart. That took guts. I owe you one."

"I know," Stuart said. As a New York politician, he could measure favors received and repaid as precisely as a Toledo scale. "That's why I'm here. I've got a problem."

Jack's face wasn't exactly stony, but like the politician *he* was, he knew just when to convey total blankness.

Stuart leaned forward confidentially. "Look, my people know all about bad unions. Believe me, paper locals, goon squads, sweetheart contracts, mobsters, you name it—this kind of stuff, we know, and we're against."

"Good," Jack said. "So am I."

Stuart shrugged away the interruption. "But at the same time, we're against union busting. We're against persecuting labor leaders, even the ones nobody likes or invites to the White House for dinner."

"Which ones have you in mind?"

"Hoffa, Mr. President."

"He's a criminal. He's sold his own people out to the mob."

"Maybe. To a lot of working people, he's a hero. What I'm saying, Mr. President, is, enough is enough. It's always Hoffa this and Hoffa that, send the son of a bitch to jail, but we don't hear about the Justice Department setting up a special task force to prosecute a banker, or the CEO of a Fortune Five Hundred company."

It was my first hint that Hoffa was a live issue. It may have been Jack's, too, for he looked surprised. "George Meany wants to see Hoffa in jail as much as Bobby does," he said.

"Mr. President, forgive me, but there are those of us who think George Meany is a fink."

Jack looked at Stuart shrewdly. "What's up, Stuart?" he said. "You don't like Hoffa. You don't want mobsters controlling unions any more than we do."

"Sometimes you have to work with mobsters, Mr. President. I'll make a deal with anybody who'll help me organize sweat-shops—and I *have*, I'm not ashamed to admit. . . ."

Stuart leaned farther forward, hands on his knees, eyes fixed on the President's, his rugged face, with the big, broken nose and the bushy eyebrows that were his trademark, set in a serious expression. "We have to live with the Teamsters, Mr. President. Okay, you don't, your brother doesn't, but if the Teamsters don't ship materials in and finished goods out, my people are out of work. You understand, Mr. President, that means they don't *eat*. Maybe I don't like Hoffa and his friends in the mob, but I got to do business with him and with them."

"You wouldn't be carrying a message from Hoffa, would you, Stuart?" Jack asked quickly.

Stuart nodded. "A guy came to see me, Mr. President, fellow you never heard of called Big Gus McKay, one of Hoffa's 'inner circle,' you might say. Nice enough guy, size of King Kong, but very soft-spoken, sort of an old Eugene Debs Wobbly type gone wrong, like a lot of the Teamster leadership. . . . He asked me to tell you that Hoffa wants to make a deal."

"He should call the Attorney General for that, Stuart."

"He doesn't trust Bobby, frankly. And it isn't that kind of deal."

"What kind is it? Just out of curiosity."

"McKay mentioned that Hoffa would keep his mouth shut about how Dave Beck got put in jail."

Jack's eyes caught mine and I shrugged. I wasn't, after all, responsible for Hoffa's behavior.

"I don't know anything about that," he said to Stuart, his face impassive. "It sounds like old stuff."

"McKay also hinted that Hoffa knows what he called 'a lot of national security stuff' involving Cuba."

"Garbage, Stuart. I can't believe you came down here with this crap." Jack was angry now, and Stuart was beginning to sweat, but I guessed that there were probably worse things in store for Stuart than Jack Kennedy's anger if he didn't deliver his full message.

Stuart wiped his face with his handkerchief. "There's one more thing, McKay told me," he said. "But it's sort of embarrassing, and, ah, *personal.* . . ."

Jack glared at him coldly.

"It's, ah, about Marilyn Monroe, Mr. President," Stuart blurted out. "Apparently, she's going around telling people you're going to divorce Mrs. Kennedy and marry her. Hoffa's got proof of it somehow. McKay says if he doesn't get a deal, he's going to take it to the papers." Stuart looked contrite. "Mr. President, I'm sorry. But I thought you ought to know."

Jack's face was ashen, but he was too good a politician to lose his temper with Stuart. He simply rose, shook his hand abruptly, and thanked him for coming.

Just as he was leaving the room, he turned, gave Stuart a look of startling intensity, and said, in a low voice, for there was an aide and a Marine guard waiting for him: "Stuart, pass this message back, will you? The President says Hoffa can go fuck himself."

Then he turned back and walked briskly out into the corridor, from the end of which we could hear, Stuart and I, the sound of a cello being tuned.

As I was leaving the White House after the concert, Jack gave me a hard look and whispered, "Don't you ever do that to me again!"

I saw Jack again in the Oval Office the next day. He was still angry about Stuart's messages. Maria had commented on the fact that he had seemed rather cold to me when we made our good-byes after the White House dinner, and he hadn't warmed up much since then.

I wasn't about to point out to him that Hoffa's attempt at blackmail had come about because Bobby, against my advice, was still trying to put him behind bars. Hoffa was Bobby's obsession, something that Jack could neither explain nor control.

Jack gave me an impatient look and said: "I've been thinking things over, David."

"What things?" I asked.

"The London embassy. I said I'd think it over, remember?"

Jack had delayed appointing an ambassador, and from time to time I had wondered if his purpose was to keep the carrot dangling in front of me. I still *wanted* it, of course—but nothing like as much as I once had. Had it been offered to me willingly when I asked for it, that would have been one thing, but I sensed that if it was going to happen now, it would be grudging, and probably hedged in with unacceptable conditions.

All the same, I felt a faint but perceptible thrill. Jack had been in office a few months, gained confidence, learned the ropes—he was in a better position to make the appointment now, I reasoned, leaning forward expectantly in my chair.

He frowned. "I can't do it," he said, with the brisk authority of a man biting the bullet.

I was momentarily taken aback. "Can't *do* it?" I asked. "Why not?" It occurred to me that Jack might be getting his revenge for my having exposed him to Stuart's visit.

"I'm not going to give you a lot of crap about your qualifications, David. We both know you're qualified. But I want a man there who has the confidence of the establishment."

"Theirs?" I was about to point out that the prewar British establishment had been outraged by his father's appointment, which didn't stop FDR, but before I could, he snapped back: *"Ours."*

He swung his chair around and stared out the window at the garden, avoiding my eyes. "The Brits are important," he said. "They're really the only allies we have in Europe we can *trust* not to make a separate deal with the Russians. . . . I need someone in London who has the confidence of our foreign policy establishment, David—the Council on Foreign Policy crowd, the people who write pieces for *Foreign Affairs*, and so on."

"They're mostly Republicans," I said. "Spiritual followers of Nelson Rockefeller. No friends of yours."

"Yes," he said distantly. "Those are exactly the people I want on my side. I'm going to send David Bruce's name to the Senate. I wanted you to hear it from me first."

I understood what was on his mind. He wanted to insure himself against criticism from the right, to co-opt the foreign policy establishment so it couldn't turn against him again, as it had over Cuba, maybe even to steal Nelson Rockefeller's "brain trust" away from him, in case Nelson won the Republican nomination in '64. . . .

It was good politics, but I still felt a deep sense of disappointment for having waited so patiently. I was angry, too. I knew Bruce, and although he was an affable enough fellow, he wasn't in my league. But you can't argue with the President of the United States. *"Thank* you," I said, not bothering to conceal my rage.

I was briefly tempted to get up and walk out, but something held me back—my friendship with Joe perhaps, or the simple fact that I could never bring myself to dislike Jack.

I would have preferred that he had simply never brought the subject of my ambassadorship up again, that somehow we had been able to let it lie, and I'm sure he did too, but of course, he was the president, so he couldn't.

Politics, I told myself, was a game for grown-ups. There was no room for hurt feelings. I should have known that better than anyone.

For a moment poor Marilyn flashed in my mind, and I wished there were some way to explain to her how dangerous it was to have a president for a friend—still worse, to love him.

"You're upset," Jack said. "I understand that. But it has to be, David. If there's anything else you want . . . I don't suppose Mexico would interest you?"

I shook my head, momentarily speechless. Mexico! What did he take me for?

"Look, you'll think of something, David. Or I will, okay? I owe you. You know that."

"I know that, Mr. President."

There was a knock on the door and his secretary appeared, summoned, I had no doubt, by a hidden button under Jack's desk.

"Duty calls," Jack said, and we rose and shook hands formally, farther apart than we had ever been before.

Once I was back in the Hay-Adams—and in control of my feelings—I called the Ambassador, in Palm Beach. I was put through to him right away, but for a moment I didn't even realize it was he. It was the voice of an old man, high-pitched, querulous, hesitant. I was shocked—ashamed too, for, caught up in the excitement of Jack's problems in the White House, I had been neglecting Joe.

"Jack gave you the news, did he?" he asked.

I suddenly wondered if Joe had been on my side. I assumed he would have been, but you could never tell with Joe, particularly where "his" ambassadorship was concerned, for he viewed it in a proprietorial way, and was always angry whenever a president appointed a new ambassador to the Court of St. James's without consulting him.

"He gave me the bad news," I said. "I'm disappointed, of course."

There was a long silence. "Yes," he said softly. "You would be." He sighed. "It's not my doing, David. I'll tell you that. Oh, don't get me wrong—I don't suppose the goddamn Brits would like a sheeny PR man any more than they liked a Mick Wall Street speculator, but I thought you'd earned the right to it. . . ."

I thought I'd earned it too, several times over in fact. What I wanted to tell Joe was that if I wasn't good enough to be Jack's ambassador to the United Kingdom, I didn't see why I should continue doing any of his dirty work with the mob, or helping to cover up the administration's more flagrant mistakes, but there was something in his voice that made me hold back. I wish I hadn't, now. If ever there was a time to make a clean break of it, this was the moment, but I listened to Joe Kennedy instead.

I had to listen hard too, to make out what he was saying, his voice was so frail. It wasn't like him to apologize, or to let slip even the smallest difference of opinion between himself and Jack. "I'm not always consulted the way I used to be," he said. There was a longish pause. "What are we talking about?" he asked. He sounded confused.

"The ambassadorship."

Another long pause. "We're old friends, David," the Ambassador said, "aren't we?"

"We are that," I agreed, wondering where this was leading.

"So I can ask you for a favor?"

"You know that."

"Don't hold this against Jack, David. He's our president now. He's not the old Jack anymore, not for you, not even for me. He has his own place in history to look out for. I wish he'd chosen you—maybe he does too. But he has to make up his own mind, and when he has, we have to back him."

"I understand," I said. I understood more than had been said. Jack was no longer consulting his father. He was his own man at last. It must have been painful for Joe, but stoic as always, he had accepted the reality of the situation. He was even determined to make sure that I accepted it—that Jack wasn't making an enemy of me.

"When are you going to come down here and see me, David?" he asked. It was a plea.

I was astonished—the Joe Kennedy I had known for thirty years, fiercely unsentimental and demanding, would never have asked such a question. I realized then that I was talking to a man who had, finally, come face-to-face with the fact of dying, and was deeply afraid of it. Joe had none of his sons' fatalism— nor his wife's, for that matter. If anybody had ever thought he was going to live forever, it was Joe Kennedy. Something had clearly taught him otherwise.

"I'll be down in a couple of weeks," I said. "I'll make a point of it."

"Fine." He tried to sound hearty, and failed. "We'll talk more about it then."

I felt even then, as I hung up the phone, a certain chill, like the drawing down of the shades on a winter afternoon—a feeling, irrational and not at all like me, of impending tragedy.

As things turned out, two weeks was leaving it too long.

38

"I THOUGHT I TOLD YOU I DIDN'T WANT TO HEAR ANY more of this crap," Robert Kennedy said impatiently.

Hoover leaned forward. "I think you ought to hear *this*," he said in an urgent voice. "Believe me, I've got your brother's best interests at heart."

Kennedy sighed. The week before, he had discovered that the New York office of the FBI was compiling its intelligence on organized crime by clipping stories from the *New York Post* and the *New York Daily News,* and he assumed that Hoover's visit was in the nature of a counterattack, to prove that he and his people were on the ball *somewhere* at least.

"This is Special Agent Kirkpatrick," Hoover said. "He is our leading expert on electronic surveillance."

The Attorney General glared at Kirkpatrick, recognizing another tough and ambitious Mick when he saw him. Kirkpatrick stared right back, a good sign. Kennedy respected men who weren't afraid of him.

Kennedy nodded glumly. Kirkpatrick placed a reel-to-reel portable tape recorder on the polished desk, plugged it in, and pushed a button. There was a faint hum, perhaps the sound of air-conditioning, then a familiar whispery voice, like a little girl's but with undertones of grown-up sexiness, spoke: . . . *I still have these dreams. . . .*

A man's voice, patient, deep, clearly a doctor's, replied. *Tell me about them.*

I keep dreaming that I'm going to marry Jack Kennedy. There was a pause. *It's not even just a dream.*

No?

I mean, it's like, in some part of my mind, I really think it's going to happen?

Yes?

. . . I'm going to marry Jack Kennedy.

There's nothing wrong with fantasy. . . . Fantasy is the safety valve of the unconscious. . . .

Yes? But you see, the problem is, I'm not sure it's just a fantasy. . . . There was a long pause, with muted sounds of traffic in the background; then Marilyn Monroe spoke very clearly: *He means it, Doctor, you see—he really means it!*

Robert Kennedy's eyes were shut, as if he was in pain. He waved his hand, to have Kirkpatrick turn the machine off.

"Thank you, Edgar," he said wearily. "I'll take it from here."

It was a hot Indian summer day, though no longer the humid heat that made people want to stay indoors with the air-conditioning on full blast.

It was the kind of weather that made Jack and Bobby Kennedy think of Hyannis Port, of sailing and clambakes on the beach—itchy to get away, as if the sea were bred in their bones. But for the present they were stuck here. As much for the need to be outdoors as for security, Jack led Bobby out into the White House Rose Garden, where they strolled, hands behind their backs, heads close together, two brothers who were now running not only the country but a large part of the world.

"Jack," Bobby said, "I *know* how you feel, but this is serious."

"You don't know how I feel."

"I've had my—adventures. I'm not exactly a goddamn virgin."

Jack laughed. "Adventures? Is that what they're called? And here all this time I thought you were a Boy Scout."

"You know better than that. But this isn't a joke like the old paternity suit Hoover keeps telling me about."

"What paternity suit?"

"Hoover claimed there was evidence you settled out of court with some girl for sixty thousand dollars. I sent someone to track her down and interview her, and she just laughed and said you still owed her the two dollars you borrowed for your taxi fare." Jack looked interested. "What was her name?"

"Giselle something. Hubert? Hulme?"

"Giselle Holmes," Jack said, grinning. "Autumn of 1950, the year I was running for a second term in Congress, waiting for Paul Dever to make up his mind whether he was going to take a second shot at the governorship or run against Lodge for the Senate. . . ."

"You're lucky he decided to go for a second term. You'd have made a terrible governor."

"You see? That's the difference between us. I wasn't thinking about politics. I was thinking about women. I met Giselle while I was campaigning, went to her apartment, spent the night. I can remember it to this day. I think she probably gave the best head in Massachusetts at the time. Anyway, in the morning I discovered I didn't have any money on me, so I borrowed two bucks off her to get back to Bowdoin Street. I guess I never paid her back. Where's she living now?"

"Springfield, Illinois. She's married to an oral surgeon."

"That figures."

"I'm not trying to cramp your style," Bobby said. "But you're playing with fire."

"I'd appreciate it if you wouldn't throw clichés at me. You *are* trying to cramp my style, and I'm not going to have it."

"We don't all have your gift for rhetoric."

"Stop it, Bobby. You and I are too close for this kind of shit to come between us. I *like* taking risks, it's part of what makes life worth living for me. And I like chasing women, as many of them as I can, because—and listen to me carefully—each and every one of them is completely different from all the others, and on the other hand, they're all the same. If that isn't a phenomenon interesting enough to spend your life exploring, I don't know what is."

"Look, I didn't come here for a sex lecture—"

"It doesn't appear you and Ethel *need* one, frankly. You seem to have got the rudiments of the thing doped out."

Bobby pushed on stubbornly. "It's political dynamite, Johnny," he said. When he addressed his brother as "Johnny," it was always serious. "Here's Marilyn Monroe, the most visible woman in the world, going around telling people the two of you are having an affair, and that you're going to *marry* her. It's a weapon in the hands of Hoover. You should *hear* the tape he's got of Marilyn talking to her analyst. She told him you'd asked her to marry you—that you'd promised to divorce Jackie."

"I know." Jack shook his head. "It seems everybody's talking about it, even our pal Hoffa, He sent word he'll make a deal—

with me, not you. Immunity, for all the usual stuff, *plus*—are you ready for this?—he won't reveal to the press that Marilyn and I are getting married!"

Bobby's face turned dark. "That *bastard!*"

"Don't worry about it. Even if he tries, I don't think anybody will print it."

"It's just what I was warning you about, Johnny, all the same." Bobby brushed the hair out of his eyes. "This thing with Marilyn, Johnny, it's going to blow up on you. I feel it in my bones."

"I'm not giving Marilyn up. I'm telling you that right now. The Leader of the Free World is entitled to some privileges, Bobby, and Marilyn happens to be one of them."

"Then tell her to shut up." Bobby paused. "Has it occurred to you she might be crazy?"

"All women are crazy."

"I'm serious!"

Jack's expression turned sadder, almost solemn. He suddenly seemed a lot older than Bobby. "Yes," he said softly, "as a matter of fact, it has."

"She could hurt you, Johnny. I hate to say it, but she could cost you your second term. Not to speak of what Jackie would say."

Jack nodded. At the mention of a second term he seemed to drift into silence, as if Bobby had finally driven the realty of it home to him. He always knew, in the end, when to listen to Bobby. Somewhere deep inside him, in that secret part of his mind where he had always hidden his real feelings and emotions, he knew that it was Bobby who was the serious one, the one who cherished responsibilities, the one who wasn't scared of the tough decisions—the one, truly, who should be president.

"I'll *think* about it," he agreed. "If I decide it's getting out of hand, I'll put an end to it, I promise. I hope to God I don't have to, though. It's funny. I really love Marilyn, you know. . . ."

He stopped and stared back at the armored glass windows of the Oval Office. "Sometimes it's not so great, being president," he said.

"I understand."

"No, you don't. But I guess you might find out yourself one day."

"There's one other thing, Johnny. . . . There's this girl you're seeing who's connected to Giancana. That's a worry too. . . ."

"Oh, come on, Bobby!" Jack said impatiently. "Judy's a whole different thing. I mean, there's nothing *personal* there. So she knows Giancana? So what? She knows a lot of guys."

"She doesn't just *know* Giancana, Jack. She's his mistress."

" 'Mistress' is a big word. Let me reassure you. I don't tell her state secrets while we're fucking, and my guess is that Giancana doesn't talk to her about his business either. She has certain valuable talents, but being Mata Hari isn't one of them. Do I make myself clear?"

"It's still a dumb risk," Bobby said stubbornly. "If it ever comes out, it's going to look terrible. I mean, how much would it cost you, frankly, to give her up? There are plenty of other girls around."

"And I hope to fuck every one of them. But I'll tell you what: I'll decide who I want to fuck, okay?"

"Okay."

The two brothers turned back toward the glass door opening out onto the garden, where a Secret Service agent stood watching them.

"Giselle Holmes," the President said with a fond smile. "Great legs. Not too much on top."

39

"OF COURSE, IT'S IMPORTANT TO BE ABLE TO DISTINGUISH fantasy from fact," Dr. Greenson said.

"My whole life I've been part of other people's fantasies. I'm entitled to my own for a change."

"Other people's fantasies?"

"Sure. Ever since my tits started to grow. All my life I've known what men think when they see me—know that when they go home to fuck their wives or jerk off, it's me they're fucking in their minds, my tits they're licking, my cunt they're coming in. . . .

"It's a weird feeling, you know? It's like I don't belong to myself at all, I belong to *them,* all those guys who fuck me in their minds. I could be dead, it wouldn't matter, they'd still be jerking off over photos of me. I'm not real, see? I'm just the girl your wife or girlfriend could never be, the one who's always ready for it, never has a headache, doesn't care if you come before she does. . . .

"Even the guys who have *married* me always had some kind of fantasy in mind, not me. It's like they were marrying Marilyn, not Norma Jean. But I'm Norma Jean, really. It's hard work being Marilyn. I don't feel like doing it every day."

"I understand that."

"That's why I love Jack. It's hard work for him, too—being Jack, I mean. Jack's in everybody's fantasies too. Women dream he's fucking them instead of their husbands, men dream of being rich and handsome like him, or of being the president, or being a war hero, or maybe being married to Jackie. . . . But once you get to know him, you realize he's as much of a fraud as I am. He's still the puny little kid with a tough big brother and an even tougher father. He desperately wants to be loved, but he's afraid to show it, and he's not too sure how to ask for it because he's been taught to despise weakness. . . . But there he is, everybody's hero. We're a pair, we are. We'll make a terrific couple."

"*Will* make?"

"I believe it, just the way I once believed I was going to marry America's greatest playwright, even though he hardly knew me, and was married with two kids, and lived twenty-five hundred miles away. . . . And that *happened,* didn't it? And when I was just a kid, picking up dates in Hollywood bars, hoping they'd buy me a hamburger before they dropped me home, *if* they dropped me home, I had this fantasy that I was going to marry America's biggest sports hero, who looked to me like the sexiest man in the world. . . . And *that* happened too, didn't it? So why shouldn't *this* happen? Tell me that? If I can go from being an orphan of LA County, with one pair of shoes, to the biggest star ever, why shouldn't I marry Jack Kennedy?"

"Mm."

"The only problem is, why do I feel like I'm not even *living*—like this is all just some kind of waiting room before they take me to the mortuary?"

"You have to learn to accept life. That's what we have to work on here."

"Oh, I *accept* it, all right. . . . I just don't *like* it much, is all."

She sat by the pool of Peter Lawford's Malibu house looking out over the picket fence that had been erected to give Jack privacy when he visited, staring at the starry sky and listening to the surf. Lawford sat beside her, smoking a joint, a glass of scotch in his hand, humming from time to time in a tuneless way. They had both taken refuge out here from a dinner party.

"Jack would be a lot happier with me," she said.

"Mm."

"You know he would."

"What on earth does that matter, darling? Marriage isn't about happiness. Least of all Jack's."

"Then what *is* it about?"

"Oh, I don't know. It's just something one *does*, isn't it? A protective screen behind which people can get on with their real lives? There's something of that in Jack's marriage. Do you know what's going to happen to you, by the way, if you keep telling people Jack is going to marry you?"

She took the joint and inhaled. "No. What?"

"Something bad, I expect. Just because Jack's a sweet chap doesn't mean he can't look after himself, if you push him hard enough. Not to speak of my dear brother-in-law Bobby. Or, God forbid, my father-in-law. Jack was in love with a Danish girl during the war. *She* told people she was going to divorce her husband to marry Jack. I heard the old man had her deported as a spy. Shot, for all I know. These are not, frankly, people to fuck with, Marilyn dear."

They sat without speaking for a few minutes. "Pat likes me," she said. "I can tell that. All Jack's sisters do."

"Yes, very likely. . . . Marilyn, you have to understand the way they've been brought up. What I'm telling you is that while the Kennedy girls are strict Catholics, no meat on Friday and all that sort of thing, they don't have any hang-ups about mistresses at all. As Jack's mistress, they may very *well* like you, but that doesn't mean they want you taking Jackie's place."

"Jack is the only thing in my life that makes any sense, Peter," she said, handing him back the joint.

His voice came to her quietly, like a ghost's, muffled by the sound of the surf and the conversation from the dinner party inside. "If Jack is the only thing in your life that makes sense, Marilyn," he said, "you're in even worse trouble than I am."

Early in the fall, she flew back to New York, since principal photography on *Something's Got to Give* was delayed until early in 1962.

It was the usual story—half a dozen different script rewrites by half a dozen different screenwriters, at a cost of several hundred thousand dollars, intended to satisfy the objections of the studio, Dino, George Cukor, and herself, had produced a script that satisfied nobody, so yet another rewrite was taking place.

She couldn't wait around in California—she knew she was going to pieces there. In New York, at least she had Dr. Kris to fall back on, as well as the Strasbergs and all her old actor friends from the Studio. Besides, New York was so big and busy that she could pass unnoticed there—she was even able to date the Slugger without anybody in the press noticing or commenting on it. She did not tell him that she planned to marry Jack Kennedy. Joe might not understand, she thought.

She spent a few days at the beach, staying in a borrowed house, and even posed for some photographs, on the condition that her surgical scar be airbrushed out. In some of the photographs seaweed and kelp clung to her, giving her the appearance of a drowning victim, in others she was covered in patches of wet sand. She liked them all.

Studying the proofs with a magnifier, she felt pretty good about the way she looked. Her tits were still resisting gravity, she still had the famous hourglass waist, her ass was as firm as ever, or almost, though she had let her hair go a little dark.

She hadn't been in town a week before she got a call asking her to the Carlyle.

*   *   *

Jack was the same, she thought, but different. He seemed to have filled out somehow. She knew he was taking cortisone, which explained the puffy cheeks—and the suggestion of breasts, which he hated so much that he kept his shirt or dressing gown on until the lights were off. . . .

What the hell—what with her surgical scars and bruises, she was just as happy herself to fuck in the dark. Maybe they were both approaching the age when it paid not to look too closely, she thought. . . .

But it wasn't so much that he had filled out *physically*—he had filled out *psychically,* as if the role of president had taken him over. The man lying beside her in the bed was first and foremost the president of the United States now—it was as if his specific gravity had changed, making him heavier, more solid, bigger than life.

She had once dreamed, in a dopey way, of making love with Lincoln, her old hero, and now, somehow, Jack had *become* Lincoln in her mind. She could sense his greatness, a certain remoteness, as if there was a part of him that could never belong to her, or any other woman, not even Jackie. Not that he was pompous about it, no, but *he* knew it had happened too. He had confronted Khrushchev in Vienna, holding his own against him, had been greeted as an equal by De Gaulle and Macmillan. He wasn't the old Jack.

She could sense, too, in him what she was sure she would have sensed in Lincoln: the loneliness of power. Civil rights protesters, the "captive nations" of Eastern Europe, people all over the world who yearned for freedom and a better life—everyone looked to this man beside her for hope and help, and everywhere from Laos to Cuba men were fighting and dying at his orders.

He stirred in bed. She thought he had been napping, though he might have been lying there thinking about who could say what world problem. But to her surprise, he had been thinking about her. "How have you been?" he asked. "Really."

" 'Really'? Would I lie to you, lover?"

"About yourself? Probably. Word has reached me that you've been feeling a little—down?"

"I missed you."

"I'm flattered. But you shouldn't, you know."

"I can't help what I feel."

"Sure you can. That's what matters most—controlling our feelings."

"You're better at it than I am. I guess that's why you're president."

"There *may* be other reasons. Look, having feelings about me is one thing. Going around feeling blue because of them, that's another. It's not part of our deal. Neither is talking about them."

"I didn't know we had a deal, Jack."

"Not in so many words, no. But there *is* one, and it goes something like this: I'm married, and have a public career I have to protect; you *used* to be married, and have a public image *you* have to protect. So we don't make waves for each other or challenge the status quo."

"Status quo?"

"The way things are."

"I'm not challenging the whatever—the way things are. I've got a right to dream things were different, though, don't I?"

"I don't think so. Dreams are dangerous. It's not a good idea to dream about things that can't happen. You start by dreaming, then you begin wanting them to happen, and pretty soon you begin to believe they're *going* to happen. . . ."

"Things like wanting to marry you?"

"Like wanting to marry me, yes. Exactly. That's definitely not part of the deal, is it?"

"I just wish—"

"Shush." He put his hand gently over her mouth. "Don't say it to me. Don't even *think* it!"

"I understand," she said. "It's going to be hard. I'm not sure I can do it."

"You can do it."

"But I love you."

He sighed. "I know," he said. "That's why you'll do it. For me."

She went down in the private elevator, accompanied by a Secret Service agent she hadn't seen before.

"We've got a car waiting for you on the side street," he said, without calling her "Miss Monroe." He gave her a wink. "That way you won't have to go through the lobby." His voice made it clear that he wasn't doing *her* any favors—he was simply protecting his boss.

She paused. "Why shouldn't I go through the lobby?"

"Because my orders are that you don't, lady."

"Well, fuck *you*," she said defiantly, and pushed the button marked "Lobby" before he could stop her.

"You can't do that!" he shouted, grabbing her arm.

"The hell I can't, asshole," she cried as the door opened. "I can do any fucking thing I *want!* I'm a free citizen! And a star!"

He tried to pull her back into the elevator, but with the quick reflexes of a trained dancer she gave him a kick in the groin—not hard, but fast enough to make him double over in self-protection—at the same time slapping him twice, back and forth, zip-zap, the way she'd learned from Robert Mitchum while making *River of No Return.* Then she was out of the elevator and in the lobby, where a dozen people, some of them in evening clothes, were staring at her.

"I'm Marilyn Monroe!" she screamed at the Secret Service agent, who was coming after her now, his cheeks flushed with embarrassment and, she hoped, pain.

He reached out for her. "I don't care *who* you are," he said. "Back in the elevator!"

She waited until he was in reach, then raised her hand and raked her fingernails hard across his face.

She hardly even heard his scream. She was out of control, her vision obscured by a film of red, as if her own eyes were full of blood. She could see the well-dressed little group—the men holding their keys, the women clutching their handbags—backing away from her, wide-eyed, wealthy people from the suburbs who had come into the city for a night out. They looked horror-struck, but she didn't care. She stood there, staring down an armed Secret Service agent in her white dress with the bolero jacket, swinging her handbag at him as if it were a dangerous weapon, the look of battle shining in her eyes.

"You touch me again and I'll *kill* you, you motherfucker!" she cried, tears of anger streaming down her face. "You hear me?"

Her voice filled the handsome lobby, with its black-and-white marble floors and working fireplaces, and brought the doorman running in from outside.

"You'd better treat me with respect," she heard herself cry, hardly recognizing the voice or the words as her own. "I'M MARILYN MONROE! I'VE BEEN FUCKING THE PRESIDENT!"

She pushed past the startled doorman, ran through the revolving doors, shielding her face against the flashguns of the inevitable paparazzi, sprinted down Madison Avenue blindly, not even sure which direction she was going in. A hand grabbed her arm, and she swung her handbag wildly again, rage and fear still controlling her, until she heard a schoolboy voice say, "Miss Monroe, please, it's Timmy—everything's going to be okay."

She was suddenly exhausted and helpless, unable to move on her own, hardly even aware of where she was.

She let Timmy Hahn, her teenage fan and follower, get her into a taxi and take her home.

The next day she felt no better. She had sent Timmy home with money for the taxi ride back to Queens—though she was pretty sure he'd save the bill rather than use it—and spent the night trying to reach Jack to explain or apologize, she wasn't sure which, but she couldn't get through, and in the morning, he was gone.

She was seized by a kind of insane restlessness despite the sleepless night, a false energy that had to be tapped, the way she sometimes felt a sudden sexual need that was almost painful in its intensity.

She called everyone she knew in New York before she realized it was a Saturday. Dr. Kris was not in her office, and everyone else was away for the weekend—for it was one of those perfect late September days, still warm, but with a crispness that promised autumn, the kind of day people in California had in mind when they talked about missing the changing seasons.

She couldn't stand being alone in the apartment, so she slipped into a pair of slacks, a blouse, and a loose jacket, pulled on a man's old felt hat—one that Milton had used as a prop in photographing her—and went shopping. The idea of plunging into the crowds appealed to her. It was a way of hiding, or pretending that she was an ordinary person, like everyone else.

Bloomingdale's was packed, which was just what she wanted. She wandered through the store, wide-eyed as a hick, for she was so seldom in stores that they always struck her as wonderful, magic places, even though there was very little in them she wanted to buy.

Some slacks caught her eye—not that she really *needed* any, but she felt obliged to buy *something*. She managed, with some difficulty, to attract the attention of the saleslady, though with a sinking heart. She *hated* New York saleslodies, she remembered too late, dragon ladies, with tinted sequined glasses, blue-rinsed hair, and relentless voices, who treated you like a piece of shit, even if you were a star. She always did her little-girlish best to charm them, which never worked, and doing it filled her with self-disgust and anger at her own weakness.

This one was clearly no exception, a prim mouth set in disapproval, eyes gleaming with impatience to get the sale made and move on to the next customer—hopefully, one who was better groomed and dressed, the woman's expression seemed to suggest. By the time she was in the dressing room, she already regretted the whole thing—didn't want the slacks, but didn't have the courage to tell the saleslady that she'd changed her mind.

She felt a mind-numbing claustrophobia come over her in the dressing room, and opened the curtain a little to make it go away. She slipped out of her own slacks, wondering what in God's name she was *doing* here alone, and was about to put on the pair she had chosen, when the saleslady thrust herself through the gap in the curtain holding another pair on a hanger.

"You might wanna try these, dear, they're a size larger—" Her eyes opened wide in shock and disgust. "You got no panties on!" she cried.

"I never wear any. Please get out."

But the saleslady pushed her way into the tiny cubicle and made a grab for the first pair of slacks. "You can't try on clothes naked, dear," the woman said. "It's *disgusting!*"

She was wedged against the back of the dressing room, naked from the waist down, without enough space to get into the slacks, which were, as the saleslady had correctly guessed, a size too small for her. "Get *out!*" she cried.

"Don't you shout at *me!*" The saleslady too seemed paralyzed by the sheer embarrassment of the situation, or perhaps by her own anger, unable to retreat. She gave a sniff of distaste. "You're not only naked, dear, you *smell.* How dare you come in like that to try on clothes?"

She didn't smell—it was a monstrous accusation, unfair, unkind, untrue. She had bathed in the morning, soaked in the tub for ages while she sipped her coffee. Any smell was her *own,* her natural juices, the personal aroma that was distinctly hers, a combination of sex and Chanel No. 5 that men adored, and that she herself could sniff for hours with pleasure.

She pushed the saleslady—not hard, just a gentle shove, more out of panic than anything else.

"Help! Help! *Help!*" The saleslady was screaming, the veins standing out on her forehead, her eyes popping—apparently riveted to the spot.

She gave her a hard shove this time, determined to get the woman out of her way. This time the saleslady was sent flying, screaming now at the top of her lungs.

She pulled the slacks up, squeezing her hips into them, and ran, in sheer terror at the sound of the woman's screams, which seemed to fill her head. She caught a glimpse of herself in a mirror—a crazy-looking woman in a funny hat, a pair of tight slacks, half unzipped, with the price tags still flapping on them, running desperately through the store, while people stared at her in horror or jumped out of her way.

Before she reached the escalator, a burly man in a blazer stepped in front of her and caught her in his arms. She lashed out furiously, as terrified of being held as a wild animal, hearing her own screams now. He held her harder, with the strength of the beat cop he had no doubt once been. She fought, struggled, kicked, bit, and swore, until a couple more security guards rushed up panting and she was pinioned roughly, her hands twisted behind her back.

"Assault and shoplifting," the man in the blazer said, dabbing at his scratches with a handkerchief.

"I wasn't shoplifting, you son of a bitch. Tell these guys to let me go or you'll be sorry."

"Those are the store's pants, lady, not yours. You haven't paid for them. That's called shoplifting. You assaulted a saleslady, and you assaulted me. We're going down to my office quietly; then I'm going to hand you over to the cops."

"She insulted me. She pushed me."

"Sure. Tell it to the judge, lady. I'm just doing my job."

"Do you know who the hell I *am*, you fucking idiot?"

He looked at her. "No," he said. "And I don't care. If it was up to me, I'd teach you not to use language like that to me or anybody else. Just because you're a woman wouldn't stop me, okay? So don't try my patience no more."

The two guards moved her to a door, away from the crowd of curious onlookers, the ex-cop unlocked it, and she was carried, helpless, into an elevator and down a long corridor at the end of which was a small, windowless office. They dumped her in a chair, while the security man sat down at the desk.

"What's your name, lady?" he asked, uncapping his pen.

"Marilyn Monroe."

He gave her a hard, humorless stare. "Sure. And I'm Fred Astaire." He reached across and grabbed her jaw in his pudgy fingers, the big Police Academy ring gouging her flesh. "A word of advice, toots. Don't get smart with me. You a pross? I don't know what I got to do to teach you girls to stay the fuck out of the store."

Rage overcame her, welled up from deep inside her, as if she were choking on her own vomit. She couldn't move, because he had her held, but she spat into his face, and a moment later, she felt the sudden, sharp pain as he brought the flat of his meaty hand against her cheek. The blow was strong enough to make her fear for her teeth—strong enough, too, to bring her to her senses.

"Open my handbag," she said.

He nodded, perhaps aware that he, too, had crossed a line beyond correct behavior, spread out her few credit cards, unfolded her California driver's license (out of date, as usual), and in a low, awed whisper said, "Holy Mary Mother of God."

It took less than an hour for a young lawyer to arrive—everybody more senior was away for the weekend—but once he was there, she was out of the store through the freight entrance in ten minutes, and into the waiting limousine, clutching her handbag, still dressed in the slacks that were too tight for her.

She went back to the apartment, tore off the slacks, and took a few pills to calm her nerves; then she decided she needed to sleep, so she opened another bottle, spilling a few capsules on the floor, which she got down on her knees to pick up; then she couldn't stand up—she was kneeling bare-assed on the white shag rug of the bathroom—and decided she might as well curl up on it and take a nap. . . .

I don't know what would have happened if I hadn't made a date to take Marilyn to a screening late that afternoon, to be followed by a steak at Gallagher's, one of her favorite places. Maria had gone to Paris for a week of shopping and was staying there with the D'Souzas, so it seemed like a perfect opportunity to catch up on what was new in Marilyn's life.

I spent one of those New York Saturdays that I love—a stroll along Madison Avenue, looking in at all the art galleries, a stop at Judd and Judd, to look at the latest books, a bone-dry martini and a chef's salad at the Carlyle Hotel, then a brisk walk home, pausing to pick out a couple of shirts at Sulka.

To say I was in a good mood when I arrived at Marilyn's would be understating it, and I was therefore irritated when she didn't answer the doorman's call.

"She's expecting me," I said.

"Yes, Mr. Leman. She mentioned it to the day man. I know she's in."

He called again. There was no reply. "Do you want to go up and try?" he asked.

I took the elevator up to her apartment, and asked the elevator man to wait. I rang several times, then banged on the metal door, but there was no sound from inside, which I thought was odd, because Marilyn always had music on—usually a stack of Sinatra records.

I knew she left a spare door key under her mat—she was always losing the one in her purse—so I dismissed the elevator man, reached under the mat, found the key, and opened the door.

"Marilyn?" I called out. There was a strange kind of silence—a heavy, unnatural silence, not that of an empty apartment but, in some way, the silence of sleep or death. I knew she was there, not just because the doorman had told me but because I could feel her presence, smell her perfume, sense that I wasn't alone.

I think I already guessed what I would find—it was one's first thought, with Marilyn. I just wasn't sure where I would find her. The bedroom was empty, although her handbag on the tangled sheets confirmed that she was home. The bathroom door was ajar, so I knocked on it, then pushed it open, realizing, to my shame, that it was the first time I had seen Marilyn naked, or almost so, for she still had on her bra and her unbuttoned blouse, as well as her white, spike-heeled shoes. She was lying on her side, eyes closed and mouth open. Her pubic hair was darker than I had expected it to be. Her skin had a bluish tone, almost violet in places, and my first thought was that she was dead.

Then she breathed, thank God—not deeply, just a gentle sigh that brought a few bubbles of saliva to her lips and made her breasts lift slightly.

I went to the bedroom, called a private ambulance service and my own doctor, then a special number at police headquarters, which would bring the police in a hurry *without* any reporters. Finally I called the doorman on the house phone to warn him of what was coming, and pledge him to silence.

After that, I went back to the bathroom, soaked a washcloth in cold water, and held it to Marilyn's face, resting her head against my knee. She didn't seem to be choking, and her breathing, though faint, was regular. Her eyelids fluttered at the touch of the cold washcloth. Her lips moved and I thought she said, "Water!" so I filled a glass from the sink tap and held it to her lips. She swallowed a couple of times, then, without any warning, threw up all over my new shirt and tie.

Perhaps that saved her life. I don't know. They pumped her stomach at Doctors Hospital anyway, and the incident never made the papers—nor did I ever ask her what the immediate cause had been.

When I went back to her apartment the next morning to pick up a few things for her, since she was being kept "under observation," there was a messengered package from Bloomingdale's.

I opened it, and found an old pair of pants from Jax, the kind Marilyn wore all the time, and her Bloomingdale's credit card, neatly cut in half.

She went back to California the day after she was released from Doctors Hospital, as if the only thing that mattered now was fleeing the city. She phoned Sulka and had them send a half-dozen silk shirts to David, but she couldn't bring herself to speak to him, besides which her throat still ached and her voice was still hoarse from the stomach pump.

Dr. Greenson himself picked her up at the airport, alerted by Dr. Kris to the seriousness of her case. Suicide attempts brought psychoanalysts to action stations, for they meant failure.

Of course, Greenson pretended that it was an overdose of prescription drugs, an "accident," but his eyes told a different story. He knew exactly what had happened, and he made plans to prevent its happening again on *his* watch, as he liked to say. First he proposed that she stay with him and his family, which she didn't want to do; then he switched to a second idea, which was to buy a house close to his—he had just the house in mind. He already had a "housekeeper" on tap, somebody she could trust, somebody *he* could trust: Eunice Murray, a lady who had a lot of experience "looking after people," as he put it.

By the end of the week, she had met Mrs. Murray—who turned out to be gently soft-spoken, but with a thrusting jaw and, behind glistening spectacles, steely eyes that promised an iron will—and hired her. Mrs. Murray's duties were elastic— she did not cook or keep house, really, but she drove the car, answered the phone, and, most important of all, kept vigil on behalf of Dr. Greenson.

It was all a great relief. She had placed herself, finally, in Greenson's hands completely: Mrs. Murray watched her at home and drove her to her sessions, Greenson's buddy Henry Weinstein was now going to produce her new picture, if it ever got off the ground, while Greenson's realtor went house-hunting for her, with instructions that the house be as close as possible to Dr. Greenson's own, and resemble it if possible. . . . As if all that weren't enough, Mrs. Murray had a daughter named Marilyn!

She felt protected at last. The house they found for her on Helena Drive in Brentwood was like a miniature version of Dr. Greenson's—really *tiny*, which was exactly what she wanted, and dark as a cave because of the encroaching tropical garden outside, which suited her present mood perfectly.

She exulted in the idea of owning it. She and Jim had rented what amounted to a shack, she and the Slugger had never bought a house of their own, the house in Roxbury was really Miller's, not hers. This one, small as it was, cramped as its rooms were, overgrown and untended as its garden might be, was *hers*.

She asked Mrs. Murray to redo the kitchen so that it would look exactly like Dr. Greenson's, with bright colors and lots of Mexican tiles, and moved in as soon as she could with her meager store of belongings, most of them still in cardboard boxes, and put her Kennedy for President poster on the bedroom wall.

She had her own pool, too, at last—not that she swam in it. Indeed, its only role in the household was as a hazard to little Maf, for she was terrified that the dog would fall in and drown. Still, she ordered pool furniture, and Mrs. Murray arranged with a service to send a man around to clean it three times a week.

Of course, there were a lot of things missing, things that nobody had thought of in the rush to move in. There were practically no cooking utensils, the heating system worked spasmodically, the phone jacks were left unchanged, which meant that her private telephone—the unlisted one, without an extension—had to be placed in the living room, and carried upstairs at the end of a long cord when she wanted to use it in her bedroom at night. . . . She didn't mind. It was home.

She was in it, dressed in her terry-cloth robe with a towel wrapped around her hair, when she heard on the radio that Ambassador Joseph P. Kennedy had suffered a massive stroke after a game of golf in Palm Beach.

The President stood in the hospital corridor, with Secret Service agents at either end. He was still wearing a winter-weight suit. He had flown down from Washington as soon as he could disengage himself, but Robert Kennedy had arrived before him.

"Christ, it's an awful thing," Jack said. "He always said this was the one thing he was afraid of, that he'd rather be dead than helpless."

"He'll get better," Bobby said fiercely. "There's therapy, rehabilitation exercises. . . . He's got the guts to come back." There were tears in his eyes.

Jack Kennedy put his arm around his brother's shoulder, and they walked the length of the corridor. "You've seen him," he said. "It was a *massive* stroke. They don't think he'll walk again. They aren't even sure he'll ever recover his speech. It's best to face facts."

"I won't face those."

"You may have to." They moved away from the window, at a gesture from the nearest agent. Already there were agents and police sharpshooters deployed against snipers on the near-by rooftops. The President grimaced and made a mental note to put a stop to this kind of display, which smacked of a police state and made him feel like a Latin American dictator. "God, I hope this doesn't happen to me," he said. "A gunshot, something quick, that's the way to go."

Bobby shook his head. "Don't talk like that," he said. His expression turned, if anything, a shade grimmer. "Did you know Marilyn sent a long telegram to Mother, telling her how sorry she was, and how much she loved Dad? She wrote that she felt as if she was a member of the family, and offered to fly out and look after him. . . ."

"Oh God."

"There's worse. She gave a press conference at Twentieth Century-Fox to say how sad she was, and how close she felt to the family."

"Shit. Is Mother upset?"

"Puzzled. But it's a real problem. David is working hard to contain the story. Still . . ."

A doctor was approaching, with the look that always spells more bad news. Jack turned toward him. "You win, Bobby," he said. "She's getting out of hand."

"This on top of what happened in New York with the Secret Service . . ."

"I know, I know. I *said* you win, so don't rub it in. It's got to be done. I understand." His voice was weary.

He held up a hand, stopping the doctor in his tracks for a moment. His eyes were full of regret, but there was also the hint of something else—relief perhaps at having finally made the tough, inevitable decision, a look Bobby had seen before when Jack called off the air strikes at the Bay of Pigs. "Go to California," he said. "See if you can get her off my back."

"Why me?"

"Because you're better at that kind of thing than I am."

Bobby nodded, his expression dark, as if he was acknowledging, without pride, that it was true.

"Do it as nicely as you can," Jack said, waving the doctor forward, already moving on to the next problem. He shook the doctor's hand, his face stern, his eyes concerned, every inch the president.

"But be firm, Bobby," he added.

PART FOUR

Legend

40

<hr>

SHE SAT BETWEEN PETER LAWFORD AND BOBBY KENNEDY at dinner, having the time of her life.

She knew Bobby, of course, but she didn't really *know* him. He had always seemed to her remote, sometimes even unfriendly, so it had come as something of a surprise when Peter told her Bobby wanted to see her. Peter was planning a dinner party for Bobby, he said, a "Welcome to LA" sort of thing, and he hoped she could make it.

Since she had nothing much to do but sit at home with Mrs. Murray, she had been only too happy to oblige. She had always wanted an opportunity to have a heart-to-heart with Bobby, and had come to the dinner with a carefully prepared list of questions. As he was a Kennedy, however, she had also prepared for the occasion by having her hair bleached white and set in a soft curl and by getting the studio makeup man to come over to the house to do her face. She had chosen a silver lamé dress with a daring V-shaped neckline that left her shoulders and her back bare, exposed her breasts almost to the nipples, and plunged down to her navel—a dress that very few women would have risked wearing, and about which even she had had doubts—not that she couldn't get away with it, but it might embarrass Bobby.

She had made a big effort to arrive on time—for her—which was to say that everybody had already had a couple of drinks and looked at their watches a few times, while Pat had gone into the kitchen once or twice to calm the cook. She timed her entrance just at the precise moment when people had begun to think she wasn't coming. She knew her business—she simply *appeared* at the top of the steps leading down into the big sunken living room and stood there, the lights reflecting off her dress, until someone looked up and said, "Marilyn!" followed by complete silence as everybody stared at her in awe, even those who knew her well.

She stood there in the silence, then flashed her smile as the room exploded into applause, cheers, and wolf whistles. This was what her life was *about,* what she knew how to do better than anyone. *Nobody* could do this to a roomful of movie people, except maybe Elizabeth Taylor, and even Liz couldn't have matched the blinding silver and platinum blaze that flashed and glittered off the world's most famous blonde, plunging everyone else in the room into the shadow.

Except Robert Kennedy. For she noticed that Bobby, slight as he was, and wearing what looked like an off-the-rack wash-and-wear summer-weight suit from Sears, his hair sticking up like a rebellious teenager's, had the *look,* the look of his brother but in spades—that mysterious star quality that made him stand out as if he were as spotlit as she was—the bright blue eyes, the compact, wiry body that exuded almost visible waves of energy.

She walked slowly down the steps, to receive a careful peck on the cheek from Lawford, who as an actor, however lousy, knew better than to smear a star's makeup. "Marilyn, *darling!*" he shouted, already a bit drunk. "You were worth waiting for!"

"Who's waiting?" she asked. "I thought I was early?"

Lawford giggled appreciatively. "You've met the Attorney General, I think," he said, doing his unsteady best to play the gracious host.

"Oh my, yes," she whispered. "Welcome to Los Angeles, Mr. Attorney General." She wasn't sure it was the right way to greet him, but it sounded respectful.

Bobby shook her hand, blushing. "Bobby, please."

She held on to his hand. "Bobby, then," she said, and she continued to hold on to him as they went in to dinner.

She had him to herself at the dinner table. At first she had an uphill struggle against what seemed to be a mulish obstinacy on his part not to be charmed by her, but by the time the soup had been served and removed, he was warming up to her. "Why can't Jack do more to help the Freedom Riders?" she asked him boldly.

"He's doing what he can."

"I think it's disgusting that the Klan and all those bigots are allowed to throw rocks and shoot people."

"It's a free country."

"Not for Negroes, apparently."

There was a flash of anger in his eyes; then he nodded. "I'm with *you*," he said. "It turns my stomach. But Jack was elected by a paper-thin majority. He can't win in '64 without the South, and that means he can't move as fast as he'd like to. He signed an order desegregating federal housing, you know, and the shit really hit the fan below the Mason-Dixon line."

"He promised to do that when he was campaigning in 1960," she said firmly.

His eyes opened wide. He was impressed. "You remember *that?*"

"Just because I'm a blonde doesn't mean I'm a dumb bunny." Her confidence was high tonight, for the first time in many months. She was pilled up, tranquillized and energized to take her beyond her normal fears, but something about Bobby—his directness, his quick grin, some hint of sadness in the depths of those bright eyes—made it possible for her to shine.

"He had to wait for the moment," he said.

"A *year?* And how about the fact that African diplomats can't stop for a meal or use a rest room when they're driving through Maryland to and from New York?"

He looked surprised. "We're looking into that."

"I heard that Jack—the President—told Angie Biddle Duke he ought to ask them to take the shuttle instead."

"That's not true. Well, okay, maybe it *is* true," he corrected himself, looking at her eyes, "but he was joking."

"But it isn't *funny*. Doesn't he *care* about these things?"

"Of course he does, you know that, but he's a practical politician. . . . Things take time. Listen, we've spent nine months getting Castro to release the Bay of Pigs prisoners, and that's something the President cared about a *lot*."

"What's the point of releasing the Cuban prisoners if Negroes can't even use a rest room in their own country?"

"We'll deal with that, too, in time."

"Does that mean you're a practical politician too, Bobby?"

He paused, his expression troubled, as if the question had somehow touched some deep, hidden part of him. "I don't know," he said at last. "In some ways, yes, I am. The problem is that I don't really *want* to be. It comes naturally to my brother, but it's harder for me."

He was silent for a moment. "So much for the ruthlessness, I guess."

She reached out and touched his hand under the table. "You never looked ruthless to me," she said.

"You could be wrong about that," he answered gruffly, an expression of infinite sadness on his face.

By the time dinner was over, she felt she knew Bobby, and liked him better than she had expected to, although there was still something about him she didn't understand, almost as if he were *afraid* of her.

Coffee was served; people were starting to drink more seriously. Bobby led her to a dark corner of the room. "I need to talk to you," he said. "In private."

For some reason, she shivered. "This is pretty private," she said.

He shook his head. "Let's go outside."

They walked out onto a terrace. "Are you up for a walk on the beach?" he asked.

She was about to point out that she was wearing a silver lamé evening gown and open-toed stiletto pumps, but something in his face made her change her mind, so she took off her shoes and left them on the terrace, then, stepping into the shadow of the doorway, she leaned over, unfastened her stockings, slipped them off, and stuffed them into her purse. "Let's go," she said, and together they walked out onto the sand and down to the shoreline, where the sea curled in phosphorescent wavelets in the moonlight. She loved the feel of sand between her toes, though her dress was so tight it made walking difficult.

"Are you cold?" Bobby asked. He touched her hand briefly, almost as if it was an accident, but she was pretty sure it wasn't. His face in the moonlight was serious, almost grim. Then he took a deep breath, like a man about to dive into cold water. "I was sent out here to talk to you, you know," he said gently, like a doctor breaking bad news.

"What about?"

"About Jack."

"What about him?"

"He's—ah—got to put some distance between himself and you, Marilyn."

She walked on, suddenly numb. She knew exactly what he had come for now, and in a way she had been expecting it, waiting for the ax to fall without daring to look at it. Well, it was falling now—one look at Bobby Kennedy's face was enough to make that obvious.

"Are you saying it's over?" she asked, trying to sound calm.

"I'm saying it's over."

"Why?"

"He's the president, Marilyn. He's got enemies. That, ah, scene in the Carlyle lobby. The letter to Mother. Talking to the press about Dad's stroke. Telling people he's going to leave Jackie and marry you. . . . That kind of thing is dangerous. I know you love him, but if you *really* love him, you'll give him up."

"And if I don't?"

"You will." His voice was harsh, and she realized it was a sentence without appeal.

"Why couldn't he tell me this himself? He owes me that." She could feel the quick rush of anger, warming her like a fire, and understood instantly why he had wanted her outside.

He stared out to sea. "Jack wanted to tell you himself. I told him not to."

"Why?"

"He's the president, Marilyn. It's my job to save him from himself, if needs be."

"What happens if I call him?"

"I don't know. I *do* know this: if you call him on the special number, you won't get him. I had it cut off today."

"He wouldn't let you!"

"He doesn't know yet." He stared at her, shaking his head. "Marilyn, Marilyn," he said softly. "In the last three weeks you called him thirty-six times. You must have known it couldn't go on."

"You superior little *prick!*" she shouted. "What the fuck do you know about it? He *loves* me."

"Yes," he said quietly, his head slightly bowed. "I believe he does." He shrugged his shoulders. "But that doesn't change anything."

"It does, it *does!*" she cried, and charged at him, splashing wet sand against the hem of her dress, fists raised to hit out at him. He dodged her easily enough, but she turned and came at him again, teeth bared, eyes blazing, and this time they collided. He grabbed her with both arms, holding her as tightly as he could, his head back, so she could only flail away impotently with her fists. She brought her head forward sharply and bit his ear, exulting in his sudden howl of pain, but he held on to her, despite her struggles, until she went limp, suddenly exhausted by her own rage.

"You carried it too far, don't you see?" he said, as softly as ever. His earlobe was bleeding, a line of blood, black in the moonlight, running down his neck and staining his collar.

"I broke the rules, you mean?"

"You broke the rules, right."

"Is he angry?" she asked.

Bobby shook his head, his hair falling over his forehead like a kid's. "No, he's not angry," he said. "He doesn't blame you. You're not to blame. He's not to blame." He kicked at the sand with his shoes. "There are people who know about this affair," he said. "People who would use it against him. I can't let that happen."

"What people?"

"People. The less you know, the better."

She shivered. Bobby took off his coat and draped it over her shoulders. "It was the best thing in my life," she said. "The thing that made the most sense. Loving Jack, I mean."

"It meant a lot to him, too."

"It wasn't just the sex. We were—I don't know—right for each other. I helped his back. He made me laugh, and sleep without pills. Our bodies fit together, you know? Like the right pieces in a jigsaw puzzle?"

"Yes?" He seemed to be turning the image over in his mind.

"I'd have done anything for him. Anything he asked. I've never felt like that about anybody before."

"He knows that. This is what he's asking you to do. Break it off."

She was shaking now, although she didn't really feel cold. She didn't feel anything much, in fact. He put his arm around her shoulder. "Are you going to be okay?" he asked.

"I don't know. I'm not going to drown myself, if that's what you mean."

"That wasn't what I meant,"

She walked into the shallow, curling surf, the waves breaking over her feet, the bottom of her silver skirt soaking wet, and for a few minutes they splashed together along the beach, the spray around them gleaming in the moonlight, the shining drops of salt water clinging to the tiny golden hairs on her arms.

"It wasn't just an illusion, was it?" she asked. "I need to know that. Jack did love me, didn't he?"

"He did. He does. If he weren't the president, it might be different, but he *is*."

She had always dreaded this moment, but now that it had come, she found, to her surprise, that she wasn't hysterical. She was calm, in control of herself—Dr. Kris and Dr. Greenson would be proud of her! She guessed that it was because she had known for a long time it would happen. Still, she felt a deep, almost bottomless sadness inside her, so big that she wasn't sure how she could live with it, or even if she *wanted* to.

They turned, in unspoken accord, and walked back toward the Lawford house.

"It's important," Bobby said, "that none of this ever happened."

"I wasn't planning to write a book."

"I didn't mean that. If there are letters, souvenirs—that kind of thing. . . . Lock them away in a bank vault, if you have to keep them."

"There isn't much. Jack never wrote."

Bobby nodded.

They were nearing the house. She wondered briefly what people must be thinking, but she didn't care.

"Dreaming that Jack and I were going to be together someday—that's been what's kept me alive, for a long time."

"It's hard. I know."

"I'm not sure you do." They were almost at the door now, the bright light from the windows blinding after the walk in the dark. She was beginning to cry—not hysterically, just a gentle, slow fall of tears. "I can't go inside," she said. "My dress is ruined. Not to mention my face and my hair."

"Do you have a car?"

She did, of course, but she shook her head. She took his hand in hers and squeezed it hard. "Take me home," she said.

"Please. I don't want to be alone yet. I'll be all right once I'm home."

There was a look of hesitation on his face—or was it something else? She couldn't be sure. "Well," he said, "I don't know. . . ."

"I've been good, haven't I?" she asked fiercely. "I haven't screamed, or shouted, or made a scene?"

He nodded, his eyes hooded in the bright light like a hawk's. It was a more complicated face than his brother's, she thought, more secretive, in some ways harsher, in others more vulnerable, the planes and angles of it more sharply cut. "You'd better get your things, then," he said.

She picked up her purse and her shoes, and followed him, barefoot, around the house and into the alleyway where a black sedan was parked. A man was sitting in it—probably a Secret Service agent. She waited in the shadows, Bobby's coat still draped over her shoulders, while he whispered something to the man in the car, who got out and handed Bobby the keys. The bottoms of Bobby's trousers were wet, and his shoes leaked puddles of water on the asphalt. He waited until the agent had vanished around the corner of the house, then waved to her.

"You'll have to show me the way," he said, opening the car door for her, then got in after she had slid across the bench seat.

Now that she was in the car, she felt the cold, and with it the first tremors of emotional shock. She was trembling uncontrollably, teeth chattering as if she had just been pulled from the coldest water after some accident.

"My Lord," Bobby said. "We'd better get you warm."

He started the car and turned the heater on, but she was still shaking, so he put his arms around her, holding her tight. She could see her face reflected in the mirror, the eyes hauntingly large, the lips parted, showing tiny, perfect teeth. Her shoulder straps had slipped, so it was almost as if she were naked, except for her bra, under his jacket.

"Oh God," she moaned. "Hold me, hold me, hold me tight."

"Okay, okay, you're going to be okay," he muttered thickly, trying to calm her. "It's going to be okay. . . ."

Okay, okay, okay. . . . She heard him say it over and over again, but his voice was muffled now, for her lips were pressed hard against his, her hands grasped his head, pulling him hard toward her, her body pressed against his too. "Hold me, *hold* me, *hold* me," she whispered, over and over again.

She had no idea how long their embrace lasted. She was trembling now, but warmer, sweat running down her torso. "Don't let me go," she pleaded. "I need to be held."

It was dark in the car, the only light coming from a street lamp a hundred feet away. She could feel his body, so much like Jack's but somehow different, slighter, more tightly muscular. There wasn't much room in the front seat of the car, but she managed to slip down, lying flat, so that he could lie between her legs, her skirt, completely ruined now, hiked up around her waist. She had one knee jammed against the dashboard, the other against the back of the seat. Her head was pillowed uncomfortably on some kind of thick vinyl notebook. The sharp edge of it cut into her neck, but she didn't care, because his face was against hers, his breath mixing with her own, his weight pressing her down. She could taste the sea salt on his lips and cheeks, smell his astringent after-shave, a different brand from Jack's, hear his breathing, heavy and deep like that of an athlete recovering from a winning effort, feel his hair, coarse like Jack's but longer. Then, with a long, gentle moan of submission, she let go of his head and lowered her hands in the dark, unzipping his trousers and closing her eyes, tried to picture Jack in her mind . . .

It was only when it was over, and they were lying in each other's arms, sweating from sexual exertion and the warmth of the car's heater, limbs messily intertwined, unable to move because his legs were trapped under the steering wheel, that she realized it hadn't worked the way she thought it would.

She had tried to picture Jack, but his image had faded as Bobby was fucking her. It had been Bobby's name on her lips as she came, and suddenly she realized that it didn't matter how it had happened, or *why* it happened, or whether it was right or wrong—whatever was meant to be, would be. . . .

Improbably, she felt at peace.

He was awake early in the morning, looking around the small, bare bedroom with curiosity.

"What *time* is it, lover?" she asked.

"Six-thirty."

"So early?"

"So late, I was thinking. The Secret Service agents must be going crazy by now."

"Fuck them, if they're anything like the one I slapped."

"What time does your housekeeper get in?"

"Not for a while. Come here and kiss me, then I'll make you coffee. I make pretty good coffee, believe it or not."

She took his hand and smiled. She could see herself in the mirror, and now glimpsed the catlike, self-satisfied smile of a woman who has captured another woman's husband. Bobby, she thought, would have some explaining to do, and not just to the Secret Service. There were the Lawfords and their guests, who must have guessed what had happened, and Ethel, whom he telephoned religiously every night when he was traveling, as all the stories about him pointed out, and Jack, she supposed. . . . She would have some explaining to do herself, not least to Dr. Greenson, who was unlikely to find her behavior evidence of sound emotional judgment. Ah well, she thought, fuck 'em. I'm alive again.

"Coffee? I believe it," he said. "You seem to do everything else pretty well."

He slipped back into bed again. He had the body of a high school athlete, neat, trim, not a scrap of superfluous fat on him. The sight of it, oddly, made her feel old, as if she had seduced a sixteen-year-old football player who had just delivered the groceries—a fantasy that made her giggle.

"What's so funny?"

"Oh, I don't know. Last night I thought my life was over, this morning I want it to go on forever. That's pretty funny, don't you think?"

"I guess so. What's not so funny is what I'm going to tell Jack."

"Because you fucked his girl?"

"No. Because I fucked up." He sighed.

She squeezed herself against him, pulled him close, her lips pressed so hard against his that he couldn't speak. From outside, she could hear the sprinklers starting up as they made love on the tangled sheets, half the pillows on the floor, the others at the wrong end of the bed, her ruined dress on the shag rug, with poor little Maf asleep on it. . . .

When they were done, he rolled over and looked into her eyes. If he felt guilt, he didn't show it. He had it under control, she decided, which was just as well, because she couldn't have handled a lot of breast-beating. But of course, she should have known better—he was a Kennedy: he didn't waste time on guilt or regret.

He held her in his arms, his lips against her ear, and in a whisper that she hardly even heard, said, "Tell me, was I as good as my brother?"

I was drafted to make sure nobody reported on Marilyn's ill-advised declaration of concern about Joe Kennedy's stroke to the press, and at the same time to minimize the seriousness of Joe's condition. We were cranking out bulletins about the Ambassador's recovery when in fact the poor man was lying paralyzed in a hospital bed, drooling from lips he could no longer control, his hands curled up like a bird's claws, the only words he could form a scary *"No, no, no, no, no, no . . ."* murmured over and over again, as if trying to repudiate what had happened to him, refusing to admit it even to himself.

Jack seemed better able to make contact with Joe than anyone else. He sat beside him for hours, talking to him as if his father could reply. It was as if Jack understood that their roles had been suddenly reversed.

Myself, I could not see Joe without breaking down and crying. Oh, he was not an easy man to like, but we had been friends a long time. Besides, like his sons, I had thought him invulnerable, and now I, like them, was suddenly face-to-face with the frailty of life, the irony of fate, which had brought Joseph P. Kennedy everything he wanted, then laid him low with the one thing that he feared most.

At the time, I didn't have the leisure to brood about what had happened, since my hands were full keeping Marilyn's name out of the papers—as well as dealing with my own feelings when I heard that Jack had made a break of sorts with her, at Bobby's urging.

I called her instantly and was surprised to find that she sounded pretty cheerful. I was prepared to hold her hand and console her, so it was a little disappointing to find that she didn't seem to need consolation.

I decided to go out to California anyway, since I had business there, but before I did, Jack called and asked me to join him in Washington for breakfast.

Jack came back from visiting his father to find the world ablaze—or so it seemed to him. There were rumors that the Diem government was about to fall in Saigon, where Buddhist monks were setting themselves on fire in time to make the evening news on American television; in the South, Negro protests had awakened the old hatreds—there were shootings, bombings, riots, threats of southern defection from the Democratic party in '64; in Europe, it looked as if the Soviets might try to grab Berlin and set off World War III. Jack looked drawn and grim as we ate. "It's gotten so I can't stand reading the papers," he said.

"Maybe you shouldn't. Ike never did. He only read the comics."

"I might give that a try."

"The good news is, the story about Marilyn isn't going to run."

"Well, that's something, at least."

"I had to give up a few markers."

"Yours or mine?"

"Yours. You're going to have to give a couple of exclusive interviews, stand still for some picture sessions, and invite one or two newspaper publishers to lunch. . . ."

Jack nodded. Nobody knew better than he did how news was managed. "Speaking of Marilyn," he said, "it turns out she wasn't inconsolable." He didn't sound any too pleased about it.

"Odd you should say that. I had the same impression. She sounded quite cheerful, for her."

The President seemed to be wrestling with deeper feelings. "Here I was worrying about how she'd take it," he said, "imagining suicide attempts and all that—and guess what?"

I shook my head.

"She's fucking Bobby now."

I stared at him in amazement, unable to believe my ears.

He shrugged. "Amazing, isn't it? Who can ever understand women? I ask you. I thought there'd be at least a big scene, maybe worse, but nothing of the kind. . . . They went for a moonlight walk. Then—are you ready for *this?*—they actually fucked in the front seat of a Secret Service car, parked in the alley behind Peter's house, like a couple of teen-age kids."

"I can't believe that!"

"It's true. Bobby told me the whole thing. He felt he owed me the truth. The Secret Service told me about it, too. They were embarrassed as hell."

"She must be out of her mind!"

For a moment I thought Jack was going to agree with me. I could tell that for once in his life he was shocked, probably even hurt, but of course, being who he was, he was determined to put up a good front. It wasn't in him to be angry with Bob-by for long, and certainly he couldn't very well be angry at Marilyn, since he had broken off with her, so I suppose he was angry with himself. All the same, he clearly needed to talk to someone about it, and he had chosen me. I was at once appalled and flattered.

"Out of her mind?" he mused. "I don't know about that, David. I think maybe I'm the one who's crazy, not Marilyn. Do you want to know the truth of it? I miss her already."

I wondered whether Jack had ever had this kind of experi-ence before. With the exception of Jackie, his love life had always run on rails—certainly he was never the one to end up feeling blue—so this kind of pain was new to him. I could see he didn't like it a bit.

"All the same, it was the right decision," I said, hoping to make him feel better—though I don't know why, since I was still smarting over the ambassadorship.

"I guess so," he said without conviction. "I sure don't feel good about it, I'll tell you that."

"I can imagine."

"What really surprises *me*," he went on, "Is that Bobby had the guts to do that to Ethel. . . . You look a little green around the gills, David. Are you okay?"

I wasn't okay, not really. I had never thought I could steal Marilyn away from Jack, but once he had broken with her, I felt, obscurely, that it was my turn. . . . Now that had been taken away from me too, along with the ambassadorship, and for the first time I felt a sense of regret, of *waste,* as if all my years of friendship with the Kennedy family had led me nowhere, won me nothing. It was no longer Jack who needed my protection now; it was Marilyn.

I waved away his concern. "I'm fine," I said.

He looked at me shrewdly. "You're pissed off about it, aren't you?"

"It's not my business."

"The hell it's not. You've been in love with Marilyn since the day you set eyes on her, six, no—Christ!—*seven* years ago."

"What you say may be true, Mr. President—"

"Don't pull that 'Mr. President' crap on me when we're having a personal conversation. Is it me you're mad at or Bobby?"

"You."

"Because I dumped her? Let me tell you, very few things in my personal life have caused me as much pain. I should have done it a long time ago, and you know it. I put it off and put it off. . . ."

It was true, and I couldn't deny it. I didn't.

The President looked out the window, as if he longed to be anywhere but here in the White House. "The presidency seemed like fun for a while," he said. "I mean, I worked hard enough to win it, so I didn't see why I shouldn't enjoy it. But now that I've settled into it, I realize winning it is nothing. What matters is how you *leave* it."

"The itch for greatness," I said. "Seizing one's 'place in history.' " I smiled. "It comes over most people who occupy this house, sooner or later."

"It does that to you," Jack agreed.

"Perhaps it should. Perhaps that's why it's worth preserving, this old house. I'm impressed. Did your father know?"

"I talked to him about it. Before the stroke, thank God. He said it was what he'd been waiting to hear."

"Yes, I can imagine." I sipped my coffee. "Of course, I hadn't realized that chastity was a requirement of presidential greatness."

"Chastity? What do you mean?"

"Actually, that's the wrong word. Monogamy? Fidelity? Are you really turning over a new leaf?"

He laughed. "No. Not yet. But I will be a little more discreet. I don't think the president's girlfriends should be giving press conferences about their relationship with him, do you?"

"Marilyn was being foolish, I agree, but she must have been terribly upset. She's fond of your father. . . ."

"I appreciate all that, but that's the kind of risk I can't afford." He sighed. "You know, Jackie's settling into *her* role too. She hates being called 'First Lady'—she says it sounds like a saddle horse—but she's a damned *good* First Lady, in fact. I think we're even getting along better. . . . Maybe Marilyn became a luxury I couldn't afford? I think that's part of it."

"And Bobby?"

"He's a grown-up. He can make up his own mind what to do. It's a little strange that he preaches caution to me, then goes and fucks Marilyn in the Lawford driveway with half of Hollywood giggling about it in the living room, but at least it proves he's just as human as the rest of us."

"Is human weakness a good thing in an attorney general?"

"No, but it's okay in my brother."

We shook hands and said good-bye, standing outside the Oval Office. "When the history of this administration is written, I want it to be about great events and great decisions," he said. "Not about pillow talk and gossip."

"Well," I said, "you've got seven more years. Time enough."

"Oh, yes," he said, laughing. "All the time in the world."

41

As LUCK WOULD HAVE IT, ONE OF THE MEMBERS OF THE 20th Century-Fox board, an old friend and client, begged me to look into things at the studio, the next time I was in California. "It's chaos," he said. "Amateur hour. It makes me almost wish Zanuck was still there, and you know how I feel about Zanuck. They're hemorrhaging money, between

Liz Taylor's illness and Marilyn Monroe's lateness. . . ."

Five minutes into lunch at the studio commissary (where the menu still featured "Fresh Sea-Food Salad à la Darryl F. Zanuck"), it was apparent to me that my client's estimate of the way things were going at Fox was, if anything, insanely optimistic. *Cleopatra* had careened totally out of control—too much money had been spent to make it feasible to stop production, but there was no end in sight. Elizabeth Taylor had recovered from her illness only to plunge into the most scandalous and public adulterous love affair of the century with Richard Burton, while nobody in the studio seemed to have the foggiest idea of what was happening with the picture.

As for *Something's Got to Give*, Marilyn's picture, principal photography had begun with a script that pleased nobody. George Cukor was writing it at night with a "friend" brought in to help him, so Marilyn, who found it difficult enough to memorize her lines in the first place, arrived on the set every morning only to find that the lines she had struggled to learn were no longer there. It took very little of that for Marilyn to decide that Cukor, despite his legendary reputation as a "woman's director," was the enemy.

Since Marilyn disliked open confrontation, she fell back on her time-honored methods of showing displeasure—illness and lateness. Sometimes she turned up on the set hours late, sometimes not at all, sending occasional health bulletins by way of intermediaries like Dr. Greenson or Mrs. Murray. When she *did* turn up, she seemed to be in a state of panic barely kept in check by medication, so that even the simplest thing took hours for her to do. Animal scenes are notoriously difficult to shoot, but in one scene where she was supposed to fondle a dog, the dog got it right on the first take while Marilyn blew *her* line twenty-three times.

All I heard at lunch were horror stories about Marilyn—this in the studio whose biggest and most profitable star she had been for ten years! Marilyn didn't even *look* like Marilyn, I was told—she had lost fifteen pounds, so that her whole wardrobe had to be remade, and she now photographed more like Audrey Hepburn than herself. She had hired writers of her own to rewrite Cukor's rewrites, she hated the kids who were playing her children in the picture, and was having trouble with the notion of Marilyn Monroe playing a mother in the first place, and so on, and so on. . . .

I decided I had better go see her as soon as possible. I found her at home, looking healthy enough for somebody who had been pleading illness for weeks.

Her new house, which she showed me proudly, was dark and cramped, the decor mysteriously Mexican (I did not know that Marilyn was attempting to duplicate her analyst's house). There were Mexican tiles everywhere, the ones around the front door with a coat of arms and the motto *"Cursum Perficio,"* which, according to my schoolboy Latin, meant "I am finishing my journey"—a message that ought to have set off alarm bells in my mind.

She opened a fresh bottle of champagne—it was noon—and we sat down in the tiny living room, although it was a beautiful day outside. "Isn't the house *great?*" she asked.

Actually, it looked as if it had been furnished out of a Mexican junk shop—primitive paintings of the kind that tourists buy on the streets of Mexico City, cheap tin-framed mirrors and sconces, "Indian" horse-blanket rugs, and heavy stained-oak furniture of vaguely Spanish design.

"I made a special trip to Mexico City, to buy all this," she said, though I would have thought there wasn't much in the house she couldn't have found in any cheap furniture warehouse in Los Angeles. "Boy, did I have fun!"

She giggled. "I met this Mexican screenwriter who showed me all the sights. . . ."

She took a couple of pills and knocked back her champagne. "The only thing is, he thinks he's going to marry me, which he's not." She showed me the pill bottle. "One thing he *does* do is send me these—Mandrax." She giggled again. " 'Randy-Mandys,' they call them. You take them with a little alcohol and you feel really warm and sexy and *relaxed,* for hours. You can buy them in Mexico without a prescription."

Now that I looked at her more closely, I could see that her eyes were unnaturally bright, the pupils dilated. She seemed to have trouble focusing on one spot, as if she were nearsighted. "I hope you're not overdoing it," I said.

She laughed. "Same old David! Always a stick-in-the-mud when everybody else is having fun."

I was hurt, and probably showed it. "I may be a stick-in-the-mud," I said, "but at least I'm *concerned* about you."

With no warning, she burst into tears. "Oh, I know," she wailed. "I'm sorry."

I took her hand, which was cold as ice, although it was a warm day. She dabbed at her eyes with Kleenex from a box on the table, dropping the used ones on the floor, which bore the stains that Maf, still imperfectly housebroken, had put there. She seemed to me to be overreacting, and I said so.

She gave a sniffle. "I know you care," she said. "I shouldn't have said you were whatever."

I waved "stick-in-the-mud" away. "That's all right. But *are* you okay? I mean *really* okay?"

She shrugged. "I guess. You know Jack ditched me?"

"I know. I saw him a couple of days ago. We talked about it."

"How *is* he? What did he say?"

"He's sad about it, Marilyn. It wasn't an easy decision for Jack. I've never known him to be as—frank—about himself. Or as presidential, somehow. He already misses you."

"I know," she said sadly. "We were good together, Jack and I, you know, all those years. Good for each other."

"Yes. I always thought so."

She looked forlorn. "You know about Bobby and me?" she asked.

I nodded. She must have guessed how I felt.

"Poor David," she said.

"How's it going with Bobby?" I asked, anxious to avoid a discussion of my own feelings.

"Oh, well, you know, it's kind of a long-distance love affair. . . . I can't go east so long as I'm stuck here making this lousy picture, and I guess the attorney general can only find so many reasons to come to LA. . . . Of course, it's only been going on a couple of weeks, but I don't know when we're going to see each other again. . . ."

She sighed. "In a lot of ways, Bobby's nicer than Jack. More—sensitive."

Bobby's dark, brooding, Celtic sensitivity was a well-known attraction, and many a heart had been broken by it on the campaign trail. That Marilyn would be bowled over was perfectly predictable: he was concerned, he loved children, he was a good father—perhaps the best and the most patient I've ever met—and he cared about everything she cared about, from blacks to orphans, the poor, and stray dogs. It was a marriage made in heaven, except that she was crazy and barely functioning, while he was married and the attorney general of the United States. As a kind of love token he had given her, she told me proudly, his private number at the Justice Department, which she had taped to her refrigerator.

"Yes," I said, "Bobby's sensitive. I'd be careful about making the same mistake twice, though."

"What mistake would that be?"

"Talking about it."

She laughed—a little unsteadily. "I *know* that," she said. "I've learned my lesson! I'm not telling a soul. Just my analyst."

I had my doubts. In my experience, people who tell their secrets to analysts have usually already divulged them to their friends. Still, there was very little I could do about it, except to warn her. She would have to learn for herself, I thought, that Bobby's view of human weakness—his own included—was harsher than Jack's.

The telephone rang. Marilyn picked it up, said, "Hello," then shook the receiver, as if something was wrong with it. She hung up, a look of mild annoyance on her face. "Ever since I moved in, I've had phone trouble," she complained. "Weird noises on the lines, or the phone rings and nobody's there. . . . It's a real *pain*."

She turned her attention back to me. "Don't look so sour," she said. "I'm happy. Really, I am. When Bobby told me about Jack, I thought, Well, this is it, I'm going to kill myself, this time I'm really going to do it. But it didn't work out that way at all. Maybe my luck's changing, David," she said. "What do you think?"

"I hope so, Marilyn."

"So do I, honey," she whispered. "God, so do I!"

But her luck didn't change. The next day, I heard, she went to the studio—late, as usual—and flubbed so many takes that even the technicians on the set—gaffers, grips, prop men, electricians, guys who got paid by the hour plus overtime so they didn't care how long it took to shoot a scene—let out a collective groan, together with a few hisses, when she stumbled over the same simple line for what might have been the twentieth or thirtieth time.

By the end of the day, the studio executives, normally invisible, were lined up behind the camera in their dark suits sweating nervously, which made everything even more difficult for her. "Don't be afraid, darling," Cukor called out encouragingly, but fear wasn't it—her problem was *panic*.

Going before the camera had become like walking the high wire without a net. Even the presence of Dr. Greenson on the set didn't help. The camera, which had made her famous, was her enemy now.

"The camera may be a phallic symbol?" Dr. Greenson suggested. He did not sound convinced.

"I'm not afraid of cocks. I've seen enough of them, God knows."

"Admittedly. The subconscious may be, however. . . ."

She lay back, eyes closed, listening. She found Dr. Greenson's voice soothing, rather like having a massage, even if he wasn't about to pull a psychiatric rabbit out of his hat.

The camera wasn't a phallus, though—she knew that perfectly well. It represented power of a different kind. All her adult life she had fought and sweated to please the studio, singing, dancing, smiling, shouting out silently with every gesture and glance, *Love me, choose me, I'm the prettiest girl of them all!* while at the same time hating and fearing their power simply to ignore her, or to push her back into the ranks of all the failed pretty blondes who waited on tables all over Los Angeles. Her stardom was a kind of slavery, and the camera was the symbol and magic totem of the slave masters.

She had explained all this to Dr. Greenson, but behind his sympathetic eyes she could sense a certain reserve, for he was, after all, part of the Hollywood establishment and found it difficult to accept the studio itself, or the picture business, as the cause of her illness.

"I always did what everyone wanted me to," she said. "I got pushed around, and bullied, and exploited, but I figured, Okay, I can take this, because I'm going to be *a star*. I thought, When I'm a star, I'll have power, then I'll show them! Only it turns out that the only power I have is the power to fuck

things up for them, by being late, by being sick, by saying
no to what they want me to do.... It's like being a wife.
The only real power you have is to say no to your husband,
right?"

"Mm."

"That's my relationship to the studio, you see? It's like a
husband. I can't fight the studio—it's bigger than I am and
stronger—but I can say no. I can have headaches. I can be
late. I can make sure the studio doesn't get laid when it wants
to get laid. Am I making any sense?"

"Yes," he said. "But in that case, my original idea remains
correct. The camera *is* a phallus—the studio's phallus—and
you're afraid of it."

"I'm *not* afraid of it. I just don't want to give it what it
wants."

"That, my dear, is called fear." He made a little steeple of
his hands. "How is the rest of your life going?"

"I miss Bobby," she said. "I guess that's one reason why I
don't care about this picture. I want to be with him."

"That would surely be difficult?"

"New York is a lot closer to Washington than LA. I think
we're getting a lot closer, you know? We have a real intimacy."

"That's good. Intimacy is what you need."

"I call him all the time—three or four times a day. We talk
every night when he's working late at the Justice Department,
sometimes for hours. He's interested in everything I do—and
he tells me all about his day, and what he's doing, and about
his family...."

"About his family?" Greenson asked doubtfully.

"Oh, yes. I told him what to buy Ethel for her birthday. And
one of his sisters even wrote to me." She pulled a couple of
pages of expensive writing paper out of her handbag, as if to
prove it. "She told me how pleased the whole family is that
Bobby and I are a thing."

A look of alarm came over Greenson's face. "I would be
careful not to show that to anyone."

"Well, of course I wouldn't. I'm just trying to show you
that this is a *good* relationship—positive, just the kind you're
in favor of. Bobby's coming out here soon. I can hardly
wait."

Greenson's expression was troubled, as if he were trying to work out what was positive about a clandestine affair between his most famous patient and the equally famous, married attorney general of the United States, but he held his tongue. His job, as he saw it, was to patch his patient up, not to discourage her.

"Yes. Well, he's got business to do as well," she went on. "He told me he's determined to nail Jimmy Hoffa—he's really *scary* on the subject. He's even scarier about Giancana, who I *met* once, did I tell you? I'd hate to be in *his* shoes, the way Bobby talks about him. . . .

"Anyway, apparently Hoffa is involved in some land swindle called the Sun Valley Retirement Community—he got the members of his own union to invest their savings in land that was worthless—and Bobby's coming out to talk to a former Teamster official who's willing to testify against him. 'Knuckles' Boyle his name is, believe it or not! I mean, if you used it in a movie, nobody would believe you. . . . Anyway, we'll spend some time together."

"Be careful," Dr. Greenson said.

"Always," she said. "Believe me, I know *that!*"

Hoffa and Giancana did not often get together. Both of them preferred to deal through intermediaries—they were the targets of so much law enforcement surveillance that any meeting was fraught with danger and difficulties.

When Hoffa demanded a sit-down, Giancana balked at first, but since Hoffa had never insisted on one before, Giancana eventually gave in—though with many complaints because it involved a long and tedious journey, changing cars at many points and zigzagging miles out of the way in order to ensure that he wasn't being followed by the FBI.

By the time Giancana arrived at Hoffa's "lodge," a small log cabin deep in the Michigan woods, he was chilled and irritable. The dark pine forest, dripping wet, depressed him, and the cabin itself didn't help, with its cheap varnished knotty pine furniture and its stone fireplace. There was a gun rack on the wall, containing a .30/30 Winchester lever action, a bolt-action rifle with a telescopic sight, and a 12-gauge Winchester pump-action shotgun. Apart from that, the only decoration was a mounted deer's head, an eight-pointer, and some color prints of fish jumping. At least, the fire was lit. He accepted a cup of coffee with a dash of brandy in it, and warmed himself for a few minutes.

Hoffa was dressed for the surroundings in a red-and-black-checked wool lumberman's shirt and old corduroy pants stuffed into laced-up boots, in contrast to Giancana's silver-gray mohair suit and custom-made shirt and tie.

"See that .270?" Hoffa asked. "That son of a bitch is the most accurate fucking rifle I've ever owned. One of these days, he don't back off, I'm gonna get that greedy little Ivy League cocksucker Bobby in the crosshairs and let him have it."

Giancana shrugged. He disliked people who made threats, and talk of violence dismayed him. Violence was very often necessary, but you never talked about it—you gave a whispered order, and that was that. Hoffa, he thought, was a dangerous guy, a loudmouth. Not for the first time, he wished he'd never involved his people with the Teamsters.

They sat down in front of the fire, facing each other, no love lost between them. Giancana's bodyguards were in the car outside, as was Hoffa's driver. The two men met alone, as was only proper, out of respect for each other.

"The reason I mention the rifle," Hoffa said, "is—never mind how I know—Bobby is coming after you."

"He's already after me."

"Yeah, but the Cuban thing, that girl of yours who was going with Jack, all that don't mean shit no more. All bets are off. Jack's listening to that little prick brother of his. No more deals. They're out for your blood. And mine."

"They wouldn't risk it. Not with what I can tell about them."

"Don't bet on it. Jack's made up his mind not to run scared anymore, that's the word I get. He probably figures if you tell the world about the whole CIA-Cuba thing, he'll deny it, maybe fire some people at the CIA, and send you to the slammer, where with any luck somebody will stick a blade in your heart. He's gonna run for a second term over our dead bodies, that's what he plans to do."

"Where does all this come from, Jimmy?"

"Here. There. I got a bug in a certain lady's house, is one place, and in her analyst's office, is another. Do you know this lady—who was fucking the President—is now fucking Bobby, that little hypocrite, who's supposed to be such a family man?"

Giancana controlled his expression carefully. He *had* heard about Marilyn and Bobby from his singer girlfriend, who was a pal of Peter Lawford's and knew all the Hollywood gossip, but he wasn't about to tell Hoffa.

"The real stroke of genius was putting a bug in the shrink's office," Hoffa said. "Plus she and Bobby are phone pals, they talk for hours, can you believe it? That Sun Valley thing, you know? That piece of shit they been trying to indict me on for years? Bobby actually *told* her the name of his new informant, the one he was going out to see in LA!"

"That's a piece of good luck," Giancana said, smiling though he thought Hoffa was a walking time bomb who couldn't shut up. "What did you do?" he asked.

Hoffa smirked. "Just what you and I are gonna do to Jack and Bobby," he snarled, leaning closer. "I'm gonna have the fucking snitch whacked, whaddya think? Jack gets a second term, we're all gonna be looking at life from behind bars."

Giancana said nothing. He knew what he knew, and he didn't need Hoffa to tell him. Still, Hoffa had a point, he had to admit. There were bad times ahead if Jack Kennedy won a second term.

But murder, he thought, was always a risk, even when it involved small fry. Things went wrong, however carefully you planned. The murder of a president was unthinkably risky, so risky that he felt himself break into a sweat at the mere thought that he was sitting here listening to Hoffa talk about it. Didn't Hoffa realize that if he could bug the Kennedys, they could bug him? That if Bernie Spindel could tape Marilyn Monroe's shrink, somebody else could tape Hoffa's cabin?

He thought about the weather outside, and the mud, then thought with regret about his custom-made five-hundred-dollar shoes. "Let's go outside for a walk," he said. "A breath of fresh air."

42

IT WAS JUST THE KIND OF WEEKEND SHE HAD HOPED FOR—
dinner at the Lawfords', the two of them pretending to be
"just friends," the star and the Attorney General. The need to
keep up appearances for several hours in front of other people heightened their desire for each other, so that by the time
they reached her house in Brentwood—Bobby had offered to
"drop her off" on the way back to the Beverly Wilshire, with
a fairly convincing display of indifference, except to those in
the know—they didn't even wait to get to the bedroom before
they pulled off each other's clothes. They fucked right there in
the living room, on the big sofa she had ordered in Mexico
City, tossing the cushions to the far ends of the room to give
themselves space.

Bobby spent the night, going downstairs once to call Ethel,
she presumed, on the house line, because he returned looking
embarrassed. She congratulated herself for not sneaking out
after him to listen in.

Her bed was small and narrow—like the house itself, it had
been designed with the needs of only one person in mind—
but that made it better in a way, for they were pressed against
each other as tightly as if they were sharing a Pullman berth,
reminding her inescapably of *Some Like It Hot.*

They talked late into the night—unlike Jack, Bobby was
one of those rare men who *didn't* close their eyes and fall
asleep the minute they'd had sex. She told him about Tippy
and the orphanage, and listened while he talked about his
childhood, which seemed to contain all the things she'd never had: a mother, a father, brothers and sisters, grandparents,
money. . . .

"I always wanted children," she told him.

"They're the best thing life has to offer, believe me. Why
didn't you have any?"

"Bad luck," she said. "There's still time." She didn't feel like telling him that she'd terminated so many pregnancies over the years that there was almost no chance of a successful one now. . . .

"I wish we could have a baby together," she whispered. "Just one. After all, Ethel's got dozens."

He laughed nervously. Sensitive he might be, but he didn't take her seriously about this. "Not dozens," he said. "Not even a dozen."

"Lots, anyway. I only want one—a boy."

"A boy? Why a boy?"

"Because boys have it made. I wouldn't want a girl. I *know* what girls have to go through, lover."

"It might not be the same."

"It's always the same."

They made love again, in the cool dawn. Before she finally fell asleep, she said, "How do you feel about middle-aged women with strong jaws and glasses?"

"They're not really my type. Why?"

"Because if you don't get dressed, you're going to meet Eunice Murray in the kitchen. It's okay with me—I don't have too many secrets from Mrs. Murray—but you might not want her to see you here."

He nodded and gave her a kiss, then she fell asleep. When she woke, he was gone, and she could hear Mrs. Murray padding about downstairs, straightening things. From the way her clothes were scattered around the living room, Mrs. Murray would certainly have guessed what had happened, though not with whom. But she was pretty unshockable, and never commented on what went on in the house or the occasional man she found there in the morning. Far from disapproving, she seemed to enjoy Marilyn's confidences, giggling and blushing like a schoolgirl. It was like having a big sister in the house, or maybe a broad-minded sorority mother, even if part of her job *was* to report on everything to Dr. Greenson, and to deal with "emergencies" if they arose.

During the day, she asked Mrs. Murray to drive her over to the market in Brentwood—given the amount of "medication" she was taking, she could no longer drive herself—and spent nearly fifty dollars on "goodies"—not that Bobby was a big eater or much of a gourmet, but she felt ashamed of the fact that her refrigerator contained nothing but a few bottles of champagne, a carton of orange juice, a box of powerful sedative suppositories bought in Mexico City, and a small carton of half-and-half for Mrs. Murray's coffee. The cupboards contained nothing but Maf's dog food.

She bought olives, crackers, several different kinds of cheese, cold cuts, nuts, potato chips, filling her cart in a kind of orgy of domesticity, imagining that she was an ordinary housewife shopping for her man—as she might have been, for in her white Capri pants and blouse, without makeup and with a scarf knotted over her hair, she could have passed for an eager young bride stocking up on delicacies to greet her husband with when he returned home from work.

This vision kept her going through the afternoon, as she and Eunice tidied up the house, dusted and vacuumed, laid out plates of hors d'oeuvres and bowls of nuts. At six, breathless with excitement, she said good-bye to Eunice, bathed herself in Chanel No. 5, changed into a filmy black negligee—giggling at the sight of herself, the quintessential seductress—and settled down to wait for Bobby.

But when he arrived—two hours late—it took only one look to know that there was a problem. His face was flushed, his eyes as cold as granite, his mouth an angry down-turned slash. He flung off his coat, with an excess of force that made it clear how furious he was.

"What's the matter?" she asked, terrified by his obvious anger. Why did a man's anger always make her feel guilty?

He unfastened his wrinkled, sweat-stained button-down shirt—none of Jack's made-to-measure, French-cuff shirts for Bobby!—and tore off his tie, as if he were trying to break his neck with it. "Hoffa. The scum he's in with. There's this fellow, Knuckles Boyle, basically a decent guy who could have put Hoffa away for years. No reason why you'd have ever heard of him. He was just an ordinary working slob. . . ."

In fact, she *had* heard all about Knuckles earlier, from Bobby himself, but the look on his face made her decide there was something to be said for playing dumb. Knuckles, she seemed to remember, had only become a "working slob" after coming to blows with Hoffa as a Teamster official.

"*Was?*" she asked.

She slipped a hand behind him and rubbed his neck, which was stiff with tension.

"Was," he said flatly. "Somebody ran over him with a forklift at the warehouse where he worked. Not more than an hour before he was supposed to meet me."

He closed his eyes. "Somehow, there was a leak, somewhere. . . . He was going to testify against Hoffa and the mob, on the Sun Valley thing. We had him ready to go the whole fucking nine yards, and now he's dead, before he could give us a thing! The worst of it is that we killed him somehow. I don't see how it happened. Hardly anybody knew. I *promised* Boyle complete confidentiality, and I betrayed him."

"It wasn't *your* fault, Bobby," she said soothingly, feeling a slight edge of panic, for he had told *her* about Boyle in detail and with great pride, and while she didn't think she had told anybody, she couldn't be sure.

"Yes it was. I gave Boyle my word, and now he's dead." He stared into the middle distance, his face a mask of hard, unforgiving Irish anger. "When I find out who's responsible for the leak, I'm going to have his balls."

She had a growing memory of having mentioned Knuckles Boyle to somebody, but she couldn't remember who. "What about the people who killed him?" she asked.

"I'll get them," he said. "I'm going to get them *all,* sooner or later. Not just Hoffa and Giancana either. I want the guys who do their dirty work, too, like this fellow Santo Trafficante in Miami, or Carlos Marcello in New Orleans, or this Johnny Roselli here, who's an out-and-out killer, probably the one who took care of poor Knuckles for Hoffa. . . . People you've probably never heard of. . . ."

She *had* heard of Johnny Roselli. As it happened, Roselli had been a pal of sorts in the old days when she was with Joe Schenck. She did not think it was a good idea to inform the Attorney General of the United States of her knowledge.

She snuggled close to him, until, finally, he started to relax. Since he didn't drink, she was obliged to loosen him up in other ways, but it didn't take her more than half an hour to get him into bed. She took a bottle of champagne into the bedroom with her—he might not need a drink, but *she* did—and put it on her night table, next to all her pills.

It was strange, she thought, that Bobby never seemed to notice her pills or her drinking. It wasn't that he deliberately ignored it, the way some men did—it was almost as if he didn't *understand* it, perhaps *couldn't* understand that anybody could be so dependent on pills or booze, and therefore simply didn't see the evidence. . . .

It wasn't, of course, that she needed booze or pills to get rid of her inhibitions, since she had none; it was just that without them she felt unable to face even the simplest of demands. Lately, it seemed to her, it had been getting worse— she was occasionally aware of stumbling when she walked, of her speech being slurred, of moments of memory loss. There were even times when she wasn't sure whether she was in bed with Bobby or with Jack.

Bobby dozed in her arms, his head cradled on her breast, breathing gently, his own particular demons temporarily at bay. She stroked his forehead with her fingertips, rejoicing in the fact that he was, for this tiny moment, *hers*—not Ethel's, or Jack's, or the people of the United States—content with her happiness.

43

"THAT'S NIXON'S PLACE."

"I know that, Chrissake."

The big powerboat cut through the mild swell off Key Biscayne, offering those on board a view of the island's most lavish homes, all of which were hidden from the road behind high hedges and walls, but whose broad lawns sloped down to the sea, revealing gardens, pools, statuary, and private docks at which multimillion-dollar yachts were moored.

None of the yachts was bigger than *Aces Wild,* which flew the Panamanian flag from her stern and was registered to a Grand Caymans corporation. Seated around a teak-and-brass table in the stern were three gentlemen in leisure clothes, yachting caps, and sunglasses, their fishing rods locked into sockets, the lines trolling unattended behind the boat. Incongruous amidst all the nautical paraphernalia, a portable tape recorder sat on the table.

Santo Trafficante—who had pointed out Nixon's place—was the host. His guests were Carlos Marcello, head of the New Orleans crime family, and Johnny Roselli.

Trafficante, de facto chief of organized crime in Miami, and Marcello had been partners in Havana—running the casinos and other interests on behalf of the five families of New York and their East Coast associates—until Castro threw them out.

Roselli operated mostly out of LA and Vegas, and had a reputation as a very heavy hitter, even among heavy hitters. The three of them did not constitute a fan club for Sam Giancana—whom, for different reasons, they all hated.

If Giancana had known the three of them were together, he would have sweated blood. For that matter, if the Feds had caught sight of them together, there would have been hell to pay; they were all convicted felons, forbidden to associate with one another. In addition, Marcello was still fighting Bobby Kennedy's attempt to have him deported again.

Here, at any rate, they were sure they weren't being bugged, either by Giancana or the FBI. The only person in earshot was the helmsman, a made man in Trafficante's family.

"You guys heard the fucking tape the same as I did," Roselli said, his voice rising above the expensive burble of the big twin V-8s like a piece of heavy earth-moving machinery working hard. "I played it the minute it arrived from Hoffa. You wanna know do I take it seriously? You bet I do! You think it's just pillow talk? I don't. Neither does Hoffa. That little cocksucker Bobby Kennedy is going to put us all away for life, his brother gets elected again." Roselli, despite his styled silver hair and Hollywood playboy tan, still talked like a professional murderer and a thug, which he was.

Trafficante shrugged, his eyes hidden by thick dark glasses. "Men speak a certain way to women, Johnny. They talk big, they boast. Not everything they say in bed is true. It's human nature." He puffed at his cigar, watching the smoke drift astern. "I'm not speaking personally, of course," he added. "Still, that's the way it is." Trafficante, though Sicilian, had acquired through his years in Havana a measure of Spanish courtesy and polish, along with a taste for fine cigars.

Marcello exchanged glances with Roselli. Both of them thought that Trafficante was a bit too much the diplomat-philosopher for his job. In the old days, he had been as quick to order a man's death as anybody else, and years ago, before his rise to don, he had done his share of killing, but lately he seemed to yearn for the respectability of elder statesman status, like Joe Bonanno.

"With respect, I think Bobby means what he says, Santo," Marcello said. "Even if he does say it in bed, to Marilyn Monroe." Somewhere along the way, Marcello had developed a deep southern accent, perhaps because he thought it was appropriate to the crime boss of New Orleans.

"It's *vendetta*, Chrissake," Roselli growled.

The three men sat silently, considering the most powerful word in their vocabulary. If Roselli was right and Bobby Kennedy had sworn *vendetta* against them, then there was only one response, and they all knew it.

"*Vendetta?*" Trafficante repeated, with cautious respect, for it was not a word to be spoken lightly. "He's Irish, not Sicilian."

Roselli snorted. "Who gives a fuck, Santo? You think the fucking harps don't unnerstan' *vendetta?* Let me tell you something. They unnerstan' *vendetta* just like us. Look at the fucking IRA. Look at the cops. Don't give me he's Irish, not Sicilian. I'm telling you it's him or us. You don't believe me, listen to the tape again."

Trafficante held up his hand, and Roselli fell silent, for Trafficante had the ear of Meyer Lansky, and Lansky was listened to with respect by the heads of each of the five families. Anyone who fucked with Santo Trafficante as good as fucked with Lansky, and anyone who fucked with Lansky was dead. "What do *you* think, Carlos?" Trafficante asked.

Marcello's face was as expressionless as an Easter Island statue's. "When a man swears *vendetta* against you," he said quietly, "what do you do?" He crossed himself quickly, for this was a serious business. "You kill him first," he said, answering his own question.

They sat in dead silence as the boat churned through the offshore swell, gently rolling at trolling speed. There was a sudden sharp crack that made them all start; then the helmsman called out, "Fish! We got a bite." He cut the throttles and pointed to one of the lines, which had snapped clear of the outrigger. He eased off the line, and shaded his eyes as the fish jumped a few hundred feet away, to seaward. "Tuna," he said.

"Fuck the tuna!" Roselli said. "I wanna tuna, I'll buy it in a fucking can."

Trafficante frowned. "Play the fish, Johnny," he said, in a voice that made it clear he was giving an order. "Somebody's watching from the shore, it wouldn't hurt we were fishing."

Roselli grunted. He moved into one of the two white vinyl-and-chrome fighting chairs, and with the help of the captain brought in a good-sized albacore. He watched as the captain gaffed it, the blood staining the surface of the sea a brief, dark red. "May Bobby Kennedy go like that," he said.

Trafficante frowned again. He didn't like that kind of talk. Business was business—there shouldn't be anything personal about it. "Let's say Johnny's right," he murmured. "I'm not saying he is or isn't, you understand, but if he is, maybe it's not Bobby we should go for."

The other two men looked at him. Trafficante might no longer be the man he once was, but nobody ever denied he was smart.

"Carlos is correct," he went on slowly, thinking it through. "A man swears *vendetta* against you, you kill him, of course. But you forgot something, Carlos—you also got to kill his family, even his children, because otherwise they grow up to kill you. We kill Bobby, his brother is going to come after us with everything he's got, and his brother is president of the United States."

He looked out at the horizon, as if it held some object of surpassing interest. "On the other hand, my friends, you kill Jack Kennedy, Bobby's got no more power. You want to kill a snake, you cut off the head, not the tail, right?"

"Kill the President?" Marcello whispered. "That's a heavy number."

Roselli laughed. "What the fuck! He's just another guy, like you or me. He's not even that hard to get to, believe me."

Marcello nodded. He came from Louisiana, a state in which assassination was virtually a normal part of the political process. "Let's say we do it," he said. "Then what?"

"Then Lyndon Johnson is president," Trafficante said. "A man we can do business with, I think. No friend of Bobby's either. Not such a bad deal all around, I would say. *If* we do it."

"I say we go for it," Marcello said. "I got better things to do with my life than spend the rest of it fighting off Bobby Kennedy." Marcello was a small man, almost gnomish, but he never seemed small to people when he looked them in the eye. He was not a man to forget that Bobby Kennedy had deported him to Guatemala, where he had been left to fend for himself in the stinking jungle.

"How would you do such a thing, Carlos?" Trafficante asked. "Just out of curiosity."

"I would not use any of our people."

Trafficante and Roselli listened intently. Marcello had a reputation as a good planner, a strategist, not a hothead. He had turned New Orleans from a honky-tonk town of pimps and whores into the center of a billion-dollar-a-year narcotics empire.

"I would look for a nut," he said. "Somebody who wants to kill the President anyway, for his own crazy reasons. Somebody with military training maybe, who can handle a rifle. . . . I wouldn't pay him or let him know he's working for us. He might want to believe he's working for the Russians, or the CIA, or just for himself, who knows? Whatever he wants to believe is what we tell him. You find the right guy, you just have to get him a gun and point him in the right direction. Hell, you don't even need to get him the fucking gun, he'll buy his own."

"Where would one find such a man, Carlos? If one wanted to?"

"There are plenty of them around, Santo—guys with some kind of a grudge. There are a couple of them in New Orleans. Probably dozens of them in Dallas or Houston. It wouldn't hurt to have a whole list of shooters so we cover most of the cities the President is going to visit, sooner or later. . . . If we had access to the Secret Service files that list people in every city who are suspected of being a threat to the President, we could pick and choose until we found the right ones. I think that would be the way to start."

Trafficante nodded. "That could be done," he said cautiously. "I have friends in the Miami United States Attorney's Office. If we decide to go ahead with this thing, that is."

The waves slapped against the hull as the boat changed course. Nobody seemed willing to be the first to talk. Then Roselli cleared his throat and said, "With all respect, we got no choice."

The other two men said nothing. Trafficante signaled to the helmsman to turn and head for home. "It's an idea," he said. "It's worth thinking about. It wouldn't hurt to start looking for the right man. Just in case."

He raised one hand in what appeared to be a papal blessing, the ring glittering in the sun.

"Let's keep in touch," he said.

J. Edgar Hoover sat alone in his office, reading a single-spaced report marked for his eyes only. It was the end of a long day, but his cuffs were as white and stiff as they had been at the beginning of it.

His desk was clear, not even a trace of dust on it. He held the papers—an original and a carbon copy—firmly in both hands. It was late. The building was silent, almost empty. Somewhere nearby, Clyde Tolson waited—impatiently, no doubt—for the Director to buzz him so they could go home and have a well-deserved drink, then dinner, served in front of the television set on the folding trays by George, the Director's faithful Negro butler—the *right* kind of Negro, Hoover thought, unlike this fellow King. . . . He was content, however, to be alone at present. The memorandum in his hands was something he couldn't share with anyone. He read it again, slowly, concentrating on every word.

It was from an FBI field agent in Miami, reporting on a regular conversation with one of his informants, a soldier in the Santo Trafficante crime family who served as the captain of a charter yacht when he wasn't smuggling narcotics into the country, or running a numbers game, or shipping truckloads of cigarettes to the North without tax stamps. This informant had overheard a conversation between Santo Trafficante himself,

Carlos Marcello, and Johnny Roselli, during what was ostensibly a day's fishing off Key Biscayne.

Hoover stared at the paper. If it was to be believed, the three mobsters intended to assassinate the President of the United States to revenge themselves on Bobby Kennedy! He did not find the idea incredible. Who knew better than he how headstrong and arrogant the President and his brother could be?

Hoover had no respect for mobsters, though he preferred them to left-wingers by a wide margin. Over the years, he had kept his men from investigating "organized crime," and had even denied before a Senate committee that the so-called "Mafia" existed, but that was because he didn't want FBI agents exposed to the inevitable corruption of mob money, which might bring them down to the same level as big-city police departments, where everybody was on the take. There was no corruption in the FBI; by concentrating his men on the threat from subversives and Communists, he had made sure there would be none.

Still, he himself knew a lot about the mob—after all, it was he who had brought down Capone! If men like Trafficante, Marcello, and Roselli were discussing the murder of the President, then it would happen, sooner or later—certainly before Kennedy's second term. He did not think Marcello's plan was a bad one either—it had a good chance of working. As for the Miami United States Attorney's Office, it was, as Hoover was well aware, a sink of corruption, which was why he had moved his Miami field office as far away from it as possible. If Trafficante thought he could get the Secret Service list of presidential threats from there, he was probably right. . . .

It was his job to pass all reports of a threat to the President's life on to the Secret Service and the Attorney General, and if he deemed it necessary, to bring it to the attention of the President himself.

He sat as if in prayer for a few moments, then made up his mind. He carefully initialed the original and the copy and made a mental note to transfer the FBI agent who had sent them to Alaska or New Mexico to deal with felonies on Indian reservations. Then he got up from behind his desk, walked into his secretary's office, and ran both copies through the shredder.

He picked up the telephone and rang Tolson's extension. "Time to go home, Clyde," he said.

44

<hr>

It was just a question of time, and she knew it, before the brass at the studio moved from concern to alarm and from alarm to sheer panic.

She had caught a cold, and seemed unable to get rid of it; then she gave her cold to Dean Martin, so he couldn't work for days.

Of course, that was only part of the story. She *hated* the script—simply couldn't believe in the character she was playing, or accept that any man would prefer Cyd Charisse to *her*. Her simmering dislike of George Cukor had turned into raging hatred, for she had heard, from one of the crew who was loyal to *her*, that Cukor actually told somebody she was "crazy, just like her mother and her grandmother."

This had precipitated a major crisis. She would not speak to Cukor, would not even *look* at him, and stayed home for days at a time nursing her cold, sending health bulletins via Mrs. Murray to assure the studio she was too sick to work—for Dr. Greenson was on vacation in Europe, with his long-suffering wife.

The picture was already a million dollars over budget, and Cukor had shot around her to the point where he could shoot no more. Of course, things had been just as bad on *The Misfits*, but she had *respected* everybody on that picture, Huston, Gable, Monty, even Eli Wallach—they had been *pros*, and they had respected and supported *her*, recognizing that without her they wouldn't have a picture. To Cukor she was just a pain in the ass, and she had already heard rumors that he had suggested replacing her with "another blonde," Kim Novak perhaps, or Lee Remick. Everybody in the cast except Dino hated her, even the dog and the children—she could feel it whenever she appeared on the set, which was increasingly rarely.

Every night, she told her problems to Bobby Kennedy on his private line at the Justice Department, almost as if she were one of his "causes," like Negroes in the South, or the urban poor.

She kept hoping he would fly out to visit her, so it surprised her when he suggested instead, as if it were the most natural thing in the world, that she should come to New York to join in the celebration of the President's birthday.

"Jack would love it," he said.

"Where is it being held?"

"Madison Square Garden. It's to raise money for Jack's reelection campaign. A kickoff for '64."

"Won't Jackie be there?"

There was a long pause.

"Ah, no. Jackie has a—ah—conflict that day."

"A conflict?"

"She's going to a horse show." He let that sink in.

"Look," he went on, "what we had in mind"—he did not say who "we" were—"is that you sing 'Happy Birthday,' that's all. Maybe with some special lyrics. You'd fly in with Peter, spend the afternoon rehearsing, do your number, and then—"

"And then what?"

"Then maybe we can spend the night together."

She giggled. Bobby had none of his big brother's persuasive charm. He said it stiffly, with a certain amount of embarrassment, but she found that charming. "It's the best offer I've had in a long time," she said.

He was silent.

"The only trouble is, I'm still a working girl. The studio will never let me go."

"For the President's birthday? Of course they will. They'll love it.

It's great publicity."

"They won't see it that way."

"I'll bet you they do," he said confidently. "You'll see."

She should have made the bet with him, because she turned out to be right.

The studio didn't give a damn about publicity at this point—they wanted the picture in the can. The notion that she was well enough to fly to New York to sing "Happy Birthday" to President Kennedy, but not well enough to take a twenty-minute limo drive to the lot, confirmed their worst fears and suspicions. Peter Levathes, the head of Fox, passed the word down to her that he would not allow her to go to New York.

The next day he found out that she had already gone.

I had been opposed to the President's "birthday bash," as Lawford called it, from the first. A black tie evening in Madison Square Garden for several thousand people, most of them fat cats who had paid through the nose for the privilege of being there, did not seem to me the right spirit in which to reconsecrate the New Frontier. Blacks were being shot and beaten throughout the South, the Soviets were pouring arms into Cuba and making threatening noises in Berlin, Southeast Asia was mired in revolution and war, and our response was to fly in Marilyn Monroe to sing "Happy Birthday" for the President.

I was even more doubtful about the wisdom of having Marilyn sing "Happy Birthday." Enough people were in on the secret—or had heard rumors of it—to make her appearance seem tasteless, particularly in Jackie's absence.

What I hadn't guessed was that Marilyn wouldn't be in any better shape to sing before a live audience than she was for George Cukor. Five minutes after I reached her suite at the St. Regis Hotel, I knew we were in bad trouble.

"She keeps asking for you," the show's producer said. He was on his way out the door, clutching his briefcase as if he were holding fast to a life vest. "Is she always like this?"

"Like what?"

He seemed a pleasant enough man, but a career of producing celebrity specials had not prepared him for dealing with Marilyn Monroe's particular brand of stage nerves. "She can't remember the words of 'Happy Birthday.' "

"The special lyrics?" I couldn't remember them myself.

He shook his head. "No," he said, "the ordinary ones. 'Happy birthday to you,' and so forth."

Since he seemed about to continue, I held up my hand to indicate that I, at least, was familiar with them. "I'll have a word with her," I said, with more confidence than I had a right to feel.

"Be my guest."

The living room was the usual chaos: a hairdresser was setting up her things, Marilyn's makeup man was unpacking his kit, while a manicurist packed up hers. The furniture had been moved to make space for a cottage industry devoted to Marilyn Monroe.

I found the center of all this activity in the bedroom, stretched out on the bed in a dressing gown with a damp washcloth over her face. "God," she said, "why did I agree to do this?"

I raised the edge of the washcloth, gave her a kiss, and sat down.

"Because you're a good sport?"

"The hell I am." She groaned. "I have a major-league hangover," she said. "I flew in from LA with Peter, and we were drinking champagne spiked with Russian vodka all the way. . . . Oh boy!" She took my hand. Her own was trembling, and hot, as if she were shaking from a fever.

"Are you sure you're okay?" I asked.

She took the washcloth off. Her eyes were vague and unfocused, or rather focused on something only she could see, the pupils like pinpoints. "I feel really *yucky*," she said wearily. "What time is it?"

"Four o'clock. You've got three or four hours to pull yourself together. Is that enough?"

She bit her lower lip. "It's going to *have* to be." With great effort she managed to swing her legs off the bed. Her robe parted, revealing her nakedness. The scars from her two operations were still raw. Her skin was pale—almost pasty— and there were mottled bruises on her thighs.

She put an arm around my shoulder and I helped her to stand. For a moment I had the feeling that if I let her go, she would fall, but gradually she managed to gain control of her feet, so that she was merely leaning on me for support.

"How about a bath?" I asked encouragingly, thinking it might bring her back to life.

"No time."

She tied up her robe and walked rather unsteadily into the living room of the suite, where her retainers instantly took her in hand like grooms around a valuable racehorse.

She sat down on a stool, while the hairdresser—I recognized him as Mr. Kenneth himself—busied himself with her hair. Now that she was back at work again, the fog seemed to have lifted from her brain. It occurred to me that this was the reality she understood best, not the performance but the preparation for it.

"I was really looking *forward* to this, you know? Even though it's the first time I've played before a live audience this size since I was in Korea. I had Jean-Louis make me a special dress—it's like this transparent nude fabric, stitched with tiny beads, skintight, so I have to be sewn into it. . . ."

"How about your lines?" I asked. "Comfortable with them?"

"Lines?"

"Well, there's 'Happy Birthday.' "

She shut her eyes. " 'Happy birthday to you, happy birthday to you.' " She opened them again, wide, with that expression of perfect innocence that nobody else could manage or imitate. " 'Happy birthday, dear Mr. President, happy birthday to you.' . . . See?"

She hadn't tried to sing. She simply recited, in a tiny voice that seemed to be coming from deep under water. Still, she *had* remembered the lines.

"Very good," I said. "How about the special lyrics?"

She gave me a wicked smile and a finger. "Don't push it, David," she said. "They're dopey, but I'll remember them."

"Well," I said, "you're in good hands. I'll order you some coffee and be on my way."

"You do that. And tell Jack not to worry."

Of course, Jack wasn't worried.

The grapevine had already alerted him to Marilyn's problems, but all Jack had said was, "She'll do fine."

I thought she would probably do fine too. When I called later in the afternoon and spoke to Marilyn, she sounded in good spirits. I had no idea she hadn't touched the coffee— that she'd been drinking champagne and popping pills as they worked on her face and her hair.

I had enough on my plate that evening that I didn't get around to worrying about Marilyn again until she was already in her dressing room at the Garden. I don't think I have ever seen more press anywhere, not even at a national convention—

the combination of Jack Kennedy and Marilyn Monroe was the most potent "draw," to use a favorite picture-business word, in history since Anthony and Cleopatra, even to those not in the know.

I had arranged for the President's birthday gala to be televised, and there were camera crews, lights, and cables everywhere, the atmosphere somewhere between that of a national convention and a circus. Unlike the circus, however, there was a pervasive spirit of amateurism about the entertainment. The people around the President had a brilliant sense of how to stage a political event, and in Jack they had a natural star performer, but they had no real knowledge of show business, and assumed that the stars would simply appear one after the other and keep the audience amused.

I made my way through the crowds of television people, photographers, and security people to her dressing room, knocked on the door, and slipped in. She was standing in front of a full-length mirror, with a team of stylists fussing over her. She could not have sat down in Jean-Louis's dress if she had wanted to—it looked as if it had been painted onto her. Her back was completely bare, right down to her buttocks, and the gossamer-thin, flesh-colored fabric was tightly molded over her breasts and stomach, so that at first glance she seemed to be nude, except for the ruffle of beaded material around her ankles, where the dress belled out as if, like Venus, she were emerging naked from the waves.

That was my first impression. My second was that Marilyn looked as if she were somehow imitating herself, dwarfed by a gleaming mass of platinum-white hair that was so stiff and bouffant it resembled cotton candy. The body was that of America's sex goddess; the face, in the harsh light, could have been that of a million women in their mid-thirties, wondering where their youth had gone and how they had gotten into their present fix.

I placed my hand on her bare shoulder and brushed my lips against her cheek, taking care not to smudge her makeup.

"You look great," I said.

"I feel like death. I think I'm coming down with a cold."

Marilyn must have noticed my expression, because she said, "Don't worry, I'm going on." She giggled and threw a salute.

"*Semper fidelis,* Mr. President," she said. "Isn't that what the Marines say?"

"It's their motto, yes." When she smiled, her face lit up—she no longer looked drawn and weary. It was a remarkable transformation, but paper-thin. "It means 'Always faithful.' "

"Oh dear," she said. "I guess it won't do for me."

I glanced at my watch. "I've got to go. It's feeding time at the zoo."

"It's funny you should say that. I thought it *smelled* like a zoo in here."

"It's the circus."

"Oh," she said. "That figures. It explains why I feel like one of the freaks tonight." She picked up her purse and shook a few pills from it, borrowed a pin from the seamstress to stick holes in them, popped them in her mouth, screwed up her face at the taste, and washed them down with a gulp of champagne from a Madison Square Garden coffee mug. "Toodle-oo, as they say in England," she said. "Give the Prez a kiss from me." Swallowing the pills seemed to have cheered her up a bit.

"I think he'd prefer if you delivered that yourself."

"I'll *bet* he would. Where's Bobby?"

"Out front, with Jack."

"Tell him to come and see me right afterwards, David. *Please.*"

She said it with terrifying intensity, her momentary good spirits vanishing as quickly as they had appeared. "Tell him I've *got* to see him."

"I will."

"I *mean* it."

Her expression was at once demanding and pleading, a combination that is probably only possible for a movie star.

"It's a promise," I said.

She gave herself a last, careful look in the mirror, professional to the last, keeping in mind that her profession consisted of looking her best. Emmeline Snively, the head of the Blue Book Model Agency, who had given her her first break, always said just that to her, in exactly those words. It was Emmeline who had sent her to Frank and Joseph's Hair Salon, on Hollywood Boulevard, in 1945, to be transformed into a bleached blonde.

The other thing that Emmeline always told "her girls" was not to get pregnant. . . .

Well, here she was, seventeen years later, she told herself, blonder than ever, and pregnant again! She took a last sip of champagne, just to clear her throat, really, and giggled. *Pregnant!* "Knocked up," as they used to say back in the days when she was hanging around with the lifeguards at the Ambassador Hotel pool, before Mr. Big Deal Ted "Me and My fucking Shadow" Lewis became the first man to knock her up, as well as the first to hand her a wad of bills and the name of a doctor on Melrose who "took care" of problems like this.

Oh, she knew the score all right, when it came to getting rid of the problem. *Thirteen* abortions at last count, she had confessed to Amy Greene, in LA, in Tijuana, in New York. . . . She could have written a book on the subject. Gynecologists shook their heads in dismay and indignation every time they examined her, as if she were some kind of object lesson on what *not* to do with the female reproductive system.

But this time things were going to be different! She was going to *have* this baby! He would grow up—she was sure it was a boy—to be as handsome and as smart as his father, maybe handsomer, for he would have some of her looks as well. She closed her eyes and tried to imagine what he would look like—the love child of Marilyn Monroe and Robert Francis Kennedy. . . .

There was a knock on the door. "Time to go, Miss Monroe," a page called out.

Not even she could be late for the President of the United States. She took one last look at herself in the mirror while Mr. Kenneth, the seamstress, and the makeup man gave her the thumbs-up sign and a patter of applause; then she stepped out into the corridor, a dimly lit shaft of painted cinder block.

She turned a corner, then another, before realizing that her page was nowhere in sight. Somewhere ahead of her she could hear the noise of a vast audience, and the familiar voice of Peter Lawford warming them up for her.

She decided not to turn back—she was obviously going in the right direction. She continued down the corridor, which seemed to zig and zag more than she would have liked, and smelled as if it had recently stabled horses, or worse, until she finally reached a big metal door marked "STAGE." She pulled at the handle, but it was firmly locked.

She began to feel panic.

"Mr. President," she heard Lawford say, his voice booming from a hundred loudspeakers, *"on this occasion of your birthday, this lady is not only pulchritudinous but punctual. . . . Mr. President—MARILYN MONROE!"*

The audience cheered, whistled, and stamped their feet, while the orchestra burst into her big song from *Some Like It Hot.* She ran down the corridor, trying door after door, all of which were locked, panic grasping her by the throat now. She turned a corner, expecting to find her dressing room door, but she had obviously taken a wrong turn again in the maze of corridors underneath the Garden.

"A woman of whom it may truly be said, she needs no introduction!" There was a roll of drums, followed by more applause, a little more hesitant now. She ran ahead as fast as her spike heels could carry her.

She could hear laughter now, as Lawford milked the situation—but of course, what *else* could he do, standing out there on stage in the spotlight in front of seventeen thousand people, left hanging high and dry?

At the end of the corridor, she found a metal staircase and clambered up it. There was a door with a red light over it, and she shoved it open, stumbling into the dark of what was clearly the backstage. She pushed through the crowd to the light, where Peter Lawford's PR man saw her and, grabbing her by the arm without ceremony, said, "Jesus Christ! Get the fuck *on!"* He pushed her toward the wing of the stage, from where she could see Lawford, sweat dripping down his face, grasping the microphone as if he were hanging on for dear life, a look of desperation on his face.

Out of the corner of his eye he must have seen her hair glittering in the spill of his spot, for he turned, shaking his head with exasperation; then, facing the audience, he grinned and shouted out: *"Mr. President, because in the history of show business, perhaps there has been no one female who has meant so much, or who has"* —he paused and winked broadly— *"has DONE more for her country and her president . . ."* The audience tittered, and as those in the know caught on, began to guffaw. Lawford joined in; then he reached out his hand toward where she waited, head throbbing, tears in her eyes, her cheeks and the back of her neck burning. *"Mr. President!"* he cried out, above the noise, bringing the audience to silence. *"Here she is—the LATE Marilyn Monroe!"*

The double entendre took her breath away. She stood there, unable to move, while the audience howled and roared. Then she was given a hefty shove, which almost knocked her flat on her face and boobs on the stage, and catching her balance, she stepped out into the bright, intense circle of the spot, smiling so hard she was afraid her jaw would break.

She blew Lawford a kiss, daggers in her eyes, and walked to the podium, blinded by the glare. She waited for a moment while her eyes adjusted to the light. She looked up and saw Jack Kennedy, in the presidential box, feet up on the rail, smoking a cigar. Bobby, hunched over beside him, was staring at her.

What would happen, she wondered, if she announced that she had fucked both of them, that even now she was carrying Bobby's child? She didn't feel any friendliness emanating from the huge arena. Her dress had caused a storm of wolf whistles and not a few gasps of shock. She sensed that the audience was getting restless now, so she pulled herself together, and clutching the sides of the podium, she sang:

> *"Happy birthday to you,*
> *Happy birthday to you,*
> *Happy birthday, Mr. President,*
> *Happy birthday to you."*

She sang slowly in a tiny voice, hesitating between each syllable, so that even with amplification, it wasn't until the third verse that the audience, a little embarrassed, started to join in.

She paused, gathering strength now, and sang the special lyrics Richard Adler had written for her, stumbling over the words as she struggled to remember them:

> *"Thanks, Mr. President,*
> *For all the things you've done,*
> *The battles you've won,*
> *The way you deal with U.S. Steel,*
> *And our problems by the ton,*
> *We thank you—so much."*

Then she held her trembling arms up, the audience rose to their feet, and she led them in another ragged chorus of "Happy Birthday."

I was sitting behind Jack and Bobby when Marilyn finally appeared on stage. Jack's relief when she finally *did* appear was short-lived. He could see, as well as I could, that her dress was a mistake, that she had crossed the line, had ceased being everybody's favorite blonde and was now an object of blatant sexuality. She simply did not represent the image the President was anxious to display to the nation on his birthday.

Marilyn, breasts as visible as if she were stark naked in Jean-Louis's flesh-colored masterpiece, was a challenge to each and every wife in the audience, the home wrecker personified. Nor was there any denying, when she started to sing in that high-pitched, breathless, little-girl-lost voice of hers, that she seemed to be drunk or drugged. Her movements not only were slow but seemed to have nothing to do with the music, and there were long pauses—*very* long pauses—between words, and even syllables.

It was like watching a film of an accident played back in slow motion, a piteous public exposure of poor Marilyn's nervous eagerness to please.

To say that Jack noticed all this would be to put it mildly. He smiled—he was no mean actor himself—but he whispered out of the corner of his mouth, "What the fuck's the matter with her, David?"

"She may have a cold," Bobby said protectively, before I could answer.

"A cold? She's fucking *stoned*, that's what she is."

He was not a leader for nothing. Before Marilyn had quite finished—and before she fell flat on her face, or did anything else embarrassing—he rose.

The spotlights turned on him instantly. "Thank you," he said, grabbing a microphone. "I can now retire from politics after having had, ah, 'Happy Birthday' sung to me in such a sweet"—he paused for a moment and grinned—"*wholesome* way!"

The audience roared with laughter, the other performers

came on stage, surrounding Marilyn and Peter Lawford, and Jack, with his usual deftness and perfect timing, brought his own gala to a conclusion.

"Remind me never to do this again," he said as we made our way out of his box past the cops and the Secret Service. "I'd rather be shot."

45

SHE DIDN'T NEED PAULA STRASBERG OR NATASHA Lytess to tell her she had fucked up—she could see it in everybody's eyes, even David's.

Still, the big advantage of being a star was that nobody had the guts to tell her to her face. The President stood on one side of her, Bobby on the other, both of them beaming as they were surrounded by well-wishers and those of the press tame enough to be allowed close. Adlai Stevenson came over to congratulate her, and Governor Harriman, and what seemed like hundreds of other, lesser mortals, and all the while, Bobby guarded her as if she were his own personal property. The President gave him a warning look a couple of times, as if to tell him to make it a little less obvious that he was having an affair with her, but Bobby, being Bobby, stuck to his guns.

She drank champagne, trying to get rid of the feeling that she had disappointed the President. He didn't *look* disappointed, but she knew him better than most people and could see the telltale signs of displeasure, which had the effect of making her drink more. It was a relief when he finally said good night, pleading fatigue, and left for the Carlyle, looking not in the least tired.

She knew somebody was waiting for him there, the way she had done in the old days from time to time, probably already snuggled up in the presidential bed. She wondered who it was, but it wasn't really any of her business. There were rumors about a certain long-legged television star who had taken her place, but she wasn't the only one. . . .

She leaned close to Bobby. "I need you," she said. "I have to be with you tonight."

He nodded, giving her a warning glance to keep her voice down.

"I want to go now," she said.

"I can't."

"Then I'm going."

She could see he was torn between the desire to go and his duty to stay, but the latter, to her disappointment, won out. "Then go," he said.

"You'll come over later?" she asked, trying not to sound as if she was pleading.

He nodded. "An hour," he said. "Two at most." Then, seeing the expression on her face: "As soon as I can."

Back at the hotel, she undressed, flinging Jean-Louis's five-thousand-dollar dress on the floor, furious that she had turned herself into a freak, as if all she had to show for twelve years of hard work and stardom was her tits and her ass. She popped open a bottle of champagne, and took a couple of pills, pacing furiously around the suite, feeling her anger come to a boil. It wasn't just that somebody else was in the President's bed at the Carlyle right now; it was that so much of her life had been spent like this, preparing for days for some event, turning up—always late—to wag her tail and show her tits for the studio, or, in this case, the President, then home in the limo alone, to remove her makeup and her borrowed finery, take her pills and wait for sleep, if it came. . . . How many times, in Hollywood, had she gone straight from the spotlight and the flashbulbs of the press to the studio to hand back her evening gown, as if Marilyn Monroe were a prop, as much a studio invention as Minnie Mouse or Lassie?

She glanced at her watch. She had lost track of the time, and the number of pills she had taken—she was no longer even sure what she was taking them for. She felt drowsy, which was something of a miracle, but of course, she didn't *want* to be drowsy for Bobby's arrival, so she took a couple of pep pills to wake her up, and a Randy-Mandy to get her juices flowing, and, on reflection, a couple of tranks to mellow out her feelings, washing them down with champagne.

She had left her makeup on, and was walking around in her bra and her high heels, occasionally bumping into the furniture—some idiot seemed to have moved it so it was in her way—leaving a trail of spilled champagne behind her, as if to mark her path, and that was the way Bobby Kennedy found her when he finally arrived—on her back on the floor, one shoe on, one shoe off, a big bruise on her thigh and her eyes shut. He thought she was dead.

She could hear his voice, but faintly, and feel his hands as he sought for a pulse or a sign of life with a layman's clumsiness. " . . . get you to a hospital," she heard.

She shook her head feebly. No hospitals, no emergency room—she didn't want that, not here in New York where the press would know it before her stomach was pumped. She was pretty sure he wouldn't want it either, since there wasn't much chance of keeping *his* name out of it.

She managed to whisper David Leman's name. She wasn't sure Bobby had heard her—she couldn't tell whether her voice was working or not—but he must have, because he went off to telephone, then came back with some ice from the champagne bucket wrapped in a hotel napkin, and held it to her head.

She *felt* the cold, which was a sign of life, but it didn't revive her. Bobby went to the bedroom and got a blanket, which he put over her. She blinked to show her gratitude, though in fact she wished he would simply leave her alone.

He sat there on the floor beside her until David's doctor arrived with his hypodermic needle and his stomach pump, to bring her back to life.

"You scared me stiff," Bobby said. He was sitting by the bed, his face haggard and exhausted. He had been up half the night while the doctor worked on her.

"I scared myself." Her throat hurt from the tube the doctor had pushed down it, and her voice was hardly more than a hoarse whisper, which sounded to her like a croak.

"Why did you do it?" His expression was puzzled, as if there was no way he could understand the notion of suicide, no way he could accept it.

Of course, she wasn't sure suicide had been on her mind at all—she never was, after one of these "episodes," as Dr. Greenson liked to call them. There was simply a point at which she not only lost control but lost interest in living, in the future, in herself. It wasn't so much that she was intent on killing herself—it was that dying didn't scare her as much as living. Sometimes she simply couldn't take the pain a moment longer.

Twice during her marriage to Arthur she had tried to kill herself, and both times he had brought her back from the brink. By the end of their marriage, he was like a psychiatric nurse, counting her pills and watching over her like a hawk— he even had the locks removed from the bathroom doors. Johnny Hyde had rescued her a couple of times too—anybody who got close to her sooner or later assumed responsibility for her life, as Bobby, with whatever reluctance, was doing now.

"I didn't do anything," she said. "It just happened, that's all."

"I don't believe that. Is it something I did?"

She shook her head. Why did men always think that? Johnny and Arthur both asked the same question. Did they suppose the only reason a girl could have for taking too many pills was a man? She wanted to tell him it had nothing to do with him, but she was too tired, and besides, that wasn't completely true. If he hadn't kept her waiting, if he'd left the party *with* her, none of it would have happened, or so she told herself.

"Stay with me," she whispered. "For the night. What's left of it." She would sleep in his arms, unafraid, and in the morning, over breakfast, when she felt a little stronger, she would tell him about the baby—*their* baby—and things would be better, the pain would finally recede. . . .

But he shook his head. "Sleep," he said. "I've got to go soon."

When she woke up, he was gone.

She left that evening for Los Angeles, bundled in the back of a limousine on the way to Idlewild Airport, staring out through the tinted glass as if she was never going to see New York again.

46

SHE WAS BACK AT WORK ON MONDAY, TO EVERYBODY'S surprise, and for a week afterward she was on her good behavior, grateful that the studio hadn't put her on suspension for going to New York.

As was so often the case after she had escaped death, she felt stronger and better now, full of new energy, though she knew it was an illusion. She had missed another period, and she could not put off telling Bobby about the baby much longer. She sensed that despite his concern for her, her "episode" with the pills in New York had made him wary of just how high the cost of his affair with her might be, in terms of scandal and bad publicity.

A week after her return to work, she had to shoot a scene in which she swam naked in her husband's pool at night, then started to climb out when he called to her from a window. She was supposed to wear a flesh-colored body stocking so the camera wouldn't actually catch her naked, but once she was in the water, she wriggled out of the suit, which was uncomfortable and silly, and on the spur of the moment, enjoying herself in front of the camera for the first time in years, she swam into movie history—for nobody had ever been filmed naked before in a mainstream Hollywood movie.

Cukor was too surprised to stop her. He called out for more lights and ordered the cameraman to start shooting as she swam back and forth, laughing at her own daring, doing a dog paddle to keep her breasts and her ass just below water. Along the edge of the pool, three still photographers, including Larry Schiller, on assignment from *Paris-Match*, kept their motorized Nikons clicking. She didn't care. She was still 37, 22, 36, even though she was about to turn thirty-six—and pregnant!— and she wanted the world to see her.

The stage was silent except for the click of the cameras, her own splashing, and a lot of heavy breathing; then she began to feel chilled. She cried out, "Here I come, ready or not," and hauled herself out as her wardrobe man rushed forward to drape her blue robe over her. For one second the photographers saw it all—Marilyn Monroe naked, from the front, blond bush and all—then she wrapped the robe tightly around her and waved good-bye.

The next week was her thirty-sixth birthday. The crew threw her a party on the sound stage, but their hearts weren't in it, and neither was hers, and she left early to go to Dodger Stadium to throw out the first ball at a benefit game for the Muscular Dystrophy Association; though she felt depressed and tired, it was a commitment she had made long before.

When she got home, she dialed Bobby on his private line at the Justice Department, where he was working late.

"Happy birthday," he said. He had sent her flowers—unlike the President, who was never a sentimentalist about that kind of thing.

"I missed you," she said.

"I wish I could have been there."

"When can you get out here?"

A pause. A slight hesitation. "It's hard to say."

"I have to see you."

"Well, I know. . . . I've been worried about you. Are you all right?"

"Bobby," she said, "I love you."

"Yes," he said, his voice sad. "I know." She knew how much he disliked being told that she loved him, and understood that it was because he was reluctant to say "I love you" back.

"You don't have to say anything, Bobby," she told him. "Really you don't. I'm not asking for that. I just want to be able to say it to you myself—that I *love* you. You don't even have to say thanks."

"I understand." His voice showed how anxious he was to get off the subject.

She took a deep breath. "Bobby, I have to tell you something very difficult."

"Yes?" His voice was cautious now, a lawyer's voice.

"It's about me." She paused. "About us."

"Look, I'll find a way to get out to LA. It's a promise."

"No, it's not that . . . I mean, that's great, I want to see you. But what I'm trying to tell you is: I'm pregnant."

"Pregnant?"

"You know, going to have a baby?"

"I know what pregnancy means," he said dryly. "How the hell did that happen?"

"Well, the usual way. . . ."

"I see."

Say you're happy about it, she begged him silently, but there was simply a long pause at the other end of the line.

"Jesus," he said at last. Then, after another pause: "You're sure?"

"Sure I'm pregnant, or sure it's yours?" she asked.

"Both."

"Yes."

He let out a long whistle of breath.

"Look," she said, "it's my problem, not yours." She did not really believe that, but she felt obliged to let him off the hook.

"What are you going to do?" he asked, without any suggestion that he might be involved in the decision.

"I think I want to have the baby," she said firmly.

"*Have* the baby?" There was shock in his voice, perhaps even the faintest trace of fear.

"I think so. It's my thirty-sixth birthday. This may be my last chance."

"I never noticed you had the maternal instinct."

"There are a lot of things about women men never notice."

"I'm just not sure it's the smartest move, Marilyn. . . ."

"You're a Catholic. I thought Catholics were against abortion."

"They are. *We* are. I am. But I'm also a politician, a married man, the father of seven children, and the brother of the President of the United States. And you're the most famous woman in the world."

"I'd give that up like a shot. Tomorrow. Tonight. Ethel doesn't love you the way I do. We could have a life together."

"That's just not possible—"

"It *is!*" she cried out fiercely. "It is if you want it to be! And even if it isn't, you could at least say you wish it was! For

God's sake, give me some *hope*, at least," she pleaded, crying now, despite her determination not to. "Tell me that you love me, that you want me, that you'll love the baby, that there's a life ahead for us somehow, that you'll be with me! Tomorrow you can tell me you didn't mean any of it, but tonight I *need* to hear it."

"Take it easy—" he began.

"No!" she shouted. "You've *got* to help me, Bobby! You've got to tell me that it's going to be all right! I swear to God, if you don't, I'm going to take care of it the way I tried to in New York, only this time you won't be around to bring me back."

"Don't even talk about it. . . ."

"You've got no right to tell me what to do!"

"I'm trying to *help* you."

"I know all about that kind of help. That's the kind of help my father gave my mother. He gave her a hundred bucks and told her to get rid of the problem, then walked out and never came back."

"Be sensible, Marilyn. . . ."

Be sensible! How many times had she heard *that*, from men who were only thinking about themselves.

"Good night," she said abruptly, and hung up.

The next day she felt too ill to go to the studio. Dr. Greenson had been told to get over to her house right away, in case of trouble, the message having been passed from Bobby Kennedy to Peter Lawford, and from Lawford to Greenson, accumulating added urgency with repetition.

Greenson had been surprised to find her wearing a black sleep mask and an old black nightgown, lying on her back, with Maf at her feet. He had clearly expected to find her dead or dying. "Everybody was worried about Nembutals," he said. "I told them I'd stopped prescribing them for you a long time ago.

"The studio is going to be upset," he went on. "I wonder, is it wise not to go in?" He pulled his chair up closer. "I hear on the grapevine," he said—she knew every grape on *that* vine!— "that Levathes is going around saying he's had it up to here." He placed the edge of his hand at his throat.

"If he doesn't have me, he doesn't have a movie."

"Maybe he doesn't care anymore. He's taking a lot of heat from New York. There are a few guys on the board who'd like to make an example out of you. Why give them the chance?"

She paid no attention. The stupid movie was the last thing on her mind at the moment. "What do you think of a fella who runs away from the woman who loves him when she gets pregnant?"

"A bad situation."

"I mean, even if the guy is really *important* he shouldn't do that, right?"

Dr. Greenson's expression was wary. "That would depend," he said.

"I mean, even if he's the attorney general of the United States, he ought to stick by her, don't you think? If he really loves her?"

"Perhaps." Greenson was sweating now. "It depends on the circumstances."

"He's a nice guy, actually," she said dreamily. "Bobby, I mean. And I really love him. But he shouldn't make a girl feel that way about him if he doesn't want her. He shouldn't tell a girl he's going to leave his wife if he doesn't mean it, should he?"

"*Did* he tell you that? I find it hard to believe."

"Well, not in so many words, I guess. . . . But I know that's what he *felt*."

Dr. Greenson sighed. "Feelings," he murmured, playing for time. "Feelings are important. You're sure you're in love with him?"

"I love him, all right."

"And how did your conversation with him go? Was he *angry*?"

"No." Bobby hadn't raised his voice. He had sounded, if anything, sad, and a little rattled, of course, which was natural under the circumstances.

"Did he tell you to get rid of the baby?"

"Not really, no," she said, for now that she thought about it, Bobby hadn't told her to do anything of the kind. He had merely asked her if she was going to have the baby—he hadn't told her *not* to. "He said he wouldn't leave Ethel and the children for me."

"One would *expect* him to say that, frankly. Besides, any man in his position—particularly a public figure—is going to be surprised and shocked by this kind of announcement."

"I asked him to play along with me, to tell me he was going to leave Ethel, that I needed to hear it, just to make it through the night, but he wouldn't. . . ."

"Possibly that was a manifestation of responsibility, of *caring*. You asked him to lie to you, and he wouldn't. It seems to me that the stand he took is admirable, if uncomforting. I'm not sure you should have hung up on him, by the way."

"You think I should call him back?" she asked hopefully.

Greenson nodded, forming his fingers into a judicial steeple before his lips. Marilyn Monroe on the telephone talking to Robert Kennedy was a better prospect for survival, he might have been thinking, than Marilyn Monroe alone in her bedroom brooding on his rejection of her.

"It couldn't hurt," he said.

Washington KL 5-8210, Washington KL 5-8210, Washington KL 5-8210—again and again she gave the number to the operator, placing a dozen or more calls in an hour, sometimes only a couple of minutes apart, desperate to reach him, desperate to hold him on the phone when she was put through.

He did not avoid her—sometimes he was unavailable, in conference, or out of the building, but his secretary, Angie Novello, was invariably polite and helpful, and when he could, Bobby always picked up the phone and talked to her, sometimes at length, though never about the subject that concerned her the most.

Dr. Greenson had been right—once the initial shock of the news of her pregnancy had worn off, Bobby was his usual caring self, listening to her troubles, telling her he would make plans to come out to California. . . . She should take care of herself and not worry. When he got there, they would talk about it. . . .

When? she asked. In a couple of weeks, tops, he told her. Things, he assumed, could wait until then? The thing that concerned her could certainly wait that long—though not much longer, as she pointed out.

She scribbled a few lines in her notebook. She had bought it years ago, with the intention of writing a diary, but she had neither the time nor the discipline to keep one. Sometimes she wrote down her thoughts—"In life death seems like an illusion; perhaps in death life seems like an illusion," she had written early on, along with poems that had caught her fancy, like the ancient Indian love poem that ended:

> *For this is the Wisdom; to love, to live,*
> *To take what fate, or the Gods, may give,*
> *To ask no question, to make no prayer,*
> *To kiss the lips and caress the hair,*
> *Speed passion's ebb as you greet its flow—*
> *To have—to hold—and—in—time—let go!*

She flipped through the notebook—there were whole periods of her life, years sometimes, when she had written nothing in it at all, others when she filled pages. Not many, she reflected ruefully, saddened by the thought that you could compress all the wisdom and the poetry of a lifetime into half the pages of a diary.

"Bobby," she wrote, and underlined it twice, then enclosed it in a heart. Then:

> *"When I'm in his arms*
> *I feel safe!*
> *When I'm in his arms*
> *I can sleep!*
> *When I'm in his arms*
> *I dream of life,*
> *Not death!!!!"*

She read it over and underlined the word "death" several times. She liked it more than the Indian poem, she decided.

Late in the afternoon, she took a couple of the cold pills that Mrs. Murray had bought for her at the Brentwood Pharmacy, and drifted off into the kind of uncomfortable doze that a bad cold produces. She woke to the sound of the telephone ringing beside her.

She picked up the receiver groggily and shoved it between her shoulder and her ear. "Hi, Bobby," she said in a sexy, sleepy voice.

There was a moment of silence at the other end, and then a voice that wasn't Bobby's said: "Ah, this is Peter Denby, Miss Monroe. Of the *Los Angeles Times*."

She came to with a start. It occurred to her, too late, that it had been some time since she had bothered to change her private number. She knew Denby, who reported on movie industry news. Denby was a Brit, and had been one of those who grilled her so relentlessly when she arrived in England to make *The Prince and the Showgirl*—she remembered a florid face above a polka-dot bow tie.

"I wondered," he went on, in his plummy English voice, "If you had any comment on tonight's news."

"What news?"

"Surely you've *heard?* Twentieth Century-Fox has fired you. You're off the picture."

"Fired? I don't believe it." She was wide awake now.

"I have it from an impeccable source. One of the Fox executives said, 'It's time to draw the line—the inmates are taking over the asylum.' Any comment on *that?*"

She couldn't think of anything to say. Was the studio saying she was *crazy?* She couldn't imagine it—there was no crueler remark anyone could have made about her. She felt . . . She wasn't sure *what* she felt—one emotion kept bubbling up on top of another in quick succession, like lava from a volcano: anger, pain, shame, fear. She could hardly even hold the telephone, she was so shaken.

"You must have seen it coming a mile away, surely?" Denby went on cheerfully. "They're weeks behind schedule." He pronounced it "shed-you-ell" to her temporary bewilderment. "At least a million dollars over budget. They screened your footage last night, all of it, and Levathes said it wasn't a performance—there was hardly anything they could use. They're going to sue you, I hear. . . . Hello?"

"Sue me?"

"Oh my, yes. Sure to, I should think. May I say that you were 'shocked and bewildered'?"

"I don't have anything to say."

" 'Shocked and bewildered, Marilyn refused to comment.' Right-o."

"No, wait!" She couldn't let him go without saying something, couldn't let the studio blacken *her* reputation without any reply from her. "You can write I said it's time some of the studio heads realized what they're doing. If there's anything wrong with Hollywood, it starts at the top. And something else. It seems to me it's time they stopped knocking their assets around."

He read her quote back to her. "Any plans for the future?" he asked.

"As soon as I'm well enough, I'm going back to work and finish this picture," she said. "This is all just bullshit."

"I can't use that," he said briskly, and hung up.

The telephone rang again instantly. She wondered why Mrs. Murray didn't pick it up. Then she remembered that Mrs. Murray had gone out to see a movie. She got up, took the phone into the living room, went back to her bedroom, and closed the door. Hundreds of journalists and columnists were surely trying to reach her, and she couldn't talk to all of them. She lay in bed listening to the constant ringing of both telephones, feeling worse and worse. To be rejected by the studio! After sixteen years of working at Fox! The studio had given her her *name*, for God's sake!

She went back into the bathroom, took a handful of pills, lay down in bed again, and covered her ears with the pillows.

The next day Peter Levathes gave a press conference, calling her "unreliable," and threatening to sue her for half a million or a million dollars because her chronic and disruptive lateness had made it impossible to complete the picture. There were even rumors that her costumes were being altered for Lee Remick so she could take her place and shooting could resume.

Bitter and hurt, she stayed at home, relying on Eunice Murray to drive her to her daily session with Dr. Greenson. Her telephone numbers had been swiftly changed, so at least she was able to call out—though the downside was that none of her friends now knew her number, and she didn't have the energy to give it to them, so the house was often as still as a tomb, just herself and Maf, with Mrs. Murray brooding silently in the kitchen.

She had hoped for some demonstration of affection and support, but there was nothing, or next to nothing—no flowers, no telegrams, no offers from other studios. True, Dino let it be known that he had signed on to do a Marilyn Monroe picture and wouldn't work with Lee Remick, which was nice, but that meant the picture had to be shelved, and in the movie industry that was as bad as things could get.

Since Bobby, happily, wasn't in show business, he had no idea of the extent of her disgrace in Hollywood. For him, it was just a labor dispute in an industry he didn't understand or take seriously. She was a star, so it would all work out, he told her every time she called.

The subject of her baby (*their* baby, she reminded herself), he avoided. He had other problems, and she was happy enough to listen to them. He was bored and restless, sorry he had ever agreed to take the job of attorney general. Everywhere he looked, he told her, he saw failure: he had been unable to get past Hoover to reform the FBI; Hoffa was still free, as were his gangster friends; the administration was dragging its feet on civil rights, so that southern blacks were beginning to talk about demonstrating against the Kennedys instead of the racists. . . .

"It's the winter of our discontent," he said sadly—he had been reading a lot of Shakespeare lately, as part of his perpetual self-improvement scheme—even though it was in fact summer.

He was to address a convention of federal prison wardens in Boulder, Colorado, toward the end of the month, he told her, and might detour to Los Angeles on his way back.

It was the only thing that kept her going in those bleak days after she was fired—the thought that Bobby was going to make things come out right for her. . . .

I was in London when I learned that Marilyn had been fired by Fox. I wasn't surprised. She had never disguised her dislike of the picture from the very beginning, and the chemistry between herself and Cukor was all wrong. I'm not sure Peter Levathes and the Fox board were to blame either—at that moment in her life it's possible that nobody could have coaxed a picture out of Marilyn. I called her immediately, but I was unable to get through.

I called again from New York, with no better luck. Much as I disliked him, I called Lawford, who told me that while Marilyn was "upset," she was basically okay, an opinion with which my friend Ike Lublin agreed. "It could be the best thing for her," Lublin said, with the built-in optimism of a show business lawyer. "That picture was a piece of shit anyhow."

I might not have taken Marilyn's problems so much to heart if I hadn't had a call from an old friend of mine in LA, one of the many liberal academics mauled by Joe McCarthy and his witch hunters, who had fled to become the host of a late-night radio call-in show. Folksy, unshockable, and intelligent, Alan Burke had become a minor cult figure in Los Angeles, at any rate among insomniacs, to his own surprise. He didn't waste words with me—once upon a time, we had known each other too well for that. "You know Marilyn Monroe, don't you?" he asked. I said I did. "You'd recognize her voice?" I said I would.

"Well, listen to this." I heard the click of a tape recorder, then that unmistakable soft, breathless little voice. *I'm going to marry a very important man in government. He's going to leave his wife for me.*

Alan spoke next. *What's your name, dear?*

Marilyn.

Like Marilyn Monroe?

A low giggle. *That's right.*

And what do you do?

I'm an actress. Or I was. Another giggle. *I just got fired.*

And who's the 'important man in government'? Can you tell me?

A pause. I could hear Marilyn's breathing on the tape. *Bobby Kennedy. . . . Whoops! I guess I shouldn't have said that.* There was a click as she hung up.

"Jesus!" I said.

"It's her, isn't it?"

"It *sounds* like her. Is this the only call?"

"No. She calls every night, sometimes a couple of times a night. She says she's pregnant and that Bobby is the father. Listen, there's more. She asked if she could *meet* me. I sounded so sympathetic on the air she *had* to see me face-to-face. . . . Well, you know, I don't like doing that at all. A lot of the people out there are cranks and loonies, so you never know who you're going to meet. . . . Still, she sounded so desperate that I said okay. Besides, I figured what the hell, it might turn out to be Marilyn. . . ."

"And did it?"

"No question. She met me in the bar of the Hollywood Brown Derby, round the corner from the studio. It was Marilyn, all right."

"What did she say?"

"We talked for a couple of hours. She told me a lot about Bobby Kennedy and the President, really intimate stuff, and it sounded to me as if she knew what she was talking about. I remember her saying, 'I've had fame, all I ever needed and more. What I want now is happiness, and I'm going to find it or die.' "

"Was she drunk, do you think?"

"No, I don't think she was drunk. She had a glass of white wine with me, that's all. She sounded like somebody who'd just landed on earth from some other planet, but not drunk, no."

"What have you done with these tapes?"

"Nothing. Listen, forget about the tapes, David. I've got an audience of half a million people out there every night, listening to her saying Bobby Kennedy is the father of her child, and that he's planning to leave Ethel for her. Sooner or later somebody's going to notice."

"Could you stop taking her calls?"

"No," he snapped with a trace of anger. "That would be unprofessional, David. Besides, I'm not sure it isn't the calls that are keeping her *alive,* frankly. This is a very crazy, very lonely lady. She needs help. That's why I'm calling. I don't want to be responsible for her killing herself, thank you."

"I wasn't suggesting that, Alan. . . ."

"Yes you were," he said without rancor. "I know who you work for. Don't forget—Bobby's not a hero to me. He's just another of the vicious little shits who drove me out of my job because I wouldn't name names to the Committee. There isn't a bit of difference between him and Roy Cohn, and Jack was just as gutless as the rest of the Senate when it came to McCarthy. If you want to worship the Kennedys, David, be my guest, but don't expect me to. I know too many people whose lives were ruined. My own among them."

"I understand."

"Then understand that I'm not going to keep Marilyn off the air to protect Bobby's reputation as a faithful husband. I'm on *her* side."

"So am I."

"In what way?"

"I don't want her to get hurt."

There was a pause as Alan digested this. "Yes," he said. "They're just the people to hurt her too, I should think. Can you stop it?"

"I don't know. I'll try."

"I won't stop taking her calls, but I'll try to steer her off the subject as much as I can."

"I'm grateful, Alan. For *her* sake. I'll be in Los Angeles tomorrow, at the Beverly Hills Hotel, if you need me."

"I thought you just got in from London."

"I did," I said grimly, at the thought of another long flight.

I tried to call Bobby, but he was in the air on the way to Hyannis. I *did* reach the President, who was already there, and testy about being disturbed with a telephone call. "I'm about to go sailing," he said. "This had better be good."

"It's not good, Mr. President. It's about Marilyn."

"I heard they fired her at the studio. That's a shame. How is she taking it?"

"It's hard to say. I thought I'd go out there and find out. Has Bobby talked to you about her?" I asked.

"He showed me a strange telegram she sent him. She was invited to a dinner Bobby and Ethel gave for Peter and Pat at Hickory Hill—which seems like a pretty dumb idea to begin with, in the circumstances—and she sent her regrets. . . . Wait a minute, Bobby gave me a copy. . . . Here it is."

There was a pause, I guessed while he put his reading glasses on. " 'Dear Attorney General and Mrs. Robert Kennedy: I would have been delighted to have accepted your invitation honoring Pat and Peter Lawford. Unfortunately I am involved in a freedom ride protesting the loss of the minority rights belonging to the few remaining earthbound stars. After all, all we demanded was our right to twinkle. Marilyn Monroe.' "

He cleared his throat nervously. "What do you make of that?"

"It may have to do with her being fired. Fox took away her right to twinkle? That would fit."

"That's what I thought."

"There's another possibility. It might have to do with Bobby."

"What's that?"

I explained to him about the calls she had been making to Alan's late-night call-in show.

"Christ!" he said. "She's gone nuts."

"It's a possibility."

"You don't think it's *true*, do you?"

"About her being pregnant? It could be, sure."

He was silent for a moment. "Just because she's having an affair with Bobby doesn't mean he's the father. We've all been through that kind of thing."

All too often, I thought, in Jack's case, remembering many scrapes with fatherhood from which his father had extricated him. "It's possible," I said. "Either way, it's not a story you want in print."

"God no!" There was another pause.

"Will you talk to Bobby about it? He's playing with fire."

I heard Jackie's voice in the background, and then the President said, "I'll take it under advisement and discuss the matter with the Attorney General." His voice was clipped and formal, the chief executive at work. "In the meantime, keep me advised of any, ah, developments."

"I guess it's not the moment to give Jackie my best."

"Thank you for your concern," Jack said crisply, and hung up.

I should have guessed—and was later to discover—that since my old friend Alan had once been associated with left-wing causes and briefly married to the daughter of what used to be called "a card-carrying" member of the Communist party, his broadcasts were regularly taped by the FBI, just in case he uttered some subversive statement on the air.

Thus Marilyn's late-night calls came to the attention of J. Edgar Hoover, who took the trouble to order a quick search of her gynecologist's files.

He was soon able to inform the President that, in this particular case at any rate, the lady wasn't lying—pregnant she definitely was, whoever the father might be.

47

OF COURSE, I DIDN'T KNOW THAT THE FBI WAS ALREADY aware of Marilyn's pregnancy—and of the presumed father—when I arrived in Los Angeles, on a day of blistering heat. I called her as soon as I was settled into my suite. When she came on the phone, she sounded astonishingly cheerful. I invited her out to dinner, and from her reaction, you would have thought nobody had asked her out for years.

Assuming that Marilyn probably wanted to stay out of the public eye, I suggested a couple of discreet little restaurants I knew she was fond of, but they turned out not to be what she had in mind at all. "Oh, come *on*, David!" she said. "You can do better than that!"

"I just thought . . ."

"I *know* what you thought. I'm tired of hiding away. Let's go out and have a little fun!"

"How about Chasen's?"

"That's your idea of fun? It's full of has-been actors having dinner with their wives. Let's eat someplace glamorous, then go dancing or something—make a *night* of it, you know?"

"Romanoff's?"

"Better—for a start, baby." She gave me a noisy kiss over the telephone. "We'll paint the town!"

Her voice was loud—alarmingly so, considering how small and soft it normally was. Most of the time when Marilyn was on the phone, I felt as if I needed a hearing aid.

"Eight?" I said.

A giggle. "Nine." She hung up.

It should not have surprised me that at nine forty-five I was still chatting with Mike Romanoff and sipping my second dry martini. "Who's joining you?" he asked.

"Marilyn Monroe."

He whistled. "Maybe you should order a shrimp cocktail,

or something. Punctual, she's not."

"I know."

I buttered another breadstick and tried not to check my watch again. I had ample time to look around the restaurant—one of the last establishments in Beverly Hills where people still dressed for the evening as if they were in New York.

It didn't seem like Marilyn's kind of place—Romanoff's was a restaurant for the "old guard." Sinatra and his pals, or Brando and *his*, wouldn't have been caught dead here. But then, I reflected, Marilyn had never wanted to be an outsider—*her* struggle was for acceptance by the Hollywood old guard. For her, Romanoff's represented some part of that world to which she had craved acceptance all her life, ever since the days when she had stared out the windows of the Los Angeles orphanage at the RKO lot next door.

There was a collective gasp from around the room, and I looked up just as Marilyn was making her entrance. Her hair was bleached a pale platinum, with hardly a trace of blond in it; her face was made up as if for filming. She was wearing a short evening dress of glittering black sequins, suspended precariously from her shoulders by the narrowest of spaghetti straps.

I stood up and gave her a kiss, unable to stop myself from thinking that I was the envy of every man in the room. "You look good enough to eat," I said.

"That was the idea." She sat down next to me on the banquette, ignoring all the people who were smiling or waving to her. This wasn't rudeness, by the way—Marilyn was shy and nearsighted, a combination that made table-hopping, or even table-waving, difficult for her. Mike popped open a bottle of Dom Pérignon for her, beaming when she tasted it as if he had trodden the grapes for it himself. She nodded at him—has there ever been such a thing, I wondered, as a *bad* bottle of Dom Pérignon, and would Marilyn have known the difference? "Do you know who first brought me here?" she asked.

I shook my head.

"Johnny Hyde. Poor little Johnny. He took me out and bought me new clothes, specially for the occasion. 'I'm gonna show you off, kid,' he told me. Did I have stage fright!" She laughed. "Johnny had *class*, you know, so he wanted *me* to have class."

She drained her champagne. There was an edge of bitterness in her voice—certainly not sentimentality or nostalgia. The captain came over, and I started to shoo him away, but she said she was hungry. She ordered a shrimp cocktail, a rare filet mignon, baked potato, and a Caesar salad—Vegas food.

"Did you have a good time?" I asked. "When Johnny took you here for the first time?"

Her eyes were sad, and strangely opaque, as if she were looking inward, still hurt and bewildered by what she saw there. "It was awful," she said, shaking her head. "Johnny had taken me to I. Magnin's, and bought me a dress, bare-shouldered, with this big wide skirt and a kind of matching wrap, and shoes the same color, sort of the Dior look, I guess, the kind of thing his wife would have bought, and I felt like a little girl dressed up in her mother's clothes. . . . And everybody in the restaurant stared at me, you know? I could almost hear them whispering, 'So *that's* the girl Johnny left his wife for!' Johnny liked to table-hop, you know—he was an agent, after all—but *nobody* came over to the table that night, and I could tell it bothered Johnny. I mean, people could accept that he had a girlfriend—what guy in his position didn't?—but here he was, bringing *me,* the girlfriend, to Romanoff's, and that wasn't *done.* Romanoff's was where you took your *wife,* see, not your girlfriend."

I thought she might be about to cry, but then her shrimp cocktail was served, and she ate it hungrily, picking up each jumbo shrimp by the tail between her long, bright red fingernails and dipping it in Russian dressing. She ate quickly, still at heart the girl from the wrong side of the tracks out on a lucky date with a big spender, afraid she might be asked to leave before she'd finished her meal.

"All the guys in my life have wanted to teach me things," she said sadly. "And I'm still the same dumb blonde I always was."

"You're not a dumb blonde."

"Not as dumb as people think, no. But I always ask myself— if men love me as much as they say they do, why is it that the first thing they want to do is change me? I'll say one thing for Jack—he never tried to teach me a thing."

"And Bobby?"

"Let's not talk about Bobby, okay? I will say this for him:

unlike Jack, Bobby's the reforming type. He figures it's his responsibility to save me."

"From what?"

She looked at me with a certain amount of pity. "From myself, sugar," she answered. "What else?"

The next course was served, and she cut her steak with quick, sharp slashes—nothing delicate in her approach to it. "You're a nice guy, David," she said between bites. "I can *talk* to you."

She resumed her reminiscence. "I cried in the ladies' room that night. Sobbed my twenty-two-year-old heart out, sitting in a toilet stall in my sapphire-blue grown-up Dior look-alike. It was supposed to be my big night, and I could tell everybody was whispering that I was just some no-talent *bimbo* who was fucking Johnny Hyde."

She finished the steak except for a few scraps, which she asked the waiter to wrap up for her. I told him to give it to my chauffeur. Marilyn might not mind walking out of a restaurant with a doggie bag of leftovers, but I did.

I ordered another bottle of champagne, and since Marilyn had signified her intention to eat what she called "a killer dessert," I asked the captain to prepare crepes suzette.

She clapped her hands together and squealed with pleasure. "You're a *mind* reader!" she cried. "I've got to go to the ladies' room." Her walk was so sexy that the entire room fell silent, but I noticed a certain unsteadiness to it.

By the time she returned, the captain was setting up his chafing dish. Marilyn's walk had become steadier—so much so that she almost seemed to float across the room, though it seemed to me that she had a little trouble navigating around obstacles.

She dropped herself onto the banquette seat so hard that she bounced. "Whoosh!" she said, just as the captain, who had been waiting for her return, put a match to the crepes, sending a burst of flames high into the air.

It caught her by surprise and she let out a blood-curdling scream that brought all conversation to an instant halt. She threw her arms around me and pressed her face against my shoulder. I could feel her breasts, only barely restrained by the thin fabric, against my chest, the nipples, perhaps from the shock, noticeably hard. Glancing down, I couldn't help noticing that her skirt had ridden up, exposing her soft, pale thighs and her stocking tops, fastened to the thin, white suspender straps of her garter belt.

I held her tightly. She looked up at me and opened one eye. "Oh, Jesus!" she wailed. "I've made a fool of myself again."

Actually, I thought her behavior was charming. I reflected that poor Johnny Hyde had been wasting his time on the Pygmalion and Galatea act so far as Marilyn was concerned.

"I do that every time," she said. She straightened up, but remained close to me, her thigh pressed against mine, an out-of-place wisp of hair across her face. She brushed it back, oohed and aahed at her crepes, and wolfed them down as if she hadn't eaten for ages.

We were most of the way through the second bottle of champagne before I brought up the question of the calls she was making. She looked at me blankly. "What calls?" she asked, eyes wide open.

The possibility that she might be genuinely crazy flashed through my mind. I dismissed it.

I mentioned Alan's name, and reminded her that she had gone to meet him. "I've never heard of him," she said.

"He said you've been calling the show every night."

"Me?" She stuck her fork in my crepes and raised an eyebrow.

I nodded. She finished the sauce off my plate with a spoon, then emptied her champagne glass, and mine.

I was about to press her further on the subject, but she leaned her head against my shoulder and said, "Let's go dancing, darling."

It was not an offer I could easily refuse. In her head Marilyn seemed to be dancing already. Her eyes closed, her arm around my waist, I could feel her body moving to a rhythm only she could hear; her lips puckered in a silent whistle, as if she were following the tune. She was unbuttoning my white vest in an absentminded way, as if not even aware that her hand was busy. I didn't move, caught between the hope that she would get to work on the buttons of my fly and the fear of her doing it in front of everyone at Romanoff's. "Loosen up," she said dreamily. "I don't know why you wear so many clothes. What's the point of a vest, anyway?"

I couldn't think of an immediate answer to that one. "It holds the stomach in, I suppose," I said. I sucked in my gut sharply, but of course, it wasn't going to stay sucked in for long.

"I think a little belly in a man is *cute*," Marilyn said, mercifully removing her fingers.

"Where does one go dancing these days?" I asked.

She laughed. " 'One'? That sounds so—British. Where do *you* like to go?"

I hadn't gone dancing in Los Angeles for many years. I had a vague memory of the Ambassador—I remembered dancing there one evening with Grace Kelly, then an unknown young actress, to the music of Freddy Martin's band, and meeting his singer afterward, a fresh-faced kid called Merv Griffin. "The last place I remember going to was the Ambassador," I admitted.

"Oh, God," she said. "The Ambassador!" She laughed, a trifle unsteadily—a high-pitched, brittle sound, not very loud, like a crystal glass breaking on a carpeted floor. "Does it still exist?"

"I don't know. Probably. But not the way it was."

"Let's go," she said. "I'll pick the place."

She was silent for a long time on the drive down Sunset Boulevard to Malibu—where she had told the driver to go—holding my hand in hers in the back of the limousine. The doggie bag for Maf was on the floor by her feet, as well as a bottle of champagne in an ice bucket, which I had asked the restaurant to place in the car. She sipped it as if refueling her spirits, which had sagged at the mention of the Ambassador Hotel. "Do you think people change?" she asked suddenly, as if she had been thinking about the question ever since we left Romanoff's.

"No. Not in my experience. Not in any way that matters."

I thought she was referring to Jack or Bobby, or some other man in her life, past or present, but I was wrong. It was herself she was thinking about. "You don't think you can just stop being whatever you were, and become something else?"

"Turn over a new leaf? I suppose. People try. But most change is on the surface, I think. In the end, we're always the same person, in a new suit, a new marriage, a new job."

"God, I hope you're wrong!" she said.

The car pulled off the Pacific Coast Highway. We stopped

at a kind of Hawaiian beach hut with a fake palm-frond roof and a carved totem pole on either side of the front door, like those that guarded the entrance to Trader Vic's. A neon sign gave the name of the place: "The Tahiti Club."

I had never heard of it, but Marilyn was obviously at home here. She swept out of the car, carrying the bottle of champagne, as I followed behind her. A grinning doorman, dressed in a faded beachcomber's outfit and a frayed straw hat, opened the door for us, releasing a blast of loud music and hot, smoky air into the cool, damp California night. Marilyn plunged into the noisy semidarkness, holding up the champagne bottle, and shouted, "Another one of these!"

We were led through the gloom to a small booth. As my eyes adjusted, I could see the place was decorated with the usual Polynesian artifacts: I had a dim impression of palm fronds, fishing nets, stuffed fish, and carved masks. From the rafters a war canoe was hung—or a papier-mâché studio prop version of one, anyway. There were half a dozen couples on the small dance floor and a live orchestra packed onto a tiny stage disguised as a beachcomber's hut. Most of the action was at the bar, which was jammed three deep.

Marilyn went off to the ladies' room, while I sat down. The place was so dark that her journey across the room hardly caused a ripple, although on the way back, as some of the lights caught her, there were a few whistles. She sat down opposite me, looking more cheerful, I thought, her eyes glittering again—though the pupils were mere pinpoints.

The captain, a swarthy fellow who looked like a hood, snapped his fingers and an ice bucket appeared, with a bottle of Dom Pérignon. "Johnny's compliments, Miss Monroe," he said.

"Who's Johnny?" I asked her as he popped it open with his thumbs.

"Johnny Roselli."

I stared at her through the hazy gloom. "Johnny Roselli? The gangster? You *know* him?"

She looked defensive. "He isn't such a bad guy."

I let that pass. Roselli was a very bad guy, even by the standards of bad guys—generally supposed to be the point man for the Chicago mob's penetration of the West Coast. Like all mobsters, he had built up a small empire of his own, which allegedly centered around narcotics and illegal gambling. "How on earth did you meet Roselli?" I asked.

Marilyn was swaying to the music, eyes half closed, drinking champagne. "I've known him for years."

"From where?" Marilyn's breadth of acquaintances fascinated me.

She frowned. "He was a friend of Joe Schenck's." She looked at me and giggled. "Well, maybe not exactly a *friend*, you know? Joe was paying off Willie Bioff—so much a month and Bioff made sure there weren't any strikes at Fox. Everybody did it. Joe just got caught, that's all."

"What did Roselli have to do with it?"

"Johnny was the bagman. He picked up the money for Bioff. Then Joe got worried that the Feds might be watching him, so he used to send me around to Johnny with the payoffs. That's how Johnny and I became friends. I used to go around to his house a couple of times a month, with a big paper bag full of money in a canvas tote."

I was speechless. From the way she was smiling, that secretive smile, eyes half closed, I could guess that she had almost certainly fucked Roselli while she was delivering Joe Schenck's money to him. The thought of the young Marilyn in the arms of such a thug dismayed me.

She grabbed my hand and pulled me onto the dance floor, then put her arms around my neck and closed her eyes. It was sexy enough—she was pressed hard against me—but I couldn't help thinking that if she didn't hold on, she would slump to the floor.

I wondered if she had taken anything while she was in the ladies' room. It also occurred to me, belatedly, that there might be something stronger than booze for sale in any nightclub owned by Johnny Roselli—that the dim lighting was probably only one of the attractions of the Tahiti Club.

"Do you come here often?" I asked.

Marilyn had a little trouble focusing on the question, but she did her best. "Used to," she said, her words slightly slurred. "Peter Lawford's house is just down the road. Came here with Jack all the time."

"Jack? Here? While he was a senator, I guess. . . ."

She giggled, and slowly drew a fingertip down my nose to my lips. "He's been here since he was elected president," she said. "The Secret Service went bananas, but he insisted. He liked to come here at night, to dance. Lunchtime, he likes it across the street, at the Sip-N-Surf Bar, where all the surfer girls hang out."

The notion of Jack dancing in a nightclub—a roadhouse, really—owned by Johnny Roselli was chilling.

We were dancing slowly now, Marilyn's head on my shoulder, her feet moving to the rhythm as if they were on automatic pilot. "Marilyn," I whispered, "talking about Jack . . . and Bobby. . . . How are things going?"

"What things?" Her voice was muffled, since her mouth was pressed against my neck.

"Well, you and Bobby. . . . This story that you're pregnant?"

"Where did you hear that?"

"On the radio."

"It's supposed to be a secret."

"So it's true?" I asked.

"Mm."

"And it *is* Bobby's?"

"Nobody else's, lamb chop. Cross my heart. I can tell."

"How?"

"It's just something I can feel happening when it happens. I felt it with Bobby and I knew we'd just made a baby."

"What does Bobby think?"

"He's thrilled."

"He is?"

"You bet. *You* don't sound too thrilled, though." There was a sharp edge to her voice.

"No, no," I said quickly, "I *am,* really! I just wondered what you plan to do."

"He's going to leave Ethel and marry me."

I held her a little more tightly as we danced, or rather swayed together, in the darkness. "Are you sure?" I asked gently. "He'd be destroying his career, you know."

"He'll do it for me," she said dreamily.

"If he *doesn't,* you know, you can always count on me."

"Mm. I know that, baby."

"I mean *really,* Marilyn. Now. Always. You know how I feel about you. . . ."

She raised her head and looked at me, a trace of suspicion

in her gray-blue eyes. "David," she said, "are you putting the make on me?"

I felt myself blush. "I guess I am."

"I thought you were my friend."

"I *am* your friend."

"No. You just want to fuck me, that's all. That's why you're telling me that Bobby isn't going to leave Ethel. That's a shitty thing to do."

It took me a moment to master my emotions. Marilyn was right—I did want to fuck her—but I also cared for her enough to want her to know the truth. I tried to get her to see reason—or what I took for reason, anyway.

"He isn't going to leave Ethel, Marilyn. You know that as well as I do."

"He *is* too!" She pulled away from my embrace, so that we were standing in the center of the dance floor, facing each other. "You're jealous," she said. "That's all. You know what your problem is.? You've wanted to fuck me ever since the night we met, at Charlie Feldman's party. And the joke is, you missed your chance when you had it."

I looked at her, puzzled. "*What* chance?" I asked.

"I would have fucked you in the library, that night at Josh Logan's party, when the president of Indo whatever the fuck it was tried to make me, but you didn't even *notice!* You missed your chance, David. You should have taken it when it was going, lover." She spoke the word "lover" with contempt.

She laughed—a loud, hurtful laugh, not the breathy, musical little laugh that I always found so sexy.

I tried to cast my mind back to that evening, so long ago, and for the life of me I couldn't remember having had even a clue that Marilyn was attracted to me. I could remember every detail of the room, I could remember exactly what she was wearing when she entered it, surprising me while I was admiring Bill Goetz's collection of bronzes—but I had no memory at all of the moment when, if Marilyn was to be believed, she had been willing to fuck me.

I was speechless with anger, at myself for having missed the one opportunity she had offered me over the years—worse, for not even having *noticed* it—at her for never giving me another chance. Over the years, I thought—how many? Six? Seven?—how often she must have laughed at me, the schmuck who had missed his chance and didn't even know it! Had she told Jack, too? Had they laughed at me together? "I don't believe you," I said furiously.

"Oh, you'd *better* believe it, David!" She glared at me. She looked demented, I thought. "You could have *had* me, right there on the sofa, I'm telling you. You've been sniffing around me all these years, and you didn't even know how close you were." She laughed hysterically.

I have a horror of scenes in public places, and in an instinctive effort to get Marilyn off the dance floor, where she was very conspicuous indeed, I grabbed her wrist. It was a mistake. Eyes blazing, she took a step back and slapped me.

I rubbed my flaming cheek, while she continued to glare at me, arms crossed in front of her chest, eyes now black as obsidian in the purple light above the dance floor.

"Bobby isn't going to leave Ethel for you," I said—sorry I'd said it even as the words came out of my mouth. "You have to know that."

"You should have fucked me, David," she said, more calmly now. "I still might not have loved you, but you'd have liked me a whole lot better than you do."

She shook her head. "I'll find my own way home," she said, and turning on her heel, she walked off into the gloom, leaving me alone on the dance floor.

They gave me a bill for the bottle of Dom Pérignon. I guess it was only a gift from the management if Marilyn stayed with me for the evening.

I slipped the money into the leather folder the bill had been presented in. "Give my best to Johnny Roselli," I said. "And see that Miss Monroe gets home safely."

The maître d's expression was carved in stone as he pocketed the folded-up bill I slipped him. "Johnny who?" he asked.

I wrote "I'm sorry" on the doggie bag from Romanoff's and asked the driver to leave it outside Marilyn's front door in Brentwood after he left me at my hotel, but she didn't call me the next day, and Mrs. Murray wouldn't put me through to her.

I flew back to New York, and tried to put the whole scene out of my mind.

48

"WHAT'S THE MANDATORY FEDERAL RETIREMENT AGE?"
Jack Kennedy asked crisply.

"Sixty-five."

The two brothers were sitting by the pool in the family compound at Hyannis Port, in swimming trunks. The President had a towel around his shoulders and a gob of sun cream on his nose. His chair was surrounded by discarded newspapers and news magazines. There was a briefcase at his feet.

"On the button," Jack said without a smile. He raised his sunglasses and rummaged briefly among the documents in his case. He held up a piece of paper. "This," he said, "is a handwritten letter from me exempting a certain federal employee from the mandatory retirement age. Can you guess who it is?"

Bobby stared glumly at the piece of paper, his Adam's apple bobbing. "I can guess," he said.

"Good for you. And can you guess *why* your president—the Leader of the Free World, who has bigger things to worry about—had to write J. Edgar Hoover a personal letter assuring him that he can remain on as director of the F-fucking-B-fucking-I until he drops?"

"Yes."

"Yes? Would that be because Hoover's men dug up the story that Marilyn is pregnant, with *your* child? That she's telling everybody you're going to leave Ethel for her?"

Bobby nodded wearily.

"It isn't just Hoover either, though that's bad enough. I had David on the phone telling me about some late-night radio show in LA she's been telling her troubles to. And she turned up at Peter's house in Malibu last night, to tell *him* her story. Pat saw her in the morning, and said she seemed 'confused.' To use Pat's exact word."

"It's all horseshit."

"Is it? She *is* pregnant. Hoover's guys, with their usual care for the constitutional niceties, broke into her gynecologist's office and photographed her file—to protect *you,* of course." He laughed mirthlessly. "*Is* it yours?"

"I don't know. I guess it might be."

"Wonderful." Jack looked across the pool at his father, who was taking the sun in his wheelchair, a Panama hat on his head, his hands grasping the arms of the chair like a bird's claws on its perch.

Jack waved to him with a big grin, but all his father could do was grimace in return. He sighed. "I don't know what *he'd* tell you to do, Bobby, but what *I'm* going to tell you is to get rid of this problem, *fast.* Tell Marilyn it's over. Be as tough as you have to, but make sure she understands it."

"And the baby?"

"And the baby? What's the *matter* with you? Christ, I always thought 'fucking your brains out' was just a *phrase.* Are you planning to stand up and acknowledge the kid, like a proud father? Are you going to ditch Ethel?"

"You know goddamn well I'm not." Bobby's face was scarlet with anger—and perhaps shame.

"Then don't sit there pissing and moaning about Marilyn's kid. Tell her to get rid of it. Tell her it isn't yours. Tell her whatever you like, *but get her to shut up!* Do I make myself clear?"

"Yes."

"Then do it." The President leaned back in the sun. In the distance there were the shouts of children playing noisily, and the sound of the waves breaking against the beach. He looked relaxed and content, but his voice when he spoke again had an edge to it. "I know it's tough," he said. "Nobody knows that better than me! You really loved her, didn't you?" He put it in the past tense with a precision that made it clear it was deliberate and not a slip of the tongue.

"Yes, I do."

Jack ignored his brother's defiance. "So did I," he continued softly. "And it's going to make you feel really *shitty,* breaking it off. All that guilt is going to hurt, believe me."

Bobby nodded. The noise of the children was coming closer, and he shaded his eyes against the sun to look for them.

"Well, that's okay," his brother said. "You *should* feel shitty. It's appropriate, and good for the soul. Look, she's a terrific girl, one of the best. Maybe *the* best. . . . It's like having an ice cream sundae—you were *entitled* to it. . . . You want my opinion, she was probably even *good* for you after all those years of doing your duty with Ethel. The problem was, you let it go too far, that's all. Everything you did was okay, except for two things. You didn't figure out she was crazy, that's number one. And you fell in love with her, that's number two."

"There's a part of me that wishes I could drop everything— everyone—and be with her." Bobby's voice was stubborn, as if this was something he had to say.

"Sure there is. But you're not going to. Maybe you'll always feel that way. Maybe I will. Maybe you'll wake up in the middle of the night every once in a while, for the rest of your life, with Ethel lying there in the bed beside you and think, Christ, why didn't I have the guts to do it? Welcome to the club, Bobby, welcome to the club."

The children appeared, running toward the pool from the beach, carrying sand pails, shovels, inflatable toys, screaming like wild Indians. The younger ones still behaved toward their grandfather as if he were perfectly healthy, perhaps unable to tell the difference. Their presence made him a little more animated, though in a manner that was painful to watch, for his facial expressions were grotesque, and the older children kept their distance.

Jack rose to his feet. "It's a tough world, Bobby," he said. "Just remember that this is what matters, and you'll be fine." He grabbed a couple of the smaller kids and tossed them in the pool. "A clean break," he shouted over his shoulder. "It's always the best. And the kindest."

He paused before diving in after them. "If that matters," he added.

It seemed to her that her whole life was on hold. Her days were full enough, but the fullness was contrived and artificial: after Mrs. Murray drove her to Dr. Greenson's for her session, her masseur would come over, and then her press agent; then she would spend the afternoon on the telephone, trying to put together some sort of plan for the evening, until the day was over.

Often enough, the evenings weren't much different. She would eat take-out food or have a cookout on the lawn with the people who had been with her during the day, then retire to her room with the phone and a pile of magazines to spend the night calling friends.

Though she had expected to be deluged with offers of work and scripts, there were still none. The only people who wanted to see her were photographers and interviewers, so she sat for as many interviews and photographic sessions as she could, if only to have something to do. Besides, she was anxious to show the world that even if Marilyn Monroe had lost her job, she hadn't lost her looks.

It gave her a sense of satisfaction—perhaps, at the moment, her *only* sense of satisfaction—that her body was as much of an attraction as ever. After every session, she pored over the contacts and the transparencies with a magnifying glass, slashing big crosses with a crayon across the ones she didn't like. She even allowed a couple of the photographers, guys she really liked and trusted like Burt Stern, to shoot her nude for the first time since her famous calendar shots sixteen years before, though she knew they couldn't be printed. She wanted to see what she looked like, to test the limits, and she wasn't displeased with the results—she even let Stern keep his negatives. She wondered what he'd say if he knew she was pregnant!

All the same, despite the photographers and the interviewers (to all of whom she told the same sad tales of her childhood, with as much emotion as if she'd never recited them before), she felt as if she were in limbo, restless and miserable. She called Bobby constantly, but increasingly she found herself talking to his secretary Angie instead, and when she *did* get through to him, he was rushed, slightly distant, the way a man might be if there was someone else in the room while he was taking a call from his girlfriend.

She needed to take a couple of Randy-Mandies after speaking to him, to calm her nerves, but soon she was taking them *before* she called him, to steady her nerves, with the result that she wasn't always sure what he'd said, and had to call back, right after hanging up, to ask him to say it again. . . . When he told her he was coming to Los Angeles, however, she heard him loud and clear. "When?" she asked.

"June twenty-sixth," he said.

She had lost track of the date, and it took a moment before it registered. She felt a jolt of discomfort. She had spoken to him yesterday, and he hadn't mentioned coming to Los Angeles. Usually his appointments and travels were fixed weeks in advance. "That's *wonderful!*" she cried, trying to sound excited enough for both of them. "How long do you have?"

"It's just for one night," he said, sounding a little cautious. "I'm having a series of meetings, cross-country, with law enforcement people, about organized crime, ending up in Los Angeles. Will you be there?"

It seemed to her an odd question. "Will I be here? Lover, I'll be wherever you *want* me to be."

"We need to talk."

"I know it." She ignored the tightness in his voice. "I'll get some food in," she said. "Can you spend the night?"

There was a long pause. He seemed to be thinking over the suggestion. Then he coughed and said, "Well, I promised Peter and Pat I'd have dinner at their house. . . . Why don't you come? They'd love to have you."

She was so hurt at the offhanded way he suggested it that she hardly knew how to react. He might, she thought, have been speaking to a total stranger. She decided there *must* be someone in his office with him. "Okay." She tried to keep the hurt out of her voice. "Then we'll get together, at my place?"

"Sure," he said, but he didn't sound sure at all.

"I love you, Bobby," she said, and waited for him to say that he loved her, but instead, he only said, "I know," so sadly that she felt like crying.

All the same, he *was* coming, and his arrival at least put an end to the lethargic routine of her days. Mrs. Murray was galvanized into getting the house spick-and-span, the refrigerator was stocked against the possibility that he might be hungry during the night, and she made appointments to have her hair done, her nails taken care of. She gave instructions for her makeup man and her hairdresser to come to the house six hours before she would have to leave for the

Lawfords', and went through her closets to find something sensational that neither Bobby nor the Lawfords had ever seen before.

For all her careful preparations, the day of Bobby's arrival began badly. Trying on dresses, she spilled coffee on the one she had chosen, and turned on Mrs. Murray (not that it had been her fault) with a rage that gave her an instant, splitting headache and obliged her to spend the rest of the day apologizing. Together—Mrs. Murray responded to any demonstration of "togetherness"—they picked out a replacement, a white off-the-shoulder dress she had bought when Yves Montand admired it in the window of Saks, and by the time she had tried it on, and picked out a bag and a pair of shoes, she and Mrs. Murray were reconciled. The manicurist gave her false nails that reminded her of the Dragon Lady in *Terry and the Pirates* and made it impossible for her to pull a zipper or fasten a button, but she had never confused glamour with practicality, and it was her intention to be glamorous tonight.

Halfway through the process, however, she changed her mind. After all, she was a mother-to-be, was she not? It wasn't as a glamorous Hollywood sexpot that she was appealing to Bobby but as the mother of his child (or yet one more of his children, to be painfully accurate) and his future wife. She proceeded to undo everything that had been done, starting with her hair, which had to be styled in loose waves, softer and more flowing.

When she glanced at herself in a hand mirror, she instantly realized how stupid she was being. Bobby wouldn't want her to be mousy and ordinary. If what he wanted was a good mother in tame clothes, one who didn't wear much makeup or go in for glamour, he would have been content with Ethel, and wouldn't have fucked *her* in the first place. "Let's go back to what we had," she said. She shook her head hard, ruining her new hairdo.

There was a collective sigh. Mrs. Murray looked at her watch nervously. "It's six o'clock," she said timidly.

People ate early in Hollywood, their habits governed by the fact that performers who were on call had to be in the studio, ready to be made up, before seven in the morning, as well as the fact that executives had to be up at dawn to take calls when people reached their desks in New York at nine a.m. Her proper ETA for the Lawfords ought to have been seven or seven-thirty, and allowing the best part of an hour to get from Brentwood to Malibu, she should have been ready to go, instead of which she was sitting here, naked beneath a smock, with work on her hair and her face only just beginning again.

It was almost eight before she was ready, standing a little unsteadily on the very highest of her spike-heeled pumps, in a dress that showed as much skin as any dress could—all of it looked pretty goddamned good, in her own opinion, and who would know better?

Her hair was like gleaming silver cotton candy, her lips were a bright, shiny red. She giggled. "*This* ought to show him," she said.

She took a couple of pills at random to steady her nerves, and poured a few into her sequined handbag, in case of emergency—though she knew there was an unlimited supply of everything she could possibly want in Lawford's bathroom medicine cabinet.

When her driver helped her out of the car, for some reason the driveway blacktop seemed to have developed a life of its own, like a slow-motion minor earthquake, and she was grateful to him for steering her to the Lawfords' front door. The maid opened the door, and she swept past her into the living room, surprised to find it empty.

"*Señorita!*" she heard the maid cry, but she was already on her way to the dining room, and taking a deep breath, she descended the couple of steps, eyes fixed on the straight lines of the sliding glass windows so as to keep her balance.

There was complete silence as everybody turned to look at her, Peter rising with his usual grin, while Pat had the embarrassed look of any middle-class hostess at the late arrival of a guest she had decided wasn't coming.

Then she saw Bobby, sitting with an empty seat at his right, and her heart fell, not at the realization that he was already eating his dessert—was she really *that* late?—but at the sight of his eyes.

They were a pale, cold blue like ice on a pond, as unforgiving as a sentence of death.

* * *

"I'm so sorry I was late," she said.

"That's okay," Bobby said nervously. During what remained of dinner, they had talked like strangers, for after all, there were guests present who presumably weren't in on the secret, and she was always conscious that Pat, however easily she accepted the sex lives of the Kennedy men, was still something of a chaperon, at least as far as her behavior in public was concerned.

They left together early—after he put on a show of making a fumbling offer to drop her off on his way back to the Beverly Hilton—and sat in silence most of the way down Sunset, holding hands like teenagers, while she watched his Adam's apple bob up and down, an unmistakable index of his nervousness and, presumably, his unwillingness to begin a conversation in front of the driver, a Justice Department cop of some kind, for she had sent her driver home.

Once they were in the house, she waited in vain for Bobby to throw his arms around her, but if he felt that kind of passion, he did nothing to show it. She stood there in her living room, until he was shamed into giving her a quick, married-couple kiss. If he'd been a drinker, he would have poured himself a drink, but he wasn't, nor a smoker either, so she went to the kitchen, poured herself a glass of champagne, and turned on the radio, then came back to the living room and sat down on the sofa, exposing her thighs, kicked off her shoes, and patted the cushions until he sat beside her, with visible reluctance. "What's the matter, baby?" she asked.

"Marilyn," he said, "I've always tried to be honest with you, haven't I? Told you the truth?"

"Do I want to hear the truth, baby?" she asked sadly.

"Probably not. Practically nobody does. It's one reason why Jack is the politician in the family, not me."

"They say you're getting better at it."

He smiled grimly. "I'm not sure it's a compliment. Listen, I've told you I love you. . . ."

"And it wasn't true?" Her voice sounded small.

"It *was* true," he said. "It is true. I love you. And I think you love me."

"Mm," she said. "You *know* I love you, baby."

"Yes, I *do* know."

He took her hand in his. "Would you love me enough to do anything I asked you to?"

"Anything?" she whispered huskily. "Anything you want, baby. I'm yours, all of me." Her cheek was close to his, she clutched his hand so hard that her fingers ached.

"If you love me as much as you say you do, there's one thing you *can* do for me, Marilyn," he said.

"Name it."

He stared into the middle distance. "Get rid of the baby."

She sat silently, eyes suddenly blurred with tears. "Why?"

His voice was patient, as if he were talking to a child. "Because I'm not going to leave Ethel. . . ."

"You love her more than you love me?"

" 'More' isn't the point. She's my wife and the mother of my children—all seven of them. I have obligations toward her I can't ignore. I have obligations toward Jack I can't ignore. I have to do what's right."

"Are you saying it wasn't right for us to fall in love? That it wasn't right for us to go to bed together?"

"It *wasn't* right. It wasn't wrong either. We're both adults. It happens, we both know that. It was a small sin. Falling in love, having a baby, those are bigger sins, with bigger consequences. Too many people are going to be hurt."

"Maybe you should have thought of that before you fucked me the first time."

"You're right," he said in a low whisper, like a small boy admitting to some fault or household misdemeanor. "We were both wrong."

"No," she said firmly. "I'm not married. And I'm willing to have the baby. I don't have anything to be guilty about, except that I fell in love with the wrong guy."

"I'm not the wrong guy."

"Oh, yes you are, but that's not your fault, honey." She laughed. "Never fall in love with a married guy who has seven children—every girl ought to know better than that!"

"Do you need any help?"

"*Help?* Christ, I've been through this before, more times than you'd want to *know*. Don't insult me, okay? You want it taken care of, I'll take care of it."

There was a long silence. "You have a right to be angry," he said at last.

"Yes, I do." She looked him in the eye. "I should have known better. That's the problem out here. We believe in happy endings, and there aren't any in real life."

"Yes there are. Sometimes."

"Not for me. . . . Bobby," she asked softly, "can we still be—friends?"

"Well, sure. . . ."

"And lovers?"

There was a moment of hesitation. It was remarkable what a bad liar he was for a man who had spent most of his adult lifetime in politics. "If you want that," he said.

"What do *you* want?"

"I want it, of course. . . ."

The words "of course" didn't ring true at all—seemed to make his statement meaningless, in fact—but she let it go. If she had to hang on to him by her fingernails, so be it, she would hang on.

She had been humiliated by the studio, and now the man she loved was giving her the brush-off.

"Stay the night, darling," she pleaded. "Don't leave me alone tonight."

"Well. . . ."

"Please." She could feel how awkward and stiff he was. Was he, as she guessed, under orders to do the deed, get out of the house, and haul his ass back to the safety of the Beverly Hilton? "You don't have to fuck me if you don't want to," she whispered. "Just stay and hold me."

"Of course I'll spend the night."

She stood up, knowing that she had never looked sexier—that perhaps *nobody* had ever looked sexier—took his hand in hers and pulled his face close against her stomach, feeling the warmth of his breath through the gossamer-thin fabric. She said to him huskily, "Unzip me, baby."

49

A BORROWED PRIVATE AIRPLANE FLEW HER TO TIJUANA, where a limo waited on the runway to take her directly to the *clínica*. It was a well-equipped, supermodern, specialized little surgical facility, safely across the border, beyond the jurisdiction of the state of California, where for the right amount of money a rich *gringa's* own American gynecologist could perform the simple procedure he could go to prison for doing at home. Only the clinic's administration and nursing staff was Mexican, all of them chosen for their discretion.

All the same, as she lay there, the pills holding the postoperative pain down to a dull ache, she felt like crying. She had given up her baby, Bobby's baby, her last chance, she knew instinctively, for motherhood, for a new life, for all the things she had traded for fame.

She was back in Los Angeles forty-eight hours after the abortion. She had confided in no one—even Mrs. Murray thought she had gone to Tahoe with the Lawfords. The moment she was home, she called Bobby at the Justice Department to tell him it was done.

His private number had been changed, so she had to go through the switchboard.

Hoffa paced restlessly. He hated this kind of shit, all the guinea bullshit about respect and honor, instead of getting down to the nitty-fucking-gritty. Palermo, with his smooth tailoring and his slicked-back hair, wasn't his favorite kind of guinea either, but he didn't have a choice: Palermo was the mob's appointed messenger, and that was that. Giancana was hiding out in Cuernavaca with his singer girlfriend, dodging subpoenas and assassins, Moe Dalitz wasn't talking to anyone, not even Dorfman; and the Lansky group—Trafficante, Marcello, and Roselli—were lying low. Just when he needed help, when that little fuck Bobby Kennedy had finally nailed him with a serious indictment, everyone was running for cover.

"Look," Palermo said, spreading his hands, "It's tough. We know that."

"Tough? It ain't you who's going to the can."

"It'll never happen, Jimmy."

"Bullshit! This time Bobby's got a case, and he *knows* it. Just remind your guys, I go down, they go down."

Palermo shook his head mournfully. "You don't want me to pass that message on, Jimmy. You really don't."

"The fuck I don't."

Palermo inspected the toe-caps of his highly polished shoes. If Hoffa wanted to commit suicide, it was none of his business. Could he be dumb enough to think the law of *omertà* didn't apply to him? Apparently.

"You put your people on notice that they'd better not try to hang me out to dry all by myself," Hoffa said grimly.

Palermo nodded. That, of course, was exactly what "his people" had in mind.

"Mind you," Hoffa said, smirking, "Bobby's got his problems too."

"Yes?" Palermo couldn't think of any problem Bobby might have that was as serious as those facing Hoffa.

Hoffa leaned across the desk until his face was close to Palermo's—a closeness Palermo disliked, since Hoffa's tawny eyes and putty-colored face close up were almost as disagreeable as Hoffa's breath. Still, he didn't flinch.

"Marilyn's just had an abortion," Hoffa said, his voice husky with contempt. "Bobby's kid! If he don't go out to California and see her, she's gonna hold a press conference and tell the world, that's what she's telling everybody."

"Is this for real?" For once, Hoffa had genuinely surprised him.

"I got it all on tape. Bobby don't know about the press conference, not yet. She called him right after she had the abortion, and he tried to calm her down, you know? But Bobby, he don't have the guts to come right out and say, 'Fuck off, lady, it's over!' He just says he's too busy right now, all that shit. . . .

"He even changed his private number on her, the little prick, and when she asks him about that, he gives her a whole sorry bunch of bullshit about how they're installing a new phone system at the Justice Department, and this and that, which she don't believe a word of. . . . What the fuck, it's the oldest story in the book, right?"

"What do you plan to do with this, Jimmy?" Palermo asked with a certain amount of skepticism. His people weren't big on sexual blackmail—they were believers in the broken kneecap or the garrote.

"I'm gonna let Bobby know that Marilyn is gonna go public with the story he made her have an abortion. And if she don't do it, I will."

"When's he going to get the news?"

Hoffa smirked again. "Any luck, he's already got it." He swiveled his big leather desk chair around so that he was looking out over the Washington skyline toward the Justice Department, the windows on the top floor still lit in the hot summer dusk.

He lifted a can of Coca-Cola in a mock toast. "Have a good evening, Bobby," he said.

The Attorney General kept late hours—later than anybody else in government. The people who were close to him understood that the job came first—if you weren't prepared to put the rest of your life, your marriage, and your kids on hold, you didn't belong on his team. Once, he had left the office with one of his assistants after midnight, both of them exhausted, and as the driver turned down Massachusetts Avenue to take them home, the Attorney General had looked up and noticed that the lights in Hoffa's office in the Teamster building were still burning. "Make a U-turn and take us back to the Justice Department," he had snapped to the driver. "If Hoffa's still working, we should be too."

He still felt the same way. His enemy was still over there, in his office, instead of behind bars where he belonged. Robert Kennedy rubbed his eyes, picked up a thick sheaf of reports, and turned on his Dictaphone machine. He was about to slip a new belt into the machine, but he realized there was already one in it. He pushed the review button to see if it contained something he had previously dictated, and heard a familiar, gravelly voice. *Hey, Bobby, listen to this!* There was a gap; then a small breathless voice, distorted by recording and transcription but recognizably Marilyn's, began to speak in a

whispery undertone, like a little girl telling secrets to a friend
on the phone. It wasn't altogether a little girl's voice, of course,
because there was a strong impression that she was drunk, or
on drugs, or both, the clear panic signal of somebody out of
control.

*He can't do this to me can he, Doctor? the voice said. He
can't make me kill my baby, then abandon me? I thought we
were going to be together, that he'd help me through all this
shit, but then he changes his fucking number so I can't even
reach him when I really need him. . . .*

*What's done is done. You terminated the pregnancy. It's
natural you should feel depressed.*

*Fuck "depressed." I'm angry! I want him here. I thought
he was my friend. I thought I could trust him. He fucked me
over, just like every other man in my life. If he doesn't come
out here to be with me, I'm going to hold a press conference
and tell the whole world what happened!*

I believe that would be a mistake, Marilyn. . . .

I don't care. I'm going to do it. I mean it. . . .

He listened, his chin cradled in his hands, the tinny voice
crackling from the dictating machine, vibrating with pain,
anger, and fear.

There was a click as she hung up, then the sound of her
dialing, and very soon she was telling the story of her abortion
all over again, in a wild rush of words, to some woman named
Dolores, who offered to come over and keep Marilyn company, and then to Aaron Diamond, the Hollywood superagent,
who gruffly told her to forget about it and call him in the
morning, at his office, then to her makeup man, who was
horrified. . . .

He switched the machine off, took the plastic belt out, and
carefully cut it into small pieces with the scissors from his
Mark Cross desk set, a gift from Ethel. Of course, it was
just a symbolic gesture. He knew where the tape had come
from, although not how it had been placed in his machine.
There would be other copies—Hoffa wouldn't have sent him
the original.

He wondered how many other people Marilyn had called
with her news, and more important, her threat. But it didn't
really matter—one was enough, or rather, too much.

On the desk in front of him was a travel folder, marked

"AG & Family—California." He stared at it and sighed. In ten days, he was taking Ethel and the children to the ranch of an old friend, near San Francisco, for an eagerly awaited long weekend, then going on to join Justice William O. Douglas on a mountain-climbing expedition in Washington.

There were things that never needed to be spoken of in any long marriage, that were just somehow, as if by mental telepathy, *known*. Ethel had never once mentioned Marilyn's name to him, but he could tell that she knew about the affair. She had made it clear enough between them that the trip to the West was something he *owed* her. She hadn't said so. She didn't need to.

Next to the travel folder was a call sheet, on which Marilyn's name appeared almost a dozen times, the calls sometimes only minutes apart.

He glanced at his watch. It was eleven p.m. in Los Angeles.

He was so tired that he closed his eyes for a moment. He opened them and rose at last from his desk, stretching. He decided to call it a night—he was simply too tired to do any useful work, and Ethel, he knew, would be waiting up for him. He looked at his calendar and sighed. He had a full day tomorrow, July 25; then the next day he flew to Los Angeles in the late afternoon to make a speech at the banquet of the National Insurance Association convention, then back to Washington on an Air Force jet, for a meeting at the White House on the Soviet buildup in Cuba. . . .

He looked again at the long list of calls from Marilyn, all of them begging him to see her, and shook his head. He couldn't—he knew that. It was too dangerous, "counterproductive" as the CIA spooks liked to say, not even fair to her. . . .

On top of that, God alone knew what kind of trouble she might make. . . .

He dialed Peter Lawford's number instead.

On July 25, though she couldn't have explained why, she cashed in her chips. She had saved up a whole sheaf of prescriptions from her many doctors and filled them all in one long pharmacy-hopping afternoon.

She knew she didn't *need* that many pills, but she was only able to relax when she had a supply on hand, plus a few secret hoards stashed away for emergencies. It was the thought that she might run out that paralyzed her with fear, that sent her from pharmacy to pharmacy in Brentwood and Santa Monica on a kind of shopping spree, until her handbag was comfortingly full of pill bottles.

It had been five days since her abortion. She had lost count of the number of times she had called Bobby Kennedy, but he had spoken to her only once. She had begged him to come to California to see her, even if only for a night, but he had pleaded work.

She had not expressed her anger to him, or her hurt—for she wanted him back. Besides, she knew Bobby. Like Jack, it was useless to threaten him. Late at night, when she was sleepless despite all the pills and champagne, she kept herself from going crazy by calling everyone she knew, letting go of all her rage and frustration, but she would never have said any of it to Bobby himself, nor did she always remember exactly what she said during those calls, let alone mean it.

She drove down Sunset to the Pacific Coast Highway, parked at the Sip-N-Surf, kicked off her shoes and walked barefoot along the beach, feeling better than she had for a long time. Maybe life would make more sense if she never thought about it, if she could simply sit on the beach and watch the waves, and let the breeze blow in her hair. . . .

She walked back to the Sip-N-Surf, slipped on her sunglasses, took a seat under the palm-frond canopy, and ordered a hamburger and a Coke. Most of the kids at the counter were in their teens, and for a moment she envied them bitterly, but then, if they had recognized who she was, they would have envied *her,* so perhaps it all evened out, she decided. . . . "Penny for your thoughts," she heard a familiar English voice say.

Lawford was sitting at the counter a couple of seats down, separated from her by two stunning girls in bikinis. He came over and gave her a hug. He was dressed for the beach in baggy shorts and an old tennis shirt, his hair tousled, his feet bare. He was genial, good-natured, grinning, and clearly a little drunk.

"Slumming, darling?" he asked, dropping down beside her.

"Since when is Malibu a slum?"

"Depends which end. . . ." He gave an admiring glance at the bare back of the girl nearest him. "Ah, youth!" he said with a sigh. "The older I get, the younger I like them. Odd that, isn't it? I suppose I'll end up a pedophile if I live long enough." He held his glass up toward the barman. "Another scotch, George," he shouted.

"His name isn't George."

"All barmen are George. Listen, when you saw me here, didn't you think, Fancy that! What a coincidence! Here's darling Peter!"

She shook her head. "No," she said. "It didn't occur to me."

"Oh dear. Because it *isn't* a coincidence, as it happens. I saw you walking along the beach, and since I've been trying to reach you for days, I thought I'd follow you and say hello."

"I've been at home."

"Really? I must have called *dozens* of times, darling."

"You can't have. . . ."

"Oh, yes, but never mind. Here you are. I was calling to ask you away for a long weekend. Rumor has it you need a change of pace. I say, what are you drinking?"

"A Coke."

"That won't do. Give the lady a glass of champagne, George."

When the barman brought her the champagne, he clicked his glass against hers. "Cheers! Listen, do say you'll come. We're flying up to Tahoe in Frank's new airplane."

"You and Pat?"

"Probably. Almost certainly." He hesitated. "Although Pat's plans aren't clear yet. . . . It's going to be quite a party—all sorts of people, really. . . ."

There was a sweaty insistence to his voice that made her nervous. He put his arm around her, as if they were the best of friends—which perhaps they *were,* she wasn't sure. . . . "It will do you the world of good," he said.

Why not? she thought. Maybe that was just what she needed—a little fun. It might teach Bobby a lesson too, that she wasn't just going to sit around calling him, or waiting for him to call. . . . She could hardly spend the rest of her life wandering around the house aimlessly, while Mrs. Murray sat in the kitchen like a bodyguard—or a nurse, which was nearer to the truth. "Okay," she said.

He gave her a broad grin, then a kiss. "Smashing!" he said.

"We might make a nice long weekend of it, what? Go up tomorrow, if the plane's free?"

Thursday was one of those days that would have made her mind up to go to Tahoe even if she'd been undecided—a day of blinding, sultry heat, with gusts of wind that brought no relief, and had the same effect as opening an oven door. Even Mrs. Murray was cross and short-tempered, while Maf, normally the most cheerful of animals, huddled in the shade beside the pool, panting.

She spent the morning fretting about what she was going to wear and pack. In the end, she did what was most comfortable and turned up at the plane in an old pair of Jax pants, a man's shirt—one of Jack's, as it happened—with the sleeves rolled up, and a scarf over her hair. Lawford poured himself a drink and slumped beside her once they were in the plane. He lit a cigarette with trembling hands.

"No smoking on takeoff," the pilot said—the door to the flight deck was open.

"Fuck off," Lawford said.

The pilot glared at him, but apparently decided that it wasn't his job to quarrel with his employer's guests.

She noticed that Lawford hadn't bothered to fasten his seat belt either. She was about to do it for him, then decided she didn't want to touch him for fear he might misunderstand the gesture. The hell with him, she decided. It wasn't up to her to be his nursemaid.

"Where's Pat?" she asked.

"Ah," he said, opening his eyes and looking around the empty cabin as if he were surprised not to see her there. "She couldn't come. Not her scene, really."

He drained his drink and fell asleep, leaving her to her own thoughts. "Not her scene"? Of course, it was *true*—the Cal-Neva Lodge *wasn't* Pat's scene. It was a place for "the boys," given over to heavy drinking, gambling, and partying. It wasn't even *her* scene, if the truth was known, but it beat being alone by a mile.

She still thought so the next day and the next night, for it was like a twenty-four-hour-a-day party, where she was surrounded by people with whom she could let her hair down and relax. Her cabin was between Frank's and Peter's, the same one she had once occupied with Jack, and she felt at home in it. She could rise late, read in bed, go for walks by herself, and somehow here, away from Los Angeles and the feeling that where she *ought* to be was the studio, she found herself beginning to relax, able, for the first time in weeks, to enjoy herself.

She joked and danced with Frank and Peter and their friends, protected by a kind of all-enveloping spirit of masculine camaraderie, her spirits kept high by an endless supply of pills from Lawford's "overnight bag," as he called the black leather doctor's satchel he never went anywhere without.

It wasn't until Sunday that she realized she'd been conned.

They had all been up until three in the morning, so it was well past noon when she joined Lawford at the pool, where he was nursing his hangover along with black coffee and juice.

With his eyes closed, he didn't notice the approach of a bellboy carrying the Sunday papers, and by the time he saw them and shouted out, "No, no, we don't want any!" it was too late. The *Los Angeles Times* had already been placed at his feet on the chaise, right side up, so she could see the top half of the front page clearly, with its large photograph of Bobby Kennedy speaking at some convention, under the headline:

> "Robert Kennedy in LA
> Vows 'War Against Crime!' "

It took her all of a second to realize why Peter Lawford had been so insistent on her coming up here for the weekend. "You fucking bastard," she said to him quietly.

A good actor might have feigned innocence, but one of the more likable things about Lawford was that he knew he wasn't a good actor, and didn't pretend to be. "We all do what we have to do," he said. "It was for your own good as much as his."

"The hell it was! He wanted me out of town, that's all. And you did it for him."

"Yes, that's true."

"Why?"

"He wanted to avoid a scene, Marilyn. I mean, what did you *expect?* You've been calling him day and night, blabbing to everyone about the fact you two were having an affair—sooner or later, he was bound to react, you must have known that."

"He could have called me himself!"

"That would have made matters worse, he thought. Listen, darling, you're lucky he didn't use the federal marshals instead of me. You keep forgetting who it is you're dealing with, baby, and that's a big mistake."

He was sitting up now, pointing his finger at her, his expression serious, without a trace of the self-mockery that usually made him bearable to her even when he was saying something hurtful. Her hand was trembling, but she didn't hesitate. She picked up the coffeepot from the outdoor table between them and sent it flying at his head.

"Marilyn went bananas, is what I'm saying."

I felt the usual palpitations at the mention of her name. In the past few weeks, since she had walked away from me at Malibu and I had flown back to New York, neither one of us had phoned the other. There seemed nothing more to say.

"Where *was* she, did you say?" I asked. Marty Glim was a client, a nice enough fellow (for a multimillionaire) who had made his pile in the wholesale plumbing fixtures business in Cleveland, then fulfilled a lifetime fantasy by moving to the West Coast to start a whole new life as an independent movie producer, leaving Mrs. Glim behind. I was in the process of transforming his image into that of a serious figure in the movie industry.

"I was at the Cal-Neva Lodge," he said. "I took a girl up there for the weekend, and we were having a good time, when Peter Lawford, who's at the next table, starts to make a pass at my girl. . . .

"Well, I wasn't about to put up with that, so I told him to knock it off, and I'm goddamned if the drunken son of a bitch doesn't get up and put his hands on my girl's tits, right there in front of everyone. Then all of a sudden Sinatra and Marilyn Monroe appear, she apologizes, he leads Lawford away, they send us champagne, and everything's hunky-dory. . . .

"Anyway, Marilyn was terrific. She handled Lawford beautifully, she was swell to this girl, and really nice to me. . . . And she seemed *happy*, too. I mean, you hear such a lot of rumors about how she's miserable, or crazy, or whatever, but here she was, right next to us, having a *great* time. . . ."

Glim was continuing, his voice boring through my thoughts—he had already picked up the Hollywood custom of talking without interruption until he or the subject was exhausted. "That's why you could have knocked me over with a feather when we saw her at the airfield," he was saying, and I realized I had missed some essential turn or detour in the conversation.

"What was that?"

"The airfield," he said with some annoyance. "Jesus, I wouldn't have recognized her as the same woman who came over to my table the night before. She was being *carried*, literally, and maybe not even *willingly*, frankly, if you can believe that. . . ."

I could believe that.

"They had a doctor there. He was walking right behind them, with his black doctor's bag. And she was struggling, fighting not to get on that plane, or maybe just to get their hands off her, who knows?"

"Did she say anything?"

"No. They pushed her onto the plane. Just *shoved* her in. Honest to God, David, it looked like a kidnapping. A hell of a thing."

I hurriedly thanked Glim, and called Marilyn right away, but it was Dr. Greenson who picked up the telephone.

"How is she?" I asked him.

"Resting, at the moment," he said. He had a pleasant voice—a perfect bedside voice. It occurred to me that he might just possibly be the only therapist in the country who made house calls.

"Look," I said, "is she all right? I hear there was some kind of problem last night, when she was leaving Tahoe."

"She went there against my advice," Greenson said rather stiffly, as if I were blaming him.

"What happened?"

"I wasn't there, Mr. Leman. I would say that the weekend was too stressful for Marilyn. Which is not so surprising, given her condition. . . ."

Dr. Greenson put a world of meaning into the word "condition." "Can anything be done to help her, Doctor?" I asked.

There was a pause. "Not a great deal, frankly. She feels abandoned, her self-esteem is shattered—it wasn't that strong to begin with, after all. . . ."

"Tell her I'll fly out there if she wants me to," I said, though I doubted I could do much good. I had flown out to California on one rescue mission that had ended badly—for me. I wasn't about to rush into another.

"I'll tell her," Greenson said. "But I don't think it's necessary at all." His confidence was reassuring.

I said good-bye to him with a certain amount of relief, and asked my secretary to send Marilyn flowers. I told her that the card should read, "I'm here if you need me, David," and then dialed Bobby's number at the Justice Department, on the theory that there was never any point in putting off what you didn't want to do.

Bobby's voice, when he finally came on the line, betrayed the obvious impatience of a man who already knows what the subject of the call is. We disposed of a certain amount of small talk; then I said, "I hear Marilyn is in a bad way."

"She's going through a tough time, poor kid," he said, as if he weren't the cause of it. His tone was sympathetic, but guarded. By this time, Marilyn's troubles must have begun to seem like a tidal wave, about to rise and engulf them all.

"I'm doing what I can, David," he went on patiently. I knew him well enough to guess what it cost him to hold back his Irish temper, but he must have decided that the calmer he was with me, the sooner I'd get off the phone and leave him alone. "I asked Peter to keep an eye on her."

"He can't look after himself half the time, let alone her. Did you know she had to be sedated and carried onto a plane last night, to get her back from Tahoe to Los Angeles?"

"The situation is under control, thank you," Bobby said. "Between Peter and Pat, Dr. Greenson and Mrs. Murray, and so on, half the city is looking after her. If you'd like to join the throng, be my guest."

"I may just do that."

"Fine," he snapped. "Do what you think best. I'll be on the West Coast myself this weekend with Ethel and the family, near San Francisco, but I'm planning to stay away from LA. And if you want my advice, so should you. She needs some time to pull herself back together again. Rushing off to see her won't help. That's her doctor's opinion too, by the way," he added, and hung up.

He was right, of course. It *was* Greenson's opinion, and exactly what all of us—certainly Bobby—wanted to hear, which Greenson must have known.

It wasn't until he had hung up that I realized Bobby hadn't once mentioned Marilyn's name himself. And that he had been speaking to Dr. Greenson.

It was Wednesday by the time she called me back, reaching me at the office just as I was about to go out to meet a client for lunch. "They were beautiful flowers," she said. "Nobody else sent me flowers."

"I'd send you flowers every day if you wanted."

"Oh, honey, that's an old line. Listen, I really behaved shittily to you and I'm sorry."

"That's okay." She didn't *sound* like a woman in trouble, I thought. Had Greenson brought about a miraculous recovery? Apparently so. My secretary tapped the face of her wristwatch significantly. I shrugged. The client could wait.

"I want to apologize to you," she said. "When are you coming out to LA again?"

There was a level of anxiety in Marilyn's voice. I put it down to the fact that she had just gone through a terrible experience. If there was an appeal to me to drop everything and fly out to see her, I didn't recognize it, to my shame. "In a week or ten days," I said.

"Oh." She sounded slightly disappointed, but she made no attempt to press me. "Can we have dinner again?"

"Sure we can. I'd like that."

"Maybe not at Romanoff's this time."

We both laughed. I thought she sounded remarkably like her old self.

"You'll let me know when you're coming?" she asked.

"Of course I will."

"Good-bye," she said. There was an eerie moment of silence, then the sound of something that might have been the wind, or a sigh.

"Good-bye," I said, but the line had already gone dead.

I rushed off to La Caravelle for my meeting. I had what

remained of a very full week in front of me. I had to be in Washington to see the President on Thursday; then I was planning to stay for a formal dinner at the White House.

I made a mental note to call Marilyn back and tell her about the White House dinner—she was still interested in hearing about anything that Jack did—but I never got around to it.

50

T HE CALL CAME ON THE SPECIAL TELEPHONE THE Signal Corps had rigged up at the Gilroy ranch house for the Attorney General. They had not wanted to damage his host's handsome living room with their wires, so they put it in the hallway—an ordinary-looking black telephone without a dial, which was connected to the White House. Wherever he went, the Attorney General had to be able to communicate with his brother. Less august callers, like his brother-in-law Peter Lawford, could be patched through the White House switchboard.

He took the call standing in the hallway, shooing the children out of the way for privacy, cradling the receiver between his ear and his shoulder, his eyes dark and hooded.

"What do you mean, she's out of control, Peter?" he asked.

There was a long pause while he listened. He faced the front door, his back toward the living room, as if to emphasize that he wanted to be left alone. "No, no, I realize you can only do so much. . . . Really, you've done well. I'm grateful."

He moved back and forth, as far as the telephone cord would let him, unable to pace as he clearly wanted to. It was as if there was so much energy contained in him that he couldn't stand still. "I don't think she'll come up here." He spoke crisply, sure of his judgment, as always. "She might do *that*, yes," he said. "Poor woman."

There was a wealth of sadness in his voice, layer after layer of pity and shame, but not self-pity, for he was a man without a trace of it. "Get the doctor there," he ordered, "what's his name. . . . Right. . . . No, no, I'll tell her myself. It's the only way."

He said good-bye, hung up, sighed, then picked up the receiver again. "Daddy, Daddy, when are you *coming?*" one of the children shouted from behind him, and he turned and flashed a huge grin. He held up a finger—a minute, he indicated, for he hated to keep children waiting—then spoke into the phone, asking the operator to transfer his call to a number at Justice. He didn't waste time on pleasantries. "Find out how I can get down to LA tonight," he snapped. "Without being seen."

He closed his eyes for a moment, as if he were suddenly exhausted. "There's a Marine base up here, isn't there?" he asked. "They must have helicopters?"

He listened impatiently. "Well, I don't care. Just *do* it."

He hung up and made a dash into the living room, engulfed in the noisy delight of his children, every trace of fatigue and concern gone.

She had spent Friday evening with the Lawfords. She remembered that she had joined them at La Scala for dinner—a party of five, with her the odd woman.

By the time dinner was served, she was bombed, and once she was bombed, she had started to talk loudly about Bobby and how he had given her the brush-off, until Peter, equally bombed and sweating bullets from sheer nervous tension, finally had to leave the table before his guests even finished the main course and drive her home. She hadn't made it easy for him either, but in the end, despite a nasty scene in front of the restaurant (in full hearing of the car jocks), she had let him bundle her into his car.

She remembered kicking off her shoes and putting her feet up on the dashboard so the breeze could cool her crotch—it was a blazing hot evening. She remembered arguing with him bitterly and angrily, while he begged her to behave sensibly, to remember who Bobby was, to think about her own career and reputation—most important of all, to stop making trouble and *shut up*.

She remembered telling him to fuck off as they pulled up in front of her house. She also remembered threatening, at the top of her voice, to go public with the whole story if Bobby didn't get his ass down to LA and see her.

"He *can't*," Lawford had wailed. There were actually *tears* in his eyes.

She threw a shoe at him, and caught him on the forehead. "I *mean* it!"

"It's over. Forget about it."

"I love him!"

"So what? He's married. He has God knows how many bloody kids. He's probably going to run for the presidency in '68. Leave him alone."

"He loves *me,* you snotty British motherfucker."

"Very likely. That doesn't matter either."

She threw the second shoe at him. It caught him on the mouth, splitting his lip. She was pleased to see that there was fear in his eyes. She wished she had something else to throw.

"Tell him I'm calling Louella, Winchell, everybody, tomorrow. I'm going to give them the whole story. Jack. Bobby. The whole thing. Tell him I have to see him, or else!"

There were lights appearing in windows all up and down the street. Dogs were barking. Lawford cowered in his car, waiting for the next missile, then he put it in gear and drove off, leaving her alone outside her front door.

In the morning, she woke early. By nine she was up, feeling curiously clearheaded, seated in the kitchen while Mrs. Murray made fresh coffee for her. During the night, she had somehow gained hope—Bobby would come, and once he set eyes on her, things would be all right.

She skipped lunch, and lay in the sun by the pool for an hour while Mrs. Murray went shopping, so there'd be something in the refrigerator for Bobby—for she was convinced he was coming, whatever Peter Lawford might think. . . .

She was so convinced, in fact, that she called a toy store on Santa Monica Boulevard and ordered toys for all seven of Bobby's children, asking the store to deliver them to her house as soon as possible. For Mary Kerry, the youngest, she ordered a big stuffed tiger, just the kind of thing she would have liked to receive herself at the age of three; for the others, a variety of stuffed animals and toy cars—she wasn't much good at knowing what kids liked at this age or that, and it seemed unlikely now that she would learn.

It had been an impulse—probably a wasted one, she thought—but she wanted Bobby to know that she loved all of him, even his family, and that he didn't have to choose between her and his children. . . . She had put too much pressure on him, she realized that now.

About one in the afternoon, a deliveryman arrived from the toy store and Mrs. Murray returned from Brentwood with the groceries. There had been no call yet from Bobby, and she was beginning to be nervous—all the more so at the sight of the toys piled in the hallway, as if it were Christmas. They reminded her of the orphanage—for as Christmas approached, there were always piles of toys in the hall, old ones, left by well-meaning donors. The thought increased her anxiety, as anything to do with her childhood did, and she was about to call Peter Lawford to ask when—if—Bobby was coming, when the telephone rang. She picked it up and heard the familiar voice. "I'm in town," Bobby said. "We have to talk."

"I know," she said, trying not to let her emotions show through. "Where are you? When did you get in?"

"I'm at Peter and Pat's house. Is it all right for me to come over?"

"Of course it is. Hurry. Please."

She rushed to her room and made herself up, as quickly as she could. She was torn between putting on a dress or wearing slacks, but she decided that a casual "at home" look would be more appropriate, as if she'd been lounging around the house of her own free will, not trapped in it, waiting for his call.

She was still dressing when he arrived. She opened the front door for him—Mrs. Murray had been sent away—and gave him a kiss there on the threshold. His face was grave. He put his arm around her, but she already felt chilled, despite the sultry heat. "You know why I'm here?" he asked. He didn't seem angry—just tired and preoccupied, but at the same time patient.

"Because you love me," she said. "Because I love you. Those are the only reasons you need."

"Yes. I love you. That's true. And I know you love me. That's why this has to stop, Marilyn."

She had made up her mind there was going to be a reconciliation scene, decided exactly how she was going to play it. She would give up the idea of his leaving Ethel, accept the role of mistress—none of that really mattered. . . .

If he wanted her to stop blaming him for the abortion, so be it, she would put it out of her mind. . . .

"You're back," she told him, running her fingers through his hair, kissing his cheek, holding on to him fiercely. "I'll do anything you say."

Gently, but forcibly, he pushed her away, guided her to the sofa, sat her down, then took up a position in front of the empty fireplace, from which he could look down at her.

"Anything? Okay. For a start, no more threats. That's number one." He held up a finger, like a schoolteacher making his points. "Number two, no more calls to radio stations. . . . Don't deny it, please. The FBI has been taping them. . . . Finally, no more communications. I'm sorry, but there it is—it's become too dangerous."

"I haven't threatened you!"

"You told Peter you were going to go public. If that isn't a threat, I don't know what is, Marilyn."

She stared at him. She hadn't really *meant* to "threaten" him—not the way *he* perceived it, anyway.

"Peter misunderstood me," she said. "You know what he's like."

"I know." His voice was grim. "But what he said was pretty simple. If I didn't come down here and see you, you planned to tell everybody about our—ah—*affair*."

He drew the word out with evident distaste, as if the whole idea disgusted him. "*Did* you say that? Or anything like it?"

There was still no anger in his voice—but no sign of affection either. Nothing in his expression or his manner suggested for an instant that this was a man whose body had become as familiar to her as her own, the man who had fathered her child. . . . He might have been a total stranger, his eyes hard, his mouth set, more like a judge than a lover—and, in fact, he *was* passing sentence, on their love: a sentence of death. "It's been a mistake," he said. "It's gone too far." He paused. "I blame myself, not you."

"There's no blame. . . ."

"Yes there is," he said sharply, eyes flashing, as if she had managed to pierce his defenses at last. "I'm to blame. I should have realized—"

"I couldn't be trusted?"

"Something like this couldn't be, ah, *contained,* is what I was *going* to say. Not in the long run. You're too famous. I'm Jack's brother. There wasn't a chance it would work, in the long run."

"There *was,*" she said. "I'm sorry."

"There's nothing to be sorry about."

"Yes there is." She fought hard for his attention, trying to get him to look her directly in the eyes, but he couldn't, or wouldn't. "When I was with Jack," she said softly, "I always thought you looked so sad."

"Sad?"

"Sad and envious. Like David, only more so. I used to think, He isn't loved, not *really* loved, the way Jack is. He's lonely, and so very, very sad. I wasn't in love with you. I just felt heartbroken *looking* at you."

He laughed uneasily. "You were wrong," he said. "Ethel loves me. The kids love me. Very few people get as much love as I do. More than I deserve."

"Oh, Bobby, that's not love. Not the kind I mean, and you know it. Except for the kids Ethel might just as well be another one of your goddamn *sisters.* All you do is worry about Ethel, and what she wants, and what she'll think. . . . I told myself the first time I set eyes on you, after Jack's back operation, He doesn't know what it's like to be loved by somebody who thinks about *him,* and worries about what *he* wants, then *does* it. . . . I told you once—whatever you want, whatever you've dreamed about in your wildest fantasies, that's what I'll do for you, lover, forever, and I meant it. I still do."

He sighed. "It's no good," he said quietly. "It isn't that I don't have feelings for you, Marilyn. I do. It isn't that I wouldn't like to go to bed with you. I would. Right now. It wouldn't take a lot for you to be able to talk me into it. But it wouldn't change anything. It has to be over. I can't see you again, I won't take your calls. If you write me, I won't open the letters. Maybe it'll break your heart. Maybe it will break *mine.* It doesn't make any difference. That's the way it is."

She covered her eyes for a moment. What *did* surprise her

was the way he said it. His tone of voice was calm. It left no room for doubt—or more important, hope.

"And I'm to keep my mouth shut, of course?" She hadn't meant to sound bitter, but she couldn't help it.

"That would help," he said. "I'd be grateful. Jack would be grateful. Still, if worse comes to worst, if you don't, I'll deny it." He looked thoughtful. "It'll be your word against mine. And Jack's."

The truth was, it didn't matter to her anymore. She didn't want to destroy Bobby, or Jack, even if she could have. They had wives, children, lives, careers that mattered to the world. "Bobby," she said, savoring his name. "Is this your decision? Or Jack's? Or Ethel's?"

"It's my decision," he said. "Jack wants it, sure. Ethel's put a certain amount of pressure on me, as you can imagine. But I'm the one who's breaking it off, Marilyn. And it's final. We won't see each other again."

She fell forward to her knees for a moment, sobbing, but he didn't trust himself enough to help her up. "You're making it harder on yourself," he said. "You're making it harder for me."

There was a knock on the door, which surprised her, for she had told Mrs. Murray not to disturb them, under any circumstances.

She looked up and saw Dr. Greenson standing there, a hypodermic needle in his hand. He wasn't looking her. He was looking at Bobby, who nodded.

She let out a cry of anger and betrayal—at Bobby for having drafted Greenson into acting as his backup, at Greenson, her own doctor, the person she trusted more than anyone in the world, for having agreed to be part of a sordid plot.

"Be reasonable—the doctor is just trying to help," Bobby said. His voice was calm—deliberately so, as if he were trying to pacify her enough so Greenson could give her a shot.

"It's just a mild sedative, Marilyn," Greenson said soothingly. He was edging into the room now, trying to get close to her with his needle, while she backed away from him.

She felt such a deep sense of disgust, at herself, at them, that she couldn't even *look* at Greenson, let alone listen to him.

She shook her head numbly, feeling sick to her stomach—though she hadn't eaten since breakfast.

"It will help you handle the stress," Greenson went on. He pressed the plunger in his hypodermic gently, to eliminate bubbles. "You'll rest," he said soothingly. "Then tomorrow, we'll talk about all this. . . ."

He reached into his pocket and produced a wad of cotton wool dipped in alcohol, the sharp smell reminding her of the hospital in which she had lost her baby—Bobby's baby—only a couple of weeks ago.

Bobby was close to the door, barring her exit, while Greenson slowly circled the room toward her. She grabbed the telephone from the floor, with its long line that allowed her to carry it all over the house. Both men backed off a little, and it occurred to her that they must have independently jumped to the conclusion that she was going to use the phone as a weapon.

She smiled at them grimly, challenging them to make a grab for her, but apparently they weren't prepared to go quite that far. "Leave me alone," she said, her voice surprisingly flat and unemotional to her own ears.

Greenson looked at Bobby, who glanced at him quickly and nodded. "You're not the man I thought you were," she said to Bobby quietly.

She walked to the far end of the room, the telephone cord snaking behind, and up a couple of carpeted steps to her bedroom door.

She was almost safe now. Greenson, she felt sure, wouldn't have the nerve to break down her door, nor would Bobby. She held the telephone up in front of herself, as if she were performing an exorcism. "Don't. Come. Near. Me," she said, very slowly, as if each word were painful to articulate.

They didn't. Greenson stood rooted to the spot, the hypodermic needle hanging uselessly at his side. Bobby stared at her from across the room.

She knew that the moment she went inside her bedroom, she would feel trapped there, but she couldn't stand looking at the two men any longer. She was determined not to cry, or to let them see that her hands were trembling. She clutched the telephone so hard her knuckles were white. All she wanted was to get safely to the other side of the door.

"You'll call me?" Greenson asked anxiously. "You'll come and see me tomorrow?"

She didn't answer. She didn't want to speak to him, and she

didn't want to think about tomorrow. Her only concern was how she was going to get through today.

She slipped into her bedroom with the telephone, and paused for a moment, looking directly down into Bobby's eyes.

"Please go now," she said. "Both of you."

Bobby was pale, his eyes fixed on her, trying to assess, she felt sure, what the damage was, whether he'd done the right thing. "Are you going to be all right?" he asked.

Again she didn't answer. It was no longer his business. She felt desperately tired, but not sleepy. "Somebody's got to pay for this," she said, not sure why she said it.

Turning away, she locked the bedroom door behind her. She did not even hear the front door slam or their cars start up as they left. She was alone.

She undressed, dropped her clothes on a chair, put Frank's *Blues in the Night* on the record changer, then stacked five more of his albums on top. She lay down on the bed naked, feeling the breeze from the window on her body. She luxuriated for a few moments in the silence of the house, broken only by the monotonous buzzing of insects in the eucalyptus trees outside, and the dry rustle of the leaves—a sound she missed whenever she was away from LA for long. Then the record dropped, the turntable spun, and Frank's voice, mellow and sad, the sexiest voice she knew, filled the room. She sang the lyrics softly along with him—"Blues in the Night," she thought, might as well have been her theme song.

She would take a few pills and rest, she decided; then she began to dial the phone. It was going to be a long, lonely afternoon and she needed to summon up support.

She no longer had Jack's private line, but she had the White House number.

She grasped the receiver and listened to the ring, waiting for someone to answer. . . .

EPILOGUE

A Prayer
For
Norma Jean

Epilogue

Two Secret Service men met me on the runway and drove me straight to Marilyn's house in Brentwood, at my request. I don't know why. There was nothing I could do there, but I somehow felt I needed to be in her home before I did anything else.

The Air Force jet had given me a fast but bumpy flight, most of it haunted by thoughts of my own guilt. Now that I was here, I realized I would have done better to go right to my office and start making calls to the media, gently guiding the story away from the Kennedys, but I couldn't. I needed a moment of communion with Marilyn first.

The little house was still surrounded by cops, but they made way at the sight of the two Treasury agents' credentials, though with visible resentment.

There was a large stuffed tiger on the lawn in front of the house. "What's that?" I asked one of the LAPD detectives, who was standing around in the hope of being photographed by the *Los Angeles Times*. He shrugged. "A toy," he said. "Brand-new. There's a whole bunch of toys in the front hall, like it was Christmas."

"I wonder why," I said. I knew Marilyn didn't collect stuffed animals.

"Beats me. You the guy from Washington?" he asked. "Leman?"

I nodded.

"Macready," he said. "I'm supposed to show you round, do the honors."

We shook hands and Macready, a large man in a rumpled seersucker suit, led me into the silent darkness of the house. "Her husband was here," he said. "Poor guy."

I raised an eyebrow. "Arthur Miller? Here?"

"No, no. Her *first* husband, Jim Dougherty. He's a sergeant in the LAPD, nice guy. I called him the minute I heard the news and told him she'd OD'd. 'Poor Norma Jean,' he said. 'She never had any luck.' I guess he was right." He opened a door. "This is where she did it."

I looked at that sad little bedroom and almost burst into tears. Marilyn's bed was almost bare—no dust ruffle, no fancy covers, just a plain striped mattress, a couple of twisted sheets, a blanket, and a pillow stained with her makeup. It might have been a bed in a cheap motel room, the kind that rents by the hour. The furniture, what there was of it, belonged in a motel room too—a cheap nightstand, a couple of chairs piled with old magazines and clothes, a telephone with its long extension cord snaking out through the door. "She was holding it when she died," Macready said. "We had to pry the receiver out of her hand when we took her away. Rigor mortis." He lit a cigarette. "She must have died while she was making a call. Hell of a way for her to go, all alone, trying to call someone. . . ."

"Did she leave any note?"

He gave me a detective's cynical stare—he knew now why I was here.

"No note," he said. "If that's what they're worried about in Washington."

"I don't know anything about Washington, Sergeant," I said. "I'm just a friend of the family."

"Which family would that be, I wonder?" He led me through the living room and back outside again. "Anything else I can do?" he asked.

I told him, and he looked at me with even greater distaste than before.

"You're the boss," he said. "I'm glad I've got my job, not yours."

Back at the hotel, I found Lawford waiting in my suite. His face was white, he was sweating despite the air-conditioning, and his hands were shaking violently.

"Jack doesn't blame me, does he?" he asked.

I shook my head. Jack wasn't blaming anybody but himself, and he could live with that. "What happened?" I asked.

"She overdosed after Bobby told her it was over between them."

"I know *that*. Why didn't Bobby stay? Why didn't Greenson calm her down?"

"Bobby decided they'd done all they could. Greenson felt the situation wasn't critical."

"Did she call you?"

He nodded miserably. "She called, yes. Her voice was slurred—the way it always was when she'd taken a few pills. I wasn't surprised, under the circumstances. Or alarmed."

"What did she say?"

"She asked if Bobby was at my house. . . . Actually it was—a little, ah, unfortunate. Bobby was right there, you see, by the pool, when I picked up the phone, and he said, 'If that's Marilyn, tell her I'm not here.' She must have heard him, because when I told her Bobby had gone, she said, 'You're a nice guy, Peter—say good-bye to Bobby for me,' and hung up on me, just like that." He snapped his fingers damply. "Then I tried calling her back, and the line was always busy, busy, busy. . . . Bobby was waiting for a helicopter, and after it came, I went back into the house and called her again. It was still busy, so I called Dr. Greenson, and eventually he went round to her house and found her dead. . . ." His eyes told me he was leaving a good deal out of the story.

He had helped himself to a tumbler of scotch, which he drank in great gulps. I had the impression his version of the events had been carefully rehearsed. "It wasn't my fault, David. Honestly," he added anxiously.

"No," I said—though in fact, I thought, he was the one person nearby who could have saved her, and he hadn't.

I poured myself a drink. "I've just come from her house," I said, as if I needed to explain to Lawford why I needed a drink.

"Ah, yes," he said. "It's depressing to see, isn't it?"

"You were *there?*"

"Oh yes, old boy. They called me when they found her, so I called Bobby, who told me to get over there fast, before the police, and see if she'd left a note. I suppose he didn't know who else to ask, and after all, I *am* family. So I went to her house and looked around. She was naked, you know, facedown on the bed with the telephone against her ear. I couldn't help feeling that if I'd made a loud noise, she'd have woken up, just like that, but of course, it was an illusion. . . ." Lawford was crying silently, tears rolling down his cheeks and wetting his shirt front. He didn't explain who "they" were and I didn't ask.

"And then?"

"I already told Bobby. No note." He sobbed. "Not a fucking thing."

I looked him in the eye. "I don't believe you."

He blew his nose. "David, it's the truth, so help me God! No note at all." He paused, snuffling. "Just a notebook full of poems."

I held my hand out. Lawford stared at me resentfully, but he probably thought of me as somebody who had been deputized by Jack, the one person in the world he was more afraid of than he was of Bobby. He reached into his pocket and produced a small notebook, the kind you can buy in any stationery store.

"Thanks, Peter," I said. "You can go now."

"You don't want to know any more?" he asked.

"No," I said. "I really don't."

And I didn't, not a word. I just wanted him out of my sight.

When he'd gone, still babbling apologies and self-justifications, I sipped my drink and flipped through the notebook. Some of the poems were familiar to me—things Marilyn had copied in her rolling, circular handwriting, because they'd captured her attention, a few of them old favorites out of the *Oxford Book of English Verse;* others were poems of her own. It was the last entry I was looking for, and I turned to the end of the book. The writing was distorted and clumsy, as if she had reached the stage when holding a pen was almost impossible for her, but it was still possible to read what she had written just before she lost consciousness.

It was not one of her poems, or even somebody else's. It was simply:

> *Dear Bobby: I loved you. That's not a crime, is it?*
> *I only wanted to be happy. Was that such a lot to*
> *ask?*
> *Wherever I'm going, I'll love you still.*
> *Take care of Jack—and yourself . . .*
>
> *Marilyn.*

Below that, as if it were a business letter, she had written out in capitals, "HON. ROBERT F. KENNEDY,

ATTORNEY GENERAL, U.S. JUSTICE DEPARTMENT, WASHINGTON, D.C."

I wondered if she had really supposed, poor woman, that the note would ever get to him. Then I thought about what the repercussions would have been if the police had found the note, and leaked it to the press. . . .

Very carefully, I tore the last page out of the notebook and shredded it into tiny pieces.

I put the book in my pocket, and left on my final errand, the one I dreaded most.

Macready was waiting for me at the morgue, looking as if he belonged there. "You *sure* you want to do this?" he asked.

I nodded.

"Up to you." In a city of palm trees, Spanish architecture, and bright colors, the morgue looked as if it had been designed by municipal architects for Cleveland or Boston a century ago. There was nothing to remind one of Los Angeles, whose citizens, when they died, were apparently fated to return to the grim, old-fashioned dampness, full of brick, vomit-colored marble, and grimy, peeling woodwork, of the cities they had fled to come here. Of course, Marilyn was *born* in LA, I reminded myself, her orphanage only a short distance from here.

Macready led me into an elevator and we descended. He lit a cigar and offered me one. I shook my head. "It helps the smell," he explained as the door opened. The smell *was* unpleasant, a combination of stale urine, formaldehyde, and decay. I didn't think it was improved by Macready's Te-Amo cigar, which smelled like a burning horse blanket.

He preceded me down an aisle between rows of stainless steel gurneys, each bearing a covered corpse, past a white-tiled room where a couple of men in surgical scrub suits were busily emptying the brains out of somebody's skull while listening to a ball game on a portable radio. I thought it was possible that Macready was testing me, but if so, he was wasting his time. I had been here before in my younger days, when I worked in the movie business—Marilyn was not the first star to commit suicide, if that was what she had done.

He opened a door and ushered me into a bright room with row after row of stainless steel doors at the far end. It was cold enough to make me shiver. There was a uniformed cop sitting against the refrigerator vault doors, his chair tilted back, reading a copy of *Playboy* and smoking a cigarette. "On your feet, Quinn, you lardass," Macready said. "She's got a visitor."

Quinn didn't take offense. Cops, as I well knew, always talked like that to each other, like large, dangerous animals that appear to be fighting when they are merely playing. "Fuck off, Macready," Quinn said amiably, and got up.

"Why's she being guarded?" I asked, beginning to be glad of Macready's cigar smoke.

"We get all kinds of sickos down here," he explained. "Photographers would pay five, six grand, maybe more, to take one picture of Marilyn Monroe in the morgue. That's why we put Quinn on guard down here. He's too fucking dumb to take a bribe."

"Up yours, Sergeant," Quinn said, opening a vault door and pulling out the tray.

Macready puffed on his cigar. "Christ," he said, "when it's a beautiful woman, we even get perverts who try to fuck the corpse. Especially if it's a star. That's another reason to put Quinn on the job. He's so afraid of his old lady he wouldn't try."

"There you go," Quinn said, ignoring Macready, and pulled back the top part of the sheet covering Marilyn.

She was as beautiful as ever—the pathologists hadn't done the autopsy yet—her blond hair slightly mussed, her face clean of makeup, her lips parted in what appeared to be a slight smile. She looked years younger, and except for a slight bluish cast to her lips, she might have been asleep.

"Could you leave me alone for a moment, Sergeant?" I asked.

Macready eyed me suspiciously, as if I might be one of the perverts he had mentioned. He didn't look happy about it, but after a moment's pause, he shrugged. "Whatever you say," he grumbled. He didn't seem in any hurry to leave, though. He reached into the pocket of his Jacket and drew out a scrap of paper. "The family might want this," he said with a knowing wink, handing it to me. Then he left the room, taking Quinn with him.

It was an official-looking list of numbers, meaningless at first; then I realized they were telephone numbers. I wasn't an expert, but I didn't need to be to guess that this was the telephone company's record of Marilyn's long-distance calls the day of her death. The morning showed nothing more than normal activity. Then, in the afternoon, standing out so clearly that they could hardly be missed, there was a long series of telephone calls to the same number, dozens of them, some only minutes apart. I recognized with a sinking heart the number of the White House. Most of the calls were short, no more than a minute or two, presumably because Marilyn wasn't being put through to the President, but the last one in the series was long—almost half an hour.

All of a sudden I knew what had happened in that cheerless little bedroom. I could picture it as if I had been there. Marilyn must have taken all her pills after Bobby left; then, as she began to realize she was slipping into a sleep from which she would never awaken, she had started to call the White House, more and more desperately reaching out to Jack, until finally the switchboard or his long-suffering secretary had put her through to the President.

She and Jack must have talked for nearly half an hour as she lay dying! Had he realized how far gone she was? Did he understand that she was saying good-bye to him, and to life? He must have, of course. Yet he had done nothing. Had he lulled her deeper into sleep, knowing that with each passing minute she was less able to call for help? Did he decide that it was time to cut his losses, that his future and Bobby's were at stake? Was he protecting Bobby, keeping Marilyn on the phone as she slipped into oblivion while Bobby headed back to his family?

Yes, I told myself, Jack was capable of that, even if it broke his heart—for he had genuinely loved her, I knew that. But in the end, he would have protected himself, protected his presidency, protected Bobby. He must have had all this in mind when he called me into the Oval Office to tell me the news—or as much of it as he thought I needed to know.

Poor Marilyn! She never had a chance. She had sought out the only world more glamorous than her own, but she never understood that in politics, unlike the movies, people play for keeps.

I wondered how Jack was going to live with himself, but I knew he would survive, a little more bitter, a little wiser, a lot harder. We don't put a president into the White House to be squeamish, after all. We expect him to make the tough decisions we wouldn't want to make for ourselves, to do the things we don't want to hear about, or even know about, and Jack Kennedy understood that better than anyone. He probably understood better than anyone the price he, too, would have to pay.

I wondered, more urgently, how I was going to live with myself. I tore the piece of paper into shreds and dropped it into a wastebasket. History would have to judge Jack Kennedy, I decided, not I.

Quinn had left his copy of *Playboy* on Marilyn's body, opened, cover up, on her stomach so he wouldn't lose his place. I didn't touch it, or her. I looked down at that perfect face for a long time. Then, at last, I allowed myself to cry.

I leaned over and kissed her, not on the forehead, coldly, as one might kiss a corpse, but boldly on the lips—the last kiss she would ever receive.

"Good-bye, Norma Jean," I whispered.

Then I pulled the sheet back over her face, and left her to Quinn's care.

MICHAEL KORDA is the author of
<u>Male Chauvinism!</u>, <u>Power!</u>, <u>Success!</u>,
<u>Charmed Lives</u>, and the bestselling novels
<u>Worldly Goods</u>, <u>Queenie</u>, <u>The Fortune</u>, and
<u>Curtain</u>. He lives with his wife Margaret in
Duchess County, New York.

The Kingdom of FRANCE
circa 1600

SCALE OF MILES
0 50 100 150

NORTH SEA

REP. OF UNITED PROVINCES

Amsterdam
Hague
Cleves
Breda
Wesel

ENGLAND

SPANISH NETHERLANDS

Dunkirk
Calais
Lille
Bruges
Ghent
Antwerp
Brussels
Cambrai
B. OF LIÈGE
Liège
Aix-la-Chapelle
LUXEMBURG
Luxemburg
TRÈVES
Trèves
MOSELLE

ENGLISH CHANNEL
Str. of Dover
Channel Is.

Dieppe
Le Havre
Rouen
Amiens
Noyon
Clermont
PICARDY
Rethel
Roucy
Reims
Crespi
MARNE
Châlons
Bar-le-Duc
Verdun
Metz
MEUSE
Toul
LORRAINE
Nancy
Saar-werden

Brest
Morlaix
Guingamp
Carentan
Caen
Lisieux
NORMANDY
Mortain
Ivry
Dreux
Chartres
ISLE OF FRANCE
Paris
Sens
CHAMPAGNE
SEINE
Troyes
Vassy
Vendre
Épinal
Münster
St. Loup

Quimper
Châtillon
Rennes
Vitré
MAINE
Mayenne
Alençon
Laval
Le Mans
SARTHE
Nemours
Orléans
Sully
Joigny
Tonnerre
Langres
BURGUNDY
Gray
SUNDGAU
Basle

Josselin
BRITTANY
VILAINE
Châteaubriant
ANGOU
Angers
LOIRE
Vendôme
TOURAINE
Tours
ORLÉANAIS
Blois
Sancerre
Bourges
BERRY
NIVERNAIS
Nevers
Dijon
FRANCHE COMTÉ
DOUBS
Neuchâtel
AARE
Berne
SWISS CONFEDERATION

Nantes

BAY OF BISCAY

Beauvoir
La Garnache
POITOU
Poitiers
VIENNE
Niort
Argenton
MARCHE
Guéret
Moulins
BOURBONNAIS
Montpensier
Autun
CHAROLAIS
SAÔNE
St. Claude
Lausanne
Lake Geneva
Sion

Île de Ré
Île d'Oléron
AUNIS
SAINTONGE
Coghac
ANGOUMOIS
Angoulême
Limoges
LIMOUSIN
Clermont
Mâcon
BRESSE
Lyons
LYONNAIS
BUGEY
Geneva

Bordeaux
Castillon
Bergerac
Périgueux
Tulle
Turenne
AUVERGNE
St. Flour
Vienne
D. OF SAVOY
Aosta
Moutiers
PR. OF PIEDMONT

Bélin
Clairac
GUYENNE
GARONNE
Albiac
Capdenac
Le Puy
ISÈRE
Grenoble
Valence
Turin

Albret
Nérac
Tournon
Cahors
Mende
Privas
DAUPHINÉ
Tallard
Cuneo

Mont de Marsan
Dax
Bayonne
GASCONY
Castelnau
BÉARN
Pau
Tarbes
Milhau
TARN
Toulouse
Castres
LANGUEDOC
RHÔNE
Viviers
Alais
uxces
Nîmes
VENAISSIN
Avignon
Nyons
Grignan
Forcalquier
Nice

St. Bertrand
FOIX
Foix
Tarascon
Carcassonne
Montpellier
Arles
Aix
PROVENCE
Marseilles
Toulon

KINGDOM OF SPAIN

MEDITERRANEAN SEA

Barbara Saunier

LIBRARY OF CONGRESS CATALOG CARD NUMBER 35-10016
MANUFACTURED IN THE UNITED STATES OF AMERICA
ISBN 0-671-01320-3
9   10   11   12   13   14   15

BY WILL DURANT

The Story of Philosophy
Transition
The Pleasures of Philosophy
Adventures in Genius

BY WILL AND ARIEL DURANT

THE STORY OF CIVILIZATION:

The Lessons of History
Interpretations of Life

THE STORY OF CIVILIZATION: PART VII

THE
AGE OF REASON
BEGINS

A History of European Civilization in the Period
of Shakespeare, Bacon, Montaigne, Rembrandt,
Galileo, and Descartes: 1558-1648

by

Will and Ariel Durant

SIMON AND SCHUSTER

NEW YORK · 1961

LIBRARY OF CONGRESS CATALOG CARD NUMBER 35-10016
MANUFACTURED IN THE UNITED STATES OF AMERICA
ISBN 0-671-01320-3
9   10   11   12   13   14   15

TO OUR BELOVED DAUGHTER
ETHEL

To the Reader

I HAD hoped to conclude my sketch of the history of civilization with a seventh volume to be called *The Age of Reason*, which was to cover the cultural development of Europe from the accession of Elizabeth I to the outbreak of the French Revolution. But as the story came closer to our own times and interests it presented an ever greater number of personalities and events still vitally influential today; and these demanded no mere lifeless chronicle, but a humanizing visualization which in turn demanded space. Hence these reams. What had begun as a final volume has swollen into three, and one of the present authors, at an unseemly age, becomes a prima donna making a succession of farewell tours.

Two of these three volumes have been completed in their first draft; one has been rewritten, and it here ventures into print. It proposes to cover the history of economic life, statesmanship, religion, morals, manners, music, art, literature, science, and philosophy in all the countries of Europe, and in the Islam of Turkey and Persia, from the accession of Elizabeth I (1558) and the births of Bacon (1561) and Shakespeare (1564) to the Treaty of Westphalia (1648) and the deaths of Galileo (1642) and Descartes (1650). In this period the basic developments were the rise of murderous nationalisms and the decline of murderous theologies.

Barring some lethal surprise to the authors or to civilization, Volume VIII, *The Age of Louis XIV*, should be ready in 1963; and if decay permits, a final volume, *The Age of Voltaire*, will appear in 1965. The unifying theme of all three volumes will be the growth of reason.

There is no attempt, in these volumes or their predecessors, to rely predominantly upon contemporary sources and documents for political or economic or military history; to do this for all the nations of Asia and Europe through all their generations and all their activities would have been physically impossible in one lifetime. But in cultural history, which is the primary concern of this record, there has been an almost complete resort to the original sources: every major religion has been studied in its main habitat, every major work of literature has been read or reread, every major work of art has been visited, every important contribution to philosophy has been explored.

Since the great debate between religion and science is the main current in the stream of modern thought, it will be recorded in these pages more frankly than may seem wise to men of the world. These have long since concluded that religious beliefs fill too vital a function in sustaining individual morality and morale, and social order and control, to justify their disturbance by public discussion. Much can be said for this point of view, and we shall find some of our dramatis personae expressing it; but obviously it cannot release the historian from his obligation to find and describe the fundamental processes in the cultural history of modern Europe. It can, however, obligate him to impartiality in selecting and presenting the facts and personalities according to their influence in shaping events and results. We shall hear Pascal and Bossuet as well as Spinoza and Voltaire.

Grateful acknowledgment is due to our daughter Ethel, who typed with patient care and skill the hardly legible second draft and corrected some of my errors; to Dr. C. Edward Hopkin, and to Flora, Sarah, Mary, and Harry Kaufman, for help in classifying the material.

Mrs. Durant's part in these concluding volumes has been so substantial that our names must be united on the title page.

WILL DURANT

Los Angeles, May 1961

1. Dates of birth and death are usually omitted from the narrative, but will be found in the Index.

2. Monetary equivalents as between past and present are guesswork, made doubly hazardous by periodic inflation. We note that an able seaman's pay per day in the England of 1540 was sixpence, and in 1880 six shillings—a twelve-fold increase (Froude, *The Reign of Elizabeth*, V, 385). Hume calculated that prices had risen threefold in England between 1492 and 1740 (*Essays*, 175); we may conservatively reckon prices to have risen another threefold between 1740 and 1960, and therefore nine times since 1492. We may in general assume that coins had, in seventeenth-century Europe, approximately ten times their present purchasing power. The reader may use the following rough equivalents, as between 1600 and 1960, in terms of the currency of the United States of America:

crown, $12.50	gulden, $10.50	pound, $50.00
ducat, $12.50	livre, $12.50	reale, $.50
écu, $8.00	louis gold, $50.00	ruble, $10.00
florin, $12.50	maravedi, $.015	scudo, $1.16
franc, $2.50	mark, $33.33	shilling, $2.50
guilder, $10.50	penny, $.20	thaler, $10.00
guinea, $52.50		

3. The location of works of art, when not indicated in the text, will usually be found in the Notes. In allocating such works, the name of the city will imply its leading gallery, as follows:

Amsterdam—Rijksmuseum
Berlin—Staatsmuseum
Bologna—Accademia di Belle Arti
Brussels—Museum
Budapest—Museum of Fine Arts
Cassel—Museum
Chantilly—Musée Condé
Chatsworth—Duke of Devonshire
    Collection
Chicago—Art Institute
Cincinnati—Art Institute
Cleveland—Museum of Art
Detroit—Institute of Art
Dresden—Gemälde-Galerie
Dulwich—College Gallery
Edinburgh—National Gallery

Ferrara—Galleria Estense
Frankfurt—Städelsches Kunstinstitut
Geneva—Musée d'Art et d'Histoire
Haarlem—Frans Hals Museum
The Hague—Mauritshuis
Kansas City—Nelson Gallery
Leningrad—Hermitage
Lisbon—National Museum
London—National Gallery
Madrid—Prado
Milan—Brera
Minneapolis—Institute of Arts
Munich—Haus der Kunst
Naples—Museo Nazionale
New York—Metropolitan Museum
    of Art

Nuremberg—Germanisches Natio-
nalmuseum
Philadelphia—Johnson Collection
Rouen—Musée Municipale
St. Louis—Art Museum
San Diego—Fine Arts Gallery
San Francisco—De Young Museum

Sarasota, Fla.—Ringling Museum of
Art
Seville—Art Museum
Stockholm—National Museum
Vienna—Kunsthistorisches Museum
Washington—National Gallery

4. Passages in reduced type are especially dull and recondite, and are not essential to the general picture of the age.

Table of Contents

BOOK I: THE ENGLISH ECSTASY: 1558–1648

List of Illustrations

THE page numbers in the captions refer to a discussion in the text of the subject or the artist, sometimes both.

The author wishes to express his gratitude to the following organizations for certain illustrative materials used in this book:
Alinari Fratelli Instituto de Edizioni Artistiche; The Bettmann Archive; British Information Services; New York Public Library; Spanish National Tourist Office.

BOOK I

THE ENGLISH ECSTASY

1558–1648

CHAPTER I

The Great Queen

1558–1603

I. THE USES OF ADVERSITY

O N November 17, 1558, a courier galloped into the court of the royal palace at Hatfield, thirty-six miles north of London, and announced to Elizabeth Tudor that she was Queen of England. Her half-sister Queen Mary, of pitiful fame, had died in the dark of that morning. In London the Parliament, receiving the news, cried out, "God save Queen Elizabeth! Long may she reign over us!"—not dreaming that it would be forty-five years. The churches, though foreboding trouble, thrilled the air with the clangor of their bells. The people of England, as they had done for Mary, spread festive tables in the streets, and that evening they colored the sky with bonfires of eternal hope.

By Saturday the nineteenth the leading lords, ladies, and commoners of the realm had gathered at Hatfield to vow their allegiance and feather their nests. To them, on the twentieth, Elizabeth spoke right royally:

> My Lords: The laws of nature move me to sorrow for my sister; the burden that has fallen upon me maketh me amazed; and yet, considering I am God's creature ordained to obey His appointment, I will thereto yield; desiring from the bottom of my heart that I may have assistance of His grace to be the minister of His heavenly will in the office now committed to me. And as I am but one body materially considered, though by His permission a body politic to govern, so shall I desire you all, my lords, chiefly you of the nobility, every one in his degree and power, to be assistant to me; that I with my ruling, and you with your service, may make a good account to Almighty God, and leave some comfort to our posterity on earth.[1]

On the twenty-eighth, clad in purple velvet, Elizabeth rode through London in public procession to that same Tower where, four years earlier, she had been a prisoner awaiting death. Now, on her route, the populace acclaimed her, choruses chanted her glory, children tremblingly recited to her the little speeches of homage they had memorized, and "such shooting of guns as never was heard afore" heralded a reign destined to abound, beyond any English precedent, in splendor of men and minds.

Twenty-five years of trials had tempered Elizabeth to mastery. It seemed, in 1533, good fortune to have been fathered by Henry VIII, but it was dangerous to have been born of Anne Boleyn. The disgrace and execution of the mother fell within the child's forgetful years (1536); yet the pain of that somber heritage outlived her youth and yielded only to the balm of sovereignty. An act of Parliament (1536) declared Anne's marriage null, making Elizabeth illegitimate; coarse gossip debated the girl's paternity; in any case, to most Englishmen she was the daughter of adultery. Her legitimacy was never re-established in law, but another act of Parliament (1544) confirmed her right, after her half-brother Edward and her half-sister Mary, to succeed to the throne. During Edward's rule (1547–53) she adhered to the Protestant worship; but when Catholic Mary acceded, Elizabeth, preferring life to consistency, conformed to the Roman ritual. After Wyatt's Rebellion (1554) had failed to unseat Mary, Elizabeth was accused of complicity and was sent to the Tower; but Mary judged her guilt unproved, and released her to live under surveillance at Woodstock. Before Mary died she recognized her sister as her successor and sent her the jewels of the Crown. We owe Elizabeth's reign to the kindliness of the "bloody" Queen.

Elizabeth's more formal education was overwhelming. Her famous tutor, Roger Ascham, boasted that "she talks French and Italian as well as she does English, and has often talked to me readily and well in Latin, moderately in Greek."[2] She had a daily stint of theology and became expert in Protestant dogma; but her Italian teachers seem to have transmitted to her something of the skepticism they had imbibed from Pomponazzi, Machiavelli, and Renaissance Rome.

She was never sure of her crown. Parliament (1553) had reaffirmed the invalidity of her mother's marriage to her father; state and Church agreed that she was a bastard; and English law, ignoring William the Conqueror, excluded bastards from the throne. The whole Catholic world—and England was still largely Catholic—believed that the legal heir to the English scepter was Mary Stuart, great-granddaughter of Henry VII. It was intimated to Elizabeth that if she made her peace with the Church the Pope would wash her free of bastardy and recognize her right to rule. She was not so inclined. Thousands of Englishmen held property that had been expropriated from the Church by Parliament under Henry VIII and Edward VI. These influential possessors, fearing that a continued Catholic restoration might enforce restitution, were prepared to fight for a Protestant queen; and the Catholics of England preferred her to civil war. On January 15, 1559, amid the acclamation of Protestant London, Elizabeth was crowned in Westminster Abbey as "Queen of England, France, and Ireland, Defender of the Faith." For English monarchs, since Edward III, had regularly claimed the throne of France. Nothing had been left undone to provide the Queen with problems.

She was now twenty-five, in all the charm of maturing womanhood. She was moderately tall, with a good figure, fair features, olive complexion, flashing eyes, auburn hair, and beautiful hands which she knew how to display.[3] It seemed impossible that such a lass should cope successfully with the chaos that encompassed her. Hostile creeds divided the land, playing for power and wielding arms. Pauperism was endemic, and vagrancy had survived the terrible penalties laid upon it by Henry VIII. Domestic trade was clogged by a dishonest currency; half a century of false coinage had left the credit of the fisc so low that the government had to pay 14 per cent for loans. Mary Tudor, absorbed in religion, had skimped on national defense, the fortresses were neglected, the coasts unprotected, the navy unfit, the army ill paid and ill fed, and its cadres unfilled. England, which under Wolsey had held the balance of power in Europe, was now a political cripple bandied about between Spain and France; French troops were in Scotland, and Ireland was inviting Spain. The Pope was holding over the Queen's head the threat of excommunication and interdict and of invasion by the Catholic states. Invasion definitely loomed in 1559, and fear of assassination was part of Elizabeth's life from day to day. She was saved by the disunion of her enemies, the wisdom of her counselors, and the courage of her soul. The Spanish ambassador was shocked by "the spirit of the woman . . . She is possessed of the Devil, who is dragging her to his place."[4] Europe had not expected to find the spirit of an emperor behind the smiles of a girl.

II. ELIZABETHAN GOVERNMENT

Her penetration proved itself at once in her choice of aides. Like her embattled father—and despite her politic speech at Hatfield—she chose men of untitled birth, for most of the older nobles were Catholic, and some thought themselves fitter than she to wear the crown. As her secretary and principal adviser she named William Cecil, whose genius for prudent policy and assiduous detail became so outstanding a factor in her success that those who did not know her thought him king. His grandfather was a prosperous yeoman become country gentleman; his father was yeoman of the wardrobe to Henry VIII; his mother's dowry raised the family to a comfortable estate. William left Cambridge without a degree, took law at Gray's Inn, sowed his wild oats in London's common fields,[5] entered the House of Commons at twenty-three (1543), and married, as his second wife, Mildred Cooke, whose grim Puritanism helped him toe the Protestant line. He served Protector Somerset, then Somerset's enemy Northumberland. He supported Lady Jane Grey to succeed Edward VI, but switched to Mary Tudor in the nick of time; he became a conforming Catholic at her suggestion, and was appointed by her to welcome Cardinal Pole into England. He was a man of affairs, who did not allow his theological somersaults to disturb his political equilibrium. When Elizabeth made him her secretary she addressed him with her usual sagacity:

> I give you this charge that you shall be of my Privy Council, and content to take pains for me and my realm. This judgment I have of you that you will not be corrupted by any manner of gift, and that you will be faithful to the state; and that without respect of my private will you will give me that counsel which you think best; and if you shall know anything necessary to be declared to me of secrecy, you shall show it to myself only. And assure yourself I will not fail to keep taciturnity therein. And therefore herewith I charge you.[6]

The test of his fidelity and competence is that she kept him as secretary for fourteen years, then as Lord Treasurer for twenty-six more, till his death. He presided over the Council, managed foreign relations, directed public finance and national defense, and guided Elizabeth in the definitive establishment of Protestantism in England. Like Richelieu, he thought the safety and stability of his country required the unifying absolutism of the monarch as against the divisive ambitions of contentious nobles, covetous merchants, and fratricidal faiths. He had some Machiavellian ways, rarely cruel, but relentless against opposition;[7] once he thought of having the Earl of Westmorland assassinated;[8] but that was an impatient moment in a half century of patient tenacity and personal rectitude. He had eyes and spies for everything, but eternal vigilance is the price of power. He was acquisitive and thrifty, but Elizabeth pardoned his wealth for his wisdom and loved the parsimony that accumulated the means for defeating the Armada. Without him she might have been misled by such lighter lights and spendthrift peacocks as Leicester, Hatton, and Essex. Cecil, reported the Spanish ambassador, "has more genius than the rest of the Council put together, and is therefore envied and hated on all sides."[9] Elizabeth sometimes listened to his enemies, and now and then treated him so harshly that he left her presence broken and in tears; but she knew, when out of her tantrums, that he was the steadiest pillar of her reign. In 1571 she made him Lord Burghley, head of the new aristocracy that, in the face of hostile nobles, upheld her throne and made her kingdom great.

Her minor aides deserve a line even in hurried history, for they served her with competence, courage, and scant remuneration, to the exhaustion of their lives. Sir Nicholas Bacon, father of Francis, was Lord Keeper of the Great Seal from the outset of the reign till his death (1579); Sir Francis Knollys was a privy councilor from 1558 and treasurer of the royal household till his end (1596); Sir Nicholas Throckmorton was her skillful ambassador in France, and Thomas Randolph in Scotland, Russia, and Germany. Only next to Cecil in devotion and craft was Sir Francis Walsingham, a Secretary of State from 1573 to his death (1590); a man of sensitive refinement, whom Spenser called "the great Maecenas of his age"; so shocked by repeated plots against the Queen's life that he formed for her protection a web of espionage that stretched from Edinburgh to Constantinople, and caught in its skein the tragic Queen of Scots. Seldom has a ruler had servitors so able, so loyal, and so poorly paid.

For the English government itself was poor. Private fortunes outshone public funds. The revenue in 1600 totaled £500,000,[10] which even now would be a paltry $25,000,000. Elizabeth seldom levied direct taxes, and she took in only £36,000 in customs dues. Ordinarily she relied on income from Crown lands, on grants in aid from the English Church, and on "loans" from the rich, which were practically compulsory but punctually repaid.[11] She honored the debts left by her father, her brother, and her sister, and acquired such a reputation for solvency that she could borrow money at Antwerp at 5 per cent, while Philip II of Spain at times could not borrow at all. She was extravagant, however, in her expenditure for dresses and finery, and in gifts of economic privileges to her favorites.

Rarely, and reluctantly, she summoned Parliament to her financial aid, for she did not patiently bear opposition, criticism, or surveillance. She put no stock in theories of popular or parliamentary sovereignty; she believed with Homer and Shakespeare that only one head should rule—and why not hers, in which ran the blood and burned the pride of Henry VIII? She held to the divine right of kings and queens. She imprisoned persons at her own sharp will, without trial or stated cause; and her Privy Council, acting as the Court of Star Chamber to try political offenders, suspended without appeal the rights of habeas corpus and jury trial.[12] She punished M.P.s who obstructed her purposes. She suggested to the local magnates who manipulated elections to Parliament that it would facilitate matters if they chose candidates with no boyish notions about free speech; she wanted pounds without palaver. Her early Parliaments yielded gracefully; her middle Parliaments yielded angrily; her later Parliaments neared revolt.

She got her will because the nation preferred her judicious absolutism to the fury of factions competing for power. No one thought of letting the people rule; politics was—as always—a contest of minorities to determine which should rule the majority. Half of England resented Elizabeth's religious policy, nearly all England resented her celibacy; but by and large the people, grateful for low taxes, flourishing trade, domestic order, and prolonged peace, returned the affection offered them by the Queen. She gave them pageants and "progresses," listened to them without visible boredom, shared in their public games, and in a hundred other ways "fished for men's souls."[13] The Spanish ambassador, while bemoaning her Protestantism, wrote to Philip: "She is much attached to the people, and is confident that they are all on her side, which is indeed true."[14] The attempts that were made on her life strengthened her popularity and power; even the Puritans whom she persecuted prayed for her safety; and the anniversary of her accession became a day of national thanksgiving and festival.

Was she the actual ruler, or only a popular front for the lower nobility of England and the mercantile oligarchy of London? Her aides, though fearing her temper, often corrected her mistakes of policy—but she often corrected theirs. They told her disagreeable truths, gave her their contradictory counsels, and obeyed her decisions; they governed, but she ruled. "She gives her orders," reported the Spanish ambassador, "and has her way as absolutely as her father."[15] Cecil himself seldom knew how she would decide, and he fretted over her frequent rejection of his laborious and meticulous advice. When he urged her not to treat with France, but to rely solely on Protestant support, she pulled him up with some asperity: "Mr. Secretary, I mean to have done with this business; I shall listen to the proposals of the French King. I am not going to be tied any longer to you and your brethren in Christ."[16]

Her statesmanship drove both friends and enemies to tears. She was maddeningly slow and irresolute in determining policy; but in many cases her indecision paid. She knew how to ally herself with time, which dissolves more problems than men solve; her procrastination allowed the complex factors in a situation to settle themselves into focus and clarity. She admired the fabled philosopher who, when importuned for an answer, silently recited the alphabet before replying. She took as her motto *Video et taceo*—"I see and am silent." She discovered that in politics, as in love, he who does not hesitate is lost. If her policy often fluctuated, so did the facts and forces to be weighed. Surrounded by perils and intrigues, she felt her way with forgivable caution, trying now one course, now another, and making no claim to consistency in so fluid a world. Her vacillation stumbled into some serious errors, but it kept England at peace until it was strong enough for war. Inheriting a nation politically in chaos and militarily in decay, her only practicable policy was to keep England's enemies from uniting against it, to encourage the Huguenot revolt against the French monarchy, the Netherlands revolt against Spain, the Protestant revolt against a Scottish Queen too closely bound to France. It was an unscrupulous policy, but Elizabeth believed with Machiavelli that scruples are not becoming in rulers responsible for states. By whatever means her subtle weakness could devise she preserved her country from foreign domination, maintained peace—with some brief intervals—for thirty years, and left England richer than ever before in matter and mind.

As a diplomat she could give the foreign secretaries of the age many a lesson in alert information, resourceful expedients, and incalculable moves. She was the ablest liar of her time. Of the four women—Mary Tudor, Mary Stuart, Catherine de Médicis, and Elizabeth—who illustrated Knox's "monstrous regiment [rule] of women" in the second half of the sixteenth century, Elizabeth was unquestionably supreme in political acumen and diplomatic skill. Cecil thought her "the wisest woman that ever was, for she understood the interest and dispositions of all the princes in her time, and was so perfect in the knowledge of her own realm that no councilor she had could tell her anything she did not know before"[17]—which, of course, requires a grain of salt. She had the advantage of conferring directly with ambassadors in French, Italian, or Latin, and was thereby independent of interpreters and intermediaries. "This woman," said the Spanish ambassador, "is possessed with a hundred thousand devils; yet she pretends to me that she would like to be a nun, live in a cell, and tell her beads from morning till night."[18] Every Continental government condemned and admired her. "If she were not a heretic," said Pope Sixtus V, "she would be worth a whole world."[19]

III. THE AMOROUS VIRGIN

The secret weapon of her diplomacy was her virginity. This condition, of course, is a recondite detail on which historians must not pretend to certainty; let us be as trustful as Raleigh naming a colony. Cecil, watching Elizabeth's long flirtation with Leicester, had some passing doubts, but two Spanish ambassadors, not loath to dishonor the Queen, concluded to her honor.[20] The gossip of the court, as reported by Ben Jonson to Drummond of Hawthornden, held that "she had a membrane on her which made her incapable of man, though for her delight she tried many. . . . A French surgeon undertook to cut it, yet fear stayed her."[21] "The people," wrote Camden in his *Annales* (1615), "cursed Huic, the Queen's physician, as having dissuaded the Queen from marrying on account of some impediment and defect in her."[22] Yet Parliament, repeatedly begging her to marry, assumed her capacity to bear. Something went wrong, in this regard, with most of Tudor royalty: probably the misfortunes of Catherine of Aragon in childbirth were due to Henry VIII's syphilis; his son Edward died in youth of some ill-described disease; his daughter Mary tried fervently to have a child, only to mistake dropsy for pregnancy; and Elizabeth, though she flirted as long as she could walk, never ventured on marriage. "I have always shrunk from it," she said; and as early as 1559 she declared her intention to remain a virgin.[23] In 1566 she promised Parliament, "I will marry as soon as I can conveniently . . . and I hope to have children."[24] But in that same year, when Cecil told her that Mary Stuart had borne a son, Elizabeth almost wept, and said, "The Queen of Scots is the mother of a fair son, and I am but a barren stock."[25] There for a moment she revealed her lasting grief—that she could not fulfill her womanhood.

The political implications deepened the tragedy. Many of her Catholic subjects believed her sterility a proper punishment for her father's sins and a promise that Catholic Mary Stuart would inherit the crown. But Parliament and the rest of Protestant England dreaded such a prospect and importuned her to find a mate. She tried, but began by losing her heart to a married man. Lord Robert Dudley, tall, handsome, accomplished, courtly, brave, was the son of that Duke of Northumberland who had died on the scaffold for trying to disinherit Mary Tudor and make Jane Grey queen. Dudley was married to Amy Robsart, but was not living with her, and rumor called him an unprincipled philanderer. He was with Elizabeth at Windsor when his wife fell downstairs at Cumnor Hall and died of a broken neck (1560). He and the Queen were suspected, by the Spanish ambassador and others, of having arranged this clumsy annulment; the suspicion was unjust,[26] but it ended for a while Dudley's hopes of becoming consort to Elizabeth. When she thought she was dying (1562), she begged that he might be appointed protector of the realm; she confessed that she had long loved him, but called God to witness that "nothing unseemly" had ever passed between them.[27] Two years later she offered him to the Queen of Scots and made him Earl of Leicester to enhance his charms, but Mary was loath to have her rival's lover in her bed. Elizabeth comforted him with monopolies, and favored him till his death (1588).

Cecil had borne this romance with dignified hostility. For a time he thought of resigning in protest, for his own plan contemplated a marriage that would strengthen England with the friendship of some powerful state. For a quarter of a century a succession of foreign suitors danced about the Queen. "There are twelve ambassadors of us," wrote one of them, "all competing for her Majesty's hand; and the Duke of Holstein is coming next, as a suitor for the King of Denmark. The Duke of Finland, who is here for his brother the King of Sweden, threatens to kill the Emperor's man, and the Queen fears they will cut each other's throat in her presence."[28] She must have felt some satisfaction when Philip II, the greatest potentate in Christendom, offered her his seasoned hand (1559).

but she rejected this device for making England a Catholic dependency of Spain. She took more time in answering a proposal from Charles IX of France, for France was meanwhile kept on good behavior. The French ambassador complained that "the world had been made in six days, and she had already spent eighty days and was still undecided"; she artfully replied that the world "had been made by a greater artist than herself."[29] Two years later she allowed English agents to propose her marriage to Charles, Archduke of Austria; but at Leicester's urging she withdrew the plan. When the international situation favored humoring France (1570), the Duke of Alençon (son of Henri II and Catherine de Médicis) was encouraged to think of becoming the sixteen-year-old husband of the thirty-seven-year-old Queen; but the negotiations were wrecked on three obstacles—the Duke's Catholic faith, his tender youth, and his pockmarked nose. Five years softened one of these deterrents, and Alençon, now Duke of Anjou, was considered again; he was invited to London, and for five years more Elizabeth played with him and France. After a final flurry (1581) this gay courtship petered out, and Anjou retired from the field waving as a trophy a garter of the Queen. Meanwhile she had kept him from marrying the Infanta and thereby allying her two enemies, France and Spain. Rarely has a woman derived so much advantage from barrenness, or so much pleasure from virginity.

IV. ELIZABETH AND HER COURT

There was more satisfaction in being courted by virile Elizabethans than in being bedded by a poxy youth, and the courtship could last as long as marriage did not stifle it. Hence Elizabeth enjoyed perennial adulation and savored it insatiably. Lords ruined themselves to entertain her; masques and pageants allegorized her glory; poets smothered her with sonnets and dedications; musicians strummed her praise. A madrigal celebrated her eyes as war-subduing orbs, and her breast as "that fair hill where virtue dwells and sacred skill."[30] Raleigh told her that she walked like Venus, hunted like Diana, rode like Alexander, sang like an angel, and played like Orpheus.[31] She almost believed it. She was as vain as if all the merits of her England were the blessed fruit of her mothering; and to a degree they were. Distrustful of her physical charms, she robed herself in costly dresses, varying them almost every day; at her death she left two thousand. She wore jewelry in her hair, on her arms and wrists and ears and gowns; when a bishop reproved her love of finery she had him warned not to touch on that subject again, lest he reach heaven aforetime.[32]

Her manners could be alarming. She cuffed or fondled courtiers, even foreign emissaries. She tickled the back of Dudley's neck when he knelt to receive his earldom.* She spat as she list—once upon a costly coat. She was usually amiable and easy of access, but she talked volubly, and she could be an unanswerable shrew. She swore like a pirate (which, by proxy, she was); "by God's death" was among her milder oaths. She could be cruel, as in playing cat and mouse with Mary Stuart, or letting Lady Catherine Grey languish and die in the Tower; but she was basically kind and merciful, and she mingled tenderness with her blows. She often lost her temper, but she soon regained control of herself. She roared with laughter when amused, which was often. She loved to dance, and pirouetted till she was sixty-nine. She gamboled and gambled and hunted, and was fond of masques and plays. She kept her spirits up even when her fortunes were low, and in the face of danger she was all courage and intelligence. She was abstemious in food and drink, but covetous of money and jewelry; with relish she confiscated the property of rich rebels; and she managed to get and to hold the crown jewels of Scotland, Burgundy, and Portugal, besides a hoard of gems presented by expectant lords. She was not renowned for gratitude or liberality; sometimes she tried to pay her servants in fair words; but there was a certain patriotism in her parsimony and her pride. When she acceded there was hardly a nation so poor as to do England reverence; when she died England controlled the seas and challenged the intellectual hegemony of Italy or France.

What sort of mind did she have? She had all the learning that a queen could carry gracefully. While ruling England she continued her study of languages; corresponded in French with Mary Stuart, bandied Italian with a Venetian ambassador, and berated a Polish envoy in virile Latin. She translated Sallust and Boethius, and knew enough Greek to read Sophocles and translate a play of Euripides'. She claimed to have read as many books as any prince in Christendom, and it was likely. She studied history almost every day. She composed poetry and music, and played forgivably on the lute and the virginal. But she had sense enough to laugh at her accomplishments, and to distinguish between education and intelligence. When an ambassador complimented her on her languages she remarked that "it was no marvel to teach a woman to talk; it were far harder to teach her to hold her tongue."[34] Her mind was as sharp as her speech, and her wit kept pace with the time. Francis Bacon reported that "she was wont to say of her instructions to great officers that they were like to garments, strait at the first putting on, but did by and by wear

---

* Aubrey tells a naughty story. Edward de Vere, "Earle of Oxford, making his low obeisance to Queen Elizabeth, happened to let a Fart, at which he was so abashed and ashamed that he went to Travell, 7 yeares. On his returne the Queen welcomed him home, and sayd, My Lord, I had forgott the Fart."[33]

loose enough."[35] Her letters and speeches were composed in an English all her own, devious, involved, and affected, but rich in quaint turns, fascinating in eloquence and character.

She excelled in intelligence rather than intellect. Walsingham pronounced her "inapt to embrace any matter of weight";[36] but perhaps he spoke in the bitterness of unrequited devotion. Her skill lay in feminine delicacy and subtlety of perception, not in laborious logic, and sometimes the outcome revealed more wisdom in her feline tentatives than in their reasoning. It was her indefinable spirit that counted, that baffled Europe and enthralled England, that gave spur and color to her country's flowering. She re-established the Reformation, but she represented the Renaissance—the lust to live this earthly life to the full, to enjoy and embellish it every day. She was no exemplar of virtue, but she was a paragon of vitality. Sir John Hayward, whom she sent to the Tower for giving rebellious notions to the younger Essex, forgave her enough to write of her, nine years after she could reward him:

> Now, if ever any person had eyther the gift or the stile to winne the hearts of people, it was this Queene; if ever she did expresse the same, it was . . . in coupling mildness with majesty as she did, and in stately stouping to the meanest sort. All her facultyes were in motione, and every motione seemed a well-guided actione; her eyes were set upon one, her ears listened to another, her judgment ran upon a third, to a fourth she addressed her speech; her spirit seemed to be everywhere, and yet so intyre in her selfe, as it seemed to bee noe where else. Some she pityed, some she commended, some she thanked, at others she pleasantly and wittingly jested, contemning no person, neglecting no office; and distributing her smiles, lookes, and graces so artificially [artfully] that thereupon the people again redoubled the testimonyes of their joyes.[37]

Her court was her character—loving the things she loved, and raising her flair for music, games, plays, and vivid speech to an ecstasy of poems, madrigals, dramas, and masques, and such prose as England has never known again. In her palaces at Whitehall, Windsor, Greenwich, Richmond, and Hampton Court lords and ladies, knights and ambassadors, entertainers and servitors moved in an exciting alternation of regal ceremony and gallant gaiety. A special Office of the Revels prepared amusements that ranged from "riddles" and backgammon to complex masques and Shakespeare's plays. Ascension Day, Christmas, New Year's, Twelfth Night, Candlemas, and Shrovetide were regularly celebrated with pastimes, athletic contests, jousts, mummings, plays, and masques. The masque was one of many Italian importations into Elizabethan England—a gaudy mixture of pageantry, poetry, music, allegory, buffoonery, and ballet, put together by playwrights and artists, presented at court, or on rich estates, with complex machinery and evolutions, and performed by masked ladies and gentlemen burdened with costly costumes and simple lines. Elizabeth was fond of drama, especially of comedy; who knows how much of Shakespeare would have reached the stage, or posterity, if she and Leicester had not supported the theater through all the attacks of the Puritans?

Not content with her five palaces, Elizabeth sallied out almost every summer on cross-country "progresses" to see and be seen, to keep an eye on her vassal lords, and to enjoy their reluctant homage. Part of the court followed her, delighted with the change and grumbling at the accommodations and the beer. Towns dressed their gentry in velvet and silk to welcome her with speeches and gifts; nobles bankrupted themselves to entertain her; hard-pressed lords prayed that she would not come their way. The Queen rode on horseback or in an open litter, greeting happily the crowds that gathered along the road. The people were thrilled by the sight of their invincible sovereign, and bewitched to fresh loyalty by her gracious compliments and infectious happiness.

The court took on her gaiety, her freedom of manners, her luxury of dress, her love of ceremony, and her ideal of the gentleman. She liked to hear the rustle of finery, and the men around her rivaled the women in molding Oriental stuffs to Italian styles. Pleasure was the usual program, but one had to be ready at any moment for martial exploits beyond the seas. Seductions had to be circumspect, for Elizabeth felt responsible to the parents of her maids of honor for their honor; hence she banished the Earl of Pembroke from the court for making Mary Fitton pregnant.[38] As at any court, intrigue wove many entangling webs; the women competed unscrupulously for the men, the men for the women, and all for the favor of the Queen and the perquisites dependent thereon. Those same gentlemen who exalted in poetry the refinements of love and morality itched in prose for sinecures, took or gave bribes, grasped at monopolies, or shared in piratical spoils; and the avid Queen looked indulgently upon a venality that eked out the inadequate pay of her servitors. Through her grants, or by her permission, Leicester became the richest lord in England; Sir Philip Sidney received vast tracts in America; Raleigh acquired forty thousand acres in Ireland; the second Earl of Essex enjoyed a "corner" on the importation of sweet wines; and Sir Christopher Hatton rose from the Queen's lapdog to Lord Chancellor. Elizabeth was no more sensitive to industrious brains than to handsome legs—for these pillars of society were not yet shrouded in pantaloons. Despite her faults she set a pace and a course to elicit the reserve energies of England's worthies; she raised their courage to high enterprise, their minds to brave thinking, their manners to grace and wit and the fostering of poetry, drama, and art. Around that dazzling court and woman gathered nearly all the genius of England's greatest age.

V. ELIZABETH AND RELIGION

But within the court, and through the nation, the bitter battle of the Reformation raged, and created a problem that many thought would baffle and destroy the Queen. She was a Protestant; the country was two-thirds, perhaps three-quarters, Catholic.[39] Most of the magistrates, all of the clergy, were Catholic. The Protestants were confined to the southern ports and industrial towns; they were predominant in London, where their number was swelled by refugees from oppression on the Continent; but in the northern and western counties—almost entirely agricultural—they were a negligible few.[40] The spirit of the Protestants, however, was immeasurably more ardent than the Catholic. In 1559 John Foxe published his *Rerum in ecclesia gestarum . . . commentarii*, describing with passion the sufferings of Protestants under the preceding reign; the volumes were translated (1563) as *Actes and Monuments;* popularly known as *The Book of Martyrs*, they had an arousing influence on English Protestants for over a century. Protestantism in the sixteenth century had the feverish energy of a new idea fighting for the future; Catholicism had the strength of traditional beliefs and ways deeply rooted in the past.

In a spreading minority the religious turmoil had generated skepticism— even, here and there, atheism. The conflict of creeds, their mutual criticism, their bloody intolerance, and the contrast between the professions and the conduct of Christians, had made some matter-of-fact minds doubtful of all theologies. Hear Roger Ascham's *Scholemaster* (1563):

> That Italian that first invented the Italian Proverb against our Englishmen Italianate, meant no more their vanity in living than their lewd opinion in Religion . . . They make more account of Tully's offices [Cicero's *De officiis*] than St. Paul's epistles; of a tale in Boccaccio than a story of the Bible. Then they count as fables the holy mysteries of the Christian Religion. They make Christ and his Gospel only serve civil policy; then neither religion [Protestantism or Catholicism] cometh amiss to them. In time they be promoters of both openly; in place again mockers of both privily . . . For where they dare, in company where they like, they boldly laugh to scorn both Protestant and Papist. They care for no Scripture . . . they mock the Pope; they rail on Luther . . . The heaven they desire is only their personal pleasure and private profit; whereby they plainly declare of

whose school . . . they be: that is, Epicures in living, and *atheoi* in doctrine.[41]

Cecil complained (1569) that "deriders of religion, Epicureans, and atheists are everywhere";[42] John Strype declared (1571) that "many were wholly departed from the communion of the church, and came no more to hear divine service";[43] John Lyly (1579) thought "there never were such sects among the heathens . . . such misbelief among infidels, as is now among scholars."[44] Theologians and others wrote books against "atheism" —which, however, could mean belief in God but disbelief in Christ's divinity. In 1579, 1583, and 1589 men were burned for denying the divinity of Christ.[45] Several dramatists—Greene, Kyd, Marlowe—were reputed atheists. The Elizabethan drama, which otherwise so widely pictures life, contains remarkably little about the strife of faiths, but makes a great play of pagan mythology.

In Shakespeare's *Love's Labour's Lost* (IV, iii, 250) are two obscure lines:

> O paradox! black is the badge of hell,
> The hue of dungeons and the school of night.

Many[46] have interpreted the last phrase as referring to the evening assemblies of Walter Raleigh, the astronomer Thomas Harriot, the scholar Lawrence Keymis, probably the poets Marlowe and Chapman, and some others, in Raleigh's country house at Sherborne, for the study of astronomy, geography, chemistry, philosophy, and theology. Harriot, apparently the intellectual leader of the group, "had strange thoughts of the Scriptures," reported the antiquary Anthony à Wood, "and always undervalued the old story of the creation . . . He made a *Philosophical Theology*, wherein he cast off the Old Testament"; he believed in God, but rejected revelation and the divinity of Christ.[47] Robert Parsons, the Jesuit, wrote in 1592 of "Sir Walter Rawleigh's school of Atheisme . . . wherein both Moyses and our Saviour, the olde and Newe Testamentes are jested at, and the schollers taught . . . to spell God backwards."[48] Raleigh was accused of having listened to Marlowe's reading of an essay on "atheism." In March 1594 a government commission sat at Cerne Abbes, Dorset, to investigate rumors of a set of atheists in the vicinity—which included Raleigh's home. The inquiry led to no action now known to us, but charges of atheism were brought against Raleigh during his trial (1603).[49] In the preface to his *History of the World* he made it a point to enlarge upon his belief in God.

Some suspicion of freethinking clings to Elizabeth herself. "No woman," said John Richard Green, "ever lived who was so totally destitute of the sentiment of religion."[50] "Elizabeth," in Froude's judgment, "was without distinct emotional conviction . . . Elizabeth, to whom the Protestant creed was as little true as the Catholic . . . had a latitudinarian contempt for theological dogmatism."[51] She called upon God—with terrible oaths that horrified her ministers—to destroy her if she did not keep her promise to marry Alençon, while in private she jested over his pretensions to her hand.[52] She declared to a Spanish envoy that the difference between the warring Christian creeds was "a mere bagatelle"—whereupon he concluded that she was an atheist.[53]

Nevertheless she took it for granted, like almost all governments before 1789, that some religion, some supernatural source and sanction of morality, was indispensable to social order and the stability of the state. For a time, till she had consolidated her position, she appeared to hesitate, and she played upon the hopes of Catholic potentates that she might be won to their public faith. She liked the Catholic ceremony, the celibacy of the clergy, the drama of the Mass, and she might have made her peace with the Church had not this involved submission to the papacy. She distrusted Catholicism as a foreign power that might lead Englishmen to put loyalty to the Church above allegiance to the Queen. She had been reared in the Protestantism of her father, which was Catholicism minus the papacy; and this is essentially what she decided to re-establish in England. She hoped that the semi-Catholic liturgy of her Anglican Church would mollify the Catholics of the countryside, while the rejection of the papacy would satisfy the Protestants of the towns; meanwhile state control of education would form the new generation to this Elizabethan settlement, and the disruptive religious strife would be quieted into peace. She made her hesitations in religion, as in marriage, serve her political purposes; she kept potential enemies bemused and divided until she could face them with an accomplished fact.

Many forces urged her to complete the Reformation. Continental reformers wrote to thank her in advance for restoring the new worship, and their letters touched her. Holders of formerly Church property prayed for a Protestant settlement. Cecil urged Elizabeth to make herself the leader of all Protestant Europe. London Protestants indicated their sentiments by beheading a statue of St. Thomas and casting it into the street. Her first Parliament (January 23 to May 8, 1559) was overwhelmingly Protestant. The funds she asked for were voted without reservation or delay, and to raise them a tax was laid upon all persons, ecclesiastical or secular. A new Act of Uniformity (April 28, 1559) made Cranmer's Book of Common Prayer, revised, the law of English liturgy, and forbade all other religious ritual. The Mass was abolished. All Englishmen were required to attend the Sunday service of the Anglican Church or forfeit a shilling for the succor of the poor. A new Act of Supremacy (April 29) declared Elizabeth to be the Supreme Governor of England in all matters, spiritual or temporal. An oath of supremacy acknowledging the religious sovereignty of the Queen was required of all clergymen, lawyers, teachers, university graduates, and magistrates, and all employees of the Church or the Crown. All major ecclesiastical appointments and decisions were to be made by an ecclesiastical Court of High Commission chosen by the government. Any defense of papal authority over England was to be punished by life imprisonment for the first offense, by death for the second (1563). By 1590 all English churches were Protestant.

Elizabeth pretended that she was not persecuting opinion; any man, she said, might think and believe as he pleased, provided he obeyed the laws; all she asked was external conformity for the sake of national unity. Cecil assured her that "that state could never be in safety where there was toleration of two religions"[54]—which did not deter Elizabeth from demanding toleration of French Protestants in Catholic France.[55] She had no objection to peaceful hypocrisy, but freedom of opinion was not to be freedom of speech. Preachers who disagreed with her views on any important subject were silenced or dismissed.[56] The laws against heresy were redefined and enforced; Unitarians and Anabaptists were outlawed;[57] five heretics were burned during the reign—which seemed a modest number in its day.

In 1563 a convocation of theologians defined the new creed. All were agreed on predestination; God of His own free will, before the creation of the world, and without regard to individual human merit or demerit, had chosen some of mankind to be elect and saved, leaving all the rest to be reprobate and damned. They accepted Lutheran justification (salvation) by faith—that is, the elect were saved not by their good works but by belief in the grace of God and the redeeming blood of Christ; however, they interpreted the Eucharist in Calvin's sense as a spiritual, rather than a physical, communion with Christ. By an act of Parliament (1566) the "Thirty-nine Articles" embodying the new theology were made obligatory on all the clergy of England; and they still express the official Anglican creed.

The new ritual too was a compromise. The Mass was abolished, but, to the horror of the Puritans, the clergy were instructed to wear white surplices in reading the service, and copes in administering the Eucharist. Communion was to be received kneeling, in the two forms of bread and wine. The invocation of saints was replaced by annual commemoration of Protestant heroes. Confirmation and ordination were retained as sacred rites, but were not viewed as sacraments instituted by Christ; and confession to a priest was encouraged only in expectation of death. Many of the prayers kept Roman Catholic forms, but took on English dress and became a noble and formative part of the nation's literature. For four hundred years those prayers and hymns, recited by congregation and priest in the spacious splendor of cathedrals or the simple dignity of the parish church, have given English families inspiration, consolation, moral discipline, and mental peace.

VI. ELIZABETH AND THE CATHOLICS

It was now the turn of the Catholics to suffer persecution. Though still in the majority, they were forbidden to hold Catholic services or possess Catholic literature. Religious images in the churches were destroyed by government order, and altars were removed. Six Oxford students were sent to the Tower for resisting the removal of a crucifix from their college chapel.[58] Most Catholics submitted sadly to the new regulations, but a considerable number preferred to pay the fines for nonattendance at the Anglican ritual. The royal Council calculated some fifty thousand such "recusants" in England (1580).[59] Anglican bishops complained to the government that Mass was being said in private homes, that Catholicism was emerging into public worship, and that in some ardent localities it was unsafe to be a Protestant.[60] Elizabeth rebuked Archbishop Parker for laxity (1565), and thereafter the laws were more rigorously enforced. Catholics who had heard Mass in the chapel of the Spanish ambassador were imprisoned; houses in London were searched; strangers found there were ordered to give an account of their religion; magistrates were commanded to punish all persons possessing books of Roman Catholic theology (1567).[61]

We must not judge this legislation in terms of the relative religious toleration earned for us by the philosophers and revolutions of the seventeenth and eighteenth centuries. The faiths were then at war, and were entangled with politics—a field in which toleration has always been limited. All parties and governments in the sixteenth century agreed that theological dissent was a form of political revolt. The religious conflict became explicitly political when Pope Pius V, after what he felt had been a long and patient delay, issued a bull (1570) that not only excommunicated Elizabeth, but absolved her subjects from allegiance to her, and forbade them "to obey her monitions, mandates, and laws." The bull was suppressed in France and Spain, which were then seeking friendship with England, but a copy of it was clandestinely posted on the door of the episcopal residence in London. The culprit was discovered and was put to death. Faced by this declaration of war, the Queen's ministers asked Parliament for stricter anti-Catholic laws. Statutes were passed making it a capital crime to call the Queen a heretic, schismatic, usurper, or tyrant, or to introduce a papal bull into England, or to convert a Protestant to the Roman Church.[62] The Court of High Commission was authorized to examine the opinions of any suspected person and to punish any of his unpunished offenses against any law, including fornication or adultery.[63]

The Catholic monarchs of Europe could not with much face protest against these oppressive measures, which so resembled their own. Most English Catholics continued to submit peaceably, and Elizabeth's government hoped that habit would generate acceptance, and, in time, belief. It was to prevent this that William Allen, an emigré Englishman, founded at Douai, then in the Spanish Netherlands, a college and seminary to train English Catholics for missionary service in England. He expounded his purpose fervently:

> We make it our first and foremost study . . . to stir up . . . in the minds of Catholics . . . zeal and just indignation against the heretics. This we do by setting before the eyes of the students the exceeding majesty of the ceremonial of the Catholic Church in the place where we live . . . At the same time we recall the mournful contrast that obtains at home: the utter desolation of all things sacred which there exists . . . our friends and kinsfolk, all our dear ones, and countless souls besides, perishing in schism and godlessness; every jail and dungeon filled to overflowing, not with thieves and villains but with Christ's priests and servants, nay, with our parents and kinsmen. There is nothing, then, that we ought not to suffer, rather than to look on at the ills that affect our nation.[64]

The college functioned at Douai till 1578, when the Calvinists captured the town; then at Reims, then again at Douai (1593). The Douay Bible— an English translation of the Latin Vulgate—was produced at Reims and Douai (1582–1610), and reached publication a year before the King James version. Between 1574 and 1585 the college ordained 275 graduates and sent 268 to labor in England. Allen was called to Rome and made a cardinal, but the work went on; 170 additional priests were dispatched to England before Elizabeth's death in 1603. Of the 438 total, ninety-eight suffered the capital penalty.

The leadership of the missionaries passed to a Jesuit, Robert Parsons, a man of enthusiasm and courage, a firebrand of polemics, and a master of English prose. He frankly announced that the bull deposing Elizabeth justified her assassination. Many English Catholics were shocked, but

Tolomeo Galli, secretary of state to Pope Gregory XIII, gave the idea his approval.*[65] Parsons urged the Catholic powers to invade England; the Spanish ambassador in England condemned the plan as "criminal folly," and Everard Mercurian, general of the Jesuit order, forbade Parsons to meddle in politics.[67] Undeterred, he decided on a personal invasion. He disguised himself as an English officer returning from service in the Netherlands; his martial swagger, gold-lace coat, and feathered hat carried him through the frontier officials (1580); he even smoothed the way for another Jesuit, Edmund Campion, to follow him in the guise of a jewel merchant. They were secretly housed in the heart of London.

They visited imprisoned Catholics, and found them leniently treated. Recruiting lay and sacerdotal aides, they began their work of inspiring Catholics to remain faithful to the Church, and reconverting recent "apostates" to the Protestant creed. Secular priests hiding in England, alarmed at the boldness of the missionaries, warned them that they would soon be caught and arrested, and that their detection would make matters worse for the Catholics, and they begged them to return to the Continent. But Parsons and Campion persisted. They moved from town to town, holding secret assemblies, hearing confessions, saying Mass, and giving their benediction to the whispering worshipers who looked upon them as messengers from God. Within a year of their coming they made—it was claimed—twenty thousand converts.[68] They set up a printing press and scattered propaganda; tracts declaring that Elizabeth, having been excommunicated, was no longer the lawful queen of England were found in London streets.[69] A third Jesuit was sent to Edinburgh to urge the Scottish Catholics to invade England from the north. The Earl of Westmorland answered a summons from the Vatican; he brought back from Rome to Flanders a mass of bullion to finance an invasion from the Netherlands; by the summer of 1581, many Catholics believed, the Spanish troops of Alva would cross into England.[70]

Warned by its spies, the English government doubled its efforts to capture the Jesuits. Parsons found his way across the Channel, but Campion was caught (July 1581). He was carried through sympathetic villages and hostile London to the Tower. Elizabeth sent for him and tried to save him. She asked, Did he consider her his lawful sovereign? He replied that he did. But to her next question, Could the Pope lawfully excommunicate her?, he answered that he could not decide an issue on which learned men were divided. She sent him back to the Tower, with instructions that

---

* A Catholic historian adds: "If the Secretary of State approved of the killing of Elizabeth, this was in conformity with the principles of law then in force. Gregory, too, with whom the Secretary of State undoubtedly consulted before he sent his letter . . . concurred in this view."[66]

he be kindly treated; but Cecil ordered him to be tortured into naming his fellow conspirators. After two days of agony he yielded a few names, and more arrests were made. Recovering his audacity, Campion challenged Protestant divines to a public debate. By permission of the Council a debate was staged in the chapel of the Tower; courtiers, prisoners, and public were admitted; and the Jesuit stood for hours on weakened legs to plead for the Catholic theology. Neither side convinced the other; but when Campion was brought to trial the charge was not heresy but conspiracy to overthrow the government by internal subversion and external attack. He and fourteen others were convicted, and on December 1, 1581, they were hanged.

Those Catholics proved right who had predicted that the Jesuit mission would exasperate the government into further persecution. Elizabeth issued an appeal to her subjects to judge between her and those who sought her throne or her life. Parliament decreed (1581) that conversion to Catholicism should be punished as high treason; that any priest who said Mass should be fined two hundred marks and be imprisoned for a year; and that those who refused to attend Anglican services should pay twenty pounds a month[71]—enough to bankrupt any but the richest Catholics. Failure to pay the fine incurred arrest and confiscation of property. Soon the prisons were so crowded with Catholics that old castles had to be used as jails.[72] Tension rose on all sides, heightened by the imminent execution of Mary Stuart and the intensified conflict with Spain and Rome. In June 1583 a papal nuncio offered Gregory XIII a detailed plan for the invasion of England by three armies at once from Ireland, France, and Spain. The Pope gave sympathetic consideration to this *disegno per l'impresa d'Inghilterra* and specific measures were prepared;[73] but English spies got wind of them, England made counterpreparations, and the invasion was postponed.

Parliament retaliated with more repressive legislation. All priests ordained since June 1559 and still refusing the oath of supremacy were required to leave the country within forty days or suffer death as treasonous conspirators; and all who harbored them were to be hanged.[74] On the basis of this and other laws, 123 priests and sixty laymen were executed during the reign of Elizabeth, and probably another two hundred died in jail.[75] Some Protestants protested against the severity of this legislation; some were converted to Catholicism; Cecil's grandson William fled to Rome (1585) and pledged obedience to the Pope.[76]

Most English Catholics were opposed to any violent action against the government. One faction among them addressed an appeal to Elizabeth (1585), affirmed their loyalty, and asked for "a merciful consideration of their sufferings." But as if to bear out the government's claim that its measures were justified by war, Cardinal Allen issued (1588) a tract designed to rouse the English Catholics to support the approaching attack on England by Spain. He called the Queen "an incestuous bastard, begotten and born in sin of an infamous courtesan," charged that "with Leicester and divers others she hath abused her body . . . by unspeakable and incredible variety of lust," demanded that the Catholics of England should rise against this "depraved, accursed, excommunicate heretic," and promised a plenary indulgence to all who should aid in deposing the "chief spectacle of sin and abomination in this age."[77] The Catholics of England answered by fighting as bravely as the Protestants against the Spanish Armada.

After that victory the persecution continued as part of the continuing war. Sixty-one priests and forty-nine laymen were hanged between 1588 and 1603; and many of these were cut down from the gibbet and were drawn and quartered—i.e., they were disemboweled and torn limb from trunk—while still alive.[78] In a remarkable address presented to the Queen in the year of her death, thirteen priests petitioned her to be allowed to remain in England. They repudiated all attacks on her right to the throne and denied the authority of the Pope to depose her, but could not in conscience acknowledge anyone but the Pope as head of the Christian Church.[79] The document reached the Queen only a few days before her death, and no result of it is recorded; but unwittingly it outlined the principles on which, two centuries later, the problem would be solved. The Queen died a victor in the greatest struggle of a reign stained with no darker blot than this victory.

VII. ELIZABETH AND THE PURITANS

Against an apparently weaker enemy, a handful of Puritans, she did not prevail. They were men who had felt the influence of Calvin; some of them had visited Calvin's Geneva as Marian refugees; many of them had read the Bible in a translation made and annotated by Genevan Calvinists; some had heard or read the blasts of John Knox's trumpet; some may have heard echoes of Wyclif's Lollard "poor priests." Taking the Bible as their infallible guide, they found nothing in it about the episcopal powers and sacerdotal vestments that Elizabeth had transferred from the Roman to the Anglican Church; on the contrary, they found much about presbyters' having no sovereign but Christ. They acknowledged Elizabeth as head of the Church in England, but only to bar the pope; in their hearts they rejected any control of religion by the state, and aspired to control of the state by their religion. Toward 1564 they began to be called Puritans—as a term of abuse—because they demanded the purification of English Protestantism from all forms of faith and worship not found in the New Testament. They took the doctrines of predestination, election, and damnation deeply to heart, and felt that hell could be escaped only by subordinating every aspect of life to religion and morality. As they read the Bible in the solemn Sundays of their homes, the figure of Christ almost disappeared against the background of the Old Testament's jealous and vengeful Jehovah.

The Puritan attack on Elizabeth took form (1569) when the lectures of Thomas Cartwright, professor of theology at Cambridge, stressed the contrast between the presbyter-ian organization of the early Christian Church and the episcopal-ian structure of the Anglican Establishment. Many of the faculty supported Cartwright, but John Whitgift, headmaster of Trinity College, denounced him to the Queen and secured his dismissal from the teaching staff (1570). Cartwright emigrated to Geneva, where, under Théodore de Bèze, he imbibed the full ardor of Calvinist theocracy. Returning to England, he shared with Walter Travers and others in formulating the Puritan conception of the Church. Christ, in their view, had arranged that all ecclesiastical authority should be vested in ministers and lay elders elected by each parish, province, and state. The consistories so formed should determine creed, ritual, and moral code in conformity with Scripture. They should have access to every home, power to enforce at least outward observance of "godly living," and the right to excommunicate recalcitrants and condemn heretics to death. The civil magistrates were to carry out these disciplinary decrees, but the state was to have no spiritual jurisdiction whatever.[80]

The first English parish organized on these principles was set up at Wandsworth in 1572, and similar "presbyteries" sprang up in the eastern and middle counties. By this time the majority of the London Protestants, and of the House of Commons, were Puritans. The artisans of London, powerfully infiltrated by Calvinist refugees from France and the Netherlands, applauded the Puritan attack on episcopacy and ritual. The businessmen of the capital looked upon Puritanism as the bulwark of Protestantism against a Catholicism traditionally unsympathetic to "usury" and the middle classes. Calvin was a bit too strict for them, but he had sanctioned interest and had recognized the virtues of industry and thrift. Even men close to the Queen had found some good in Puritanism; Cecil, Leicester, Walsingham, and Knollys hoped to use it as a foil to Catholicism if Mary Stuart reached the English throne.[81]

But Elizabeth felt that the Puritan movement threatened the whole settlement by which she had planned to ease the religious strife. She thought of Calvinism as the doctrine of John Knox, whom she had never forgiven for his scorn of women rulers. She despised the Puritan dogmatism even more heartily than the Catholic. She had a lingering fondness for the crucifix and other religious images, and when an iconoclastic fury destroyed paintings, statuary, and stained glass early in her reign,[82] she awarded damages to the victims and forbade such actions in the future.[83] She was not finicky in her own language, but she resented the description which some Puritan had given of the Prayer Book as "culled and picked out of that popish dunghill, the Mass Book," and of the Court of High Commission as a "little stinking ditch."[84] She saw in the popular election of ministers, and in the government of the Church by presbyteries and synods independent of the state, a republican threat to monarchy. Only her monarchical power, she thought, could keep England Protestant; popular suffrage would restore Catholicism.

She encouraged bishops to trouble the troublemakers. Archbishop Parker suppressed their publications, silenced them in the churches, and obstructed their assemblies. Puritan clergymen had organized groups for the public discussion of Scriptural passages; Elizabeth bade Parker put an end to these "prophesyings"; he did. His successor, Edmund Grindal, tried to protect the Puritans; Elizabeth suspended him; and when he died (1583) she advanced to the Canterbury see her new chaplain, John Whitgift, who dedicated himself to the silencing of the Puritans. He demanded of all English clergymen an oath accepting the Thirty-nine Articles, the Prayer Book, and the Queen's religious supremacy; he subpoenaed all objectors before the High Commission Court; and there they were subjected to such detailed and insistent inquiry into their conduct and belief that Cecil compared the procedure to the Spanish Inquisition.[85]

The Puritan rebellion was intensified. A determined minority openly seceded from the Anglican communion, and set up independent congregations that elected their own ministers and acknowledged no episcopal control. In 1581 Robert Browne, a pupil (later an enemy) of Cartwright, and chief voice of these "Independents," "Separatists," or "Congregationalists," crossed over to Holland, and he published there two tracts outlining a democratic constitution for Christianity. Any group of Christians should have the right to organize itself for worship, formulate its own creed on the basis of Scripture, choose its own leaders, and live its religious life free from outside interference, acknowledging no rule but the Bible, no authority but Christ. Two of Browne's followers were arrested in England, were judged in contempt of the Queen's religious sovereignty, and were hanged (1583).

In the campaign for election to the Parliament of 1586 the Puritans waged oratorical war upon any candidate unsympathetic to their cause. One such was branded as a "common gamester and pot companion"; another was "much suspect of popery, cometh very seldom to his church, and is a whoremaster"; those were days of virile speech. When Parliament convened, John Penry presented a petition for reform of the Church, and charged the bishops with responsibility for clerical abuses and popular paganism. Whitgift ordered his arrest, but he was soon released. Antony Cope introduced a bill to abolish the entire episcopal establishment and reorganize English Christianity on the presbyterian plan. Elizabeth ordered Parliament to remove the bill from discussion. Peter Wentworth rose to a question of parliamentary freedom, and four members supported him; Elizabeth had all five lodged in the Tower.

Frustrated in Parliament, Penry and other Puritans took to the press. Eluding Whitgift's severe censorship of publications, they deluged England (1588–89) with a succession of privately printed pamphlets, all signed "Martin Marprelate, Gentleman," and attacking the authority and personal character of the bishops in terms of satirical abuse. Whitgift and the High Commission deployed all the machinery of espionage to find the authors and printers; but the printers moved from town to town, and public sympathy helped them to escape detection until April 1589. Professional writers like John Lyly and Thomas Nash were engaged to answer "Martin" and gave him good competition in scurrility. Finally, as billingsgate ran out, the controversy subsided, and moderate men mourned the degradation of Christianity into an art of vituperation.

Stung by these pamphlets, Elizabeth gave Whitgift a free hand to check the Puritans. The Marprelate printers were found, arrests multiplied, executions followed. Cartwright was sentenced to death, but was pardoned by the Queen. Two leaders of the "Brownian Movement," John Greenwood and Henry Barrow, were hanged in 1593, and soon thereafter John Penry. Parliament decreed (1593) that anyone who questioned the Queen's religious supremacy, or persistently absented himself from Anglican services, or attended "any assemblies, conventicles, or meetings under cover or pretense of any exercise of religion" should be imprisoned and—unless he gave a pledge of future conformity—should leave England and never return, on pain of death.[86]

At this juncture, and amid the turmoil and fury, a modest parson raised the controversy to the level of philosophy, piety, and stately prose. Richard Hooker was one of two clergymen assigned to conduct services in the London Temple; the other was Walter Travers, Cartwright's friend. In the morning sermon Hooker expounded the ecclesiastical polity of Elizabeth; in the afternoon Travers criticized that church government from the Puritan view. Each developed his sermons into a book. As Hooker was writing literature as well as theology, he begged his bishop to transfer him to a quiet rural parsonage. So at Boscombe in Wiltshire he completed the first four books of his great work *Of the Laws of Ecclesiastical Polity* (1594); three years later, at Bishopsbourne, he sent Book V to the press; and there, in 1600, age forty-seven, he died.

His *Laws* astonished England by the calm and even-tempered dignity of its argument and the sonorous majesty of its almost Latin style. Cardinal Allen praised it as the best book that had yet come out of England; Pope Clement VIII lauded its eloquence and learning; Queen Elizabeth read it gratefully as a splendid apology for her religious government; the Puritans were mollified by the gentle clarity of its tone; and posterity received it as a noble attempt to harmonize religion and reason. Hooker astonished his contemporaries by admitting that even a pope could be saved; he shocked the theologians by declaring that "the assurance of what we believe by the Word of God is to us not so certain as that which we perceive by sense";[87] man's reasoning faculty is also a divine gift and revelation.

Hooker based his theory of law on medieval philosophy as formulated by St. Thomas Aquinas, and he anticipated the "social contract" of Hobbes and Locke. After showing the need and boon of social organization, he argued that voluntary participation in a society implies consent to be governed by its laws. But the ultimate source of the laws is the community itself: a king or a parliament may issue laws only as the delegate or representatives of the community. "Law makes the king; the king's grant of any favor contrary to the law is void . . . For peaceable contentment on both sides, the assent of those who are governed seemeth necessary . . . Laws are not which public approbation has not made so."[88] And Hooker added a passage that might have warned Charles I:

> The Parliament of England, together with the [ecclesiastical] Convocation annexed thereunto, is that whereupon the very essence of all government within this kingdom doth depend; it is even the body of the whole realm; it consisteth of the king and of all that within the land are subject to him, for they are all there present, either in person, or by such as they voluntarily have derived [delegated] their power unto.[89]

To Hooker religion seemed an integral part of the state, for social order and therefore even material prosperity depend on moral discipline, which collapses without religious inculcation and support. Consequently every state should provide religious training for its people. The Anglican Church might be imperfect, but so would be all institutions made and manned by the children of Adam. "He that goeth about to persuade a multitude that they are not so well off as they ought to be, shall never want attentive and favorable hearers; because they know the manifold defects whereunto every kind of regiment [government] is subject, but the secret lets and difficulties, which in public proceedings are innumerable and inevitable, they have not ordinarily the judgment to consider."[90]

Hooker's logic was too circular to be convincing, his learning too scholastic to meet the issues of his time, his shy spirit too thankful for order to understand the longing for liberty. The Puritans acknowledged his eloquence, but went on their way. Compelled to choose between their country and their faith, many of them emigrated, reversing the movement of Continental Protestants into England. Holland welcomed them, and English congregations rose at Middelburg, Leiden, and Amsterdam. There the exiles and their offspring labored, taught, preached, and wrote, preparing with quiet passion for their triumphs in England and their fulfillment in America.

VIII. ELIZABETH AND IRELAND

Ireland had been conquered by the English in 1169–71, and had been held ever since on the ground that otherwise it would be used by France or Spain as a base for attacks on England. At Elizabeth's accession direct English rule in Ireland was confined to the eastern coast—"the Pale"—around and south of Dublin; the rest of the island was governed by Irish chieftains only nominally acknowledging English sovereignty. The perennial conflict with the English disrupted the tribal administration that had given Ireland chaos and violence, but also poets, scholars, and saints. Most of the land was left to woods and bogs; transport and communication were heroic enterprises, and the native Celtic population of some 800,000 souls lived in a half-lawless misery on the edge of barbarism. The English in the Pale were almost as poor, and they made Elizabeth's problem worse by debauchery, peculation, and crime; they robbed the London government as sedulously as they plundered the Irish peasantry. Throughout the reign English settlers drove Irish proprietors and tenants from "clearances"; the dispossessed fought back with assassinations; and life for conquerors and conquered alike became a persisting fever of force and hate. Cecil himself thought that "the Flemings had not such cause to rebel against the oppression of the Spaniards" as the Irish against English rule.[91]

Elizabeth's Irish policy was based on the conviction that a Catholic Ireland would be a peril to a Protestant England. She ordered a full enforcement of Protestantism throughout the island. Mass was prohibited, the monasteries were closed; public worship ceased outside the narrow Pale. Priests survived in hiding, and administered the sacraments furtively to a few. Morality, deprived of both religion and peace, almost disappeared; murder, theft, adultery, and rape flourished, and men changed wives without grudge or qualm. Irish leaders appealed to the popes and Philip II for protection or aid. Philip feared to invade Ireland, lest the English should invade and help the rebellious Netherlands, but he established centers and colleges for Irish refugees in Spain. Pius IV sent to Ireland an Irish Jesuit, David Wolfe (1560); with the courage and devotion characteristic of his order, Wolfe established clandestine missions, brought in other disguised Jesuits, and restored Catholic piety and hope. The chieftains took heart, and one after another rose in revolt against English rule.

The most powerful of them was Shane (i.e., John) O'Neill of Tyrone. Here was such a man as legend could sing of and Irishmen could fight for. He fiercely defended his title of *the* O'Neill against a usurping brother. He ignored the Commandments and adored the Church. He foiled all English efforts to subdue him, risked his head to visit London and win Elizabeth's alliance and support, and returned in triumph to rule Ulster as well as Tyrone. He fought the rival O'Donnell clan ferociously, was finally defeated by it (1567), and was killed when he took refuge with the MacDonnells, Scottish immigrants whose settlement at Antrim he had formerly attacked.

The history of Ireland after his death was a parade of rebellions, massacres, and lords deputy. Sir Henry Sidney, father of Sir Philip, served Elizabeth faithfully in that ungrateful office for nine years. He joined in defeating O'Neill, hunted Rory O'More to the death, and was recalled (1578) because of the high cost of his victories. In two years as Lord Deputy, Walter Devereux, first Earl of Essex, distinguished himself by a massacre on the island of Rathlin, off the Antrim coast. Thither the rebel MacDonnells had sent for safety their wives and children, their aged and ailing, with a protective guard. Essex dispatched a force to capture the island. The garrison offered to surrender if they might be allowed to sail for Scotland; the offer was refused; they surrendered unconditionally; they and the women and children, the sick and the old, numbering six hundred, were put to the sword (1575).[92]

The great revolt of the reign was that of the Geraldine clan in Munster. After many captivities and escapes, James Fitzmaurice Fitzgerald crossed to the Continent, raised a troop of Spaniards, Italians, Portuguese, Flemings, and English Catholic emigrés, and landed them on the coast of Kerry (1579), only to lose his life in an incidental war with another clan. His cousin Gerald Fitzgerald, fifteenth Earl of Desmond, carried on the revolt, but the neighboring Butler clan, under the Protestant Earl of Ormonde, declared for England. The Catholics of the Pale organized an army and defeated the levies of the new Lord Deputy, Arthur, Lord Grey (1580). Reinforced, Grey besieged Desmond's main force by land and sea on a promontory in Smerwick Bay. Finding themselves defenseless against Grey's artillery, the six hundred surviving rebels surrendered and begged for mercy; all were slaughtered, women and men, except for officers who could promise substantial ransoms.[93] The war of English against Irish, and of clan against clan, so ravaged Munster that (said an Irish chronicler) "the lowing of a cow, or the voice of a plowman, was not to be heard that year from Dingle to the Rock of Cashel"; and an Englishman wrote (1582) that "there hath died by famine . . . thirty thousand in Munster in less than half a year, besides others that are hanged and killed."[94] For "to kill an Irishman in that province," wrote a great English historian, "was thought no more of than to kill a mad dog."[95] Almost denuded of Irish, Munster was divided into plantations for English settlers (1586)—one of them Edmund Spenser, who there completed *The Faerie Queene.*

The desperate Irish rose again in 1593. Hugh O'Donnell, Lord of Tyrconnel, joined forces with Hugh O'Neill, second Earl of Tyrone. Spain, now at open war with England, promised help. In an interregnum between lords deputy, O'Neill routed an English army at Armagh, captured Blackwater, an English stronghold in the north (1598), and sent a force to renew the Munster revolt. The English colonists fled, abandoning their plantations. Hope and joy spread in Ireland, and even the English expected that Dublin itself would fall.

It was in this crisis that Elizabeth appointed the youthful Robert Devereux, second Earl of Essex, as her Lord Deputy in Ireland (March 1599). She gave him an army of 17,500 men—the greatest that England had ever sent to the island. She bade him attack O'Neill in Tyrone, make no peace without consulting her, and not return without her permission. Arrived in Dublin, he dallied through the spring, undertook a few skirmishes, let his army waste away with disease, signed an unauthorized truce with O'Neill, and returned to England (September 1599) to explain his failure to the Queen. Quickly replacing him, Charles Blount, Lord Mountjoy, faced with courage and skill a combination of tricky O'Neill, fearless O'Donnell, and a fleet landing at Kinsale with troops and arms from Spain and indulgences from Clement VIII for all who would defend Ireland and the faith. Mountjoy rushed south to meet the Spaniards, and defeated them so decisively that O'Neill submitted; the revolt collapsed, and a general amnesty brought a precarious peace (1603). Meanwhile Elizabeth had died.

Her record in Ireland subtracted from her glory. She underestimated the difficulty of conquering, in an almost roadless country, a people whose love of their land and their faith was their only bond to life and decency. She scolded her deputies for failures that were due in part to her own parsimony; they were unable to pay their troops, who found it more profitable to rob the Irish than to fight them. She vacillated between truce and terror, and never followed one policy to a decision. She founded Trinity College and Dublin University (1591), but she left the people of Ireland as illiterate as before. After the expenditure of £10,000,000, the peace achieved was a desert of desolation over half the lovely isle, and, over all of it, a spirit of unspeakable hatred that only bided its time to kill and devastate again.

IX. ELIZABETH AND SPAIN

The Queen was at her best in her management of Spain. She allowed Philip to think she might marry him or his son; and in his hopes of winning England with a wedding ring, he played the game of patience till his friends were alienated and Elizabeth was strong. Pope and Emperor and a hapless Scottish Queen might beg him to invade England, but he was too doubtful of France, too troubled in the Netherlands, to venture upon so incalculable a throw of the political dice. He had no assurance that France would not pounce upon the Spanish Netherlands the moment he became embroiled with England. He was loath to encourage revolution anywhere. He trusted, in his heavy procrastinating way, that Elizabeth would in due time find one or another of the many exits that an ingenious nature has provided from our life; and yet he was in no haste to give the throne of England to a Scottish lass in love with France. For years he held back the Pope from promulgating the excommunication of Elizabeth. He bore in somber silence her treatment of Catholics in England, and her protests against the treatment of English Protestants in Spain. For almost thirty years he kept the peace while English privateers made war upon Spanish colonies and trade.

The nature of man confesses itself in the conduct of states, for these are but ourselves in gross, and behave, for the most part, as men presumably did before morals and laws were laid upon them by religion and force. Conscience follows the policeman, but there were no police for states. On the seas there were no Ten Commandments, and trade existed by permission of piracy. Small pirate craft used the inlets of the British coast as lairs and thence sallied forth to seize what they could; if the victims were Spanish the English could enjoy the religious fervor of plundering a papist. Bold men like John Hawkins and Francis Drake fitted out substantial privateers and took all the oceans for their province. Elizabeth disowned but did not disturb them, for she saw in the privateers the makings of a navy, and in these buccaneers her future admirals. The Huguenot port of La Rochelle became a favorite rendezvous of English, Dutch, and Huguenot vessels, which "preyed on Catholic commerce under whatever flag it sailed,"[96] and, in need, on Protestant commerce too.

From such piracy the buccaneers passed to that lucrative trade in slaves which the Portuguese had opened up a century before. In the Spanish colonies of America the natives were dying out from toil too arduous for their climate and constitutions. A demand arose for a sturdier breed of laborers. Las Casas himself, defender of the natives, suggested to Charles I of Spain that African Negroes, stronger than the Caribbean Indians, should be transported to America, to do the heavy work for the Spaniards there.[97] Charles consented, but Philip II condemned the trade and instructed the Spanish-American governors to prevent the importation of slaves except under license—costly and rare—by the home administration.[98] Aware that some governors were evading these restrictions, Hawkins led three ships to Africa (1562), captured three hundred Negroes, took them to the West Indies, and sold them to Spanish settlers in exchange for sugar, spices, and drugs. Back in England, he induced Lord Pembroke and others to invest in a second venture, and persuaded Elizabeth to put one of her best vessels at his disposal. In 1564 he headed south with four ships, seized four hundred African Negroes, sailed for the West Indies, sold them to Spaniards under threat of his guns if they refused to buy, and returned home to be hailed as a hero and share his spoils with his backers and the Queen, who made 60 per cent on her investment.[99] In 1567 she lent him her ship the *Jesus;* with this and four other vessels he sailed to Africa, captured all the Negroes his holds could stow, sold them in Spanish America at £160 a head, and was homeward bound with loot valued at £100,000 when a Spanish fleet caught him off the Mexican coast at San Juan de Ulúa, and destroyed all of his fleet but two small tenders, in which Hawkins, after a thousand perils, returned empty-handed to England (1569).

Among the survivors of that voyage was Hawkins' young kinsman Francis Drake. Educated at Hawkins' expense, Drake became, so to speak, a native of the sea. At twenty-two he commanded a ship on Hawkins' futile expedition; at twenty-three, having lost everything but his reputation for bravery, he vowed vengeance against Spain; at twenty-five he received a privateer's commission from Elizabeth. In 1573, aged twenty-eight, he captured a convoy of silver bullion off the coast of Panama and returned to England rich and revenged. Elizabeth's councilors kept him in hiding for three years while Spain cried out for his death. Then Leicester, Walsingham, and Hatton fitted out for him four small vessels, totaling 375 tons; with these he sailed from Plymouth on November 15, 1577, on what turned out to be the second circumnavigation of the globe. As his fleet issued from the Straits of Magellan into the Pacific, it ran into a heavy storm; the ships were scattered and never reunited; Drake alone, in the *Pelican,* moved up the west coast of the Americas to San Francisco, raiding Spanish vessels on the way. Then he turned boldly westward to the Philippines, sailed through the Moluccas to Java, across the Indian Ocean to Africa, around the Cape of Good Hope, and up the Atlantic to reach Plymouth on September 26, 1580, thirty-four months after leaving it. He brought with him £600,000 of booty, of which £275,000 were handed over to the Queen.[100] England hailed him as the greatest seaman and pirate of the age. Elizabeth dined on his ship and dubbed him knight.

All this time England had been technically at peace with Spain. Philip lodged repeated protests with the Queen; she made excuses, hugged her spoils, and pointed out that Philip also was violating international "law" by sending help to the rebels in Ireland. When the Spanish ambassador threatened war she threatened marriage with Alençon and alliance with France. Philip, busy conquering Portugal, ordered his envoy to keep the peace. As usual, good luck supplemented the vacillating genius of the Queen. What would have happened to her if Catholic France had not been cut in two by civil war, if Catholic Austria and the Emperor had not been harassed by the Turks, if Spain had not been embroiled with

Portugal, France, the papacy, and its rebellious subjects in the Netherlands?

For years Elizabeth played fast and loose with the Netherlands, shifting
her policy with fluid circumstance, and no charges of irresolution or
treachery could make her move in blinders on one course. She had no
more liking for Dutch Calvinism than for English Puritanism, and no more
liking than Philip for abetting revolution. She recognized the importance,
to the English economy, of uninterrupted trade with the Netherlands. She
planned to support the revolt of the Netherlands sufficiently to keep them
from surrendering to Spain or bequeathing themselves to France. For as
long as the revolt continued Spain would stay out of England.

A blessed windfall allowed the Queen to help the rebels at a delectable
profit to her treasury. In December 1568 several Spanish vessels, carrying
£150,000 to pay Alva's troops in the Netherlands, were driven by English
privateers into Channel ports. Elizabeth, who had just heard of Hawkins'
disaster at San Juan de Ulúa, recognized a providential opportunity to
make up for what England had lost in that defeat. She asked Bishop Jewel
whether she had a right to the Spanish treasure; he judged that God, being
surely a Protestant, would be pleased to see the papists plundered. Moreover, the Queen learned, the money had been borrowed by Philip from
Genoese bankers, and Philip had refused to take title to it until its safe
delivery in Antwerp. Elizabeth had the money transferred to her vaults.
Philip complained; Alva seized all English nationals and goods that he
could lay hands upon in the Netherlands; Elizabeth arrested all Spaniards
in England. But the necessities of trade gradually restored normal relations.
Alva refused to prod Elizabeth into alliance with the rebels. Philip kept
his temper. Elizabeth kept the money.

The uneasy peace dragged on until continued English raids on Spanish
shipping, and the appeals of the imprisoned Mary Stuart's friends, involved
Philip in a plot to assassinate the Queen.[101] Convinced of his participation,
Elizabeth expelled the Spanish ambassador (1584) and gave open aid
to the Netherlands. English troops entered Flushing, Brill, Ostend, and
Sluys; Leicester was sent to command them; they were defeated by the
Spaniards at Zutphen (1586). But now at last the issue was drawn. Both
Philip and Elizabeth prepared with all their resources for the war that
would decide the mastery of the seas and the religion of England, perhaps
of Europe, perhaps of the New World.

Spain had risen to wealth by grace of Columbus and Pope Alexander
VI, whose arbitration decrees of 1493 had awarded nearly all of the Americas to his native Spain. With those voyages and bulls the Mediterranean
ceased to be the center of the white man's civilization and power, and the
Atlantic age began. Of Europe's three great Atlantic nations France was

debarred by civil war from the contest for oceanic dominion. England and Spain remained, jutting out like grasping promontories toward the promised land. It appeared impossible to dislodge Spain from her pre-eminence in America; by 1580 she had hundreds of colonies there, England none; and each year immense riches passed from the mines of Mexico and Peru to Spain. It seemed manifest destiny that Spain should rule all the Western Hemisphere, and make both the Americas in her political and religious image.

Drake was not content with this prospect. For a time the war for the world was between himself and Spain. In 1585, financed by his friends and the Queen, he fitted out thirty vessels and sallied forth against the Spanish Empire. He entered the Estuary of Vigo in northwest Spain, plundered the port of Vigo, disrobed a statue of the Virgin, and carried away the precious metals and costly vestments of the churches. He sailed on to the Canary and Cape Verde islands, pillaged the largest of them, crossed the Atlantic, raided Santo Domingo, took £30,000 as a *douceur* not to destroy the Colombian city of Cartagena, plundered and burned the town of St. Augustine in Florida, and returned to England (1586) only because yellow fever had killed a third of his crew.

This was war without its name. On February 8, 1587, the English government put to death the Scottish Queen. Philip informed Sixtus V that he was now ready to invade England and dethrone Elizabeth. He asked the Pope to contribute 2,000,000 gold crowns; Sixtus offered 600,-000, to be paid to Spain only if the invasion actually occurred. Philip bade his best admiral, the Marquis of Santa Cruz, to prepare the largest armada so far known in history. Ships were gathered or built at Lisbon, stores were assembled at Cádiz.

Drake urged Elizabeth to give him a fleet to destroy the Armada before it could take irresistible form. She consented, and on April 2, 1587, with thirty ships, he hurried out from Plymouth before she could change her mind. She did, but too late to reach him. On April 16 he ran his fleet into Cádiz harbor, maneuvered out of range of the batteries on the shore, sank a Spanish man-of-war, raided the transports and storeships, captured their cargoes, set all enemy vessels on fire, and departed unharmed. He anchored off Lisbon and challenged Santa Cruz to come out and fight. The Marquis refused, for his ships were not yet armed. Drake moved north to La Coruña and seized great stores collected there; then to the Azores, where he took a Spanish galleon. With it in tow he returned to England. Even the Spaniards marveled at his audacity and seamanship, and said that "were it not that he was a Lutheran, there was not the like man in the world."[102]

Philip patiently rebuilt his fleet. The Marquis of Santa Cruz died (January 1588); Philip replaced him with the Duke of Medina-Sidonia, a grandee with more pedigree than competence. When finally the Armada was complete, it numbered 130 vessels, averaging 445 tons; half the ships were cargo carriers, half were men-of-war; 8,050 sailors manned them, 19,000 soldiers sailed. Philip and his admirals thought of naval warfare in ancient terms—to grapple and board the enemy and fight man to man; the English plan was to sink the enemy's ships, with their crowded crews, by broadside fire. Philip instructed his fleet not to seek out and attack the English squadrons, but to seize some English beachhead, cross to Flanders, and take on board the 30,000 troops that the Duke of Parma had ready there; so reinforced, the Spanish were to march on London. Meanwhile a letter composed by Cardinal Allen (April 1588) was smuggled into England, bidding the Catholics join the Spanish in deposing their "usurping, heretic, prostitute" Queen.[103] To help restore Catholicism in England, hundreds of monks accompanied the Armada, under the vicar general of the Inquisition.[104] A devout religious spirit moved the Spanish sailors and their masters; they sincerely believed they were on a sacred mission; prostitutes were sent away, profanity subsided, gambling ceased. On the morning when the fleet sailed from Lisbon (May 29, 1588), every man on board received the Eucharist, and all Spain prayed.

The winds favored Elizabeth; the Armada ran into a damaging storm; it took refuge in the harbor of La Coruña, healed its wounds, and set forth again (July 12). England awaited it in a feverish mixture of divided counsels, hurried preparations, and desperate resolve. Now the time had come for Elizabeth to spend the sums that she had saved through thirty years of skimping and deviltry. Her people, Catholic as well as Protestant, came manfully to her rescue; volunteer militia trained in the towns; London merchants financed regiments and, asked to fit out fifteen ships, provided thirty. For ten years now Hawkins had been building men-of-war for the Queen's navy; Drake was now a vice-admiral. Privateers brought their own vessels to the fateful rendezvous. Early in July 1588 the full complement of eighty-two ships, under command of Charles, Lord Howard of Effingham, as Lord High Admiral of England, gathered at Plymouth to greet the advancing foe.

On July 19* the vanguard of the Armada was sighted in the mouth of the Channel. The defending fleet sailed out of Plymouth, and on the twenty-first the action began. The Spaniards waited for the English to come close enough for grappling; instead, the light English vessels— built to low lines and narrow beam—scurried around the heavy Spanish galleons, firing broadsides as they went. The Spanish decks were too high; their guns fired too far above the English vessels, doing only minor

---

* Old Style, ten days earlier than by the Gregorian calendar, which was adopted by Spain in 1582, but not by England till 1751.

damage; the English boats ran beneath the fire, and their maneuverability and speed left the Spaniards helpless and confused. As night fell they fled before the wind, leaving one of their ships to be taken by Drake. Another was blown up, reportedly by a mutinous German gunner, and the wreck fell into English hands. Luckily, both ships contained ammunition, which was soon transferred to the Queen's fleet. On the twenty-fourth more ammunition came, but still the English had only enough for a day's fighting. On the twenty-fifth, near the Isle of Wight, Howard led an attack; his flagship sailed into the center of the Armada, exchanging broadsides with every galleon that it passed; and the superior accuracy of the English fire broke the Spanish morale. "The enemy pursue me," wrote Medina-Sidonia that night to the Duke of Parma; "they fire on me from morn till dark, but they will not grapple . . . There is no remedy, for they are swift and we are slow."[105] He begged Parma to send him ammunition and reinforcements, but Parma's ports were blockaded by Dutch ships.

On the twenty-seventh the Armada anchored in Calais roads. On the twenty-eighth Drake set fire to eight small and dispensable vessels and placed them in the wind to sail amid the Spanish fleet. Fearing them, Medina-Sidonia ordered his ships to put out to sea. On the twenty-ninth Drake attacked them off the French coast at Gravelines, in the main action of the war. The Spaniards fought bravely, but with poor seamanship and gunnery. At noon Howard's squadron came up, and the full English fleet poured such fire into the Armada that many of its ships were disabled and some were sunk; their wooden hulls, though three feet thick, were penetrated by the English shot; thousands of Spaniards were killed; blood could be seen flowing from the decks into the sea. At the close of that day the Armada had lost four thousand men; four thousand more were wounded, and the surviving vessels were with difficulty kept afloat. Seeing that his crews could bear no more, Medina-Sidonia gave orders to withdraw. On the thirtieth the wind carried the broken fleet into the North Sea. The English followed them as far north as the Firth of Forth; then, lacking food and ammunition, they returned to port. They had lost sixty men and not one ship.

For the remnants of the Armada there was no haven nearer than Spain itself. Scotland was hostile, and Irish ports were held by English troops. Desperately the injured ships and starving men made their way around the British Isles. The water was rough and the wind was wild; masts were shattered and sails were torn; day after day some vessel sank or was abandoned, dead men were dropped into the sea. Seventeen ships were wrecked on the rugged Irish shores; at Sligo alone 1,100 drowned Spaniards were washed up on the beach. Some of the crews made landings in Ireland and begged for food and drink; they were refused, and hundreds, too weak to fight, were massacred by the half-savage denizens of the coasts. Of the 130 vessels that had left Spain, 54 returned; of 27,000 men, 10,000, most of them wounded or sick. Philip, learning of the prolonged disaster day by day, shut himself up in his Escorial cell, and none dared speak to him. Sixtus V, pleading that no invasion of England had occurred, sent not one ducat to bankrupt Spain.

Elizabeth was as careful with ducats as the Pope. Wary of peculation in the navy, she demanded account of every shilling spent by navy and army before, during, and after the battle; Howard and Hawkins made up out of their own pockets whatever discrepancies they could not explain.[106] Elizabeth, expecting a long war, had kept the crews and troops on short rations and low pay. Now a violent disease, akin to typhus, ran through the returning men; on some vessels half the crew died or were disabled; and Hawkins wondered what England's fate would have been had the epidemic preceded the enemy.

The naval war continued till Philip's death (1598). Drake took a fleet and fifteen thousand men to help the Portuguese in their revolt against Spain (1589); but the Portuguese hated Protestants more than Spaniards, the English drank themselves drunk on captured wine, and the expedition ended in failure and disgrace. Lord Thomas Howard led a fleet to the Azores to intercept the Spanish *flota* bringing silver and gold to Spain; but Philip's new Armada put Howard's ships to flight—except th' *!evenge*, which, caught lagging behind the rest, fought fifteen Spanish ps heroically until overcome (1591). Drake and Hawkins made another sally to the West Indies (1595), but they quarreled and died on the way. In 1596 Elizabeth sent still another fleet to destroy ships in Spanish ports; at Cádiz it found nineteen men-of-war and thirty-six merchantmen; but these escaped to the open sea while Essex plundered the town. This expedition too was a failure, but it demonstrated again the English mastery of the Atlantic.

The defeat of the Armada affected almost everything in modern European civilization. It marked a decisive change in naval tactics; grappling and boarding gave way to cannonading from shipside and deck. The weakening of Spain helped the Dutch to win their independence, advanced Henry IV to the throne of France, and opened North America to English colonies. Protestantism was preserved and strengthened, Catholicism waned in England, and James VI of Scotland ceased to flirt with the popes. Had the Armada been more wisely built and led, Catholicism might have recovered England, the Guises might have prevailed in France, Holland might have succumbed; the great burst of pride and energy that raised up Shakespeare and Bacon as the symbols and fruit of a triumphant

England might never have been; and the Elizabethan ecstasy would have had to meet the Spanish Inquisition. So wars determine theology and philosophy, and the ability to kill and destroy is a prerequisite for permission to live and build.

X. RALEIGH AND ESSEX: 1588–1601

Though Cecil and Walsingham, Drake and Hawkins had been the immediate instruments of glory and victory, Elizabeth personified triumphant England, and at sixty she was at the top of her fame and power. Her face was a bit wrinkled, her hair was detachable, some teeth were missing and some were black, but in her awesome finery of lacy headdress, flying ruff, padded sleeves, and hoopskirt, all asparkle with encrusted gems, she stood proud and straight and undeniably a queen. Parliament grumbled at her royal ways, but submitted; old councilors offered advice with the timidity of young suitors; and young suitors fluent with adoration surrounded the throne. Leicester and Walsingham paid their debt to nature, Drake and Hawkins would soon be swallowed by the sea they had thought to rule. Cecil—the "Atlas of this commonwealth," Bacon called him[107]— was now old, and he creaked with gout; presently Elizabeth would nurse him in his final illness and feed him his last food with her own hand.[108] She grew sad with these amputations, but she did not let them darken the splendor of her progresses or the vivacity of her court.

New faces shone about her, bringing her some vicarious youth. Christopher Hatton was so handsome that she made him Chancellor (1587). She waited nine years before accepting Burghley's advice to make his sagacious hunchbacked son, Robert Cecil, her Secretary of State. She relished more the fine features and rattling sword of Walter Raleigh, and did not mind his private theological doubts; she had some of her own.

Raleigh was almost the complete Elizabethan man: gentleman, soldier, mariner, adventurer, poet, philosopher, orator, historian, martyr; here was the *uomo universale* of Renaissance dreams, who touched genius at every point, but never let the part become the whole. Born in Devonshire in 1552, entered at Oxford in 1568, he fled from books into life and joined a gallant group of pedigreed volunteers who crossed to France to fight for the Huguenots. Six years in those wars may have taught him some of the unscrupulous violence of action and reckless audacity of speech that molded his later fate. Back in England (1575), he forced himself to study law, but in 1578 he went off again as a volunteer to help the Dutch against Spain. Two years later he was in Ireland as a captain in the army that put down Desmond's rebellion, and he played no hesitant part in the Smerwick massacre. Elizabeth rewarded him with twelve thousand acres in Ireland and favor at her court. Pleased with his figure, his compliments,* and his wit, she listened with less than her customary skepticism to his proposal for English colonies in America; she gave him a charter, and in 1584 he sent out, but did not accompany, the first of several expeditions that tried—and failed—to establish a settlement in Virginia; only the name survived, as a lasting memorial to the Queen's inaccessibility. Elizabeth Throckmorton, a maid of honor, proved more approachable; she accepted Raleigh as her lover, and secretly married him (1593). As no member of the court might marry without the Queen's consent, the ardent couple received an unexpected honeymoon in the Tower. Raleigh earned release —with banishment from the court—by writing to Burghley a letter describing the Queen as an amalgam of all the perfections in history.

He retired to his Sherborne estate, planned voyages and discoveries, played with atheism, and wrote poetry whose every line had a characteristic tang and sting. But two years of quiet exhausted his stability. With the help of Lord Admiral Howard and Robert Cecil, he fitted out five vessels and headed for South America, seeking El Dorado—a fabled land of golden palaces, rivers running gold, and Amazons with undiminished charms. He sailed a hundred miles up the Orinoco, but found no female warriors and no gold. Baffled by rapids and falls, he returned to England empty-handed; but he told how the American natives had marveled at the beauty of the Queen when he showed them her portrait; and soon he was readmitted to the court. His eloquent account *The Discovery of the Large, Rich, and Beautiful Empire of Guiana* reaffirmed his faith that "the sun covereth not so much riches in any part of the world" as the region of the Orinoco. Tirelessly he preached the desirability of getting America's wealth out of Spanish into English hands; and he phrased the doctrine of sea power perfectly: "Whoever commands the sea commands the trade; whoever commands the trade of the world commands the riches of the world, and consequently the world itself."[109]

In 1596 he joined the expedition to Cádiz, fought as vigorously as he wrote, and received a wound in the leg. The Queen now "used him graciously" and made him captain of the guard. In 1597 he commanded part of the fleet that Essex led to the Azores. Separated from the rest by a storm, Raleigh's squadron encountered and defeated the enemy. Essex never forgave him for pre-empting victory.

Robert Devereux, second Earl of Essex, surpassed even Raleigh in fascination. He had Walter's ambition and verve and pride, a little more of his

---

* The tale of his coat in the mud beneath her feet is a legend.

hot temper, a little less of his wit, much more of generosity and *noblesse oblige*. He was a man of action enamored of intellect—victor in jousts and on the athletic field, distinguished for bravery and audacity in war, yet also the helpful and appreciative friend of poets and philosophers. When his mother became Leicester's second wife, Leicester advanced him at court to offset Raleigh's ingratiating charm. The Queen, fifty-three, fell maternally in love with the high-strung, handsome lad of twenty (1587); here was a son to console her childlessness. They talked, rode, heard music, played cards together, and "my Lord," said a gossip, "cometh not to his own lodging till birds sing in the morning."[110] Her aging heart suffered when he secretly married Philip Sidney's widow; but she soon forgave him, and by 1593 he was a member of the Privy Council. However, he was poorly fitted for court life or statesmanship; "he carried his love and hate always on his face," said his servant Cuffe, "and knew not how to hide them."[111] He made enemies of Raleigh, William Cecil, Robert Cecil, finally of the ungrateful Bacon and the reluctant Queen.

Francis Bacon, who was destined to have more influence on European thought than any other Elizabethan, had been born (1561) in the very aura of the court, at York House, official residence of the Lord Keeper of the Great Seal, who was his father, Sir Nicholas; Elizabeth called the boy "the young Lord Keeper." His frail constitution drove him from sports to studies; his agile intellect grasped knowledge hungrily; soon his erudition was among the wonders of those "spacious times." After three years at Cambridge he was sent to France with the English ambassador to let him learn the ways of state. While he was there his father unexpectedly died (1579) before buying an estate that he had intended for Francis, who was a younger son; and the youth, suddenly reduced to meager means, returned to London to study law at Gray's Inn. Being a nephew of William Cecil, he appealed to him for some political place; after four years of waiting, he sent him a whimsical reminder that "the objection of my years will wear away with the length of my suit."[112] Somehow, in that year 1584, he was elected to Parliament, though still but twenty-three. He distinguished himself by favoring more toleration of the Puritans (his mother was one). The Queen ignored his arguments, but he restated them bravely in a privately circulated *Advertisement Touching the Controversies of the Church of England* (1589). He proposed that no man should be molested for his religious faith who promised to defend England against any foreign power—including the papacy—that threatened England's full sovereignty and freedom. Elizabeth and Cecil thought the young philosopher a bit forward; and in truth he was ahead of his times.

Essex relished the keenness of Bacon's mind and invited his advice. The young sage counseled the young noble to seem, if he could not be, modest; to moderate his expenditures; to seek civil rather than military office, since setbacks in politics could be sooner redeemed than defeats in war; and to regard his popularity with the populace as a danger with the Queen.[113] Bacon hoped that Essex would mature into a statesman and give his mentor some opportunity to rise. In 1592 he appealed again to Cecil in famous lines:

> I wax now somewhat ancient; one-and-thirty years is a great deal of sand in the hourglass . . . The meanness of my estate doth somewhat move me . . . I confess that I have as vast contemplative ends as I have moderate civil ends: for I have taken all knowledge to be my province . . . This, whether it be curiosity, or vainglory, or nature . . . is so fixed in my mind as it cannot be removed.[114]

When Essex importuned the Cecils and Elizabeth to give Bacon the vacant office of attorney general, his appeals were in vain; Edward Coke, older and technically more fit, was chosen instead. Essex took the blame handsomely, and gave Bacon an estate at Twickenham with £1,800.[115] Before Bacon could use this he suffered a brief and genteel imprisonment for debt.[116] In 1597 he was appointed to the "Learned Council" of lawyers who advised the Privy Council.[117]

Despite Bacon's advice, Essex joined the war party, and planned to make himself head of the army. His dashing bravery at Cádiz made him too popular for the Council's taste; failure at the Azores and his undiminished pride, extravagance, and sharp tongue alienated the court and irritated the Queen. When she flatly rejected his recommendation of Sir George Carew for office in Ireland, he turned his back on her with a gesture of contempt. Furious, she boxed his ears and cried, "Go to the Devil!" He grasped his sword and shouted at her, "This is an outrage that I will not put up with. I would not have borne it from your father's hands." He rushed in anger from the room, and all the court expected him to be clapped into the Tower (1598).[118] Elizabeth did nothing. On the contrary—or was it to get rid of him?—a few months later she appointed him Lord Deputy for Ireland.

Bacon had cautioned him not to seek that ungrateful task of countering a faith by force; but Essex wanted an army. On March 27, 1599, he left for Dublin amid the acclamations of the populace, the misgivings of his friends, and the satisfaction of his enemies. Six months later, having failed in his mission, he hurried back to England without permission of the Queen, rushed unannounced into her dressing room, and tried to explain his actions in Ireland. She listened to him with patient wrath, and had him committed to the custody of the Lord Keeper at York House until the charges against him could be heard.

The people of London murmured, for they were ignorant of his failure and remembered his victories. The Privy Council ordered a semipublic trial, and commissioned Bacon—as a member of the Learned Council and as a lawyer pledged to defend the Queen—to draw up a statement of the charges. He asked to be excused; they insisted; he consented. The indictment he formulated was moderate; Essex acknowledged its truth and offered humble submission. He was suspended from his offices and was told to remain in his own home till the Queen should be pleased to free him (June 5, 1600). Bacon pleaded for him, and on August 26 Essex was restored to liberty.

Now in his own Essex House, he continued his search for power. One of his intimates was Shakespeare's patron, Henry Wriothesley, Earl of Southampton; him Essex sent to Ireland to propose that Mountjoy, now Lord Deputy there, should return to England with the English army and help Essex take control of the government. Mountjoy refused. Early in 1601 Essex wrote to James VI of Scotland, asking his aid and promising to support him as successor to Elizabeth; James sent him a letter of encouragement. Wild rumors spread through the excited capital: that Robert Cecil was planning to make the Spanish Infanta queen of England; that Essex was to be immured in the Tower; that Raleigh had vowed to kill him. Perhaps to force Essex to show his hand, the younger Cecil induced the Queen to send Essex a message requiring him to attend the Council. His friends warned him that this was a ruse to seize him. One friend, Sir Gilly Merrick, paid the Chamberlain's company to stage, that evening in Southwark, Shakespeare's *Richard II*, showing a sovereign justly deposed.[119]

The next morning (February 7, 1601) some three hundred supporters of Essex, fervent and armed, gathered in the courtyard of his home. When the Lord Keeper and three other dignitaries came to ask the cause of this illegal assembly, the crowd locked them up and swept the hesitant Earl on with them to London and revolution. He had hoped that the people would rise to his cause, but the preachers bade them stay indoors, and they obeyed. The forces of the government were on guard and routed the rebels. Essex was captured and lodged in the Tower.

He was quickly brought to trial on a charge of treason. The Council bade Bacon help Coke in preparing the government's case. His refusal would have ruined his political career; his consent ruined his posthumous reputation. When Coke faltered in presenting the indictment, Bacon rose and stated the matter with convincing, convicting clarity. Essex confessed his guilt and named his accomplices.[120] Five of these were arrested and beheaded. Southampton was sentenced to life imprisonment; James I later released him. Legend told how Essex sent the Queen a ring once given him by her with a promise to come to his aid if he should ever return it in his hour of need. If sent, it did not reach her.[121] On February 25, 1601, aged thirty-five, Essex went gallantly to the fate that was the seal of his character. Raleigh, his enemy, wept when the blow fell. For a year the Tower displayed the severed and decaying head.

XI. THE MAGIC FADES: 1601–3

The sight of that head, or the knowledge that it was staring down upon her night and day, must have shared in the somber mood of Elizabeth's final years. She sat alone for hours in silent, pensive melancholy. She maintained the amusements of her court and made at times a brave pretense of gaiety, but her health was gone and her heart was dead. England had ceased to love her; it felt that she had outlived herself and should make room for younger royalty. The last of her Parliaments rebelled more vigorously than any before against her infringement of parliamentary freedom, her persecution of Puritans, her rising demands for funds, her gifts of trade monopolies to her favorites. To everyone's surprise, the Queen yielded on the last point and promised to end the abuse. All the members of the Commons went to thank her, and they knelt as she gave what proved to be her last address to them, her wistful "Golden Speech" (November 20, 1601):

> There is no jewel, be it of never so rich a price, which I prefer before . . . your love. For I do esteem it more than any treasure . . . And though God has raised us high, yet this I count the glory of my crown, that I have reigned with your loves . . .[122]

She bade them rise and then continued:

> To be a king and wear a crown is a thing more glorious to them that see it than it is pleasant to them that bear it . . . For my own part, were it not for conscience' sake to discharge the duty that God hath laid upon me, and to maintain His glory, and keep you in safety, in mine own disposition I should be willing to resign the place I hold to any other, and glad to be freed of the glory with the labors; for it is not my desire to live or to reign longer than my life and reign shall be for your good. And though you have had and may have many mightier and wiser princes sitting in this seat, yet you never had, nor shall have, any love you better.[123]

She had postponed as long as she could the question of a successor, for while the Queen of Scots lived, as legal heir to her throne, Elizabeth could not reconcile herself to letting Mary undo the Protestant settlement. Now that Mary was dead, and Mary's son, James VI of Scotland, was heir apparent, it was some comfort to know that, however vacillating and devious, he was Protestant. She knew that Robert Cecil and others of her court were secretly negotiating with James to ease his accession and feather their nests, and were counting the days when she should die.

Rumors moved across Europe that she was dying of cancer. But she was dying of too much life. Her frame could not bear any more the joys and sorrows, the burdens and blows of the relentless years. When her godson, Sir John Harington, tried to amuse her with witty verses, she sent him off, saying, "When thou dost feel creeping time at thy gate, these fooleries will please thee less."[124] In March 1603, having exposed herself too boldly to the winter cold, she caught a fever. Through three weeks it consumed her. She spent them mostly in a chair or reclining on cushions. She would have no doctors, but she asked for music, and some players came. Finally she was persuaded to take to her bed. Archbishop Whitgift expressed a hope for her longer life; she rebuked him. He knelt beside the bed and prayed; when he thought it was enough, he tried to rise, but she bade him continue; and again, when "the old man's knees were weary," she motioned to him to pray some more. He was released only when, late at night, she fell asleep. She never woke. The next day, March 24, John Manningham wrote in his diary: "This morning, about three o'clock, her majesty departed this life, mildly like a lamb, easily like a ripe apple from a tree."[125] So it seemed.

England, which had long awaited her passing, felt the blow nevertheless. Many men realized that a great age had ended, a powerful hand had fallen from the helm, and some, like Shakespeare, feared a chaotic interlude.[126] Bacon thought her such a great queen that

> if Plutarch were now alive to write lives by parallels, it would trouble him . . . to find for her a parallel among women. This lady was endued with learning in her sex singular, and rare even among masculine princes . . . As for her government . . . this part of the island never had forty-five years of better times; and yet not through the calmness of the season, but through the wisdom of her regiment. For if there be considered, of the one side, the truth of religion established, the constant peace and security; the good administration of justice; the temperate use of the prerogative . . . the flourishing state of learning . . . and if there be considered, on the other side, the differences of religion, the troubles of neighbor countries, the ambition of Spain, and opposition of Rome; and then that she was solitary and of herself: these things I say considered, as I could not have chosen an[other] instance so recent and so proper, so I suppose I could not have chosen one more remarkable or eminent . . . concerning the conjunction of learning in the prince with felicity in the people.[127]

Looking back now in the hindsight of time, we should shade the portrait a little, noting and forgiving the faults of the incomparable Queen. She was no saint or sage, but a woman of temper and passion, lustily in love with life. The "truth of religion" was not quite established, and not all her subjects could, as Shakespeare may have thought, "eat in safety, under their own vines, what they planted, and sing the merry songs of peace."[128] The wisdom of her rule was partly that of her aides. The vacillations of her mind proved often fortunate, perhaps by the chance of change; sometimes they brought such weakness of policy that the internal troubles of her enemies had to help her to survive. But survive she did, and she prospered, by fair means or devious. She freed Scotland from the French and bound it with England; she enabled Henry of Navarre to balance his Mass in Paris with the Edict of Nantes; she found England bankrupt and despised, and left it rich and powerful; and the sinews of learning and literature grew strong in the wealth of her people. She continued the despotism of her father, but moderated it with humanity and charm. Denied husband and child, she mothered England, loved it devotedly, and used herself up in serving it. She was the greatest ruler that England has ever known.

CHAPTER II

Merrie England¹

1558–1625

I. AT WORK

WHAT sort of England was it that gave Elizabeth her power and victory, and Shakespeare his language and inspiration? What kind of people were these Elizabethan Englishmen, so recklessly aggressive, so outspoken and exuberant? How did they live and labor, dress and think, love and build and sing?

In 1581 they numbered some five million. Most of them were farmers. Most of these were sharecroppers; some were tenants paying a fixed rent; a rising proportion were freeholding yeomen. Enclosures of common lands continued, as pasturage proved more profitable than tillage. Serfdom was almost gone, but evictions of tenants by enclosures and combinations were generating an unhappy class of laborers who sold their brawn precariously from farm to farm, or from shop to shop in the expanding towns.

Except for the capital, however, the towns were still small. Norwich and Bristol, the largest after London, had little more than twenty thousand souls each. There was a pleasant side to the matter: townsmen were neighborly, and even in London most homes had gardens, or were near to open fields, and could gather the varied flowers that Shakespeare litanied. Houses were heated by burning wood; most industry used charcoal as fuel power; but the price of firewood soared in the sixteenth century, and the rising demand of the towns for coal prompted landowners to explore the deposits of their soil. German operators were imported to improve mining and metallurgy. Elizabeth forbade the use of coal in London, but her imperative proved less categorical than economic need.² Textile shops expanded as weavers and fullers fled to England from Alva's oppression in the Netherlands; Huguenots brought from France their artisan and mercantile skills; it was an Englishman, however, the Reverend William Lee, who invented (1589) the semi-automatic "stocking frame" for knitting. Fishing was the most flourishing industry, for the government encouraged it to inure men to seamanship and provide a reserve for the navy; hence Elizabeth, bowing to the Roman Church, ordered her people to abstain from meat on two days a week and on the traditional fast days of Lent.

The guilds, hamstrung by their medieval regulations, continued to lose

Fig. 1—Anonymous: *Queen Elizabeth*. National Portrait Gallery, London PAGE 3

FIG. 2—ATTRIBUTED TO ZUC-
CARO: *Sir Walter Raleigh.*
National Portrait Gallery,
London (Bettmann Archive)
PAGE 38

FIG. 3—ANONYMOUS: *Robert
Devereux, Second Earl of Essex.*
National Portrait Gallery, Lon-
don (Bettmann Archive)
PAGE 39

FIG. 4—ANONYMOUS: *William Cecil, First Lord Burghley*. National Portrait Gallery, London

PAGES 5, 61

FIG. 5—*Burghley House*, Stamford, England. British Information Services Photo

PAGE 62

Fig. 8—*The Signatures of Shakespeare.* From E. K. Chambers, *William Shakespeare,* Oxford University Press, 1930   PAGE 87

Fig. 9—Attributed to P. Oudry: *Mary, Queen of Scots*. National Portrait Gallery, London

PAGE 110

Fig. 10—Cornelis Boel: *Title Page of the King James Bible, 1611.*

PAGE 143

THE HOLY BIBLE,

Conteyning the Old Testament,

AND THE NEW.

Newly Translated out of the Originall
tongues: & with the former Translations
diligently compared and reuised, by his
Maiesties speciall Comandement

Appointed to be read in Churches.

Imprinted at London by Robert
Barker, Printer to the Kings
most Excellent Maiestie.

ANNO DOM. 1611.

FIG. 11—CORNELIUS JANSSEN: *Sir William Harvey*. From Abraham Wolf, *History of Science, Technology and Philosophy in the 16th and 17th Centuries*, Macmillan Company   PAGE 167

FIG. 12—ANONYMOUS: *Benjamin Jonson*. National Portrait Gallery, London   PAGE 146

FIG. 13—PAUL VAN SOMER: *Francis Bacon.*
National Portrait Gallery, London (Bettmann Archive)   PAGE 169

FIG. 14—SIMON VAN DE PASSE:
*Title Page of Bacon's "Instau-
ratio Magna," 1620*   PAGE 172

FIG. 15—ANTHONY VANDYCK: *King Charles I.* Louvre, Paris   PAGE 200

FIG. 16—ALESSANDRO ALLORI: *Torquato Tasso*. Uffizi, Florence

PAGE 259

FIG. 17—SASSOFERRATO: *Pope Sixtus V*. Lateran Gallery, Rome

PAGE 240

FIG. 18—GUIDO RENI: *St. Joseph.* Corsini
Gallery, Rome   PAGES 233, 266

FIG. 19—BERNINI: *Tomb of Pope Urban
VIII.* St. Peter's, Rome   PAGE 272

FIG. 20—TITIAN: *Philip II.* Prado, Madrid
(Bettmann Archive)   PAGE 277

FIG. 21—*The Escorial*, Spain. Spanish National Tourist Office Photo   PAGE 279

FIG. 22—JUAN DE JUAREGUI: *Cer-vantes* (Bettmann Archive)

PAGE 298

FIG. 23—VELÁZQUEZ: *Philip IV of Spain*. The Frick Collection, New York

PAGE 288

FIG. 24—EL GRECO: *Burial of Count Orgaz*. Church of Santo Tomé, Toledo, Spain

PAGE 318

FIG. 25—EL GRECO: *The Assumption of the Virgin*. The Art Institute of Chicago, Gift of Nancy Atwood Sprague in memory of Albert Arnold Sprague   PAGE 317

markets in this individualistic and innovating age. Clever promoters gathered capital, bought up raw materials, distributed these to shops and families, bought the product, and sold it for all that the traffic would bear. Capitalism in England began in the home, with the work of father, mother, daughter, and son for the entrepreneur; now that "domestic system" took its rise which would prevail until late in the eighteenth century. Nearly every house was a miniature factory, where women wove and spun flax and wool, sewed and embroidered, prepared herb medicines, distilled liquor, and almost succeeded in developing an art of cookery in England.

The Elizabethan state legislated as zealously for the economy as for religion. Aware that municipal restrictions on manufacture and trade were hampering commerce and industry, it replaced communal by national regulation. The famous Statute of Apprentices (1563) established a laborious code of governmental supervision and compulsion that remained the law of England till 1815. Proposing to banish idleness and unemployment, it required every able-bodied youngster to serve as apprentice for seven years, for "until a man grow into twenty-three years, he for the most part, though not always, is wild, without judgment, and not of sufficient experience to govern himself."[3] Every willfully unemployed man under thirty not having an income of forty shillings a year could be forced to take employment as directed by the local authorities. In the countryside all well men under sixty could be compelled to join in harvesting. All workmen were to be hired by yearly contract, at a kind of guaranteed annual wage. The justices of the peace were empowered to fix maximum and minimum remuneration for every employment in their territory; for London laborers the pay was fixed at ninepence a day. Masters unduly dismissing employees were to be fined forty shillings; men unlawfully quitting their jobs were to be jailed; and no employee was to leave his town or parish without permission of his employer and the local magistrate. Hours of work were defined as twelve per day in summer and through daylight in winter. Strikes of any kind were forbidden under penalty of imprisonment or heavy fines.[4]

All in all, the statute had the effect of protecting the employer against the employee, agriculture against industry, and the state against social revolt. A guild of bricklayers at Hull inscribed at the head of its ordinances the consoling proposition that "all men are by nature equal, made all by one Workman of like mire";[5] but nobody believed it, least of all Cecil and Elizabeth; and it was probably Cecil who directed the economic legislation of 1563. Its results for the working classes was to make poverty compulsory. It proposed to readjust wages periodically to the price of basic foods, but the magistrates commissioned to do this belonged to the

employing class. Wages rose, but far more slowly than prices; between
1580 and 1640 the price of necessities climbed 100 per cent, wages 20
per cent.[6] During the century from 1550 to 1650 the conditions of artisans
and laborers worsened from day to day.[7] The outskirts of London "filled
up with a comparatively poor and often vicious class, dwelling in meanest
tenements,"[8] and living in some parts by theft and beggary. At the funeral
of the Earl of Shrewsbury (1591) some twenty thousand beggars applied
for a dole.[9]

The government attacked these evils with ferocious laws against mendi-
cancy, and a comparatively humane series of Poor Laws (1563–1601) that
acknowledged the responsibility of the state for keeping its people from
starvation. In every parish a tax was collected to care for the unemployable poor and to put the employable to work in workhouses managed by
the state.

The rise of prices proved as stimulating to industry and commerce as it
was tragic to the poor. The main causes were the mining of silver in
Europe, the importation of precious metals from America, and the debasement of currencies by governments. In the period from 1501 to 1544 the
total amount of silver imported or produced in Europe was worth some
$150,000,000 in terms of 1957; for the period from 1545 to 1600 it was
worth some $900,000,000.[10] Elizabeth struggled nobly against debasement
of the English coinage. She accepted the advice of her canny councilor,
Sir Thomas Gresham, who warned her (1560), in words that became
"Gresham's law," that bad money drives out good—that coins with an
honest content of precious metal will be hoarded or sent abroad, while
coins without proper content will be used for all other purposes, especially
for taxes, the state being "paid in its own coin." Elizabeth and Cecil reformed the currency that her father and brother had debased, and restored
the gold or silver content of English coins. Prices rose nevertheless, for
the influx or production of silver and gold, and the circulation of
currency, outran the production of goods.

Monopolies shared in raising prices. Elizabeth permitted them for the
manufacture or sale of iron, oil, vinegar, coal, lead, saltpeter, starch, yarns,
skins, leather, glass. She granted these patents partly to encourage capital
in importing products and establishing new industries, partly as remuneration for offices and services not otherwise sufficiently paid. When complaints against these monopolies rose to the pitch of parliamentary revolt,
Elizabeth agreed to suspend them until their operation had been investi-
gated and approved (1601). Some were maintained.

So hampered, domestic trade developed more slowly than foreign commerce. Except at fairs, no one was allowed to sell goods in any town of
which he was not a resident. Such fairs were periodical in many localities,

and numbered several hundred a year; the most popular was the Bartholomew Fair, held each August near London, with a circus to draw the people to the merchandise. Goods moved by water rather than by road; the rivers were alive with traffic. Roads were bad but improving, and men could ride a hundred miles on them in a day; the messenger who brought to Edinburgh the news of Elizabeth's death traveled 162 miles on his first day out. Postal service, established in 1517, was for the government only; private mail went by friends, envoys, couriers, or other travelers. Land travel was mostly on horseback. Coaches were introduced about 1564; they remained till 1600 a luxury of the few; but by 1634 they were so numerous that a proclamation forbade their use by private persons because of congestion of traffic.[11] Inns were good, and so were their waitresses, except on demand; but the wayfarer had to watch his purse and conceal his route.[12] You had to be on your toes in Elizabeth's England.

Foreign commerce grew as industry developed. The export of finished products was the preferred way of paying for the import of raw materials and Oriental luxuries. The market was expanding from commune to nation to Europe, even to Asia and America, and the scope and power of national governments grew with the reach and problems of trade. England, like Spain and France, wished to export goods and import gold, for the "mercantilist" theory then prevalent measured a nation's wealth by the precious metals it held. Francis Bacon was apparently the first to speak of a favorable "balance of trade,"[13] by which he meant an excess of exports over imports, and therefore an intake of silver or gold. Cecil declared his aim "by all policies to abridge the use of foreign commodities as be not necessary for us."[14] He knew that silver and gold cannot be eaten or worn, but they were an international currency that could in an emergency buy almost anything, even enemies. Home industries had to be protected in time of peace, lest the nation be dependent on foreign products in time of war. Hence governments discouraged imports by tariffs and encouraged exports with subsidies. "Merchant companies" were formed to sell English products abroad; English "merchant adventurers" developed an export outlet at Hamburg, Anthony Jenkinson led trade missions to Russia (1557) and Persia (1562), another went to India (1583–91), an English Turkey Company was set up in 1581, the Muscovy Company was founded in 1595, and the historic East India Company on December 31, 1600. The stage was prepared for Hastings and Clive. Men in love with the sea or money ventured across oceans to find new trade routes; the science of geography was in part a by-product of their zeal. A fury of shipbuilding was engendered by the quest for markets and colonies; English forests became masts and hulls, Britannia began to rule the waves, and the British Empire was born in fact and phrase.

As commerce spread its sails, financial institutions developed to expedite it. Banks multiplied. In 1553 the Merchant Adventurers organized a joint-stock company for trade with Russia; 240 shares were issued, at £25 each; after each expedition profits were distributed and the invested capital was refunded.[15] The East India Company financed its voyages likewise; and the 87½ per cent profit realized on its first venture led to a rush of subscribers—courtiers, judges, clergymen, knights, widows, spinsters, tradesmen—to share in the next enterprise. Men and women loved money as passionately then as now. Interest on loans had been forbidden by Parliament as late as 1552 as "a vice most odious";[16] but the growing strength of business forces in the Commons led to the Usury Bill of 1571, which distinguished interest from usury and legalized a 10 per cent return. As stock transactions mounted, bourses were formed for the exchange of ownership in shares or goods, and additional currency was coined to facilitate the sale and purchase of commodities. In 1566 Gresham built the Royal Exchange to cover such mercantile and financial operations. In 1583 it issued the earliest life insurance policy.[17]

The commercial spirit grew as London became one of the thriving marts and centers of the world. The unlit streets were brightened with goods; a traveler to many countries judged the London goldsmiths' establishments as the most sumptuous anywhere.[18] Businessmen were cramped for quarters, and some used the nave of St. Paul's Cathedral as temporary offices, confident that Christ had changed His mind since Calvin; lawyers dealt with clients there, men counted out money on the tombs, and in the courtyard hucksters sold bread and meat, fish and fruit, ale and beer. Pedestrians, peddlers, coaches, and carts swarmed in the narrow and muddy streets. The Thames served as the main thoroughfare, carrying barges, ferries, and pleasure craft; at almost any point a waterman could be found with a boat ready to transfer goods or passengers across the river or upstream or down; hence their lusty cries, "Eastward Ho!" and "Westward Ho!"—which gave titles to Jacobean plays. When its odors abated, the river was a blessing to commerce, recreation, and amours, the setting for stately pageants and rich homes. London Bridge, built in 1209, was the pride of the town and the only road between its north and south sides. The south specialized in taverns, theaters, brothels, and jails. The north was the chief center of business; here the merchant was master, the titled lord entered on sufferance; royalty and nobility lived mostly in palaces outside London. Westminster, where Parliament met, was then a separate city. There too the businessman made himself heard; by 1600 he could frighten the Queen, and a half century later he beheaded the King.

II. IN THE SCHOOLS

The age of Shakespeare was not addicted to education. It had little Latin and less Greek, more of Italian and French. It read books avidly but rapidly, rushing to test them with experience. It went to school to life, and talked back to its teacher with unheard-of insolence.

The language that it used was not that of schools. It was the whole spoken heritage of Celtic, Roman, Saxon, Norman England; it was swollen with the linguistic spoils of France and Italy; it snatched up slang from the London streets,* and dialects from the provinces; and, not content, it made words breed words and let exuberant imagination riot in originative speech. Was there ever a language so vivid, powerful, flexible, and rich? It could not stop to spell consistently; there were, before 1570, no dictionaries to guide orthography, and Shakespeare never decided how to spell his name. Shorthand was used, but did not cool the impatience of bustling business or precipitate poetry.

All organized education of girls had been ended by Henry VIII's dissolution of the nunneries; but primary education was offered gratis to any boy in reach of a town. Elizabeth opened 100 free grammar schools; James I and Charles I would found 288 more. For lads of pedigree there were already established "public" schools at Winchester, Eton, St. Paul's, and Shrewsbury; now were added Rugby (1567), Harrow (1571), and the Merchant Taylors' School (1561), where Richard Mulcaster left a great pedagogical name. The curriculum was classical plus flogging, and the Anglican religion was compulsory in all schools. At Westminster School classes began at seven and ended at six, with humane interludes for breakfast at eight and a cat nap and short recess in the afternoon. Parents were resolved that the school should fill to the full one of its main functions—to relieve them of their children.

Oxford and Cambridge still monopolized university education. They had fallen, during the turmoil of the Reformation, from their medieval authority and myriad registrations, but they were recovering, and each had some 1,500 students in 1586. At Cambridge Sir Walter Mildmay endowed Emmanuel College (1584), and Frances, Countess of Sussex and aunt of Philip Sidney, founded Sidney Sussex College (1588). At Oxford, Jesus College was set up by governmental and other funds (1571), and Wadham (1610) and Pembroke (1624) were added under James I. Cambridge was thrilled in 1564 by a visit from the Queen. She listened with modest demurrers to a Latin oration in her praise; at Trinity College she replied in Greek to a Greek address; on the streets she bandied Latin with the students; finally she herself made a Latin speech expressing the hope that she might do something for learning. Two years later she visited Oxford, gloried in the lovely halls and fields, and, departing, cried out fervently, "Farewell, my good subjects! farewell, my dear scholars! and may God prosper your studies!"[19] She knew how to be a queen.

Other Englishwomen rivaled her in erudition. The daughters of Sir Anthony

* In Shakespeare's time *prat* was already popular for "buttocks," and *duds* for "clothes."

Coke were famous for their learning, and Mary Sidney, Countess of Pembroke, made her mansion at Wilton a salon of poets, statesmen, and artists, who found in her a mind capable of appreciating their best. Such women received most of their education from tutors at home. Grammar schools were open to both sexes, but public schools and universities were for men only.

It was a sign of the times when Elizabeth's ablest financier set up in London (1579) Gresham College for law, medicine, geometry, rhetoric, and other studies useful to the business class; he specified that the lectures were to be given in English as well as in Latin, since "merchants and other citizens" would attend.[20] Finally, for the moneyed or titled class, education was completed by travel. Students went to Italy to finish their medical and sexual training or make acquaintance with Italian literature and art, and many learned to like France on the way. Language was then no barrier, for every educated man in Western and Central Europe understood Latin. Nevertheless, when the travelers returned, they brought home some rubbing of Italian and French, and a special fondness for the easy morals of Renaissance Italy.

III. VIRTUE AND VICE

"Every schoolboy" knows Roger Ascham's denunciation of the "Italianate" Englishman (1563):

> I take going thither [to Italy] . . . to be mervelous dangerous . . . Vertue once made that countrie mistress over all the worlde. Vice now maketh that countrie slave to them that before were glad to serve it . . . I know diverse that went out of England, men of innocent life, men of excellent learnyng, who returned out of Italie . . . neither so willing to live orderly, nor yet so liable to speak learnedlie, as they were at home before they went abroad . . . If you think we iudge amiss . . . heare what the Italian sayth . . . *Englese Italianato e un diabolo incarnato* . . . I was once in Italie myself, but I thanke God my abode there was but ix days. And yet I saw in that litle tyme, in one Citie, more libertie to sinne, than ever I hard tell of in our noble Citie of London in ix years.[21]

Elizabeth's tutor was not the only one who strummed this tune. "We have robbed Italy of wantonness," wrote Stephen Gosson in *The Schoole of Abuse* (1579); "compare London to Rome, and England to Italy, you shall find the theaters of the one, and the abuses of the other, to be rife among us." Cecil advised his son Robert never to allow his sons to cross the Alps, "for they shall learn nothing there but pride, blasphemy, and atheism."[22] Philip Stubbs, a Puritan, in *The Anatomie of Abuses* (1583), described the Elizabethan English as wicked, vainly luxurious, and proud of their sins. Bishop Jewel, in a sermon before the Queen, lamented that men's morals in London "make a mockery of God's Holy Gospel, and so become more dissolute, more fleshly, more wanton than ever they were before . . . If our life should give testimony and report to our religion . . . it crieth out . . . 'There is no God.' "*[23]

Much of the jeremiads was the exaggeration of moralists fuming against men and women who no longer took to heart the terrors of hell. Probably the bulk of the population was no worse or better than before. But just as the Puritan minority tightened its morals, purses, and lips, so a pagan minority agreed with many Italians that it was better to enjoy life than fuss about death. Possibly Italian wines, popular in England, helped to broaden morals as well as arteries, and more lastingly. From Italy, France, and classical literature may have come a franker sense of beauty, though saddened with a keener consciousness of its brevity. Even the beauty of the youthful male aroused the Elizabethan soul and pen; Marlowe made Mephistopheles praise Faust as fairer than the skies,[24] and Shakespeare's sonnets fluttered between homosexual and heterosexual love. Woman's loveliness was now no mere poetic conceit, but an intoxication that ran through the blood, the literature, and the court, and turned pirates into sonneteers. For at the court women added wit to cosmetics and captured men's minds as well as their hearts. Modesty was an invitation to the chase and doubled beauty's power. Litanies to the Virgin were lost in deprecations of virginity. Romantic love burst into song with all the ardor of denied desire. Women gloried in seeing men fight for them, and gave themselves, in marriage or without, to the victor. It was significant of the decline in the authority of religion that no church sanction or ceremony was now required for the validity of marriage, though the admission was considered an offense to public morals as distinct from law. Most marriages were arranged by the parents after a mutual courtship of properties; then the dizzy goddess of the hour became a disillusioned housekeeper, dedicated to children and chores, and the race survived.

A worse laxity of morals marked public life. Graft, petty or magnificent, ran through the official services; Elizabeth connived at it, as excusing her from raising salaries.[25] The war treasurer made £16,000 a year besides his pay; by a time-honored swindle the captains kept dead soldiers

---

* Aubrey tells a tale that gives point to Ascham: "Sir Walter Raleigh, being invited to dinner with some great person . . . His son sat next to his father, and was very demure at least half dinner time. Then said he: 'I, this morning, not having the fear of God before my eyes . . . went to a whore. I was very eager of her . . . and went to enjoy her, but she thrust me from her and vowed I should not, "For your father lay with me but an hour ago." ' Sir Walt, being so strangely surprised . . . at so great a table, gives his son a damned blow over the face; his son, as rude as he was, would not strike his father, but strikes over the face of the gentleman that sat next to him, and said, 'Box about, 'twill come to my father anon.' "—Brief Lives, 256.

on the list, pocketed their stipends, and sold the uniforms allotted to them;[26] a soldier was worth more dead than alive. Men in high places took large sums from Philip II to turn English policy to Spanish ends.[27] Admirals practiced piracy and sold slaves. Clergymen sold ecclesiastical emoluments.[28] Apothecaries could be persuaded to concoct poisons, and some doctors to administer them.[29] Tradesmen adulterated goods to the point of international scandal; in 1585 "more false cloth and woolen was made in England than in all Europe besides."[30] Military morals were primitive; unconditional surrender was in many cases rewarded with massacre of soldiers and noncombatants alike. Witches were burned, and Jesuits were taken down from the scaffold to be cut to pieces alive.[31] The milk of human kindness flowed sluggishly in the days of Good Queen Bess.

IV. JUSTICE AND THE LAW

The nature of man, despite so many centuries of religion and government, still resented civilization, and it voiced its protest through a profusion of sins and crimes. Laws and myths and punishments barely stemmed the flood. In the heart of London were four law schools, the Middle Temple, the Inner Temple, Lincoln's Inn, and Gray's Inn, collectively known as the Inns of Court. Law students resided there as other students dwelt in the halls or colleges of Oxford and Cambridge. Only "gentlemen" of blood were admitted; all graduates were sworn to the service of the Crown; their leading or easily led lights became judges in the Queen's courts. Judges and lawyers, in action, wore impressive robes; the majesty of the law was half sartorial.

The courts were by common consent corrupt. One member of Parliament defined a justice of the peace as "an animal who, for half-a-dozen chickens, would dispense with a dozen laws";[32] Francis Bacon required higher inducements. "Plate sin with gold," said Shakespeare's saddened Lear, "and the strong lance of justice hurtless breaks."[33] As judges were removed at the Queen's pleasure, they weighed it in their judgments, and royal favorites accepted bribes to induce her interference with decisions of the courts.[34] Jury trial was maintained except for treason, but the juries were often intimidated by the judges or other officers of the Crown.[35] Treason was loosely defined to include all actions endangering the life or majesty of the sovereign; such cases could be summoned before the Star Chamber—the Privy Council in its judicial capacity; there the defendant was denied jury trial, counsel, and habeas corpus, he was subject to exhausting interrogation or torture, and he was usually condemned to imprisonment or death.

Criminal law relied on deterrents rather than surveillance or detection; laws being weak, punishments were severe. Death was the statutory penalty for any of two hundred offenses, including blackmail, cutting down young trees, and stealing more than a shilling; in an average Elizabethan year eight hundred persons were hanged in Merrie England for crime.[36] Minor crimes were punished by the pillory, the stool, whipping at the cart's tail, burning a hole in the ears or the tongue, cutting out the tongue, or cutting off an ear or a hand.[37] When John Stubbs, a Puritan lawyer, wrote a pamphlet condemning Elizabeth's proposed marriage to Alençon as a surrender to Catholicism, his right hand was cut off by order of a magistrate. Holding up the bleeding stump, and raising his hat with his left hand, Stubbs cried, "Long live the Queen!"[38] Philip Sidney sent Elizabeth a protest against the barbarity, and Cecil, ashamed, gave Stubbs a government sinecure. Torture was illegal, but the Star Chamber used it. We perceive that despite the profound and powerful literature of the age, its general level of civilization had not yet reached that of Petrarch's Italy or Avignon, much less that of Augustus' Rome.

V. IN THE HOME

English life began by risking infantile mortality, which was high. Sir Thomas Browne was a leading physician, yet six of his ten children died in childhood.[39] Then there were epidemics, like the "sweating sickness" of 1550 and the plague visitations of 1563, 1592–94, and 1603. Tenure of life must have been low; one calculation places it at eight and a half years.[40] Men matured and grew old faster than today. Those who survived were the hardy, and their adventures with death toughened them for stratagems and spoils.

Sanitation was improving. Soap was graduating from a luxury to a necessity. About 1596 Sir John Harington invented a flush toilet. Private bathrooms were few; most families used a wooden tub placed before an open fire. Many towns had public baths, and Bath and Buxton provided fashionable bathing establishments for the upper classes. "Hot houses" offered sweat baths and facilities for meals and assignations. Only the well-to-do had their own domestic water supply; most families had to fetch water from public conduits opening at ornamental spouts.

Houses in villages and towns were built of plaster and brick, under roofs thatched with straw; Anne Hathaway's cottage near Stratford-on-Avon is a well-restored example. In the cities dwellings usually adjoined each other, used more brick and stone, and had tiled roofs; mullioned bay windows and overhanging upper stories make them attractive to unfamiliar eyes. Interiors were decorated with carvings and pilasters; fireplaces gave the main room or "great hall" dignity and warmth; and ceilings—of timber or plaster—might be cut into symmetrical or fanciful designs. Chimneys took off the smoke that had formerly sought exit through a hole in the ceiling, and stoves were helping the hearth. Glass windows were now common, but night lighting was still by torch or candle power. Floors were covered with rushes and herbs, sweet-smelling when fresh, but soon malodorous and sheltering insects; carpets were forty-five years in the future. Walls were adorned with tapestries, which, under Charles I, would give way to paintings. Most people sat on benches or stools; a chair with a back was a luxury reserved for an honored guest or the master or mistress of the house; hence to "take the chair" came to mean to preside. Otherwise the furniture was strong and admirable: buffets, cabinets, tables, chests, four-posters were cut and mortised in walnut or oak to last for centuries; some beds, with thick mattresses of feather, embroidered coverings, and silk canopies, cost a thousand pounds and were the proudest heirloom of the home. Around or behind the house, in nearly all classes, a garden provided trees, shrubs, shade, and such flowers as women used to grace their homes and hair, and Shakespeare to scent his verse—primrose, hyacinth, honeysuckle, larkspur, sweet William, marigold, Cupid's-flower, love-lies-bleeding, love-in-a-mist, lily of the valley, roses white or red, Lancaster or York. "God Almighty first planted a garden," said Bacon, "without which buildings and palaces are but gross handiworks."[41]

Ornamentation of the person was often more costly than decoration of the home. No age surpassed Elizabethan England in splendor of dress. "Costly thy habit as thy purse can buy," advised Polonius. In moneyed ranks all the fashions of France, Italy, and Spain were merged to redeem the human figure from the depredations of appetite and time. Portia laughed at young Falconbridge—"I think he bought his doublet in Italy, his round hose in France, his bonnet in Germany, and his behavior everywhere."[42] Elizabeth set an example and a vogue of finery, so that in her reign fashions changed repeatedly as common imitation blurred class distinction. "The fashion," mourns a character in *Much Ado about Nothing*, "wears out more apparel than the man."[43] Sumptuary laws tried to end this sartorial chorea; so a statute of 1574, to heal "the wasting and undoing of a great number of young gentlemen" who were wearing their acres on their backs, decreed that none but the royal family, dukes, marquesses, and earls should wear purple, silk, cloth of gold, or sable furs; none but barons and their betters should sport furs, crimson or scarlet velvets, imported woolens, gold or silver or pearl embroidery.[44] Such laws were soon evaded, for the ambitious bourgeoisie denounced them as not only invidious but restraining trade, and in 1604 they were repealed.

Hats were of any shape or color, of velvet, wool, silk or fine hair. Outside the home and the court men wore them nearly always, even in church, doffing them ceremoniously on meeting a lady, but at once covering again. Men wore their hair as long as the women, and grew fancy beards. Around the neck both sexes wore a ruff, a collar of linen and cambric built upon a frame of pasteboard and wire, and stiffened into broad sharp pleats by "a certain liquid matter which they call starch,"[45] which was then making its debut in England. Catherine de Médicis had introduced this noose into France (1533) as a small frill, but fashion expanded it into a pillory reaching to the ears.

Clothing made women a temporarily impenetrable mystery. Half their day must have been taken up with taking on and taking off; "a ship is sooner rigged than a woman."[46] Even hair could be put off·or on, for Elizabeth gave the example of wearing a wig, dyed to resemble the golden curls of her youth. False hair was common; poor women, said Shakespeare, sold their locks "by the weight."[47] Instead of hats most women preferred a tiny cap or a transparent net, which let their hair display its allure. Cosmetics colored the face and penciled the eyebrows; ears were pierced for pendants or rings; jewelry sparkled everywhere. The female ruff was as in men, but the bosom was sometimes bare to a point.[48] Elizabeth, narrow-chested and long-bellied, set a fashion of prolonging the bodice or jacket triangularly to a sharp apex below the corseted waist. The skirt was spread out from the hips by a "farthingale" or hoop. Gowns of delicate material and elaborate design covered the legs. Silk stockings were introduced by the Queen. Skirts trailed, sleeves bulged, gloves were embroidered and perfumed. In summer a lady could speak with a jeweled fan, and utter thoughts too kind for words.

But life in the home was seldom in full dress. Breakfast at seven, dinner at eleven or twelve, supper at five or six redeemed the day. The main meal was near noon and plentiful. "The English," said a Frenchman, "stuff their sacks."[49] Fingers still served in place of forks, which came into their present use in the reign of James I. Silver plate adorned prosperous homes; the hoarding of it was already a hedge against inflation. The lower middle classes had vessels of pewter; the poor got along with dishes of wood and spoons of horn. Meat, fish, and bread were the staple foods, and nearly everybody who could afford it suffered from gout. Dairy products were popular only in the countryside, for means of refrigeration were still scant in the towns. Vegetables were widely used only by the poor, who grew them in their garden plots. Potatoes, introduced from America by Raleigh's expeditions, were a garden product, not yet a crop in the fields. Puddings were an English specialty, relished beyond dessert. Sweets were as favored as now; hence Elizabeth's black teeth.

These hearty meals required liquid lubricants—ale, cider, beer, and wine. Tea and coffee were not yet Anglicized. Whiskey* came into general use throughout Europe in the sixteenth and seventeenth centuries, being distilled from grain in the north, from wine in the south. Drunkenness was a protest against the damp climate; the phrase "drunk as a lord" suggests that this remedy rose in favor along the social scale. Tobacco was brought into England by Sir John Hawkins (1565), by Drake, and by Sir Ralph Lane; Raleigh made smoking of it fashionable at court, and took a puff or two before he went to the scaffold. In Elizabeth's time it was too costly for its use to be widespread; at social gatherings a pipe might be passed around to let each guest get his quota. In 1604 King James sent forth a mighty *Counterblast to Tobacco*, lamenting its introduction into England and warning against "a certain venomous quality" in it.

> Is it not both great vanity and uncleanness that at the table, a place of respect, of cleanliness, of modesty, men should not be ashamed to sit tossing of Tobacco pipes, and puffing the smoke one to another, making the filthy smoke and stink thereof to exhale athwart the dishes and infect the air? . . . The public use whereof, at all times and in all places, hath now so far prevailed as divers men . . . have been at least forced to take it also, without desire . . . ashamed to seem singular . . . Moreover, which is a great iniquity . . . the husband shall not be ashamed to reduce thereby his delicate, wholesome, and clean complexioned wife to that extremity, that either she must also corrupt her sweet breath therewith, or else resolute to live in a perpetual stinking torment . . . A custom loathesome to the eye, hateful to the nose, harmful to the brain, dangerous to the lungs, and, in the black stinking fume thereof, nearest resembling the horrible Stygian smoke of the pit that is bottomless.[50]

Despite this and heavy taxes, there were seven thousand tobacco shops in London. Lighting and puffing did not take the place of conversation. Both sexes spoke freely of matters now confined to smoking rooms, street corners, and scientists; and women vied with men in oaths that verged on blasphemy. In the Elizabethan drama whores rub elbows with heroes, and *doubles-entendres* sprinkle high tragedy. Manners were ceremonious rather than polite; words often graduated into blows. Manners, like morals, came from Italy and France, and also manuals of courtesy that strove to make gentlemen of aristocrats and ladies of queens. Modes of salutation were effusive, often osculatory. Homes were more cheerful with light and jollity than before under medieval terror or afterward under Puritan gloom. Festivals were frequent; any excuse served for a procession or parade; wed-

---

* From Gaelic *uisque-beatha,* "water of life," *eau-de-vie.*

dings, lyings-in, even funerals, gave occasion for festivities, at least for meals. Games of all sorts were played in homes and fields and on the Thames. Shakespeare mentions billiards, and Florio speaks of cricket. Blue laws and blue Sundays were laughed at; if the Queen set the merry pace, why should not her people keep step with her? Nearly everybody danced, including, said Burton, "old men and women that have more toes than teeth." And all England sang.

VI. ENGLISH MUSIC: 1558–1649

No one who knows only post-Puritan England can feel the joyous role of music in Elizabethan days. From the home, the school, the church, the street, the stage, the Thames, rose sacred or profane song—masses, motets, madrigals, ballads, and delicate little lyrics of love such as those that found a setting in Elizabethan plays. Music was a main course in education; at Westminster School it received two hours a week; Oxford had a chair of music (1627). Every gentleman was expected to read music and play some instrument. In Thomas Morley's *Plaine and Easie Introduction to Practicall Musicke* (1597) an imaginary untutored Englishman confesses this shame:

> Supper being ended, and musicke bookes, according to the custome, being brought to the table, the mistresse of the house presented me with a part, earnestly requesting me to sing; but when, after many excuses, I protested unfeignedly that I could not, everyone began to wonder, some whispering to others, demanding how I was brought up.[51]

Barbershops provided instruments for waiting customers to play.

Elizabethan music was predominantly secular. Some composers, like Tallis, Byrd, and Bull, remained Catholic despite the laws and wrote for the Roman ritual, but such compositions were not publicly performed. Many Puritans objected to church music as diverting piety; Elizabeth and the bishops saved church music in England, as Palestrina and the Council of Trent rescued it in Italy. The Queen supported with her wonted determination the chapelmasters who organized large choirs and formal music for the royal chapel and the cathedrals. The Book of Common Prayer became a magnificent libretto for English composers, and the Anglican services almost rivaled the Continental Catholic in polyphonic splendor and dignity. Even the Puritans, following Calvin's lead, approved psalm singing by the congregations; Elizabeth laughed at these "Geneva jigs," but they matured into some noble hymns.

Since the Queen was a profanely secular spirit and loved to be courted, it was fitting that the musical glory of her reign should be the madrigal—love in counterpoint, a part song unaccompanied by instruments. Italian madrigals reached England in 1553 and set the key. Morley tried his hand at the form, expounded it in his graceful dialogue, and invited imitation. A madrigal for five voices, by John Wilbye, suggests the themes of these "ayres":

> Alas, what a wretched life this is, what a death,
> Where the tyrant love commandeth!
> My flowering days are in their prime declining,
> All my proud hope quite fallen, and life entwining;
> My joys each after other in haste are flying
>   And leave me dying
>   For her that scorns my crying;
> Oh, she from here departs, my Love restraining,
> For whom, all heartless, alas, I die complaining.[52]

William Byrd was the Shakespeare of Elizabethan music, famous for masses and madrigals, for vocal and instrumental compositions alike. His contemporaries honored him as *homo memorabilis*; Morley said he was "never without reverence to be named among the musicians."[53] Almost as highly rated and versatile were Orlando Gibbons and John Bull, royal-chapel organists. These and Byrd joined (1611) in producing the initial book of keyboard music in England, *Parthenia, or The Maydenhead of the first musicke that ever was printed for the Virginalls*. Meanwhile the English sustained their reputation for composing solo songs of a wholesome freshness redolent of the English countryside. John Dowland, renowned as a virtuoso of the lute, won praise for his *Songes or Ayres*, and Thomas Campion gave him close rivalry. Who does not know Campion's "Cherry Ripe"?[54]

Musicians were organized in a strong union, disturbed under Charles I by internal strife.[55] Instruments were nearly as various as today: lute, harp, organ, virginal or spinet, clavichord or harpsichord, flute, recorder (our flageolet), hautboy, cornet, trombone, trumpet, drums, and many forms of viol, which was now giving place to the violin. The lute was favored for virtuoso performance and to accompany songs; the virginal, modest mother of the piano, was popular with young women, at least before marriage. Instrumental music was intended chiefly for the virginal, the viol, and the lute. A kind of chamber music was composed for an ensemble or "consort" of viols varying in size and range. Campion, in a masque for James I's Queen Anne, used an orchestra of lutes, harpsichords, cornets, and nine viols (1605). Much instrumental music by Byrd, Morley, Dowland, and others has come down to us. It is largely based on dance forms, follows Italian models, and excels in a delicate and tender beauty rather than in vigor or range. Fugue and counterpoint are developed, but no thematic variation, no ingenuity in modulation, no resolved discords or chromatic harmonies. And yet when our nerves are frayed with the pounding stimuli of modern life, we find something cleansing and healing in Elizabethan music; no bombast, no rasping dissonances, no thundering finales, only the voice of an English youth or girl singing plaintively or merrily the timeless canticles of impeded love.

VII. ENGLISH ART: 1558–1649

The Elizabethan was a minor age in art. Metalworkers turned out some lovely silverware, like the Mostyn salt cellar, and majestic grilles like that in St. George's Chapel at Windsor. The making of Venetian glass was domiciled in England about 1560; vessels of such glass were by many valued above corresponding pieces in silver or gold. Sculpture and pottery were undistinguished. Nicholas Hilliard developed a school of miniature painting, and Elizabeth granted him a monopoly in so reproducing her features. Portrait painters were importees: Federigo Zuccaro from Italy, Marcus Gheeraerts and his son of the same name from the Netherlands. The son has left us an imposing portrait of William Cecil in resplendent, voluminous robes as a Knight of the Garter.[56] Otherwise there was no great painting in England between Holbein and Vandyck.

Only architecture was a major art in the England of Elizabeth and James, and it was almost entirely secular. While Europe was fighting the battle of the faiths, art, like conduct, neglected religion. In medieval centuries, when the profoundest poetry and art had their roots in the sky, architecture dedicated itself to church building, and made homes a form of life imprisonment. In Tudor England religion departed from life into politics; the wealth of the Church passed into lay hands and was transformed into civic structures and lordly palaces. Style changed accordingly. In 1563 John Shute returned from Italy and France bursting with Vitruvius, Palladio, and Serlio; soon he published *The First and Chief Grounds of Architecture*, lauding the classic styles; so the Italian scorn of Gothic entered England, and Gothic verticals fought for air amid the encompassing horizontals of the Renaissance.

In civic architecture the age could boast some handsome achievements: the gate of honor of Caius College and the quadrangle of Clare College at Cambridge, the Bodleian Library at Oxford, the Royal Exchange in London, and the Middle Temple. As lawyers, since Wolsey, had replaced bishops in the administration of England, it was fitting that the civic masterpiece of Elizabethan Renaissance architecture should be the great hall of a law school, finished in the Middle Temple in 1572. No woodwork in England was finer than the oak screen at the inner end of that hall. It was demolished by bombs in the Second World War.

When Elizabethan magnates could afford it they built palaces rivaling the châteaux of the Loire. Sir John Thynne raised Longleat House; Elizabeth, Countess of Shrewsbury, had her Hardwick Hall; Thomas, Earl of Suffolk, built Audley End at a cost of £190,000, "mainly procured from Spanish bribes";[57] Sir Edward Phillips reared Montacute House in chaste Renaissance style; and Sir Francis Willoughby erected Wollaton Hall. William Cecil poured part of his gleanings into an immense château near Stamford; and his son Robert spent almost as much on Hatfield House, whose long gallery is one of the grandest interiors in all the architecture of the age. Such long galleries, on an upper floor, replaced in Elizabethan palaces the timbered great hall of the manor house. Magnificent chimney pieces, massive furniture in walnut or oak, majestic stairways, carved balustrades, and timbered ceilings gave these palatial chambers a warmth and dignity missing in the more brilliant rooms of the French châteaux. So far as we know, the designers of these palaces were the first to receive the title of architect. The epitaph of Robert Smythson, creator of Wollaton Hall, called him "architector," i.e., master builder; now at last the great profession found its modern name.

Now, too, English art became personal, and a man stamped his work with his character and his will. Born in Smithfield in 1573, Inigo Jones showed in youth such a flair for design that an earl sent him to Italy (1600) to study Renaissance architecture. Back in England (1605), he prepared the scenery of many masques for James I and his Danish Queen. He visited Italy again (1612–14) and returned an enthusiast for the classic architectural principles that he had studied in the English translation (1567?) of Vitruvius, and which he found illustrated in the buildings of Palladio, Peruzzi, Sanmicheli, and Sansovino in Venice and Vicenza. He rejected the anomalous mixtures of German, Flemish, French, and Italian forms that had predominated in Elizabethan architecture; he proposed a pure classic style, in which the Doric, Ionic, and Corinthian orders would be kept apart or combined in a congenial sequence and unity.

In 1615 he was put in charge of all royal construction as surveyor general of the works. When the banqueting hall in the palace of Whitehall was burned down (1619), Jones was commissioned to build a new hall for the King. He planned an immense congeries of structures—all in all, 1,152 feet by 874—which, if completed, would have given the British ruler a vaster home than the Louvre, the Tuileries, the Escorial, or Versailles. But James preferred drinking for the day to building for centuries; he confined his outlay to the new banqueting hall, which, deprived of its intended setting, presented an unprepossessing façade of classical and Renaissance lines. When Archbishop Laud asked James to repair the old Cathedral of St. Paul the architect committed the crime of encasing the Gothic nave in a Renaissance exterior. Fortunately this structure was destroyed in the Great Fire of 1666. Jones's Palladian fronts gradually replaced the Tudor style, and it dominated England till the middle of the eighteenth century.

Jones not only served as chief architect for Charles I, but learned to love that luckless gentleman so visibly that when the Civil War broke out he buried his savings in the Lambeth marshes and fled to Hampshire (1643). Cromwell's soldiers captured him there, but gave him his life for £1,045.[58] During this absence from London he designed a country house in Wiltshire for the Earl of Pembroke. The façade was simple Renaissance, but the interior was a model of grandeur and elegance; the "double-cube" hall, sixty by thirty by thirty feet, has been judged the most beautiful room in England.[59] As royal armies consumed aristocratic wealth, Jones lost patronage as well as popularity; he retired into obscurity and died in poverty (1651). Art slept while war remade the government of England.

VIII. ELIZABETHAN MAN

How can we understand the Elizabethan Englishman from the supposedly staid and silent Briton of our youth? Can it be that national character is a function of place and time and change? Puritanism and Methodism intervened between the two ages and types; centuries of Eton, Harrow, and Rugby; and reckless conquerors quiet down when they sit supreme.

All in all, the Elizabethan Englishman was a scion of the Renaissance. In Germany the Reformation overwhelmed the Renaissance; in France the Renaissance rejected the Reformation; in England the two movements merged. Under Elizabeth the Reformation triumphed; *in* Elizabeth, the Renaissance. There were some stolid—not speechless—Puritans there, but they did not set the key. The dominant man of the age was a charge of energy released from old dogmas and inhibitions and not yet bound to new; boundless in ambition, longing to develop his capacities, unshackled in humor, sensitive to literature if it breathed life, given to violence of action and speech, but struggling, amid his bombast, vices, and cruelties, to be a gentleman. His ideal hovered between the amiable courtesies of Castiglione's *Courtier* and the ruthless immoralism of Machiavelli's *Prince*. He admired Sidney, but he aspired to be Drake.

Meanwhile philosophy made its way through the cracks of crumbling faith, and the best minds of the age were the most disturbed. There were orthodox and conservative souls, timid and gentle souls, amid this undammed flux; there were good men like Roger Ascham, desperately preaching the virtues that had served the past. But their students were in a venturesome mood. Hear Gabriel Harvey on Cambridge:

> The Gospel taught, not learned; Christian Key cold; nothing good but by imputation; the ceremonial law, in word abrogated; the judicial in effect disannulled; the moral indeed abandoned . . . All inquisitive after news, new books, new fashions, new laws . . . some after new heavens, and hells too . . . Every day fresh span new opinions: heresy

in divinity, in philosophy, in humanity, in manners . . . The Devil not
so hated as the pope.[60]

Copernicus had upset the world and sent the earth whirling dizzily
through space. Giordano Bruno came to Oxford in 1583 and talked of the
new astronomy and infinite worlds, the sun dying of its own heat, the
planets decaying into atomic mist. Poets like John Donne felt the earth
slipping beneath their feet.

In 1595 Florio began to publish his translation of Montaigne; after that
nothing was certain, and doubt was the air men breathed; as Marlowe is
Machiavelli, so Shakespeare is Montaigne. While wise men doubted, young
men schemed. If heaven seemed lost in a philosophic cloud, youth could
resolve to suck this life dry and sample all truth however lethal, all beauty
however fleeting, all power however poisonous. So Marlowe conceived his
Faust and Tamburlaine.

It was this plowing up of old ideas, this liberation of the mind for the
impassioned utterance of new hopes and dreams, that made Elizabethan
England memorable. What would we have cared for its political rivalries,
its religious disputes, its martial triumphs, its thirst for gold, if its literature, confined to these passing things, had not voiced the longings, hesitations, and resolves of thoughtful souls in every age? All the influences of
that exciting time came to the Elizabethan ecstasy: the voyages of conquest and discovery that expanded the globe, the market, and the mind;
the wealth of the middle classes enlarging the scope and goals of enterprise;
the revelation of pagan literature and art; the upheaval of the Reformation;
the rejection of papal influence in England; the theological debates that
unwittingly led men from dogma to reason; education and the widening
audience for books and plays; the long and profitable peace, and then the
arousing challenge and exhilarating victory over Spain; the great crescendo
of confidence in human power and thought: all these were the stimuli that
prodded England into greatness, these the germs that made her big with
Shakespeare. Now, after almost two silent centuries since Chaucer, she
burst into a passion of prose and poetry, drama and philosophy, and spoke
out bravely to the world.

CHAPTER III

On the Slopes of Parnassus

1558–1603

I. BOOKS

THEY were a swelling legion. "One of the great diseases of this age," wrote Barnaby Rich in 1600, "is the multitude of books that doth so overcharge the world that it is not able to digest the abundance of idle matter that is every day hatched and brought into the world." "Already," wrote Robert Burton (1628), "we shall have a vast chaos and confusion of books; we are oppressed with them, our eyes ache with reading, our fingers with turning."[1] Both these plaintiffs wrote books.

The aristocracy, having learned to read, rewarded with material patronage authors who had softened them with dedications. Cecil, Leicester, Sidney, Raleigh, Essex, Southampton, the earls and the Countess of Pembroke were good patrons, who established between English nobles and authors a relation that continued even after Johnson lectured Chesterfield. Publishers paid authors some forty shillings for a pamphlet, some five pounds for a book.[2] A few authors managed to live by their pens; the desperate profession of "man of letters" now took form in England. Private libraries were numerous among the well-to-do, but public libraries were rare. On the way home from Cádiz in 1596 Essex stopped at Faro, in Portugal, and appropriated the library of Bishop Jerome Osorius; he gave it to Sir Thomas Bodley, who included it in the Bodleian Library that he bequeathed to Oxford (1598).

The publishers themselves led a harried existence, subject to state law and public whim. There were 250 of them in Elizabeth's England, for publishing and bookselling were still one trade. Most of them did their own printing; the separation of printer and publisher began toward the end of this reign. Publishers, printers, and booksellers united (1557) in a Stationers' Company; registry of a publication with this guild constituted copyright, which, however, protected not the author but only the publisher. Normally the company would register only such publications as had obtained a legal license to be printed. It was a felony to write, print, sell, or possess any material injurious to the reputation of the Queen or the government, to publish or import heretical books or papal bulls or briefs, or to possess a book that upheld the supremacy of the popes over the

English Church.[3] There were several executions for violation of these decrees. The Stationers' Company was empowered to search all printing establishments, to burn all unlicensed publications, and to imprison their publishers.[4] Elizabethan censorship was more severe than any before the Reformation, but literature flourished; as in eighteenth-century France, wits were sharpened by the peril of print.

Scholars were few; it was an age of creation rather than criticism, and the humanistic current had run dry in those hot theological years. Most historians were still chroniclers, dividing their narratives by years; Richard Knolles, however, surprised Burghley with the comparative excellence of his *General History of the Turks* (1603). Raphael Holinshed's *Chronicles* (1577) gave him an unearned increment of fame by supplying Shakespeare with stories of the English kings. John Stow's *Chronicles of England* (1580) was dressed up with "some colors of wisdom, invitements to virtue, and loathing of naughty facts,"[5] but its scholarship was lamentable, and its prose had a powerful *virtus dormitiva*. His *Survey of London* (1598) was more scholarly, but brought him no more bread; in old age he had to be given a license to beg.[6] William Camden, in good Latin, recorded the geography, scenery, and antiquities of England in *Britannia* (1582); and his *Rerum Anglicarum et hibernicarum annales regnante Elizabetha* (1615–27) based its story on conscientious study of original documents. Camden glorified the great Queen indiscriminately, lauded Spenser, ignored Shakespeare, and praised Roger Ascham, but mourned that so fine a scholar had died poor through love of dicing-and cockfighting.[7]

Ascham, secretary to "Bloody Mary" and tutor to Elizabeth, left at his death (1568) the most famous of English treatises on education, *The Scholemaster* (1570), primarily on the teaching of Latin, but containing, in strong, simple English, a plea for the replacement of Etonian severity with Christian kindness in education. He told how, at a dinner with men high in Elizabeth's government, the conversation had turned on education through flogging; how Cecil had favored gentler methods; and how Sir Richard Sackville had privately confessed to Ascham that "a fond [foolish] schoolmaster . . . drave me, with fear of beating, from all love of learning."[8]

The major and most fruitful function of the scholars was to impregnate the English mind with foreign thought. In the second half of the sixteenth century a wave of translations swept over the land from Greece, Rome, Italy, and France. Homer had to wait till 1611 for George Chapman, and the lack of English versions of Greek plays probably shared in giving the Elizabethan drama a "romantic" rather than a "classical" form. But there were translations of Theocritus' idyls, Musaeus' *Hero and Leander*, Epictetus' *Enchiridion*, Aristotle's *Ethics* and *Politics*, Xenophon's *Cyropaedia* and *Oeconomicus*, the speeches of Demosthenes and Isocrates, the histories of Herodotus, Polybius, Diodorus Siculus, Josephus, and Appian, the novels of Heliodorus and Longus, and Sir Thomas North's racy translation (1579) of Amyot's French translation of Plutarch's *Lives*. From the Latin came Virgil, Horace, Ovid, Martial, Lucan, the plays of Plautus, Terence, and Seneca, the histories of Livy, Sallust, Tacitus, and Suetonius. From Italy came Petrarch's sonnets, Boccaccio's *Filocopo* and *Fiammetta* (but no *Decameron* till 1620), the histories of Guicciardini and Machiavelli, the *Orlandos* of Boiardo and Ariosto, Castiglione's *Libro del cortegiano,* the *Gerusalemme liberata* and *Aminta* of Tasso, Guarini's *Pastor fido,* and many fabulous *novelle* by Bandello and others, gathered into such collections as William Painter's *Palace of Pleasure* (1566). Machiavelli's *Il Principe* was not done into English till 1640, but its substance was familiar to the Elizabethans; Gabriel Harvey reported that at Cambridge "Duns Scotus and Thomas Aquinas, with the whole rabblement of Schoolmen . . . were expelled the University," and were replaced with Machiavelli and Jean Bodin.[9] From Spain came one of the longest romances, *Amadis de Gaula;* one of the first picaresque novels, *Lazarillo de Tormes;* one of the classic pastorals, the *Diana* of Montemayor. The best spoils from France were the poems of the Pléiade, and the essays of Montaigne, nobly Englished by John Florio (1603).

The influence of these translations upon Elizabethan literature was immense. Classical allusions began—and for two centuries continued—to encumber English poetry and prose. French was known to most memorable Elizabethan authors, so that translations were not indispensable. Italy fascinated England; English pastorals looked back to Sannazaro, Tasso, and Guarini, English sonnets to Petrarch, English fiction to Boccaccio and the *novelle*; these last gave plots to Marlowe, Shakespeare, Webster, Massinger, and Ford, and Italian locales to many Elizabethan plays. Italy, which had rejected the Reformation, had gone beyond it to break down the old theology, even the Christian ethic. While Elizabethan religion debated Catholicism and Protestantism, Elizabethan literature, ignoring that conflict, returned to the spirit and verve of the Renaissance. Italy, struck down for a time by a change in trade routes, handed the torch of the Rebirth to Spain, France, and England.

II. THE WAR OF THE WITS

In this Elizabethan exuberance both poetry and prose poured down in a turbulent flood. We know the names of two hundred Elizabethan poets. But until Spenser introduced his *Faerie Queene* (1590), it was prose that caught the ear of Elizabethan England.

John Lyly did it first with his fanciful *Euphues, or the Anatomy of Wit* —i.e., of intelligence—in 1579. Lyly proposed to show how a fine mind and character can be formed through education, experience, travel, and wise counsel. Euphues (Good Speech) is a young Athenian whose adventures provide the scaffolding for wordy discourses on education, manners, friendship, love, atheism. What made the book the best seller of its time was its style—a flux of antitheses, alliterations, similes, puns, balanced clauses, classical allusions, and conceits that took the court of Elizabeth by storm and held the fashion for a generation. For example:

> This young gallant, of more wit than wealth, and yet of more wealth than wisdom, seeing himself inferior to none in pleasant conceits, thought himself superior to all in honest conditions, insomuch that he deemed himself so apt to all things that he gave himself almost to nothing.[10]

Whether Lyly caught this disease from the Italian Marini or the Spaniard Guevara or the *rhetoriker* of Flanders is in dispute. In any case Lyly welcomed the virus and transmitted it to a host of Elizabethans; it spoiled Shakespeare's early comedies, tinged Bacon's *Essays*, and gave a word to the language.

It was a word-conscious age. Gabriel Harvey, a Cambridge tutor, exerted all his influence to turn English poetry from accent and rhyme to classic meters based on syllabic quantities. At his urging, Sidney and Spenser formed in London a literary club, the Areopagus, which strove for a time to force Elizabethan vitality into Virgilian forms. Thomas Nash parodied Harvey's "hopping" hexameters and laughed them literally out of court. When Harvey added insult to pedantry by condemning the morals of Nash's friend Greene, he became the prime target in a pamphlet war that brought into England all the resources of Renaissance vituperation.

Robert Greene's life summarized a thousand literary Bohemian careers from Villon to Verlaine. He was a fellow student at Cambridge with Harvey, Nash, and Marlowe; there he spent his time among "wags as lewd as" himself, with whom he "consumed the flower of his youth."

> I was drowned in pride; whoredom was my daily exercise, and gluttony with drunkenness was my only delight. . . . I was so far from calling upon God that I seldom thought on God, but took much delight in swearing and blaspheming the name of God. . . . If I may have my desire while I live, I am satisfied; let me shift after death as I may. . . . I feared the judges of the bench no more than I dread the judgments of God.[11]

He traveled in Italy and Spain, and there, he tells us, he "saw and practiced such villainy as is abominable to declare." Returning, he became a familiar figure in London taverns, with his red hair, pointed beard, silk stockings, and personal bodyguard. He married and wrote tenderly of marital fidelity and bliss; then he forsook his wife for a mistress, upon whom he spent his wife's fortune. From his firsthand knowledge he described the arts of the underworld in *A Notable Discovery* [uncovering] *of Cozenage* (1591) and warned rural visitors to London against the wiles of swindlers, cardsharpers, pickpockets, panders, and prostitutes; whereupon the underworld tried to kill him. It surprises us that in a life so assiduously devoted to vice he found time to write, with journalistic haste and verve, a dozen novels (in *Euphuestic* style), thirty-five pamphlets, and many successful plays. As his vigor and income declined, he saw some sense in virtue, and repented as eloquently as he had sinned. In 1591 he published a *Farewell to Folly*. In 1592 he composed two tracts of some moment. One, *A Quip for an Upstart Courtier*, attacked Gabriel Harvey. In the other, *Greene's Groatsworth of Wit Bought with a Million of Repentance*, he attacked Shakespeare and called upon his fellow lechers—apparently Marlowe, Peele, and Nash—to quit their sinning and join him in piety and remorse. On September 2, 1592, he sent to his forsaken wife an appeal to reimburse with ten pounds a shoemaker without whose charity "I had perished in the streets."[12] The next day, in the house of this shoemaker, he died—according to Harvey, from "a surfeit of pickled herring and Rhenish wine." His landlady, forgiving his debts for his verse, crowned his head with a laurel wreath and paid for his funeral.[13]

Of all the Elizabethan pamphleteers, Greene's friend Tom Nash had the sharpest tongue and the widest audience. Son of a curate and tired of decency, Nash graduated from Cambridge into London's Bohemia, buttered his bread with his pen, and learned to write "as fast as [his] hand could trot." He established the picaresque novel in England with *The Unfortunate Traveller, or The Life of Jack Wilton* (1594). When Greene died, and Harvey assailed both Greene and Nash in *Four Letters*, Nash retaliated with a series of pamphlets culminating in *Have with You to Saffron Walden*—Harvey's birthplace—in 1596.

> Readers, be merry, for in me there shall want nothing I can do to make you merry . . . It shall cost me a fall, but I will get him hooted out of the University . . . ere I give him over. What will you give me when I bring him upon the stage in one of the principalest colleges in Cambridge?[14]

Harvey survived this experience, outlived the Bohemians, and died at eighty-five in 1630. Nash completed his friend Marlowe's play *Dido*, collaborated with Ben Jonson in *The Isle of Dogs* (1597), was indicted for sedition, and subsided into a cautious obscurity. At the age of thirty-four (1601) he crowned a fast life with an early death.

III. PHILIP SIDNEY: 1554–85

Far from this maddened crowd, Sidney rode serenely to an even earlier end. Facing us still in the National Portrait Gallery of London, he seems too delicate for a man: slender of face, with auburn hair, and "not a morsel too much of health," said Languet;[15] "extremely beautiful," said Aubrey,[16] "not masculine enough, yet . . . of great courage." Some grumblers thought him a bit pompous[17] and felt that he carried perfection to excess; only his heroic end won him pardon for his virtues.

But who would not be proud to have had for his mother Lady Mary Dudley, daughter of that Duke of Northumberland who had ruled England under Edward VI; and to have had for his father Sir Henry Sidney, Lord President of Wales and thrice Lord Deputy of Ireland; and to have received his Christian name from King Philip II of Spain as his godfather? Part of his fleeting life was lived in spacious Penshurst Place, whose oak-beam ceilings, picture walls, and crystal chandelier are among the fairest relics of that time. At the age of nine he was appointed lay rector to a church benefice, which brought him sixty pounds a year. At ten he entered Shrewsbury School, which was not too far from Ludlow Castle, his father's residence as Lord President of Wales. To the boy of eleven Sir Henry wrote loving words of wisdom.[18]

Philip learned these lessons well and became a favorite with his uncle Leicester and his father's friend William Cecil. After three years at Oxford he was sent to Paris as a minor member of an English mission. He was received at the court of Charles IX and witnessed the Massacre of St. Bartholomew. He traveled leisurely in France, the Netherlands, Germany, Bohemia, Poland, Hungary, Austria, and Italy. At Frankfurt he began a lifelong friendship with Hubert Languet, one of the intellectual leaders of the Huguenots; at Venice he had his portrait painted by Paolo Veronese; at Padua he imbibed the traditions of the Petrarchan sonnet. Back in England, he was welcomed at court and for almost two years danced attendance on the Queen, but he forfeited her favor for a time by opposing her prospective marriage with the Duke of Alençon. He had all the knightly qualities—pride of bearing, skill and bravery in tournament, courtesy in court, honor in all dealings, and eloquence in love. He studied Castiglione's *Courtier* and tried to model his conduct on that gentle philosopher's ideal of a gentleman, and others modeled themselves on Sidney. Spenser called him "the President of Noblesse and of Chivalry."

It was a mark of the times that the aristocracy, which had once scorned literacy, now wrote poetry and suffered poets to come to them. Sidney, though not rich, became the most active literary patron of his generation.

He helped Camden, Hakluyt, Nash, Harvey, Donne, Daniel, Jonson, and, above all, Spenser, who thanked him as "the hope of all learned men and the patron of my young muse."[19] It was quite out of order that Stephen Gosson should dedicate to Sidney his *Schoole of Abuse* (1579), whose title page described it as "a pleasant invective against poets, pipers, players, jesters, and such like caterpillars of the commonwealth." Sidney took up the gauntlet and wrote the first of the Elizabethan classics—*The Defence of Poesy*.

Taking a lead from Aristotle and Italian critics, he defined poetry as "an art of imitation . . . representing, counterfeiting, or figuring forth . . . a speaking picture" designed "to teach and delight."[20] Placing morals far above art, he justified art as teaching morality by pictured examples:

> The philosopher . . . and the historian . . . would win the goal, the one by precept, the other by example; but both, not having both, do both halt. For the philosopher, setting down with thorny arguments the bare rule [of morals], is so hard of utterance, and so misty to be conceived, that one that hath no other guide but him shall wade in him till he be old, before he shall find sufficient cause to be honest. For his knowledge standeth so upon the abstract and the general that happy is that man that may understand him . . . On the other side the historian, wanting the precept, is tied, not to what should be but to what is . . . that his example draweth no necessary consequence, and therefore a less fruitful doctrine.
>
> Now doth the peerless poet perform both, for whatsoever the philosopher said should be done, he gives a perfect picture of it by some one by whom he supposeth it was done, so as he completeth the general notion with the particular example. A perfect picture, I say, for he yieldeth to the powers of the mind an image of that whereof the philosopher bestoweth but a wordish description, which doth neither strike, pierce, nor possess the sight of the soul so much as that other doth.[21]

Poetry, therefore, in Sidney's view, includes all imaginative literature—drama, verse, and imaginative prose. "It is not rhyming and versifying that maketh poetry. One may be a poet without versifying, a versifier without poetry."

He added example to precept. In the same year 1580 that produced the *Defence*, he began to write *The Countess of Pembroke's Arcadia*. This Countess, his sister, was one of the best-flattered ladies of the century. Born in 1561 and therefore seven years younger than Philip, she received all the education she could stand, including Latin, Greek, and Hebrew, but her charm survived. She became a member of Elizabeth's household and accompanied the Queen on the royal progresses. Her uncle Leicester advanced part of the dowry that enabled her to marry Henry, Earl of Pembroke. "She was very salacious," according to Aubrey, and took some lovers to supplement her husband; but this did not deter Philip from adoring her and writing the *Arcadia* at her request.

Following the example of Sannazaro's *Arcadia* (1504), Sidney imagined, at length and ease, a world of brave princes, exquisite princesses, knightly combats, mystifying disguises, and fascinating scenery. "The loveliness of Urania is the greatest thing the world can show, but the least that may be praised in her";[22] and Palladius had "a piercing wit quite devoid of ostentation, high erected thoughts seated in a heart of courtesy, an eloquence as sweet in the uttering as slow to be uttering, a behavior so noble as gave majesty to adversity";[23] clearly Sidney had read *Euphues*. The story is an amorous maze: Pyrocles disguises himself as a woman to be near the fair Philoclea; she frustrates him by loving him as a sister; her father falls in love with him, thinking him a woman; her mother falls in love with him, perceiving him to be a man; however, everything ends according to the Ten Commandments. Sidney did not take the tale very seriously; he never corrected the sheets he had dashed off for his sister; on his deathbed he ordered them burned. They were preserved, edited, and published (1590), and were for a decade the most admired work in Elizabethan prose.

While writing this romance and the *Defence*, and amid his life as diplomat and soldier, Sidney composed a sonnet sequence that paved the way for Shakespeare's. For this he needed some unsuccessful love. He found it in Penelope Devereux, daughter of the first Earl of Essex; she welcomed his sighs and rhymes as lawful game, but married Baron Rich (1581); Sidney continued to address sonnets to her, even after his own marriage to Frances Walsingham. Few Elizabethans were shocked by this poetic license; no one expected a man to write sonnets to his own wife, whose generosity stilled the muse. The sequence was published (1591) after Sidney's death under the title of *Astrophel and Stella*—star lover and star. It followed the style of Petrarch, whose Laura had strangely anticipated the eyes, hair, brow, cheeks, skin, and lips of Penelope. Sidney was quite aware that his passion was a poetic mechanism; he himself had written: "If I were a mistress, [sonneteers] would never persuade me they were in love."[24] Once accepted as fair play, these sonnets are England's best before Shakespeare's. Even the moon is sick with love:

> With how sad steps, O Moon, thou clim'st the skies,
>   How silently, and with how mean a face!
> What, may it be that even in heavenly place
> That busy Archer his sharp arrows tries?

> Sure, if that long-with-love-acquainted eyes
>   Can judge of love, thou feel'st a lover's case,
>   I read it in thy looks, thy languish'd grace
> To me, that feel the like, thy state descries.
> Then, even of fellowship, O Moon, tell me,
>   Is constant love deemed there but want of wit?
> Are beauties there as proud as here they be?
>   Do they above love to be loved, and yet
> Those lovers scorn whom that love doth possess?
> Do they call virtue there ungratefulness?[25]

In 1585 Sidney was sent by Elizabeth to aid the Netherland rebels against Spain. Though not yet thirty-one, he was made governor of Flushing. He displeased the pinching Queen by asking for more supplies and better wages for his soldiers, who were being paid in debased currency.[26] He led his men to the capture of Axel (July 6, 1586) and fought in the front of the action. But in the battle of Zutphen (September 22) he was too brave. His horse having been killed in a charge, Sidney leaped upon another and fought his way into the enemy's ranks. A musket ball entered his thigh. His horse, out of control, fled back to Leicester's camp.* Thence Sidney was taken to a private home in Arnhem. For twenty-five days he suffered under incompetent surgeons. Gangrene set in, and on October 17 the "wonder of our age" (so Spenser mourned him) welcomed death. "I would not change my joy," he said on that last day, "for the empire of the world."[28] When his corpse was brought to London it received such a funeral as England would not see again before Nelson's death.

IV. EDMUND SPENSER: 1552–99

"Sidney is dead," wrote Spenser, "dead is my friend, dead is the world's delight."[29] It was Sidney who had given Spenser the courage to be a poet. Edmund had begun unpropitiously as the son of a journeyman clothmaker, too distantly related to the aristocratic Spensers to allow the boy to be noticed. Charitable funds sent him to the Merchant Taylors' School, then to Pembroke Hall in Cambridge, where he worked for his board. By seventeen he was writing—even publishing—poetry. Harvey tried to guide him into classic molds and themes; Spenser tried humbly to please him, but soon rebelled against the bonds that uncongenial meters placed upon his muse. In 1579 he showed Harvey the first portion of *The Faerie Queene*;

---

* A story not sufficiently verified relates that when a bottle of water was offered to the wounded Sidney, he handed it to a dying soldier nearby, saying, "Thy need is greater than mine." (Fulke Greville, *Life of the Renowned Sir Philip Sidney*.)[27]

Harvey had no fancy for its medieval allegorical content, no appreciation for its fine metrical form. He advised the poet to abandon the project. Spenser continued it.

It was the gruff and bellicose Harvey who secured for Spenser a place in the service of the Earl of Leicester. There the poet met Sidney, loved him, dedicated to him *The Shepherd's Calendar* (1579). The form echoed Theocritus, but followed the plan of popular almanacs, allotting the tasks of shepherds according to the season of the year. The theme was the unrequited love of the shepherd Colin Clout for the cruel Rosalind. It is not recommended reading, but Sidney's praise won Spenser some acclaim. To butter his bread, the poet accepted the post of secretary to Arthur, Lord Grey, the new Lord Deputy of Ireland (1579); accompanied him to war, and saw and approved Grey's slaughter of the surrendering Irish and Spaniards at Smerwick. After seven years of clerical service to the English government in Ireland he was granted, from the confiscated property of Irish rebels, the Castle of Kilcolman, on the road between Mallow and Limerick, and three thousand acres.

There Spenser settled down to gentleman farming and genteel poetry. He commemorated Sidney's death in an eloquent but lengthy elegy, *Astrophel* (1586). Then he polished and elongated *The Faerie Queene*. Warm with enthusiasm, he crossed to England in 1589, was presented by Raleigh to the Queen, and dedicated the first three "books" to her "to live with the eternity of her fame." To ensure a wide reception he prefaced the poem with laudatory verses addressed to the Countess of Pembroke, Lady Carew, Sir Christopher Hatton, Raleigh, Burghley, Walsingham, Lords Hunsdon, Buckhurst, Grey, and Howard of Effingham, and the earls of Essex, Northumberland, Oxford, Ormonde, and Cumberland. Burghley, feuding with Leicester, called Spenser an idle rhymer, but many hailed him as the greatest poet since Chaucer. The Queen relaxed enough to award him a pension of fifty pounds a year, which Burghley, as Lord Treasurer, delayed in paying. Spenser had hoped for something more substantial. Disappointed, he returned to his Irish castle and continued his idealistic epic amid barbarism, hatred, and fear.

He had planned the poem to be in twelve books; he published three in 1590 and three more in 1596, and proceeded no further; even so *The Faerie Queene* is twice the length of *The Iliad*, thrice that of *Paradise Lost*. Each book was offered as an allegory—of holiness, temperance, chastity, friendship, justice, courtesy; the whole was intended "to fashion a gentleman or noble person in virtuous and gentle discipline"[30] by giving him formative instances; all this accorded with Sidney's conception of poetry as morality conveyed by imagined examples. So dedicated to decency, Spenser could allow himself only a few voluptuous passages; he glances once at a "snowy breast bare to ready spoil,"[31] but goes *ne plus ultra*. Through six cantos he sings the high note of chivalric love as unselfish service to fair women.

To us, who have forgotten chivalry and are bored by knights and confused by allegories, *The Faerie Queene* is at first quaintly delightful, at length unbearable. Its political allusions, which contemporaries enjoyed or resented, are lost upon us; the theological battles that it adumbrates are the subsiding tremors of our infancy; its narratives are at best melodious echoes of Virgil, Ariosto, and Tasso. No poem in the world's literature surpasses *The Faerie Queene* in artificial conceits, awkward inversions, pretentious archaisms and neologisms, and romantic grandiosities unleavened with Ariosto's smile. And yet Keats and Shelley loved Spenser and made him "the Poets' poet." Why? Was it because, here and there, some sensuous beauty of form redeemed a medieval absurdity, some splendor of description adorned an unreality? The new nine-line Spenserian stanza was a difficult medium, and Spenser often startles us with its rounded perfection and flowing ease; but how many times he spoils its reason for a rhyme!

He interrupted the *Queene* to write some briefer poems that perhaps justify his fame. His *Amoretti*, "little loves" in sonnet form (1594), may have been Petrarchan fantasies, or may have reflected his year-long courtship of Elizabeth Boyle. He married her in 1594 and sang his wedding joy in his finest poem, *Epithalamium*. He shares her charms with us unselfishly:

> Tell me, ye merchants' daughters, did ye see
> So fayre a creature in your towne before,
> So sweet, so lovely, so mild as she,
> Adornd with beautyes grace and vertues store,
> Her goodly eyes like saphyres shining bright,
> Her forehead yvory white,
> Her cheekes like apples which the sun hath rudded,
> Her lips like cherryes charming men to byte,
> Her breast like to a bowl of cream uncrudded,
> Her paps like lyllies budded,
> Her snowie necke lyke a marble toure,
> And all her body like a palace fayre . . .

When the wedding and feasting are over he bids his guests depart without delay:

> Now cease, ye damsels, your delights forepast;
> Enough is it that all the day was yours;
> Now day is doen, and night is nighing fast.
> Now bring the bryde into the brydall bowres . . .

And in her bed her lay;
Lay her in lilies and in violets,
And silken curteins over her display,
And odoured sheets, and Arras coverlets . . .
But let the night be calme and quietsome,
Without tempestuous storms or sad afray,
Lyke as when Jove with fayre Alcmena lay . . .
And let the mayds and yongmen cease to sing;
Ne let the woods them answer, nor their echo ring.

Was ever maid brought to fulfillment more melodiously?

Spenser sustained this flight in *Four Hymns* (1596) honoring earthly love, earthly beauty, heavenly love, and heavenly beauty. Following Plato, Ficino, and Castiglione, and leading to Keats's *Endymion*, he cried *peccavi* over his "many lewd layes," and bade his soul pierce through physical loveliness to find and feel the divine beauty that hides in divers degrees in all earthly things.

Living on a volcano of Irish misery, Spenser's life was every day near death. Just before the volcano of resentment erupted again, he wrote in fine prose (for only a poet can write good prose) his *View of the Present State of Ireland*, advocating a better deployment of English funds and forces for the thorough subjugation of the island. In October 1598 the dispossessed Irish of Munster rose in wild revolt, drove out English settlers, and burned down the Castle of Kilcolman. Spenser and his wife barely escaped with their lives and fled to England. Three months later, all funds and passion spent, the poet died (1599). The young Earl of Essex, destined soon to follow him, paid for the funeral; nobles and poets walked in the procession, and threw flowers and elegies into the Westminster Abbey grave.

A craze for sonnets now ran through England, rivaling the drama's fury —nearly all excellent in form, stereotyped in theme and phrase, nearly all addressed to virgins or patrons and bemoaning their strait-laced or tight-fisted frugality. Beauty is urged to let itself be reaped before it rots on the stalk; sometimes an original note intrudes, and the lover promises the lady a child as reward for expeditious conjugation. Every poet seeks and finds a Laura—Daniel's Delia, Lodge's Phillis, Constable's Diana, Fulke Greville's Caelia. Most famous of these sonneteers was Samuel Daniel; however, Ben Jonson, who was more tough than "rare," called him "an honest man, but no poet."[32] Michael Drayton's Pegasus roamed through all forms of poetry with his feet of prose, but one of his sonnets struck a fresh note, stinging the lass out of her stinginess by bidding her farewell— "Since there's no help, come, let us kiss and part!"

All in all, outside the drama, Elizabethan literature was still a generation behind the French. The prose was vigorous, flexible, often involved, verbose, and fanciful, but sometimes moving with a royal dignity or a stately rhythm; it produced no Rabelais or Montaigne. The poetry echoed foreign models timidly, except for the *Epithalamium* and *The Faerie Queene*. Spenser never found an audience on the Continent, but neither did Ronsard in England; poetry makes of language and feeling a music that cannot be heard across the frontiers of speech. Ballads noticed and reached the people more intimately than the poetry of the palace and the court; they were posted on house and tavern walls, and were sung and sold in the streets; "Lord Randall" still moves us with its dirge.[33] Perhaps it was this popular poetry, and not the pretty artifices of the sonneteers, that prepared the Elizabethans to appreciate Shakespeare.

V. THE STAGE

How, then, did English literature, so negligible in the long drought between Chaucer and Spenser, rise to Shakespeare? Because of wealth growing and spreading; because of a long and fruitful peace, a stimulating and triumphant war; because of foreign literature and travel broadening the English mind. Plautus and Terence were teaching England the art of comedy, Seneca the technique of tragedy; Italian actors played in England (1577f.); a thousand experiments were made; between 1592 and 1642 England saw 435 comedies performed. Farces and interludes developed into comedies; mysteries and moralities gave way to secular tragic dramas as the once sacred myths lost their hold on belief. In 1553 Nicholas Udall produced in *Ralph Roister Doister* the first English comedy in classic form. In 1561 the lawyers of the Inner Temple staged there *Gorboduc*, the first English tragedy in classic form.

For a time that form, descended from Rome, seemed destined to mold the Elizabethan drama. University scholars like Harvey, lawyer-poets like George Gascoyne, men of classical learning like Sidney, pleaded for the observance of the three "unities" in a play: that there should be only one *action* or plot, and that this should occur in one *place*, and represent no longer *time* than a day. These unities, so far as we know, were first formulated by Lodovico Castelvetro (1570) in a commentary on Aristotle's *Poetics*. Aristotle himself requires only unity of action; he recommends that the action should fall "within a single revolution of the sun"; and he adds what might be called unity of mood—that comedy, as "a representation of inferior people," should not be mingled with tragedy, as "a representation of heroic action."[34] Sidney's *Defence of Poesy* took the doctrine of the dramatic unities from Castelvetro and applied it with rigor and yet good humor to Elizabethan plays, in whose highhanded geography

> you shall have Asia of the one side, and Africa of the other, and so many other under kingdoms, that the player, when he comes in, must ever begin with telling where he is. . . . Now of time they are much more liberal; for ordinary it is, that two young princes fall in love; after many traverses she is got with child; delivered of a fair boy; he . . . groweth a man, falleth in love, and is ready to get another child; and all this in two hours' space.[35]

France followed the classic rules and produced Racine; England rejected them, gave its tragic drama romantic freedom and naturalistic scope, and produced Shakespeare. The ideal of the French Renaissance was order, reason, proportion, propriety; the ideal of Renaissance England was liberty, will, humor, life. The Elizabethan audience, composed of lordlings, middlings, and groundlings, had to have a rich and varied diet; it demanded action, not lengthy reports of hidden actions; it had a belly for laughter and did not mind gravediggers bandying philosophies with a prince; it had an untamed imagination that could leap from place to place and cross a continent at the bidding of a sign or the hint of a line. The Elizabethan drama expressed the Elizabethan English, not the Periclean Greeks or the Bourbon French; hence it became the national art, while arts that followed alien models took no English root.

The English drama had to fight another battle before it could proceed to Marlowe and Shakespeare. The nascent Puritan movement rejected the Elizabethan stage as a home of paganism, obscenity, and profanity; it denounced the presence of women and prostitutes in the audience, and the propinquity of brothels to the theaters. In 1577 John Northbrooke published a furious diatribe against "dicing, dancing, plays, and interludes," writing:

> I am persuaded that Satan hath not a more speedy way and fitter school to work and teach his desire, to bring men and women into his snare of concupiscence and filthy lusts of wicked whoredom, than those plays and theaters are; and therefore it is necessary that those places and players should be forbidden and dissolved, and put down by authority, as the brothels and stews are.[36]

Stephen Gosson's *Schoole of Abuse* was relatively moderate, and acknowledged some plays and actors to be "without rebuke"; but when Lodge replied to him Gosson abandoned all distinctions, and in *Players Confuted in Five Actions* he described plays as "the food of iniquity, riot, and adultery," and actors as "masters of vice, teachers of wantonness."[37] Critics saw in the comedies demoralizing pictures of vice and rascality, and in tragedies stimulating examples of murder, treachery, and rebellion.[38] In the earlier years of Elizabeth's reign, Sunday was the usual day for plays; trumpets announced them just as church bells called the people to afternoon prayer, and clergymen were dismayed to find their congregations skipping services to crowd the theater. "Will not a filthy play, with the blast of a trumpet," asked a preacher, "sooner call thither a thousand than an hour's tolling of a bell bring to a sermon a hundred?"[39] And Northbrooke proceeded: "If you will learn . . . to deceive your husbands, or husbands their wives, how to play the harlot . . . how to flatter, lie . . . murder . . . blaspheme, sing filthy songs . . . shall you not learn, at such interludes, to practice them?"[40]

The dramatists replied with pamphlets, and by making fun of Puritans in the plays, as of Malvolio in *Twelfth Night*. "Dost thou think, because thou art virtuous," asks Sir Toby Belch of the clown in that play, "there shall be no more cakes and ale?" And the clown replies, "Yes, by Saint Anne, and ginger shall be hot i' the mouth, too!"[41] The playwrights, even Shakespeare, continued to salt their tales with violence, rage, incest, adultery, and prostitution; one scene in Shakespeare's *Pericles* shows a room in a brothel, whose general manager complains that his personnel "with continual action are even as good as rotten."[42]

The city authorities of London—some of them Puritans—thought the Puritans had the better of the argument. In 1574 the Common Council forbade the performance of plays except after censorship and licensing; hence Shakespeare's line about "art made tongue-tied by authority."[43] Fortunately, Elizabeth and her Privy Council enjoyed the drama; several lords had companies of players, and under this royal protection and a lax censorship six troupes were licensed to produce plays in the city.

Before 1576 theatrical performances had taken place chiefly on temporary platforms in the courtyards of inns, but in that year James Burbage built the first permanent theater in England. It was called simply The Theatre. To escape the jurisdiction of the London magistrates, it was located just outside the City proper, in the suburb of Shoreditch. Soon other theaters rose: the Curtain (1577?), the Blackfriars (1596), the Fortune (1599). In this last year Richard and Cuthbert Burbage demolished their father's Theatre and raised the famous Globe in Southwark, just across the Thames. It was octagonal in outer form but probably circular within; hence Shakespeare could call it "this wooden O."[44] All the London theaters were of wood before 1623. Most of them were large amphitheaters, seating some two thousand spectators in several tiers of encircling galleries, and allowing another thousand to stand in the "yard" around the stage;

these latter were the "groundlings," whom Hamlet rebuked for their "dumb-shows and noise."[45] In 1599 the price of standing room was one penny, of a seat in the galleries two or three pence; a little more bought a seat on the stage. This was a spacious platform projecting from one wall into the center of the yard. At its rear was a "tiring," or attiring, room, where the actors donned their costumes and the "stage-keeper" managed the properties. These included tombs, skulls, box trees, rosebushes, caskets, curtains, caldrons, ladders, weapons, implements, phials of blood, and some severed heads. Machines could let gods and goddesses down from heaven or raise ghosts or witches up through the floor; "rain" could be produced at the pull of a string, and "double girts" could hang the sun in the sky.[46] These properties had to make up for the absence of scenery; the open and uncurtained stage forbade any rapid change of the setting. In recompense the action transpired in the very midst of the audience, which could almost feel itself a part of the event.

The audience was no minor portion of the spectacle. Caterers sold tobacco, apples, nuts, and pamphlets to the spectators; in later days, if we may believe the Puritan William Prynne, the women were offered pipes.[47] Women came to the plays in considerable number, not deterred by pulpit warnings that such mingling was an invitation to seduction. Sometimes— the class war interrupting the drama—the groundlings threw the leavings of their collations at the dandies on the stage. To understand an Elizabethan play we must remember that audience: the sentiment that welcomed a love story, the hearty humor that wanted clowns with kings, the swagger that relished rhetoric, the rough vitality that enjoyed scenes of violence—and the nearness of the three-sided stage, inviting soliloquies and asides.

Actors abounded. Strolling players might be seen in almost any town on festival days, performing in the village square, the tavern courtyard, a barn or a palace, and at wakes. There were in Shakespeare's day no actresses; female parts were played by boys, and sometimes an Elizabethan audience could see a boy representing a woman disguised as a boy or a man. In the aristocratic public schools the students presented dramas as part of their training. Companies of such boy actors competed with adult troupes by giving performances in private theaters for public and paying audiences. Shakespeare complained of this competition,[48] and after 1626 it ceased.

To avoid being classed as vagrants, the adult actors were organized in companies under the patronage and protection of opulent nobles—Leicester, Sussex, Warwick, Oxford, Essex. The Lord Admiral had a company; so did the Lord Chamberlain. The actors were paid by their patrons only for performances in the baronial halls; for the rest they lived precariously on the earnings of their shares in their company. Shares were unevenly divided; the manager took a third, and the leading actors received the lion's share of the rest. Richard Burbage, the most famous of these "stars," left property bringing £300 a year; his rival, Edward Alleyn, founded and endowed Dulwich College, London. The celebrities of the stage were rewarded also with public idolatry and a succession of mistresses. In his diary for March 1602, John Manningham tells a famous story:

> Once upon a time, when Burbage played *Richard III*, there was a citizen gone so far in liking with him that before she went from the play she appointed him to come that night unto her by the name of Richard III. Shakespeare, overhearing their conclusion, went before, was entertained and at his game before Burbage came. Then, message being brought that Richard III was at the door, Shakespeare caused return to be made that William the Conqueror was before Richard III.[49]

VI. CHRISTOPHER MARLOWE: 1564–93

The dramatists did not fare so well as the actors. They sold their plays outright to one of the theatrical companies for some four to eight pounds; they retained no rights to the manuscript, and usually the company prevented publication of the text lest it be used by a rival troupe. Sometimes a stenographer would record a play while it was being acted, and a printer would publish from this report a pirated and garbled edition, which brought the author nothing but hypertension. Such editions did not always bear the author's name; hence some plays, like *Arden of Faversham* (1592), have survived centuries of anonymity.

After 1590 the English stage was alive with plays of some moment, though only a few exceeded a day's run. John Lyly graced his comedies with charming lyrics; the fairy enchantments of his *Endymion* prepared for *A Midsummer Night's Dream*. Robert Greene's *Friar Bacon and Friar Bungay* (1589?), dealing with the marvels of magic, may have exchanged ideas with Marlowe's *Doctor Faustus* (1588? 1592?). Thomas Kyd's *Spanish Tragedy* (1589?) told a bloody tale of homicide, leaving hardly anyone alive at the end; its success inspired the Elizabethan playwrights to rival the generals and the doctors in shedding blood. Here, as in *Hamlet*, we have a ghost demanding revenge, and a play within a play.

Christopher Marlowe was christened just two months before Shakespeare. Son of a Canterbury shoemaker, he might have missed a university education had not Archbishop Parker given him a scholarship. During his college years he was engaged as a spy by Sir Francis Walsingham to check on plots against the Queen. His study of the classics unsettled his theology, and his acquaintance with Machiavelli's ideas gave his skepticism a cynical turn. Moving to London after receiving his M.A. (1587), he shared a room with Thomas Kyd, and joined the freethinking circle of Raleigh and Harriot. Richard Barnes, a government agent, reported to the Queen (June 3, 1593) that Marlowe had declared that "the first beginning of religion was only to keep men in awe . . . that Christ was a bastard . . . that if there be any good religion, then it is in the Papists, because the service of God is performed with more ceremonies . . . that all Protestants are hypocritical asses . . . that all the New Testament is filthily written." Furthermore, said Barnes, "this Marlowe . . . almost in any company he cometh, persuadeth men to atheism, willing them not to be afraid of bugbears and hobgoblins, and utterly scorning both God and His ministers."[50] For good measure Barnes (who was hanged in 1594 for a "degrading" offense) added that Marlowe defended homosexuality.[51] Robert Greene, in his dying appeal to his friends to reform, described Marlowe as given to blasphemy and atheism.[52] And Thomas Kyd, arrested on May 12, 1593, stated (under torture) that Marlowe was "irreligious, intemperate, and of cruel heart," accustomed to "jest at the divine Scriptures" and "gibe at prayers."[53]

Long before these reports were made to the government, Marlowe had written and staged powerful dramas hinting at his unbelief. Apparently *Tamburlaine the Great* was composed in college; it was produced in the year of his graduation, and its exaltation of knowledge, beauty, and power reveal the Faustian temper of the poet.

> Our souls, whose faculties can comprehend
> The wondrous architecture of the world,
> And measure every wandering planet's course,
> Still climbing after knowledge infinite,
> And always moving as the restless spheres,
> Will us to wear ourselves, and never rest
> Until we reach the ripest fruit of all.[54]

The two plays about Timur are crude with immaturity. The characterization is too simplified—each person is one quality; so Tamburlaine is pride of power, and the pride is rather the conceit of a collegian swollen with undigested novelties than the calm self-confidence of a victorious sovereign. The story runs on rivers of blood, obstructed with improbabilities. The style inclines to bombast. What, then, made this play the greatest success, so far, of the Elizabethan stage? Presumably its violence, bloodshed, and bombast, but also, we may believe, its heresies and its eloquence. Here were thoughts more boldly ranging, images more deeply felt, phrases more aptly turned, than the Elizabethan stage had yet heard; here were scores of those "mighty lines" that Jonson was to praise, and passages of such melodious beauty that Swinburne thought them supreme in their kind.

Quickened with acclaim, Marlowe wrote with all the intensity of his spirit his greatest play, *The Tragical History of Doctor Faustus* (1588?). Medieval ethics, perhaps recognizing that "the joy of understanding is a sad joy,"[55] and that "in much wisdom is much grief,"[56] had branded the unchecked lust for knowledge as a great sin; yet medieval aspirations had braved this prohibition, even to calling upon magic and Satan for the secrets and powers of nature. Marlowe represents Faustus as a learned and famous physician of Wittenberg who frets at the limits of his knowledge, and dreams of magic means that will make him omnipotent:

> All things that move between the quiet poles
> Shall be at my command . . .
> Shall I make spirits fetch me what I please,
> Resolve me of all ambiguities,
> Perform what desperate enterprise I will?
> I'll have them fly to India for gold,
> Ransack the oceans for orient pearl,
> And search all corners of the new-found world
> For pleasant fruits and princely delicates;
> I'll have them read me strange philosophy,
> And tell the secrets of all foreign kings.[57]

At his call Mephistophilis appears and offers him twenty-four years of limitless pleasure and power if he will sell his soul to Lucifer. Faustus agrees, and signs the contract with blood from his cut arm. His first requisition is the fairest maid in Germany to come to be his wife, "for I am wanton and lascivious"; but Mephistophilis dissuades him from marriage and suggests instead a succession of courtesans. Faustus calls for Helen of Troy; she comes, and he swells into ecstasy.

> Was this the face that launch'd a thousand ships,
> And burnt the topless towers of Ilium?
> Sweet Helen, make me immortal with a kiss. . . .
> O, thou art fairer than the evening air
> Clad in the beauty of a thousand stars . . .

The final scene is rendered with great power: the despairing appeal to God for mercy, for at least a term to damnation—"Let Faustus live in hell a thousand years, a hundred thousand, and at last be sav'd!"—and the disappearance of Faustus, on the stroke of midnight, in a fury of clashing, blinding clouds. The chorus sings his epitaph—and Marlowe's:

> Cut is the branch that might have grown full straight,
> And burnéd is Apollo's laurel-bough.

In these plays Marlowe might have purged his own passions for knowledge, beauty, and power; the catharsis, or cleansing effect, that Aristotle ascribed to tragic drama could better purge the author than the audience. In *The Jew of Malta* (1589?) the will to power takes the intermediate form of greed for wealth, and defends itself in the Prologue spoken by "Machiavel":

> Admired I am of those that hate me most.
> Though some speak openly [publicly] against my books,
> Yet they will read me, and thereby attain
> To Peter's chair; and when they cast me off,
> Are poison'd by my climbing followers.
> I count religion but a childish toy,
> And hold there is no sin but ignorance.

Barabas the moneylender is again one quality personified, greed raised to hatred of all who hinder his gains, an unpleasant caricature redeemed by majestic vices.

> I learn'd in Florence how to kiss my hand,
> Heave up my shoulders when they call me dog,
> And duck as low as any barefoot friar,
> Hoping to see them starve upon a stall.[58]

Contemplating his jewels, he thrills at their "infinite riches in a little room."[59] When his daughter recovers his lost money bags he cries out, in a confusion of affections anticipating Shylock, "O my girl, my gold, my fortune, my felicity!"[60] There is a power, almost a fury, in this play, a sting of epithet and force of phrase, that lead Marlowe now and then to the very verge of Shakespeare.

He came still closer in *Edward II* (1592). The young King, just crowned, sends for his "Greek friend" Gaveston, and lavishes kisses, offices, and wealth upon him; the neglected nobles rise and depose Edward, who, driven to philosophy, calls to his remaining comrades:

> Come, Spencer, come, Baldock, come sit down by me;
> Make trial now of that philosophy
> That in our famous nurseries of arts
> Thou suck'dst from Plato and from Aristotle.

From this well-constructed drama, this poetry of sensitivity, imagination, and power, these characters distinctly and consistently drawn, this King

so mingled of pederasty and pride and yet forgivable in his young simplicity and grace, it was but a step to Shakespeare's *Richard II*, which followed it by a year.

What would this twenty-seven-year-old dramatist have accomplished
had he matured? At that age Shakespeare was writing trifles like *Love's
Labour's Lost, Two Gentlemen of Verona*, and *A Comedy of Errors*.
In *The Jew of Malta* Marlowe was learning to make every scene advance
an orderly plot; in *Edward II* he was learning to conceive character
as more than a single quality personified. In a year or two he might have
purged his plays of bombast and melodrama; he might have risen to a
broader philosophy, a greater sympathy with the myths and foibles of
mankind. His distorting defect was lack of humor; there is no genial
laughter in his plays, and the incidental comedy does not, as in Shakespeare, serve its proper function in tragedy—to ease the hearer's tension
before lifting him to greater tragic intensities. He could appreciate the
physical beauty of women, but not their tenderness, solicitude, and grace;
there is no vivid female character in his plays, not even in the unfinished
Dido, Queen of Carthage.

What remains is the poetry. Sometimes the orator overcame the poet,
and declamation shouted "a great and thundering speech."[61] But in many
a scene the lucid verse flows with such vivid imagery or melody of speech
that one could mistake the lines for some Shakespearean stream of fantasy.
In Marlowe blank verse proved itself as the English drama's proper vehicle,
sometimes monotonous, but usually varied in its rhythm, and achieving a
seemingly natural continuity.

His own "tragical history" was now suddenly closed. On May 30, 1593,
three government spies, Ingram Frizer, Nicholas Skeres, and Robert Poley,
joined the poet—perhaps himself still a spy—at dinner in a house or tavern
in Deptford, a few miles from London. According to the report of William Danby, coroner, Frizer and Marlowe "uttered one to the other
divers malicious words for the reason that they could not . . . agree about
the payment" for the meal. Marlowe snatched a dagger from Frizer's belt
and struck him with it, inflicting some superficial cuts. Frizer seized Marlowe's hand, turned the weapon upon him, and "gave the said Christopher
then and there a mortal wound over his right eye, of the depth of two
inches . . . of which the aforesaid Christopher Morley then and there instantly died"; the blade had reached the brain. Frizer, arrested, pleaded
self-defense, and he was released after a month. Marlowe was buried
on June 1, in a grave now unknown.[62] He was twenty-nine years old.

He left, besides the *Dido*, two fragments of high excellence. *Hero and
Leander* is a romantic version, in heroic couplets, of the story Musaeus had
told, in the fifth century, of the youth who swam the Hellespont to keep
a tryst. "The Passionate Shepherd to His Love" is one of the great Eliz-

abethan lyrics. Shakespeare made handsome acknowledgments to Marlowe by putting snatches of that poem into the mouth of Sir Hugh Evans in *The Merry Wives of Windsor* (III, i), and by a tender reference in *As You Like It* (III, v):

> Dead Shepherd, now I find thy saw of might,
> "Who ever loved that loved not at first sight?"

—which is line 76 of *Hero and Leander*.

Marlowe's achievement was immense in its brief moment. He made blank verse a flexible and powerful speech. He saved the Elizabethan stage from the classicists and the Puritans. He gave their definite forms to the drama of ideas and that of English history. He left his mark on Shakespeare in *The Merchant of Venice*, in *Richard II*, in love poetry, and in a tendency to magniloquent rhetoric. Through Marlowe, Kyd, Lodge, Greene, and Peele the way had been opened; the form, structure, style, and material of the Elizabethan drama had been prepared. Shakespeare was not a miracle, he was a fulfillment.

CHAPTER IV

William Shakespeare

1564–1616

I. YOUTH: 1564–85

LET US, for the adequacy of this record, summarize what half the world knows about Shakespeare. Now that devout scholarship has rummaged among his relics for three centuries, it is remarkable how much we do know—far more than enough to set aside, as not meriting debate, all doubts about his authorship of nearly all the plays ascribed to his name.

However, we are not sure about his name. Elizabeth allowed more freedom of spelling than of religion; the same document might use different spellings of the same word, and a man might sign his name variously according to his haste or mood. So contemporaries wrote Marlowe as Marlo, Marlin, Marley, Morley; and Shakespeare's six surviving signatures appear to read Willm Shaksp, William Shakespē, Wm Shakspē, William Shakspere, Willm Shakspere, and William Shakspeare; the now prevalent spelling has no warrant in his autographs. The last three signatures are all on the same will.

His mother was Mary Arden, of an old Warwickshire family. She brought to John Shakespeare, son of her father's tenant, a goodly dowry in cash and land, and gave him eight children, of whom William was the third. John became a prosperous businessman in Stratford on Avon, bought two houses, served his town as ale taster, constable, alderman, and bailiff, and contributed liberally to the poor. After 1572 his fortunes fell; he was sued for thirty pounds, he failed to answer, and an order was issued for his arrest. In 1580, for reasons unknown, he was required by the court to give security against a breach of the peace. In 1592 he was listed as "not coming monthly to church according to her Majesty's laws"; some have concluded from this that he was a "recusant" Catholic, others that he was a Puritan, others that he dared not face his creditors. William later restored his father's finances, and when the father died (1601) two houses in Henley Street remained in the Shakespeare name.

The Stratford parish church registered William's baptism on April 26, 1564. Nicholas Rowe, his first biographer, recorded in 1709 the Stratford tradition, now generally credited, that the father "bred him . . . for some time at a free school . . . But the narrowness of his circumstances, and the want of his assistance at home, forced his father to withdraw him from thence."[1] Ben Jonson, in the elegy prefixed to the First Folio edition of the plays, addressed his dead rival, "Thou hadst small Latin and less Greek." Apparently the Greek dramatists remained Greek to Shakespeare, but he learned enough Latin to clutter his lesser plays with Latin odds and ends and bilingual puns. If he had learned more he might have become another scholar, laborious and unknown. London was to be his school.

Another tradition, recorded by Richard Davies about 1681, described young William as "much given to all unluckiness in stealing venison and rabbits, particularly from Sir [Thomas] Lucy, who had him oft whipped and sometimes imprisoned."[2] On November 27, 1582, when said miscreant was eighteen, he and Anne Hathaway, then about twenty-five, obtained a marriage license. Circumstances indicate that Anne's friends compelled Shakespeare to marry her.[3] In May 1583, six months after the marriage, a daughter was born to them, whom they named Susanna. Later Anne presented the poet with twins, who were christened Hamnet and Judith on February 2, 1585. Probably toward the end of that year Shakespeare left his wife and children. We have no record of him between 1585 and 1592, when we find him an actor in London.

II. DEVELOPMENT: 1592–95

The first reference to him there is uncomplimentary. On September 3, 1592, Robert Greene issued from his deathbed a warning to his friends that they were being displaced in the London theater by "an upstart Crow, beautified with our feathers, that with his Tygers hart wrapt in a Players hyde [parody of a line from *3 Henry VI*] supposes he is as well able to bombast out a blanke verse as the best of you; and being an absolute *Johannes fac totum*, is in his own conceit the only Shake-scene in a countrey."[4] This morsel was prepared for the press as part of *Greene's Groatsworth of Wit* by Henry Chettle, who in a later epistle offered an apology to *one* of the two persons (probably Marlowe and Shakespeare) who had been attacked by Greene:

> With neither of them that take offence was I acquainted, and with one of them I care not if I never be. [As to] the other . . . I am sorry . . . because myself have seen his demeanour no less civil than he was excellent in the quality [calling] he professes. Besides, divers of worship have reported his uprightness of dealing, which argues his honesty, and his facetious [agreeable] grace in writing, that approves his art.[5]

There seems no doubt that Greene's attack and Chettle's apology referred to Shakespeare. By 1592, then, the former poacher of Stratford had become an actor and playwright in the capital. Dowdall (1693) and Rowe (1709) related that he "was received into the playhouse as a servitor" in "a very mean rank,"[6] which is probable. But he fretted with ambition, "desiring this man's art and that man's scope," with "not a thought but turned on dignity."[7] Soon he was acting minor parts, making himself "a motley to the view";[8] then he played the kindly Adam in *As You Like It* and the Ghost in *Hamlet*. Probably he rose to higher roles, for his name headed the list of actors in Jonson's *Every Man in His Humour* (1598), and in Jonson's *Sejanus* (1604) he and Richard Burbage were specified as the "principal tragedians."[9] By the end of 1594 he was a shareholder in the Chamberlain's company of players. It was not as a dramatist, but as an actor and shareholder in a theatrical company, that Shakespeare made his fortune.

However, by 1591 he was writing plays. He seems to have begun as a play doctor, editing, touching up, and adapting manuscripts for his company. From such work he passed to collaboration; the three parts of *Henry VI* (1592) appear to have been such a composite production. Thereafter he wrote plays at the rate of almost two per year—thirty-six or thirty-eight in all. Several early ones, *A Comedy of Errors* (1592), *Two Gentlemen of Verona* (1594), and *Love's Labour's Lost* (1594) are lighthearted trifles, frothy with now tiresome badinage; it is instructive to see that Shakespeare had to grow into greatness by hard work. But the growth was rapid. Taking a hint from Marlowe's *Edward II*, he found in English history many a dramatic theme. *Richard II* (1595) equaled the earlier play; *Richard III* (1592) had already surpassed it. In some measure he fell into the fault of making a whole man out of one quality—the hunchback King out of treacherous and murderous ambition; but he lifted the play now and then out of Marlowe's reach by depth of analysis, intensity of feeling, and flashes of brilliant phrase; soon "A horse! A horse! My kingdom for a horse!" was a London cliché.

Then, in *Titus Andronicus* (1593), genius flagged; imitation took the lead and presented a repulsive dance of death. Titus kills his son, and others kill his son-in-law, on the stage; a bride, raped behind the scenes, comes on the boards with her hands cut off, her tongue cut out, her mouth bubbling blood; a traitor chops off Titus' hand before the groundlings' avid eyes; the severed heads of two of Titus' sons are displayed; a nurse is killed on stage. Reverent critics have labored to burden collaborators with part or all of the responsibility for this slaughter, on the mistaken theory that Shakespeare could not write nonsense. He wrote reams of it.

It was at about this point in his development that he composed his narrative poems and his sonnets. Perhaps the plague that caused the closing of all London theaters between 1592 and 1594 left him with penurious leisure, and he thought it advisable to cast a hopeful line to some patron of poetry. In 1593 he dedicated *Venus and Adonis* to Henry Wriothesley, third Earl of Southampton. Lodge had adapted the tale from Ovid's *Metamorphoses;* Shakespeare adapted it from Lodge. The Earl was young, handsome, and addicted to venery; perhaps the poem was spiced to his taste. Much of it seems jejune to jaded years; but in this proliferated seduction there are passages of sensuous beauty (e.g., lines 679–708) such as England had rarely read before. Encouraged by public applause and a gift from Southampton, Shakespeare issued in 1594 *The Ravyshement of Lucrece,* where the seduction was accomplished with a greater economy of verse. This was the last of his voluntary publications.

About 1593 he began to write, but kept from the press, the sonnets that first established his pre-eminence among the poets of his time. Technically the most nearly perfect of Shakespeare's works, they borrow heavily from the Petrarchan treasury of sonnet themes—the transitory beauty of the beloved, her cruel hesitations and inconstancy, the dreary crawl of unused time, the jealousies and the panting thirst of the lover, and the poet's boast that in his rhymes the lady's loveliness and fame would shine forever. Even some phrases and epithets are appropriated from Constable, Daniel, Watson, and other sonneteers, who themselves were links in a chain of pilferings. No one has succeeded in arranging the sonnets in any consistent narrative order; they were the casual labor of scattered days. We must not take too seriously their hazy plot—the love of the poet for a young man, his passion for a "dark lady" of the court, her rejection of him and acceptance of his friend, the winning of that friend by a rival poet, and Shakespeare's despairing dalliance with thoughts of death. It is possible that Shakespeare, acting before the court, cast looks of distant longing at the Queen's ladies in waiting, so intoxicatingly perfumed and gowned; it is unlikely that he ever spoke to them or followed the scent to the prey. One such lady, Mary Fitton, became the mistress of the Earl of Pembroke. She appears to have been blond, but this may have been merely a passing dye. However, she was unmarried, whereas Shakespeare's lady broke her "bed-vow" in loving the poet and his "boy."[10]

In 1609 Thomas Thorpe published the sonnets, apparently without Shakespeare's consent. As the author supplied no dedication, Thorpe provided one, to the puzzlement of centuries: "To the onlie begetter of these ensuing sonnets Mr. W. H. all happinesse and that eternitie promised by our ever-living poet, wisheth the well-wishing adventurer in setting forth." The signature, "T. T.," presumably meant Thomas Thorpe, but who was "W. H."? The initials might mean William Herbert, third Earl of Pembroke, who had seduced Mary Fitton and was destined, with his brother

Philip, to receive the dedication of the posthumous First Folio as "the greatest Maecenas, to learned men, of any peer of his time or since." Herbert was only thirteen when the sonnets began (1593), but their composition extended to 1598, by which time Pembroke was ripe for love and patronage. The poet speaks ardently of his "love" for the "boy"; "love" was then often used for friendship; but Sonnet 20 calls the lad "the master-mistress of my passion" and ends with an erotic play on words; and Sonnet 128 (apparently addressed to the "lovely boy" of 126) talks of amorous ecstasy. Some Elizabethan poets were literary pederasts, capable of winding themselves up to rapturous love for any man of means.

The important point about the sonnets is not their story but their beauty. Many of them (e.g., 29, 30, 33, 55, 64, 66, 71, 97, 106, 117) are rich in lines whose depth of thought, warmth of feeling, glow of imagery, or grace of phrase has made them ring for centuries through the English-speaking world.

III. MASTERY: 1595–1608

But the artifices and restraint of the sonnet clipped the wings of fancy, and Shakespeare must have rejoiced in the fluent freedom of blank verse when, still young and ardent, he let himself go in one of the great love poems of all time. The story of Romeo and Juliet came to England from the *novelle* of Masuccio and Bandello; Arthur Brooke rephrased it in narrative verse (1562); and Shakespeare, following Brooke and perhaps an earlier play on the subject, staged his *Romeo and Juliet* about 1595. The style is cloyed with conceits that may have clung to his pen from his sonneteering, the metaphors run wild, Romeo is weakly drawn beside the effervescent Mercutio, and the denouement is a concatenation of absurdities. But who that remembers youth, or has a dream left in his soul, can hear that honeyed music of romance without jettisoning all canons of credibility and rising breathless at the poet's bidding into this world of precipitate ardor, trembling solicitude, and melodious death?

Almost yearly now Shakespeare won a dramatic victory. On June 7, 1594, Elizabeth's Jewish physician, Rodrigo López, was executed on the charge of having accepted a bribe to poison the Queen. The evidence was inconclusive, and Elizabeth long hesitated to sign the death warrant; but the London populace took his guilt for granted, and anti-Semitism ran hot in the pubs.[11] Possibly Shakespeare was moved or commissioned to tap this mood by writing *The Merchant of Venice* (1596?). He shared in some measure the feelings of his audience;* he allowed Shylock to be

---

* Cf. *Two Gentlemen of Verona*, V, ii, 3,6; *Merry Wives of Windsor*, II, i.

represented as a comic character in slovenly dress and with a vast artificial nose; he rivaled Marlowe in bringing out the moneylender's hatred and greed; but he gave Shylock some lovable qualities that must have made the injudicious grieve, and he put into his mouth so bold a statement of the case for the Jews that competent critics still debate whether Shylock is pictured as more sinned against than sinning.[12] Here, above all, Shakespeare showed his skill in weaving into one harmonious tapestry divers threads of story coming from the Orient and Italy; and he made the converted Jessica the recipient of such moonstruck poetry as only a spirit of supreme sensitivity could have conceived.

For five years Shakespeare gave himself chiefly to comedy; perhaps he had learned that our harassed species reserves its richest rewards for those who can distract it with laughter or imagination. *A Midsummer Night's Dream* is powerful nonsense, only redeemed by Mendelssohn; *All's Well That Ends Well* is not salvaged by Helena; *Much Ado about Nothing* lives up to its title; *Twelfth Night* is bearable only because Viola makes a very handsome boy; and *The Taming of the Shrew* is boisterously incredible; shrews are never tamed. All these plays were potboilers, sops to the groundlings, ways of keeping the herd in the pit and the wolf from the door.

But with the two parts of *Henry IV* (1597–98) the great magician rose again to mastery, and mingled clowns and princes—Falstaff and Pistol, Hotspur and Prince Hal—with a success that would have given Sidney pause. London relished this serving of royal history garnished with rogues and tarts. Shakespeare carried on with *Henry V* (1599), at once moving and amusing his audience with dying Falstaff's "babbling o' green fields," rousing it with the fanfare of Agincourt, and delighting it with the bilingual courtship of Princess Kate by the invincible King. If we may believe Rowe, the Queen was not content to let Falstaff rest; she bade his creator revive him and show him in love;[13] and John Dennis (1702), relating the same story, adds that Elizabeth desired the miracle to be accomplished in two weeks. If all this be true, *The Merry Wives of Windsor* was an astonishing tour de farce; for though the play is noisy with slapstick and punctured with puns, it has Falstaff at the height of his verve, until he is cast into the river in a hamper of wash. The Queen, we are told, was pleased.

It is startling to find a dramatist capable of producing in one season (1599–1600?) such nugatory nonsense as this and then so ethereal an idyl as *As You Like It*. Perhaps because it took a lead from Lodge's novel *Rosalynde* (1590), the play has a music of refinement in it—still hobbled with arid badinage, but tender and delicate in feeling, gay and elegant in speech. What pretty friendship is here between Celia and Rosalind—and Orlando carving Rosalind's name into the bark of trees, "hanging odes upon hawthorns and elegies on brambles"; what a Fortunatus' fund of eloquence spilling immortal phrases on every page—and songs that have been welcome on a million lips: "Under the greenwood tree," "Blow, blow, thou winter wind," "It was a lover and his lass." The whole outpour is such delectable foolery and sentiment as cannot be matched in any literature.

But amid this cornucopia of sweets Monsieur Melancholy Jaques mingles some bitter fruit, announcing that life's "wide and universal theatre presents more woeful pageants than do the scene we play" upon the boards, that nothing is certain except death, usually after a toothless, eyeless, tasteless old age.

> And so, from hour to hour we ripe and ripe,
> And then from hour to hour we rot and rot,
> And thereby hangs a tale.[14]

So the Swan of Avon warned us that *As You Like It* was the swan song of his gaiety, and that thereafter, till further notice, he proposed to flay the surface of life and show us its bloody reality. Now he would open his vein of tragedy and mingle gall with his ambrosia.

In 1579 Sir Thomas North's Plutarch exposed a treasure trove of drama. Shakespeare took three of the *Lives* and molded them into *The Tragedy of Julius Caesar* (1599?). He found North's translation so spirited that he appropriated several passages word for word, merely measuring the prose into blank verse; however, the speech of Antony over Caesar's corpse was the poet's own invention, a masterpiece of oratory and subtlety, and the sole defense he allows to Caesar. His admiration for Southampton, Pembroke, and the young Essex may have moved him to see the assassination from the standpoint of endangered and conspiring aristocrats; so Brutus becomes the center of the play. We, who have Mommsen's details as to the odorous corruption of the "democracy" that Caesar overthrew, are more inclined to sympathize with Caesar, and are taken aback to find the title character dead at the outset of Act III. The past is helpless in the hands of the present, which repeatedly remolds it to the hour's whim.

In writing *Hamlet* (1600?), as in *Julius Caesar*, Shakespeare had the aid and challenge of an earlier play on the theme; a *Hamlet* had been performed in London only six years before. We do not know how much he took from that lost tragedy, or from François de Belleforest's *Histoires tragiques* (1576), or from the *Historia Danica* (1514) of the Danish historian Saxo Grammaticus; nor can we say if Shakespeare read *Of the Diseases of Melancholy*, the recent English translation of a French medical work by Du Laurens. Doubting stoically every attempt to turn the plays into autobiography, we are yet warranted in asking whether some personal grief—in addition to the sobering of time—entered into the pessimism that cried out in *Hamlet* and grew bitterer in succeeding plays. It might have been a second disillusionment with love. Was it the first arrest of Essex (June 5, 1600), or the collapse of Essex' revolt, the arrest of Essex and Southampton, the execution of Essex (February 25, 1601)? Presumably these events moved the sensitive poet who had so warmly praised Essex in the prologue to the last act of *Henry V* and, in the dedication to *Lucrece*, had pledged himself to Southampton forever. In any case, Shakespeare's greatest plays were written during or after these calamities. They are subtler in plot, deeper in thought, more magnificent in language than their predecessors, but also they voice against life the bitterest reproaches in all literature. Hamlet's vacillating will, and almost his "noble and most sovereign reason," are disordered by discovering the reality and the nearness of evil, and by feeding on the venom of revenge till he himself sinks to feelingless cruelty, and sends Ophelia not to a nunnery but to madness and death. In the end the slaughter is general. Only Horatio survives, too simple to be mad.

Meanwhile Elizabeth too had found the final balm, and James VI of Scotland became James I of England. Soon after his accession he confirmed and extended the privileges of Shakespeare's company, which became "the King's Men." Shakespeare's plays were regularly performed before the King and met with ample royal encouragement. The three seasons between 1604 and 1607 brought the poet to the fullness of his genius and his bitterness. *Othello* (1604?) is as powerful as it is incredible. The audience was moved to pity by the devotion and the death of Desdemona and fascinated by the intelligent malignancy of Iago; but in picturing such unmixed and unmotived evil in a man Shakespeare fell into Marlowe's fault of monolithic characters, and even Othello, despite his union of generalship and stupidity, lacks that rich admixture of elements which makes Hamlet and Lear, Brutus and Antony human.

Macbeth (1605?) is a still more macabre contemplation of unmitigated evil. Shakespeare could cite Holinshed for the stark facts, but he made the story darker with his passionate disillusionment. The mood reached its nadir, the art its apogee, in *King Lear* (1606?). The tale had been elaborated by Geoffrey of Monmouth, carried down by Holinshed, and lately staged by a now unknown dramatist in *The True Chronicle of King Lear* (1605); plots were common property. The earlier play had followed Holinshed in giving Lear a happy ending, through reunion with Cordelia and restoration to the throne; Shakespeare is apparently guilty of the King's madness and dethroned death, and he added the bloody blinding of Gloucester on the stage. Bitterness is the organ tone of the play. Lear bids fornication thrive and adultery increase, "for I lack soldiers";[15] all virtue, in his darkened view, is a front for lechery, all government is bribery, all history is humanity preying upon itself. He goes mad perceiving the profundity and the apparent victory of evil, and he sheds all faith in a sustaining Providence.

Antony and Cleopatra (1607?) reaches lesser heights and depths. There is something nobler in Antony's defeat than in Lear's rage, something more believable and bearable in the Roman's infatuation with the Egyptian Queen than in the Briton's unlikely cruelty to a daughter absurdly frank; and Cleopatra, cowardly in battle, is magnificent in suicide. Here too Shakespeare had previous plays to work on, and again he bettered them, renewing and brightening the oft-told tale with subtler analyses of character and the unwearied magic and sparkle of his speech.

In *Timon of Athens* (1608?) the pessimism is sardonic and unrelieved. Lear aims his shafts at women, but feels some tardy pity for mankind; the hero of *Coriolanus* (1608?) despises the people as the fickle, sycophantic, brainless spawn of carelessness; but Timon denounces all, high or low, and curses civilization itself as having demoralized mankind. Plutarch in his life of Antony had mentioned Timon as a famous misanthrope; Lucian had put him in a dialogue; and an English play had been written about him some eight years before Shakespeare, with an unknown collaborator, took up the theme. Timon is an Athenian millionaire, surrounded by receptive flattering friends. When he loses his money and sees his friends vanish overnight, he kicks the dust of civilization from his feet and retires—a Jaques in dour earnest—to a forest solitude, where, he hopes, he "shall find the unkindest beasts more kinder than mankind."[16] He wishes Alcibiades were a dog, "that I might love thee something."[17] He lives on roots, digs, finds gold. Friends appear again; he drives them off with lashing scorn; but when prostitutes come he gives them gold, on condition that they will infect as many men as possible with venereal disease:

> Consumptions sow
> In hollow bones of man; strike their sharp shins,
> And mar men's spurring [marriages]. Crack the
> lawyer's voice,
> That he may never more false title plead,
> And sound his quillets [quibbles] shrilly; hoar
> the flamen [priest],
> That scolds against the quality of flesh,
> And not believes himself; down with the nose,
> Down with it flat; take the bridge quite away ...
> And let the unscarr'd braggarts of the war
> Derive some pain from you: plague all;
> That your activity may defeat and quell

The source of all erection.—There's more gold;
Do you damn others, and let this damn you . . .[18]

In an ecstasy of hatred he bids nature cease to breed men, and hopes
that vicious beasts may multiply to wipe out the human race. The excesses
of this misanthropy make it seem unreal; we cannot believe that Shakespeare felt this ridiculous superiority to sinful men, this cowardly incapacity
to stomach life. Such a *reductio ad nauseam* suggests that the disease was
purging itself, and that Shakespeare would soon smile again.

IV. ARTISTRY

How did a man of so little education come to write plays of such varied
erudition? But it was not really erudition. In no field except psychology
was it extensive or accurate. Shakespeare knew the Bible only so far as
his boyhood studies might have opened it to him; his Biblical references are
incidental and ordinary. His classical learning was casual, careless, and apparently confined to translations. He knew most of the pagan deities, even
the lesser or looser ones, but this knowledge could have been from the
English version of Ovid's *Metamorphoses*. He made little errors that
Bacon, for example, could never have made: called Theseus a duke, had
Hector of the eleventh century B.C. refer to Aristotle of the third,[19] and
let a character in *Coriolanus*[20] (fifth century B.C.) quote Cato (of the first).
He had little French and less Italian. He had some knowledge of geog-
raphy, and gave his plays exotic locales from Scotland to Ephesus; but
he gave Bohemia a seacoast,* and he sent Valentine by sea from Verona to
Milan,[23] and Prospero from Milan in an ocean-going vessel.[24] He took
much of his Roman history from Plutarch, of his English history from
Holinshed and from earlier plays. He made historical *faux-pas* unimportant
to a dramatist: put a clock in Caesar's Rome, billiards in Cleopatra's Egypt.
He wrote *King John* without mentioning Magna Charta, and *Henry VIII*
without bothering about the Reformation; again we see the past changing
with each present. In outline the English historical plays are correct from
our current view; in detail they are untrustworthy; in standpoint they are
colored by patriotism—Joan of Arc, in Shakespeare, is merely a wanton
witch. Nevertheless many Englishmen, like Marlborough, confessed that
most of their knowledge of English history came from Shakespeare's
plays.
Like other Elizabethan dramatists, Shakespeare used many legal terms,

---

* Ben Jonson pounced upon this in his talks with Drummond at Hawthornden.[21] Shakespeare took it from a novel by Robert Greene—a university graduate. Under Ottokar II
(r. 1253–78) Bohemia extended her rule to the Adriatic shores.[22]

sometimes improperly; he could have gleaned them in the Inns of Court—the law schools in which three of his plays were staged—or in the several lawsuits engaged in by his father or himself. He is rich in musical terms and was evidently sensitive to music—"Is it not strange that sheeps' guts should hale souls out of men's bodies?"[25] He lovingly remembers the flowers of England, strings them on a rosary in *The Winter's Tale*, and decks Ophelia with them in her delirium; he alludes to 180 different plants. He was acquainted with the sports of the field and the points of a horse. But he had little interest in science, which was soon to fascinate Bacon. Like Bacon, he retained the Ptolemaic astronomy.[26] At times (Sonnet 15) he seems to accept astrology, and he speaks of Romeo and Juliet as "star-crossed lovers";[27] but Edmund in *Lear* and Cassius in *Julius Caesar* vigorously reject it: "The fault, dear Brutus, is not in our stars, but in ourselves, that we are underlings."[28]

All in all, the evidence indicates that Shakespeare had the incidental learning of a man of affairs too busy with acting, managing, and living to sink his head into books. He knew the more startling of Machiavelli's ideas, he referred to Rabelais, he borrowed from Montaigne; but it is unlikely that he read their works. Gonzalo's description of an ideal commonwealth[29] is taken from Montaigne's essay "On Cannibals"; and Caliban, in the same play, may be Shakespeare's satire on Montaigne's idealization of the American Indians. Whether the skepticism of Hamlet owed anything to Montaigne's genial doubts is an unsolved problem; the play was published in 1602, a year before the printing of Florio's translation, but Shakespeare knew Florio and may have seen the manuscript. Montaigne's subtle criticism of traditional ideas may have helped to deepen Shakespeare, but there is nothing in the Frenchman that corresponds to Hamlet's soliloquy, or to the bitter indictment of life in *Lear, Coriolanus, Timon*, and *Macbeth*. Shakespeare is Shakespeare—pilfering plots, passages, phrases, lines anywhere, and yet the most original, distinctive, creative writer of all time.

The originality is in the language, the style, the imagination, the dramatic technique, the humor, the characters, and the philosophy. The language is the richest in all literature: fifteen thousand words, including the technical terms of heraldry, music, sports, and the professions, the dialects of the shires, the argot of the pavement, and a thousand hurried or lazy inventions—*occulted, unkenneled, fumitory, burnet, spurring* . . . He relished words and explored the nooks and crannies of the language; he loved words in general and poured them forth in frolicsome abandon; if he names a flower he must go on to name a dozen—the words themselves are fragrant. He makes simple characters mouth polysyllabic circumlocutions. He plays jolly havoc with the grammar: turns nouns, adjectives, even adverbs into verbs, and verbs, adjectives, even pronouns into nouns;

gives a plural verb to a singular subject or a singular verb to a plural subject; but there were as yet no grammars of English usage, no rules. Shakespeare wrote in haste, and had no leisure to repent.

The marvelous style, "manneristic and baroque,"[30] has the faults of its lawless wealth: phrases fancifully artificial or involved, farfetched images, word plays tiresomely elaborate; puns amid tragedy, metaphors falling over one another in contradictory confusion, repetitions innumerable, sententious platitudes, and, now and then, hilarious, nonsensical bombast filling the unlikeliest mouths. Doubtless a classical training would have chastened the style, silenced the *doubles-entendres;* but then consider what we should have lost. Perhaps he was thinking of himself when he made Ferdinand describe Adriano as a man

> That hath a mint of phrases in his brain;
> One whom the music of his own vain tongue
> Doth ravish like enchanting harmony . . .
> But, I protest, I love to hear him lie . . .[31]

From this mint issued an almost universal currency of phrases: the winter of our discontent;[32] piping time of peace;[33] wish father to the thought;[34] tell the truth and shame the devil;[35] sits the wind in that corner?;[36] uneasy lies the head that wears a crown;[37] paint the lily;[38] one touch of nature makes the whole world kin;[39] what fools these mortals be!;[40] the Devil can quote Scripture to his purpose;[41] midsummer madness;[42] the course of true love never did run smooth;[43] wear my heart upon my sleeve;[44] every inch a king;[45] to the manner born;[46] brevity is the soul of wit[47] . . . but this is a hint to stop. And of metaphors another thousand, of which one may serve—"to see the sails conceive and grow big-bellied with the wanton wind."[48] And entire passages now almost as familiar as the phrases: Ophelia's disordered herbal of flowers, Antony over dead Caesar, Cleopatra dying, Lorenzo on the music of the spheres. And a whole repertoire of songs: "Who is Silvia?,"[49] "Hark, hark! the lark at heaven's gate sings,"[50] "Take, O take those lips away."[51] Probably Shakespeare's audience came for his plumage as well as for his tale.

"The lunatic, the lover, and the poet are of imagination all compact";[52] Shakespeare was two of these and may have touched the third. He creates a world with every play, and, not content, he fills imagined empires, woods, and heaths with childlike magic, scurrying fairies, awesome witches and ghosts. His imagination makes his style, which thinks in images, turns all ideas into pictures, all abstractions into things felt or seen. Who but Shakespeare (and Petrarch) would have made Romeo, exiled from Verona, fume with envy that its cats and dogs might gaze on Juliet and he be disallowed? Who else (but Blake) would have made the banished Duke, in *As You Like It*, regret that he must live by hunting beasts so often more beautiful than man? Little wonder that a spirit so keen in every sense should have reacted passionately against the ugliness, greed, cruelty, lust, pain, and grief that seemed at times to dominate the panorama of the world.

His originality is least in dramatic technique. As a man of the theater he knew the tricks of his trade. He began his plays with scenes or words calculated to jolt the attention of his nut-cracking, card-playing, ale-swilling, woman-ogling audience. He took full advantage of the abundant "properties" and machinery of the Elizabethan stage. He studied his fellow actors and created parts suitable to their physical and mental peculiarities. He used all the jugglery of disguises and recognitions, all the shifts of scenery and the complications of a play within a play. But in his craftsmanship he shows some scars of haste. Sometimes the plot within the plot tears the tale in two; what has Gloucester's tragedy to do with Lear's? Almost all the stories turn on improbable coincidences, concealed identities, highly opportune revelations; we may be reasonably asked to make believe, in drama as in opera, for the sake of the story or the song, but an artist should reduce to a minimum the "baseless fabric" of his dream. Less important are the inconsistencies of time or character;[53] presumably Shakespeare, thinking of rapid production, not of careful publication, judged that these flaws would pass unnoticed by an excited audience. Classical norms and modern taste alike condemn the violence that often dyes Shakespeare's stage; this was another concession to the pit, and an effort to meet the competition of the slaughterhouse school of Elizabethan-Jacobean dramatists.

As he developed, Shakespeare redeemed the violence with humor and learned the difficult art of intensifying tragedy with comic relief. The early comedies are wit and humor unrelieved, the early historical plays are stodgy for lack of humor; in *Henry IV* tragedy and comedy alternate but are not well integrated; in *Hamlet* the integration is achieved. Sometimes the humor seems too broad; Sophocles and Racine would have turned up their classical noses at the jokes about human flatulence[54] or equine micturition.[55] An erotic quip now and then is more to the modern taste. Generally, Shakespeare's humor is good-natured, not the savage misanthropy of Swift; he felt that the world was better for a clown or two; he suffered fools patiently, and emulated God in seeing little difference between them and world-explaining philosophers.

His greatest clown rivals Hamlet as Shakespeare's supreme achievement in the creation of character—which is the supreme test of a dramatist. Richard II and Richard III, Hotspur and Wolsey, Gaunt **and Gloucester,**

Brutus and Antony rise out of the limbo of history into a second life. Not in Greek drama, not even in Balzac, are imagined persons so endowed with consistent character and vital force. Most real are those creations that only seem contradictory because of their complexity—Lear cruel and then tender, Hamlet thoughtful and impetuous, hesitant and brave. Sometimes the characters are too simple—Richard III merely villainy, Timon merely cynicism, Iago merely hate. Some of the women in Shakespeare seem plucked from the same mold—Beatrice and Rosalind, Cordelia and Desdemona, Miranda and Hermione—and lose reality, and then at times a few words make them live; so Ophelia, told by Hamlet that he had never loved her, answers without recrimination, but with sad and moving simplicity, "I was the more deceived." Observation, feeling, empathy, astonishing receptivity of senses, penetrating perception, alert selection of significant and characteristic detail, tenacious remembering, come together to people this living city of dead or imagined souls. Play after play these personae grow in reality, complexity, and depth, until, in *Hamlet* and *Lear*, the poet matures into a philosopher and his dramas become the glowing vehicles of thought.

V. PHILOSOPHY

"Hast any philosophy in thee, shepherd?"[56] So Touchstone asks Corin, and we ask Shakespeare. One of his confessed rivals gave a negative answer to the question;[57] and we may accept that judgment as Bernard Shaw meant it—that there is no metaphysics in Shakespeare, no view as to the ultimate nature of reality, no theory of God. Shakespeare was too wise to think that a creature could analyze his creator, or that even *his* mind, poised on a moment of flesh, could comprehend the whole. "There are more things in heaven and earth, Horatio, than are dreamt of in your philosophy."[58] If he made a guess he kept it to himself, and perhaps thereby proved himself a philosopher. He speaks with no reverence of professed philosophers, and doubts that any of them ever bore the toothache patiently.[59] He laughs at logic and prefers imagination's light; he does not offer to solve the mysteries of life or mind, but he feels and visions them with an intensity that shames or deepens our hypotheses. He stands aside and watches the dogmatists destroy one another or disintegrate in the catalysis of time. He hides himself in his characters and is hard to find; we must beware of attributing an opinion to him unless it is expressed with some emphasis by at least two of his creations.

He is at first sight more of a psychologist than a philosopher; but again not as a theorist but, rather, as a mental photographer, catching the secret

thoughts and symptomatic actions that reveal the nature of a man. However, he is no surface realist; things do not happen, people do not speak, in
life as in his plays; but in the sum we feel that through these improbabilities
and extravagances we are nearing the core of human instinct and thought.
Shakespeare knows as well as Schopenhauer that "reason panders will";[60]
he is quite Freudian in putting erotic ditties into the virgin mouth of the
starved and crazed Ophelia; and he reaches beyond Freud to Dostoevski
in studying Macbeth and his "worser" half.

If we interpret philosophy not as metaphysics but as any large perspective of human affairs, as a generalized view not only of the cosmos and
the mind but as well of morals, politics, history, and faith, Shakespeare is
a philosopher, profounder than Bacon, as Montaigne is deeper than Descartes; it is not form that makes philosophy. He recognizes the relativity
of morals: "There's nothing good or bad but thinking makes it so,"[61] and
"our virtues lie in the interpretation of the time."[62] He feels the puzzle
of determinism: some men are bad by heredity, "wherein they are not
guilty, since nature [character] cannot choose his origin."[63] He knows the
Thrasymachus theory of morals: Richard III holds that "conscience is but
a word that cowards use, devised at first to keep the strong in awe; our
strong arms be our conscience, swords our law";[64] Richard II judges that
"they well deserve to have, that know the strong'st and surest way to
get";[65] but both these Nietzscheans are brought to a sorry fate. Shakespeare
notes, too, the feudal-aristocratic ethic of honor and gives it many a
noble phrase, but he deprecates, as in Hotspur, its bent toward pride and
violence, "defect of manners, want of [self-]government."[66] In the end
his own ethic is one of Aristotelian measure and Stoic control. Measure
and reason are the theme of Ulysses' speech reproving Ajax and Achilles.[67]
Reason alone, however, is not enough; a stoic fiber must strengthen it:

> Men must endure
> Their going hence even as their coming hither:
> Ripeness is all . . .[68]

Death is forgivable if it comes after we have fulfilled ourselves. Shakespeare
welcomes Epicurus, too, and admits no inherent contradiction between
pleasure and wisdom. He snaps at the Puritans, and makes the maid Maria
tell Malvolio, "Go shake your ears"[69]—i.e., "You're an ass." He is as lenient
as a pope to sins of the flesh, and puts into the mad Lear's mouth a hilarious
paean to copulation.[70]

His political philosophy is conservative. He knew the sufferings of the
poor and made Lear voice them feelingly. A fisherman in *Pericles* (1609?)
notes that fishes live in the sea

as men do a-land,—the great ones eat up the little ones. I can compare
our rich misers to nothing so fitly as to a whale; a' plays and tumbles,
driving the poor fry before him, and at last devours them all at a
mouthful: such whales have I heard on o' the land, who never leave
gaping till they've swallowed the whole parish, church, steeple,
bells, and all.[71]

Gonzalo, in *The Tempest*, dreams of an anarchistic communism where
"all things in common nature should produce," and there should be no
laws, no magistrates, no labor, and no war;[72] but Shakespeare smiles this
utopia away as made impossible by the nature of man; under every constitution the whales will eat the fish.

What was Shakespeare's religion? Here especially the search for his
philosophy is difficult. He expresses through his characters almost every
faith, and with such tolerance as must have made the Puritans think him
an infidel. He quotes the Bible often and reverently, and lets Hamlet, supposedly skeptical, talk believingly of God, prayer, heaven, and hell.[73]
Shakespeare and his children were baptized according to Anglican rites.[74]
Some of his lines are vigorously Protestant. King John speaks of papal
pardons as "juggling witchcraft," and quite anticipates Henry VIII:

> . . . no Italian priest
> Shall tithe or toll in our dominions;
> But as we, under heaven, are supreme head,
> So, under Him, that great supremacy,
> Where we do reign, we will alone uphold . . .
> So tell the Pope, all reverence set apart
> To him and his usurpt authority.[75]

Though, of course, John goes to Canossa in the end. A later play,
Henry VIII, only partly by Shakespeare, gives very favorable pictures of
Henry and Cranmer and ends with a eulogy of Elizabeth—all chief architects of the Reformation in England. There are some pro-Catholic touches,
as in the sympathetic portrayal of Catherine of Aragon and Friar Lawrence;[76] but the latter character had come to Shakespeare as formed in
the *novelle* of Italian Catholics.

Some faith in God survives throughout the tragedies. Lear in his bitterness thinks that

> As flies to wanton boys are we to the gods,—
> They kill us for their sport.[77]

But: "The gods are just," answers the good Edgar, "and of our pleasant
vices make instruments to plague us";[78] and Hamlet affirms his faith in "a

divinity that doth shape our ends, rough-hew them how we will."[79] Despite this struggling faith in a Providence that deals with us justly there is, in Shakespeare's greatest plays, a spreading cloud of unbelief in life itself. Jaques sees in all the "seven ages" of man nothing but slow riping and fast rotting. We hear the same refrain in *King John*:

> Life is as tedious as a twice-told tale
> Vexing the dull ear of a drowsy man;[80]

and in Hamlet's scorn of the world:

> Fie on't! O, fie! 'tis an unweeded garden,
> That grows to seed; things rank and gross in nature
> Possess it merely;[81]

and in Macbeth's

> Out, out, brief candle!
> Life's but a walking shadow; a poor player
> That struts and frets his hour upon the stage,
> And then is heard no more: it is a tale
> Told by an idiot, full of sound and fury,
> Signifying nothing.[82]

Does any sense of immortality soften this pessimism? Lorenzo, after describing to Jessica the music of the spheres, adds that "such harmony is in immortal souls."[83] Claudio, in *Measure for Measure*, visions an afterlife, but in somber terms of Dante's Inferno or Pluto's Hades:

> Ah, but to die, and go we know not where;
> To lie in cold obstruction, and to rot;
> This sensible warm motion to become
> A kneaded clod; and the delighted spirit
> To bathe in fiery floods, or to reside
> In thrilling region of thick-ribbed ice;
> To be imprison'd in the viewless winds,
> And blown with restless violence round about
> The pendent world . . . 'tis too horrible![84]

Hamlet speaks casually of the soul as immortal,[85] but his soliloquy affirms no faith; and his dying words in the older version of the play, "Heaven receive my soul," were changed by Shakespeare to read, "The rest is silence."

We cannot say with confidence how much of this pessimism came from the demands of tragic drama and how much voiced Shakespeare's mood; but its repetition and emphasis suggest that it expressed the darker moments of his philosophy. The sole mitigation of it in these culminating plays is a hesitant recognition that amid the evils of this world there are blessings and delights, amid the villains many heroes and some saints—for every Iago a Desdemona, for every Goneril a Cordelia, for every Edmund an Edgar or a Kent; even in Hamlet a fresh wind blows from Horatio's faithfulness and Ophelia's wistful tenderness. After the tired actor and playwright leaves the chaos and crowded loneliness of London for the green fields and parental consolations of his Stratford home he will recapture the strong man's love of life.

VI. RECONCILIATION

However, he had no obvious reason to complain of London. It had given him success, acclaim, and fortune. There are over two hundred references to him, almost all favorable, in the surviving literature of his time. In 1598 Francis Meres's *Palladis Tamia: Wits Treasury* listed Sidney, Spenser, Daniel, Drayton, Warner, Shakespeare, Marlowe, and Chapman, in that order, as England's leading authors, and ranked Shakespeare first among the dramatists.[86] In that same year Richard Barnfield, a rival poet, declared that Shakespeare's work (of which the best was yet to come) had already placed his name in "Fame's immortal Book."[87] He was popular even with his competitors. Drayton and Jonson and Burbage were among his closest friends; and though Jonson criticized his inflated style, his careless facility in composition, and his outrageous neglect of classic rules, it was Jonson who, in the First Folio, rated Shakespeare above all other dramatists ancient or modern and judged him to be "not of an age, but for all time." In the papers that Jonson left at his death he wrote, "I loved the man . . . this side idolatry."[88]

Tradition joins Jonson with Shakespeare in the meetings of literary men at the Mermaid Tavern in Bread Street. Francis Beaumont, who knew them both, exclaimed:

> What things have we seen
> Done at the Mermaid!—heard words that have been
> So nimble and so full of subtle flame
> As if that everyone from whence they came
> Had meant to put his whole wit in a jest,
> And had resolved to live a fool the rest
> Of his dull life.[89]

And Thomas Fuller's *Worthies of England* (1662) reported:

> Many were the wit combats betwixt Shakespeare and Ben Jonson, which two I behold like a Spanish great galleon and an English man-of-war. Master Jonson (like the former) was built far higher in learning, solid but slow in his performances. Shakespeare . . . lesser in bulk but lighter in sailing, could turn with all tides, tack about, and take advantage of all winds by the quickness of his wit and invention.[90]

Aubrey, about 1680, continued the easily credible tradition of Shakespeare's "very ready and pleasant smooth wit," and added that he "was a handsome, well-shaped man, very good company."[91] The only extant likenesses of him are the bust placed over his tomb in the Stratford church and the engraving prefixed to the First Folio; they agree well enough, showing a man half bald, with mustache and (in the bust) beard, sharp nose, and meditative eyes, but giving no sign of the flame that burns in the plays. Perhaps the plays mislead us about his character; they suggest a man of high-strung energy and passion fluctuating between the summits of thought and poetry and the depths of melancholy and despair; while his contemporaries describe him as civil and honest, slow to take offense, "of an open and free nature,"[92] enjoying life, careless of posterity, and showing a vein of practicality unbecoming a poet. Whether by thrift or gift, he was already rich enough in 1598 to join in financing the Globe theater; and in 1608 he and six others built the Blackfriars. His shares in these enterprises, added to his earnings as actor and playwright, gave him a substantial income—diversely estimated between £200[93] and £600[94] a year. The latter figure seems better able to explain his purchases of Stratford realty.

"He was wont," says Aubrey, "to go to his native country once a year."[95] Sometimes he stopped on the way at Oxford, where a John Davenant kept an inn; Sir William Davenant (poet laureate in 1637) liked to suggest that he was the unpremeditated result of Shakespeare's dalliance there.[96] In 1597 the dramatist, for sixty pounds, bought New Place, the second-largest house in Stratford, but he continued to live in London. His father died in 1601, leaving him two houses in Henley Street, Stratford. A year later, for £320, he bought near the town 127 acres of land, which he probably leased to tenant farmers. In 1605 he bought for £440 a share in the prospective ecclesiastical tithes of Stratford and three other communities. While he was writing his greatest plays in London he was known in Stratford chiefly as a successful businessman, frequently engaged in litigation about his properties and investments.

His son Hamnet had died in 1596. In 1607 his daughter Susanna married John Hall, a prominent Stratford physician, and a year later she made the poet a grandfather. He had now new ties to draw him homeward. About 1610 he retired from London and the stage and moved into New Place. Apparently it was there that he composed *Cymbeline* (1609?), *The Winter's Tale* (1610?), and *The Tempest* (1611?). Two of these are of minor rank, but *The Tempest* shows Shakespeare still master of his powers. Here is Miranda, who at the outset reveals her nature when, seeing a shipwreck from the shore, she cries out, "Oh, I have suffered with those that I saw suffer!"[97] Here is Caliban, Shakespeare's answer to Rousseau. Here is Prospero, the kindly magician, surrendering the wand of his art and bidding his airy world a fond goodbye. There is an echo of the poet's melancholy in the undiminished eloquence of Prospero's lines:

> Our revels now are ended. These our actors,
> As I foretold you, were all spirits, and
> Are melted into air, into thin air:
> And, like the baseless fabric of this vision,
> The cloud-capp'd towers, the gorgeous palaces,
> The solemn temples, the great globe itself,
> Yea, all which it inherit, shall dissolve,
> And, like this insubstantial pageant faded,
> Leave not a rack behind. We are such stuff
> As dreams are made on; and our little life
> Is rounded with a sleep.[98]

But this is not now the dominant mood; on the contrary, the play is Shakespeare relaxing, talking of brooks and flowers, singing songs like "Full fathom five" and "Where the bee sucks, there suck I." And, despite all cautious demurrers, it is the aging poet who speaks through Prospero's farewell:

> . . . graves at my command
> Have waked their sleepers, oped, and let 'em forth
> By my so potent art. But this rough magic
> I here abjure . . . I'll break my staff,
> Bury it certain fathoms in the earth,
> And deeper than did ever plummet sound
> I'll drown my book.[99]

And perhaps it is Shakespeare again, rejoiced by his daughters and his grandchild, who cries out, through Miranda:

> O wonder!
> How many goodly natures are there here!
> How beauteous mankind is! O brave new world
> That hath such people in it![100]

On February 10, 1616, Judith married Thomas Quiney. On March 25 Shakespeare made his will. He left his property to Susanna, £300 to Judith, small bequests to fellow actors, and his "second-best bed" to his estranged wife. Perhaps he had arranged with Susanna to take care of her mother. Anne Hathaway survived him by seven years. In April, according to John Ward, vicar (1662–81) of Stratford Church, "Shakespeare, Drayton, and Ben Jonson had a merry party, and it seems drank too hard, for Shakespeare died of a fever there contracted."*[101] Death came on April 23, 1616. The body was buried under the chancel of the Stratford church. Nearby on the floor, graved on a stone bearing no name, is an epitaph which local tradition ascribes to Shakespeare's hand:

> GOOD FRIEND, FOR JESUS SAKE FORBEARE
> TO DIGG THE DUST ENCLOASED HEARE.
> BLESE BE YE MAN YT [THAT] SPARES THES STONES,
> AND CURST BE HE YT MOVES MY BONES.

VII. POST-MORTEM

He had, so far as we know, taken no steps to have his plays published; the sixteen that severally appeared in his lifetime were printed, apparently, without his co-operation, usually in quarto form, and in various degrees of textual corruption. Stirred by these piracies, two of his former associates, John Heming and Henry Condell, issued in 1623 the First Folio, containing in one tall volume of some nine hundred double-column pages the authoritative text of thirty-six of the plays. "We have but . . . done an office to the dead," said the foreword, ". . . without ambition either of self-profit or fame; only to keep the memory of so worthy a friend . . . alive as was our Shakespeare." The volume could then be bought for a pound; each of the approximately two hundred extant copies is now valued at £17,000, more highly than any book except Gutenberg's Bible.

Shakespeare's reputation fluctuated curiously in time. Milton (1630) praised "sweetest Shakespeare, Fancy's child," but during the Puritan interval, when the theaters were closed (1642–60), the fame of the bard faded. It revived with the Restoration. Sir John Suckling, in his portrait by Vandyck (in the Frick Gallery, New York), holds the First Folio open at *Hamlet*. Dryden, the oracle of the later seventeenth century, commended Shakespeare as having, "of all modern, and perhaps ancient, poets . . . the largest and most comprehensive soul . . . always great when some great occasion is presented to him," but "many times flat, insipid, his comic

---

* "There is no reason to reject this report."—Sir E. K. Chambers, *William Shakespeare*, I, 89.

art degenerating into clenches, his serious swelling into bombast."[102] John
Evelyn noted in his diary (1661) that "the old plays disgust this refined
age, since his Majesty's being so long abroad"—i.e., since Charles II
and the returning royalists had brought to England the dramatic norms
of France; soon afterward the Restoration theater produced the bawdiest
dramas in modern literature. Shakespeare's plays were still performed,
but usually in "adaptation" by Dryden, Otway, or other models of Restoration taste.

The eighteenth century restored the plays to Shakespeare. Nicholas
Rowe published (1709) the first critical edition and the first biography;
Pope and Johnson issued editions and commentaries; Betterton, Garrick,
Kemble, and Mrs. Siddons made Shakespeare popular on the stage as
never before; and Thomas Bowdler made his own name a verb by publishing (1818) an expurgated version omitting parts "which cannot with
propriety be read aloud in a family." In the early nineteenth century the
romantic movement took Shakespeare to its heart, and the superlatives of
Coleridge, Hazlitt, De Quincey, and Lamb transformed him into a tribal
god.

France demurred. By 1700 its literary standards had been formed by
Ronsard, Malherbe, and Boileau in the Latin tradition of order, logical
form, polite taste, and rational control; it had adopted, in Racine, the
classical rules of drama; it was disturbed by Shakespeare's windy word
play, his bubbling torrent of phrases, his emotional storms, his coarse
clowns, his mingling of comedy with tragedy. Voltaire, returning from
England in 1729, brought with him some appreciation of Shakespeare
and "first showed the French a few pearls which I found in his enormous
dunghill";[103] but when someone ranked the Englishman above Racine,
Voltaire rose to the defense of France by calling Shakespeare "an amiable
barbarian."[104] His *Philosophical Dictionary* (1765) made some amends:
"In this same man there are passages which exalt the imagination and
penetrate the heart. . . . He reaches sublimity without having searched
for it."[105] Mme. de Staël (1804), Guizot (1821), and Villemain (1827)
helped France to bear with Shakespeare. Finally the translation of the plays
into good French prose by Victor Hugo's son François won Shakespeare
the respect of France, though never the devout admiration there accorded
to Racine.

The bard had a better press in Germany, where no native playwright
contested the prize. It was Germany's first great dramatist, Gotthold Les-
sing, who in 1759 informed his countrymen that Shakespeare was superior
to all other poets, ancient or modern; and Herder supported him. August
von Schlegel, Ludwig Tieck, and other leaders of the Romantic school
raised the Shakespearean banner, and Goethe contributed an enthusiastic

discussion of *Hamlet* in *Wilhelm Meister* (1796).[106] Shakespeare became popular on the German stage; and for a time German scholarship snatched the lead from England in the clarification of Shakespeare's life and plays.

For those brought up in the aura of Shakespeare an objective estimate or comparison is impossible. Only one who knows the language, the religion, the art, the customs, and the philosophy of the Periclean Greeks will feel the unequaled dignity of the Dionysian tragic drama, the stark simplicity and inexorable logic of its structure, its proud self-restraint in word and deed, the moving commentary of its choral chants, the high enterprise of seeing man in the perspective of his cosmic place and destiny. Only one who knows the French language and character, and the background of the *grand siècle*, can feel, in the plays of Corneille and Racine, not merely the majesty and music of their verse, but as well the heroic effort of reason to overspread emotion and impulse, the stoic adherence to difficult classic norms, the concentration of the drama into a few tense hours summarizing and deciding lives. Only one who knows English in its Elizabethan fullness, who can ride with gusto the Elizabethan winds of rhetoric, lyric, and vituperation, who puts no bounds to the theater's mirroring of nature and release of imagination, can bring to Shakespeare's plays their merited acceptance with open arms and heart; but such a man will tremble with delight at the splendor of their speech, and he will be moved to the depths of his spirit to follow and fathom their thought. These are the three epochal gifts of the world's drama, and we must, despite our limitations, welcome them all to our deepening, thanking our heritage for Greek wisdom, French beauty, and Elizabethan life.

(But, of course, Shakespeare is supreme.)

CHAPTER V

Mary Queen of Scots

1542–87

I. THE FAIRY QUEEN

WITHIN the interlocking dramas of the Scottish Reformation and Elizabethan politics the tragedy of Mary Stuart moved with all the fascination of beauty, passionate love, religious and political conflict, murder, revolution, and heroic death. Her ancestry almost assured a violent end. She was the daughter of the Stuart James V of Scotland and of Mary of Guise, Lorraine, and France; she was the granddaughter of Margaret Tudor, who was the daughter of Henry VII of England; she was therefore niece, loosely called cousin, of "Bloody Mary" and Elizabeth; by common consent she was the legitimate heir to the English crown if Elizabeth should die without issue; and for those who—like all Catholics (and, at one time, Henry VIII)—considered Elizabeth a bastard and therefore ineligible to rule, Mary Stuart, and not Elizabeth Tudor, should have succeeded to the throne of England in 1558. To make tragedy certain, Mary, on becoming Queen of France (1559), allowed her followers and her state papers to call her Queen of England. It had long been a vain pretense of French kings to be also kings of England, and of English kings to be also kings of France; but in this case the pretense came close to a generally acknowledged claim. Elizabeth could not be sure of her crown as long as Mary lived. Only common sense could have saved the situation, and sovereigns rarely stoop so low.

Mary was offered kingdoms within a year of her birth. Within a week of her birth her father's death made her Queen of Scots. Henry VIII, hoping to unite Scotland as an appanage to England, proposed that the infant be betrothed to his son Edward, be sent to England, and be there brought up, presumably as a Protestant, to be Edward's Queen. Her Catholic mother accepted, instead, the offer of Henry II of France (1548) to give her in marriage to his son the Dauphin. To guard her against being kidnaped into England, Mary, aged six, was hurried off to France. She remained there thirteen years, was educated with the royal children, and became completely French in spirit, being already half French in blood. As she matured into youth she developed all the charms of young womanhood in beauty of features and form, sprightliness of mind, and merry grace of ways and speech. She sang sweetly, played the lute well, talked Latin, and wrote poetry that poets affected to praise. Courtiers throbbed to "the snow of her pure face" (Brantôme),[1] "the gold of her curled and plaited hair" (Ronsard),[2] the slender elegance of her hands, the fullness of her bust; and even the grave and sober L'Hôpital thought that such loveliness must be the vesture of a god.[3] She became the most attractive and accomplished figure at the most polished court in Europe. When, aged sixteen, she married the Dauphin (April 24, 1558), and still more when, aged seventeen, she became through his accession Queen of France, all the hopes of a fanciful dream seemed to have come true.

But Francis II died (December 5, 1560) after two years of rule. Mary, a widow at eighteen, thought of retiring to an estate in Touraine, for she loved France. But meanwhile Scotland had gone Protestant; it was in danger of being lost to France as an ally. The French government held it to be Mary's duty to go to Edinburgh and lead her native land back to the French alliance and the Catholic faith. Unwillingly, Mary reconciled herself to leaving the comforts and brilliance of French civilization for life in a Scotland which she could barely remember, and which she pictured as a land of barbarism and cold. She wrote to the leading Scottish nobles, affirming her fidelity to Scotland; she did not tell them that in her marriage contract she had deeded Scotland to the kings of France if she died without issue. The nobles, Protestant as well as Catholic, were charmed; the Scottish Parliament invited her to come and possess her throne. She asked Elizabeth for a safe-conduct through England; it was refused. On August 14, 1561, Mary sailed from Calais, bidding France a tearful farewell, and gazing at the receding coast till nothing remained but the sea.

Five days later she disembarked at Leith, the port of Edinburgh, and discovered Scotland.

II. SCOTLAND, 1560–61

It was a nation of ancient roots and rooted ways: bound by the rough highlands of the north to a feudal regime of almost independent nobles organizing and exploiting a half-primitive culture of hunting, herding, and tenant tillage; favored in the south by lovely lowlands fertile with rain but darkened by long winters and crippling cold; a people struggling to create a moral and civilized order out of illiteracy, illegitimacy, corruption, lawlessness, and violence; riddled with superstition, and sending witches to the stake; seeking in a tense religious faith some hope of a less arduous life. To offset the divisive power of the barons, the kings had

supported the Catholic clergy, and had dowered these with wealth leading to venality, lethargy, and concubines.[4] The nobles itched for the
riches of the Church; they debased the clergy by filling ecclesiastical offices with their worldly sons; they declared for the Reformation and made
the Scottish Parliament, which they controlled, the master alike of Church
and state.

External danger was the strongest incentive to internal unity. England
felt unsafe in an island shared with her by untamed Scots; time and again
she sought, by diplomacy, marriage, or war, to bring Scotland under
English rule. Fearful of absorption, Scotland allied herself with a France
traditionally hostile to England. Cecil advised Elizabeth to support the
Protestant nobles against their Catholic Queen; so Scotland would be
divided and would cease to be a peril to England or a support to France.
Moreover, the Protestant leaders, if successful, might reject Mary, enthrone a Protestant noble, and make all Scotland Protestant; privately
Cecil dreamed of uniting such a Scotland to England by persuading Elizabeth to marry such a king.[5] When France sent a force into Scotland to
suppress the Protestants, Elizabeth dispatched an army to protect them
and drive out the French. Beaten in the field, the French representatives
in Scotland signed at Edinburgh (July 6, 1560) a fateful treaty requiring
not only that the French should leave Scotland but that Mary should
cease to claim the throne of England. On the advice of her husband,
Francis II, Mary refused to ratify the treaty. Elizabeth took note.

The religious situation was equally confused. The Scottish "Reformation Parliament" of 1560 officially abolished Catholicism, and established
Calvinist Protestantism, as the religion of the state; but these acts did not
receive from Mary the royal ratification then required to make parliamentary decrees the law of the land. Catholic priests still held most of
the Scottish benefices; half the nobles were "papists," and John Hamilton,
of royal blood, still came to Parliament as the Catholic primate of Scotland. In Edinburgh, however, and in St. Andrews, Perth, Stirling, and
Aberdeen, a large proportion of the middle classes had been won to Calvinism by devoted preachers under the lead of John Knox.

In the year before Mary's coming Knox and his aides drew up a Book
of Discipline defining their doctrine and purposes. Religion was to mean
Protestantism; "the godly" were to mean Calvinists alone; "idolatry" was
to include "the Mass, invocation of saints, adoration of images, and the
keeping . . . of the same," and "the obstinate maintainers and teachers
of such abominations ought not to escape the punishment of the civil
magistrate." All doctrine "repugnant to" the Gospel was to "be utterly
suppressed as damnable to man's salvation."[6] Ministers were to be elected
by the congregations, were to establish schools open to all godly children,

and were to have control of the Scottish universities—St. Andrews, Glasgow, and Aberdeen. The wealth of the Catholic Church and the continued ecclesiastical tithes were to be devoted to the needs of the ministers, the education of the people, and the relief of the poor. The new Kirk, and not the secular state, was to legislate on morals and prescribe penalties for offenses—drunkenness, gluttony, profanity, extravagance of dress, oppression of the poor, obscenity, fornication, and adultery. All who resisted the new doctrine or persistently absented themselves from its services were to be turned over to the secular arm, with the Kirk's recommendation that they be put to death.[7]

However, the lords who dominated Parliament refused to accept the Book of Discipline (January 1561). They had no relish for a powerful and independent Kirk, and they had their own plans for using the wealth of the superseded Church. The Book remained the goal and guide of the Kirk's development.

Defeated in his attempt to establish a theocracy—a government by priests claiming to speak for God—Knox labored with massive tenacity to organize the new ministry, to find funds for its support, and to spread it throughout Scotland in the face of a still functioning Catholic clergy. The dogmatic force of his preaching and the enthusiasm of his congregation made him a power in Edinburgh and in the state. The Catholic Queen would have to reckon with him before she could consolidate her rule.

III. MARY AND KNOX: 1561–65

She had arranged to arrive in Scotland a fortnight before she was expected, for she had feared some opposition to her landing. But word of her arrival at Leith spread through the capital, and soon the streets were crowded with people. They were surprised to find that their Queen was a pretty and vivacious girl not yet nineteen years old; most of them cheered her as she rode gracefully on her palfrey to Holyrood Palace; and there the lords, Protestant and Catholic, welcomed her, proud that Scotland had so charming a ruler, who might someday, in person or through a son, bring England under a Scottish sovereign.

The two portraits[8] that have come down to us support her reputation as one of the most beautiful women of her time. We cannot tell how far the now nameless painters idealized her, but in both cases we see the finely molded features, the lovely hands, the luxuriant chestnut hair that entranced barons and biographers. Yet those pictures hardly reveal to us the real attractiveness of the young Queen—her buoyant spirit, her "laughing mouth," her nimble-witted speech, her fresh enthusiasm, her capacity for kindness and friendliness, her longing for affection, her reckless admiration of strong men. It was her tragedy that she wished to be a woman as well as a queen—to feel all the warmth of romance without abating the privileges of rule. She thought of herself in terms of chivalric tales—of proud yet gentle beauties, at once chaste and sensuous, capable of ardent longing and sensitive suffering, of tender pity, incorruptible loyalty, and a courage rising as danger rose. She was an expert horsewoman, leaped fences and ditches rashly, and could bear the hardship of campaigns without weariness or complaint. But she was neither physically nor mentally fit to be a queen. She was frail in all but nervous vigor, she was subject to fainting fits that looked like epilepsy, and some undiagnosed ailment often hampered her with pain.[9] She had not the masculine intelligence of Elizabeth. She was often clever, but rarely wise; repeatedly she let passion ruin diplomacy. At times she showed remarkable self-control, patience, and tact, and then again she would let go with hot temper and sharp tongue. She was cursed with beauty, unblessed with brains; and her character was her fate.

She tried hard to meet the manifold dangers of her situation, poised between grasping lords, hostile preachers and a decadent Catholic clergy that did no honor to her trusting faith. She chose as leaders of her Privy Council two Protestants: her bastard half-brother Lord James Stuart, later Earl of Murray (or Moray), aged twenty-six, and William Maitland of Lethington, thirty-six, who had more intellect than his character could handle, and who shifted from side to side in compromises till his death. The goal of Lethington's diplomacy was admirable—the union of England and Scotland as the only alternative to a consuming hostility. In May of 1562 Mary sent him to England to arrange an interview between herself and Elizabeth; Elizabeth consented, but her Council demurred, fearing that even the most indirect admission of Mary's claim to the succession would encourage Catholic attempts to assassinate Elizabeth. The two queens corresponded with diplomatic affection, while each sought to play cat to the other's mouse.

Mary's first three years of rule were a success in everything but religion. Though she could never reconcile herself to the climate or the culture of Scotland, she sought, with dances, masques, and charm, to make Holyrood Palace a little Paris in a subarctic zone, and most of the lords thawed under the sun of her gaiety; Knox growled that they were bewitched. She allowed Murray and Lethington to administer the kingdom, which they did reasonably well. For a time even the religious problem seemed to be solved by her concessions. When papal agents urged her to restore Catholicism as the official religion of the land she replied that this was at present impossible; Elizabeth would forcibly intervene. To appease the Scottish Protestants she issued (August 26, 1561) a proclamation forbidding the Catholics to attempt changes in the established religion, but she asked to be allowed to practice her own worship privately and to have Mass said for her in the royal chapel.[10] On Sunday, August 24, Mass was there celebrated. A few Protestants gathered outside and demanded that "the idolatrous priest should die";[11] but Murray barred their entry into the chapel, while his aides led the priest to safety. On the following Sunday Knox denounced the lords for permitting the Mass, and told his congregation that to him one Mass was more offense than ten thousand armed foes.[12]

The Queen sent for him and strove to win his tolerance. On September 4, in her palace, the two faiths met in a historic interview, whose details are known to us only from Knox's report.[13] She reproached him for having stirred up rebellion against the duly constituted authority of her mother, and for having written his "blast" against "the monstrous regiment of women"—which had denounced all female sovereigns. He answered that "if to rebuke idolatry be to raise subjects against their princes, then cannot I be excused, for it has pleased God . . . to make me one (amongst many) to disclose unto this realm the vanity of the papistical religions, and the deceit, pride, and tyranny of that Roman Antichrist," the Pope. As for the blast, "Madam, that book was written most especially against that wicked Jezebel of England," Mary Tudor. Knox's report continues:

> "Think ye (quod she) that subjects may resist their princes?"
> "If (he [Knox] replied) their princes exceed their bounds . . . it is no doubt they may be resisted, even by power."
> . . . The Queen stood as it were amazed . . . At length she said:
> "Well, then, I perceive that my subjects shall obey you, and not me."
> "God forbid (answered he) that ever I take upon me to command any to obey me, or yet to let subjects at liberty to do what pleaseth them. But my travail is that both princes and subjects obey God . . . And this subjection, Madam, unto God and unto His troubled Church, is the greatest dignity that flesh can get upon this earth."
> "Yea (quod she), but ye are not the Kirk that I will nourish. I will defend the Kirk of Rome, for I think it is the true Kirk of God."
> "Your will (quod he), Madam, is no reason; neither doth your thought make that Roman harlot to be the true and immaculate spouse of Jesus Christ. And wonder not, Madam, that I call Rome a harlot, for that Church is altogether polluted with all kind of spiritual fornication . . ."
> "My conscience (said she) is not so."

If this conversation is faithfully reported, it was a dramatic confrontation of monarchy with theocratic democracy, of Catholicism with Calvinism. If we may believe Knox, the Queen took his reproofs without retaliation, merely saying, "Ye are oure sain [overmuch sore] for me"; she went off to dinner, and Knox to his ministry. Lethington wished "Mr. Knox would deal more gently with her, being a young princess unpersuaded."[14]

His followers did not feel that he had been too hard with her. When she appeared in public some called her idolater, and children informed her that hearing Mass was a sin. The Edinburgh magistrates issued a decree of banishment for "monks, friars, priests, nuns, adulterers, and all sic filthy persons."[15] Mary deposed the magistrates and ordered new elections. At Stirling the priests who tried to minister to her were driven off with bloody heads, "while she wept helplessly."[16] The General Assembly of the Kirk demanded that she should be forbidden to hear Mass anywhere, but the lords of the Council refused to comply. In December 1561 a hot dispute arose between the Council and the Kirk over the distribution of ecclesiastical revenues: the Protestant ministers were allotted a sixth, the Queen a sixth, the Catholic clergy (still in the great majority) two thirds. Knox summarized the matter by saying that two parts were given to the Devil and the third was divided between the Devil and God.[17] The ministers received, on an average, one hundred marks ($3,333?) per year.[18]

Throughout the ensuing year the clergy of the Kirk continued to denounce the Queen. They were scandalized by the masques and revels, the singing, dancing, and flirting, that went on at Mary's court. She diminished her amusements in deference to the protests, but the ministers felt that she had yet far to go, for she still heard Mass. "John Knox," wrote a contemporary, "thundereth out of the pulpit, so that I fear nothing so much as that one day he will mar all. He ruleth the roost, and of him all men stand in fear."[19] Here again the Reformation came to grips with the Renaissance.

On December 15, 1562, Mary summoned Knox. Before Murray, Lethington, and others she accused him of teaching his followers to hate her. He answered, he says, that "princes . . . are more exercised in fiddling and flinging than in reading or hearing of God's most blessed word; and fiddlers and flatterers . . . are more precious in their eyes than men of wisdom and gravity, who, by wholesome admonition, might beat down in them some part of that vanity and pride whereunto all are born, but in princes take deep root and strength by wicked education." According to Knox, the Queen replied (with unwonted meekness), "If ye hear anything of myself that mislikes you, come to myself and tell me, and I shall hear you"; and he answered, "I am called, Madam, to a public function within the Kirk of God, and was appointed by God to rebuke the sins and vices of all. I am not appointed to come to every man in particular to show him his offense, for that labor were infinite. If your Grace please to frequent the public sermons, then doubt I not but that ye shall fully understand both what I like and mislike."[20]

She let him go in peace, but the war of faiths went on. At Easter of 1563 several Catholic priests who had violated the law by saying Mass were seized by local agents and were threatened with death for idolatry.[21] Some were jailed, some escaped and hid in the woods. Mary sent for Knox once more and interceded for the imprisoned priests; he replied that if she would enforce the law he would guarantee Protestant docility; otherwise he thought the papists deserved a lesson. "I promise to do as you require," she said, and for a moment they were friends. At her order the Archbishop of St. Andrews and forty-seven other priests were tried for saying Mass and were sentenced to prison. The ministers rejoiced, but a week later (May 26, 1563), when Mary and her ladies attended Parliament in their best raiment and some of the people cried "God bless that sweet face!" the ministers denounced "the targetting [tasseling] of their tails," and Knox wrote, "Such stinking pride of women . . . was never seen before in Scotland."[22]

Shortly thereafter he heard that Lethington was trying to arrange a marriage between Mary and Don Carlos, son of Philip II. Feeling that such a marriage would be fatal to Scottish Protestantism, Knox spoke his mind on the subject in a sermon preached to the nobles attending Parliament:

> And now, my Lords, to put an end to all, I hear of the Queen's marriage . . . This, my Lords, will I say: Whensoever the nobility of Scotland professing to Lord Jesus consents that an infidel (and all papists are infidels) shall be head to your sovereign, ye do so far as in ye lieth to banish Christ Jesus from this realm.[23]

The Queen lost her temper. She summoned him and asked (he reports), "What have ye to do with my marriage? Or what are ye in this commonwealth?" He made a famous reply: "A subject born within the same, madam. And albeit I neither be earl, lord, nor baron within it, yet has God made me (how abject that ever I be in your eyes) a profitable member within the same."[24] Mary broke into tears and bade him leave her.

His boldness reached its peak in October (1563). A crowd again gathered about the royal chapel to protest against the Mass that was about to be said there. Andrew Armstrong and Patrick Cranstoun entered the chapel and frightened the priest into retiring. The Queen, who had not been present, ordered the trial of the two Calvinists for invading her premises. On October 8 Knox sent out a letter bidding all "my brethren, of all estates [classes], that have preferred the truth," to attend the trial. The Queen's Council judged this call to be treason, and cited Knox to stand trial before her. He came (December 21, 1563), but so great a crowd of his supporters gathered in the courtyard and on the stairs and "even to the chamber door where the Queen and her Council sat," and he defended himself so skillfully, that the Council acquitted him, and the Queen said, "Mr. Knox, you may return to your home for this night." "I pray God," he replied, "to purge your heart from papistry."[25]

On Palm Sunday, 1564, the indomitable prophet, aged fifty-nine, married his second wife, Margaret Stuart, aged seventeen, a distant relative of the Queen. A year later the Queen too married a second time.

IV. THE QUEEN IN LOVE: 1565–68

Whom could she marry without a diplomatic mess? A Spaniard? But France and England would protest, and Protestant Scots would rage. A Frenchman? But England would oppose, even to war, any renewal of the Scottish-French alliance. An Austrian—the Archduke Charles? But Knox from the pulpit already thundered against union with a Catholic "infidel," and Elizabeth let Mary know that marriage with a Hapsburg—old foes of the Tudors—would be construed as a hostile act.

In a moment of passion Mary cut the diplomatic knot. Matthew Stuart, Earl of Lennox, who held himself to be the next in line to Mary for the Scottish throne, had lost his estates by supporting Henry VIII against Scotland, and had fled to England to elude the Scots' revenge; now (October 1564) he thought it timely to return. Soon thereafter came his nineteen-year-old son Henry Stuart, Lord Darnley, who through his mother was (like Mary) descended from Henry VII of England. Mary was charmed by the beardless youth; she admired his skill at tennis and on the lute; she forgave his vanity as the due of his good looks, and rushed into love before she could discern his lack of mind. On July 29, 1565, over the protests of Elizabeth and half her own Council, Mary made the lad her husband and named him king. Murray retired from the Council and joined the enemies of the headstrong Queen.

She enjoyed a few months of troubled happiness. Her need for love had mounted in her four years of widowhood; it was pleasant to be desired! She gave her love unstintedly, and without stint she lavished gifts upon her mate. "All dignities that she can indue him with," reported Elizabeth's ambassador, Thomas Randolph, "are already given and granted. No man pleases her that contenteth not him. . . . She hath given over unto him her whole will."[26] Good fortune turned the boy's head; he became dictatorial and insolent, and he demanded joint powers of rule with the Queen. Meanwhile he caroused, drank heavily, alienated the Council, had fits of jealousy, and suspected Mary of adultery with David Rizzio.

Who was Rizzio? An Italian musician, he had come to Scotland in 1561, aged twenty-eight, in the train of the ambassador from Savoy. Mary, fond of music, attached him to her service as organizer of musical fetes. She enjoyed his wit, his quick intelligence, his varied Continental culture. As he knew French and Latin well and wrote a fine Italian hand, she used him also as secretary. Soon she let him draft as well as write her foreign correspondence; he became an adviser, a power; he shared in directing policy; he ate with the Queen; sometimes he sat closeted with her far into the night. The Scottish nobles, seeing themselves superseded, and suspecting Rizzio of serving the Catholic cause, plotted to destroy him.

At first Darnley himself had been captivated by the clever Italian. They had played together, slept together. But as Rizzio's functions and honors grew, and Darnley's foolishness reduced him to political impotence, the affection of the King for the servant-become-minister descended the gamut of feeling to hatred. When Mary became pregnant Darnley thought she was bearing Rizzio's child. Randolph believed it; and, a generation later, Henri Quatre quipped that James I of England *must* be "the modern Solomon," since his father was the harpist David.[27] Having warmed his courage with whiskey, Darnley joined with the Earl of Morton, Baron Ruthven, and other nobles in a plot to murder Rizzio. They signed a "band" pledging themselves to uphold Protestantism in Scotland and to give Darnley the "crown matrimonial"—full rights as Scotland's king—and the right of succession should Mary die. Darnley promised to protect the signers from the consequences "of whatever crime," and to restore Murray and other banished lords.[28]

On March 6, 1566, Randolph revealed the plot to Cecil.[29] On March 9 it was carried out. Darnley entered the boudoir where Mary, Rizzio, and Lady Argyll were at supper; he grasped and held the Queen; Morton, Ruthven, and others rushed in, dragged Rizzio from the room over Mary's helpless protests, and stabbed him to death on the stairs—fifty-six wounds for good measure and sure. Someone rang the town tocsin; a crowd of armed citizens marched on the palace, proposing to cut Mary "to collops,"[30] but Darnley persuaded them to disperse. All that night and the next day Mary remained in Holyrood Palace, a prisoner of the assassins. Meanwhile she played upon Darnley's terror and love, and he helped and accompanied her when, on the following night, she escaped and fled to Dunbar. There, vowing revenge, she issued an appeal to all loyal supporters to come to her defense. Perhaps to divide her enemies, she recalled Murray to her Council.

The most effective of those who offered her protection was James Hepburn, fourth Earl of Bothwell. A strange and fateful character: not handsome, but strong of body, passions, and will; an adventurer on land and sea, skilled with sword and rapier; cowing men with his cool audacity, alluring women with his talk, his recklessness, and his reputation for seducing them; but also a man of superior education, a lover of and author of books in an age when many a noble Scot could not write his name. At first the Queen had disliked him, for he had spoken ill of her; but that is one way of winning a woman's interest. Then, seeing his martial qualities, she had appointed him Lieutenant of the Border; hearing of his familiarity with ships, she had made him Lord Admiral; learning of his desire for Lady Jane Gordon's hand, she promoted their marriage.

Now, fearing the assassins of Rizzio and suspecting her husband's complicity, she turned to Bothwell for protection and advice. She did not take to him precipitately, but his masculine qualities of courage, vigor, and confidence were those that her feminine nature had longed for and had not found in Francis II or Darnley. She noted how respect for his sword and his troops drove the conspirators into hiding or submission; soon she felt secure enough to return to Holyrood. Though Knox had approved the murder of Rizzio, Mary quieted the ministers for a while by making better provision for their maintenance. The common Scots, never in love with the lords, sympathized with her, and for a few months more she enjoyed a general popularity. "I never saw the Queen so much beloved, esteemed, and honored," wrote the French ambassador, "or so great harmony among her subjects."[31] Nevertheless, as she approached her confinement she was obsessed with the thought that she would be murdered or deposed in her helplessness.[32] When she safely gave birth to a boy (June 19, 1566), all Scotland rejoiced, as if foreseeing that this lad would be king of both Scotland and England. Mary was in apogee.

But she was miserable with Darnley. He resented her renewed trust in Murray and her rising admiration for Bothwell. There was talk that Bothwell would kidnap the royal infant and rule in its name.[33] Darnley accused the nobles of killing Rizzio and claimed innocence; in revenge they sent to the Queen proof of his participation.[34] Argyll, Lethington, and Bothwell proposed to the Queen that she should divorce him; she objected that this might endanger the succession. Lethington replied that they would find some means of freeing her from Darnley without prejudice to her son. She did not approve; she offered rather to retire from Scotland to let Darnley rule; and she ended the interview with a caution: "I will that ye do nothing whereby any spot may be laid to my honor or conscience; and therefore, I pray you, let the matter be as it is, abiding till God of His goodness put remedy thereto."[35] Several times now she talked of suicide.[36]

In or about October 1566, Argyll, Sir James Balfour, Bothwell, and perhaps Lethington signed a pact to get rid of Darnley. The Earl of Lennox got wind of the plot and warned his son; Darnley, who had been living apart from Mary, joined his father in Glasgow (December 1566). There he fell ill, apparently from smallpox, though rumors of poison rose. Meanwhile Mary's developing intimacy with Bothwell put her under suspicion of adultery; Knox openly called her a whore.[37] She seems to have approached Archbishop Hamilton about arranging a divorce of Bothwell from his wife. She offered to visit Darnley; he sent her an insulting reply; she went to him nevertheless (January 22, 1567), asserted her fidelity, and reawakened his love. She begged him to return to Edinburgh, where, she promised, she would nurse him back to health and happiness.

Here the "Casket Letters" enter upon the scene, and the rest of the story hinges in part on their authenticity, which is still in dispute after four hundred years. They were allegedly found in a silver casket which was presented by Mary to Bothwell and was taken from a servant of Bothwell on June 20, 1567, by agents of the nobles who were then seeking to dethrone the Queen. The casket was opened on the following day by Morton, Lethington, and other members of the Privy Council. As exhibited soon thereafter to the Scottish Parliament, and later to the English commission that tried Mary in 1568, the contents were eight letters and some fragmentary poems, all in French, undated and unaddressed but allegedly from Mary to Bothwell. The lords of the Council swore to the Scottish Parliament that the letters were genuine and had not been tampered with; Mary claimed that they had been forged. Her son apparently considered them authentic, for he destroyed them;[38] only copies remain. Continental rulers, shown copies, acted as if believing them genuine.[39] Elizabeth at first questioned, then hesitantly accepted, their authenticity. Our first impulse on reading them is to doubt that a woman meditating the murder of her husband would so carelessly and extensively express her intentions in letters entrusted to carriers who might be intercepted or corrupted; it appears improbable that letters so incriminating to Bothwell should have been preserved by him; and it is equally improbable that anyone in Scotland, even the clever Lethington (who is especially suspected), could have forged any substantial part of these letters in the single day between the capture of the casket and the display of the letters to the Council or the Parliament. The most incriminating letter—the second—is strangely long, taking up ten pages in print; if it was forged it is a most remarkable forgery, for its emotional content seems as true to Mary's nature as its writing is like her hand. It shows Mary as a pitying, hesitating, and ashamed accomplice in the murder of Darnley.*

---

* Critical opinion inclines to describe the letters as mostly genuine, with some interpolations. Lord Acton, informed, Catholic, and honest, thought four of the letters genuine, the second forged.[40] Their text can be read in Andrew Lang's *Mystery of Mary Stuart,* 391–414.

The ailing, fearful, trusting King allowed himself to be carried across Scotland in a litter and placed in the old parsonage of Kirk o' Field on the outskirts of Edinburgh. Mary explained that she could not at once take him to Holyrood, lest he infect their child. For two weeks he lay there. Mary visited him daily and nursed him so sedulously that his strength returned, and he wrote to his father (February 7, 1567), ". . . my good health is the . . . sooner come through the good treatment of . . . the Queen, which I assure you hath all this while, and yet doth, use herself like a natural and loving wife. I hope yet that God will lighten our hearts with joy that have so long been afflicted with trouble."[41] Why she should have nursed him back through tedious weeks if she knew that he was to be killed is part of the mystery of Mary Stuart. On the evening of February 9 she left him to attend the wedding of one of her maids at Holyrood. That night an explosion occurred in the Kirk o' Field house, and in the morning Darnley was found dead in the garden.

Mary at first behaved like an innocent woman. She mourned and lamented and vowed vengeance; she had her room draped in black and curtained from the light, and she remained there in darkness and solitude. She ordered a judicial inquiry, and proclaimed a reward in money and land for information leading to the capture of the criminals. When placards appeared on city walls charging Bothwell with the murder, some implicating the Queen, a proclamation called upon the accusers to come forth with their evidence and promised the informers protection and rewards. The author(s) of the placards refused to appear, but the Earl of Lennox urged the Queen to bring Bothwell to trial at once. Bothwell seconded their demand. On April 12 he stood trial; Lennox, either lacking proofs or fearing Bothwell's soldiers in the capital, remained in Glasgow; Bothwell was acquitted, and the Parliament officially declared him innocent. On April 19 he persuaded Argyll, Huntly, Morton, and a dozen other nobles to sign "Ainslee's band," attesting their faith in his innocence, pledging themselves to defend him, and approving his marriage with Mary. She now favored Bothwell publicly and added to the many costly presents that she had already given him.

On April 23 she visited her son at Stirling; she was fated never to see him again. On her way back to Edinburgh she and Lethington were waylaid by Bothwell and his soldiers and were carried by force to Dunbar (April 24). Lethington protested; Bothwell threatened to kill him. Mary saved him and he was released; thereafter he joined the enemies of the Queen. At Dunbar negotiations were resumed for Bothwell's divorce. On May 3 he and Mary returned to Edinburgh; she declared herself free from constraint; on May 7 he was granted a divorce, and on the fifteenth, her Catholic confessor having refused to marry them, they were married according to the Protestant rite by the once Catholic Bishop of Orkney. Catholic Europe, formerly devoted to Mary, now turned against her as a lost soul. The Catholic clergy of Scotland stood aloof from her; the Protestant ministry called for her deposition; the populace was hostile; a sympathetic few attributed her reckless infatuation to a love potion given her by Bothwell.

On June 10 an armed band surrounded Borthwick Castle, where Mary and Bothwell were staying. They escaped, Mary dressed as a man. At Dunbar Bothwell gathered a thousand men, and with them he and Mary sought to force their way back to Edinburgh. They were opposed at Carberry Hill (June 15) by an equal force bearing a banner painted with figures of Darnley dead and the child James VI. Bothwell offered to settle the issue by single combat; Mary refused to allow him; she agreed to surrender if Bothwell were permitted to escape; later she claimed that the rebel leaders had promised loyalty to her if she joined them peacefully.[42] Bothwell fled to the coast and made his way to Denmark; there, after ten years of imprisonment by the Danish King, he died at the age of forty-two (1578).

Mary accompanied her captors to Edinburgh amid cries of soldiers and populace: "Burn the whore! Burn her!" "Kill her!" "Drown her!"[43] She was placed under guard in the provost's house; under her window, where she appeared disheveled and half clad, the crowd continued to threaten her with the coarsest epithets. On June 17, over her wild protests, she was removed to a remote and more secure imprisonment on an island in Loch Leven, a lake some thirty miles north of the capital. There, according to her secretary Claude Nau, she gave birth prematurely to twins.[44] She sent an appeal to the French government; it refused to interfere. Elizabeth instructed her envoy to promise Mary protection and to threaten the nobles with dire punishment if they should harm the Queen. Knox called for Mary's execution, and predicted that God would scourge Scotland with a great plague if Mary should be spared.[45] On June 20 the lords secured the Casket Letters. She appealed to the Parliament for a hearing; it refused, on the ground that the letters sufficiently disposed of her case. On July 24 she signed her abdication, and Murray was made regent for her son.

For almost eleven months she remained a captive in Lochleven Castle. Gradually the rigor of her confinement was relaxed; she ate with the family of William Douglas, lord of the castle; his younger brother George fell in love with her and helped her to escape (March 25, 1568). She was captured, but on May 2 she tried again and succeeded. Protected by young Douglas, she reached the mainland, where she was met by a party of Catholics. They rode through the night to the Firth of Forth, crossed it, and found refuge in the home of the Hamiltons. In five days six thousand men gathered there, sworn to set her again on the throne. But Murray called the Protestants of Scotland to arms; at Langside, near Glasgow, the two forces met (May 13); Mary's ill-disciplined army was overwhelmed. She took flight once more and rode wildly through three nights to Dundrennan Abbey on Solway Firth. Now she returned to its donor the diamond that Elizabeth had once given "her dearest sister," and she added a message: "I send back to its Queen this jewel, the token of her promised friendship and assistance."[46] On May 16, 1568, she crossed Solway Firth in an open fishing boat, entered England, and left her fate to her rival.

V. EXPIATION: 1568–87

From Carlisle she dispatched another message to Elizabeth, asking for an interview in which she might explain her behavior. Elizabeth, on principle averse to supporting rebellion against a legitimate sovereign, was inclined to invite her, but her Council confused her with cautions. If Mary were allowed to proceed to France, the French government would be tempted to send an army to Scotland to restore her and make Scotland again a Catholic ally of France and a thorn in England's rear; Mary's claim to the throne of England would then be supported by French arms as well as by English Catholics. If Mary remained free in England she would always be a possible source and center of Catholic revolt, and England was at heart still predominantly Catholic. If England should force the Scottish nobles to re-enthrone their Queen, their lives would be endangered and England would lose her Protestant allies in Scotland. Cecil would probably have agreed with Hallam that the forcible detention of the Queen of Scots violated all law, "natural, public, and municipal,"[47] but he felt that his overriding responsibility was to protect England.

As one function of diplomacy is to dress realism in morality, Mary was told that before her request for an interview with Elizabeth could be granted she must clear herself of various charges before a trial commission. Mary replied that she was a queen and could not be judged by lay commissioners, especially of another nation, and she demanded freedom to return to Scotland or go to France. She asked to meet Morton and Lethington in Elizabeth's presence, and promised to prove them guilty of Darnley's death. The English Council ordered her removed from Carlisle (as too near the border) to Bolton Castle, near York (July 13, 1568). Mary submitted to loose imprisonment there on Elizabeth's promise, "Put yourself in my hands without reserve; I will listen to nothing which shall be said against you; your honor shall be safe, and you shall be restored to your throne."[48] So mollified, Mary consented to appoint representatives to an examining commission. She tried to please Elizabeth by pretending to accept the Anglican faith and creed, but she assured Philip of Spain that she would never abandon the Catholic cause.[49] From that time onward Mary and Elizabeth ran an equal race in duplicity, the one excusing herself as a betrayed and royal prisoner, the other as an endangered queen.

The trial commission met at York October 4, 1568. Mary was represented by seven men, chiefly John Leslie, Catholic Bishop of Ross, and the Catholic Lord Herries of the western marches of Scotland; Elizabeth had appointed three Protestants: the Duke of Norfolk, the Earl of Sussex, and Sir Ralph Sadler. Before them appeared Murray, Morton, and Lethington, who privately showed the Englishmen the Casket Letters. If, they said, Mary would recognize Murray as regent and agree to reside in England on a large pension from Scotland, the letters would not be made public. Norfolk, who dreamed of marrying Mary and thereby becoming King of England on Elizabeth's death, refused, and Sussex wrote to Elizabeth that Mary seemed likely to prove her case.[50]

Elizabeth ordered the trial transferred to Westminster. There Murray laid the Casket Letters before her Council. Opinion remained divided as to the authenticity of the documents; but Elizabeth ruled that she could not receive Mary until the authenticity had been disproved. Mary asked to be shown the letters, either originals or copies; the commissioners refused, and Mary never saw either copies or originals.[51] The commission disbanded without announcing a decision (January 11, 1569); Murray was received by Elizabeth and then returned to Scotland with the letters; Mary, angry and defiant, was removed to stricter custody at Tutbury on the Trent. Foreign governments protested; Elizabeth replied that if they saw the evidence that had been presented to the commission they would consider her treatment of Mary rather lenient than severe.[52] The Spanish ambassador advised Philip to invade England and promised the collaboration of Catholic north England. Philip was skeptical of such aid, and Alva warned him that Elizabeth might order Mary's death at the first sign of invasion or revolt.

Revolt came. On November 14, 1569, the earls of Northumberland and Westmorland led a rebel army of 5,700 men into Durham, overthrew the Anglican Communion board, burned the Book of Common Prayer, restored the Catholic altar, and heard Mass. They planned a dash into Tutbury to release Mary, but Elizabeth balked them by transferring Mary to Coventry (November 23, 1569). The Earl of Sussex, with an army largely composed of Catholics, rapidly suppressed the rebellion. Elizabeth ordered all captured insurgents and their conniving servants to be hanged, and "the bodies were not to be removed, but remain till they fell to pieces where they hung."[53] Some six hundred men were so disposed of, and their property was confiscated by the Crown. Northumberland and Westmorland escaped to Scotland. In February 1570 Leonard Dacres led another uprising of Catholics; he too was defeated and fled across the border.

In January 1570 Knox wrote to Cecil advising him to order Mary's death at once, for "if ye strike not at the root, the branches that appear to be broken will bud again."[54] He had now finished his *History of the Reformation of Religioun within the Realme of Scotland*—a book making no pretense to impartiality, a narrative inaccurate but vivid and vital, a style quaint and idiomatic, sharp with the tongue of a preacher who called a whore a whore. A bitter man but a great man, building his dream to power more complete than Calvin's, hating heartily, fighting bravely, consuming to the last flicker the incredible energy of a tenacious will. By 1572 he had worn himself out. He could no longer walk unsupported, but he had himself aided every Sunday to his pulpit at St. Giles's. On November 9, 1572, he preached for the last time, and the entire congregation escorted him to his home. He died on November 24, aged sixty-seven, almost as poor as he had been born; he "had not made merchandise of the Word of God." He left posterity to judge him. "What I have been to my country, albeit this unthankful age will not know, yet the ages to come will be compelled to bear witness to the truth."[55] Few men have had so decisive an influence upon the beliefs of a people; few of his time equaled him in encouragement given to education, fanaticism, and self-government. He and Mary divided the soul of Scotland between them: he was the Reformation, she was the Renaissance. She lost because she did not know, like Elizabeth, how to marry them.

Mary, like some restless tiger caged, tried every corner and possibility of escape. In March 1571 Roberto di Ridolfi, a Florentine banker active in London, made himself an intermediary between Mary, the Spanish ambassador, the Bishop of Ross, Alva, Philip, and Pope Pius V. He proposed that Alva should send Spanish troops into England from the Netherlands, that a Catholic force should simultaneously invade England from Scotland, that Elizabeth should be dethroned, that Mary should be made Queen of England and Scotland, and that Norfolk should marry her. Norfolk was told of the plan, did not clearly approve of it, did not reveal it. Mary tentatively consented.[56] The Pope gave Ridolfi money for the enterprise and promised to recommend it to Philip;[57] Philip made his own approval conditional on Alva's; Alva ridiculed the project as visionary, and nothing came of it but tragedy for Mary's friends. Letters of Ridolfi and Norfolk were found on arrested servants of Mary and the Duke; Norfolk, Ross, and several Catholic nobles were imprisoned; Norfolk was tried for treason and convicted. Elizabeth hesitated to sign the death warrant of so prominent a noble, but Cecil, the English Parliament, and the Anglican hierarchy called for the execution of both Norfolk and Mary. Elizabeth compromised by sending Norfolk to the block (June 2, 1572). When news reached England of the Massacre of St. Bartholomew (August 22), there were revived cries for the death of Mary,[58] but Elizabeth still refused.

Only by remembering that Mary's captivity lasted almost nineteen years can we understand her desperation and her sense of bitter wrong. Her place of imprisonment was repeatedly changed, lest the sympathy felt for her in the neighborhood and among her custodians should beget or abet new plots. The conditions of her confinement were humane. She was permitted to receive her French pension of £1,200 a year; the English government gave her a substantial sum for food, medical treatment, servants, and entertainment; she was allowed to attend Mass and other Catholic services. She tried to pass the long hours with embroidery, reading, gardening, and play with her pet spaniels. As her hope of freedom faded, she lost interest in caring for herself; she took less exercise and became flaccid and fat. She suffered from rheumatism; sometimes her legs were so swollen that she could not walk. By 1577, when she was only thirty-five, her hair had turned white, and thereafter she covered it with a wig.

In June 1583 she offered, if released, to withdraw all claim to the English crown, never more to communicate with conspirators, to live anywhere in England according to Elizabeth's choice, never to go more than ten miles from that residence, and to submit to surveillance by neighboring gentlemen. Elizabeth was advised not to trust her.

Mary resumed her schemes for escape. By a variety of desperate devices she managed to correspond secretly with the French and Spanish ambassadors and governments, with her adherents in Scotland, and with representatives of the Pope. Letters were smuggled in and out, in the washing, in books, in sticks, in wigs, in the lining of shoes. But the spies of Cecil and Walsingham uncovered every plot in time. Even among the students and priests at the Jesuit college in Reims Walsingham had an agent who kept him informed.

The romantic aura of the captive Queen touched the sympathy of many young Englishmen, and aroused the ardor of Catholic youths. In 1583 Francis Throckmorton, Catholic nephew of Elizabeth's late ambassador to France, organized another plot to release her. He was soon detected; tortured into confession, he moaned, "I have disclosed the secrets of her who was the dearest to me in all the world."[59] He died under the executioner's ax at the age of thirty.

A year later William Parry, a spy in Cecil's service, induced a papal nuncio in Paris to forward to Gregory XIII a request for a plenary indulgence on the ground that he was entering upon a dangerous attempt to free Mary Stuart and bring England back to the Catholic Church. The papal secretary of state replied (January 30, 1584) that the Pope had seen Parry's petition, rejoiced at his resolve, was sending him the desired indulgence, and would reward his efforts.[60] Parry took this reply to Cecil. Another English spy, Edmund Neville, accused Parry of urging him to assassinate Elizabeth. Parry was arrested, confessed, was hanged, and, still alive, was cut down and dismembered.[61]

Angered by a long succession of conspiracies, and frightened by the assassination of William of Orange, Elizabeth's Council drew up (October 1584) a "Bond of Association" pledging the signers never to accept, as successor to their Queen, any person in whose behalf Elizabeth's life had been attempted, and to prosecute to the death any person involved in such an enterprise. The bond was signed by the Council, by most members of Parliament, and by prominent men throughout England. A year later Parliament gave it the sanction of law.

It did not deter further plots. In 1586 John Ballard, a Roman Catholic priest, induced Anthony Babington, a rich young Catholic, to organize a conspiracy for the assassination of Elizabeth, the invasion of England by armies from Spain, France, and the Low Countries, and the enthronement of Mary. Babington wrote to Mary about the plot, told her that six Catholic nobles had agreed to "get rid of the usurper of the throne," and asked her approval of the plan. In a letter of July 17, 1586, Mary accepted Babington's proposals, gave no explicit consent to the assassination of Elizabeth, but promised rewards for the success of the undertaking.[62] The messenger to whom her secretary entrusted this reply was a secret agent of Walsingham; he had the letter copied and sent the copy to Walsingham and the letter itself to Babington. On August 14 Babington and Ballard were arrested; soon three hundred prominent Catholics were jailed; the two leaders confessed, and Mary's secretary was induced to acknowledge the authenticity of Mary's letter.[63] Thirteen of the conspirators were executed. Bonfires were lighted throughout London, bells rang, and children sang psalms, in thanksgiving for the preservation of Elizabeth's life. All Protestant England cried out for Mary's death.

Mary's rooms were searched and all her papers were seized. On October 6 she was transferred to Fotheringay Castle. There she was tried by a commission of forty-three nobles. She was not allowed a defender, but she defended herself resolutely. She admitted complicity in the Babington plot, but denied having sanctioned assassination. She protested that, as a person unjustly and illegally imprisoned for nineteen years, she had a right to free herself by whatever means. She was unanimously condemned, and Parliament asked Elizabeth to order her death. Henry III of France made a polite plea for mercy, but Elizabeth thought that such a plea came with poor grace from a government that had massacred thousands of Protestants without trial. Most of Scotland now defended its Queen, but her son made only a halfhearted intercession, for he suspected that, because of his Protestantism, she had disowned him in her will. His agent in London suggested to Walsingham that James VI, though anxious that his mother should not be beheaded, might be reconciled to much if the English Parliament would confirm his title to succeed Elizabeth, and if Elizabeth would increase the pension she had been sending him. The very canny Scot dallied so greedily that the citizens of Edinburgh hooted him in the streets.[64] Nothing remained between Mary and death but Elizabeth's hesitation.

The harassed Queen allowed almost three months to drag by before she made up her mind, and then she did not. She was capable of generosity and mercy, but she was tired of living every day in fear of assassination by the adherents of a woman who had claimed her throne. She considered the danger of invasion from France, Spain, and Scotland in protest against the execution of a queen; and she calculated the possibility that she herself might suffer a natural or violent death in time to let Mary and Catholicism inherit England. Cecil urged her to sign the death warrant and promised to take full responsibility for the results. She thought to avoid decision by intimating that Sir Amias Paulet, Mary's keeper, could clear up the confusion by ordering Mary's execution on a merely verbal understanding that the Queen or her Council desired it; but Paulet refused to act without a written order from Elizabeth. Finally she signed the warrant; her secretary, William Davison, delivered it to the Council, which at once dispatched it to Paulet before Elizabeth could change her mind.

Mary, who during this long delay had begun to hope, met the news at first with unbelief, then with courage. She wrote a touching letter to Elizabeth, asking her to "permit my poor desolated servants . . . to carry away my corpse, to bury it in holy ground, with the other queens of France." On the morning of her execution, we are told, she wrote a little Latin poem having all the grace and fervor of a medieval hymn:

> O Domine Deus! speravi in te.
> O care mi Jesu! nunc libera me.
> In dura catena, in misera poena, desidero te;
> Languendo, gemendo, et genu flectendo,
> Adoro, imploro, ut liberes me.*[65]

---

* O Lord God! I have hoped in Thee.
O my dear Jesus! now free me.
In cruel chains, in bitter pain, I desire Thee.
Longing, moaning, and bending the knee,
I adore, I implore, that you set me free.

She asked to be allowed to confess to her Catholic chaplain; she was refused. Her jailers offered her an Anglican dean instead; she rejected him. She robed herself royally to meet death, arranged her false hair carefully, and covered her face with a white veil. A golden crucifix hung from her neck, an ivory crucifix was in her hand. She inquired why her attendant women were forbidden to be present at her execution; she was told that they might make a disturbance; she promised that they would not, and she was allowed to take two of them and four men. Some three hundred English gentlemen were admitted to the scene in the great hall of Fotheringay Castle (February 8, 1587). Two masked executioners asked and received her forgiveness. When her women began to cry she checked them, saying, "I promised for you." She knelt and prayed, then laid her head upon the block. The wig fell from her severed head and disclosed her white hair. She was forty-four years old.

Pardon is the word for all. Pardon for Mary, who labored bravely to be a just as well as a joyful queen; we cannot believe that she who tended her husband so long and brought him back to health had consented to his murder; we can forgive the young woman who gave up everything for a love however foolish; we must pity the desolate woman who came to England for refuge and found, instead, nineteen years of imprisonment; and we can understand her wild attempts to regain her liberty. But we can also forgive the great Queen, whose councilors insisted on Mary's confinement as vital to England's security, who saw her life and policy continually threatened by plots to free and enthrone her rival, and who prolonged that cruel captivity only because she could not bring herself to end it with a warrant for Mary's execution. They were both noble women: one noble and hastily emotional, the other noble and hesitantly wise. Fitly they lie near each other in Westminster Abbey, reconciled in death and peace.

CHAPTER VI

James VI and I

1567–1625

I. JAMES VI OF SCOTLAND: 1567–1603

JAMES VI was crowned King of Scotland (July 29, 1567) at the age
of thirteen months, while his mother lay captive at Lochleven. He was
eight months old when his presumptive father, Darnley, was killed, ten
months old when he saw his mother for the last time; she could never be
anything more to him than a name and an imagination blurred with
contumely and far-off tragedy. He was brought up by self-seeking lords
and by teachers hostile to his mother. He received ample education in
the humanities, too much in theology and too little in morals, and he became the most learned hard drinker in Europe.

Four regents in succession ruled Scotland in his name—Murray, Lennox,
Mar, Morton; all but one died by violence. Rival noble bands fought for
the King's person as the aegis of power. In 1582 some Protestant lords, supported by the Kirk, confined him in Ruthven Castle for fear that he might
submit to the influence of his Catholic relative Esmé Stuart. Released, he
promised to defend Protestantism, signed an alliance with Protestant England, and, aged seventeen, undertook to be actual king (1583).

He was unique among sovereigns. His manners were rough, his gait ungainly, his voice loud, his conversation a cross of coarseness with pedantry.
One not too kindly to him judged that "in languages, sciences, and affairs
of state he has more learning than any man in Scotland."[1] But the same
observer added, "He is prodigiously conceited"; perhaps this trait was a
life preserver in a sea of troubles, as well as the warped perspective of one
who could never recall when he had not been king. He must have had
some saving intelligence to keep his crown on his head in Scotland and
wear a greater one in England to a natural death. He was a bit unsteady
about sex; he married the Danish Catholic Princess Anne, but he had little
taste for women, and indulged his friendliness with favorites to the point
of giving gossip a lead.

He had to weave his way craftily amid the furious dogmatisms of his
time. The Guises in France, Philip in Spain, the Pope in Rome, pleaded
with him to bring Scotland back to the Catholic Church, but the Scottish
Kirk watched his every word lest he deviate from the Calvinist line. He

burned no bridges behind him. He corresponded politely with Catholic powers and was inclined to soften the laws against Catholic worship; he secretly released a captured Jesuit and connived at another's escape.[2] But Catholic plots angered him, England's victorious Protestantism impressed him; he cast in his lot with the Kirk.

It was no comfortable bedfellow. By 1583 its ministers formed the great majority of the Scottish clergy. Poor in income and in secular learning, they were rich in devotion and courage. They labored to restore neglected churches, they organized schools, administered charity, defended the peasants against the lords, and preached long sermons which their congregations absorbed in place of printed material. In the kirk sessions, the provincial synods, and the General Assembly the new clergy now enjoyed a power rivaling that which the Catholic hierarchy had wielded before them. Claiming divine inspiration and therefore infallibility in faith and morals, they assumed over public and private conduct a control much more rigorous than under the lax guardians of the older creed. In many towns they levied fines on Scots who failed to attend kirk services. They prescribed public penitence, sometimes physical penalties, for detected sins.[3] Alarmed by the prevalence of fornication and adultery, they commissioned the elders to watch with especial severity over sexual deviations, and to report these to the sessions and the synods of the Kirk. Shocked by the license of the English stage, they sought to prohibit theatrical performances in Scotland; and failing in this, they forbade their people to attend them. Like their predecessors, they made heresy a capital crime. They pursued witches with burning zeal and voted firewood for the pyres.[4] They persuaded the Parliament to decree the death penalty for any priest who thrice said Mass; this edict, however, was not enforced. On hearing of the Massacre of St. Bartholomew, the Kirk called for a massacre of Catholics in Scotland, but the state neglected to co-operate.[5]

Except for the ministerial claim to inspiration and infallibility, the Kirk was one of the most democratic institutions of its time. The parish parson was chosen by the elders, subject to the approval of the congregation, and the laity shared in the sessions, the synods, and the General Assembly. These democratic tentatives irritated the aristocratic Parliament and the anointed King. Arguing—perhaps believing—that he ruled by divine right, James complained that "some fiery-spirited men in the ministry got such a guiding of the people . . . that, finding the gust [taste] of government sweet, they began to fancy a democratic form . . . I was calumniated in their sermons not for any vice in me but because I was king, which they thought the highest evil."[6] The medieval struggle between Church and state was resumed.

Now it took the form of an attack by the ministers on the bishops. These, a Catholic legacy to the Kirk, were formally chosen by the ministers, but were actually nominated, and often forced upon the clergy, by the Regent or the King, and they handed over a large part of their ecclesiastical revenues to the state. The ministers saw no warrant in Scripture for episcopacy, and resolved to run it out of Scotland as incompatible with the popular organization of the Kirk.

Their leader, Andrew Melville, was a fiery Scot equipped by nature to inherit the mantle of John Knox. After a university education at St. Andrews, he continued his studies in Paris and then imbibed the Calvinist gospel from Bèze in Geneva. Returning to Scotland (1574), he was at once appointed, at the age of twenty-nine, principal of Glasgow University, and he ably reorganized its curriculum and discipline. In 1578 he shared in compiling the Second Book of Discipline, which denounced episcopacy in the name of ministerial equality. He argued for the definite separation of spheres between Church and state, and this influenced their separation in the United States; but he claimed the right of the ministers to teach the civil magistrates how to exercise their powers "according to the word."[7] James, however, wanted to be an absolute ruler like Henry VIII or Elizabeth; he believed in bishops as necessary in ecclesiastical administration, and as convenient intermediaries between Church and state.

In 1580 the General Assembly of the Kirk "damned" the office of bishops as a "folly of men's invention"; all bishops were commanded, under penalty of excommunication, to cease their functions, and to apply to the Assembly for admission as simple ministers. The government rejected the Second Book of Discipline and held that no excommunication should be valid unless ratified by the state. In 1581 Lennox, then regent, nominated Robert Montgomerie to be Archbishop of Glasgow. The Glasgow ministry refused to elect him; he insisted on officiating nevertheless; the General Assembly, led by Melville, excommunicated him (1582); Montgomerie yielded and withdrew. Melville, accused of sedition, rejected a civil, demanded an ecclesiastical, trial; condemned for contempt of court, he fled to England (1584). James persuaded the Parliament to declare treasonable any refusal to submit to secular jurisdiction, any meddling of ministers in affairs of state, any resistance to the episcopate, any convocations unlicensed by the King. Many ministers, rather than accept these decrees, followed Melville into exile. James, savoring his sovereignty, indulged himself in a reign of terror: ministers were punished because they prayed for their exiled brethren; two men were put to death for communicating with them; two others were executed on a charge of conspiracy.

The clergy and their congregations resisted with Scottish tenacity. Pamphlets of undiscovered origin blackened the King, ballads sang the shame of his tyranny, even women wrote diatribes committing him to hell.

His bishops received less and less money, transmitted ever less to the state; James found himself starved of coin—the very sinews of his will. Year by year he weakened, until the Parliament of 1592, with his dour consent, voted a charter of liberty to the Kirk, restoring to it all its powers of jurisdiction and discipline, and abolishing the episcopate. The exiles returned.

Melville, bolder than ever, called James to his face "God's silly vassal," and gave the theocratic gospel to him in 1596 as firmly as Gregory VII to Emperor Henry IV five hundred years before (1077): "There are two kings and two kingdoms in Scotland: there is Christ Jesus and His Kingdom the Kirk, whose subject King James VI is . . . not a king, nor a head, nor a lord, but a member."[8] David Black, minister at St. Andrews, told his congregation (1596) that all kings were children of the Devil, Elizabeth was an atheist, and James was Satan himself.[9] The English ambassador protested. The Privy Council summoned Black to trial. He refused to appear, saying that an offense in the pulpit was subject only to a court of the Kirk, and that, besides, he had received his message from God. James ordered him tried in absentia. A committee of ministers came to the King; he yielded nothing; on the contrary, he demanded that acts of the ecclesiastical Assembly, as of Parliament, must be subject to his ratification. The ministers proclaimed a general fast, and declared ominously that, whatever happened, "they were free of his Majesty's blood."[10]

A riotous crowd gathered about the building where James was staying (December 17, 1596). He fled to Holyrood Palace, and next morning removed with all his court from Edinburgh. He declared to its people, by a herald, that it was not fit to be a capital, and that he would never return except to execute judgment on rebels; and he ordered all clergy and nonresidents to leave the city. The rioters, having no one to kill, dispersed. The merchants bemoaned the loss of court trade; the citizens wondered whether the dispute was worth economic martyrdom; James returned in angry triumph (January 1, 1597). The General Assembly, meeting at Perth, offered the Kirk's submission; it agreed that no ministers were to be appointed in the chief cities without the consent of the King and the congregation; that ministers were not to preach about acts of Parliament or the Privy Council, and that no man was to be personally attacked from the pulpit. The ministers were allowed to re-enter the capital (1597), but the episcopate was restored. A sullen truce settled down upon the ancient war between Church and state.

Two figures stand out in the Scottish literature of this period: the King himself and the most famous of his teachers. George Buchanan had an astonishing career. Born in Stirlingshire in 1506, he studied in Paris, served as a soldier in France and Scotland, caught scholastic and political fire from the lectures of John Major, returned for love and learning to Paris, came back to Scotland a satirical heretic, was imprisoned by Cardinal Beaton, escaped to Bordeaux, taught Latin there, wrote poems and dramas in remarkably good Latin, saw his pupil Montaigne act in one of these plays, headed a college in Coimbra, was imprisoned by the Spanish Inquisition for making fun of friars, went back to Scotland, to France, to Scotland, tutored Mary Queen of Scots (1562), was made moderator of the General Assembly (1567), pronounced the Casket Letters authentic, was accused of forging part of them,[11] condemned Mary without mercy in his *Detectio Mariae Reginae* (1571), tutored her son over her protests, and gave up the ghost in 1582. His *Rerum Scoticarum historia* (1579) labored to free his country's history from "English ties and Scottish vanity." His treatise *De iure regni apud Scotos* (1579) boldly reaffirmed, in the face of his soon-to-be-autocratic pupil, the medieval doctrine that the sole source of political power, under God, is the people; that every society rests on an implicit social contract of mutual obligations and restraints between the governed and the governors; that the will of the majority may rightly rule the whole; that the king is subject to the laws passed by the representatives of the people; and that a tyrant may justly be resisted, deposed, or killed.[12] Here was the social-contract myth a century before Hobbes, two centuries before Rousseau. The book was condemned by the Scottish Parliament and burned by the University of Oxford, but it had a powerful influence. Samuel Johnson thought that Buchanan was the only man of genius that Scotland had produced.[13] Hume modestly gave this plume to Napier; Carlyle, being Knox *redivivus*, offered it to Knox; and James VI had his own views on the matter.

The King was as proud of his books as of his regalia. In 1616 he published, in a huge folio, *The Works of the Most High and Mighty Prince James*, which he dedicated to Jesus Christ. He wrote poems, advice to poets, a translation of the Psalms, a study of the Apocalypse, a treatise on demons, and, in the *annus mirabilis* 1598, two royal octavos in defense of absolute monarchy. One, the *Basilikon Doron* (1598), or *Kingly Gift*, was a book of advice to his son Henry on the art and the duties of sovereignty; it emphasized the ruling of the Kirk as "no small part of the king's office." The other volume, *The True Law of Free Monarchies*, expounded absolutism with considerable eloquence: kings were chosen by God, since all important events were dictated by His Providence; their divine appointment and anointment constituted a mystery as holy and ineffable as any sacrament; therefore their rule had every right to be absolute, and resistance to it was a folly, a crime, and a sin bound to cause more harm than any tyranny. What to Elizabeth had been a useful myth became to James a passionate principle, born of being born of a queen. His son Charles inherited the doctrine and paid the penalty.

England, however, did not in 1598 foresee 1649. After James had pledged himself to Protestantism, the leaders of Elizabeth's Privy Council recognized him as heir, through Mary, to the English crown. Four days after Elizabeth's death James began (April 5, 1603) a festive progress from Edinburgh to London; he stopped leisurely en route to be feted by the English nobility; on May 6 he reached a London which was all decked out to welcome him—crowds genuflecting before him, lords kissing his hands. After a millennium of useless strife the two nations (not till 1707 the two parliaments) were united under one king. So fruitful had been Elizabeth's barren womb.

II. JAMES I OF ENGLAND: 1603–14

What sort of a man had he become in thirty-seven years? Of middle stature, weak legs, slightly swollen paunch, padded doublet and breeches to impede assassins' knives; brown hair, ruddy cheeks, knobby nose, a look of suspicion and sadness in the blue eyes, as if the god were conscious of his clay. A little lazy, resting on Elizabeth's oars. Profane in his language, coarse in his amusements; stammering and absolute, wagging too loosely his burry tongue. Vain and generous, timorous and deceitful because often endangered and deceived; ready to take and give offense, to grant and sue for pardon. When John Gib denied having lost some precious documents, James lost his temper, kicked him; then, having found the papers, he knelt down before his humiliated aide and would not rise till Gib had forgiven him. Tolerant amid intolerance, sometimes hard, usually kind and affectionate, suspecting his son Henry as too popular, loving his son Charles to foolishness; unblemished in his relations with women, but given to fondling handsome young men. Superstitious and learned, silly and shrewd, taking demons and witches seriously but favoring Bacon and Jonson; jealous of scholars and enamored of books. One of his first acts as King of England was to empower Oxford and Cambridge to send representatives to Parliament. When he saw the Bodleian Library he cried out, "If I were not a king, I would be a university man; and if it were so that I must be a prisoner, if I might have my wish, I would desire to have no other prison than that Library, and to be chained together with so many good authors and dead masters."[14] All in all, a man a bit off balance and key, but at bottom good-natured, good-humored, ridiculed by the clever, but forgiven by his people because, till near his melancholy end, he gave them security and peace.

He was so unfriendly to water that he resented having to use it for washing. He drank to excess and allowed some court festivities to end in a general and bisexual intoxication. Extravagance in dress and entertainment prevailed at his court even beyond Elizabethan precedent. Masques had been favored by Elizabeth; but now, when Ben Jonson wrote the lines and Inigo Jones designed the costumes and scenery, and the roles were played by gorgeous lords and ladies swathed in the revenues of the kingdom, the fabulous, fantastic art reached its apogee. The court became gayer than ever, and more corrupt. "I do think," says a lady in one of Jonson's plays, "if nobody should love me but my poor husband, I should e'en hang myself."[15] Courtiers accepted substantial "gifts" to use their influence in getting charters, patents, monopolies, or offices for applicants; Baron Montagu paid £20,000 for appointment as Lord Treasurer;[16] one tender soul, we are told on not the best authority, grew sick and died when he learned how much his friends had paid to have him made recorder.[17]

James took all such matters in his stride, and did not trouble himself too laboriously with government. He left administration to a Privy Council of six Englishmen and six Scots, headed by Robert Cecil, whom he made Earl of Salisbury in 1605. Cecil had every advantage of heredity except health. He was crippled with a humped back and made a lamentable appearance to the world; but he had all his father's acumen in the selection and ordering of men, and a silent tenacity and crafty courtesy that outwitted domestic rivals and foreign courts. When "my little beagle" died (1612), James fell under the sway of handsome young Robert Carr, made him Earl of Somerset, and allowed him to supersede, in policy and administration, such older and far more accomplished men as Francis Bacon and Edward Coke.

Coke was the embodiment and the watchdog of the law. He rose to fame by his tenacious prosecution of Essex in 1600, Raleigh in 1603, the Gunpowder Plotters in 1605. In 1610 he issued a historic opinion:

> It appears in our books that in many cases the common law will control [override] acts of Parliament, and sometimes adjudge them to be utterly void. For when an act of Parliament is against common right and reason . . . or impossible to be performed, the common law will control it and adjudge such an act to be void.[18]

Parliament may not have relished this, but James made Coke chief justice of the King's Bench (1613), and a member of the Privy Council. From being the King's man he became the King's gadfly, condemning inquisitions into private opinions, upholding parliamentary freedom of speech, and puncturing the royal absolutism with sharp reminders that kings are

the servants of the law. In 1616 Bacon, his rival, brought charges of malfeasance against him. Coke was dismissed, but he was returned to Parliament; continuing to lead the resistance to the King, he was sent to the
Tower (1621), but was soon released. He died impenitent (1634), obstinately faithful to the letter and rigor of the law, and leaving behind him
four volumes of *Institutes* that still stand as a pillar and monument of English jurisprudence.*

Meanwhile James had been carrying on with Parliament the debate that
in his son's reign would eventuate in civil war and regicide. He did not
merely assume all the powers that Henry VIII and Elizabeth had wielded
over their cowed or grumbling legislators; he formulated his claims as
divine imperatives. To the Parliament of 1609 he announced:

> The state of monarchy is the supremest thing upon earth. For kings
> are not only God's lieutenants on earth, and sit upon God's throne,
> but even by God Himself are called gods. . . . Kings are justly called
> gods, for that they exercise a manner or resemblance of divine power
> on earth; for if you will consider the attributes of God, you shall see
> how they agree in the person of a king. God hath power to create or
> destroy, make or unmake at His pleasure, to give life or send death,
> to judge all and be judged nor accountable to none . . . And the like
> power have kings; they make and unmake their subjects, they have
> power of raising and casting down, of life and death; judges over all
> their subjects and in all causes, and yet accountable to none but God
> only. They have power to . . . make of their subjects like men at the
> chess—a pawn to take a bishop or a knight—and to cry up or down
> any of their subjects, as they do their money.[20]

This was quite a step backward, for medieval political theory had regularly made the king a delegate of the sovereign people; only the popes had
professed to be the viceroys of God. To put the best philosophical front
on this claim we must assume that the popes, as the final heads of authority
in the Middle Ages, had believed the individualistic impulses of men to be
so powerful that social order could be maintained only by inculcating in
the people a traditional reverence for ecclesiastical authority, and for the
popes as the voice and vicars of God. The weakening or destruction
of papal authority by the Reformation had left the political powers primarily or ultimately responsible for social order; and they too judged that
a purely human authority would be too challengeable to restrain effectively,

---

* Aubrey informs us that Coke's second wife, the widow of Sir William Hatton, "was
with child when he married her. Laying his hand on her belly (when he came to bed),
and finding a child to stir, 'What,' said he, 'flesh in the pot?' 'Yea,' quoth she, 'or else I
would not have married a cook.' "[19]—for so his name was pronounced. We might add that
she had already refused Bacon.

or economically, the antisocial proclivities of men. Hence the doctrine of the divine right of kings grew side by side with the development of nationalism and the reduction of papal power. The Lutheran princes of Germany, having assumed the spiritual powers of the old Church in their realms, felt justified in transferring to themselves the divine aura which almost all rulers before 1789 considered indispensable to moral authority and social peace. James made the mistake of expressing this assumption too clearly, and in the most extreme form.

Parliament might have yielded (with private smiles) some theoretical acceptance of this royal absolutism if, as in Elizabeth's heyday, its members had been great landowners largely indebted to the Tudors for their title deeds. But the House of Commons now included among its 467 members many representatives of the rising mercantile classes—who could not stomach a limitless royal power over their money—and many Puritans who repudiated the claim of the King to rule their religion. The House defined its rights in bold disregard of James's divinity. It declared itself the sole judge in contested elections to its membership. It demanded freedom of speech and security from arrest during its sessions; without these, it argued, Parliament would be meaningless. It proposed to legislate on matters religious, and denied the authority of the king to decide such issues without parliamentary consent; the Anglican bishops, however, claimed for their Convocation the right to rule in ecclesiastical affairs, subject only to the approval of the king. The Speaker of the Commons informed James that the king could not institute any law, but could only ratify or reject the laws that Parliament had passed. "Our privileges and liberties," declared the Commons (June 1604), "are our rights and due inheritance, no less than our very lands and goods . . . They cannot be withheld from us . . . but with apparent wrong to the whole state of the realm."[21]

So the lines were drawn for that historic struggle between the "prerogative" of the king and the "privilege" of Parliament—which, after a hundred victories and defeats, would create the democracy of England.

III. THE GUNPOWDER PLOT: 1605

Above the economic and political strife, but deeply rooted in it, the religious warfare raged. Half the pamphlets that bruised the air were blasts of Puritans against Anglican bishops and ritual, of Anglicans against Puritan rigor and intransigence, or of both against Catholic plots to restore England to papal obedience. James underrated the intensity of these hatreds. He dreamed of an *entente demi-cordiale* between Puritans and Anglicans, and for that purpose called their leaders to a conference at

Hampton Court (January 14, 1604). He presided like another Constantine, and astonished both parties by his theological learning and his debating skill, but he insisted on "one doctrine and one discipline, one religion in substance and ceremony,"[22] and declared episcopacy indispensable. The Bishop of London thought the King divinely inspired, "the like of whom had not been seen since the time of Christ";[23] but the Puritans complained that James had acted like a partisan rather than a judge; and nothing came of the conference except the unexpectedly historic decision to make a new translation of the Bible. The Convocation of 1604 issued canons requiring conformity of all clergymen to Anglican worship; those refusing to comply were dismissed, and several were imprisoned; many resigned; some migrated to Holland or America.

James disgraced himself by having two Unitarians burned for doubting the divinity of Christ despite the proofs which he offered them (1612), but he distinguished himself by never thereafter allowing an execution for religious dissent; these were the last men to die for heresy in England. Slowly, as secular rule improved, the idea that religious toleration was compatible with public morals and national unity was making headway against the almost universal conviction that social order required a faith and a Church which were unchallengeable. In 1614 Leonard Busher's *Religious Peace* argued that religious persecution intensified dissent, compelled hypocrisy, and injured trade; and he reminded James that "Jews, Christians, and Turks are tolerated in Constantinople and yet are peaceable."[24] However, Busher thought that persons whose religion was "tainted with treason"—probably meaning such Catholics as put the pope above the king—should be forbidden to hold assemblies or to live within ten miles of London.

For the most part James was a tolerant dogmatist. He offended the Puritans by permitting—encouraging—Sunday sports, provided one had first attended Anglican services. He was inclined to relax the laws against Catholics. Over the heads of Robert Cecil and the Council he suspended the recusancy laws; he allowed priests to enter the country and say Mass in private homes. He dreamed, in his loose and philosophic way, of reconciling Catholic and Protestant Christendom.[25] But when Catholics multiplied in this sunshine and the Puritans denounced his lenience, he allowed the Elizabethan anti-Catholic laws to be renewed, extended, and enforced (1604). To send anyone abroad to a Catholic college or seminary was made punishable by a fine of one hundred pounds. All Catholic missionaries were banished, all Catholic teaching prohibited. Persons neglecting Anglican services were fined twenty pounds per month; any default in paying such fines involved forfeiture of property, real and personal; all the cattle on the delinquent's lands, all his furniture and wearing apparel, were to be seized for the Crown.[26]

Some half-crazed Catholics thought there was now no remedy but assassination. Robert Catesby had seen his father suffer imprisonment for recusancy under Elizabeth; he had joined in Essex' rebellion against the Queen; it was he who now conceived the Gunpowder Plot to blow up Westminster Palace while the King, the royal family, the Lords, and the Commons were assembled there for the opening of Parliament. He brought into the conspiracy Thomas Winter, Thomas Percy, John Wright, and Guy Fawkes. The five men swore one another to secrecy and sealed their oaths by taking the Sacrament from a Jesuit missionary, John Gerard. They engaged a house adjacent to the palace; sixteen hours a day they labored to dig a tunnel from one cellar to the other; they succeeded and placed thirty casks of gunpowder directly under the meeting chamber of the House of Lords. Repeated postponements of Parliament kept the project in precarious abeyance; through a year and a half the conspirators had to feed the fires of their wrath. At times they doubted the morality of an enterprise in which many innocent persons would perish with those whom the Catholics thought mercilessly guilty. To reassure them, Catesby asked Henry Garnett, provincial of the Jesuits in England, whether in war it was permissible to share in actions that would bring death to innocent noncombatants; Garnett answered that divines of all faiths agreed in the affirmative, but warned Catesby that any plot against the lives of governmental officials would only bring greater suffering to English Catholics. The provincial conveyed his suspicions to the Pope and the general of the Jesuits; they bade him keep aloof from all political intrigues and discourage all attempts against the state.[27] To another Jesuit, Oswald Greenway, Catesby in confession revealed the plot, which now included measures for a general rising of Catholics in England. Greenway reported the plot to Garnett. The two Jesuits hesitated between betraying the conspirators to the government and remaining silent; they chose to keep silent, but to do all in their power to dissuade the conspirators.

Catesby sought to quiet the qualms of his associates by arranging that on the morning of the appointed day friendly members of Parliament should receive urgent messages to call them away from Westminster. A minor figure in the plot warned his friend Lord Monteagle several days before the session was to begin. Mounteagle laid the matter before Cecil, who told the King. Their agents entered the cellars, found Fawkes there and the explosives in due place. Fawkes was arrested (November 4, 1605); he confessed his intentions to blow up Parliament the next day, but, despite extreme torture, refused to name his accomplices. These, however, revealed themselves by taking up arms and attempting flight. They were pursued and gave battle; Catesby, Percy, and Wright were mortally wounded, and several subalterns were hunted and secured. When the prisoners were tried they freely acknowledged the conspiracy, but no threat or torment could induce them to implicate the Jesuit priests. Fawkes and three others were drawn on hurdles from the Tower to Parliament House and were there executed (January 27, 1606). England still celebrates November 5 as Guy Fawkes Day, with bonfires and fireworks and the carrying of "guys," or effigies, through the streets.

Gerard and Greenway escaped to the Continent, but Garnett was captured, and with him another Jesuit, Oldcorne. In the Tower these two found means of what they supposed to be secret conversation, but spies reported their words. Separately accused of these conferences, Garnett denied them, Oldcorne admitted them; Garnett confessed that he had lied. Breaking down, he conceded that he had had knowledge of the plot; but as this had come to him from Greenway, and Greenway had received it under the seal of confession, he had not felt free to reveal it; however, he had done all in his power to discourage it. He was pronounced guilty, not of the plot but of concealing it. For six weeks the King delayed signing the death warrant. Garnett, falsely informed that Greenway was in the Tower, sent him a letter; it was intercepted; asked if he had communicated with Greenway, he denied it; confronted with the letter, he argued that equivocation was permitted to a person to save his life. On May 3, 1606, he was hanged, drawn, and quartered.[28]

Parliament felt justified in intensifying the statutes against Catholics (1606). They were barred from the practice of medicine or law, and from serving as executors or guardians; they were forbidden to travel more than five miles from their houses; and a new oath was demanded of them which not only denied the power of the popes to depose secular rulers, but branded the assertion of that power as impious, heretical, and damnable.[29] Pope Paul V forbade the taking of this oath; a majority of English Catholics obeyed him; a large minority accepted it. In 1606 six priests were executed for refusing it and for saying Mass; between 1607 and 1618 sixteen more were put to death.[30] The prisons held several hundred priests, several thousand Catholic laymen. Despite these terrors, Jesuits continued to enter England; there were at least 68 there in 1615, 284 in 1623.[31] Some Jesuits found their way into Scotland; one of them, John Ogilvie, was put to death there in 1615, after having his legs crushed in torture by "the boots," and being kept awake for eight consecutive days and nights by the insertion of pins into his flesh.[32] All the sins of the old Church were visited upon her by the new certainties and powers.

IV. THE JACOBEAN STAGE

The English ecstasy continued in literature as well as in religion. To the age of James I belong the better half of Shakespeare's plays, much of

Chapman, most of Jonson, Webster, Middleton, Dekker, Marston, some of Massinger, all of Beaumont and Fletcher; in poetry Donne, in prose Burton and, noblest of all, the King James version of the Bible: these are glories enough for any reign. The King had a taste for drama; in one Christmas season fourteen plays were acted at his court. The Globe theater was burned to the ground in 1613 by the firing of two cannons in a production of *Henry VIII*, but it was soon rebuilt, and by 1631 there were seventeen theaters in or near London.

George Chapman was five years older than Shakespeare and outlived him by eighteen, spanning three reigns (1559–1634). He took his time maturing; by 1598 he had successfully completed Marlowe's *Hero and Leander*, and had published seven books of *The Iliad*; but his translation of Homer was not finished till 1615, and his best plays came between 1607 and 1613. He opened a new field to English drama by taking a theme from recent French history in his *Bussy d'Ambois* (1607?)—five acts of blusterous oratory rarely redeemed with magic of phrase, but rising to corrosive power in a page where Bussy and his enemy exchange ironic compliments as indigestible as truth. Chapman never recovered from his education; his much Greek and more Latin sat stiflingly upon his muse, and to read his plays is now a labor of lore, hardly of love. Nor do we thrill as Keats did "on first looking into Chapman's Homer." There is a sturdy vigor in these heptameters that here and there lifts them above Pope's generally better version, but the music of poetry dies in translation; the leaping hexameters of the original carry us on with swifter melody than the measured, fettered feet of rhyming verse. No long English poem in rhyme has escaped the somnolence of a barcarolle. Chapman changed to "heroic couplets"— ten-syllable lines in rhyming pairs—for his rendering of *The Odyssey*, with similar lulling power. King James must have slept, under these massive blankets, beyond Homer's casual nods, for he neglected to pay the three hundred pounds which the late Prince Henry had promised Chapman when the translation should be complete; but the Earl of Somerset rescued the aging poet from poverty.

Shall we tarry with Thomas Heywood, Thomas Middleton, Thomas Dekker, Cyril Tourneur, and John Marston, or beg them to let us off with a humble salute to their flickering fame? John Fletcher cannot be so scrimped, for in his heyday (1612–25) England honored him, in the drama, only next to Shakespeare and Jonson. Son to a Bishop of London, nephew or cousin to three poets of a sort, he was nursed on verse and reared with rhyme; and to all this heritage he added the privilege of collaborating with Shakespeare on *Henry VIII* and *The Two Noble Kinsmen*, with Massinger on *The Spanish Curate*, and, with most success, with Francis Beaumont.

"Frank" was also to the manner born, being the son of a prominent judge, and brother to a minor poet who eased by a year the way for Frank's entrance into the world. Failing to graduate from Oxford or the Inner Temple, Beaumont tried his hand at voluptuous poetry, and joined with Fletcher in writing plays. The two handsome bachelors shared bed and board, goods and clothes, mistresses and themes; "they had one wench between them," says Aubrey, and "a wonderful consimility of phansey."[33] For ten years they collaborated in producing such plays as *Philaster, or Love Lies a-Bleeding*, *The Maid's Tragedy*, *The Knight of the Burning Pestle*. The dialogue is vigorous but windy, the plots artfully tangled but artificially resolved, the thought seldom reaching to philosophy; nevertheless, toward the end of the century (Dryden assures us) these dramas were twice as popular on the stage as Shakespeare's.[34]

Beaumont died at thirty, in the year of Shakespeare's death. Thereafter Fletcher wrote, alone or with others, a long series of plays successful and forgotten; some of his comedies of involved and boisterous intrigue stemmed from Spanish models, and in turn, with their accent on adultery, led to the Restoration drama. Then, tiring of these bloody or bawdy scenes, he issued (1608) a pastoral play, *The Faithful Shepherdess*, as nonsensical as *A Midsummer Night's Dream*, and sometimes rivaling it in poetry. Clorin, her shepherd lover dead, retires to a rustic bower by his grave, and vows to stay there intact till her death:

> Hail, holy earth, whose cold arms do embrace
> The truest man that ever fed his flocks
> By the fat plains of fruitful Thessaly!
> Thus I salute thy grave; thus do I pay
> My early vows and tribute of mine eyes
> To thy still-lovéd ashes; thus I free
> Myself from all ensuing heats and fires
> Of love; all sports, delights, and jolly games,
> That shepherds hold full dear, thus put I off:
> Now no more shall these smooth brows be begirt
> With youthful coronals, and lead the dance;
> No more the company of fresh fair maids
> And wanton shepherds be to me delightful,
> Nor the shrill pleasing sound of merry pipes
> Under some shady dell, when the cool wind
> Plays on the leaves: all be far away,
> Since thou art far away, by whose dear side
> How often have I sat crowned with fresh flowers
> For summer's queen, whilst every shepherd's boy
> Puts on his lusty green, with gaudy hook,
> And hanging scrip of finest cordevan.
> But thou art gone, and these are gone with thee,
> And all are dead but thy dear memory;

> That shall outlive thee, and shall ever spring,
> Whilst there are pipes or jolly shepherds sing.

The idyl had one performance and disappeared from the stage. What chance had such a paean to chastity in an age still simmering with the Elizabethan fire?

The most powerful and disagreeable of the Jacobean dramatists is John Webster. We know almost nothing of his life, and it is just as well. We gather his mood from the preface to his best play, *The White Devil* (1611), where he calls the audience "ignorant asses," and deposes that "the breath that comes from the incapable multitude is able to poison . . . the most sententious [profound] tragedy." The story is that of Vittoria Accoramboni, whose sins and trial (1581–85) had stirred Italy in Webster's childhood. Vittoria feels that her husband's income does no justice to her beauty. She accepts the attentions of the moneyed Duke of Brachiano, and suggests that he dispose of her husband and his own wife. He attends to the matter at once, with the aid of Vittoria's pander brother Flamineo, who provides for these crimes the most cynical obbligato in all English literature. She is arrested on suspicion, but defends herself with such audacity and skill as scares a lawyer out of his Latin and a cardinal out of his hat. She is kidnaped from justice by Brachiano; they are pursued; finally pursuers and pursued, the just and the unjust, are slaughtered in a dramatic holocaust that left Webster's blood lust sated for a year. The plot is well managed, the characters are consistently drawn, the language is often virile or vile, the crucial scenes are powerful, the poetry rises at times to Shakespeare's eloquence. But to a taste made squeamish by civilization the play is deformed by the forced and gutter coarseness of Flamineo, by the hot curses that pour even from pretty mouths ("Oh, could I kill you forty times a day, and use 't four years together, 'twere too little!"),[35] by the pervasive obscenity, the word *whore* on every second page, the endless double meanings that would have made even Shakespeare blush.

Webster returned to the shambles in *The Duchess of Malfi* (1613). Ferdinand, Duke of Calabria, forbids his young widowed sister, the Duchess of Amalfi, to marry again, for if she dies mateless he will inherit her fortune. She mourns her enforced chastity:

> The birds that live i' the field
> On the wild benefit of nature, live
> Happier than we, for they may choose their mates,
> And carol their sweet pleasures to the spring.[36]

Excited by lust and prohibition, she lures her steward, Antonio, into a secret marriage and a precipitate bed. Ferdinand has her killed. In the final act someone is slain almost every minute; doctors are ready with poisons, ruffians with daggers; no one has the patience to wait for a legal execution. The worst villain of the piece—who kills the Duchess, steals her property, takes a mistress and then murders her—is a cardinal; Webster was no papist. Here, too, are *doubles-entendres* of quite urological candor, a resolve to exhaust the vocabulary of execration, and a wild, indiscriminate condemnation of human life. Only in the remote corners of this dark canvas do we find nobility, fidelity, or tenderness. Ferdinand forgets himself and is soft for a line as he looks upon his sister, still beautiful in death:

Cover her face! Mine eyes dazzle, she died young . . .[37]

But he soon recalls himself to barbarism.

Let us hope to find something sweeter than all this in the man who could write "Drink to me only with thine eyes."

V. BEN JONSON: 1573?–1637

He was a posthumous product, being born in Westminster a month after his father's death. He was christened Benjamin Johnson; he dropped the *h* to distinguish himself, but the printers continued to use it, over his dead body, till 1840; it still appears in the plaque on Westminster Abbey's walls. The mother, having had a minister for her first husband, took a bricklayer for her second. The family was poor; Ben had to scrape for an education; only the kindness of a discerning friend financed his entry into Westminster School. There he had the luck to come under the influence of its "undermaster," the historian and antiquarian William Camden. He took to the classics with less than normal animosity, made intimates of Cicero, Seneca, Livy, Tacitus, Quintilian, and later claimed, apparently with justice, to know "more in Greek and Latin than all the poets of England."[38] Only his excitable "humour" and the rough-and-tumble of the London world kept his learning from ruining his art.

After graduating from Westminster, he attended Cambridge, "where," says his earliest biographer, "he continued but a few weeks for want of further maintenance."[39] His stepfather needed him as apprentice bricklayer, and we picture Ben sweating and fretting for seven years as he laid bricks and meditated poetry. Then suddenly he was off to the wars, caught in the draft, or rushing to them as livelier than bricks. He served in the Netherlands, fought a duel with an enemy soldier, killed and despoiled him, and came home to tell expanding tales. He married, begot many children, buried three or more of them, quarreled with his wife, left her for five years, rejoined her, and lived with her incompatibly till her death. Clio herself knows not how he buttered the family's bread.

The mystery deepens when we learn that he became an actor (1597). But he was bursting with bright ideas and happy lines, and merely reciting other men's thoughts could not long contain him. He rejoiced when Tom Nash invited him to collaborate on *The Isle of Dogs*, and doubtless he contributed his share to the "very seditious and slanderous matter" that the Privy Council found in the play. The Council ordered the performance stopped, the theater closed, the authors arrested. Nash, an old hand at such scrapes, lost himself in Yarmouth; Jonson found himself in jail. As the custom of the prison required him to pay for his food, his lodging, and his shackles, he borrowed four pounds from Philip Henslowe, and, released, joined Henslowe's (and Shakespeare's) theatrical company (1597).

A year later he wrote his first important comedy, *Every Man in His Humour*, and saw Shakespeare act in it at the Globe. Perhaps the great dramatist did not relish the prologue, which proposed, despite current example, to follow the classic unities of action, time, and place, and not

> To make a child, now swaddled, to proceed
> Man, and then shoot up, in one beard and weed,
> Past threescore years . . . You will be pleased to see
> One such today as other plays should be,
> Where neither chorus wafts you o'er the seas,
> Nor creaking throne comes down, the boys to please . . .
> But deeds and language such as men do use,
> And persons such as comedy should choose
> When she would show an image of the times,
> And sport with human follies, not with crimes.

So Jonson turned his back upon the aristocratic badinage of Shakespeare's early comedies, and upon the miraculous geography and chronology of the "romantic" drama; he brought the slums of London to the stage, and concealed his erudition in a remarkable reproduction of lower-class dialects and ways. The characters are caricatures rather than complex philosophical creations, but they live; they are as worthless as in Webster, but they are human; they are mentally unkempt, but they are not murderers.

The Latins had used *umor* to mean "moisture" or "a fluid"; the Hippocratic medical tradition had used *humor* to designate four fluids of the body—blood, phlegm, black bile, and yellow bile; according to the predominance of one or another of these in a person, he was said to be of a sanguine, phlegmatic, melancholic, or choleric "humour," or temperament. Jonson defined his own interpretation of the term:

> As when some one peculiar quality
> Doth so possess a man that it doth draw
> All his affects [feelings], his spirits, and his powers,
> In their confluctions, all to run one way—
> That may be truly said to be a humour.[40]

The word came to life in the hilarious portrayal of Captain Bobadil, a direct descendant of Plautus' *miles gloriosus*, but reeking with his own peculiar "humour" and unconscious humor—always brave except in peril, bursting to fight except when challenged, a master of the sheathed sword.

The play was well received, and Ben could sow his wild oats less niggardly. He was now bouncy with confidence, proud as a poet, talking to lords without servility, standing his ground stubbornly, absorbing life hurriedly at every chance and pore, relishing forthrightness and rough humor, seducing women now and then, but finally (he told Drummond) preferring "the wantonness of a wife to the coyness of a mistress."[41] He left off acting and lived rashly by his pen. For a time he prospered by writing masques for the court; the light fantastic lines he wrote fitted well the scenes that Jones designed. But Ben, hot-tempered, quarreled widely. In the year of his first success he fell out with Gabriel Spencer, an actor, dueled with him, killed him, and was jailed for murder (1598). To make matters worse for himself, he was converted to Catholicism in prison. Nevertheless he received a fair trial, and he was allowed to plead "benefit of clergy" because he read the Latin psalter "like a clerk"; he was released, but only after having the letter *T* stamped with a hot iron on his thumb so that he might be readily identified as a second offender if he killed again; all the rest of his life he was a branded felon.

After a year of liberty he was returned to jail for debt. Henslowe again bailed him out, and in 1600 Jonson wooed solvency by writing *Every Man out of His Humour*. He weighted the comedy with classical tags; added to the dramatis personae three characters who served as a commenting chorus; rained invectives upon Puritans who had "religion in their garments, and their hair cut shorter than their eyebrows"; and brandished his lore at playwrights who were wrecking the Aristotelian unities. Instead of impossible romances about incredible lords, he proposed to show London mercilessly to itself, to

> oppose a mirror
> As large as is the stage whereon we act,
> Where they shall see the time's deformity
> Anatomized in every nerve and sinew
> With constant courage, and contempt of fear.[42]

The play made more enemies than royalties, and it is not recommended reading today. Dissatisfied with the noisy audience at the Globe, Jonson wrote his next comedy, *Cynthia's Revels* (1601), for a company of boy actors and a smaller, choicer audience at the Blackfriars theater. Dekker and Marston felt themselves satirized in the play; in 1602 the Chamberlain's company, angered by the competition of the Blackfriars' boys, produced Dekker's *Satiromastix* (i.e., the satirist flogged), which pilloried Jonson as a puny, pockmarked, conceited pedant, murderer, and bricklayer. The quarrel ended in an exchange of eulogies, and for a time fortune smiled. A prospering lawyer took Ben into his home, and the Earl of Pembroke sent the poet twenty pounds "to buy books."[43] So fortified, he tried his hand at tragedy. He took as his subject Sejanus, the evil favorite of Tiberius. He based his narrative carefully upon Tacitus, Suetonius, Dio Cassius, and Juvenal; he achieved a scholarly masterpiece, some moving scenes (e.g., V, x) and stately lines; but the audience resented the long speeches, the tedious moralism of lifeless characters; the play was soon withdrawn. Jonson printed the text and in the margin gave his classical sources, with notes in Latin. Lord Aubigny, impressed, gave the sorrowing author asylum for five years.

He returned to the arena in 1605 with his greatest play. *Volpone, or The Fox* attacked with burning satire the money lust that raged in London. As usual with comedies—from Plautus to *The Admirable Crichton*—a clever servant is the brains of the plot. Mosca (Italian for fly) brings to his miser master, Volpone, who pretends to be seriously ill, a succession of legacy hunters—Voltore (vulture), Corbaccio (crow), Corvino (raven)— who leave substantial presents in the hope of being named Volpone's heir. The "fox" accepts each gift with grasping reluctance, even to borrowing Corbaccio's wife for a night. Mosca finally deceives Volpone into making the servant sole legatee. But Bonario (good nature) exposes the trick, and the Venetian Senate sends nearly all the cast to jail. The play at last brought the Globe audience to Jonson's feet.

He moved hurriedly from success to adversity. He collaborated with Marston and Chapman on *Eastward Ho!* (1605); the government arrested the authors on the ground that the comedy insulted the Scots; the prisoners were threatened with circumcision of their noses and ears, but they were released intact, and such dignitaries as Camden and Selden joined in the banquet given by the liberated triumvirate. Then, on November 7, 1605, Ben was summoned to the Privy Council as a Catholic who might know something about the Gunpowder Plot. Though he had dined with a chief conspirator, Catesby, a month before, he escaped implication; but on January 9, 1606, he was hailed to court as a delinquent recusant. Since he was too poor to be profitably fined, the charge was not pressed. In 1610 he re-

turned to the Anglican fold, and "with such enthusiasm that he drank all
the wine in the cup when he attended" Communion.[44]

In that year he staged his most famous play. *The Alchemist* satirized not
merely alchemy, which was a flagging quest, but half a dozen impostures
that harried London with quackery. Sir Epicure Mammon is sure that he
has found the secret of alchemy:

> This night I'll change
> All that is metal in my house to gold,
> And, early in the morning, will I send
> To all the plumbers and the pewterers,
> And buy their tin and lead up, and to Lothbury
> For all the copper . . . I'll purchase Devonshire and Cornwall,
> And make them perfect Indies . . . For I do mean
> To have a list of wives and concubines
> Equal with Solomon, who had the stone
> Alike with me; and I will make me a back,
> With the elixir, that shall be as tough
> As Hercules, to encounter fifty a night
> . . . And my flatterers
> Shall be the pure and gravest of divines
> That I can get for money . . .
> My meat shall all come in in Indian shells,
> Dishes of agate set in gold, and studded
> With emeralds, sapphires, hyacinths, and rubies;
> The tongues of carps, dormice, and camel's heels . . .
> Old mushrooms, and the swelling unctuous paps
> Of a fat pregnant sow, newly cut off . . .
> For which I'll say unto my cook, "There's gold;
> Go forth, and be a knight."[45]

Sir Epicure is a rare morsel, but the others of the cast are dregs, and their
talk is sticky with scatological filth; it is a pity to see scholarly Ben so
erudite in scum and in the argot of the slums. The Puritans forgivably attacked such plays. Jonson retaliated by caricaturing them in *Bartholomew
Fair* (1614).

He produced many more comedies, full of life and lees; *non ragionam
di lor.* At times he rebelled against his own coarse realism, and in *The Sad
Shepherd* he let his imagination roam quite recklessly.

> Her treading would not bend a blade of grass
> Or shake the downy blowball from his stalk,
> But like the soft west wind she shot along,
> And where she went the flowers took thickest root,
> As she had sowed them with her odorous foot.[46]

But he left the play unfinished, and, for the rest, confined his romanticism to pretty lyrics scattered in his comedies like jewels set in dross. So, in *The Devil Is an Ass* (1616), suddenly he sings:

> Have you seen but a bright lily grow
>   Before rude hands have touched it?
> Ha' you marked but the fall o' the snow
>   Before the soil hath smutched it?
> Ha' you felt the wool of beaver,
>   Or swan's down ever?
> Or have smelt o' the bud o' the briar,
>   Or the nard in the fire?
> Or have tasted the bag of the bee?
>   O so white! O so soft! O so sweet is she!

Still finer, of course, is the song "To Celia," which he pilfered from the Greek of Philostratus and transformed, with perfect scholarship and skill, into "Drink to me only with thine eyes."

After Shakespeare's death Jonson was the acknowledged head of the poetic guild. He became the uncrowned poet laureate of England—not officially so named, but most often recognized by the government, and receiving from it a pension of one hundred marks a year. The many friends who gathered round him at the Mermaid Tavern saw his rough good nature behind his bad temper and sharp tongue; they fed on his juicy speech and let him play the lead almost as presidentially as his namesake of the next century. Ben was now as corpulent as Samuel would be, and no handsomer; he mourned his "mountain belly" and "rocky face" pocked with scurvy; he could hardly visit a friend without breaking a chair. In 1624 he moved his dais to the Devil Tavern in Fleet Street; there the Apollo Club, which he had founded, met regularly to feast on victuals, wine, and wit; and Jonson, at one end of the room, had a raised seat, with a handrail that guided his magnitude into the throne. Tradition called his followers the Tribe of Ben, and numbered among them James Shirley, Thomas Carew, and Robert Herrick, who called him "Saint Ben."[47]

He needed a saintly and uncongenial patience to bear with the poverty and sickness of his disintegrating years. He reckoned that all his plays had brought him less than two hundred pounds. He spent in haste and starved at leisure; he had none of the financial sense that had made Shakespeare an expert in realty. Charles I continued his pension, but when Parliament stinted the royal funds the pension was not always paid. Charles, however, sent him one hundred pounds in 1629, and the dean and the chapter of Westminster Abbey voted five pounds for "Mr. Benjamin Johnson in his sickness and want."[48] His last plays failed, his fame waned, his friends disappeared, his wife and children were dead. By 1629 he lived alone, bed-ridden with paralysis, with only one old woman to take care of him. He lingered in pain and penury for eight years more. He was buried in West-minster Abbey, and John Young carved, upon the stone that faced the grave, a famous epitaph:

O RARE BEN JOHNSON

Only the first two words remain, but every educated Englishman can fill out the rest.

VI. JOHN DONNE: 1573–1631

At the Hampton Court Conference a Puritan delegate proposed a new translation of the Bible. The Bishop of London objected that existing versions were good enough; King James overruled him and ordered "special pains taken for a uniform translation, which should be done by the best learned in both universities, then reviewed by the bishops, presented to the Privy Council, lastly ratified by royal authority, to be read in the whole Church, and no other."[49] Sir Henry Savile and forty-six other scholars undertook the task, leaning on earlier translations by Wyclif and Tyndale, and completed it in seven years (1604–11). This "Authorized Version" became official in 1611 and began its immense influence on English life, literature, and speech. A thousand pithy phrases passed from it into the language. The adoration of the Bible, already so strong in Protestant lands, took on fresh fervor in England, raising the Puritans, then the Quakers, then the Methodists, to a knowledge and worship of the text equaled only by Moslem devotion to the Koran. The influence of the translation on English literary style was completely beneficent: it broke up the long and fanciful involutions of Elizabethan prose into sentences short and strong and clear and natural; it replaced foreign terms and constructions with racy Anglo-Saxon words and English idioms. It made a thousand mistakes in scholarship, but it transformed the noble Hebrew and the common Greek of the Testaments into the finest monument of English prose.

Two other works of distinguished prose honored the reign: Sir Walter Raleigh's *History of the World* (of which more later), and Robert Burton's *Anatomy of Melancholy* (1621)*—the massive matrix in which the vicar of St. Thomas' at Oxford set his garnered fragments of theological,

---

* Some undistinguished prose acquired historical distinction: the newssheets that fluttered about Jacobean London graduated in 1622 into the first English newspaper, *The Weekly Newes*.

astrological, classical, and philosophical lore. The dons at first thought him "very merry and facete," but later in life he became so melancholy that nothing could make him happy but the ribaldry of the bargemen on the Thames.[50] To relieve his "black bile" Burton "devoured authors" supplied to him by the Bodleian Library. With these, and his manuscript, and astrology, and priestly ministrations, he passed his gloomy days and starry nights. He calculated his own horoscope, and predicted therefrom the day of his death with such accuracy that Oxford lads suspected him of having hanged himself to prove his prescience.[51]

He is very much alive in his book. Setting out to examine and prescribe for hypochondria, he finds digression more pleasant than his plan. With eccentric humor Rabelaisian only in its pathless wandering, he discusses everything as casually as Montaigne, peppering his pages with Latin and Greek, and genially beckoning his reader on and on to nowhere. He disclaims originality; he feels that all authorship is pilfering: "We can say nothing but what has been said; the composition and method is ours only."[52] He confesses that he knows the world only through books, and through the news that filters into Oxford:

> I hear new news every day, and those ordinary rumors of war, plagues, fires, inundations, thefts, murders, massacres, meteors, comets, spectrums, prodigies, apparitions, of towns taken, cities besieged in France, Germany, Turkey, Persia, Poland, etc., daily musters and preparations, and such like, which these tempestuous times afford, battles fought, so many men slain . . . shipwrecks, piracies, and sea fights; peace, leagues, stratagems, and fresh alarms. A vast confusion of vows, wishes, actions, edicts, petitions, lawsuits, pleas, laws, proclamations . . . opinions, schisms, heresies . . . weddings, masquings, mummeries, entertainments, jubilees . . . burials[53]—

and he feels (like Thoreau) that if he reads the news of one day he may take it for granted the rest of the year, merely changing names and dates. He doubts that man progresses, yet "I will make an Utopia of mine own . . . in which I will freely domineer," and he describes it in fanciful detail; actually, however, he prefers browsing at peace in his study or on the banks of the Thames to going forth to reform mankind. Meanwhile all the authors in the world bring sweetmeats to his feast. He gets clogged with quotations, becomes dismal again, and after 114 fat pages he resolves to come to grips with the causes of melancholy, which are sin, concupiscence, intemperance, demons, witches, stars, constipation, venereal excess . . . and its symptoms, which include "wind rumbling in the guts . . . sour belchings . . . troublesome dreams."[54] Having completed two hundred digressions, he prescribes cures for melancholy: prayer, diet, medicine, laxatives, diuretics, fresh air, exercise, games, shows, music, merry company, wine, sleep, blood-letting, baths; and then he digresses again, so that every page is a disappoint-ment and a delight—if time would stop.

Now, in poetry, the sonneteers subside and the "metaphysical poets" come: Richard Crashaw, Abraham Cowley, John Donne, George Herbert —who phrased with gentle grace the peace and piety of an Anglican parsonage. Samuel Johnson called them metaphysical only partly because they inclined to philosophy, theology, and argument, chiefly because they adopted—from Lyly or Góngora or the Pléiade—a style of linguistic novelties and conceits, verbal wit and involutions, classical excerpts and labored obscurities. All of which did not prevent Donne from becoming the finest poet of the age.

Like Jonson and Chapman, he overspread three reigns. Under Elizabeth he wrote of love, under James of piety, under Charles of death. Brought up a Catholic, educated by Jesuits, Oxford, and Cambridge, he knew the sting of persecution and the brooding of concealment. His brother Henry was arrested for harboring a proscribed priest, and died in jail. Sometimes John fed his melancholy on the mystical writings of St. Teresa and Luis de Granada. But by 1592 his proud young intellect had rejected the marvels of his faith, and the third decade of his life revolved around martial ad-ventures, erotic pursuits, and skeptical philosophy.

For a time he dedicated his muse to candid promiscuity. In Elegy XVII he celebrated "Love's sweetest part, Variety"—

> How happy were our sires in ancient time,
> Who held plurality of love no crime![55]

In Elegy XVIII he swam "the Hellespont between the Sestos and Abydos of her breasts." In Elegy XIX, "To His Mistress Going to Bed," he un-dressed her poetically and bade her "licence my roving hands." He mixed entomology with love and argued that since a flea, by biting both, had mingled his blood with hers, they were now married in blood and might sport in sinless ecstasy.[56] Then, surfeited with surfaces, he found fault un-generously with generous women, forgot their dated charms, and saw only the tricks they had learned in a heartless world; he flayed his Julia with a raging litany of execrations, and counseled his reader to choose a homely mate, since "love built on beauty soon as beauty dies."[57] Now, singing antistrophe to Villon, he drew up a poetic testament in which each stanza struck a blow at "love."

He shipped with Essex in 1596, helped raid Cádiz, and shipped with him again in 1597 to the Azores and Spain. Back in England, he found a good berth as secretary to Sir Thomas Egerton, Lord Keeper of the Great Seal; but he ran away with the Lord Keeper's niece, married her (1600), and set himself to support her with poetry. Children came as easily as rhymes; often he could not feed or clothe them; his wife's health broke down; he wrote a defense of suicide. At last relenting, Egerton sent the family an allowance (1608), and in 1610 Sir Robert Drury gave them an apartment in his mansion in Drury Lane. A year later Sir Robert lost his only daughter, and Donne published anonymously, as an elegy for her, his first major poem, "An Anatomy of the World." He enlarged the death of Elizabeth Drury into the decay of man and the universe:

> So did the world from the first hour decay . . .
> And new philosophy calls all in doubt.
> The element of fire is quite put out;
> The sun is lost, and th' earth, and no man's wit
> Can well direct him where to look for it.
> And freely men confess that this world's spent,
> When in the Planets and the Firmament
> They seek so many new, then see that this
> Is crumbled out again . . .
> 'Tis all in pieces, all coherence gone,
> All just supply, and all relation.[58]

He mourned to see "how lame and cripple" this earth is, once the scene of divine redemption, now, in the new astronomy, a mere "suburb" of the world. In one mood he had exalted the "sacred hunger of science"; in another he wondered whether science would destroy mankind:

> With new diseases on ourselves we war,
> And with new Physic a worse Engine far.[59]

And so he turned to religion. His repeated illnesses, the ominous death of friend after friend, led him to the fear of God. Though his reason still questioned theology, he had learned to distrust reason too as but another faith, and he decided that the old creed should be accepted without further argument, if only to bring peace of mind and security of bread. In 1615 he became an Anglican priest; and now he not only preached sermons in somber and stirring prose, but composed some of the most moving religious poetry in the English language. In 1616 he was made chaplain to James I; in 1621 he became dean of St. Paul's. He had never published the erotic lyrics of his youth, but he had allowed copies to circulate in manuscript; now he "repenteth highly," Ben Jonson reported, "and seeketh to destroy all his poems."[60] He wrote, instead, "Holy Sonnets" and, whistling in the dark, challenged death:

> Death, be not proud, though some have called thee
> Mighty and dreadful, for thou art not so;
> For those whom thou thinks't thou dost overthrow
> Die not, poor Death, nor yet canst thou kill me . . .
> Our short sleep past, we wake eternally,
> And death shall be no more; Death, *thou* shalt die.[61]

In 1623, recovering from a serious illness, he wrote in his diary some famous lines: "Any man's death diminishes me, because I am involved in mankind; and therefore never send to know for whom the bell tolls; it tolls for thee."[62] On the first Friday in Lent, 1631, he rose from a sickbed to preach what men were soon to call his own funeral sermon; his aides had tried to dissuade him, seeing how (said his devoted friend Izaak Walton) "his sickness had left him but so much flesh as did only cover his bones."[63] Having delivered his sermon, eloquent in the confidence of resurrection, and "being full of joy that God had enabled him to perform this desired duty, he hastened to his house; out of which he never moved till . . . he was carried by devout men to his grave."[64] He died in the arms of his mother, who had borne patiently with his sins and lovingly with his sermons, March 31, 1631.

It was a full, tense life, running the gamut of lust and love, of doubt and decay, and ending in the warm comfort of old faith. We of today, who sleep so readily over Spenser, find ourselves startled on almost every page by this strangely fanciful realist and modern medieval soul. His verse is rough, but he wished it so; he rejected the affected graces of Elizabethan speech, and relished unworn words and arresting prosody; he liked harsh discords that could be resolved into unwonted harmonies. There was nothing trite in his verse, once he had graduated from the stews; and this man, who had polished obscenity like another Catullus, grew to such delicacy and depth of feeling and thought, such originality of phrase and sentiment, as no other poet could match, in that amazing age, but Shakespeare himself.

VII. JAMES SOWS THE WHIRLWIND: 1615–25

Love and diplomacy are treacherous bedfellows. In 1615 King James fell in love, in his kindly ambidextrous way, with handsome, dashing, rich George Villiers, twenty-three. He made him Earl, then Marquis, then Duke of Buckingham and, after 1616, allowed him to direct the policies of the state. Buckingham's wife, Lady Katherine Manners, outwardly conforming to the Anglican rite, was at heart a Roman Catholic, and may have inclined him to friendship with Spain.

James himself was a man of peace, and did not allow theology or piracy to keep him embroiled with the Continent. Soon after his accession he ended the long war that England had waged with Spain. When Frederick, Prince of the Palatinate and husband to James's beloved daughter Elizabeth, lost his principality at the outset of the Thirty Years' War, James played with the hope that the Hapsburg King of Spain, properly appeased, would influence the Hapsburg Emperor, Ferdinand II, to let Frederick regain his throne. To the disgust of his people, James proposed to Philip IV the marriage of Philip's sister, The Infanta Maria, with Prince Charles.

Raleigh came to his bloody end as a sacrifice to this Spanish policy. He had privately opposed James's succession, and bitterly opposed James's supporter Essex. Soon after reaching London James dismissed him from all governmental posts. With characteristic passion and rashness, Raleigh allowed himself to be implicated in several attempts to unseat the King.[65] He was sent to the Tower, protested his innocence, and attempted suicide. He was tried, was convicted on dubious evidence, and was condemned to die, December 13, 1603, with all the tortures of a traitor. On December 9 he wrote to his wife a letter[66] warm with such tenderness and piety as he had seldom shown to the world. James rejected the pleas of the Queen and Prince Henry to forgive him, but permitted the prisoner to live on for fifteen years more, always keeping the death penalty over his head. Raleigh's wife was allowed to come and dwell with him in a little house that he built within the Tower precincts. He was supplied with books by his friends; he made experiments in chemistry, composed some excellent poems, and wrote his *History of the World*. As published in 1614, it began with a pious preface involved and verbose, revealing a mind harassed and distraught. The narrative opened with Nineveh, passed on through Egypt, Judea, Persia, Chaldea, Greece, and Carthage, and ended with Imperial Rome. Raleigh was not anxious to reach recent times, for "whosoever, in writing a modern history, shall follow truth too near the heels, it may haply strike out his teeth."[67] His style improved as he went on, attained a noble splendor in describing the battle of Salamis, and came to a climax in the concluding apostrophe to "eloquent, just, and mighty Death."[68]

But he was not reconciled to defeat. In 1616, having raised £1,500, he bribed the Duke of Buckingham to intercede for him with the King.[69] He promised that, if released, he would sail to South America, find what he alleged to be the rich gold deposits of Guiana, and bring back royal spoils for the thirsty treasury. James freed him provisionally, and agreed to let him and his partners keep four fifths of any treasure he might capture from "heathen and savage people"; but the canny ruler held the death sentence still in force as an inducement to good behavior. The Count of Gondomar, the Spanish ambassador, pointed out that there were Spanish settlements in Guiana and hoped they would not be disturbed. James, anxious for peace and marriage with Spain, forbade Raleigh, on pain of immediate execution of his death sentence, to interfere with Christian communities anywhere, particularly the Spanish.[70] Raleigh consented in writing to these restrictions.[71] Gondomar still protesting, James vowed that if Raleigh violated his instructions the death penalty would be enforced.[72]

With the aid of his friends Raleigh equipped fourteen ships, and with these he sailed (March 17, 1617) to the mouth of the Orinoco. A Spanish settlement, Santo Tomás, barred the way up the river to the supposed— quite legendary—mines. Raleigh's men (he himself staying on board) landed, attacked and burned the village, and killed its governor. Then, discouraged by further Spanish resistance, the depleted force abandoned the gold quest and returned empty-handed to the ships. Raleigh was disheartened to learn that his son had been slain in the assault. He reproved his second in command, who thereupon committed suicide. His men lost confidence in him; vessel after vessel deserted his fleet. Returning to England and finding that the King was in a rage against him, he negotiated for escape to France; he was arrested; he tried again to escape and got as far as Greenwich; there a French agent betrayed him. He was captured and sent to the Tower, and the King, pressed by Gondomar, ordered the death sentence carried out.

Tired at last of life and welcoming the boon of a sudden death, Raleigh walked to his execution (October 29, 1618) with a calm dignity that made him the hero of a people that hated Spain. "Let us dispatch," he asked the sheriffs. "At this hour mine ague comes upon me; I would not have mine enemies to think I quaked from fear." He tested with his thumb the edge of the ax. "This," he said, "is a fair sharp medicine to cure me of all diseases and miseries."[73] His loyal widow claimed the corpse and had it buried in a church. "The Lords," she wrote, "have given me his dead body, though they denied me his life. God hold me in my wits."[74]

Raleigh's expedition was one of many that took James's subjects hopefully to America. Peasants hungry for land of their own, adventurers seeking fortunes in trade or spoils, criminals fleeing the cruelty of the law, Puritans resolved to plant the flag of their faith on virgin soil—these and others bore the risks and the tedium of the sea to make new Englands everywhere. Virginia was settled in 1606–7, Bermuda in 1609, Newfoundland in 1610. "Separatist" clergymen refusing to accept the Prayer Book and the ritual of the Anglican Church fled to Holland with their followers (1608). From Delft (July 1620), Southampton, and Plymouth (September) these "Pilgrims" took sail across the Atlantic; after three months of ordeal, they set foot on Plymouth Rock (December 21).

In Asia the English East India Company, confined to £30,000 and seventeen ships, tried in vain to capture trading ports and routes from the Dutch East India Company, sailing sixty ships and sinewed with £540,000. But in 1615 the mission of Sir Thomas Roe resulted in the establishment of trade depots at Ahmadabad, Surat, Agra, and elsewhere in India; and Fort St. George was built and armed to protect them (1640). The first steps had been taken toward the British Empire in India.

Despite all temptations of mercantile interests, parliamentary prodding, and popular chauvinism, James for sixteen years kept to his policy of peace. The House of Commons begged him to enter the Thirty Years' War on the side of the endangered Protestants of Bohemia and Germany. It pleaded with him to marry his sole surviving son not to a Spanish but to a Protestant princess. It condemned James's relaxation of the anti-Catholic laws, urged him to order all Catholic children to be separated from their parents and brought up as Protestants, and warned him that toleration would lead to the growth of a Catholic Church frankly pledged to intolerance.[75]

In 1621 the divergence of views between Parliament and King almost rehearsed the conflict (1642) between the Long Parliament and Charles I. The Commons denounced the extravagance of the court and the persisting monopolies in restraint of trade; it fined and banished monopolists, rejecting their plea that a nascent industry had to be protected from competition. When James rebuked it for meddling in executive business, it issued (December 18) a historic "Great Protestation," which again affirmed that "the liberties, franchises, privileges, and jurisdictions of Parliament are the ancient and undoubted birthright and inheritance of the subjects of England," and added that "the arduous and urgent affairs concerning the king, state, and defense of the realm . . . are proper subjects and matter of council and debate in Parliament."[76] James angrily tore from the journal of the Commons the page containing this protestation; he dissolved the Parliament (February 8, 1622), ordered the imprisonment of four parliamentary leaders, Southampton, Selden, Coke, and Pym, and defiantly proceeded with Buckingham's plea for a marital alliance with Spain.

The reckless minister now urged the King to let him take Prince Charles to Madrid to show him off, to see the Infanta, and to conclude the match. James consented reluctantly, for he feared that Philip would send Charles back to England the laughingstock of Europe.

Arrived in Madrid (March 1623), Prince and Duke found the lovely Infanta unapproachable, and the Spanish populace as furious at the thought of her marrying a Protestant as the English were at the idea of Charles bringing home a Catholic. Philip and his minister Olivares gave the visitors every courtesy; Lope de Vega wrote a play for the welcoming festivities; Velázquez painted a portrait of Charles; and Buckingham wooed the

Spanish beauties almost to the point of honor. But it was made an indispensable condition of the marriage that English Catholics should receive religious freedom. Charles at once, James at last, agreed; the marriage treaty was signed; but when James further required Philip to promise the use of Spanish arms, if needed, to restore the Palatinate to Frederick, Philip refused to commit himself, and James ordered his son and his favorite home. We see the human side of a king in his letter to Charles (June 14, 1623): "I now repent me sore that ever I suffered you to go away. I care [neither] for match nor nothing, so I may once have you in my arms again. God grant it! God grant it! God grant it!"[77] The Infanta, in bidding Charles farewell, made him promise that he would have a care for the Catholics of England.[78] The returning Prince was hailed by England as a hero because he brought no bride. He brought a set of Titians instead.

And now Buckingham, angry at having made a fool of himself in Spain (as Olivares had assured him), turned to France for a marital alliance, and secured for Charles the youngest daughter of Henry IV—that Henrietta Maria whose Catholic faith was to be one of many thorns in the side of coming Parliaments. Then the rash young minister regained popularity with the House of Commons by importuning James—failing in health and in mind—to declare war against Spain. Reassembled in February 1624, Parliament followed policies formed in part by mercantile interests eager to capture Spanish booty, colonies or markets, and in part by a resolve to deflect Spain from lending aid to the Catholic Emperor against the Protestants of Germany. The people, having called James a coward for loving peace, now called him a tyrant for conscripting men to military service. The regiments raised, the funds voted, were inadequate, and James had the bitterness of concluding a peaceful reign with a futile war.

His ailments crowded upon him in these final years. He had poisoned his organs with Gargantuan and indiscriminate food and drink; now he suffered from catarrh, arthritis, gout, stone, jaundice, diarrhea, and hemorrhoids; he had himself bled every day until the least royal of his troubles made this superfluous.[79] He refused medicine, received the sacraments of the Church of England, and died (March 27, 1625) murmuring the last consolations of his faith.

Despite his vanity and coarseness, he was a better king than some who excelled him in vigor, courage, and enterprise. His absolutism was mainly a theory, tempered with a timidity that often yielded to a powerful Parliament. His pretensions to theology did not impede a will to tolerance far more generous than that of his predecessors. His brave love of peace gave England prosperity, and checked the venal bellicosity of his Parliament and the vicarious ardor of his people. His flatterers had called him the British Solomon because of his worldly wisdom, and Sully, failing to embroil him in Continental strife, termed him "the wisest fool in Christendom." But he was neither philosopher nor fool. He was only a scholar miscast as a ruler, a man of peace in an age mad with mythology and war. Better the King James Bible than a conqueror's crown.

CHAPTER VII

The Summons to Reason

1558–1649

I. SUPERSTITION

ARE people poor because they are ignorant, or ignorant because they are poor? It is a question that divides political philosophers between conservatives stressing heredity (inborn inequalities of mental capacity) and reformers relying on environment (the power of education and opportunity). In societies knowledge grows, and superstition wanes, with the increase and distribution of wealth. And yet even in a widely prosperous country—and especially among the harassed poor and the idle rich—thought has to live in a jungle of superstitions: astrology, numerology, palmistry, portents, the evil eye, witches, goblins, ghosts, demons, incantations, exorcisms, dream interpretations, oracles, miracles, quackery, and occult qualities, curative or injurious, in minerals, plants, and animals. Consider, then, the intellectual miasma poisoning the roots and wilting the flowers of science in a people whose wealth is scant or centered in a few. To the poor in body and mind superstition is a treasured element in the poetry of life, gilding dull days with exciting marvels, and redeeming misery with magic powers and mystic hopes.

Sir Thomas Browne, in 1646, required 652 pages to list and briefly treat the superstitions current in his day.[1] Nearly all these occultisms flourished among the Britons under Elizabeth and the early Stuarts. In 1597 King James VI published an authoritative *Demonologie*, which is one of the horrors of literature. He ascribed to witches the power to haunt houses, to make men and women love or hate, to transfer disease from one person to another, to kill by roasting a wax effigy, and to raise devastating storms; and he advocated the death penalty for all witches and magicians, and even for their customers.[2] When a tempest nearly wrecked him on his return from Denmark with his bride, he caused four suspects to be tortured into confessing that they had plotted to destroy him by magic means; and one of them, John Fain, after the most barbarous torments, was burned to death (1590).[3]

In this matter the Kirk agreed with the King, and lay magistrates lenient to witches were threatened with excommunication.[4] Between 1560 and 1600 some eight thousand women were burned as witches in a Scotland having hardly a million souls.[5] In England the belief in witchcraft was almost universal; learned physicians like William Harvey and Sir Thomas Browne shared it; the hardheaded Elizabeth allowed her laws of 1562 to make witchcraft a capital crime; eighty-one women were executed for it in her reign.[6] James moderated his fanaticism after passing from VI to I; he insisted on fair trials of the accused, exposed false confessions and accusations, and saved the lives of five women charged by a hysterical boy.[7] The hunt nearly ceased after Charles I, but it was resumed, and reached its height, under the rule of the Long Parliament, when in two years (1645–47) two hundred "witches" were consumed.[8]

One voice, amid the fury, appealed to reason. Reginald Scot, an Englishman despite his name, published at London in 1584 *The Discouerie of Witchcraft*, second only to Johann Wier's *De praestigiis daemonum* (Basel, 1564) in the dangerous attempt to moderate the sadistic superstition. Scot described the "witches" as poor old women who could harm no one; even if Satan did work through them they were rather to be pitied than to be burned; and to ascribe miracles to these crones was an insult to the miracles of Christ. He exposed the awful tortures that made witchcraft confessions worthless, the lax irregularity and injustice of trial procedure, the incredibilities gulped down by judges and inquisitors. The book had no effect.

In this atmosphere science tried to grow.

II. SCIENCE

Nevertheless, the expansion of commerce and industry were compelling the development of science. The Platonic and artistic strains in the Renaissance hardly harmonized with the swelling economy; the demand grew for a mental procedure that would deal with facts and quantities as well as with theories and ideas; the Aristotelian empiricism revived, shorn of its Alexandrian and medieval masks. The emphasis of Italian humanism on the glories of ancient literature and art made way for a less ethereal stress on current practical needs. Men had to count and calculate, measure and design, with competitive accuracy and speed; they needed tools of observation and recording; demands arose which were met by the invention of logarithms, analytical geometry, calculus, machines, the microscope, the telescope, statistical methods, navigational guides, and astronomical instruments. Throughout Western Europe lives were henceforth dedicated to meeting these needs.

In 1614 John Napier in Scotland and in 1620 Joost Bürgi in Switzerland independently proposed a system of logarithms (i.e., a logic of numbers) by which products, quotients, and roots could be quickly calculated from the tabulated relation of the given numbers as powers of a fixed number used as a base. Henry Briggs (1616) modified the method for common computation by proposing 10 as a base, and published tables giving the logarithms of all numbers from one to 20,000. Now two numbers could be multiplied by finding, in such tables, the number whose "log" was the sum of the logs of the numbers to be multiplied; and a could be divided by b by finding the number whose log was the log of b subtracted from the log of a. William Oughtred (1622) and Edmund Gunter (1624) constructed slide rules by which the results of logarithmic calculations could be read in a few seconds. These inventions halved the time given to arithmetical work by mathematicians, astronomers, statisticians, navigators, and engineers, and in effect lengthened their lives.[9] Kepler, who used the new method in computing planetary motions, addressed an enthusiastic panegyric to the Laird of Merchiston (1620), not knowing that Napier was then three years dead. Napier himself had made a little miscalculation, having figured that the world would come to an end between 1688 and 1700.[10]

Mathematicians and astronomers were still closely allied, for the reckoning of celestial motions, the charting of the calendar, and the guidance of navigation required complex manipulations of astronomic measurements. As a mathematician, Thomas Harriot established the standard form of modern algebra, introduced the signs for root, "greater than" and "less than," replaced clumsy capitals with small letters to indicate numbers, and hit upon the beneficent trick of placing all the quantities in an equation on one side and zero on the other. As an astronomer, he discovered the spots on the sun, and his observations of Jupiter's satellites were made independently of Galileo's. George Chapman, himself a monster of learning, thought Harriot's knowledge to be "incomparable and bottomless."[11]

Astronomy was still dripping with astrology. "Horary" astrology decided whether the stars favored the enterprise of the hour; "judicial" astrology foretold affairs in general, usually with judicious ambiguity; "natural" astrology disclosed the destiny of an individual from his horoscope—an examination of the position of the stars at the moment of his birth; all these are found in Shakespeare (though not proving his belief), and in our time. The moon, in astrological theory, produced tides, tears, madmen, and thieves (cf. Shakespeare, *I Henry IV*, I, ii, 15), and each sign of the zodiac controlled the character and fate of specific organs in the human anatomy (*Twelfth Night*, I, iii, 146–51). John Dee symbolized the time by mingling astrology, magic, mathematics, and geography: he engaged in crystal gazing, wrote a *Treatise of the Rosie Crucean Secrets*, was charged with practicing sorcery against Queen Mary Tudor (1555), drew up geographical and hydrographical charts for Elizabeth, proposed a northwest passage to China, invented the phrase "the British Empire," lectured on Euclid before large audiences in Paris, defended the Copernican theory, advocated the adoption of the Gregorian calendar (170 years before England resigned itself to such a papistical contraption), and died at eighty-one; here was a full life! His pupil, Thomas Digges, promoted the acceptance of the Copernican hypothesis in England, and anticipated Bruno's notion of an infinite universe.[12] Thomas and his father, Leonard Digges, used "perspective glasses" which were probably forerunners of the telescope; and William Gascoigne invented (c. 1639) the micrometer, which enabled observers to adjust a telescope with unprecedented accuracy. Jeremiah Horrocks, a poor Lancashire curate who died at twenty-four, ascribed an elliptical orbit to the moon, and predicted—and observed (1639) for the first recorded time—the transit of Venus across the sun. His speculations on the forces moving the planets helped Newton to the theory of universal gravitation.

Meanwhile the study of terrestrial magnetism was also preparing for Newton. In 1544 Georg Hartmann, a German clergyman, and in 1576 Robert Norman, an English compass maker, independently discovered the tendency of the magnetic needle, when freely suspended at its center of gravity, to "dip" from a horizontal position to one at an angle to the earth's surface. Norman's book, *The Newe Attractive* (1581), suggested that the "joynt Respective" to which the needle dipped lay within the earth.[13]

This fascinating lead was followed by William Gilbert, physician to Elizabeth. After seventeen years of research and experiment—financed by his inherited fortune, and sometimes watched by the Queen—he set forth his results in the first great book of English science, *De magnete . . . et de magno magnete tellure* (1600)—*On the Magnet . . . and the Great Magnet the Earth.* He laid a pivoted compass needle successively at different points upon a globular lodestone, he marked with lines on the globe the directions in which the needle successively set, he prolonged each line to form a great circle around the stone, and he found that all these circles crossed at two diametrically opposite points on the globe; these were the magnetic poles, which, in the case of the earth, Gilbert mistakenly identified with the geographical poles. He described the earth as an enormous magnet, explained thereby the behavior of the magnetic needle, and showed that any iron bar left for a long time in a north-and-south position would become magnetized. A magnet placed at either pole of the globular lodestone took a position vertical to the globe; placed at any point midway between the poles (such points constituting the magnetic equator), the magnet lay horizontal. Gilbert concluded that the dip of the needle would be greater the nearer it was placed to the geographical poles of the earth; and though this was not quite correct, it was approximately confirmed by Henry Hudson in his exploration of the Arctic in 1608. From his own observations Gilbert drew up directions for calculating latitude from the degree of the magnetic dip. He suggested that "from about a magnetic body the virtue magnetical is poured out on every side"; he ascribed the rotation of the earth to the influence of this magnetic field. Passing on to the study of electricity—wherein little had been done since antiquity—he proved that many other substances besides amber could, when rubbed, generate frictional electricity; and from the Greek for *amber* he formed the word *electric* to denote a power to deflect a magnetic needle. He believed that all heavenly bodies are endowed with magnetism; Kepler was to use this idea to explain the motion of the planets. Most of Gilbert's work was an admirable example of experimental procedure, and its effects on science and industry were immeasurable.

The advance of science appeared more dramatically in the efforts of adventurous or acquisitive spirits to explore the "great magnet" for geographical or commercial purposes. In 1576 Sir Humphrey Gilbert (no kin to William) published a suggestive *Discourse . . . for a New Passage to Cataia*—i.e., "Cathay," or China—proposing a northwest sailing through or around Canada. Sir Martin Frobisher, in that year, set out with three small vessels to find such a route. One of his ships foundered, another deserted; he went ahead in the tiny twenty-five-ton *Gabriel;* he reached Baffin Land, but the Eskimos fought him, and he returned to England for more men and supplies. His later voyages were diverted from geography by a vain hunt for gold. Gilbert took up the quest for a northwest passage, but was drowned in the attempt (1583). Four years later John Davys pushed through the strait now named for him; then he fought the Armada, went off to the South Seas with Thomas Cavendish, discovered the Falkland Islands, and was killed by Japanese pirates near Singapore (1605). Cavendish explored southern South America, accomplished the third circumnavigation of the globe, and died at sea (1592). Henry Hudson navigated the Hudson River (1609), and, in another voyage, reached Hudson Bay; but his crew, maddened with hardships and longing for home, mutinied and set him adrift, with eight others, in a small open boat (1611); they were never heard of again. William Baffin explored the bay and the island that bear his name, ventured as far north as 77° 45′—a latitude not reached again for 236 years—and had the further distinction of first finding longitude by observation of the moon. Richard Hakluyt saw in such ships and hearts of oak an epic of courage and terror surpassing any *Iliad*, and he gathered their narratives into successive volumes, the best-known of which are those published as *The Principal Navigations, Voyages, and Discoveries of the English Nation* (1589, 1598–1600); Samuel Purchas expanded the record in *Hakluytus Posthumus, or Purchas his*

Pilgrimes (1625). So, by the greed for gold or trade, and the zest for far-off peril and scenes, geography unwittingly grew.

The best work of this age in physics, chemistry, and biology was done on the Continent; in England, however, Sir Kenelm Digby discovered the necessity of oxygen to plant life, and Robert Fludd, mystic and medico, advocated vaccination 150 years before Jenner. Medical prescriptions continued to rely on their repulsiveness for their effect; the official London pharmacopoeia of 1618 recommended bile, blood, claws, cockscomb, fur, sweat, saliva, scorpions, snakeskin, wood lice, and spider web as medicaments; and bloodletting was a first resort.[14] Nevertheless this period boasts of Thomas Parr ("old Parr"), who was presented to Charles I in 1635 as still in good health at the alleged age of 152. Parr did not profess to know his exact age, but his parish authorities dated his birth in 1483; he claimed to have joined the army in 1500, and he recalled in detail the dissolution of the monasteries by Henry VIII (1536). "You have lived longer than other men," said Charles I. "What have you done more than they?" Parr replied that he had fertilized a wench when he was over a hundred years old and had done public penance for it. He had subsisted almost entirely on potatoes, greens, coarse bread, and buttermilk, with rarely a taste of meat. For a while he became a lion in London parlors and pubs, and he was so handsomely feasted that he died within a year of meeting the King. Sir William Harvey performed a post-mortem on him, found him free of arteriosclerosis, and diagnosed his death as due to change of air and food.[15]

It was Harvey who provided the scientific climax of the age by explaining the circulation of the blood—"the most momentous event in medical history since Galen's time."[16] Born at Folkstone in 1578, he studied at Cambridge, then at Padua under Fabrizio d'Acquapendente. Returning, he settled down to medical practice in London, and became personal physician to James I and Charles I. Through patient years he carried on experiments and dissections on animals and cadavers, and particularly studied the flow and the course of blood in wounds. He came to his main theory in 1615,[17] but belatedly published it at Frankfurt in 1628 as a modest *Exercitatio anatomica de motu cordis et sanguinis in animalibus*—the first and greatest classic in English medicine.

The steps to his discovery illustrate the internationalism of science. For over a thousand years the functions of heart and blood had been interpreted as by Galen in the second century A.D. Galen had supposed that blood flowed to the tissues from the liver as well as the heart; that air passed from the lungs to the heart; that the arteries and veins carried twin streams of blood, which were propelled and received by the heart in tides of ebb and flow; and that blood passed from the right to the left side of the heart through pores in the septum between the ventricles.

Leonardo da Vinci (c. 1506) questioned the view that air passed from lungs to heart; Vesalius (1543) denied the existence of pores in the septum, and his masterly sketches of arteries and veins revealed their terminals as so minute and neighborly as almost to suggest passage and circulation; Fabrizio showed that valves in the veins made it impossible for venous blood to flow from the heart. The Galenic theory faded away. In 1553 Michael Servetus, and in 1558 Realdo Colombo, discovered the *pulmonary* circulation of the blood—its passage from the right chamber of the heart through the pulmonary artery to and through the lungs, its purification there by aeration, and its return via the pulmonary vein to the left chamber of the heart. Andrea Cesalpino (c. 1571) tentatively—as we shall see—anticipated the full theory of circulation. Harvey's work turned the theory into a demonstrated fact.

While Francis Bacon, his patient, was extolling induction, Harvey proceeded to his illuminating conclusion by a striking combination of deduction and induction. Estimating the amount of blood pressed out of the heart by each systole, or contraction, to be one half a fluid ounce, he calculated that in half an hour the heart would pour into the arteries over 500 fluid ounces—a larger quantity than the entire body contained. Where did all this blood come from? It seemed impossible that so great a quantity should be produced, hour after hour, from the digestion of food. Harvey concluded that the blood pumped out of the heart was returned to it, and that there was no other apparent avenue for this but the veins. By simple experiments and observations—as by pressing a finger upon some superficial vein—it was readily shown that venous blood flowed away from the tissues and toward the heart.

> When I surveyed my mass of evidence, whether derived from vivisections and my previous reflections on them, or from the ventricles of the heart and the vessels that enter into and issue from them . . . and frequently and seriously bethought me . . . what might be the quantity of blood which was transmitted . . . and not finding it possible that this could be supplied by the juices of the ingested aliment without the veins on the one hand becoming drained, and the arteries on the other getting ruptured through the excessive charge of blood, unless the blood should somehow find its way from the arteries into the veins, and so return to the right side of the heart; when, I say, I surveyed all this evidence, I began to think whether there might not be *a motion as it were in a circle* . . . And now I may be allowed to give my view of the circulation of the blood.[18]

He had long hesitated to publish his conclusions, knowing the conservatism of the medical profession of his time. He predicted that no one over forty years of age would accept his theory.[19] "I have heard him say," reported Aubrey, "that after his book of the *Circulation of the Blood* came out, he fell mightily in his practice, and 'twas believed by the vulgar that he was crack-brained."[20] Not until Malpighi in 1660 demonstrated the existence of capillaries conveying blood from the arteries to the veins did the learned world concede the circulation to be a fact. The new view illuminated almost every field of physiology, and affected the old problem of the interrelation between body and mind. Said Harvey:

> Every affection of the mind that is attended with either pain or pleasure, hope or fear, is the cause of an agitation whose influence extends to the heart . . . In almost every affection [emotion] . . . the countenance changes, and the blood appears to course hither and thither. In anger the eyes are fiery and the pupils contracted; in modesty the cheeks are suffused with blushes . . . in lust how quickly is the member distended with blood![21]

Harvey continued to serve Charles I almost to the latter's bitter end. He accompanied Charles when revolution drove the King from London, was with him at the battle of Edgehill, and narrowly escaped death.[22] Meanwhile the rebels sacked his London house and destroyed his manuscripts and anatomical collections. Perhaps he had made a variety of enemies by his sharp temper and views. He rated man as "but a great mischievous baboon," says Aubrey, and thought that "we Europeans knew not how to order or govern our Woemen," and that "the Turks were the only people who used them wisely."[23] Still vigorous at seventy-three, he published a treatise on embryology, *Exercitationes de generatione animalium* (1651). Rejecting the prevalent belief in the spontaneous generation of minute organisms out of decaying flesh, Harvey held that "all animals, even those that produce their young alive, including man himself, are evolved out of an egg"; and he coined the phrase *Omne animal ex ovo*—"Every animal comes from an agg." He died six years later of paralysis, bequeathing most of his fortune of twenty thousand pounds to the Royal College of Physicians, and ten pounds to Thomas Hobbes "as a token of his love."

III. THE RISE AND FALL OF FRANCIS BACON: 1561–1621

We come now to the greatest and proudest intellect of the age. We have already noted his birth and lineage, his education in letters, diplomacy, and law, his unexpected poverty, his unheard pleas for office, his futile cautioning and reluctant prosecution of his beneficent, guilty friend. Learning and ambition so consumed him that he had no lust left for women; he had, however, a liking for young men.[24] Finally, at forty-five (1606), he married Alice Barnham, who brought him £220 a year. But he gave no "hostages to fortune"—he had no children.

On the accession of James I, Bacon, in a letter of adulation profuse in the manner of the time, suggested himself to the King as fit and due for a governmental post. Son of a Lord Keeper of the Great Seal, nephew or cousin to the Cecils, he felt that his long wait for office reflected some hostility on the part of the commanding ministers; and perhaps his impatient opportunism was an effect as well as a cause of his tardy admission to place. He had already served in Parliament for nineteen years, usually defending the government, and winning repute for wide learning, constructive thought, and clear and striking speech. Periodically he sent to the King "memories" eloquent with prudent advice: how to improve mutual understanding and co-operation between Commons and Lords, to unite the parliaments of England and Scotland, to end persecution for religious diversity, to pacify Ireland by conciliating its Catholics, to give greater freedom to Catholics in England without opening the door to papal claims, and to find a compromise between Anglicans and Puritans. "To carry out this program," in the judgment of the historian who has most thoroughly studied the politics of this period, "would have been to avert the evils of the next half-century."[25] James put the proposals aside as impracticable in the current state of opinion, and contented himself with including Bacon in the three hundred knighthoods that he distributed in 1603. Sir Francis still cooled his heels.

Nevertheless his skill as a lawyer slowly raised him to affluence. By 1607 he estimated his wealth at £24,155.[26] On his luxurious estate at Gorhambury, manned with select and expensive servants and alert secretaries like Thomas Hobbes, he could enjoy the beauty and comfort that he loved wisely but too well. He nursed his health by gardening, and built amid his gardens a costly retreat for his scholastic privacy. He wrote like a philosopher and lived like a prince. He saw no reason why reason should be penniless, or why Solomon should not be king.

He did not fall far short. In 1607 James, valuing him at last, made him solicitor general; in 1613, attorney general; in 1616, a member of the Privy Council; in 1617, Lord Keeper of the Great Seal; in 1618, Chancellor. New dignities were added to grace his powers: in 1618 he was created first Baron Verulam; in January 1621, Viscount St. Albans. When James went to Scotland he left his Chancellor to rule England. Bacon "gave audience in great state to ambassadors," and lived in such splendor at Gorhambury that it "seemed as if the court was there, and not in Whitehall or St. James."[27]

All was won save honor. In the pursuit of place Bacon had repeatedly sacrificed principle. As attorney general he used his influence to secure judicial verdicts desired by the King.[28] As Keeper of the Seal he defended and protected the most oppressive monopolies, apparently to keep the good will of Buckingham. As judge he accepted substantial presents from persons suing in his court. All this was in the loose custom of the age: public officials were poorly paid, and they recompensed themselves with "gifts" from those whom they aided; James confessed, "If I were . . . to punish those who take bribes, I should soon not have a single subject left"; and James himself took bribes.[29]

The Parliament that assembled in January 1621 was in angry revolt against the King. It hated Bacon as James's best advocate, who had ruled that monopolies were legal. If it could not yet depose the King it could impeach his minister. In February it named a committee to inquire into the courts of justice. In March the committee reported that it had found many irregularities, especially in the conduct of the Lord Chancellor. Twenty-three specific cases of corruption were charged against him. He appealed to the King to save him, predicting that "those who now strike at the Chancellor will soon strike at the Crown."[30] James advised him to acknowledge the charge and so set an example deterrent to further venality in office. On April 22 Bacon sent in his confession to the House of Lords. He admitted taking gifts from litigants, as other judges did; he denied that his decisions had been thereby influenced—in several cases he had ruled against the giver. The Lords condemned him "to pay a fine of £40,000; to be imprisoned in the Tower during the King's pleasure; to be forever incapable to holding any public office . . . in the Commonwealth; never to sit in Parliament nor come within the verge of the Court." He was taken to the Tower on May 31, but was released within four days by order of the King, who also remitted the ruinous fine. The chastened Chancellor retired to Gorhambury and tried to live more simply. In cipher, on a paper left by Bacon at his death, his first biographer, Rawley, found the famous statement, "I was the justest judge that was in England these fifty years. But it was the justest censure in Parliament that was these 200 years."[31]

The effects of the impeachment were good. It lessened corruption in office, especially in the courts; and it set a precedent for the responsibility of the King's ministers to Parliament. It turned Francis Bacon back from politics, where he had been a liberal in views and a reactionary in practice, to his alternative pursuit of science and philosophy, where he would "ring the bell that called the wits together," and would proclaim, in majestic prose, the revolt and program of reason.

IV. THE GREAT RENEWAL

Philosophy had long been his refuge from affairs, if not his secret love and happiest aptitude. He had already, in 1603–5, published a noble work, *The Proficience and Advancement of Learning*, but that seemed to him rather a prospectus than a performance. In 1609 he had written to the Bishop of Ely, "If God give me leave to write a just and perfect volume of philosophy . . .";[32] and in 1610 to Casaubon, "To bring about the better ordering of man's life . . . by the help of sound and true contemplations—this is the thing I aim at."[33]

During those harassed years of office he had conceived—with a rash assumption of abundant days—a magisterial plan for the renovation of science and philosophy. Seven months before his fall he announced the plan in a Latin work addressed to all Europe, boldly entitled *Instauratio Magna (The Great Renewal)*. The title page itself was a challenge: it showed a vessel passing full sail through the Pillars of Hercules into the Atlantic; and where a medieval motto had set between those pillars the warning *"Ne plus ultra"* ([Go] no farther beyond), Bacon wrote, *"Multi pertransibunt, et augebitur scientia"* (Many will pass through, and knowledge will be increased). The proud proemium added, "Francis of Verulam reasoned thus with himself, and judged it to be for the interest of the present and future generations that they should be made acquainted with his thoughts."[34]

Finding that "in what is now done in the matter of science there is only a whirling round about, and perpetual agitation, ending where it begins," he concluded that

> there was but one course left . . . to try the whole thing anew upon a better plan, and to commence a total reconstruction of sciences, [practical] arts, and all human knowledge, raised upon the proper foundation; . . . Moreover, because he knew not how long it might be before these things would occur to any one else . . . he resolved to publish at once so much as he had been able to complete . . . that in case of his death there might remain some outline and project of that which he had conceived . . . All other ambition seemed poor in his eyes compared with the work which he had in hand.[35]

He dedicated the entire project to James I, with apologies for "having stolen from your affairs so much time as was required for this work," but hoping that the result would "go to the memory of your name and the honor of your age"—and it did. James was a man of considerable learning and good will; if he could be persuaded to finance the plan, what progress might not be made? As Roger Bacon, far back in 1268, had sent to Pope Clement IV his *Opus majus* seeking aid for a proposed expansion of knowledge, so now his namesake appealed to his sovereign to undertake, as a "royal work," the organization of scientific research and the philosophical unification of the results for the material and moral benefit of mankind. He reminded James of the "philosopher kings"—Nerva, Trajan, Hadrian, Antoninus Pius, and Marcus Aurelius—who had given good government to the Roman Empire for a century (A.D. 96–180). Was it because of his need and hope for state funds that he had consistently and ruinously supported the King?

A further preface asked the reader to look upon current science as porous with error and shamefully stagnant, for

> the greatest wits in each successive age have been forced out of their own course; men of capacity and intellect above the vulgar had been fain, for reputation's sake, to bow to the judgment of the time and the multitude; and thus, if any contemplations of a higher order took light anywhere, they were presently blown out by the winds of vulgar opinions.[36]

And to pacify the theologians, who were powerful with the people or the King, he cautioned his readers to "confine the sense" of his undertaking "within the limits of duty in respect of things divine." He disclaimed any intention to deal with religious beliefs or affairs; "the business in hand . . . is not an opinion to be held, but a work to be done . . . I am laboring to lay the foundation not of any sect or doctrine, but of human utility and power."[37] He urged others to come forward and join him in the work, and trusted that successive generations would carry it on.

In an imperial prospectus, *Distributio operis*, he offered a plan of the enterprise. First, he would attempt a new classification of existing or desirable sciences, and would allot to them their problems and fields of research; this he accomplished in *The Advancement of Learning*, which he translated and expanded in *De augmentis scientiarum* (1623) to reach a Continental audience. Second, he would examine the shortcomings of contemporary logic, and seek a "more perfect use of human reason" than that which Aristotle had formulated in his logical treatises collectively known as the *Organon*; this Bacon did in his *Novum Organum* (1620). Third, he would begin a "natural history" of the "phenomena of the universe"—astronomy, physics, biology. Fourth, he would exhibit, in a "Ladder of the Intellect" (*Scala intellectus*), examples of scientific inquiry according to his new method. Fifth, as "Forerunners" (*Prodromi*), he would describe "such things as I myself have discovered." And sixth, he would begin to expound that philosophy which, from sciences so pursued, would be developed and certified. "The completion, however, of this last part is . . . both above my strength and beyond my hope." To us who now flounder and gasp in the ocean of knowledge and specialties, Bacon's program seems majestically vain; but knowledge was not then so immense and minute; and the brilliance of the parts performed forgives the presumption of the whole. When he told Cecil, "I have taken all knowledge to be my province," he did not mean that he could embrace all sciences in detail, but only that he purposed to survey the sciences "as from a rock," with a view to their co-ordination and encouragement. William Harvey said of Bacon that he "wrote philosophy like a lord chancellor";[38] yes, and planned it like an imperial general.

We feel the range and sharpness of Bacon's mind as we follow him in *The Advancement of Learning*. He offers his ideas with unwonted modesty, as "not much better than that noise . . . which musicians make while they are tuning their instruments";[39] but he strikes here nearly all his characteristic notes. He calls for the multiplication and support of colleges, libraries, laboratories, biological gardens, museums of science and industry; for the better payment of teachers and researchers; for ampler funds to finance scientific experiments; for better intercommunication, co-operation, and division of labor among the universities of Europe.[40] He does not lose his perspective in the worship of science; he defends a general and liberal education, including literature and philosophy, as promoting a wise judgment of ends to accompany the scientific improvement of means.[41] He tries to classify the sciences in a logical order, to determine their fields and bounds, and to direct each to major problems awaiting inquiry and solution. Many of his demands have been met by the sciences—for better clinical records, for the prolongation of life by preventive medicine, for the careful examination of "psychical phenomena," and for the development of social psychology. He even anticipated our contemporary studies in the technique of success.[42]

The second and boldest part of the Great Renewal was an attempt to formulate a new method of science. Aristotle had recognized, and occasionally preached, induction, but the predominant mode of his logic was deduction, and its ideal was the syllogism. Bacon felt that the old *Organon* had kept science stagnant by its stress on theoretical thought rather than practical observation. His *Novum Organum* proposed a new organ and system of thought—the inductive study of nature itself through experience and experiment. Though this book too was left incomplete, it is, with all its imperfections, the most brilliant production in English philosophy, the first clear call for an Age of Reason. It was written in Latin, but in such lucid, pithy sentences that half of it radiates epigrams. The very first lines compacted a philosophy, announcing the inductive revolution, foreshadowing the Industrial Revolution, and giving the empirical key to Hobbes and Locke and Mill and Spencer.

> Man, being the servant and interpreter of Nature, can do and understand so much, and so much only, as he had observed, in fact or in thought, of the course of Nature; beyond this he neither knows anything nor can do anything . . . Human knowledge and human power meet in one; for where the course is not known, the effect cannot be produced. Nature, to be commanded, must be obeyed.*

And as Descartes seventeen years later, in the *Discourse on Method*, would propose to begin philosophy by doubting everything, so Bacon here demands an "expurgation of the intellect" as the first step in the Renewal. "Human knowledge as we have it is a mere medley and ill-digested mass, made up of much credulity and much accident, and also of the childish notions which are at first imbibed."[44] Therefore we must, at the start, clear our minds, so far as we can, of all preconceptions, prejudices, assumptions, and theories; we must turn away even from Plato and Aristotle; we must sweep out of our thought the "idols," or time-honored illusions and fallacies, born of our personal idiosyncrasies of judgment or the traditional beliefs and dogmas of our group; we must banish all logical tricks of wishful thinking, all verbal absurdities of obscure thought. We must put behind us all those majestic deductive systems of philosophy which proposed to draw a thousand eternal verities out of a few axioms and principles. There is no magic hat in science; everything taken from the hat in works must first be put into it by observation or experiment. And not by mere casual observation, nor by "simple enumeration" of data, but by "experience . . . sought for, experiment." Thereupon Bacon, so often belittled as ignoring the true method of science, proceeds to describe the actual method of modern science:

> The true method of experience first lights the candle [by hypothesis], and then by means of the candle shows the way, commencing as it does with experience duly ordered . . . and from it educing axioms ["first fruits," provisional conclusions], and from established axioms again new experiments . . . Experiment itself shall judge.[45]

However, Bacon was wary of hypotheses; they were too often suggested by tradition, prejudice, or desire—i.e., again by "idols"; he distrusted any procedure in which hypothesis, consciously or not, would

---

* The famous phrase "Knowledge is power" does not occur, in that form, in Bacon's extant works; but in a fragment of his *Meditationes sacrae* he writes, ". . . *ipsa scientia protestas est*"—knowledge itself is power.[43] The idea, of course, runs all through Bacon's writings.

select from experience confirmatory data and gloss over, or be blind to, contrary evidence. To avoid this pitfall, he proposed a laborious induction by accumulation of all facts pertinent to a problem, their analysis, comparison, classification, and correlation, and, "by a due process of exclusion and rejection," the progressive elimination of one hypothesis after another, until the "form" or underlying law and essence of a phenomenon should be revealed.[46] Knowledge of the "form" would give increasing control of the event, and science would gradually remake the environment and possibly man himself.

For this, Bacon felt, is the ultimate aim—that the method of science shall be applied to the rigorous analysis and resolute remolding of human character. He urges a study of the instincts and emotions, which bear the same relation to the mind as winds to the sea.[47] But here especially the fault lies not merely in the seeking of knowledge but in its transmission. Man could be remade by an enlightened education, if we were willing to draw first-rate minds into pedagogy by giving them adequate remuneration and honor.[48] Bacon admires the Jesuits as educators and wishes they were "on our side."[49] He condemns compendiums, approves college dramatics, and pleads for more science in the curriculum. Science and education so conceived would be (as in *The New Atlantis*) not the tool and handmaid, but the guide and goal, of government. And the confident Chancellor concludes, "I stake all on the victory of art over Nature in the race."

V. A STATESMAN'S PHILOSOPHY

Here, we feel, is a powerful mind—a man, one in a century, at home equally in philosophy and politics. It would be interesting to know what this philosopher thought in politics, and what this politician thought in philosophy.

Not that he had any system in philosophy, or left any orderly exposition of his thought, except in logic. The trend of his ideas is clear, but their form is that of a man who had to rush repeatedly out of the calm of philosophy to try a case in law, to fight an opposition in Parliament, or to counsel an unteachable King. We must gather his views from incidental remarks and literary fragments, including his *Essays* (1597, 1612, 1625). With the vanity inherent in authorship, Bacon wrote, in dedicating these to Buckingham, "I do conceive . . . [the] volume may last as long as books last." In his letters his style is labored and involved, so that his wife confessed, "I do not understand his enigmatical folded writing";[50] in the *Essays* he concealed still intenser labor, disciplined his pen to clarity, and achieved such compact force of expression that very few pages in English prose can match them for significant matter pressed with luminous similes into perfect form. It is as if Tacitus had taken to philosophy, and had condescended to be clear.

Bacon's wisdom is worldly. He leaves metaphysics to the mystical or the rash; even his vaulting ambition rarely leaped from the fragment to the whole. Sometimes, however, he seems to plunge into a determinist materialism: "In nature nothing really exists besides individual bodies performing pure individual acts according to a fixed law";[51] and "inquiries into nature have the best result when they begin with physics and end in mathematics";[52] but "nature" here may mean only the external world. He preferred the skeptical pre-Socratic philosophers to Plato and Aristotle, and he praised the materialistic Democritus.[53] But then he accepts a sharp distinction between body and soul,[54] and anticipates Bergson's chiding of the intellect as a "constitutional materialist": "The human understanding is infected by the sight of what takes place in the mechanical arts . . . and so imagines that something similar goes on in the universal nature of things."[55] He rejects in advance the mechanistic biology of Descartes.

With careful ambivalence he "seasons" his philosophy "with religion as with salt."[56] "I had rather believe all the fables in the [Golden] Legend, and the Talmud, and the Alcoran, than that this universal frame is without a mind."[57] He puts atheism in its place in a famous passage twice repeated.[58] His analysis of the causes of atheism illuminates the theme of this volume:

> The causes of atheism are divisions in religion, if they be many; for any one main division addeth zeal to both sides, but many divisions introduce atheism. Another is scandal of priests. And lastly, learned times, specially with peace and prosperity; for troubles and adversities do more bow men's minds to religion.[59]

He lays it down as a rule that "all knowledge is to be limited by religion."[60] According to his chaplain, Rawley, he "repaired frequently, when his health would permit him, to the services of the church . . . and died in the true faith established in the Church of England."[61] Nevertheless, like his great predecessor William of Ockham, he availed himself of the distinction between theological and philosophical truth: faith might hold to beliefs for which science and philosophy could find no evidence, but philosophy should depend only on reason, and science should seek purely secular explanations in terms of physical cause and effect.[62]

Despite his zest for knowledge, Bacon subordinates it to morality; there would be no gain to humanity if the extension of knowledge brought no gain in benevolence. "Of all virtues and dignities of the mind, goodness is the greatest."[63] However, his usual enthusiasm subsides when he speaks of the Christian virtues. Virtue should be practiced in moderation, for the wicked may take advantage of the indiscreetly good.[64] A little dissimulation is necessary to success, if not to civilization. Love is a madness, and marriage is a noose. "He that hath wife and children hath given hostages to fortune; for they are impediments to great enterprises . . . The best works, and of the greatest merit for the public, have proceeded from the unmarried or childless men." Like Elizabeth and Hildebrand, Bacon approved of clerical celibacy. "A single life doth well with churchmen, for charity will hardly water the ground when it must first fill a pool."[65] (Note his flair for metaphor and Anglo-Saxon brevity.) Friendship is better than love, and married men make unsteady friends. Bacon talks of love and marriage in the strain of a man who has sacrificed the tender emotions to ambition, and who could rule a kingdom better than his home.

His political philosophy faced conditions rather than theories. He had the courage to say a good word for Machiavelli, and candidly accepted the principle that states are not bound by the moral code taught to their citizens. He felt, like Nietzsche, that a good war halloweth any cause. "Neither is the opinion of some of the Schoolmen to be received, that a war cannot be justly made but upon a precedent injury or provocation . . . A just fear of an imminent danger, though there be no blow given, is a lawful cause of war." In any event, "a just and honorable war is the true exercise" to keep a nation in trim.[66] "For empire and greatness it is of most importance that a nation profess arms as their principal honor, study, and occupation." A powerful navy is a guarantee of neighborly respect; "to be master of the sea is the very epitome of monarchy."[67] "In the youth of a state arms do flourish; in the middle age of a state, learning; and then both of them together for a time; in the declining age of a state, mercantile acts and merchants."[68] Townsmen make poor warriors, peasants better, yeomen best. Hence Bacon, like More, condemned enclosures, as reducing the proportion of landowners in the population. He deprecated the concentration of wealth as a chief cause of sedition and revolt. Of these

> the first remedy or prevention is to remove by all means possible that material cause . . . which is want and poverty. . . . To which purpose serveth the opening and well-balancing of trade; the cherishing of manufactures; the banishing of idleness; the repression of waste and excess by sumptuary laws; the improvement and husbanding of the soil; the regulating of prices of things vendible; the moderation of taxes . . . Above all things good policy is to be used that the treasures and monies in a state be not gathered into a few hands . . . Money is like muck, not good except it be spread.[69]

Bacon distrusted Parliament as composed of uneducated and intolerant landowners and merchants or their agents; he thought James I by comparison informed and humane; even the King's theoretical absolutism seemed benevolent as the alternative to greedy factions and violent creeds. Like his contemporary Richelieu, he considered the centralization of authority in the king, and the royal subordination of the great landlords, a necessary step in the evolution of orderly government; and like Voltaire, he thought it easier to educate one man than a multitude. His own great wealth did not disturb him, and James proved obdurately wedded to extravagance, taxes, and peace.

Bacon had smiled at "the philosophers" who "make imaginary laws for imaginary commonwealths; their discourses are as the stars, which give little light because they are so high." But in his tired age he yielded to the temptation to picture the kind of society in which he would have men live. He had doubtless read More's *Utopia* (1516); Campanella had just published his *City of the Sun* (1623); now (1624) Bacon wrote *The New Atlantis*. "We sailed from Peru (where we had continued for the space of one whole year) for China and Japan by the South Sea." A long calm, failing rations, a providential isle, a people living happily under laws made for them by a late King Salomon. Instead of a parliament, a Salomon's House—an aggregation of observatories, laboratories, libraries, zoological and botanical gardens—manned by scientists, economists, technicians, physicians, psychologists, and philosophers, chosen (as in Plato's *Republic*) by equal tests after equal educational opportunity, and then (without elections) governing the state, or, rather, ruling nature in the interest of man. "The end of our Foundation," one of these rulers explains to the barbarians from Europe, "is the knowledge of causes and secret motions of things, and the enlarging of the bounds of Human Empire, to the effecting of all things possible."[70] Already, in this South Pacific enchantment, the Salomonic wizards have invented microscopes, telescopes, self-winding clocks, submarines, automobiles, and airplanes; they have discovered anesthetics, hypnosis, and ways of preserving health and lengthening life; they have found ways of grafting plants, generating new species, transmuting metals, and transmitting music to distant places. In Salomon's House government and science are bound together, and all the tools and organization of research that Bacon had begged James to provide are there part of the equipment of the state. The island is economically independent; it avoids foreign trade as a snare to war; it imports knowledge, but not goods. So the humbled philosopher replaces the proud statesman, and the same man who had advised an occasional war as a social tonic now in his closing years dreams of a paradise of peace.

VI. THE CHANTICLEER OF REASON

He continued working to the end. A year after his retirement he published a *History of the Reign of Henry VII*. It set a new standard for historiography: a clear account, in fine, strong prose, of issues, policies, and events; a just, impartial, penetrating sketch of a ruler unidealized, illuminatingly real.[71] A medley of treatises followed: *History* [i.e., a study] *of Winds, History of Density and Rarity, History of Life and Death, Sylva Sylvarum,* and further essays. He had unexpected leisure now—no place, no children, no friends, for the place seekers who had crowded about him in his days of power were scraping before other doors. "What comrades have you in your work?" he asked a correspondent. "As for me, I am in the completest solitude."[72]

Seeking to test how long snow could keep flesh from putrefaction, he interrupted a journey one day in spring to buy a fowl. He killed it and stuffed it with snow, then found himself chilled. He went to the nearby home of Lord Arundel and was there put to bed. He thought the trouble would soon pass; he wrote that the experiment had "succeeded excellently well." He had preserved the fowl—but he lost his life. Fever consumed him, phlegm choked him; on April 9, 1626, he died, aged sixty-five, the glowing candle suddenly snuffed out.

He was not, as Pope thought, "the wisest, brightest, meanest of mankind."[73] Montaigne was wiser, Voltaire brighter, Henry VIII meaner; and Bacon's enemies called him kindly, helpful, and quick to forgive. He was self-seeking to the verge of servility, and proud enough to anger the gods; but we share these faults sufficiently to pardon his humanity for the light that he shed. His egotism was the wind in his sails. To see ourselves as others see us would be crippling.

He was not a scientist, but a philosopher of science. His range of observation was immense, but his field of speculation was too vast to allow him much time for special investigations; he attempted some, with little result. He fell far behind the progress of contemporary science. He rejected the Copernican astronomy, but gave excellent reasons for doing so.[74] He ignored Kepler, Galileo, and Napier. He often noted (as in *The New Atlantis*), but still underrated, the role of imagination, hypothesis, and deduction in scientific research. His proposal for a patient collection and classification of facts worked well in astronomy, where the stellar observations and records of thousands of students gave Copernicus inductive material for his revolutionary deductions; but it bore small resemblance to the actual methods that in his time discovered the laws of planetary motions, the satellites of Jupiter, the magnetism of the earth, and the circulation of the blood.

He did not claim to have discovered induction; he knew that many men had practiced it before him. He was not the first to "overthrow Aristotle"; men like Roger Bacon and Petrus Ramus had been doing this for centuries past. And the Aristotle whom they deposed was not (as Francis Bacon sometimes realized) the Greek who had often used and praised induction and experiment, but the transmogrified *ille philosophus* of the Arabs and the Scholastics. What Bacon wanted to overthrow was the mistaken attempt to deduce medieval creeds from ancient metaphysics. In any event, he helped to free Renaissance Europe from too cramping a deference to antiquity.

He was not the first to emphasize knowledge as the road to power; Roger Bacon had done it, and Campanella had said, with Baconian pithiness, "*Tantum possumus quantum scimus*"—Our power is proportioned to our knowledge.[75] Perhaps the statesman stressed unduly the utilitarian ends of science. Yet he recognized the value of "pure" as compared with "applied" science—of "light" as distinct from "fruits." He urged a study of ends as well as of means, and knew that a century of inventions would create greater problems than it solved if it left human motives unchanged. He might have discovered in his own moral laxity the abyss created by the progress of knowledge beyond the discipline of character.

What remains after all these hindsight deductions? This: that Francis Bacon was the most powerful and influential intellect of his time. Shakespeare, of course, stood above him in imagination and literary art; but Bacon's mind ranged over the universe like a searchlight peering and prying curiously into every corner and secret of space. All the exhilarating enthusiasm of the Renaissance was in him, all the excitement and pride of a Columbus sailing madly into a new world. Hear the joyful cry of this Cock Robin announcing the dawn:

> Thus have I concluded this portion of learning touching Civil Knowledge; and with civil knowledge have concluded Human Philosophy; and with human philosophy, Philosophy in General. And being now at some pause, looking back into that I have passed through, this writing seemeth to me, as far as a man can judge of his own work, not much better than that noise or sound which musicians make while they are tuning their instruments; which is nothing pleasant to hear, but yet is a cause why the music is sweeter afterwards. So have I been content to tune the instruments of the muses that they may play that have better hands. And surely, when I set before me the condition of these times, in which learning hath made her third visitation or circuit, in all the qualities thereof; as the excel-

lency and vivacity of the wits of this age; the noble helps and lights
which we have by the travails of ancient writers; the art of printing,
which communicateth books to men of all fortunes; the openness of
the world by navigation, which hath disclosed multitudes of experiments, and a mass of natural history; . . . I cannot but be raised to
this persuasion, that this third period of time will far surpass that of
the Græcian and Roman learning. . . . As for my labours, if any, if
any man shall please himself or others in the reprehension of them,
they shall make that ancient and patient request, *Verbere sed audi*
[Strike me if you will, only hear me]; let men reprehend them, so
they observe and weigh them.[76]

Because he expressed the noblest passion of his age—for the betterment
of life through the extension of knowledge—posterity raised to his memory
a living monument of influence. Scientists were stirred and invigorated
not by his method but by his spirit. How refreshing, after centuries of
minds imprisoned in their roots or caught in webs of their own wishful
weaving, to come upon a man who loved the sharp tang of fact, the vital-
izing air of seeking and finding, the zest of casting lines of doubt into the
deepest pools of ignorance, superstition, and fear! Some men in that age,
like Donne, thought the world was decaying, hastening to a consumed
or shattered end; Bacon announced to his times that they were the youth
of a world rampant with effervescent life.

Men would not listen to him at first; in England, France, and Germany
they preferred to carry the competition of faiths to the arbitrament of
arms; but when that fury had cooled, those who were not fettered with
certainties organized themselves in the spirit of Bacon for the enlargement
of man's empire not over men but over the conditions and hindrances of
human life. When Englishmen founded the Royal Society of London for
Improving Natural Knowledge (1660), it was Francis Bacon who was
honored as its inspiration, and Salomon's House in *The New Atlantis*
probably pointed the goal.[77] Leibniz hailed Bacon as the regenerator of
philosophy.[78] And when the *philosophes* of the Enlightenment put together their world-shaking *Encyclopédie* (1751), they dedicated it to
Francis Bacon. "If," said Diderot in the prospectus, "we have come to it
successfully, we shall owe most to the Chancellor Bacon, who proposed
the plan of a universal dictionary of sciences and arts at a time when, so
to speak, neither arts nor sciences existed. That extraordinary genius, at
a time when it was impossible to write a history of what was known, wrote
one of what it was necessary to learn." And d'Alembert, in a frenzy of
enthusiasm, called Bacon "the greatest, the most universal, and the most
eloquent of philosophers." When the Enlightenment had burst into the
French Revolution the Convention had the works of Bacon published at

the expense of the state.[79] The tenor and career of British thought from Hobbes to Spencer—excepting Berkeley and Hume and the English Hegelians—followed Bacon's line. His tendency to conceive the external world in Democritean terms gave Hobbes the impetus to materialism; his emphasis on induction spurred Locke to an empirical psychology in which the study of the mind would be freed from the metaphysics of the soul; and his stress on "commodities" and "fruits" shared with the philosophy of Helvétius in leading Bentham to identify the useful and the good. The Baconian spirit prepared England for the Industrial Revolution.

Therefore we may place Francis Bacon at the head of the Age of Reason. He was not, like some of his successors, an idolator of reason; he distrusted all cogitations unchecked by actual experience, and all conclusions tainted with desire. "The human understanding is no dry light, but receives an infusion from the will and affections; whence proceed sciences which may be called 'sciences as one would.' For what a man had rather were true he more readily believes."[80] Bacon preferred "that reason which is elicited from facts. . . . From a closer and purer league between these two faculties, the experimental and the rational . . . much may be hoped."[81]

Nor did he, like the *philosophes* of the eighteenth century, propose reason as an enemy of religion or as a substitute for it; he made room for both of them in philosophy and life. But he repudiated the reliance upon traditions and authorities; he required rational and natural explanations instead of emotional presumptions, supernatural interventions, and popular mythology. He raised a banner for all the sciences, and drew to it the most eager minds of the succeeding centuries. Whether he willed it or not, the enterprise that he called for—the comprehensive organization of scientific research, the ecumenical expansion and dissemination of knowledge—contained in itself the seeds of the profoundest drama of modern times: Christianity, Catholic or Protestant, fighting for its life against the spread and power of science and philosophy. That drama had now spoken its prologue to the world.

CHAPTER VIII

The Great Rebellion

1625–49

I. THE CHANGING ECONOMY

THE revolution that enthroned Parliament and killed a king—144 years before Louis XVI atoned for his ancestry—had its roots in economic conflict and religious rivalry.

Feudalism was an organization and dependency of agriculture; monarchy, in Western Europe, was an organization and culmination of feudalism; it was tied by its roots to an economy of landlords and land. In England two economic developments cut these feudal roots. One was the growth of the "gentry," the untitled owners of minor estates, who, on the land, ranked between the titled nobility and the yeomanry, or peasant proprietors. They fretted under a king, a court, and a code of laws still thinking or fashioned in feudal terms; they bought or captured seats in the House of Commons; they longed for a government submissive to a Parliament submissive to themselves. The other development was the expanding wealth of the bourgeoisie—bankers, merchants, manufacturers, lawyers, physicians—and its demand for political representation commensurate with its economic power. These revolutionary factors had no common interest; they collaborated only in the attempt to check the pedigreed landlords, the snobbish court, and a king who considered a hereditary aristocracy the necessary source of economic and political order and stability.

Year by year the English economy was changing its base and fulcrum from static land to movable money. Before 1540 a brass factory required an investment of $300 (in United States currency of 1958); in 1620, $125,000. By 1650 capitalistic undertakings involving large outlays of funds had developed alum factories in Yorkshire, paper manufactures at Dartford, cannon foundries at Brendeley, and deep-level mines that were called upon for more and more coal, copper, tin, iron, and lead. In 1550 only a few English mines produced more than 300 tons a year; in 1640 several gave 20,000 tons each. Artisans using metal depended on mining and metallurgical industries concentrated under capitalistic control. Textile organizations furnished material to shops employing 500 to 1,000 workers, and to weavers and sewers scattered among thousands of houses in towns and villages. Agriculture itself was sharing in the capitalistic conversion of production: capitalists bought and enclosed large tracts of land to provide meat for the towns and wool for factories at home and abroad. England's foreign commerce grew tenfold between 1610 and 1640.

Not in England's memory had the gap been so wide between rich and poor. "The laborer's service sank to the worst scale of remuneration during the first half of the seventeenth century, for the price of food increased while wages remained stationary."[1] Taking 100 as a base, the real wages of English carpenters stood at 300 about 1380, at 370 in 1480, at 200 under Elizabeth, at 120 under Charles I—the lowest in four hundred years.[2] Unemployment was so great in 1634 that Charles compelled the demolition of a newly erected mechanical sawmill because it threw so many sawyers out of work.[3] War with France raised taxes, war in France disrupted the export trade, bad harvests (1629–30) inflated prices to the verge of starvation;[4] the swelling economy burst in depressions (1629–32, 1638). All these factors collaborated with religious strife to drive many English families to America, and to plunge England into a civil war that changed the face and destiny of the nation.

The class war became also a conflict of regions and moral codes. The north was overwhelmingly agricultural and largely Catholic, however clandestinely; London and the south were increasingly industrial and Protestant. The new business class, while cherishing its monopolies and protective tariffs, demanded a free economy, in which wages and prices would be determined by the supply of labor and goods; in which there would be no feudal or governmental control of production, distribution, profit, or property; and in which no stigma would be attached to commercial occupations, the charging of interest, or the manipulation of wealth. The barons and their peasants clung to the feudal concept of mutual obligation and group responsibility, of state regulation of wages and prices, of limits by custom and law to conditions of employment and profit. The barons protested that the new mercantile economy, producing for a national or international market, was disrupting class relations and social stability. They (and the gentry and the government) felt their own solvency threatened by the effects of inflation on the value of the traditional dues, rents, or taxes upon which they depended. They looked with angry disdain upon the lawyers who shared so prominently in administration, and the merchants who ruled the cities. They dreaded the power of mercantile London, which, with a population of some 300,000 out of England's 5,000,000, was able to finance an army and a revolution.

II. THE RELIGIOUS CALDRON: 1624-49

The new King, raised in the old feudal and social code of the land, and lost in the London of merchants and Puritans, was troubled beyond patience by the variety and the intensity of religious beliefs. The right of individual judgment, which every new opinion preached until it came to power, united with the spread of the Bible to encourage the diversity of sects. One pamphleteer (1641) listed twenty-nine; another (1646), 180. Besides the cleavage between Catholics and Protestants, there was the tense division of Protestants into Anglicans, Presbyterians, and Puritans, and of Puritans into Independents who dreamed of a republic, Quakers who opposed war, violence, and oaths, Millenarians—or Fifth Monarchy Men—who believed that Jesus would soon come to establish His personal rule on earth, Antinomians who argued that the elect of God were exempt from human laws, and Brownist Separatists, and Seekers, and Ranters. A member of Parliament complained that "mechanical men" (artisans) were setting up pulpits and preaching their own hot brands of faith, many of them clothing economic or political demands in Scriptural texts. And there were Anabaptists, who administered baptism only to adults; and Baptists, who separated from the Separatists (1606) and divided (1633) into General Baptists rejecting, and Particular Baptists accepting, the Calvinist doctrine of predestination.

The multiplication of sects, and their spirited debates, led a small minority to doubt all forms of Christianity. Bishop Fotherby mourned (1622) that "the Scriptures (with many) have lost their authority, and are thought only fit for the ignorant and the idiotic."[5] And the Reverend James Cranford (1646) spoke of "multitudes" who "have changed their faith either to Skepticism . . . or Atheism, to believe nothing."[6] A pamphlet entitled *Hell Broke Loose: A Catalogue of the Many Spreading Errors, Heresies, and Blasphemies of These Times* (1646) cited, as the first heresy, the opinion "that the Scripture, whether a true manuscript [an authentic text] or no . . . is but humane [man-made], and not able to discover [reveal] a divine God."[7] Another heresy declared that "right Reason is the rule of Faith, and . . . we are to believe the Scriptures, and the doctrines of the Trinity, Incarnation, Resurrection, so far as we see them agreeable to reason, and no further."[8] A large number of doubters denied hell and the divinity of Christ. A growing number of thinkers, who came to be called deists, sought a compromise between skepticism and religion by proposing a Christianity confined to the belief in God and immortality. Edward, Lord Herbert of Cherbury, gave this *via media* a philosophical formulation in a remarkable essay on truth, *De veritate* (1624). Truth, said Herbert, is independent of Scripture, and cannot be decreed by a church or any other authority. The best test of truth is universal assent. Consequently the wisest religion would be a "natural" rather than a revealed religion, and would limit itself to doctrines generally accepted by the different creeds: that there is a Supreme Being, that He should be worshiped chiefly by virtuous living, and that good conduct will be rewarded, and bad conduct punished, either here or in a life hereafter. Herbert, says Aubrey, died "serenely," after being refused the sacraments.[9]

Parliament was more worried about Catholicism than about heresy. In 1634 the Catholics in England were probably a quarter of the population,[10] and, despite all laws and perils, there were still some 335 Jesuits there.[11] Prominent nobles accepted the old faith. George Calvert, Lord Baltimore, announced his conversion in 1625; in 1632 Charles gave him a charter to found the colony that became Maryland. The Catholic Queen, Henrietta Maria, sent an emissary to Rome (1633) to solicit a cardinal's hat for a British subject. The Anglican King offered to allow a Catholic bishop to reside in England if Urban VIII would support Charles's plan for some diplomatic marriages (1634); the Pope refused. The Catholics called for religious tolerance, but Parliament—remembering Catholic intolerance, the Massacre of St. Bartholomew, and the Gunpowder Plot, and loath to risk inquiry into Protestant titles to once Catholic property —demanded instead the full enforcement of the anti-Catholic laws. A strong "no popery" sentiment, especially in the gentry and the middle class, opposed alike the influx of Catholic priests into England and the growing approximation of Anglican to Catholic ritual and thought.

The Established Church enjoyed the full protection of the state. The Anglican creed and worship were legally compulsory; even the Thirty-nine Articles were made law of the land (1628). The Anglican bishops claimed the Apostolic Succession—that is, that they had been ordained by an Apostle; and they rejected the Presbyterian and Puritan assertion that others than bishops might validly ordain a minister. Many Anglican ecclesiastics in this age were men of great learning and good will. James Ussher, Archbishop of Armagh, was a real scholar despite his famous calculation (in his *Annales Veteris Testamenti*, 1650) that God had created the world on October 22, 4004 B.C.—a chronological slip that was made semiofficial in editions of the Authorized Version.[12] John Hales, chaplain to an English embassy in Holland, preached doubt, reason, and toleration:

> The ways that lead us to . . . any knowledge . . . are but two: first, experience, secondly ratiocination. They that come and tell you what

to believe, what you are to do, and tell you not why, they are not physicians but leeches . . . The chiefest sinew and strength of wisdom is not easily to believe. . . . Those things which we reverence for antiquity, what were they at their first birth? Were they false? Time cannot make them more true. The circumstance of time . . . is merely impertinent . . . It is not the variety of opinions but our own perverse wills—who think it meet that all should be conceited [of the same thought] as ourselves are—which hath so inconvenienced the Church. Were we not so ready to anathematize each other where we concur not in opinion, we might in hearts be united . . . Two parts there are that do completely make up a Christian man—a true faith and an honest conversation [conduct]. The first, though it seems the worthier, and gives us the name of Christians, yet the second, in the end, will prove the surer . . . There is no kind of man . . . though he be an heathen and idolater, unto whom the skirts of Christian compassion do not reach.[13]

Hale's generosity was not reciprocated by some "idolators." A Jesuit, writing under the name "Edward Knott" a tract entitled *Charity Mistaken* (1630), maintained that, barring accidents, no Protestant could be saved.[14] The condemned were reassured by William Chillingworth, whose *The Religion of Protestants a Safe Way to Salvation* (1637) was the outstanding theological treatise of the time. Chillingworth knew both sides: he had been converted to Catholicism, had returned to Protestantism, and still had his reservations; he had, said Clarendon, "contracted such a habit of doubting that by degrees he grew confident of nothing, and a skeptic, at least, in the greatest mysteries of religion."[15]

The most eloquent of these Caroline Anglicans was Jeremy Taylor. His sermons are still readable, and more moving than Bossuet's; even a Frenchman has been stirred by them.[16] Taylor was an ardent Royalist, a chaplain in the army of Charles I. When the Presbyterians and the Puritans controlled Parliament and abused the once intolerant Anglicans intolerantly, he issued *The Liberty of Prophesying* (1646), a timid call for toleration: any Christian who accepted the Apostles' Creed should be received within the amity of the Church, and Catholics were to be left free unless they insisted on papal sovereignty over England and kings.* Taylor was captured and imprisoned by the Parliamentary party in the Civil War, but after the Restoration he was raised to the episcopacy, and his ardor for toleration cooled.

The growing influence of Catholicism appeared in the predominant Anglican of the age. William Laud was a man of ideas and will, born to

---

* In 1631, in Massachusetts Bay Colony, Roger Williams advocated unlimited toleration for Catholics, Jews, and infidels.

rule or die, strictly virtuous, severely strict, and resolute to the point of irascible inflexibility. Like a good churchman, he took it for granted that a unified religious belief was indispensable to successful government, and that a complex ceremonial was necessary for a tranquilizing and effectual faith. To the sorrow of Presbyterians and Puritans, he proposed to recall the arts to the service of the Church, to beautify the altar, the pulpit, and the baptismal font, to restore the cross to the ritual and the surplice to the priest. As a special mountain of offense, he ordered the Communion table, which heretofore had been placed in the center of the chancel (where it had sometimes served as a hat stand), to be put behind a railing at the eastern end of the church. These changes were mostly a revival of Elizabethan customs and laws, but to the Puritans, who loved simplicity, they represented a backsliding to Catholicism and the renewal of a class separation between priest and congregation. Laud seems to have felt that the Catholic Church was right in surrounding religion with ceremony and endowing the priest with an aura of sanctity.[17] The Roman Church appreciated his views, even to offering him a cardinal's hat.[18] He courteously refused, but the offer appeared to support the reproaches of the Puritans. They called him the forerunner of Antichrist. Charles made him Archbishop of Canterbury (1633) and a commissioner of the treasury. Another archbishop was made Chancellor of Scotland. People complained that ecclesiastics were returning to political power, as in the heyday of the medieval Church.

From his Lambeth Palace the new Primate of All England set himself to remolding English ritual and morals. He made a hundred new enemies by levying, through the Court of High Commission (a judiciary body set up by Elizabeth, and now predominantly ecclesiastical), severe fines from persons convicted of adultery; and the victims found little comfort in his devoted use of the fines to repair the decaying St. Paul's Cathedral and to drive lawyers, hucksters, and gossipers from its naves.[19] Ministers who rejected the new ritual were deprived of their benefices; writers and speakers who repeatedly criticized it, who questioned the Christian creed, or who opposed the institution of bishops were to be excommunicated, and were to stand in the stocks and perhaps lose their ears.

The brutality of the punishments exacted under Laud's regime must be visualized to understand his fate. In 1628, at his instigation, a Puritan minister, Alexander Leighton, was indicted before the Star Chamber as the admitted author of a book that called the institution of bishops anti-Christian and satanic. He was put in irons and was kept in solitary confinement for fifteen weeks in an unheated cell "full of rats and mice, and open to snow and rain." His hair fell out, his skin peeled off. He was tied to a stake and received thirty-six stripes with a heavy cord upon his naked back; he was placed in the pillory for two hours in November's frost and snow; he was branded in the face, had his nose slit and his ears cut off, and was condemned to life imprisonment.[20] In 1633 Ludowyc Bowyer, who had charged Laud with being a Catholic at heart, was fined, branded, mutilated, and sentenced to imprisonment for life.[21] William Prynne, firebrand of the Puritans, in *News from Ipswich* (1636) denounced Laud's bishops as servants of the pope and the Devil, and recommended hanging for bishops; he was branded on both cheeks, had his ears cut off, and was jailed till the Long Parliament freed him (1640). A woman who insisted on keeping Saturday as the Sabbath was imprisoned for eleven years.[24]

Laud's chief enemies, the Puritans, agreed with him on the necessity of intolerance. They thought it a reasonable conclusion from the divine origin of Christianity and the Scriptures; anyone who opposed a faith so founded must be a criminal or a fool, and society should be protected from the many damnations that would follow from his teaching. The Presbyterians pleaded with Parliament (1648) to legislate life imprisonment for all who continued to teach Catholic, Arminian, Baptist, or Quaker views, and death for all who denied the doctrines of the Trinity or the Incarnation. Cromwell's Independents, however, offered toleration to all who would accept the fundamentals of Christianity, but they excluded Catholics, Unitarians, and defenders of prelacy.[25]

There were so many parties among the Puritans that it is a rare generalization that can hold of them all. Most of them adhered to a strict Calvinism, to individual political liberty, to the right of congregations to run their own affairs without episcopal supervision, and to a worship unceremonious, egalitarian, and divorced from the distractions of religious art. They agreed with the Presbyterians in theology, but rejected presbyteries as tending to exercise episcopal power. They insisted on a literal interpretation of Scripture, and condemned the pretense of reason to sit in judgment on revealed truth. They attached as much reverence to the Old Testament as to the New; they applied to themselves the Judaic conception of the chosen people; they baptized their children with the names of Old Testament patriarchs and heroes; they thought of God in terms of a stern Yahveh, and added the Calvinistic conviction that most men were the "children of wrath," doomed before their birth, by the arbitrary will of a relentless deity, to everlasting hell; and they ascribed the salvation of the few "elect" not to good works but to divine grace granted at divine whim. Some of them thought they talked to God; some, thinking themselves damned, went about the streets groaning in anticipation of their eternal sufferings. The thunderbolts of God seemed always to hang over the heads of men.

In this self-imposed Terror "Merrie England" almost disappeared. The humanism of the Renaissance, the lusty naturalism of the Elizabethans, yielded to a sense of sin, a fear of divine vengeance, which looked upon most pleasures as wiles of Satan and challenges to God. The old monastic fears of the flesh returned, perhaps to a larger proportion of the people than ever in known history before. Prynne declared all embraces "lewd," all mixed dancing "lascivious."[26] To most Puritans music, stained glass, religious images, surplices, anointed priests were obstacles to direct communion with God. They studied the Bible with devoted diligence and quoted its phrases in nearly every speech, in almost every paragraph; some zealots embroidered their clothing with Scriptural texts; the especially godly added "Verily" or "Yea, verily" to attest sincerity or truth. Good Puritans prohibited the use of cosmetics and banned hairdressing as vanity; they earned the nickname "Roundheads" because they cut their hair close to the head. They denounced the theater as scandalous (it was), the baiting of bears and bulls as barbarous, the morals of the court as pagan. They condemned festival jollities, ringing bells, gathering around the Maypole, drinking healths, playing cards. They forbade all games whatever on the Sabbath; that day was to be kept for God, and it was no longer to bear the heathen name Sunday. They—Milton among them—cried out in anger when Charles I and Laud, renewing an edict of James I, issued (1633) a "Declaration of Sports" sanctioning Sunday games after Sunday prayers. The Puritans extended their Sabbatarianism—the advocacy of blue Sundays—to Christmas; they lamented the style of celebrating the birth of Christ with merrymaking, dancing, and games; they rightly ascribed many Christmas customs to pagan origins; they demanded that Christmas should be made a solemn day of fasting and atonement; and in 1644 they prevailed upon Parliament to sanction this view by law.

As Protestantism had stressed the sermon beyond Catholic precedent, so Puritanism expanded it even beyond Protestant custom. A hunger for sermons gnawed at some hearts; the mayor of Norwich moved to London to hear more preaching; a mercer resigned from a congregation because it provided only one sermon per Sunday. Special "lecturers" arose to ease this hunger—laymen hired by a parish to preach a Sunday sermon additional to what the regular minister offered. Most Puritan preachers took their function with high seriousness; they terrified their audiences with descriptions of hell; some of them denounced sinners publicly by name; one pointed out the drunkards in his congregation and, talking of whores, specified as an example the wife of a chief parishioner; another told his auditors that if adultery, swearing, cheating, and Sabbath breaking could lead a man to heaven, the whole parish would be saved.[27] The Puritan ministers felt it their duty to prescribe or proscribe the conduct, dress, studies, and amusements of the people. They forbade the observance of the holydays established by pagan custom or the Catholic Church, and so added some fifty working days to the year.[28] A call to duty sounded throughout the Puritan ethic, and with it a stern inculcation of courage, self-reliance, prudence, thrift, and work. It was an ethic congenial to the middle class; it made for industrious workers and gave a religious sanction to mercantile enterprise and private property. Poverty, not wealth, was a sin; it revealed lack of personal character and divine grace.[29]

Politically, the Puritans aspired to a democratic theocracy in which there would be none but moral and religious distinctions among men, no ruler but Christ, no law but God's Word. They resented the heavy taxes that supported the Anglican Church; their businessmen felt themselves milked by that expensive and superior Establishment; the "trading part of a nation," said one pamphleteer, "is devoured in this Prelatical Gulph."[30] The Puritans defended wealth, but scorned the idle luxury of the nobility. They carried morality to excess, as later ages carried liberty; but perhaps their inhuman code was a necessary corrective to the loose morals of Elizabethan England. They produced some of the strongest characters in history—Cromwell and Milton, and the men who conquered the American wilderness. They defended and transmitted to us parliamentary government and trial by jury. To them, in part, England owes the solid sobriety of the British character, the stability of the British family, and the integrity of Britain's official life. Nothing is lost.

III. THE PURITANS AND THE THEATER

The first victory of the Puritans was in their war against the theater. Everything that distinguished them—their theology of "elect" and "reprobate," their strict morality, their solemn mood and Biblical speech—had been ridiculed on the stage with gross and unforgivable caricature. And in 1629 came the culminating crime: a French actress dared to replace a boy in taking a female part in a play at the Blackfriars. She was pelted with apples and rotten eggs.

The new dramatists might have appeased the Puritan party, for, though now and then they stooped to conquer the groundlings with ribaldry, by and large they were gentlemen. Philip Massinger's *A New Way to Pay Old Debts* (1625) satirized not prim virtue but monopolistic greed; there was no soaring poetry in it, no crackling wit, no winging imagery; but the unscrupulous extortioner was brought to justice in the end, and five acts transpired without a trull. John Ford angled for an audience by entitling a play *'Tis Pity She's a Whore*, but this and *The Broken Heart* (both 1633) kept a decent pitch, and might still hold the boards if modern audiences could stomach the holocausts of their denouements.

The Puritans fired their hottest shot against the theater when their most fearless protagonist, William Prynne, sent to the press (1632) his *Histrio-mastix, the Players Scourge*. Prynne was a lawyer and made no claim to impartiality; he presented a thousand-page brief for the plaintiff. By quotations from the Bible, from the Fathers of the Church, and even from the pagan philosophers, he proved that the drama had been invented by Satan and had begun as a form of devil worship. Most plays are blasphemous and obscene, full of amorous embraces, wanton gestures, and lust-arousing music, song, and dance; all dancing is devilish, and its every pace is a step to hell; most actors are profane and godless criminals. "The Church of God, not the playhouse, is the only 'proper' school; the Scriptures, sermons, and devout and pious books . . . are the only lectures" (reading) fit for Christians. And if they need diversion,

> they have the several prospects of the sun, the moon, the planets, the stars, with all the infinite variety of creatures, to delight their eyes. They have music of all birds . . . to please their ears; the incomparably delicate odoriferous scents and perfumes of all herbs, all flowers, fruits to refresh their noses; the savoury tastes of all edible creatures . . . the pleasures that orchards, rivers, gardens, ponds, woods . . . can afford them; the comfort of friends, kindred, husbands, wives, children, possessions, wealth, and all other external blessings that God hath bestowed upon them.[31]

The argument was learned and eloquent, but it called all actresses whores, and the Queen had just imported some actresses from France and was herself rehearsing a part in a court masque. Henrietta Maria took offense, and Laud indicted Prynne for seditious libel. The author protested that he had had no intention of libeling the Queen; he apologized for the intemperance of his book; nevertheless, with a severity which the Puritans long remembered, he was debarred from the practice of law, was fined the impossible sum of £5,000 ($250,000?), and was sentenced to life imprisonment. He was placed in the pillory, and both his ears were cut off.[32] From his prison he issued *News from Ipswich* (1636), in which he denounced Anglican prelates as devilish traitors and ravenous wolves, and recommended that these bishops be hanged. He was pilloried again, and the stumps of his ears were shorn away. He remained in jail until the Long Parliament freed him in 1640.

In 1642 the Parliament ordered all the theaters of England closed. This was at first a war measure, apparently limited to "these calamitous times," but it remained in force till 1656. The long career of the Elizabethan drama came to an end amid a drama greater than any that the English stage had ever played.

IV. CAROLINE PROSE

There were at least two men in England who could look out upon the seething scene with perspective and calm. John Selden was so learned that men said, *"Quod Seldenus nescit nemo scit"*—What Selden does not know, nobody knows. As an antiquarian he collected state records of pre-Norman England and compiled an authoritative *Titles of Honor* (1614); as an Orientalist he made a European reputation with his study of polytheism, *De diis Syris* (1617); as a jurist he expounded rabbinical law and wrote a *History of Tythes* refuting the claim of the divine origin of tithes; as an M.P. he took part in impeaching Buckingham and Laud and in drawing up the Petition of Right; he was twice imprisoned. He attended the Westminster Assembly as a lay delegate "to see wild asses fight," and pleaded for moderation in religious disputes. After his death his *Table Talk*, recorded by his secretary, became an English classic. Shall we sample him?

> 'Tis a vain thing to talk of an heretic, for a man can think no otherwise than he does think. In the primitive times there were many opinions. One of these being embraced by some prince . . . the rest were condemned as heresies . . . No man is the wiser for his learning; it may administer matter to work in . . . but wit [intelligence] and wisdom are born with a man . . . Wise men say nothing in dangerous times. The lion . . . called the sheep to ask her if his breath smelled; she said Yes; he bit off her head for a fool. He called the wolf and asked him; he said No; he tore him to pieces for a flatterer. At last he called the fox, and asked him. Why [said the fox], he had got a cold and could not smell.[33]

Sir Thomas Browne was a fox. Born in London (1605), educated at Winchester School, Oxford, Montpellier, Padua, and Leiden, absorbing arts and sciences and history at every turn, he resigned himself to the practice of medicine at Norwich. He sublimated his uroscopies by jotting down his ideas *de omnibus rebus et quibusdam aliis* ("on all things and a few others"), and eloquently concealed his theology in *Religio medici* (1642), one of the milestones in English prose. Here is a British Montaigne, quite as quaint and fanciful, as undulant and diverse, perhaps borrowing from him in the pages of friendship,[34] subordinating his skepticism to conformity, relishing reason and professing faith, congested with classical allusions and derivatives, but loving the art and the music of words, and using style as "the antiseptic of decay."

He was by education inclined to doubt. His longest work, *Pseudodoxia epidemica* (1646), explained and chastised hundreds of "false opinions epidemic" in Europe—that a carbuncle gives light in the dark, that an elephant has no joints, that the phoenix regenerates itself from its own ashes, that the salamander can live in fire, that the unicorn has a horn, that swans sing before their death, that the forbidden fruit was an apple, that "the toad pisseth and this way diffuseth its venom."[35] But, like every iconoclast, he had his icons. He accepted angels, demons, palmistry, and witches;[36] in 1664 he shared in the condemnation as witches of two women, who were soon thereafter hanged protesting their innocence.[37]

He had no fancy for women, and thought sex ridiculous:

> I was never yet once, and commend their resolutions who never marry twice . . . I could be content that we might procreate like trees, without conjunction, or that there were any way to perpetuate the world without this trivial and vulgar way of union; it is the foolishest act a wise man commits in all his life; nor is there anything that will more deject his cool'd imagination, when he shall consider what an odd and unworthy piece of folly he hath committed.[38]

As to his titular topic, he is apologetically Christian:

> For my religion, though there be several circumstances that might persuade the world I have none at all (as the general scandal of my profession, the natural course of my studies, the indifferency of my behavior and discourse in matters of religion, neither violently defending one, nor with that common ardor and contention opposing another), yet, in despite hereof, I dare without usurpation the honorable style of Christian. Not that I merely owe this title to the font, my education, or the clime wherein I was born . . . but having in my riper years and confirmed judgment seen and examined all.[39]

He feels that the marvels and the order of the world declare a divine mind—"nature is the art of God."[40] He confesses to having entertained some heresies, and he slips into some doubts about the Biblical account of Creation;[41] but now he feels the need of an established religion to guide wondering, wandering men; and he deplores the vanity of heretics who disturb the social order with their hot infallibilities.[42] Puritans were not to his taste; he remained quietly faithful to the first Charles during the Civil War and was knighted for his pains by the second.

In his later years he was moved to meditation on death by the unearthing of some ancient sepulchral urns in Norfolk, and he recorded his thoughts in a desultory masterpiece of English prose, *Hydriotaphia, Urne-Buriall* (1658). He recommends cremation as the least vain method of disencumbering the earth of ourselves. "Life is a pure flame, and we live by an invisible Sun within us"; but we flicker out with ignominious haste. "Generations pass while some trees stand, and old families last not three oaks."[43] The world itself is probably nearing its end in "this setting part of time." We need the hope of immortality to gird us against this brevity; it is a precious prop to feel ourselves immortal—but a great pity that we must be scared into decency by visions of hell.[44] Heaven is no "empyreal vacuity" but "within the circle of this sensible world," in a condition of mental content and peace. Then, hurrying back from the verge of heresy, he ends his *Religio* with a modest prayer to God:

> Bless me in this life with but peace of my conscience, command of my affections, the love of Thyself and my dearest friends, and I shall be happy enough to pity Caesar. These are, O Lord, the humble desires of my most reasonable ambition, and all I dare call happiness on earth; wherein I set no rule or limit to thy Hand or Providence. Dispose of me according to the wisdom of Thy pleasure. Thy will be done, though in my undoing.[45]

V. CAROLINE POETRY

Meanwhile a bevy of minor bards—each of whom is someone's major love—amused the leisurely with amorous rhymes and tuneful piety; and because the King liked them and they sang his cause through all vicissitudes, history knows them as the Cavalier Poets. Robert Herrick apprenticed his pen to Ben Jonson, and thought for a time that a bowl of wine would make a book of verse; he drank to Bacchus for hours on end, and then studied for the ministry. He took courses in love, pledged himself to prefer mistresses to marriage,[46] and counseled virgins to "gather rosebuds" while they bloomed. His "Corinna" received further prodding:

> Get up, get up for shame! The blooming morn
> Upon her wings presents the god unshorn.
>   See how Aurora throws her fair
>   Fresh-quilted colors through the air;
>   Get up, sweet Slug-a-bed, and see
>   The dew bespangling herb and tree . . .
> Come, let us go, while we are in our prime,
> And take the harmless folly of the time!
>   We shall grow old apace, and die
>   Before we know our liberty . . .
> Then while time serves, and we are but decaying,
> Come, my Corinna, come, let's go a-Maying.[47]

And so in many of the wanton poems that he published in 1648 in the collection *Hesperides*; even in our loose days they need expurgation to suit Everyman. But eating is also necessary, so Herrick left his beloved London (1629), and—taking Catullus with him—went sorrowfully to be vicar of a modest parsonage in distant Devonshire. Soon he began to write *Noble Numbers, or Pious Pieces*, and first a prayer for absolution:

> For those my unbaptised rhymes,
> Writ in my wild unhallowed times,
> For every sentence, clause, and word,
> That's not inlaid with Thee (my Lord),
> Forgive me, God, and blot each line
> Out of my book that is not Thine.[48]

In 1647 the Puritans deprived him of his benefice. He starved loyally through the dour days of the Commonwealth, but was restored by the Restoration to his vicarage, and died there at eighty-four, Corinna lost in the dusk of memory.

Thomas Carew did not live so long, but he too found time for mistresses. Drunk with the inexplicable charms of woman, he sang them in such rapt detail ("A Rapture"), and with such cavalier contempt for chastity, that other poets reproved him for his licentious exactitude. The Puritans could not forgive Charles I for making him a gentleman of the privy chamber, but perhaps the King pardoned the matter for the form; in these Caroline poets all the Gallic finesse of Ronsard and the Pléiade is imported to grace with delicate art the indelicacies of desire.

Sir John Suckling crowded much living into his thirty-three years. Born in 1609, he inherited a great fortune at eighteen, made the Grand Tour, was knighted by Charles I, fought under Gustavus Adolphus in the Thirty Years' War, returned to England (1632) to become by his good looks, his wit, and his generous wealth a favorite at the court. He was, says Aubrey, "the greatest gallant of his time, and the greatest gamester, both for bowling and cards . . . His sisters would come to the . . . bowling green, crying for fear he should lose all their portions."[49] He invented cribbage. He never married, but entertained "a great number of ladies of quality"; at one party he served the ladies, as dessert, silk stockings, then a great luxury.[50] His play *Aglaura* was produced with lavish scenery, paid for from his purse. He raised his own troops to fight for the King and risked his life in an attempt to rescue the King's minister, Sir Thomas Wentworth, Earl of Strafford, from the Tower. Frustrated, he fled to the Continent, and there, deprived of his fortune, he took poison and died.

Richard Lovelace too served the King in war and verse, and he too was rich and handsome, "the most amiable and beautiful person that ever eye beheld"[51]—so Anthony à Wood saw him at Oxford. In 1642 he headed a delegation from Kent to petition the Long Parliament (transiently Presbyterian) for the restoration of the Anglican liturgy. For this audacious orthodoxy he was imprisoned for seven weeks. His Althea came to comfort him, and he made her immortal with a line:

> When Love with unconfined wings
>   Hovers within my gates,
> And my divine Althea brings
>   To whisper at the grates;
> When I lie tangled in her hair
>   And fettered to her eye,
> The birds that wanton in the air
>   Know no such liberty. . . .
>
> Stone walls do not a prison make,
>   Nor iron bars a cage;
> Minds innocent and quiet take
>   That for an hermitage;
> If I have freedom in my love
>   And in my soul am free,
> Angels alone, that soar above,
>   Enjoy such liberty.[52]

He went off to the wars again in 1645—and apologized to his betrothed (Lucy Sacheverell) in "To Lucasta, Going to the Wars":

> Tell me not, sweet, I am unkind
>   That from the nunnery
> Of thy chaste breast and quiet mind
>   To war and arms I fly. . . .
>
> Yet this inconstancy is such
>   As thou too shalt adore;
> I could not love thee, dear, so much,
>   Loved I not honour more.[53]

On the false report of his death in battle, Lucasta (chaste Lucy) married another suitor. Having lost both his lady and his fortune in the Royalist cause, Lovelace was reduced to depend upon the charity of his friends for food, and he who had worn cloth of silver and gold now dressed in rags and lived in slums. He died of consumption in 1658, aged forty.

He might have learned the art of survival from Edmund Waller, who managed to be active for sixty years on both sides of the Great Rebellion, became the most popular poet of his time, outlived Milton, and died in bed at eighty-one (1687). He entered Parliament at sixteen, went mad at twenty-three, recovered, married a London heiress at twenty-five, buried her three years later, and soon wooed "Sacharissa" (Lady Dorothy Sidney) with a fresh variant of an ancient theme:

> Go, lovely Rose!
> Tell her, that wastes her time and me,
> That now she knows,
> When I resemble her to thee,
> How sweet and fair she seems to be.
>
> Tell her, that's young,
> And shuns to have her graces spied,
> That hadst thou sprung
> In deserts, where no men abide,
> Thou must have unrecommended died. . . .
>
> Then die! that she
> The common fate of all things rare
> May read in thee;
> How small a part of time they share
> That are so wondrous sweet and fair!

One other hardly minor poet enters this period. Richard Crashaw burned with religious ardor rather than with the fevers of the flesh. His father, an Anglican clergyman, wrote tracts against Catholicism and filled his son with fears of popery; Richard became a Catholic. He was expelled from Cambridge (1644) for supporting the King; he fled from England to Paris, where he consoled his poverty with visions of God. The Spanish mystics were to him a revelation of religious intensity and devotion. Standing before a picture of St. Teresa, he envied her transfixion by the dart of Christ, and begged her to accept him as her selfless disciple:

> By the full kingdom of that final kiss
> That seized thy parting soul, and sealed thee His;
> By all the heavens thou hast in Him
> (Fair sister of the seraphim);
> By all of Him we have in thee,
> Leave nothing of myself in me.
> Let me so read thy life that I
> Unto all life of mine may die.

This and other poems he gave to the world in *Steps to the Temple* (1646), an ambivalent mixture of pious ecstasies and poetic conceits. Through him and a like but later poet, Henry Vaughan, we perceive that not all England was in those hectic days divided into Puritans and Cavaliers, but that amid the fury of poetical and theological war some spirits found religion neither in massive shrines and hypnotic ritual, nor in fearful dogmas and proud election, but in the childlike, trustful communion of the baffled and surrendering soul with a humane and forgiving God.

VI. CHARLES I VERSUS PARLIAMENT: 1625–29

And now this tragic King over whom all England was to fight, what sort of man and monarch was he? Before the storm soured the milk of human kindness in him, he was a reasonably good man—a loving son, an unusually faithful husband, a loyal friend, a father idolized by his children. He had begun the struggle of life by fighting a congenital weakness of physique; he could not walk till he was seven. He overcame this defect by resolute pursuit of vigorous sports, until in maturity he could ride and hunt with the best. He suffered from an impediment of speech; until ten he could hardly speak intelligibly; his father thought of having an operation performed on the boy's tongue. Charles gradually improved, but to the end of his life he stammered and had to counter his difficulty by speaking slowly.[54] When his popular brother Henry died, leaving him heir apparent, Charles was suspected of complicity in the death; the charge was unjust, but it shared in darkening the Prince's mood. He preferred a studious solitude to the bibulous hilarity of his father's court. He became proficient in mathematics, music, and theology, learned something of Greek and Latin, spoke French, Italian, and a little Spanish. He loved art; he cherished and expanded the collection left by his brother; he became a discriminating collector, and a generous patron of artists, poets, and musicians. He invited the Italian painter Orazio Gentileschi to his court, then Rubens, Vandyck, and Frans Hals; Hals declined, and Rubens came chiefly as ambassador; but all the world knows Charles as the proud and handsome king, with Vandyke beard, repeatedly painted by Vandyck. William Dobson, pupil of Vandyck, continued the idealization of the royal family.

Charles's parentage and marriage contributed to his ruin. He inherited his father's conception of the royal prerogative as absolute, with power to make as well as administer laws, to rule without Parliament, and to override laws enacted by Parliament. This view seemed justified by precedents and was taken for granted in France and Spain; it was encouraged in Charles by Buckingham, the court, and the Queen. Henrietta Maria had been reared at the French court in the very days when Richelieu was making her brother Louis XIII absolute over everybody but Richelieu. She had come to England as an avowed Catholic, bringing priests in her bridal train, and her faith had been made more intense by the disabilities she saw it suffer there. She had all the allure of beauty, vivacity, and wit, and the full Medicean flair for politics. Inevitably she urged her devoted husband to alleviate the lot of English Catholics; doubtless she dreamed of converting the King himself. She gave him six children; it must have cost him many a struggle to resist her wish that they might be brought up Catholic. But he had developed a sincere attachment to the Anglican Church, and he realized that his England was predominantly Protestant and hostile to a threatening papacy.

Charles's first Parliament met on June 18, 1625. One hundred lords— peers and bishops—sat in the upper house; five hundred men, three fourths of them Puritan,[55] had been elected to the Commons by various forms of financial or political skulduggery;[56] there was no pretense of democracy. Probably the level of ability in this Parliament was higher than an adult suffrage would have returned; here were Coke, Selden, Pym, Sir John Eliot, Sir Thomas Wentworth, and others marked for history. The total wealth of the Commoners exceeded threefold the wealth of the lords.[57] The Commons showed its temper by demanding the full enforcement of the anti-Catholic laws. The King asked for an appropriation for governmental expenses and the war with Spain; Parliament granted him £140,000 ($7,000,000?), which was purposely inadequate; the fleet alone required twice that sum. For two centuries the English monarchs had been granted, for the duration of their reigns, the right to levy export and import duties, usually of two to three shillings per tun (a large cask), and six to twelve pence per pound; now the Parliament's "tonnage and poundage" bill allowed Charles this right for one year only. It argued that previous appropriations had been squandered in the extravagance of James's court; it complained that taxes had been levied without its consent; it was resolved to compel hereafter an annual summoning of Parliament and an annual examination, by Parliament, of governmental expenditures. Charles took umbrage at these economies and intentions, and when plague threatened London he seized the excuse to dissolve the Parliament (August 12, 1625).

The government was now in the hands of Buckingham. Charles had not merely inherited the amiable, reckless Duke from his father; he had been brought up with him, had traveled with him, in a companionship that made it difficult for the King to see in his friend an unwise and disastrous counselor. Buckingham, with the support of Parliament, had led James into war with Spain; Parliament now refused to finance the war. The Duke organized an armada to go out and capture Spanish spoils or ports; it failed utterly, and the returning soldiers, unpaid and demoralized, spread rape, robbery, and defeatism in the coastal towns.

Desperate for funds, Charles resigned himself to calling his second Parliament. The opposition grew stronger with his needs. The House warned him not to levy taxes without parliamentary sanction. Eliot, once a friend of the Duke, excoriated him as a corrupt incompetent who had grown richer with each failure of strategy or policy. Parliament appointed a committee to investigate Buckingham; Charles rebuked it, saying, "I would not have the House to question my servants, much less one that is so near me." Eliot advised Parliament to withhold any grant of funds until the King admitted its right to demand the removal of a minister; Charles angrily reminded Parliament that he could at any time dismiss it; the Commons replied by formally impeaching Buckingham—accusing him of treason and demanding his dismissal (May 8, 1626); it informed the King that until this was done it would grant no funds. The King dissolved the Parliament (June 15). The issue of ministerial responsibility was left to the future.

But Charles was again destitute. A large quantity of royal plate was sold. "Free benevolences"—gifts to the King—were asked of the country; the yield was slight; British money was pro-Parliament. Charles ordered his agents to collect tonnage and poundage dues despite lack of Parliamentary consent, and to seize the goods of merchants who failed to pay; he commanded the ports to maintain the fleet; he allowed his agents to impress men into military service. English and Danish troops, fighting for Protestantism in Germany, were being overwhelmed by the Imperialists; England's Danish allies demanded the subsidy she had promised them. Charles ordered a forced loan—every taxpayer was to lend the government one per cent of the value of his land, five per cent of the worth of his personal property. Rich opponents were jailed, poor opponents were hustled into the army or the navy. Meanwhile English merchants delivered materials at Bordeaux and La Rochelle to Huguenots embattled with Richelieu; France declared war on England (1627). Buckingham led a fleet to attack the French at La Rochelle; the expedition failed. The £200,000 raised by the loan was soon spent, and Charles was again at his money's end. He summoned his third Parliament.

It met on March 17, 1628. Coke, Eliot, Wentworth, and John Hampden were returned, and, for the first time, Huntingdon Borough sent up a sturdy squire named Oliver Cromwell. Charles, in his speech from the throne, sternly called for funds, and added, with reckless insolence, "Take not this as threatening; I scorn to threaten any but my equals."[58] Parliament proposed £350,000, but, before voting it, required the King's consent to a "Petition of Right" (May 28, 1628) which became a historic landmark in the rise of Parliament to mastery:

To the King's Most Excellent Majesty:

> We humbly show unto our sovereign lord the King . . . that whereas it is declared and enacted by a statute . . . of Edward I . . . that no tallage or aid shall be laid or levied by the King . . . without the good will and assent of the archbishops, bishops, earls, barons, knights, burgesses, and other the freemen of the commonalty . . . your subjects have inherited this freedom, that they should not be compelled to contribute to any tax, tallage, aid, or other like charge not set by common consent in Parliament.

The petition went on to protest against forced loans, and the King's violation of the rights of habeas corpus and trial by jury as embodied in the Magna Charta of 1215. "We shall know by this [petition] if Parliaments live or die," said Coke. Charles gave it an ambiguous consent; Parliament demanded a clearer reply, and still held up the appropriation; Charles gave formal consent. London felt the significance of the surrender; there broke out such ringing of bells as had not been heard there for years.

Parliament, moving forward, requested the King to dismiss Buckingham; Charles refused. Suddenly both sides were startled to find this issue taken out of their hands. John Felton, a wounded ex-soldier weighed down with debts, angry at the arrears of his pension, and inflamed by pamphlets, bought a butcher's knife, walked sixty miles from London to Portsmouth, plunged the weapon into Buckingham's breast, and yielded himself to the authorities (August 23, 1628). Buckingham's wife, soon to give birth, collapsed at sight of the corpse. Felton, overcome with remorse, sent her his apologies and begged her forgiveness; she gave it. He was executed without torture.

The Parliament admonished the King that his continued collection of tonnage and poundage dues violated the Petition of Right; Charles replied that such dues had not been mentioned in the document; Parliament encouraged merchants to refuse to pay them.[59] Reasserting its right to legislate for religion despite the ecclesiastical supremacy of the king, it proclaimed a strictly Calvinist, anti-Arminian interpretation of the Thirty-nine Articles as the law of England; it proposed, of its own authority, to enforce religious conformity on this basis, and to deal out penalties to Catholics and Arminians alike.[60] Charles ordered the Parliament to adjourn; the Speaker, obeying, left the chair; but Parliament refused to adjourn, and members compelled the Speaker to resume the chair. Sir John Eliot now (March 2, 1629) offered three resolutions which made it a capital crime to introduce "Popery, or Arminianism, or other opinions disagreeing from the true and orthodox Church," to counsel, or take any share in, the collection of tonnage or poundage dues not sanctioned by Parliament, or to pay such unsanctioned dues. The Speaker refused to put the motions to a vote; a member put them; the House acclaimed and passed them. Then, learning that the King's troops were about to enter and dismiss the Parliament, it moved its own adjournment and dispersed.

On March 5 Charles ordered the imprisonment of Eliot, Selden, and seven other members of Parliament on charges of sedition. Six of them were soon released; three were condemned to heavy fines and long imprisonment; Eliot died in the Tower, aged thirty-eight (1632).

VII. CHARLES ABSOLUTE: 1629–40

Eleven years—the longest such interval in English history—were to pass without the assembling of Parliament. Charles was now free to be an absolute king. Theoretically he was claiming no more than James, Elizabeth, and Henry VIII; practically he was claiming more, for they had never stretched the royal prerogative so near the breaking point as Charles was doing by levying unsanctioned taxes, forcing loans, billeting soldiers on citizens, making arbitrary arrests, denying prisoners the rights of habeas corpus and trial by jury, extending the tyranny and severity of the Star Chamber in political, and of the Court of High Commission in ecclesiastical, trials. But Charles's basic mistake was his failure to recognize that the wealth now represented by the House of Commons was much greater than that wielded by or loyal to the King, and that the power of Parliament must be increased accordingly.

Amid this crisis, before it drew the nation's blood, the economy prospered, for Charles, like his father, was a man of peace and, through most of his reign, kept England out of war, while Richelieu exhausted France and Germany became a wilderness. The harassed King did what he could to mitigate the natural concentration of wealth. He ordered a halt to enclosures, annulled all those made in five Midland counties between 1625 and 1630, and fined six hundred recalcitrant landlords.[61] He had the wages of textile workers raised in 1629, 1631, 1637; he bade the justices of the peace exercise better control over prices; he appointed commissions to protect the wage scale and supervise poor relief; and Laud made new enemies by warning employers not to "grind the faces of the poor."[62] But at the same time the government granted, and profited from, monopolies in soap, salt, starch, beer, wine, and hides; it kept to itself a monopoly in coal, buying it at eleven shillings a caldron and selling it for seventeen in summer and nineteen in winter;[63] and these monopolies too ground the faces of the poor. During this period over twenty thousand Puritans emigrated to New England.

Charles pleaded that he had to find some ways to pay the costs of government. In 1634 he tried, disastrously, a new tax. Precedents existed for requiring coastal cities, in return for the protection afforded them by the navy, to fit out vessels for it in time of war, or, instead, to contribute "ship money" to the government for the maintenance of the fleet. Charles now (1635), without precedent, exacted this ship money from all England in time of peace, alleging the (quite real) need to rebuild the dilapidated navy for emergency and to protect British commerce from Channel piracy. Many resisted the new levy. To test its legality John Hampden refused to pay it; he was indicted, but was left free. He was a well-to-do Puritan of Buckinghamshire, no firebrand, but a quiet man (said the Royalist Clarendon) of "extraordinary sobriety and strictness,"[64] who hid firmness in courtesy and leadership in modesty.

His trial was long delayed, but came to court at last in November 1637. The lawyers for the Crown cited precedents for the ship-money tax, and held that the king, in time of peril, had the right to call for financial aid without waiting to assemble Parliament. Hampden's attorneys replied that there was no emergency, there had been plenty of time to call Parliament, and the exaction violated the Petition of Right accepted by the King. The judges voted seven to five for the Crown, but public sentiment supported Hampden, and questioned the impartiality of judges subject to royal retaliation; Hampden was soon released. Charles continued till 1639 to collect ship money, and he used most of it to build the navy that fought victoriously against the Dutch in 1652.

Meanwhile he had extended his blunders to Scotland. He shocked the Presbyterian Scots by marrying a Catholic and extending the authority of the bishops over the presbyteries of the Kirk. He alarmed half the nobility by an "Act of Revocation" (1625) revoking all grants of Church or Crown lands made to Scottish families since the accession of Mary Stuart. He named to the Privy Council of Scotland five bishops and an archbishop, John Spottiswoode, and (1635) made this prelate Chancellor— the first churchman to be appointed to that office since the Reformation. When, after irritating delays, he came to Scotland to be crowned (1633), he allowed the bishops to carry out the ritual with the almost Catholic ceremonies of the Anglican Church—vestments, candles, altar, and crucifix. Determined to enforce their authority over the presbyteries, the Scottish bishops drew up a set of liturgical rules, which, because emended and approved by the Archbishop of Canterbury, came to be known as "Laud's Canons." These gave the king full jurisdiction over all ecclesiastical matters, forbade assemblies of the clergy except at the king's call, restricted the right of teaching to persons licensed by a bishop, and limited ordination to candidates accepting these canons.[65] Charles sanctioned the canons and ordered them proclaimed in all Scottish churches. The Presbyterian ministers protested that half the Reformation was thereby annulled, and they warned that Charles was preparing to submit Britain to Rome. When an attempt was made, in St. Giles's Church, Edinburgh, to conduct a service according to the new formulas, a riot broke out; sticks and stones were hurled at the officiating dean; Jenny Geddes flung her stool at his head, crying, "Thou foul thief, wilt thou say Mass at my lug [ear]?"[66] Petitions from all classes were sent to Charles to revoke the canons; he replied by branding such petitions treasonable. Scotland now set the pace in revolt against the King.

On February 28, 1638, representatives of the Scottish ministry and laity signed at Edinburgh the National Covenant, reaffirming the Presbyterian faith and ritual, rejecting the new canons, and pledging themselves to defend the Crown and the "true religion." Nearly all Scotland, urged on by the ministers, subscribed to this covenant. Spottiswoode and all but four of the bishops fled to England. The General Assembly of the Kirk at Glasgow repudiated all bishops, and declared the Kirk to be independent of the state. Charles sent orders to the Assembly to disperse or be charged with treason; it continued its sittings. The King mustered an unenthusiastic army of 21,000 men and advanced toward Scotland; the "Covenanters" raised 26,000 men aflame with patriotic and religious fervor. When the two forces came face to face Charles agreed to submit the issues to a free Scottish Parliament and an unhindered Assembly of the Kirk; a truce was signed at Berwick (June 18, 1639), and the "First Bishops' War" ended without shedding blood. But the new Assembly, convened at Edinburgh (August 12, 1639), confirmed the "treasonable" decisions of the Glasgow conference, and the Scottish Parliament ratified the acts of the Assembly. Both sides prepared for the "Second Bishops' War."

In this crisis Charles called to his aid a man as resolute and thorough (this word was his motto) as the King was vacillating and incompetent. Thomas Wentworth had reached Parliament at twenty-one (1614), and had often voted against the King. Charles won him over by making him president of the Council of the North, rewarded his vigorous enforcement of the royal policies by appointing him to the Privy Council, and sent him as Lord Deputy to Ireland (1632), where his "Thorough" policy of merciless efficiency stamped out rebellion and created an angry peace. In 1639 he was made Earl of Strafford and chief counselor to Charles. He advised the King to raise a large army, suppress the Covenanters, and face a recalcitrant Parliament with an irresistible force. But a large army required large funds, which could hardly be raised without Parliament. Reluctantly, Charles summoned his fourth Parliament. When this "Short Parliament" met (April 13, 1640), he displayed to it an intercepted letter in which Covenanters had solicited the aid of Louis XIII;[67] against such treason,

Fig. 26—Velázquez: *Pope Innocent* X. Galleria Doria, Rome (Bettmann Archive)

PAGE 325

Fig. 27—Velázquez: *Las Meninas*. Prado, Madrid
PAGE 326

Fig. 28—Velázquez: *Self-portrait*. Detail from *Las Meninas*. Prado, Madrid (Bettmann Archive)
PAGE 326

FIG. 29—MURILLO: *A Beggar Boy*. Louvre, Paris   PAGE 331

FIG. 30—AFTER CLOUET: *Charles IX.*
Bibliothèque Nationale, Paris
PAGE 346

FIG. 31—SCHOOL OF
CLOUET: *Catherine de
Médicis.* Louvre, Paris
PAGE 338

FIG. 34—*Michel de Montaigne*. Musée de Condé, Chantilly (Bettmann Archive) PAGE 399

FIG. 35—POUSSIN: *Et Ego in Arcadia*. Louvre, Paris PAGE 433

Fig. 36—Philippe de Champaigne: *Cardinal Richelieu.* Louvre, Paris   page 380

FIG. 37—ATTRIBUTED TO WILLEM
KEY: *Duke of Alva.* Rijksmuseum,
Amsterdam (Bettmann Archive)

PAGE 444

FIG. 38—MICHIEL JANSZOON VAN
MIEREVELT: *William the Silent.*
Rijksmuseum, Amsterdam
(Bettmann Archive)

PAGE 437

Fig. 39—School of Rubens: *Ambrogio Spinola*. The Frick Collection, New York   PAGE 458

Fig. 40—Rubens: *Rubens and Isabella Brandt*. Alte Pinakothek, Munich
          PAGE 468

FIG. 41—FRANS HALS: *The Laughing Cavalier*. Reproduced by permission of the Trustees of the Wallace Collection, London   PAGE 485

FIG. 42—FRANS HALS: *The Women Regents*. Frans Halsmuseum, Haarlem   PAGE 486

FIG. 43—ANTHONY VANDYCK: *Self-portrait*. The Jules S. Bache Collection, 1949;
The Metropolitan Museum of Art, New York (Bettmann Archive)   PAGE 473

FIG. 44–REMBRANDT: *The Artist's Father*. Mauritshuis, The Hague   PAGE 487

FIG. 45—REMBRANDT: *The Artist's Mother*. Kunsthistorisches Museum, Vienna

FIG. 46—REMBRANDT: *Self-portrait*. Kunsthistorisches Museum, Vienna   PAGE 487

Fig. 47—Rembrandt: *Anatomy Lesson of Dr. Tulp*. Mauritshuis, The Hague (Bettmann Archive)

PAGE 488

argued the King, he had the right to organize an army. John Pym secretly communicated with Covenanters, decided that their cause was akin to Parliament's case against the King, and persuaded the Parliament to deny the King the subsidies and arrange an alliance with the Scots. Charles dissolved the Short Parliament as traitorous (May 5, 1640). Riots broke out in London; a mob attacked the palace of Archbishop Laud; not finding him, it killed a Catholic who refused to join in Protestant worship.[68]

Charles moved north with an improvised army. The Scots came down over the border, defeated the English (August 20, 1640), and took possession of northern England. The helpless monarch agreed to pay them £850 a day until a satisfactory treaty could be concluded; he could not pay, and the Scottish army remained around Newcastle as a decisive ally of the English Parliament in its war with the King. Bewildered and desperate, Charles called a council of peers to meet him at York. They advised him that his authority was on the verge of collapse, and that he must find some accommodation with his enemies. For the last time he summoned a Parliament, the longest and most fateful in English history.

VIII. THE LONG PARLIAMENT

It assembled at Westminster November 3, 1640. The House was composed of some five hundred men, the "flower of the English gentry and the educated laity . . . an aristocratic and not a popular house,"[69] representing the wealth rather than the people of England, but standing clearly for the future against the past. The majority of the Short Parliament were returned, brooding revenge. Selden, Hampden, and Pym were again on hand, and Oliver Cromwell, though not yet a leader, was a man of mark.

It is impossible, at this distance, to picture him objectively, for since his rise and till today historians have described him as an ambitious hypocrite[70] or a statesman-saint.[71] A personality so ambivalent probably encloses—sometimes he harmonizes—in his character the opposite qualities that beget such contradictory estimates. This may be the key to Cromwell.

He was one of those landowners without pedigree who stood outside the glamour of government, but paid uncomfortably for its maintenance. And yet he too had ancestors. His father, Robert Cromwell, had a modest estate in Huntingdon, worth three hundred pounds a year; his great-grandfather, Richard Williams, the nephew of Henry VIII's minister Thomas Cromwell, changed his name to Cromwell, and received, from minister or King, manors and revenues confiscated from the Catholic Church.[72] Oliver was one of ten children and was the only one who survived infancy. His grammar-school instructor was a fervent preacher who wrote a treatise proving the pope to be Antichrist, and another recording the divine punishment of notorious sinners. In 1616 Oliver entered Sidney Sussex College, Cambridge, where the headmaster was Samuel Ward, who died in prison (1643) for taking a strong Puritan stand against Laud's innovations and Charles's "Declaration of Sports." Apparently Oliver left Cambridge without graduating. Later (1638) he accused himself of some youthful wickedness:

> You know what my manner of life hath been. Oh, I have lived in a loved darkness, and hated light; I was a chief, the chief, of sinners. This is true: I hated godliness; yet God had mercy on me. Oh, the riches of His mercy! Praise Him for me—pray for me, that He who hath begun a good work would perfect it in the day of Christ.[73]

He experienced all the ecstasies of repentance; he had hallucinations of death and other mental terrors that left him permanently touched with melancholy, and for the rest of his life he spoke in terms of Puritan piety. He settled down, married, had nine children, and became so model a citizen that in 1628, aged twenty-eight, he was chosen to represent Huntingdon in Parliament. He sold his Huntingdon property for £1,800 in 1631 and moved to St. Ives, later to Ely. When Cambridge returned him to Parliament in 1640 he was described by another member as "very ordinarily appareled" in "a plain cloth suit . . . His linen not very clean . . . a speck or two of blood upon his little [neck] band," his face "swollen and reddish," his voice "sharp and untunable," his temper "exceeding fiery," but under firm control.[74] He bided his time, talked with God, and had the strength of ten. As yet, however, God chose other instruments.

It was John Pym who revealed the angry mood of the Parliament by denouncing Strafford as a secret papist plotting to bring in an army from Ireland, to overthrow Parliament, and to "alter law and religion."[75] On November 11, 1640, the House of Commons—which had never forgiven his desertion to the King—impeached the Earl as a traitor and had him sent to the Tower. On December 16, having declared the new Anglican canons illegal, it impeached Archbishop Laud on grounds of "popery" and treason, and had him too sent to the Tower. Selden later confessed, "We charge the prelatical clergy with popery to make them odious, though we know they are guilty of no such thing."[76] Charles was so bewildered by these uncompromising moves that he took no action to protect his aides. The Queen justified the Parliament's fears by asking her confessor to solicit aid from the Pope.[77]

Excitement and passion mounted on both sides. A "Root and Branch" faction among the London radicals—which included Milton—petitioned

Parliament to abolish episcopacy and restore the government of the Church to the people; it branded as abominable the opinion of some bishops "that the pope is not Antichrist . . . and that salvation is attainable in that [Catholic] religion."[78] The House rejected the petition, but voted the debarment of the clergy from all legislative and judicial functions. The Lords agreed, with the proviso that bishops should retain their seats in the upper house. This, however, was precisely what the Commons wished to end, for it expected that the bishops in the Lords would always vote for the King. Pamphlets defending or attacking episcopacy made the issue boil. Bishop Joseph Hall claimed divine right for it on the ground that it had been established by the Apostles or Christ; five Presbyterian publicists replied in a famous pamphlet under the pseudonym "Smectymnuus," composed of their initials; five later blasts were contributed by Milton. On May 27, 1641, Cromwell again proposed the total abolition of the episcopacy; the bill was passed by the House, rejected by the Lords. On September 1 the Commons resolved that "scandalous pictures" of the Trinity, all images of the Virgin Mary, all crosses and "superstitious figures" should be removed from English churches, and that all "dancing and other sports" were to be avoided on the Lord's Day. Another wave of iconoclasm swept over England; altar rails and screens were taken down, stained-glass windows were smashed, statues were demolished, pictures were cut to shreds.[79] The House again passed a bishops' exclusion bill on October 23. The King appealed to the Lords, declaring that he was resolved to die in the maintenance of the existing doctrine and discipline of the Anglican Church; he did. His intervention secured the defeat of the bill, but hostile crowds prevented the bishops from attending Parliament. Twelve of them signed a protest, declaring that any legislation passed in their absence would be null and void. Parliament impeached and imprisoned them. Finally the Lords ratified the exclusion bill (February 5, 1642), and bishops no longer sat in Parliament.

The victorious Commons proceeded to consolidate its power. It borrowed money from the city of London to finance its maintenance. It passed bills requiring triennial Parliaments and forbidding the dissolution of any Parliament within fifty days of its convening, or of the present Parliament without its consent. It reformed taxation and the judiciary. It abolished the Star Chamber and the Court of High Commission. It ended monopolies and the levy of ship money, and rescinded the verdict against Hampden. It granted the King the right to collect tonnage and poundage dues, but only for periods specified by Parliament. Charles agreed to these measures, and the Parliament passed from reform to revolution.

In March 1641 it brought Strafford to trial; in April it pronounced him guilty of treason and sent the bill of attainder to the King for signature.

Against Laud's advice, Charles appeared in the Lords and declared that though he was ready to disqualify Strafford from office he would never consent to condemn him for treason. The Commons pronounced this royal appearance a violation of parliamentary privilege and freedom. On the next day "great multitudes" gathered about the House of Lords and the palace of the King, crying "Justice! justice!" and demanding Strafford's death. The frightened Privy Council begged Charles to yield; he refused. The Archbishop of York added his plea for signature; nobles warned the King that his own life and the lives of the Queen and his children were in danger; he still refused. Finally the condemned man himself sent him a message advising him to sign, as the only alternative to mob violence.[80] Charles signed and never forgave himself. On May 12, 1641, Strafford was led out to execution. Laud stretched out his hands through the bars of his cell window to bless him as he passed. "Thorough" died without whimpering, before a hostile crowd.

His execution sharpened the division of the House into what later came to be the rival parties of Whigs and Tories—those who favored and those who opposed the further transference of power from king to Parliament. Men like Lucius Cary (Viscount Falkland) and Edward Hyde (future Earl of Clarendon), both of whom had supported Parliament, wondered now whether the King, having been so severely chastened, might not be a desirable bulwark against mob rule in London, Puritan rule in religion, and a runaway Parliament that would disestablish the Church, threaten private property, and imperil the whole class structure of British life. Pym, Hampden, and Cromwell might have admitted these dangers, but there was another that touched them more closely: they had gone so far that they feared for their lives if Charles should recover power. At any moment the King might bring over a half-Catholic army from Ireland as Strafford had proposed to do. For its own safety Parliament decided to maintain the friendly army of Scots in the north of England. It sent the Scots an initial gift of £300,000 and pledged a monthly subsidy of £25,000.[81]

The fears of the Parliament were sharpened by the sudden outbreak of a wild revolt in Ireland (October 1641). Phelim O'Neill, Rory O'More III, and other leaders called for a war of liberation—of Ulster from its English colonists, of Catholics from oppression, of Ireland from England. Inflamed by the memory of merciless persecutions and brutal evictions, the rebels fought with a fury that made them barbarous; the English in Ireland, defending what now seemed to them their legitimate property as well as their lives, returned barbarity with ferocity, and every victory became a massacre. The English Parliament wrongly suspected the King of having fomented the revolt to restore Catholicism in Ireland and later in England; it refused his request for funds to raise an army to rescue the English in the Pale; such an army might be turned against Parliament itself. The Irish revolt continued throughout the English revolution.

The revolution took a further step when Charles advanced two of the excluded and impeached bishops to higher place. Indignant Commoners proposed a "Grand Remonstrance" which would summarize and publicize the case of Parliament against the King, and would compel him to give Parliament the right to veto his appointments to important posts. Many conservatives felt that the measure would transfer executive power to the Parliament and reduce the King to impotence. The division of parties became acute, the debate more violent; members clutched their swords to emphasize their words; Cromwell later declared that if the bill had lost he would have taken ship to America.[82] It passed by eleven votes, and on December 1, 1641, it was presented to the King. It began by affirming its loyalty to the Crown. It proceeded to list in detail the offenses which the King had given Parliament and the injuries he had inflicted upon the country. It reviewed the abuses which parliamentary reforms had corrected; it charged "papists . . . bishops, and the corrupt part of the clergy," and self-seeking councilors and courtiers, with plotting to make England Catholic. It pointed to repeated violations of the Petition of Right and to highhanded dissolutions of elected Parliaments. It asked the King to call an assembly of divines to restore the Anglican worship to its pre-Laudian form. It proposed that he remove from his Council all opponents of the Parliament's policies, and employ hereafter only "such counselors, ambassadors, and other ministers . . . as the Parliament have cause to confide in; without which they could not give his Majesty such supplies for his own support, or such assistance for the Protestant party beyond the seas, as was desired."[83]

Charles took his time answering this ultimatum. On December 15 Parliament went over his head to the people by ordering publication of the Grand Remonstrance. Charles then replied. He agreed to call a synod to repress all invasions of "popery"; he refused to deprive the bishops of their votes in Parliament; he insisted on his right to call to his Council, and to public employment, such men as he thought fit; and he again asked for funds. Instead, the Commons proposed a "Militia Bill" which would give it control of the army.

Charles, so regularly irresolute, now rushed into a bold stroke that Parliament denounced as an act of war. On January 3, 1642, his attorney general, before the Lords, indicted, in the King's name, five members of the lower house—Pym, Hampden, Holles, Heselrige, Strode—on a charge of treason for seeking to turn the army from obedience to the King and for encouraging a "foreign power" (Scotland) to invade England and make war upon the King. On the next day Charles, supported by three hundred soldiers whom he left at the door, entered the House of Commons to arrest the five men; they were not there, having taken refuge in friendly homes; "I see," said the baffled King, "all the birds are flown." As he walked out he was rebuked with cries of "Privilege!"; for such royal and armed invasion of Parliament was manifestly illegal. In fear of whole-sale arrest, the Commons moved to the Guildhall, under protection of the citizens. When Charles left London for Hampton Court, the Commons, including the five indicted men, returned to Westminster. Queen Henrietta fled secretly to France with the Crown jewels to buy aid for the King. Charles left for the north with the Great Seal. He tried to enter Hull and secure the military supplies there; the town refused to admit him; he moved on to York. Parliament ordered all armed forces to obey only Parliament (March 5, 1642). Thirty-five peers and sixty-five Commoners seceded from Parliament and joined Charles at York. Edward Hyde now became chief adviser to the King.

On June 2 Parliament transmitted to Charles nineteen propositions whose acceptance it held to be essential to peace. He was to turn over to Parliament control of the army and all fortified places. Parliament was to revise the liturgy and the government of the Church. It was to appoint and dismiss all ministers of the Crown and the guardians of the King's children, and was to have authority to exclude from the upper house all peers hereafter created. Charles rejected the proposals as in effect a destruction of the monarchy. As if rehearsing the French Revolution, Parliament appointed a Committee of Public Safety, and ordered that "an army shall be forthwith raised" (July 12). Cromwell and others left for their home boroughs to organize volunteers. In an appeal to the nation (August 2), Parliament based its revolt not on the desirability of parliamentary sovereignty, but on the imminence of a Catholic uprising in England; and it warned the country that victory for the King would be followed by a general massacre of Protestants.[84] On August 17 its agents seized the military stores at Hull. On August 27, 1642, Charles unfurled his standard at Nottingham and began the Civil War.

IX. THE FIRST CIVIL WAR: 1642–46

England was now divided as seldom in known history before. London, the ports, the manufacturing towns, in general the south and the east, most of the middle class, part of the gentry, and practically all Puritans were for Parliament. Oxford and Cambridge, the west and the north, most of the aristocracy and the peasantry, and nearly all Catholics and episcopalian Anglicans stood with the King. The House of Commons was itself divided:

some 300 members were on the rebel side, some 175 were Royalists. In the Lords 30 of the 110 peers sided at first with Parliament. The balance of wealth fell against the King; London had half the money of the nation and lent heavily to the revolution; Charles could not borrow anywhere; the navy was against him, and it blocked foreign aid; he had to rely upon gifts and men from the great estates, whose owners felt that their landed interest depended on his victory. Some chivalric virtues and sentiment survived in the old families; they gave their loyalty to the King without stint; they fought and died like gentlemen. The colorful Cavaliers, their hair in ringlets, their horses in gay accouterment, had all the romance of the war on their side, and all the poets but Milton. The money was with Parliament.

The gauge of blood began at Edgehill (October 23, 1642). Each army had some 14,000 men. The Royalists were led by Prince Rupert, the twenty-two-year-old son of Charles's sister, Elizabeth of Bohemia; the "Roundheads," by Robert Devereux, third Earl of Essex. The result was indecisive, but Essex withdrew his forces, and the King marched on to make Oxford his headquarters. Nehemiah Wallington, a fervent or politic Puritan, called it a great victory for Parliament and God:

> Herein we see God's great mercy . . . for, as I hear, the slaughter was in all 5,517; but ten of the enemy's side were slain to one of ours. And observe God's wonderful works, for those that were slain of our side were mostly of them that ran away; but those that stood most valiantly to it, they were most preserved. . . .
> If I could relate how admirably the hand of Providence ordered our artillery and bullets for the destruction of the enemy! . . . Oh, how God did guide their bullets . . . that some fell down before them [of our side], some grazed along, some bullets went over their heads, and some one side of them! Oh, how seldom or never were they hurt, that stood valiant to it, by their bullets! . . . This is the Lord's doing, and it is marvelous in my eyes.[85]

However, matters went poorly for Parliament in the ensuing spring. Queen Henrietta stole back to England with arms and ammunition and joined Charles at Oxford. Essex dallied while his army was eroded by desertion and disease. Hampden was mortally wounded in a skirmish at Chalgrove Field. A Parliamentary force was defeated at Adwalton Moor (June 30, 1643), another was destroyed at Roundway Down (July 13); Bristol fell to the King. In this nadir of its fortunes, Parliament turned to Scotland for help. On September 22 it signed with Scottish commissioners a "Solemn League and Covenant" which pledged the Scots to send an army to Parliament's aid in return for £30,000 a month, on condition that Parliament establish in England and Ireland the Presbyterian form of

Protestantism—church government by presbyteries free from episcopal control. In the same month Charles made peace with the Irish insurgents, and imported some of them to fight for him in England. English Catholics rejoiced, Protestants turned increasingly against the King. In January 1644 the Irish invaders were defeated at Nantwich, and the Scottish invaders advanced into England. The Civil War now involved three nations and four faiths.

On July 1, 1643, the Westminster Assembly—121 English divines, thirty English laymen, and (later) eight Scottish delegates—met to define the new Presbyterian Protestantism of England. Hampered by Parliamentary domination, it dragged out its conferences through six years. A few members, favoring episcopacy, withdrew; a small group of Puritan Independents demanded that each congregation should be free from presbyteries as well as from bishops; the majority, following the pledge and the will of Parliament, favored the rule of religion in England and Ireland, as in Scotland, by presbyters, presbyteries, provincial synods, and general assemblies. Parliament abolished the Anglican episcopacy (1643), adopted and legislated the Presbyterian organization and creed (1646), but gave itself a veto power over all ecclesiastical decisions. In 1647 the Assembly issued the Westminster Confession of Faith, Larger Catechism, and Smaller Catechism, reaffirming the Calvinistic doctrine of predestination, election, and reprobation.* The decisions of the Westminster Assembly were set aside by the restoration of the Stuart dynasty and the Anglican Church, but the confession and the catechisms have remained in theoretical force in the Presbyterian churches of the English-speaking world.

The Assembly and the Parliament agreed in rejecting the plea of the minor sects for religious toleration. The incorporated city of London petitioned Parliament to suppress all heresies. In 1648 the Commons passed bills punishing with life imprisonment the opponents of infant baptism, and with death those who denied the Trinity, or the Incarnation, or the divine inspiration of the Bible, or the immortality of the soul.[87] Several Jesuits were executed between 1642 and 1650; and on January 10, 1645, Archbishop Laud, aged seventy-two, was led from the Tower to the block. Parliament felt that it was engaged in a war to the death and that it was no time for amenities. Cromwell, however, stood out for some measure of

---

* Excerpts from the Westminster Confession, ch. III: "By the decree of God, for the manifestation of His glory, some men and angels are predestined unto everlasting life, and others foreordained to everlasting death. . . . Those of mankind that are predestined unto life, God, before the foundation of the world was laid, according to His eternal and immutable purpose, and the secret counsel and good pleasure of His will, hath chosen in Christ unto everlasting glory, out of His mere free grace and love, without any foresight of faith or good works, or perseverance in either of them . . . and all to the praise of His glorious grace . . . The rest of mankind God was pleased, according to the unsearchable counsel of His own will, whereby He extendeth or withholdeth mercy as He pleaseth, for the glory of His sovereign power over His creatures, to pass by, and to ordain them to dishonour and wrath for their sin, to the praise of His glorious justice."[88]

toleration. In 1643 he organized at Cambridge a regiment which came to be called the Ironsides—a name originally given by Prince Rupert to Cromwell himself. Into this company he welcomed men of any faith—except Catholics and Episcopalians—"who had the fear of God before them and made some conscience of what they did."[88] When a Presbyterian officer wished to cashier a lieutenant colonel as an Anabaptist, Cromwell protested, "Sir, the state, in choosing men to serve it, takes no notice of their opinions; if they be willing to serve it faithfully, that suffices."[89] He asked Parliament (1644) to "endeavour the finding out some way how far tender consciences, who cannot in all things submit to the common [ecclesiastical] rule . . . may be borne with according to the Word."[90] Parliament ignored the request, but he continued to practice a comparative toleration in his regiments, and during his ascendancy in England.

Cromwell's development as a general was one of the surprises of the war. He shared with Lord Ferdinando Fairfax the honors of a victory at Winceby (October 11, 1643). At Marston Moor (July 2, 1644) Fairfax was routed, but Cromwell's Ironsides saved the day. Other Parliamentary leaders, the earls of Essex and Manchester, suffered reverses or failed to follow up their successes; Manchester frankly admitted his unwillingness to overthrow the King. To get rid of these titled generals, Cromwell proposed a "Self-denying Ordinance" (December 9, 1644) by which all members of Parliament were to resign their commands. The proposal was defeated; it was revived and passed (April 3, 1645); Essex and Manchester retired; Sir Thomas Fairfax, son of Ferdinando, was made commander in chief, and he soon appointed Cromwell lieutenant general in charge of the cavalry. Parliament ordered the formation of a "New Model" army of 22,000 men. Cromwell undertook to train it.

He had had no military experience before the war, but his force of character, his steadiness of purpose and will, his skill in playing upon the religious and political feelings of men, enabled him to mold his regiments into a unique discipline and loyalty. The Puritan faith equaled the Spartan ethic in making invincible soldiers. These men did not "swear like a trooper"; on the contrary, no oaths were heard in their camp, but many sermons and prayers. They stole not, nor raped, but they invaded churches to rid them of religious images and "prelatical" or "papistical" clergymen.[91] They shouted with joy or fury when they encountered the enemy. And they were never beaten. At Naseby (June 14, 1645), when the Royalists were routing Sir Thomas Fairfax's infantry, Cromwell with his new cavalry turned the defeat into so thorough a victory that the King lost all his infantry, all his artillery, half his cavalry, and copies of his correspondence, which were published to show that he planned to bring more Irish troops into England and to repeal the laws against Catholics.

From that time Charles's affairs rapidly worsened. The Marquis of Montrose, his heroic general in Scotland, after many victories, was routed at Philiphaugh and fled to the Continent. On July 30, 1645, the Parliamentary army took Bath; on August 23 Rupert surrendered Bristol to Fairfax. The King turned in all directions for help, in vain. On every side and pretext his troops, feeling their cause hopeless, went over to the enemy. By separate and devious negotiations he tried to divide his foes—the Independents from the Parliament, Parliament from the Scots—and failed. He had already sent his pregnant wife across hostile country to find ship for France; now he bade Prince Charles escape from England by whatever possible means. He himself, disguised and with but two attendants, made his way to the north and surrendered to the Scots (May 5, 1646). The First Civil War was in effect at an end.

X. THE RADICALS: 1646–48

Charles had been led to hope that the Scots would treat him as still their King; they preferred to consider him their prisoner. They offered to help him regain his throne if he would sign the Solemn League and Covenant making the Presbyterian form of Christianity compulsory throughout the British Isles; he refused. The English Parliament sent commissioners to the Scots at Newcastle, proposing to accept Charles as King on condition that he accept the Covenant, consent to the proscription of leading Royalists, and allow Parliament to control all armed forces and name all high officials of the state; he refused. Parliament offered the Scots £400,000 to pay their arrears and expenses if they would return to Scotland and surrender the King to English commissioners. The Scottish Parliament agreed. It accepted the money not as a price for the King, but as just reimbursement for its outlay in the war; Charles, however, felt that he had been bartered for gold. He was removed to Holmby House in Northamptonshire (January 1647) as prisoner of the English Parliament.

The English army, now encamped at Saffron Walden, forty miles from London, reviewed its victories and called for commensurate rewards. The cost of maintaining these thirty thousand men had compelled Parliament to raise taxes to twice their maximum under Charles; even so it owed the soldiers from four to ten months of back pay. Moreover, the Puritan Independents, defeated in Parliament, were gaining the upper hand in the army, and Cromwell, their leader, was suspected of ambitions inconsistent with the sovereignty of Parliament. Worse yet, there were in his regiment "Levelers" who rejected all distinctions of rank in Church and state, and who called for manhood suffrage and religious liberty. A few of them were anarchist communists; William Walwyn declared that all things should be in common; then "there would be no need for government, for there would be no thieves or criminals."[92] John Lilburne, the most undiscourageable of the Levelers after every arrest and punishment, was "the most popular man in England" (1646).[93] Cromwell was attacked as a Leveler, but, though sympathetic with them, he was hostile to their ideas, feeling that in the England of that day democracy would lead to chaos.

Parliament, now Presbyterian, resented the threat implied in the nearness of so large and troublesome an army so potently Independent. It passed a bill to disband half of it and to enroll the rest as volunteers for service in Ireland. The soldiers demanded their arrears; Parliament voted them a part in cash, the remainder in promises. The army refused to disband until fully paid. Parliament reopened negotiations with the King, and nearly reached an agreement with him to restore him on his consenting to accept the Covenant for three years. Warned of this, a squad of cavalry raided Holmby House, captured the King, and took him to Newmarket (June 3-5, 1647). Cromwell hurried to Newmarket and made himself head of a Council of the Army. On January 10 the army began a leisurely march upon London. En route it sent to Parliament a declaration formulated chiefly by Cromwell's able son-in-law Henry Ireton, which condemned the absolutism of Parliament as no better than the King's, and demanded the election of a new Parliament by a wider suffrage. Parliament was between two fires, for the merchants, the manufacturers, and the populace of London, fearing occupation by the army, clamored for the restoration of the King on almost any terms. A city crowd invaded Parliament (July 26), and compelled it to invite the King to London and to put the militia under Presbyterian command. Sixty-seven Independents left Parliament for the army.

On August 6 the troops entered London, bringing the King with them. The sixty-seven Independents were escorted back to their places in Parliament. From that time until Cromwell took supreme authority, the army dominated Parliament. It was not chaotic or unprincipled; it maintained order in the city and within its own ranks; and its demands, though probably impracticable at the time, were sanctioned by posterity. In the pamphlet *The Case of the Army Truly Stated* (October 9, 1647) it called for freedom of trade, abolition of monopolies, and restoration of common lands to the poor, and urged that no man be forced to testify against himself in court.[94] In *An Agreement of the People* (October 30) it proclaimed that "all power is originally and essentially in the whole body of the people"; that the only just government is through representatives freely chosen by manhood suffrage; that therefore kings and lords, if allowed to exist, should be subordinate to the House of Commons; that no man should be exempt from the laws; and that all should enjoy full religious liberty.[95]

"Every man born in England, the poor man, the meanest man in the kingdom," said Colonel Rainsborough, ought to have a voice in choosing those
who made the laws of the land by which he was to live and die.[96]

Cromwell quieted the debate by summoning its leaders to prayer. The
Levelers charged him with hypocrisy and with secret negotiations for
restoring the King, and he confessed that he still believed in monarchy.
He explained to the democrats that the resistance to their proposals would
be too formidable to be overcome by mere "fleshly strength," and after
long argument he persuaded the leaders to reduce their demand for universal suffrage to a request for an extension of the franchise. Some soldiers
refused to compromise; they wore the *Agreement* in their hats, and
ignored Cromwell's command to remove it. He had three ringleaders arrested; they were tried by court-martial and condemned to death; he
ordered them to throw dice for their lives; the one who lost was shot.
Discipline revived.

Meanwhile the King escaped from his army captors, made his way to
the coast and the Isle of Wight, and found friendly lodging in Carisbrooke
Castle (November 14, 1647). He was heartened by news of Royalist rebellions against Parliament in the countryside and in the fleet. Scottish commissioners in London secretly offered a Scottish army to re-enthrone him
if he would adopt Presbyterian Christianity and suppress other forms of
religion. He accepted this "engagement," but limited it to three years.
The commissioners left London to raise an army. The Scottish Parliament
ratified their plan for an invasion of England, and issued a manifesto (May
3, 1648) requiring all Englishmen to take the Covenant, to suppress all
forms of religion except the Presbyterian, and to disband the Independent
army. The English Parliament saw itself superseded and England subordinated to Scotland if these proposals came into force. It hurriedly made its
peace with Cromwell and persuaded him to lead his troops against the
Scots; doubtless it was glad to put him at a distance and in peril. After three
days of pleading he prevailed upon the army to follow him back to battle.
It went reluctantly, and some leaders vowed that if they again saved England, it would be their "duty . . . to call Charles Stuart, that man of blood,
to account for the blood he had shed."[97]

XI. FINIS: 1648–49

Cromwell's energy made short work of the Second Civil War. While
Fairfax put down Royalist revolts in Kent, Oliver turned west and cap-
tured a Royalist stronghold in Wales. The Scots crossed the Tweed on
July 8 and moved with alarming speed to within forty miles of Liverpool.

At Preston, in Lancashire, Cromwell's nine thousand men met twice that number of Scots and Cavaliers and overwhelmed them (August 17).

While Cromwell and his army were saving Parliament, it plotted to protect itself from them by reopening negotiations for the restoration of the King. But it insisted that he should sign and enforce the Covenant; he would not. The returning army offered to support his restoration with severe limitations on the royal prerogative; he refused (November 17). To prevent his being restored by Parliament, the army captured him again and lodged him in Hurst Castle, opposite the Isle of Wight. Parliament condemned the action and voted to accept the King's latest terms as a basis for settlement. The army leaders, anticipating death if Charles were restored, declared that none might be permitted to pass into the House but such as had continued "faithful to the public interest." Early on December 6 Colonel Thomas Pride and a troop of soldiers surrounded and invaded the House of Commons and barred or expelled 140 Royalist and Presbyterian members; forty who resisted were jailed.[98] Cromwell approved the action, and joined in voting for the speedy trial and execution of the King.

Of the five hundred members who in 1640 had composed the House of Commons only fifty-six now remained. This "Rump Parliament," by a majority of six, passed an ordinance declaring it treason for a king to make war upon Parliament. The Lords rejected the ordinance as beyond the authority of the Commons; the Commons thereupon (January 4, 1649) resolved that the people were, "under God, the original of all just power"; that the Commons, as representing the people, had "the supreme power in this nation"; and that therefore its enactments, without the consent of the Lords or the king, had the force of law. On January 6 they named 135 commissioners to try the King. One commissioner, Algernon Sidney, told Cromwell they had no legal authority to try a king. Cromwell lost his temper. "I tell you," he cried, "we will cut off his head with the crown upon it."[99] The army leaders made a last attempt to avoid regicide; they offered to acquit Charles if he would agree to the sale of the bishops' lands and resign the power to veto the ordinances of Parliament. He said he could not, for he had sworn to be faithful to the Church of England. There was no question of his courage.

The trial began on January 19, 1649. The sixty or seventy impromptu judges who consented to act sat on a raised dais at one end of Westminster Hall, soldiers stood at the other, spectators thronged the galleries; Charles was seated in the center, alone. The presiding officer, John Bradshaw, stated the charge and asked the King to answer. Charles denied the authority of the court to try him, or that it represented the people of England, and claimed that government by a Rump Parliament dominated by the army was a worse tyranny than any he had ever shown. The galleries cried,

"God save the King!" The pulpits condemned the trial; Bradshaw feared for his life in the streets. Prince Charles dispatched from Holland a sheet bearing only his signature, and promised the judges to abide by any terms they would write over his name if they would spare his father's life.[100] Four nobles offered to die in Charles's stead; they were refused.[101] Fifty-nine judges, including Cromwell, signed the death sentence. On January 30, before a vast and horror-stricken crowd, the King went quietly to his death. His head was severed with one blow of the executioner's ax. "There was such a groan by the thousands then present," wrote an eyewitness, "as I never heard before and desire I may never hear again."[102]

Was the execution legal? Of course not. On the basis of existing law, the Parliament progressively and rudely appropriated royal rights sanctioned by the precedents of a hundred years. By definition a revolution is illegal; it can advance to the new only by violating the old. Charles was sincere in defending the powers he had inherited from Elizabeth and James; he was sinned against as well as sinning; his fatal error lay in not recognizing that the new distribution of wealth required, for social stability, a new distribution of political power.

Was the execution just? Yes, so far as war is just. Once law is set aside by trial at arms, the defeated may ask for mercy, but the victor may exact the ultimate penalty if he judges it necessary as a preventive of renewed resistance, or as a deterrent to others, or as protection for the lives of himself and his followers. Presumably a triumphant King would have hanged Cromwell, Ireton, Fairfax, and many more, perhaps with the tortures regularly allotted to persons convicted of treason.

Was the execution wise? Probably not. Cromwell apparently believed that a live king, no matter how securely imprisoned, would be a stimulus to repeated Royalist revolts. But so would the King's son, unreachable in France or Holland, as yet unblemished with his father's faults, and soon to be glorified with romance. The execution of Charles I led to a foreseeable revulsion of national feeling, which in eleven years restored his line. Subsequent history suggests that mercy would have been wisdom. When Charles's son James II gave equally great offense, the Glorious Revolution of 1688, managed with aristocratic finesse, deliberately allowed him to escape to France; and the results of that deposition were permanent. However, it was the earlier Rebellion that made the later Revolution possible in all its swift effectiveness.

The Great Rebellion corresponded both to the Huguenot uprisings in sixteenth-century France and, despite many differences, to the French Revolution of 1789—in the first case the insurrection of a stern and simple Calvinism, sinewed by mercantile wealth, against a ritualistic Church and

an absolutist government; in the second case the revolt of a national assembly, expressing the power of the purse and the middle class, against a
landed aristocracy led by a well-meaning but blundering ruler. By 1789
the English had digested their two rebellions, and could look with horror
and eloquence upon a revolution that, like its own, incarnadined a country
and killed a king because the past had tried to stand still.

BOOK II

THE FAITHS FIGHT FOR POWER

1556–1648

CHAPTER IX

Alma Mater Italia

1564–1648

I. THE MAGIC BOOT

AFTER the double fury of Renaissance and Reformation, Italy was subsiding into a Spanish subjection harassed with poverty, solaced with religion, and gilded with peace. The Treaty of Cateau-Cambrésis (1559) had awarded the duchy of Savoy to Emmanuel Philibert. Genoa, Lucca, Venice, and San Marino survived as independent republics. Mantua remained obedient to the Gonzaga dukes, Ferrara to the Estensi, Parma to the Farnese. The Medici ruled Tuscany—Florence, Pisa, Arezzo, Siena— but their ports were under Spanish control. Through her viceroys Spain governed the duchy of Milan and the Kingdom of Naples, which included Sicily and all Italy south of the Papal States. These, running across the center of the peninsula from the Mediterranean to the Adriatic, were ruled by popes hemmed in by Spanish power.

That power was not militarily aggressive; it did not interfere in the internal affairs of the states, except Milan and Naples; but its distaste for commerce and its fear of the free intellect cast a pall over Italian life. The capture of Oriental and American trade by the Atlantic nations transferred to them the wealth that had once financed the Renaissance and now nourished the cultural blooming of Spain, England, and the Netherlands. Italy suffered further from the decline of papal revenues consequent upon the Reformation. The patient peasantry toiled and prayed, the innumerable monks prayed, the merchants lost caste and fortune, the aristocracy spent itself in the pursuit of titles and in extravagant display.

And yet amid this political debacle Italy produced the greatest scientist of the age, Galileo; the adventurous and prophetic philosophy of Bruno; the greatest sculptor, Bernini; the most influential composer, Monteverdi; the bravest missionaries; one of her greatest poets, Tasso; and, in Bologna, Naples, and Rome, schools of painting rivaled only in the opulent Netherlands. Culturally Italy was still supreme.

1. In the Foothills of the Alps

It is pleasant to traverse again, if only with mind and pen and haste, the garden and gallery called Italy. Turin became a major capital under the able rule of Emmanuel Philibert and the encouragement given to literature and art by his consort, Margaret of France and Savoy. Milan, though subject, was still magnificent; Evelyn described it in 1643 as "one of the most princely cities in Europe, with 100 churches, 71 monasteries, 40,000 inhabitants . . . sumptuous palaces, and rare artists."[1] After a fire gutted the Basilica of San Lorenzo Maggiore (1573), Carlo Borromeo, the saintly Archbishop of Milan, commissioned Martino Bassi to rebuild the interior in the stately Byzantine style of San Vitale's at Ravenna. Carlo's nephew, Cardinal Federigo Borromeo, raised the Palazzo Ambrosiano (1609), and established in it the famous Biblioteca Ambrosiana. The Palazzo di Brera, begun for a Jesuit college in 1615, has been since 1776 the home of the Accademia di Belle Arti, and since 1809 that of the renowned Brera Gallery, seriously injured in the Second World War but now handsomely restored. There one may find much of the work of the Procaccini and the Crespi, the two families that dominated Milanese painting in this age.

Genoa, La Serenissima, still proudly surveyed, from her palace-decorated hills, a Mediterranean dotted with Genoese ships. The merchant republic had lost its Eastern possessions to the Turks, and some of her trade with the Orient had passed to the Atlantic states; but her great mole gave her so fine a harbor that she remained (and is) the chief Italian port. Here the princes of commerce or finance built some of the richest homes in Italy. Evelyn thought that the Strada Nova, or New Street, planned by Rubens and faced by palaces of polished marble, was "far superior to any in Europe."[2] Galeazzo Alessi and his pupils designed many of these lordly mansions, which were famous for their art galleries, their stately stairways, their paneled or frescoed walls, and their luxurious furniture—"whole tables and bedsteads of massive silver"; the Genoese magnates were adepts at turning sweat into gold. In 1587 Giacomo della Porta raised the Basilica of the Santissima Annunziata, whose fluted columns, perfect pulpit, and ornate vault were the pride of Genoese piety. This and many another of Genoa's churches and palaces were largely ruined in the Second World War.

As late as Vasari, Florence was still termed the Athens of Italy, for she was fertile in literature, scholarship, and science as well as art. Everything prospered there except chastity. Under Grand Duke Francesco I (1574-87) the great Medici family deteriorated into a mess of intemperance and adultery. Cardinal Ferdinando de' Medici resigned his ecclesiastical orders to become Grand Duke Ferdinand I; for twenty-two years (1587-1609) he gave Tuscany a just and enlightened rule, he expanded Tuscan commerce by making Livorno (Leghorn) a free port open to all traders and faiths, and he restored the morals of his people by the morality of his life. His successors Cosimo II and Ferdinand II distinguished themselves by financing Galileo. Bartolommeo Ammanati carved the great fountain of Neptune for the Piazza della Signoria in Florence, and designed the Palazzo Ducale in Lucca. Giovanni da Bologna finished in 1583 the *Rape of the Sabines* that stands in the Loggia dei Lanzi, and cast the statue of Henry IV which Cosimo II presented to Marie de Médicis to adorn the Pont Neuf in Paris. Alessandro Allori and his son Cristofano continued, diminuendo, the chromatic fantasy of Florentine painting, and Pietro da Cortona skirted mastery in frescoes picturing, on the ceilings of the Pitti Palace, the virtues of Duke Cosimo I.

Parma in this period had a renowned duke, Alessandro Farnese, who was kept so busy leading Spanish armies in the Netherlands that he never occupied his throne. Under his son Ranuccio the University of Parma attained European fame, and Aleotti built (1618) the Teatro Farnese, accommodating seven thousand spectators in a semicircular amphitheater rivaled only, in modern Italy, by the Teatro Olimpico of his teacher, Palladio.

Mantua now entered upon a period of prosperity recalling the great days of Isabella d'Este. A flourishing textile industry made Mantuan cloth popular even in rival England and France. The house of Gonzaga, which had ruled the duchy since 1328, was still producing able men. Duke Vincenzo I again incarnated the qualities of a Renaissance prince: handsome and gracious, patron of happy Rubens and miserable Tasso, collector of ancient and Chinese art, of musical instruments, Flemish tapestries, Dutch tulips, and beautiful women, lover of poetry and gambling, brave in battle and bold in statesmanship, but wearing himself out in adultery and war, and dying at fifty in 1612. Three sons ruled in turn; the last, Vincenzo II, left no children, and the competition of France, Austria, and Spain to determine and control his successor made the duchy the helpless theater of a devastating War of the Mantuan Succession (1628-31), which almost blotted Mantua from history.

Verona idled culturally through this epoch, resting on the Renaissance. In Vicenza the classic façades of Palladio were setting a style for Christopher Wren. Vincenzo Scamozzi completed Palladio's Teatro Olimpico and designed the Palazzo Trissino-Barton. A flair for ornament, hardly suppressed in Palladio, made Scamozzi a living bridge from classicism to baroque.

2. Venice

The Queen of the Adriatic, like ancient Rome, had a long and stately decline. She was losing to Portugal her sea trade with India and would soon feel the competition of the Dutch. She bore the brunt of Turkish maritime expansion; her navy and her commanders were major factors in the victory over the Turks at Lepanto (1571), but she yielded Cyprus a few months later, and thereafter her commerce with the eastern Mediterranean was subject to Turkish permission and terms. She struggled valiantly to meet the challenge of change. By connecting at Aleppo with caravans from Central Asia, she made up in some measure for the lessening of her seaborne trade with the East. Her vessels still controlled the Adriatic. She shared in the profits of the slave trade that was now disgracing Portugal, Spain, and England. Her mainland dependencies—Vicenza, Verona, Trieste, Trent, Aquileia, Padua—prospered in economy and increased in population. Her industries continued to excel in glass, silk, lace, and artistic luxuries. Her Banco di Rialto, established in 1587 after the failure of many private banks, put the strength of the state behind Venetian finance, and served as a model for similar institutions in Nuremberg, Hamburg, and Amsterdam. Travelers marveled at the beauty of her architecture and her women, the cleanliness of her streets, and the tenacious stability of her government.

Her foreign policy aimed to keep a balance of power between France and Spain, lest one or the other absorb the weakened republic; hence her early recognition of Henry IV to strengthen war-torn France. In 1616 the Spanish viceroy at Naples, the Duke of Osuna, entered into a conspiracy with the Spanish ambassador at Venice to overthrow the Senate and make the republic a dependency of Spain. Philip III, after the delicate fashion of governments, gave the enterprise his blessing, but bade Osuna proceed "without letting anyone know that you are doing it with my knowledge, and make believe that you are acting without orders."[3] The Venetian Signory had the best spies in Europe; the plot was detected, the local conspirators were seized, and one morning the people were edified to see them hanging in St. Mark's Square, gazing with dead eyes upon happy doves.

This quiet and austere oligarchy, holding commerce with—and giving religious freedom to—men of any creed, took a remarkably independent attitude toward the papacy. It taxed the clergy, subjected them to the civil law, and forbade, without its consent, the erection of new shrines or monasteries and the deeding of land to the Church. A party of Venetian statesmen, led by Leonardo Donato and Nicolo Contarini, especially resisted the claims of the papacy to power in temporal affairs. In 1605 Camillo Borghese became Pope Paul V; a year later Donato was chosen doge; these two men, who had been friends when Donato was Venetian envoy at Rome, now confronted each other in a struggle between Church and state, echoing across five centuries the contest between Gregory VII and the Emperor Henry IV. And Pope Paul was shocked to find that the intellectual leader of the anticlerical party in Venice was another Paul, Fra Paolo Sarpi, a Servite monk.

Sarpi, said Molmenti, was "the loftiest intellect that Venice ever produced."[4] Son of a merchant, he entered the Servite order at thirteen, absorbed knowledge passionately, and at eighteen defended 318 theses in a public disputation at Mantua, so successfully that its Duke made him court theologian. At twenty-two he was ordained priest and became a professor of philosophy; at twenty-seven he was elected provincial of his order for the Venetian Republic. He continued his studies in mathematics, astronomy, physics, everything. He discovered the contractility of the iris. He wrote scientific treatises that are now lost, and took part in the investigations and experiments of Fabrizio d'Acquapendente and Giambattista della Porta, who said that he had never met a "more learned man, or one more subtle in the whole circle of knowledge."[5] Perhaps these profane studies injured Paolo's faith. He welcomed some Protestants to friendship, and charges were lodged against him before the Venetian Inquisition—the same body that was soon to capture Giordano Bruno. Thrice he was nominated to bishoprics by the Senate; thrice the Vatican rejected him; and the memory of these rebuffs accentuated his hostility to Rome.

In 1605 the Senate arrested two priests and convicted them of serious crimes. Pope Paul V demanded that the men be turned over to ecclesiastical jurisdiction, and also ordered the repeal of the laws against new churches, monasteries, and religious orders. The Venetian Signory courteously refused. The Pope gave the Doge, the Signory, and the Senate twenty-seven days within which to comply. They called in Fra Paolo as counselor in canon law; Sarpi advised resistance on the ground that papal power extended only to spiritual concerns; the Senate adopted his view. In May 1606 the Pope excommunicated Donato and the Signory and laid an interdict upon all religious services in Venetian territory. The Doge instructed the Venetian clergy to ignore the interdict and continue their functions; they did, except the Jesuits, the Theatines, and the Capuchins. The Jesuits, pledged by their constitutions to obey the popes, left Venice in a body, despite the Signory's warning that if they left they would never be allowed to return. Meanwhile Sarpi, answering Cardinal Bellarmine, published tracts limiting the papal power, and proclaiming the superior authority of general councils over the popes.

Paul V appealed to Spain and France. But Spain had often rejected papal edicts, and Henry IV of France was grateful to Venice. However, Henry sent to Venice the judicious Cardinal de Joyeuse, who devised the necessary face-saving formulas. The priests were released to the French ambassador, who soon released them to Rome; the Senate refused to repeal the protested laws, but (hoping for papal aid against the Turks) it promised that the Republic would "conduct itself with its accustomed piety." The Pope suspended his censures, and Joyeuse absolved the excommunicates. "The claims of Paul V," says a Catholic historian, "were too medieval in character to be made good."⁶ This was the last time that an entire state was placed under an interdict.

On October 5, 1607, Sarpi was attacked by assassins, who left him for dead. He recovered, and is said to have remarked, in an epigram almost too good to be true, "*Agnosco stilum curiae Romanae*" (I recognize the pointed style of the Roman court).*⁷ The assassins found protection and acclaim in the Papal States.⁸ Henceforth Sarpi lived quietly in his cloister saying Mass every day; but his own *stilus* was not idle. In 1619 he published, under a pseudonym and through a London firm, his *Istoria del Concilio Tridentino,* a voluminous indictment of the Council of Trent. He gave a quite Protestant account of the Reformation, and condemned the Council for making the schism irreconcilable by yielding completely to the popes. The Protestant world hailed the book with enthusiasm, and Milton called its author "the great unmasker." The Jesuits commissioned a learned scholar of their order, Sforza Pallavicino, to write a counter-history (1656–64), which exposed and rivaled Sarpi's bias and inaccuracy.⁹ Despite their *parti pris*, these two books marked an advance in the collection and use of original documents, and Sarpi's vast brief has the added and dangerous attraction of fiery eloquence. He was far ahead of his time in advocating a complete separation of Church and state.

Under that proud government, on and between those placid and odorous canals, Venice continued to pursue money and beauty, appeasing Christ with architecture and the Virgin with litanies. Every week had some festival, for which any saint provided excuse; we see such collective raptures in the paintings of Guardi; and in the portraits we note the sensuous, Oriental prodigality of costumes and jewelry. Almost any evening one could hear music coming from the gondolas. If you stepped into such a magic bark and gave no directions, the gondolier would, with no word spent, take you to the house of some associated courtesan. Montaigne, who had as few prejudices as any man, was surprised at the abundance and freedom of the Venetian *filles de joie.* They paid a tax to the state, which in return allowed them to live where they liked and dress as they pleased; and it defended them against defaulting customers.¹⁰

The Grand Canal and its tributaries grew fairer year by year with lordly churches, gay new palaces, or a graceful bridge. In 1631 the Senate commissioned Baldassare Longhena to build the noble Church of Santa Maria della Salute as a votive offering to the Virgin for restoring the health of the city after a great plague. In 1588–92 Antonio da Ponte re-

---

* *Stilus* meant originally a pointed iron; then an iron point used in writing on wax tablets; then a pen; then a manner of writing, a style. The Italian diminutive *stiletto* meant both an engraving tool and a small dagger.

placed an old wooden bridge with a new Ponte di Rialto, spanning the Grand Canal with a single marble arch ninety feet in length, flanked by shops on either side. About 1600 the Bridge of Sighs (the Ponte dei Sospiri) was built high over a canal between the Palazzo dei Dogi and the Prigioni di San Marco—"a palace and a prison on each hand."[11] Scamozzi completed Palladio's Church of San Giorgio and Sansovino's Libreria Vecchia; Scamozzi and Longhena raised the Procuratie Nuove (1582–1640), adjoining St. Mark's Square, as new offices for the Venetian administration. Some famous palaces now rose along the Grand Canal: the Balbi, the Contarini degli Scrigni, and the Mocenigo, where Byron lived in 1818. Those who have seen only the exterior of the Venetian palaces can never visualize the luxury—redeemed with taste—of their interiors: the frescoed or coffered ceilings, the painted or tapestried walls, the satin-covered chairs, the carved seats, tables, and chests, the cabinets inlaid with marquetry, the stairs majestically broad and built for centuries. Here a jealous oligarchy of a few hundred families enjoyed all the wealth of merchant princes and all the discriminating standards of old aristocracies.

Only one Venetian sculptor, Alessandro Vittoria, stands out in this period, but Venetian painting produced two men of the second rank. Across the generations Palma Vecchio (d. 1528) handed the colors to his grandnephew Palma Giovane—i.e., Jacopo Palma the Younger— who died just a hundred years later. Giovane is put down as a decadent because he painted with careless haste, but some of his pictures, like the *Pope Anaclytus* in the Church of the Crociferi, come close to greatness; and in some lines of Molmenti's this careless Younger leaps to life:

> Palma il Giovane had no other object . . . than his work, from which the profoundest grief was powerless to distract him. In his art he sought consolation for the death of his two sons, one of whom died in Naples, the other ended in a life of debauchery. As his wife was being borne to the tomb he set himself to paint to escape from his pain.[12]

Bernardo Strozzi straddled the top of the Magic Boot, getting born in Genoa, dying in Venice (1644), and leaving pictures for almost every gallery between. For a time he was a Capuchin monk; he unfrocked himself, but could never shed the nickname Il Cappucino. After many trials he found tolerance and prosperity in Venice, and there he produced his best work. One example must suffice: his *Portrait of a Dominican Friar* (Bergamo)—the high beret setting off the spacious forehead, the eyes frowning and intent, the nose and mouth breathing character, the fine hand proclaiming pedigree; Titian himself could hardly have done better. These heirs of the giants would have been giants in any other land.

3. From Padua to Bologna

Padua's glory was now all in her university; there in this period Harvey studied and Galileo taught. At Ferrara Alfonso II (r. 1559–97) showed no slackening of vigor in that Este family that had ruled the principality since 1208. An anonymous print in the British Museum gives him a powerful head, authoritative beard, eyes expressing a resolute and somber intelligence. He could be merciless to those who crossed him, kind to others, patient with Tasso's tantrums, fearless in battle, limitless in taxation. He continued the Estensi tradition of favoring literature, science, and art, and gathering their products into the culture, splendor, and gaiety of his court. The people had to be content with subsistence, and to enjoy vicariously the fruits of their toil. With all his power, and three successive wives, Alfonso failed to beget a son; and by an agreement made in 1539 Ferrara, long a papal fief, became in 1598 a papal state. Her cultural history came to an end.

Bologna, under papal rule since 1506, had in this age a second flowering, in a school of painting that dominated Italy for two centuries and spread its influence into Spain, France, Flanders, and England. Lodovico Carracci, son of a prosperous butcher, returned to Bologna after studying art in Venice, Florence, Parma, and Mantua. Tintoretto had warned him that he had no genius for painting, but Lodovico felt that industry could substitute for genius, and that he had genius too. He stirred with his enthusiasm his cousins Agostino and Annibale Carracci—one a goldsmith, the other a tailor. The two went off to Venice and Parma to study Titian and Correggio. When they came back they joined with Lodovico in opening (1589) the Accademia degli Incamminati—"of those setting out on the road." They provided instruction in the elements, the history, and the technique of art, and a careful study of the masters; they rejected the "manneristic" stress on the mannerisms or peculiarities of any individual master; they proposed, rather, to unite the feminine tenderness of Raphael, the delicate eloquence of Correggio, the masculine vigor of Michelangelo, the chiaroscuro of Leonardo, and the warm coloring of Titian all in one comprehensive style. This "Eclectic school" made Bologna rival Rome as the art capital of Italy.

The pictures bequeathed by the Carracci are countless; many of them are in the Bolognese Accademia di Belle Arti; some are in the Louvre; but one finds them anywhere. Lodovico's own product is the least attractive, but appears at its best in a luminous *Annunciation* and an excellent *Martyrdom of St. Ursula*, both in the *pinacoteca* of the academy. Agostino is represented by a powerful

Communion of St. Jerome—which did not prevent him from meeting a wide demand for obscene prints. Annibale was technically the most gifted of the clan, having derived from Correggio a refinement of line and color rarely achieved by his cousins; see the voluptuous elegance of his *Bacchante* in the Uffizi Gallery, the perfect female form in *The Nymph and the Satyr* in the Pitti Palace, and the perfect male form in *The Genius of Fame* in Dresden; and in *Christ and the Samaritan Woman* (Vienna) he produced one of the masterpieces of this period—figures worthy of Raphael, a landscape anticipating Poussin.

In 1600 Annibale and Agostino accepted the invitation of Cardinal Farnese to come and paint the gallery of his palace in Rome. They chose an appropriate subject and painted *The Triumph of Bacchus*, a Rubensian riot of feminine charms. Thence Agostino went to Parma, where he painted a great fresco for the Casino; and Annibale proceeded to Naples, whose Museo Nazionale still shows his characteristic counterpoint of *The Holy Family* with *Venus and Mars*. The three cousins, so long united in art, were far apart in death: Agostino in Parma (1602), Annibale in Rome (1609), Lodovico still faithful to Bologna—the first to come and the last to go (1619).

The new school trained several of the most famous painters of the period. One of them, Guido Reni, had the largest following of any painter in Europe. After his early budding under the care of the Carracci, he yielded to the lure of Rome (1602), worked there for twenty years, then returned to Bologna to produce pictures whose pious sensuality and sentimental grace made them a welcome bridge between the orthodoxy of the faith and the heresies of the flesh. Guido himself seems to have been sincerely religious, and is reputed to have kept himself virginally intact to the end. The self-portrait in the Capitoline Museum shows him in youth, pretty as a girl, with blond hair, fair complexion, and blue eyes. His masterpiece is the *Aurora* frescoed on the ceiling of the Rospigliosi Palace in Rome: the goddess of the dawn flying through the air, followed by gallant horses drawing a disheveled Phoebus in his chariot, and accompanied by dancing females of lovely face and form, representing the hours, with a winged cherub giving a Christian imprimatur to a pagan ecstasy. Guido painted other mythologies—the *Rape of Helen* in the Louvre, the *Apples of the Hesperides* in Naples, the voluptuous *Venus and Cupid* in Dresden. From the Old Testament he took his famous *Susannah and the Elders* (Uffizi). But for the most part he was content to picture again the old themes dear to the people and the Church, the story of Christ and his mother, all suffused with what merciless critics denounce as a maudlin* exaggeration of sentiment. He did well, however, with the Apostles, as in the *St. Matthew* of the Vatican; he painted a magnificent head of St. Joseph (Brera), and in the Vatican's *Martyrdom of St. Peter* he tried the harsh realism of Caravaggio. Returning to sentiment, he painted for the galleries his

---

* Note that this word is a corruption of *Magdalen*—which is still pronounced "maudlin" in the names of Magdalen College, Oxford, and Magdalene College, Cambridge. The Magdalen herself did not escape the devoted pursuit of Guido's sensuous brush.

famous *St. Sebastian*, showing the saint calmly receiving arrows into his perfect frame. In all this *oeuvre* we perceive the skill of well-trained technique;
but when we compare these saccharine sanctities with Raphael's Stanze or
Michelangelo's Sistine ceiling, we are moved not by the fullness of color and
the smoothness of line, but by the "loss of nerve" in Reni's art. He dreamed
forgivably when he wrote, "I should like to give to the figure I am about to
paint such beauty as that which dwells in Paradise";[13] but he gave himself
away when he boasted that he had "two hundred ways of making the eyes
look up to heaven."[14]

Domenichino (Domenico Zampieri) followed Guido's policy of pleasing
at once the pagans and the devotees; and as these two were often one, it proved
a profitable plan. He was more complex than Guido, modest and shy, in love
with music and his wife. He too learned his art in Bologna and then sought the
fauna and florins of Rome. His success there aroused the envy of his local
competitors; they accused him of plagiarism; he retired to Bologna, but
was recalled by Gregory XV to be chief architect, as well as chief painter,
to the Vatican. With some of the old Renaissance versatility he designed the
now vanished Villa Ludovisi at Rome and part of the Villa Aldobrandini at
Frascati. Moving on to Naples, he began a series of frescoes in the cathedral.
Despite difficulties multiplied by the Neapolitan painters, he had almost completed his assignment when he died (1641), aged sixty, still in the vigor of his
art. His greatest picture is *The Last Communion of St. Jerome*, in the Vatican.
On the basis of this chef-d'œuvre Poussin ranked Domenichino second only
to Raphael among painters;[15] we respect the enthusiasm more than the judgment. Ruskin thought Domenichino "palpably incapable of doing anything
good, great, or right in any field, way, or kind whatsoever";[16] we admire
neither the judgment nor the rhetoric.

The last of the three famed pupils of the Carracci was lamentably called
Guercino—"Squint-eyed"—from an accident that distorted his eye in infancy;
but his mother called him Giovanni Francesco Barbieri. He was already a
painter, influenced by the masculine style of Caravaggio, before he came to
study with the Carracci; so he mediated in art between Bologna and Rome.
Like Guido he remained unmarried, lived semimonastically, and displayed the
best qualities of the Catholic Reformation in his quiet and decent life. He has
left us many pleasing pictures, scattered from Rome to Chicago. He was the
weakest and most lovable of the Bolognese school.

The basic theory of the Eclectic school, that a great artist can be
formed by trying to unite the diverse excellences of his predecessors, was
surely a mistake, for it is often the character of genius to express a personality and strike out new paths; but the Accademia degli Incamminati
served well to transmit a tradition and a discipline without which genius
may run to excesses and bizarreries. The prosperity of the school was due
in part to its ready co-operation with the needs of the Church. The reformed papacy and the expanding Jesuits required fresh representations of

the Christian story, and vivid incitations to piety and faith. The Bolognese painters touched every chord of feeling in the worshiper; their Madonnas and Magdalens spread throughout Catholic Christendom. Who shall deny that the people were grateful for these inspirations, or that in providing them the Church proved herself the most understanding psychologist in history?

4. Naples

The Papal States had long since absorbed Forlì, Ravenna, Rimini, and Ancona; Urbino was added in 1626, Pesaro in 1631. Thence southward through Foggia, Bari, and Brindisi to the heel—and through Taranto, Crotone, and Reggio Calabria to the toe—of the Magic Boot, and across from Scylla to Charybdis through Sicily, and northward along the west coast to Capua, was the Kingdom of Naples, since 1504 a viceroyalty of Spain. A population of three million passionate souls labored in burning poverty throughout that sprawling realm to finance the splendor of its brilliant capital. Evelyn saw and described Naples in 1645:

> The chief magistrates, being prodigiously avaricious, do wonderfully enrich themselves out of the miserable people's labor . . . The structure of the city is, for its size, the most magnificent of any in Europe: the streets exceeding large, well paved, having many subterranean passages for the sewerage; which renders them very sweet and clean . . . To it belongeth more than 3,000 churches and monasteries, and these the best built and adorned in Italy. The people greatly affect the Spanish gravity in their habit; delight in good horses; the streets are full of gallants on horseback, in coaches and sedans . . . The women are generally well-featured, but excessively libidinous.[17]

Everybody seemed jovial, full of music, romance, and piety; but under that singing surface, and under the eyes of the Inquisition, heresy and revolution brewed. In this *regno* the philosopher Telesio lived and died (1588); in Nola, near Naples, Bruno was born (1548). In 1598 Campanella took part in a rebellion that aimed to make Calabria an independent republic; the plot failed, and the poet-philosopher spent the next twenty-seven years in jail.

In 1647 Naples went hysterical with one of those operatic uprisings that periodically disturbed agrarian exploitation in Italy. Tommaso Aniello, popularly known as Masaniello, was a fish hawker whose wife had been heavily fined for smuggling corn. When the Spanish governor laid a tax on fruit to finance a navy, and the growers and the vendors of fruit refused to pay the imposition, Tommaso called for an armed revolt. A hundred thousand Italians followed him as he marched to the viceregal palace to demand withdrawal of the tax. The frightened Viceroy yielded; Tommaso, aged twenty-four, became master of Naples, and he ruled it for ten days. Fifteen hundred opponents were executed in a delirium of dictatorship; a lower price was decreed for bread, and a baker who failed to comply was roasted alive in his own oven[18]—but Tommaso's enemies wrote the history. We are told that Masaniello dressed in cloth of gold, transformed his humble home into a palace seething with authority, and cruised about the bay in a sumptuous gondola. On July 17 he was assassinated by desperadoes in the pay of Spain. His dismembered body was recovered and reunited by his followers, who gave him a lordly funeral. The leaderless revolt died away.

A somber religious art maintained itself under the archbishops and the viceroys. In 1608 the Church spent a million florins to build, in the Cathedral of San Gennaro, the Cappella del Tesoro as a shrine for the two phials containing the coagulated blood of St. Januarius, patron of Naples. Twice a year, the people were told, the blood must liquefy and flow in order that Naples should prosper and be safe from Vesuvius.

Painting in Naples was for a time controlled by a triumvirate of jealous artists, Corenzio, Caracciolo, and Ribera, determined that all Neapolitan painting should be done by themselves or their friends. They sent such threats to Annibale Carracci that he fled to Rome, where he died soon afterward from the effects of a hectic journey under a hot sun.[19] When Guido Reni came to decorate the Chapel of the Treasure he received a warning to leave Naples or die; he left almost at once, his work hardly begun. Two of his assistants, who stayed behind, were put on a galley and never heard of again. Domenichino came, completed four frescoes in the Chapel despite repeated erasures of his work, and then fled before Ribera's threats; he returned under the Viceroy's pledge of protection, but died shortly afterward, possibly by poison.[20]

With all his crimes, José or Giuseppe Ribera must be commemorated as the greatest painter of this period in Italy. Spain claims him through his birth at Xátiva, near Valencia (1588); he studied for a time under Francisco de Ribalta; but in early youth he made his way to Rome. There he lived in ragged poverty, copying frescoes and gathering crusts, until one of those art-loving cardinals who still felt the afflatus of the Renaissance took him into his palace and gave him bed and board, colors and clothes. Sedulously Giuseppe copied the works of Raphael in the Vatican and of the Carracci in the Farnese Palace. Then, finding his passion dulled by comfort, Lo Spagnoletto—"the little Spaniard"—ran away to Parma and Modena to study Correggio. He returned to Rome, quarreled with

Domenichino, and moved to Naples. There or at Rome he fell under the influence of Caravaggio, whose brutal style confirmed him in the dark naturalism that he may already have learned from Ribalta. A rich picture dealer took a fancy to him and offered him a pretty daughter in marriage. The penniless Giuseppe thought the proposal a joke, but when it was repeated he leaped into marriage and prosperity.

Now he painted *The Flaying of St. Bartholomew*, with such bloody verisimilitude that when it was exposed to public view it drew a crowd of gazers more interested in blood than in art. The Viceroy—that same Osuna who conspired against Venice—asked for the picture and its author, was fascinated, and gave Ribera charge of all decorations in the palace. The insatiable Spaniard frightened off all competitors until the commission to fresco the Chapel of the Treasure was given to Giovanni Lanfranco, his friend. He himself executed the altarpiece, representing the incombustible St. Januarius issuing unsinged from a fiery furnace.

Thereafter Ribera was the unchallenged master of his art in Naples. He seemed able at will to rival the tenderness of Raphael and Correggio without falling into the sentimentality of Guido Reni or Murillo, and to raise the realism of Caravaggio to a higher power by the intensity of his conception and the depth of his coloring. Let us instance only the *Pietà* and the *Lamentation* in the church and monastery of San Martino —"a work before which, as an embodiment of the solemn majesty of grief, all similar representations of that century sink to mere theatrical spectacles."[21] Or, from the mythologies, take the *Archimedes* in the Prado —precisely such a wrinkled old Sicilian as one might find in Syracuse today. Stepping out from the Bible and history into the streets, Ribera found variety for his art in realistic snatches from common life; and in the *Barefoot Boy* of the Louvre he gave a lead to Velázquez and Murillo.*

Ribera's defects leap to the eye—an exaggerated violence, a fondness for wrinkles and ribs, and a thirst for blood; Byron noted that

> Spagnoletto tainted
> His brush with all the blood of all the sainted.[22]

His dark colors and somber emphasis frighten and depress us, but in a Naples inured to Spanish rule and moods this *tenebroso* style found a ready acceptance. Every new church or monastery competed for him; Philip IV and the Neapolitan viceroys were avid customers; Ribera's paintings and etchings were more widely diffused in Spain than those of Velázquez—who visited him twice in Italy. His home was one of the

---

* The museum traveler will find sixty-three Riberas in the Prado and half a roomful in the vestibule of the Salon Carré in the Louvre. New York has *The Holy Family* in the Metropolitan Museum of Art and a *Magdalen* in the Hispanic Society.

finest in Naples, and his two daughters were paragons of brown loveliness. One of them had the distinction of being seduced by another Don Juan, Philip IV's natural son, who carried her off to Sicily and, soon tiring of her, abandoned her to a Palermo nunnery. Ribera almost succumbed to grief and shame; he sought consolation by giving to pictures of the Virgin the remembered features of his lost Maria Rosa; but within four years of her tragedy he died (1652).

II. ROME AND THE POPES

The capital of the Papal States* and of the Roman Catholic world was now a city of the second rank, with some 45,000 souls in 1558, rising to 100,000 under Sixtus V (1590). Montaigne, coming to it in 1580, thought it more extensive than Paris, but having only one third as many houses. Criminals and prostitutes (before Sixtus V) constituted a sizable part of the population; many a noble had a standing staff of ruffians. Poverty was general but genial, alleviated by papal charity, ecclesiastical ceremonies, religious hopes. The old aristocratic clans—Orsini, Colonna, Savelli, Gaetani, Chigi—had declined in income and power, though not in claims and pride; younger families—Aldobrandini, Barberini, Borghese, Farnese, Rospigliosi—were taking the lead in fortune and influence, usually through connections with the popes. Papal nepotism had another heyday: the Aldobrandini reaped a harvest from the election of Clement VIII, the Ludovisi from Gregory XV, the Barberini from Urban VIII, the Borghese from Paul V. Paul's nephew, Cardinal Scipione Borghese, enjoying plural benefices and 150,000 scudi per year, laid out the Villa, and built the Casino, Borghese (1615), founded its rich art collections, and earned a moderate immortality in marble from his protégé Bernini. Many of the cardinals used their wealth to support literature and art.

A succession of strong popes now helped the Roman Church to survive despite the loss of Germany, the Netherlands, Scandinavia, and Britain to the Reformation. The Council of Trent had confirmed and enhanced the supremacy of the popes over the councils, and the young and vigorous Society of Jesus—the Jesuits—was pledged and devoted to the papacy. Antonio Ghislieri, Dominican friar and Grand Inquisitor, became Pope Pius V in 1566 at the age of sixty-two. The saintliness of his personal life seemed to him fully consistent with his severity in pursuing heresy. He withdrew from the Bohemian Catholics the right previously granted them

---

* Chiefly the following cities and their environs: Rome, Ostia, Viterbo, Terni, Spoleto, Foligno, Assisi, Perugia, Gubbio, Urbino, Loreto, Ancona, Pesaro, Rimini, Forlì, Ravenna, Bologna, and Ferrara.

to receive Communion in wine as well as bread. He excommunicated Elizabeth of England and released the English Catholics from her allegiance. He urged Charles IX of France and Catherine de Médicis to prosecute war against the Huguenots till these should be utterly and mercilessly destroyed.[23] He commended the harsh measures of Alba in the Netherlands.[24] He labored with his dying strength to prepare the armada that defeated the Turks at Lepanto. He never mitigated a penal sentence;[25] he encouraged the Inquisition to enforce its rules and penalties.

He was equally strict in compelling ecclesiastical reform. Bishops who neglected to reside in their dioceses were deposed; monks and nuns were to remain completely secluded from the public; all malfeasance in ecclesiastical office was to be ferreted out and punished. When some discharged supernumeraries of the court complained that they would die of hunger, Pius replied that it would be better to die of hunger than to lose one's soul.[26] His appointments and nominations were determined by fitness, not favoritism or nepotism. He himself worked assiduously, sitting through long hours as judge, seldom sleeping more than five hours in a day, and giving an example to the clergy by the ascetic simplicity of his private life. He fasted frequently, and kept the coarse woolen shirt of a friar under his papal robes. He wore himself out with his severities; at sixty-eight he looked ten years older—lean and haggard, with sunken eyes and snow-white hair. Though hardly able to walk, he insisted upon making, mostly on foot, a pilgrimage to the seven basilicas of Rome. Nine days later, after a month of suffering, he died, clothed in the habit of St. Dominic. "To few popes," wrote a great Protestant historian, "does Catholicism owe more than to Pius V; for while pitiless in his persecution of heresy, his recognition of the need of reform, and his unbending resolution to effect it, regained for the Church much of the respect which it had forfeited."[27] Pius was canonized in 1712.

Gregory XIII (1572–85) continued, in a milder spirit, the reform of the Church. We think of him as the man who gave us our calendar and who celebrated the Massacre of St. Bartholomew with a Mass of thanksgiving to a merciful God. Nevertheless he was a man of good morals, temperate habits, and kindly character. He had had a natural son before entering the priesthood, but that peccadillo was forgiven by the lusty Romans. He was generous in charity, tireless in administration. His appointments have won Protestant praise.[28] Montaigne saw him in 1580 as "a handsome old man, a face full of majesty, a long white beard. Over seventy-eight years old, yet healthy and vigorous . . . Of a gentle nature, exciting himself little over the affairs of the world."[29]

However, his enterprises—financing Jesuit schools, suppressing Hugue-

nots, deposing Elizabeth—required ducats. To raise them Gregory ordered the letter of the law to be applied to the owners and the title deeds
of estates in papal territory; many properties that should have lapsed to
the papacy through failure in the direct line of succession, or in the payment of dues required from papal fiefs, were now confiscated by the
Pope. Actual or prospective victims armed their retainers, resisted expro-
priation, and retaliated with brigandage. Men of aristocratic lineage, like
Alfonso Piccolomini and Roberto Malatesta, led bands of outlaws who
captured towns and controlled roads. Taxes could no longer be collected;
the flow of gold to Rome was dammed; soon the papal administration
was in chaos. Gregory suspended his confiscations, made peace with
Piccolomini, and died in humiliating defeat.

Emergencies make men, and this one made Felice Peretti, as Sixtus V
(1585-90), one of the greatest popes. He first saw the light at Grotta-
mare, near Ancona, in a cottage so ill thatched that the sun shone through
the roof; later he jested that he was *"nato di casa illustre"*—born of an
illustrious (or well-lighted) house.[30] Schooled at a Franciscan monastery
in Montalto, earning a doctorate in theology by his studies in Bologna
and Ferrara, he rose rapidly by his pulpit eloquence and administrative
capacity; and when, at sixty-four, he was chosen pope, it was because
the conclave recognized in him the resolute character needed to restore
safety and solvency to the Papal States.

His relatives crowded around him with outstretched palms, and he
could not resist them; nepotism was renewed. But where his family was
not concerned, he was inflexible. His appearance itself gave pause: short,
broad, strongly built, with a great forehead, a thick white beard, big nose
and ears, vast eyebrows, and piercing eyes that could silence opposition
without a word. His florid complexion went with a violent temper, his
large head suggested unbending will. With all his severity he had a well
of good humor, and often a penetrating wit; he predicted that Henry IV
would defeat Mayenne because Henry spent less time in bed than Mayenne
did at meals.[31] He himself slept little and worked hard.

He resolved, first of all, to suppress the victorious brigands. He began
by enforcing the existing prohibition, heretofore largely ignored, against
carrying murderous weapons. On the day before his coronation four
youths were arrested for violating this ordinance; Sixtus ordered them
hanged forthwith. Their relatives pleaded for pardon or delay; he replied,
"While I live, every criminal must die"; soon, amid the coronation festivities, their bodies hung on one gallows near the Sant' Angelo Bridge. It
was Sixtus' inaugural address, a statement of policy on crime.

The Pope commanded the nobles to dismiss their *bravi*; he promised
pardon and reward to any bandit who would deliver to him another

bandit alive or dead; and the reward was to be paid by the captured bandit's family or commune. When one bandit issued a defiance, Sixtus ordered the outlaw's family to find him and bring him in or suffer death themselves. The Duke of Urbino pleased the Pope[32] by loading mules with poisoned food and directing the drivers to pass by a bandit's lair; the bandits robbed the pack, ate, and died. No consideration was given to holy orders or social rank; offenders belonging to "first families" were executed without mercy or delay; a priest outlaw dangled with the rest. Soon the countryside was dotted with corpses swaying in the wind, and the wits of Rome calculated that more severed heads were nailed to the Sant' Angelo Bridge than there were melons in the market stalls.[33] The people murmured that the Pope was barbarously cruel, but ambassadors told him that "in every part of his states through which their road had led, they had traveled through a land blessed with peace and security."[34] The proud pontiff had coins struck with the inscription *Noli me tangere*. In a fury of virtue he ordered a priest and a boy burned for homosexual acts, and compelled a young woman to witness the hanging of the mother who had sold her into prostitution. All detected adulteries were to be punished with death. Men were arrested for crimes dating so far back that a placard quoted St. Peter as trembling with fear lest Sixtus should indict him for cutting off Malchus' ear on the occasion of Christ's arrest.

Amid this mad pursuit he found time for government and reform. He ended the war of confiscations that Gregory XIII had waged against the nobles. He reconciled those ancient foes the Orsini and the Colonna by uniting them in marriage. He distributed the cardinals among eleven new and four old "congregations," and divided among these the administration of the Curia. He commanded the clergy to observe all the reform decrees of the Council of Trent, and required periodical visitation and correction of monasteries by the bishops. Fornication with a nun was to be punished by the death of both parties. He revived to full activity the University of Rome. To accommodate the great increase of books he commissioned Domenico Fontana to design a sumptuous new home for the Vatican Library. He personally supervised an improved edition of Jerome's Vulgate—which is as splendid a translation of the Bible into Latin as the King James version is into English.

He did not share the respect that his Renaissance predecessors had felt for the remains of pagan art. He completed the ruin of the Septizonium of Severus to provide columns for St. Peter's. He proposed to raze the tomb of Caecilia Metella. He threatened to demolish the Capitol itself if the statues of Jupiter Tonans, Apollo, and Minerva were not removed; he allowed Minerva to remain, but rechristened her Roma and replaced her spear with a cross. He exorcised the columns of Trajan and Marcus

Aurelius by topping them with statues of St. Peter or St. Paul and re-
naming the columns accordingly. To further symbolize the subjection of
paganism to Christianity, he engaged Domenico Fontana to transfer to
St. Peter's Square the obelisk that Caligula had brought from Heliopolis
and that Nero had set up in the Circus Maximus. The monolith of red
granite was eighty-three feet high and weighed over a million Roman
pounds. Masterful architects like Antonio da Sangallo and Michelangelo
had pronounced its removal to be beyond the capacity of Renaissance
engineers. Domenico and his brother Giovanni took a year to accomplish
the task (1585–86). Immense machines lowered and transported the monument; eight hundred men, fortified by the Sacrament, and 140 horses
pulled forty-four ropes, each as thick as a man's arm, to raise it aloft on
its new site. Domenico, succeeding, became the hero of Rome; Sixtus
struck commemorative medals and sent official announcements to foreign
governments. The ball at the top was replaced with a cross containing a
piece of the "true cross" on which Christ had died. Sixtus felt that Christianity had resumed its sway after its interruption by the Renaissance.

The indefatigable Pope, in his brief quinquennium, renovated secular
Rome. He brought in a fresh supply of good water—feeding twenty-seven
new fountains—by rebuilding the ruined Acqua Alessandria, which he
renamed, after himself, Acqua Felice. He cleared the air by financing the
drainage of the marshes; good progress was made and 9,600 acres were
reclaimed, but the enterprise was abandoned at his death. At his bidding
Domenico Fontana opened up new avenues on the classic plan of straight
lines; the Via Sistina was prolonged as the Via Felice; the noble Church
of Santa Maria Maggiore became the center of several radial thorough-
fares; Rome began to assume its modern form. To finance his undertakings
Sixtus, starting with an empty treasury, taxed even the necessaries of life,
debased the coinage, sold appointments, and issued annuity insurance
(*monti*) for life in return for gifts to the papal exchequer. He administered his funds with competence and care, and left five million crowns
in his coffers at his death.

His greatest concern was foreign policy. He never abandoned hope of
regaining England and Germany and uniting all Christendom against
Islam. He admired Elizabeth's statesmanship, but lent his aid to plots to
depose her. He promised to contribute to the expense of the Spanish
Armada, but he distrusted Philip's dallying, and shrewdly made his aid
conditional on the actual landing of Spanish troops in England. France
was his greatest problem. The Huguenots, supposedly exterminated in
1572, were advancing upon Paris under the undiscourageable Henry of
Navarre. Philip II was financing the League to save France for Catholicism—and for Spain; Sixtus faced the choice of letting France go Prot-

estant or helping Philip to turn France into a Spanish dependency. But a balance of power between France and Spain seemed indispensable to papal freedom from secular domination. In 1589 Sixtus offered to join in war against Henry; but when Henry promised to become a Catholic, Sixtus withdrew from the plan. Philip threatened to detach Spain from the papal obedience, and a Spanish Jesuit denounced the Pope as abetting heresy, but Sixtus held his ground and welcomed Henry's ambassador. In the end his faith in Henry was justified: France was saved to the Church and continued as a balance against Spain.

This was his last triumph, and perhaps the strain of it exhausted him. Neither the cardinals nor the nobles nor the people regretted his death (1590); the cardinals had winced under his severity; the nobles had been forced, against the most time-honored customs, to obey the laws; the people, taxed to the limit and disciplined to unwonted peace, tried to demolish the statue that had been raised to Sixtus on the Capitol. But after the blows he dealt had lost their sting, posterity could balance his achievements against his cruelty, his pride, and his love of power. A rationalist historian, Lecky, judged him, "though not the greatest man, by far the greatest statesman, who has ever sat on the papal throne."[35]

Among his successors in this period two are especially memorable. Clement VIII (1592–1605) was almost a Christian. "Of all the popes that have for a long time past sat in the see of Rome," said the Huguenot Sully, he "was most free from party prejudices, and had more of that gentleness and compassion which the Gospel prescribed";[36] however, he refused mercy to Beatrice Cenci (1599), and allowed the Inquisition to burn Giordano Bruno at the stake (1600). Urban VIII (1623–44) at first aided Spain and Austria in the Thirty Years' War; but when they tried to absorb Mantua he feared encirclement, and turned his diplomatic maneuvers to co-operation with Richelieu in using the Protestant armies of Gustavus Adolphus to weaken the Hapsburg power. Infected with the military spirit of the age, he subordinated spiritual concerns to the extension of his rule as a secular prince; he acquired Urbino, and heavily taxed it—and his other states—to finance a papal army for war against the Duke of Parma. The army proved worthless, and his death left the papal realm "in such a condition of decay and exhaustion," reported a Venetian ambassador, "that it is impossible for it ever to rise or recover."[37] The ambassador was mistaken. Elements of recovery appeared everywhere in the Church, and mounted to the papacy. The plain people of Italy, solacing immemorial hardship with intense and imaginative piety, still crowded their hallowed shrines, marched solemnly in religious processions, told one another of new miracles, and with painful ecstasy climbed the Scala Santa on their knees. Saints like Philip Neri, Francis of

Sales, and Vincent de Paul revealed the capacity of the old Church to inspire an absorbing devotion; so the Jesuit Aloysius Gonzaga died at the age of twenty-three while ministering to the victims of pestilence in Rome (1591). Worldliness and corruption in the Curia gave way before the assaults of Protestant reformers, the exhortations of saints, the inspiring example of prelates like St. Charles Borromeo of Milan. From pope to pope the movement of self-reform, however halting, grew. Old religious orders were reinvigorated, new ones multiplied—the Oratorians (1564), the Oblates of St. Ambrose (1578), the Regular Clerks Minor (1588), the Lazarists (1624), the Sisters of Charity (1633), and many more. Seminaries were established throughout Catholic Christendom to train an educated secular clergy. Catholic missionaries went to every non-Christian land, facing hardships and perils, tending the sick, educating the young, and preaching the faith. And everywhere, battling Protestants in Germany, plotting politics in France, dying for their cause in England, carrying the creed to "heathens" in five continents, moved the incredible, indomitable Jesuits.

III. THE JESUITS

1. In Europe

After the death of Diego Laynez (1565), the Society of Jesus chose as its general Francisco Borgia, whose character and career were an earnest of the time. Born rich, grandson of Pope Alexander VI, rising to be Duke of Gandia, Viceroy of Catalonia, and friend of kings, he joined the new order in 1546, gave it all his personal wealth, and earned canonization by the austere sanctity of his life. Everard Mercurian, who followed him as general, left no mark on history; but Claudio Aquaviva guided the society with such wisdom and tact through thirty-four troubled years (1581–1615) that many Jesuits now rank him highest of all their generals since Loyola. When he took command there were some five thousand Jesuits; when he died there were thirteen thousand.

Under his direction a committee of Jesuit scholars drew up (1584–99) the *Ratio studiorum*, which continued till 1836 to determine the order and method of studies in Jesuit colleges. Taking boys of eleven to fourteen years of age, the six-year course gave them three years of the Greek and Latin languages and literatures; the remaining years were devoted to philosophy in its broadest sense, as including natural science, logic, metaphysics, and ethics. The consensus of evidence is that all these subjects were admirably taught. The philosophy was Scholastic, but as yet there was no acceptable substitute. Biology and modern secular history, as in nearly all schools of that time, were largely ignored, perhaps because the awful sight of the struggle for existence among animals, and the almost uninterrupted pageant of war among men, offended the trustful simplicity of faith. All in all, the *Ratio* was a skillful compromise between the Middle Ages and the Renaissance. With remarkable adaptability, the Jesuits welcomed the rebirth of the drama; they translated, wrote, and staged plays, and discovered in student dramatics a lively means of teaching speech and eloquence; in stage management and scenery they were ahead of their times. They used debates to sharpen wits and reason, but they discouraged originality of ideas in teacher and pupil alike. Their aim was apparently to produce an educated but conservative elite capable of intelligent and practical leadership, yet untroubled by doctrinal doubts and immovably rooted in the Catholic creed.

In almost all cases the Jesuit schools were founded and endowed by secular authorities, ecclesiastical leaders, or moneyed individuals, but the Jesuits kept full control. Though a few of their colleges were specifically established for the sons of the nobility, nearly all were open, without tuition fees, to any qualified student, rich or poor.[38] The teachers, usually members of the order, were better trained than their Protestant analogues; they were devoted and unpaid, and their priestly garb and bearing gave them a revered authority that enabled them to keep discipline without resorting to fear or corporal punishment. Many Protestants sent their sons to Jesuit colleges,[39] hoping to get for them not only a sound education in the classics, but also a superior discipline of morals, manners, and character. "As for the pedagogical part," wrote Francis Bacon, "the shortest rule would be, 'Consult the schools of the Jesuits,' for nothing better has been put in practice."[40] In 1615 the Jesuits had 372 colleges; in 1700 they had 769, and twenty-four universities, scattered throughout the world. In Catholic countries secondary education fell almost entirely into their hands, giving them an immense influence in shaping the national mind.

At the other end of the scale they sought the ear of kings. Aquaviva forbade them to become royal confessors and discouraged their participation in politics; nevertheless, even in Aquaviva's lifetime, Father Coton accepted Henry IV's invitation to be his spiritual director; and thereafter the Jesuits agreed with their most brilliant pupil, Voltaire, that the best way to mold a nation is to mold its king. By 1700 they were confessors to hundreds of prominent personalities. Women were especially sensitive to their good manners and their tolerant acceptance of the world; and as confessors to important women the subtle fathers reached important men.

Frankly declaring their intent to mingle with mankind instead of isolating themselves in monasteries, they adapted their moral precepts to the incorrigible ways of mankind. In their judgment the strict Christian ethic was possible only for hermits and saints; the realities of human nature required some mitigation of the perfect rule. Such adjustments of the ethical code had been made by Aristotle in reaction against the perfectionism of Plato, and by the rabbis in fitting the old Hebraic laws to the novel conditions of urban life. Though in their doctrine—and usually in their own practice —the Jesuits despised the flesh, they understood the flesh, and they gave it some moral leeway lest sinners be driven into rebellion and be lost to the Church. To reduce the strain between the code of Christ and the nature of man, Jesuit and other theologians developed casuistry—the application of moral doctrines to particular cases. But let us leave this subtle science till we come to its greatest enemy, Blaise Pascal.

Generally, in their theology, the Jesuits leaned to liberal views. Some, like Fathers Less and Hamel at Louvain (1585), thought it unnecessary to believe that every word or every doctrine in the Bible was inspired by God.[41] Nearly all Jesuits emphasized the Scholastic tenet that secular governments derive their power from the people; and not a few, like Mariana and Busenbaum, preached the right of the people, through their lawful representatives, to depose, even to kill, a "bad" king; but "bad" in this connection meant heretical, and the democratic emphasis may have come from the desire of the Jesuits, in their "ultramontanist" loyalty to Rome, to exalt the uniquely divine and supreme authority of the pope. The Jesuits upheld, against Luther, the efficacy of good works in earning salvation; they deprecated the emphasis on original sin, and they offset the dark predestinarianism of Paul, Augustine, Luther, Calvin, and Jansen with a reaffirmation of free will. Luis Molina, a Portuguese Jesuit, roused a theological furor by arguing that man, through his own will and works, can determine his eternal fate, and that man's free choice can co-operate with or overcome divine grace. Dominican theologians demanded that Molina be condemned as a heretic; Jesuits came to his defense; and the controversy rose to such a temperature that Clement VIII ordered both sides to hold their peace (1596).

The comparatively humane ethics of the Jesuits combined with their radical ideas, conservative associations, and spreading power to make them unpopular with the secular Catholic clergy and hated with special warmth by the Protestants. St. Charles Borromeo charged them with being scandalously lenient with influential sinners.[42] If, said Sarpi, St. Peter had been directed by a Jesuit confessor, he might have arrived at denying Christ without sin.[43] Mutio Vitelleschi, who succeeded Aquaviva as general of the Jesuits, warned his order that its anxiety to accumulate wealth was arousing wide reproach.[44] Protestant divines in England, committed to the doctrine that their kings ruled by divine right, were shocked by Jesuit ideas of popular sovereignty and occasional regicide. Robert Filmer denounced Cardinal Bellarmine's opinion that "secular or civil power is . . . in the people, unless they bestow it on a prince."[45] German Protestants fought the Jesuits as "creatures of the Devil, whom hell has vomited forth," and some demanded that they be burned at the stake as witches.[46] In 1612 there appeared in Poland *Monita secreta*, purporting to be confidential instructions to Jesuits in the art of winning legacies and political power. The book went through twenty-two editions before 1700. It was believed until almost our time, but it is now generally classed as a clever satire or an impudent forgery.[47]

2. In Partibus Infidelium

In the eyes of Catholic populations the faults of the Jesuits were far outweighed by their merits as educators and their courage as missionaries. Other religious orders shared in the devout adventure of spreading the faith; but what could compare with the audacity, enterprise, and martyrdoms of the Jesuits in India, China, Japan, and the Americas? In India the enlightened Mogul Emperor Akbar invited some Jesuits to his court at Fatehpur Sikri (1579); he listened to them with curiosity and sympathy, but refused to dismiss his harem. An Italian aristocrat, Roberto de' Nobili, entered the Society of Jesus, went to India as a missionary (1605), studied the Hindu creeds and rituals, adopted the dress and rules of the Brahmin caste, composed works in Sanskrit, and made some converts to Christianity. Other Jesuits became yogis and worked among the lower classes. Jesuit missionaries crossed the Himalayas into Tibet about 1624 and gave Europe its first—and for a long time its last—reliable information concerning that hidden world.

As early as 1549 the Jesuits entered Japan; by 1580 they claimed 100,000 converts; in 1587 they were ordered to leave the islands; in 1597 they and the Franciscan friars suffered a furious persecution, in which priests, monks, and thousands of Japanese Christians were crucified—a new technique which the killers claimed to have learned from the Gospels. About 1616 a fresh group of Jesuits entered Japan and garnered new converts in considerable number. But Dutch and English merchants, believing that the Jesuits were paving the way for Portuguese or Spanish trade, prodded the government into renewed persecution;[48] thirty-one Jesuits were put to death, and by 1645 Christianity had disappeared from Japan.

China was a challenging peril, for the emperors had promised death to any Christian daring to enter the "Middle Kingdom." We have seen elsewhere how the Jesuit Francis Xavier died (1552) almost in sight of the

China that he had resolved to convert. In 1557 Portuguese merchants established a settlement at Macao, on the southeast coast of China. There some Jesuits devoted themselves to learning Chinese dialects and ways. Finally two of them, Matteo Ricci and Michele Ruggieri, entered the province of Kwantung, armed with languages, astronomy, mathematics, clocks, watches, books, maps, and instruments. The provincial viceroy was charmed with these novelties; and as Ricci and Ruggeri assumed Chinese names and dress, lived simply, worked hard, and conducted themselves with the modesty that the Chinese expected from the children of so young and immature a civilization as Europe's, they were allowed to remain. Ricci made his way to Canton, where he impressed the mandarins with his scientific and geographical knowledge. He constructed sundials, drew convenient and trustworthy maps, and made difficult astronomical calculations. He initiated his new friends into Christianity by writing a catechism in which the basic Christian beliefs were explained and supported by quotations from classical Oriental texts. Emboldened by the toleration he received, he moved to a suburb of Peking (1601) and sent a clock to the Emperor K'ang-hsi. When the clock stopped and no Chinese scholar could start it again, the "Son of Heaven" sent for the donor. Ricci came, fixed the clock, and introduced other scientific instruments to the curious ruler; soon Ricci and other Jesuits were established at the Ming court. The genial Emperor raised no obstacle to the conversion of many upper-class Chinese. After Ricci's death (1610) another Jesuit, Johann Adam Schall von Bell, carried on the scientific and proselytizing work of the mission. He reformed the Chinese calendar, made superior cannon for the Chinese armies, became an intimate and honored friend of the Emperor, dressed in mandarin silks, lived in a palace, played politics, was demoted to a jail, and died within a year after his release.

The sequel of the story, reaching into the eighteenth century, might amuse a philosophical historian. The Jesuits in China, so versed in science, had shed the dogmatism of theology. When they studied the Chinese classics they were moved by the high wisdom they discovered there. The Chinese worship of ancestors appeared as an admirable inducement to moral and social stability; and there was plenty in Confucius to warrant his veneration. But other missionaries complained to the Roman Inquisition (1645) that the Jesuits were minimizing the crucifix and the doctrine of divine redemption, as likely to shock Chinese unaccustomed to the idea of men killing a god; that the Jesuits read the Mass not in Latin but in Chinese; that they allowed their converts to retain many rites of the native religion; and that Jesuit missionaries were acquiring wealth as physicians, surgeons, merchants, moneylenders, and advisers to generals and emperors. The Jesuits in their turn were appalled by Dominican and

Franciscan insistence on telling the Chinese that Christianity was the sole escape from eternal damnation, and that the ancestors whom they worshiped were burning in hell. Innocent X ordered the Jesuits to forbid the sacrifices of meat and drink offered to the shades of ancestors. Meanwhile the Jesuit fathers were sending to Europe those descriptions of Chinese life, religion, and thought which were to share in disturbing Christian orthodoxy in the eighteenth century.

In South America the Jesuit missionaries won the respect and trust of the natives by opening schools and medical centers, and laboring to mitigate the brutality of the Spanish masters. They compiled dictionaries and grammars, explored the dangerous interiors, and immensely advanced geography. They sent to Europe the Peruvian bark which, as quinine, became the standard drug for treating malaria. And in Paraguay they set up a communistic Utopia.

There, in the pampas and woods bordering the Uruguay River, and above dangerous waterfalls that discouraged colonists, they organized their own Indian settlements. With the permission of Philip III of Spain, they excluded all white men except Jesuits and the colonial governor. They claimed to have found the inhabitants to be of a childlike and friendly disposition—"two hundred thousand Indians in every way fitted for the Kingdom of God."[49] They learned the language of the natives, but taught them no Spanish or Portuguese; they discouraged all intercourse with colonists. They coaxed the people into Christianity by charity, humanity, and music. They established schools for musical training; they formed orchestras that played all the major European instruments and nearly every variety of composition, even to selections from Italian operas. Soon the natives were singing massive chorales, and we are assured that in a chorus of a thousand voices not one false note was heard. A band of musicians led the natives to and from work, and accompanied their labor in shops and fields. Christian festivals were celebrated with singing, dancing, and athletic games. The Jesuit fathers composed comedies, which their flocks were taught to perform.

The economy, as well as the government, was entirely under Jesuit control. The natives showed remarkable aptitude in duplicating European products, even complex watches, delicate lace, and musical instruments. Work was compulsory, but youths were allowed to choose their trades, and leisure was provided for recreation and cultural development. The average workday was eight hours. The Jesuits fixed the hours of work, sleep, prayer, and play. Part of the soil was individually owned; most of it was communal property. The product of communal labor was turned over to the government; part of it was set aside for sowing or for bad years; part went to pay a head tax to the Spanish king; most of it was discributed to the twenty thousand families according to their need; presumably some part went to support, on a modest level,[50] the 150 Jesuits who served as directors, overseers, physicians, teachers, and priests. A royal decree, suggested by the Jesuits, forbade them to share in the profits of the economy, and required them to render a periodic accounting to their provincial head. Law was administered by native judges and police. Penalties included flogging, imprisonment, and banishment, but there was no capital punishment. Each settlement had its own hospital, college, church, and facilities for the old or infirm. It was a theocratic communism: the natives received sustenance, security, peace and a limited cultural life, in return for accepting Christianity and discipline.

Whence had the Jesuits derived the idea for this remarkable regime? Perhaps in part from More's *Utopia* (1516), in part from the Gospels, in part from the constitution of their own society, which was itself a communistic isle in an individualistic sea. In any case the system proved popular with the natives; it was established by persuasion without force; it maintained itself for 130 years (c. 1620–1750); and when it was attacked from without it defended itself with an ardor that astonished its assailants. Even the skeptics of the French Enlightenment were impressed. "By means of religion," wrote d'Alembert, "the Jesuits established a monarchical [?] authority in Paraguay, founded solely on their powers of persuasion and on their lenient methods of government. Masters of the country, they rendered happy the people under their sway." Voltaire described the experiment as "a triumph of humanity."[51]

It ended in disaster because it could not isolate itself from outside humanity. Spanish traders reproached the Jesuits with engaging in commerce; Spanish colonists resented their exclusion from an area inviting exploitation of resources and men.[52] Slave-hunting bands repeatedly attacked the Jesuit settlements. The fathers and their subjects evacuated the regions that were most exposed to these raids. When the raids penetrated farther, the Jesuits secured permission from the King of Spain to arm their natives with European weapons; thereafter the raids were successfully resisted. More dangerous to the colony was the course of European politics and thought. The persistent political intrigues of Jesuits in France, Spain, and Portugal combined with the rise of free thought and anticlericalism to lead to the expulsion of the order from nearly all countries in the second half of the eighteenth century. The Marquis of Pombal, as ruling minister in Portugal, was especially active in the movement against the Jesuits. In 1750 he arranged a treaty by which Portugal ceded to Spain the colony of San Sacramento, at the mouth of the Rio de la Plata, in exchange for Spanish lands farther north—which included seven Jesuit settlements containing thirty thousand Indians. Meanwhile a false rumor was circulated that the lands in question contained gold which the Jesuits were hoarding. The Portuguese authorities ordered the fathers and the natives to leave the seven settlements within thirty days. The Jesuits (one excepted) counseled submission; the Indians preferred to resist, and they held off Portuguese attacks through five years. In 1755 the Portuguese army brought up artillery; hundreds of the Indians were massacred; the remainder fled to the forests or surrendered; the Jesuits were ordered by their European superiors to return to Spain. The experiment in what Muratori called *Cristianesimo felice*[53] came to an end.

The story of the Jesuit missionaries in North America is better known to us, and need only be noted to round out the perspective of Jesuit activity in this age. They entered Mexico in 1572 and shared in the rapid conversion of the natives to Christianity, but the main burden of that enterprise was borne by the Dominicans and the Franciscans; these last left a trail of lovely missions and mendicant beneficence all the way from Mexico to the fascinating city that bears their founder's name. Many Jesuits suffered torture and violent death in the attempt to win the Indians to Catholicism. Isaac Jogues was mutilated, enslaved, and slain; Jean de Brébeuf, Gabriel Lalemant, Anthony Daniel and other Jesuits were burned at the stake or were boiled to death in the two years 1648–49. We may not agree with the theology that these men sought to inculcate, but we must honor their humanity and devotion, if only as a pitiful offset to the cruelty and greed of the slave-hunting, slave-driving Christian settlers who complained that the humanitarian activities of the missionaries were unfitting the Indians for civilization.

IV. ITALIAN DAYS AND NIGHTS

"The people of Rome," said Montaigne, seeing them in 1581, "seem less religious than in the good towns in France, but much more given to ceremony."[54] The ceremonies of Holy Week included processions of bleeding self-flagellants, the public pronouncement of papal excommunications, and an exhibition of the veil with which Veronica had wiped the sweat from the brow of Christ. "On Easter Eve I saw, in the Church of St. John Lateran, the heads of St. Paul and St. Peter, which are on show there, and which still have their flesh, complexion, and beard, as if they were alive."[55] Exorcisms were performed with impressive ritual, perhaps as mass psychotherapy. Catholicism in Italy deliberately ignored the minds of the elite and offered to the masses of the people a beneficent but unwelcome moral code wrapped up in poetry, drama, symbolism, catharsis, and hope.

Montaigne bore witness to a general improvement of morals, but much of the old laxity remained in the relations of the sexes. The Italian theater was so loose in action and dialogue that the Venetian Senate, which winked at prostitution, expelled all actors from its territory (1577).[56] Obscene literature could be bought in any large town, as now almost anywhere in Christendom. Pius V made homosexual actions a capital crime, to the dismay of noble Roman youths. Eight Portuguese inverts entered into a formal marriage; they were arrested and burned at the stake.[57] Pius also decreed the expulsion of prostitutes from the Papal States (1566). Businessmen complained that the edict would depopulate the city; the Pope allowed a few courtesans to remain in a segregated quarter, and gave substantial help to women who tried to transfer to a younger profession. Sixtus V, who conquered the bandits, won only Pyrrhic victories against the courtesans, as evidenced by his repeated edicts of 1586, 1588, and 1589.

Since romantic love was still an extramarital vagary, and marriage was a mating of dividends, and divorce was forbidden by the Church, imaginative spouses indulged in adultery. Pius V thought of making it a capital crime; a report of August 25, 1568, said, "The threat of the death penalty for adultery is expected, so that everyone will have to become moral or leave the city." Pius, relenting, contented himself with milder penalties: a noble Roman lady was sentenced to life imprisonment; a prominent banker was publicly whipped; many other offenders were banished.

Toward the end of the sixteenth century the *cicisbeatura* came in from Spain through Naples and Milan: a husband, in the upper classes, might allow a friend to be the *cicisbeo*, or *cavaliere servente* (gentleman attendant), of his wife; apparently the custom had arisen in Spain in times of frequent wars and long absences of the husband from home. The knightly servitor waited on a lady from her rising to her bedding, but convention did not yet condone the adultery that often attended the custom in the Italy of the eighteenth century.

Despite theological deterrents, crime flourished. *Bravi* in noble homes, brigands on the highway, pirates in the Mediterranean, political and amorous assassinations abounded. Paolo Giordano Orsini, like another Othello, strangled Isabella de' Medici in her bed; Piero de' Medici murdered his wife on suspicion of adultery; we have seen how John Webster turned the bloody story of Vittoria Accoramboni into *The White Devil*; and Shelley was to do likewise with Beatrice Cenci. Her father, Francesco Cenci, was a paragon of vice and brutality. In 1594 he was tried on a charge of sodomy, but escaped with a fine of 100,000 scudi. His first wife died after giving him twelve children. Having quarreled with his sons, he left Rome with Beatrice and his second wife, Lucrezia Petroni, and removed to a lonely castle on the road to Naples. There he imprisoned them in the upper rooms and treated them with great cruelty—though there is no evidence of incestuous relations with his daughter. Beatrice found means of having a liaison with Olimpio Calvetti, keeper of the castle. At the instigation, or in the pay, of Beatrice, of her stepmother, and of her brothers Giacomo and Bernardo, the keeper, with the aid of a professional assassin, killed the father in his bed (1598). The conspirators were arrested and tried; they pleaded unbearable provocation, and many citizens begged Clement VIII for clemency; he refused. Beatrice and Lucrezia were beheaded, and Giacomo was tortured to death.[58]

Nevertheless, morals were improving, manners were softening, and Italian society had charms and graces that only the French could rival. Dress, in the upper ranks, was a colorful fancy of velvets, satins, and silks. About this time aristocratic women began to frame their faces, crown their heads, and drape their shoulders with the black silk *mantiglia* already popular in Spain. Men of social pretension still walked in high hose, but commoners and merchants, familiar with Turkish garb, were slipping into trousers. Italian comedy satirized the custom in the stock comic character Pantaleone, who became *pantaloons* and *pants*.

As in most Latin countries, amusements were plentiful. Rome had its annual carnival before Lent; the streets, as Evelyn saw them in 1645, "swarm with prostitutes, buffoons, and all manner of rabble";[59] there were races in the Corso, with fleet steeds from Barbary, riderless but prodded by spurs hanging against their sides, and races of asses, buffaloes, old men, naked men, and boys; and plays were performed on movable stages in the open air. The arts of the dance, conversation, and flirtation graced homes, gardens, and streets. And was there an Italian who could not sing?

V. THE BIRTH OF THE OPERA

Religion, love, the dance, the court, even work shared in generating music. Evelyn found the rural Italians "so jovial and addicted to music that the very husbandmen almost universally play on the guitar . . . and will commonly go to the field with their fiddle."[60] Every ducal court had its choir and *maestro di cappella*; at Ferrara a female quartet famous as the "Concert of Ladies" moved Tasso to tears and rhymes. Madrigals of love wove their polyphonic plaints, making the adoration of woman, till married, almost as reverent as the litanies to the Mother of God. Masses, vespers, motets, and hymns rolled from a thousand organs; choirs of emasculated boys (*evirati, castrati*) began, about 1600, to thrill the naves; a Protestant visitor described Catholic church music "sung by eunuchs and other rare voices, accompanied by theorboes, harpsichords, and viols, so that we were even ravished."[61] Monks and nuns were trained into choruses that could stir even the savage breast to orthodoxy. Andrea Gabrieli, Claudio Merulo, and Andrea's nephew Giovanni Gabrieli in succession drew thousands to St. Mark's in Venice to hear their organ-playing, their orchestras, and their choirs. When Girolamo Frescobaldi played the great organ at St. Peter's as many as thirty thousand crowded in or around the church to hear. His varied compositions, complex with their difficult experiments, influenced Domenico Scarlatti, and prepared for the harmonic evolutions of Johann Sebastian Bach.

Musical instruments were almost as diverse as today. Toward the middle of the sixteenth century the violin, evolving out of the lyre, began to replace the viol. The first great violinmakers, Gasparo da Salò and his pupil Giovanni Maggini, worked at Brescia; from them, it seems, Andrea Amati learned the art and took it to Cremona, where his sons handed it down to the Guarneri and the Stradivari. The innovation encountered opposition from those who preferred the softer and gentler tones of the viols; for a century the viols, the lutes, and the violins competed; but when the Amati found ways of tempering the shrillness of the violin, the new instrument, helped by the growing predominance of soprano voices in vocal music, rose to unchallenged leadership.

Compositions were still for the voice rather than for instruments. To this period belongs the romantic figure of Carlo Gesualdo, Prince of Venosa, who graced pedigree with music and murder with madrigals. Born in Naples (c. 1560), he became a virtuoso of the lute, married a high-born lady, had her and her lover killed on suspicion of adultery, fled to Ferrara, married Donna Eleonora d'Este, and published five books of madrigals whose adventurous harmonies and sharp modulations moved from Renaissance to modern polyphonic forms. In February 1600 Emilio de' Cavalieri, in the Oratory, or prayer chapel, of St. Philip Neri in Rome, produced a semidramatic allegory, with only symbolic action, but with orchestra, dancing, chorus, and soloists; this "first oratorio" preceded by only eight months, and in many ways resembled, Peri's opera *Euridice*. A generation later Giacomo Carissimi composed oratorios and cantatas whose monodic chants influenced the development of operatic recitatives.

Many other lines of musical growth converged to produce the opera. Some medieval *sacre rappresentazioni* had added music and song to the action; in these, as in her Passion music, the Church was mother or nurse of opera as of so many other arts. Recitatives accompanied by music had been heard in late medieval courts. Renaissance scholars had pointed out that parts of Greek tragedies had been sung or recited to instrumental accompaniments. At the court of Mantua, in 1472, Angelo Poliziano united music and drama in his brief *Favola di Orfeo*; now that sad fable began its long odyssey through opera. The masque, so popular in sixteenth-century courts, provided another road to opera; probably the ballet, the lavish scenery, and the sumptuous costumes of modern opera descend from the dancing, the pageantry, and the gorgeous dress that predominated over the action in Renaissance masques.

Toward the close of the sixteenth century a group of musical and literary enthusiasts, meeting in the home of Giovanni Bardi in Florence, proposed to revive the music drama of the Greeks by freeing song from the heavy polyphony and drowned-out language of the madrigals, and restoring it to what was believed to be the monodic style of ancient tragedy. One member, Vincenzo Galilei, father of the astronomer, set to monodic music parts of Dante's *Inferno*. Two other members, the poet Ottavio Rinuccini and the singer Jacopo Peri, composed the libretto and the score for what may be reckoned the first opera, *Dafne*, which was produced in the home of Jacopo Corsi in 1597.[62] The performance was so applauded that Rinuccini was invited to write the words, and Peri and Giulio Caccini the music, of a more substantial composition to celebrate the marriage of Henry IV and Maria de' Medici at Florence (October 6, 1600). The *Euridice* there performed is the oldest opera still extant. Peri apologized for the imperfections of his hurried work, and hoped to "have opened the path for the talent of others, for them to walk in my footsteps to that glory to which it has not been given me to attain."[63]

It was attained by one of the major figures in the history of music. Claudio Monteverdi became an expert violinist in his native Cremona. At twenty-two (1589) he was made violinist to the Duke of Mantua; at thirty-five he was *maestro di cappella*. Critics hotly denounced his five books of madrigals (1587–1605) for double discords, "licentious modulations," "illegal" harmonic progressions, and broken rules of counterpoint. "These new composers," wrote Giovanni Artusi in *Delle imperfezioni della musica moderna* (1600–3), "seem to be satisfied if they can produce the greatest possible tonal disturbance by bringing together completely unrelated elements and mountainous collections of cacophonies."[64]

Turning his reckless hand to the new form that he had heard in Florence, Monteverdi produced at Mantua his first opera, another *Orfeo* (1607), with an enlarged orchestra of thirty-six pieces. The music and action marked a great advance over Peri's *Euridice*. In Monteverdi's second opera, *Arianna* (1608), the action was still more dramatic, the music more appealing; all Italy began to intone the deserted Ariadne's lament, "*Lasciate mi morire*" (Let me die). In his expansion and reorganization of the orchestra, in his leitmotiv signalization of each character with a specific musical theme, in the overtures (*sinfonie*) with which he prefaced his operas, in the improvement of recitatives and arias, in the complex and intimate union of music and drama, Monteverdi marked as decisive an advance in opera as his contemporary Shakespeare was making in the theater.

In 1612 Monteverdi moved to Venice as *maestro di cappella* at St. Mark's.

He composed more madrigals, but altered that declining form into such declamation that critics accused him of subordinating music (as Bernini would be accused of subordinating sculpture) to drama; and unquestionably Monteverdi—like nearly all opera—is musical baroque. In 1637 Venice opened the first public opera house, the Teatro di San Cassiano; there Monteverdi's *Adone* ran from 1639 till Carnival of 1640, while at times his *Arianna* was filling another theater. When he produced his last opera, *L'incoronazione di Poppea* (1642), Italy was happy to see that at the age of seventy-five Monteverdi (like Verdi with *Otello* at seventy-four) was still in the fullness of his powers. A year later he died, leaving the world of music inspired and rejuvenated by a creative revolution.

VI. LETTERS

It is astonishing to see the genius of Italy bubbling over in every field, even in this period of supposed decline. In abundance and fervor this was a fruitful age in the literature of Italy. Only a lack of time, space, and knowledge keeps us from doing it justice here.

Italian scholarship naturally declined after the exhaustion of the Renaissance afflatus; one could not go on rediscovering Greece and Rome forever. The care of letters was now left to literary academies, whose very organization made them conservative. Almost every city in Italy had such a society, dedicated to the cultivation of literature and the mutual toleration of poetry. The Accademia della Crusca (i.e., of Chaff), founded in Florence in 1572, anticipated the French Academy by compiling a dictionary of the language (1612f.) and attempting to regulate literary style and taste.

Italian historians were the best of the age. We have noted Sarpi's passionate *History of the Council of Trent*. Cardinal Guido Bentivoglio produced a remarkably sympathetic account of the revolt in the Netherlands. He might have done more, but he died in conclave just as he seemed about to be chosen pope—done to death, said Nicius Erythraeus, by the snoring of a cardinal in the next cell, which deprived him of sleep for eleven successive nights.[65] Cardinal Caesar Baronius compiled a massive history of the Church (*Annales ecclesiastici*, 1588–1607) in twelve folio volumes, which later scholars extended to thirty-eight; Ranke pronounced them quite free of charm,[66] but Gibbon found them helpful, and the Cardinal made a laudable effort to be fair. "I shall love with a special love," he wrote, "the man who most rigidly and severely corrects my errors."[67] Isaac Casaubon undertook to do this, but desisted after writing an introductory fragment of eight hundred folio pages.

The theater prospered, while drama declined. Few memorable plays were composed, but many were produced, and with a scenic lavishness and histrionic skill that made Inigo Jones marvel and learn. Italian actors were in demand throughout the Continent. While in England female parts were taken by boys, in Italy they were played by women. Actresses were already deified; Tasso indited a sonnet to Isabella Andreini, who was not only a beautiful performer but a passable poetess and a good wife.

Two plays stand out in this period, partly because they established a new genre on the stage—the pastoral drama. Tasso gave it impetus with his *Aminta* (1573); Giovanni Battista Guarini produced the classic example in *Il pastor fido* (1585). "If he had not read *Aminta*," said Tasso, "he had not excelled it."[68] Cardinal Bellarmine rebuked Guarini for the licentiousness of the play, saying that it had done more harm to Christendom than all the heresies of Luther and Calvin; however, a sedulous search has found no saucier scene than the pretty Corisca offering the "two apples" of her breast to the unappreciative Silvio, a hunter who "takes more joy in one beast caught . . . than in the love of all the nymphs that are."[69] Barring Silvio, the play, like nearly all the Italian poetry of the time, has a sensual temperature, fusing all life into love. The action transpires in a pastoral Arcadia, in that "fair Golden Age when milk was the only food," no vice or grief stained humanity, and love was free from all censures and chains.[70] What with *Aminta* and this *Faithful Shepherd*, and Montemayor's *Diana enamorada*, and Sidney's *Arcadia*, and Fletcher's *Faithful Shepherdess*, half the reading population of Europe was sent out to pasture.

Crescimbeni listed 661 sonneteers who in the Italy of the sixteenth century had no trouble finding resonant rhymes for their variations of Petrarch.[71] Some of the finest sonnets of the time were thrown off by Campanella and Bruno as sparks from their philosophic fire. Alessandro Tassoni satirized the sonneteers and the idolators of Petrarch, Marini, and Tasso in one of the most famous of Italian poems, *La secchia rapita* (*The Stolen Bucket*). As its victim was a powerful noble, no one would publish it; but the demand was so great that scribes prospered by copying it and selling it at eight crowns per manuscript; finally it was printed in France and smuggled into Italy. What charmed Italian readers was not only the aptness and sharpness of the barbs, but the episodes of pure poetry that interrupted the hilarity—the love story of Endymion delicately told, almost side by side with the picture of a senator traveling to heaven on a toilet stool.

Only two Italian poets surpassed Tassoni's acclaim in this epoch—Tasso and Giovanni Battista Marini. Born at Naples and bred for the law, Giovanni abandoned pleading for rhymes, and for a time enjoyed a vagabond life. The Marquis Manso, forgiving the licentiousness of Marini's lyrics, gave him a room in his palace, where, at a respectful distance, the youth could look upon the somber decaying Tasso. For helping a friend to abduct a girl, he was thrown into prison. Released, he went to Rome, where the genial Cardinal Pietro Aldobrandino made him his private secretary. The Cardinal took him to Turin and there lost him to Charles Emmanuel, Duke of Savoy. For a while Marini sipped the wine and vinegar of court life. He made fun of a rival poet, Gasparo Murtola, who waylaid him, shot at him, missed him, but wounded a servant of the Duke. Murtola was sentenced to death; Marini had him pardoned, and won his rival's warmest ingratitude. Imprisoned for satires too personally pointed, Marini accepted an invitation from Marie de Médicis to adorn her court at Paris (1615). The Italians in her retinue welcomed him as their voice in France; he was idolized, and he received fat sinecures; lords and ladies paid him well for pre-publication copies of his epic *Adone*. One such copy reached Cardinal Bentivoglio, who appealed to Marini to purge the poem of its lascivious passages; we do not know how far the author tried. *Adone* was published in Paris in 1623, was put on the Index, and became the rage and the theme of Italy. When Marini returned to Naples (1624) highwaymen pelted his coach with roses, noblemen came out to escort him, and beauties melted toward him from their balconies. A year later he died, aged fifty-two, at the apex of his wealth and fame.

The *Adone* is an outstanding poem even in a country where poetry is almost as congenital as song. Its size deters us—a thousand pages, 45,000 lines. Its style indulges in all those tricks of speech that delighted Lyly in England, Guevara and Góngora in Spain, and some *précieuses ridicules* of the Hôtel de Rambouillet in France; *marinismo* was part of a European plague. The clever Italian had an almost sensual passion for words; he tossed them about in crackling antitheses, fanciful conceits, artful circumlocutions, even facile puns. But the Italian public of the sixteenth century, itself bubbling with hot speech, took no offense from this love of the wiles and jugglery of words. And what did such verbal conjuring matter in an epic that was a paean to sex in all its forms—normal, bestial, homosexual, incestuous? Here were the love myths of Hellas elegantly told; Mars and Vulcan sport with Aphrodite, and Zeus seduces Ganymede. The charms of the male body are the running theme, and the sense of touch is praised as the astonishing source of man's keenest delights. The hero, Adonis, dowered with all the beauty of a girl, is courted by women, men, and beasts. Venus woos him with her smoothest arts; a bandit chief seeks to make him his mistress; at last the helplessly lovable lad is mortally wounded in the groin by a boar with the most amorous intentions. Was this effeminate concentration on sex a relief and escape from too much religion and too much Spain?

VII. TASSO

Torquato Tasso had many inducements to poetry. He was born at Sorrento (1544), where the sea is an epic, the sky a lyric, and every hill an ode. His father Bernardo was a poet, a courtier, a man of sensitivity and passion, who plotted against the Viceroy, was banished from the Kingdom of Naples (1551), and wandered from court to court, leaving wife and child impoverished behind him. Torquato's mother, Porzia de' Rossi, came of an old Tuscan family with culture in its blood. For three years the boy studied in a Jesuit school at Naples. He imbibed Latin and Greek in nerve-racking doses, and was trained to a profound piety that gave him in alternation theological tremors and an indescribable peace. At ten he joined his father in Rome; his mother's death two years later left him deeply moved and long disconsolate. He accompanied his father to Urbino and Venice; there Bernardo published his own *Amadigi* (1560), which set medieval romance into verse.

Torquato himself was now agitated with poetry. He was dispatched to Padua to study law, but the father's example was more powerful than his precepts; the youth neglected statutes, and concatenated rhymes. He had long since fallen under Virgil's spell; now he resolved to apply the Mantuan's noble and serious style to those chivalric legends that Ariosto had treated with a twinkle in his eye. So he surprised his father by sending him *Rinaldo,* a romance in twelve cantos. Bernardo was saddened and pleased; he foresaw the vicissitudes of a poet with nothing but genius, yet he beamed to see his son, aged eighteen, rivaling in delicacy and imaginative verse the best poets of the time. He had the little epic published (1562), warmed his soul in the acclaim it received, and allowed Torquato to abandon law at Padua for philosophy and literature at Bologna. There the youth's talent proved troublesome; he wrote prickly epigrams upon his teachers, was threatened with a libel suit, and returned precipitately to Padua.

Bernardo persuaded Cardinal Luigi d'Este, brother to Duke Alfonso II of Ferrara, to engage Torquato as secretary (1565). The poet gladly joined a court then regarded as the finest flower of Italian culture. There he found an environment alive with music, dancing, literature, art, intrigue, and love. Two sisters of the Cardinal caught Tasso's fancy: Lucrezia, lofty, beautiful, and thirty-one, and Leonora, twenty-nine, a pious invalid whose quarrels with Alfonso made her the idol of the court. Legend (as in Goethe's drama and Byron's *Lament of Tasso*) describes the poet as falling in love with Leonora; certainly he addressed impassioned poems to her, as custom demanded, and both ladies admitted him to a friendship haloed with the aura of pedigree; but one sister was his senior by eleven years, the other by nine, and neither seems ever to have given him anything cozier than an ear. Tasso never married; he could love only princesses, and they could marry only property. Perhaps, as diffident of his powers as he was proud of his poetry, he feared the obligations and restraints of marriage.

In 1569 his father died penniless; Tasso had to borrow to bury him. A year later Cardinal d'Este took the youth to Paris. Torquato was shocked to find Charles IX associating amiably with Huguenot leaders; he openly criticized the government for consorting with heretics. The Cardinal, anxious to keep the favor of the King, sent his troublesome secretary back to Italy; Tasso never forgave him.

Alfonso consoled the poet by attaching him to his own household with an annual stipend and no responsibilities except to dedicate to the Duke the epic that he was known to be writing about the First Crusade. These years were relatively happy. In the summer of 1573 Tasso produced at the court his pastoral drama *Aminta*, and was heartened by its success. The lords and ladies of Ferrara, who lived by exploiting the peasantry, were thrilled to see the bliss of rustics—on the stage; and all the gallants of the court rejoiced in the picture of a golden age when everything pleasant was lawful and good.

O bel età dell' oro	O lovely age of gold!
Non già perchè di latte	Not that the rivers rolled
Sen corse il fiume,	With milk, or that the
* e stillò mele il bosco . . .*	woods wept honeydew . . .
Ma sol perchè quel vano	But solely that that vain
Nome senza oggetto	And breath-invented pain,
Quel idolo d'errori,	That idol of mistake, that
* idol d'inganno,*	worshiped cheat,
Quel che dal volgo insano	That honor—since so called
Onor poscia fu detto,	By vulgar minds appalled—
Chi di nostra natura 'l	Played not the tyrant
* feo tiranno,*	with our nature yet.
Non mischiava il suo affano	It had not come to fret
Fra le liete dolcezze	The sweet and happy fold
Delle amoroso gregge;	Of gentle humankind;
Nè fu sua dura legge	Nor did its hard law bind
Nota a quell' alme	Souls nursed in freedom; but
* in libertate avvezze,*	that law of gold,
Ma legge aurea e felice	That glad and golden law, all
Che Natura scolpì,	free, all fitted,
* "S'ei piace, ei lice."*[72]	Which Nature's own hand wrote:
	"What pleases is permitted."[73]

That unwonted boldness of spirit left him when (1574) he found himself finishing his epic, *Gerusalemme liberata*. This was the culminating

effort of his life. If it failed, or if the Church condemned it as licentious
or heretical, he would never be happy again. Fearfully he sent the manuscript to seven critics and asked their judgment on the poem's plot, characters, diction, and morality. They passed so many censures upon it that,
not knowing how to please them all, he put the poem aside. For five years
it lay unpublished. The poet, conscious that he had written a masterpiece,
demanded too much of his critics, and of life. He confessed that "he could
not bear to live in a city where the nobles did not yield him the first place,
or at least admit him to absolute equality." This last he surely merited, but
he added that he "expected to be adored by friends, served by serving-
men, caressed by domestics, honored by masters, celebrated by poets, and
pointed out by all."[74] A party grew up at Ferrara that criticized his poetry,
his character, and his claims. He began to dream of softer berths in kinder
courts.

Physical and mental disturbances had shaken his nerves: malarial fever,
repeated headaches, the cumulative shocks of his father's exile, his mother's
death, his father's dying destitution. Moreover, theological doubts—of hell,
of immortality, of Christ's divinity—darkened his mind with a sense of sin
and drove him to frequent confession and Communion.[75] He was convinced that he had experienced the power of black (Satanic) magic. He
had horrible visions of the Last Judgment and saw God driving the condemned into everlasting fire.[76] He had delusions of persecution—suspected
his servants of betraying his secrets, believed that he had been denounced
to the Inquisition, and daily expected to be poisoned. He was a difficult
guest.[77]

Alfonso dealt with him sympathetically, for, after all, the greatest poem
of the age was dedicated to him and gave half a canto (XVII) to celebrating his lineage. He excused the poet from attendance at court, and sent him
to the pleasant villa of Belriguardo for change and quiet. But his patience
was strained when he found that Tasso was secretly negotiating with
Francesco de' Medici—Alfonso's keenest rival and enemy—with a view to
acceptance as a pensioner at the Florentine court. In November 1575 the
poet left Ferrara, saying that he was going to Rome to get the indulgence
of the jubilee. He went, but visited Florence twice en route. The Grand
Duke did not take to him. Francesco wrote to a friend (February 4, 1576),
"I hardly know whether to call him a mad, or an amusing and astute,
spirit"; and a year later he decided that "he did not want to have a madman at his court."[78] Tasso returned sadly to Ferrara.

He asked Alfonso for the post of historiographer; he received it. In
January 1577 he appeared before the Inquisition at Bologna and confessed
that he had sinfully entertained doubts of the Catholic faith; the Inquisition sent him back with words of comfort and good cheer. In June of that
year, while in the apartments of Lucrezia d'Este, he drew his knife upon a

servant who had aroused his suspicion. Alfonso ordered the poet to be confined in a room of the castle, but soon released him and took him to Belriguardo. The Duke behaved, wrote Tasso, "almost as if he had been a brother, and not as a sovereign."[79] The poet asked to be sent to the Monastery of San Francesco; Alfonso so ordered, and he recommended a purge. Tasso submitted; but at the monastery he broke out into a frenzy, charging that his wine had been doctored; the monks asked that he be taken off their hands. He was returned to the ducal castle and put under guard. He escaped, disguised himself as a peasant, and wandered on foot and alone across the Apennines to the home of his sister Cornelia in Sorrento. She received him with loving tenderness.

He might have won some clarity and happiness there had he not worried about the great poem, still unpublished, that he had left behind him in Ferrara; and perhaps, long accustomed to court life, he missed the comforts that had accompanied his tribulations. He went to Rome and begged the Ferrarese ambassador to intercede for him with Alfonso. The Duke sent money to take care of him and consented to his return, on condition that he promise to be quiet and submit to medical treatment. Arrived at Ferrara (1578), he was given a private apartment outside the palace; a servant was provided, and meals were sent from the ducal table. Tasso accepted sedatives and purges obediently and continued to write fine poetry. But he had hoped to be again a favorite at the court; instead, nearly everyone treated him as a madman. Neither the Duke nor the princesses any longer admitted him to their presence. The worst insult of all was that Alfonso ordered the poet's manuscripts, including the *Gerusalemme*, to be taken from him, lest he destroy them.

In June 1578 Tasso again fled from Ferrara. He went to Mantua, Padua, Venice, Urbino, Turin. There Duke Charles Emmanuel received him with honors and gave him all the comforts he had known at Ferrara. But after three months the restless poet, perhaps anxious to recover his manuscripts, petitioned Alfonso to take him back. Alfonso agreed, and in February 1579 Tasso was again lodged in the palace of Cardinal Luigi d'Este. But Alfonso, longing for heirs, was being married for the third time, and had no ear for poets; Tasso was not invited to the festivities. For two weeks he bore neglect fretfully; then (March 12, 1579) he left the Cardinal's quarters and broke into the Palace of the Bentivogli, crying out against the Duke, the new Duchess, and the whole court. He ran to the Castello, insisting on seeing the Duchess and recovering his manuscripts. The Duke ordered him removed to the nearby Sant' Anna mental hospital. There he was confined for over seven years.

He was not entirely mad. He had lucid intervals, in which he wrote poetry and received friends; Montaigne claimed to have visited him. Several ladies of the court came to comfort him, and once Lucrezia took him to her villa at Belvedere; but his violence frightened her, and she had him sent back to the hospital. The broken mind was cast into intermittent terror by hallucinations of spectral voices heard, of supernal spirits invading his room and stealing his poems.

Now, at last, his epic was published. Those who had possession of the manuscript, learning that book pirates had copied it, sent it to the printers (1580). The critics still found fault with it, but Italy acceped it enthusiastically, and Church authorities praised its theme and piety. Edition followed upon edition; two thousand copies were sold in a day; homes and courts echoed its melody. Men debated whether Tasso should be ranked with Ariosto or Petrarch; Voltaire, with no Christian prejudice, preferred the poem to *The Iliad*;[80] Elizabeth of England, hearing parts of it translated into Latin, envied the Duke of Ferrara for having found a Homer to immortalize him.[81]

If we prod our historic sense we can begin to understand why Europe responded so warmly to this stirring narrative of the First Crusade. It was hailed as the long-awaited, sorely needed épic of Christendom. For when Tasso commenced his poem Europe was amassing the fleet that met the Turks at Lepanto; the great battle was fought while the poet wrote; it was won, but the rapid recovery of the Turks was threatening Europe, especially Italy; Rome, the citadel of Christianity, was in danger as the poem reached completion. The fear of Islam was then as pervasive in Christendom as Europe's dread today of a revitalized Orient. In that atmosphere men and women read, in seductive verse, the heartening story of how Godfrey of Bouillon, in 1099, had led a battered but triumphant Christian host to the capture of Jerusalem.

So Tasso, remembering and challenging Virgil's *arma virumque cano*, proudly begins:

> *Canto l'arme pietose, e 'l capitano*
> *Che il gran sepolcro liberò di Cristo—*

"I sing the pious arms, and the captain who freed the great sepulcher of Christ." He calls upon the Muse to inspire celestial ardors in his breast, and dedicates his poem to "*magnanimo* Alfonso" for rescuing him from the squalls of fortune and giving him a pleasant port. God sends the Archangel Gabriel to bid Godfrey cease dallying and press on to Jerusalem. As the Christians near the city, its Turkish governor, Aladin, orders his men to transfer a statue of the Virgin from a Christian church to a Moslem mosque, believing that the image will bring victory to its possessor. The statue is recaptured and concealed by Christians; Aladin decrees the massacre of all the remaining Christians in Jerusalem. The lovely maiden Sophronia offers herself as a sacrifice for her people; she falsely tells Aladin that she has stolen and burned the image; he condemns her to die at the stake. Her unrequited lover Olindo seeks to die in her place and assumes the guilt; they are both condemned to death, but they are rescued by the Moslem heroine Clorinda. Pluto, god of the nether world, calls a council of his followers to consider means of defeating the Christian besiegers. As their instrument they choose the fair Armida, a Damascene damsel with bewitching powers. Rinaldo and other knights are ensnared into her enchanted garden, and Rinaldo relaxes in her arms. Tancred, the perfect Christian knight, chivalrous and brave, admires Clorinda's courage and falls in love with her across the barriers of creed. In one of the liveliest cantos (XII) of the poem Clorinda disguises herself and fights Tancred to her death; dying, she begs him to christen her into his own faith. Godfrey sends soldiers to find Rinaldo and the lost knights; they discover Armida's castle, turn away from the "naked beauties" swimming in her pool, and free the captives. Angry at Rinaldo's desertion of her, Armida offers herself as prize to anyone who will kill him. Tisiphernes takes the task, but Rinaldo pierces him through from fore to aft. Armida proposes suicide, but Rinaldo dissuades her with revived love; she consents to conversion and surrenders to him with the Virgin's phrase, "*Ecco l'ancilla tua.*"[82] The Christians scale the walls, slaughter the Moslem hosts, and give thanks to God. The story does not go on to the incineration of the Jews.

Ariosto had smiled at the chivalric romance; Tasso revived it in fullest gravity, adding medieval magic and marvels to the classical machinery of intervening divinities. The Counter Reformation had for a time repressed the lusty Italian sense of humor; a lack of humor prepared Tasso for insanity. The cosmos must not be taken too seriously. Tasso, in his epic, is faith unquestioned and sentiment unrelieved. He adorns the poem with such conceits that Galileo compared it to a museum of curiosities,[83] and wrote angry criticisms in the margin of his copy.[84] The imitations are obvious: of Homer in the battle scenes, of Virgil in the visit to hell, of Ariosto in the amours, of Virgil, Dante, and Petrarch in ideas and whole lines. The magic is childish, the Amazons are absurd. The *Gerusalemme* may not be as majestic as *The Iliad*, nor as captivating as *The Odyssey*, nor as noble as *The Aeneid*; yet it sustains interest as well as any epic, its style is studded with happy turns and flows of melody, its characters are alive, its episodes are skillfully fused with the central theme. Many of its scenes and incidents inspired famous paintings. Its verse and mood helped to form Spenser's *Faerie Queene*. Its stanzas, put to music, have solaced the weary rhythm of Venetian gondoliers.

Tasso, in his lucid intervals, took little pleasure and less profit from the success of his poem. Not a penny came to him from the publishers. As with most authors, an ounce of censure outweighed a pound of praise. He winced to read the strictures of some critics—that his rhymes were too often jingles, his love scenes too sensuous, his Moslems too admirable, his heroines too often like men. But the remainder of Italy hailed him as Virgil reborn, and voices were raised demanding some better treatment for the stricken poet. Those who visited him, however, saw that he needed careful supervision, and that Alfonso was handling the matter as considerately as could be expected of a man often offended, and busy with government.

The condition of the poet improved. In July 1586 Vincenzo Gonzaga, heir apparent to the duchy of Mantua, secured his release on a promise to take care of him. For a month Tasso lived at Mantua; then he left it for Bergamo, Modena, Bologna, Loreto, Rome, selling his poems and praises to any who would pay. He was well received in Rome, but soon he wandered away again, to Siena, to Florence, again to Mantua, again to Naples, where Marquis Manso befriended him, and once more to Rome, where Cardinals Cinzio and Aldobrandino housed him in their rooms in the Vatican (1594). He wished to return to Ferrara to die there; Alfonso refused to let him come. Pope Clement VIII assigned him a pension and made plans to crown him poet laureate. But in April 1595 the worn-out poet, old and infirm at fifty-one, had to be taken to the Monastery of San Onofrio, in Rome, for better supervision. There, after one more out-burst of passion, he died (April 25), murmuring, *"In manus tuas, Domine."* The laurel wreath that he had never lived to wear was placed upon his bier. The body was borne in procession to St. Peter's and back again, fol-lowed by the papal court and the nobles and scholars of Rome; it was buried in the monastery church and was marked with a simple epitaph: *Hic jacet Torquatus Tassus.* The cell he had occupied became a goal of pilgrimage, as it is today.

VIII. THE COMING OF BAROQUE: 1550–1648

Classical art—the Parthenon and its frieze, the sculptures of Myron and Polyclitus, the Roman Forum, *The Aeneid*, the Vatican Stanze of Raphael, the Medici Chapel figures of Michelangelo—had been the reduction of chaos to order, of the manifold to unity, of movement to stability, of feeling to thought, of the indiscriminate to the significant, of the complex and obscure to the simple and clear; it was matter forged into form. But even perfection palls when it is long continued. Change is necessary to life, sensation, and thought; an exciting novelty may seem by its very novelty to be beautiful, until the forgotten old returns on the wheel of time and is embraced as young and new. So the Renaissance drove Gothic out of

Italy as barbarous, until artists and patrons, irked by pretty proportions and cramping symmetry, and laughing like cathedral gargoyles at classic columns, architraves, and pediments, brought the Gothic spirit back in the exuberant irregularities and elaborations of baroque.*

Classical art had sought to reveal the objective, the impersonal, the perfect; baroque allowed the individual artist, even his passing humor, to find embodiment in work that represented not so much an object realistically portrayed (as in Dutch painting), but an impression or feeling objectified through partly imaginary forms. So El Greco's elongations were not Spain's men but his own memories or moods; the tender Madonnas of Murillo and Guido Reni were not the harassed mothers whom they knew but the exemplary piety they had been asked to represent. Moreover, an Italy that had felt the seismic shock of the Reformation, and that had been stirred to fresh intensities of religious emotion by Loyola, Teresa, Xavier, and Charles Borromeo—this post-Luther Italy could no longer rest in the calm, proud peace of the classic ideal. It reaffirmed its faith, displayed its symbols defiantly, adorned its shrines, and poured into art a new warmth of color and sensibility, a fresh diversity and incalculable freedom of structure and movement, released from classic rule, restraint, and line. Art became the expression of feeling through ornament, not the compression of thought into form.

Architecture was no longer Greek mathematics or Roman engineering, it was music, sometimes opera, like the Opéra in Paris. Designers and builders turned from stability to fluidity and rhythm; they rejected a static symmetry for deliberate disbalance and disunity; they willfully carved or twisted columns and architraves; they were weary of plain surfaces and heavy masses; they interrupted cornices, broke pediments in two, and scattered sculpture at every turn. The sculptors themselves were tired of perfect limbs, immobile features, the stiff frontal pose; they placed their figures in unexpected attitudes, inviting the eye to take diverse views; they introduced the effects of painting into statuary, carving light and shade into the stone, movement into the body, thought and feeling into the face. Painters left pure line, clear light, and an innocuous serenity to Perugino, Correggio, and Raphael; they bathed the world in color like Rubens, shaded it with mysticism like Rembrandt, roused it into sensuality like Reni, or troubled it with suffering and ecstasy like El Greco. The woodworkers littered furniture with decoration, the metalworkers turned their material into bizarre or humorous forms. When, in 1568, the Jesuits engaged Vignola to design their church, Il Gesù, in Rome, they saw to it that it should gather all the arts into a profusion of columns, statues, pic-

---

* From the Portuguese *barroco*, an irregularly shaped shell often used as decoration.

tures, and precious metal, designed not to illustrate geometry, but to inspire and irradiate faith.

Because in art Italy still led Europe, the new style of ornament, sentiment, and expression passed not only into Catholic Spain, Flanders, and France, but even into Protestant Germany, where it achieved some of its gayest forms. Literature felt the baroque influence in the extravagant word play of Marini, Góngora, and Lyly, in the high-flown language of Shakespeare, in Marlowe's *Doctor Faustus* and Goethe's *Faust*. Opera is music baroquefied. The new style won no general victory. The Dutch preferred a quiet realism to the excitements of baroque. Velázquez at his best was classical or realist, and Cervantes, after a romantic life, wrote *Don Quixote* with classic poise and calm. Corneille, Racine, and Poussin were devotedly classical. But were the classics always classical? Could anything be more baroque than the ugly struggling *Laocoön?* History smiles at all attempts to force its flow into theoretical patterns or logical grooves; it plays havoc with our generalizations, breaks all our rules. History is baroque.

One powerful factor remained constant in Italian art: the Church was still the most active and formative patron. There were, of course, other patrons and influences: princely houses and cultured cardinals built private palaces, and in ornament carried on some pagan themes; so Odoardo Farnese had the Carracci paint for him *The Triumph of Bacchus* and *The Rule of Love.* But the Council of Trent and the Catholic Reformation that followed it had set a sterner tone; nudes retired from Italian art, and pious subjects no longer served as sensual vehicles. Only the supplications of Roman artists dissuaded Pope Clement VIII from completely covering Michelangelo's *Last Judgment,* Daniele da Volterra's breeches and all. The Council had defended religious images against the attacks of Huguenots and Puritans, but it had insisted that such symbols should inspire worship rather than stir the blood. Whereas the reformers had discountenanced the adoration of Mary and the invocation of saints, the painters and sculptors of Counter-Reformation Italy told again, sometimes with crude realism, the sufferings of the martyrs, and, with conscious sentiment, the story of the Virgin Mother of God. The anxiety of the Church to depaganize art and to inculcate doctrine and piety co-operated with the political and economic reverses of Italy to make this age the last echo of the Renaissance.

IX. THE ARTS IN ROME

Rome was still the art capital of the world. The great age of Roman painting was over, and no Italian painter now could rival Rubens or Rembrandt, but

Roman architecture prospered, and Bernini was for a generation the most famous artist in Europe. Though Bologna had stolen the lead in painting, the stars of that school came to Rome for their final flourishing, and Vasari arrived in 1572 to fresco the Sala Regia of the Vatican. Painters whom fond minorities still reverence peopled the *botteghe* of Rome: Taddeo and Federigo Zuccaro, Girolamo Muziano, Francesco de' Salviati, Giovanni Lanfranco, Bartolommeo Manfredi, Domenico Fetti, Andrea Sacchi. Most of these are usually classed as "mannerists"—artists who imitated the manner of one or another of the masters of the High Renaissance. We may include "mannerism" (1550–1600) as the first stage of baroque.

Federigo Zuccaro unfurled his colors in four nations. In Florence he completed the frescoes that Vasari had begun in the cathedral dome; in Rome he painted the Capella Paolina of the Vatican; in Flanders he designed a series of cartoons; in England he made famous portraits of Queen Elizabeth and Mary Stuart; in Spain he shared in decorating the Escorial; and back in Rome he founded the Academy of St. Luke, whose organization suggested to Reynolds the English Royal Academy of Arts. Of all Italian painters in that generation Zuccaro was in greatest demand, but posterity has preferred Pietro Berrettini da Cortona. With Renaissance versatility Pietro designed the Barberini and Pamfili palaces in Rome, and painted, in the Pitti Palace at Florence, frescoes crowded with fantastic figures in the full profusion of baroque.

The real master of Roman painting in this age was Michelangelo Merisi da Caravaggio. He was a man of Cellinian spirit. Son of a Lombard stonemason, he studied in Milan, moved to Rome, enjoyed a dozen quarrels, killed a friend in a duel, escaped from prison, fled to Malta, Catania, and Syracuse, and died of sunstroke on a Sicilian shore at the age of forty-four (1609). In the intervals he effected a near-revolution in the mood and the technique of Italian painting. He liked violent contrasts of light and shade, played such tricks as illuminating a scene from a hidden hearth, modeled his figures with light, brought them out from a dark background, and began the reign of the *tenebrosi*—Guercino, Ribera, and Salvator Rosa—in Italy. Scorning the idealistic sentimentality of the Bolognese painters, he startled the age with his almost brutal realism. When he took religious subjects he made the Apostles and the saints look like burly workers borrowed from the docks. His *Card Players* (now in the Rothschild Collection in Paris) won him international fame. His *Musicians*—three singers and a lovely lutanist—gathered dirt for three centuries before it was found in a north-of-England antique shop about 1935; it was sold to a surgeon for £100 and was bought for $50,000 by the Metropolitan Museum of New York (1952). The Church usually rejected Caravaggio's religious pictures as too plebeian and lacking in sublimity; today they are the prizes of connoisseurs. Rubens so admired the Italian's *Madonna del Rosario* that he collected 1,800 gulden among the artists of Antwerp to buy it and present it to the Church of St. Paul.[85] *The Supper at Emmaus* (London) is not as profound as Rembrandt's, but it is a powerful rendering of peasant figures. *The Death of the Virgin* (Louvre)—again a peasant scene—was one of the pictures that established the school of *naturalisti* in Italy and realists in Spain and the Netherlands. Too often Caravaggio stressed the melodrama of violence and crudity; but history, like oratory, seldom makes a point without exaggeration. An age that had exhausted the themes of sentiment shuddered at these brawny longshoremen, and then accepted them as an invigorating entry of forgotten men into art. Ribera took up Caravaggio's darkened brush and equaled him; Rembrandt captured the chiaroscuro of the Italian and bettered it; and even the painters of the nineteenth century felt that stormy influence.

Architecture now saw both the advent and the zenith of baroque. Pope after pope transmuted the sweat and pennies of the willing faithful into the glory of Rome. Pius IV completed the Belvedere and other rooms in the Vatican. Gregory XIII built the Collegio Romano and began the Quirinal Palace—which in 1870 became the residence of the King. Domenico Fontana, favorite architect of Sixtus V, designed the new Lateran Palace, the Sistine Chapel in the Church of Santa Maria Maggiore, and, in that chapel, the very baroque tomb of Pius V. Meanwhile cardinals and nobles added new palaces to Rome (Giustiniani, Lancelotti, Borghese, Barberini, Rospigliosi) and new villas (Pamfili, Borghese, Medici). Destruction went on, too; in this period Paul V demolished the Baths of Constantine, which had survived, almost intact, since the first Christian Emperor.

Good architects were plentiful. There was Giacomo della Porta, who ably completed several buildings left unfinished by his master, Vignola, like the façade of Il Gesù and the cupola of St. Peter's; in that same immensity he designed the majestic Cappella Gregoriana; he gave the final touches to the Palazzo Farnese, which Michelangelo had begun; and to him are due two of the magnificent fountains that give Rome the freshness of eternal youth. The loveliest of the fountains is the Fontana delle Tartarughe (tortoises), which Taddeo Lundini set up before the Palazzo Mattei. Martino Lunghi the Elder shared with della Porta in raising from Michelangelo's sketches the Palazzo de' Conservatori, and himself began the Borghese Palace, which Flaminio Ponzio completed for Paul V. Domenico Fontana contributed the Fontanone dell' Acqua Felice and the Fontana dell' Acqua Paolina, and erected the beautiful Loggia of the Benediction on the north portico of St. John Lateran. His nephew Carlo Maderna succeeded him as architect of St. Peter's, changed its basic plan from the Greek cross of Michelangelo to the Latin cross, designed the façade of the great shrine, and found in the baths of Caracalla and Diocletian the inspiration for its immense nave. Maderna's disciple Francesco Borromini rebuilt magnificently the interior of St. John Lateran, and began, as his masterpiece, the sumptuous Church of Sant' Agnese, which rivals Il Gesù as illustrating Roman baroque.

The Church of Jesus—Il Gesù—was planned (1568) by Giacomo da Vignola to meet the desire of the Jesuits for an architecture whose magnificence would awe, inspire, and uplift the worshiper. The architect and his successors designed a spacious nave without aisles, with ornate pillars, spandrels, capitals, and cornices; an imposing altar, a luminous cupola, and brilliant decoration with pictures, statuary, marble, silver, and gold; and in 1700 Andrea del Pozzo, himself a Jesuit, added the noble tomb and altar of St. Ignatius. The Jesuit attitude to life differed from that of some other Catholic churchmen, and was at opposite pole to the Puritan view; art was to be chastened of secular sensuality, but it was to be welcomed in the adornment of life and faith. However, there was no specific "Jesuit style." Il Gesù was baroque petrified, and many Jesuit churches, especially in Germany, were baroque, but each church followed local and current forms and moods.

The final achievement of Roman art was the completion of St. Peter's. Michelangelo had left a model of the dome, but the drum alone had been laid when Sixtus V came to the papacy. The drum was 138 feet in diameter. Only Brunelleschi, at Florence, had dared to cover so great an area without intervening supports. Architects and engineers quailed before the task proposed by Buonarotti; financiers moaned that it would take a million ducats and ten years' time. Sixtus ordered the work to proceed, hoping to celebrate Mass under the new dome before he died. Giacomo della Porta took charge, with Domenico Fontana as his aide. Eight hundred men labored night or day, Sundays excepted, from March 1589 till, on May 21, 1590, three months before the doughty pontiff's death, Rome was informed that "to his everlasting glory, and the shame of his predecessors, our holy Pope Sixtus V has completed the vaulting of the dome of St. Peter's."[86]

The effect of the dome, except from a distance, was diminished by the baroque façade that Maderna set up in 1607–14. The church itself was finally consecrated in 1626, 174 years after its first planning. In 1633 Bernini cast in bronze the gaudy *baldacchino*, or canopy, over the "tomb of St. Peter" and the high altar. The great sculptor redeemed himself by enclosing the approach to the shrine in a massive elliptical colonnade (1655–67) that helps to make St. Peter's the most sublime building on earth, as its dome is the crowning achievement of modern art.

X. BERNINI

Giovanni Lorenzo Bernini summed up in one dominating life (1598–1680) the art of seventeenth-century Rome. From his Florentine father, a sculptor, he learned his art; from his Neapolitan mother he may have derived his emotional intensity and ardent faith. In 1605 the father was summoned to Rome to work on the Church of Santa Maria Maggiore. There "Gian" grew up in an atmosphere of classic statuary and Jesuit piety. He was thrilled by the Vatican *Antinoüs* and the *Apollo Belvedere;* but he was more deeply moved by the Spiritual Exercises of St. Ignatius, which he practiced till he felt the terror and devotion of one who had experienced the pains of hell and the love of Christ. Every day he heard Mass; twice a week he took the Sacrament.

He tried his hand at painting, even to producing a hundred pictures. Of these the *Sts. Andrew and Thomas* in the Barberini Collection at Rome has won most praise, though we might prefer the self-portrait in the Uffizi Gallery—a dark, handsome youth tending to melancholy meditation. He did better in architecture. For Maffeo Barberini he completed the Barberini Palace; and when this patron became Pope Urban VIII, Bernini, aged thirty-one, was appointed chief architect of St. Peter's. There, besides the colonnade and the *baldacchino,* he built in the apse the ornate Cathedra Petri, enshrining the wooden chair which the faithful believed to have been used by the Apostle; around it he grouped four powerful figures of Church Fathers; and over the whole bizarre structure he scattered angelic statuary with the abandon of a man who had a mint of masterpieces in his brain. Near it he placed a massive tomb for his beloved Urban VIII. He designed the balconies, and many of the statues adorning the piers that support the dome. Under the dome he placed a monumental figure of St. Longinus, and in the right aisle he raised a lavish memorial to Countess Matilda of Tuscany. Outside the church, in a chaster style, he remodeled the Scala Regia, which leads up past stately columns to the Vatican Palace, and in an alcove of this Royal Stairway he set up an equestrian statue of Constantine seeing in the sky his summons to Christianity; the emotionalism of this figure set a pattern for the baroque age. Toward the end of his life he built in the Chapel of the Sacrament in St. Peter's an altar whose brilliant marbles and crowning ciborium, temple, cupola, and angels rapt in adoration seemed to him not too gorgeous an embodiment for the Eucharistic mystery of the Mass. All this work in and around St. Peter's impresses a modern artist as theatrical excess and a specious appeal to the senses; to Bernini it seemed the exuberant vehicle of an ecstatic and communicable faith.

Everywhere he mingled architecture and statuary. He dreamed of an art that would unite architecture, sculpture, and painting into one soul-stirring ensemble. In the Church of Santa Maria della Vittoria he brought together precious marbles—green, blue, and red—and loosed his decorative fancy to build the Cornaro Chapel, with fluted pillars and graceful

Corinthian columns; there he placed one of his most arresting and emotional sculptures: St. Teresa, limp and unconscious in an ecstatic trance, with a delectable seraph preparing to pierce her heart with a flaming arrow, a symbol of the saint's union with Christ. The seemingly lifeless figure of Teresa is one of the triumphs of Italian baroque, and the darting angel is a song in stone.

Bernini had some rivals. Montaigne was strongly impressed by Giacomo della Porta's statue of Justice on the tomb of Paul III in St. Peter's. Torrigiano cast a powerful and realistic bust of Sixtus V, now in the Victoria and Albert Museum. Borromini, like Bernini, mingled sculpture with architecture, as in the tomb of Cardinal Villamarino in the Church of Santi Apostoli in Naples. Alessandro Algardi equaled Bernini in carving three figures for the tomb of Leo XI in St. Peter's, and surpassed him in sculptural relief with the *alto relievo* of *The Meeting of Pope Leo I and Attila*, also in St. Peter's; and Algardi's bust of Innocent X in the Palazzo Doria Pamfili is more satisfying than Bernini's, and almost as powerful as Velázquez' portrait. But no one in this age matched Bernini in artistic fertility, imagination, and total achievement.

He delighted Rome with bizarre fountains: the Fontana del Tritone, the Fontana dei Fiumi—where minor sculptors carved four figures representing the Danube, the Nile, the Ganges, and the Plata. From competitive plans submitted for this fountain, Innocent X chose Bernini's, saying, "One must not look at his designs unless one is prepared to adopt them."[87] Bernini's flair for sumptuous sepulchral monuments must have given his patrons some pleasant anticipations of death. Urban VIII lived long enough to see the tomb in St. Peter's that was prepared for his remains.

Cardinal Scipione Borghese rivaled Urban in giving Bernini scudi and tasks. For him the sculptor made the vivid *Rape of Proserpine*, a dream of masculine muscles and feminine contours; *David* slinging his shot at Goliath; and *Apollo and Daphne*—too ideal a representation of male and female youth. These figures (now all in the Borghese Gallery) brought upon Bernini the charge of mannerism and theatrical exaggeration. The Cardinal himself was transmitted to us in two busts, the personification of good nature and good appetite. Naturally more attractive is the bust of the lovely Constanza Buonarelli in the Museo Nazionale at Florence; she was the wife of Bernini's aide, but Bernini, said his son, made her into stone while hotly enamored of her flesh—*fieramente innamorato*.[88]

More than any other artist, Bernini illustrates the faults of baroque. He made too obvious an appeal to emotion. He mistook the theatrical for the dramatic, prettiness for beauty, sentiment for sympathy, size for grandeur. He appropriated to sculpture the intense facial expression usually a privilege of painting. By too meticulous a realism of detail he sometimes dulled the psychological impact of his work. He rarely achieved in his figures the repose that gives a timeless quality to the sculptures of Periclean Athens. But why must a statue always express repose? Why should not the movement, feeling, and zest of life invade and animate marble and bronze? It is a virtue, not a fault, in baroque sculpture that it made stone feel and speak. Bernini observed the Horatian precept and felt what he expressed—the smooth texture of a girl's skin, the agile vitality of youth, the cares and labors of leaders, the piety and ecstasy of saints.

For almost fifty years he was accepted as the greatest architect of his age. In 1665, when Colbert and Louis XIV proposed to remodel and extend the Louvre, they invited Bernini to come to Paris and undertake the task. He came, and designed not wisely but too well—too grandly for French taste and funds. Perrault's severer façade was preferred, and Bernini returned to Rome a disappointed man. Now (1667) he made his remarkable chalk drawing of himself, at present in Windsor Castle—white locks receding over a powerful head, a face lined and gnarled with work, the once gentle eyes become hard and fearful, as if seeing whither the paths of glory lead. But he was not yet defeated; for thirteen more years he built and carved *con furia*, "sharp in spirit, resolute in his work, ardent in his wrath."[89] When his fire flickered out (November 28, 1680), he had outlived the Italian Renaissance.

Milton, visiting Italy in 1638, reported that Italian scholars themselves felt that the glory of their country had departed with the coming of Spanish dominance and the Counter Reformation. Probably subjection and censorship had injured the mind and art of Italy—though Cervantes, Calderón, and Velázquez were flourishing under a severer Inquisition in Spain. But it was a Portuguese mariner, not a Spanish general or an Index Expurgatorius, that ended the Italian Renaissance. Vasco da Gama had found an all-water route to India, a long route, but cheaper than the Venetian and Genoese trade avenues that had made Italy rich. Portuguese and Dutch commerce was supplanting Italian; Flemish and English textiles were taking markets from the Florentines. And the Reformation had cut in half the flow of German and English gold to Rome.

Italy shone in her decline. Art had fallen from the heights of Raphael and Michelangelo, political thought had lost the depth and courage of Machiavelli. But there was no decline, there was a rise, in statesmanship from Leo X to Sixtus V, there was a rise in science from Leonardo to Galileo, in philosophy from Pomponazzi to Bruno, in the music drama from Politian to Monteverdi, only a debatable decline in poetry from Ariosto to Tasso. Meanwhile, like a nourishing mother, Italy was pouring her art and music, her science and philosophy, her poetry and prose, over the Alps to France and Flanders, over the Channel to England, and over the sea to Spain.

CHAPTER X

Grandeur and Decadence of Spain

1556–1665

I. SPANISH LIFE

THOSE of us who have been brought up on the English historians easily forget that after as well as before the defeat of the Armada Spain was the greatest, richest, farthest-flung empire on earth, and that she considered herself, not without reason, superior to Elizabethan England in literature and to contemporary Italy in art. When Philip II came to the throne (1556), the Spanish monarchy ruled Spain, Roussillon, Franche-Comté, Ceuta, Oran, the Netherlands, the duchy of Milan, the Kingdom of Naples, Sicily, Sardinia, the Philippines, the West Indies, most of South America, part of North America, all of Central America; add (1580–1640) Portugal and the Portuguese possessions in Asia, Africa, and Brazil; add also a protectorate over Savoy, Parma, and Tuscany, and an alliance with the Holy Roman Empire ruled by Philip's uncle, Ferdinand I. Spain had an army of fifty thousand men noted for their bravery and discipline, and led by the best generals of the age; a navy of 140 vessels; an annual revenue ten times that of England. The gold and silver of America flowed into Spanish ports. The Spanish court in this age was the most splendid, and the Spanish aristocracy the proudest, in the world. The Spanish language was spoken by millions of people outside Spain, and in many countries the educated classes learned Spanish as in the eighteenth century they would learn French. Spanish architecture adorned cities in five continents.

Spain had now some eight million population. Agriculture languished as more and more land was turned to pasture sheep for the production of wool. About 1560 there were fifty thousand textile workers in Toledo alone. The demands of her colonies stimulated Spain's industries; Seville became one of the busiest ports in Europe; and the colonies in return sent cargoes of silver and gold. The influx of precious metals raised prices hectically—in Andalusia 500 per cent in the sixteenth century; wages clambered in feverish, and finally futile, pursuit of living costs. Much of the industry was manned by Moriscos—Moors superficially converted to Christianity. Domestic service was largely left to slaves captured in African raids or in wars against "infidels." The Spanish commoners scorned labor, and were philosophically content with little; to sleep in a hut, bask in the sun, strum a guitar, and mourn the stinginess of beauty seemed better than to sweat like a slave or a Moor. The expulsion of the Moriscos in 1609 shared with the high prices of Spanish products in the decline of Spanish industry.

The expulsion of the Jews in 1492 had left a vacuum in the commercial and financial structure of Spain. The Genoese and the Dutch became the chief carriers of Spain's foreign trade. Spain, governed by grandees more adept in diplomacy and war than in economic affairs, allowed her wealth to depend upon the import of gold; for a time the government grew richer while the people remained poor; but much of the gold was poured out for war, much of it was taken by foreign merchants carrying Spain's trade, until the government was almost as poor as the people. Spain repeatedly repudiated its debts (1557, 1575, 1596, 1607, 1627, 1647) or compelled their conversion into new loans; it was these financial crises that forced her to end her war with Henry II in 1559, with Henry IV in 1598, and with the United Provinces in 1609. In history we must *chercher* not *la femme* but *le banquier*.

In Spain we must also look for the priest. Nowhere else on the globe had religion such power over the people, and therefore over the government. Spain rejected not only the Reformation, but—except for an Erasmian moment—the Renaissance as well. It remained medieval amid modernity, and contentedly so. The poverty of the people gloried in the wealth of the Church. Everybody was pious, from the kings who were "more Catholic than the pope,"[1] to the bandits who were never found without religious medallions or scapulars. In 1615 some forty thousand Spaniards marched in a demonstration demanding that the Pope make the Immaculate Conception of the Virgin (i.e., her freedom from the stain of original sin) a *de fide* dogma—a belief obligatory on all Catholics.[2] Priests, monks, and friars were everywhere, not smiling on the joys of life and love as in Italy or France, but casting an aura of El Greco somberness over all affairs except bullfights. Spain had now 9,088 monasteries, 32,000 Dominican and Franciscan friars,[3] and a rising number of Jesuits. Churches were dark, rich in awesome relics, and adorned with realistic terrors in their art. Stories of the saints and their miracles were the cherished poetry of the people. The lyrics of St. John of the Cross and the writings of St. Teresa made mysticism popular. The Church herself had to protest against the claims of "Quietists" to divine communion and beatific visions; in 1640 the Inquisition laid its claws upon a sect of Alumbrados—"Enlightened Ones"—who claimed that their mystical union with God cleansed them of sin even in their erotic ecstasies. We must bear in mind this pervasive and perfervid piety if we are to understand why the Spanish people could look with passionate approval upon the burning of heretics, and bleed itself to bankruptcy and exhaustion in fighting for the faith in Germany and the Netherlands. There was something noble in this insanity. It was as if the nation felt that unless its faith were true, life would be a meaningless absurdity.

So the Inquisition continued its conscientious ferocity. It checked with "moderate" punishments—such as a hundred lashes—such heresies as that fornication is no sin, or that marriage is as holy as monastic celibacy. But for "relapsed" Marranos—converted Jews who secretly returned to Judaism—death or life imprisonment was the standard expiation. When Philip II arrived in Spain (1559) he was welcomed at Valladolid with an auto-da-fé in which 200,000 persons, presided over by the King, saw ten heretics strangled and two burned alive.[4] One of the condemned appealed to Philip for mercy; he refused it, and won the admiration of the people by saying, "If my own son were such a wretch as you are, I myself would carry the faggots to burn him."[5] Philip occasionally checked the tendency of the Inquisition to extend its authority at the expense of the civil power, but by and large he encouraged the institution as an instrument of national fervor and unity. It was of some convenience to him that the condemned could be used as galley slaves,[6] and that in one year (1566) he received 200,000 gold ducats as the government's two thirds of Inquisition fines and confiscations.

The Inquisition prided itself on preserving the medieval faith undiluted, and on saving Spain from the religious disunity that was convulsing France. Its emphasis on belief rather than conduct left the protection of morals to the clergy—who were themselves notoriously lax in their behavior—and to civil officials whose authority with the public was impaired by their subjection to Inquisition imprisonment and fines. Female purity was guarded not only by religion and law, but by the *punto*, or point of honor, which required every male to defend or avenge by the sword the threatened or violated chastity of any woman in his family. Dueling was illegal but popular. Decent women were usually kept at home in a semi-Arabic seclusion; they dined apart from the men, seldom accompanied them in public, and used closed coaches when they stirred outside their homes. Suitors made their plea with music from the streets to maidens behind grated windows; they were rarely admitted into the house until the parents on both sides had come to an agreement; nevertheless there were many love marriages.[7] Under Philip II the level of morality was kept as high as the beauty of the women or the imagination of the men allowed; the natural venality of officials was moderated by the watchfulness of the King; and until the defeat of the Armada the morale of the nation was sustained by the belief that Spain was leading a holy war against Islam, the Netherlands, and England. When that dream broke, Spain collapsed in body and soul.

Meanwhile Spanish life had its characteristic splendor and charm. Charity was widely spread, and good manners ran through every class. Half the nation claimed noble blood, tried to live up to the pretense of chivalric courtesy, and insisted on dressing like the uppermost tenth. Under Philip II dress was fairly simple: the men wore ruffs, doublets, tight dark hose, and buckled boots; the ladies (all were ladies) covered their curves with stiff, flat corsages, veiled from the other sex all of their faces except their eyes (which are especially inflammatory in Spanish women), and so coyly hid their feet that a glimpse of these was among the most exciting rewards of a lover's prayers.[8] In the relaxing of morals that followed Philip's death, female dress became fancier, fans were flaunted in wordless badinage, rouge glowed on faces, shoulders, bosoms, and hands, and mysterious legs were concealed in hoopskirts so ample that theater owners charged each such inflated woman for two seats.

The bullfight continued to be the favorite spectacle. Pope Pius V issued a bull against it in 1567, but Philip II protested that such a prohibition would loose a revolution in Spain, and the edict was ignored. Religious processions added a solemn poetry to prosaic days, and carnival masks covered a multitude of sins. Music was a passion only secondary—and closely allied—to religion and love. The guitar-shaped vihuela strummed hypnotic obbligatos to amours, and madrigals enjoyed a passing popularity. In church music Spain rivaled Italy. Tomás Luis de Victoria, the Velázquez of Spanish music, grew up in St. Teresa's Ávila and may have felt her influence. He had a voice and a vocation; probably he was ordained to the priesthood in 1564; certainly, a year later, Philip gave him an allowance to study music in Italy. By 1571 he was choirmaster in the Collegium Germanicum in Rome. In 1572, aged thirty-two, he issued a book of motets containing the inspired *O vos omnes* setting to Jeremiah's lamentation over Jerusalem. Returning to Spain (1583), he presented to Philip II a book of Masses including one of his noblest compositions, the Mass *O quam gloriosum*. For the obsequies of Philip's sister Maria, widow of Emperor Maximilian II, he wrote a deeply moving Requiem Mass which a distinguished historian of music has ranked as "one of the most magnificent compositions of the entire literature."[9] He called it his swan song; after its publication (1603) he gave himself wholly to his duties as a priest. He was among the outstanding ornaments of Spain's most famous reign.

II. PHILIP II: 1555–98

Here is one of the strangest, strongest figures in history, fanatical and conscientious, hotly hated outside Spain, passionately loved within it, a challenge to any student struggling for objectivity. His ancestry was his fate: his father was Charles V, who left him a kingdom and an obligation to bigotry; his paternal grandmother was Juana la Loca, the insane daughter of Ferdinand the Catholic; mysticism and madness were in his blood, dogma and absolutism were in his heritage. His mother, Isabella of Portugal, had two other sons, both of whom died of apoplexy in their childhood; she herself died at thirty-six, when Philip was twelve. He was born at Valladolid in 1527, at the very time when his father's troops were sacking Rome and imprisoning the Pope. He was brought up by priests and women who immersed him in piety and convinced him that the Catholic Church was the indispensable support of morality and monarchy. Whereas his father, reared in Flanders, had become a man of the world, Philip, living mostly in Spain, became, despite his fair skin and silken yellow hair, a Spaniard in face and creed, body and mind.

He had almost no youth, for at thirteen he was made governor of Milan and at sixteen regent of Spain—and this last in no merely nominal sense. Charles appointed advisers for him, explained their characters penetratingly, bade him play one councilor against another, and urged him to keep all real power and all final decisions for himself—which Philip did to the end of his days. In that year 1543 Philip married his cousin Princess Maria of Portugal; she died in 1545, shortly after presenting him with a "star-crossed" son, Don Carlos. Philip now contracted a morganatic marriage with Isabel de Osorio, by whom he had several children. His father urged him to have this union annulled; it was the obligation of every Hapsburg prince to help establish, by marriage or war, a ring of allies around the ancient enemy, France. To safeguard Spanish power in the Netherlands from English meddling, Philip should swallow his esthetic sense, marry England's Catholic Queen Mary Tudor, and give her sons who would keep England Catholic. So in 1554 he crossed the Channel, married plain, ailing, hopeful Mary (eleven years older than himself), did his best to make her pregnant, failed, and departed (1555) to become governor of the Netherlands.

Year by year his responsibilities grew. In 1554 he had been made governor of the double kingdom of Naples and Sicily. In 1556 Charles resigned to him the crown of Spain. For four years Philip ruled his scattered realms from Brussels. He struggled to adjust his Spanish solemnity to Flemish jollity and Dutch finance. He had no taste for war, but his generals won for him, at St.-Quentin (1557), a battle that induced the French to sign the Peace of Cateau-Cambrésis. To establish some friendship with France Philip married Elizabeth of Valois, daughter of Henry II and Catherine de Médicis. Then, thinking matters stabilized, he bade farewell to the Netherlands, and sailed from Ghent (August 1559) to immure himself for the rest of his life in Spain.

He transferred the capital from Toledo to Madrid (1560), and soon afterward, loving solitude, and ill at ease in crowds, he commissioned Juan Bautista and Juan de Herrera to build for him, twenty-seven miles northwest of Madrid, an architectural ensemble including a royal palace, an administrative center, a college, a seminary, a monastery, a church, and a mausoleum—for Philip was now as religious as politics would permit. In the battle of St.-Quentin his cannon had demolished a church dedicated to St. Lawrence; in repentance of this sacrilege, and in gratitude for his victory, he had vowed to raise a shrine to the saint in Spain. So he named the vast assemblage of structures El Sitio Real de San Lorenzo—the royal seat of St. Lawrence; time, however, has christened it Escorial, from a town nearby, which itself took its name from the *scoriae*, or slag, of the local iron mines.[10] As St. Lawrence was believed to have been burned to death on an iron grill, Juan Bautista designed the ground plan as a gridiron crisscrossed by halls from side to side, dividing the inner space into sixteen courts.

Driving out to it from Madrid, one wonders how, in an age with no faster communication than horses' feet, Philip could have governed his global realm from such a sanctuary, lost in gloomy hills; but Madrid was still farther remote from the world. The great pile is left desolate today except for the monks and their services; but in its prime, with its Renaissance façade 744 feet long, its towers and spires, and the massive dome of the church, it served as an awesome symbol of Spanish power, garnished with piety and art. Here half of Christendom was ruled; religion and government were united in one labyrinth of policy and stone; here the King could live, as he longed to do, not among courtiers but among priests and monks and saintly relics, and hearing many times a day the bells of the Mass. Here the Panteón was to receive the remains of Spain's kings and queens; the library was to become one of the richest in Europe; the picture gallery would soon harbor masterpieces by Raphael, Titian, Tintoretto, Veronese, El Greco, and Velázquez; here Pellegrino Tibaldi, Bartolommeo Carducci, and Federigo Zuccaro came from Italy to join Juan Fernández Navarrete, Luis de Morales, Luis de Carbajal, and other Spanish artists in frescoing the endless walls and vaults. The royal palace was left entirely simple, but the church, though of sternly Doric order, had an altar gleaming with porphyry, agate, and gold, and backed with a *retablo* elaborate in its ornament. The hall for the reception of dignitaries was vast and ornate, but Philip's own room was the poorest chamber in the building, as modest as a hermit's cell.[11] The building symbolized Philip's power, the room expressed his character.

He tried hard to be a saint, but could not forget that he was a king. He knew that he was the mightiest ruler on earth and felt a politic obligation to *hauteur;* but he dressed so simply that some strangers, coming

upon him in the Escorial, mistook him for an attendant and allowed him
to be their cicerone.[12] His protrusive Hapsburg chin should have betrayed
him, for it was an outstanding challenge to the world. In 1559, before time
and trials had hardened him, he was described by a Venetian ambassador
as "always showing such gentleness and humanity as no prince could surpass,"[13] and an English ambassador reported him (1563) as "of good disposition, soft nature, and given to tranquillity."[14] No one found any
public humor in him; heartless enemies said that in all his life he had smiled
only once—on hearing of the Massacre of St. Bartholomew; privately,
however, he relished pranks and jests and laughed heartily enough.[15] He
collected books with taste and zeal, but preferred art to literature; he was
a discriminating patron of Titian and critic of El Greco; he loved music
and played the guitar when the world was not looking. He had all the
Spanish courtesy of manners, but was awkward with shyness and stiffened
with ceremony. He made a handsome figure till his penchant for pastry
and sweets crippled him with gout. From his youth he was subject to ill
health, and if he rounded out his threescore years and ten it was only by
an obstinate resolve to complete his tasks. He took government as a sacred
duty, and labored at it day after day for fifty years. He seems really to
have believed that God had chosen him to stem the Protestant tide; hence
his grim tenacity and his reluctant cruelty; "he had no natural preference
for violent courses."[16] He never forgot a favor (Egmont's case excepted)
or an injury. He was sometimes vengeful, often magnanimous. He distributed alms with conscientious generosity.[17] In a corrupt age he was incorruptible; no bribe or gift could bend him from his pious persecutions.

In political morality he compared well enough with his contemporaries.
He hated war, never began one, and bore almost a full generation of injuries from England before commissioning the Armada. He was capable,
even beyond most rulers, of sanctimonious dissimulation. Apparently he
joined in a conspiracy to kill Elizabeth, as a last resort to save Mary Stuart.[18]
His government of Spain was autocratic but just. He "had an immense
solicitude for his subjects, and remedied whatever social injustices he
could find time to discover."[19]

His private morals were above those of most sixteenth-century kings.
In his youth at Brussels, if we may believe his enemies, "he was grossly
licentious," and "it was his chief amusement to issue forth at night disguised, that he might indulge in vulgar and miscellaneous incontinence
in the common haunts of vice."[20] Years later William of Orange, leading
the Netherlands revolt, accused the hermit of the Escorial of having
murdered his own son and poisoned his third wife;[21] but an indignant man
makes a poor historian. However, an unquestionably great and brave historian, the Spanish Jesuit Mariana, renders a like hostile verdict: while

crediting Philip with "liberality, resolution, vigilancy, and abstemiousness in eating and drinking," he charged him with "lust, cruelty, pride, perfidy, and several other vices."[22] A recent Dutch historian concludes, "Philip II could not be reproached with wantonness . . . dissipation and immorality . . . After his return to Spain he led, so far as we know, an austerely moral life"[23] as a faithful husband and a solicitous father. When his third wife, Elizabeth of Valois, fell ill of smallpox (then often fatal), Philip seldom left her side, though his ministers pleaded with him not to run such risk of infection. After Elizabeth's death Philip undertook another diplomatic marriage (1570), with one of many Annes of Austria; Anne died in 1580, and thereafter Philip spent his warm domestic affections upon his daughters. His letters to them are human with humor and love.[24] Isabel Clara became his closest companion and his chief solace amid the cares and defeats of old age. In his will he called her the light of his eyes. He had no comfort in his sons.

Legend and literature* and human pity have made Philip's first son better known than his father. Carlos was constitutionally weak, subject to intermittent fever, melancholy, and outbursts of temper and pride. He was prodigally generous and fiercely brave; he amused his grandfather, the once great Charles V, by reproaching him for having fled from Maurice of Saxony at Innsbruck (1552)—"*I* never would have fled!"[25] In the preliminaries to the Treaty of Cateau-Cambrésis Carlos, then fourteen, had been promised in marriage to Elizabeth of Valois; but in the treaty itself Philip, widowed by the death of Mary Tudor, took the Princess as his own wife, to divert French friendship from England to Spain. A year later (1560) the bride came to Madrid; Carlos, seeing her demure beauty, may have resented his father's variation of the *droit du seigneur*, but there is no evidence of any romance between him and the fourteen-year-old Queen.[26]

Despite Carlos' illness, he was formally recognized as heir to the crown. In 1561 he was sent to the University of Alcalá. There he fell down a flight of stairs while in amorous pursuit of a girl, fractured his skull, and fell into delirium. The great Vesalius trepanned the cranium and so saved the boy's life; but the improvement was ascribed by the people to the bones of a holy Franciscan friar—dead a century before—which had been taken from their coffin and laid in bed beside the Prince. During the youth's long convalescence Philip remained in Alcalá and spent much time at the bedside. Carlos was taken back to Madrid, where he regained sufficient strength to join young nobles in street violence against men and women. His tempestuous cruelties encouraged suspicion that his fall had irrevocably injured his brain. It did not help him with Philip that he expressed

* Don Carlos was made the subject of plays by Schiller, Alfieri, Otway, Marie Joseph de Chénier, Juan Pérez de Montalván, etc.

sympathy with the Netherland rebels. When Alva was appointed to command in the Low Countries, Carlos protested that the mission should have been assigned to him; he forbade Alva to go, and attacked him with drawn dagger when the Duke insisted.[27] Apparently the Prince thought for a time of fleeing to the Netherlands and putting himself at the head of the revolt.[28] Philip commissioned unwilling ministers to watch him. Carlos made plans to escape, sent out agents to collect funds, amassed 150,000 ducats, and ordered eight horses for his flight (January 1568). He confided his plan to Don Juan of Austria, who revealed it to the King. Fearing that his son, if allowed to leave Spain, would be used by Elizabeth of England or William of Orange as a contender to depose him, Philip ordered a stricter watch over the Prince. Carlos threatened suicide; Philip deprived him of all weapons and confined him in the royal palace at Madrid.

Thus far Philip's conduct admitted of defense; but now bigotry intensified the tragedy. Suspecting his son of heresy, the King ordered that no books should be allowed him but a breviary and some manuals of devotion. Carlos spurned the books and neglected all religious observances. A priest warned him that the Inquisition might be led to inquire whether he was a Christian. Carlos tried to kill himself, but was prevented; however, he accomplished his purpose by rejecting all food for three days, then gorging himself with meat and ice water. A severe dysentery set in; the Prince welcomed death, accepted the last sacrament, forgave his father, and died, aged twenty-three (July 24, 1568). Antonio Pérez, Philip's exiled enemy, accused him of having poisoned Carlos; most of Europe believed it, research has disproved it.* But the severity of the youth's imprisonment stands as one of many dark spots on the record of the King.

His conduct toward his half-brother, Don Juan of Austria, casts another shadow over the picture. The natural son of Charles V and Barbara Blomberg seems to have excited in Philip an admiration troubled with jealousy. Nevertheless he raised Juan to the rank of prince, and commissioned him to organize an expedition against the pirates of Algeria. Juan acquitted himself brilliantly. Philip gave him command of the land forces against the rebel Moriscos of Granada; Juan accomplished his mission with no time or mercy wasted. Philip appointed him—aged twenty-four—admiral in chief of the combined navies in the "last crusade"; Juan defeated the Turks at Lepanto and became the hero of Christendom. He felt that he deserved a kingdom, and he fretted when Philip made him merely governor general of the Netherlands.

---

* "In the painful episode of the imprisonment and death of Don Carlos, Philip behaved honorably."—*Encyclopaedia Britannica*, XVII, 722c. Cf. Martin Hume, *Spain, Its Greatness and Decay*, 150, and R. Trevor Davies, *The Golden Century of Spain*, 149n.

The silent King, always too proud to explain or defend himself in the forum of public opinion, received the full blame for another tragedy. He had raised to his Council a clever and elegant commoner, Antonio Pérez, who was believed to be the natural son of Philip's most trusted friend, Ruy Gómez, Prince of Eboli. When Gómez died (1573), Pérez became the confidant—probably the lover[29]—of the doubly intriguing widow, Ana de Mendoza, Princess of Eboli. Philip himself was said to have had a liaison with this one-eyed beauty eleven years before, but here "history" is probably romancing.[30] Pérez conspired with her to profit from their knowledge of state secrets. When Juan de Escobedo threatened to reveal their dubious trafficking, Pérez persuaded Philip that Escobedo had plotted treason, and the King gave Pérez an order for Juan's assassination. Pérez kept the order to himself for six months; then, to Philip's surprise and embarrassment, he had it carried out (1578). A year later the secret papers of Don Juan of Austria convinced Philip of Escobedo's innocence. He arrested Pérez and confined the Princess to her palace. Pérez confessed under torture and agreed to restore 12,000,000 maravedis to the treasury. With the help of his wife he escaped to Aragon, where the Inquisition, at Philip's urging, pursued him as a heretic. He fled to France, ascribed his persecution to the King's lingering passion for La Eboli, betrayed Spain's military and financial weaknesses to the French and English governments, and spurred Essex to raid Spanish ships and coasts. He died in Paris in 1611, after vain attempts to win pardon and asylum from Philip III.[31]

Philip found good reason for following the advice that his father had given him not to trust his aides. The grandees, like the French nobles, were jealous of the royal power, and were not above conspiring against the King. He kept them at odds among themselves, played them against one another, received summaries of their rival views, and made his own decisions. Losing faith in his subordinates, he labored personally on details of administration in every field—papal policy, public works, local abuses, roads and bridges, dredging rivers for navigation, establishing libraries, reforming and codifying Spanish law, and directing an extensive geographical, historical, and statistical survey of Spain, whose fifteen folio volumes are still unpublished.[32] Undertaking more than even his industry could manage, he fell into a philosophy of procrastination; many problems, he noted, lost urgency or meaning if resolutely deferred; in several cases, however, as in the Netherlands, the course of events decided against him while he weighed or pigeonholed pros and cons. In his royal cubicle he dictated or wrote with his own hand instructions for his appointees in five continents. He assumed that kingly power should be absolute; he ignored or overrode the *cortes,* or provincial assemblies, except in Aragon; he issued decrees, even of death, without public trial; and he comforted his autocracy with the conviction that only so could he protect the poor against the rich.[33] Within his despotism he built up, in a Europe almost universally corrupt, a bureaucracy and a judiciary comparatively competent and just.[34]

He respected the Church as the traditional molder of morals and guardian of kings, but he kept religion as subject to the state in Spain as Henry VIII or Elizabeth I in England. He placed so high a value on religious unity as an organ of government that he counted it "better not to reign at all than to reign over heretics."[35] Convinced that the Moriscos, while pretending Catholicism, were still practicing the Islamic ritual, he issued (1567) a pragmatica forbidding all Moorish customs, the use of the Arabic language, and the possession of Arabic books. The Moriscos rose in revolt (1568), captured a large region south of Granada, massacred Christians, tortured priests, and sold women and children into Berber slavery in exchange for powder and guns. The rebellion was suppressed after two years of competitive atrocities. All Moriscos were expelled from the province of Granada and were scattered among Christian communities in Castile; their children were placed in Christian homes, and school attendance was made compulsory for all children—the first such requirement in Europe.[36] Philip, at war with the Turks, suspected the Moriscos remaining in Valencia and Catalonia of plotting with the enemy, but his hands were so full that he left the final stage of the problem to his successor.

His father had bequeathed to him the defense of Christendom against Islam as a major part of Hapsburg policy. In 1570 he joined with Venice and the papacy in a crusade to end the Turkish mastery of the Mediterranean. Cyprus fell to the Turks while Philip formulated plans and the three allies assembled a fleet. By the summer of 1571 they had collected at Messina 208 galleys, 50,000 seamen, and 29,000 soldiers; a crucifix was at every prow, banners were blessed, prayers rose en masse to the sky, and the inspiring young Admiral issued the crusading call: "Christ is your general, you fight the battle of the Cross." On September 16, 1571, the fleet sailed off to a victory that ended Turkish predominance in the Mediterranean. As Spain had furnished more than her share of ships and men, the glamour of Lepanto fell upon Don Juan and the King, and Philip neared the crest of his curve. The zenith came when he fell heir to the throne of Portugal (1580) and added that strategic land to his swelling realm.

His abiding grief was the revolt in the Netherlands. He learned with wrath that Coligny, the Protestant leader, had almost convinced Charles IX that France should ally itself with the rebels. When news came that

Charles had let loose the Massacre of St. Bartholomew upon the Huguenots, Philip rejoiced, and he hardened his heart against the Netherlands.
He urged and paid for the assassination of William of Orange. He tried
to buy the friendship of Henry of Navarre, but Henry proved unpur-
chasable. So Philip bought the Guises and the Catholic League, and
dreamed of making his daughter the queen of France; then Spain and
France, joining forces, would subdue the Netherlands, make Mary Stuart
queen of England, and end Protestantism everywhere. When Elizabeth sent
aid to Holland (1585) and Mary to her death (1587), Philip, after years
of bearing with politic patience the harrying of Spanish vessels, coasts,
and treasure by Elizabeth's privateers, turned to war and bankrupted
his government to finance the Armada. All Spain supported the effort and
prayed for victory, feeling that the fate of that fleet would determine the
history of Europe.

Philip took the ignominious catastrophe with outward stoicism, saying
that he had sent the ships to fight men, not winds. But it broke his spirit
and almost broke Spain, though he survived and fought through ten years
more and Spain took a century to admit her ruin. He could hardly believe
that God had abandoned him after thirty years of fighting for the faith; yet
the dark truth must have come to him at last that after taxing his people
into poverty he had failed in everything except the accidental acquisition of
Portugal and the temporary repulse of the Turks—who had recaptured
Tunis and were recovering power. Henry IV was moving to victory in
France; the Netherlands were in irreconcilable revolt; the Pope refused
to bear a penny of the Armada's cost; Protestantism held the prosperous
north; England was taking control of the seas, therefore soon of America
and the East; and that incredible virago, Elizabeth, was sitting triumphant
on her moated throne, having outwitted all the kings of her time.

Bereavements, isolation, and disease joined to humble the once proud
and confident King. His fourth wife had died in 1580; of the three children
that she had borne him only one survived, a mediocre lad to whom must
be transmitted the first empire upon which the sun never set. The people
still reverenced Philip, despite his errors and defeats; they were convinced that he had labored in a sacred cause and had played the game
of power no more unscrupulously than his enemies, and they bore without reproach the misery into which his economic policies, his taxation, and
his failures had depressed them. In his old age his father's last bequest,
gout, racked his limbs with pain and crippled him with paralysis; one eye
had gone bad with a cataract; repulsive sores mangled his skin. In June 1598
he was borne in a litter to the Escorial, into that favorite room through
whose window he could see the high altar of the church. For fifty-three
days he lay rotting, bearing all in the trust that these were God's tests of

his faith, keeping that faith to the awful end, clutching and kissing a crucifix, and repeating, repeating prayers. He ordered the release of some prisoners as a final act of mercy. He sent for his son, counseled him always to be merciful and just, and bade him see the humbling finale of earthly power. His sufferings ended on September 13, 1598.

He had done the best he could with an intelligence too cramped by education, too narrow for his empire, too inflexible for his diverse responsibilities. We cannot know that his faith was false; we only feel that it was bigoted and cruel, like almost all the faiths of the age, and that it darkened his mind and his people while it consoled their poverty and supported his pride. But he was not the ogre that the fervent pens of his foes have pictured. He was as just and generous, within his lights, as any ruler of his century except Henry IV. He was decent in his married life, loving and loved in his family, patient under provocation, brave in adversity, conscientious in toil. He paid to the full for his rich and damning heritage.

III. PHILIP III: 1598–1621

His heir was quite another Philip. The father, seeing the youth's improvident lassitude, had mourned, "God, who has given me so many kingdoms, has not granted me a son fit to govern them."[37] Philip III, now twenty, was even more pious than his sire, so that gossip doubted that he had ever committed even a venial sin. Timid and meek, and quite unable to command, he handed over all the powers and perquisites of government to Francisco Gómez de Sandoval y Rojas, Duke of Lerma.

The Duke was a man of some benevolence, for he promoted nearly all his relatives to lucrative offices. He did not neglect himself; in his twenty years as chief minister he grossed so fat a fortune that popular resentment estimated it at the impossible sum of 44,000,000 ducats.[38] He spared to the treasury enough to equip two armadas against England (1599, 1601); both were shattered by unsympathetic winds. Lerma had the good sense to welcome the pacific overtures of James I, and after nineteen years of war Spain and England signed the Peace of London (1604). The war in the Netherlands continued, draining gold from Spain faster than it could come from America; Lerma found it beyond his ingenuity to satisfy, out of the revenues of an exhausted country, the needs of his hampered generals and his private purse. Realizing the futility of further efforts to deny independence to the United Provinces, he signed with them a twelve-year truce (1609).

But his next enterprise was as costly as war. He was a native of Valencia, where there were thirty thousand Morisco families; he had enough piety to hate these farmers and craftsmen, whose industry and thrift kept them prosperous amid the proud and shiftless penury of the Christians. He knew that these Christianized Moors, resenting their persecution by Philip II, maintained treasonous contacts with the Moslems of Africa and Turkey, and with Henry IV of France, who hoped to raise timely revolts in Spain.[39] It was unpatriotic of the Moriscos to avoid wine and eat so little meat; in this way the burden of the taxes on these commodities fell almost wholly upon the Spanish Christians. Cervantes expressed the fear that the Moriscos, who, rarely celibate, had a higher birth rate than the "Old Christians," would soon dominate Spain.[40] Juan de Ribera, Archbishop of Valencia, presented memorials to Philip III (1602) urging the expulsion of all Moriscos above seven years of age; the disasters that had befallen Spain, including the destruction of the Armada, were (he explained) God's punishments for harboring infidels; these pretended Christians should be deported, or sent to the galleys, or shipped to America to work as slaves in the mines.*[41] Over the warnings of the Pope, and despite the protests of landlords who profited from their Morisco tenants, Lerma issued (1609) an edict that—with some exceptions—all Moors of Valencia province were to embark within three days on ships provided for them and be transported to Africa, taking with them only such goods as they could carry on their backs. The scenes that had marked the expulsion of the Jews 117 years before were now repeated. Desperate families found themselves forced to sell their property at great losses; they marched in misery to the ports; many were robbed, some were murdered, on the way or on board ship. Reaching Africa, they rejoiced to touch Moslem soil, but two thirds of them died of starvation there or were killed as Christians.[42] During the winter of 1609–10 similar expulsions cleared the other provinces of Moriscos; altogether 400,000 of Spain's most productive inhabitants were expropriated and banished. In the eyes of the people this was the most glorious accomplishment of the reign, and simple Spaniards looked forward to a more prosperous era now that God had been appeased by ridding Spain of infidels. The proceeds from the confiscation of Morisco property rejoiced the court. Lerma pocketed 250,000 ducats, his son 100,000, his daughter and son-in-law 150,000.[43]

By 1618 the greed and carelessness of Lerma, the extravagance of the King and the court, the venality of officials, and the disruption of the economy by the Morisco exodus had reduced Spain to a condition where even the *fainéant* King saw the need of a change. In a flurry of resolution he dismissed Lerma (1618), only to accept Lerma's son, the Duke of Uceda, as chief minister. Lerma retired gracefully, received a cardinal's hat, and

* Juan de Ribera was canonized in 1960.

lived seven years more in piety and wealth. In 1621 the Council of Castile warned the King that his realm was being "totally ruined and destroyed owing to the excessive burdens, taxes and imposts,"[44] and it besought him to moderate his expenditures. He agreed—and then marched off on a royal progress lavishly equipped and maintained. In that same year he died, leaving to his son a realm enormous and impotent, a government corrupt and incompetent, a populace reduced to destitution, beggary, and theft, a nobility too proud to pay taxes, and a Church that had stifled the thought and broken the will of the people, and had transmuted their superstitions into hoards of gold.

IV. PHILIP IV: 1621–65

The son differed from his father in everything but extravagance. We know him externally from the many portraits of him by Velázquez: in the Metropolitan Museum of Art at New York he is nineteen (1624), handsome, blond, already expanding; in the National Gallery at London he is blithe and confident at twenty-seven, stout and somber at fifty; in the Prado we can see him in five stages of glory and decay; he is also in Florence, Turin, Vienna, Cincinnati—he must have spent half his life in Velázquez' studio. But those portraits show only his official features; he was not really so solemn and proud; we imagine him more justly by studying his children in Velázquez' portraits; presumably he loved them beyond reason, as we do ours. In reality he was a kindly man, generous to artists, authors, and women; no semi-saint like his father, but enjoying food and sex, plays and pictures, the court and the hunt, and resolved to get the most out of life even in a dying Spain. Perhaps because he savored life so fully, poetry and drama, painting and sculpture flourished under him as never in Spain before or again. When his pleasures seemed too promiscuous he multiplied his prayers, and he relied on his good intentions to pave the road to heaven. He had thirty-two natural children, of whom he acknowledged eight.[45] Having little time left for government, he delegated his powers and tasks to one of the predominant personalities in the diplomacy of the seventeenth century.

The career of Don Gaspar de Guzmán, Count of Olivares, ran remarkably parallel and counter to Richelieu's. For twenty-one years (1621–42) the great Count played against the wily Cardinal a bloody game of wits and war for the hegemony of Europe. Velázquez has revealed Olivares to us without fear and without reproach, in all the pugnacity of power, his prim mustachios curling like some ferocious scimitar, his robes and bands and chains and keys of state proclaiming authority.[46] His faults of imperial pride, quick irritability, and stern implacability alienated all but those who knew, too, his dedicated zeal and industry in serving Spain, his forthright honesty in a venal milieu, his contempt of worldly pleasures except as devices to bemuse the King, his frugal board and simple private life, his warm support of literature and art. He strove sincerely to abate abuses, to stop corruption, to recapture past peculations for the treasury, to moderate the cost of the royal establishment, to enjoin economy and modesty in dress and equipage, even to check the cruelty of the Inquisition. He took upon himself all the burdens of administration, policy, diplomacy, and war. He began his day's labors before dawn and continued them when prostrate with fatigue. It was his curse that Richelieu, with equal devotion, was slowly, subtly, inexorably sapping the Hapsburg power in Austria and Spain. To meet that deadly challenge armies were needed in Catalonia, Portugal, France, Naples, Mantua, the Valtelline passes, and the Netherlands, and in the vast and bloody trough of the Thirty Years' War. But armies needed money, and money required taxes. The *alcabala,* or sales tax, was raised to 14 per cent, choking trade; and the collectors embezzled two thirds of the taxes before the remnant reached the treasury. So, with patriotic resolution, Olivares bled Spain of her economic life to save her political power.

We must not follow all the moves of that sanguinary chess; they add nothing to our knowledge or estimation of mankind. It was a contest of strength, not of principles, each side shelving religion for military victory: Richelieu financing Protestant armies in Germany against Catholic Austria, Olivares sending 300,000 ducats yearly to the Duke of Rohan to prolong the Huguenot revolt in France.[47] In the end Spain was crushed; her power on the seas was ended by the Dutch in the battle of the Downs (1639), and her power on land was ended by the French at Roussillon (1642) and Rocroi (1643). In Spain's debility Portugal and Catalonia wrenched themselves free (1640); and for nineteen years the Catalán Republic, aided by France, waged war against Castile. At last the amiable King, who had trusted his minister through a hundred calamities, reluctantly dismissed him (1643). Olivares fled from hostile Madrid to voluntary exile in distant Toro; and there, two years later, he died insane.

Philip now for a time took personal charge. He reduced his own expenditures and devoted himself conscientiously to government. But the causes of Spain's decline were beyond his understanding or control. War continued, taxes were not lowered; production and population fell. At the Peace of Westphalia (1648) Spain was helpless, and had to concede independence to the United Provinces after nearly a century of wasted war. The Peace of the Pyrenees (1659) gave official sanction to French ascendancy in Europe. Amid these disasters Philip's loyal and patient wife,

Isabel of Bourbon, died (1644); and two years later she was followed by her sole surviving son, Don Baltasar Carlos, whom Velázquez had pictured so alluringly. The King was left with only one legitimate child, María Teresa, whom he gave in marriage to Louis XIV. Longing for an heir, Philip, aged forty-four, married (1649) his fourteen-year-old niece, Mariana of Austria, who had been betrothed to Baltasar. She rewarded him with two sons: Philip Prosper, who died at the age of four, and the future Carlos Segundo, Charles II. The tired King, racked with gallstones, weakened with hemorrhages, and harassed by magic-mongering monks, resigned himself to death (1665), comforted with the thought of an heir and spared the knowledge that his half-idiot son would bequeath all Spain to France.

V. PORTUGAL: 1557–1668

Three events marked these years in Portugal: she lost and rewon her independence, and Camões wrote *The Lusiads*.

She shared with Spain the ecstasy of expansion and the ferocity of dogma, and preceded her in decline. The rapidity of her colonial development had drained overseas her most enterprising sons; agriculture was neglected or left to spiritless slaves; Lisbon reeked with corrupt officials, covetous merchants, and penniless proletaires, all living ultimately on imperial exploitation or foreign trade. Young King Sebastian, inspired by the Jesuits with religious zeal, proposed to his uncle, Philip II, a joint conquest and Christianization of Morocco. Philip demurred, having his hands full; Sebastian proposed to undertake the enterprise unaided; Philip warned him that the resources of Portugal were too small for such a campaign; when Sebastian insisted Philip said to his Council, "If he wins, we shall have a good son-in-law; if he loses, we shall have a good kingdom."[48] Sebastian invaded Morocco and was overwhelmed and killed (1578) at the battle of Al-Kasr-al-Kabir (Alcázarquivir). A dedicated celibate, Sebastian left no heir; the throne was taken by his great-uncle, Cardinal Henry; but Henry himself died without issue in 1580, ending the royal Aviz dynasty that had ruled Portugal since 1385.

This was the opportunity that Philip had waited for. As grandsons of King Manuel of Portugal, he and Philibert Emmanuel of Savoy were the most direct heirs to the vacant throne. The Cortes of Lisbon recognized Philip; some rival claimants resisted his entry; the redoubtable Alva overcame them; and in 1581 Philip II entered Lisbon as Philip I of Portugal. By courtesy and bribery he strove to win the friendship of the nation. He forbade his armies to pillage the countryside, and Alva hanged so many of his troops for such offenses that he feared a shortage of rope. Philip promised to keep Portuguese territory under Portuguese administrators, to appoint no Spaniards to office in Portugal, and to maintain the privileges and liberties of the people. These promises were kept as long as he lived. So, with astonishing ease, Philip inherited the Portuguese navy and the Portuguese colonies in Africa, Asia, and South America. The old papal line of demarcation between Spanish and Portuguese possessions disappeared; and the most powerful of European kings, now made more powerful still, was ready to destroy himself by invading England.

While Portugal's empire was passing to Spain and the Dutch, her greatest poet was singing the glory of her conquests. Again the barriers of nationality and language defeat our desire to understand. How can those who were not bred on Portuguese history, and who do not feel the sense and music of Portuguese speech, do justice to Luiz Vaz de Camões—our Camoëns?

He lived his song before writing it. One of his ancestors was a soldier-poet like himself; his grandmother was a relative of Vasco da Gama, who is the hero of *The Lusiads;* his father, a poor captain, was shipwrecked near Goa, and died there shortly after Luiz was born in Lisbon or Coimbra. The youth probably studied at the university, for his poem rings with echoes of Catullus, Virgil, Horace, and Ovid. His personal romance began in a church, in a moment of adoration: he saw a beautiful woman with "snow-white face and hair of gold," and was stirred to poetry. Some of his lines must have offended the court; he was banished to a village on the upper Tagus, and there dreamed of an epic that "should increase the glory of Portugal and make Smyrna envious despite her being the birthplace of Homer."[49] The unappreciative government sent him into exile or military service in Ceuta, where, in battle or quarrel, he lost an eye. Back in Lisbon, he defended some friends in a brawl, stabbed a courtier, was jailed for eight months, and was released probably on his promise to enlist for foreign service. On March 26, 1553, aged twenty-nine, he sailed for India as a common soldier on the flagship of Fernão Álvares Cabral.

He bore the tedium of humid nights on the half-year voyage by composing the first of two cantos of *The Lusiads.* In September his ship reached Goa, the Portuguese Sodom in India. He took part in many campaigns: on the Malabar Coast, off the shores of Arabia, at Mombasa, in the East Indies, and at Macao, the Portuguese Sodom in China. He describes himself as brandishing a sword in one hand and a pen in the other; his comrades called him Trincafortes—the Swashbuckler—and probably respected his sword more than his pen. A grotto at Macao is still shown as the place where Camões wrote part of his poem. An uncertain story pictures him as brought back from Macao in chains, having been arrested for causes now unknown. Another story (shedding his chains) tells how his ship was wrecked off the Cambodian coast and Luiz swam ashore with his epic between his teeth;[50] in that wreck, however, he lost his beloved Chinese concubine. After months of misery he found his way to Goa, only to be cast into prison. Released, he was jailed again, this time for debt. A friendly viceroy freed him, and for a brief interlude the poet could enjoy life and a kaleidoscope of diversely colored mistresses. In 1567 he borrowed money and took passage for Portugal; his funds ran out in Mozambique, where he dallied in destitution for two years. Some transient friends paid his debts and his fare and brought him at last (1570) to Lisbon. His only possession was his poem. King Sebastian gave him a modest pension; the poem finally reached print (1572), and Camões was allowed to live in penurious peace for eight years. He died in Lisbon in 1580, and was buried with other plague victims in a common grave. Portugal celebrates his anniversary, June 10, as a memorial holiday, and cherishes as its national epic *Os Lusiadas,* whose title means "the Portuguese." Camões took the term Lusia from the old Roman name for the western part of Spain, Lusitania.

The meandering narrative winds itself about the historic voyage (1497–99) of Vasco da Gama from Portugal around the Cape of Good Hope to India. After an invocation to King Sebastian and the "nymphs of Tagus," the story proceeds with da Gama's fleet up the east coast of Africa. Feeling an obligation to imitate Homer and Virgil, the poet pictures a conclave of the gods debating whether they should allow the expedition to reach India. Bacchus votes No, and rouses the Moors of Mozambique to attack the Portuguese who are landing for water. Venus intercedes with Jupiter in the sailors' behalf; the Moors are repulsed, and Mercury bids da Gama to get along. The fleet stops on the Kenya coast and is hospitably received; the native king falls into Camões' plan by asking Vasco to tell him the history of Portugal. The admiral responds at length, recounts the tragedy of Inés de Castro, describes the fateful battle of Aljubarrota (1385), where the Portuguese first won their freedom from Spain, and ends with the sailing of his own expedition from Lisbon. As the new Argonauts cross the Indian Ocean Bacchus and Neptune stir up a typhoon against them, and Camões, having lived through such a storm, rises to an exciting description. Venus stills the waves, and the fleet triumphantly reaches Calicut.

On the return voyage Venus and her son Cupid arrange a feast for the weary crew; at her bidding lovely Nereids rise out of the sea, load palace tables with delicacies and flowers, and comfort the sailors with food and drink and love.

> What famished kisses were there in the wood!
> What gentle sound of pretty lamentation!

> What sweet caress! What angry modest mood
> That into bright mirth knew sweet transformation!
> From dawn till noon such pleasures they pursued
> As Venus kindled to a conflagration,
> Which men would rather taste of than condemn,
> Rather condemn who cannot taste of them.[51]

Lest some such Portuguese should complain that these lines insulted monogamy, Camões assures us that the affair was quite allegorical, and that the nymphs were "nothing more than honors . . . whereby life is exalted and refined."[52] In any case the sailors allegorically stumble back to their ships, and the fleet finds its way back to Lisbon. The poem concludes with a plea to the King to reward merit everywhere, and not least this patriotic song.

Even through the mist of translation an alien can feel the rippling music and lyrical ecstasies of this remarkable poem, the warm blood of a soldier-poet who conveys to us the lusty mettle and adventurous history of the Portuguese in those expansive days. Tasso is reported to have named Camões as the only contemporary poet against whom he would not confidently measure himself; and Lope de Vega, when Spanish and Portuguese were not so far apart as now, ranked *The Lusiads* above both *The Iliad* and *The Aeneid*.[53] Today the poem is a bond of unity, a flag of pride and hope, wherever Camões' language is spoken—in lovely Lisbon, in decadent Goa and Macao, in thriving, burgeoning, spirited Brazil.

Camões, hearing that Philip was taking Portugal, is reported to have said, almost as his last words, "I loved my country so much that I shall die with her."[54] So long as Philip lived, the captive country fared reasonably well; but his successors violated his vows. Olivares proposed to merge the two nations and languages into one; Spain took most of the gains from Portugal's colonies and trade; and the English and the Dutch, at war with Spain, captured or pillaged Portuguese as well as Spanish possessions, markets, and fleets. Spaniards crowded into Portuguese offices, Spanish ecclesiastics into Portuguese sees. The Inquisition laid a pall upon Portuguese literature and thought.

Popular discontent rose as national income declined, until at last the nobility and the clergy led the infuriated nation in revolt. Encouraged by England and Richelieu, the patriots declared John, Duke of Braganza, to be the King of Portugal (1640). France and the Dutch sent protective fleets into the Tagus, and France pledged itself never to make peace with Spain until the independence of Portugal was recognized. Spain was so harassed with foreign war that she had hardly any men or money to put down the resurgence of her neighbor; but when other pressures eased she sent two armies, totaling 35,000 troops, against the new government (1661). Portugal could raise only 13,000; but Charles II of England, in return for Catherine of Braganza, a more beautiful dowry, and a lucrative treaty of free trade with Portuguese ports in all continents, dispatched to Portugal a force under the brilliant General Friedrich Schomberg. The Spanish invaders were defeated at Évora (1663) and Montes Claros (1665), and in 1668 exhausted Spain acknowledged that Portugal was free.

CHAPTER XI

The Golden Age of Spanish Literature

1556–1665

I. EL SIGLO DE ORO

"GREAT is the number of divine geniuses who live in our Spain to-day," wrote Cervantes in 1584.[1] Probably he alone then knew that he was the greatest of them; he had not yet written *Don Quixote* (1604). By that later time the "Century of Gold" (1560–1660) was in full course and splendor.

What caused this cultural explosion, this brilliant concourse of luminaries in literature and art? Probably the political, economic, and religious victories of Spain—the conquest and exploitation of the Americas, the power and profits of Spain in Italy, the Netherlands, Portugal, and India, and the triumph over the Moors in Spain and the Turks at Lepanto. We today, far from the crises of the Spanish soul, can hardly understand how both the dangers and the successes of those exciting years warmed the ardor of the Catholic faith, and made most Spaniards as proud of their religion as of their blood. Censorship and the Inquisition, which we should have thought stifling, were accepted by the nation as war measures necessary for national unity in the crusade against Islam; and the Spanish mind, forbidden to stray from the hallowed creed, soared within its narrowed bounds into an exalted world of fiction, poetry, drama, architecture, sculpture, and painting.

But it was also an age of conscientious scholars and bold historians, of notable works in theology, government, law, economics, geography, and classical and Oriental studies. The learned Hallam judged that "learning was farther advanced under Philip II than under Elizabeth."[2] Certainly education was more abundant. Poor as well as rich found their way into the many universities; twenty new universities were in this period added to those already renowned; and Salamanca alone had 5,856 students in 1551.[3] "No one could call himself a *caballero* [gentleman] who was not a man of letters as well."[4] Kings, ministers, nobles, and prelates opened their purses to scholars, poets, artists, and musicians. There were, however, some discords in the crescendo: the Church held a whip over all teachers,

and Philip II, to keep Spanish universities full and Spanish minds theologi-
cally pure, forbade Spanish youth to study in any foreign universities
except Coimbra, Bologna, and Rome. After the Century of Gold this
intellectual endogamy may have played a part in the cultural sterility
of Spain.

Two remarkable Jesuits enter the picture at this point. Baltasar Gracián,
director of a Jesuit college at Tarragona, found time to write (1650–53)
a three-volume novel, *El criticón*, describing the shipwreck of a Spanish
gentleman on the island of St. Helena, his education of the solitary savage
whom he found there (a source for *Robinson Crusoe?*), their travels together in the world, and their penetrating criticism of European civilization. Their pessimism and misogyny delighted Schopenhauer, who called
this "one of the best books in the world."[5] A friend gave Gracián international currency by selecting from his works three hundred paragraphs
and publishing these as *Oráculo manual y arte de prudencia* (1653)—*A
Handy Oracle and Art of Worldly Wisdom*. Schopenhauer made one of
the many translations. Some sample oracles:

> Avoid outshining the master . . . Superiority has always been
> detested, and most thoroughly when greatest. A little care will serve to
> cloak your ordinary virtues, as you would hide your beauty in careless
> dress.[6]

> Mediocrity gets further with industry than superiority without it.[7]

> There are rules to luck, for to the wise not all is accident.[8]

> The perfect does not lie in quantity but in quality. . . . Some judge
> books by their knees, as though they had been written to exercise
> the arms.[9]

> Think as the few, speak as the many. . . . The truth is for the few
> . . . Let the wise man take refuge in silence; and when at times he
> permits himself to speak, let it be in the shelter of the few and the
> understanding.[10]

> Know how to say No . . . Refusal should never be flat, the truth
> appearing by degrees. . . . Employ courtliness to fill the void of the
> denial.[11]

> Maturity may be recognized in the slowness with which a man
> believes.[12]

> There is always time to add a word, but none in which to take one
> back.[13]

The Spanish historians were at this time the best in Europe. Philip II
gathered into archives at Simancas an extensive collection of official papers

and other documents, because, he said, "chroniclers and historians were ill informed in matters of state, and it was desirable, in order to obviate that defect, to assemble all such materials as might prove serviceable."[14] These archives have been a treasure for historians ever since. Jerónimo de Zurita consulted thousands of original documents in preparing his *Anales de la Corona de Aragón* (1562–80), and earned a European reputation as *exactissimus scriptor*.

The greatest of the Spanish historians, Juan de Mariana, began as the natural son of a canon at Talavera. Left in youth to shift for himself, he sharpened his wits on hard necessity and grinding poverty. The Jesuits, always quick to recognize talent, gave him a rigorous education. When he was twenty-four they sent him to teach in their college at Rome; later to Sicily; then to Paris, where his lectures on Aquinas drew enthusiastic audiences. His health broke down, and at the age of thirty-seven (1574) he was allowed to retire to the house of his order in Toledo, which he seldom left in his remaining forty-nine years. There he wrote some important treatises, one of which (as we shall see later) caused an international furor; another, *On the Coinage of the Realm*, was a brave attack upon Lerma's debasement of the currency; still another, which he left unprinted, expounded *The Errors in the Government of the Society of Jesus*. The main industry of his final forty years was the composition of *Historiae de rebus Hispaniae* (1592), which he wrote in Latin so that all educated Europe might learn how Spain had risen to leadership and power. At the urging of Cardinal Bembo he translated most of it into purest Castilian as *Historia de España* (1601), which is the proudest achievement of Spanish historiography, vivid in narrative, beautiful in style, masterly in characterizations, fearless in honesty—"the most remarkable union of picturesque chronicling with sober history that the world has ever seen."[15]

As, in such works, the old chronicles graduated into history as a form of literature and philosophy, so Spanish fiction, in this age, passed from the chivalric and pastoral romance to reach at one bound the highest point in the history of the novel. Romances of chivalry still abounded; everyone in Spain from St. Teresa to Cervantes read them hungrily. Perhaps for some readers they were a relief from the exalted intensity of Spanish religion, for the creed of the romances was love, and the devotion of the knights was not to the Virgin but to the ladies of their choice or fancy; to defend or possess these they would break many a lance, and not a few laws of God or man. But the rage for such stories was subsiding when Cervantes wrote; Montaigne and Juan Luis Vives had already ridiculed them; and the Cortes of Castile long ago (1538) had complained that "much harm" was "done to men, boys, girls, and others" by the romances, and that many were "seduced by them from the true Christian doctrine."[16]

One other development led to the summit. In 1553 an author of uncertain identity had written, in *Lazarillo de Tormes*, the first novel in the *gusto picaresco*, the "roguish style" that made a hero of some jolly rascal (*pícaro*), who redeemed his poverty with lawlessness and his lawlessness with wit. In 1599 Mateo Alemán published a rollicking *Vita del pícaro Guzmán de Alfarache*. Five years later Cervantes took the two moods—the fading dream of the chivalrous knight and the humorous wisdom of the common man—and brought them together, soul to soul, in the most famous of all novels, and the best.

II. CERVANTES: 1547–1616

According to Spanish custom, which tended to name each child for the saint commemorated on the day of its birth, the creator of Don Quixote and Sancho Panza was baptized Miguel de Cervantes at Alcalá October 9, 1547. He—and perhaps his father—added the name Saavedra, from the Castilian family with which his Galician ancestors had intermarried in the fifteenth century. The father was an unlicensed physician, hard of hearing and short of funds, who traveled from town to town setting bones and alleviating minor injuries; apparently young Miguel accompanied him to Valladolid, Madrid, and Seville. Nothing is known of the boy's education; though born in a university town, he seems to have had no college training; he remained unchastened and uncluttered by classics, and had to pick his knowledge of life from living.

The first fact that we have of him after his baptismal record is that in 1569 a Madrid schoolmaster published a volume that included six poems by "our dear and beloved pupil," Cervantes. In September of that year a Myguel de Zerbantes was arrested for dueling, and was banished from Spain for ten years on penalty of losing his right hand. In December we find our Miguel serving in the household of a high ecclesiastic in Rome. On September 16, 1571, the same Miguel, probably (like Camões) choosing military service to escape jail, sailed from Messina on the ship *Marquesa* in the armada of Don Juan of Austria. When that fleet encountered the Turks at Lepanto Cervantes lay ill with fever in the hold; but as he insisted on playing his part, he was put in charge of twelve men in a boat by the ship's side; he received three gunshot wounds, two in the chest and another that permanently maimed his left hand—"for the glory of the right," he said. He was returned to a hospital in Messina and was paid eighty-two ducats by the Spanish government. He took part in other military actions—at Navarino, Tunis, and Goletta (La Goulette). Finally he was allowed to return to Spain; but on the voyage homeward he and his brother Rodrigo were captured by Barbary corsairs (September 26, 1575) and were sold into slavery in Algiers. The letters that he carried from Don Juan and others persuaded his captors that Miguel was a man of some worth; they placed a high ransom on his head, and, although his brother was released in 1577, Miguel was kept in bondage for five years. Repeatedly he tried to escape, only to have the severity of his treatment increased. The Dey, the local ruler, declared that "if he could keep that lame Spaniard well guarded, he should consider his capital, his slaves, and his galleys safe."*[17] His mother struggled to raise the five hundred crowns demanded for his release; his sisters sacrificed their marriage dowries for the same cause; at last (September 19, 1580) he was freed, and after an arduous journey he rejoined his mother's family at Madrid.

Penniless and maimed, he found no way of making ends meet except to re-enlist in the army. There are indications that he saw service in Portugal and the Azores. He fell in love with a lady eighteen years his junior and rich only in names—Catalina de Palacio Salazar y Vozmédiano of Esquivias. Goaded by love and penury, Cervantes wrote a pastoral romance, *Galatea*, which he sold for 1,336 reales ($668?). The lady now married him (1584), after which he introduced to her, and persuaded her to rear as her own, an illegitimate daughter who had been born to him by a transient belle a year before.[18] Catalina herself bore him no children. She berated him periodically for his poverty, but remained apparently loyal to him, survived him, and, dying, asked to be buried at his side.

The *Galatea* brought no further reales; its shepherds proved too eloquent, except in their poetry; and though Cervantes had planned a continuation, and to the end thought it his masterpiece, he never found time or spur to complete it. For twenty-five years he tried his hand at playwriting, and he composed some thirty plays; he considered them excellent, and assures us that they "were all acted without any offering of cucumbers";[19] but none of them touched the public fancy or a vein of gold. He resigned himself to a modest place in the commissary of the army and navy (1587), and in that capacity he traveled to a score of towns, leaving his wife at home. He helped to provision the Invincible Armada. In 1594 he was appointed taxgatherer for Granada. He was imprisoned at Seville for irregularities in his accounts, was released after three months, but was dismissed from the government service. He remained for several years in obscure poverty in Seville, trying to live on pen and ink. Then, wandering through Spain, he was arrested again, at Argamasilla. There

---

* The story of the captive in *Don Quixote* (Part I, Book IV, chapters 12–14) is largely autobiographical.

in jail and in misery, says tradition, he continued writing one of the most cheerful books in the world. Back in Madrid, he sold to Francisco de Robles the manuscript of *The Life and Adventures of the Renowned Don Quixote de la Mancha*. It was published in 1605, and now at last, after fifty-eight years of struggling, Cervantes touched success.

Everyone except the critics hailed the book as a feast of humor and philosophy. Philip III (says an old tale), "standing one day on the balcony of the palace at Madrid, observed a student, with a book in his hand, on the opposite bank of the Manzanares. He was reading, but every now and then he interrupted his reading and gave himself violent blows upon the forehead, accompanied with innumerable motions of ecstasy and mirthfulness. 'That student,' said the King, 'is either out of his wits or reading . . . *Don Quixote*.' "[20]

As in every masterpiece, there are some flaws in these eight hundred pages. The plot is not very ingenious—a string of episodes, thickened with irrelevant interpolated tales, and as planless as the knight, who "rode on, leaving it to his horse's discretion to go which way it pleased." Some threads of the plot are left at loose ends or get tangled up, like the loss and unexplained reappearance of Sancho's ass. Now and then the lively narrative grows dull, the grammar lax, and the language coarse; and geographers pronounce the geography impossible. But what does it matter? More and more, as we read on, carried by a genial pull through sense and nonsense, the wonder mounts that Cervantes, amid all his tribulations, could have put together such a panorama of idealism and humor and could have brought the two distant poles of human character into such illuminating apposition. The style is as it should be in a long narrative— not a fatiguing torrent of eloquence, but a clear and flowing stream, sparkling now and then with a pretty phrase ("he had a face like a blessing"[21]). The inventiveness of incident continues to the end, the well of Sancho's proverbs is never exhausted, and the last bit of humor or pathos is as good as the first. Here, in what Cervantes calls "this most grave, high-sounding, minute, soft, and humorous history," are the life and the people of Spain, described with a love that survives impartiality, and through a thousand trivial details that create and vitalize the revealing whole.

Adapting an old device, Cervantes pretends that his "history" is taken from the manuscript of an Arabian author, Cid Hamet Ben-Engeli. The preface declares his purpose clearly: to describe in "a satire of knight-errantry . . . the fall and destruction of that monstrous heap of ill-contrived romances . . . which have so strangely infatuated the greater part of mankind." Chaucer had done something like this in *The Canterbury Tales* ("The Rhyme of Sir Topas"), Rabelais in *Gargantua*, Pulci in *Il Morgante maggiore;* Teofilo Folengo and other "macaronic" poets had burlesqued the knights, and Ariosto, in *Orlando furioso*, had made fun of his heroes and heroines. Cervantes does not reject the romances outright; some, like *Amadis da Gaula* and his own *Galatea*, he saves from the fire; and he inserts a few chivalric romances into his story. In the end his chivalrous Don, after a hundred defeats and ignominious catapults, is seen to have been the secret hero of the tale.

Cervantes pictures him as an imaginative country gentleman—*ingenioso hidalgo*—so bemused by the fiction that he has accumulated in his library that he arms himself cap-a-pie in knightly costume and sallies forth on his Rozinante to defend the oppressed, to right iniquities, and to protect virginity and innocence. He hates injustice, and dreams of a golden past when there was no gold, when "those two fatal words, *thine* and *mine*, were distinctions unknown; all things were in common in that holy age . . . all then was union, all love and friendship in the world."[22] As chivalric custom requires, he dedicates his arms, nay, his life, to a lady, La Dulcinea del Toboso. Never having seen her, he can picture her as the perfection of demure purity and gentle grace. "Her neck is alabaster, her breasts are marble, her hands are ivory; and snow would lose its whiteness near her bosom."[23] Hardened with this marble and warmed with this snow, Don Quixote moves to attack a world of wrongs. In this battle against great odds he does not feel outnumbered, for "I alone am worth a hundred." As Cervantes keeps him company through inns and windmills, filthy ditches and stampeding swine, he comes to love the "Knight of the Woeful Figure" as a saint as well as a madman; in all those misadventures and painful falls the Don remains the soul of courtesy, compassion, and generosity. At last the somber lunatic is transformed by his author into a philosopher who, even in the mud, talks kindly good sense and forgives the world that he cannot understand; and we begin to take offense when, to hew to his charted line, Cervantes continues to dash him to the ground. We feel for the disillusioned knight when Sancho assures him that the only Dulcinea del Toboso known to her town is "a strapping wench . . . a sizable, sturdy, manly lass" of lowly stock. The knight answers him with a golden phrase, "Virtue ennobles the blood."[24] "Every man," he tells Sancho, "is the son of his own works."[25]

What the Don lacks is humor, which is the better half of philosophy. Therefore Cervantes gives him, as an attendant squire, a sturdy town laborer and son of the soil, Sancho Panza. The knight secures his services by promising him food and drink, and the governorship of some province in the realms they are to conquer. Sancho is a man of simple sense and hearty appetite, who, though always on the verge of starvation, remains fat to the last page; a kindly fellow, who loves his mule as his alter ego and values its "sweet company." He is not a typical Spanish peasant, for he is long on humor and short on dignity; but, like any Spaniard free from theological rabies, he is goodhearted and charitable, wise without letters, and faithful to his master this side of flagellation. He soon concludes that the Don is mad, but he too comes to love him. "I have stuck close to my good master and kept him company this many a month," he says toward the end, "and now he and I are all one."[26] It is true, for they are two sides of one humanity. The knight in his turn comes to respect the wisdom of his squire as better rooted, if not as noble, as his own. Sancho expresses his philosophy through proverbs, which he strings end to end almost to the suffocation of his thought: "A hen and a woman are lost by rambling"; "Between a woman's yea and nay I would not engage to put a pin's point, so close they be to one another"; "A doctor gives his advice by the pulse of your pocket"; "Everyone is as God made him, and often worse."[27] Cervantes probably used an anthology of such proverbs, which he defined as "short sentences framed on long experience."[28] Sancho excuses his adagiorrhea on the ground that these saws clog his windpipe and must fly out, "first come, first served." The Don resigns himself to the flood. "In faith," he says, "it would seem that thou art no saner than I am . . . I pronounce thee *noncompos;* I pardon thee, and have done."[29]

The success of *Don Quixote* brought Cervantes two patrons, the Count of Lemos and the Cardinal of Toledo, who gave him a small pension; now he could support his wife, his natural daughter, his widowed sister, and a niece. A few months after the publication of his book he and his whole family were arrested for possible complicity in the murder of Gaspar de Ezpeleta at Cervantes' door. Gossip said that Gaspar had loved the daughter, but inquiry proved nothing, and all were released.

Leisurely Cervantes proceeded with Part Two of *Don Quixote.* In 1613 he interrupted this fond labor by publishing twelve *Novelas ejemplares.* "I have given these stories the title of Exemplary," said the preface, "and if you look closely there is not one of them that does not offer a useful example."[30] The first is of a gang of thieves operating in exemplary unison with the constable of Seville; another (*Colloquy of the Dogs*) describes the manners and morals of that city. In the Prologue to the *Novelas* Cervantes pictured himself:

> The man you see here with the acquiline countenance, the chestnut hair, the smooth, untroubled brow, the bright eyes, the hooked yet well-proportioned nose, the silvery beard that less than a score of years ago was golden, the big mustache . . . the teeth that are scarcely worth counting . . . the body of medium height . . . the slightly stoop-

ing shoulders, the somewhat heavy build—this, I may tell you, is the author of *Galatea* and *Don Quixote de la Mancha*.[31]

He was surprised in 1614 by the appearance of Part Two of *Don Quixote*, not by himself but by an unidentified poacher who took the name of Avellaneda. The preface made fun of Cervantes' wounds, and rejoiced at the neat trick that would ruin Cervantes' own Part Two. The harassed author hurried to finish his continuation and published it in 1615. Literate Spain was delighted to find this extension of remarks quite up to the first part in imagination, vigor, and humor; through these additional half-thousand pages the interest was kept up to the sad if not bitter end; and the mishaps of the Don and his squire at the court of the Duke, the reign of Sancho over his province, and the painful tale of his beaten buttocks seemed to some to make the second the better half. When Sancho is made governor of Barataria everyone expects him to surpass all records of gubernatorial fatuity. On the contrary, his good heart and common sense, his simple and just regulations and reforms, and his wise decision in a case of rape[32] put to shame the actualities of contemporary government. But the forces of heartless evil are too strong for him; finally they harass him to the point where he surrenders his office and returns with relief to his life as squire to the Don.

It remains only for the knight to make a similar escape from dreams to fact. He sets out for new adventures, but meets with a culminating defeat, in which the victor exacts from him a pledge that he will go home and live for a year in unknightly peace. The tired warrior consents, but his disillusionment dries up the sources of his life. He calls his friends to his bedside, distributes gifts, makes his will, disavows knight-errantry, and lets his spirit doubly ebb away. Sancho goes back to his family, and cultivates his garden in the content of a man who has seen enough of the world to appreciate his home. In the end his good-natured realism appears to triumph over the generous but fanciful idealism of his master. But it is not quite so. The soul of the knight has the last word, in the epitaph that he left for his tomb: "If I did not accomplish great things, I died in their pursuit." The realist survives till his death, but the idealist then begins to live.

In the year that remained to him Cervantes published eight plays; time has not confirmed his estimate of them, but has given high rank to his *La Numancia*, a dramatic poem of power and beauty, celebrating the resistance of that Spanish city to Roman siege (133 B.C.). Like his knight he had his sustaining delusion; he thought that posterity would honor him above all for his dramas, and he spoke with unbecoming but forgivable jealousy of the incredibly successful Lope de Vega. And with almost his last breath, after ridiculing most romances, he wrote another of his own, *Pérsiles y Sigismunda*. Four days before his death he dedicated it to the Count of Lemos:

> Yesterday I received extreme unction, and today I pen this dedication. The time is short, my agony increases, hopes diminish . . . And so farewell to jesting, farewell my merry humors, farewell my gay friends; for I feel that I am dying, and have no desire but to see you happy in the other life.[33]

He died April 23, 1616.*

In his characteristic Quixotic way he had predicted a sale of thirty million copies of his *Don Quixote;* the world smiled at his naïveté, and bought thirty million copies. The great story has been translated into more languages than any book except the Bible. In Spain the simplest villagers know about Don Quixote; and generally, again outside of the Bible, he is "the most living, the most endearing, and the best known character in all literature,"[34] more real than a thousand proud notables of history. By making his story a picture of manners Cervantes established the modern novel and opened the way for Lesage, Fielding, Smollett, and Sterne; and he raised the new form to philosophy by making it reveal and illuminate the moral gamut of mankind.

III. THE POETS

The masculine resonance of the Castilian tongue, like the melodious grace of Tuscan Italian, lent itself willingly to music and rhyme; and the spirit of the people responded more congenially to poetry than to prose. Poets were as plentiful as priests. In his *Laurel of Apollo* (1630), Lope de Vega described a feast and joust of poetry, where, in his fancy, the three hundred poets of contemporary Spain fought for the laurel crown. Such poetical contests were almost as popular with the people as the burning of heretics. There were soporific didactic poems, homilies in verse, romances in rhyme, pastoral poetry, mock-heroic poetry, ballads, lyrics, epics; and not all authors had the courage of Francisco de Figueroa, who condemned his verses to an auto-da-fé.

The best of the epics was *La Araucana* (1569–89), describing the revolt of an Indian tribe in South America; it was written by Alonso de

---

* Only apparently on the same day as Shakespeare. England was still using the Julian calendar; by the Gregorian, which Spain had adopted, Shakespeare's death fell on May 3, 1616.

Ercilla y Zuñiga, who fought with distinction as a Spanish soldier in that war. Perhaps the finest of the lyric poets was an Augustinian monk, Luis Ponce de León, whose partly Jewish ancestry did not prevent him from expressing the tenderest aspects of Christian piety. More remarkable was the union in him of poet and theologian; at thirty-four he was appointed professor of divinity at Salamanca, and he never ceased to be attached to that university; yet his scholarly pursuits and austere life did not stop his lyric flights. The Inquisition hailed him before its tribunal (1572) for translating the Song of Songs into the form of a pastoral eclogue. For five years he suffered imprisonment; released, he resumed his lectures at the university with wry words: "As we remarked when we last met . . ."[35] He agreed with his superiors that poetry did not become a theologian; he left his verses unpublished, and they did not reach print till forty years after his death. They are by common consent the most nearly perfect productions of the Castilian tongue.

Luis de Góngora and Francisco Gómez de Quevedo y Villegas were still more famous, for they stirred the air with controversy as well as rhymes, and left behind them the warring schools of *gongorismo* and *conceptismo* as philosophies of style. Cervantes, who had a good word to say for all his rivals except Lope and Avellaneda, called Góngora "a rare and lively genius, without a second."[36] We catch a distant echo of the poet's cry of hate in this stanza from his "Ode to the Armada":

> O Island! once so Catholic, so strong,
> Fortress of faith, now Heresy's foul shrine,
> Camp of train'd war, and Wisdom's sacred school;
> The time hath been, such majesty was thine,
> The luster of thy crown was first in song.
> Now the dull weeds that spring by Stygian pool
> Were fitting wreath for thee. Land of the rule
> Of Arthurs, Edwards, Henries! Where are they?
> Their mother where, rejoicing in their sway,
> Firm in the strength of Faith? To lasting shame
> Condemned, thou guilty blame
> Of her who rules thee now.
> O hateful Queen! so hard of heart and brow,
> Wanton by turns, and cruel, fierce, and lewd,
> Thou distaff on the throne, true virtue's bane,
> Wolf-like in every mood,
> May Heaven's just flame on thy false tresses rain![37]

Here was a pen worth wooing. No wonder Philip IV made the fiery poet (now become a priest) his royal chaplain, binding his talents to the throne. Góngora labored to acquire polish of style and subtlety of phrase; he declared war upon such hasty writing as Lope de Vega's, and insisted that every line should be filed and purified into a gem. In his fervor he carried art to artificiality, burdened his lines with extravagant metaphors, epithets, inversions, and antitheses, outdoing the euphuism of Lyly and the affectations of Marini. So, of a lass's entrancing charms:

> Her twin-born sun-bright eyes
> Might turn to summer Norway's wintry skies;
> And the white wonder of her snowy hand
> Blench with surprise the son of Ethiopian land.

Spanish poets now divided into three camps: those who followed *gongorismo* (or *cultismo*); those who adopted the *conceptismo* of Quevedo; and those who, like Lope de Vega, resisted both plagues.

At Alcalá Quevedo took honors in law, theology, Latin, Greek, French, Arabic, Hebrew, and dueling. Though he was shortsighted and clubfooted, he was a peril with both rapier and pen, and his satires were as cutting as his sword. After killing several opponents, he fled to Sicily and Naples. At thirty-five he served there as finance minister; he shared in Osuna's plot against Venice (1618); when it failed he was imprisoned for three years. Back in Madrid, he was not silenced by a sinecure as secretary to Philip IV; his verses scalded the King, the Pope, Olivares, women, and monks. His scandalous little book *El perro y la calentura—The Dog and the Fever*—(1625) barked at all things, poured upon them a storm of proverbs thicker than Sancho Panza's and sourer; and his final advice, which he never took, was to stand aside from the battle and "let the swill pass."[38] Greedy for enemies and butts, Quevedo attacked the *cultismo* of the *gongoristas* and countered it with *conceptismo*: instead of hunting for fanciful phrases and words, the poet should seek ideas— and not obvious notions staled with time or soiled by common use, but concepts of subtlety, grandeur, dignity, and depth.

He was wrongly charged with writing letters that warned the King to cease extravagance and dismiss incompetent ministers. He was imprisoned for four years in a damp cell; when he was freed his health was ruined, and three years later he died (1645). This was no peaceful literary career, but a life in which ink was blood and poetry was war. Ending it, he warned his country that it too was dying:

> I saw the ramparts of my native land,
>   One time so strong, now dropping in decay,
>   Their strength destroyed by this new age's way
> That has worn out and rotted what was grand.

> I went into the fields; there I could see
> The sun drink up the waters newly thawed;
> And on the hills the moaning cattle pawed;
> Their miseries robbed the light of day for me.
> I went into my house, I saw how spotted,
> Decaying things made that old home their prize;
> My withered walking-staff had come to bend;
> I felt the age had won; my sword was rotted;
> And there was nothing on which to set my eyes
> That was not a reminder of the end.[39]

IV. LOPE DE VEGA: 1562–1635

The dramatists, in that lively age, were as numerous as the poets. Heretofore, as in contemporary England, the stage had been an impromptu contraption; strolling players peddled their art impecuniously in the towns; and the Inquisition, struggling to control the coarseness of their comedies, placed an interdict upon all plays (1520). When Madrid became the royal residence (1561), two troupes of actors asked the King's permission to establish themselves permanently there. Permission was given, the ecclesiastical ban was lifted (1572), and two theaters were built, the Teatro de la Cruz and the Teatro del Príncipe—the two names expressing the main loyalties and powers of Spain. By 1602 there were theaters also in Valencia, Seville, Barcelona, Granada, Toledo, and Valladolid; by 1632 there were a thousand actors in Madrid and seventy-six dramatists in Castile; tailors, tradesmen, and shepherds were writing dramas; by 1800 Spain had heard thirty thousand different plays. No other country in history—not even Elizabethan England—had such a theatrical ecstasy.

The form of the theater evolved from the courtyards—surrounded by houses and temporary stands—in which the earlier plays were performed; so the permanent theaters were designed as tiers of seats and boxes surrounding a corral. Costumes were Spanish, whatever the place or period of the piece. The audiences were of all classes. Women came, but sat in a special section and wore heavy veils. The actors lived in a demoralizing insecurity between famines and feasts, consoling their poverty and rootlessness with promiscuity and hopes. A few male "stars" rose to wealth and head-turning fame; they paraded the main avenues of Madrid, adjusting their swords and mustaches; and some prima donnas slept with kings.

The monarch of the Spanish stage was Lope Félix de Vega Carpio. In 1647 the Inquisition had to suppress a published credo which began: "I believe in Lope de Vega the Almighty, the poet of heaven and earth."[40] Probably no other writer in history ever enjoyed such contemporary fame; only the difficulty of translating rhymed poetry has confined that fame mostly to Spain; even so, during his lifetime his plays were performed in Spanish in Naples, Rome, and Milan; and in France and Italy his name was prefixed to plays not his, in order to lure an audience.

He was born in Madrid, two years before Shakespeare, of a poor but (we are assured) a noble family. At fourteen he ran away from home and college, enlisted in the army, and saw some bloody action in the Azores. He fell in love, but extricated himself with some minor wounds; he penned mean epigrams on the lady, was arrested for libel, was banished from Madrid. Re-entering the city secretly, he eloped with Isabel de Urbina, married her, was pursued, and, to escape the law, joined the Armada; he shared in its defeat, and his brother, killed in the battle, died in Lope's arms. The death of his wife released him for other entanglements. He begot two children by the actress Micaela de Lujan,[41] married again, became an official of the Inquisition (1609), lost his second wife, was ordained a priest (1614?), and fell into new amours.[42]

Spain forgave him his mistresses for his plays. He wrote some eighteen hundred, in addition to four hundred short *autos sacramentales* ("sacramental acts") for performance in religious festivals. He was reputed to have composed ten plays in one week, and one before breakfast. Cervantes gave up before this avalanche, and called his rival a "monster of nature." Lope was a *commedia dell' arte* in himself, composing as he improvised. Breeding with such careless fertility, he made no pretense to art or philosophy. In his *New Art of Making Plays* he confessed amiably that he wrote to butter his bread, and so catered to public taste.[43] He might not have printed his plays except for piratical publishers who sent to his performances men of miraculous memory; after three hearings these men could recite a play by heart and provide a garbled text to printers, who paid the author nothing. Once Lope's cast refused to go on with the play until one such mnemonic marvel had been thrown out[44]—publication might lessen attendance. But Lope published with loving care his poetic romances —*Arcadia, San Isidro, Jerusalén conquistada, La hermosura de Angélica, La Dorotea*—all melodious and mediocre.

The plot in his plays is everything. The characters are seldom studied intimately, and one might say of these dramas what Thoreau said of newspapers—that if you merely change the names and dates, the contents are always the same. Nearly always the story turns on two hinges: the point of honor and the question who shall sleep with the lady. The public never tired of variations on the latter theme, not being allowed any of its own. Meanwhile it enjoyed the incidental humor, the lively dialogue, the lyric verses that fell trippingly from the tongues of fair women and brave men. The spirit of the romances, never extinct, took new life on the Spanish stage.

The most famous of Lope's plays is *The Star of Seville* (*La estrella de Sevilla*). Sancho the Bold, King of Castile, comes to Seville, praises the splendor of its streets, but asks his councilor Arias to tell him more particularly about its women.

> KING: And its ladies, divinely fair, why do you not mention them?
> . . . Tell me, are you not aflame in the light of such glories?
> ARIAS: Doña Leonor de Rebera seemed heaven itself, for in her countenance shone the light of the springtime sun.
> KING: She is too pale. . . . I want a burning sun, not freezing.
> ARIAS: The one who threw roses to you is Doña Mencia Coronél.
> KING: A handsome dame, but I saw others lovelier. . . . One I saw there full of grace, whom you have left unmentioned. . . . Who is she who on her balcony drew my attention, and to whom I doffed my hat? Who is she whose two eyes flashed lightning like Jove's thunderbolts and sent their deadly rays into my heart? . . .
> ARIAS: Her name is Doña Stella Tabera, and Seville in homage calls her its star.
> KING: And it might call her its sun. . . . My guiding star brought me to Seville. . . . What means, Don Arias, will you find for me to see her and speak with her? . . . O vision that inflames my inmost soul![45]

Stella, however, is in love with Don Sancho Ortiz, and she indignantly repels Arias' proposal to let the King enjoy the *droit du seigneur*. Arias bribes the maid to admit the King to her mistress' room; Stella's devoted brother Bustos enters on the very point of honor, stops the King, and is about to kill him; but, awed by royalty, he lets him pass, scorned but intact. An hour later the King sees hanging on his palace wall the corpse of the maid who had accepted the bribe. He sends for Ortiz, asks if his loyalty to his king knows no bounds, receives a proud and satisfactory answer, and bids him kill Bustos. Ortiz meets Bustos, receives from him Stella's message that she returns his love and accepts his suit; he thanks him, kills him, and almost goes insane. Fearing public revolt, the King hides the fact that the assassination was by his command. Ortiz is arrested and is about to be executed when Stella finds means to free him. But there is no happy ending; the lovers agree that the murder has poisoned their love forever.

After producing a thousand such plays, Lope became the idol of Madrid. Nobles and commoners showered him with admiration; the Pope sent him the Cross of Malta and the degree of Doctor of Theology. When he appeared on the streets he was surrounded by eager crowds; women and children kissed his hands and begged his blessing. His name was given to any object supreme in its kind: there were Lope horses, Lope melons, Lope cigars.[46] A critic who had found fault with him lived in daily fear of death from the poet's devotees.

Even so, Lope was not happy. He had been paid reasonably well for his plays, but he had spent or given away his earnings as fast as they had come; after so many successes he was poor and had to appeal for aid to Philip IV—who, out of his bankruptcy, sent him a generous dowry. But bereavements cut more deeply than poverty. His daughter Marcela entered a convent; his son Lope joined the navy and was drowned; his daughter Antonia eloped with Cristóbal Tonorio, taking with her a considerable quantity of paternal valuables; Lope disowned her, Cristóbal deserted her. Thinking these tribulations to be divine punishments for his sins, Lope locked himself in a room and macerated his flesh till the walls were stained with his blood. On August 23, 1635, he composed his last poem, "El siglo de oro." He died four days later, aged seventy-three. Half of Madrid joined the funeral procession, which turned aside to pass the convent where his daughter could bid him farewell from the window of her cell. His apotheosis was enacted on a public stage.

We cannot, like Voltaire, place him beside Shakespeare; but we may say of him that by his abounding genius, his effervescent verse, his lovable character shining through a thousand plays, he rose to the literary pinnacle of that Golden Age, where only Cervantes and Calderón could reach him.

V. CALDERÓN: 1600–81

Others briefly challenged Lope's supremacy. Guillén de Castro composed (1591) Las mocedades del Cid (The Youth of the Cid), which some have preferred to Corneille's more famous imitation. Luis Vélez de Guevara absented himself from his law practice long enough to write four hundred plays, including El diablo cojuelo, source of Lesage's Le Diable boiteux (The Lame Devil). And Tirso de Molina staged at Barcelona (1630) El burlador de Sevilla y convidado de pietra (The Mocker of Seville and the Stone Guest), which established Don Juan as a sensual blasphemer, provided the plot for Molière's Le Festin de pierre and Mozart's Don Giovanni, and suggested Byron's Don Juan. In these few lines are some hints of the immense influence of Spanish drama abroad. And in 1803 August Wilhelm von Schlegel startled Germany by announcing that in modern drama Pedro Calderón de la Barca was second only to Shakespeare.

Calderón, like Murillo, concluded and outlived the Golden Age. Son of a finance minister under Philip II and III, he received at Salamanca all the education that the Jesuits could give and allow; the religious emphasis in his training strongly colored his work and his life. He studied law at Salamanca, but abandoned it on discovering that he could write successfully for the stage. One piece contained too clear a reference to gongoristic verbiage in the sermons of an influential preacher; Calderón was jailed for a time, but his reputation was made. A volume of his plays, containing *La vida es sueño*, was published in 1636 and won him at once the leadership of the Spanish theater. Philip appointed him in that year to succeed Lope de Vega as court dramatist. In 1640 he joined a company of mounted cuirassiers and won distinction by his gallant courage at Tarragona; in Spain, as in Islam, the man of letters has often realized his secret dream of being a man of deeds. Calderón's health failing after two years of war, he was retired on a military pension. Bereavements turned him to religion; he became a lay member of the Franciscan order, was ordained a priest (1651), and for ten years served a parish in Toledo while continuing to write occasionally for the stage. After receiving all the honors of this world, he died at the age of eighty-one, in high hopes of some reward for having composed hundreds of *autos sagramentales* and having had only one mistress.

His religious dramas are the finest of their kind, for there his lyric power was sustained by sincere devotion. His secular dramas had for a long time a wider international repute than Lope's, being equally beautiful as poetry and superior in thought. He lacked some of Lope's incredible vitality and variety; yet he too turned out "cloak-and-sword" plays (*comedias de capa y espada*) with verve and skill. Only one familiar with the Castilian tongue can appreciate him fully, but we note that two English poets felt his genius and struggled to evoke it from its linguistic crucible. Shelley, who agreed with Schlegel about Calderón, freely translated parts of *El mágico prodigioso*, and Edward Fitzgerald, in *Six Dramas of Calderón* (1853), tried and failed to do for the Spanish dramatist what six years later he did so well for Omar Khayyám.

The Monstrous Magician is a variant of the Faust legend. Cyprian, renowned scholar of Antioch, interrupts a duel between two of his students, who both desire Justina; he sheathes their swords by agreeing to go to her and ascertain her preference; he goes, and he falls in love with her at sight; she dismisses him scornfully, and then longs for him. The students, also rejected, console themselves with her sister Livia, but Cyprian cannot exorcise his memory of Justina's loveliness.

> So beautiful she was—and I,
> Between my love and jealousy,
> Am so convulsed with hope and fear,

Unworthy as it may appear—
So bitter is the life I live,
That—hear me, Hell!—I now would give
To thy most detested spirit
My soul, forever to inherit,
To suffer punishment and pine,
So that this woman may be mine.[47]

"I accept it," says the Devil, but he finds Justina difficult. Finally he brings her to Cyprian; but as the scholar seeks to embrace her Justina's veil opens and reveals nothing but a skull. Lucifer confesses that only the power of Christ could have played such a trick upon him. In the end, as both Cyprian and Justina are carried away to Christian martyrdom, she confesses her love.

Among the plays translated by Fitzgerald *El alcalde de Zalamea* (*The Mayor of Zalamea*) has won high praise for its technical excellence. But *La vida es sueño* (*Life Is a Dream*) has deeper undertones. It puts aside the old themes of honor and love, and boldly brings to the stage an almost Oriental problem: How permanent and real are the vicissitudes and victories of life? Or are they surface illusions, maya, part of the veil that hides the basic, lasting reality? Basileus, King of Poland, imprisons his recently born son, of whom the stars prognosticate rebellion against his father. Sigismund is brought up in chains among forest animals, and grows to manhood more savage than any unharassed beast. The King, aging, relents and invites his son to come and share the throne; but Sigismund, ill-trained for rule, lays about him with such thoughtless violence that he has to be drugged into submission. When he recovers his senses he finds himself back in his woodland den and chains. He is told that his recent royalty was but a disordered dream, and, believing it, he talks like Shakespeare's defeated Richard II:

'Tis plain,
In this world's uncertain gleam,
That to live is but to dream:
Man dreams what he is, and wakes
Only when upon him breaks
Death's mysterious morning beam.
The king dreams he is a king,
And in this delusive way
Lives and rules with sovereign sway;
All the cheers that round him ring,
Born of air, on air take wing.
And in ashes (mournful fate!)

> Death dissolves his pride and state.
> Who would wish a crown to take,
> Seeing that he must awake
> In the dream beyond death's gate? . . .
> And in fine, throughout the earth,
> All men dream, whate'er their birth. . . .
> What is life? A thing that seems,
> A mirage that falsely gleams,
> Phantom joy, delusive rest,
> Since is life a dream at best,
> And even dreams themselves are dreams.[48]

Then, by another transformation very inadequately explained, Sigismund grows out of his savagery into reason; and when a revolution gives him the throne, he becomes a good king, humbly conscious that this exaltation is again a dream, an insubstantial bubble in the froth of life.

The speeches are painfully long, and a gongorism of fanciful phrases waters the poetic wine; but it is a powerful play nevertheless, mingling action with thought and sustaining dramatic suspense to the end. If we had been differently domiciled and indoctrinated, and could understand Castilian well, we should probably consider this one of the world's great plays.

It is impossible for us now to pull ourselves up by the bootstraps of imagination out of the prison of our time and place, and realize how lively a role the drama played in seventeenth-century Spain, and what influence it enjoyed. In Italy it almost drove the native tragic drama from the boards. In France it provided plots for Hardy, Corneille, Molière, and a dozen others; it molded the form of French tragedy before Racine, stressing honor and spilling rhetoric. When we recall also the influence of Cervantes and other Spanish novelists upon Lesage, Defoe, Fielding, and Smollett, and through them upon Dickens and Thackeray, and when we compare the art of Elizabethan England, or even that of contemporary France, with the architecture, the sculpture, and the painting of Spain in that heyday, we may begin to understand why the Spanish-speaking peoples of the world yield to none in the pride of their heritage and their blood.

CHAPTER XII

The Golden Age of Spanish Art*

1556–1682

I. ARS UNA, SPECIES MILLE

HOW shall we explain that in this period, when Spain lost command of the seas to England and of the land to France, and when all her material enterprises seemed to collapse in failure and bankruptcy, she could build the cathedral of Segovia, guide the sculpture of Hernández and Montañes, and inspire the painting of El Greco, Zurbarán, Velázquez, and Murillo? Was it because the Spanish Church was still rich, the Spanish court was still extravagant, American gold still entered Seville, and Spanish artists, nourished by faith and fees, still felt the glow of a glory not yet quite gone?

The splendor was least in architecture, for there the triumphs of the past met all the needs of piety. At Seville the Church certified its victory over the Moors by topping a Moslem minaret with a Christian belfry that perfected the grace of the Giralda (1567); and a year later Bartolomé Morel crowned the whole with a figure of La Fé (Faith), weighing a ton, yet so lightly poised that it turns with every breath of wind to survey its worshipful domain. At Valladolid Juan de Herrera, architect of the Escorial, began in 1585 the austere Cathedral of the Assumption, on so vast a scale that it is still unfurnished. On a hill dominating Segovia two centuries of architects and craftsmen began in 1522 the monumental cathedral that proudly symbolizes the dominant and immovable devotion of Spain. At Salamanca Juan Gómez de Mora designed for the Jesuits, in Palladian Doric plus dome, the immense Seminario Conciliar (1617–1755).

But even Spain was becoming secular, and palaces as well as churches were calling for art. At Aranjuez Philip II built (1575) a summer residence whose cool gardens could rescue him from the heat and solemnity of the Escorial. Philip III, as a center for his haunts, added the Palace of El Pardo, whose ornate Hall of Ambassadors is famous for its chandeliers. Philip IV and Olivares almost anticipated Versailles by building at the eastern gate of Madrid a pleasure garden, Buen Retiro (1631–33); in its court theater many plays of Lope and Calderón were staged. Stately town halls—*ayuntamientos*—were raised in this age at León and Astorga; and one at Toledo was designed by El Greco.

---

* All Spanish pictures mentioned in this chapter are in the Prado unless otherwise stated.

Sculpture was almost wholly ecclesiastical in form and mood. The Gothic style was modified by Italian influence and baroque ornament, but the portrait bust so popular in Italy was discountenanced in Spain with an almost Mohammedan taboo. Painters—even masters like Zurbarán and Murillo—lent their art to make sculpture impress the worshiper with the realism of crucifixions and martyrdoms; nearly all statues were in polychrome wood. Sir William Stirling-Maxwell, the erudite Scot who so loved and annaled Spanish art, thought Juan de Juni "the best sculptor of Spain."[1] Juan earned his renown by an altar in the Church of Nuestra Señora de la Antigua at Valladolid and, in another church there, the *Mater Dolorosa*, a statue so cherished by the people that, in the pathetic depth of their faith, they pleaded to be allowed to clothe it in costly raiment. Spain usually ranks still higher Gregorio Hernández; he too carved at Valladolid a *Mater Dolorosa*; with characteristic realism he painted bloodstains on her robe and set tears of glass into her face; this *Sorrowful Mother*, with the dead Christ lying in her lap, may be the supreme work of Spanish sculpture in this age.

The greatest of these sculptors was Juan Martínez Montañes. He was only eighteen when he and his wife came (1582) to the Monastery of Dulce Nombre de Jésus at Seville, presented to it a figure of the Virgin, and received in grateful exchange free residence there for life. He pleased the Jesuits with statues of Ignatius and Xavier, and delighted the Hieronymite monks with his *St. Jerome*. The cathedral of Seville still shows his *Crucifix*, ranked by one historian of art as "perhaps the supreme rendering of the divine Victim."[2] When Pope Paul V, responding to popular demand, made belief in the Immaculate Conception obligatory on all Catholics, Spain was especially happy since, like France, it had concentrated its piety upon the Virgin. Montañes rose to the occasion by carving his chef-d'oeuvre (now in the Seville cathedral) —the young Mother of God meditating on the mystery of her freedom from original sin; this too has been ranked among the masterpieces of the world's sculpture,[3] but the Andalusian maiden seems too calm and satisfied, though weighed down with drapery.

The picture of Spanish art, to be fair in spite of brevity, would have to enumerate and celebrate its minor glories: the gratings, screens, and gates in iron or bronze; the woodwork on many a reredos, and such choir stalls as those carved by Pedro de Mena for the cathedral of Málaga; the lamps, crosses, chalices, pyxes and tabernacles wrought in silver or gold, like the world-famous *custodias* of Juan de Arfe; the figurines in wood, ivory, alabaster, or bronze; the embroideries and brocades that graced altars and women; the enameled glass of Barcelona, and Talavera's tin-glazed wares.

In painting, before Velázquez, the Church was almost the sole patron and arbiter. The somber passion of Spanish theology and piety, reflecting, perhaps, the gloomy crags and the burning heat of the terrain, allowed little humor, lightness, or elegance in treating themes, banished the nude, frowned upon portraits and landscapes, and encouraged a harsh realism that stressed the frightening rather than the comforting phases of the faith; pictures were to instill the creed and burn it into the soul with flaming imagery and monastic severity. At last the painters themselves saw visions and claimed divine in-spiration. Philip II rivaled the Church as a patron of painters, but the subjects remained religious; when nobles commissioned paintings they usually obeyed the same rule; only with Velázquez and Philip IV did secularization begin. Some foreign influences entered to modify this ecclesiastical influence. Carducci and Zuccaro and some eighteen other Italians brought a softer mood into Spanish art; Anthonis Mor came from Flanders in 1572; Spanish painters visiting the Low Countries were touched by the spirit of Vandyck; and the exuberant Rubens himself, sweeping down upon Madrid in 1603, begged the native artists to look at life rather than death.

Besides the four masters who dominated Hispanic painting in this age there were many of milder fire: Alonso Sánchez Coello, who made portraits, in Flemish style, of Philip II's Infante Don Carlos and Infanta Isabel; Coello's pupil Juan Pantoja de la Cruz, who left us a somber *Felipe II*[4] and a powerful *St. Augustine;* Francisco de Ribalta, whose *tenebroso* style of light surrounded by darkness appears in *The Sick St. Francis Comforted by an Angel;* and Francisco Pacheco, who taught Velázquez, gave him a daughter in marriage, and expounded the principles of Spanish painting in his *Arte de la pintura* (1649). "The chief end of art," he wrote, "is to persuade men to piety and incline them to God."[5] In 1611 he visited El Greco in Toledo and condemned the Greek's pictures as *crueles borrones*—rough sketches.[6] Let us see.

II. EL GRECO: 1548?–1614

In Crete, where he was born, he called himself Kyriakos Theotokopoulos —i.e., the Lord's divine son; in Italy he was called Domenico Teotocopulo; in Spain Domingo Teotocópuli; he signed himself, in Greek letters, Domenikos Theotokopoulos; time has shortened him to El Greco, the nickname given him in Spain. We know nothing of his life in Crete. His ancestors may have emigrated to Crete from Constantinople after the Moslem conquest of that Greek city (1453); in any case he could feel in Crete, as later in Venice, the austere influence of Byzantine mosaics. In his day Crete belonged to Venice; not unnaturally the young artist, hearing of painting's heyday there, took ship in excited hopefulness to the lagoons, and probably joined the large colony of Greeks in that cosmopolitan capital. He studied under Titian for two or more years, admired Tinto-retto's art of grouping figures in a crowded picture, and may have caught Veronese's flair for rich and colorful robes. He copied famous paintings with patient humility in Venice, Reggio Emilia, Parma, and Florence, and he arrived in Rome not long after Michelangelo's death (1564).

The first definite notice we have of him is in a letter written at Rome November 16, 1570, by Giulio Clovio to Cardinal Alessandro Farnese:

There has arrived in Rome a young man from Candia, a pupil of Titian, who is, I think, a painter of rare talent. . . . He has painted a portrait of himself which is admired by all the painters in Rome. I should like him to be under the patronage of your revered lordship, without any other contribution to his living than a room in the Farnese Palace.[7]

The Cardinal consented, and El Greco rewarded Clovio with a masterly portrait.[8] When talk arose about the nudes in Michelangelo's *Last Judgment*, Domenico offered, if the whole picture were taken down, to replace it with another just as good and better clothed.[9] His standing with Roman artists fell. Some Spanish prelates in Rome told him that Philip II was looking for painters to decorate the Escorial. In 1572 he moved to Spain, shaking the dust of Rome from his shoes, but taking on his brush something of the distortions of Italian mannerism.

We have no record of him thereafter till 1575, when we find him both designing and adorning the Church of Santo Domingo el Antiguo in Toledo, the ecclesiastical capital of Spain. For its altar he painted the magnificent *Assumption of the Virgin* that now holds so prominent a place in the Chicago Art Institute—partly modeled on Titian's *Assunzione* in the Frari at Venice, and still in the Italian style of healthy youthful forms and majestic old heads. For the cathedral at Toledo he painted (1577) a famous *Espolio de las vestiduras del Señor*—despoiling of the garments of the Lord. A commission appointed to judge the picture complained that the tunic of Jesus was too glaringly red, and that the women at the lower left—the three Marys—were out of place there, since the Scriptures said they had looked on from afar; nevertheless the judges prophetically pronounced the painting "inestimable, so great is its value."[10] One of the Marys was the painter's mistress, Doña Jerónima de las Cuevas, whose sad and lovely face appears in most of El Greco's Virgins. Despite his loyalty to her and the Church he never married her; this was not an old Spanish custom, but one long sanctified in artists' studios.

A writer of the next generation, José Martínez, described Domenico as already confident of immortality:

He settled in . . . Toledo, introducing such an extravagant style that to this day nothing has been seen to equal it; attempting to discuss it would confuse the soundest minds. . . . He gave it to be understood that there was nothing superior to his works. . . . His nature was extravagant like his painting. . . . He used to say no price was high enough for his works, and so he gave them in pledge to their owners, who willingly advanced him what he asked for them. . . . He was a famous architect, and very eloquent in his speeches. He had few disciples, as no one cared to follow his capricious and extravagant style, which was only suitable to himself.[11]

Toward 1580 Philip II sent for El Greco and asked him to paint *St. Maurice and the Theban Legion*. After four years of labor the artist presented the result to the King. Philip found the grouping of the figures too confused; the picture was paid for but not accepted, and El Greco returned grieving to Toledo, which, so far as we know, he never left again. It was just as well, for now he was free to be his mystic self.

As if in revenge, he painted for the Church of Santo Tomé (1586) his most famous picture, one of the high points of pictorial art. The contract stipulated that he should show the clergy commemorating the tradition that saints had descended from heaven to bury Don Gonzalo Ruiz, Count Orgaz; St. Stephen and St. Augustine (in episcopal vestments) were to be shown lowering the body to the tomb, amid a reverent assemblage of notables; and over these figures the heavens, opening, were to reveal the Son of God in glory. All this was done to the letter, and much more, for almost every head is a finished portrait, the robes are a marvel of gold and green and white, the demascened armor of the Count gleams with light; and, for good measure, behind St. Stephen may be seen El Greco himself. The masterpiece of this masterpiece is the bearded, mitered head of St. Augustine. Or should we prefer the handsome corpse? Or the lovely face of St. Stephen? Or the bald priest reading the burial service? Or El Greco's eight-year-old son Jorge Manuel proudly holding a torch and letting a handkerchief emerge from his pocket to display El Greco's signature? In Francisco de Pisa's *History of Toledo* (1612) we read what we should have surmised: this *Burial of Count Orgaz* "is one of the very finest [paintings] in all Spain. Men come from foreign lands to see it, with especial admiration; and the people of Toledo, far from tiring of it, continually find in it new matter to gaze at. In it may be seen, realistically portrayed, many of the illustrious men of our time."[12] However, the parish council haggled over the fee; the hot-tempered Greek took the matter to court, won his case, and received two thousand crowns.

He had no dearth of commissions now. He had found himself; he no longer thought of Titian or Tintoretto; and he could experiment with the elongation of forms, not because he suffered any defect of eyesight, but probably because he felt that he might in this way symbolize the spiritual exaltation of his figures—bodies stretched out by heaven-seeking souls. In the *St. Andrew* and *St. Francis* of the Prado this emaciation seems unintelligible unless we consider such symbolism, and recall Gothic statuary slenderized for architectural limitations. All is forgiven when we come to the *St. Ildefonso* painted for the Caridad Hospital at Illescas; here in the reverend spirit, the absorbed mind, the ascetic face, the thin white hairs, and the delicate hands of the medieval archbishop is one of El Greco's profoundest conceptions. "This one picture would repay the journey to Spain."[13]

We do not gather, from the little we know about El Greco's life, that he was Hispanically pious; he seems to have inclined to pleasure rather than sanctity. When he painted *The Holy Family* for the Tavera Hospital he endowed the Virgin with sensual beauty, not maternal dedication. *The Crucifixion* is anatomically erudite but emotionally cold; Grünewald felt that tragedy far more deeply. In his religious pictures El Greco is at his best in the incidental portraits—as of himself, with white beard and bald head, in *The Pentecost*. In a city crowded with ecclesiastics he had no difficulty in getting powerful personalities to sit for him: his friend the Trinitarian Paravicino (Boston), with a face half scholar, half Inquisitor; or the Grand Inquisitor himself, Cardinal Niño de Guevara (New York) —not quite as good as Velázquez' imitation portrait of Innocent X. El Greco himself surpassed it in *The Cardinal of Tavera*, whose gaunt face, all bones and somber eyes, express again the artist's conception of ecclesiastical consecration. But the best of all the portraits are of the brothers Covarrubias: one, Antonio, secular, grizzled, disillusioned, weary, forgiving; the other, Diego, in priestly garb, but looking much more worldly, more humorous, quite well adjusted. Only a few Rembrandts and Titians, and Raphael's *Julius II*, excel these profound studies.

They are among the treasures gathered in the Casa del Greco Museum at Toledo. There, too, is the *Plan of Toledo*, in which the artist surveys, as from a cloud, the whole city and its encompassing hills. He represented it again, late in his life, in the *View of Toledo* under stormy skies (New York)—an impressionist picture utterly disdaining realist accuracy. By 1600 "the Greek" had become one of the town's most famous citizens, known to all for his proud and capricious spirit, a mystic with a taste for money, occupying twenty-four rooms in an old palace, hiring musicians to play for him at his meals, gathering about him the intellectuals of Toledo, and honored as an "eminent philosopher."[14] About 1605 he painted what is presumed to be his self-portrait (New York)—bald, gray, almost haggard. In 1611 Pacheco found him too weak to walk. Though he still kept his twenty-four rooms, he could not pay his debts; the city council repeatedly voted him substantial sums. He died in 1614, aged seventy-three.

His standing in the world of art has been a posthumous adventure. Góngora wrote a sonnet eulogy, and Velázquez recognized his genius, but his strange art inspired no imitation, founded no school. By 1650 he was lost in the glare of Velázquez' fame. For two centuries he was almost forgotten. Then Delacroix rediscovered him, Degas, Manet, and Cézanne took a lead from his rendering of moods; van Gogh and Gauguin saw in him their own progenitor. In 1907 Julius Meier-Graefe's *Spanish Journey* raised El Greco far above Velázquez to the highest place in Spanish painting. Such oscillations of fame are precarious, being subject to "the wild vicissitudes of taste."[15] But El Greco will remain for many centuries to come a stimulating example of an artist who reached beyond objects to ideas and feelings, and beyond bodies to souls.

III. ZURBARÁN: 1598–1664

After El Greco, for a generation, Spanish painting marked time with lesser men, who did their best and disappeared. Then, almost simultaneously, Francisco de Zurbarán and Diego Velázquez flooded Spain with great art. During thirty years these two served as complements to each other: Zurbarán painting like a monk frightened into adoration and near to God, Velázquez prospering in the world and close to his King.

Zurbarán was baptized at Fuente de Cantos, in southwestern Spain, November 7, 1598, son of a shopkeeper successful enough to send him to develop his talent in Seville. After two years of study he signed his first dated picture (1616), an *Immaculate Conception* which should have ruined his career. A year later he moved to Llerema, fifteen miles from his birthplace. The neighborhood was dotted with convents, churches, and hermitages, from which Francisco took his modest commissions and his inspirations. There he married María Pérez, nine years his senior, in order to legitimize his child; she died after giving him two more. In 1625 he married a widow ten years his senior, but with a charming dowry; by her he had six children, of whom five died in childhood. After her death he married a prosperous widow; she gave him six children, of whom five died in childhood. Love labored to keep a step ahead of death.

In art his creative period began with a contract to paint, in six months, twenty-one pictures for the Dominican Monastery of San Pablo el Real at Seville (1626). Having completed this assignment, Zurbarán appears to have visited Madrid and felt the influence of Velázquez. Heretofore his paintings had reflected the dark and massive style of Caravaggio, and perhaps of Ribera; now he added to his rugged naturalism a new subtlety of shadows and a refinement of finish. Soon thereafter we find him in Seville, painting twenty-two immense canvases for the Mercedarian monks—the Order of Our Lady of Mercy, devoted to ransoming captive Christians. The four pictures that remain from this group are not masterpieces; but memorable is a boyish face in one of them, perhaps the artist's son Juan. Seville must have liked these paintings, for in 1629 it officially asked Francisco to make his home there—"Seville would be honored . . . considering that the art of painting is one of the major embellishments of the state."[16] Zurbarán consented.

In 1630, for the Franciscan Church of San Buenaventura, he painted some of his greatest works. One is *St. Bonaventura Pointing St. Thomas Aquinas to the Crucifix*: the great theologian—unfortunately a Dominican—is gently admonished that religion consists not in philosophical theory but in the contemplation of Christ. This—the theme picture of Zurbarán's art—was stolen from Spain by Marshal Soult (1810), found its way into the Kaiser Friedrich Museum in Berlin, and was destroyed in the Second World War. Another in the series, *St. Bonaventura on His Bier*, also taken by Soult, was sold to the Louvre in 1858 and is still there; the four figures at the left are masterly. Still finer is *The Apotheosis of St. Thomas Aquinas*, which Zurbarán painted for a Dominican college in Seville; the mind passes in astonishment from one profound face to another—Ambrose, Gregory, Jerome, Augustine, Charles V. However, Jerónimo Velázquez was paid six times as much for the frame as Zurbarán for the picture.

Moving on to the Carmelite Church of San Alberto (1630), the busy painter showed St. Francis absorbed in humble devotion, and St. Peter Thomas, a monk wrinkled and haggard with waiting for Paradise. Returning to the Mercedarian monastery (1631), he painted some of its most revered monks; among these portraits is the magnificent *Fray Pedro Machado*. The year 1633 was hectic with commissions: twelve Apostles for a church in Lisbon, three pictures for the Carthusians at Seville, and ten for the Chapel of St. Peter in the great cathedral; one of these, *St. Peter Repentant*, still in its original place, is a striking essay in realism, perhaps remembering Ribera.

Zurbarán was now in such wide demand that he delegated much of his work to his aides. For the Monastery of Guadalupe in Estremadura he painted *The Temptation of St. Jerome*, in which the head and the hands of the saint are technical wonders, and the gentle ladies playing music hardly deserve to have their temptations resisted. Even from Peru and Guatemala orders came; one series of Apostles went to Lima, another to Antigua; and to Mexico City went *Christ at Emmaus*, picturing the risen Christ as a hale and happy peasant at a meal. Some of these canvases were done in haste or by proxy, and Zurbarán had to sue Lima for his fee.

From 1645 his ascendancy at Seville was challenged by the young Murillo, who supplied churches and convents with such tender illustrations of the Christian story that the demand for Zurbarán's disconcerting realism sharply declined. The older artist tried to soften his terrors, and for a time he strove to rival Murillo in pious and domestic sentiment, as in *The Virgin and Child with St. John* (now in San Diego, California); but this new style was uncongenial to his art and mood. He moved to Madrid (1658) to repair his fortunes, but Philip IV, himself penniless, found nothing better for him to do than to decorate a hunting lodge. Velázquez was kind to him, but suddenly Velázquez died. Zurbarán outlived his friend and his fame.

His reputation hardly surmounted the Pyrenees until Napoleon's generals took a fancy to Zurbarán's monumental monks and somber saints and kidnaped some of them to France. When the Spanish monasteries were secularized in 1835 more of his work came to Paris, and in 1838 King Louis Philippe opened in the Louvre a Spanish Gallery with four hundred paintings, of which eighty were ascribed to Zurbarán. Our present taste finds his range too narrow and monastic, his spirit too gloomy and entranced. We miss in him the ragamuffins of Murillo and the philosophers and pretty princesses of Velázquez. And yet there is in his work a solid sincerity, a depth of dedication, a power of color and form, that lift him beyond the realm of transient preferences and ensure his place in the remembrance of men.

IV. VELÁZQUEZ: 1599–1660

His paternal grandfather was a Portuguese noble who, all fortune lost, moved with his wife from Oporto to Seville. To their son Juan de Silva and to Doña Jerónima Velázquez the artist was born, in the same year as Vandyck, one year after Zurbarán and Bernini, eighteen before Murillo. He was named Diego Rodríguez de Silva y Velázquez; usually he called himself by his mother's name, a practice common in southern Spain. He received a good education, learned some Latin and philosophy, and for a while tried science; then he turned to painting, studied briefly with Juan de Herrera, longer with Pacheco. "I married him to my daughter," Pacheco tells us, "induced by his youth, integrity and good qualities, and the prospects of his great natural genius."[17]

Velázquez set up his own studio, and soon attracted attention by his predilection for profane subjects. He mingled with the lowly, and delighted to put their thoughts and biographies into their faces. When he was still a lad of twenty he painted a great picture, *The Water Carrier of Seville*;[18] here, in rags and patience, is the dignity of honest poverty. And at twenty-three he portrayed with already mature insight the poet Góngora (Boston)—eyes and nose piercing the world.

Presumably this was done during Velázquez' first visit to Madrid (1622). Seville and its ecclesiastics were too narrow a field for him; some heat of ambition drove him to the capital, with his *Water Carrier* under his arm. There he courted the court unsuccessfully, for Philip IV and Olivares were busy with politics, marriages, and wars, and a dozen other artists were climbing the same stairs. Diego returned to Seville. A year passed; Prince Charles Stuart came to Madrid, wooed an infanta, and showed a taste for art; now Olivares sent for Velázquez. The black-eyed, black-haired youth rode up again to the capital, was made court painter, and took the fancy of the King by picturing him as an intrepid horseman on a prancing charger. Philip not only posed for Velázquez a dozen times, but encouraged the royal family (brothers, wives, children) and the court (ministers, generals, poets, jesters, dwarfs) to take their turn before that immortalizing brush. Diego was given a studio in the royal palace; and there, or near it, he spent nearly all the remaining thirty-seven years of his life. It was a magnificent opportunity and a narrowing imprisonment.

Two major influences broadened him. Rubens, then the most famous artist in the world, visited Madrid again in 1628—a master of light and shade, a reckless painter of pagan deities and voluptuous nudes; Velázquez was stirred. Rubens advised him to go to Italy, especially to Venice, and study those geniuses of coloring. Diego pleaded with Philip and was granted *congé* and four hundred precious ducats for the trip. We get a sample of maritime speeds in that age when we learn that Velázquez left Barcelona August 10, 1629, and reached Genoa August 20. He crossed Italy to Venice and sat for days before the great canvases of Tintoretto and Veronese, the portraits and the mythologies of Titian. He passed on to Ferrara and Rome, copied the ancient marbles in the Forum, and envied the drawing in the frescoes of Michelangelo on the Sistine Chapel ceiling. Those majestic forms helped Velázquez to pass from the dark shadows of Caravaggio to a sharper rendering of figures in clear light. Then he moved south to Naples to visit Ribera; and from Naples he sailed back to Spain (January 1631).

Was it vanity—the sustaining shadow of every self—that prompted Philip to sit so often for an artist of such penetrating vision and meticulous veracity, or was it to give his portrait to soliciting friends? Sad is the change from the fine tall youth of the early pictures to the later revelations of color gone from the face and painted into the hair, of somber autocracy persisting, through years and defeats, in the cold blue eyes and the prehensile Hapsburg chin. If there is something superficial in these royal portraits it may be because there was nothing beneath the visible surface. When there was something there, as in the portraits of Góngora and Olivares, it came out on the canvas.

Between the King's pictures came Queen Isabel, then Queen Mariana, and Philip's sister Queen Maria of Hungary, sitting to no great result. Philip's younger brother, the Cardinal Infante Ferdinand, posed as a hunter, with a dog all muscle, nerve, and alert devotion. Olivares mounted a black charger for his picture in the Prado, and a white charger for the same pose in the painting in the Metropolitan Museum of Art at New York, leaving no doubt as to who was in the saddle in Spain. The most pleasing of these court portraits are those of the young Don Baltasar Carlos, in whom all the hopes of the dynasty rested. Velázquez painted this lovely child again and again, with transparent delight: in 1631 with an attendant dwarf;[19] in 1632 as already the charm of the court;[20] in 1634 as swinging a marshal's baton and (aged five) proudly bestriding a tremendous horse; in 1635 as a hunter carefully grasping his gun, but clearly too gentle to kill or rule; that guileless face answers those who thought that Velázquez rendered only surfaces. And so the series progressed, from Carlos' second to his sixteenth year, when the beloved Prince fell into a fever and died.

The dwarf seen in one of these pictures was among several who gave the failures at Philip's court a comforting sense of superiority and magnitude. The custom had come down from Imperial Rome and the still more ancient East. Even the papal court had dwarfs; Cardinal Vitelli collected forty-four to wait upon his guests. The first Duke of Buckingham presented Queen Henrietta Maria with a pie that contained a dwarf eighteen inches tall.[21] For their own satisfaction, and the general amusement, Philip IV's dwarfs were dressed in sumptuous raiment flashing jewelry and gold. Velázquez painted them with sympathy and humor: one, called Antonio el Ingles (the Englishman), proudly taller than his dog, though not half so handsome; another, Sebastián de Morra, scowling in his massive beard and clenching his fists against his fate. There were jesters too at the court. Velázquez painted five of them; one, whose portrait is called *The Geographer*[22] because he points to a globe, looks more rational than Olivares; a second, *Barbarossa*, draws a ferocious sword; a third has dressed himself as Don Juan of Austria; a fourth struggles with an enormous book; a fifth, portrayed in *The Idiot*, is harmlessly, almost ingratiatingly insane.

Though always a courtier, and unmistakably a gentleman, Velázquez found relief from protocol by studying the life of those stately commoners who still adorn the Spanish scene. Early in his career (1629) he persuaded two handsome youths and half a dozen peasants to pose for *Los borrachos* (*The Drinkers*): a nearly naked Bacchus, sitting on a barrel, crowns with vines a kneeling figure, while about them gather rough devotees of the grape, some worn with work, some grizzled with age; this is perhaps the only memorable bacchanal in Spanish art of the Golden Century. Even more remarkable than these topers are the two strange paintings that Velázquez labeled *Aesopus*, the portrait of an old sad author, destitute and half blind, carrying his fables down the years, and *Menippus*, that of a Cynic philosopher of the third century B.C.; these are unforgettable faces. And not least in the world that Velázquez has left us are the animals: horses that now seem to us ungainly stout, but redeemed by proud heads and flashing eyes; a stag's head with philosophic countenance resigned to human ferocity; and dogs on the *qui vive* for action or alertly asleep.

These were the byplays of Velázquez' brush, perhaps a relief from the perils of painting without compliment the dignitaries of the court. Our estimate of the seventeenth-century Spaniards rises when we see these nobles, unassumingly robed, yet confronting with proud faith a world in which their beloved country seemed palsied with decay. Don Diego del Corral y Arellano, Cardinal Gaspar de Borja y Velasco,[23] the sturdy sculptor Montañes, the supercilious *Knight of Santiago*,[24] the handsome and diffident Francesco II d'Este,[25] the magnificent, lordly Don Juan Francisco Pimental—these are portraits that reach the soul. And if the *Portrait of a Man* in the Capitoline Gallery of Rome is really of Velázquez himself, it is impossible not to love him—the carelessly curly hair, the modest dress, the soft and meditative eyes.

It is remarkable how, in Velázquez, the court crowded out the Church and the hallowed religious themes. He could not rival El Greco or Zurbarán in picturing wrinkled old Apostles and saints; only *The Coronation of the Virgin* among his religious paintings evoked all his powers. He was much happier in secular scenes. In *Las lanzas*, which we know better as *The Surrender of Breda*, he spread himself out lavishly, making it one of the largest (120 by 144 inches), but also one of the most detailed, canvases in the history of art. In the long war of Spain against the rebels in the Netherlands, Ambrosio de Spinola had recaptured for Spain (1625) the strategic city of Breda, in northern Brabant. Velázquez had met Spinola in 1629 on the voyage from Italy; he had been struck by the knightly nobility of the great general; now he signalized this in a masterpiece that showed the victorious Spanish lancers raising their pikes aloft, the captured city burning, the defeated and surrendering general, Justin of Nassau, offering the keys of the town to Spinola, and the chivalrous victor complimenting the loser on the bravery of his defense. In the striking contrasts of colors, and the individualization of the attendant figures, Velázquez achieved a triumph, which Philip IV was happy to display in the Palace of Buen Retiro.

In 1649, as reward for twenty-six years of work, Philip financed Velázquez' second visit to Italy and commissioned the artist to secure castings of classic statuary and to purchase paintings by the Italian masters. Velázquez found prices already awesome; hardly any major work by the great Venetians could be bought at any price; for five pictures he had to pay 12,000 crowns ($150,000?). Were millionaires and others already using art as a hedge against inflation?

The best painting done in Italy in that year 1650 was Velázquez' portrait of Innocent X. When the Pope consented to sit for him the artist, feeling out of practice, prepared his hand and eye by making a portrait of his mulatto slave, Juan de Pareja.*26 This picture met with universal acclaim among the artists of Rome, who at once elected Velázquez to their Academy of St. Luke. The Pope gave him only a few sittings; Velázquez made preliminary studies of the head, and one of these, in the National Gallery at Washington, is almost indistinguishable from the finished portrait that passed down as an heirloom in the Doria family to which the Pope belonged; it was preserved in the Palazzo Doria Pamfili, where

---

* Pareja, after years of preparing Velázquez' brushes, colors, and palettes and watching his mind and work, secretly used the materials himself, and finally painted so well that Philip IV, having mistaken one of Pareja's canvases for a Velázquez, freed him; nevertheless Juan remained as a scholar and servant in the artist's family till his own death.27

Reynolds, viewing it, judged it "the most beautiful picture in Rome."[28] Coming upon it there today, one feels in it a power, both of character and of art, that places it alongside Raphael's *Julius II* and Titian's *Paul III*, among the most impressive portraits of all time. Innocent X was seventy-six when he posed for this picture; he died five years later. But for his pontifical dress and ring, one could mistake him for one of the bandit leaders who had troubled so many popes; but then, studying those hard and resolute features, we realize that Innocent was what he had to be—a ruler governing a state of unruly Italians, a pontiff guiding a Church of unchristian Christians reaching from Rome to the Philippines, from Rome to Paraguay; he had to have iron in his blood, steel in his eyes, mastery in his face; and Velázquez saw and placed them there. Seeing the portrait, the Pope made one wry comment: "Too true!"[29] Roman artists admired the compact composition, the striking harmony of red, white, and gold, the suspicious, searching, sidelong glance of the blue-gray eyes, the hands themselves announcing character. When Velázquez left Italy (June 1651), it was not as a pupil seeking old masters, but as himself the acknowledged master of the age. For Rubens now was dead, and no one dreamed that an obscure Dutchman, struggling with debts and soon to retire to an Amsterdam ghetto, would rise from the grave after centuries to challenge that supremacy.

Returning to Madrid, Velázquez made the outstanding blunder of his life: he applied for, and obtained, appointment as *aposentador del rey*—manager of the royal palace. Perhaps he was tired of painting, or felt that he had reached the limit of his possibilities in that field. The post was no sinecure; it involved personal supervision of the palace, of its furniture and decoration, heating and sanitation; moreover, he was expected to make arrangements for court plays, balls, and tournaments, and to provide quarters for the court on royal tours. He had to accompany the King on all major journeys, for pleasure or politics or war. Could anything be more absurd for a man who had painted Innocent X? The pride of place had surmounted, in Velázquez, the consciousness of genius.

In the nine years that remained to him he gave to painting only such time as could be spared from his official chores. He resumed the portrayal of the royal family, of distinguished courtiers, and of the King himself. He made three lovely pictures of the Infanta Margarita, and painted her again as the center of one of his masterpieces, *Las meninas—The Maids of Honor*; servants, dwarf, and dog gather around the Princess, and Velázquez himself is seen in the background, putting them all on canvas. He portrayed her again in the great blue skirt that made her legs thenceforth a sacred and inscrutable mystery;[30] and shortly before his death he pictured her as a miracle of innocence in lace. In 1657 he digressed from the court to paint

Las hilanderas—The Tapestry Weavers—magnificent figures caught in the turmoil and dignity of work. In that same year he dared the Inquisition, and scandalized and delighted Spain, by painting the shapely back and buttocks of *The Rokeby Venus*, so called from its long stay in the home of an English family that bought it for £500 and sold it to the London National Gallery for £45,000. A suffragette, angry at such an exposure of trade secrets, slashed that rosy back in six places, but it was sewed up again alluringly.

In *Las meninas* we see Velázquez as he saw himself in his final years—hair abounding, proud mustache, slightly somber eyes. The mouth seems sensual, yet we hear nothing, in his record, of those sexual diversions and personal conflicts that use up so much of so many artists. He had a high standing at the court for his fine manners, his sense of humor, his decent family life. He has left us portraits of his wife Juana and his daughter Francisca;[31] perhaps the subject of *The Lady with the Fan*[32] is again Francisca. Her husband, Juan Bautista del Mazo, painted *The Family of the Artist*,[33] showing Velázquez, in a studio background, and five children who helped to keep the family one.

His death resulted from his office. In the spring of 1660 he arranged the complex ceremonies and festivities that were to accompany, on an island in the boundary river Bidassoa, the signing of the Treaty of the Pyrenees and the betrothal of the Infanta María Teresa to Louis XIV. Velázquez had to provide for the transit of the court halfway across Spain to San Sebastián, and for four thousand pack mules carrying furniture, pictures, tapestry, and other decoration. The painter, now lost in the official, returned to the capital "tired with traveling by night and working by day," as he reported to a friend. On July 31 he was put to bed with tertian fever. On August 6, or, in the words of his first biographer, "on the Feast of the Lord's Transfiguration . . . he resigned his soul to God, who had created it to be a wonder of the world."[34] Eight days later his wife was laid beside him in the earth.

Those of us who do not know the technique of painting can only enjoy Velázquez' works, not judging their quality, but letting them show us an age, a court, a *roi fainéant*, and a proud but gentle soul. Even so we may relish the classic clarity, simplicity, dignity, and truth of these pictures; we can surmise the labor and the skill that underlay their triumphs, the tentative sketches, the experimental distribution of figures, the apposition, depth, and transparency of colors, the molding play of light and shade. Critics, tired of hackneyed adulation, have pointed out the defects of the Spanish master: minor faults like the silly headdresses of his Infantas, the barrel bellies of his horses, the disproportionate mirrored face in *The Rokeby Venus*; and major blemishes like his lack of emotion, imagination, idealism, or sentiment, his almost feminine absorption in personalities rather than ideas, his apparent blindness to anything unseen by his eyes.[35] Even in Velázquez' days one of his rivals, Vincenzo Carducci, accused him of a myopic naturalism that mistook the conscientious representation of external reality as the highest function of pictorial art.

Who shall reply for Velázquez (who would never have replied) that he was not responsible for those headdresses and those equine bellies; that controlled emotion is more moving than emotion expressed; that the portraits of Baltasar Carlos and the princesses, the pictures of the maids of honor, and *The Surrender of Breda* show a delicate sentiment; that *Aesopus* and *Menippus* are studies in philosophy; that the portraits of Góngora, Olivares, and Innocent X are not imitations of surfaces but evocations of souls? There is no obvious pursuit of beauty in Velázquez, but rather a quest for the revealing type; few females smoothed with loveliness, but many men lined and charactered with life.

Always honored in Spain as her greatest painter, Velázquez was hardly known north of the Pyrenees—perhaps because so much of him was in the Prado—until Raphael Mengs proclaimed him to Germany in 1761, and the Napoleonic wars in Spain revealed him to England and France. Manet and the Impressionists hailed him as their precursor in the study and representation of light and atmosphere; and for half a century Velázquez was ranked with the highest. Whistler called him "the painter's painter," as the teacher of them all; Ruskin declared *ex cathedra* that "everything that Velázquez does may be regarded as absolutely right." Then Meier-Graefe went to Spain to seek Velázquez in the Prado, found El Greco in Toledo, and announced that Velázquez "stopped where El Greco began," and "always remained in the antechamber of art."[36] Suddenly half the world believed Velázquez to be second-rate.

Fame is a fashion. We tire of wearing old admirations on our pens, and find it exhilarating to discard worn idols from our fancy, to take down the dead mighty from their seats, and to put on the praises of new gods, blown up by our originality or exhumed by some fresh renown. There is no telling how great Velázquez will seem when the vanes of taste veer again.

V. MURILLO: 1617–82

There was a time, in our believing youth, when Murillo's *Immaculate Conception of the Virgin* stood as high in repute as Raphael's *Sistine Madonna*; now none so poor to do it reverence. The decline of Christian faith in Europe and America has taken half their beauty from pictures that we thought inherently beautiful. Murillo is one victim of that denudation.

But first a courtesy to Alonso Cano. A strange man—priest, duelist, painter, sculptor, architect. Born in Granada, he migrated to Seville, studied painting (beside Velázquez) with Pacheco and sculpture with Montañes. He designed, carved, and painted retables for the College of San Alberto and the Church of Santa Paula, where he competed successfully against Zurbarán. For the church of Lebrija he carved religious statuary that drew students from foreign lands to admire and imitate. He fought a duel, severely wounded his adversary, fled to Madrid, and won the protection of Olivares through the intercession of Velázquez. His paintings in and near the capital earned him a court appointment. In 1644 his wife was found murdered in bed; he accused his servant, but was himself charged with the crime. Again he fled from success; he hid in a remote monastery, was found, arrested, tortured; bore all pains without admitting guilt; was freed, and began again. In 1651, aged fifty, he returned to Granada, where he became a priest and a canon of the cathedral, and made for it statues, paintings, a lectern, and a portal of such excellence that his arrogance found pardon. Commissioned by the royal auditor in Granada to model a statue of St. Anthony of Padua, he finished it to the satisfaction of the official, who, however, haggled about the price. Cano asked one hundred doubloons ($3,200?). "How many days has it taken you?" the official asked. "Twenty-five," said Cano. "Then," said the auditor, "you esteem your labor at four doubloons a day?" "You are a bad accountant, for I have been fifty years learning to make such a statue as this in twenty-five days." "And I have spent my youth and my patrimony on my university studies, and now, being auditor of Granada, a far nobler profession than yours, I earn each day a bare doubloon." "Yours a nobler profession than mine!" cried the sculptor. "Know that the King can make auditors of the dust of the earth, but that God reserves to Himself the creation of an Alonso Cano"; and at once, in fury, he smashed the statue to bits.[37] For a time it was thought that the Inquisition would imprison him, but Philip IV protected him, and Cano continued to paint pictures and carve statues—nearly all religious—that moved admirers of his multiple genius to call him the Michelangelo of Spain. He spent his earnings as fast as they came, usually in charities, and grew old in such poverty that the cathedral chapter had to vote funds for his relief. On his deathbed he rejected the crucifix offered him, because, he said, it was badly carved.

Bartolomé Esteban Murillo was quite another man—modest, gentle, pious, the idol of his pupils, the beloved of his competitors, the cornucopia of charity. Seville, then the metropolis of Spanish art, saw his birth in 1617, the last of fourteen children. He studied painting under Juan de Castillo, but, as his parents died poor when he was fourteen, the orphan earned his bread by painting coarse and hasty pictures for a weekly fair. Hearing that Philip IV was kind to artists, he made his way to Madrid(?), where, according to an uncertain tradition,[38] Velázquez befriended him, lodged him in his own home, secured his admission to the royal galleries, and encouraged him to study the works of Ribera, Vandyck, and Velázquez.

However, we find him in 1645 again at Seville. A Franciscan monastery there had offered a resistible sum for seven large pictures; established artists scorned the fee; Murillo agreed to it, and produced his first masterpiece, *The Angels' Kitchen*,[39] showing angels coming from heaven, bringing food, cooking it, laying tables, and feeding the pious in a famine; Murillo, though he tried to follow the masculine style of Ribera and Zurbarán, told the story with his own turn for tender sentiment. This picture and *The Death of Santa Clara*[40] made the artist's fame; half of literate Seville came to admire, and commissions mounted. As these were nearly all ecclesiastical, Murillo poured out Virgins, Holy Families, and saints in happy profusion, peopling the Christian legends with such fair women, handsome men, charming gamins, rosy colors, and mystic atmosphere that Catholic Europe warmed to him as the most lovable expositor of the most lovable creed.

So fed, Murillo, aged thirty, ventured into marriage, filled his home with the noise, quarrels, and delight of nine children, and labored for them contentedly till his death. The cathedral chapter paid him ten thousand reals for the *St. Anthony of Padua* that still hangs there. A story suspiciously recalling a legend told of Zeuxis,[41] but printed eleven years before Murillo's death, assures us that birds flying into the cathedral tried to perch on the lilies in the picture, and pecked at the fruit.[42]

Though his subjects were nearly all religious, he made them human rather than ecclesiastical. If all Roman Catholic Europe took to its heart the many copies he sent out of his *Immaculate Conception of the Virgin*,[43] it was not only because they celebrated a theme especially dear to Spain and that age, but because it enthroned womanhood in a cloud of idealism and sanctity. The lovely and modestly sensual women of Andalusia inspired *The Madonna of the Rosary*,[44] *The Gypsy Madonna*,[45] and the darkly beautiful *Holy Family with the Bird*.[46]

And who has painted children better? The Prado *Annunciation* shows us a girl just entering her teens, diffident and delicate, the very chef-d'-œuvre of life. For the many forms in which Murillo pictured Christ as a child, he found models in the pretty children around him in his home and his street; probably it was they who interested him, rather than the set theme; and he painted them as charmingly as any *bambini* of the Italian Renaissance. If he could not squeeze children into his religious pictures he painted them independently. The Haus der Kunst in Munich has a wall full of them: boys throwing dice, boys eating melons as a bearable way of washing their faces, a boy munching bread while his mother picks lice from his hair. *A Boy Leaning out of a Window*[47] makes it plain that money and happiness have quarreled and parted; let him be *A Boy with a Dog*,[48] and the world is his oyster. In the *Beggar Boy* of the Louvre the idealist painter takes leave of the supernatural, looks at life on earth, and finds it lovable even in rags. In his realism Murillo is still the idealist.

He lived, as he painted, without tragedy, except at the very end. Climbing a scaffold to finish a painting in a church at Cádiz, he lost his footing, fell, and ruptured himself so severely that poisoning set in, and soon the favorite son of all Andalusia died (1682), so suddenly that he could not complete his will. Over his tomb, by his instructions, were inscribed his name, a skeleton, and two words, *Vive moriturus*—"Live as though about to die."

Through two centuries his reputation remained high for those who cared more for what a picture said than for how it said it. Napoleon's generals spread his fame by stealing his works and selling them as legitimate loot. Incompetent copyists multiplied his paintings and stirred criticism to question his art. He knew the technique of his trade, but his range was too restricted by his success with the Church; he lent himself too readily to the feminine and sentimental side of life; and what began by being beautiful became, through stereotyped repetition, unimpressively pretty. His saints looked up to heaven so persistently that when Europe turned from heaven it lost sight of Murillo. For the same reason it lost sight of Spanish painting in general after 1680. While Europe debated Christianity, Spain clung to her medieval heritage, and not till Goya would her art startle the world again.

During Murillo's life a hundred fatal factors ended the Century of Gold. Gold itself, and its foreign quest, were factors: the youth and vigor of Spain broke from the prison of the Peninsula to explore and exploit the Americas; and the gold they sent back corrupted Spanish life, encouraged sloth, raised prices, or fell into Dutch or Genoese bottoms carrying Spanish trade. The government hoarded the precious metals, debased the currency, expelled the productive Moriscos, multiplied and sold offices, taxed everything to the point of economic apathy, and squandered wealth in martial expeditions and court extravagance while industry languished, unemployment spread, commerce dwindled, population shrank, and cities decayed. The narrowly aristocratic government lost all dignity, put collection boxes in the streets, and solicited money from door to door to finance its domestic incompetence and its foreign defeats.[49] Spanish armies garrisoning Sicily, Naples, and Milan, forcing their way through New World jungles and wilderness, wasting themselves in the Thirty Years' War, fighting a losing battle against the incredible pertinacity of the Netherlands, drained away the human and material resources of a small, half-arid and mountainous state shackled by its boundaries in a sea controlled by commercial competitors and naval enemies. Only the monasteries and the churches remained, clinging to their enormous, inalienable, untaxable properties, and multiplying monks in costly idleness. While religion appeased poverty with promissory notes on Paradise, stifled thought, and invited Spain to live on its past, France and England rewarded industry, captured commerce, and entered the future. Adjustment to a changing environment is the essence of life, and its price.

CHAPTER XIII

The Duel for France

1559–74

I. THE RIVAL FORCES

AS long as he fears or remembers insecurity, man is a competitive animal. Groups, classes, nations, and races similarly insecure compete as covetously as their constituent individuals, and more violently, as knowing less law and having less protection; Nature calls all living things to the fray. In the broil of Europe between the Reformation (1517) and the Peace of Westphalia (1648), this collective competition used religion as a cloak and a weapon for economic or political ends. When, after a century of struggle, the combatants laid down their arms, Christianity barely survived among the ruins.

France suffered first and recovered first; her "religious wars" of 1562 to 1594 were to her what the Thirty Years' War (1618–48) was to be to Germany, and the Civil Wars (1642–48) to England. When Henry II died in a tragic joust (1559) and his fifteen-year-old son succeeded him as Francis II, the nation had been led to bankruptcy by the long contest between the Hapsburgs and the Valois kings. The gross annual revenue of the government was then 12,000,000 livres; the public debt was 43,000,000. Many magistrates had been unpaid for four years past. The French people could not be persuaded to pay taxes.[1] A financial crash threw Lyon into economic chaos in 1559. The flow of American silver and gold through Spain and Portugal into France depreciated the currency, inflated prices, and set on foot an angry race between wages and prices, in which no one gained but the informed and speculative financiers. In 1567 and 1577 the government tried by edict to fix maxima for prices and wages, but the economic scramble overrode the laws,[2] and inflation went on, perhaps as an impious way to pay for pious wars. The only prosperous organization in the country was the Catholic Church, with its 94,000 ecclesiastics (in 1600), its 80,000 nuns, its 70,000 monks or friars, its 2,500 Jesuits, its august cathedrals and stately episcopal sees, its extensive and well-cultivated lands. A third—some said two thirds—of the riches of France belonged to the Church.[3] Behind the religious wars lay the desire to retain or obtain this ecclesiastical wealth.

Fortunately for the Church, Charles de Guise, who had been made

Cardinal of Lorraine at thirty-five, was now chief minister to Francis II. The ducal family of the Guises took its name from their castle near Laon, but had its main seat in Lorraine, which had only recently been absorbed into France. The Cardinal was handsome, of alert intelligence and decent life, a good administrator, eloquent in Latin, French, and Italian; but his taste for wealth and power, his suave duplicity, his readiness to persecute dissent and avenge opposition, his courageous retrenchment of governmental outlays, made him enemies in almost every class. His older brother, Francis, Duke of Guise, had already earned renown in strategy and battle and was now minister of war; but as the national bankruptcy counseled peace, Francis had to nurse his ambitions in a galling idleness. He loved glory, fine raiment, and cavalier display, but his courtly manners and grace of person and carriage made him the idol of Catholic France. He was intolerant of heresy and proposed to exterminate it by force.[4] He and his brother were convinced that if France, like Germany and England, adopted Protestantism, the Church would be near its end, and France would lose the religious ardor that had supported its social order and its national unity. In defense of their faith and their power the Guises braved many perils, suffered premature death, and shared responsibility for the harrowing of France.

The Huguenots were no longer a small and helpless minority of French Protestants led and inspired by Calvin from Geneva, but a spreading doctrinal and social revolt against the Church. Calvin reckoned them to be 10 per cent of the French people in 1559;[5] Michelet estimated their numbers to have doubled by 1572.[6] They had centers in every province from Dauphiné to Brittany, above all in southwest France, where, three centuries back, the Albigensian heresy had met with apparent extermination. Despite the repressive legislation of Francis I and Henry II, they held their prayer meetings, fed on solemn sermons preaching predestination, issued a fire of pamphlets on the abuses of the Church and the tyranny of the Guises, and held a general synod in Paris (May 26, 1559) under the very nose of the King. They professed loyalty to the French monarchy, but they organized on republican lines the regions where they prevailed. Like any persecuted minority, they formulated a temporary ideology of liberty, but they agreed with the Catholics that the state should enforce the "true religion" throughout France. Their ethical theory was stricter than the time-relaxed code of their enemies; they avoided dancing, fancy dress, and the theater; and they denounced with indignation the morals of the court, where, as Jeanne d'Albret told her son, "it is not the men who invite the women, but the women who invite the men."[7]

The Queen Mother, Catherine de Médicis, thought that in both parties "religion is a cover which serves merely to mask ill will . . . and yet they have nothing less than religion in their hearts."[8] She may have put it too strongly, but unquestionably social and economic factors underlay the religious strife. The peasantry remained Catholic; it had no material stake in the contest, and saw no substitute in a stern predestinarian Protestantism for the comforting myths and festival alleviations provided by the ancient faith. The proletariat, small numerically but big with revolt, denounced its employers, and gave a sympathetic hearing to "the Reform" as promising some change; and as in the England of the Lollards and the Puritans and the Germany of the Peasants' War, the Gospel became a textbook of revolution.[9] The middle classes too gave ear to the courageous preachers that Geneva trained and sent to France. The businessmen, who at the great fairs met prosperous Germans, Englishmen, and Swiss, noted the successful alliance of these merchants with Protestant rulers and ideas. They had long suffered contumely under bishops and barons disdainful of commerce and tied to feudal ways; they learned with pleasure and envy that Calvin was well disposed toward business and finance, and that he gave a share to the laity in the control of morals and the church. They resented ecclesiastical wealth and tithes, and feudal tolls on trade. They could not forgive the monarchy for subjecting to the central government the municipal communes that had for centuries been their political preserve.[10] Even bankers smiled on the Huguenots, who raised no eyebrows at the taking of interest, upon which the Church had immemorially frowned, though lately winking a solemn theological eye.

Many nobles were taking up the rebel cause. They too were unreconciled to the centralization of power in a unified state. They must have heard of territorial German princes who, in league with Protestantism, had been able to defy emperors and popes, and had enriched themselves with the spoils of the Church. What if these doughty Huguenots could serve as a timely tool for chastening and subordinating the king? The nobles controlled the fields, the crops, and the peasantry of France, they organized and led her regiments, they held her fortresses, they governed her provinces. If the Reform won the aristocracy it would have a nation-wide power at its back. Already in 1553 the Cardinal of Lorraine had warned Henry II that the nobility were defecting to the Huguenots. In Normandy, Brittany, Poitou, Anjou, Maine, Saintonge, by 1559, nobles were openly leading the Huguenot revolt.

Proud Bourbon families had not forgiven the ruling Valois dynasty for driving Charles, Duke of Bourbon, to treason and an early death (1527); nor did they relish their exclusion from the French government by the clannish Guises, whom they looked upon as foreigners from a Lorraine that was far more German than French. Louis I de Bourbon, Prince of Condé, descended from King Louis IX, was of royal blood, far superior in rank to the Guises; he joined the Huguenots, and died in the attempt to rise to power on the wave of their faith. His brother, Antoine de Bourbon, titular King of Navarre—but actually ruling only the province of Béarn, in southwest France—played on the Huguenot side for a while, largely under the influence of his wife, Jeanne d'Albret. Jeanne was the aggressive daughter of the gentle Marguerite of Navarre, who had remained out-wardly orthodox in deference to her brother, Francis I, but had protected many a heretic and Huguenot. As the mother had represented the Renais-sance in love of life and poetry, so Jeanne exemplified the role and the character of women in the French Reformation—fervent in their religion to the point of intolerance, rearing and dedicating their children to carry on the holy war to death or victory. She brought up her famous son, the future Henri Quatre, to every Spartan and Puritan virtue, and did not live to see him revert to the lax gaiety of the Renaissance. She must have ad-mired intensely Gaspard de Coligny, for he was all that she idealized: a nobleman in title and character, a prudent but loyal leader of the Huguenot cause, a stern soldier-statesman whose blameless morals shamed the gilded infidelities of the court.

Calvin had cautioned his Huguenot followers against violent resistance to the government,[11] but their patience withered in the heat of persecution. Henry II had ordered all judges to issue the death penalty against per-sistent Protestants (June 1559). Francis II, urged on by the Guises, re-newed this edict, and added that all buildings in which Reformed assemblies met should be demolished; that all persons, even relatives, who sheltered a condemned heretic, or failed to report him to the magistrates, should also suffer death. In the last five months of 1559 eighteen persons were burned alive for unrepentant heresy, or for refusing to attend Mass or receive Catholic Communion. Hundreds of French Huguenots fled to Geneva, where Calvin succored them. Those who remained in France began to organize themselves for civil war.

On December 23, 1559, Anne du Bourg, who had dared in the Parlement of Paris to condemn persecution for heresy, was burned at the stake. Soon thereafter Gaspard de Heu was strangled in the Château de Vincennes by order of the Guises. His brother-in-law, Godefroi de Barri, Seigneur de La Renaudie, conspired with nobles and others to capture and depose the Guises in a *coup de main* to be effected at Amboise. The Cardinal of Lor-raine discovered the plot, mobilized troops, overcame and arrested the con-spirators, hanged some, beheaded some, flung others into the Loire in sacks. "For a whole month," said a contemporary chronicle, "there was nothing but hanging or drowning folks. The Loire was covered with corpses" (March 1560).[12] Condé was summoned to the royal court to answer charges of complicity; he came, denied them, and challenged any accuser to trial by combat. No evidence was adduced against him, and he was left free.

Disturbed by this "Tumult of Amboise," the high rank of the conspirators, the ferocity of the suppression, and the fever of revenge that agitated Huguenots and nobles, Catherine persuaded the weakling King and the reluctant Guises to allow a trial of toleration. She called Michel de L'Hôpital to the post of chancellor (May 1560) and bade him pacify France. As a student in Italy Michel had learned to be a humanist rather than a dogmatist; as a magistrate in France he had treated Catholics and Protestants with equal mercy and consideration. Now he proposed to the Parlement the views which had led Du Bourg to the stake: "Every man hath made a religion for himself. Some . . . desire that *their* religion should be accepted, and the faith of the rest hunted down. . . . We must try to deal gently with one another, to invent a *modus vivendi*."[13] Following his lead, Catherine summoned an Assembly of Notables, consisting of both Catholics and Protestants, which met at Fontainebleau on August 21, 1560. Coligny there presented to the King a petition from the Huguenots, affirming their loyalty but asking for full freedom of worship. Some bishops called for moderation on both sides and urged the clergy to reform their morals. The Assembly decided that the problems involved required a convocation of delegates from all sections and classes of France. The King ordered such a States-General to meet on December 10, and meanwhile forbade any trials for heresy till the new gathering could pass upon the basic issues that were dividing the country.

The Huguenot Bourbons, fearing arrest, had refused to attend the Assembly of Notables. Skeptical of conciliation, the Prince of Condé and Antoine de Bourbon plotted to raise an army and set up an independent state with Lyon as its capital. One of Condé's couriers was intercepted by the government; papers found on him revealed the conspiracy; Condé was arrested, tried, and condemned to be executed on December 10. The Guises resumed dictatorial power.

Suddenly the situation was changed by the death of Francis II (December 5), aged sixteen. His brother, Charles IX, succeeded to his formal power, but, being only ten years old, he accepted the regency of his mother, who now joined Elizabeth of England and Philip II of Spain in guiding the chaos of Europe to their rival ends.

II. CATHERINE DE MÉDICIS

She is still a puzzle, after four centuries of conflicting interpretations. Descended from Lorenzo the Magnificent, grandniece of Pope Leo X, she was a typical Medici, with government in her heritage and subtlety in her blood. Born in Florence (1519) of parents who both died of syphilis before she was a month old, she remained a helpless and movable pawn in the diplomacy of her embattled relatives until her uncle, Pope Clement VII, gave her, aged fourteen, in marriage to the future Henry II of France. For ten years she remained barren while her somber mate devoted himself to Diane de Poitiers. Then children emerged from her almost annually, ten in all. She hoped and schemed to get them thrones. Three of them died in childhood; three became kings of France; two became queens. Nearly all of them tasted tragedy, but herself most of all, who lived through the deaths of her husband and three successive royal sons. Queen or Queen Mother, she bore the vicissitudes of four reigns, and survived them by prudence, self-control, and unscrupulous duplicity.

A contemporary described her as "a beautiful woman when her face is veiled"[14]—that is, she had a fine figure; and Brantôme assures us that her bosom was "white and full," her "thigh very beautiful," and her hands and fingers exquisite.[15] But her features were rugged, her eyes too big, her lips too thick, her mouth too large. If she seduced men it was by proxy. Rumor accused her of keeping about her an *escadron volant*, or flying squadron, of pretty women who might bring men around to her purposes;[16] but this was apparently a fiction.[17] Wounded by Diane's dominance in policy as in love, she found revenge, after Henry's death, by making herself for thirty years the power behind the throne. Her finesse had to atone for the incompetence of her sons; they resented her interference, but their failure as kings compelled it. Cast into the maelstrom of a religious revolution, surrounded by aggressive nobles and intolerant dogmatisms, she fought with the only weapons she had—Medicean money, Italian acumen, Machiavellian diplomacy. Machiavelli had dedicated *The Prince* to her father; Catherine hardly needed its instruction, for she had seen its principles practiced everywhere in Italy and France. Like Elizabeth of England, she outplayed all the statesmen around her, beat them at lying, "had more wiles than all the Council of the King."[18] She worked hard and ably at administration. "Nothing is done without her knowing it," said an Italian observer; "scarcely has she time to eat"[19]—though somehow she achieved obesity. Her personal morals were above her time. She seems to have been faithful to her unfaithful husband and to his memory; after his death she wore mourning to the end of her life. Her greatest successor, Henry IV, judged her leniently:

> I ask you, what could a woman do, left by the death of her husband with five little children on her arms, and two families in France who were thinking of grasping the crown—ours [the Bourbons] and

the Guises? Was she not compelled to play strange parts to deceive
first one and then the other, in order to guard, as she did, her sons,
who successively reigned through the wise conduct of that shrewd
woman? I am surprised that she never did worse.[20]

We may accept this as a fair appraisal of Catherine's behavior before
1570. Surrounded by these rival families and forces, she played them off
against each other. "God willing," she wrote, "I shall not let myself be
governed either by one party or the other, having learned only too well
that they all love God, the King, and myself less than their profit . . . and
the satisfaction of their ambition."[21] She was too much of a Renaissance
Italian to savor the predestinarian severity of the Huguenots; besides, she
was asking the Church for a loan to stave off state bankruptcy;[22] nevertheless she was ready, for France's sake, to marry her daughter Marguerite to
the Huguenot Henry of Navarre, and her son Henry to the excommunicated Elizabeth. She saw the situation in dynastic and political rather than
in religious or economic terms. She had to protect her divided country
against the Hapsburg union of Spain and Austria. The Treaty of Cateau-
Cambrésis had left the Spanish power supreme in Flanders and encroaching dangerously upon northeastern France. At any moment the old war of
Valois and Hapsburg might flame again, and then France would need
Huguenot as well as Catholic blood and arms. External danger demanded
internal peace.

In this frame of mind she and her Chancellor L'Hôpital prepared to
meet the States-General at Orléans. The "states" were not regions but
classes: the nobility, the clergy, and, as the *tiers état*, the remainder of
France—principally the bourgeoisie or middle classes of the towns or
boroughs (*bourgs*), but also, in some modest representation, the peasantry
and the incipient proletariat. Chosen by local and class powers rather than
by any wide suffrage, the delegates had in theory no legislative authority,
but only the right to advise the monarch; however, his need for funds gave
the advice some force.

L'Hôpital opened the session (December 13, 1560) with an idealistic
appeal for mutual toleration. It was the function of government, he urged,
to maintain peace, order, and justice among all citizens impartially, without regard to their religious opinions. It was desirable that all Frenchmen
should have the same religion, for this would favor national unity and
strength; but if such a general agreement could not be peacefully reached,
toleration became advisable. Who, after all, he asked, knows what is heresy
and what is truth? "You say your religion is the better; I say mine is;
is it any more reasonable that I should adopt your opinion than that you
should adopt mine? . . . Let us end these diabolical names, these partisan

tags and factions and seditions—Lutherans, Huguenots, Catholics; let us change our name to Christians!"[23]

The response was not cordial. A doctor of the Sorbonne—then the faculty of theology in the University of Paris—demanded the death penalty for all heretics, and the papal nuncio advised Catherine to begin by burning all the Huguenot delegates, then all the Huguenots in Orléans.[24] The Huguenot delegates proposed to the Queen Mother a variety of reforms: that all pastors should be chosen by their congregations; that bishops should be chosen by the pastors and the nobles of the diocese; that a third of ecclesiastical revenues should go to relief of the poor, and another third to the building of churches, hospitals, and schools; and that the doctrine of the Church should be limited to Scripture.[25] This was a bit too advanced for Catherine, who needed Church money desperately. She appeased the Huguenots by freeing the imprisoned Condé and urging Pius IV to allow the removal of religious images from churches, and the administration of the Sacrament in wine as well as bread.[26] On January 28, 1561, she released all persons arrested for religious "offenses," and ordered an end, till further notice, of all prosecutions for religion. On the thirty-first she prorogued the States-General to reassemble in May and meet her needs for funds.

The Huguenots expanded in this sunshine. On March 2 they held at Poitiers their second national synod. Protestant ministers preached freely in the apartments of Condé and Coligny at the court at Fontainebleau. At Castres in south France a municipal election (January 1, 1561) gave all offices to Protestants; soon thereafter all citizens were ordered to attend Protestant services;[27] Catholic services were forbidden; religious images were officially condemned to be destroyed.[28] At Agen and Montauban the Huguenots took over unused Catholic churches. The old Constable Anne de Montmorency formed with the Duke of Guise and Marshal de Saint-André a "triumvirate" to protect the Catholic interest (April 6, 1561). Riots flared up at Paris, Rouen, Beauvais, and elsewhere. The Queen issued an "Edict of July" (1561) forbidding violence and public Huguenot services. The Huguenots ignored the edict; in various towns they attacked Catholic processions, entered Catholic churches, burned relics, and smashed images.[29] At Montpellier, in the autumn of 1561, all the sixty churches and convents were sacked, and many priests were killed; at Montauban the Convent of the Poor Claires was burned down, and the nuns were dispersed with the advice to get themselves husbands.[30] At Carcassonne the Catholics slaughtered all available Protestants.[31] At Nîmes the Huguenots expelled all priests, appropriated or destroyed all Catholic churches, burned down the cathedral, and trampled the consecrated Host underfoot (February 1562).[32] Generally, in Languedoc and Guienne, the Huguenots, when they gained the upper hand, seized Catholic churches and property and expelled the Catholic clergy.[33] Huguenot ministers, though more exemplary in their personal morals than the Catholic priests, quite equaled them in intolerance;[34] they excommunicated Huguenots who were married by Catholic priests or who allowed their children to marry Catholics.[35] Neither side saw any sense in toleration.

The States-General resumed its sittings on August 1, 1561, this time at Pontoise. It offered funds to the government on condition that its consent should thereafter be prerequisite to any levy of new taxes or any declaration of war. The Third Estate, now chief provider of funds, added a bold request—that the entire property of the Catholic Church in France should be nationalized, that the clergy should be paid by the state, and that out of the surplus of 72,000,000 livres thus obtained 42,000,000 should go to the liquidation of the public debt. The Catholic clergy, frightened, made a hurried peace with Catherine by offering her 16,600,000 livres, to be paid cautiously in ten annual installments. She accepted, and the States-General was dissolved.

Meanwhile L'Hôpital, with Catherine's consent and over the protest of the Pope, had invited Catholic and Protestant clergymen to meet and seek some formula for pacification. Six cardinals, forty bishops, twelve doctors of the Sorbonne, twelve canonists, ten Protestant ministers from France, one from England, Théodore de Bèze from Geneva, and twenty Protestant laymen met at Poissy, eleven miles west of Paris, for the famous "Colloquy of Poissy" (September 9, 1561). The King, the Queen Mother, the princes of the blood, and the Council of State attended in all their dignity. Bèze, representing the aged Calvin, was received with almost royal honors; he held a Reformed service and preached in Catherine's palace. He spoke at first moderately and charmed all with his perfect French; but when he remarked that in the Eucharist "the body of Christ is as far removed from the consecrated bread as heaven is from earth," the Catholic delegates cried out in protest, and turmoil ensued. The bishops urged the banishment of all preachers who questioned the Real Presence,[36] and the colloquy broke up with the conflict of dogmas embittered and unappeased.

It was the merry wont of the Huguenots to hold their meetings in a public square confronting a Catholic church, and to disturb the Mass with lusty psalms; the Catholics in turn drowned out the psalmody by ringing the steeple bell. At Paris a Protestant assemblage before the Church of St.-Médard was nullified by a mighty clangor from the campanile; a Protestant who entered the church to protest was killed; in fury the Protestants sacked the building and smashed the statues and the crucifix. In the resultant battle eighty worshipers were wounded (December 27, 1561).

Catherine thought to mollify the Catholics by her "Edict of January" (1562), which required the Huguenots to surrender all ecclesiastical buildings to their former owners and to hold their assemblies only outside the town walls. The Catholic leaders agreed with Bèze that this was in effect an edict of toleration, which recognized Protestantism as a legal religion in France; Parlement leaders told Catherine to her face that they would die rather than register the edict. When Montmorency and Saint-André condemned her policy, Catherine dismissed them from the court; and when Cardinal de Tournon fulminated against her she retired him to his diocese. Catholic preachers denounced her as a Jezebel—the same term that Protestant Knox was then applying to the Catholic Queen of Scots.

On Sunday, March 1, 1562, Francis, Duke of Guise, passing with a band of two hundred armed retainers through the village of Vassy, some forty miles northwest of Dijon, stopped in a church there to hear Mass. The psalm singing of Huguenots meeting in a nearby barn disturbed the service. He sent a messenger to ask them to defer their songs for fifteen minutes, till the Mass should be finished. They found this too inconvenient. While Guise continued his worship some of his retainers exchanged sectarian compliments with the Huguenots; the retainers drew their swords, the Huguenots threw stones; one stone struck Guise as he left the church, and drew ducal blood; his followers dashed into the assemblage of five hundred men, women and children, killed twenty-three, and wounded a hundred.[37] The "Massacre of Vassy" roused the Protestants of France to martial fever; the Catholics, especially in Paris, hailed it as a timely chastening of a troublesome minority. Catherine ordered Guise to come to her at Fontainebleau; he refused and went on to Paris; Montmorency and Saint-André joined him on the way with two thousand men. Condé ordered his Protestant levies to assemble in arms at Meaux. The Catholic triumvirate marched in force to Fontainebleau, captured the Queen Mother and the royal family, and compelled them to stay at Melun, twenty-seven miles from Paris; they formed a new Privy Council, chiefly of Guise's men and excluding L'Hôpital. Condé led his 1,600 warriors to Orléans and called upon all Reformed congregations to send him troops. The first of the "Religious Wars" began (April 1562).

III. ARBITRAMENT OF BLOOD: 1562–70

Both sides sought and received foreign aid, the Catholics from Spain, the Protestants from England and Germany. Elizabeth, bribed by the promise of Calais, sent 6,000 men; 2,000 of these took Rouen, but Guise captured and sacked the city (October 26, 1562), and his spoils-hungry soldiers pillaged and slaughtered Catholic and Protestant inhabitants impartially. In these actions Antoine de Bourbon, who had joined the Catholic faith and forces, was mortally wounded. The Huguenots took control of most towns in south France, sacking churches and smashing images religiously. Their main body of 17,000 men, under Condé and Coligny, marched toward Normandy to unite with the English reinforcements. At Dreux they were intercepted by a Catholic army of 17,000 under the triumvirs; on December 19 a furious battle was fought, which left 6,000 dead on the field; Saint-André was killed, Montmorency was wounded and captured by the Huguenots, Condé was wounded and captured by the Catholics. For a time French courtesy prevailed: Montmorency was treated as a hero, who, though commander in chief of the King's armies, had always fought in the ranks and had been wounded in seven battles; and the Duke of Guise used Condé as an honored guest, dined with him, and shared with him the only bed available in the camp.[38] The indecisive victory went to the Catholics, but Paris and the royal family for a time believed that the Huguenots had won. Catherine took the news calmly, saying, "Very well, then, we shall pray to God in French."[39]

Guise himself met death in the aftermath of victory. While deploying his army to besiege Orléans he was shot in ambush by Jean Poltrot de Méré (February 18, 1563), a nineteen-year-old Huguenot. The Duke died after six days of pain. Poltrot, brought before Catherine, asserted that Coligny had hired him, for a large sum, to murder Guise, and that Bèze had promised him Paradise if he succeeded. Catherine wrote to Coligny asking for his answer to the charge. He denied any part in the assassination plan; he had often warned the Duke to beware of assassins; he admitted that he had heard Poltrot declare his intention, and had done nothing to deter him; he had given Poltrot one hundred crowns, but for other purposes; however, he was not sorry that the plot had succeeded, "for . . . fortune can deal no better stroke for the good of the Kingdom and the Church of God, and most especially it is good for myself and my house."[40] Poltrot was torn apart by horses on March 18; in his dying agony he renewed his accusation of Coligny.[41] Henry, now third Duke of Guise, swore to avenge his father's death.

Catherine continued to work for peace; it was quite clear that either faction, if decisively victorious, would set her aside and possibly depose her son. She called L'Hôpital back to her Council, arranged a meeting of Montmorency and Condé, and persuaded them to sign the Edict of Amboise, ending the First Religious War (March 19, 1563). The terms were a victory for the Huguenot nobles only: liberty of conscience and practice of the religion "called reformed" were granted "for all barons and lords high justiciary in their houses, with their families and dependents," and "for nobles having fiefs without vassals and living on the King's lands, but for them and their families personally." The Huguenot worship was to be allowed in towns where it had been practiced before March 8, 1563; otherwise it was to be confined to the outskirts of a single town in any seneschalty or bailiwick; in Paris it was altogether forbidden. Coligny charged Condé with having sacrificed the Huguenot rank and file to protect his class.

On September 15 Charles IX, who was not yet fourteen, was declared of age; Catherine surrendered her regency, but not her leadership. In March 1564 she led the King and the court on a progress through France, partly to show the nation its new monarch, partly to consolidate the fragile peace. At Roussillon she issued an edict of partial toleration, calling upon each faith to respect the liberty of the other. After fourteen months of royal touring, the party reached Bayonne (June 3, 1565), where Catherine greeted with joy her daughter Elizabeth, now Queen of Spain, and conferred with the Duke of Alva in secret parleys that alarmed the Huguenots. They rightly suspected that Alva counseled full forcible measures against them, but his extant letters to Philip make it clear that Catherine rejected his proposals, refused to dismiss L'Hôpital, and still clung to her policy of peace.[42] Soon after her return to Paris (December 1565) she used all her influence to reconcile Coligny, Montmorency, Condé, and the Guises.

In 1564 the Jesuits entered France; their sermons roused the ardor of the Catholics, and in Paris especially they converted a number of Huguenots. In the provinces a strong Catholic reaction nullified many Protestant gains. The edicts of toleration were repeatedly violated, and barbarity flourished under both dispensations. It was not unusual for Catholic magistrates to hang citizens merely for being Huguenots.[43] At Nîmes the Protestants massacred eighty Catholics (1567).[44] Between 1561 and 1572 there were eighteen massacres of Protestants, five of Catholics; and there were over thirty assassinations.[45] Catherine imported mercenaries from Switzerland and gave no satisfactory answer when Condé asked for what use she intended them. Believing that their own lives were in danger, Condé and Coligny, with armed followers, tried to seize the King and the Queen Mother at Meaux (September 1567), but Montmorency foiled the attempt. Catherine now feared Coligny as once she had feared Guise.

Coligny and Condé felt that a second war was needed to restore even the limited rights of the Huguenots. They in their turn imported mercenaries, chiefly from Germany, to reinforce their depleted armies; they captured Orléans and La Rochelle and marched on Paris. Catherine asked Alva for reinforcements; he sent them at once, and at St.-Denis, just outside the capital, Montmorency led sixteen thousand men against Condé's troops in one of the bloodiest and least decisive battles of these wars. Montmorency died of his wounds. France again wondered what religion was this that led men to such slaughter; and L'Hôpital seized the opportunity to arrange the Peace of Longjumeau (March 23, 1568), which restored the modest toleration granted in the Edict of Amboise.

The Catholics denounced the treaty and refused to carry out its terms. Coligny protested to Catherine; she pleaded impotence. In May 1568 the Spanish ambassador at Rome, Juan de Zuñiga, reported that he had heard from Pope Pius V that the French government was considering the assassination of Coligny and Condé.[46] The two Huguenot leaders may have had similar information. They fled to La Rochelle, where they were joined by Jeanne d'Albret and her son, now fifteen years old and itching for action. A new Huguenot army was formed, a fleet was collected, the walls were fortified, and all attempts of government forces to enter the city were repulsed. English private vessels accepted Condé's commission, flew his flag, and made a prey of any Catholic property they could seize.[47] Condé was now virtually sovereign south of the Loire.

Catherine looked upon this Third Religious War as a revolution, as an attempt to divide France into two nations, one Catholic, the other Protestant. She reproached L'Hôpital for the failure of his conciliation policies; he resigned; she replaced him as chancellor with an uncompromising partisan of the Guises. On September 28, 1568, the government repealed the edicts of toleration and outlawed the Reformed faith from France.

All that winter the rival forces prepared for a decisive engagement. On March 3, 1569, they met at Jarnac, near Angoulême. The Huguenots were defeated; Condé, exhausted with wounds, surrendered, but was shot from the rear and died. Coligny took command and reorganized the troops for an orderly retreat. At Moncontour the Huguenots were again defeated, but Coligny recovered by strategy what had been lost in battle; and without victories, almost without food, the undiscourageable Huguenots advanced to within a few hours' march of Paris (1570). Despite subsidies from Rome and Spain, the government found it difficult both to finance its armies and to keep the Catholic nobles in the field for more than a month or two at a time. Meanwhile hordes of mercenaries devastated the country, pillaging Catholics and Protestants indiscriminately, and killing all who dared resist.

Catherine offered Coligny a renewal of the Treaty of Longjumeau; he refused it as inadequate and continued his advance. At this point the youthful Charles IX suddenly asserted his authority and signed at St.-Germain (August 8, 1570) a peace that gave the oft-defeated Huguenots more than they had ever gained before: freedom of worship except in Paris or near the court, full eligibility to public office, and, as a guarantee that these terms would be honored in practice, the right to hold four cities under their independent rule for two years. The Catholics fumed and wondered why such a surrender followed so many victories. Philip and the Pope protested.

Catherine turned them off with the assurance that she was only biding her time.*

Nevertheless she proceeded to strengthen the new peace by offering to marry her daughter Marguerite of Valois to Henry, King of Navarre, now, since Condé's death, the titular head of the Huguenots. It was Catherine's last and boldest stroke. No matter that she and Jeanne d'Albret were sworn foes; no matter that Henry had already slain his quota of Catholics in war. He was young and malleable; perhaps the magic of a beautiful and vivacious princess would woo him from his heresies. There would be a magnificent wedding feast at Paris; men and women of either faith would be invited. The gay Renaissance would revive amid the bitter Reformation; there would be a moratorium on theology and war and massacre.

IV. MASSACRE

But would Henry's mother consent? Jeanne d'Albret was Huguenot in body and soul. Coming to the court in 1561, she declared that "she would not go to Mass if they killed her; she would sooner throw her son and her kingdom into the sea than yield";[48] on the contrary, she had her Huguenot chaplain preach to her with all doors open, and defiantly ignored the recriminations of the Parisian populace. When her husband was converted to Catholicism she left him and the court (1562), returned to Béarn, and raised money and troops for Condé. After her husband's death she made Protestantism compulsory in Béarn (which included the cities of Pau, Nérac, Tarbes, Orthez, and Lourdes); Catholic clergymen were dispossessed and were replaced by Huguenot ministers;[49] for fifty years thereafter no Mass was heard in Béarn.[50] Pope Pius IV excommunicated her and wished to depose her, but Catherine dissuaded him.[51] When Jeanne accepted the offer to bind Valois and Bourbon in marriage she may have remembered this, and Catherine's long struggle for peace. Besides, Catherine's sons were sickly; might they not all die and leave the throne of France to Henry of Navarre? Had not the soothsayer Nostradamus prophesied that the Valois dynasty would soon end?

The sickliest of the sons, Charles IX, might have been a lovable youth except for occasional fits of cruelty and temper that blazed out at times into a passion verging on insanity. Between such storms he was a reed in the wind, seldom having a mind of his own. Perhaps he weakened himself by sensual indulgence. He was married to Elizabeth, daughter of the Emperor

---

* The view that for two years past she had considered the feasibility of removing the Huguenot leaders by murder is ably defended by the Catholic historian Lord Acton in *The History of Freedom* (London, 1907), pp. 101–49.

Maximilian II; but his illicit and lasting love was for his Huguenot mistress, Marie Touchet. He was sensitive to art, poetry, and music; he loved to recite Ronsard's lyrics, and he wrote in Ronsard's honor verses as pretty as Ronsard's own:

> Tous deux également nous portons des couronnes,
> Mais roi je la reçus; poète, tu la donnes;
> Ta lyre, qui ravit par de si doux accords,
> Te soumet les esprits, dont je n'ai que les corps;
> Elle amollit les coeurs, et soumet la beauté;
> Je puis donner la mort, toi l'immortalité.*

When Coligny joined the court at Blois (September 1571), Charles took to him as weakness welcomes strength. Here was a man all the world away from so many who had been pirouetting around the throne: a gentleman, an aristocrat, but quiet and sober, carrying half of France in the power of his word. The young King called the aging commander *"mon père,"* appointed him commander of the fleet, gave him from the royal purse a grant of 100,000 livres to reimburse him for his losses during the wars. Coligny joined the Council and presided over it in the absence of the King.[52] Charles had always been jealous and fearful of Philip II; he resented the dependence of Catholic France upon Spain. Coligny proposed to him that a war with Spain would give France a unifying cause, and would rectify that northeastern boundary upon which Spain was encroaching. Now was the time, for William of Orange was leading a revolt of the Netherlands against their Spanish overlord; one good push, and Flanders would be French. Charles listened sympathetically. On April 27 he wrote to Count Louis of Nassau, who was leading the Protestant rebellion in Hainaut, that "he was determined . . . to employ the powers which God had put into his hands for the deliverance of the Low Countries from the oppression under which they were groaning."[53] Louis and his brother William of Orange offered to surrender Flanders and Artois to France in return for decisive aid against Spain.[54] In the fall of that year Charles negotiated with the Elector Augustus of Saxony for a defensive alliance of France and Protestant Germany.[55]

Catherine condemned Coligny's proposals as fantastically impracticable. Now that she had the peace that France so needed, it would be folly to unleash the hounds of war so soon again. Spain was as bankrupt as France,

---

* We both wear diadems; but I my crown
  Received as king, you, poet, made your own;
  Your lyre, which charms with concourse of sweet sounds,
  Subdues the soul, while flesh my empire bounds.
  It softens hearts, holds loveliness in fee.
  I can give death; you, immortality.

but she was still the strongest power in Christendom; she had just covered herself with glory in the defeat of the Turks at Lepanto; she would have all Catholic Europe—and most of Catholic France—to support her if France entered a Protestant league. In such a war Coligny would be commander in chief, and, through his influence on the impressionable Charles, he would in effect be king; Catherine would be relegated to Chenonceau, if not to Italy. Henry of Guise and Henry of Anjou—brother of the King —learned with dismay that Charles was allowing Coligny to send Huguenot troops to join Louis of Nassau; Alva, forewarned by his friends at the French court, overwhelmed this force (July 10, 1572). A full meeting of the King's Council heard Coligny defend his proposals for war with Spain (August 6–9, 1572); they were unanimously rejected; Coligny persisted. "I have promised on my own account," he said, "my assistance to the Prince of Orange; I hope the King will not take it ill if, by means of my friends, and perhaps in person, I fulfill my promise." He said to the Queen Mother, "Madame, the King is today shunning a war which would promise him great advantages; God forbid that there should break out another which he cannot shun."[56] The Council broke up in excited resentment of what seemed a threat of another civil war. "Let the Queen beware," warned Marshal de Tavannes, "of the King her son's secret counsels, designs, and sayings; if she do not look out the Huguenots will have him."[57] Catherine took Charles aside and reproached him for having surrendered his mind to Coligny; if he persisted in the plan for war against Spain she would ask his leave to withdraw with her other son to Florence. He asked her forgiveness and promised filial obedience, but he remained Coligny's devoted friend.

It was in this atmosphere that Jeanne d'Albret came to Blois to prepare for the marriage that was to unite Catholic and Protestant France. She insisted that Cardinal de Bourbon should perform the ceremony not as a priest but as a prince, not in a church but outside it, and that Henry should not accompany his wife into the church to hear Mass. Catherine agreed, though this would raise more trouble with the Pope, who had refused dispensation for Marguerite to marry the Protestant son of an excommunicated Protestant. Then Jeanne went on to Paris to shop, fell sick of pleurisy, and died (June 9, 1572). The Huguenots suspected that she had been poisoned, but this hypothesis is no longer entertained.[58] Despite his own suspicions and grief, Henry of Navarre came from Blois to Paris in August, accompanied by Coligny and eight hundred Huguenots. Four thousand armed Huguenots followed them into the capital,[59] partly to see the festivities, partly to protect their young King. Catholic Paris, aroused by this influx and a hundred inflammatory sermons,[60] denounced the marriage as a surrender of the government to Protestant force. Nevertheless the ceremony took place (August 18), without papal dispensation; Catherine took measures to prevent the post from bringing a papal prohibition. Henry led his wife to the portals of Notre Dame, but did not enter with her; Paris was not yet worth a Mass. Provisionally he lodged with Marguerite in the Louvre.

Seldom had Paris seethed with such excitement. Coligny, still pressing for open aid by France to the revolting Netherlands, was believed ready to leave for the front. Some Catholics warned Catherine that Huguenots were planning another attempt to kidnap her and the King.[61] The hammering of anvils throughout the city revealed the hurried forging of weapons. At this juncture, according to her son Henry, Catherine gave her consent to the murder of the Admiral.[62]

On August 22, as Coligny was walking from the Louvre to his house, two shots from a window cut off the first finger of his left hand and ripped his arm to the elbow. His companions rushed into the building, but found only a smoking arquebus; the assailant had escaped by the rear. Coligny was carried to his rooms. The King, informed, cried out angrily, "Am I never to have any peace?" He sent his personal physician, the Huguenot Ambroise Paré, to treat the wounds, assigned royal guards to Coligny's house, commanded the Catholics to leave the adjoining premises, and allowed Huguenots to move in.[63] The Queen, the King, and his brother Henry came to comfort the wounded man, and Charles swore the "most terrible oath" to revenge the attack. Coligny again urged Charles to enter the war for the acquisition of Flanders.[64] Taking him aside, he whispered some secret. As the royal family returned to the Louvre, Catherine insisted that the King reveal the secret. "Very well, then, by the death of God," he answered, "since you *will* know, this is what the Admiral said to me: that all power has gone to pieces in your hands, and that evil for me would come of it." In a state of frenzy the King shut himself up in his private apartment. Catherine brooded in fearful resentment.[65]

Henry of Navarre came to Coligny and discussed measures of defense. Some members of the Admiral's retinue wished to go at once and assassinate the Guise leaders; he forbade them. "If ample justice be not done," said the Huguenots, "they would certainly do it themselves."[66] All that day Huguenots moved about the Louvre; one of them told the Queen that if justice were not soon executed they would take the law into their own hands.[67] Bands of armed Huguenots passed repeatedly by the Hôtel de Lorraine, where the Guises were staying, and shouted threats of death.[68] The Guises appealed to the King for protection and barricaded themselves in their house. Charles, suspecting them of having hired the assassin, arrested several of their servants and menaced the Duke of Guise. Henry and his brother the Duke of Aumale asked permission to leave Paris; it was granted;

they went as far as the Porte St.-Antoine; then they turned back and secretly made their way to the Hôtel de Lorraine.

On August 23 the Council met to inquire into the crime. They learned that the house from which the shots had been fired was owned (though not occupied) by the Dowager Duchess of Guise, who had vowed to avenge the murder of her husband, Francis; that the assassin had escaped on a horse taken from the stables of the Guises; that the weapon had belonged to one of the Duke of Anjou's guardsmen. The assassin was never apprehended. According to Anjou's later account, he and Henry of Guise now decided that Coligny and some other Huguenots must be killed. While Catherine and some members of the Council were assembled in the Tuileries, Anjou's agent Bouchavannes rushed in with the announcement that the Huguenots in Coligny's lodgings were planning violent revolt, probably for the next evening.[69] To Catherine's dislike of the Admiral, her anger at what seemed to her his seduction of the King from her guidance, her conviction that the policy of war with Spain would be disastrous for France and her dynasty, there was now added the fear that her life was in immediate danger, and that all power might soon pass into the hands of Coligny and his friends. She agreed that the leading Huguenots should be killed.[70]

But the consent of the King was desirable, if not necessary; and he was still demanding the prosecution of all concerned in the attack upon Coligny. About ten o'clock in this evening of August 23 the Queen Mother sent Count de Retz to warn Charles of the supposed insurrection. Soon Catherine and her councilors surrounded the young ruler, whose excitement now brought him close to insanity. Catherine assured him that thirty thousand Huguenots were planning to seize him on the morrow and carry him off to some Protestant stronghold, where he would be captive and impotent; had they not twice before attempted such a stroke? If victorious, they would kill her on suspicion of having ordered or allowed the attack upon the Admiral. The boy of twenty-three was told to choose between his mother's life and the lives of six Huguenots. If he refused consent, and Catholic Paris should overcome the revolt, he would be set aside as a coward and a fool. He resisted these arguments; he asked why it would not suffice to arrest the Huguenot leaders and try them legally; the councilors answered that it was too late to avert revolt by such action. Catherine threatened to withdraw to Italy and leave him to his fate. Finally, toward midnight, in a fit of nervous breakdown and rage, Charles shouted, "By the death of God, since you choose to kill the Admiral, I consent! But then you must kill all the Huguenots in France, so that not one shall be left to reproach me. . . . Kill them all! Kill them all!" Uttering blasphemies, he fled from his councilors and shut himself up in his room.

If the conspirators had plotted to kill only a few, they now took advantage of the King's mad order to make the slaughter of the Huguenots as thorough as possible. Catherine insisted on protecting Henry of Navarre; the young Prince of Condé—Henry I—and the Montmorencys were excepted as too noble for slaughter; the surgeon Ambroise Paré was saved by the King; but word was sent out to the district captains of Paris to arm their men and be ready for action at the tolling of church bells at three o'clock in the morning, August 24, St. Bartholomew's Day. Carte blanche was given the Guises to execute their long-delayed revenge upon the Admiral. Henry of Guise sent word to the officers of the militia that at the tocsin's sound their men were to slay every Huguenot they could find. The gates of the city were to be closed to prevent escapes.

While it was yet night Guise himself led three hundred soldiers to the building where Coligny lay asleep. Near him were Paré his physician, Merlin his secretary, Nicolas his servant. They were awakened by the clatter of soldiers approaching; they heard shots and cries—Coligny's guards were being killed. A friend burst into the room crying, "We are lost!" The Admiral replied, "I have long been prepared for death. Save yourselves. I do not wish those who hold you dear to be able to reproach me with your death. I commend my soul to the mercy of God." They fled. Guise's soldiers broke in the door. They found Coligny kneeling in prayer. A soldier ran him through and slashed his face; others stabbed him; still alive, he was tossed through the window to fall upon the pavement below at Guise's feet. After making sure that Coligny was dead, the Duke ordered his men to scatter through Paris and spread the word, *"Tuez! Tuez!—* Kill! Kill! The King commands it." The head of the Admiral was severed from his body and sent to the Louvre—some said to Rome;[71] the body was given up to the multitude, which mangled it ferociously, cut off the hands and the genitals to offer them for sale, and strung up the rest by the heels.[72]

Meanwhile the Queen, feeling some remorse or fear, sent orders to the Guises to halt the massacre; they answered that it was too late; Coligny being dead, the Huguenots must be killed or they would surely revolt. Catherine yielded and ordered the tocsin to be rung. There followed such slaughter as cities have seldom known even in the frenzy of war. The populace rejoiced at the freedom given to its suppressed impulses to strike, to inflict pain, and to kill. It hunted out and slew from two to five thousand Huguenots and others; murders previously meditated could now be perpetrated with impunity; harassed or ambitious wives or husbands took the opportunity to rid themselves of unwanted mates; merchants were slain by competitors; relatives too slow to die were pointed out as Huguenots by prospective heirs.[73] Ramus the philosopher was killed at the urging of a jealous professor. Every house suspected of harboring Huguenots was invaded and searched; Huguenots and their children were dragged into the streets and slain; embryos were torn from dead mothers and smashed.[74] Soon corpses littered the pavement; urchins played games on them. The Catholic Swiss guards of the King entered the fray and slew indiscriminately out of pure joy of slaughter. The Duke de La Rochefoucauld, who had played tennis with the King the day before, was killed by masked men who, he supposed, had come to invite him to some royal frolic. Huguenot nobles and officers who had been lodged in the Louvre as the King of Navarre's retinue were called into the courtyard and were shot one by one as they came. Henry himself, rising at dawn, went off to play tennis. Charles sent for him and Condé and gave them a choice of "the Mass or death." Condé chose death, but was saved by the Queen. Navarre promised compliance and was allowed to live. His bride, Marguerite, sleeping fretfully, was awakened by a wounded Huguenot who rushed into her room and her bed; she persuaded his pursuers to spare him. "As I write," reported the Spanish ambassador, "they are killing them all, they are stripping them naked . . . sparing not even the children. Blessed be God!"[75] Now that the law itself had become lawless, pillage ran free, and the King was informed that members of his court had joined in the sack of the capital. Toward midday some horrified citizens pleaded with him to have the slaughter stopped, and a party of the town police offered to help restore order. He issued commands to halt the massacre; he bade the police imprison Protestants for their own protection; some of these he saved, others, at his bidding, were drowned in the Seine. For a while the carnage abated. But on Monday the twenty-fifth a hawthorn blossomed, quite out of season, in the Cemetery of the Innocents; the clergy hailed this as a miracle; the church bells of Paris rang out to acclaim it; the populace mistook the clangor as a call to renew the slaughter; murder took on new life.

On the twenty-sixth the King went in state with his court, through the streets still littered with corpses, to the Palace of Justice, and proudly certified to the Parlement of Paris that he had ordered the massacre. The president replied with a long address of congratulation. Parlement voted that Coligny's heirs should be outlawed, his home at Châtillon demolished, the remainder of his property confiscated by the Duke of Anjou. On the twenty-eighth the King, the Queen Mother, and the court visited several churches in a religious festival of thanksgiving for the redemption of France from heresy and the escape of the royal family from death.

The provinces imitated Paris in their amateur way. Inspired by news from the capital, Lyon, Dijon, Orléans, Blois, Tours, Troyes, Meaux, Bourges, Angers, Rouen, Toulouse staged ecstatic massacres (August 24–26). Jacques de Thou reckoned 800 victims at Lyon, 1,000 at Orléans.

The King encouraged and then discouraged these holocausts. On the twenty-sixth he sent verbal instructions to provincial governors to kill all leading Huguenots;[76] on the twenty-seventh he sent them written orders to protect peaceful and law-abiding Protestants. At the same time he wrote his agent at Brussels to invite the Duke of Alva's co-operation:

> The Duke has many of my rebellious subjects in his hands, and the means of taking Mons and punishing those [besieged] in it. If he answers you that this is tacitly to require him to kill these prisoners and to cut to pieces those in Mons, you are to say that this is what he must do.[77]

Alva rejected the invitation. When he captured Mons he allowed the French garrison to depart unharmed. Privately he scorned the Massacre of St. Bartholomew as a base means of waging war; publicly he ordered a celebration of the massacre as a triumph for the only true Christianity.[78]

Some provincial governors kept their populace under civilized control. There were no killings in Champagne, Picardy, or Brittany, and few in Auvergne, Languedoc, Burgundy, or Dauphiné. At Lyon many Catholics denounced the slaughter, and the soldiers refused to take part in it; at Vienne the bishop took the Protestants under his protection, and Catholic families gave hiding to endangered Huguenots.[79] But at Troyes and Orléans the bishops gave full rein to the massacre;[80] at Bordeaux a Jesuit announced that the Archangel Michael had ordered the killings, and he condemned the tardiness of the magistrates in ordering the executions. Probably the provinces contributed 5,000 victims and Paris some 2,000; but estimates of the total range from 5,000[81] to 30,000.[82]

Catholics generally condoned the massacre as an explosion of resentment and revenge after years of Huguenot persecution of Catholics.[83] Philip II laughed beyond his dour wont when he heard the news; now there would be no danger of France's interfering in the Netherlands. The papal nuncio at Paris wrote to Rome: "I congratulate His Holiness from the depths of my heart that it has pleased the Divine Majesty, at the beginning of his pontificate, to direct the affairs of this kingdom so felicitously and so honorably, and to have so protected the King and the Queen Mother that they would destroy this pestiferous root with such prudence and at such an opportune moment when all their rebels were locked in the cage."[84] When the tidings reached Rome the Cardinal of Lorraine, out of ungovernable happiness, gave the bearer a thousand crowns. Soon all Rome was illuminated; salvos were fired from Castel Sant' Angelo; bells rang joyously; Gregory XIII and his cardinals attended a solemn Mass of thanksgiving to God for "this signal favor shown to Christian people," which had saved France and the Holy See from great peril. The Pope ordered a special medal struck to commemorate *Ugonotorum strages*—the defeat or slaughter of the Huguenots[85]—and he engaged Vasari to paint, in the Sala Regia of the Vatican, a picture of the massacre, bearing the words *Pontifex Colignii necem probat*—"The Pope approves the killing of Coligny."*[86]

Protestant Europe branded the massacre as dastardly barbarism. William of Orange told the French envoy that Charles IX would never be able to wash the blood from his hands. In England Elizabeth was beset with demands for revenge, and bishops advised her that the only way to quiet the public fury was to put to death at once all Catholics who were in prison for having refused to take the oath of allegiance; at least the Queen of Scots should be executed at once.[88] Elizabeth kept her head. She robed herself in deep mourning to receive the French ambassador and met with visible unbelief his protestations that the massacre had been necessitated by imminent Huguenot conspiracy. But she continued to play France against Spain, and to dally with Alençon's suit for her hand; and in November she consented to act as godmother to the daughter of Charles IX.

Catherine emerged from the shambles cheerful and refreshed; the King was now again her vassal, and the Huguenot problem seemed solved. She was mistaken. Though many French Protestants had accepted conversion as an alternative to death, these recantations proved transitory; within two months of the massacre the Huguenots opened the Fourth Religious War; La Rochelle and several other towns closed their gates to royalist troops and successfully resisted siege. On July 6, 1573, Charles signed the Peace of La Rochelle, guaranteeing the Huguenots religious liberty. Politically the massacre had accomplished nothing.

And now the Huguenot intellectuals, who had heretofore professed loyalty to the King, turned in horror from Charles IX and questioned not only the divine right of kings but the institution of monarchy itself. François Hotman, a Huguenot jurist, had fled to Switzerland after the massacre; a year later he published a passionate attack upon Charles, *De furoribus Gallicis:* the crimes of that King had released his people from their oath of loyalty; he was a felon and should be deposed. Before the year was out Hotman sent forth from Geneva his *Franco-Gallia*, the first modern attempt at constitutional history. The Gallo-French monarchy, he argued, had been elective; the king had been, till Louis XI, subject to a national assembly of one kind or another; the now abject *parlements* and the long neglected States-General were the weakened remnants of that elective

---

* The Catholic historian Pastor, while not excusing the massacre, attempts to explain the papal jubilation as relief after fear that the triumph of Coligny would have brought an end to Catholicism in France, and the union of France with Protestant England, Holland, Scandinavia, and northern Germany in a war of extermination (such as Luther had called for) of Catholicism everywhere.[87]

power; and that power had been delegated to these bodies by the people. "To the people alone belongs the right to elect and depose kings."[89] He demanded the periodic assembly of the States-General; this body alone should have the authority to issue laws and make war or peace, to appoint to major offices, to regulate the succession, and to depose bad kings. Here already was the thunder of 1789.

Life itself soon deposed Charles IX. Good and evil in him had struggled to the point where a constitution congenitally botched had broken down from the strain. Sometimes he gloated over the hardihood and the extremity of his crime; at other times he accused himself for having consented to the massacre, and the cries of butchered Huguenots kept ringing in his ears, murdering sleep. He began to reproach his mother: "Who but you is the cause of all this? God's blood, you are the cause of it all!" She complained that she had a lunatic for a son.[90] He became melancholy and somber, thin and pale. He had always tended to tuberculosis; now, his resistance weakened, it destroyed him; by 1574 he was spitting blood. In the spring his hemorrhages grew more violent, and he again had visions of his victims. "What bloodshed, what murders!" he cried to his nurse. "What evil counsel have I followed! O my God, forgive me! . . . I am lost!"[91] On his dying day, May 30, 1574, he called for Henry of Navarre, whom he embraced affectionately. "Brother," he said, "you are losing a good friend. Had I believed all that I was told, you would not be alive. But I always loved you. . . . I trust in you alone to look after my wife and daughter. Pray God for me. Farewell." Soon afterward he died. He was not yet twenty-four.

CHAPTER XIV

Henry IV

1553–1610

I. LOVE AND MARRIAGE

HENRY'S grandmother was Marguerite of Angoulême, Valois, and Navarre, the lovable, sensitive, pious sister of the amorous, gallant, dashing Francis I. His mother was the rebellious, unmanageable, heretical Jeanne d'Albret. His father, Antoine de Bourbon, a descendant of St. Louis, was handsome, brave, debonair, vain, with a tendency to fluctuate from creed to creed. When Henry struggled into the world (December 14, 1553) at Pau in Béarn, he may have carried in him all these ancestral qualities except piety. His happy grandfather, sure that it would be a fine omen, persuaded Jeanne, in her pains, to sing a song to the Virgin; and, as a baptism into Béarn, he rubbed the lips of the babe with garlic and made him drink wine. The hero sucked eight nurses dry.

He did not relish education. He disliked writing, fled from grammar, and learned to write a fascinating style. He read Plutarch as his bible of heroism. He was brought up almost wholly out of doors; majored in running, romping, wrestling, riding, pummeling; ate black bread, cheese and onions; enjoyed summer and winter with a relish that laughed pessimism out of face. He was reared as a Huguenot, but he never allowed religion to hobble life. Summoned at the age of nine to live at the court and learn its graces and morals, he readily adopted Catholicism; returning to Béarn at thirteen, he resumed the Huguenot faith as if he were adjusting his clothes to the climate. With greater facility he passed from love to love —La Petite Tignonville, Mlle. de Montagu, Arnaudine, La Garce (the Wench), Catherine de Luc, Anne de Cambefort. He molted creeds and mistresses without distressing his conscience or shifting his aim.

His aim was to be king of France. At nineteen, his father having died, Henry became King of Navarre, but that was only a teasing taste of royalty. When he went to Paris to marry Marguerite of Valois, he was received as next only to the Duke of Anjou and the Duke of Alençon in line for the throne. When massacre followed on marriage, he kept and saved his head by timely apostasy.

His bride, "Margot," was the most fascinating and accommodating woman in France. No one questioned her beauty; Ronsard sang it; Brantôme intoned ecstasies about her fine cosmetic skin, her waving hair or varied wigs, her eyes darting humor, anger, or deviltry, her figure shapely as a courtesan's and stately as a queen's, her lively feet leading the dances of the court, her contagion of vivacity in an age of strife and gloom; all these magnets drew a dozen lovers to her lair, and gossip credited her with tactful, even incestuous, capitulations.[1] Henry could hardly complain, having himself a roving eye; but when Margot, who had married him against her will, resumed her fluctuations after a brief obeisance to monogamy, he began to wonder who would be the father of his children. He took a mistress; he fell ill; Margot generously nursed him, though she ascribed his disorder to "excesses with women." But soon their mutual suspicion so estranged them that she wrote, "*Nous ne couchions plus, ni ne parlions plus ensemble*" (We neither slept nor spoke with each other any more).[2]

For three years he remained unwillingly at the court. One night (1575), while hunting, he galloped out of bounds; then he fled in disguise across France, found his way through a dozen perils to Nérac, and governed Béarn and Guienne with justice and wit. He abandoned Catholicism, restored the Protestants to power in Béarn, and protected them in Guienne. Three years later Margot joined him, and the young King, when not following the hunt or fighting Catholics, helped her to make the festivities of her little court outface their infidelities. In 1582, tired of helping his mistresses in their confinements, she returned to Paris; but there her escapades were so flagrant that her brother, Henry III, bade her hurry back to her husband. After two years more in Béarn she retired to Agen. The two kings—now two Henrys—agreed to her practical imprisonment in the Château d'Usson, and allowed her a fair pension (1587–1605). She turned her prison into a salon, entertained poets, artists, scholars, and lovers, and composed her gossipy memoirs. Richelieu commended her style, Montaigne dedicated essays to her, preachers praised her charity. After substantial inducements she consented to an annulment of her marriage, and was allowed to return to Paris and the court (1605). There she resumed her romances and her salon, became fat and penitent, took Vincent de Paul as her chaplain, founded a convent, and died in peace and piety (1615) at the age of sixty-two. So ended, said a contemporary, "Marguerite, sole remains of the race of the Valois, a princess full . . . of good intentions . . . who did no harm to anyone but herself."[3]

II. HENRY III: 1574–89

The Duke of Anjou, after a brief tenure of the Polish throne, returned, aged twenty-four, to be Henry III, the last Valois king of France. An anonymous portrait in the Louvre shows him tall, lank, pale, wistful—

a man of good will confused by bad heredity. He was physically weak, emotionally unstable, easily fatigued; he had to avoid riding and hunting, and a few minutes of active love left him bedded for days. His skin itched incurably, his head and stomach ached, his ear ran. Before he was thirty-six his hair was white and his teeth were gone. His apparent haughtiness was really diffidence, his cruelty was fear; normally he was gentle and cautious. Unfortunately, he had a passion for feminine raiment. He appeared at a ball in a low-necked dress, with a circlet of pearls around his throat; he wore jewels on his ears and bracelets on his arms. He gathered about him a dozen *mignons*, youths who frizzed their long hair, painted their faces, adorned themselves with fancy garb, and sprinkled themselves with perfumes that scented their trail. With these uncertain men he would on occasion—disguised as a woman—romp through the streets at night, playing pranks upon the citizens. In a country nearing bankruptcy and anarchy he emptied the treasury upon his male favorites, spending eleven million francs on the wedding of one, and doubling the price of judgeships to buy a marriage gift for another. Some of his people's money he spent to good purpose—building the Pont Neuf, improving the Louvre, and raising parts of Paris out of squalor into architecture and cleanliness. He supported literature and the theater. He labored fretfully at administration. To square all his accounts he made pilgrimages on foot to Chartres and Cléry; in Paris he walked from church to church fingering large rosaries, zealously accumulating paternosters and Ave Marias; he marched in the ghostly nocturnal processions of the Blue Penitents, his body enclosed in a sack with holes for feet and eyes. He had no children. His mother, who had brought the seeds of degeneracy to him from diseased parents, looked with sorrow on the decadence and the imminent extinction of her stock.

The political situation was confused beyond Henry's understanding. He was not made for war, and Catherine, aging, longed for peace; but the Huguenots, desperate yet unsubdued, were still in revolt. His brother, the Duke of Alençon, was flirting with a Protestant queen in England, with Protestant rebels in the Netherlands, and with Henry of Navarre in Béarn. A minority of Catholic leaders, called "Politiques" by their critics, took up the ideas of L'Hôpital (who had died in grief in 1573), proposed mutual toleration between the warring faiths, and defended the idea, so unpopular in both camps, that a nation could survive without unity of religious belief. If (they argued) the popes forbade such a compromise, France should sever its religious bonds with Rome. Frightened by the co-operation of Politiques and Huguenots, and by the inroads of German troops coming to reinforce the Protestants, Henry ended (1576) the Fifth Religious War by signing the "Peace of Monsieur" at Beaulieu, and issuing an edict of pacification—the Edict of Beaulieu—which gave the Huguenots full freedom of worship everywhere in France, made them eligible to all offices, and allowed them eight cities in which they were to have complete political and military dominance.

Most French Catholics, and above all the ardently orthodox populace of Paris, were shocked by these concessions to a party supposedly destroyed. In 1562 the Cardinal of Lorraine had proposed a *ligue sainte* whose members should swear to defend the Church by whatever means and at whatever cost; Henry of Guise had organized such a band in Champagne in 1568; now similar associations were formed in many provinces. In 1576 the Duke openly proclaimed the Holy League, and took the field with a vow to crush the Huguenots once and for all.

We must not follow the trajectories of the Sixth, Seventh, and Eighth Religious Wars except as they affected the flow of ideas or the character of France. Now again philosophy entered the fray. In 1579 an unidentified author—perhaps Philippe Duplessis-Mornay, one of Navarre's councilors —sent out from Basel a stirring pronunciamento entitled *Vindiciae contra tyrannos* (*A Vindication* [of public rights] *against Tyrants*). It was written in Latin, but was soon translated into vernaculars. Its influence lasted for a century; it was used by the Huguenots in France, by the Dutch against Philip, by the Puritans against Charles I, by the Whigs to justify the dethroning of James II. The old theory of an implicit "social contract" between a nation and its ruler here took definite form; we shall see it again in Hobbes, Locke, and Rousseau. Government is first of all a covenant between God, the people, and the king to uphold and obey the "true religion"—in this case Protestantism; any king failing to do this may be deposed. Secondly, government is a pact between king and people: the one to rule justly, the other to obey peaceably. King and people alike are subject to natural law—that is, a law of reason and natural justice conformable to the divine moral code and superior to all "positive" (man-made) law. The function of the king is to maintain the law, positive, natural, and divine; he is the instrument, not the dictator, of the law. "Subjects . . . , considered in a body, ought to be esteemed absolute lords and owners of the kingdom." But who shall determine whether the king is a tyrant? Not the people as a multitude, "that monster with countless heads"; rather, let the magistrates decide, or some such assembly as the States-General of France. It will not do for each private individual to follow his own conscience; he would mistake his desires for his conscience, and chaos would ensue; but if the magistrate summons him to armed rebellion he must obey the call. If however, the tyrant is a usurper, he may justly be killed by anyone.[4]

The conflict of forces and ideas was sharpened when the Duke of Alençon died (1584) and Henry III recognized Henry of Navarre as heir presumptive to the throne. Overnight the Huguenots ceased to talk of tyranny and deposition and became ardent supporters of legitimacy, expecting the fragile Valois King to collapse soon and yield France to their Bourbon Protestant. The *Vindiciae*, so recently a Huguenot manifesto, was frowned upon, and Hotman himself proclaimed that resistance to Henry of Navarre was a sin.[5] But most of France shuddered at the thought of a Huguenot king. How could a Protestant be anointed at Reims by the Church? And could anyone, without such unction, ever be a rightful monarch of France? The orthodox clergy, led by fervent Jesuits, denounced the succession and called all Catholics to the League. Henry III, swept away by the tide, joined the League and ordered all Huguenots to accept Catholicism or leave France. Henry of Navarre appealed to Europe to recognize the justice of his cause, but Pope Sixtus V excommunicated him, and declared that as a persistent heretic he could not inherit the throne. Charles, Cardinal de Bourbon, now declared himself heir presumptive. Catherine again tried for peace, offering to support Navarre if he would renounce Protestantism; he refused. He took the field with an army partly Catholic, captured half a dozen cities in as many months, and defeated at Coutras a League army twice as large as his own (1587).

The Huguenots, numbering about a twelfth of the population,[6] now held half the major towns of France.[7] But Paris was the heart of France, and Paris was passionately for the League. Dissatisfied with Henry III's halfhearted support, the League set up in the capital a revolutionary government composed of representatives from the sixteen wards; the "Sixteen" negotiated with Spain for a Spanish invasion of England and France and planned to seize the person of the King. Henry sent for Swiss guards; the Sixteen called upon the Duke of Guise to take control of Paris; the King forbade it; the Duke came and was hailed by the populace as head of the Catholic cause in France. Henry III, humiliated and vowing vengeance, fled to Chartres. Then, again losing his nerve, he disowned Henry of Navarre, appointed Henry of Guise commander in chief of the royal armies, and summoned the States-General to meet at Blois.

When the delegates assembled, the King noted with anger the almost royal honors paid to Guise. In a day of frenzied resolution he persuaded some of his aides to kill the Duke. He invited him to a private conference; as the young noble approached the King's room nine assailants stabbed him to death; and the King, opening a door, gazed in excited satisfaction upon his accomplished aim (December 24, 1588). He ordered the imprisonment of the League leaders and the death of the Duke's brother, the Cardinal of Guise. In pride and terror he reported his vicarious exploits to his mother. She wrung her hands in despair. "You have ruined the kingdom," she told him.

Twelve days later she died, aged sixty-nine, worn out with responsibilities, anxieties, intrigues, and probably remorse. Hardly anyone paused to mourn her. She was buried in a common grave at Blois, for when a proposal was made to let her remains occupy the tomb she had prepared in St.-Denis, the Sixteen announced that if her body were brought to Paris they would throw it into the Seine. Half of France denounced Henry III as a murderer; students paraded the streets demanding his dethronement; the theologians of the Sorbonne, supported by the Pope, absolved the people from allegiance to the King, and priests called for armed resistance to him everywhere. Supporters of the King were arrested; men and women crowded the churches for fear of being taken as royalists. The pamphleteers of the League took over the political ideology of the Huguenots: the people were declared sovereign, with the right, through the Parlement or the magistrates, to depose a tyrant; any future king should be subject to constitutional limitations, and his prime duty should be to enforce the true religion—in this case Catholicism.[8]

Henry III, now at Tours with some nobles and soldiers, found himself between two terrors. The army of the League, under the Duke of Mayenne, was advancing upon him from the north; the army of Navarre, taking town after town, was advancing from the south; one or the other force must capture him. Henry the Huguenot seized his opportunity; he sent Duplessis-Mornay to offer the King alliance, protection, and support. At Plessis-les-Tours the two Henrys met and pledged mutual fidelity (April 30, 1589). Together their armies defeated Mayenne and marched upon Paris.

In the frenzied capital a Dominican monk, Jacques Clément, listened fervently to denunciations of Henry III as an assassin. He was assured that a great deed in a divine cause would clear away all the guilt of his sins; and the grief and beauty of Catherine, Duchess of Montpensier, sister of the slain Guises, agitated him. He bought a dagger, found his way into the royal camp, stabbed the King in the stomach, was killed by the guards, and died in the confidence of Paradise. Henry of Valois died on the morrow (August 2, 1589), beseeching his followers to cleave to his cousin of Navarre. Chaos swept through the besieging army; much of it melted away; the proposed attack on Paris was postponed. Within the city the joy of the League and its followers reached delirium. Some churches placed the monk's picture on the altar;[9] devotees hailed the assassination as the noblest act of God since the Incarnation of Jesus Christ.[10] Clément's mother was brought from the provinces, preached in the churches, and was hailed with a sacred chant: "Blessed be the womb that bore thee, and the paps that gave thee suck."[11]

III. THE ROAD TO PARIS: 1589-94

Henry of Navarre was at the crisis of his life. Suddenly he was, in law and by tradition, King of France; but almost as suddenly half his troops deserted him. The nobles who had clung to Henry III rode off to their estates; most of the Catholics in his army disappeared. Two thirds of France rejected forcibly the notion of a Protestant king. The Politiques had for the time been silenced by the two assassinations; the Parlement of Paris recognized Cardinal de Bourbon as king of France; Philip of Spain pledged to the League the gold of the Americas to keep France Catholic. Meanwhile, not quite to Philip's chagrin, the disruption of French production and trade had brought the country to such desolation that no comfort was left it but the consuming ecstasy of hate.

It was out of the question for Navarre to attack a city so overwhelmingly hostile as Paris with an army so disorganized and reduced. Cautiously, and with a generalship impeded more by his mistresses than by the enemy, he withdrew his forces northward to receive help from England, and Mayenne followed as rapidly as his corpulence would permit. At Arques, just south of Dieppe, the two armies met, Henry with 7,000 men, Mayenne with 23,000 (September 21, 1589). We may gather the result from Henry's message to his comrade at arms Crillon: *"Pends-toi, brave Crillon; nous avons combattu à Arques, et tu n'y étais pas"* (Hang yourself, brave Crillon; we have fought at Arques, and you were not there). The victory heartened Henry's secret supporters everywhere. Several towns opened their gates to him cheerfully; the Republic of Venice recognized him as King; Elizabeth, as anxious as Venice to keep Spain from dominating France, sent him four thousand troops, £22,000 in gold, 70,000 pounds of gunpowder, and cargoes of shoes, food, wine, and beer. Philip retaliated by sending a detachment from Flanders to Mayenne. The reinforced armies fought at Ivry, on the Eure, March 14, 1590. Henry stuck a white plume —hardly to be termed a white feather—in his helmet and told his soldiers, "If the heat of battle disperse you for a while, rally . . . under those pear trees you see up yonder to my right, and if you lose your standards do not lose sight of my white plume—you will always find it in the path of honor and, I hope, of victory too." As usual, he fought in the fore of the fray; his right arm was swollen and his sword beaten out of shape with the blows they gave. His reputation for mercy served him well, for thousands of unpaid Swiss in Mayenne's service surrendered. Henry's victory left the League without an army; almost unhindered he advanced to besiege Paris again.

From May to September, 1590, his hungry and penniless soldiers camped around the capital, eager to assault and plunder it, but checked by Henry's refusal to sanction a slaughter that might have been worse than the St. Bartholomew. After a month of siege the Parisians were eating horses, cats, dogs, and grass. Henry relented and let provisions enter the city. The Duke of Parma, Philip's governor in the Netherlands, came to the relief of Paris with a well-equipped army of Spanish veterans; Henry, outmaneuvered, retreated to Rouen; Parma followed him in a duel of strategy; sickness disabled the Duke, and Henry's army once more sat down before the capital.

Now he faced the decisive question: Could he, as a Protestant, win and *keep* the throne of a country 90 per cent Catholic? Even his army was predominantly Catholic. Doubtless it was no small item in his thoughts that he was running out of funds and could no longer pay his troops. He called in his aides and confessed that he was thinking of conversion to Catholicism. Some approved the plan as the only road to peace; some condemned it as a cruel and scandalous desertion of Huguenots who had given him blood and money in the hope of having a Protestant king. To these Henry replied, "If I were to follow your advice, in a little while there would be neither king nor kingdom in France. I wish to give peace to my subjects and rest to my soul. Take council among you as to what you need for your security. I shall always be ready to satisfy you."[12] He added, "Perhaps between the two religions the difference is great only through the animosity of those who preach it. Someday, by my authority, I shall try to arrange all that."[13] And he defined his own essential faith: "Those who unswervingly follow their conscience are of my religion, and I am of the religion of all who are brave and good."[14] Duplessis-Mornay, Agrippa d'Aubigné, and many other Protestant leaders abandoned the King, but Henry's most trusted adviser, the Duke of Sully, while himself remaining staunchly Protestant, agreed with his master's decision, *"Paris vaut bien une messe"* (Paris is well worth a Mass).[15]

On May 18, 1593, Henry sent word to the Pope and the Paris hierarchy that he desired instruction in the Catholic faith. Gregory XIV had renewed his excommunication, but the French hierarchy, never obsequious to Rome, prepared to groom the new penitent to be a pious king. He was no easy pupil. He would give no pledge to make war against heresy, and refused to sign or believe "rubbish which he was quite sure that the majority of them did not believe" themselves.[16] He graciously agreed to the doctrine of purgatory because "it is the best part of your revenues."[17] On July 25 he wrote to his current mistress, *"Je vais faire le saut perilleux"* (I am going to make the perilous leap). He went to the abbey church of St.-Denis, confessed, received absolution, and heard Mass.

Thousands of voices, in both camps, denounced him as a hypocrite. The Jesuits repudiated his conversion, and the League leaders continued to resist. But the deaths of the Duke of Parma and Cardinal de Bourbon had weakened the League, and the Sixteen had lost standing with French patriots by supporting Philip's plan to have his daughter made queen of France. Many of the nobility inclined to Henry as a general who could keep Philip in check, and as a humane ruler who could restore health to a land disordered to the verge of dismemberment. A clever periodical, *Satyre Ménippée* (1593–94), voiced the sentiments of the Politiques and the bourgeoisie, ridiculed with wit and irony the Jesuits and the League, and declared, "There is no peace so unjust that it is not worth more than the most just war."[18] Even fanatical Paris was crying for peace. Minor hostilities continued for eight months more, but on March 22, 1594, Henry marched into Paris and hardly a man hindered him; such crowds acclaimed him that when he wished to enter Notre Dame he had to be lifted over the heads of the multitude. Established as king in the same Louvre where, twenty-two years before, he had been a prisoner and near death, he surrendered himself to joy, and issued, in his buoyant way, an amnesty to all, even to the Guises and the Sixteen. Some enemies he brought over by ready forgiveness and gallant courtesy; some he bribed with borrowed funds.

Not all were won over. At Lyon Pierre Barrière bought a knife, had it sharpened, and started out for Paris proclaiming his intent to assassinate the King. He was arrested at Melun and summarily strangled. "Alas," said Henry, "if I had known it I would have pardoned him." Pope Clement VIII sent the King absolution, but the Jesuits continued to preach against him. On December 27 Jean Châtel, aged nineteen, struck at the King with a dagger, but inflicted only a cut lip and a broken tooth. Again Henry proposed to pardon the fanatic, but the authorities subjected Châtel to all the tortures required by the law against regicides. He proudly admitted his desire to kill the King as a dangerous heretic, and professed his readiness to make another attempt for his own salvation's sake. He confessed that he was a pupil of the Jesuits, but would not further implicate them in his enterprise. The Spanish Jesuit Juan de Mariana (whom we shall meet again) was quoted as having approved the assassination of bad kings, of Henry III especially; and the French Jesuit Jean Guignard was found to have written that Henry IV should have been killed in the Massacre of St. Bartholomew, and that he ought now to be got rid of "at any price and in any way whatsoever."[19] Early in 1595 the Parlement of Paris, on petition of the secular clergy of the Sorbonne, ordered the Jesuits to leave France.

IV. THE CREATIVE KING: 1594–1610

Henry found the task of reconstruction more arduous than the conquest of power. Thirty-two years of "religious" wars had left France almost as devastated and chaotic as after the Hundred Years' War the century before. The French merchant marine had practically vanished from the seas. Three hundred thousand homes had been destroyed. Hatred had declared a moratorium on morals and had poisoned France with the lust for revenge. Demobilized soldiers harried the roads and villages with robbery and murder. The nobles plotted to exact, as the price of their loyalty, a return to feudal seignorial sovereignties; the provinces, long left to their own resources, were dividing France into autonomous states; and the Huguenots were clamoring for political independence as well as religious liberty. The League still had a hostile army in the field; Henry bought its leader, Mayenne, to truce and finally to peace (January 1596). The terms having been signed, Henry walked the fat Duke into panting exhaustion, and then assured him that this was the only revenge he would take.[20] When one of his own generals, Charles de Gontaut, Duke of Biron, led a conspiracy against him, Henry offered him pardon for a confession; this being refused, Henry had him tried, convicted, and beheaded (1602). By this time France realized that Navarre was King. The people of France, tired of anarchy, allowed him—the business classes begged him—to make the new Bourbon monarchy absolute. Royal absolutism, which was the cause of civil war in England, was the effect of civil war in France.

Since the first necessity of government is money, Henry collected taxes. The existing Council of Finance emitted more than the normal odor of corruption; Henry made the fearless Sully superintendent of finance, and gave him a free hand to clear the air and the road between taxes paid and those received. Maximilien de Béthune, Baron of Rosny, Duke of Sully, had been Henry's faithful friend for a quarter of a century, had fought at his side for fourteen years; now (1597), still only thirty-seven, he attacked embezzlers and incompetents with such uncompromising energy that he became the most valuable and unpopular member of the royal Council. His portrait, by Dumonstier, hangs in the Louvre: large head, massive brow, sharp suspicious eyes; here was the practical genius needed to check the romantic spirit of a king who was too busy as Casanova to be quite Charlemagne. Sully made himself the watchdog of the administration. As superintendent of finance, highways, communications, public buildings, fortifications, and artillery, as governor of the Bastille and surveyor general of Paris, he was everywhere, supervised everything, insisted on efficiency, economy, and integrity. He worked through every waking hour, lived austerely in a simple room bearing pictures of Luther and Calvin on the walls. He guarded the interests of his fellow Huguenots. He stabilized the currency, reorganized and disciplined the bureaucracy, and forced thieving officials to disgorge. He reclaimed for the state all property and revenues that

had been appropriated by individuals during the wars. He compelled 40,-
000 tax dodgers to pay their taxes. He had found the national treasury
in debt by 296,000,000 livres; he paid off these obligations, balanced the
budget, and gathered a surplus of 13,000,000 livres. He protected and
encouraged all phases of economic life; built roads and bridges, planned
the great canals that were to join the Atlantic and the Mediterranean, the
Seine and the Loire;[21] he declared all navigable rivers to be part of the
royal domain, forbade obstructions in them, and renewed the flow of
goods through the land.

With the help of such wisely chosen ministers Henry proceeded to re-
create France. He restored to the courts and the *parlements* their lawful
functions and authority; and if he allowed the bureaucratic officials, for a
price, to transmit their positions to their sons, it was not merely to raise
money, but to ensure stability of administration and to raise up the middle
classes—in particular the legal fraternity, or *noblesse de la robe*—as offsets
and balances to the hostile aristocracy. Usually too eager for life and work
to read a book, the King studied carefully Olivier de Serres' *Les Théâtre
d'agriculture* (1600), which suggested more scientific methods of farming; he established these improvements on the crown lands as examples and
prods to the vegetative peasantry; he longed, as he said, to see *la poule au
pot*, a chicken in every pot on Sunday.[22] He forbade nobles to ride over
vineyards or cornfields on their hunts; he suppressed the ravages of troops
on peasant lands. He canceled twenty million livres of tax arrears owed
by the peasants (perhaps because he knew he could never collect them),
and lowered the poll tax from twenty to fourteen million livres. Anticipating Colbert, he protected existing industries with tariffs, and introduced new industries like the making of fine pottery and glass, and
the culture of silk; he planted mulberry trees in the gardens of the
Tuileries and Fontainebleau and required that ten thousand should be
planted in every diocese. He helped and enlarged the tapestry works of
the Gobelins. To evade the restrictive policies of the masters in the guilds,
he reorganized French industry on a corporative basis—employers and employees united in each craft and subject to regulation by the state. Poverty
continued, partly because of war, pestilence, and taxes, partly because the
natural inequality of ability, amid the general equality of greed, ensures
in each generation that the majority of goods will be absorbed by a minority of men. The King himself lived economically, extravagant only with
his mistresses. To occupy the unemployed and clear the countryside of
idle and voracious veterans, he financed a large variety of public works:
streets were broadened and paved, canals were dug, trees were planted
along the highways; parks and squares—like the Place Royale (now the
Place des Vosges) and the Place Dauphine—were opened to let Paris

breathe. For the disabled destitute the King founded the Hôpital de la Charité. Not all these reforms matured before his sudden death, but by the end of his reign the country was enjoying such prosperity as it had not known since Francis I.

Above all, Henry ended the Religious Wars, and taught Catholics and Protestants to live in peace. Not in amity, for no thoroughgoing Catholic would admit the right of a Huguenot to exist, and no fervent Huguenot could view the Catholic worship as anything but pagan idolatry. Taking his life in his hands, Henry issued (April 13, 1598) the historic Edict of Nantes, authorizing the full exercise of the Protestant faith, and freedom of the Protestant press, in all of the eight hundred towns of France except seventeen, in which (as in Paris) Catholicism was overwhelmingly predominant. The eligibility of Huguenots to public offices was confirmed; two were already in the Council of State, and the Huguenot Turenne was to be a marshal of France. The government was to pay the salaries of Protestant ministers and of the rectors of Protestant schools. Protestant children were to be admitted, on an equality with Catholics, to all schools, colleges, universities, and hospitals. Towns already controlled by the Huguenots—such as La Rochelle, Montpellier, and Montauban—were to remain so, and their garrisons and forts were to be maintained by the state. The religious liberty so granted was still imperfect; it included only Catholics and Protestants; but it constituted the most advanced religious toleration in Europe. It took a man of doubtful faith to turn "His Most Christian Majesty" into a Christian.

Catholics throughout France cried out against the edict as a betrayal of Henry's promise to support their creed. Pope Clement VIII condemned it as "the most accursed that can be imagined, whereby liberty of conscience is granted to everybody, which is the worst thing in the world."[23] Catholic writers proclaimed anew that a heretic king might justly be deposed or slain; and Protestant authors like Hotman, who under Henry III had defended popular sovereignty, now praised the virtues of absolutism—in a Protestant king.[24] The Parlement of Paris long refused to give the edict that official registration without which, according to custom, no royal decree could become accepted law. Henry summoned the members and explained that what he had done was indispensable to peace and the reconstruction of France. The Parlement yielded, and it received six Huguenots into its membership.

Perhaps to quiet the Catholic opposition and placate the Pope, Henry allowed the Jesuits to return to France (1603). Sully argued stoutly against the move. The Jesuits, he urged, were "men of genius, but full of cunning and artifice"; they were committed to the cause of the Hapsburgs, therefore of France's enemies, Spain and Austria; they were pledged and inclined to unconditionally obey the pope, who was a geographical prisoner and financial dependent of the Hapsburgs; they would sooner or later dictate Henry's policies, or, failing therein, they would persuade some fanatic to "take away your life by poison or other means." Henry replied that the support of the Jesuits would be a great help to him in unifying France, and their continued exile and hostility would be more dangerous to his life and policies than their re-entry into France.* He accepted the Jesuit Pierre Coton as his confessor, found him likable and faithful, and devoted himself to the administration of France and the turbulence of love.

V. THE SATYR

In the Condé Museum at Chantilly there is a delectable portrait, by Frans Pourbus the Younger, showing Henry in full maturity of power and pride: lithe of build, simply dressed in baggy breeches and black doublet and hose, left arm akimbo, a ruff under his gray beard, a majestic nose, a firm mouth, eyes alert, skeptical, and humane. His many years of campaigning had given him the bearing, morals, and odor of a soldier: strong, active, tireless, too busy to indulge in cleanliness or to duly change his clothes; sometimes, said a friend, "he stank like a corpse."[25] After a day of marching or fighting he would alarm his aides by organizing a hunt. He was a paragon of courage, but he had a tendency to diarrhea when battle neared,[26] and in his final seven years he suffered from dysentery, dysuria, and gout. His mind was as mettlesome and resilient as his body. He saw through buncombe readily, seized the essence of matters at once, wrote letters still quick with life, and brightened France and history with his wit. When he named La Vieuville to an office and the grateful recipient said, Biblically, "Lord, I am not worthy," Henry replied, "I know it quite well, but my nephew asked me to appoint you."[27] Once, on his way to dinner, he was stopped by a petitioner who began pompously, "Sire, Agesilaus, King of Lacedaemon—" "*Ventre saint-gris!*" moaned Henry. "I have heard of him; but he had dined, and I haven't."[28] "He was," says a French historian, "the most intelligent of French kings."[29]

He was also the most beloved. Not yet the most popular; half of France still accepted him grudgingly. But those who knew him closely were ready to go to the stake for him, some inclusively. He was the most approachable of rulers, unpretentious, natural, good-natured, not quick to take offense, never tardy to forgive. His court complained of his unwillingness to put on the majesty of a king. He allowed poets and playwrights to make fun of

---

* Sully, *Memoirs*, III, 10-11. We have no way of determining the accuracy of this report of a private conversation.

him, though he liked it better when Malherbe made him a god of virtue and charm. He went to see the farces that satirized him, and he dulled their barbs with his laughter. He took no revenge on those who had opposed him by deed or speech—"All the forests in my kingdom would not provide enough gibbets if all who have written or preached against me were to be hanged."[30] He was as sensitive as a poet, and felt the poverty of the people almost as keenly as the beauty of women. He was no stoic; control of his emotions was not among his virtues. He had many faults. He could be thoughtlessly rude and gaily coarse. He had a Rabelais in him—he enjoyed risqué stories and told them beyond compare. He gambled too much at cards, lost heavily, cheated often, but always restored his lawless gains.[31] He neglected the pursuit of a retreating enemy to pursue a retreating woman.

We must not list all his loves. Three women in particular marked his road to the throne. To "La Belle Corisande" he wrote burning *billets:* "I devour your hands . . . and kiss your feet a million times . . . It would be a desolate spot indeed where we two would be bored together."[32] By 1589 he was bored, and he discovered Esther Ymbert de Boislambert. A year later, aged thirty-seven, and undeterred by gonorrhea,[33] he lost his heart to Gabrielle d'Estrées, then a girl of seventeen, whom a poet endued with "golden hair, starry eyes, lily throat, pearly fingers, and alabaster breasts."[34] Her lover, Bellegarde, recklessly described her beauty to the King; Henry galloped twelve miles, in disguise, through enemy terrain, to see her. She laughed at his long nose; he fell at her feet; Bellegarde withdrew. She yielded to the charms of francs and royalty and bore Henry three children. He took her to court and on his hunts, caressed her in public, thought of marrying her if Margot would give him a divorce. Huguenot and Catholic preachers joined in condemning him as an arrant adulterer, and brave Sully reproached him for wasting state funds on courtesans. He begged forgiveness on the plea that, having labored so arduously in war and government, and having fared so ill in marriage, he was entitled, like a good soldier, to some recreation.[35] For eight years he loved Gabrielle as uxoriously as was possible to a spirit so *ondoyant et divers*. But Gabrielle became fat and acquisitive. She intrigued against Sully, called him "valet"; Henry raged, told her that he valued such a minister above ten such mistresses. He relented and again talked of marrying her, but on April 10, 1599, she died in giving birth to a dead child. He mourned her bitterly and wrote, "The plant of love within me is dead."[36]

It revived two months later when he met Henriette d'Entragues, daughter of that Marie Touchet who had served Charles IX. Mother, father, and half-brother forbade her to capitulate except for a wedding ring. Henry wrote her a promise of marriage, conditional on her bearing him a son; Sully tore it up before his face; Henry wrote another and delivered it with twenty thousand crowns. The lady's conscience cleared, and she became the royal mistress. Some of the King's diplomats thought it time for him to settle down. They persuaded Margot to consent to a divorce, provided Henry would not marry his mistress. Clement VIII agreed to grant a divorce on the same terms, and offered as a bride Maria de' Medici, daughter of the Grand Duke of Tuscany; the Florentine bankers proposed to cancel the huge debt France owed them if Henry made Maria his queen.[37] The marriage was celebrated by proxy at Florence (October 5, 1600). Henry tore himself away from a battlefield to go as far as Lyon to greet his wife; he found her tall and fat and imperious, gave her every royal courtesy, begot Louis XIII, and returned to Mlle. d'Entragues. Periodically, however, he performed his marital duties. Marie de Médicis (as France called her) bore him seven children in ten years. Henry brought them up, together with his offspring by Gabrielle and Henriette, at St.-Germain-en-Laye.

Henriette was presented to the Queen and was lodged in a palace near the Louvre; but, having borne a son to the King, she insisted that she, not Marie, was the rightful queen. Her father and half-brother plotted to kidnap her and her son to Spain and to have Philip III acknowledge him as the true dauphin of France (1604). The plot was discovered, the brother was arrested, the father was released on returning Henry's promise of marriage. Henry continued to pursue Henriette like a famished satyr; she returned his caresses with disgust and hatred, and accepted bribes from Philip III to serve as a spy for Spain.[38]

VI. ASSASSINATION

Amid these incredible absurdities the King schemed to break the cordon with which the Hapsburgs had imprisoned France—the iron circle of the Spanish Netherlands, Luxembourg, Lorraine, Franche-Comté, Austria, the Valtelline passes, Savoy, Italy, and Spain. Sully, in writing his memoirs, claimed to have proposed to Henry and to James I of England a "Grand Design": France, England, Scotland, Denmark, Sweden, the United Provinces (Holland), Protestant Germany, Switzerland, and Venice were to unite against the Hapsburgs, wrest America from Spain, free Germany from the Emperor, and drive the Spaniards from the Netherlands; then the victors were to divide all Europe except Russia, Turkey, Italy, and Spain into a federated "Christian Republic" of fifteen autonomous states trading with one another without tariffs, and submitting their foreign policies to a federal council armed with supreme military force.[39] Henry himself seems never to have entertained this grandiose conception; probably the limit of his hope was to extend France to "natural boundaries" at the Rhine, the Alps, the Pyrenees, and the sea, and to liberate her from fear of Spain and Austria. For these ends he resorted to any available means: he sought alliances with the Protestant powers, he helped the Dutch in their revolt against Spain, he planned to support an uprising of Moriscos in Valencia, he encouraged the Turks to attack Austria.[40]

A trivial dispute offered to spark this Bourbon-Hapsburg enmity into a European war. On March 25, 1609, there died, without issue, Duke John William of the little triune principality of Jülich-Cleves-Berg, near Cologne. The Emperor Rudolf, as its suzerain, claimed the right to name a Catholic to this petty throne. Henry protested that the further subjection of the duchy to the Hapsburgs would endanger the eastern boundary of France. He joined Brandenburg, the Palatinate, and the United Provinces in determination to appoint a Protestant successor to John William; and when Archduke Leopold of Austria occupied Jülich with Imperial troops Henry prepared for war.

His final romance harmonized fetchingly with this call to Armageddon. Though he was now fifty-six and looked older, he developed in 1609 an uncontrollable longing for Charlotte de Montmorency, then sixteen. She rejected his advances, but consented, at his behest, to marry the new Prince of Condé. "Are you not very wicked," his mistress Henriette is said to have taunted him, "to want to bed with the wife of your son? For you well know that you have told me that he [the Prince] was your offspring."[41] Condé fled with his bride to Brussels; Henry itched to pursue her, and Malherbe stitched the royal itches into rhyme. Villeroi, Henry's foreign minister, begged Archduke Albert of the Netherlands to extradite the Princess to Paris; the Archduke, encouraged by Philip III of Spain, refused; Villeroi threatened a war "that may set fire to the four corners of Christendom."[42] It seemed providential to Henry that Brussels was on the way to Jülich: he would conquer the lady—and the Spanish Netherlands—as a prelude to shattering the Empire and humbling Spain. He hired Swiss mercenaries and prepared to raise an army of thirty thousand men. James I of England promised four thousand more.

Catholic France was alarmed. It gave too much credit to the gossip that the charms of the Princess were the real *casus* belly; it noted with dismay that the King's allies and generals were mostly Protestants; it wondered what the fate of Catholicism and the papacy would be in a Europe where the Catholic south had been conquered by the Protestant north and a so-recently-Huguenot King. The taxes levied to finance the dreaded war lowered Henry's always precarious popularity; even the court turned away from him as a man too foolish to realize that he could no longer be Lothario and Alexander in one. Prophecies were bandied about—perhaps as hopeful provocations to the suggestible—that he would soon be killed.

François Ravaillac of Angoulême heard the prophecies. Arrested for a crime that he had not committed, he brooded in his prison, had visions, studied theology, read tracts defending tyrannicide. Strong of arm, weak of mind, he dallied with the idea that God had chosen him to fulfill the prophecies, to save France from Protestant doom. Released, he went to Paris (1609), lodged with Mme. d'Escoman, a friend of Henriette d'Entragues, and confessed to her that he had thoughts of killing the King. A warning was sent to Henry, but he was so accustomed to such alarms that he took no notice of it. As Henry passed through the streets Ravaillac tried to approach him; soldiers stopped him; he said he wished to ask the King if it was true that he was planning war against the Pope, and that the Huguenots were preparing to massacre the Catholics. He tried to enter a monastery and to join the Jesuits; he was rejected. He went back to Angoulême to perform his Easter duty; he received the Sacrament and, from a monk, a little bag containing, he was told, a fragment of the cross on which Christ had died. He bought a knife and returned to Paris. Mme. d'Escoman sent a warning to Sully, who transmitted it to the King.

Henry was preparing to join his army at Châlons. On May 13, 1610, he appointed the Queen as regent during his absence. On the fourteenth the Duke of Vendôme, his natural son, begged him to stay at home, for predictions of his assassination had named this as the fatal day. In the afternoon he decided to take a carriage ride, visit the sick Sully, and get "a breath of air." To avoid being noticed he dismissed his guards, but he was accompanied by seven members of the court. Ravaillac, who had been watching the Louvre, followed the carriage. At a point in the Rue de la Ferronnerie it was stopped by a traffic tangle. Ravaillac leaped upon the step and struck the King so powerfully that the blade pierced the heart. Henry died almost instantly.

Ravaillac, put to the torture, took full responsibility for his action, denied that he had any abettors or accomplices, mourned the violence of his act, but professed confidence that God would forgive it as in a sacred cause. His limbs were torn from his body by four horses, his trunk was burned in a public square. Many accused the Jesuits of having inflamed the assassin's mind; it was pointed out that Mariana's *De rege*, justifying tyrannicide, had been openly sold in Paris shops. The Jesuits replied that this book had been explicitly condemned by an assembly of Jesuits held in Paris in 1606. The Sorbonne judged the Jesuits guilty of dangerous doctrines and officially burned Mariana's book.[43] Marie de Médicis, as regent, protected the Jesuits from harm, and accepted their guidance in faith and policy.

France was confused and divided by Henry's final enterprise and sudden death. A minority accepted the assassination as an act of God in defense of the Church. But the great majority, Catholic as well as Protestant, mourned the passing of a king whose labors for his people far outweighed his errors, follies, and sins. Frenchmen had not forgotten the poverty and desolation, the religious turmoil, the official corruption and incompetence that he had inherited with the throne; and they saw now a nation cleansed and orderly, prosperous despite high taxation, and powerful enough to challenge the long ascendancy of Spain. They remembered fondly Henry's simplicity of dress and conduct and speech, his good humor and kindly nature, his gay courage in war, his tact in friendship and diplomacy; and their own moral laxity condoned those amorous escapades in which he had but shown himself a man after their own desires. He had with warrant called himself "a loyal king, faithful and true";[44] he was also the most human and humane of French kings; and he was the savior of France. His plan to extend France to natural boundaries may have seemed impracticable, but Richelieu, twenty years later, followed it, and Louis XIV carried it through. Soon after his death Europe agreed in calling him Henry the Great. In the French Revolution all the French kings who succeeded him were condemned, but Henry IV remained supreme in the affections of the people.

CHAPTER XV

Richelieu

1585–1642

I. BETWEEN TWO KINGS: 1610–24

THE sudden death of Henry IV left France in a renewed disorder, many-rooted in the struggle of the nobles against the monarchy, of the middle classes against the aristocracy, of the Catholics against the Huguenots, of the clergy against the state, of the young King Louis XIII against his mother, and of France against Austria and Spain. The fascinating and demonic genius who resolved all this chaos into order, defeated the feudal reaction, pacified the Huguenots, subordinated the Church to the state, saved Protestant Germany from collapse, broke the power of the encompassing Hapsburgs, and raised the French monarchy to domestic omnipotence and European supremacy was a Catholic priest, the greatest, subtlest, and most ruthless statesman in the history of France.

It was part of Henry's tragedy that at his death his heir, Louis XIII, was a helpless boy of eight, and that the widow to whom he had left the regency was a woman of more courage than intelligence, willing to surrender the government to Italian favorites provided she might enjoy the sweets of life in swelling amplitude. She abandoned Henry's plan of a war to the death against the Hapsburgs; on the contrary, she allied France with Spain by marrying her children to those of Philip III—her son Louis to Anne of Austria, her daughter Elizabeth to the future Philip IV. The will of Richelieu was to prove stronger than this mingled blood.

Henry and Sully had left 41,345,000 livres in the treasury. Concino Concini, his wife Leonora Galigai, the Duke of Épernon, and other thirsty courtiers gathered around this hoard and prepared to consume it. Sully protested but was overruled; he resigned in disgust, retired to his estates, and wrote memoirs of his beloved King.

The nobles saw in the corrupt incompetence of the central government a chance to restore their old feudal sovereignties. They demanded and obtained a convocation of the States-General, assuming that it would be, as usually in the past, their voice and weapon against the monarchy. But when it met, at Paris in October 1614, they were disconcerted by the strength and the proposals of the Third Estate—the untitled, untonsured mass of the people, represented then, as now, by lawyers, and expressing the power and the wishes of the middle class. Nobles and clergy, rating birth and ointment above wealth and law, challenged the new heritability of judicial offices, which was creating a rival nobility of the robe. The *tiers état* retaliated by asking for an investigation of the spacious gifts and pensions recently received by nobles from the government; it called for the correction of abuses in the Church; it objected to the application, in France, of the rigorous decrees of the Council of Trent; it demanded that the clergy be subject to the same laws and courts as the laity, that a check be put upon the further acquisition of realty by the untaxable Church, and that the clergy baptize, marry, and bury the people without charge; finally, it defended the absolute authority and divine right of the king over the claims of nobles to rule him and of the popes to depose him. This was an unexpected revolution. The troublesome delegates were placated with promises, and the assembly was dissolved (March 1615). The promises were for the most part forgotten, peculation and mismanagement were resumed, and no further States-General was called until monarchy, nobility, and clergy alike collapsed in 1789.

Nevertheless the French Catholic clergy now honored itself with sincere and effective self-reform. It was not always responsible for the abuses that disordered the Church, since many of these stemmed from the appointment of bishops and abbots by kings or nobles half pagan in life and sometimes skeptical in creed.[1] Henry IV gave Huguenot Sully four monasteries for his private support, and made his mistress "Corisande" abbess of Châtillon-sur-Seine. Noble lords bestowed episcopacies, abbacies, and nunneries upon their younger sons, their illegitimate children, their brave soldiers, their favorite women. As the reform decrees of the Council of Trent were not yet accepted in France, there were few seminaries for the training of priests; any tonsured youth who could read the Latin missal and acquire the elements of liturgy was eligible for the sacerdotal office; and many bishops, who had been easy-living men of the world before being rewarded with sees, appointed to pastorates men of little education and less holiness. "The name of priest," said a priest, "has become the synonym for ignorance and debauchery."[2] "The worst enemies of the Church," said St. Vincent de Paul, "are her unworthy priests."[3]

Père Bourdoise attacked the moral side of the problem by establishing (1610) the Communauté des Prêtres, which required all the priests of a parish to live together in simplicity and fidelity to their vows. In 1611 Père de Bérulle founded the Congregation of the Oratory, on the model of a similar foundation by St. Philip Neri in Italy; it became a seminary for training young priests to better education and dedication. In 1641 Père Jean Jacques Olier organized the Sulpician order to prepare men for the priesthood, and in 1646 he opened the seminary and church of St.-Sulpice in Paris. In 1643 Père Jean (St. John) Eudes formed the Congregation of Jesus and Mary to fit men for the priesthood and missions. So were formed Bossuet, Bourdaloue, and Malebranche of the next generations, and the power and splendor of the Church under Louis XIV.

New religious orders revealed and revived the piety of the people. The Ursuline nuns entered France toward 1600 and undertook the education of girls; within a century they had 1,000 houses and 350 congregations. The Order of the Brothers of Mercy, founded (1540) in Spain by Juan de Dios (St. John of God), was welcomed into France by Marie de Médicis and soon provided thirty hospitals. In 1610 Jeanne Frémiot, Baroness of Chantal (St. Chantal), helped by François de Sales (St. Francis of Sales), established the Congregation of the Visitation of Our Lady for the care of the sick and the poor; by 1640 it had a hundred convents; by 1700 one branch alone had four hundred nunneries. All in all there were in France in 1600 some eighty thousand nuns.[4]

Two men stand out with special prominence in this Catholic revival of the seventeenth century. François de Sales took part of his name from the town of his birth, near Annecy, in Savoy. He studied law at Padua and became an official of the Savoy Senate. But religion was in his blood; he was ordained a priest, and undertook (1594) the difficult task of winning back to Catholicism the Chablais region, south of Lake Geneva, which had been Calvinist since 1535. In five years the mission was accomplished, partly by exiling the unconverted, but mostly by François' persuasive piety, patience, and tact. Raised to a bishopric, he gave himself to teaching children and adults. When he visited Paris highborn women fell reverently in love with him, and for a time piety became fashionable.

The career of Vincent de Paul followed less traditional grooves. He began as a swineherd, but somehow he found his way to a Franciscan college in Gascony. His father, longing, like every Catholic parent, to get his family into Paradise by dedicating a child to the Church, sold a yoke of oxen to send his boy to study theology at the University of Toulouse. There Vincent was ordained priest (1600). On a voyage in the Mediterranean he was captured by pirates, and he was sold as a slave in Tunis. He escaped, went to Paris, served King Henry's divorced Margot as chaplain, and then became spiritual director to Mme. de Gondi. With funds provided by this lady he organized missions among the peasantry; after nearly every mission he established a *conférence de charité* for the relief of the local poor; and to provide for the continuance of these foundations he organized the Congregation of the Priests of the Mission—often called the Lazarists from the Priory of St. Lazarus that served as their headquarters in Paris. As M. de Gondi was commandant of the French galleys, Vincent took to preaching to the galley convicts. Shocked by their hardships and diseases, he opened hospitals for them at Paris and Marseille, and aroused the conscience of France to better treatment of the prisoners. He persuaded well-to-do women to give periodic service in the hospitals; he raised large sums for charitable distribution; and to administer these, and help his "Ladies of Charity," he organized (1633) the Sisters (whom he preferred to call the Daughters) of Charity—now serving humanity and their Church in many quarters of the world.

Physically unattractive, poorly garbed, resembling some wrinkled, bearded rabbi, "Monsieur Vincent," by his labors for the poor, the sick, the criminal, won the hearts of nearly all who knew him. He collected great sums, established hospitals, asylums, seminaries, homes for the aged, retreats for laymen and priests; volumes have swollen with accounts of his benefactions. During the Fronde of 1648–53 and the blockade of Paris he supervised the feeding of fifteen thousand destitute persons; here, however, dogma overcame charity, and he required a confession of Catholic faith as a condition of receiving food.[5] He joined in the campaign against Port-Royal, but tried to soften the persecution of its nuns.[6] When he died, half of Paris mourned him; and satisfaction was universal when the Church (1737) enrolled him among her saints.

Through him, and François de Sales, and the undiscourageable Jesuits, and the ardent service of innumerable women, French Catholicism experienced under Louis XIII a rebirth of vigor and devotion. Old monastic orders returned to their rules; nunneries reformed themselves; now began Port-Royal and its Jansenist saints. Mysticism found new advocates and practitioners of absorption in direct contemplation of God. The young King, caught in the fervor of the age, solemnly placed France under the protection of the Virgin Mary, "in order," said the royal edict, "that all his loyal subjects might be received into Paradise . . . such being his good will and pleasure."[7] Watchmen continued, as in medieval France, to awaken the Parisians each morning with a call to prayer for the departed dead:

Réveillez vous, gens qui dormez,
Priez Dieu pour les trépassés.[8]

But the conflict of creeds continued bitterly. Marie de Médicis adhered faithfully, despite her piety, to the Edict of Nantes, but neither Catholics nor Huguenots were disposed to tolerance. The Pope, his nuncio, and the Catholic clergy denounced the government for permitting heresy. Where Catholics dominated they disrupted Protestant services, destroyed Protestant churches, homes, sometimes lives;[9] children were forcibly taken from Huguenot parents on the ground that the parents prevented them from fulfilling their desire to become Catholics.[10] Where Protestants dominated they retaliated in kind. They excluded the Mass from some 250 towns under their rule;[11] they demanded that the government prohibit Catholic processions in Protestant territory; they ridiculed, disturbed, sometimes attacked such processions; they forbade Protestants to attend Catholic baptisms, marriages, or funerals; and their ministers declared that they would withhold the Sacrament from parents whose children married Catholics.[12] Said a famous freethinker, "While the Catholics were theoretically more bigoted than the Protestants, the Protestants became more bigoted than the Catholics."[13] The preachers rivaled the Catholic clergy in suppressing heresy and criticism; they excommunicated and "delivered up to Satan" (but did not burn) Jérémie Ferrier for having made fun of ecclesiastical assemblies; and their writings attacked Catholicism in "works which, for bitterness of feeling, have hardly ever been equaled, and which it would certainly be impossible to surpass."[14] Fearing repeal of the Edict of Nantes, and resenting the alliance of France with Spain, the Huguenots strove to make their part of France politically independent and militarily secure, with its own army and its own laws.

When Louis XIII visited Pau (1620) he was shocked to find not one Catholic church in which to perform his devotions.[15] The young King looked with alarmed resentment upon a faith that threatened to divide not merely the soul but also the body of France. He searched anxiously, amid his court, for a man with enough iron in his blood to transform this sundering chaos of creeds and powers into a strong and united nation.

II. LOUIS XIII

He knew that he himself lacked the physical health and mental force needed to meet these challenges. Begotten in the forty-eighth year of a father perhaps weakened by sexual exuberance, he suffered from tuberculosis, intestinal inflammation, and an embarrassing impediment in his speech. Through long periods he was too weak to indulge in sports; he played and composed music, grew peas for the market, put up preserves, and helped in the kitchen. Heredity and disease left him no charms of figure or face; he was precariously thin, his head and nose were oversized, his pendulous underlip left his mouth always partly open; and his long, livid countenance harmonized with his deliberately drab costume. He suffered no more from nature than from his physicians, who in a single year bled him forty-seven times, gave him 215 enemas, and poured 212 drugs down his throat.[16] He survived by engaging in sports when he could, hunting, joining his army, sleeping in the open air, and eating the soldiers' simple food.

Beaten repeatedly by his teachers, he abominated education, and seems never to have read a book except for prayer. He read the canonical hours every day, accepted without question the faith taught him in his growing years, and always joined and accompanied to its end any procession that bore the consecrated Host. A neurotic tendency to occasional cruelty tarnished a disposition basically kind. He was shy, secretive, and morose, not much loving a life that had not loved him. His mother considered him feeble-minded, neglected him, and openly preferred his younger brother, Gaston; he responded by hating her and worshiping the memory of his father. He developed an aversion to women, and after some timid contemplation of Mlle. de Hautefort's beauty he gave his affections to young men. Married politically to Anne of Austria, he had to be prodded into her bed. When she miscarried he left her intact for thirteen years. The court advised him to take a mistress, but he had other tastes. Then at thirty-seven, yielding to the demands of all France for a dauphin, he tried again, and grateful Anne gave the world Louis XIV (1638). Two years later she bore Philippe I of Orléans, who continued his father's appreciation of male charms.

Louis was some inches a king. Suddenly, still a lad of sixteen, tired of Concini's impudence and peculations, he gave secret orders for his assassination (1617); and when the Queen Mother protested against this termination of her favorite, he banished her to Blois and chose as his chief minister Charles d'Albert, who had suggested the stroke, and who was now made Duke of Luynes. Pressed by the Duke and Pope Paul V, Louis ordered the Huguenots to restore all property that they had appropriated from the Church. When Béarn ignored the decree, he marched into the province, compelled obedience, and brought Béarn and Navarre—once his father's personal realm—under the direct rule of the king. The Huguenots made no immediate resistance; but in 1620 their General Assembly, meeting in their strongest city, La Rochelle, demanded the return of the restored property, as belonging to the people rather than to the Church; moreover, it apportioned France into eight "circles," and appointed for each of them a chief administrator and a council to levy taxes and raise troops. Louis declared that France could not tolerate such a state within a state. In April 1621 he led one army, and his generals led three others, against the Protestant citadels. Several of these were taken, but Montauban, under Henri, Duke of Rohan, held out successfully. Incompetent generals allowed the war to drag on for a year and a half. The peace treaty of October 9, 1622, forbade Protestant assemblies, but left Montauban and La Rochelle in Huguenot hands. During these campaigns Luynes died (1621), and Richelieu climbed to power.

III. THE CARDINAL AND THE HUGUENOTS

How does a man make his way to the top? In those days it helped to be wellborn. Armand Jean du Plessis de Richelieu had for mother the daughter of an advocate in the Parlement of Paris, and for his father the Seigneur de Richelieu, Grand Provost of the Royal Household under Henry IV. The ancient Poitou family inherited the right to recommend to the king a candidate for the bishopric of Luçon. Armand, twenty-one, was so nominated by Henry (1606). Two years too young for episcopacy, he hastened to Rome, lied about his age, and delivered before Paul V so handsome a Latin harangue that the Pope surrendered the see. This *fait* being *accompli*, Richelieu confessed his lie and asked for absolution. The Pope complied, remarking, *"Questo giovane sarà un gran furbo"* (This youth will be a great knave).[17]

The young bishop described his bishopric as the "poorest and nastiest" see in France, but there was some money in the family, and he soon had his coach and his silver plate. He did not take his office as a lazy sinecure; he devoted himself assiduously to his duties, but he found time to flatter every influence and pull every wire. When the clergy of Poitou chose a delegate to the States-General (1614), Armand was their man. In that assembly his grave face, his tall, slim figure, his almost legal ability to grasp an issue clearly and present it persuasively, impressed everyone, especially Marie de Médicis. Through her and Concini he was made a secretary of state (1616). A year later Concini was killed and Richelieu lost his post. After a brief service with the banished Queen Mother at Blois he returned to Luçon. Marie plotted to escape; Richelieu was suspected of complicity; he was exiled to Avignon (1618); his political career seemed finished. But even his enemies recognized his abilities; and when Marie let herself out by night from a window of her castle at Blois and joined a force of rebel aristocrats, Luynes recalled the young bishop and commissioned him to win the Queen Mother back to reason and the King. He succeeded; Louis secured a cardinal's hat for him and appointed him to the Council of State. Soon Richelieu's superiority of mind and will made itself evident, and in August 1624, aged thirty-nine, he became prime minister.

The King found in him precisely the objective intelligence, the clear purpose, the tenacity of ends, and the flexibility of means wherein he himself was wanting; and he had the wisdom to accept the Cardinal's guidance in the triple task of subduing the Huguenots, the nobles, and Spain. In his memoirs Richelieu remarked appreciatively, "The ability to let himself be served [to delegate authority] is not among the least qualities of a great king."[18] Louis did not always agree with his minister; sometimes he rebuked him; always he was jealous of him; now and then he thought of dismissing him. But how could he reject a man who was making him absolute in France and supreme in Europe, and who was bringing in more taxes than even Sully had gleaned?

The spirit of the Cardinal showed itself first in his treatment of religion. He accepted without discussion the doctrines of the Church, and added a few superstitions surprising in so powerful a mind. But he ignored the claim of the "Ultramontanist" party that the popes had full dominion over kings; he preserved the "Gallican liberties" of the French Church as against Rome; and in things temporal he subordinated the Church to the state as resolutely as any Englishman. He banished Father Caussin, who, as the royal confessor, had intervened in politics; no religion, in his view, should mingle with affairs of state. The alliances he formed for France were made with Protestant and Catholic powers indifferently.

He applied his principles firmly to Huguenots playing politics. Despite the peace of 1622, they had made La Rochelle a virtually sovereign city, under the control of its merchants, ministers, and generals. From that strategic port the merchants plied their trade with the world, and pirates sailed out to seize any booty or any ship, even those of France; through this port, given Huguenot permission, any enemy of France might enter. Louis too had violated the treaty; he had promised to demolish Fort Louis, which was a standing threat to the city; instead he strengthened it, and assembled a small fleet in the nearby harbor of Le Blavet. Benjamin (brother to Henri) de Rohan, Seigneur de Soubise, commanding a Huguenot squadron, captured this royal fleet and towed it in triumph to La Rochelle (1625). Richelieu built another fleet, organized an army, and accompanied the King to the siege of the Huguenot stronghold.

Soubise persuaded the Duke of Buckingham to send an armada of 120 vessels to protect the city. It came, but suffered so sorely from the artillery of the royal forts on the island of Ré that it crept back to England in disgrace (1627). Meanwhile Richelieu, acting as general for his sick King, had captured all the land approaches to La Rochelle; it remained only to blockade it by sea. He ordered his engineers and his soldiers to build a mole of masonry, 1,700 yards long, across the entrance to the harbor, leaving an opening for the movement of the tides. These were so strong, rising and falling twelve feet, that the enterprise seemed impracticable; every day half the stones laid that day were washed away. The King grew weary of this bloodless warfare and went off to Paris; many courtiers expected him to dismiss Richelieu for failing to take the city by assault. But at last the mole was complete and began its scheduled work. Half the population of La Rochelle died of hunger. Only the richest could get a little meat; they paid forty-five livres for a cat, two thousand for a

cow. Jean Guiton, the mayor, threatened to kill with his own dagger anyone who spoke of yielding. Nevertheless, after thirteen months of famine
and disease, the city capitulated in despair (October 30, 1628). Richelieu
entered on horseback, followed by soldiers mercifully distributing bread.

Half of France clamored for the total extinction of the Huguenots. Exhausted, they could only pray. Richelieu surprised them with peace terms
that seemed to the Catholics outrageously lenient. La Rochelle lost its
municipal independence, its forts, and its walls, but the persons and property of the inhabitants were spared, the surviving Huguenot troops were
allowed to depart with their arms, and the free exercise of both the Protestant and the Catholic worship in the city was guaranteed. Other Huguenot towns, surrendering, received similar terms. Catholic property expropriated by Protestants had to be restored, but the temporarily homeless
Huguenot ministers were compensated by a state subsidy of 200,000 livres,
and, like the Catholic clergy, they were exempted from the head tax, or
taille.[19] A general amnesty was granted to all who had shared in the rebellion. Henry IV's Edict of Nantes was confirmed in every essential by
Richelieu's Edict of Grace (June 28, 1629). Positions in the army, navy,
and civil service were kept open to all without question of creed. Europe
was startled to see French Catholics following and honoring Protestant
generals like Turenne, Schomberg, and Henri de Rohan. "From that time,"
said Richelieu, "differences in religion never prevented me from rendering
to the Huguenots all sorts of good offices."[20] With a wisdom tragically
lacking in Louis XIV, the great Cardinal recognized—as Colbert was to
do—the immense economic value of the Huguenots to France. They
abandoned revolt, gave themselves peacefully to commerce and industry,
and prospered as never before.

IV. THE CARDINAL AND THE NOBLES

He proceeded with equal resolution, and less lenience, against the nobles
who still held France to be many and not one. Feudalism was by no means
dead. It had fought in the religious wars for control of the central government. The great nobles still had their fortified castles, their armed forces,
their private wars, their private courts, their officers of law; they still had
the peasantry at their mercy, and charged obstructive tolls on commerce
traversing their domains. France, dismembered by feudalism and religion,
was not yet a nation; it was an unstable and agitated assemblage of proud
and semi-independent barons capable at any moment of disrupting the
peace and the economy of the state. Most of the provinces were ruled by
dukes or counts who claimed their governorships for life and handed them
on to their sons.

It seemed to Richelieu that the only practicable alternative to this enfeebling chaos was to centralize authority and power in the king. Conceivably he might have labored to balance this by restoring some measure of municipal autonomy. But he could not restore the medieval commune, which had rested on the guilds and a protected local economy; the passage from a city to a national market had undermined the guilds and the communes, and required central rather than local legislation.* To minds frozen in the perspective of today, the royal absolutism desired by Richelieu seems but a reactionary despotism; in the view of history, and of the great majority of Frenchmen in the seventeenth century, it was a liberating progress from feudal tyranny to unified rule. France was not ripe for democracy; most of its population were ill-fed, ill-clothed, illiterate, darkened with superstitions and murderous with certainties. The towns were controlled by businessmen who could think in no other terms than their own profit or loss; and these men, hampered at every step by feudal privileges, were not disposed to unite with the lesser nobles, as in England, to establish a parliament checking the royal power. The French *parlements* were not representative and legislative parliaments; they were superior courts, nurtured and mortised in precedent; they were not chosen by the people, and they became citadels of conservatism. The middle classes, the artisans, and the peasants approved the absolutism of the king as the only protection they could see from the absolutism of the lords.

In 1626, in the name of the King, Richelieu issued an edict that struck at the very base of feudalism: he ordered the destruction of all fortresses except on the frontiers, and forbade, in future, the fortification of private dwellings. In the same year (his older brother having been killed in a duel) he made dueling a capital crime; and when Montmorency-Bouteville and the Count des Chapelles dueled nevertheless, he had them put to death. He confessed himself "much troubled in spirit" by this procedure, but he told his master, "It is a question of breaking the neck of duels or of your Majesty's edicts."[21] The nobles vowed vengeance and plotted the minister's fall.

They found an eager ally in the Queen Mother. Once the patron of Richelieu, she came to hate him when she saw him opposing her policies. When Louis fell gravely ill (July 1630), she and the Queen nursed him back to semihealth and asked, as their reward, the Cardinal's head. In her own palace, the Luxembourg, Marie de Médicis, thinking Richelieu far away, repeated the demand with passionate urgency, and offered, as a willing replacement, Michel de Marillac, Keeper of the Seals. Richelieu, coming by a secret passage, entered the room unannounced and confronted the Queen Mother; she confessed that she had told the King that either she

---

* A like development weakened "states' rights" in the United States in the twentieth century.

or he, Richelieu, must go. The harassed King withdrew and rode off to his hunting lodge at Versailles. Courtiers flocked around Marie, rejoicing in her expected victory. But Louis sent for Richelieu, confirmed him as prime minister, assured him of the royal support, and signed an order for Marillac's arrest. The plotting nobles were thrown into angry confusion by that "Day of Dupes" (November 10, 1630). Marillac was allowed to live, but his younger brother, a marshal of France, was later indicted on a charge of peculation and was rather summarily put to death (1632). Louis ordered his mother to retire to her château at Moulins and to withdraw from politics. Instead, she fled to Flanders (1631), formed a court in exile at Brussels, and continued to work for Richelieu's fall. She never saw the King again.

Her other son, "Monsieur," Gaston, Duke of Orléans, raised an army in Lorraine and led it in open rebellion against his brother (1632). He was joined by several nobles, among them the highest in France—Henri, Duke of Montmorency, governor of Languedoc. Thousands of the aristocracy rallied to the revolt. Near Castelnaudary (September 1) the thirty-seven-year-old Montmorency engaged the forces sent against him by Richelieu. He fought till brought down by seventeen wounds; his and Gaston's army, rich in titles but poor in discipline, fell to pieces under attack, and Montmorency was captured. Gaston surrendered and, as the price of pardon, named his accomplices. Louis ordered the Parlement of Toulouse to try Montmorency for treason; its verdict was death. The last of the ducal Montmorencys died without fear or complaint, saying, "I hold this decree of the King's justice for a decree of God's mercy."[22] Most of France condemned the Cardinal and the King for unfeeling severity; Louis replied, "I should not be king if I had the feelings of private persons"; and Richelieu defended the execution as a necessary notice to the aristocracy that they too were subject to the laws. "Nothing so upholds the laws," he said, "as the punishment of persons whose rank is as great as their crime."[23]

Two further obstacles remained to Richelieu's supremacy: the governors and the *parlements*. Resenting the loss of provincial revenue through malversation and incompetence in noble governors and in bourgeois or petty-noble magistrates, the Cardinal sent to each district "intendants" to supervise the administration of finance and justice and the enforcement of the laws. These royal appointees took precedence over local officials of whatever rank; local autonomy declined, efficiency and tax collections rose. Anticipated in some measure by Henry IV, suppressed by the nobles in the Fronde, consolidated by Louis XIV, adapted by Napoleon, this system of intendants became a major feature of the centrally controlled bureaucracy that henceforth administered the laws of France.

The Parlement of Paris thought it opportune, under a weak monarchy, to extend its functions from the registration and interpretation of the laws to the role of an advisory council to the king. Richelieu would not brook such rivalry to his Council of State; probably under his prodding, and with his sharp phrasing, Louis summoned the leaders of the Parlement and told them, "You are constituted only to judge between Master Peter and Master John; if you go on as at present I will pare your nails so close that you will be sorry."[24] The Paris Parlement yielded, and the provincial *parlements* followed suit. Even their traditional functions were curtailed; Richelieu set up "extraordinary commissions" to try special cases. France became a police state; the Cardinal's spies were everywhere, even in the salons; *lettres de cachet* (orders in secret) became a frequent instrument of government. Richelieu was now, in effect, king of France.

V. THE CARDINAL SUPREME

With this concentrated power in his hands, he did everything for France, little for the people. He thought of France as a power, not as a sum of living individuals; he did not idealize the common man, and he probably thought it *dulce et decorum* that such men should die for their country; he would sacrifice them to make the future France secure from Hapsburg encirclement. He labored far into the night at the business of the state, but almost always on foreign policy. He had no time to improve the economy, except to ferret out tax evaders and bring revenue and "intelligence" to Paris with less leakage on the way. In 1627 he organized a public post.

Taxes were still collected by financiers to whom they had been "farmed"; these men had exacted twice, sometimes thrice, the amount they transmitted to the government. The nobility and the clergy were exempt from the major taxes; clever businessmen and the hoards of officials found ways of avoiding or appeasing the collectors; towns paid a small composition to escape the poll tax; the brunt of the burden fell upon the peasantry; Richelieu bled it to destitution to make France the strongest power in Christendom. Like Henry IV, he preferred to conquer enemies with money rather than with blood; many of the treaties with which he waged war included subsidies to allies and *douceurs* to potential foes. At times, desperate for funds, he advanced his own money to the treasury; once he hired an alchemist to make gold.[25] Taxation and the state *corvée*—unpaid labor on the roads—co-operated with drought, famine, pestilence, and ravages by soldiery to bring peasants near to suicide; several killed their families and themselves; starving mothers killed and ate their infants (1639).[26] In 1634, according to a probably exaggerated report, a fourth of the population of Paris begged.[27] Periodically and sporadically the poor rose in revolts that were mercilessly suppressed.

Richelieu used the taxes to build armies and a navy; right would not be heard unless it spoke with guns. Having purchased the office of grand admiral, he fulfilled its functions resolutely. He repaired and fortified harbors, established arsenals and provision depots at the ports, built eighty-five ships, founded pilot schools, trained marine regiments. He raised a hundred regiments of infantry, three hundred troops of cavalry; he restored discipline in the army; he failed only in his efforts to banish its prostitutes. With his revitalized armament he faced the chaos of foreign relations bequeathed by the regency of Marie de Médicis, returned to the policy of Henry IV, and directed all his forces to one goal—the liberation of France from the cordon of Hapsburg power in the Netherlands, Austria, Italy, and Spain.

Marie had allied France to Spain—i.e., in Richelieu's view, she had submitted to the enemy; and she had alienated those on whom Henry IV had relied as friends—the English, the Dutch, and the Protestants of Germany. With the quick strategic eye of a general, Richelieu saw in the Valtelline passes that connected Austria and Spanish Italy the key to the united power of Spain and the Empire to exchange supplies and troops. For twelve years he struggled to win those passes; his wars against the Huguenots and the nobles distracted and defeated him; but he retrieved with diplomacy far more than he had lost in war. He had won to his faithful service François Le Clerc du Tremblay, who had taken the name Joseph on becoming a Capuchin monk; "Father Joseph" was sent everywhere on delicate diplomatic missions, and performed them skillfully; and France began to pair the gray-garbed monk as Éminence Grise—his Gray Eminence—with the red-robed Richelieu as Eminence Rouge. So aided, the Cardinal vowed that he would "prove to the world that the age of Spain is passing, and the age of France has come."[28]

In 1629 the epochal conflict in Germany seemed about to end in the complete triumph of the Catholic Hapsburg Emperor over the Protestant princes. Richelieu turned the tables with money. He signed with Gustavus Adolphus (1631) a treaty by which the virile King of Sweden, aided by a million livres a year from France, was to invade Germany and rescue the Protestant states. The ultramontanists of France denounced the minister as a traitor to the faith; he retorted that neutrality was treason to France. When Gustavus died in victory at Lützen (1632) and most German princes yielded to the Emperor, Richelieu actively entered the war. He expanded the French armies from 12,000 in 1621 to 150,000 in 1638; he helped the revolt of the Catalans in Spain; his diplomacy gave him control of Trier,

Coblenz, Colmar, Mannheim, and Basel; his troops took Lorraine and forced their way through Savoy to Milan, the center of Spanish power in North Italy.

Then the pendulum of fortune veered, and all these victories seemed meaningless. In July and August, 1636, a strong force of Spanish and Imperial troops crossed the Netherlands into France, took Aix-la-Chapelle (Aachen) and Corbie, advanced to Amiens, laid waste the green valleys of the Somme and the Oise. Richelieu's armies were far away; the road to Paris lay open and defenseless to the enemy. The Queen Mother in Brussels, the Queen in St.-Germain, and her pro-Spanish party in France rejoiced, and counted the days before the Cardinal's expected fall. In Paris angry multitudes pullulated in the streets, calling for his death. But when he appeared among them, outwardly calm on his stately horse, no one dared touch him, and many prayed God to give him strength to save France. Then appeared not only his courage, but his foresight and industry: he had long ago organized the citizens of Paris into a reserve militia; he had stored up arms and materials for them; now he inspired them with fervor, and they responded to his call; the Parlement of Paris, the corporations, and the guilds voted funds; in a few days a new army was on the march, and it laid siege to Corbie. Gaston of Orléans, in command, dillydallied; Richelieu came up, took charge, ordered assault. On November 14 Corbie was taken, and the Hapsburg troops retreated into the Netherlands.

In 1638 Bernhard of Saxe-Weimar, leading a German army financed by Richelieu, took Elsass; dying a year later, he bequeathed it to France; Elsass and Lothringen became Alsace-Lorraine and began to be French. In 1640 Arras was taken. In 1642 a force under the command of the King and the Cardinal captured Perpignan, and the surrounding province of Roussillon was detached from Spain. Everywhere Richelieu seemed now the organizer of victory.

The unreconciled nobles, the Spanish faction at the court, the highborn ladies palpitating with intrigue, made a last effort to unseat the minister. In 1632, after long serving the Cardinal in diplomacy and war, the Marquis of Effiat died, leaving a widow and a handsome twelve-year-old son, Henri Coiffier de Ruzé, Marquis of Cinq-Mars. Richelieu took the lad under his protection and introduced him to the King; perhaps he thought with this toy to distract Louis from Mlle. de Hautefort, who was among the *intriguantes*. It so transpired. The King was charmed by the youth's looks and wit and insolence, made him Master of the Horse, begged him to share the royal bed.[29] But Cinq-Mars, maturing to twenty-one, preferred the pretty courtesan Marion Delorme and the exalted Marie de Gonzague, future Queen of Poland, now one of the Cardinal's loveliest enemies. Probably at her suggestion, and inflamed by her strategic retreats, the youth importuned Louis for admission to the royal Council and for a command in the army. When Richelieu discountenanced these proposals, Cinq-Mars begged the King to dismiss the minister. Refused, he joined Gaston of Orléans, the Duke of Bouillon, and others in a plot to surrender Sedan to a Spanish army; with this army at their back the conspirators were to enter Paris and take possession of the King; and Gaston pledged himself to arrange the assassination of the Cardinal on the way to Perpignan. Cinq-Mars' friend, Jacques Auguste de Thou, solicited the co-operation of the Queen. But Anne of Austria, expecting Louis' early death and her elevation to power as regent, sent a hint of the scheme to Richelieu. He pretended to have a copy of the agreement with Spain; Gaston, believing it, confessed and, as usual, betrayed his associates. Cinq-Mars, de Thou, and Bouillon were arrested; Bouillon, as the price of pardon, confirmed Gaston's confession. The two youths were tried by a court at Lyon; they were unanimously condemned, and they dignified their treason with a stoic death. The King hurried back to Paris to protect his power. Richelieu, mortally ill, was carried in a litter through a France dying of victories and crying out for peace.

VI. EPITAPH

What was he like, this Cardinal who was hardly a Christian, this great man who felt that he could not afford to be good? Philippe de Champaigne sent him down the ages in one of the most famous paintings in the Louvre: the tall figure saved from absurdity by raiment, given authority by red robe and hat, posing as if in some forensic plea, proclaiming his nobility in his clear-cut features and delicate hands, challenging his enemies with his sharp eyes, but pale with exhausting years and saddened with the consciousness of inexorable time. Here is the worldliness of power crossed with the asceticism of dedication.

He had to be strong to keep his faults from defeating his purposes. He began his career at court with an ingratiating humility, which he later avenged with a pride that admitted only one superior. Once, when the Queen visited him, he remained seated—a discourtesy permitted only to the King. He was (like most of us) vain of his appearance, avid of titles, resentful of criticism, eager for popularity. Jealous of Corneille, he wished to be known also as a dramatist and a poet; actually he wrote excellent prose, as his memoirs show. As readily as Wolsey he reconciled the following of Christ with a cautious attention to Mammon. He refused bribes and took no salary, but he appropriated the income of many benefices, alleging his need to finance his policies. Like Wolsey, he built himself so splendid a palace that before he died he thought it wise to present it to the Dauphin; so the Palais Cardinal became the Palais Royal; we may suppose that it was built for an administrative staff and diplomatic show rather than for personal extravagance. He was no miser; he enriched his relatives and could be generous with the money of the state. He bequeathed half of his personal hoard to the King, advising him to use it "on occasions which cannot abide the tardiness of financial forms."[30]

What appears as his unfeeling cruelty was to him a necessity of rule: he took it for granted that men—certainly states—could not be managed by kindness; they had to be intimidated by severity. He loved France, but Frenchmen left him cold. He agreed with Cosimo de' Medici that a state cannot be governed with paternosters, and with Machiavelli that the ethics of Christ cannot be safely followed in ruling or preserving a nation. "A Christian," he wrote, "cannot too soon forgive an injury, but a ruler cannot too soon punish it when it is a crime against the state. . . . Without this virtue [of severity]—which becomes mercy insofar as the punishment of one culprit prevents a thousand from forgetting it—states cannot survive."[31] It was Richelieu who gave currency to the phrase *raison d'état*: i.e., the ethical code must give way to reasons of state.[32] He seems never to have questioned the identification of his policies with the needs of France; hence he persecuted his personal enemies as firmly as he punished the foes of the King.

Within his castle and his diplomatic front he was human, longed for friendship, and felt the loneliness of the exalted. Tallemant's gossipy *Historiettes* would have us believe that Richelieu tried to make a mistress of Marie de Médicis, who was twenty years older than he;[33] it is highly improbable. There are other legends of the Cardinal's secret amours, even with Ninon de Lenclos; and it would not have violated the mores of the time if the harassed statesman had consoled himself with contours. All that we know clearly of his affections is that he was profoundly attached to his niece, Marie-Madeleine de Combalet. Widowed soon after marriage, she wished to enter a convent, but Richelieu persuaded the Pope to forbid it; he kept her near him to manage his household, and he received from her a devotion intenser than most loves. She dressed like a nun and concealed her hair. Richelieu conducted himself toward her with all due propriety, but the Queens refused her the benefit of any doubt, and gave a lead to gossip that added another sting to the Cardinal's tale. He loved "not man, nor woman neither," and both took their revenge.

What he had above all was will. Few lives in all history have been so unified in their aim, so undeviating in its pursuit; the laws of motion could not be more constant. We must admire his devotion to his tasks, his wearing himself out in them through years of labor and nights without sleep.

He dedicated those labors to those who could sleep without fear under cover of his sleepless care. We must concede him a surpassing courage, which faced powerful nobles and scheming women, stood them off, killed them off, dauntlessly, amid repeated plots against his life. He risked his head time and again on the issue of his policies.

He was seldom well. Having contracted a fever from the marshes of Poitou, he was subject to repeated headaches, which sometimes lasted for days on end. Probably his nervous system was genetically weak or congenitally injured; one sister was feeble-minded, one brother was for a while insane, and court rumor said that the Cardinal himself had fits of epilepsy and mad hallucinations.[34] He suffered from hemorrhoids, boils, and a disease of the bladder; as in Napoleon's case, his political crises were occasionally complicated by inability to urinate.[35] More than once his illnesses led him to think of retiring; then, imprisoned in his will, he took hold again and fought on.

We cannot judge him fairly unless we see him wholly, including features that will take form as we proceed. He was a pioneer of religious toleration. He was a man of wide and sensitive culture: a connoisseur of music, a discerning collector of art, a lover of drama and poetry, a helpful friend of men of letters, the founder of the French Academy. But history properly remembers him above all as the man who freed France from that Spanish dominance which had resulted from the Religious Wars and which, in the League, had made France a pensioner, almost a dependency, of Spain. He achieved what Francis I and Henry IV had longed and failed to do: he broke the *cordon strangulaire* with which Hapsburg powers had encircled France. Later pages must detail the far-seeing strategy whereby he decided the Thirty Years' War, saved German Protestantism as the ally of Catholic France, and made it possible for Mazarin to mold the constructive Peace of Westphalia. For France itself he created unity and strength at the cost of a dictatorship and a royal absolutism that in time generated the Revolution. If it is a statesman's prime duty to make his people happy and free, Richelieu fell far short; Cardinal de Retz—a shrewd but not impartial judge—condemned him as having "established the most scandalous and dangerous tyranny that perhaps ever enslaved a state."[36] Richelieu would have replied that the statesman is required to consider the happiness and freedom of future generations as well as of his own, that he must make his country strong to guard it against alien invasion or domination, and that for this purpose he may justly sacrifice a present generation for the security of its successors. In this sense Richelieu's Spanish rival, Olivares, rated him "the ablest minister that Christendom has possessed these last thousand years";[37] Chesterfield ranked him as "the ablest statesman of his time, and perhaps of any other."[38]

His return from his final victory at Roussillon was the funeral procession of a still living man. From Tarascon to Lyon he took a barge on the Rhone; at Lyon he remained till Cinq-Mars and de Thou were tried and dead; then, weak from the pain of an anal fistula, he had himself carried to Paris in a litter borne by twenty-four men of his bodyguard, and large enough to contain a bed for the dying man, a table, a chair, and a secretary to take dictation of army orders and diplomatic messages. Six weeks that death march took; and along the road people gathered to get a glimpse of the man to whom they could give not love but fear, respect, and reverence, as the awesome embodiment of both Church and state, the vicar of God and king. Arrived in Paris, he was moved into his palace without leaving his couch. He sent in his resignation to his master, who refused to accept it. Louis came to his bedside, nursed him, fed him, wondered what he would do if this incarnate will should cease. The Cardinal's confessor, giving him the last sacrament, asked him if he had forgiven his enemies; he answered that he had never had any except the enemies of France. After a day of coma he died, December 4, 1642, aged fifty-seven. The King decreed an entire week of funeral ceremonies; through a day and a half sight-seers filed by his corpse. But in many provinces people kindled bonfires in gratitude that the iron Cardinal was dead.[39]

He continued for a time to rule France. He had recommended Giulio Mazarini as successor to his ministry; Louis complied. He left ten volumes of memoirs, recording the actions of the state as if they had been not his but the King's. In his final years he had dedicated to Louis a *Testament politique*, "to serve after my death for the administration and conduct of your realm." Here, amid some platitudes, are precise and pithy maxims of government, in a style rivaling any other prose of the time. He advises the King to avoid war, as something for which his Majesty was by nature unfit. "It is more profitable, and more glorious, to reconcile a dozen enemies than to ruin one."[40] Besides (he confided), the French are not constituted for war; at the start they are all ardor and bravery, but they lack the patience and *flegme* to await the propitious moment; as time goes on "they lose interest, and become soft to the point where they are less than women."[41] A king, like a general, must have a masculine courage capable of resisting emotional inclinations. He should give women no voice in government, for they follow their moods and passions rather than their reason.[42] However, intellect in a woman is unbecoming; "I have never seen a woman of much learning who was not marred by her knowledge."[43] Women cannot keep secrets, and "secrecy is the soul of statesmanship."[44] "A prudent statesman will talk little and listen much."[45] He will watch lest he give offense by some careless word; he will never speak ill of anyone unless the interest of the state requires it.[46] The King should get "a general knowledge of the history and constitution of all states, especially his own."[47] And the author asks some understanding for his ministry and his character. "Great men who are appointed to govern states are like those condemned to torture, with only this difference, that the latter receive the punishment of their crimes, the former of their merits."[48]

The King survived him by five months. Louis' brief rule was gratefully remembered, for he released political prisoners, suffered exiles to return, and allowed France to breathe. He complained that the Cardinal had not permitted him to act as he wished. His mother had died a few months before Richelieu; he had her remains brought from Cologne and gave them stately burial, and in his last moments he repeatedly prayed that God and man would pardon the harshness he had shown to her.

He saw himself failing, but rejoiced in the vigor and beauty of his four-year-old son. "What is your name?" he asked playfully. "Louis the Four-teenth," answered the boy. "Not yet, my son, not yet," said the King, smiling. He bade the court accept the regency of the Queen until his son should come of age. When he was told that death was near, he said, "Then, my God, I consent, with all my heart."[49] He died on May 14, 1643, aged forty-one. "People went to his funeral as to a wedding," Tallemant re-ported, "and appeared before the Queen as at a tourney."[50] The terrible Cardinal had made everything ready for *le grand monarque* and *le grand siècle*.

CHAPTER XVI

France Beneath the Wars

1559–1643

I. MORALS

THE religion whose varieties gave specious excuses for so many wars was beginning to suffer from its political employment; there was a growing number of men who questioned the divinity of doctrines that argued by the competitive shedding of blood; and in the upper classes doubts of the Christian ethic began to mingle with skepticism of the creed. It was a sign of the times when a good priest, Pierre Charron, explained the respectability of sex and its absurd apparatus.[1]

The peasants retained their faith, and honored the Christian code even when violating it; they might kill one another in passing ecstasy, they might diverge from monogamy when opportunity called and surveillance slept, but otherwise they led a tolerably decent life, heard Mass regularly, and, at least once a year, consumed the body and the blood of the Lord. The middle classes—Catholic or Huguenot—gave the best example of Christian morality: they dressed modestly, married once, attended to their business and their children, went to church, and gave the state its priests, physicians, lawyers, magistrates, and stability. Even in the aristocracy there were exemplary women; Charles IX called his wife, Elizabeth of Austria, the most virtuous woman in the world. But generally, in the leisure classes of the capital and in the artisans of the towns, erotic matters were getting out of hand. It was an age of frankly physical drive. Something of the platonic love that had amused Bembo and Castiglione in Italy and Marguerite of Navarre in France survived in the circle of Mme. de Rambouillet (herself an Italian), but it was mostly a feminine device, a resistance in depth to glorify the citadel.

So far as we know, Catherine de Médicis was a faithful wife and solicitous mother, but gossip accused her of training pretty women to seduce her enemies into obedience,[2] and Jeanne d'Albret (something of a prude) described Catherine's court as "the most corrupt and accursed society that ever was."[3] Brantôme was a scandalmonger, but his testimony should enter the picture:

> As for our fair women of France . . . they have in the last fifty years learned so much gentleness and delicacy, so much attraction and

charm in their clothes, in their fair looks and wanton ways . . . that now none can deny that they surpass all other women in every respect. . . . Moreover, the wanton language of love is in France more wanton, more exciting and sweeter-sounding, than in other tongues. And more than all, this blessed liberty which we have in France . . . renders our women more desirable and captivating, more tractable and easy of access than all others; and further, adultery is not so generally punished as in other lands . . . In a word, it is good to make love in France.[4]

The kings set the fashion. Francis II died too soon for sinning. Charles IX had his Marie Touchet. Henry III passed from *mignonettes* to *mignons*. Henry IV was faithfully heterosexual. Neither he nor his mistress Gabrielle d'Estrées seems to have objected to her being portrayed naked to the waist.[5] When his daughter Henrietta Maria of France, aged seventeen, married Charles I, she had had so many liaisons that her confessor advised her to take the Magdalen as her model and England as her penance.[6]

Even so, the complaisance of the women lagged behind the eagerness of the men, and prostitutes labored to meet the swelling demand. Paris recognized three types: the *chèvre coiffée* (she-goat with a hairdo) for the court, the *petrel* (chattering bird) for the bourgeoisie, and the *pierreuse*, who served the poor and lived in a stone basement. There were educated tarts for aristocrats, like Marion Delorme, who, dying, confessed ten times, since after each shriving she reminded herself of untold sins.[7] Charles IX and Henry III issued edicts outlawing brothels, and an ordinance of Louis XIII (1635) required that all detected prostitutes should be "whipped, shaved, and banished," and that all men concerned in the traffic should be sent to the galleys for life.[8] Several men, including Montaigne and a Huguenot clergyman, protested against such measures, and advocated the legalization of brothels in the interest of public morals.[9] These laws remained on the statute books till the late eighteenth century, but were seldom enforced. Other decress fought in vain against nature's perversions and vagaries; Montaigne tells of a girl who at twenty-two was changed into a man.[10] Obscene literature found a ready market, and print-shop windows displayed erotic pictures without incurring any now known interference.

Social and political morality suffered from the wars. The sale of public offices was extended to a nearly universal venality. The financial administration, before Sully cleansed it, was corrupt to the point of chaos.[11] War was not as indiscriminately devastating as it was soon to be under Louis XIV; yet we hear of armies, Huguenot as well as Catholic, engaging in wholesale massacre, pillage, and rape, stringing citizens up by the thumbs, or kindling a fire under their feet, to extort hidden gold. Dueling became more frequent in the sixteenth century, perhaps because the sword became a regular part of male dress. It was forbidden by Charles IX, under the urging of Michel de L'Hôpital, but it became almost an epidemic under Henry III; seconds as well as principals were expected to fight; duels, said Montaigne, were now battles. Richelieu's edict against dueling differed from its predecessors in being vigorously and impartially enforced. After his death the practice revived.

Crime was frequent. Nocturnal Paris was mostly unlit; robbery and murder flourished; violent brawls disordered the streets, and travel in the countryside endangered life as well as limb. Penalties were barbarous; we are not sure that they were effective deterrents, but probably crime would have been still worse without them. Imprisonment was genteel for gentlemen; aristocrats sent to the Bastille could pay for comfortable quarters equipped with their own furniture and wives. Common criminals might be sent to stifling dungeons or be deported to colonies or condemned to the galleys. Traces of this last penalty go back to 1532, but its earliest known enactment in French law belongs to 1561. The *galériens* were usually sentenced for ten years; the letters GAL were branded on their backs. In winter they remained in their docked galleys or were herded into prisons, chiefly at Toulon or Marseille. During the Religious Wars many captured Huguenots were sentenced to the galleys, where they received such brutal treatment that death must have seemed a boon. Epidemics of suicide broke out in those bitter decades, above all among the women of Lyon and Marseille.

II. MANNERS

Manners improved while morals declined. Catherine de Médicis had brought Italian politeness with her, a sense of beauty, a taste for elegance, a refinement in appointments and dress. Brantôme thought her court the finest that had ever been, "a veritable earthly Paradise," sparkling with "at least three hundred ladies and damoiselles"[12] dressed to the height of taxation. French court ceremonial, established by Francis I, now displaced the Italian as the model of Europe. Henry III created the office of Grand Master of the Ceremonies of France and issued an edict detailing the ritual and protocol of court behavior, specifying the persons who were to be admitted to the king's presence, the manner of addressing him, of serving him at his rising, his toilette, his meals, and his retiring, who might accompany him on his walks or hunts, who might attend the court balls. Henry III, timid and finicky, insisted on these rules; Henry IV violated them freely, Louis XIII ignored them, Louis XIV expanded them into a liturgy rivaling High Mass.

Court dress became increasingly costly and ornate. Marshal de Bassompierre wore a coat made of cloth of gold, laden with pearls weighing fifty pounds and costing fourteen thousand écus.[13] Marie de Médicis at the baptism of her son wore a robe covered with three thousand diamonds and thirty-two thousand other precious stones.[14] A courtier considered himself poor unless he had twenty-five costumes of divers styles. Sumptuary laws were numerous and soon ignored. One, issued by Henry IV, forbade "all inhabitants of this kingdom to wear either gold or silver on their clothes, except prostitutes and thieves,"[15] but even this clever correlation failed. Preachers complained about the calculated risk that ladies took in only partly covering their curves; if we may believe Montaigne, who was not often guilty of wishful thinking, "our ladies (dainty-nice though they be) are many times seen to go open-breasted as low as the navel."[16] To accentuate white skin or rosy cheeks, women began in the seventeenth century to adorn them with spots or patches which the prosaic called *mouches*, or flies. They stiffened stays with whalebone and spread their hoopskirts with wire. They tossed their hair up in a dozen tempting shapes. Men wore theirs in long and flowing curls, and crowned themselves with broad hats gaily plumed. Louis XIII, becoming prematurely bald, made the wig fashionable. The sexes rivaled each other in vanity.

Their fine manners did not deter them from eating with their fingers. Even in the nobility forks did not replace fingers before 1600, hardly before 1700 in other ranks. A fashionable restaurant, La Tour d'Argent, where Henry III dined on his way back from the hunt, achieved fame by supplying forks. Already in the seventeenth century the French were eating frogs and snails. Wine was their favorite drink. Coffee was coming into use, but was not yet indispensable. Chocolate had come in through Spain from Mexico; some physicians condemned it as an inopportune laxative; others prescribed it for venereal disease; Mme. de Sévigné told of a pregnant lady who indulged in it so immoderately that she gave birth to a charming little blackamoor—*un petit garçon noir comme le diable*.[17]

The improvement in manners was reflected in transportation and amusements. Public coaches were now common in Western Europe, and in France the well-to-do began to move about in splendid *carrosses* equipped with curtains and glass. Tennis was the rage, and dancing claimed all classes. The stately *pavane* came in from Spain, taking its name from the Spanish for peacock—*pavo*; its proud and graceful evolutions gave it an aristocratic flair, and the kissing that was part of it helped to circulate the blood. Under Catherine de Médicis the ballet became the crown of court entertainments, combining music and the dance to tell a tale in verse or pantomime; her loveliest ladies took part, in costumes and settings artistically designed; one such ballet was performed in the Tuileries on the day after the Massacre of St. Bartholomew.

Musicians were the heroes of the passing hour. They exercised such fascination on the French that one courtier, at a concert in 1581, clapped his hand on his sword and swore that he must challenge the first man he met; thereupon the conductor led his orchestra into a gentle strain that soothed the savage breast.[18] The lute was still the favorite instrument, but in 1555 Balthazar de Beaujoyeux, the first famous violinist in history, brought a band of violinists to Catherine's court and made violin music popular. In 1600 Ottavio Rinuccini followed Marie de Médicis into France and introduced there the idea of opera. Singing was still the favorite music, and Père Mersenne rightly judged that no other sound in nature could match the beauty of a woman's voice.[19]

Music, literature, fine manners, and cultured conversation now came together in one of the most basic contributions of France to civilization—the salon. Italy, alma mater of modern arts, had shown the way in such urbane gatherings as those ascribed to Urbino in Castiglione's *Courtier*; it was from Italy that the salon—like the violin, the château, ballet, opera, and syphilis —came to France. Its founder in France was born in Rome (1588) to Jean de Vivonne, French ambassador to the papacy, and Giulia Savelli, an Orsini heiress. Catherine de Vivonne received an education exceptional for a girl of the sixteenth century. At twelve she was married to Charles d'Angennes, who, as Marquis of Rambouillet, held high office under Henry IV and Louis XIII. The young Marquise complained that French speech and manners fell short of the Italian in correctness and courtesy, and she noted with disapproval the separation between the intellectual classes— poets, scholars, scientists, savants—and the nobility. In 1618 she designed for her family the Hôtel de Rambouillet in the Rue St.-Thomas-du-Louvre in Paris. One room was hung with panels of blue velvet bordered with silver and gold; in this spacious *salon bleu* the Marquise received her guests in what became the most celebrated salon in history. She took care to invite men and women of congenial manners but diverse interests: nobles like the Great Condé and La Rochefoucauld, ecclesiastics like Richelieu and Huet, generals like Montausier and Bassompierre, highborn dames like the Princess of Conti, the duchesses of Longueville and Rohan, lettered ladies like Mmes. de La Fayette and de Sévigné and Mlle. de Scudéry, poets like Malherbe, Chapelain, and Guez de Balzac, scholars like Conrart and Vaugelas, wits like Voiture and Scarron. Here Bossuet preached a sermon at the age of twelve, and Corneille read his plays. Here aristocrats learned to take interest in language, science, scholarship, poetry, music, and art; men learned from women the graces of courtesy; authors learned to hide their vanity, savants to humanize their erudition; wit rubbed elbows with pedigrees; correct speech was debated and acquired, and conversation became an art.

The Marquise managed these lions and tigers with a tact that painlessly trimmed their claws. Despite bearing seven children, she kept her beauty long enough to inspire passion in Voiture and Malherbe, who, being poets, kindled into flame at every smile; despite these fires she was respected by all for her fidelity to her dull husband; despite ill health, she gave her guests an example of good cheer and sprightly intelligence; despite losing two sons to death and three daughters to religion, she silenced her melancholy till she wrote her epitaph. In an age of sexual license and untamed speech she spread about her a contagion of manners and decency. Good taste—*bon ton*, good tone—became a passport to her salon. Marshals and poets left their swords and shafts in the vestibule; politeness turned the edge of difference; discussion flourished, dispute was banned.

At last the refinement was carried to excess. The Marquise drew up a code of correctness in speech and deed; those who practiced it too precisely were called *précieux* or *précieuses*; and in 1659, when the Marquise was retired and solitary, Molière pounced upon these fanciful residues of her art and finished them off with ridicule. But even the excess had its use; the *précieuses* helped to clear the meaning and connotations of words and phrases, to cleanse the language of provincialisms, bad grammar, and pedantry; here in germ was the French Academy. In the Hôtel de Rambouillet Malherbe, Conrart, and Vaugelas developed those principles of literary taste that led to Boileau and the classic age. The *précieuses* contributed to that analysis of the passions which elongated the romances and lured Descartes and Spinoza; they helped to embroider the relations of the sexes with that strategy of retreat, and consequent idealization of the elusive treasure, which made for romantic love. Through this and the later salons French history became more than ever bisexual. The status of women rose; their influence increased in literature, language, politics, and art. The respect for knowledge and intellect increased, and the sense of beauty spread.

But would the salons and the Academy have made Rabelais impossible? Would they have closed the French mind to the gay physiology, the easy ethic, the proliferating pedantry of Montaigne? Or would they have forced and raised these geniuses to a subtler and higher art?

We have gone too far forward. Montaigne was twenty-six years dead when Mme. de Rambouillet opened her salon. Let us turn back in our course and listen for an hour to the greatest writer and thinker of France in this age.

III. MICHEL DE MONTAIGNE: 1533–92

1. Education

Joseph Scaliger described Montaigne's father as a seller of herring. The great scholar skipped a generation; it was the grandfather, Grimon Eyquem, who exported wines and dried fish from Bordeaux. Grimon inherited the business from Michel's great-grandfather Ramon Eyquem, who made the family fortune so, and bought (1447) the mansion and estate known as Montaigne on a hill outside the city. Grimon expanded his patrimony with a judicious marriage. His son Pierre Eyquem preferred war to herring; he joined the French army, soldiered in Italy with Francis I, returned with scars and a rubbing of the Renaissance, and rose to be mayor of Bordeaux. In 1528 he married Antoinette, daughter of a wealthy merchant of Toulouse who was Jewish by birth, Christian by baptism, and Spanish by cultural background. Michel Eyquem, who became the Sieur de Montaigne, was born to Pierre and Antoinette with Gascon and Jewish blood in his brain. To further broaden his outlook, his father was a pious Catholic, his mother was probably a Protestant, and a sister and a brother were Calvinists.

Pierre had ideas on education. "That good father," Michel tells us, "even from my cradle sent me to be brought up in a poor village of his, where he kept me so long as I sucked, and somewhat longer, breeding me after the meanest and simplest common fashion."[20] While the boy was still nursing he was given a German attendant who spoke to him only in Latin. "I was six years old before I understood more of French than of Arabic."[21] When he went to the Collège de Guienne his teachers (except George Buchanan) were loath to talk Latin to him, he spoke it so glibly. Such mastery he had acquired "without books, rules, or grammar, without whipping or whining."

Perhaps the father had read Rabelais on education. He tried to rear his son on libertarian principles, substituting affection for compulsion. Montaigne relished this regimen and recommended it in a long letter on education,[22] professedly written for Lady Diane de Foix; but in a later essay he recanted it and recommended the rod as a convincing supplement to reason.[23] Nor did he follow his father in giving priority to Latin or the classics. Though his own memory bubbled over with classical quotations and instances, he deprecated a merely classical education, scorned book learning and bookworms, and stressed, rather, the training of the body to health and vigor and of the character to prudence and virtue. "We have need of little learning to have a good mind,"[24] and a game of tennis may be more instructive than a diatribe against Catiline. A boy should be made hardy and brave, able to bear heat and cold without whimpering, and to relish the inevitable risks of life. Montaigne quoted Athenian authors, but preferred Spartan ways; his ideal was a manly virtue, almost in the Roman sense that made such a phrase redundant—to which he added the Greek ideal of "nothing in excess." Temperance in everything, even in temperance. A man should drink moderately, but be able, if occasion should require, to drink abundantly without becoming stupefied.

Travel can form a vital part of education, if we leave our prejudices at home. "It was told to Socrates that a certain man had been no whit improved by travel. 'I believe it well,' said he, 'for he carried himself with him.' "[25] If we can keep our minds and eyes open, the world will be our best textbook, for "so many strange humors, sundry sects . . . diverse opinions, different laws, and fantastical customs teach us to judge rightly of ours."[26] Next to travel, the best education is history, which is travel extended into the past. The student "shall, by the help of histories, inform himself of the worthiest minds that were in the best ages. . . . What profit shall he not reap . . . reading the *Lives* of our Plutarch?"[27] Finally, the student should get some philosophy—not the "thorny quiddities of logic," but such philosophy as "teaches us how to live . . . what it is to know, and not to know; what valor, temperance, and justice are; what difference there is between ambition and avarice, bondage and freedom; by what marks a man may distinguish true and perfect contentment; and how far one ought to fear . . . death, pain, or disgrace. . . . A child coming from nurse is more capable of them [such lessons] than he is to learn to read or write."[28]

After seven years at the Collège de Guienne Montaigne proceeded to university and the study of law. No subject could have been less congenial to his discursive mind and limpid speech. He never tired of praising custom and berating law. He noted with joy that Ferdinand II of Spain had sent no lawyers to Spanish America, lest they should multiply disputes among the Indians; and he wished that physicians too had been forbidden there, lest they make new ailments with their cures.[29] He thought those countries worst off that had most laws, and he reckoned that France had had "more than the rest of the world besides." He saw no progress in the humaneness of the law, and doubted if any such savagery could be found among barbarians as togaed judges and tonsured ecclesiastics practiced in the torture chambers of European states.[30] He gloried that "to this day [1588?] I am a virgin from all suits of law."[31]

2. Friendship and Marriage

Nevertheless, we find him in 1557 councilor in the Court of Aids at Périgueux and in 1561 a member of the Bordeaux Parlement—the municipal court. There he met and loved Étienne de La Boétie. We have seen elsewhere how, about the age of eighteen, this young aristocrat wrote, but did not publish, a passionate *Discours sur la servitude volontaire*, which came to be called *Contr'un*—i.e., against one-man rule. With all the eloquence of Danton, it called upon the people to rise against absolutism. Perhaps Montaigne himself felt some republican ardor in his youth. In any case, he was drawn to the noble rebel, who, three years older, seemed a paragon of wisdom and integrity.

> We sought one another before we had seen one another, and, by the reports we heard of one another . . . I think by some secret ordinance of the heavens we embraced one another by our names. And at our first meeting, which was by chance at a great feast and solemn meeting of a whole township, we found ourselves so surprised, so . . . acquainted, and so . . . bound together, that from thenceforward nothing was so near to us as one unto another.[32]

Why this profound attachment? Montaigne answered, "Because it was he, because it was I"[33]—because they were so different that they completed each other. For La Boétie was all idealism, warm devotion, tenderness; Montaigne was too intellectual, prudent, impartial to be so dedicated; this very friend described him as "equally inclined to both outstanding vices and virtues."[34] Perhaps the deepest experience of Montaigne's life was watching his friend die. In 1563, during a plague at Bordeaux, La Boétie fell suddenly ill with fever and dysentery. He bore his lingering death with a stoic fortitude and a Christian patience never forgotten by his friend, who stayed at his bedside during those final days. Montaigne inherited the manuscript of the dangerous essay and concealed it for thirteen years; a copy was printed in a pirated edition (1576); thereupon he published the original, and explained that it was the rhetorical exercise of a boy of "sixteen."

That friendship made every later human relationship seem insipid to Montaigne. He wrote, again and again, that half of him had died with La Boétie. "I was so accustomed to be ever two, and so inured to be never single, that methinks I am but half myself."[35] In the warmth of that memory he placed friendship above the love between father and son, maid and youth, husband and wife. He himself seems to have had no romantic passion for any woman: "In my youth I opposed myself to the notions of love, which I felt to usurp upon me; and I labored to diminish its enjoyment, lest in the end it might . . . captivate me to its mercy."[36] Not that he lacked erotic hours; on the contrary, he acknowledges premarital relations of proud scope and frequency.[37] He described sexual love as no "other than a tickling delight of emptying one's seminary [sic] vessels, as is the pleasure which nature giveth us to discharge other parts"; and he thought it absurd that nature "hath pell-mell lodged our joys and filths together."[38]

He agreed with most philosophers that the itch to detumesce is no reason for marriage. "I see no marriages fail sooner, or more troubled, than such as are concluded for beauty's sake, or huddled up for amorous desires."[39] Marriage should be arranged by "a third hand"; it should reject the company and conditions of [sexual] love" and should try "to imitate those of friendship"; marriage must become friendship to survive. He inclined to the view of Greek thinkers that a man should not marry before thirty. He avoided the tie as long as he could. Still single at twenty-eight, he traveled to Paris, fell in love with it,[40] enjoyed the life of the court for a while (1562), saw some American Indians at Rouen, hesitated between the rival charms of civilization and savagery, returned to Bordeaux, and married (1565) Françoise de Chassaigne.

He seems to have married for strictly rational reasons: to have a home and a family, to transmit his estate and his name. Amid all his fifteen hundred pages he says almost nothing of his wife—but that may have been good manners. He claims to have been faithful to her: "Licentious as the world reputes me, I had (in good faith) more strictly observed the laws of wedlock than either I had promised or hoped."[41] She made allowances for the self-absorption of genius; she took competent care of the household, the land, even the accounts, for he had no mind for business. For his part, he gave her full respect, and now and then a sign or word of love—as when he responded gratefully to her quick aid after his fall from a horse, and when he dedicated to her his edition of La Boétie's translation of Plutarch's *Letter of Consolation*. It was a successful marriage, and we must not take very seriously the quips against women in the *Essays*; they were a fashion among philosophers. Françoise bore him six children, all girls; all died in childhood but one, of whom he speaks tenderly.[42] When he was fifty-four he adopted into the family a twenty-year-old girl, Marie de Gournay, "truly of me beloved with more than a fatherly love, and as one of the best parts of my being, enfeoffed in my home and solitariness."[43] He was not above the common feelings of humanity.

3. The Essays

In 1568 his father died, and Michel, as the oldest son, inherited the estate. Three or four years later he resigned from the Parliament of Bordeaux, and retired from the bedlam of the city to the boredom of the countryside. Even there peace was precarious, for religious war was dividing France, its cities, and its families. Soldiers raided villages, entered homes, stole, raped, and killed. "I have a thousand times gone to bed . . . imagining I should, the very same night, have been either betrayed or slain in my bed."[44] As a dissuasion to violence, he left his doors unlocked and gave orders that if marauders came they were to be received without resistance. They stayed away, and Montaigne was left free to live in his corner of philosophy amid the clatter of creeds and arms. While Paris and some provinces murdered Protestants in the Massacre of St. Bartholomew, Montaigne wrote the supreme work of French prose.

His favorite retreat was the library on the third floor of the tower that rose in the façade of his château. (The château was destroyed by fire in 1885, but the tower survived.) He loved his library as himself, his alter ego.

> The form of it is round, and hath no flat side but what serveth for my table and chair; in which . . . manner at one look it offers me the full sight of all my books . . . There is my seat, there is my throne. I endeavor to make my rule therein absolute, and to sequester that only corner from the community of wife, of children, and of acquaintance.[45]

Seldom has a man so relished solitude, which is almost our direst dread.

> A man must sequester and recover himself from himself . . . We should reserve a storehouse for ourselves . . . altogether ours . . . wherein we may hoard up and establish our true liberty. The greatest thing in the world is for a man to know how to be his own.[46]

In that library he had a thousand books, most of them bound in tooled leather. He called them "*meas delicias*" (my delights). In them he could choose his company and live with the wisest and the best. In Plutarch alone, "since he spoke French" (through Amyot), he could find a hundred great men to come and talk with him, and in Seneca's *Epistles* he could savor a pleasant Stoicism melodiously phrased; these two (including Plutarch's *Moralia*) were his favorite authors, "from whom, like the Danaïdes, I draw my water, incessantly filling as fast as emptying[47] . . . The familiarity I have with them, and the aid they afford me in my old age, and my book merely framed of their spoils, binds me to maintain their honor."[48]

He never quotes the Bible (perhaps as too well known), though he frequently cites St. Augustine. For the most part he prefers the ancients to the moderns, the pagan philosophers to the Christian Fathers. He was a humanist insofar as he loved the literature and the history of old Greece and Rome; but he was no indiscriminate idolater of classics and manuscripts; he thought Aristotle superficial and Cicero a windbag. He was not quite at home with the Greeks. He quoted the Latin poets with roaming erudition, even one of Martial's most privy epigrams. He admired Virgil, but preferred Lucretius. He read Erasmus' *Adagia* predaceously. In the early essays he was a pedant, adorning himself with classical tags. Such excerpts were in the manner of the age; readers who had no competence for the originals relished these samples as little windows glimpsing antiquity, and some complained that there were not more.[49] From all his pilfering Montaigne emerged uniquely himself, laughing at pedantry and making up his own mind and speech. He looks like scissors and paste, and tastes like ambrosia.

So, leisurely, page by page and day by day, after 1570, he wrote his *Essais.** He seems to have invented the term,[50] almost the type; for though there had been *discorsi* and *discours*, they were formidably formal, not the informal, meandering conversations of Montaigne; and this easygoing, buttonholing style has tended to characterize the essay since his death, making it a predominantly modern genre. "I speak to paper," he said, "as I do to the first person I meet."[51] The style is the man, natural, intimate, confidential; it is a comfort to be spoken to so familiarly by a seigneur of the mind. Open him at any page, and you are caught by the arm and swept along, never knowing, and seldom caring, where you will go. He wrote piecemeal, on any subject that struck his thought or matched his mood; and he diverged anarchically from the initial topic as he rambled on; so the essay "On Coaches" rattles off into ancient Rome and new America. Of the three volumes, three consist of digressions. Montaigne was lazy, and nothing is so arduous as producing and maintaining order in ideas or men. He confessed himself *divers et ondoyant*—wavering and diverse. He made no fetish of consistency; he changed his opinions with his years; only the final composite picture is Montaigne.

Amid the confused flux of his notions his style is as clear as the soul of simplicity. Yet it sparkles with metaphors as surprising as Shakespeare's,

---

* The first edition, 1580, contained Books I and II; the second, 1588, expanded these and added Book III; the third, containing his final revision and edited by Mlle. de Gournay, appeared in 1595, after his death. The nine editions between 1580 and 1598 attest their popularity.

and with illuminating anecdotes that instantaneously transform the abstract into the real. His probing curiosity snatches at such instances anywhere, admitting no moral hindrance. He carefully hands down to us the remark of the Toulouse woman who, having been handled by several soldiers, thanked God that "once in my life I have had my bellyful without sin."[52] *Nihil naturae alienum putat.*

4. The Philosopher

He claims to have only one subject—himself. "I look within myself; I have no business but with myself; I incessantly consider . . . and taste myself."[53] He proposes to study human nature at first hand, through his own impulses, habits, likes, dislikes, ailments, feelings, prejudices, fears, and ideas. He does not offer us an autobiography; he says almost nothing, in the *Essays*, about his career as a councilor or mayor, about his travels, his visits to the court. He does not wear his religion or his politics on his sleeve. He gives us something more precious—a frank and penetrating analysis of his body, mind, and character. He expounds his faults and vices with pleasure and at length. To accomplish his purpose he asks permission to speak freely; he will violate good taste to exhibit a man naked in body and soul. He talks with noisy candor about his natural functions, quotes St. Augustine and Vives on melodic flatulence, and meditates on coitus:

> Each one avoideth to see a man born, but all run hastily to see him die. To destroy him we seek a spacious field and full light; but to construct him we hide ourselves in some dark corner and work as close as we may.[54]

Even so, he claims to have practiced some reticence. "I speak truth, not my bellyful, but as much as I dare."[55]

He tells us a great deal about his physical self, and he nurses his health from page to page. Health is the *summum bonum.* "Renown or glory is overdearly bought by a man of my humor, in God's name."[56] He records the vicissitudes of his bowels in affectionate detail. He sought the philosopher's stone and found it lodged in his bladder. He hoped to pass these pebbles in some amorous ecstasy, but found, instead, that they "do strangely diswench me,"[57] threatening him with inopportune disablement. He consoled himself with his proud capacity to "hold my water full ten hours,"[58] and to be in the saddle long hours without exhausting fatigue. He was stout and strong, and he ate so avidly that he almost bit his fingers in his greed. He loved himself with indefatigable virtuosity.

He was vain of his genealogy, his coat of arms,[59] his fine dress, and his distinction as a Chevalier of St. Michael—and wrote an essay "Of Vanity." He pretends to most of the vices, and assures us that if there is any virtue in him it entered by stealth. He had many nevertheless: honesty, geniality, humor, equanimity, pity, moderation, tolerance. He tossed explosive ideas into the air, but caught and extinguished them before they fell. In an age of dogmatic slaughter he begged his fellow men to moderate their certainties this side of murder; and he gave the modern world one of its first examples of a tolerant mind. We forgive his faults because we share them. And we find his self-analysis fascinating because we know that it is about us that the tale is told.

To understand himself better he studied the philosophers. He loved them despite their vain pretensions to analyze the universe and chart man's destiny beyond the grave. He quoted Cicero as remarking that "nothing can be said so absurd but that it has been said by one of the philosophers."[60] He praised Socrates for "bringing human wisdom down from heaven, where for a long time it had been lost, to restore it to man again,"[61] and he echoed Socrates' advice to study natural science less and human conduct more. He had no "system" of his own; his ideas were in such restless evolution that no label could pin down his philosophic flight.

In the brave morning of his thought he adopted Stoicism. Since Christianity, splitting into fratricidal sects and bloodying itself with war and massacre, had apparently failed to give man a moral code capable of controlling his instincts, Montaigne turned to philosophy for a natural ethic, a morality not tied to the rise and fall of religious creeds. Stoicism seemed to have approached this ideal; at least it had molded some of the finest men of antiquity. For a time Montaigne made it his ideal. He would train his will to self-mastery; he would shun all passions that might disturb the decency of his conduct or the tranquillity of his mind; he would face all vicissitudes with an even temper and take death itself as a natural and forgivable fulfillment.

Some Stoic strain continued in him to the end, but his effervescent spirit soon found another philosophy to justify itself. He rebelled against a Stoicism that preached the following of "Nature" and yet strove to suppress nature in man. He interpreted Nature through his own nature, and decided to follow his natural desires whenever they did no perceivable harm. He was pleased to find Epicurus no coarse sensualist but a sane defender of sane delights; and he was astonished to discover so much wisdom and grandeur in Lucretius. Now he proclaimed with enthusiasm the legitimacy of pleasure. The only sin that he recognized was excess. "Intemperance is the pestilence which killeth pleasure; temperance is not the flail of pleasure, it is the seasoning thereof."[62]

From the oscillation of his views, and the degradation of contemporary Christianity in France, he came to the skepticism that thereafter colored most of his philosophy. His father had been impressed by the *Theologia naturalis* of the Toulouse theologian Raymond of Sabunde (d. 1437?), who had continued the noble effort of the Scholastics to prove the reasonableness of Christianity. The father asked his son to translate the treatise; Montaigne did, and published his translation (1569). Orthodox France was edified, but some critics objected to Raymond's reasoning. In 1580 Montaigne inserted into the second "book" of his *Essais* a two-hundred-page "Apologie de [Defense of] Raimond Sebond," in which he proposed to answer the objections. But he did so only by abandoning his author's enterprise, arguing that reason is a limited and untrustworthy instrument, and that it is better to rest religion on faith in the Scriptures and in Holy Mother Church; in effect Montaigne demolished Raymond while purporting to uphold him. Some, like Sainte-Beuve, have judged this "Apology" as a tongue-in-cheek argument for unbelief.[63] In any case, it is the most destructive of Montaigne's compositions, perhaps the most thoroughgoing exposition of skepticism in modern literature.

Long before Locke, Montaigne affirms that "all knowledge is addressed to us by the senses,"[64] and that reason depends upon the senses; but the senses are deceptive in their reports and severely limited in their range; therefore reason is unreliable. "Both the inward and the outward parts of man are full of weakness and falsehood."[65] (Here, at the very outset of the Age of Reason, a generation before Bacon and Descartes, Montaigne asks the question that they would not stop to ask, that Pascal would ask eighty years later, that the philosophers would not face till Hume and Kant: Why should we trust reason?) Even instinct is a safer guide than reason. See how well the animals get along by instinct—sometimes more wisely than men. "There is a greater difference between many a man and many another man than between many a man and many an animal."[66] Man is no more the center of life than the earth is the center of the universe. It is presumptuous of man to think that God resembles him, or that human affairs are the center of God's interest, or that the world exists to serve man. And it is ridiculous to suppose that the mind of man can fathom the nature of God. "O senseless man, who cannot make a worm and yet will make gods by the dozen!"[67]

Montaigne arrives at skepticism by another route—by contemplating the variety and fluctuation of beliefs in laws and morals, in science, philosophy, and religion; which of these truths is truth? He prefers the Copernican to the Ptolemaic astronomy, but: "Who knows whether, a thousand years hence, a third opinion will rise, which haply may overthrow these two," and "whether it be not more likely that this huge body, which we call the

World, is another manner of thing than we judge it?"[68] "There is no science," only the proud hypotheses of immodest minds.[69] Of all the philosophies the best is Pyrrho's—that we know nothing. "The greatest part of what we know is the least part of what we know not."[70] "Nothing is so firmly believed as that which is least known," and "a persuasion of certainty is a manifest testimony of foolishness."[71] "In few words, there is no constant existence, neither of our being nor of the objects. And we and our judgment, and all mortal things else, do incessantly roll, turn, and pass away. Thus can nothing be certainly established. We have no communication with being."[72] Then, to heal all wounds, Montaigne ends by reaffirming his Christian faith and singing a pantheistic paean to the unknowable God.[73]

Thereafter he applied his skepticism to everything, always with an obeisance to the Church. "*Que sais-je?* What do I know?" became his motto, engraved on his seal and inscribed on his library ceiling. Other mottoes adorned the rafters: "The for and against are both possible"; "It may be and it may not be"; "I determine nothing. I do not comprehend things; I suspend judgment; I examine."[74] Something of this attitude he took from Socrates' *Ouden oida*, "I know nothing"; something from Pyrrho, something from Cornelius Agrippa, much from Sextus Empiricus. Henceforth, he said, "I fasten myself on that which I see and hold, and go not far from the shore."[75]

Now he saw relativity everywhere, and nowhere absolutes. Least of all in standards of beauty; and our lusty philosopher revels in noting the diverse opinions among divers peoples as to what constitutes beauty in a woman's breasts.[76] He believes that many beasts surpass us in beauty and thinks we were wise to clothe ourselves. He perceives that a man's religion and his moral ideas are usually determined by his environment. "The taste of good or evil greatly depends upon the opinion we have of them," as Shakespeare was to say; and: "Men are tormented by the opinions they have of things, not by the things themselves."[77] The laws of conscience proceed not from God but from custom. Conscience is the discomfort we feel when violating the mores of our tribe.[78]

Montaigne had better sense than to suppose that because morals are relative they may therefore be ignored. On the contrary, he would be the last to disturb their stability. He talks boldly about sex, and claims much freedom—for men; but when you cross-examine him you find him suddenly orthodox. He recommends chastity to youth, on the ground that energy spent in sex comes from the common store of force in the body; he notes that athletes training for the Olympic games "abstained from all venerean acts and touching of women."[79]

It was part of his humor to extend his skepticism to civilization itself, and to anticipate Rousseau and Châteaubriand. The Indians he had seen at Rouen inspired him to read the reports of travelers; from these accounts he composed his essay "Of Cannibals." Eating dead people, he thought, was less barbarous than torturing live ones. "I find nothing in that nation [Indian America] that is either barbarous or savage, unless men call that barbarism which is not common among themselves."[80] He imagined these natives as rarely sick, as nearly always happy, and as living peaceably without laws.[81] He praised Aztec art and Inca roads. He put into the mouth of his Rouen Indians an indictment of European wealth and poverty: "They had perceived there were men amongst us full gorged with all sorts of commodities, and others that were dying of hunger; and they marveled that the needy ones could endure such an injustice and took not the others by the throat."[82] He compared the morals of the Indians with those of their conquerors, and charged that "the pretended Christians . . . brought the contagion of vice to innocent souls eager to learn and by nature well disposed."[83] For a moment Montaigne forgot his geniality and burst into noble indignation:

> So many goodly cities ransacked and razed; so many nations destroyed or made desolate; so infinite millions of harmless people of all sexes, status, and ages, massacred, ravaged, and put to the sword; and the richest, the fairest, the best part of the world topsyturvied, ruined, and defaced for the traffic of pearls and peppers! Oh, mechanical victories, oh, base conquest![84]

Was his obeisance to religion sincere? Obviously his classical foraging had long since weaned him from the doctrines of the Church. He retained a vague belief in God conceived sometimes as Nature, sometimes as a cosmic soul, the incomprehensible intelligence of the world. At times he presages Shakespeare's Lear: "The gods play at handball with us, and toss us up and down";[85] but he ridicules atheism as "unnatural and monstrous"[86] and rejects agnosticism as another dogmatism—how do we know that we shall never know?[87] He waives aside as pretentious futilities all attempts to define the soul or to explain its relation to the body.[88] He is willing to accept the immortality of the soul on faith, but finds no evidence for it in experience or reason;[89] and the idea of eternal existence appalls him.[90] "Except for faith, I believe not miracles";[91] and he anticipates Hume's famous argument: "How much more natural and likely do I find it that two men should lie than that one man in twelve hours should be carried by the winds from East to West?"[92] (He might seek another example today.) He steals a march on Voltaire by telling of the pilgrim who judged that Christianity must be divine to have maintained itself so long despite the corruption of its administrators.[93] He notes that he is a

Christian by geographical accident; otherwise "I should rather have taken part with those who worshiped the sun."[94] So far as one reader can recall, he mentions Christ but once.[95] The lovely saga of the Mother of Christ made only a moderate appeal to his unsentimental soul; however, he crossed Italy to lay four votive figures before her shrine at Loreto. He lacked those marks of the religious spirit—humility, a sense of sin, remorse and penance, a longing for divine forgiveness and redeeming grace. He was a freethinker with an allergy for martyrdom.

He remained a Catholic long after he had ceased to be a Christian.[96] Like some sensible early Christian bowing transiently to a pagan deity, Montaigne, the most pagan of Christians, turned aside now and then from his selected Greeks and Romans to honor the cross of Christ, or even to kiss the foot of a pope. He did not, like Pascal, pass from skepticism to faith, but from skepticism to observance. And not merely through caution. He probably realized that his own philosophy, paralyzed with hesitations, contradictions, and doubt, could safely be the luxury only of a spirit already formed to civilization (by religion?), and that France, even while bathing its creeds in blood, would never exchange them for an intellectual labyrinth in which death would be the only certainty. He thought a wise philosophy would make its peace with religion:

> Simple minds, less curious, less well instructed, are made good Christians, and through reverence and obedience hold their simple belief and abide by the laws. In intellects of moderate vigor and capacity is engendered the error of opinions. . . . The best, most settled, and clearest-seeing spirits make another sort of well-believers, who by long and religious investigation, penetrate to a more profound and abstruse meaning in the Scriptures and discover the mysterious and divine secrets of our ecclesiastical polity. . . . The simple peasants are honest folk, and so are the philosophers.[97]

So, after all his barbs at Christianity, and because all faiths alike are cloaks to cover our shivering ignorance, he advises us to accept the religion of our time and place. He himself, true to his geography, returned to the ritual of his fathers. He liked a sensory, fragrant, ceremonial religion, and so he preferred Catholicism to Protestantism. He was repelled by the Calvinist emphasis on predestination;[98] being of Erasmian lineage, he liked the genial and worldly cardinals of Rome more than the Loyola of Geneva or the lion of Wittenberg. He regretted particularly that the new creeds were imitating the intolerance of the old. Though he laughed at heretics as fools who raised a fuss over competitive mythologies, he saw no sense in burning such mavericks. "After all, it is setting a high value on our opinions to roast people alive on account of them"[99] or to let people roast us.

In politics too he ended as a comfortable conservative. There is no use changing forms of government; the new one will be as bad as the old, because it will be administered by men. Society is so "vast a frame," so complex a mechanism of instinct, custom, myth, and law, slowly fashioned by the trial-and-error wisdom of time, that no individual intellect, however powerful and brilliant, can take it apart and put it together again without incalculable confusion and suffering.[100] Better submit to current rulers, bad as they are, unless they attempt to chain thought itself; then Montaigne might screw his courage up to revolt, for "my reason is not framed to bend or stoop; my knees are."[101] A wise man will avoid public office, while respecting it; "the greatest vocation is to save the commonwealth and be profitable to many"; but "as for me, I depart from it."[102] However, he served his terms.

He mourned that half his life had been lived during the ruination of France,[103] "in an age so corrupt and times so ignorant." "Read all ancient stories, be they never so tragical, you shall find none to equal those we daily see practiced."[104] He was not neutral in the duel for France, but "my interest has not made me forget either the commendable qualities of our adversaries or the reproachful qualities of those whom I have supported."[105] He would not shoulder a gun, but his pen was with the Politiques, those peace-preferring Catholics who advocated some compromise with the Huguenots. He lauded Michel de L'Hôpital for farsighted humanitarian moderation, and he rejoiced when his friend Henry of Navarre moved to victory on the policies of L'Hôpital. Montaigne was the most civilized of Frenchmen in that savage age.

5. The Rolling Stone

The stones in his bladder bothered him more than the wars of France. In June 1580, shortly after the first publication of the Essays, he set out on an extended tour of Western Europe, partly to see the world, partly to visit medicinal springs in the hope of alleviating the "colic" (as he called it) that repeatedly incapacitated him with pain. He left his wife behind to take care of the estate; but he took with him a younger brother, a brother-in-law, the Baron of Estissac, and a secretary to whom he dictated part of his travel diary; add a retinue of servants and muleteers, and we no longer wonder that these memoirs are intellectually thin. They were meant rather for remembrance than for publication; Montaigne, returning, hid them in a chest, where they were discovered 178 years after his death.

The party went first to Paris, where the proud author presented a copy of the Essays to Henry III; then by easy stages to Plombières, where

Montaigne for nine days drank two quarts of medicinal waters daily and succeeded in passing some small stones with great pain.[106] Then through Lorraine to Switzerland. "He had infinite pleasure," says the third-person diary, "in observing the freedom and good government of this nation."[107] He took the waters at Baden-Baden and advanced into Germany. He attended Calvinist and Lutheran as well as Catholic services, and discussed theology with Protestant clergymen. He tells of one Lutheran minister who vowed that he would rather hear a thousand Masses than partake of one Calvinist Communion[108]—for the Calvinists denied the physical presence of Christ in the Eucharist. Moving into the Tirol, he felt the grandeur of the Alps long before Rousseau. From Innsbruck the party mounted to the Brenner Pass, Montaigne passing on the way "a stone of middling size." Then through Trent to Verona, Vicenza, Padua, and Venice, where he contributed "two big stones" to the Grand Canal. He thought the city not so wonderful as he had expected, nor the prostitutes as beautiful. On to Ferrara, where (according to the *Essays*, not the diary) he visited the insane Tasso; to Bologna and Florence, where the Arno received "two stones and a quantity of gravel,"[109] and through Siena to Rome, where he "passed a stone as big as a pine kernel."[110] All in all, these recorded accretion-excretions would have built a pretty pyramid.

In Rome he visited a Jewish synagogue, witnessed a circumcision, and discussed with the rabbis their religious rites. He exchanged philosophies with the Roman courtesans. He was not (as Stendhal thought) insensitive to the art in Rome.[111] He wandered day after day among the classic remains, never ceasing to marvel at their grandeur. But the great event was a visit to Gregory XIII. Like any son of the Church, Montaigne knelt to kiss the papal shoe, which the Pope kindly raised to ease the operation.[112] Meanwhile the customs officials had found a copy of the *Essays*, which they turned over to the Inquisition. Montaigne was summoned to the Holy Office and was gently admonished that some passages smelled of heresy; would he not change or delete them in future editions? He promised. "I thought I left them very well satisfied with me"; indeed, they invited him to come and live in Rome. (He kept his promise indifferently, and in 1676 his book was placed on the Index.) Perhaps to reassure them and himself, he journeyed across Italy to the shrine of the Virgin at Loreto and dedicated a votive tablet to her. Then he recrossed the Apennines to take the waters at Lucca.

There (September 7, 1581) a message came, saying that he had been chosen mayor of Bordeaux. He asked to be excused, but Henry III bade him accept, and the tradition of public service left him by his father could not be ignored. He took his time getting back to France; he did not sight his château till November 30, seventeen months after beginning the tour.

The duties of the mayoralty were light; the emoluments were honors without pay. He functioned sufficiently well, for he was re-elected (August 1583) for another two years. In December 1584 Henry of Navarre, with a mistress and forty followers, visited him, and the future king of France slept in the philosopher's bed. Toward the end of the second term plague struck Bordeaux, and Montaigne, like nearly all public officials, left the city for rural retreats. On July 30, 1585, he turned over the insignia of his office to a successor and retired to his home.

He was only fifty-two, but his stones periodically disabled him, sometimes preventing him for days from passing water.[113] Early in 1588 he was strong enough to make a third trip to Paris. While there he was arrested, as an adherent of Henry III, by the League then dominating the capital; he was lodged in the Bastille (July 10, 1588), but was released the same evening through the intercession of Catherine de Médicis. In October he attended the States-General at Blois, but he returned to Bordeaux just in time to escape involvement in the vicissitudes of Henry III after the assassination of the Duke of Guise.

In his final and finest essay, "Of Experience," he included a description of his physical decay. His teeth, for example, seemed to have reached "the natural term of their continuance."[114] He endured his "going hence" without bitterness. He had lived his life very much as he had planned it, and he could write with pride: "View all antiquity over, and you shall find it a hard matter to choose out a dozen men that have directed their lives unto one certain, settled . . . course, which is the sweetest drift of wisdom."[115] Told that his end was near, he gathered his household and his legatees about him, and gave them in person the sums or objects he had bequeathed them in his will. He received the sacraments of the Church as piously as if he had never written a doubting word. He died September 13, 1592, aged fifty-nine.

His influence pervaded three centuries and four continents. Richelieu accepted with pleasure the dedication of Mlle. de Gournay's final edition of the *Essays*. His friend and disciple Charron, as early as 1603, developed them into a formal and orderly philosophy. Florio made them into an English classic (1603), but overlaid his author's brief simplicity with erudite verbosity. Shakespeare may have seen that translation and been helped to form and phrase the skepticism of his greatest tragedies; we have noted his specific debts. Perhaps Ben Jonson had Shakespeare in mind when he accused English writers of stealing from Montaigne.[116] Bacon felt that influence, and Descartes may have found in the *Essays* the stimulus to his initial universal doubt. Pascal went almost insane trying to salvage his faith from Montaigne's questionings. From Montaigne stemmed Bayle,

Vauvenargues, Rousseau, Diderot, Voltaire—Rousseau from Montaigne's confessions and his essays "Of Education" and "Of Cannibals," Voltaire from all the rest. Montaigne was the grandfather, as Bayle was the father, of the Enlightenment. Mme. du Deffand, the least deceived woman of her brilliant age, wished to "throw into the fire all the immense volumes of the philosophers except Montaigne, who is the father of them all."[117] Through Montaigne the psychological analysis of mind and character entered into French literature, from Corneille and Molière, La Rochefoucauld and La Bruyère to Anatole France. Thoreau took much at this fountainhead, and Emerson bathed himself in it before writing his own *Essays*. Of Montaigne, as of few authors before the eighteenth century, it may be said that he is read today as if he had written yesterday.

The world has long since recognized and forgiven his faults. He admitted so many that he almost depleted the armory of his critics. He knew quite well that he was garrulous and vain. We tire, now and then, of his classical quotations, and for a moment fall into Malebranche's unjust judgment of the *Essays* as "nothing but a tissue of historical anecdotes, little stories, bon mots, verses, and apothegms . . . proving nothing."[118] Unquestionably Montaigne jumbles his wares into a lazy disarray, so lessening their impact and point. He contradicts himself in a hundred subjects; he is bound to be right, since he says everything and its opposite. There is something paralyzing in universal skepticism; it preserves us from theological homicide, but it takes the wind out of our sails and drains us of fortitude. We are more deeply moved by Pascal's desperate attempt to save his faith from Montaigne than by Montaigne's willingness to have no faith at all.

We cannot put our hearts into such criticism; it interrupts only passingly our joy in the *gaya ciencia*, the laughing learning, the *allegro pensieroso*, of this unsilenceable gossiper. Where again shall we find so animated a synthesis of wisdom and humor? There is a subtle similarity between these two qualities, since both may come from seeing things in perspective; in Montaigne they make one man. His loquacity is redeemed by quaintness and clarity; there are no shopworn phrases here, no pompous absurdity. We are so weary of language used to conceal thought or its absence that we can overlook the egoism in these self-revelations. We are surprised to see how well this amiable *causeur* knows our hearts; we are relieved to find our faults shared by so wise a man, and by him so readily absolved. It is comforting to see that he too hesitates and does not know; we are delighted to be told that our ignorance, if realized, becomes philosophy. And what a relief it is, after St. Bartholomew, to come upon a man who is not sure enough to kill!

Finally, and despite his onslaught upon reason, we perceive that

Montaigne begins in France, as Bacon in England, the Age of Reason. Montaigne, the critic of reason, was nothing if not reason itself. With all his curtsies to the Church, this irrationalist was a rationalist. He consented to conform only after he had sown the seeds of reason in the mind of France. And if, like Bacon, he tried to do this without disturbing the consolatory faith of the poor, we must not hold his caution or tenderness against him. He was not made for burning. He knew that he too might be wrong; he was the apostle of moderation as well as of reason; and he was too much of a gentleman to set his neighbor's house on fire before he had any other shelter to give him. He was profounder than Voltaire because he sympathized with that which he destroyed.

Gibbon reckoned "in those bigoted times but two men of liberality [of free and generous ideas] in France: Henry IV and Montaigne."[119] And Sainte-Beuve, after viewing Montaigne unsympathetically through the eyes of Pascal,[120] ended by pronouncing him, in a rare burst of enthusiasm, *"le Français le plus sage qui ait jamais existé"*—"the wisest Frenchman that ever lived."[121]

IV. IMMORTALS FOR A DAY

After Montaigne French literature rested on his oars for a generation. He had almost succeeded in escaping the Religious Wars, hiding himself in himself till they passed by. Elsewhere the martial-theologic fever blighted letters in France: between Montaigne and Corneille she fell behind England and Spain in literature, just as England fell behind France after the Civil War. A succession of gaseous comets crossed the firmament, leaving no fixed stars. Richelieu tried to nurse genius with pensions, but he hampered it with censorship and suborned it to his praise. When he died the pensions were canceled by Louis XIII with a shrug of the pen: "We're not going to be troubled with that any more." More stimulating to literature were the literary soirees of the Hôtel de Rambouillet and Richelieu's establishment of the French Academy.

The Academy began in gatherings of scholars and authors in a private home—that of Valentin Conrart, a secretary to the King (1627). Richelieu, alert to letters as well as war, envying the academies of Italy and the literature of Spain, offered to constitute the group as a public body recognized by the state. Some members opposed the plan as a bribe to orthodoxy; but the poet Chapelain (who was enjoying a pension from the Cardinal) reminded them that "they had to do with a man who willed in no half-hearted way whatever he willed."[122] Chapelain's caution prevailed; the group unanimously resolved to "accede to the pleasure of his Eminence,"

and was incorporated (1635) as the Académie Française. Its statutes declared that

> it seems that naught was wanting to the happiness of the kingdom but to take this language, which we speak, out of the list of barbarous tongues . . . that, already more perfect than any other living language, it might at length fairly succeed to the Latin as the Latin had to the Greek, if more care were taken than hitherto; that the functions of the Academicians should be to purify the language from the defilements which it had contracted, whether in the mouths of the people, or in the crowds of the law courts . . . or by the bad habits of ignorant courtiers.[123]

One of the original thirty members, Claude Vaugelas, was charged with compiling a dictionary; fifty-six years were to elapse before its first publication (1694). Meanwhile the Academy raised significantly the status of literary men; to be one of the (by 1637) forty "Immortals" became as great an honor as to stand high in the government; no nation has so honored letters as France. Frequently the Academy, composed mostly of old men, acted as a conservative brake upon literary developments or linguistic growth; now and then it closed its doors to genius (Molière, Rousseau); but it kept its head above the factions, and taught its members a courteous tolerance of diverse ideas; and France rewarded it with a permanence that stood the shocks of change while so much else gave way.

Having corralled the poets and the scholars, Richelieu cast his watchful eye upon the journalists. In May 1631 Théophraste Renaudot, aided by the Cardinal, began publication of the first French newspaper, afterward called the *Gazette de France*. Appearing weekly as a sheet folded into eight pages, it gave such official news as Richelieu permitted or supplied, and it added some pages of *nouvelles ordinaires*. Louis XIII was a frequent contributor; in the *Gazette* he answered the critics of the government and defended his banishment of his mother; sometimes he took his paragraphs in person to supervise their graduation into type; even a king is fascinated when he finds himself in print. From its beginning the French press was an agent of propaganda—in this case a means of explaining to the literate minority the policies of the state. The people soon distrusted the *Gazette* and bought, rather, the scurrilous sheets sold on the streets by the pensioners of the Cardinal's foes.

The most widely read production of the age was a romance. The chivalric romance was going out of fashion, not merely because Cervantes and others ridiculed it, but because feudalism, now subordinated to royalty, was losing more and more of its privileges and prestige. Tales of when knighthood was in flower were replaced by agonizing romances of impeded desire. Every possessor of letters and leisure under Louis XIII read the *Astrée* (1610–19) of Honoré d'Urfé. The author's genius grew from a wound in love. His wife, well named Diana, preferred the venery of the hunt to the venery of mar-riage; she had her dogs eat at table with her and share her bed. She was delivered of an abortion annually.[124] Honoré retired to his estate and disguised his plaintive autobiography as a pastoral romance. He found this cure by expression so satisfactory that he stretched it out to 5,500 pages in five volumes issued at intervals from 1610 to 1627. In the story of the shepherd Céladon's love for the shepherdess Astrée we hear an interminable echo of Montemayor's *Diana enamorada* and Sannazaro's and Sidney's *Arcadias*; but the echo was melodious, the shepherds and shepherdesses had all the grace and lace of the French court, the language met all the demands of the Rambouillet Hôtel, the varieties of amorous experience rivaled Henry IV's, and the adoration of woman pleased the goddesses of the salons, who made the book a code of manners for platonic love. Here was the gushing spring from which streamed the sentimental romances of Mlle. de Scudéry, Abbé Prévost (Antoine Prévost d'Exiles), Samuel Richardson, Jean Jacques Rousseau—who professed to have read the book once a year through most of his life. For nearly a century the lords and ladies of the French, German, and Polish courts took the names and played the parts of *L'Astrée*; and half the prose written in France cultivated romance.

The other half contained some memorable prose. Jean Louis Guez de Balzac's *Lettres* (1624f.) were really essays, designed to impress the *précieuses*, sharing with Vaugelas and Malherbe in purifying the language, and helping to give French prose the form and logic of the classic age. . . . Pierre de Bourdeilles de Brantôme, after a gay life in the army and at the court, left at his death (1614) a bundle of memoirs retailing with gusto the amours of the French ladies, the virtues of Catherine de Médicis, the beauty of Mary Stuart, and the wit of Marguerite of Valois; it is a pity that his most fascinating stories are unverifi-able. "It is not good," he thought, "to grow old in the same hole, and no man of spirit ever did so; one must adventure boldly in all directions, in love as in war." In a more judicious moment he acknowledged that "the greatest bless-ing God can grant us in our marriage is fair issue, not concubinage." . . . Jacques Auguste de Thou, magistrate and councilor of state under his friend Henry IV, helped to draft and negotiate the Edict of Nantes, and devoted half his life to writing *Historia sui temporis* (1604-8), or *History of His Own Time*, a book distinguished by its scholarship, its impartiality, and its courage in branding the Massacre of St. Bartholomew as "an outburst of fury unex-ampled in the annals of any nation." . . . The Duke of Sully, in his old age and with the help of secretaries, composed the famous *Mémoires des sages et royales économies domestiques, politiques, et militaires de Henri le Grand*, which he dedicated "to France, to all good soldiers, and to all the French peo-ple." . . . In the final year of Louis XIII a group of Flemish Jesuits, led by Jean de Bolland, began to publish the *Acta Sanctorum*, giving with cautious criticism the lives of the saints in the order of their commemoration by the Catholic Church. Despite the vicissitudes of the Society, the labor was zealously pursued, until in 1910 it ran to sixty-five volumes. Some mythmongers protested, but the work stands as a credit to the scholarship of the most scholarly of religious orders. Finally, we must list again the ubiquitous and incredible Richelieu, who dipped his pen into every literary well and left us his *Mémoires* —a bit prejudiced in favor of the Cardinal, but standing high in that remarkable sequence of French memoirs which has no rival in any other tongue.

Minor poets were never so plentiful. Théophile de Viau, Vincent Voiture, and Honorat de Bueil, Marquis of Racan, are still read by loyal Frenchmen, if only in school. Théophile's libertine loves and scandalous doubts made him the Villon of the age, condemned to the stake and then let off with banishment. Voiture's breezy wit made him the *bel esprit* (we had almost dared to say the prime ribber) of the Hôtel de Rambouillet. When Bossuet, aged twelve, preached at midnight in that salon, Voiture said he had never heard a sermon delivered so early and so late.

Two major poets honored these reigns. François de Malherbe illustrated the principle that each age, to relish itself, must denounce and reverse the past. The great Ronsard was still singing in Malherbe's youth; he and his Pléiade had chastened French verse by directing it to classic models and themes; but their successors were now sonneteering France and their mistresses to sleep with archaic terms, fanciful phrases, Italian *concetti*, clumsy inversions, obscure allusions, recondite mythology. Malherbe decided that there had been enough of this. Born at Caen (1555), he studied at Basel and Heidelberg, spent years in travel, and was already fifty when he reached the court of France. Despite his impudences and impieties, he made his way and became the favorite poet of Henry the Great, who, however, gave him "more compliments than money."[125] He lived by selling his verses to the highest bidder, and he promoted his wares by eviscerating his predecessors. Like the *précieuses* of the salon Rambouillet, he declared war on words that smacked of rural coarseness or the less poetical operations of the human bag; he banished inversions, ambiguities, colloquialisms, provincialisms, Gasconisms (which was hard on the King), padding, cacophony, solecisms, importations, Latinisms, technicalities, poetic license, imperfect rhymes. Now there should be dignity of ideas, simplicity and clarity of expression, harmony of rhythm, consistency of metaphors, order in exposition, logic in phrase. Good writing must breathe well and must be welcome to the ear; hiatus ("a historian") is an auditory offense, a respiratory disease. Malherbe tried his verses on his butler's ears.[126]

Let us breathe one of his poems—a "Consolation" addressed to a friend who mourned the passing of a daughter:

> Mais elle était *du monde, où les plus belles choses*
> *Ont le pire destin,*
> *Et rose elle a vécu ce que vivent les roses,*
> *L'espace d'un matin . . .*
> *La mort a des rigueurs à mille autre pareilles;*
> *On a beau la prier,*
> *La cruelle qu'elle est se bouche les oreilles,*
> *Et nous laisse crier.*

Le pauvre en sa cabane, où le chaume le couvre,
Est sujet à ses lois;
Et la garde qui veielle aux barrières du Louvre
N'en défend point nos rois.*[127]

Malherbe's practice was less effective than his principles; his verses suffered a chill from his rules; and Guez de Balzac, who was at this time reforming prose, saw only good prose in Malherbe's poetry. But the Hôtel de Rambouillet took him to its bosoms, the Academy adopted his precepts, and Boileau inherited them as the foundation of the classic style. They became for two centuries a stoic saintly shirt of hair and mail for the lyric bards of France. In old age Malherbe swelled into a very pontiff of poetry, an oracle on questions of language and style; some of his admirers saluted him as "the most eloquent man of all time," and he agreed that "what Malherbe writes will last eternally."[128] On his deathbed (1628), he roused himself from his final stupor to reprove his nurse for using incorrect French.[129]

Mathurin Régnier thought him a bore, ignored his rules, and, like Villon, sent up poetry steaming from the stews. Tonsured and destined for the priesthood, he so lost himself in Venusberg that he became old and gray while young. At thirty-one he was infirm with gout and syphilis. He still found that "every woman is to my taste," but they were more discriminating. He wrote some of the most vigorous verse in the language, recklessly venereal, savagely satirical, rivaling Horace in form and Juvenal in vinegar, and alive with persons and places felt or seen. He laughed at the linguistic purism of the *précieuses* and the classic rigor of Malherbe; impassioned ardor from an inner flame seemed to him more vital to poetry than grammatical, rhetorical, prosodical orthodoxy; here at the dawn of the classic age romanticism stirred. Even science and philosophy got their comeuppance for their vaunts:

Philosophes rêveurs, discourez hautement;
Sans bouger de la terre allez au firmament;
Faites que tout le ciel branle à votre cadence,
Et pesez vos discours même dans sa balance . . .
Portez une lanterne aux cachots de nature;
Sachez qui donne aux fleurs cette aimable peinture . . .
Déchiffrez les secrets de nature et des cieux:
Votre raison vous trompe aussi bien que vos yeux.†[130]

---

* "But she was of the world, where the loveliest things have the saddest destiny. Herself a rose, she lived as lives the rose, a morning's hour . . . Death has compulsions nowhere paralleled; we pray to it in vain; cruelly it closes its ears and lets us cry. The poor man in his cabin, under a thatched roof, is subject to its laws; and the watch that guards the Louvre's gates cannot keep him from our kings."

† Dreaming philosophers, prattle loftily; without budging from the earth-leap to the stars; make the whole firmament dance to your tune, and weigh your discourses in the scale of the sky. . . . Carry a lantern into the recesses of nature; know who gives the flowers their lovable hues; . . . decipher the secrets of heaven and earth: your reason deceives you as well as your eyes."

In 1609 he became court poet to Henry IV. Four years later, aged thirty-nine, he died, worn out with melodious lechery. He had composed his epitaph:

> J'ai vécu sans nul pensement,
> Me laissant aller doucement
> À la bonne loi naturelle,
> Et ne saurais dire pourquoi
> La mort daigna penser à moi,
> Qui n'ai daigné penser à elle.*[131]

V. PIERRE CORNEILLE: 1606–84

The literary star in Richelieu's firmament was Pierre Corneille, for with him French drama became literature, and French literature, for a century, became predominantly drama.

Many experiments had prepared for him. Étienne Jodelle had staged the first French tragedy in 1552. Similar imitations of Seneca followed, all based on the Senecan scheme of tales of violence, psychological studies, and bursts of rhetoric, shorn of the classic chorus, but cramped into the supposedly Aristotelian unities of one *action* represented as occurring in one *place* in one day's *time*. Aristotle (as we have seen in discussing the Elizabethan drama) had required unity of action or plot; he had not asked for unity of place, he had not insisted on unity of time. But the *Poetices libriseptem* (1561) of the learned Julius Caesar Scaliger required of all dramatists adherence to Greek and Latin forms; Jean Chapelain repeated the demand in 1630; the arguments that in England had fallen before the wild genius of a man who had small Latin and less Greek won a complete victory in a France inheriting the Latin language and culture; and after 1640 the Senecan form of three unities held the French tragic stage through Corneille and Racine, through Voltaire and the eighteenth century, through the Revolution, the Empire, and the Restoration, till in Hugo's *Hernani* (1830) the romantic drama won its historic, tardy victory.

The French drama had no regular home in the sixteenth century, but had to nurse itself in colleges and had to wander from court to court, from hall to hall. In 1598 the first permanent French theater was established at the Hôtel de Bourgogne in the Rue Mauconseil, and in 1600 the Théâtre des Marais was opened in the present Rue Vieille du Temple. In both cases the form was a long central parterre, or pit, where the less opulent classes stood, ate, drank, gambled, quarreled, and watched the performance and their purses; while along the walls ran two tiers of boxes, in which the

---

* "I have lived without a thought, letting myself go sweetly by nature's good law; and I know not why death should think of me, who never deigned to think of her."

moneyed gentry sat. Before the reign of Richelieu only a few women with nothing to lose attended the plays. The stage, raised at one end of the rectangle, was so far from half the audience that the representation of thought or feeling by facial expression was almost useless to the actors, and a premium was placed upon rhetoric that could reach the farthest ear. Performances were given in the afternoon, usually from five to seven; the law required them to end before dark, for both theaters were in dangerous quarters of the town. The actors, before Molière, were generally imported from Italy and Spain. Female parts were taken by women, and in the comedies the need for revenue laid a bold emphasis on sex. Church and Parlement tried in vain to cleanse or suppress the comic theater. Richelieu raised the moral level of the French drama by taking some of the dramatists under his patronage and surveillance, by attending performances himself, and by collaborating with Rotrou, Scarron, and others in the composition of plays. Gradually, under his all-seeing eye, the predecessors of Corneille —Garnier, Hardy, and Rotrou—prepared the way for the epochal success of *Le Cid*.

Corneille had the usual vicissitudes en route to mastery. Born in Rouen (1606), he had the handicap of growing up in a provincial capital distant from the literary stimulations and opportunities of Paris; but his father was a distinguished magistrate able to give Pierre the best available education in the local college of the Jesuits. These zealous educators used drama as a tool of instruction; the students were taught to act in Latin, classical and other plays, and this Jesuit practice influenced the French drama in theme, technique and style. Of course no one intended Pierre to become a dramatist; he was trained for the law, and he practiced it for a time; and the art and habit of forensic eloquence may have shared in molding the oratory that resounds in his tragedies.

At twenty-one, almost simultaneously, he fell into love and poetry: the lady rejected him, and he found refuge in rhymes. Wounded into lasting melancholy and timidity, he acted in ink the dramas forbidden to his blood. Eleven years passed before he found a wife (1640)—and then only through Richelieu's aid; but meanwhile he conceived a dozen tragedies or comedies of amorous or heroic gallantry. In 1629 he took to Paris his first piece, *Mélite*; it was performed at the Hôtel de Bourgogne; it was an absurd quadrangle of love and intrigue, but its lively dialogue carried it to success, and Corneille warmed himself before a blaze of fame. Richelieu engaged him, along with four others, to write plays on topics and lines suggested by the Cardinal. Corneille transformed too independently a sketch so submitted to him; his Red Eminence frowned; Corneille withdrew in a huff to Rouen, but continued to receive from Richelieu a pension of five hundred crowns a year.

Stirred and piqued by the success of Mairet's tragedy *Sophonisbe,* he abandoned comedy, studied Seneca, and took to Paris in 1635 his *Médée.* Here for the first time appeared his basic qualities—power of thought and nobility of speech. Henceforth, with some lapses, he would people his stage with men and women of high station, dower them with lofty sentiments, and express these in splendid language and forceful reasoning. The contemporary English poet Waller, hearing *Médée,* hailed a new master. "The others," he said, "make . . . verses, but Corneille is the only one who can think."[132]—the highest art is art impregnated with philosophy. From the heroic drama of Rome and Greece, from his Jesuit teachers, from his own somber and solitary meditations—stately Alexandrines marching in his dreams—Corneille achieved a plane of thought and style never before known in French drama, and seldom since.

There was another dramatic literature that drew and formed him. He could derive little from the Elizabethan stage, for that was too negligent of classic rules to fit a classic mold. But Spain, in this age, was mad with theater, showering honors upon Lope de Vega and Tirso de Molina and Calderón de la Barca as the only worthy heirs of Sophocles and Euripides, Terence and Seneca. And in the Spanish drama Corneille found a naturally dramatic theme—that code of honor which required a death for every insult or seduction. He learned Spanish, read Guillén de Castro's *Las mocedades del Cid* (1599?), borrowed the plot with no more apology than Shakespeare, and wrote the most famous play in French literature.*

Le Cid was performed in 1636. The audience felt that nothing so powerful as this had yet appeared on Gallic boards. "It is so fine," said a contemporary, "that it has inspired even the coldest ladies with love, so that their passion has sometimes broken out in the public theater. People have been seen in the boxes who seldom leave their gilded halls and fleur-de-lis–covered armchairs."[133] Not many knew that the plot had been borrowed, though Corneille frankly confessed it; all marveled at its entangled subtlety. Highborn Chimène and noble Rodrigue are tremblingly in love. But Chimène's father, Don Gomès, quarrels with and insults Rodrigue's old and ailing father, Don Diègue. Rodrigue feels bound in honor to avenge his father; he challenges Gomès and kills him. Chimène, still loving Rodrigue, feels bound in honor to beg King Fernand to behead or banish him; the conflict in her between the "point of honor" and the call of the mate gives the story and her divergent passions an extraordinary force and intensity. Rodrigue offers Chimène his sword and invites her to kill him, but she cannot make up her mind. He goes off to fight the Moors, returns to Seville trailing captured kings and clouds of glory; all Seville sings his

---

* *El Cid* (i.e., *Sayyid,* noble) was the title given by the Moors to Rodrigo Díaz, the half-legendary hero who shared (c. 1085) in restoring Spain to Christ.

name, but Chimène still demands his death. As Fernand refuses, she pledges her hand to anyone who will challenge and kill the man she loves. Sancho takes the task. Rodrigue proposes to let Sancho kill him. Chimène repents of her revenge, begs him to defend himself; he overcomes Sancho, but spares him; at last the code of honor is satisfied; Chimène accepts her lover, and all is well.

For half a season Paris celebrated the beauty and debated the sanity of Chimène. Political overtones were heard. Richelieu had forbidden duels, and in this play duels seemed part of the highest law. The nobles, hating Richelieu, gloried in the representation of an aristocracy that still took the law into its own hands. Nor was the Cardinal quite pleased with the success of one who had balked at receiving his literary directives. He asked his newborn Academy to issue a judicial critique of the play, and hardly concealed his hope that the judgment would be adverse. The Academy prolonged its discussions to let tempers cool; finally, after five months, it published its "Sentiments." All in all, the verdict was moderate and just. It objected to the apparent exaltation of romantic love, it thought the denouement lacking in verisimilitude, and it saw something indecent and absurdly vain in Chimène's final words to Rodrigue as he went to fight Sancho, "*Sors vainqueur d'un combat dont Chimène est le prix*" (Come victor from a combat of which Chimène is the prize). This criticism was handsomely salved with the Academy's conclusion

> that even learned men must grant some indulgence to the irregularities of a work which would not have had the good fortune to please the community so much if it had not possessed uncommon beauties . . . and that the naturalness and vehemence of its passions, the force and delicacy of many of its thoughts, and the indescribable charm which mingles with all of its defects, have gained for it a high rank among French poems of the same character.[134]

The Academy never again assumed the office of literary judge. Corneille eased the situation by dedicating the published *Cid* to the Cardinal's beloved niece, and to the Cardinal himself his next masterpiece, *Horace* (1640). Livy[135] had told the legend in his *History*. On the same day, in separate cities, twin sisters gave birth to male triplets—one set fathered by Horatius at Rome, the other by Curiatus at Alba Longa. A generation later the two families were further allied by the marriage of Sabina, daughter of Curiatus, to Horace, a son of Horatius, and by the love of Camilla, daughter of Horatius, for one of the Curiati triplets. But then the two cities stumble into war; their armies come face to face; Sabina and Camilla tremble in the Roman camp, and Sabina sets the feminine theme of the composition:

> *Je suis Romaine, hélas! puisque Horace est Romain;*
> *J'en ai reçu le titre en recevant sa main;*
> *Mais ce nœud me tiendrait en éclave enchaînée*
> *S'il m'empéchait de voir en quel lieux je suis née.*
> *Albe, où j'ai commencé de respirer le jour,*
> *Albe, mon cher pays, et mon premier amour;*
> *Lorsqu'entre nous et toi je vois la guerre ouverte,*
> *Je crains notre victoire autant que notre perte.*
> *Rome, si tu te plains que c'est là te trahir,*
> *Fais-toi des ennemis que je puisse haïr.*
> *Quand je vois de tes murs leur armée et la nôtre,*
> *Mes trois frères dans l'une, et mon mari dans l'autre,*
> *Puis-je former des vœux, et sans impiété*
> *Importuner le ciel pour ta félicité?**[136]

So Corneille displays as his subject no mere battle of arms and men, but the conflict of passionate loyalties, the tragedy of right contending with right; and thus inspired, his pen strikes off phrases of compact power, and lines that march with martial step and resounding harmonies.

The Alban commander reminds the Romans that they and the Albans (did Corneille have Catholics and Huguenots in mind?) are of one blood and land, and that it is criminal to dismember Italy (France?) with civil strife; and he proposes to settle the war by a combat of three Albans and three Romans. The offer is accepted, and the women have an hour of fearful happiness. But the Alban chief chooses the Curiati triplets, the Roman chooses the Horatii. The women mourn, and the heroes are for a moment softened by their tears; but Horatius the father, sounding the masculine theme, reproves them for wasting time with women while honor calls:

> *Faites votre devoir, et laissez faire aux dieux.*
>
> Do your duty, and leave the rest to the gods.[137]

The gods fumble. The three Curiati are slain; Horace alone of the Horatii survives. His sister, Camilla, reproves him for killing her betrothed and denounces Rome and its code of honor and war. Still drunk with battle, he slays her as unworthy to be a Roman. His wife, Sabina, upbraids his cruelty,

---

* "I am a Roman, alas, since Horace is a Roman; I took that title in receiving his hand; but this bond would hold me a chained slave if it closed my eyes to the place of my birth. Alba, where I first breathed the day, Alba, my dear land and my first love, when I see war declared between you and ourselves, I dread our victory as much as our defeat. If, Rome, you complain that this is to betray you, give yourself such foes as I may hate. When I see from your walls their army and ours, my three brothers in the one and my husband in the other, how can I form my prayers and, without impiety, importune Heaven for your felicity?"

laments her lost brothers, and invites Horace to kill her too. He tries to persuade her that patriotism is higher than love.

The plot, of course, is incredible, but hardly more so than in Shakespeare. The dramatic is by definition exceptional; dramas would be ruined if they impartially described reality; they rise to art if, by ignoring the irrelevant and selecting the significant, they can deepen us with a fuller understanding of life. Corneille inherited the Renaissance exaltation of ancient Rome; he upheld the stoic conception of duty against those laxities of love that had dominated the French stage before him; his heroes were to be not lovers primarily, but patriots or saints.

He took a saint from the Catholic calendar to dominate a still stronger play. "All the world knows *Polyeucte*, knows it by heart," said Sainte-Beuve.[138] Here the construction is severely classical, accepting all the unities, yet building within them a complex tragedy of concentrated power. Only the eloquence of the play reaches us in our studies today; we must hear it rolling from the tongues of French actors moving in stately figures over the stage, or under the stars in the court of the Invalides or the Louvre; and even then we must have the French language and French souls, and we must reclothe ourselves in our youthful faith. The plot centers around the resolve of Polyeucte, a proud and cultured Roman newly converted to Christianity, to smash the altar of the pagan gods. The time is the Decian persecution (249–51 A.D.); the place is Melitene, a Roman outpost in Armenia; the scene of the entire drama is the palace of Felix, the Roman governor. All Christians, on pain of death, have been ordered to join in an Empire-wide prayer and sacrifice to the ancient deities for divine support of Roman arms against the invading, encompassing barbarians. Burning with a convert's zeal, Polyeucte desires by some dramatic action to encourage Christian resistance to the Imperial edict. He is held back by love for his wife, Pauline, daughter of the governor, but, like a true Corneillean hero, he sacrifices love to duty. In the presence of Felix himself he and a friend interrupt the pagan rites; they appeal to the worshipers to turn from the adulterous Jupiter to the God of the Christians, the one and "absolute monarch of earth and sky"; and to expose the "impotent monsters" of the Roman pantheon they mount the altar and dash to the ground the ritual vessels and the statue of Jove. Felix has the violators arrested. Pauline pleads with Polyeucte to repent his sacrilege; instead, he challenges her to join in his new faith. She appeals to her father to pardon him; he refuses; she announces her conversion and prepares to accompany her husband to death. Felix is so impressed that he resigns his office and becomes a Christian. Suddenly the persecution ends; Felix is reappointed, but meanwhile Polyeucte has suffered martyrdom.

All but the martyrdom and the desecration of the altar is Corneille's embellishment of history; his, too, are the proud insolence of the saint and the violence of the deed. When the author read the play at the Hôtel de Rambouillet, several auditors, including a bishop, condemned Polyeucte as unnecessarily harsh and extreme. Corneille for a time thought of suppressing the play. Its success on the stage brought him to the zenith of his career (1643). He still had forty-one years of life left him, which we shall see him spending in rivalry with Racine; but he could not know that he had already written his three greatest plays—some would say the best in all the history of the French stage. They are so different from the "romantic" drama of Elizabethan England or nineteenth-century France that imagination must aid history to explain their hold upon their time and the theater today. There is romance too in Corneille, as much as in Shakespeare, and passions studied with more than the care and subtlety of Descartes; but, following the classic ideals of the age, the passions, though vigorously expressed, are subjected to "reason"—or to argument. Superabundance of argument is the ballast of these plays, so that they rarely reach the flights so numerous in Racine. Action is kept off the boards; there all is narration, exhortation, eloquence; in Corneille every character is an accomplished *raisonneur*. For Frenchmen these faults disappear in the splendor of the style and the majesty of the themes. If, in any work of art, we seek nobility, some thought or feeling to lift us above ourselves and the day, we shall find it frequently in Corneille. He wrote as if for statesmen and philosophers; he molded his lines as if composing music; he carved phrases that still haunt the memory of France. Now the classic and aristocratic spirit—of reason checking passion, of form dominating matter—merged with Stoic self-control, Spanish honor, and French intelligence to produce a theater all the world apart from the Elizabethan, and yet, with Racine and Molière, as precious and brilliant in the legacy of mankind.

VI. ARCHITECTURE

Was the victory of the classic mood visible in art as well as literature? It stares at us in almost every French façade of the age. Some Gothic churches were Gothically restored, like the cathedral at Orléans; but more often old churches—like those of St.-Gervaise and St.-Étienne-du-Mont—were refurnished with Renaissance fronts. New churches might show a neo-Italian style throughout; so Jacques Lemercier designed the Church of the Sorbonne on the model of St. Peter's—columns, pediment, and dome. In architecture, as in morals, letters, and philosophy, the pagan revival gave a bold new face to Christianity.

Even the Jesuits were caught in the Renaissance current, all the more readily since, as an order, they had no binding medieval roots. In their first generations, under Loyola and Laynez, they had been austere and fearless missionaries, devoted defenders of orthodoxy and the popes; but they had saved some measure of humanism at the Council of Trent; and as in their colleges they made the ancient classics the core of their curriculum, so in architecture they chose semiclassic façades for their outstanding shrines. From their brilliant church in Rome, the Gesù, they carried their style of luxuriant decoration across the Alps and over the Pyrenees. They were not uniformly pledged to copious ornament; their most famous architect—who raised the transept façade of the Orléans cathedral—designed churches and colleges on lines of severe simplicity congenial to his character and his funds. But when the order prospered it built with a happy exuberance. In 1627 it began the handsome church familiarly known to Paris as Les Jésuites—the façade Roman, the interior exquisitely carved in capitals, arches, and cornices, the choir vaults meeting harmoniously to support a luminous dome; John Evelyn, touring Paris in 1644, called this church "one of the most perfect pieces of architecture in Europe."[139] It was not unpleasantly baroque; it contained nothing distorted or bizarre. In France baroque was sobered by aristocratic taste—as Ronsard and Malherbe chastened the enormities of Rabelais.

Religious architecture languished during the Religious Wars, and in the intervals of peace civil architecture grew. City halls rose at La Rochelle, Lyon, Troyes, and Reims. In Paris Catherine de Médicis, wishing to leave the Louvre to Charles IX and his Queen, hired Philibert Delorme to build for her and her aides the Tuileries (1564), which took its name from the tile (*tuile*) potteries nearby. The new palace, fronted in Renaissance style with Corinthian pillars, rose west of the Louvre at the present Place du Carrousel, and ran for 807 feet along the Seine. It was burned down in the fury of the Commune in 1871; only the gardens remain— the delectable Jardins des Tuileries.

Civic building recovered rapidly under Henry IV. The Pont Neuf, opened to traffic in 1604, became the most popular of the bridges spanning the Seine. The Hôtel de Ville, finished in Henry's dying year, remained till 1871 the rival of Notre Dame and the Louvre in the pride of the people. Like Francis I and Louis XIV, Henry gathered artists under his wing, understood them, and co-ordinated their work. For him they extended the Louvre by the Pavillon de Flore and connected it with the Tuileries by the Grande Galerie. At Fontainebleau they built the chapel, the Galerie des Cerfs, the Cour and Salon Ovale, the Porte Dauphine, and the Galerie de Diane. Fontainebleau under Henri le Grand was the fulfillment of the French Renaissance.

His widow, Marie de Médicis, before running afoul of Richelieu, engaged Salomon de Brosse to design her own Palais du Luxembourg, in the Rue Vaugirard south of the Seine (1613–20). When Louis XIII and Richelieu freed themselves from her they commissioned Lemercier to again extend the Louvre as the seat of government; now the Pavillon de l'Horloge was completed, the great wings were extended, and the lordly building took essentially its present form. From Lemercier's plans Richelieu built in Paris the sumptuous Palais Cardinal, into which he gathered his collections of painting, sculpture, and other arts; here were Mantegnas, da Vincis, Veroneses, and Michelangelo's *Slaves*. Most of this treasure passed to Louis XIII and XIV, to the Louvre, and to us.

In domestic architecture François Mansart reshaped the skyline of Paris by developing the mansard roof—having two slopes, the lower one steeper than the other, readily shedding snow and rain, and allowing greater space in the top floor; many a Paris student or artist has lived in a *mansarde* or attic room. Mansart designed several churches in Paris, and many châteaux in France—most successfully at what is now Maisons Laffitte, a suburb of the capital. In 1635 "Monsieur" Gaston d'Orléans commissioned him to rebuild the family château at Blois; Mansart finished only the northwest wing; its Renaissance façade and magnificent stairway remain the chef-d'oeuvre of "the most skillful architect France has ever produced."[140]

VII. MANY ARTS

In the same mood of classic tradition softened by French refinement and feeling, the sculptors adorned the churches, mansions, gardens, and tombs of the great. Germain Pilon inherited the Renaissance grace of Cellini, Primaticcio, and Jean Goujon, but he remembered too the Gothic merger of tenderness and strength. His masterpieces are three tombs. One, in the abbey church of St.-Denis, reunited in death Catherine de Médicis and her occasional husband Henry II—the Queen dowered with an idealized beauty that would have warmed her solitary heart. Another, now in the Louvre, honored René de Birague, Chancellor to Francis II and Charles IX—a picture of pride humbled to piety, a marvel of pliant drapery caught in bronze. Beside this is the tomb of René's wife, Valentine Balbiani: above, the lady in her prime, glorified with figured robes; below, the same beauty ruthlessly carved as a corpse, with bony face, hands, and legs, corrugated chest, and sunken empty breasts; this is a powerful outcry of anger against time's sardonic desecration of loveliness. These tombs alone would have raised Pilon above any other French sculptor of the age; but he added to them an abundance of statuary, all of arresting merit, and now mostly gathered into France's inexhaustible treasury, the Louvre.

There, too, within a few paces, one may see works of Pilon's successors: a life figure of Henry IV by Barthélemy Tremblay, with a smile as puzzling as

Mona Lisa's; the tomb of Anne de Montmorency by Barthélemy Prieur; and a lively *Renommée (Fame)* by Pierre Briard—a nude blowing from puffed cheeks and writing in the air, as if to say, improving on Keats, "Here lies one whose name was writ in wind." In the chapel at Chantilly is a memorable monument to Cardinal de Bérulle by Jacques Sarazin. Some of these sculptors studied in Rome and brought back from Bernini a baroque tendency to excessive ornament, movement, and emotion, but these excesses soon vanished under the cold eye of Richelieu and the classic taste of Louis XIV. The smooth perfection of *le grand siècle* already appears in the medallions of Jean Varin, who came from Liège to live in France, and who reached, in his minuscule portraits of Richelieu, Mazarin, and Anne of Austria, an excellence no later medalist has ever surpassed.

If France had left us no sculpture, architecture, or painting she would still command our loving homage for her achievements in the lesser arts. Even in this harassed interval between Francis I and Louis XIV, the drawings, engravings, enamels, goldsmithery, gem cutting, ironwork, woodwork, textiles, tapestries, and garden designs of France rivaled—some would say surpassed—the like products of her contemporaries from Flanders to Italy. Jacques Callot's drawings of gypsies, beggars, and tramps carry the very odor of life, and his series of etchings *The Miseries of War* stole a march of two centuries on Goya. Let the iron artistry of the age be judged from the grille leading to the Galerie d'Apollon in the Louvre. Tapestry was as much a major art as sculpture or painting. Jean Gobelin had opened dye works in Paris in the fifteenth century; in the sixteenth the firm added a tapestry factory; Francis I established another at Fontainebleau, Henry II a third in the capital. When Catherine de Médicis went to meet the Spanish envoys at Bayonne she took with her twenty-two tapestries woven for Francis I to display the wealth and art of France. The art-craft declined under Henry II, but Henri Quatre restored it by bringing a new generation of Flemish designers, dyers, and weavers to the Gobelin plant in Paris. Five distinguished specimens from his reign—*The Hunt of Diana*—adorn the Morgan Library in New York.

Interior decoration felt the baroque influence seeping in from Italy. Chairs, tables, chests, buffets, cabinets, dressers, bedsteads were curved and carved luxuriantly, often inlaid with ebony, lapis lazuli, jasper or agate, or adorned with statuettes. In the Louis Treize period many chairs were upholstered in velvet, needlework, or tapestry. Walls, cornices, and ceilings might be carved or painted with a frolic of plant or animal forms. Fireplaces lost some of their medieval ruggedness, and were sometimes embellished with delicate arabesques in polychrome.

In pottery it was the heyday of two old men: Léonard Limousin, who continued till 1574 to produce such enamels as had made him famous under Francis I,* and Bernard Palissy, who, born in 1510, survived till 1589. Palissy was a man mad about pottery, with a passionate curiosity spilling

---

* Note the fine specimens in the Wallace Collection in London and the Frick Collection in New York.

over into agriculture, chemistry, and religion, interested in everything from the formation of stones to the nature of deity. He studied the chemistry of diverse soils to get the best clay for his kiln, and he experimented for years to produce a white enamel that would take and hold delicate hues. He burned half his belongings to feed his ceramic furnace, and told the story as if challenging Cellini. Too poor to hire help, he did all the work himself; he cut his hands so frequently that, he said, "I was forced to eat my soup with my hands bound up in rags." And: "After working like this for ten years, I was so thin that no muscles appeared on my arms or legs; my legs were so thin that the garters with which I hold up my stockings [no longer held them] . . . When I walked my stockings fell to my ragged shoes."[141] His neighbors accused him of practicing magic and neglecting his family. Finally, about 1550, he found the mixture he sought, made an enamel of iridescent glaze, and used it to fashion vessels and figurines brilliantly adorned with fishes, lizards, snakes, insects, birds, stones— all the plethora of nature. Catherine de Médicis delighted to place these artificial fossils in her garden and flower beds; she gave the old potter a workshop in the Tuileries, and in his new environment he added naiads and nymphs to his decorations. Though a zealous Huguenot, he was exempted from the Massacre of St. Bartholomew, for Catherine and her court were fascinated by his vases, cups, plates, candlesticks, and quaint ideas. But in 1588 the Catholic League ordered a new prosecution of Protestants, and Palissy was sent to the Bastille. A diarist wrote in 1590:

> In this year [actually in 1589] there died in the dungeons of the Bastille Maître Bernard Palissy, a prisoner on account of his religion, aged eighty years; he succumbed to misery, ill-treatment, and want. . . . The aunt of this good man having gone to inquire how he was, . . . the jailer told her that if she wished to see him she would find him a corpse with the dogs along the ramparts, where he had caused him to be thrown like the dog that he was.[142]

VIII. POUSSIN AND THE PAINTERS

French painting was still in bondage to Flanders and Italy. Flemish *tapissiers* dominated their art in Paris, and Flemish painters prospered in Paris, Lyon, Toulouse, Montpellier, and Bordeaux. The best French portraits of this period were by Flemings in France: the lovely *Elizabeth of Austria* (now in the Louvre) by François Clouet, the proud *Henry IV* (in Chantilly) by Frans Pourbus the Younger, and, above all, the *Richelieu* of Philippe de Champaigne.

But the mastering influence on French painting in this period was Italian. Art students went to Rome, sometimes at the French government's expense, and came back hesitating between the idealism of the sixteenth-century Florentines and the dark realism of the seventeenth-century Bolognese or Neapolitans. Simon Vouet, from the age of fourteen (1604), made such a name for himself as a painter that three countries competed for him. Charles I tried to keep him in London, but the Baron of Sancy took him on an embassy to Constantinople, where Simon made a remarkable likeness of Ahmet I from a secret study of the Sultan's features in an hour's audience given to the ambassador. Returning through Italy, Vouet fell in love with Venice and Veronese, then with Caravaggio in Rome, whose dukes and cardinals so favored him that he remained in Italy fifteen years. In 1627 Louis XIII, who had been paying him an annual pension of four thousand livres, summoned him to France to be court painter, and gave him an apartment in the Louvre. Soon all France wanted him. He decorated the chapel of Richelieu's château, made an altarpiece for the Church of St.-Eustache, furnished designs for royal tapestries, and painted portraits for the court. Buried in commissions, he gathered aides into a school which grew into the Royal Academy of Painting and Sculpture; there he trained and employed Le Sueur, Mignard, Le Nôtre, Bourdon, and Le Brun. His surviving works hardly vindicate his fame, but he has in French history the pivotal place of preparing the painters of the culminating age.

Three brothers, Antoine, Louis, and Mathieu Le Nain, varied the canvases of their time by picturing the life of the peasants with somber pity, finding in them the silent poverty and grim strength of seventeenth-century France. Georges de La Tour (recently exhumed by critical acclaim) also gave his brush to the lowly; his matching portraits *A Peasant Man* and *A Peasant Woman* stand near the top of paintings in these reigns; we may judge his current *réclame* by the $500,000 or more paid for his *Fortuneteller* by the New York Metropolitan Museum of Art (1960). Akin to this turning from court to cottage was the specific achievement of French painting in this age—the development of landscape as a major element in pictorial art.

The father of Nicolas Poussin was a soldier in the army of Henry IV. Quartered in the home of Nicolas Delaisement after the battle of Ivry, he married Nicolas' daughter—a peasant woman who could not write her name—and tilled a farm near Les Andelys in Normandy. Their son learned to love fields and woods, and to catch some moment of them with pencil or pen. Quentin Varin came to Les Andelys to decorate a church; young Nicolas watched him eagerly and coaxed lessons from him in drawing and painting. When Varin departed, Nicolas, aged eighteen (1612), ran away to Paris to study art. There his months of near-starvation were glorified by

finding Raimondi's engravings of Raphael's works. Here were two revelations for Nicolas: that line, not color, was the tool of art, and that Rome
was art's capital. For eight struggling years he tried to reach that citadel.
Once he got as far as Florence, but, penniless, despondent, and ill, he
returned to Paris. He tried again, but was stopped at Lyon by a creditor;
he crept back to pay his debts and butter his bread by some minor painting
in the Luxembourg Palace. In 1622 the Italian poet Giovanni Battista Marini,
coming to Paris, employed him to illustrate the poem *Adone*. Poussin's
drawings won Marini's approval, and some commissions. Nicolas painted
portraits grudgingly and saved his francs reverently, and in 1624 he at
last saw Rome.

Marini recommended him to Cardinal Francesco Barberini: "You will
find here a youth who has demonic fury in him"—a young man "mad
about painting" (to vary Hiroshige's self-analysis). He was mad about
Italy too, but not so much about the paintings of the Renaissance masters
as about the perfection of fragments in the Roman Forum, and not about
the frescoes surviving from antiquity but about Rome herself—her vistas,
fields, trees, hills, her very soil. Like some later enthusiasts, he must have
wondered why God had not let him be born in Italy.

Cardinal Barberini tested him with a commission to paint *The Death of
Germanicus;* the result pleased, and soon Poussin had all he could do to
meet the calls on his art. His patrons, lay or churchly, yearned for nudes;
and for a time he appeased them with such feminine displays as *The
Triumph of Flora** for Cardinal Omodeo, and *A Bacchanalian Scene* for
Richelieu. He settled down in Rome, married at thirty-six a girl of seventeen, and spent ten years of happiness with her and his oils. Then (1640)
Richelieu and Louis XIII summoned him to Paris. "I shall go," said Poussin,
"like one sentenced to be sawn in half."[143] He was given high honors and
a pension of a thousand crowns, but he was ill at ease in the rancorous competition of the Parisian artists. Surrendering rich prospects, he hurried back
to Italy (1643). He bought a house on the Pincian Hill, next to Claude
Lorrain's, and there he remained till his death, quiet, domestic, absorbed,
content.

His life, like his pictures, was a classic composition, a model of order,
measure, and self-restraint. He had few marks of the artist except his
tools; he was not an avid lover like Raphael, nor a man of the world like
Titian, nor (despite Marini) a demonic genius like Michelangelo; he was
a bourgeois who took care of his family and paid his debts. Cardinal Mas-
simo, seeing his modest establishment, remarked, "How I pity you for having no servant!"—to which Poussin replied, "How I pity you for having
so many!"[144] Every morning he walked on his hill; then all day he painted,

---

* All Poussin pictures named are in the Louvre unless otherwise indicated.

relying on labor rather than inspiration. When, later, someone asked him how he had reached mastery, he answered, "I neglected nothing."[145]

Considering his laborious and unaided methods, his production was immense. He must have painted four hundred pictures, for we know that some were lost, and 342 remain; add thirteen hundred drawings, of which Windsor Castle cherishes a hundred for their precision and purity of line. He did not excel in variety. Often his nudes are lifeless statues; we should have relished more sensuality. He was a sculptor using a brush; he tended to look upon women as sculptural figures—though at times he recognized them as the divine originals of art. "The pretty girls whom we see in the streets of Nîmes," he said, "please our eyes and souls no less than the lovely columns of the Maison Carré, since these are only old copies of those."[146] Nor was he at home in Biblical subjects. Some he did well— *The Philistine Struck Down at the Gates*, and *The Blind Men of Jericho*; and how lovely, yet stately, are the women in *Eliezer and Rebecca!* His forte was classical mythology pictured amid classical ruins against a landscape of classic calm. He drew not from living models but from an imagination steeped in the love and illusion of an antiquity in which all men were strong and all women beautiful. See the perfection of the one female figure in *The Shepherds of Arcady*, which Poussin, on Colbert's order, painted for Louis XIV. And note, in passing, the inscription on the shepherd's tomb: *Et ego in Arcadia*—"I too [was once] in Arcadia"; was this Poussin dreaming that he too had lived in Greece with Orpheus and the gods?

The Funeral of Phocion is the most powerful of Poussin's mythologies, but *Orpheus and Eurydice* is the most moving, perhaps because we recall Gluck's despairing strains. The romantic soul is disturbed to find the story so lost in the landscape. For in truth it was not man that Poussin loved, nor woman either, it was the chastening expanse of fields, woods, and sky—all that encompassing panorama in which change is leisurely or shamed by permanence, and human ills are swallowed up in the perspectives of space and time. Therefore his greatest pictures are landscapes, in which man is as minor an incident as in Chinese painting or modern biology.

These landscapes are majestic, but monotonous. We should hardly distinguish one from another if Poussin had not thrown in some identifying figures or a careless title. He loved line wisely but too well; he neglected the gamut of color, playing too much on brown; no wonder later artists have rebelled against this "brown sauce" dripping from his trees. And yet those softly lighted, softly colored vistas, so unsatisfying to a Ruskin fascinated by Turner's glare,[147] are a relief after the ideological fermentation of painting in our time. Here is the classic conception of beauty as the

harmony of parts in a whole, not the youthful idea of art as "expression"—
which might be a child's daub or a hawker's cry. Amid mannerism and
baroque, and against the force and sentiment of Italian painting in the
seventeenth century, Poussin clung to the classic ideal of nothing in excess:
no shouting colors, no tears, no bizarreries, no theatrical contrasts of light
and shade. It is a masculine art, resembling Corneille rather than Racine,
and Bach more than Beethoven.

The self-portrait that he made in 1650 shows his eyes a bit weary, perhaps with painting or reading by scant light. He read much, seeking to
know the life of ancient Greece and Rome in sedulous detail; not since
Leonardo had an artist been so learned. As he entered old age he found
his eyes weakening, his hand unsteady. The death of his wife at fifty-one
(1664) cut a living bond; he survived her but a year. "Apelles is dead,"
wrote a friend. On or near the tomb in the parish church of San Lorenzo,
Châteaubriand (1829) raised a marble monument as one mortal immortal
to another:

> *F. A. de Châteaubriand*
> *à*
> *Nicolas Poussin*
> *Pour la gloire des arts et l'honneur de la France*

His closest rival as a landscape painter was his neighbor but friend,
Claude Gellée, named Lorrain from the province of his birth. He too felt
the urge to Italy, accepting any position, however menial, to get there and
live there, where every turn of the seeking eye revealed some monument
of Christian art or some inspiring fragment of antiquity. In Rome he
apprenticed himself to Agostino Tassi, mixed colors for him, cooked for
him, learned from him. He made a thousand tentative drawings, and etchings now prized by connoisseurs. He worked slowly and scrupulously,
sometimes a fortnight over one detail. At last he too was a painter, fed
with commissions from appreciative cardinals and kings. Soon he had his
own home on the Pincian Hill, and he shared with Poussin in meeting the
new demand for natural scenes.

He responded willingly, for he loved the land and sky of Rome so passionately that often he rose before dawn to watch the daily creation of light,
to catch the stealthy changes of light and shade made by each emerging
inch of the sun. Light was to Claude no mere element in a picture; it was
his major subject; and though he did not care, like Turner, to look into
the very face of the sun, he was the first to study and convey the spreading
integument of light. He grasped the intangible play of air upon fields, foliage, water, clouds; every moment of the sky was new, and he seemed bent

on having each fluid moment still itself in his art. He loved the tremor of sails meeting the wind, the majesty of ships riding the sea. He felt the lure of distance, the logic and magic of perspective, the longing to see, beyond the visible, the infinity of space.

Landscapes were his only interest. On Poussin's advice he inserted classical structures—temples, ruins, pedestals—into his pictures, perhaps to give the dignity of old age to a passing scene. He consented to add some human figures to Nature's panorama, but his heart was not in these excrescences. The figures "were thrown in for nothing"; he "sold his landscapes and gave away his figures."[148] The titles and the stories they suggested were concessions to minds that could not feel the miracle of light and the mystery of space without the grace of Christian legend or some tag of classical tales. But in reality there was for Claude only one theme— the world of morning, noon, and eventide. He dowered the galleries of Europe with fond variations, whose names mean nothing, but whose pantheism is a mystic marriage of poetry and philosophy.

We may admit to Ruskin[149] that Claude and Poussin show Nature deceptively in her gentler moods, missing her grandeur and ignoring her furies of pitiless destructiveness. But through their work a great tradition of landscape painting had been established. Now more and more this would compete with figures and portraits, with Biblical and mythical scenes. The way was opened for Nature's procession from the Ruisdaels to Corot.

Richelieu and national unity, Corneille and the Academy, Montaigne and Malherbe, de Brosse and Mansart, Poussin and Lorrain—this was no scanty harvest from a land at war. Louis XIV would now stand on that rising heritage and preside over France in her greatest age.

CHAPTER XVII

The Revolt of the Netherlands

1555–1648

I. MISE-EN-SCÈNE

ON October 25, 1555, the Emperor Charles V transferred the sovereignty of the Netherlands to his son Philip. On the twenty-sixth, before the States-General at Brussels, Philip received oaths of allegiance, and swore to maintain the rights and privileges of the seventeen provinces according to tradition, treaty, and law. Those mutual pledges set the stage for one of the great dramas in the history of freedom.

The scene was complex. The Netherlands—i.e., the lowlands—then comprised the present Belgium as well as the existing Kingdom of the Netherlands. Dutch—Low German—was the language not only of the seven northern provinces (Holland, Zeeland, Utrecht, Friesland, Groningen, Overijssel, and Gelderland) but also of four provinces (Flanders, Brabant, Mechlin, and Limburg) in northern "Belgium"; while Walloon, a dialect of French, was spoken in six southern provinces (Artois, Walloon Flanders, Cambrai, Tournai, Hainaut, and Namur). All these, and the neighboring duchy of Luxembourg, were under Hapsburg rule.

The people, in 1555, were overwhelmingly Catholic,[1] but their Catholicism was of the humane humanist kind preached by Erasmus a half-century back and generally practiced in Renaissance Rome—not the somber, uncompromising type developed in Spain by centuries of war against Moslem "infidels." After 1520 Lutheranism and Anabaptism seeped in from Germany, and then, more numerously, Calvinism from Germany, Switzerland, and France. Charles V tried to stem these inroads by importing the papal or episcopal form of the Inquisition and by proclaiming, through "placards," the most terrible penalties for any serious deviation from Catholic orthodoxy; but after the weakening of his power by the Peace of Passau (1552) these penalties were rarely enforced. In 1558 a Rotterdam crowd forcibly rescued several Anabaptists from the stake. Alarmed by the growth of heresy, Philip renewed the placards and their penalties. Fear spread that he intended to introduce the Spanish form of the Inquisition in all its severity.

Calvinism was congenial to the mercantile element in the economy. The ports of Antwerp and Amsterdam were the central ganglia of north-European commerce, alive with importation, exportation, speculation, and every form of finance; insurance alone kept six hundred agents in affluence.[2] The rivers Rhine, Maas, Ijssel, Waal, Scheldt, and Lys and a hundred canals bore in silence a dozen varieties of transport. The winds of trade fed the fires of craft and factory industry in Brussels, Ghent, Ypres, Tournai, Valenciennes, Namur, Mechlin, Leiden, Utrecht, Haarlem. The businessmen who controlled these towns respected Catholicism as a tradition-rooted pillar of political, social, and moral stability; but they had no relish for its pompous heirarchy, and they liked the role given to the educated laity in the management of Calvinist congregations and policy. More immediately they resented the taxes laid upon the Netherlands economy by the Spanish government.

The peasantry suffered most and benefited least from the revolt. The greater part of the land was owned by magnates resembling the feudal lords of Germany and France, and it was these who organized the struggle for independence. Philippe de Montmorency, Count of Horn, held vast tracts in the southern provinces. Lamoral, Count of Egmont, had spacious estates in Flanders and Luxembourg, and could afford to marry a Bavarian duchess. In several campaigns he fought with such dashing valor that he became a favorite of Charles and Philip; it was he who led Philip's army to victory at St.-Quentin (1557). In his princely palace he displayed a generous but extravagant hospitality and slipped embarrassingly into debt. Such men, and many lesser nobles, looked hungrily upon the wealth of the Church and heard with envy of German barons who had enriched themselves by seizing ecclesiastical property.[3] "They thought that the King would do well to carve a round number of handsome military commanderies out of the abbey lands," so creating "a splendid cavalry . . . in place of a horde of lazy epicureans telling beads."[4]

The richest and ablest of the great landowners was William of Nassau, Prince of Orange. The family owned large properties in the German province of Hesse-Nassau and in the district around Wiesbaden as well as in the Netherlands, while it derived its title from its little principality of Orange in southern France. Born in German Dillenburg (1533), William was brought up as a Lutheran till he was eleven; then, to be eligible to inherit the lands of his cousin René, he was moved to Brussels and reconditioned as a Catholic. Charles V took a fancy to him, secured for him the hand of Anne of Egmont (heiress of the Count of Buren), and chose him as chief attendant at the historic abdication in 1555. Philip sent him—still a youth of twenty-two, but already a master of Flemish, German, Spanish, French, and Italian—as one of his plenipotentiaries to negotiate the Peace of Cateau-Cambrésis; there William handled himself with solid judgment and such watchful tongue that the French called him *le taciturne*, the Silent.

Philip made him a state councilor, a Knight of the Golden Fleece, and stadholder of Holland, Zeeland, and Utrecht. But William developed a mind of his own, and Philip never forgave him.

The young prince had graces of person as well as of purse. He was tall and athletic, carried no useless weight, and charmed all but his enemies by his eloquence and courtesy. As a military leader he was a consistent failure, but as a political strategist his flexible persistence and patient courage transmuted his defects into the establishment of a new state against the opposition of the strongest political and religious forces in Europe. He handled men better than armies, and in the long run this proved the greater gift. His foes charged him with changing his religion to suit his personal or political needs.[5] It was probably so; but all the leaders of that century used religion as an instrument of policy.* Many found fault with his marriages. His first wife having died, he negotiated for the hand of another wealthy Anne, daughter of the Protestant Maurice, Elector of Saxony; he married her with Lutheran rites in 1561, but did not declare himself a Protestant till 1573. Anne went semi-insane in 1567 and was deposited with friends. While she was still alive, William secured from five Protestant ministers permission to marry Charlotte de Bourbon, of the royal house of France (1575), who had fled from a nunnery and had embraced the Reformed faith. She died in 1582. After mourning her for a year William took a fourth wife, Louise de Coligny, daughter of the admiral who had perished in the Massacre of St. Bartholomew. Despite—perhaps because of—these marriages, William was rich only in lands, poor in money. By 1560 he was almost a million florins in debt.[7] In a flurry of economy he dismissed twenty-eight of his cooks.[8]

Philip fumbled ruinously in handling the Netherlands nobles. His father, reared in Brussels, knew these men, spoke their language, managed them judiciously. Philip, brought up in Spain, could speak neither French nor Dutch; he found it difficult to bend to the magnates graciously, to respect their customs and their debts; he frowned upon their extravagance, their drinking, and their easy ways with women; above all, he could not understand their claims to check his power. They on their part disliked his somber pride, his penchant for the Inquisition, his appointment of Spaniards to lucrative posts in the Netherlands, his garrisoning of their towns with Spanish troops. When he asked for funds from the nobles and businessmen who constituted the States-General, they listened coldly to his plea—through interpreters—that his father and the recent wars had left the treasury with great deficits; they were alarmed by his request for 1,300,000 florins and a further tax of one per cent on realty and two per

---

* "The princes who have established, protected, or changed religions have very rarely had any of their own."—Voltaire.[6]

cent on movable property; they refused to sanction these levies, but voted him only such sums as they deemed adequate for current needs. Three years later he summoned them again and asked for three million guilders. They yielded, but on condition that all Spanish troops be withdrawn from the Netherlands. He made this concession, but canceled its conciliatory effect by getting papal permission to establish eleven new bishoprics in the Low Countries and nominating to these sees men willing to enforce his father's decrees against heresy. When he sailed for Spain on August 26, 1559, never to see the Netherlands again, the economic and religious outlines of the great struggle were taking form.

II. MARGARET OF PARMA: 1559-67

Philip had appointed as his regent Margaret, Duchess of Parma, a natural daughter of Charles V by a Flemish mother. She had been brought up in the Netherlands and, despite long residence in Italy, she could understand the Flemings if not the Dutch. She was neither bigoted nor intolerant, but was a devout Catholic who, annually in Holy Week, washed the feet of twelve maidens and gave them marriage dowries. She was an able and kindly woman, uncomfortably lost in a maelstrom of revolution.

Her authority was limited by advisers whom Philip had designated. Egmont and Orange were in her Council of State, but, finding themselves consistently outvoted by the three other members, they ceased to attend. In the resultant triumvirate the dominant personality was Antoine Perrenot, Bishop of Arras, known to history as Cardinal de Granvelle. He was a man of good character according to his lights; like Margaret, he was inclined to peaceful means in dealing with "heresy," but he was so dedicated to Catholicism and monarchy that he found it hard to understand dissent. He and the Regent were handicapped by Philip's insistence that no important measure could be taken without the royal consent, which took weeks to transmit from Madrid to Brussels. The Cardinal sacrificed popularity by obeying the King. He privately opposed the multiplication of bishoprics, but yielded to Philip's insistence that four sees were not enough for seventeen provinces. The Protestant minority noted with anger that the new bishops were spreading and intensifying the papal Inquisition. In March 1563 Orange, Egmont, and Horn, themselves Catholics, wrote to Philip charging Granvelle with violating provincial rights that the King was pledged to maintain; they thought the Cardinal responsible for the new bishops, and they urged his removal from office. Margaret herself did not relish his assumption of powers; she longed for some accord with the dissatisfied nobles, who were important to her in preserving social order; finally (September 1563) she too recommended that Granvelle be sent to other pastures. After long resistance, Philip yielded, and invited the lordly minister to enjoy a leave of absence. Granvelle left Brussels (March 13, 1564), but he continued to be one of the King's most trusted counselors. The nobles returned to Margaret's Council of State. Some of their appointees sold offices, justice, and pardons, and the Regent seems to have shared in the spoils.[9]

The Inquisition spread. Philip watched it from Spain, urged it on, and sent Margaret the names of suspected heretics. Hardly a day passed without an execution. In 1561 Geleyn de Muler was burned at Audenaarde; Thomas Calberg was burned alive at Tournai; an Anabaptist was hacked to death with seven blows of a rusty sword in the presence of his wife, who died with horror at the sight.[10] Enraged by these barbarities, Bertrand le Blas invaded the cathedral of Tournai during Christmas Mass, rushed to the altar, snatched the Host from the priest, trampled it underfoot, and cried out to the congregation, "Misguided men, do ye take this thing to be Jesus Christ, your Lord and Saviour?" He was put to torture, his right hand and foot were burned away to the bone, his tongue was torn out, he was suspended over a fire and was slowly roasted to death. At Lille Robert Ogier, his wife, and his sons were burned because they called the worship of the consecrated Host a blasphemous idolatry.*

The Torquemada of the Netherlands was Peter Titelman, whose methods were so arbitrary and brutal that the city council of Bruges, all Catholic, denounced him to the Regent as a barbarian who dragged people from their homes, tried them without any legal checks, forced them to say whatever he wished, and then condemned them to death; and the magistrates of Flanders, in an earnest address to Philip, begged him to end these enormities. Margaret timidly asked the Inquisitor to conduct himself "with discretion and modesty," but the executions continued. Philip supported Titelman, and bade the Regent enforce without mercy or delay the decrees recently issued by the Council of Trent (1564). The Council of State protested that several of these decrees violated the recognized privileges of the provinces, and it suspended their publication.

William of Orange, anxious to keep the Netherlands united in the preservation of their traditional political liberties, proposed a policy of toleration far in advance of his time. "The King errs," he told the Council of State, "if he thinks that the Netherlands . . . can indefinitely support these sanguinary edicts. However strongly I am attached to the Catholic religion, I cannot approve of princes attempting to rule the consciences of their subjects and wanting to rob them of the liberty of faith."[11] Catholics

---

* For these cases we have only Protestant authorities, as quoted in Motley, *Rise of the Dutch Republic*, I, 283-90.

joined with Protestants in branding the edicts as tyrannical.[12] Egmont was sent to Madrid to ask for a mitigation of the edicts; Margaret privately seconded the request. Egmont was feted in Spain, but came back empty-handed. The bishops of Ypres, Namur, Ghent, and St.-Omer addressed a petition to Philip (June 1565), begging him to soften the edicts and "to admonish the people by gentleness and fatherly love, not by judicial severity."[13] To all such protests Philip replied that he would rather sacrifice a hundred thousand lives than change his policy,[14] and in October 1565 he sent this plain directive to the agents of the Inquisition:

> As to the Inquisition, my will is that it be enforced . . . as of old, and as is required by all law, human and divine. This lies very near my heart, and I require you to carry out my orders. Let all condemned prisoners be put to death, and suffer them no longer to escape through the neglect, weakness, and bad faith of the judges. If any are too timid to execute the edicts, I will replace them by men who have more heart and zeal.[15]

Margaret obeyed Philip and ordered full enforcement of the edicts (November 14, 1565). Orange and Egmont again withdrew from her Council. Orange, other nobles, and many magistrates refused to enforce the edicts. Protestants poured forth pamphlets and broadsheets denouncing the persecution. Foreign merchants, sensing revolution in the air, began to leave the Low Countries. Stores closed, trade languished, Antwerp seemed dead. Many Netherland Protestants fled to England or Germany. In England they helped to develop those textile industries which in the seventeenth century competed with the United Provinces, and in the eighteenth led the Industrial Revolution.

Many of the lesser nobles secretly adopted the Protestant creed. In December 1565 some of these—Louis, Count of Nassau (the chivalrous younger brother of William), Philip van Marnix, Lord of St.-Aldegonde, his brother Jean van Marnix, Lord of Tholouse, Hendrik, Count of Brederode, and others—met in the palace of the Count of Culemborch in Brussels, drew up a "Compromise" denouncing the introduction of the Inquisition into the Netherlands, and formed a league pledged to drive it from the country. On April 5, 1566, some four hundred of these minor nobles marched to the palace of the Regent, and presented to her a "Request" that she ask the King to end the Inquisition and the edicts in the Netherlands, and that all enforcement of the edicts be suspended until Philip's reply was received. Margaret replied that she would communicate their petition to the King, but that she had no authority to suspend the edicts; however, she would do all in her power to mitigate their operation. One of her councilors, seeing her frightened by the number and the resolution of the petitioners, reassured her: "What, madam, is your Highness afraid of these beggars [*ces gueux*]?" The confederates defiantly accepted the name; many of them adopted the coarse gray costume, the wallet and bowl then characteristic of mendicants; "*Vivent les Gueux!*" became the battle cry of the revolution, and for a year it was these younger nobles who led and nourished the revolt.

Margaret apprised Philip of the "Request" and its wide popular support, and renewed her efforts to bring him around to moderation. He answered in an apparently conciliatory mood (May 6, 1566): he hoped that heresy could be suppressed without further ·shedding of blood, and he promised to visit the Netherlands soon. The Council of State sent to him Florent de Montmorency, Baron of Montigny, and the Marquis of Bergheon to reinforce the Regent's plea. Philip received them handsomely; wrote to Margaret (July 31) consenting to the abolition of the episcopal Inquisition in the Netherlands, and offering a general pardon to all for whom the Regent should recommend it.

The Calvinists, Lutherans, and Anabaptists of the Netherlands took advantage of this lull in the storm to bring their worship out in the open. Protestant refugees returned in considerable number from England, Germany, and Switzerland; preachers of all kinds—ex-monks, learned theologians, ambitious hatters, curriers, and tanners—addressed large gatherings of fervent men and women, many of them armed, all chanting psalms and crying, "*Vivent les Gueux!*" Near Tournai Ambrose Wille, who had studied with Calvin, preached to six thousand (June 28, 1566); two days later, on the same spot, another minister addressed ten thousand; a week later, twenty thousand.[16] Half of Flanders seemed to have gone Protestant. On Sundays the churches and towns were almost empty while the townspeople attended the Protestant assemblies. When word went about the province of Holland that the eloquent Peter Gabriel was to preach at Overeen, near Haarlem, Protestants by the thousands flocked there and shook the fields with their psalms. Near Antwerp the Protestant assemblages numbered fifteen thousand—some said thirty thousand—nearly every man armed. The Regent ordered the magistrates of Antwerp to prevent such gatherings as a danger to the state; they replied that their militia was inadequate and unreliable. Margaret herself, since the departure of the Spanish garrisons, had no troops at her disposal. Antwerp was in such turmoil that economic life was seriously impeded. The Regent asked William of Orange to go there and arrange some peaceful settlement between Catholics and Protestants. He quieted the strife by persuading the preachers to confine their assemblies to the suburbs and to keep them unarmed.

In this same month (July 1566) two thousand "Beggars," led by Count

Louis of Nassau, gathered at St.-Trond, in the bishopric of Liége, and, amid much joyous roistering, laid plans to advance their cause. They resolved to communicate with German Protestants and to raise among them an army that would come to the aid of the Netherland Protestants in case these should be attacked. On July 26 Louis and twelve others, garbed as beggars, presented to the Regent a demand that she convene the States-General, and that meanwhile she be guided by Orange, Egmont, and Horn. Her answer being noncommittal, they intimated that they might be obliged to seek foreign aid. Louis at once proceeded, with the connivance of his more cautious brother William, to raise in Germany four thousand cavalry and forty companies of infantry.[17]

On August 9 Philip signed a formal instrument declaring that his offer of pardon had been wrung from him against his will and did not bind him, and on August 12 he assured the Pope that the suspension of the Inquisition was subject to papal approval.[18] On August 14 a Protestant crowd, aroused by preachers who denounced religious images as idols, broke into one after another of St.-Omer's churches, smashed the images and the altars, and destroyed all decorations. In that week similar mobs accomplished like denudations in Ypres, Courtrai, Audenaarde, and Valenciennes. At Antwerp, on the sixteenth and seventeenth, mobs entered the great cathedral, broke up the altars, shattered stained glass, the crucifixes and other images, destroyed organs, embroideries, chalices, and monstrances, opened sepulchers, and stripped corpses of ornaments. They drank the sacramental wine, burned costly missals, and trampled upon masterpieces of art. Having sent for ladders and ropes, they hauled statues down from niches and smashed them with sledge hammers. Shouting in triumph, the crowd passed through Antwerp, destroyed the images and ornaments in thirty churches and monasteries, burned monastic libraries, and drove monks and nuns from their convents.[19] When the news of this "Calvinist Fury" reached Tournai the iconoclastic ecstasy was let loose there, and every church was sacked. In Flanders alone four hundred churches were cleansed of their imagery. At Culemborch the jolly Count presided over the devastation, and fed his parrots with consecrated Hosts;[20] elsewhere some former priests toasted the wafers on forks.[21] From Flanders the Fury passed into the northern provinces, to Amsterdam, Leiden, Delft, Utrecht, at last into Groningen and Friesland. Most Protestant leaders condemned these ravages, but some of them, noting that very little violence had been done to persons, judged the destruction of statues and pictures as less criminal than the burning of live "heretics."

Margaret of Parma shrank before this storm. "Anything and everything is now tolerated in this country," she wrote to Philip, "except the Catholic religion."[22] Philip bided his time for revenge, but the Regent, faced with armed mobs and audacious leaders, felt compelled to make concessions. On August 23 she signed with the representatives of the Gueux an "Accord" by which Calvinist worship was to be permitted wherever it was already practiced, on condition that it should not interfere with Catholic services, and that the Protestants should leave their weapons at home. The confederate spokesmen agreed to disband their league if the government lived up to this accord. The persecution halted, and for a moment there was peace.

Neither William of Orange nor the King of Spain was satisfied to let matters rest. William saw in the growth of a passionate Protestantism an instrument with which to win independence for the Netherlands. Though still nominally a Catholic, he resigned all his state offices, organized his own system of espionage, and went to Germany (April 22, 1567) to seek soldiers and funds. Five days later the Duke of Alva left Spain, commissioned by Philip to raise and use sufficient troops to avenge the Calvinist riots and stamp out, by uncompromising force, all heresy, rebellion, and freedom in the Netherlands.

III. ALVA IN THE NETHERLANDS: 1567–73

Fernando Álvarez de Toledo, Duke of Alba, or Alva, now fifty-nine years old, was a figure out of El Greco: straight, tall, thin, with dark eyes, yellow skin, silver beard. At twenty he had inherited his illustrious title and extensive estates. He had entered early upon a military career, in which he distinguished himself by courage, intelligence, and severity. Philip attached him to his innermost council and listened congenially to his advice. In this emergency his judgment was that of a soldier trained in Spanish discipline and piety: crush the rebels without mercy, for every concession strengthens the opposition. Philip gave him full powers and bade him Godspeed.

Alva crossed to Italy and assembled there, chiefly from Spanish garrisons in Naples and Milan, a select army of ten thousand men. He dressed them in proud splendor, gave them the latest arms and armor, and solaced them with two thousand prostitutes properly enrolled and assigned. He led them over the Alps and through Burgundy, Lorraine, and Luxembourg, and entered Brussels on August 22, 1567. Egmont met him with all submission and a gift of two rare horses. Margaret met him with regret, feeling that her brother had superseded and overruled her just when she had restored a humane order. When Alva garrisoned the larger towns with his Spanish troops she protested, but the Duke coldly replied, "I am ready to take all the odium upon myself." Margaret asked Philip's permission to resign; he granted it with a comfortable pension, and in

December she left Brussels for her home in Parma, mourned by the Catholics, who revered her, and by the Protestants, who foresaw how mild her greatest rigor would soon appear beside Alva's calculated brutality.

The new Regent and Governor General installed himself in the citadel at Antwerp and prepared to cleanse the Netherlands of heresy. He invited Egmont and Horn to dinner, feted them, arrested them, and sent them under strong guard to a castle in Ghent (September 7). He appointed a "Council of Troubles," which the terrified Protestants rechristened the "Council of Blood"; seven of its nine members were Netherlanders, two were Spaniards; but only these two had a vote, and Alva reserved to himself the final decision in any case that specially interested him. He ordered the council to ferret out and arrest all persons suspected of opposition to the Catholic Church or the Spanish government, to try them privately, and to punish the convicted without tenderness or delay. Agents were sent out to spy; informers were encouraged to betray their relatives, their enemies, their friends. Emigration was forbidden; shipmasters aiding emigration were to be hanged.[23] Every town that had failed to stop or punish rebellion was held guilty, and its officials were imprisoned or fined. Thousands of arrests were made; in one morning some 1,500 persons were seized in their beds and carried off to jail. Trials were summary. Condemnations to death were sometimes voted upon groups of thirty, forty, or fifty at a time.[24] In one month (January 1568) eighty-four residents of Valenciennes were executed. Soon there was hardly a family in Flanders that did not mourn a member arrested or killed by the Council of Troubles. Scarcely anyone in the Netherlands dared protest; the slightest criticism would have meant arrest.

Alva felt his success tarnished by inability to lure William of Orange within his reach. The Council of Troubles drew up an indictment of the Prince, his brother Louis, his brother-in-law Count van den Berg, the Baron of Montigny, and other leaders as having encouraged heresy and revolt. Montigny was still in Spain; Philip had him jailed. William's son, Philip William, Count of Buren, was a student in the University of Louvain; he was arrested, was sent to Spain, and was brought up as a fervent Catholic, who repudiated his father's principles. William was declared an outlaw whom anyone might kill with legal impunity.

He proceeded with the organization of an army, and directed his brother Louis to do likewise. He asked aid of the Lutheran princes, who responded feebly, and of Queen Elizabeth, who held back cautiously; sums came to him from Antwerp, Amsterdam, Leiden, Haarlem, Flushing; Counts van den Berg, Culemborch, and Hoogstraaten sent 30,000 florins each; he himself sold his jewelry, plate, tapestries, and rich furniture and contributed 50,000 florins. Soldiers were plentiful, for mercenaries released by a lull in the religious wars of France had returned to Germany penniless. Toleration was a necessary policy for William: he had to win Lutherans as well as Calvinists to his banner, and he had to assure the Catholics of the Netherlands that their worship would not be impeded by liberation from Spain.

He planned simultaneous action by three armies. A force of Huguenots from France was to attack Artois in the southwest; Hoogstraaten was to lead his men against Maastricht in the south; Louis of Nassau was to enter Friesland from Germany in the northeast. The Huguenot and Hoog-straaten invasions were repulsed, but Louis won a victory over the Spanish soldiery at Heiligerlee (May 23, 1568). Alva ordered the execution of Egmont and Horn (June 5) to release for action the 3,000 troops that had guarded them and Ghent. With these reinforcements he advanced into Friesland, overwhelmed Louis' weakened army at Jemmingen (July 21), and killed 7,000 men. Louis escaped by swimming an estuary of the Ems. In October William led 25,000 men into Brabant, resolved to meet Alva in a decisive battle. Alva, with men less numerous but better disciplined, outgeneraled him, and avoided battle except in destructive rearguard attacks. William's troops, unpaid, refused to fight. He led them to safety in France and disbanded them. Then, disguised as a peasant, he made his way from France to Germany, where he moved from one town to another to avoid assassination. With these disastrous campaigns began the "Eighty Years' War" waged with unprecedented perseverance by the Netherlands till their final triumph in 1648.

Alva was for the time proud master of the field, but he too was penniless. Philip had arranged with Genoese bankers to send Alva, by sea, 450,000 ducats; but the vessels were forced by English privateers into Plymouth harbor, and Elizabeth, not averse to helping William for such a fee, seized the money with the blandest of apologies. Alva summoned the States-General of nobles and burgesses to Brussels, and proposed to them (March 20, 1569) an immediate tax of one per cent to be levied upon all property, a perpetual tax of 5 per cent on every transfer of realty, and a perpetual tax of 10 per cent on every sale. The assembly protested that since many articles changed ownership several times a year, such a sales tax would approach confiscation. It referred the proposals to the provincial assemblies, and there the opposition was so bitter that Alva had to defer the 10 per cent tax till 1572, and content himself meanwhile with the one per cent tax and a grant of two million florins yearly for two years. Even the one per cent tax was hard and costly to collect. Utrecht refused to pay it; a regiment of soldiery was quartered upon the households; resistance continued; Alva declared the whole district treasonous, abolished its charters and privileges, and confiscated all the property of the inhabitants for the King.

It was this taxation, and the measures taken to enforce it, that defeated the hitherto undefeated Alva. Now nearly the entire population, Catholic as well as Protestant, opposed him, and with rising anger as his impositions hampered and discouraged the business activity upon which the Netherlands had built their prosperity. More skilled in war than in finance, Alva retaliated for Elizabeth's appropriation of the Genoese funds by seizing English property in the Netherlands and forbidding trade with England. Elizabeth thereupon confiscated Netherland goods in England and diverted English trade to Hamburg. Soon the Netherlands felt the torpor of commercial decay. Shops closed, unemployment mounted, and the powerful business classes, which had borne so patiently the hanging of Protestants and the sacking of churches, secretly meditated, at last financed, revolt. Even the Catholic clergy, fearing the collapse of the national economy, turned against Alva and warned Philip that the Duke was ruining the state.[25] Pope Pius V, who had rejoiced over Alva's victories, joined with Cardinal de Granvelle in deploring Alva's severity,[26] and recommended a general amnesty to all repentant rebels and heretics. Philip agreed and so notified Alva (February 1569), but the Duke asked for delay, and the amnesty was not proclaimed till July 16, 1570. In that year the Pope bestowed the blessed hat and sword upon Alva and the Golden Rose upon Alva's wife,[27] and Philip put the imprisoned Montigny to death (October 16, 1570).

Meanwhile a new force had entered upon the scene. In March 1568 a band of desperate men known as the Wild Beggars turned their ardor to pillaging churches and monasteries and cutting off the noses or ears of priests and monks, as if resolved to rival the barbarities of the Council of Blood.[28] In 1569-72 another group, calling themselves Beggars of the Sea, seized control of eighteen vessels, received commissions from William of Orange, raided the Netherland coast, plundered churches and monasteries, preyed upon Spanish shipping, and replenished their provisions in friendly English ports—and even in distant La Rochelle, then held by Huguenots. Wherever a coastal town was left without a Spanish garrison, the Beggars of the Sea rushed in, captured strategic posts, and, by their power to open the dykes, made it dangerous for Spanish forces to approach. Alva could no longer receive supplies by sea. The principal cities of Holland, Zeeland, Gelderland, and Friesland, so protected, gave their allegiance to William of Orange and voted him supplies for war (July 1572). William moved his headquarters to Delft and declared himself *"calvus et Calvinista,"* bald and Calvinist, which was truer of his head than of his creed. Now Philip van Marnix wrote the song "Wilhelmus van Nassouwen," which became and still is the national hymn of the Netherlands.

So encouraged, William organized another army and invaded Brabant.

At the same time Louis of Nassau, supported by Coligny, raised a force in France, entered Hainaut, and captured Valenciennes and Mons (May 23, 1572). Alva marched to recapture Mons, hoping thereby to discourage further support of Louis by France. William advanced southward to help his brother; he won some minor victories, but too soon exhausted his funds; his troops paid themselves by plundering churches and amused themselves by killing priests.[29] Catholic opposition rose; when William's army neared Brussels it found the gates closed and the citizens armed to resist. Resuming its march, it was but a league from Mons when it was surprised in its sleep by six hundred Spanish soldiers; eight hundred of William's men were slaughtered before they could organize for defense; William himself barely escaped, fleeing with a remnant of his forces to Mechlin in Brabant. Meanwhile the murder of Coligny and the Massacre of St. Bartholomew ended all hope of aid from France. On September 17 Mons fell to Alva, who allowed Louis and his surviving troops to leave unharmed; but Alva's general, Philippe de Novarmes, on his own authority, hanged hundreds of the inhabitants, confiscated their property, and bought it in at bargain rates.[30]

William's failure in strategy, the excesses of his uncontrollable troops, and the barbarities of the Beggars frustrated his hopes of uniting Catholics, Calvinists, and Lutherans to oppose Alva's tyranny. The Beggars, who were nearly all ardent Calvinists, showed against Catholics the same ferocity that the Inquisition and the Council of Blood had shown against rebels and heretics. In many instances they gave Catholic captives a choice between Calvinism and death, and they unhesitatingly killed, sometimes after incredible tortures, those who clung to the old faith.[31] Both sides in the conflict put to death many prisoners of war. Wrote a Protestant historian:

> On more than one occasion men were seen hanging . . . their own brothers, who had been taken prisoners in the enemy's ranks. . . . The islanders found a fierce pleasure in these acts of cruelty. A Spaniard had ceased to be human in their eyes. On one occasion a surgeon at Veer cut the heart from a Spanish prisoner, nailed it on a vessel's prow, and invited the townsmen to come and fasten their teeth in it, which many did with savage satisfaction.[32]

It was these merciless Beggars who defeated Alva. Resting from his campaigns, he bequeathed to his son Don Federigo Álvarez de Toledo the task of recovering and punishing the cities that had declared for William or had surrendered to him. Álvarez began with Mechlin, which offered only a few shots of resistance; priests and citizens came out in a penitent procession to beg that the town be spared. But Alva had ordered an exemplary revenge. For three days Don Federigo's troops sacked homes, monasteries, and churches, stole the jewels and costly robes of religious statuary, trampled consecrated wafers underfoot, butchered men and violated women, Catholic or Protestant. Advancing into Gelderland, his army overcame the feeble defenses of Zutphen, put nearly every man in the town to death, hanging some by the feet, drowning five hundred by tying them in couples back to back and throwing them into the Ijssel. Little Naarden, after a brief resistance, surrendered; it greeted the conquering Spaniards with tables set with feasts; the soldiers ate and drank, then killed every person in the town. They passed on to Haarlem, a Calvinist center which had shown especial enthusiasm for the revolt. A garrison of four thousand troops defended the city so resolutely that Don Federigo proposed to withdraw. Alva threatened to disown him if he desisted from the siege. Barbarities multiplied; each side hanged captives on gibbets facing the enemy, and the defenders infuriated the besiegers by staging on the ramparts parodies of Catholic rites.[33] William sent three thousand men to attack Don Federigo's army; they were destroyed, and all further efforts to relieve Haarlem failed. After a siege of seven months, and after being reduced to eating weeds and leather, the city surrendered (July 11, 1573). Of the garrison only 1,600 survived; most of these were put to death; four hundred leading citizens were executed; the rest were spared on agreeing to pay a fine of 250,000 guilders.

This was the last and most costly victory of Alva's regime. Over twelve thousand of the besieging army had died of wounds or disease, and hateful taxes had poured their proceeds fruitlessly into the sieve of war. Philip, who counted pennies rather than lives, discovered that Alva was not only unpopular but expensive, and that his general's methods were uniting the Netherlands against Spain. Alva felt the veering of the wind and asked to be relieved. He boasted that he had executed eighteen thousand rebels;[34] but the heretics were as strong as when he came; moreover, they controlled the ports and the sea, and the provinces of Holland and Zeeland were completely lost to the King. The Bishop of Namur estimated that Alva in seven years had done more harm to Catholicism than Luther and Calvinism had done in a generation.[35] Alva's resignation was accepted; he left the Netherlands (December 18, 1573), was well received by Philip, and, aged seventy-two, led the Spanish armies in the conquest of Portugal (1580). Returning from that campaign, he fell into a lingering fever, and was kept alive only by drinking milk from a woman's breast. He died December 12, 1582, having lived a year on milk and half a century on blood.

IV. REQUESÉNS AND DON JUAN: 1573–78

To replace him Philip sent Don Luis de Requeséns, lately Spanish Viceroy of Milan. The new governor was surprised by the number and the spirit of the rebels. "Before my arrival," he wrote to the King, "I did not understand how they could maintain such considerable fleets, while your Majesty could not support a single one. It appears, however, that men who are fighting for their lives, their firesides, their property, and their false religion—for their own cause, in short—are contented to receive rations only, without receiving pay."[37] He begged Philip to allow him to grant a general amnesty to all but persisting heretics, to allow these to emigrate, and to abolish the 10 per cent tax on sales. William of Orange saw in these proposals merely a play for time and a new device for extirpating Protestantism from the Netherlands; he would accept peace only on full freedom of worship, the restoration of provincial privileges, and the withdrawal of all Spaniards from civil and military posts. The war continued. In the battle of Mook (April 13, 1574) William's brothers Louis, aged thirty-six, and Henry, aged twenty-four, lost their lives.

Two events helped the revolt at this point: Philip went bankrupt (1575), and Requeséns died while besieging Zierikzee (March 5, 1576). The King appointed his half-brother, Don Juan of Austria, to the ungrateful post, but Juan did not reach Luxembourg till November. During this interval the representatives of Holland and Zeeland signed at Delft (April 25) an Act of Pacification, which gave William supreme command on land and sea, the power of appointment to all political posts, and even, in emergency, the right to confer the protectorate of the confederation upon a foreign prince. Speaking with his new authority, he appealed to the other provinces to join in expelling the Spaniards from the Netherlands. He promised liberty of conscience and worship to Catholics and Protestants alike.

His appeal would probably have met with little response in the southern provinces had not the Spanish soldiery, cheated of pillage at Zierikzee, mutinied (July) and begun a campaign of indiscriminate plunder and violence that terrorized Flanders and Brabant. The Council of State at Brussels reprimanded them; they defied it; the Council declared them outlaws, but had no force to oppose them. William offered to send military protection, and renewed his pledge of religious freedom. The Council hesitated; the people of Brussels overthrew it and set up another Council under Philippe de Croy, who opened negotiations with the Prince. On September 26 Ghent welcomed a body of troops sent by William to protect it from the Spanish mutineers. On October 19 delegates from Brabant,

Flanders, and Hainaut met at Ghent; they were reluctant to ally their states with the outlawed Prince; but on the twentieth the mutineers sacked Maastricht; on the twenty-eighth the conferees, to secure the protection of William's troops, signed the "Pacification of Ghent," which recognized him as governor of Holland and Zeeland, suspended all persecution for heresy, and agreed to co-operate in expelling all Spanish soldiers from their provinces. The States-General of the southern provinces, meeting at Brussels, refused to sign the Pacification, considering it a declaration of war against the King.

Once more the mutineers reinforced William's arguments. On November 4, 1576, they seized Antwerp and subjected it to the worst pillage in Netherland history. The citizens resisted, but were overcome; seven thousand of them were killed; a thousand buildings, some of them master-pieces of architecture, were set on fire; men, women, and children were slaughtered in a delirium of blood by soldiers crying, "*Santiago! España! A sangre, a carne, a fuego, a sacco!*" (Saint James! Spain! To blood, to flesh, to fire, to sack!) All through that night the soldiers plundered the rich city; nearly every house was robbed. To extort confessions of hidden hoards, real or imaginary, parents were tortured in their children's presence, infants were slain in their mother's arms, wives were flogged to death before their husbands' eyes. For two days more this "Spanish Fury" raged on, until the soldiers were sated with gold and jewelry and costly clothing, and began to gamble their gains with one another in streets still littered with the dead. On November 28 the States-General ratified the Pacification of Ghent.

It was a timely victory for the Prince. When Don Juan sent word from Luxembourg that he was about to enter Brussels, the States-General replied that it would not receive him as governor unless he accepted the Pacification, restored the charters of the provinces, and dismissed all Spanish troops from the Netherlands. The Don, brave in battle, muddled in diplomacy, soldierless and penniless, fretted the winter through in Luxembourg, then (February 12, 1577) signed the "Perpetual Edict," which committed him to the Pacification and the provincial liberties. On March 1 Juan made a ceremonial entry into Brussels, and the city was delighted to have so handsome and powerless a governor. The Spanish troops departed, and peace smiled for a moment upon the ravaged land.

Juan's dreams were larger than his purse. After his exploits at Lepanto and Tunis this helpless majesty chilled his romantic blood. Nearby, in England, the lovely Mary Stuart was a prisoner of that ogress Elizabeth. Why not collect an army and some ships, cross the water, depose one queen, marry the other, be king of England and Scotland, and bring those benighted regions back to Mother Church? Philip, who feared the gap between ducats and dreams, set his brother down as a fool. Juan proved it by suddenly leaving Brussels (June 11), putting himself at the head of a Catholic Walloon regiment, and repudiating the Pacification. After fruitless negotiations with Juan, the States-General invited William to the capital. On his arrival (September 23) he was welcomed by a large part of the Catholic citizenry as the only man who could lead the Netherlands to freedom. On October 8 the States-General notified Don Juan that it no longer recognized him as governor, but would accept, in his place, a prince of the blood. On December 10, 1577, all the provinces except Namur bound themselves together in the "Union of Brussels." The Catholic members of the States-General, fearing William's Calvinism, asked Matthias, Archduke of Austria, to accept the government of the Netherlands. The youth of twenty came and was installed (January 18, 1578), but William's supporters persuaded the new governor to appoint him as his lieutenant—actually the master of administration and policy.

Only mutual toleration of religious diversity could have preserved this association, and intolerance shattered it. The Calvinists of Holland, like the Catholics of Spain, held that only unbelievers could practice toleration. Many of them openly called William of Orange an atheist.[38] The Calvinist preacher Peter Dathenus charged him with making the state his god and changing his religion as others changed their clothes.[39] The Calvinists were (and till 1587 remained) only a tenth of the population in the province of Holland, but they were active and ambitious, and they were armed. They won control of the political assemblies; they replaced Catholic with Protestant magistrates; in 1573 the Estates, or provincial council, forbade all Catholic worship in Holland,[40] on the ground that every Catholic was a potential servant of Spain. By 1578 Calvinism was almost universal in Zeeland, and was politically—not numerically—dominant in Friesland. Waves of image-breaking swept over Holland and Zeeland in 1572, and after 1576 in other provinces, even in Flanders and Brabant. All association of religion with art was repudiated as idolatrous or profane. Churches were stripped of pictures, statues, crucifixes, and decoration; gold and silver vessels were melted down; bare walls remained. The Beggars tortured Catholic priests and put some to death.[41]

William condemned these procedures, but connived[42] at the seizure of political power by armed Calvinist minorities in Brussels, Ypres, Bruges, and all northern Flanders.[43] At Ghent the victorious Calvinists imprisoned the councilors, sacked and gutted churches and monasteries, confiscated ecclesiastical property, prohibited all Catholic services, burned monks in the market place,[44] and set up a revolutionary republic (1577). At Amsterdam (May 24, 1578) armed Calvinists entered the town hall, banished the magistrates, replaced them with Calvinists, and gave the denuded churches to the Reformed worship. On the following day a similar uprising transformed Haarlem. At Antwerp, which was now William's headquarters, the Protestants drove priests and monks from the city (May 28); the Prince berated his followers for their violence and persuaded them to let Catholic services be resumed, but in 1581 all Catholic worship was forbidden in Antwerp and Utrecht. The Calvinists charged that the priests had deceived the people with bogus relics and manipulated miracles —exhibiting fragments of the "true cross," holding up old bones for adoration as those of saints, and secreting oil in the heads of statues to make them opportunely sweat.[45]

William mourned to see his years of labor for unity ending in division, chaos, and hate. The Calvinist democracy that had captured several cities was falling into such anarchy that men of property, Protestant as well as Catholic, began to wonder whether the new dispensation was not, for them, worse than the old, placards and all. William met this rising demand for order by negotiating with François, Duke of Anjou, to take over the governorship from the incompetent and negligible Matthias, but Anjou proved treacherous and worthless. As a culminating misfortune for the Prince, a new Spanish army of twenty thousand well-trained men was marching north under the ablest general of the age. In December 1577 Alessandro Farnese, Duke of Parma, brought his army to Don Juan in Luxembourg. On January 31, 1578, they defeated the undisciplined forces of the States-General at Gembloux. Louvain and a dozen minor towns opened their gates to the new conqueror. The States-General of the Netherlands fled from Brussels to Antwerp. Don Juan, smelling new glory, caught a malignant fever, and died at Namur October 1, 1578, aged thirty-three. Philip appointed Farnese governor general, and a new chapter began.

V. PARMA AND ORANGE: 1578–84

Alessandro Farnese, now thirty-three, was the son of the former Regent, Margaret of Parma. Brought up in Spain, he swore loyalty to Philip, fought at Lepanto, and gave the last fourteen years of his life to saving the southern Netherlands for the King. In 1586 he was to inherit the duchy of Parma and its title, but he never took the ducal throne. Sharp eyes, dark features, cropped black hair, eagle nose, and bushy beard revealed only a part of his ability, courage, and subtlety. He had all the military art of Alva, less of his cruelty, immeasurably more skill in negotiation and address. The battle for the Netherlands now became a duel between the Duke of Parma's diplomacy and arms, supported by Catholic funds and hopes, and the heroic perseverance of the Prince of Orange, financed by Dutch merchants and helped and hindered by the fanaticism of his friends.

On January 5, 1579, a group of Catholic nobles from Hainaut, Douai, Artois, and Lille, inspired by the Bishop of Arras, formed the League of Arras for the protection of their religion and property. On January 29 the provinces of Holland, Zeeland, Groningen, Utrecht, and Gelderland formed the Union of Utrecht for the defense of their faith and liberties; soon they were joined by Friesland and Overijssel; these seven "United Provinces" became the Dutch Netherlands of today. The remaining provinces became the "Spanish Netherlands" and, in the nineteenth century, Belgium. The division of the seventeen provinces into two nations was determined partly by the predominance of Catholicism in the south and of Protestantism in the north, but also by the geographical separation of the lowlands by the great inlets and rivers which, by their breadth and their controllable dykes, offered defensible ports and barriers to Spanish fleets and arms.

On May 19 the League of Arras signed an agreement with Parma by which it bound itself to tolerate no religion but the Catholic, and accepted Spanish sovereignty on condition that the privileges of the provinces and communes should be restored. By persuasion, bribery, or force, the Duke soon regained almost all the southern provinces for Spain. The Calvinist leaders at Brussels, Ghent, and Ypres abandoned their conquests and fled to the Protestant north. On March 12, 1579, Parma led a large army against Maastricht, strategically situated on the river from which it took its name. Prodigies of heroism and barbarity were performed on both sides. The attackers dug miles of subterranean passages to mine and invade the city; the defenders—women joining the men—dug passages to meet them, and battles were fought to the death in the bowels of the earth. Boiling water was poured into the tunnels, fires were lit to fill them with smoke; hundreds of besiegers were scalded or choked to death. One of Parma's mines, exploding prematurely, killed five hundred of his men. When his soldiers tried to scale the wall they were met with firebrands, and burning pitch-hoops were quoited around their necks. After four months of effort and fury, the besiegers made a breach in the wall, entered through it silently at night, caught the exhausted defenders sleeping, and massacred 6,000 men, women and children. Of the city's 30,000 population only 400 now survived. Parma repeopled it with Walloon Catholics.

It was a major disaster for the Protestant cause. William, who had tried in vain to succor the city, was with some reason blamed for incompetence and delay. The same extremists who had frustrated his unifying policies by their intolerance and violence now charged him with treason to their cause in his negotiations with the Catholic Duke of Anjou, and they pointed out that he had attended no religious service during the past year. Philip seized the moment to promulgate a ban (March 15, 1581) against Orange. After detailing all the ingratitude, disloyalty, marriages, and crimes of the Prince, he proceeded:

> Therefore . . . for all his evil doings as chief disturber of the public peace, and as a public pest, we outlaw him forever, and forbid all our subjects to associate with him or communicate with him in public or in secret, or to administer to him victuals, drink, fire, or other necessaries. We declare him an enemy of the human race and give his property to all who may seize it. In order the sooner to remove our people from his tyranny and oppression, we promise, on the word of a king and as God's servant, that if one of our subjects be found so generous of heart . . . that he shall find means of executing this decree and ridding us of the said pest, either by delivering him to us dead or alive, or by depriving him at once of life, we will give him and his heirs landed property or money, as he will, to the amount of 25,000 gold crowns. If he has committed any crime, of any kind whatsoever, we will pardon him. If he be not noble we will ennoble him.[46]

The provincial Estates replied to this ban by appointing William stadholder, or chief magistrate, of Holland and Zeeland (July 24, 1581); and two days later the representatives of Holland, Zeeland, Gelderland, Utrecht, Flanders, and Brabant signed at the Hague an "Act of Abjuration" solemnly renouncing allegiance to the King of Spain. In a document as famous in Dutch history as Parliament's Declaration of Rights (1689) in the history of England, they proclaimed that a ruler who treats his subjects as slaves and destroys their liberties should no longer be accounted their legitimate sovereign, and may lawfully be deposed.[47] William's own reply to the ban took the form of an *Apologia* written for him by his chaplain and sent to the States-General and to every European court. He welcomed the ban as a distinction. He charged Philip with incest, adultery, and the murder of his own wife and son. He expressed his readiness to resign his offices, to withdraw from the Netherlands, even to surrender his life, if he might thereby benefit his country. He signed the document with his motto, *Je maintiendrai*—"I will hold fast."

Soon afterward (March 18, 1582) Philip reaped the first fruits of the ban. Jean Jaureguy, spurred on by the promised reward, armed himself with a pistol, begged God's help, promised the Virgin a portion of his spoils, made his way to William of Orange at Antwerp, and shot him through the head. The bullet entered under the right ear, passed through the palate, and emerged through the left cheek. The assassin was caught and killed at once by William's attendants, but the mission seemed accomplished; for weeks the Prince seemed near death. Farnese invited the rebel provinces, now that their obstinate leader was dead, to make their peace with their merciful King. But William slowly recovered under the devoted care of his wife Charlotte, who died of exhaustion and fever on May 5. In July two obscure conspirators laid a plan to poison both the Prince of Orange and the Duke of Anjou; the plot was detected and the criminals were arrested; one killed himself in jail, the other was sent to Paris, was tried and found guilty, and was torn to pieces by means of four horses.

During this year 1582 Anjou collected some French soldiers about him at Antwerp. Dissatisfied with his ducal title, he dreamed of making himself a king. Suddenly, on January 17, 1583, his followers, shouting "Long live the Mass!" attempted to seize control of the city. The people resisted them; nearly two thousand lives were lost in this "French Fury"; the uprising failed, Anjou fled, and William suffered further loss of popularity for having so long supported him. In March another attempt was made upon his life. Feeling unsafe in Antwerp, he moved his headquarters to Delft. The provinces of Groningen and Gelderland now made their peace with Parma. Only two of the "united" provinces still adhered to William, but these two, Holland and Zeeland, testified their loyalty by making the stadholdership hereditary in his family (December 1583). So were laid the foundations of the house of Orange, which in 1688 would half conquer, half inherit, England.

Assassins persisted. In April 1584 Hans Hanszoon of Flushing tried to blow up the Prince; he failed and was put to death. Balthasar Gérard, of Burgundy, burned with religious zeal and the thought of twenty-five thousand crowns.* Going to the Duke of Parma, he offered to kill the Prince of Orange. Parma judged the youth of twenty unfit for such an enterprise, refused him the modest advance requested, but promised him the full reward if he succeeded.[48] Gérard went to Delft, disguised himself as a poor and pious Calvinist, received an alms of twelve crowns from William, and poured three bullets into the Prince's body (July 10, 1584). William cried, "My God, have pity on my soul. . . . Have pity on this poor people." He died within a few minutes. Gérard was caught, was tried by the city magistrates, expressed joy over his success, and was put to extreme torture and death. William was buried at Delft with the highest honors as "Father of His Country." Having sacrificed nearly all his belongings in promotion of the revolt, he left his twelve children almost penniless—a silent testimony of the nobility into which he had matured.

The full reward was paid to Gérard's parents. The Catholics of the

---

* That Gérard was encouraged by a Jesuit is affirmed by Ranke (*History of the Popes*, I, 472) and by Motley (*Rise of the Dutch Republic*); it is denied by Pastor (*History of the Popes*, XX, 19-20).

Netherlands rejoiced, calling the crime God's vengeance for the desecration of churches and the murder of priests. They sent the assassin's head to Cologne as a precious relic, and for half a century they labored to have him declared a saint.[49]

VI. TRIUMPH: 1584–1648

The death of their leader broke the spirit of such followers as William still had in Flanders and Brabant. Parma took Bruges, Ghent, Brussels, Mechlin, Antwerp; by the end of 1585 all the Netherlands south of the Maas—except Ostend and Sluys—had fallen to Spain. The Beggars, however, still controlled the ports and the sea.

The northern provinces had repeatedly appealed to Elizabeth for aid. Now she responded. She knew that the revolt of the Netherlands had kept Spain from declaring war upon England; she could not afford to have that blessing cease; moreover, the Dutch controlled the market for English wool. In December 1585 she sent to Holland a substantial force under Leicester and Sir Philip Sidney. Leicester, as governor general of the rebel provinces, assumed almost sovereign power. Seeing that the southern provinces imported the necessaries of life from the northern, he forbade all trade with any Spanish possession. But the Dutch merchants lived on that trade; they exported goods to Spain during their war with Spain; they refused to obey Leicester's prohibitions. Defeated at Zutphen (September 22, 1586), Leicester left Holland in disgrace and disgust. For a year chaos reigned in the north. The little republic was saved by Parma's absorption in Philip's plan for the invasion of England; by Parma's diversions against Henry of Navarre in France; by Dutch control of the waters; by the wealth and the persistence of the Dutch merchants; by the political genius of Jan van Oldenbarneveldt; and by the military genius of Maurice of Nassau, William the Silent's son.

Soon after his father's death, Maurice was chosen stadholder of Holland and Zeeland. In 1588, aged twenty-one, he was made captain general and admiral of the United Provinces. In 1590 Utrecht, Overijssel, and Gelderland conferred their stadholderships upon him. Profiting from the Leiden lectures of Simon Stevin on mathematics, Maurice applied the latest science to ballistics, engineering, and siege. He trained the Dutch army to new cohesion and discipline. In a series of campaigns (1590–94) remarkable for swift movement and surprising strategy, he recaptured Zutphen, Deventer, Nijmegen, and Groningen. Parma, having wasted his skill and funds in Philip's vain sallies against England and Henry IV, died at Spa of exhaustion and wounds (February 20, 1592).

To succeed him Philip appointed Archduke Ernest of Austria, who soon died; then Cardinal Archduke Albert, who resigned his religious dignities and married the King's daughter Isabel Clara Eugenia. Shortly before his own death (1598), Philip bestowed upon Albert and Isabel sovereign rights in the Netherlands, with the proviso that if they died childless the sovereignty was to revert to Spain. They proved to be capable and kindly rulers, unable to subdue the northern provinces, but establishing in the south a civilized regime under which ecclesiastical arts flourished in genial harmony with Rubens' nudes.

A new figure appeared upon the scene in 1603. Albert had besieged Ostend for two years without success. An Italian banker, Ambrosio de Spinola, placed his fortune at the service of Spain, raised and equipped a force of eight thousand men, besieged and took Ostend. But even his immense riches could not offset the wealth of the Dutch merchants. They persisted in building and financing fleets that harassed Spanish shipping and threatened the line of gold between America and Spain. Tired of blockade and slaughter, Albert and Isabel urged negotiations with the Dutch, and Philip III, tired of bankruptcy, consented. Oldenbarneveldt, over the protests of Maurice, persuaded the Dutch to conciliation. A truce was signed (1609) that gave the Netherlands twelve years' rest from war.

Internal concord varies inversely with external peace. Maurice resented the dominance of Oldenbarneveldt in the affairs of the republic. Technically the grand pensionary—chief paid official—of Holland had authority in that province alone; but since Holland had as much wealth, and paid to the States-General as much in taxes, as all the rest of the United Provinces together, he wielded in the federation a power commensurate with that wealth, and with the force of his mind and character. Moreover, the landowners who ruled the provinces and the rich merchants who ruled the communes felt drawn to Oldenbarneveldt, who, like them, rejected democracy. "Better overlorded," he said, "than ruled by a mob."[50] Maurice, turning to the people for support, found that he could win them if he made the Calvinist ministers his friends.

The religious issue that now inflamed the republic was threefold: the growing opposition between Church and state, the conflict between Catholics and Protestants, and the war of doctrine within the Protestant fold. Calvinist synods sought to determine political policy and to use the government as an agent for the enforcement of their creed; the States-General distrusted the Calvinist congregations as dangerous examples and seedplots of democracy, and Oldenbarneveldt made many enemies by bidding the clergy leave government to the civil powers. Strange to say, even in the northern provinces the population in 1609 was still predominantly Catholic.[51] The laws forbade Catholic worship, but were not enforced; 232 priests conducted Catholic services.[52] The provincial council of Utrecht ordered the priests to marry their housekeepers, but compliance was sporadic and spiritless.

Within the Protestant communities the struggle lay between the Calvinists and a minority of "libertines." The latter were so called not as loose livers but as favoring religious liberty, even for Catholics, and a liberal and humane interpretation of the Protestant theology. These heirs of the Erasmian tradition (to whom William of Orange had belonged) were denounced as secret "papists" by the Precisians, or orthodox Calvinists, who adhered to strict predestinarianism and felt that their faith should be made compulsory throughout the United Provinces.[53] Dirck Coornhert, who had served as secretary to the Prince of Orange, argued for freedom of worship in writings that established the literary language of Holland. An Amsterdam preacher, Jacobus Arminius, was assigned to refute Coornhert's views; he was converted to them as he studied to answer them, and when he was appointed professor of theology at Leiden he shocked the Precisians by questioning predestination and asserting, against Luther and Calvin, that man is saved by good works as well as faith. He admitted that virtuous heathen might escape hell, and surmised that in the end all men would be saved. His fellow professor Franciscus Gomarus branded him an insidious heretic.

Arminius died in 1609. By that time he had won an influential following, including Oldenbarneveldt and Hugo Grotius, the pensionary of Rotterdam. In 1610 these "libertines" drew up a *Remonstrantie* against the doctrines of predestination, election, and reprobation, and proposed a national synod of clergymen and laymen to redefine the Reformed faith. The Precisians formulated a *Contra-Remonstrantie* reaffirming the Calvinist theology:

> God had, after Adam's fall, reserved a certain number of human beings from destruction, and . . . destined them to salvation through Christ. . . . In this election God does not consider belief or conversion, but acts simply according to his pleasure. God sent his son Christ for the salvation of the elect, and of them alone.[54]

The Gomarists insisted that such questions could be dealt with only by clergymen; and they so successfully labeled the Remonstrants as papists, Pelagians, or Unitarians that a large majority of the Protestant population rallied to the Precisian side. Maurice of Nassau moved from a scornful disregard of theological disputes to a tentative association with the orthodox party, as offering him a popular basis for an attempt to regain national leadership.

A battle of sermons and pamphlets ensued, of more than warlike bitterness. Violent disturbances broke the peace of the truce. "Libertine" houses
were raided in The Hague, orthodox Calvinist preachers were driven from
Rotterdam. Holland mustered an army to defend its theology; other provinces followed suit; civil war seemed about to destroy the republic so
lately born. On August 4, 1617, Oldenbarneveldt put through the council
of Holland a *"scherpe resolutie"*—which Maurice thought sharp indeed—
proclaiming the supremacy of the state in matters of religion, and directing
the cities of the province to arm themselves for protection against Calvinist violence. Passing to Utrecht, he persuaded its provincial council to raise
troops in support of Holland. On July 25, 1618, Maurice of Nassau, as
legal head of the army, entered Utrecht at the head of an armed force,
and compelled its new regiments to disband. On August 29 the States-General of the United Provinces ordered the arrest of Oldenbarneveldt, Grotius, and other Remonstrant leaders. On November 13 a synod of the
Reformed Church met at Dordrecht (Dort), gave the Remonstrant theologians a hearing, condemned them as heretics, and ordered all Remonstrant
ministers dismissed from ecclesiastical or educational posts. The Arminians,
like the Catholics, were placed under a ban and were forbidden to hold
public assemblies or services. Many of them fled to England, where they
were well received by the Established Church and strongly influenced the
Latitudinarian Anglicans.

Oldenbarneveldt was tried by a special court, which allowed him no
legal aid. He was charged with having treasonably divided and endangered
the Union, having sought to set up a state within the state. Outside the
court a flurry of pamphlets advertised to the multitude the faults of his
private life. He defended himself with such eloquence and force that his
children raised a Maypole before his prison and confidently celebrated
his coming release. On May 12, 1619, the court pronounced him guilty, and
the sentence of death was carried out the next day. Grotius was condemned
to life imprisonment, but through the ingenuity of his wife he escaped and
lived to write a memorable book.

Despite this triumph of intolerance, religious liberty grew in the provinces. The Catholics were too numerous to be suppressed, and the doctrinal
decrees of the Synod of Dort could not be enforced. In this same year
1619 the Mennonites freely founded at Rijnsburg their Quakerlike sect of
Collegianten, with whom Spinoza would find safe refuge. In 1629 Descartes
was to praise the intellectual freedom that he enjoyed in Amsterdam, and
by the end of the century Holland was to be the haven of heretics from
many lands.

On August 9, 1621, the war with Spain was resumed. The Archduke Albert having died childless, the southern Netherlands reverted to Spain.

Spinola attacked the Dutch border towns. Maurice marched against him, but years of strife had worn him out, and suddenly, aged fifty-seven, he was dead (1625). Spinola captured Breda, so opening the road to Amsterdam and giving a theme to Velázquez.

The Dutch recovered obstinately. Frederick Henry, who succeeded his brother as stadholder, surprised enemies and friends by his hitherto hidden talents as statesman and general. Through the diplomacy of Francis Aerssens, he secured an annual subsidy of a million livres from Richelieu; he raised a new army; after long sieges he took 's Hertogenbosch, Maastricht, Breda; fortunately, Spinola had been recalled to Lombardy.

Meanwhile the Dutch merchants turned money into ships, for every victory on the sea expanded trade. In 1628 a Dutch flotilla under Piet Hein captured a Spanish squadron carrying gold from Mexico. Another Dutch fleet attacked a Spanish force of thirteen vessels on the River Slaak, destroyed it, and took 5,000 prisoners (1631). The most brilliant of these naval victories was won by Lieutenant Admiral Maarten Harpertszoon Tromp in the Downs—the English Channel between Dover and Deal. The Spaniards, resolved to regain control of the Netherlands ports from the Dutch, had assembled a new armada of seventy-seven ships, manned by 24,000 men. Sighting it in the Channel, Tromp sent for reinforcements; on October 21, 1639, with seventy-five vessels, he sailed in to close quarters with the enemy and sank, disabled, or captured all but seven of the Spanish ships; 15,200 of the Spanish crews were killed in battle or were drowned. This Battle of the Downs ranks in Dutch history as the defeat of the Armada does in the history of England; it ended all claim of Spain to control the seas, cut the lifeline between Spain and her colonies, and shared with the French victory over the Spanish army at Rocroi (1643) in closing the era of Spanish ascendancy in Europe.

Deeply involved in the Thirty Years' War, Spain decided to yield everything to the Dutch in order to be free to fight the French. At Münster, January 30, 1648, the Spanish plenipotentiaries signed the Treaty of Westphalia, ending the "Eighty Years' War" in the Netherlands. The United Provinces were declared free of all bond to Spain; their conquests were recognized; Rhine commerce was to reach the North Sea through Dutch ports alone; and freedom of trade was conceded to Dutch merchantmen in the Indies East and West. So triumphantly ended the longest, bravest, and most cruel struggle for freedom in all history.

CHAPTER XVIII

From Rubens to Rembrandt

1555–1660

I. THE FLEMINGS

IT IS surprising that in so small a segment of Europe as the Netherlands two such diverse cultures developed as the Flemish and the Dutch, two faiths so uncongenial as Catholicism and Calvinism, two artists so opposed in mood and method as Rubens and Rembrandt, as Vandyck and Hals.

We cannot explain the contrast through language, for half of Flanders,* like all the United Provinces, spoke Dutch. Some of the difference may have derived from the proximity of Holland to Protestant Germany, of Flanders to Catholic France. Part of it came from the closer association of Catholic, royalist, aristocratic Spain with Brussels and Antwerp. Flanders inherited medieval religion, art, and ways, while Holland was yet too poor to have a culture of its own. Possibly the greater sunshine in the southern provinces inclined their population to a sensual, morally easy life and an indulgent Catholicism, while the mists and hardships of the north may have encouraged a stern and stoic faith. Or was it, rather, that the Spanish armies won in the south and, harassed by intervening rivers and Dutch money, lost in the north?

Antwerp must have been beautiful when its cathedral was complete in all its spires, façade, and decorative art, while nearby the Bourse throbbed with all the vitality and chicanery of commerce, and the waters danced with the shipping of the world. But then war came: Alva's fury and the Inquisition drove Protestant artisans and merchants into Holland, Germany, and England, the Calvinist Fury gutted the churches, the Spanish Fury rifled the homes and burned the palaces, the French Fury drowned its failure in blood, and the fourteen months' siege by Farnese starved Catholics and Protestants impartially. At last the Catholics joined the Protestants in exodus, and Antwerp's trade passed to Amsterdam, Rotterdam, Haarlem, Hamburg, London, and Rouen.

But man's ferocity is intermittent, his resilience endures. It is a consolation to note how quickly some nations and cities have recovered from

---

* Let us, for convenience, use *Flanders* and *Flemish* as applying to all the Spanish Netherlands, and *Holland* and *Dutch* for all the northern, or United, Provinces.

FIG. 50–JAN MATEJKO: *King Stephen Bathory of Poland*. From Stanislaw Witkie-
wicz, *Matejko*, Lwow, 1912   PAGE 507

Fig. 51–*Shah Abbas the Great*. From Sir John Malcolm, *History of Persia*, vol. i:
John Murray and Longman & Co., London, 1815　　　　　　　　PAGE 527

FIG. 52—*Mosque of Sultan Ahmed*, Istanbul. From Ulga Vogt-Göknil, *Türkische Moscheen:* Origo Verlag, Zürich, 1953   PAGE 521

FIG. 53—*Masjid-i-Shah, Portal to Sanctuary*, Isfahan. From Arthur Upham Pope and Phyllis Ackerman, *Survey of Persian Art*, vol. iv: Oxford University Press, 1958   PAGE 529

FIG. 54—*Poet Seated in Garden*. Museum of Fine Arts, Boston   PAGE 534

Fig. 55—*Safavid Tile Wall Panels*, probably from Palace Chihil Sutun in Isfahan. (ABOVE, BELOW, BELOW LEFT). Rogers Fund, 1903; The Metropolitan Museum of Art, New York

PAGE 535

FIG. 56—*Persian Rug*, from the Ardebil Mosque, Persia. Hewitt Fund, 1910; The
Metropolitan Museum of Art, New York   PAGE 536

FIG. 57—ANTHONY VANDYCK: *Wallenstein*. Alte Pinakothek, Munich

PAGE 558

FIG. 58—SUSTERMANS: *Galileo*. Pitti Gallery, Florence (Bettmann Archive)

PAGE 600

Fig. 59—Frans Hals: *Descartes*. Louvre, Paris

PAGE 636

the destructiveness of war. So it was with Flanders after 1579. The textile industry survived, Flemish lace was still in demand, the rains still nourished the land, and the toil of the people supplied the splendor of the court. Under the archdukes, luxury-loving but humane, Antwerp and Brussels enjoyed a remarkable resurrection. Flanders returned to its cathedrals, its religious festivals, its pagan kermis. Perhaps Rubens exaggerated this in the wild *Kermis* of the Louvre, but hear the report of the Cardinal Infante Ferdinand from Antwerp to Philip IV in 1639: "Yesterday they held their great festival . . . a long procession moved out to the countryside with many triumphal cars. After the parade they all went to eat and drink, and in the end they were all drunk; for without that they do not think it a festival."[1] The Cardinal himself, when he came from Spain to Brussels (1635), had been received with several days of pageantry, amid gorgeous decorations designed by Rubens himself. The Flemish towns, before the revolt, had been described by an Italian visitor as having "a constant succession of gay assemblies, nuptials, and dances, while music, singing, and cheerful sounds prevailed in every street";[2] and not all of that spirit had yielded to the war. The games that Brueghel had pictured were still played in the streets, and the churches heard again such polyphonic Masses as had once made Flemish singers the desired of every court. Flanders entered its most brilliant age.

II. FLEMISH ART

The court and the Church, the nobles and the burghers, co-operated to finance the revival of Flemish art. Albert and Isabel supported many artists besides Rubens; for a time Antwerp was the art center of Europe. Brussels tapestries regained their excellence, aided by Rubens' heroic designs. Venetian glassmakers had brought their art to the Netherlands in 1541; now native artisans reproduced the fragile miracles, some so cherished that they have survived centuries of turbulence. Workers in metal fashioned marvels of their own, like the magnificent reliquaries that may still be found in the Catholic churches of Belgium. The merchant aristocracy ordered objects of art, sat for pictures, and built princely palaces and town halls—such as that which Cornelis de Vriendt raised to the glory of Antwerp (1561–65) before the storm. When fanaticism had denuded the churches of their art, they became eager patrons of the studios, demanding statues and pictures to visualize the creed for the people.

Sculpture struck no spark here, for François Duquesnoy of Brussels did most of his work in Rome, where he carved a mighty *St. Andrew* for the interior of St. Peter's. Very few tourists who make it a point to see "the oldest citizen of Brussels," the fountain of the *Manneken-Pis* (1619)—the bronze boy who adds to the city's water out of his own resources—know that this is the most enduring of Duquesnoy's creations.

But of Flemish painters there is no count. Apparently every house in the Netherlands had to have some original picture; a thousand artists were kept busy in a hundred studios painting portraits, landscapes, animals, victuals, mythologies, Holy Families, Crucifixions, and, as their distinctive contributions to the history of art, group pictures of municipal bodies and genre pictures of domestic or village life. At first these painters submitted to the prestige of Italian modes. Italian ships sailed every day into Antwerp, Italian traders set up shops there, Italian artists came to scoff and remained to paint. Many Flemish painters went to study in Italy; some settled there; so Justus Sustermans of Antwerp became a favorite portrait painter for the grand dukes of Tuscany; some of the finest portraits in the Pitti Palace are by this lusty Fleming. Frans Floris, returning from his studies with Michelangelo in Rome, called himself frankly a "Romanist," relished anatomy, and subordinated color to line. For a generation (1547-70) his studio at Antwerp was the center and summit of Flemish painting. It is almost worth going to Caen to see in its museum his jolly mountainous *Wife of the Falcon Hunter*. Frans lived in wealth, built himself a palace, gave and drank freely, and died in poverty. Cornelis de Vos was the ablest in a large family of painters; when too many notables begged to sit for Rubens he sent some of them to Vos, assuring them that they would fare just as well. We can still see Cornelis, his wife, and two pretty daughters, hanging comfortably in the Brussels Museum.

Toward the end of the sixteenth century the Italian infatuation faded, and Flemish artists resumed native themes and ways. David Teniers the Elder, though he studied in Rome, returned to Antwerp to paint a *Dutch Kitchen* and a *Village Kermis*,[3] and then taught his son to surpass him. The descendants of Old Droll Peasant Pieter Brueghel formed a dynasty of painters devoted to local landscapes and village scenes: his sons Pieter "Hell" Brueghel and Jan "Velvet" Brueghel, his grandsons Jan II and Ambrose, his great-grandson Abraham, his great-great-grandson Jan Baptist Brueghel—they run over two centuries (1525-1719), but let us clear the slate of them here. They took from their powerful ancestor a flair for rural prospects and village festivities, and some of them painted landscape backgrounds for busy Rubens.

The artists of the Netherlands brought art out of the church and the monastery into the home, the fields, and the woods. Daniel Seghers painted flowers and fruit in loving detail, devoted his pictured wreaths to the Virgin, and joined the Jesuits. Frans Snyders gave life and fragrance to a score of museums with exciting, sometimes gory, hunting scenes, and many a dish of venison and fruit; he still remains, as Rubens ranked him, the greatest painter of animals; no one has rivaled him in catching the play of light upon the fur of beasts or the plumage of birds.

Adriaen Brouwer returned to Brueghel's peasants and pinned them on his brush as they dined, drank, sang, danced, played cards, cast dice, fought, caroused, and slept. Adriaen himself, in his thirty-two years, sampled many lives: studying for a while with Hals in Haarlem; then, aged twenty-one, already a registered master in the painters' guild at Antwerp; spending beyond his income, and soon entangled in debt; imprisoned by the Spaniards for causes now unknown, but living sumptuously in jail; achieving freedom and paying his debts with little pictures so full of life, so technically excellent in sensitive drawing and subtle play of light, that Rubens bought seventeen of them and Rembrandt eight. His peasants seem never happy except when stupefied with strong tobacco or cheap drink, but Brouwer preferred a peasant singing in his cups to a silken hypocrite flattering a prince. In 1638, aged thirty-two, he was found dead outside a tavern door.

Jacob Jordaens was a soberer man, who inscribed upon one of his pictures a warning to his thirst: *Nihil similius insano quam ebrius*—"Nothing is liker to a lunatic than a drunkard." He chose to picture people who could drink without drooling and women who could rustle silk majestically. Born in 1593, he lived to the sensible old age of eighty-five. He pictured himself for us in *The Artist and His Family*:[4] a man erect, self-confident, handsome, prosperous, holding a lute; a wife at ease in her choking ruff; a pretty daughter just beginning to bloom Flemishly; and a little girl happy in a comforting home and creed—see her pendant cross. Jordaens was converted to Protestantism, but only at sixty-two. He painted several religious pictures, but he preferred genre and mythologies, where he could bring out the powerful heads and effulgent breasts of the men and women he had seen in Antwerp homes, as in *The King Drinks*[5] or, better, in *The Allegory of Fertility*;[6] here, amid fruit (painted by Jacob's friend Snyders) and satyrs, we are startled by a magnificent nude, seen only in rear elevation but in all the grace of youth; where in Rubens' Flanders did Jordaens find so slender a model?

III. RUBENS: 1577–1640

The greatest of the Flemings was born in 1577 of a long line of successful businessmen; he continued the line. His father, Jan Rubens, studied law at Padua, married Maria Pypelinckx, and was elected an alderman at Antwerp at thirty-one. Accused of Protestantism and excluded by name from the amnesty of 1574, he fled with his wife and four children to Cologne. Chosen as legal adviser by Anne of Saxony (the separated wife of William of Orange), he committed adultery with her and was imprisoned by the Prince at Dillenburg. Maria forgave her husband, wrote him tender and touching letters,* pleaded and labored for his liberation, and obtained it after two trying years, on condition that Jan live under surveillance at Siegen in Westphalia. She joined him in 1573, and it was probably there that Peter Paul was born. He was baptized by Lutheran rites, but while he was still a child the family was converted to Catholicism. In 1578 Jan moved with his family to Cologne, where he practiced law and prospered. When he died (1587) Maria and the children went to live in Antwerp.

Rubens received formal education only till fifteen, but he added to it much reading and experience. For two years (1590–91) he served as page to the Countess of Lalaing at Audenaarde; there, presumably, he learned French and the fine manners that distinguished him from most artists of his time. His mother, perceiving his flair for drawing, apprenticed him to Tobias Verhaecht, then to Adam van Noort, then to Otho Vaenius, a man of wide culture and courtly speech. After eight years with this admirable teacher, Rubens, now twenty-three, went to Italy to study the masterpieces whose fame agitated all pictorial souls. At Venice he showed his own work to a gentleman in the retinue of Vincenzo Gonzaga, Duke of Mantua; soon Rubens was living in the ducal palace of Mantua as court painter. Two pictures that he made there already touched mastery: *Justus Lipsius and His Pupils*,[8] in which the pupils of the famous scholar include Peter and his brother Philip; and a *Self-Portrait*,[9] showing Rubens half bald at twenty-five, but bearded, bold, and alert. He made trips to Rome to copy pictures for the Duke, and to Florence, where he saw (and later idealistically painted) the marriage of Maria de' Medici to the absent Henry IV. In 1603 the Duke sent him with a diplomatic mission to Spain, bearing gifts to the Duke of Lerma; the minister accepted as originals the copies that Rubens had made, and the artist returned to Mantua as a successful diplomat. On a second trip to Rome he settled there permanently with his brother, who was librarian to a cardinal. Pieter now painted a multitude of saints; one of these pictures, *St. Gregory Worshiping the Madonna*,[10] he rated as his first great picture. In 1608, hearing that his

---

* E.g.: "Dear and beloved husband . . . A letter from you . . . gave me joy, because I see from it that you are satisfied with my forgiveness. . . . I never thought that you would have believed that there would be any difficulty about that from me, for in truth I made none. How could I have the heart to be angry with you in such peril, when I would give my life to save you? . . . How could so much hatred have succeeded so quickly to our long affection, as to make it impossible for me to pardon a slight trespass against myself, when I have to pray to God to forgive the many grave trespasses I commit against Him every day?"[7]

mother was ill, he rushed north to Antwerp and was deeply moved to find her dead. Her wise and patient love had helped to give him the cheerful disposition that blessed his life. Meanwhile he had learned much in Italy. The luscious color of the Venetians, the sensualism of Giulio Romano's frescoes at Mantua, the pliant grace of Correggio's female figures at Parma, the pagan art of pagan and Christian Rome, the reconciliation of Christianity with the enjoyment of wine, women, and song—all these passed into his blood and art. When Archduke Albert made him court painter at Antwerp (1609), Gothic remnants disappeared from Flemish painting, and the fusion of Flemish with Italian art was complete.

It was part of his unconscious wisdom that he had been away from the Netherlands during eight years of war, and that he received his appointment in the first year of the truce. It was precisely in the next twelve years that Antwerp and Brussels restored their cultural life. Rubens was no small part of that revival; his biographer lists 1,204 paintings and 380 drawings,[11] and probably many others escaped history. This fertility is unparalleled in the history of art; and almost as remarkable were the diversity of subjects and the rapidity of execution. "My talent is of such a kind," Rubens wrote, "that no commission, however great in size or varied in subject matter, ever daunted me."[12] He finished in twenty-five days the three panels of *The Descent from the Cross* for the Antwerp cathedral, and in thirteen days the immense *Adoration of the Kings* now in the Louvre. In addition to his court salary of five hundred florins a year, he received payment for each individual product, and he charged at a lordly rate; e.g., 3,800 florins ($47,500?) for the two masterpieces just named—i.e., one hundred florins ($1,250?) per day.[13] Part of this, of course, went to his numerous assistants, several of whom were themselves registered as masters in the artists' guild. Jan "Velvet" Brueghel painted flowers in Rubens' pictures, Jan Wildens painted landscapes and accessories, Paul de Vos painted minerals and fruit, Frans Snyders evoked the fine-pointed head of a dog in *Diana Returning from the Chase*,[14] and we do not know how much is Snyders and how much is Rubens in the powerful hunting scenes in the Dresden and Munich galleries and the Metropolitan Museum in New York. In some cases Rubens drew the figures and left the painting to his aides. To his clients he gave a conscientious account of the degree in which the pictures he sold them were by his own hand.[15] Only in this way could he meet the demands made upon him. His studio became a factory, reflecting the business methods of the Netherlands economy. His fertility and celerity sometimes lowered the quality of his product, but he neared perfection often enough to become the god of Flemish art.

Now he felt secure enough to marry (1609). Isabella Brant was the daughter of an Antwerp lawyer and alderman, and therefore a fit mate for the son of an Antwerp lawyer and alderman. Rubens went to live in her father's house till his own palatial home on the Wappens Canal was finished. In one of his finest paintings[16] Peter and Isabella are pictured in the happiness of early marriage: she hidden in overflowing robes and laced in flowered bodice, her hand laid trustfully and possessively upon his, her proud face rising out of an enormous blue ruff, her head crowned with a cavalier hat; he in ripe manhood and success, with sturdy legs, blond beard, handsome features, and ribboned hat. Isabella was allowed only seventeen more years of life; but she gave him children whom he raised and portrayed lovingly; see the curlyheaded boy in the Berlin Kaiser-Friedrich Museum, plump and happy, playing with a dove, and see him again, sobered by full seven years, in *The Sons of the Artist.*[17] Only a good man could have painted these portraits.

At the same time he was basically a pagan, unabashedly in love with the human body, male as well as female, in all the intoxication of athletic strength or easeful curves. It is a symbol of his Flanders that it enjoyed his profane mythologies—riots of unimpeded flesh—while the churches welcomed his interpretations of religious themes. He could not quite make up his mind between Mary and Venus; probably he felt no contradiction between them, for both of them brought money. In *The Worship of Venus*[18] the pagan element is unrestrained—a parkful of bacchantes modestly hiding an elbow or a knee and embraced by goaty satyrs, while a dozen infants dance around a statue of the goddess of love. Though these pagan subjects echo his stay in Italy, his Venuses lack all classic line; they cannot live in the north on sun and air and wine, as in the south; they must eat and drink to cushion themselves from rain and mists and cold; Teutonic flesh, like British whiskey—English or Scotch—is a climatic defense. One of Rubens' pictures—three bulging nudes—is entitled *Without Wine and Bread Venus Is Cold;*[19] he was too courtly to say "without meat and beer." So he saw nothing out of scale in a *Shepherd Making Love,*[20] which shows a shepherd trying to seduce three hundred pounds; there's nothing good or bad, beautiful or ugly, but environment makes it so. In *The Rape of the Sabines*[21] it is all that two mighty Romans can do to lift one of their ravishing ravished captives upon a horse. Even in *The Consequences of War*[22] there is no emaciation. *Diana Returning from the Chase*[23] is no Greek goddess trim and chaste, but a Flemish housewife, broad-shouldered, muscular, matronly; in all that massive picture only the dog is slim. The Rubensian woods are full of satyrs squeezing avoirdupois, as in *Ixion and Hera*[24] and *The Four Corners of the World;*[25] and, as we might have expected, *The Origin of the Milky Way*[26] is no nebular hypothesis, but a fat *Hausfrau* squirting streams of milk from a congested breast. The *Three Graces,*[27] however, are relatively svelte, and in *The*

Judgment of Paris[28] two of the ladies conform to later fashions; one is among the fairest female figures in art. Usually, in these pagan pictures, there is far more than flesh; Rubens poured into them the rich abandon of his fancy, a hundred accessories filling out the scene, delineated with careless care, and leaping to the eye with color, warmth, and life. Nor is there any prurience in the billowy display; it is merely animal vitality, *mens plena in corpore pleno;* not one of these pictures offers erotic stimulus. Rubens himself was anomalously well-behaved for an artist necessarily high-strung and sensitive to color and form; he was known as a good husband, a "solid family man," untouched with any scandal of gallantry or intrigue.[29]

The ecclesiastics of Flanders, Italy, and Spain recognized the innocence of his sensuality, and had no qualms in asking him to illustrate again the story of Mary, Christ, and the saints. He accommodated them, but in his own unhackneyed way. Which of his countless predecessors visualized with fuller imagination, or painted with subtler skill, the ancient theme of *The Adoration of the Kings?**[30] Who would have dared to center the composition upon the fat belly of a bronzed and turbaned Ethiopian looking in colorful disdain upon the pale faces around him? Who would have dreamed that this pagan peering with eye and brush into every nook and cranny of the female form would love the Jesuits, would join their Marian Congregation, and would perform the exercises prescribed by Ignatius Loyola to cleanse the soul with visions of hell?[31] In March 1620 he contracted with the Jesuits to design, before the end of the year, thirty-nine pictures to cover the ceilings of the splendid baroque church that they had begun to build in Antwerp in 1614. He made the drawings, Vandyck and others turned these into paintings, nearly all of which were destroyed in 1718. For the high altar Rubens himself painted two major works, *Ignatius Healing the Possessed* and *The Miracles of St. Francis,* both now in the Vienna Kunsthistorisches Museum.

Nevertheless, Rubens was a Catholic only in the Renaissance sense, and a Christian only by location. His paganism survived within his piety. He was not quite comfortable with Virgins and saints; his Madonnas are robust women clearly fitter to manage a man than to beget a god. In *The Madonna in a Garland of Flowers*[32] Mary holds up not a divinity but a handsome boy displaying his equipment to the world; and *The Return from Egypt*[33] shows Christ as a curlyheaded lad, and Mary dressed like a Flemish matron wearing her new hat on a Sunday walk in the park. Even in *The Elevation of the Cross* (in the Antwerp cathedral) Rubens' interest in anatomy dominates the religious motif: Christ is a virile athlete, not a dying god. In *The Blow of the Lance*[34] everything again is anatomy:

---

* This picture brought $770,000 at an auction in London in 1959.

Christ and the thieves are massive figures, every straining muscle shown; the women at the foot of the Cross are posing for the artist rather than fainting with grief; Rubens has not felt the scene.

At least five times Rubens challenged Titian with an *Assumption of the Virgin;* in the most famous of these efforts[35] the Madonna seems lifeless, and the living creatures are the Magdalen and the startled Apostles at the empty tomb. Finer is the great triptych[36] commissioned by the Archduchess Isabel for the Confraternity of St. Ildefonso in Brussels. In the central panel the Virgin, descended from heaven, presents to the Archbishop of Toledo a chasuble direct from Paradise; the saint is all humility, "breathless with adoration"; while in the side panels Isabel and Albert lay aside their crowns and kneel in prayer; here for a time Rubens gave life to piety. And in *St. Ambrose and the Emperor Theodosius*[37] he caught and conveyed the mysterious power and authority of the Church: the Archbishop of Milan, armed only with priests and an acolyte, but with a head of majesty, drives from the cathedral the Emperor backed with awesome guards but burdened with unshriven cruelty. Rubens rarely failed with old men, for in them, especially, the face is an autobiography, and offers visible character to perceiving art. See the patriarch's head in *Lot and His Family Leaving Sodom*[38]—one of the finest Rubens pictures in America.

He returned with gusto to secular subjects, mixed with mythology, when Marie de Médicis offered him the most tempting contract of his career. On February 16, 1622, he signed an agreement to paint, within four years, twenty-one large pictures and three portraits commemorating events in the life of Marie and her husband, Henry IV. The Queen invited him to come and live at the French court; he had the good sense to stay home. In May 1623 he took the first nine panels to Paris. Marie liked them, Richelieu admired them. The series was completed in 1624; Rubens took the remainder to Paris and saw them set up in the Luxembourg Palace. In 1802 the pictures were transferred to the Louvre, where nineteen of them now enjoy a room all their own. Those who have seen and studied them will not grudge the twenty thousand crowns ($250,000?) paid to Rubens for his work, and doubtless shared by him with his aides. All in all, these paintings are his supreme achievement. If we allow for some marks of haste, and accept the incredible story as we do in Ovid, Shakespeare, and Verdi, we shall find all of Rubens here except his occasional piety. He loved the splendor of court ritual, the majesty of royal power; he never tired of plump women, rich raiment, and gorgeous drapery; he had lived half his days with the gods and goddesses of classical mythology; now he brought all these together in a flowing narrative, with an inventiveness of episode, an opulence of color, a mastery of composition and design, that made the series an epic and opera in the history of painting.

Only two more honors were wanting to Rubens' apotheosis—to be made a diplomat and to receive a patent of nobility. In 1623 the Archduchess Isabel used him as negotiator in hopes to renew the truce with Holland; Rubens had his own reason for promoting peace, since his wife aspired to inherit a fortune from her Dutch uncle.[39] These efforts failed; nevertheless Isabel persuaded Philip IV to ennoble him (1624), and made him "Gentleman of the Household of Her Most Serene Highness"—i.e., herself. Later the King protested against her employing "so mean [unpedigreed] a person" to receive foreign envoys and discuss "affairs of such great importance";[40] yet Isabel sent Rubens to Madrid a year later (1628) to help arrange a peace between Philip IV and Charles I. He took some of his paintings with him; the King revised his notion of pedigree and sat to Rubens for five portraits, as if Velázquez were not making enough. The two artists became good friends, the Spaniard, then twenty-nine, modestly deferring to the genial Fleming, then fifty-one. Finally Philip appointed the "mean" Rubens as his envoy to England. In London the artist successfully concluded a treaty of peace, despite the emissaries and the bribes of Richelieu to the contrary. Rubens painted some English portraits—the Duke and Duchess of Buckingham,[41] and the magnificent face, beard, and armor of Thomas Howard, Earl of Arundel.[42] Having paved the way for Vandyck, he returned to Antwerp (March 1630) with a degree from Cambridge and a knighthood from Charles.

Meanwhile his first wife had died (1626), and, as Flemish custom required, the funeral was celebrated with a lavish banquet that cost the artist-diplomat 204 florins ($2,800?) "on food and drink and hired plate";[43] death in Flemish society was an almost prohibitive luxury. Rubens drowned his loneliness in diplomacy. In 1630, aged fifty-three, he married Helena Fourment, aged sixteen. He needed beauty about him, and she had already the warm coziness that filled his art and his dreams. He painted her again and again, in every garb and none: in her wedding costume,[44] holding a glove,[45] happy under a saucy hat,[46] hiding only her hips in a fur coat,[47] and, best of all, walking with Rubens in their garden[48]—this last is one of the peaks of Flemish painting. Then he showed her with their first-born,[49] and later with their two children[50]—a presage of Renoir; not to speak of the pictures in which she posed voluptuously as Venus or demurely as the Mother of God.

He painted his beloved rulers, Albert and Isabel, without flattery; we see them in the Vienna and Pitti galleries probably as they were—governing a troubled land with all the good will compatible with Spanish ideals. He found fine types of manhood and womanhood in Flanders; he pictured them in his painting of Jean Charles de Cordes and his pretty pouting wife,[51] and in the portrait of Michael Ophovius,[52] Bishop of 's Hertogenbosch; and he left us a powerful image of the invincible Spinola.[53] But portraiture was not Rubens' forte; he gives us no subtle insights like Titian, no revelations from the depths as in Rembrandt. The greatest of his portraits is that which he painted of himself in 1624 for the future Charles I:[54] immense gold-tasseled hat, revealing only the great forehead of the bald head; penetrating eyes in quizzical glance; the long sharp nose that seems to go with genius; the bristling mustache and fine red beard; this is a man well aware that he is at the top of his craft. Yet something of the physical vitality, sensuous enjoyment, and calm content that had shone in the picture of himself with Isabella Brant has gone with the years. Only failure wears out a man faster than success.

He was rich, and he lived in grand style; his costly home in Antwerp was one of the sights of the city. In 1635 he bought for 93,000 florins an extensive estate and feudal castle in the lordship of Steen, eighteen miles out, and took the title Lord of Steen. He spent his summers there, painted landscapes, and tried his polyphonic hand at genre. Amid his luxuries, with three maidservants, two grooms, and three horses, he continued to work hard, finding his happiness in his family and his work. His wives, children, patrons, aides loved him for his serenity of spirit, his generosity, his warm-hearted sympathy.[55]

Others more competent must analyze the technical qualities of his art, but we may safely describe him as the chief exemplar of pictorial baroque —sensuous color, incalculable movement, rich imagination, luscious orna-ment, as against classic placidity and restraint of thought and line. But amid this confusion of beauty, the critics tell us, there is superb draftsman-ship. Rubens' drawings fed a brilliant school of engravers, who made the master's paintings known to Christian Europe as Raimondi had done with Raphael's designs. From Rubens' hand or studio came famous cartoons for the tapestry weavers of Paris and Brussels; they made royal gifts or decoration for Louis XIII, Charles I, and the Archduchess Isabel.

His final decade was one of universal triumph darkened by physical de-cline. Only Bernini equaled him in artistic fame; in painting no one dreamed of questioning his supremacy. Pupils ran to him from all quarters; com-missions came from half a dozen courts, even from Stadholder Frederick Henry across the lines of war. In 1636 Philip IV asked him to paint scenes from Ovid's *Metamorphoses* for the Pardo hunting lodge; Rubens' studio produced fifty pictures for the series, of which thirty-one are in the Prado; one of them, *The Judgment of Paris*, seemed to the Cardinal Infante Ferdi-nand "the best picture Rubens ever painted."[56] We may prefer the riotous *Kermis*[57] that he painted in 1636—a Brueghel of mad pursuit, in which no woman is so old or ample but some man snatches her.

The self-portrait at sixty[58] is the other side of these concluding years: a man still proud, hand on his sword of nobility, but face thinning, skin hanging, crow's-feet under the eyes—a brave and honest picture. In 1635 gout put him to bed for a month; in 1637 it disabled his hand for a time; in 1639 it prevented him from signing his name; by 1640 both hands were paralyzed. On May 30, 1640, aged sixty-three, he died from arthritis and arteriosclerosis.

It was an astonishing career. He was not the *uomo universale* of the Renaissance ideal; yet he realized his ambition to play a role in the state as well as the studio. He was not a universal artist, like Leonardo and Michelangelo; he left no sculpture, designed no building except his home. But in painting he reached high excellence in every field. Religious pictures, pagan revels, gods and goddesses, nudity and raiment, kings and queens, children and old men, landscapes and battle scenes all poured from his brush as from a kaleidoscopic cornucopia of color and form. Rubens ended the subjection of Flemish to Italian painting, not by rebellion, but by absorption and union.

He was not as deep as Rembrandt, but wider; he shied away from the dark depths that Rembrandt revealed; he preferred the sun, the open air, the dance of light, the color and zest of life; he repaid his own good fortune by smiling upon the world. His art is the voice of health, as ours today sometimes suggests sickness in the individual or national soul. When our own vitality lags, let us open our Rubens book anywhere and be refreshed.

IV. VANDYCK: 1599–1641

It was just like Rubens to hail and encourage the precocious talent of the young Adonis who joined his studio about 1617. Anthony Vandyck (or Vandyke) had been apprenticed, at the age of eight, to Hendrik van Balen, the teacher of Snyders; at sixteen he had pupils of his own; at nineteen he was a registered master, not so much a pupil of Rubens as a highly valued aide. Rubens rated an early painting by Vandyck as equal in worth to his own *Daniel* of the same year; he kept for his own collection Vandyck's *Christ Crowned with Thorns* and only later, reluctantly, surrendered it to Philip IV for the Escorial.[59] In religious pictures Vandyck came too amiably under Rubens' influence and, lacking the older artist's vitality of movement and color, fell short of him in all but portraiture. In the early *Self-Portrait* of 1615 (?)[60] he revealed the qualities that were to mark and limit his genius—grace, finesse, and a soft beauty almost unbecoming in a man. His fellow artists were happy to sit for him as an added hedge against oblivion; he made admirable portraits of Snyders,[61] Duquesnoy,[62] Jan Wildens,[63] Jan de Wael,[64] Gaspar de Crayer,[65] and Marten Pepijn;[66] it was one of the many lovable qualities of Vandyck that he liked his rivals. These portraits suggest in Rubens' studio a pleasant spirit of comradeship not always present in the realm of art.

In 1620 the Earl of Arundel received from Antwerp a letter: "Vandyck lives with Rubens, and his works are being esteemed almost as highly as those of his master."[67] He invited the young artist to England. Vandyck went, received a piddling pension of £100 from James I, painted a few portraits, rebelled at the menial copying required of him by the King, asked for an eight months' leave of absence, received it, and stretched it to twelve years. At Antwerp he made provision for his mistress and her baby; then he hurried down into Italy (1621).

There for the first time he struck his stride, and he left fine portraits at almost every stop. He pored over the great Venetians, not so much to study their color and massive scope, as Rubens had done, but to ferret out the secrets of poetic portraiture in Giorgione, Titian, and Veronese. He went on to Bologna, Florence, Rome, even to Sicily. At Rome he stayed with Cardinal Guido Bentivoglio and repaid him with a portrait.[68] His courtly manners were resented by the Flemish artists who were starving in Italy; they dubbed him *"il pittore cavalleresco"* and made things so unpleasant that he gladly accompanied Lady Arundel to Turin. He was especially welcomed in Genoa, which remembered Rubens and had heard of Vandyck's flair for ennobling nobility, making every sitter seem a prince. The Metropolitan Museum of Art in New York has a sample of these Genoese aristocrats in *The Marchesa Durazzo*—sensitive face and (as always in Vandyck) fine hands; the National Gallery in Washington has *The Marchesa Balbi*, and *The Marchesa Grimaldi*—proud and pregnant; Berlin and London have other examples; and Genoa managed to keep, in her Palazzo Rosso, *The Marchese and Marchesa di Brignole-Sale*. When Vandyck returned to Antwerp (1628) his pockets were full and his lace was exquisite.

His native city called him back from nobles to saints. To fit himself for these he repented of his promiscuity, willed his young fortune to two nun sisters, joined the Jesuit Confraternity of the Unmarried, and turned his hand to religious themes. He could not rival Rubens in this field, but he avoided the exuberant master's exaggerations and carnal effulgence, and gave to his pictures a touch of the elegance he had learned in Italy. Reynolds thought Vandyck's *Crucifixion*, in the Mechlin cathedral, one of the world's greatest paintings; however, that may have been Sir Joshua's way of repaying a debt.

Vandyck tried his hand at mythological pictures, but though he had pursued many women he was not at home with nudes. His forte was always portraiture, and during these four years in Antwerp he gave some respite from oblivion to Baron Philippe Le Roy and a devoted dog;[69] to

General Francisco de Moncada and his horse;[70] to Count Rhodokanakis,[71] looking like Swinburne; to Jean de Montfort,[72] looking like Falstaff; and—most beautiful of these Vienna Vandycks, young Rupert, Prince Charming Palatine, soon to be fighting for Charles I in England. Alluring, too, is the portrait of Maria Luisa of Tassis,[73] lost in her swelling robes of black satin and white silk. And as good as any of these is Vandyck's etching of Pieter "Hell" Brueghel (the Younger), an old man still seething with the unspent sap of an amazing dynasty.

Some of these portraits he took with him when Charles I invited him to try England again. Charles, unlike his father, had a sure taste in art. He surmised that this handsome Fleming was just the man to do for him what Velázquez was doing for Philip IV. Vandyck came and transmitted the King, Queen Henrietta Maria, and their children to posterity, indelibly marked with the Vandyck elegance. Most famous of the five royal portraits is the one in the Louvre—the proud incompetent King posing in riding costume, one arm akimbo, sword prominent, jaunty hat, and Vandyke beard; but the tired horse, champing the bit between hunts, can be more easily loved. In Dresden and Turin are rival paintings of Charles's children, as yet harmless and innocent. Charles was more human than he pretended; his capacity for warm affection showed in his fondness for Vandyck; he knighted him, gave him expensive homes in London and the country, a yearly pension of £200, additional payment for each picture, and every welcome at the court.

The happy artist lived up to his income, loved fine clothing, had his coach-and-four, his thoroughbreds and his mistresses, and filled his homes with music and art. He bettered Rubens' instruction in delegating work—left the painting of costumes to assistants, painted a portrait in an hour from a sketch made at one sitting, and made hay while the sun played hide-and-seek. Once (story says) Charles I, suffering from parliamentary parsimony, asked the extravagant artist if he knew what it meant to be short of funds. "Yes, Sire," answered Vandyck. "When one keeps an open table for his friends and an open purse for his mistresses, he soon reaches the bottom of his money chest."[74]

If at times he sank into debt, it was not for lack of patronage. Half the English aristocracy waited in turn to receive his imprimatur: James Stuart, Duke of Lennox,[75] as handsome as his dog; Robert Rich, Earl of Warwick;[76] Lord Derby and his family;[77] Thomas Wentworth, Earl of Strafford,[78] challenging fate. Poets too had their hour—Carew, Killigrew, Suckling. And finally there was Old Parr,[79] claiming to be 150 years old and looking it. Vandyck painted three hundred portraits in England, almost all distinguished by the grace and dignity that he saw in a lord even when they were not there.

His mistress, Margaret Lemon, competed expensively with the aristocracy for his services. The King suggested that marriage would be cheaper,
and he helped Vandyck to secure (1639) the hand of Lady Mary Ruthven,
of a family famous in Scottish history. The artist painted a handsome picture of his bride,[80] but it could not compare with the lovely face he gave
himself in the *Self-Portrait*[81] that all the world knows—rich wavy hair,
sharp eyes, refined features, scissored beard, gold chain proclaiming his
knighthood. Did Vandyck flatter Sir Anthony? If so, it was of no use, for
his health, consumed too lavishly, had already begun to fail. Loath to be
remembered only for portraits, he asked Charles to let him paint historic
scenes on the walls of the banqueting hall at Whitehall, but Charles was
living from an empty purse. Vandyck crossed to Paris (1640), hoping for
the commission to paint the Grande Galerie of the Louvre; Louis XIII had
already chosen Poussin, and when Poussin relinquished the assignment it
was too late for Vandyck. He fell ill, rushed back to London to his lying-in
wife. He died (1641) eleven days after she gave birth to a daughter. He
was not yet forty-two.

He founded no school and left no mark upon Continental art, but in
England his influence was overwhelming. Local painters like William
Dobson, Robert Walker, and Samuel Cooper made haste to copy his flattering, lucrative style; and when a great burst of portraiture came with
Reynolds and Gainsborough, it was the Vandyck legacy that provided
schooling and stimulus. Vandyck's portraits were not profound; he was
too hurried to search for the soul, and sometimes he stopped at the face
or the beard. The Cavaliers who surrounded Charles I were known for
their fine manners, but it is unlikely that so many of them looked like
poets; and some of the romance that we find in their brave stand for their
King may have come to us from seeing them through Vandyck's eyes. It
would be unfair to expect from so frail and fortunate a youth the robust
vitality of Rubens or the *de profundis clamavi* of Rembrandt; but we shall
continue to cherish these Genoese, Flemish and English portraits as bright
and "precious minims" in our inheritance.

V. THE DUTCH ECONOMY

What a leap it is from those perfumed English lords to the stout, tough
burghers of Haarlem, The Hague, and Amsterdam! It is a unique world
behind the dykes, a world of water rather than land, a life of ships and
commercial ventures rather than of courts and chivalry. There is hardly
anything more startling in economic history than the rise of the Dutch to
world power, or more comforting in cultural history than the way in
which this wealth so soon graduated into art.

The United Provinces had some three million population in 1600. Only half of it tilled the land; by 1623 half of it lived in cities, and much of the land was owned by urban landlords who trusted that commercial profits could be deodorized by putting them into the soil. Even in agriculture Dutch energy and skill had taken the lead in Europe; new dykes and dams were ever reclaiming "polders" from the sea; canals fertilized farms and trade; intensive horticulture complemented extensive stockbreeding; and Dutch engineers in the late sixteenth century brought the windmill to perfection just as Dutch painters were bringing it into art. Half of industry was still handicraft, but in mining and treating metals, weaving cloth, refining sugar, brewing beer it was advancing to a larger, less happy, more remunerative scale. Every year 1,500 "doggers"—two-masted fishing vessels— sailed from Dutch ports to snare herring. Shipbuilding was a major industry. During the truce with Spain (1609–21) the Netherlands sent out 16,000 vessels, averaging fifty-seven tons, with crews totaling 160,000 men —more than England, Spain, and France combined.[82]

Anxious for trade outlets and raw materials, Dutch captains explored uncharted seas. In 1584 Dutch merchants established themselves at Archangel, and advanced against the Arctic ice in a vain effort to find a "Northeast Passage" to China and thereby win a prize of 25,000 florins offered by the government of Holland. Dutch names on modern maps of the Spitsbergen Archipelago recall the voyages in which Willem Barents lost his life during a winter on the ice of Novaya Zemlya (1697). In 1593 the adventurous Dutch sailed into the rivers of the Guinea Gold Coast of Africa, made friends with the natives, and inaugurated a busy trade.

Till 1581 Dutch merchants had bought Oriental products on the docks of Lisbon to resell them in northern Europe. But in that year Philip II, having conquered Portugal, forbade trade with the Dutch, who thereupon decided to make their own voyages to India and the Far East. Jewish refugees from Spain and Portugal, or their descendants, were well informed about Portuguese trading posts in the East, and the Dutch profited from this knowledge.[83] In 1590 Dutch merchantmen, even during the war with Spain, passed through the Straits of Gibraltar; soon they were trading with Italy, then with the Arabs, sturdily ignoring religious differences. They made their way to Constantinople, signed a treaty with the Sultan, sold goods to both the Turks and their enemies the Persians, and moved on to India. In 1595 Cornelis de Houtman led a Dutch expedition around the Cape of Good Hope and via Madagascar to the East Indies; by 1602 sixty-five Dutch ships had made the return voyage to India. In 1601 the Dutch East India Company was organized, with a capital of 6,600,000 florins— forty-four times more than the English East India Company, formed three months before.[84] In 1610 Dutch merchants opened trade with Japan, in 1613 with Siam; in 1615 they secured control of the Moluccas, in 1623 of

Formosa. In one generation they conquered an empire of islands, and they ruled it from their Java capital, Jakarta, which they named Batavia. In that generation the company returned an average of 22 per cent annually to its shareholders. Pepper was imported from the "Spice" Islands and sold in Europe for ten times the price paid to the native producers.[85]

Taking the planet for their province, the Dutch sent ships to seek a Northwest Passage to China. In 1609 they hired an English captain, Henry Hudson, to explore the Hudson River. Twelve years later they organized the Dutch West India Company. In 1623 they established the colony of New Netherland, comprising the present states of Connecticut, New York, New Jersey, Pennsylvania, and Delaware. In 1626 they bought "New Amsterdam" (Manhattan) from the Indians for trinkets valued at twenty-four dollars. They were rapidly clearing and developing these lands when their North American possessions fell as a prize of war into English hands (1664). Similar Dutch acquisitions in South America were surrendered to the Spanish and the Portuguese; only Surinam remained, as Dutch Guiana.

Despite these losses, the Dutch Empire shared abundantly with Dutch trade in Europe to give the merchants of Holland a financial base for their political power, their splendid homes, and their patronage of art. During the first half of the seventeenth century the United Provinces held the commercial leadership of Europe, and their wealth per capita was greater than that of any other country in the world. Raleigh was dismayed by the superiority of the Dutch to the English in living standards and business enterprise.[86] A Venetian ambassador (1618) thought that every Hollander was in comfortable circumstances, but he had probably little acquaintance with the lower classes, whose poverty Rembrandt knew so well. "Millionaires" were numerous in Holland; some of them made fortunes by selling shoddy materials to the Dutch army and navy defending Holland;[87] and such men labored zealously to prevent the outbreak of peace.[88]

Most Dutch wealth was in the province of Holland, whose commerce, from the neighboring sea, was many times greater than that of the other northern provinces. Several towns in Holland had a prosperous bourgeoisie —Rotterdam, The Hague, Haarlem, Utrecht—but none could rival Amsterdam. The growth of its population tells the tale: 75,000 in 1590, 300,000 in 1620. Merchants, craftsmen, and bankers had flocked to it from war-ravaged Antwerp. After 1576 the Jews of Antwerp transferred to Amsterdam their financial activities, their commerce, their jewel industry— the diamond cutters of Amsterdam still lead the world. The merchant rulers of the city allowed considerable religious freedom, for only in this way could trade be encouraged with peoples of diverse faiths. The Bank of Amsterdam, founded in 1609, was in this age the strongest financial institution in Europe. Dutch currency was sought and trusted everywhere.

VI. DUTCH LIFE AND LETTERS

The Dutch were charged by their rivals with undue commercialism, a fever of money-making, and the coarseness of manners sometimes connected with absorption in economic life. Dutch historians amiably admit these allegations.[89] And yet can we call a culture commercial that so loved cleanliness, tulips, music, and art, that set up a school in every village and wiped out illiteracy, that created an intellectual atmosphere electric with controversy and ideas, and allowed such freedom of thought, speech, and press as soon made Holland the international refuge of rebel minds? "There is no country," said Descartes, "in which freedom is more complete, security greater, crime rarer, the simplicity of ancient manners more perfect than here."[90] And in 1660 another Frenchman wrote:

> There is not today a province in the world that enjoys so much liberty as Holland. . . . The moment a seigneur brings into this country any serfs or slaves they are free. Everybody can leave the country when he pleases, and can take all the money he pleases with him. The roads are safe day and night, even for a man traveling alone. The master is not allowed to retain a domestic against his will. Nobody is troubled on account of his religion. One is free to say what he chooses, even of the magistrates.[91]

The basis of this freedom was order, and the clarity of the mind was mirrored in the neatness of the home. Courage, industry, and obstinacy characterized the men; domestic assiduity and mastery marked the women; calm temper and a bluff good humor were in both sexes. Many Dutch businessmen retired after making a reasonable fortune, and gave themselves to politics, literature, golf,* music, and domestic felicity. The Dutch "hold adultery in horror," wrote Lodovico Guicciardini. "Their women are extremely circumspect, and are consequently allowed much freedom. They go out alone to make visits, and even journeys, without evil report. . . . They are housekeepers, and love their homes."[93] There were many women of fine culture, like Maria Schuurman, "the Minerva of Holland," who read eleven languages, spoke and wrote seven, practiced painting and sculpture well, and was adept in mathematics and philosophy. Maria Tesselschade's poetry was almost as beautiful as her person; she translated Tasso's *Gerusalemme liberata* to universal praise; she painted, carved, and etched; she played the harp and sang so well that half a dozen notables, including Constantijn Huygens, Joost van den Vondel, and Gerbrand

---

* This game was probably of Dutch origin, passing to Scotland in the fifteenth century. The word is from the Dutch *kolf,* which is the German *Kolb,* the English *club.*[92]

Bredero, laid proposals at her feet; she married a sea captain, became a devoted housewife and mother, and left behind her a tradition, still dear to Dutch memory, of intelligence, accomplishments, and nobility.[94]

The love of music was even more widely spread than the appreciation of art. Jan Pieterszoon Sweelinck of Amsterdam, the greatest of Dutch organists, taught Heinrich Scheidemann, who taught Johann Adam Reinken, who taught Johann Sebastian Bach. Along with all this excellence went some corruption in Dutch commerce, much drunkenness, many brothels, and a taste for gambling in all its forms,[95] even to speculation in the future prices of tulips.[96]

Haarlem was the center of the tulip culture. The bulbs had been imported from Italy and South Germany toward the end of the fifteenth century. Paris too made the flower a fashion and distinction; in 1623 one fancier refused 12,000 francs ($30,000?) for ten tulip bulbs.[97] In 1636 nearly the entire population of Holland took to speculating in tulips; special bourses existed where one could buy or sell tulip crops or futures; tulips had their own financial "crash" (1637). In that year an auction of 120 precious bulbs for the benefit of an orphanage brought 90,000 florins; *credat qui vult.*

Into this genial atmosphere the refugees from Flanders, France, Portugal, and Spain, and foreign merchants from half the world, imported a stimulating variety of exotic ways. The universities of Leiden, Franeker, Harderwijk, Utrecht, and Groningen gathered world-famous scholars, and produced others in turn. Justus Lipsius, Joseph Scaliger, Daniel Heinsius, and Gerard Vossius were all professing at Leiden in the first half century (1575–1625) of its career; by 1640 Leiden was the most renowned seat of learning in Europe. Among the general public of the United Provinces literacy was probably higher than anywhere else in the world. The Dutch press was the first free press. The Leiden weekly *News* and the Amsterdam *Gazette* were read throughout Western Europe because they were known to speak freely, while elsewhere the press was at this time governmentally controlled. When a king of France asked to have a Dutch publisher suppressed he was astonished to learn that this was impossible.[98]

Men of letters were many in Holland, but it was their misfortune that they wrote either in Latin, which was dying, or in Dutch, which narrowed their audience; the Dutch could not make their language, like their marine, a common carrier. Dirck Coornhert and Hendrik Spiegel upheld the lusty vernacular as a literary vehicle, and struggled to free it from uncongenial accretions. Coornhert—artist, writer, statesman, and philosopher—was the first and most virile figure in the cultural blossoming that crowned the political revolt. He drew up, as city secretary at Haarlem, the manifesto of 1566 for William of Orange, was imprisoned at The Hague, escaped to

Cleves, earned his living as a skilled engraver, translated *The Odyssey*, Boccaccio, Cicero, and the New Testament. Back in Holland, he labored for religious toleration, and symbolized the intellectual history of the next —seventeenth—century by losing the faith that he saw so mangled in bloody disputes. He became an agnostic, confessing that man will never know the truth.[99] His principal book, *Zedenkunst* (*The Art of Well-Living*), proposed a Christianity without theology, a system of morality independent of religious creeds. By some oversight he was allowed to die a natural death (1590).

It was characteristic of Holland that businessmen often mingled literature with their material affairs. Roemer Visscher, wealthy merchant of Amsterdam, gave help and hospitality to young writers, made his home a salon rivaling those of France, and himself wrote poetry that won him the title of the Dutch Martial. Pieter Hooft made his Castle of Muiden, on the Zuider Zee, a haven for the Dutch Renaissance; into his Muiderkring, or Muiden Circle, he welcomed poets, scientists, diplomats, generals, and physicians; and he himself, in his last twenty years, wrote the *Nederlandsche Historien*, telling the story of the Netherlands revolt in prose so strong and beautiful that Holland celebrated him as its Tacitus.

Three among a hundred poets brought the vernacular to its literary peak. Jacob Cats, for twenty-two years grand pensionary of Holland, expounded proverbial wisdom in popular verse, salted with spicy anecdotes; for centuries the works of "Father Cats" were in every literate Dutch home. Joost van den Vondel climbed over misfortunes and enemies to the supreme place in the literature of Holland. His father, a hatter, was banished from Antwerp for Anabaptist opinions, and Joost was born in Cologne. In 1597 the family settled in Amsterdam, where the father, going from one extreme to the other, opened a hosiery shop. Joost inherited the business, but left its operation to his wife and son while he made up for lack of formal education by studying Latin, Greek, Italian, French, and German. His twenty-eight plays were formed on Greek and French models, carefully obeying the unities. His satires ridiculed predestination and the debates among the Protestant sects. He felt the aesthetic appeal of Roman Catholic ritual, and of Maria Tesselschade, who was both Catholic and beautiful. After her husband died (1634) and Vondel's wife died (1635), the two poets entered into close friendship. In 1640 he was received into the Catholic faith. He continued to flay religious animosity, economic chicanery, and political corruption, and won a warm place in Dutch hearts by singing the courage and glory of the Netherlands. In 1657 the hosiery business, which his son had mismanaged, went bankrupt. The son fled to the East Indies, the poet sold all his modest possessions to satisfy the creditors, and for ten years he earned his bread as a pawnbroker's clerk. At last his government pensioned him, and he spent the last thirteen of his ninety-two years in peace.

The most attractive figure in the literature of the Netherlands in this age was Constantijn Huygens, a Dutchman with all the versatility of the Italian Renaissance. His father, Christian Huygens, was secretary to the Council of State at The Hague; his son, Christian Huygens, was to be the greatest of Continental scientists in the age of Newton; between them Constantijn well maintained the family's remarkable progression of ability. He was born at The Hague in 1596. There and at Leiden, Oxford, and Cambridge he received an ample education. He wrote Latin and Dutch poetry, excelled in athletics, and became a good musician and artist. At twenty-two he joined a diplomatic mission to England, played the lute before James I, and fell in love with John Donne, whose poems he later translated into Dutch. At twenty-three he was sent on a diplomatic mission to Venice; on his return he nearly lost his life scaling the topmost spire of the Strasbourg cathedral. In 1625 he became secretary to a succession of stadholders; in 1630 he was appointed to the Privy Council. Meanwhile he issued several volumes of poetry, distinguished by grace of style and delicacy of feeling. His death at the age of ninety (1687) marked the close of the Netherlands' most brilliant age.

VII. DUTCH ARTS

The Dutch Protestants felt that medieval church architecture and decoration had been forms of indoctrination perpetuating legends and discouraging thought; they decided to worship God with prayer and sermons rather than with art; the only art they kept in their ritual was song. So their ecclesiastical architecture aimed at an almost stark simplicity. Even the Catholics raised no memorable churches in the United Provinces. Overseas merchants, in the sixteenth century, brought in, perhaps from Syria or Egypt, the idea of bulbous cupolas; the fashion spread from Holland and Russia into Germany, and became a feature of Central European baroque.

Businessmen, not the clergy, dominated Dutch architecture. And first of all they built themselves sturdy dwellings—almost all alike, not instilling fear, like the Florentine palace, nor arousing envy; the luxury and art were all inside, and in the flower gardens carefully tended. Their civic buildings allowed more ornament and pride. Lieven de Key brought French, German, and Renaissance elements into a remarkable harmony in the *Rathaus*, or town hall, that he built for Leiden. The Hall of the Butchers' Guild at Haarlem, also by Lieven de Key, is as proud as a Gothic cathedral. The town hall at The Hague shows the classic style completely domesticated in Holland.

The Michelangelo of Dutch architecture and sculpture in this age was Hendrik de Keyser, who became city architect of Amsterdam at the age of twenty-nine (1594). There he designed the Westerkerk, the Exchange, and the East India House, all in Italian-Dutch Renaissance style. At Delft he built the town hall and the monument to William I; and in 1627, at Rotterdam, he cast in bronze his masterpiece, the noble statue of Erasmus which for some years sat calmly intact amid the ruins of the Second World War. Some of the loveliest Dutch structures dating from this period lost their lives in that failure of statesmanship.

Pottery shone among the minor arts. In Rotterdam and Delft tiles were an industry that good taste made an art. Delft raised its faïence to a place in nearly every home in the Netherlands. About 1610, soon after the opening of Dutch trade with the Orient, Delft potters began to imitate Chinese ware, and produced a thin blue majolica called *Hollandsch porseleyn*.[100] Soon half the West-European world displayed Delft pottery on its walls or shelves.

The one major art in the Netherlands was painting. Never elsewhere in known history—not excepting Renaissance Italy—did an art win such pervasive popularity. For the years between 1580 and 1700 the art catalogues list fifteen thousand Dutch paintings.[101] Italian influence dominated Flemish art, but in the northern provinces the successful resistance to Spanish power aroused a nationalistic spirit and pride that needed only the wealth derived from overseas trade to produce a cultural explosion. Art was turned into new channels of domesticity and realism by the almost complete withdrawal of ecclesiastical and aristocratic patronage. The new patrons were merchants, burgomasters, lawyers, corporations, guilds, communes, hospitals, even almshouses; hence the portraits, group pictures, and genre. Nearly every Dutch city had its school of artists, nourished by local patronage: Haarlem, Leiden, Utrecht, Amsterdam, Dordrecht, Delft, The Hague. Simple citizens who in other lands might have been, in art, illiterate dependents of the Church, adorned their homes with pictures, sometimes bought at considerable cost; so a baker proved his good taste by paying 600 florins ($7,500?) for a single figure by Vermeer.[102] Secularization was almost complete: saints went out as subjects, merchants came in; the home and the fields triumphed over the church. Realism flourished; the bourgeois sitter appreciated a little idealization of himself and his wife, but dykes and dunes, windmills and cottages, sailing ships and cluttered docks pleasantly refreshed, on the walls, the memory of actual and common things. Jolly topers, tavern tipplers, even *bordeeltjes* were welcomed into homes that a century earlier might have shown saintly martyrs, historic heroes, or pagan gods. Nudes were out of style; in that damp climate, with those stout forms, nudity was no delight. The Italian cult of beauty, refinement and dignity seemed out of place in this new environment, which asked nothing more of art than the reproduction of daily life and familiar scenes.

There was a sad side to this picture of a nation mad about pictures: the artists who painted them lived for the most part in poverty and low esteem. In Flanders the Archduke, the lords, and the bishops paid their chosen artists well. But in Holland the painters, competing individually, produced for the common market, and they reached customers largely through dealers who grew up between producer and purchaser and who knew how to buy cheap and sell dear. Dutch artists rarely received high prices: at the crest of his fame Rembrandt earned only 1,600 guilders by *The Night Watch*, van Goyen only 600 by his *View of The Hague* and much less for the rest; Jan Steen painted three portraits for twenty-seven guilders, Isaac van Ostade sold thirteen of his pictures for a like sum. Many Dutch artists had to do extraneous work to butter their bread: van Goyen sold tulips, Hobbema was a tax collector, Steen kept an inn.[103] The artists themselves were so numerous that they glutted their market. A list of the famous ones would fill pages, and a list of their treasured works would crowd a book. Shall we thank them in a footnote?*

VIII. FRANS HALS: 1580–1666

His ancestors had lived for two centuries in Haarlem; his father was a magistrate there; but for unknown reasons Frans was born in Antwerp; not till he was nineteen did he return to live in Haarlem. We hear no more of him till 1611, when the registry of a Haarlem church notes the baptism of

---

* Aelbert Cuyp: *Piping Shepherds* (New York).
  Carel Fabritius: *Portrait of a Young Man* (Rotterdam).
  Jan van Goyen, the greatest in this group: masterly landscapes in a dozen museums, including the Corcoran Gallery in Washington.
  Dirk Hals, younger brother of Frans: *The Merry Company* (London).
  Gerard van Honthorst: *The Concert* (Leningrad).
  Thomas de Keyser (son of Hendrik): fine portraits in Dresden, Naples, the Louvre, New York; his *Anatomy Lesson of Dr. Vrij* (1619) long preceded Rembrandt's *Anatomy Lesson of Professor Tulp* (1632).
  Karel van Mander wrote a *Schilderboek* (1604), or *Book of Painters of the Netherlands*, almost rivaling his model, Vasari.
  Michiel van Mierevelt: portraits in many museums.
  Adriaen van Ostade: *The Old Fiddler* and *The Smokers* (both in New York).
  Isaac van Ostade: *A Market Place* (Wallace Collection).
  Frans Pourbus the Elder: *Portrait of a Gentleman* (Wallace Collection).
  Frans Pourbus the Younger: *Portrait of a Youth* (Pitti Gallery).
  Pieter Pourbus: *An Allegorical Feast* (Wallace Collection).
  Hercules Seghers: *View of Rhenen* (Berlin).

Herman, son of Frans Hals and his wife Anneke. The next record is from a police court (1616), telling how Frans Hals, arrested for undue beating of his wife, was severely reprimanded, and was dismissed on his undertaking to be more gentle and to avoid drunken company. Seven months later Anneke died; five months thereafter (1617) Frans married Lysbeth Reyniers; nine days later she gave him the first of ten children.[104] He has left us an admirable picture of himself and this second wife.[105] She lived with him through his remaining forty-seven years, putting up with all his impecuniosity and drunken bouts. There was nothing very attractive about him except that he was a great painter and a jolly soul.

He was already thirty-six when he achieved a major success, *The Banquet of the Officers of St. Joris' Shooting Guild*[106]—the first of the five *Doelen* pictures that give Hals his rank. The *doelen* were the headquarters of volunteers who practiced marksmanship, held competitions and social gatherings, and served as communal militia. Occasionally the officers of such guilds would pay an artist to paint their portraits as a group, each individual insisting that his prominence in the picture should be proportioned to his grade in the company and his contribution to the cost. Here, then, are these officers, decked out in their best finery, gathered around a feast, with one of them carrying the colorful standard of the company. Hals earned his fee, for each of these heads is an individual and powerful portrait, each different, each a biography and a masterpiece.

We do not hear of another such assignment till eleven years later, but in the interval he produced pictures that are among the prizes of Dutch art: *The Herring Seller*[107]—again a history in a face; *The Merry Trio* and *Junker Ramp and His Girl*, both in New York; the famous *Laughing Cavalier*[108]—self-confidence incarnate, with all his fortune on his back in ruff and frills and flowered cloak, and a smile almost as subtle as La Gioconda's. And in this period (1624?) Frans painted his *Self-Portrait*[109]—a strong and handsome face, with wistful eyes denying the pride of the fine clothes and folded arms. The man was a bruised shuttlecock between the hunger for perfection and the thirst for drink.

In 1627 came the second *Doelen* group, another *Officers of St. Joris' Guild*,[110] not so clear and bright as the first; Hals deliberately turned for a time from the easy brilliance of strong colors to the more difficult manipulation of the minor keys—half tones, gray shadows, softer outlines. Another *Doelen* of that year, *St. Adriaen's Shooting Guild*,[111] is also in subdued tones. The shooters must have been pleased, for they commissioned Hals to paint them again (1633);[112] now the artist recalled his colors and displayed his genius for making every face interesting and unique. In 1639 he painted still another *Officers of St. Joris' Guild*,[113] but here the individual is lost in the crowd. All in all, these *Doelen* are among the outstanding group pictures of all time. They illustrate the emergence of the middle class into proud prominence in Dutch history and art.

In his second period (1626–50) Hals painted portraits that cry out for remembrance: *The Jolly Toper*,[114] under a hat large enough to cover a multitude of drinks; *The Sand Runner*,[115] disheveled and ragged and charming; *The Gypsy* (or *La Bohémienne*), smiling and bulging in the Louvre; *The Jester* in Amsterdam; the fanciful *Balthazar Coymans* in Washington; and, as the climax of this maturity, Hals's supreme picture, *The Regents of St. Elizabeth's Hospital*,[116] so like, so unlike, Rembrandt's *Syndics of the Drapers' Guild*, painted twenty-one years afterward.

Frans's incalculable carouses, though they do not seem to have injured his art, had hurt his standing even in a land and a time that took occasional intoxication as an ode to joy. He continued to paint pictures that would have made any artist famous: *Hille Bobbe*,[117] "the witch of Haarlem"; the disenchanting *Descartes*[118]—enormous eyebrows, enormous nose, eyes saying "*Dubito*"; and (painted at the age of eighty) *Young Man in a Slouch Hat*.[119] But meanwhile disasters multiplied. In 1639 Hals's son Pieter was sent to an insane asylum at municipal expense. In 1641 his wayward eldest daughter, at her mother's request, was put into a workhouse. By 1650 Frans was destitute. In 1654 the local baker sued him for a debt of two hundred gulden, and attached the painter's goods. In 1662 the broken old man applied for and received poor relief. Two years later the Haarlem council voted him a yearly pension and an immediate gift of three loads of peat to fire his hearth.

Probably as additional alms he was given, in this year 1664, a commission to paint two pictures: *The Regents of the Almshouse* and *The Women Regents of the Almshouse*. The male group shows the unsteady hand of the artist's eighty-four years; many features are daubed in vaguely. But in the companion piece, the *Regentessen*, the old skill has surprisingly returned; here are five souls drawn out into their obedient faces, five old women wasted with unwanted tasks, prim and stern with their puritan code, forgetting the joys and frolics of their youth; yet through those grim features somehow shines a timid kindliness, a weary sympathy. These final pictures, last flames of the painter's fire, now, with the great *Doelen* canvases, hang in the Frans Hals Museum that Haarlem built on the site of that almshouse.

He died a pauper (1664), but he was given honorable burial in the chancel of St.-Bavon's in the city whose fame rests upon a long-resisted siege and the works of her greatest son. For two centuries thereafter he was almost forgotten. His pictures sold for pittances, or by auction, or not at all. If historians of art remembered him it was to note the narrowness of his range—no religious pictures, no mythologies, no histories, no land-scapes, no nudes; or the apparently careless haste of his method—no pre-liminary sketches, but rapid daubs and slashes of color that relied on sug-gestion and the beholder's memory to fill in details. Today a possibly exaggerated acclaim balances that long neglect, and one generous critic considers Hals "the most brilliant executant of portraits the world has seen."[120] Where time, the safest judge, so vacillates in its judgment, let us be content to admire.

IX. REMBRANDT HARMENSZ VAN RIJN: 1606-69

He was born at Leiden to a prosperous miller, Gerrit Harmens, who added "van Rijn" to his name, probably because his house overlooked the Rhine. The artist must have loved his father, for he painted him eleven times or more: in lordly hat and chain,[121] and as a money-changer,[122] and as *A Noble Slav*[123]—a strong, well-modeled face bristling with character—and, in 1629, as a man sombered with age.[124] His mother too he pictured a dozen times, most memorably in the *Old Woman* of the Vienna Gallery, worried and worn. In the Rijksmuseum at Amsterdam we see her poring over a Bible. If, as some believe, she was a Mennonite, we can better under-stand Rembrandt's predilection for the Old Testament, and his closeness to the Jews.

At fourteen he entered the University of Leiden. But he thought in other forms than ideas or words; after a year he withdrew and persuaded his father to let him study art. He did so well that in 1623 he was sent to Amsterdam as pupil to Pieter Lastman, who was then rated the Apelles of the age. Lastman had returned from Rome to Holland with a classic emphasis on correct drawing; from him, probably, Rembrandt learned to be a superlative draftsman. But after a year in Amsterdam the restless youth hurried back to Leiden, eager to paint after his own fashion. He drew or painted almost everything that he saw, including hilarious ab-surdities and shameless obscenities.[125] He improved his art with fond experiments in self-portraiture; the mirror became his model; he has left us more self-portraits (at least sixty-two) than many great painters have left paintings. Among these early *autoritratti* is a charming head in The Hague: Rembrandt at twenty-three, handsome of course (for all mirrors show us handsome), hair carelessly tossed about with young superiority to conventions, eyes alert and proud with the confidence of proved ability.

In fact, he had already established himself. In 1629 a connoisseur paid him a hundred florins for a picture—quite a fee for a young competitor in a land where painters were as numerous as bakers, and not so amply fed.

His first themes, after himself and his parents, were Biblical. *Jeremiah Mourning the Destruction of Jerusalem*[126] has the mystic aura that distinguishes Rembrandt's religious pictures, and *Simeon in the Temple*[127] catches completely the spirit of *Nunc dimittis servum tuum, Domine*. So many commissions came from Amsterdam that Rembrandt went back to it in 1631 and lived there the rest of his life.

Within a year of his arrival he painted one of the world's masterpieces, *The Anatomy Lesson of Professor Nicolaes Tulp*.[128] There had already been several anatomies in Dutch painting. No precedents were broken, no modesty violated, when the distinguished surgeon, four times burgomaster of Amsterdam, commissioned Rembrandt to picture him giving a demonstration in anatomy in the Hall of the Surgeons' Guild; he planned to present the painting to the guild as a memorial to his professorship. It was probably Dr. Tulp who chose the seven "students" to share the picture with him—obviously not pupils but men of maturity and standing either in medicine or in another field; and Rembrandt made full use of the opportunity to show faces illuminated with character and intelligence. The cadaver seems unduly inflated, and two of the onlookers are posing for posterity; Dr. Tulp himself takes the affair quite calmly, as one inured and confident; but the two men peering over the head of the corpse are curiosity and attention vivified; and the play of light upon flesh and ruffs announces Rembrandt's specialty.

Commissions now flowed in—in two years, forty. With money in his pocket and hunger in his blood, the artist was ripe for marriage (1634). Saskia Uylenborch had a lovely face, dancing eyes, hair of silk and gold, a comfortable figure and fortune; what could be lovelier than the *Saskia* in Cassel? She was the orphaned daughter of a wealthy lawyer and magistrate. Perhaps her cousin, an art dealer, had induced her to sit to Rembrandt for a portrait. Two sittings sufficed for a proposal. Saskia brought a dowry of forty thousand guilders, which made the future bankrupt one of the richest artists in history. She became a good wife despite her money. She bore patiently with her mate's absorbed genius; she sat for many pictures, though they revealed her expanding form; she let him deck her out in strange costumes for the rosy *Flora* now in London and the simpler, wistful *Flora* in New York. We see his happiness in a Dresden painting where he holds her on his knee, irradiates the canvas with his smile, and raises a tall tumbler to his physical and financial ecstasy.

In these grateful years (1634-42) he turned out one masterpiece after another. He continued to picture himself: in the *Self-Portrait* (1634) in the Louvre, handsome and jolly, with jewels in his hat and a gold chain on his chest; and again that year in *An Officer*[129]—magnificent in a world-conquering hat; and in 1635 with a gorgeous hat whose plume tickles the sky. Looking for character rather than beauty, he painted (1634) the *Old Lady* who looks down upon us, from the walls of the National Gallery in London, with a face corrugated by the years, and, a year later, the *Old Woman in an Armchair* in New York. Among the human ruins of Amsterdam he found an octogenarian whom he dressed in turban and robes and pictured in *An Oriental*.[130] He had a penchant for collecting costumes, jewelry, swords, fancy hats and shoes; see them (except the sword) in *Martin Daey*[131]—with lace on his gloves, frills on his pants, and shields on his shoes. Now, too, he painted timeworn religious subjects with a fresh sincerity, taking his models from the old men and young women whom he met in the streets—each picture so remarkable in technique, so striking in its manipulation of light, and so moving in the intensity of its feeling, that any one of them might be defended as the artist's best; let *The Sacrifice of Abraham*[132] and *The Angel Raphael Leaving Tobias*[133] serve as examples. From these blessed years came some famous portraits, like *The Lady with a Fan*[134] and *A Man with Gloves*[135]—both defying words.

The last achievement of this period, and perhaps the greatest picture that Rembrandt ever painted, was the immense canvas (fourteen by twelve feet) that history knows as *The Night Watch*, but that is more properly named *Captain Cocq's Company of Harquebusiers* (1642).[136] No detail is unfinished in that vast expanse, no shade of darkness or incidence of light is uncalculated, no contrast of color is unexplored. In the center the proud captain stands in brown and white and red; at his left a lieutenant in golden yellow boots and coat and hat; swords gleam, pikes flash, pennants wave; at the right the fife-and-drum corps; the company emerges from its headquarters, apparently for some festival parade. Rembrandt had signed a contract with each of the sixteen persons to be painted, each paying one hundred florins. Many felt that equal pay had not been rewarded with equal prominence in the picture; some complained that he had put them too deeply in shadows, or had neglected to make them recognizable by their friends. Few further group commissions came to his studio, and his prosperity began to wane.

It must have been high in 1639, for in that year he bought a spacious house in the Joden-Breedstraet, a street inhabited by well-to-do Jews. It cost him thirteen thousand florins, an enormous sum, which he never succeeded in paying off. Probably it was intended to shelter not only his family but his pupils, his studio, and his growing collection of antiquities, curiosities, and art. After paying half the purchase price in the first year of occupancy, he let the rest remain as a debt, on which the unpaid interest rose to a point that eventually drove him to bankruptcy.

Meanwhile his beloved Saskia was declining in health. She had borne him three children, but each died in childhood, and their painful birth and tragic end weakened her hold on life. In 1641 she gave birth to a son, Titus, who survived; but in 1642 she passed away. Her will left all her possessions to Rembrandt, with the proviso that on his remarriage the remainder of her legacy should be transferred to her son. A year after her death Rembrandt painted her from loving memory.

That loss darkened his mood; thenceforth he seemed obsessed with thoughts of death. Though deeply affectionate within his family, he had always preferred privacy to company; now he courted a somber solitude. When he was painting he brushed premature viewers away, telling them, "The smell of paint is not good for the health."[137] He was not a cultured man of the world, like Rubens. He read little, hardly anything but the Bible. He lived in a wordless realm of color, shadow, and light, as varied as the world of letters, but alien to it and unique. He had difficulty in donning the social graces when sitters came, and in making small talk to keep them amused and still. They came in less number when they found that Rembrandt, like most of his predecessors, was not content to make a sketch from a sitting or two and then paint from the sketch, but preferred to paint directly on the canvas, which required many sittings; moreover, he had an impressionistic way of painting what he thought or felt, rather than merely what he saw, and the result was not always flattering.

It did not help him that his house was in the Jewish quarter. He had long since made friends with many Jews; he had engraved a portrait of Manassah ben Israel in 1636; now (1647) he painted on wood the dark face of the Jewish physician Ephraim Bonus. Almost surrounded by Hebrews, and evidently liking them, he found subjects increasingly among the Portuguese and Spanish Jews of Amsterdam. Perhaps he knew Baruch Spinoza, who lived in that city from 1632 till 1660. Some have thought that Rembrandt himself was Jewish; this is improbable, for he was christened and reared in a Protestant faith, and his features were completely Dutch. But he had no perceivable prejudice in religion or race. There is an especial depth of sympathetic understanding in his pictures of Jews. He was fascinated by their old men, their beards dripping wisdom, their eyes remembering grief. Half the Hebrew Calvary is in the face of *An Old Jew* (1654) in the Leningrad Hermitage, and in the *Portrait of a Rabbi* (c. 1657) in London. This last is the rabbi who, after Rembrandt's bankruptcy, gave him spiritual comfort and material aid.

In 1649 we find him painting *Hendrikje Stoffels in Bed*,[138] and we perceive that he has taken a mistress. She had been Saskia's maid; she stayed with the widowed artist, took faithful care of him, and soon consoled him with the warmth of her body. He did not marry her, for he was loath to relinquish Saskia's legacy to Titus, still a boy of eight. As he painted Hendrikje in 1652,[139] she was tolerably fair, with eyes of haunting wistfulness. It was probably she who posed for two studies in nudity, in 1654,

Bathsheba at the Bath[140] and *A Woman Wading*,[141] both of them glories of color and amplitude. In July of that year she was summoned before the elders of the parish church, was severely reprimanded for adultery, and was excluded from the Sacrament. In October she bore him a child; Rembrandt acknowledged it as his and managed to get it safely baptized. He learned to love his mistress as deeply as he had loved his wife; how else could he have put such tenderness in her face when he painted her in 1658 in the red robe that matched her hair?[142] She was a good stepmother to Titus, who was growing up into a bewitching lad. See him in the Metropolitan Museum of Art, aged fourteen, as lovely as a girl, with the wondering eyes of youth, mystified by life and only half secure under paternal love; or, again, in the Wallace Collection, a year older. We can weakly imagine what a solace he must have been to Rembrandt, who in this year found economic realities crashing about his head.

He labored to make ends meet. Some great religious pictures belong to this period (1649–56) of adultery and debt: *Jacob Blessing His Grandchildren*,[143] *Christ at the Fountain*,[144] *Christ and the Woman of Samaria*,[145] and a *Descent from the Cross*.[146] However, in Protestant Holland ecclesiastical subjects were not in demand. He tried his hand at mythologies, but succeeded only when he could clothe the figures; *Danaë*[147] is uninviting, but *Athene*[148] and *Mars*[149] are unsurpassed in their kind. He continued to paint portraits of arresting character. *Nicolaes Bruyningh*[150] is snatched directly from a vivid moment of life and thought; and *Jan Six*[151] is the Dutch burgomaster at his strongest and best. And about this time Rembrandt painted some nameless figures profoundly studied: *The Man with the Golden Helmet*,[152] *The Polish Rider*,[153] *The Centurion Cornelius*;[154] beside these, most portraits seem surface sheen.

Rembrandt was fifty when disaster came. He had seldom bothered to count his debits and credits; he had recklessly bought house and art, even shares in the Dutch East India Company;[155] now, as patronage lagged far behind maintenance, he found himself hopelessly in debt. In 1656 the Orphans' Chamber of Amsterdam, to protect Titus, transferred the house and grounds to the son, though the father was for a while allowed to live there. In July Rembrandt was declared bankrupt. His furniture, paintings, drawings, and collections were sold in costly haste (1657–58), but the proceeds fell far short of his obligations. On December 4, 1657, he was evicted. He moved from one house to another, until at last he settled on the Rozengracht, in the Jewish ghetto. Out of the wreck some seven thousand florins were salvaged for Titus. He and Hendrikje, to protect Rembrandt, formed a partnership by which they could sell his remaining works without letting them go to his creditors. They seem to have taken loving care of the aging artist.

Amid these tribulations he continued to spawn masterpieces: the *Man on*

Horseback, recently sold to the National Gallery, London, for $400,000; the wonderful *Head of an Old Man*[156]—a Karl Marx in octogenarian disillusionment; the astonishingly vivid and natural *Woman Cutting Her Nails*[157]—perhaps part of the religious ritual that required cleansing of the whole body on the eve of the Sabbath. Now, too, he painted some startling self-portraits: *Rembrandt with His Sketch-Book* (1657), in Dresden; the stern face and enveloped corpulence of the more famous portrait (1658) in the Frick Collection at New York; the full-figure portrait (1659) in Vienna; the worried face (1659) in Washington.

In his final decade (1660–69) he was kept alive by his son and his mistress, but his quarters were cramped, his studio was badly lighted, his hand must have lost some of its decisiveness as the result of age and drink. *St. Matthew the Evangelist*[158] is coarse in its texture, but the angel whispering in his ear is none other than Titus, now twenty and still as fair as a bride. And then, in that year 1661, came the master's last triumph, *The Syndics of the Drapers' Guild*.[159] The *staelmeesters*—examiners and controllers of cloth—commissioned the old artist to commemorate them in a group picture to be hung in the hall of their corporation. We would have forgiven some hesitancy in the composition, some crudity in details, some carelessness in the incidence of light; but criticism is at a loss to find fault there. The subdued foreground and background make the five main figures leap to the eye, each of them "a single and separate person," but all caught in the living moment of their common thought. In many paintings of these broken years the connoisseurs find signs of failing energy and technique—simplicity of colors, neglect of details, a hasty sweep and crudity of the brush. And yet even then we have such arresting pictures as *The Return of the Prodigal*[160]—an unforgettable portrayal of loving forgiveness—and *The Jewish Bride*.[161] This is wondrous fruit to come from a dying tree.

But we have said nothing of his landscapes, his drawings, and his etchings. Only a few of the landscapes stand out, but the drawings are at the top of their kind. Famous are the pen-and-ink *View of Amsterdam*, in Vienna, and *An Old Woman Sitting*, in Berlin. Rembrandt's etchings are prized as highly as any in the history of that painstaking art. One of them, *Christ Healing the Sick*, came to be known as "The Hundred-Guilder Piece" because it was bought for that unprecedented price ($1,250); in 1867, however, a copy of it brought 25,000 francs ($20,000?).

Three hundred etchings, 2,000 drawings, 650 paintings—this is the surviving *œuvre* of Rembrandt, almost as widely known as Shakespeare's plays, almost as varied, original, and profound. Nearly all were from his own hand, for though he had aides, none of them shared his secret for revealing the invisible.[162] Some of his work was careless, some of it repulsive, like the *Flayed Ox* in the Louvre. At times he was engrossed in technique,

at times he skimped it for the vision's sake. He was as neutral as nature between beauty and ugliness, for to him truth was the ultimate beauty, and a
picture representing ugliness truthfully was beautiful. He refused to idealize
the figures in his Biblical paintings; he suspected that those Old Testament
Hebrews looked pretty much like the Jews of Amsterdam; he pictured
them so, and in consequence they rise from myth or history into life. More
and more, as he grew older, he loved the simple people around him rather
than men dehumanized by the pursuit of gain. Where artists like Rubens
sought their subjects among the beautiful, the happy, or the powerful,
Rembrandt lavished his sympathetic art on the outcasts, the sick, the miserable, even the deformed; and though he made no show of religion, he
seemed to embody, unconsciously, the attitude of Christ and Whitman
toward those who had failed, or had refused to compete, in the war of
each against all.

We take a last look at him in the self-portraits of his old age. There is
no vanity here; on the contrary, these are the autobiography of defeat.
As he pictured himself in 1660,[163] he was still facing life with a blend of
courage and resignation; the pudgy unshaved face was quizzical but not
sad; he was still moving forward. But in another portrait[164] of the same
year a worried look darkens and ridges the face around the rubicund nose.
In 1661 he saw himself[165] as baffled, but shrugged his wrinkles philosophically. And in his last year he pictured himself[166] as having found peace in
accepting the limits and the wry humor of life. Hendrikje died in 1662,
but Titus still blessed him with the sight of youth; and in 1668 the old man
rejoiced in the marriage of his son. When, in that same year, the son followed the mistress, the artist lost his hold on life. On October 8, 1669, the
death register of the Westerkerk recorded: "Rembrandt van Rijn, painter
. . . Leaves two children."

His contemporaries hardly noticed his passing. None of them dreamed of
ranking him with Rubens, or even with Vandyck. Joachim von Sandrart,
his contemporary, wrote of him: "What he chiefly lacked was knowledge
of Italy, and of other places which afford opportunities for the study of
the antique and of the theory of art. [This now seems to us the secret of
his greatness.] Had he managed his affairs more prudently, and shown
more amenity in society, he might have been a richer man. . . . His art
suffered from his predilection for the society of the vulgar."[167] Ruskin
agreed with the German historian of art: "Vulgarity, dullness, or impiety
will always express themselves through art in brown and grays as in Rembrandt. . . . It is the aim of the best painters to paint the noblest things they
can see by sunlight. It was the aim of Rembrandt to paint the foulest things
he could see—by rushlight."[168] But Eugène Delacroix, reflecting democratic
developments in France, thought, "Perhaps we shall one day find that Rem-

brandt is a greater painter than Raphael. I write down—without taking sides—this blasphemy, which will cause the hair of the Academicians to stand on end."[169] The tendency among art critics today is to rate Rembrandt above Raphael and Velázquez, equaled only by El Greco.[170] "Truth," we perceive, is a function and vassal of time.

From Rubens to Rembrandt, what a gamut and chasm!—between joyous light and somber shadow, between the abyss and the court, between the happy sensuality of the Antwerp noble, at home in palaces and with kings, and the Amsterdam bankrupt who knew the lower depths and was acquainted with grief. To see these two men as the contrapuntal elements of a mighty harmony is to feel in another way the greatness of the little nation that had fought a giant empire, to feel the complexity of a civilization that could produce, at one end, a Catholic culture gladly adorning its unquestioned creed with myths and its beloved shrines with art, and, at the other, a Protestant culture that could nourish the greatest artist and the greatest philosopher of the age.

CHAPTER XIX

The Rise of the North

1559-1648

I. DENMARK AS A GREAT POWER

LET us look at the map, for maps, like faces, are the signatures of history.

When Frederick II ascended its throne in 1559, Denmark was one of the strongest and most far-reaching states in Europe; it had not yet learned how clever it is to be small. In the perennial contest with Sweden for control of the commerce between the North Sea and the Baltic, Denmark was at first the victor, even extending its rule across the Skagerrak to and throughout Norway, and across the Kattegat into what is now south Sweden. It held the strategic cities of Copenhagen and Helsingör on the west side, and Malmö and Helsingborg on the east side, of the Öresund, or Sound—the swirling waters, in one place only three and a half miles wide, that now separate Denmark from Sweden. Farther east it held, through most of this period, the islands of Bornholm, Gotland, and Ösel, thereby controlling the Baltic Sea. On the south it included the duchies of Schleswig and Holstein, and far away in the northwest it ruled Iceland and Greenland. The tolls charged by Denmark on commerce passing through the straits between the seas were the chief source of the kingdom's revenues and wars.

Political power resided in the eight hundred nobles who owned half the land, kept the peasants in serfdom, elected the king, and ruled the country through the Rigsdag, or National Diet, and the Rigsraad, or Council of State. They had profited from the Reformation by absorbing most of the property formerly belonging to the Catholic Church. In return for exemption from taxation, they were expected, but they often refused, to arm and lead their peasants in war at the call of the king. The Protestant clergy, shorn of wealth, had a minor social standing and little political influence; however, they controlled education and held a censorship over literature, which consequently produced mainly theology and hymns. The general population, numbering a million, enjoyed heavy meals and heavy drinking. A barber-surgeon advised his clients: "It is very good for persons to drink themselves intoxicated once a month, for the excellent reasons that it frees their strength, furthers sound sleep, eases the passing of water, increases perspiration, and stimulates general well-being."[1]

Two Danes in this period have a special claim on history: Tycho Brahe, the greatest astronomer of his generation, and Christian IV, who not only was King of Denmark for sixty years (1588–1648) but would have been a leader of men even without the advantage of royal birth. We pass by his father, Frederick II, merely noting that for him the Flemish architect Anthonis van Obberger designed (1574–85) the fortress of Kronborg Castle at Helsingör—Hamlet's Elsinore.

When Frederick died (1588), Christian was a boy of eleven; a regency of four nobles ruled for eight years; then Christian took the reins. For the next half century he lived the abundant life with such exuberance and versatile energy that all Europe marveled. He bettered the instruction of the aforesaid barber-surgeon, for he regularly required to be helped home after an evening's carouse. His profanity set a standard that few of his subjects surpassed. The number of his bastards created a problem in accountancy. His people laughed these popular faults away and loved him, for he danced at their weddings, joined in their labor, and risked his life repeatedly in their service. To all this he added a knowledge of Latin and science, an educated taste in the arts, and a simple religious faith that raised no sophomoric questions about credibility and no qualms about fun. In his spare time he helped to make Copenhagen (Kφbmannehavn, merchants' harbor) one of Europe's most attractive capitals. His building program doubled the circumference of the city.[2] In his reign Schloss (Castle) Rosenborg took form; soon thereafter the Bourse spread its vast façade and raised its twisted steeple high. He reformed the government of Norway, developed its industries, and rebuilt its capital, which for three centuries bore his name as Christiania. (It was renamed Oslo in 1925.) In Denmark he improved administration, promoted manufactures, organized commercial companies, founded colleges and towns, and raised the condition of the peasants on the Crown estates.

Ambition toppled him, for he dreamed of reuniting all Scandinavia under one head, his own. The nobles objected that Sweden was unconquerable, and they refused their support. Chiefly with foreign mercenaries he waged against Sweden the Kalmar War (1611–13). When the Thirty Years' War came he found himself uncomfortably allied with Sweden in defense of the Protestant cause. That peril over, he resumed the struggle with Sweden (1643), though he was now sixty-seven years old. He led his inadequate forces with romantic ardor. In the naval battle of Kolberg (1644) he fought all through the day, despite twenty wounds and a blinded eye, and won a temporary victory. In the end Sweden proved stronger, and the Peace of Brömsebro (1645) freed Sweden from paying dues for her commerce in the Sound, and ceded to her Gotland, Ösel, and three provinces on the Scandinavian peninsula. When Christian IV died, after fifty years of constructive labor and destructive wars, his kingdom was smaller than at his accession, and the ascendancy of Denmark had passed away.

II. SWEDEN: 1560–1654

1. The Rival Faiths: 1560–1611

Between Gustavus Vasa, the founder of modern Sweden, and Gustavus Adolphus, the savior of Protestantism, Swedish history is clouded by the contest of religious creeds for political power. The first Vasa had freed Sweden from Denmark and had united his country under a strong hereditary monarchy, while noble oligarchies kept Denmark and Poland feudal and weak. The Swedish peasantry was free, and was represented, along with the nobles, the clergy, and the towns, in the Riksdag, or Diet; the same word *bonde* that in Denmark had come to mean serf was in Sweden the proud title of a freeman tilling his own soil. But the resources of the land were severely limited by climate, by inadequate population, and by Danish control of three peninsular provinces and the Sound. The nobles chafed in their new subordination to the king, and the Catholic Church, despoiled of her Swedish wealth, plotted patiently to recapture the people, her property, and the throne.

Vasa's son Eric XIV (1560–68) was unfitted to meet these problems. He had courage and ability, but his violent temper stultified his diplomacy, and led him to murder and madness. He infuriated the nobles by killing five of their leaders, one with his own hand. He carried on against Denmark the "Northern Seven Years' War" (1563-70), and prepared future wars by conquering Livonia. He alienated his brother John by obstructing a marriage that would have made John heir to the Polish crown; and when John nevertheless married Princess Catharine Jagellon, Eric shut him up in the fortress of Gripsholm. Catharine came to share the rigors of John's imprisonment, and inclined his ear to the Catholic faith. In 1568 Eric's brothers compelled him to abdicate, and after six years in confinement he was put to death by order of the Riksdag and the new King.

John III (1568-92) made peace with Denmark and his nobles, and renewed the conflict of the faiths. His wife pleaded with him, more by night than by day, to accept Catholicism. With his permission Jesuits entered Sweden in disguise, and the ablest of them, Antonio Possevino, undertook the conversion of the King. John's conscience burned with the memory that he had consented to his brother's death; for such a fratricide the fires of hell seemed an inevitable punishment; this, Possevino urged, could be escaped only by confession and absolution in the Church which all believed to have been founded by Christ. John yielded; he received the Sacrament according to the Roman rite, and promised to make Catholicism the religion of the state provided the Pope would allow the Swedish clergy to marry, the Mass to be celebrated in the vernacular, and the Eucharist to be administered in wine as well as bread. Possevino went to Rome; the Pope rejected the conditions; Possevino returned empty-handed. John ordered the Jesuits to receive the Sacrament in both kinds and recite the Mass in Swedish. They refused and departed. In 1584 Catholic Catharine died; a year later John married a Protestant lady, who, more by night than by day, brought him back to the Lutheran faith.

In August 1587 his Catholic son was elected to the Polish throne as Sigismund III. By the Statute of Kalmar father and son agreed that after John's death Sigismund should reign over both Poland and Sweden; but Sigismund pledged himself to respect Sweden's political independence and Protestant faith. When John died (1592) the Riksdag, under the lead of his brother Duke Charles, met at Uppsala (February 25, 1593) with three hundred clergymen and three hundred laymen—nobles, burgesses, miners, and peasants—and adopted the Lutheran Augsburg Confession of 1530 as the official creed of the Swedish Church and state. The historic synod (Uppsala-möte) declared that no religion but Lutheranism was to be tolerated in the nation, that none but orthodox Lutherans were to be appointed to ecclesiastical or political office, and that Sigismund would be crowned in Sweden only after he had accepted these principles. Meanwhile Duke Charles was recognized as regent in the absence of the King.

Sigismund, who had been educated by the Jesuits, dreamed of bringing Sweden and Russia into the Catholic fold. When he landed at Stockholm (September 1593) he found the Swedish leaders almost unanimous in demanding his solemn guarantee to obey the Uppsala declarations. For five months he sought to win a compromise; the leaders were obdurate, and Duke Charles collected an army. Finally Sigismund gave the required pledge, and a Lutheran bishop crowned him at Uppsala (February 1594). Soon thereafter he issued a statement protesting that his pledge had been given under duress. He appointed six lords lieutenant to protect the remaining Catholics in Sweden, and in August he returned to Poland.

Duke Charles and Archbishop Angermannus of Uppsala prepared to enforce the synod's decrees. The Diet of Süderköping (1595) called for an end to all Catholic worship and the banishment of "all sectaries opposed to the evangelical religion." The Archbishop ordered that whoever neglected to attend Lutheran services was to be beaten with rods, and in his visitation of the churches he personally attended such punishments.[3] All surviving monasteries were closed, and all Catholic shrines were removed.

Sigismund's advisers begged him to invade Sweden with a large army. He thought five thousand men would suffice; with these he landed in Sweden in 1598. At Stegeborg Duke Charles gave him battle and was defeated; in a second engagement, at Stängebro, Charles won; Sigismund again agreed to the Uppsala declarations and returned to Poland. In July 1599 the Swedish Diet deposed him, and Duke Charles, still as regent, became the actual ruler of the state. The Diet of 1604 passed a succession act entailing the crown upon such male or female members of the Vasa family as accepted the established Lutheran religion, and enacting that no dissenters from that religion should be allowed to dwell or hold property in Sweden. "Every prince who should deviate from the Confession of Augsburg should *ipso facto* lose the crown."[4] So the road was opened to the accession of Charles's son Gustavus Adolphus, and to the abdication of his granddaughter Christina. In 1607 Charles IX was crowned King.

He reformed the disordered government, vigorously promoted education, commerce, and industry, and founded the cities of Karlstad, Filipstad, Mariestad, and Göteborg; this last settlement gave Sweden clear access to the North Sea, circumventing Danish control of the straits. Christian IV declared war (April 1611) and invaded Sweden. Charles, aged sixty-one, challenged Christian to single combat; Christian refused. At the height of the conflict (October 1611) Charles died; but before his death he laid his hand upon the head of his son, saying, "*Ille faciet*" (He will do it).[5] He did.

2. Gustavus Adolphus: 1611–30

The most romantic figure in Swedish history was now sixteen. His mother was a German, daughter of Duke Adolphus of Holstein-Gottorp. Father and mother gave him a rigorous education in the Swedish and German languages and in Protestant doctrine. By the age of twelve he had learned Latin, Italian, and Dutch; later he picked up English, Spanish, even some Polish and Russian; to which was added as strong a dose of the classics as comported with training in sports, public affairs, and the arts of war. At the age of nine he began to attend the sessions of the Riksdag; at thirteen he received ambassadors; at fifteen he ruled a province; at sixteen he fought in battle. He was tall, handsome, courteous, generous, merciful, intelligent, brave; what more could history ask of a man? His popularity was so universal in Sweden that even the sons of nobles whom Charles IX had executed for treason came willingly to serve him.

He did not display the Vasa tendency to personal temper and violence, but it appeared in his relish for war. He inherited from his father the Kalmar War with Denmark; he waged it zealously, but he felt that it was leading him in the wrong direction, and in 1613 he gave Denmark a million thalers ($10,000,000?) in exchange for peace and the free passage of Swedish vessels through the straits and the Sound. At this stage of his career he was more interested in keeping Russia out of the Baltic. "If at any time," he wrote to his mother, "Russia should . . . learn her strength, she would be able not only to attack Finland [then part of Sweden] on both sides, but also to get such a fleet on the Baltic as would endanger our Fatherland."⁶ He sent his most resourceful general, Jacob de la Gardie, to conquer Ingria, and in 1615 he himself laid siege to Pskov. The Russian resistance was troublesome, but by threatening to ally himself with Poland Gustavus persuaded Czar Michael Romanov to sign a peace (1617) recognizing Swedish control of Livonia, Esthonia, and northwestern Ingria, including what is now Leningrad. For the time being Russia was blocked from the Baltic. Gustavus boasted that without Swedish permission Russia could not launch a single boat upon that sea.

Now he turned his attention to Poland, whose Sigismund III still claimed the Swedish throne. Catholicism was by this time victorious in Poland and was eager for another chance to capture Sweden; moreover, Poland, with great ports at Danzig, Memel, Libau, and Riga, was then a stronger competitor than Russia for control of the Baltic. In 1621 Gustavus led 158 ships and 19,000 men to the siege of Riga, through which a third of Polish exports passed. Its population was predominantly Protestant and might not resent a Lutheran overlord. When it capitulated, Gustavus dealt with it leniently to attach it to his cause. During a three-year truce with Poland he strengthened the spirit and discipline of his army and, like his contemporary Cromwell, made piety an instrument of martial morale. He studied the military art of Maurice of Nassau and learned how to win campaigns by swift movement and farseeing strategy. He brought in technicians from Holland to instruct his men in siege tactics and the use of artillery. In 1625 he crossed the Baltic again, captured Dorpat, confirmed Swedish control of Livonia, and completely shut out Lithuania from the Baltic Sea. A year later his armies subdued both East and West Prussia, which were fiefs of the Polish Crown; only Danzig held out. The conquered regions became provinces of Sweden, the Jesuits were expelled, Lutheranism was made official. All Protestant Europe now looked to Gustavus as a possible savior in the great war that was then devastating Germany.

In the intervals of peace, he had faced with less genius than in war the problems of internal administration. During his absence on campaigns he left the government to the nobles, and to ensure their fidelity he allowed them to monopolize office and to buy from the Crown vast estates at little cost. But he found time to stabilize finances, to reorganize the courts, the postal service, the hospitals, and poor relief. He established free schools, founded the University of Dorpat, and richly re-endowed the University of Uppsala. He prodded mining and metallurgy, and it was no small item in his successes that Sweden had materials and skill to manufacture armament. He promoted foreign commerce by granting monopolies and gave a charter to a Swedish South Sea Company. His minister Oxenstierna, known for his calm in crises, was appalled by his master's energy. "The King," he said, "controls and steers mines, commerce, manufactures, and customs just as a steersman steers his ship."[7] He begged Gustavus to cool down. "If we were all as cold as you," answered the King, "we should freeze." "If we were all as hot as your Majesty," the minister retorted, "we should burn."[8]

Now the consuming fever of the Swedish knight was to get into the Thirty Years' War. "All wars in Europe hang together," he said.[9] He had noted with deep anxiety the victories of Wallenstein, the advance of Hapsburg armies into northern Germany, the collapse of Danish resistance, the alliance of Catholic Poland and Catholic Austria; soon the Hapsburg power would seek control of the Baltic, and the commerce, religion, and life of Sweden might be at the mercy of the Empire and the papacy. On May 20, 1629, Gustavus sent to the Swedish Diet a warning of Wallenstein's plan to make the Baltic a Hapsburg sea. He recommended offense as the best defense, and asked the nation to support and finance his entry into the Armageddon that was about to determine the fate of theologies. Sweden was already heavily burdened by his campaigns, but the Diet and the people responded to his call. With the help of Richelieu he persuaded Poland to a six-year truce (September 1629). Nine months he spent collecting ships, provisions, troops, and allies. On May 30, 1630, he addressed the Diet in an eloquent and moving farewell, as if surmising that he would not see Sweden again. On June 26–28 his forces disembarked on an island off the Pomeranian coast, and Gustavus went forth to glory and death.

3. Queen Christina: 1632–54

Since his daughter, heiress to his throne, was a child of four, he appointed as regent one of the ablest statesmen of that genius-crowded age— Count Axel Oxenstierna. Christina later described him: "He had studied much in his youth, and continued to do so in the midst of business. His capacity and knowledge of the world's affairs and interests were very great; he knew the strong and weak points of every state in Europe. . . . He was ambitious, but faithful and incorruptible, withal a little too slow and phlegmatic."[10] He had a reputation for silence, but to say nothing, especially when speaking, is half the art of diplomacy. For two years he ruled Sweden well while Gustavus fought on alien fields. Then, as regent for Christina, he directed the armies of Sweden in Germany as well as affairs at home, and no country in Europe had in those twelve years a better government. In 1634 he drew up a "Form of Government" specifying the composition, powers, and duties of each department in the administration; this is the earliest known example of a written constitution.

In 1644 Christina, now eighteen, assumed control. She felt herself fit to rule this vibrant nation, grown to a million and a half souls; and indeed she had all the abilities of a precocious male. "I came into the world," she said, "all armed with hair; my voice was strong and harsh. This made the women think I was a boy, and they gave vent to their joy in exclamations which at first deceived the King."[11] Gustavus took the discovery of her sex like a gentleman, and came to love her so dearly that he seemed quite content to have her as heir to his power; but her mother, Maria Eleanora of Brandenburg, never forgave her for being a girl. Perhaps this maternal rejection shared in making Christina as much of a man as her physique would allow. She conscientiously neglected her person, scorned ornament, swore manfully, liked to wear male dress, took to masculine sports, rode astride at top speed, hunted wildly, and bagged her game at the first shot; but: "I never killed an animal without feeling pity for it."[12]

Despite all this she had some feminine charms. Pierre Huet, afterward Bishop of Avranches, reported (1653): "Her face is refined and pretty, her hair golden, her eyes flash. . . . She carries modesty written on her face, and shows it by the blushes which cover it at an immodest word."[13] "She cannot bear the idea of marriage, because she was born free and will die free," reported the Jesuit confessor of the Spanish ambassador.[14] She seems to have felt that coitus was, for a woman, a form of subjection; and doubtless, like Elizabeth of England, she knew that her husband would want to be king. She was sensitively aware of her faults, and acknowledged them bravely. "I was distrustful, suspicious, ambitious to excess. I was hot-tempered, proud, and impatient, contemptuous and satirical. I gave no quarter. I was too incredulous, and little of a devotee."[15] But she was generous to extravagance, and faithful to her tasks. "She spends only three or four hours in sleep," said the Jesuit. "When she wakes she spends five hours in reading. . . . She never drinks anything but water; never has she been heard to speak of her food, whether it was well or ill cooked. . . . She attends her Council regularly. . . . During a fever twenty-eight days long she never neglected her state affairs. . . . Ambassadors treat only with her, without ever being passed on to secretary or minister."[16]

She wished to rival not only the youths in sports and the courtiers in politics, but also the scholars in learning, and these not merely in languages and literature but in science and philosophy as well. By the age of fourteen she knew German, French, Italian, and Spanish; by eighteen she knew Latin; later she studied Greek, Hebrew, and Arabic. She read and loved the French and Italian poets, and envied the bright vivacity of French civilization. She corresponded eagerly with scholars, scientists, and philosophers in several lands. She brought together a splendid library, including rare ancient manuscripts which students came from many countries to consult. At her death connoisseurs were impressed by the fine taste she had shown in purchasing pictures, statues, enamels, engravings, and antiques. She collected savants as she collected art; she longed to have pundits and thinkers about her; she drew to her court Claudius Salmasius, Isaac Vossius, Hugo Grotius, Nicolaas Heinsius, and rewarded all of them lavishly. Those scholars who could not come sent her their books and paeans— Scarron, Guez de Balzac, Mlle. de Scudéry; and the grave Milton, while blasting her Salmasius, declared her "fit to govern not only Europe but the world."[17] Pascal sent her his calculating machine, with a remarkably beautiful letter complimenting her on being a queen in the realm of mind as well as of government.[18]

Her penultimate passion was for philosophy. She corresponded with Gassendi, who, like a hundred others, congratulated her on realizing Plato's dream of philosopher-kings. René Descartes, the outstanding philosopher of the age, came, saw, and marveled to hear her deduce his pet ideas from Plato.[19] When he tried to convince her that all animals are mechanisms, she remarked that she had never seen her watch give birth to baby watches.[20] But of this more later on.

She did not neglect native talent. Sweden had then a true polymath, Georg Stjernhjelm, linguist, jurist, scientist, mathematician, historian, philosopher, the father of Swedish poetry and the center of Swedish intellectual life in this age. Gustavus Adolphus so admired him that he raised him to the peerage; Christina made him court poet, until he joined her enemies.[21]

Attracted by the pedagogical theories of John Comenius, she brought him to Stockholm to reform the school system of Sweden. Like Elizabeth at Oxford and Cambridge, she visited Uppsala to encourage by her presence the teachers and pupils at the university; she listened there to Stjernhjelm and others discourse on the Hebrew text of the Old Testament. She built a college at Dorpat and gave it a library; she founded six other colleges; she developed into a university the college that her father had founded at Åbo (Turku) in Finland. She sent students to study abroad, some to Arabia to learn Oriental scholarship. She imported Dutch printers to establish a publishing house in Stockholm. She urged Swedish scientists to write in the vernacular, so that knowledge might spread among her people. She was, without question, one of the most enlightened rulers in history.

Did she have a mind of her own, or was she the undiscriminating receptacle of the intellectual currents eddying about her? The unanimous testimony is that in government she did her own thinking, made her own decisions, ruled as well as reigned.[22] We shall see, in a later chapter, how she vetoed Oxenstierna's martial policy, labored for peace, and helped to end the Thirty Years' War. Her fragmentary memoirs are vital and fascinating. The maxims which she left in manuscripts have nothing hackneyed about them. E.g.:

> One is, in proportion as one can love.
>
> Fools are to be more feared than knaves.
>
> To undeceive men is to offend them.
>
> Extraordinary merit is a crime never forgiven.
>
> There is a star which unites souls of the first order, though ages and distances divide them.
>
> More courage is required for marriage than for war.
>
> One rises above all, when one no longer esteems or fears anything.
>
> He who loses his temper with the world has learned all he knows to no purpose.
>
> Philosophy neither changes men nor corrects men.[23]

In the end, after sampling a dozen philosophies, perhaps after ceasing to be a Christian, she became a Catholic. She was accused of having imbibed atheism from her physician Bourdelot.[24] A Swedish historian, echoed by Voltaire,[25] thought her conversion a conscious farce: on this theory she had come to the conclusion that since truth cannot be known, one might as well adopt the religion that appeals most to the heart and the aesthetic sense,[26] and gives most comfort to the people. But conversion to Catholicism is often a sincere reaction after extreme skepticism; in the depths of doubt mysticism may sink its well. There were mystic elements in Christina; her memoirs are intimately addressed to God. Belief is a protective garment; its complete divestiture leaves an intellectual nudity that longs to be clothed and warmed. And what warmer raiment than the colorful, sensuous Catholicism of France and Italy? "How," she asked, "can one be a Christian without being a Catholic?"[27]

She pondered long over the question, and over the many complications involved in conversion. If she abandoned Lutheranism she must, by the laws of her realm and her beloved father, abandon not only her throne but her country. What an anticlimax such a change of faith would be to her father's heroic defense of Protestant Europe! But she was tired of her official duties, of the harangues of preachers and councilors, of the pedantic trivia of scholars, antiquaries, and historians. And perhaps Sweden was tired of her. Her alienation of Crown lands, her costly gifts to her favorites, had impoverished and consumed her revenues. A majority of the nobles were leagued against her policies. In 1651 there was a flurry of rebellion; the leaders were hastily executed,[28] but an active resentment survived. Finally, she was sick. She had injured her health, probably by too much work and study. Frequently she suffered dangerous fevers, with symptoms of inflamed lungs. Several times she fainted, sometimes remaining unconscious for an hour. In 1648, during a severe illness, she says, she "made a vow to quit all and become a Catholic, should God preserve my life."[29] She was a Mediterranean soul shivering in the wintry north. She dreamed of Italian skies and French salons. How pleasant it would be to join the cultured women who were beginning their unique function of nursing the intellect of France! If she could take a substantial fortune with her . . .

In 1652 she secretly sent to Rome an attaché of the Portuguese embassy to ask for Jesuits to come and discuss Catholic theology with her. They came in disguise. They were discouraged by some of the questions she asked—whether there was really a Providence, whether the soul could survive the body, whether there was any actual distinction between right and wrong except through utility. Then, when they were about to abandon her as lost, she comforted them: "What would you think if I were nearer to becoming a Catholic than you suppose?" "Hearing this," said one of the Jesuits, "we felt like men raised from the dead."[30]

To become a Catholic before abdicating was legally impossible. But before abdicating she desired to protect the hereditary character of the Swedish monarchy by persuading the Diet to ratify her choice of her cousin, Charles Gustavus, as her successor. Long negotiations delayed her abdication till June 6, 1654. The final ceremony was almost as moving as the abdication of Charles V ninety-nine years before. She took the crown from her head, discarded all regal insignia, removed her royal mantle, stood before the Diet in a dress of plain white silk, and bade her country and her people farewell in a speech that brought taciturn old nobles and phlegmatic burgesses to tears. The Council provided for her future income, and allowed her to keep the rights of a queen over her retinue.

She left Stockholm at nightfall five days after her abdication, stopped at Nyköbing for a last visit with her mother, went on, sleepless, for two days, fell sick with pleurisy, recovered, and rode on to Halmstad. There she wrote to Gassendi, awarding him a pension and sending him a chain of gold. At the last moment she received an offer of marriage from the new-crowned Charles X; she refused it courteously. Then, disguised as a man and under the name of Count Dohna, she took ship for Denmark, not knowing that for thirty-five years more she would play a part in history.

III. POLAND GOES TO CANOSSA: 1569–1648

Poland too, in this age, made her peace with the Roman Church, and it is instructive to see how Catholicism so quickly recovered in that kingdom nearly all the ground it had lost in the Reformation. But first let us note, with our usual haste, the political background of the cultural evolution.

1. The State

The period begins with an outstanding achievement of statesmanship. Southeast of Poland lay the grand duchy of Lithuania, ruled by its own dukes, and extending from the Baltic through Kiev and the Ukraine to Odessa and the Black Sea. The growth of Russian power threatened Lithuania with the loss of its autonomy. Though its Greek Orthodox Christianity largely agreed with Russia's, it reluctantly decided that a merger with Roman Catholic Poland would better preserve its self-rule than an embrace by the Russian bear. Sigismund II signalized his reign by signing the historic Union of Lublin (July 1, 1569). Lithuania acknowledged the King of Poland as its grand duke, sent delegates to the Sejm at Warsaw, and accepted that diet, or parliament, as its government in all external relations; but it kept its own religion, its own laws, its own control of its internal affairs. Poland, so enlarged, had now a population of eleven million from Danzig to Odessa, from sea to sea. It was unquestionably one of the Great Powers.

The death of Sigismund II (1572), leaving no male heir, brought to an end that Jagellon dynasty which had begun in 1386 and had given Poland a line of creative kings and a civilization of religious toleration and humanistic enlightenment. The nobles had always resented hereditary monarchy as a violation of their feudal rights and liberties; now they resolved to keep power in their own hands by making the monarchy elective; they established a republic of nobles and made Poland's future kings the servants of the Sejm. Since the Sejm included not only the greater nobles, or magnates, but also the gentry (szlachta), or lesser nobility, the plan seemed to realize

Aristotle's ideal of a government mingling monarchical, aristocratic, and democratic elements in mutual checks and balances. In the context of the time, however, the new constitution meant a feudal reaction, a fragmentation of authority and leadership while Poland's Baltic competitors, Sweden and Russia, were being forged into martial unities by hereditary monarchies privileged to think in terms of generations. Every royal election now became an auction of noble votes to the highest bidder among rival candidates financed, usually, by foreign powers. So French agents, by distributing gifts with both hands, bought the Polish crown for the degenerate Henry of Valois (1573)—only to have him called back a year later to misrule France as Henry III.

The electoral Diet redeemed itself when, after a chaotic interregnum, it chose Stephen Báthory as king (1575). As Prince of Transylvania he had already made a name for himself in politics and war. His agents in Warsaw had promised that if elected he would pay the national debt, put 200,000 florins into the treasury, recover all territory that Poland had lost to Russia, and sacrifice his life on the battlefield, if necessary, for Poland's honor and glory. Who could resist such an offer? Whereas a few rich nobles supported the candidacy of Maximilian II of Austria, seven thousand members of the electoral Diet cried out for Báthory. He rode up with 2,500 troops, won many hearts by marrying Anna Jagellon, led an army against Danzig (which had refused to acknowledge him), and forced the proud port to pay a fine of 200,000 gulden into the national treasury.

Even so, the nobles were not sure that they liked the new King, with his sharply penetrating eyes, his realistic mind, his frightening mustache and authoritative beard. He despised pomp and ceremony, dressed simply, wore patches, and made beef and cabbage his favorite dish. When he called for funds for a campaign against Russia they granted him inadequate supplies grudgingly. Relying upon subsidies from Transylvania, he advanced with a small army and laid siege to Pskov, then the third in size of Russian cities. Ivan IV, though Terrible to his people, felt too old to meet so vigorous a foe. He sued for peace, yielded Livonia to Poland, and allowed Russia to be cut off from the Baltic (1582). When Ivan died (1584) Báthory proposed to Sixtus V to conquer all Russia, unite it with Poland, drive the Turks from Europe, and bring all Eastern Europe to the papal obedience. The Pope made no objections, but amid laborious preparations for this crusade Báthory died (1586). When he had ceased to trouble her, Poland recognized him as one of her greatest kings.

After a year of bargaining the Diet gave the throne to Sigismund III, who, as heir to the Swedish crown, might unite the two countries to control the Baltic and check the expansion of Russia. Half his reign, as we have seen, was consumed in vain efforts to establish his authority, and the Catholic faith, in Sweden. The sudden death of Boris Godunov (1605), plunging Russia into a defenseless chaos, gave Sigismund another opportunity. Without consulting the Sejm, he announced his candidacy for the Muscovite throne and advanced with an army into Russia. While he spent two years besieging Smolensk, his general Stanislas Zolkiewski defeated the Russians at Klushino, marched to Moscow, and persuaded the Russian nobles to accept Sigismund's son Ladislas as their king (1610). But Sigismund repudiated this arrangement; he, not his son, should be czar. Having at last taken Smolensk (1611), he marched toward Moscow. He never reached it, for winter caught up with his dilatory advance. His unpaid soldiers rebelled, and in December 1612, two centuries before Napoleon, his army retreated, amid disorder and suffering, from Russia into Poland. All that remained from the costly campaigns was the possession of Smolensk and Severski, and a strong infusion of Polish influence into Russian life.

The rest of Sigismund's reign was a succession of disastrous wars. His alliance with the Hapsburgs involved him, to the Emperor's delight, in an expensive struggle with the Turks, in which Poland was saved only by the skill of her generals and the courage of her troops. Gustavus Adolphus took advantage of Poland's preoccupation in the south to invade Livonia; and the Peace of Altmark (1629) left Sweden master of Livonia and the Baltic Sea. Sigismund died a broken man (1632).

The Diet gave the crown to his son, for Ladislas (Wladyslaw) IV, now thirty-seven, had shown his mettle as a general and had won many friends by his frank and cheerful character. He offended the Pope by tolerating Protestantism in Poland and the Greek Orthodox Church in Lithuania; and at Thorn (Toruń) he allowed a peaceful public debate of Catholic, Lutheran, and Calvinist clergymen (1645). He encouraged art and music, bought Rubens pictures and Gobelin tapestries, established the first permanent Polish theater, and staged Italian operas. He corresponded with the imprisoned Galileo, and invited the Protestant scholar Grotius to his court. He died (1648) just as a great Cossack revolt threatened the life of the Polish state.

2. The Civilization

The Polish economy was still medieval. Internal trade was in the peddler stage; foreign commerce was largely confined to Danzig and Riga; the merchant class was negligible in wealth and rarely found admittance to the Sejm. The nobles controlled the Diet, the king, and the economy. The large estates were tilled by peasants subject to feudal regulations in some ways more severe than on the manors of medieval France. The noble owner made these regulations himself and enforced them with his own soldiery. He forbade his tenants to leave his jurisdiction without his consent; he transferred them from place to place; he increased or diminished their lands at his own will; he exacted several days of unpaid labor from them yearly; he obliged them to buy and sell only from or to him; he compelled them to buy from him a certain annual quantity of badly brewed ale; he could conscript their children to serve him in peace or war. Legally they were free; they could own and bequeath property; but the Jesuit Father Skarga described them as slaves.[31]

Life was mostly rural. The nobles gathered in Warsaw to vote their collective will, but they lived on their estates, hunting, quarreling, loving, feasting, giving one another openhanded hospitality, and training themselves for war. Marriages were arranged by the parents; the girl was rarely asked, and she rarely resisted; it was assumed that love generated by marriage and parentage would be more enduring than marriage generated by love. Women were modest and industrious. Sexual morality was firmly maintained; we hear of no extramarital love affairs before the eighteenth century.[32] Men, rather than women, molded manners, except that Cecilia Renata, who married Ladislas IV in 1637, refreshed the Italian influences imported by artists and clergymen in earlier times; and Louise Marie de Gonzague, whom he married in 1648, brought with her a wave of French manners and speech that lasted till the twentieth century. Polish dances had a grave grace that as early as 1647 led a Frenchman to speak with admiration of the polonaise.

Polish art could not keep the pace that Veit Stoss had set at Cracow in 1477. The splendid tapestries of Sigismund II were woven in Flanders. Architects and sculptors from Italy raised the monuments to Sigismund and Báthory and Anna Jagellon in the Cracow cathedral, the baroque churches of the Jesuits in Cracow and Nieśwież, and the famous Sigismund III Column in Warsaw. Painting languished under the Protestant attack upon religious images, but Martin Kober made a revealing portrait of Báthory.

Education, like the graphic arts, suffered from the religious turmoil. The University of Cracow was in passing decay, but Báthory founded the University of Wilno (1578), and at Cracow, Wilno, Poznań, Riga, and elsewhere the Jesuits established colleges of such excellence that many Protestants favored them for the mental and moral training of their sons. Better still was the Unitarian school at Rakow, which attracted a thousand students from all the creeds. Jan Zamojski, the humanist Chancellor of Báthory, organized in Zamość a new university devoted chiefly to the classical curriculum.

There was an abundant literature. Religious controversy was often rude in epithets but polished in form; so Stanislas Orzechowski, who defended

Catholicism, laid about him with violent intolerance, but "in wonderful Polish, among the best in our history."[33] Equally noted for its style was *The Polish Courtier* (1566), by Lukasz Gornicki, an adaptation of Castiglione's *Cortegiano*. The Jesuit Peter Skargo was eminent in prose and verse, in education and politics. He passed from the presidency of Wilno University to be for twenty-four years the Bossuet of Poland as the leading preacher at the royal court; and he denounced without fear the corruption that surrounded him. He predicted that unless the nation could evolve a more stable and centralized government it would fall a prey to foreign powers; but he called for a responsible monarchy limited and restrained by law. The poetry of Jan Kochanowski remained unrivaled in his own field and tongue till the nineteenth century, and is still popular today. He reached the height of his inspiration in his *treny* (threnody or lament) for his daughter Ursula, dead in the full charm of childhood.

All Polish culture in this age was disturbed by the conflict of creeds. In the first half of the sixteenth century Protestantism seemed destined to capture Poland as well as Germany and Sweden. Many nobles were won to it as a rebellion against royal authority and ecclesiastical corruption, and as a means of appropriating Church property.[34] Sigismund II granted a wide religious toleration. A year after his death a committee of the Diet drew up (January 28, 1573) the "Confederation of Warsaw," guaranteeing religious liberty to all *dissidentes de religione* without exception. When put to a vote it was opposed by the episcopal members of the Diet, but it was unanimously approved by the ninety-eight lay members, including forty-one Catholics.[35] It represents a landmark in the history of toleration, for no previous official proclamation had gone so far. Under this broad protection a variety of sects flourished: Lutherans, Calvinists, Zwinglians, Anabaptists, Bohemian Brethren, Anti-Trinitarians. In 1579 Faustus Socinus came to Poland and began to organize a church on Unitarian lines; but the Cracow populace dragged him from his house, destroyed his library, and would have killed him had not the Catholic rector of the university come to his aid (1598).[36] The Calvinists united with the Lutherans in demanding the expulsion of the "Socinians" from Poland. The Diet in 1638 ordered the closing of the Unitarian schools, and in 1658 banished the sect from the country. They fled to Transylvania, Hungary, Germany, Holland, England, and at last to America, to find their most genial voice in Emerson.

Popular intolerance, Jesuit pedagogy, Catholic discipline, and royal politics joined with Protestant sectarianism to destroy Protestantism in Poland. The new sects fought one another as vigorously as they opposed the ancient creed. The peasants clung to the old faith because it was old; it had the comfort of custom on its side. When the kings—Báthory and Sigismund III—rallied to it, many Protestant converts or their children found it pleasant to make their peace with the Church. The fact that most of the Germans in Poland were Protestants gave Catholicism the help of nationalist sentiment. And the Church actively co-operated with these extraneous aids to reclaim Poland for the papacy. She sent some of her most subtle diplomats and most enterprising Jesuits to win the kings, the women and children, even the Protestant nobles themselves. Ecclesiastical statesmen like Cardinal Stanislas Hosius and Bishop Giovanni Commendone warned the kings that no stable social, moral, or political order could be based upon the fluid and clashing Protestant creeds. The Jesuits proved themselves well able to defend the old incredibilities against the new. Meanwhile the Catholic clergy, submitting to the decrees of the Council of Trent, underwent a rigorous and impressive reform.[37]

The Catholics too had a problem. The union of Lithuania with Poland brought the Greek Orthodox Church into irritating contact with the Roman. Their creeds differed slightly, but the Orthodox services used the Slavonic ritual, and the Orthodox priests had wives. In 1596 Jan Zamojski, by the Union of Brześć (Brest Litovsk), formed a middle group of clergy and laity into a Uniat Church, which adhered to clerical marriage and the Slavonic rite, but accepted the Roman creed and the papal supremacy. Roman Catholic leaders hoped that the compromise would gradually win the Greek and Russian communions to the papal obedience, but the new church encountered passionate resistance, and its archbishop at Polock was murdered by the Orthodox populace.

The Polish kings continued throughout the sixteenth century a religious toleration more advanced than in any other Christian country, but the Catholic population frequently returned to the old policy of violent hostility. They attacked a Protestant church in Cracow and exhumed and scattered corpses from Protestant graves (1606–7). They destroyed a Protestant church in Wilno and beat—some say killed—the ministers (1611). In Poznań they burned down a Lutheran church and demolished a conventicle of the Bohemian Brethren.[38] The Catholic clergy took no part in these popular theological demonstrations, but they profited from them. All circumstances conspired to favor the old Church, and by 1648 her victory was complete.

IV. HOLY RUSSIA: 1584–1645

1. The People

"You have only to look upon a map of the world," said Nadiezdin in 1831, "to be filled with awe before the destiny of Russia." As early as 1638 it had reached through Siberia to the Pacific, and along the Volga to the

Caspian; not yet, however, to the Black Sea—hence many wars. The population was only ten million in 1571.[39] The soil might easily have fed these millions, but reckless tillage exhausted farm after farm, and the peasants moved on to fresher fields.

This migratory tendency seems to have shared in bringing serfdom. Most tenants received advances from their boyar landlords to clear, equip, and plant their farms; they paid as much as 20 per cent on such loans;[40] many of them, unable to repay their borrowings, fell into servitude to their landlords, for a law of 1497 made a delinquent debtor the slave of his creditor till the debt was redeemed. To escape such servitude some peasants fled to Cossack camps in the south; some won freedom by agreeing to develop new and difficult terrain—and so Siberia was settled; some migrated to the towns to join the craftsmen there, or work in the mines or in the metallurgical or ammunition industries, or to serve the merchants, or peddle goods in the streets. The landowners complained that the desertion of farms by tenants —usually leaving debts unpaid—disrupted agricultural production, and made it impossible for the owners to pay the rising taxes demanded by the state. In 1581 Ivan the Terrible, to assure continuous cultivation, forbade the tenants of his administrative class (the *oprichniki*) to leave their farms without the owner's consent. Though that class was now losing its distinctive existence, the serfdom so established continued on its estates, and was soon demanded of their tenants by the nobles and the clergy who owned the greater part of Russia's land. By 1648 most Russian peasants were in fact, if not in law, serfs bound to the soil.[41]

Russia was still close to barbarism. Manners were coarse, cleanliness was a rare luxury, literacy was a class privilege, education was primitive, literature was largely monkish chronicles, priestly homilies, or liturgical texts. Of five hundred books published in Russia between 1613 and 1682, nearly all were religious.[42] Music played a prominent role in religion and in the home, and art was the handmaid of the Orthodox faith. Architecture built complex churches bulging with chapels and apses and bulbous domes, like the Church of the Virgin of the Don in Moscow. Painting adorned churches and monasteries with frescoes, now mostly covered over, or raised iconostases (icon panels) rich in pictorial invention rather than artistic skill,[43] as in the Church of the Miracle of St. Michael at Cracow. By 1600 icon painting had ceased to be an art and had become an industry, producing stereotyped pieces on a large scale for domestic piety. The outstanding art product of the age was the hundred-meters-high bell tower of Ivan Veliki (John the Great), raised by a German architect in the Kremlin Square (c. 1600) as part of Boris Godunov's program of public works to relieve unemployment.

In the picturesque churches, bright with costly ornaments, somber with calculated gloom, hypnotic with solemn ceremony and sonorous chants and prayers, the Orthodox clergy molded the people to piety, obedience, and humble hope. Seldom has a religion so closely co-operated with the government. The czar gave the example of faithful religious observance and beneficence to the Church; in return the Church invested him with awesome sanctity, made his throne an inviolable altar, and inculcated submission and service to him as a duty owed to God. Boris Godunov established the patriarchate of Moscow as independent of Constantinople (1598); and for almost a century the metropolitan of Moscow rivaled the dignity, sometimes challenged the power, of the czar. When (1594) an embassy came to Moscow from Pope Clement VIII to propose a union of the Orthodox and Latin churches under the papacy, Boris rejected the plan with scorn. "Moscow," he said, "is now the true orthodox Rome"; and he caused prayers to be offered up for himself as "the only Christian ruler on earth."[44]

2. Boris Godunov: 1584–1605

As yet he was ruler in fact only. The Czar was Feodor I Ivanovich (1584–1598), the feeble son of Ivan IV the Terrible, and the last of the Rurik line. Feodor had seen his elder brother die under his father's demonic blow; he had allowed his own will to be broken; he took refuge from the dangers of the palace in devotion to religion; and though his people called him a saint, they recognized that he lacked the iron to govern men. Ivan IV had appointed a council to guide the youth; one member of it, Feodor's brother-in-law, Boris Godunov, made himself dominant and became the ruler of the reign.

Ivan IV, by the last of his seven wives, had left another son, Dmitri Ivanovich, who was now (1584) three years old. To protect the child from intrigues other than their own, the Council sent him and his mother to live in Uglich, some 120 miles north of Moscow. There, in 1591, the young Czarevich died, by means not yet determined. A commission headed by Prince Vasili Shuiski (a member of the Council) went to Uglich to investigate; it reported that the boy had cut his throat in an epileptic fit; but Dmitri's mother charged that he had been killed by an order of Godunov.[45] Boris' guilt was never established, and is questioned by some historians.[46] The mother was forced to take the veil, and her relatives were banished from Moscow. Dmitri was added to the calendar of Orthodox saints, and was temporarily forgotten.

Like Richard III of England, Boris ruled more successfully as regent than later on the throne. Though lacking formal education, and perhaps illiterate, he had a shrewd ability, and seems to have labored earnestly to meet the problems of Russian life. He reformed internal administration, checked judicial venality, favored the lower and middle classes, undertook public works to give employment to the urban poor, mitigated the lot and the dues of the serfs, and—says a contemporary chronicle—was "beloved of all men."[47] He enjoyed the respect and confidence of foreign powers.[48] When Czar Feodor I died (1598), the Zemski Sobor, or national assembly, unanimously asked Godunov to take the crown. He accepted it with coy protestations of unworthiness, but there is some suspicion that the assembly had been prepared by his agents. Several nobles, resenting his defense of the commonalty,[49] contested his right to the throne, and conspired to depose him. Boris imprisoned some, exiled some, and compelled Feodor Romanov (father of the first Romanov czar) to become a monk. Several of the defeated group died so conveniently for Boris that he was accused of having them murdered. Living now in suspicion and fear, he spread spies everywhere, deported suspects, confiscated their property, put men and women to death. His early popularity faded, and the poor harvests of 1600–04 left him without the support of the starving populace against the persisting intrigues of the nobility.

One intrigue became famous in history, literature, and music. In 1603 a young man appeared in Poland who claimed that he was the supposedly dead Dmitri, the legitimate heir to the throne of Feodor Ivanovich. Boris, on good grounds,[50] identified him as Grishka Otrepieff, an unfrocked monk who had been in the service of the Romanov family. The Poles, fearful of expanding Russia, were pleased to find in their midst, available to their use, a claimant to the crown of Muscovy; they were further delighted when "Dmitri" married a Polish girl and joined the Roman Church. King Sigismund III, who had just signed (1602) a truce with Russia for twenty years, connived at Dmitri's recruiting of Polish volunteers. The Jesuits warmly espoused the pretender's cause. In October 1604 Dmitri crossed the Dnieper with four thousand men, including Russian exiles, German mercenaries, and Polish knights. The Russian nobles, professing neutrality, gave him secret support; fugitive peasants joined the advancing force; the starving people, longing to be deceived, accepted the new Dmitri at his word, and carried his banner as the symbol of monarchical legitimacy and their desperate hopes. While the shouting, praying mob moved upon Moscow from the west, the Cossacks, always ready for a fray, dashed up from the south. The movement became a revolution.

Seeing it as a Polish invasion, Boris sent his army westward. It defeated a detachment of Dmitri's forces, but missed the rest. In his Kremlin chambers Godunov received no news but of the swelling and advancing mob, the spreading disaffection, the toasts drunk by the boyars even in Moscow to the health of Dmitri, whom they heralded to the people as the holy czarevich chosen by God to be czar. Suddenly, after doubts and agonies known to Pushkin and Moussorgsky rather than to history, Boris died (April 13, 1605). He had commended his son Feodor to the care of Patriarch Basmanov and the boyars; but the priest and the nobles went over to the pretender. Godunov's son and widow were killed, and in a delirium of national ecstasy the "False Dmitri" was hailed and crowned as Czar of All the Russias.

3. "Time of Troubles": 1605–13

The new Czar was not a bad ruler as kings go. Unimposing in stature, unprepossessing in face, he could nevertheless handle a sword and ride a horse like a born boyar. He had a perceptive and furnished mind, eloquent address, genial manners, and an unaffected simplicity that shocked the protocol of palace life. He surprised his staff by assiduity in administration, and his army by training it in person. But his superiority to his environment was too conscious and manifest. He openly expressed his scorn of boyar coarseness and illiteracy; he proposed to send noble sons to be educated in the West; he planned to import foreign teachers to establish high schools in Moscow. He laughed at Russian customs and neglected Orthodox ritual; he failed to salute the images of the saints, he dined without having the table sprinkled with holy water, he ate veal, which was considered ritually unclean. He concealed—perhaps he had never taken seriously—his conversion to Catholicism, but he brought to Moscow his Polish Catholic wife, escorted by Franciscan friars and a papal legate; he himself had Poles and Jesuits in his entourage. He spent too freely the revenues of the treasury, doubling the pay of army officers and allotting to his friends the estates confiscated from the Godunov family. Restless and martial, he planned a campaign against the Khan of the Crimea, and practically declared war by sending the Moslem ruler a pigskin coat. When he almost denuded Moscow of soldiers by ordering them south, the boyars feared that he was opening the capital to Polish invasion.

A few weeks after Dmitri's accession a boyar faction under Shuiski conspired to depose him. Shuiski confessed that he had recognized the pretender only to get rid of Godunov; now the tool must be cast aside and a real boyar enthroned.[51] Dmitri discovered the plot and had the leaders arrested. Instead of summarily executing them, as tradition demanded, he granted them a trial by the Zemski Sobor—which, for the first time, was now chosen from all ranks and classes. When it condemned Shuiski and others to death, he commuted the sentence to banishment, and after five months he allowed the exiles to return. Many who had believed him to be the son of Ivan the Terrible felt that such unorthodox clemency cast doubt on his royal parentage. The pardoned conspirators renewed their conspiracy; the Romanov family, upon which Dmitri had rained plums of patronage, joined in the plot. On May 17, 1606, Shuiski and his followers invaded the Kremlin with their armed retainers. Dmitri defended himself well, killing several of his assailants with his own hand, but he was overcome and slain. His body was exposed on the place of executions; a ribald mask was thrown over his face, a flute was placed in his mouth; later his corpse was burned, and a cannon shot his ashes to the winds to discourage further resurrections.

The victorious boyars proclaimed Shuiski Czar Vasili IV. He bound himself to put no man to death, to confiscate no property, without consent of the Duma—the assembly of boyars; and he solemnly vowed, in the Uspenski Cathedral, "that ill shall unto no man be done without the Council"— i.e., the Zemski Sobor, or assembly of all classes. These guarantees, though often violated, formed a historic step in the evolution of the Russian government.

They failed to appease those large elements of the population that mourned the deposition of Dmitri. A rebellion broke out in the north; a second False Dmitri was set up as its leader, and Sigismund III of Poland gave him unofficial support. Shuiski solicited the aid of Sigismund's enemy, Charles IX of Sweden; Charles sent a Swedish force into Russia; Sigismund declared war upon Russia; his general Zolkiewski took Moscow. Shuiski was deposed (1610), was carried off to Warsaw, and was forced to become a monk. A faction of the boyars agreed to recognize Sigismund's fourteen-year-old son Ladislas as czar, on condition that the independence of the Orthodox Church be maintained and that the Polish army help the nobles to suppress the social revolt that was threatening aristocratic government in Russia.

The revolt was first of all a religious and patriotic repudiation of a Polish czar. Hermogenes, Orthodox Patriarch of Moscow, forbade the people to swear allegiance to a Roman Catholic sovereign. The Poles arrested him; he soon died in his cell, but his proclamation made Ladislas' rule impossible. Religious leaders called upon the people to drive out the Poles as Roman Catholic heretics. Government seemed to dissolve, and Russia fell into turmoil. A Swedish army held Novgorod and proposed a Swedish prince for the Russian throne. Peasants in the north and the south, Cossacks in the south, repudiated Ladislas and set up their own rule in the provinces. Bands of brigands pillaged villages and towns and tortured all who resisted. Agriculture was disrupted, food production fell, transportation was hazardous, famine rose, and in some districts the population resorted to eating human flesh.[52] A rebel mob entered Moscow, and in the confusion most of the city was burned to the ground (March 19, 1611). The Polish garrison retreated into the Kremlin and waited in vain for Sigismund to come to its support.

At Nizhni Novgorod a butcher, Kosma Minin, organized another rebel army, inspired by Orthodox devotion. He called upon each family to give up a third of its possessions to finance an advance upon the capital; it was done. But the people would follow only a titled leader. Minin invited Prince Dmitri Pozharski to serve as their general. He consented, and the new army marched upon Moscow, fasting and praying. Arrived, they laid siege to the Polish garrison in the Kremlin. It held out till it was reduced to eating rats and men and boiling Greek manuscripts for broth; then (October 22, 1612) it surrendered and fled. That year was long celebrated in Russian memory as the year of liberation, and when, two centuries later, the French were driven from Moscow, the victorious Russians set up in their again incinerated capital a monument to Minin and Pozharski, the butcher and the prince who had set them so heroic an example in 1612.

Pozharski and Prince Dmitri Troubetskoy invited lay and ecclesiastical representatives from all regions of the empire to a council for the election of a new ruler. Various boyar families pulled various wires; finally the Romanovs prevailed; the council chose Michael Romanov, then only fifteen, and the Moscow populace, quickly gathered and quickly coached, acclaimed him Czar (February 21, 1613). The people, having saved the state, humbly returned it to the nobility.

The new government suppressed social disorder and revolt, confirmed and extended serfdom, pacified Sweden by ceding Ingria, and signed a fourteen-year truce with Poland. The truce freed from long captivity Michael's father, Feodor Romanov, whom Boris had forced to become the monk Philaret. Michael made him Patriarch of Moscow, and welcomed him as a councilor so powerful that the people called Philaret "the Second Czar." Under the combined rule of father and son, despite more uprisings and wars, Russia achieved, after a generation of turmoil, an unsteady and discontented peace. The Time of Troubles (*Smutnoe Vremia*), which had begun with Boris' death, ended with Michael's accession; and this in turn began the Romanov dynasty, which was to rule Russia till 1917.

CHAPTER XX

The Islamic Challenge

1566-1648

I. THE TURKS

AMID the internal conflicts of Christendom, political or theological, some thoughtful men were disturbed by the apparent neutrality with which Providence looked upon the greater contest between Christianity and Mohammedanism. That faith had been driven from Spain, but *Daru'l-Islam* ("the world of Islam") was still immense. It included Indonesia and northern India; indeed, this was the age of the brilliant Mohammedan Mogul dynasty at Delhi (1526–1707). It embraced Afghanistan, much of Central Asia, and all of Iran, where in this period Persian art would display its sunset glory. West of Persia the Islamic realm was the Ottoman or Turkish Empire, then rivaled in extent only by the empire of Spain. It kept in its grasp all the coasts of the Black Sea, controlled the mouths of the Danube, the Dnieper, and the Dniester, and helped its allies, the Tatar khans, to control the Crimea and the mouth of the Don. It took in Armenia, Asia Minor, Syria, Arabia—all the Near East. There it held the most famous cities of the ancient and medieval world: Babylon, Nineveh, Baghdad, Damascus, Antioch, Tarsus, Smyrna (İzmir), Nicaea (İznik), Mecca, and Jerusalem, where by Moslem permission Christians worshiped at the tomb of Christ. In the eastern Mediterranean it secured the great islands of Cyprus, Rhodes, and Crete. North Africa was overwhelmingly Moslem, from the Red Sea to the Atlantic: Egypt was governed by pashas appointed by the sultans; Tripoli, Tunisia, Algeria, and Morocco were ruled by local Mohammedan dynasties whose submission to the sultans varied inversely with their distance from Constantinople. This was the age of the Saadian dynasty (1550–1668) in Morocco, when its capital, Marrakech, hummed with commerce and shone with art. In Europe the Ottoman power extended from the Bosporus through Hellas (usually including Athens and Sparta), the Balkans, and Hungary to within a hundred miles of Vienna; through Dalmatia to the gates of Venice; through Bosnia and Albania to just a leap across the Adriatic into papal Italy. There, and at besieged Vienna, the great debate was not between Protestants and Catholics, but between Christianity and Islam. Within that Moslem cordon Christendom lived its divided life.

No matter how far west Islam reached, it remained Oriental. Constantinople was a window on Europe, but Ottoman roots stretched too far back into Asia to let proud Turkey ape the West. In some parts of Islam the heat of the desert or the tropics burned out the vital spirits; the uninhabited distances discouraged commerce; men could not bestir themselves so acquisitively as the West Europeans; they cultivated immobility and were more readily content. The unchanging crafts of Islam were exquisite, but required time and taste and did not lend themselves to large-scale industry. The caravans were patient, but they could not compete with the commercial fleets of Portugal, Spain, England, and the Netherlands, which used all-water routes to India; however, some ports on the Mediterranean, like Smyrna, prospered from the transfer of goods between ships and caravans. The Mohammedan religion inspired men to hopeful bravery in war, but to an enervating fatalism in peace; it lulled them with dervish dances and mystic dreams; and though it had in its youth allowed great science, it had now frightened philosophy into a scholasticism of barren pedantry. The ulema—the scholar-theologians who wrote the laws on the basis of the Koran—formed the children in faithful orthodoxy, and saw to it that no Age of Reason should raise its head in Islam. There the conflict between religion and philosophy gave religion a decisive victory.

Moreover, that religion made easy conquests in lands won from Christendom. In Constantinople, Antioch, Jerusalem, and Alexandria the Eastern Christian Church still had patriarchs, but the Christian population was rapidly diminishing. In Asia Minor the Armenians and in Egypt the Copts remained Christian, but generally in Asia, Africa, and the Balkans the masses had gone over to Mohammedanism. Probably the reasons were practical: if they remained Christian they were excluded from public office, they paid a substantial tax in lieu of military service, and of every ten children they had to surrender a son to be reared as a Moslem Janissary for the army or the bureaucracy.

Otherwise the Christians in Islam enjoyed a religious toleration such as no Christian ruler would have dreamed of according to Mohammedans in Christian states. At Smyrna, for example, the Moslems had fifteen mosques, the Christians seven churches, the Jews seven synagogues.[1] In Turkey and the Balkans the Greek Orthodox Church was protected by Turkish authorities from any molestation in their worship.[2] Pepys thought that most of Hungary yielded to the Turks because it had more religious liberty under Ottoman rule than under the Catholic emperors.[3] This was certainly true of heterodox Christians. "The Calvinists of Hungary and Transylvania, and the Unitarians of the latter country," reported Sir Thomas Arnold, "preferred to submit to the Turks rather than fall into the hands of the fanatical House of Hapsburg," and "the Protestants of Silesia looked with

longing upon Turkey, and would gladly have purchased religious freedom
at the price of submission to Muslim rule."[4] More striking still is the judgment of the leading Christian authority on the history of modern Greece:

> Many Greeks of high talent and moral character were so sensible
> of the superiority of the Mohammedans that, even when they escaped
> being drafted into the sultan's household as tribute children, they vol-
> untarily embraced the faith of Mahomet. The moral superiority of
> Ottoman society must be allowed to have had as much weight in
> causing these conversions . . . as the personal ambition of individuals.[5]

This "moral superiority" of the seventeenth-century Ottomans is difficult
to assess. Tavernier, who traveled and traded in Moslem lands in 1631–33,
1638–43, and later, reported, "Turkey is full of thieves, that keep in troops
together, and waylay merchants on the road."[6] The Turks were known
for their calm benevolence, but the same religion that tamed their unsocial
impulses in peace released them violently in war with "infidels." The en-
slavement of captured Christians was sanctioned, and there were slave-
capturing raids by Turks on Christian lands near Ottoman frontiers;[7] however, in number and cruelty the Turkish trade in slaves lagged far behind
the Christian slave raids in Negro Africa. Sexual indulgence was apparently
more abundant and enervating in Islam than in Christendom, though it was
usually kept within the orderly limits of polygamy. Turkish society was
almost exclusively male, and since there was no permitted association of
men with women outside the home, the Moslems found companionship in
homosexual relationships, platonic or physical. Lesbianism flourished in
the zenana.[8]

Among a large minority there was an active though circumscribed intellectual life. Literacy was probably higher in European Turkey, in the
seventeenth century, than in Christendom. We may judge the abundance
of the literature from a bibliography that Hajji Khalfah compiled (1648)
of over 25,000 books in the Arabic, Turkish, and Persian languages. Hundreds of volumes were available on theology, jurisprudence, science, medicine, rhetoric, biography, and history.[9] Prominent among the historians was
Ahmed ibn Muhammad, whose *History of the Mohammedan Dynasties of
Spain* has often buttressed our story; we have known him chiefly as al-
Maqqari, so named from his native village in Algeria. Most of his book is
made up of passages transcribed or abridged from earlier narratives, yet it
is a remarkable production for its time, giving an account not merely of
politics and war, but of morals, law, women, music, literature, and medicine,
and bringing the record to life with vivid details and humanizing anecdotes.

Nearly every literate Turk wrote poetry, and (as in Japan) the rulers

competed zealously in the game. Mehmet Suleiman Oglou, more melodiously known as Fuzuli, composed the finest love lyrics of the age; they
sound silly in the poor translation available in English, but we catch his
meaning—that the young women of Baghdad were warm and soft and
smooth to the touch, timid and tender till yoked. Mahmud Abdu'l Baqi
(d. 1600), greatest of Ottoman lyric poets, after being the favorite singer
of Suleiman the Magnificent, continued to warble for thirty-four years
after his patron's death. Nefi of Erzurum (d. 1635) wrote satires with a
sting, one of which must have reached Allah, for while Murad IV was
reading it a thunderbolt fell at the royal feet; so the Sultan tore up the
volume and banished the poet from Constantinople. He was soon recalled;
but another satire pricked Vizier Beyram Pasha, who had him beheaded.[10]

Ottoman art still produced masterpieces. The Mosque of Ahmed I rose
in 1610 to dominate the capital with its six soaring minarets, its succession
of swelling domes, the massive fluted columns of its interior, its mosaic
arches, lordly script, and shining ornament. Five years later Ahmed dedicated to his favorite wife the lovely Yeni-Validé-Jamissi Mosque. Two
majestic mosques were added to Damascus in this period; and in Adrianople
the unrivaled architect Sinan, who had designed the Mosque of Suleiman,
built for Selim II a temple that some rank higher than any in Constantinople.

No civilization has surpassed Islam in the making of artistic tiles. See, for
example, those in the Mosque of Ahmed I, or, still more beautiful, those
that adorn the entrance to the mausoleum of Selim II, near St. Sophia's:
bouquets of white and blue flowers in a field of green, blue, and red sprays
and foliage; living flowers could not be fairer, and might envy this
permanence. In this age Iznik—where, thirteen centuries back, Constantine
had presided over the historic council that fixed the Christian creed—was
famous for its lustered tiles; there are convincing samples in the Metropolitan Museum of Art.

Miniature painting in Turkey echoed that of Persia, which we shall look
at presently. Calligraphy was in so high repute (story had it that a line
of handwriting by Mir Imad was sold for a gold piece even in his lifetime)[11]
that no book was printed in Turkey before 1728. In textiles too the Turks
were pupils of the Persians, but they yielded to no others in excellence.
Turkish rugs were not quite as delicate in texture, intricate in design, or
rich in color as the Persian, but they stand high in the history of this art.
Already in the fifteenth century Turkish rugs had won renown in the
West, for we see them in the paintings of Mantegna, and later in Pinturic-
chio, Paris Bordone, and Holbein. Many Tudor mansions were carpeted
with Turkish rugs; even the hardy Cromwell had twenty-two;[12] and we
find them represented in the Gobelin tapestries illustrating the life of Louis
XIV. The West was learning that the East had arts as well as guns.

II. LEPANTO

The rulers of the West, however, had to watch the guns, for Ottoman sultans had announced their intention of making all Europe Moslem. The manpower and the wealth of their sprawling realm gave them the largest and best-equipped army in Europe. The Janissaries alone numbered over fifty thousand. Perhaps the salvation of the West, and of Christianity, lay in the very vastness of the Ottoman Empire; distances were too great to bring the scattered resources to a point. And the sultans, though they constituted a more enduring dynasty (1288–1922) than any Christian ruling family, were deteriorating through the opportunities of the harem, and were delegating their government to transitory viziers whose insecurity tempted them to cushion their fall by feathering their nests.

So Selim II, who succeeded Suleiman the Magnificent in 1566, was a dissolute idler, whose one stroke of genius lay in entrusting both administration and policy to his able vizier, Mohammed Sokolli. The Turkish assaults upon the Holy Roman Empire were interrupted; Emperor Maximilian II bought peace with an annual tribute of thirty thousand ducats, and Sokolli turned to nearer game. Arabia had preserved its independence religiously, but now (1570) it was conquered for the Porte. The Aegean Sea was still dotted with Venetian possessions hampering Turkish fleets and trade; Lala Mustafa was sent against Cyprus with sixty thousand men. Venice appealed to the Christian powers for help; only the Pope and Spain responded. Pius V had not forgotten that in 1566 a Turkish fleet had threatened Ancona, the papal port and fortress on the Adriatic. Philip II knew that the Moors of Spain, suffering under his blows, had appealed to the Sultan for help (1569), and that their embassy had been favorably received. The diplomatic situation was illuminating. The Emperor would not join in war against Turkey, for he had just signed a treaty of peace and could not honorably or safely break it. France opposed any plan that would raise the power or prestige of Spain, and she cultivated the friendship of the Turks as an aid against the Emperor. England feared that a common enterprise with Philip would leave her at the mercy of Catholic Spain in case of victory. Venice worried lest victory bring Spanish power into the Adriatic and end Venetian monopoly of that sea. Pius labored for a year to overcome these hesitations; he had to consent to the use of ecclesiastical revenues by Venice and Spain; finally (May 20, 1571) the three powers joined in a Holy League and prepared for war.

During these negotiations the Turkish attack upon Cyprus had proceeded with great losses on both sides. Nicosia was taken after a siege of forty-five days; twenty thousand of its inhabitants were put to the sword. Famagusta resisted for almost a year; when it fell (August 6, 1571) its heroic defender,

Marcantonio Bragadino, was flayed alive, and his skin, stuffed with straw, was sent to Constantinople as a trophy.

So prodded, the Holy League gathered its forces. Savoy, Florence, Parma, Lucca, Ferrara, Urbino, and Venice's old enemy, Genoa, contributed vessels and men. At Naples Don Juan of Austria received the admiral's flag in solemn ceremony from Cardinal de Granvelle. On September 16, after the sailors and soldiers had been given the Eucharist by the Jesuits and Capuchins who were attached to the expedition, the armada sailed from Messina past the toe and heel of Italy across the Strait of Otranto to the island of Corfu. Here the news came of the massacres and atrocities that had attended the fall of Cyprus. The thirst for revenge animated the crews, and shouts of *"Vittoria! Vittoria! Viva Cristo!"* rose from the fleet as Don Juan gave the order to advance to battle.

On October 7, 1571, the armada moved through the Gulf of Patras into the Gulf of Corinth. There, off the port of Lepanto, the Turkish navy was waiting, with 222 galleys, 60 smaller vessels, 750 cannon, 34,000 soldiers, 13,000 sailors, 41,000 rowers. The Christians had 207 galleys, 6 greater Venetian galleasses mounting heavy guns, 30 smaller vessels, 1,800 cannon, 30,000 soldiers, 12,900 sailors, 43,000 rowers.[13] The Christian fleet carried a standard of Christ crucified; the Turkish carried the Sultan's standard, bearing the name of Allah embroidered in gold. The right wing of the Christians gave way before the Turks, but the left wing, under the Venetians, turned sturdy resistance into disciplined attack, and the artillery of the galleasses killed thousands of Turks. Don Juan ordered his flagship to steer straight for that of the Ottoman admiral, Muesinade Ali. When they met, the Don's 300 Spanish veterans boarded the Turkish galley; a Capuchin monk led them to the assault, waving a crucifix aloft; the battle was decided when the vessel was captured, and Ali's severed head was hoisted upon his own flagstaff.[14] The morale of the Turks collapsed. Forty of their ships escaped, but 117 were captured and 50 others were sunk or burned. Over 8,000 Turks died in the battle, 10,000 were taken prisoner, and most of these were distributed as slaves among the victors. Some 12,000 Christian slaves, rowing in the Turkish galleys, were freed. The Christians lost 12 galleys and 7,500 men killed, including members of the oldest and most prominent families in Italy. It was unquestionably the greatest naval battle of modern times. Cervantes, who was among the 7,500 wounded Christians, described it as "the most memorable occasion that either past or present ages have beheld, and which perhaps the future will never parallel."*[15]

It should have been the most decisive battle in modern history, but the

---

* Hardly a hundred miles to the northwest, near Actium on the present Gulf of Arta, Octavian with 400 warships had snatched the mastery of the ancient Mediterranean world from Antony and Cleopatra and their 500 men-of-war (September 2, 31 B.C.).

exhaustion of the rowers, the damaged condition of the victorious fleet, and the rise of a violent storm prevented pursuit of the Turks. Quarrels sprang up among the Christians over the distribution of the glory and the spoils. As Spain had contributed half the ships and expense, Venice a third, and the papacy a sixth, the booty was divided accordingly. The Turkish prisoners were allotted in like proportion; Philip II received 3,600 slaves in chains, and out of the Pope's share Don Juan was granted 174 slaves as an honorarium.[16] Some Christian leaders wished to keep as slaves the Christians freed from the Turkish galleys, but Pius V forbade it.[17]

All Catholic Europe rejoiced when news of the triumph arrived. Venice decked itself with garlands and art; men kissed each other when they met in the street; Titian, Tintoretto, and Veronese painted vast pictures of the battle, and the Venetian leader, Sebastiano Veniero, was feted for days and nights and at last was chosen doge. Rome, where, since the departure of the armada from Messina, clergy and laity had spent hours each day in anxious prayer, broke out in Te Deums of joy and relief; and Pius V, organizer of victory, almost canonized Don Juan by applying to him the words of the Gospel: "There was a man sent from God, whose name was John" (John i, 6). Masses were said, fireworks were set off, salvos of artillery were fired. The Pope begged the victors to assemble another fleet; he besought the rulers of Europe to seize the opportunity by uniting in a crusade to drive the Turks out of Europe and the Holy Land. He appealed to the Shah of Persia and Sheik Mutahat of Arabia Felix to join the Christians in the attack upon the Ottomans.[18] But France, jealous of Spain, proposed to the Sultan, soon after Lepanto, a direct alliance against Philip II.*[19] Intelligence of this offer shared with other factors in dissuading Philip from further enterprise against the main Turkish power. He was involved in disputes with England and in the mess that Alva was making in the Netherlands; he resented Venetian insistence on monopolizing trade in the Adriatic, and he feared that another victory over the Turks would rehabilitate the crumbling empire of Venice and strengthen her as a rival to Spain. Pius V, worn out with victory and defeat, died on May 1, 1572, and the Holy League died with him.

III. DECLINE OF THE SULTANS

Meanwhile the Turks, with an energy that dismayed the West, built another fleet, as great as that which had been almost destroyed. Within

---

* In 1536 France had obtained the first Turkish "capitulations," and these had been renewed in 1569. They were not surrenders but a treaty—named from its chapters or headings (*capitula*)—chiefly agreeing that French subjects in Turkish lands should be governed and tried by French law ("extraterritorial jurisdiction"). Turkey signed similar capitulations with England in 1580 and with the United Provinces in 1613.

eight months after Lepanto a Turkish flotilla of 150 ships roamed the seas looking for the Christian armada, which was too disorganized to venture from its havens. Encouraged by all to continue the war, but helped by none, Venice made peace with the Porte (March 7, 1573), not only ceding Cyprus but paying the Sultan an indemnity that covered the cost of the island's conquest. The Turks had lost the battle and won the war. How far they were from enfeeblement appears in the confident proposal made by Sokolli to Venice (1573) that if she joined Turkey in war against Spain, they would help her to conquer the Kingdom of Naples as rich amends for losing Cyprus. Venice rejected the proposal as inviting the Turkish domination of Italy and Christendom. In October Don Juan refurbished his glory by capturing Tunis for Spain; but within a year the Turks, now with a fleet of 250 vessels, recaptured the city, and massacred the Spaniards who had newly settled there; for good measure they raided the coasts of Sicily. Selim II died in 1574, but Sokolli carried on the administration and the war.

It is a problem for philosophers that historians see a decline of Ottoman power in the reign of Murad III (1574–95), who loved philosophers. But he loved women too, and he begot 103 children from not quite so many wives. His favorite wife, "Baffo" the Venetian slave, enslaved him with her charms, mingled in affairs of state, and accepted bribes to use her influence. Sokolli's authority was undermined, and when he aroused fanatical opposition among the populace by proposing to build an observatory in Stamboul, he was assassinated (1579), probably at Murad's behest. Chaos ensued. The currency was debased; the Janissaries mutinied against being paid in bad coin; bribery corroded the bureaucracy; a pasha boasted that he had bribed the Sultan. Murad abandoned himself to venery and died of debauchery.

"Baffo" wielded almost as much influence over her son Mohammed III (1595–1603) as she had over his father. He began his reign in orthodox fashion by murdering nineteen of his brothers as an inducement to domestic peace; but Murad's fertility had made this problem difficult; many of his sons were left dangerously alive. Corruption and disorder spread. War with Austria and Persia annulled victories with defeats. Ahmed I (1603–17), facing the rise of Shah Abbas I as a powerful leader in Persia, decided to concentrate Turkish forces on the eastern front. To free them in the West he ordered his agents to sign with Austria the Peace of Zsitva-Török (1606), the first treaty that the proud Turks condescended to sign outside Constantinople. Austria paid the Sultan 200,000 ducats, but was excused from any further tribute. Transylvania now voluntarily accepted Ottoman suzerainty. Persia too made peace (1611), giving Turkey, as a war indemnity, a million pounds of silk. Altogether this reign was marked with success and sanity, except for continued revolts of the Janissaries.

Ahmed was a man of piety and good will. He tried, and failed, to end the rule of imperial fratricide.

Othman II (1617–22) proposed to discipline and reform the Janissaries; they demurred and killed him. They forced his imbecile brother Mustafa I to take the throne, but Mustafa was sane enough to abdicate (1623) in favor of his twelve-year-old nephew Murad IV (1623–40). The Janissaries chose the grand viziers and slew them whenever it seemed time for a change. They invaded the royal palace and compelled Sultana Kussem to open the treasury vaults to appease them. In 1631 they came again, pursued the young Sultan into his private apartments, and demanded the heads of seventeen officials. One of them, Hafiz, offered himself to the crowd as a sacrifice; they cut him to pieces. Murad, as yet impotent, faced them with what seemed an idle threat: "So help me God, ye men of blood, who fear not Allah, nor are ashamed before his Prophet, a terrible vengeance shall overtake you."[20] He bided his time, formed a corps of loyal troops, and arranged the assassination of one after another of the men who had led the mutinies. Further attempts at rebellion were crushed with savage feroc- ity, and occasionally the Sultan, like Peter the Great, shared personally in carrying out the sentences of death. He killed all of his brothers but one, whom he thought harmlessly imbecile. Reveling in royal authority, he decreed the capital penalty for using tobacco, coffee, opium, or wine. Altogether, we are told, 100,000 persons were executed in his reign, not counting deaths in war.[21] For a moment social order and administrative integrity were restored. Feeling now reasonably secure, Murad took the field against the Persians, accepted himself the challenge of a Persian war- rior to single combat, slew him, captured Baghdad (1638), and concluded a victorious peace. When he returned to Constantinople the populace re- ceived him with wild acclaim. A year later he died of gout brought on by drunkenness. He was twenty-eight years old.

After him the Turkish decline was resumed. Ibrahim I (1640–48) had escaped death from his brother by being, or pretending to be, feeble- minded. Under his careless rule anarchy and corruption were renewed. He made war on Venice and sent an expedition against Crete. The Vene- tians blockaded the Dardanelles. The people of Constantinople began to starve. The army revolted and strangled the Sultan. The Christian West, recalling the story of Rome's Praetorian Guard, concluded that Turkish power need no longer be feared. Within thirty-five years the Turks were again at Vienna's gates.

IV. SHAH ABBAS THE GREAT: 1587-1629

It was a boon to the Christian West that from 1577 to 1638, while first France and then Germany were crippled by the wars of religion, the Turks, who might have pushed their western frontier to Vienna, directed their energies against Persia. Here too religion offered a pretext to disguise the lust for power. The Turks, following the Sunna, or traditional forms of Mohammedanism, denounced as heretics the Persians, who accepted the heterodox Shi'a, and condemned as usurpers all caliphs since Ali, the Prophet's son-in-law. The real *casus belli*, of course, was more abdominal than theological—the desire of ruling minorities for additional land, resources, and taxable population. By a series of persistent wars the Ottoman Turks advanced to the Euphrates, the Caucasus, and the Caspian Sea, absorbing the new Persian capital, Tabriz, and the old Arab capital, Baghdad. Pedro Teixeira described Baghdad, about 1615, as a substantial city of Arabs, Persians, Turks, and Jews, living in twenty thousand brick houses, amid a crowded movement of pack bullocks, camels, horses, asses, and mules; the men cleanly dressed, "many of the women handsome, and nearly all have fine eyes, peering over or through their veils."[22] One public official was entirely devoted to protecting strangers.

East of Baghdad and the Euphrates lay the disunited states of Iran, reaching to the Caucasus and the Caspian on the northwest, to Turkistan on the northeast, Afghanistan on the east, the Indian Ocean on the south, the Persian Gulf on the southeast. These scattered members waited for a unifying soul.

Abbas the Great was the fifth Shah, or king, of that Safavid dynasty which Ismail I had founded at Tabriz in 1502. During the long reign (1524-76) of the second Shah, Tamasp I, the new state suffered many incursions by the Turks. After his death they invaded and annexed the Persian provinces of Iraq, Luristan, and Khuzistan. Meanwhile the Uzbeks came down from Transoxiana, captured Herat, Mashhad, and Nishapur, and overran Persia's eastern provinces. When Abbas, aged thirty, succeeded to the throne without a capital (1587), he made peace with the Turks and marched eastward to meet the lesser foe. After years of war he recaptured Herat and drove the Uzbeks from Persia. He was now eager to face the Turks, but his army was depleted by losses, disordered by tribal jealousies, and lacking in the latest means of inflicting death.

About this time (1598) two adventurous Englishmen, Sir Anthony Sherley and his younger brother Robert, arrived in Persia on a trade mission from England. They brought valuable presents, military experience, and an expert founder of cannon. With their help Shah Abbas reorganized his army, equipped it with muskets as well as swords, and soon had five hundred pieces of artillery. He led this new force against the Turks, drove them from Tabriz (1603), and recovered Erivan, Shirvan, and Kars. The Turks sent against him an avalanche of 100,000 men; Abbas, with 60,000, defeated them (1605); Azerbaijan, Kurdistan, Mosul, and Baghdad were recovered, and Abbas ruled from the Euphrates to the Indus.

Even before these arduous campaigns he had begun (1598) to build a new capital farther removed than Tabriz from invaders, and less desecrated with alien memories and Sunni feet. Isfahan was already two thousand years old (though not under that name), and had 80,000 population. About a mile from this ancient city the Shah had his engineers lay out a rectangular space as the Maidan-i-Shah, or Royal Square, 1,674 feet long, 540 wide, and bordered with trees. On two sides ran promenades covered against rain and sun. On the south side rose the Masjid-i-Shah, the Royal Mosque; on the east, the Mosque of Lutf Allah and a royal palace; the remainder of the periphery was occupied by shops, inns, and schools. West of the *maidan* ran an avenue two hundred feet wide, the Chahar Bagh ("Four Gardens"), flanked by trees and gardens, and adorned with pools and fountains. On either side of this parkway were the palaces of the ministers of state. Through the city flowed the River Zayand, spanned by three masonry bridges; one of these, the Allah Verdi Khan, was a picturesque structure 1,164 feet long, with a broad paved roadway and on each side arcades for pedestrians. The new town was watered and cooled with streams, reservoirs, fountains, and cascades. The whole design was as excellent a piece of town planning as that age anywhere knew.[23]

When Chardin visited Isfahan in 1673 he was astonished to find a great metropolis of administration, commerce, crafts, and arts, with 1,500 villages surrounding it and an urban population of 300,000 souls. The city and its suburbs had 162 mosques, 48 colleges, 273 public baths, and 1,800 cara-vanserais, or inns. Tavernier, seeing Isfahan in 1664, described it as equaling Paris in extent, but only a tenth as populous, for every family had its own house and garden, and there were so many trees that it seemed "rather a forest than a city."[24] It is a pleasant picture, but Tavernier adds, "There are before every door certain troughs to receive the filth and ordure of each family, which the peasants come daily to carry away to dung their grounds. . . . You shall also meet with little holes against the walls of the houses in the open street, where the Persians are not ashamed to squat and urinate in sight of all the world."[25]

Alert to the fact that Western Europe was grateful to him for keeping the Turks busy in the East, Shah Abbas sent Sir Anthony Sherley and others on missions to establish relations with Christian governments, and to open up exports of Persian silk free from Turkish intermediaries. When

European envoys came to Isfahan he housed them palatially and gave them full religious freedom. Having captured five thousand Armenians in his Turkish campaigns, he did not enslave them, but allowed them to develop their own center at Julfa, near Isfahan; and he profited from their commercial activity and finesse. There they built their own church and decorated it with a mixture of Christian iconography and Moslem decoration. Sometimes Abbas played with the idea of fusing all religions into one and "imposing peace in heaven and on earth."[26] In a more realistic mood he used the Shi'a fervor of the Persians as a means of national morale. He encouraged his people to make pilgrimages to Mashhad as the Mecca of Persian Islam, and he himself walked the eight hundred miles from Isfahan to Mashhad to offer his devotions and gifts.

Therefore the architecture with which he made Isfahan gleam was chiefly religious; like the medieval Church in the West, he would transmute the pennies of the poor into temples whose grandeur, beauty, and peace would be a pride and a possession for all. The most impressive structure in the new capital was the Masjid-i-Shah, which Abbas built in 1611–29. The *maidan* is its majestic plaza and approach; the whole square seems to lead to that embracing portal. The eye is caught first by the flanking minarets and their lacery of overhanging turrets, from which the muezzin proclaims the unity of God; then by the resplendent faïence that covers the portal frame, and by the inscription frieze offering this shrine as a gift from Abbas to Allah; in Persia even the alphabet is art. Within the arch the walls are clustered with stalactites spangled with white flowers. Then the inner court, open to the sun; then through further arches into the sanctuary under the great dome. One must go outside again to study the dome, its majestic Kufic lettering, its swelling and yet graceful form, faced with enameled tiles of blue and green flowing in arabesques over an azure ground. Despite the enmity of time this is "even now one of the most beautiful buildings in the world."[27]

Less imposing, more delicate, is the mosque that Shah Abbas raised (1603–18) in honor of his saintly father-in-law, the Masjid-i-Sheikh-Lutf-Allah: an elegant portal, a sanctuary and mihrab of exquisite faïence, but, above all, an interior of incredible beauty—arabesques, geometrical figures, flowers, and scrolls in perfect, unified design. Here is abstract art, but with a logic and structure and consequence that offer the mind no bewildering chaos, but intelligible order and mental peace.

On the east side of the *maidan* the Shah built an open throne under a great arch, the Ala Kapi, or Sublime Portal; there he gave audience, or watched the horse races or polo matches in the *maidan*.* Behind this gate

---

* The marble goalposts still stand in the square. The game of polo came to Europe from Persia.

were the royal gardens, containing several palaces used by the Shah for special purposes. One of these survives, much chastised by time: the Chihil Sutun (Forty Columns), an audience chamber and throne room supported by twenty plane-tree columns faced with mirror glass, and a long gallery adorned with oil paintings depicting events in the life of the Shah. The doors of the palace were of lacquered wood decorated with garden scenes and floral scrolls; two of these doors are in the Metropolitan Museum of Art. Still in place is the brilliant stucco decoration, in gilt and colors, of the audience chamber ceiling; here again abstract art is brought to perfection in logic and design.

From his many palaces, and from his camp, Shah Abbas directed the life of his expanding realm. Like most great rulers, he interested himself in every phase of his people's life. He built roads and bridges and had miles of road paved with stone. He encouraged manufactures, foreign trade, and the extraction of minerals from the soil. He built dams, spread irrigation, brought clean water to the towns. He restored injured cities—Mashhad, Qasvin, Tabriz, Hamadan. "He often disguised himself," said Tavernier, "and went about Isfahan like an ordinary inhabitant, under pretense of buying and selling, making it his business to discover whether merchants used false weights or measures. . . . Finding two culprits, he had them buried alive."[28] This was the Oriental way of establishing law: in the imperfection of surveillance and police, severity of punishment aimed to check the natural lawlessness of men. Probably a long career in war accentuated in Shah Abbas this use of cruelty as deterrent or revenge; he killed one of his sons and blinded another.[29] Yet this same man composed poetry, financed many charities, and supported many arts.

His death (1629) ended the zenith of Safavid art and rule, but the order that his co-ordinated energy had built endured for almost another century. Despite a succession of weak shahs, the Safavid dynasty maintained itself till its cataclysmic collapse under the Afghan conquest of Persia (1722–30). And even in that period of political decline Safavid art continued to rank among the most refined products of human taste and skill.

V. SAFAVID PERSIA: 1576–1722

Let us look at the Safavid period from the death of Tamasp I (1576) to its end in 1722, for this is a cultural development that cannot be cut to fit European chronology. Several Occidental travelers have left us illuminating accounts of Persia in this age: Pedro Teixeira, who was there in 1600; the Jesuit Father Kiusinski, who lived in Isfahan from 1702 to 1722 and wrote a *History of the Revolution of Persia*, covering the whole Safavid dynasty;

Jean Tavernier, who described at length his travels (1631–68) in Turkey, Persia, India, and the East Indies; and Jean Chardin, who reported in ten volumes his stay in Persia from 1664 to 1677. Though he encountered the simoon near the gulf, Chardin fell in love with Iran; he preferred Isfahan to Paris in summertime, and found such "an exquisite beauty in the air of Persia" that, he wrote, "I can neither forget it myself, nor forbear mentioning it to everybody"; he thought that the clear Persian sky had influenced Persian art to brilliance of luster and color and had happily affected the Persians in body and mind.*[30] He believed that the Persians had profited from their mixture with the people of Georgia and the Caucasus, whom he rated the handsomest and bravest in the world—but not quite as handsome as a Persian horse.[31]

This once fertile Eden, home of jeweled caliphs and melodious poets, had been ruined by Mongol incursions, disruptions of government, the neglect and silting of lifeblood canals, the shifting of trade routes; and the discovery of an all-water passage from Western Europe to India and China had left Persia commercially becalmed. Some trade, however, moved down the rivers to the Persian Gulf. In 1515 the Portuguese captured Hormuz, the leading gulf port, and they held it for a century; but in 1622 the army of Shah Abbas, aided by the ships of the English East India Company, expelled the Portuguese from Hormuz; the Shah built another commercial depot nearby at Bandar Abbas (the Port of Abbas), and the trade that developed there helped to finance the art and luxury of his reign. Caravans still passed from the West to the East through Persia, and left some wealth in the towns on their way. Teixeira described Aleppo as a city of 26,000 homes—many of them built of well-wrought stone, and some fit for princes—with a population of Moslems, Christians, and Jews; it had clean and handsome public baths, and several streets were paved with marble slabs.[32]

Most industry was still in the handicraft stage—medieval, painstaking, artistic, slow; but Aleppo had a silk factory, and tobacco was grown throughout the land. According to Chardin the Persians had a filter system for smoking: they passed the smoke through water, and thereby it was "purged of all the oily and gross qualities of the tobacco."[33] Smoking became a necessity to the Persians; "they had rather go without their dinners than their pipes."[34] Shah Abbas was an exception; he despised the habit and tried to cure his courtiers of it with a trick. He had horse manure dried and substituted for tobacco in the vessels from which they filled their pipes; he explained that this was a costly product presented to him by the vizier of Hamadan. They smoked it and praised it to the skies; "it smells

---

* Cf. Cicero (De fato, 7) on "Athens' clear air," which "is said to have contributed to the keenness of the Attic mind."

like a thousand flowers," vowed one guest. "Cursed be that drug," cried
Shah Abbas, "that cannot be distinguished from the dung of horses."[35]

Any man gifted with ability and courtesy could rise to a place in the
Shah's court; there was no aristocracy of birth.[36] In all classes and sexes
dress was essentially the same: a robe reaching to the knees, tight sleeves,
a broad girdle (sometimes of flowered silk) around the waist, a silk or
cotton shirt under the robe, breeches gathered at the ankles, and a turban
topping all. The women were "very richly habited," wrote Tavernier, and
"little otherwise than the men. . . . They wear breeches like the men."[37] The
women lived in the privacy of the zenana, seldom stirring from their
homes, and then rarely on foot. There were three sexes. Much of the love
poetry was addressed by men to boys, and Thomas Herbert, an Englishman
at Abbas' court, saw "Ganymede boys in vests of gold, rich bespangled
turbans, and choice sandals, their curled hair dangling about their shoulders,
with rolling eyes and vermilion cheeks."[38]

Chardin noted a decrease in population in his time and ascribed it to

> *First*, the unhappy inclination which the Persians have, to commit
> that abominable sin against nature, with both sexes.
> *Secondly*, the immoderate luxury [sexual freedom] of the country.
> The women begin there to have children betimes, and continue fruit-
> ful but a little while; and as soon as they get on the wrong side of
> thirty they are looked upon as old and superannuated. The men like-
> wise begin to visit women too young, and to such an excess, that
> though they enjoy several, they have never the more children for
> it. There are also a great many women who make themselves abortive,
> and take remedies against growing pregnant, because [when] they
> have been three or four months gone with child, their husbands take
> to other women, holding it . . . indecency to lie with a woman so far
> in her time.[39]

Despite polygamy there were many prostitutes. Drunkenness was widespread, though Mohammedan law forbade wine. Coffee shops abounded;
the plant received its European from its Arabic name, *qahwah*.[40] Cleanliness
was more common in person than in speech; bathhouses were numerous
and were sometimes artistically adorned, but there was much profanity and
obscenity.[41] "Great dissemblers and flatterers," Tavernier called them, and
they were much given to cheating, reports Chardin, but he adds, "They
are the most kind people in the world," tolerant and hospitable, with "the
most engaging ways, the most complying temper, the smoothest . . . tongues
. . . altogether the most civilized people of the East."[42] They were fond of
music, and usually their poets sang the poems they had composed.

We may judge the excellence of the Persian poets from their popularity at the court of the Moguls in Delhi, but none of them in this period found a Fitzgerald to phrase them for Western ears. We learn that Urfi of Shiraz was at the top of Persian poetry in the sixteenth century; he thought himself at least superior to Sa'di; but which of us provincials has ever heard of him? His verses were better liked than himself, as we gather from the "friends" who came to enjoy his mortal illness:

> My body hath fallen into this state, and my eloquent friends
>   stand like pulpits round my bed and pillow.
> One draws his hand through his beard and cocks his neck,
>   saying, "O life of thy father! To whom is fortune constant?
> One should not set one's heart on ignoble rank and wealth;
>   where is the Empire of Jamshid and the name of Alexander?"
> Another, with soft voice and sad speech, begins, drawing his
>   sleeve across his moist eyes:
> "O my life! All have this road by which they must depart;
>   we are all travelers on the road, and time bears forward
>   the riders."
> Another, adorning his speech with smoother words, says . . .
> "Collect thyself . . . let not thy heart be troubled, for I
>   will with single purpose collect thy verse and prose.
> After copying and correcting it, I will compose an introduction
>   like a casket of pearls in support of thy claims." . . .
> May God . . . give me health again, and thou shalt see what
>   wrath I will pour on the heads of these miserable
>   hypocrites![43]

Urfi's rival in rhyme was Sa'ib of Isfahan. He followed the fashion of migrating to Delhi, as French and Flemish artists of that age went to Rome. But after two years he returned to Isfahan, and became poet laureate to Shah Abbas II (1642–66). He was something of a philosopher, fertile in fragments of measured wisdom:

> All this talk of infidelity and religion finally leads to one place;
> The dream is the same dream, only the interpretations differ . . .
> The cure for the unpleasant constitution of the world is to ignore it;
> Here he is awake who is plunged in heavy sleep . . .
> The wave is ignorant of the true nature of the sea;
> How can the temporal comprehend the eternal? . . .
> The only thing that troubles me about the Resurrection Day is this,
> That one will have to look again upon the faces of mankind.[44]

If the music of Persian poetry eludes us, the enjoyment of Safavid art is not beyond our reach, for here is a speech that all can understand. The skill, finesse, and taste that had been formed in Iran through two thousand years now flowered in architecture, pottery, illumination, calligraphy, woodcarving, metalwork, textiles, tapestries, and rugs, that are among the prizes of the world's museums today. The best architecture of the age, as we have noted, was under Abbas I at Isfahan. There the second of his name built the Talar Ashraf (1642); and there, in the twilight of the Safavids, Shah Husein raised the Madrasa Madar-i-Shah—the College of the Mother of the Shah—which Lord Curzon rated "one of the stateliest ruins in Persia."[45] But other cities boasted new architectural achievements: the Madrasa-i-Khan at Shiraz, the great mausoleum of Kwaja Rabi at Mashhad, the now ruined but still lovely shrine of Qadam-Gah at Nisha-pur, and the Blue Mosque of Erivan.

Shah Abbas I founded at Isfahan an academy of painting, where students were required, as part of their discipline, to copy famous miniatures, in which beauty of design and delicacy of drawing predominated over the subjects and the figures. Now—apparently under European influence—the secular painters allowed themselves to deviate from orthodox Moham-medan custom by making miniatures in which a human figure stood out as the major theme. Here the sequence inverted the Italian; in the painting of the Renaissance the landscape was at first neglected, then it became incidental background, then (perhaps as individualism declined under the Counter Reformation) it predominated over the figures; but in Islamic painting the human figure was at first excluded, then it was permitted as incidental, and only in the later stages (perhaps as individualism grew with wealth) did it predominate in the design. So in *The Falconer*[46] a green-robed noble sports a bird on his wrist, against a minor background of golden flowers; and in *The Poet Seated in a Garden*[47] every detail reveals the characteristic Persian elegance. Another innovation developed mural painting, of which we have seen an example in the Chihil Sutun. But the great masters still devoted themselves chiefly to the adornment of the Koran, or the illustration of literary classics like Firdausi's *Shahnama* or Sa'di's *Gulistan*—which Mawlana Hasan of Baghdad illuminated in liquid gold.

Supreme in the painting of this second Safavid period was Riza-i-Abbasi, who added the Shah's name to his own in gratitude for royal patronage. For a generation his renown was brighter than Bihzad's. After him the art declined; the sensitivity of the artist and the refinement or subtlety of his design passed into effeminate excess. Meanwhile the Persian style, having itself felt a Chinese influence, affected in turn the miniature painting at the court of the Moguls, and even their architecture. Grousset thought that the Taj Mahal was "but a new chapter in the art of Isfahan."[48]

Calligraphy was still a major art in Persia; Mir Imad was almost as loved by Shah Abbas for his meticulous copies of older manuscripts as Riza-i-Abbasi for his miniatures. Books were cherished for their form as well as their content; a beautiful binding delighted eyes and touch quite as much as a delicate vase. Artists signed covers as proudly as paintings; so a gold-stamped leather binding of the early seventeenth century is inscribed "the work of Muhammud Salih Tabrizi";[49] and a cover of papier-mâché, painted in lacquer, is signed "Ali Riza" and is dated 1713.[50] Both are temptingly beautiful.

In the Persian cities it is the painted tiles that, next to the domes, or on them, strike the eye; and their age arouses wonder at the ceramic art that could give such permanence to such brilliance. This immortalizing of color by glazing it with fire was an old skill in Persia; the glazed tiles of Achaemenid Susa (400 B.C.) were already perfect in their kind. Alloys of gold, silver, copper, and other metals were fused to make more lustrous colors, especially in ruby red and turquoise blue; and a double firing hardened the clay and the glaze against the bite of centuries. The Armenians probably employed Persian potters to make the tiles in their Christian church at Julfa—as delicate in design as a miniature. Even more beautiful are the painted tiles in the Kevorkian Collection, ascribed to Isfahan and the second half of the seventeenth century.[51]

The potters continued, at Isfahan, Kashan, and elsewhere, to make luster-ware—bottles, bowls, vases, plates, flagons, cups—painted under glaze in varied colors on divers grounds. Mosaic faïence became a favorite material to cover the walls of mosques and palaces. Shah Abbas imported Chinese porcelain and his potters tried to duplicate it, but they lacked the precise soils and skills. Again under the prodding of the ruler, attempts were made at Isfahan and Shiraz to rival Venetian glass. The metalworkers excelled in carving and inlaying brass; a good example, dated 1579, is a Persian candlestick in the Metropolitan Museum of Art. In the Hermitage at Leningrad is a saber sheath of gold encrusted with large and finely cut emeralds.

Textiles were a major industry and art. Designers, weavers, and dyers occupied a large section of Isfahan and were numbered in the thousands. Their products formed the staple of the export trade, giving Persia a world-wide reputation for satins, velvets, taffetas, embroideries, and silks. When Abbas wished to confer a special gift he usually chose some masterpiece of the Persian looms; "The numbers of garments he thus bestows is infinite," reported Chardin.[52] The Shah and his court were dressed, on ceremonial occasions, in silks and brocades whose beauty seemed to Chardin unequaled by any court costumes in Europe. "The art of dyeing," he wrote, "seems to have been more improved in Persia than in Europe, their colors being much more solid and bright, and not fading so soon."[53] The velvets of Kashan were unrivaled anywhere; some fragments are among the trophies in the museums of Boston, New York, San Francisco, and Washington. One of the prizes captured by the Christian armies in the repulse of the Turks from Vienna (1683) was a carpet of brocaded silk velvet, apparently made in Isfahan under Shah Abbas.[54]

Persian textiles reached their apogee in the design and weaving of rugs, and the age of Shah Abbas saw the final glory of this art in Iran. A carpet was almost as necessary to a Persian as his clothing. Thomas Herbert reported, in the seventeenth century: "In their houses they have little furniture or household stuff, except it be their carpets and some copper works. . . . They eat on the ground, sitting on carpets cross-legged, as do tailors. There is no man so simple but he sitteth on a carpet better or worse; and the whole house or room . . . is wholly covered with carpets."[55] Colors ran now to deep scarlet or wine red; but to balance this exuberance the design was restful, if only because it carried out with satisfying logic some basic theme. This might be geometrical, and endless were the variations that here made Euclid beautiful. More often the design was floral, bringing to the eye, in rich but orderly array, the favorite products of a Persian garden— flowers in vases or loosely strewn, or flowers imagined rather than seen, with leisurely, gracefully trailing arabesques. Sometimes the garden itself provided the design: trees, shrubs, flower beds, and flowing water were disciplined into geometry. Or the design was centered around a large medallion dangling pendants to each end; or it might display animals in frolic or the chase.

Then came infinite labor and patience: stretching the threads in a vertical warp on the loom, interweaving them with the horizontal threads of the weft, and sewing little knots of colored wool or silk into the warp to form the "pile" and the design; there might be 1,200 knots in a square inch, or 90,000,000 in a rug twenty-three feet square.[56] Slavery seems woven into this art, but the worker prided himself on the accuracy and finesse of his work, transforming the chaos of his materials into an order and harmony and hierarchy of parts in a whole. Such rugs were made at a dozen centers in Persia, Afghanistan, and the Caucasus, to grace palaces, mosques, and homes, and to serve as precious gifts to potentates or friends.

Persian carpets and Persian illumination went through similar developments in the sixteenth and seventeenth centuries: they received a Chinese influence in "cloud" and other designs, they in their turn influenced the arts in Turkey and India, and they reached their final peak of excellence under the Safavids. By 1790 the production of Persian rugs was on a quantity basis, hurriedly designed and woven for a larger and less exacting market, chiefly European. Even then, however, there were some exceptional pieces unequaled in texture, color, and design anywhere in the world.

Such was Persia, such was Islam, in this last flowering of their power and art—a civilization profoundly unlike ours of the West, and at times contemptuously hostile, denouncing us as polytheists and materialists, laughing at our matriarchal monogamy, and sometimes coming in avalanches to batter down our gates; we could not be expected to understand it, or admire its art, when the great debate was between Moslem and Christian, not yet between Darwin and Christ. The competition of the cultures is not over, but for the most part it has ceased to shed blood, and they are now free to mingle in the osmosis of mutual influence. The East takes on our industries and armaments and becomes Western, the West wearies of wealth and war and seeks inner peace. Perhaps we shall help the East to mitigate poverty and superstition, and the East will help us to humility in philosophy and refinement in art. East is West and West is East, and soon the twain will meet.

CHAPTER XXI

Imperial Armageddon

1564-1648

I. THE EMPERORS

IN 1564 the Holy Roman Empire, though, as Voltaire said, it was none of these, was an imposing motley of semi-independent states: Germany, Luxembourg, Franche-Comté, Lorraine, Switzerland, Austria, Bohemia, Moravia, and part of Hungary. All these acknowledged as their head Emperor Maximilian II of the ancient house of Hapsburg, which had ruled the Empire since 1438 and would continue to rule it till 1808. After the abdication of Charles V (1555–56) the family divided half of Europe between its two branches: the Austrian Hapsburgs reigned over the Empire, the Spanish Hapsburgs reigned over Spain and its dependencies. Rarely in history has one family held power so long over so many men.

The rule of the Hapsburgs was more liberal in the Empire than in Spain, because the constituent states differed so widely in government, economy, language, religion, and ethnic character that even Hapsburg power and prestige could not keep these centrifugal forces from making the Empire a loose association of proudly self-governed units. The Imperial Diet, meeting occasionally, found it easier to check the authority of the emperor than to make laws that would be accepted by all the states; and the seven Imperial electors who chose the emperor controlled him by the pledges exacted from him as the price of his election. These electors were the king of Bohemia, the rulers of Saxony, Brandenburg, and the Palatinate, and the "spiritual electors"—the archbishops of Cologne, Trier, and Mainz. The emperor ruled directly only Austria, Styria, Carinthia, Carniola, and the Tirol, at times also Bohemia, Moravia, Silesia, and western Hungary. His independent revenues were from these lands; for anything more he had to come hat in hand to the Imperial Diet, which held the power of the purse.

When Ferdinand I (brother of Charles V) died in 1564, the electors transmitted the Imperial crown to his son Maximilian II, who had already received the crowns of Bohemia and Hungary. He was too lovable to be an emperor. Everyone basked in the sunshine of his good nature and good humor, his kindness and courtesy to all classes, his open mind and heart; add his intelligence and toleration, his encouragement of science, music, and

art, and a picture emerges of a gentleman incredibly crowned. He had
endangered his accession by preferring Lutheran to Catholic preachers, and
insisting on wine as well as bread in receiving the Sacrament; and only
when he had to choose between returning to the Roman Church and retiring to private life did he conform, outwardly, to the Catholic observance.
Meanwhile he protected the Protestants from persecution. He condemned
the Massacre of St. Bartholomew as mass murder,[1] and allowed William of
Orange to levy troops in Germany to fight Alva in the Netherlands. In
an age of intolerance and war he gave to the states and creeds of the
Empire a remarkable example of toleration without indifference and of
peace without cowardice. On his deathbed (1576) he refused to receive
the last rites from the Church of Rome, but all the Empire joined in
blessing his memory.

He had persuaded the electors to accept his son Rudolf as his successor,
though he must have seen in him some traits of character, or effects of
education, dangerous to religious concord. Rudolf II was by temperament
suspicious and somber. As a possible heir to Philip II he had been sent to
Spain for part of his schooling, and the Jesuits there had disabled him for
toleration. Soon after his accession he severely restricted the freedom and
the area of Protestant worship, alleging, with some reason,[2] that the
violence of religious controversy and the mutual intolerance of the
Protestant sects were undermining the peace and stability of the Empire.
But he was not entirely wanting in the qualities that had made his father
loved. He lived in a modest simplicity, assuming no imperial airs. When one
of his brothers condemned his familiarity with people of humble station,
he replied, "Though elevated above others by our dignity and birth, we
ought not to forget that we are allied to the rest of mankind by our weaknesses and defects."[3]

Indeed, he preferred to be a savant rather than an emperor. He learned
half a dozen languages, practiced almost every science and art, made
valuable collections of pictures and statuary, botanical varieties and zoological specimens. He helped poets and historians, and founded many
schools. He became proficient in mathematics, physics, chemistry, astronomy, and medicine, but also in alchemy and astrology; he financed the
astronomic researches of Tycho Brahe and Kepler, who dedicated to him
their Rudolphine tables of the stars. Absorbed in science in his palace at
Prague—which he made his capital—he found no time for marriage,
and not much for government. After 1594 he attended no meeting of the
Diet; after 1598 he refused to sign official papers and delegated his authority
to incompetent favorites. As his years mounted his mind deteriorated, not
into insanity, but into a brooding, melancholy isolation haunted by fear of
assassination. He had dreamed—or Tycho Brahe had read in the stars[4]—

that his murderer would be a monk; so he came to distrust all Catholic ecclesiastics, and especially the Jesuits.[5] Under compulsions internal and
external, he resigned to his younger brother Matthias in 1608 the government of Austria, Hungary, and Moravia, and in 1611 the throne of Bohemia
and all his remaining powers. In 1612 he died.

Matthias was already fifty-five, too wearied with campaigns to enjoy
active rule. He entrusted both administration and policy to Melchior Klesl,
the able and conscientious Bishop of Vienna. Klesl offended the Catholics
by concessions to the Protestants, and offended the Protestants by conced-
ing too little. Matthias' cousin Ferdinand, Archduke of Styria, imprisoned
Klesl (1618), and secured his own election to the Imperial authority soon
after Matthias' death (1619). By that time Armageddon had begun.

II. THE EMPIRE

Switzerland was only formally a part of the Empire; lusty victories
against the emperors and the archdukes had left the cantons free to quarrel
among themselves. Savoy and Spain joined the Catholic cantons, led by
Lucerne, in diplomatic or martial efforts to recover the Protestant cantons
for the Roman Church. The Jesuits, from their college at Lucerne, began in
1577 a resolute campaign of education, preaching, and intrigue. Papal
nuncios in Switzerland reformed abuses in the Catholic clergy, ended clerical concubinage, and stemmed the Protestant influences that were spreading from Zurich, Geneva, and Bern.

Geneva was slowly recovering from Calvin. Théodore de Bèze succeeded his master (1564) as head of the Venerable Company (of pastors)
and the Consistory (of pastors and laymen), and through them he carried
on the work of the Reformed Church with tact and courtesy that only
the *odium theologicum* could disrupt. He traveled into France to attend
Calvinistic synods, and we have seen him presenting the case for Protestantism in the Colloquy of Poissy. At home he strove, not quite successfully,
to maintain the austere morality that Calvin had imposed. As business
leaders diverged more and more from that code, Bèze led the clergy in
denouncing usury, monopoly, and profiteering; and when the city council
suggested that preachers confine themselves to religion, Bèze argued
that nothing human should be alien to religious control.[6] He was the only
one of the great Reformation leaders to survive into the seventeenth century, dying in 1608 at the age of eighty-nine.

Austria's role in the Empire was central. It was usually the home of the
emperors; it was the bulwark of Western civilization against the ambitious

Turks; it was a bastion of the Counter Reformation, and the seat of Catholic power in the Thirty Years' War. And yet it had for a time wavered between Catholicism and Protestantism, even between Christianity and unbelief. During the reign of Ferdinand I (1556–64) the Lutheran catechism was adopted in most Austrian parishes; Lutheranism prevailed in the University of Vienna; the Austrian Diet allowed Communion in both kinds and the marriage of the clergy. "It was considered a sign of an enlightened mind to despise Christian interment, and to be buried without the assistance of a priest . . . and without a cross." A preacher reckoned in 1567, "Thousands and tens of thousands in the towns—yea, even in the villages—no longer believe in God."[7] Fearing the collapse of religious support to the Austrian government and the Hapsburg power, Emperor Ferdinand summoned Peter Canisius and other Jesuits to the University of Vienna. Under their lead Catholicism began to recover ground, for these trained men combined patient subtlety of intellect with an impressive simplicity of life. By 1598 the Roman Church was again predominant.

A like transformation came over Christian Hungary. Two thirds of Hungary had been under Turkish rule since 1526; the Turkish frontier was less than a hundred miles from Vienna, and peace with Turkey was preserved only by an annual tribute paid till 1606 by the emperors to the sultans. Transylvania, lying northeast of Turkish Hungary, paid similar tribute, but in 1606 its prince, Stephen Bocskay, dying childless, bequeathed the province to the Hapsburgs.

The Diet of Austrian Hungary, controlled by nobles eager to appropriate Catholic Church property,[8] had since 1526 favored the Reformation. Under the religious freedom that they maintained, Protestantism won ascendancy among the literate classes. Soon it divided into Lutheranism, Calvinism, and Unitarianism, and the Unitarians divided into smaller sects over the propriety of addressing prayers to Christ. The nobles, now secure in their appropriations, saw no further reason for Protestantism. They welcomed Peter Pazmany and other Jesuits, accepted exemplary conversion, expelled Protestant pastors,[9] and replaced them with Catholic priests. In 1618 Archduke Ferdinand of Styria became King of Hungary, and actively furthered the Counter Reformation. In the Diet of 1625 the Catholics regained the majority. Pazmany, son of a Calvinist, became a cardinal and one of the most eloquent Hungarian authors of the age.

Bohemia and its dependencies—Moravia, Silesia, and Lusatia—were in 1560 predominantly Protestant. All four states acknowledged the king of Bohemia as their sovereign, but each had its own national assembly, laws, and capital—Prague, Brünn (Brno), Breslau, Bautzen. Prague was already one of the most flourishing and picturesque cities in Europe. In the Bohemian Diet only the 1,400 landed proprietors could vote, but its membership included burgher and peasant representatives whose control of the purse gave them an influence beyond words. Most of the nobles were Lutherans; most of the burghers were Lutherans or Calvinists; most of the peasants were Catholics, but a minority were "Utraquists" who in 1587 renounced their Hussite traditions, insisted only on receiving the Sacrament in both kinds, and finally (1593) made their peace with the Roman Church. Most sincere of the religious groups was the Unitas Fratrum—the Bohemian or Moravian Brethren—who took the Sermon on the Mount seriously, shunned all modes of life but agriculture, and lived in peaceful Tolstoyan simplicity.

In 1555 Ferdinand I brought the Jesuits into Bohemia. They established a college at Prague, brought up a cadre of fervent Catholics, and won over many nobles who had married Catholic wives.[10] Rudolf II issued edicts banishing first the Bohemian Brethren, then the Calvinists, but he lacked the means to enforce these decrees. In 1609 the Protestants prevailed upon him to sign a famous *Majestätsbrief*, or Royal Charter, guaranteeing the freedom of Protestant worship in Bohemia. Two years later Rudolf yielded the crown to Matthias, who removed the Imperial capital to Vienna, leaving Prague offended and rebellious. In 1617 the Bohemian Diet, increasingly Catholic though the country was still predominantly Protestant,[11] acknowledged as king of Bohemia Archduke Ferdinand of Styria, who had been educated by the Jesuits and had vowed to eradicate Protestantism wherever he ruled. The Bohemian Protestants prepared for war.

Germany was a confusion within a complexity: not a nation but a name, a medley of principalities agreeing in language and economy, but jealously diverging in customs, government, currencies, and creeds.* Each of these units acknowledged no superior except the emperor, and ignored him fifty weeks in the year. Some foreigners found consolation in this division of Germany; "If it were entirely subject to one monarchy," wrote Sir

---

* In the sixteenth century Germany was divided into seven administrative "circles":
1. Franconia, including Würzburg, Bamberg, and Bayreuth.
2. Bavaria, including Munich, Regensburg (Ratisbon), and Salzburg.
3. Swabia, including Baden, Stuttgart, Augsburg, and the duchy of Württemberg.
4. Upper Rhine, including Frankfurt am Main, Cassel, Darmstadt, Wiesbaden, the county of Nassau, the landgraviate of Hesse, the duchy of Lorraine, and part of Alsace.
5. Lower Rhine, including Westphalia, Jülich and Cleves, the Palatinate, and the archbishoprics of Cologne, Trier, and Mainz.
6. Lower Saxony, including Mecklenburg, Bremen, Magdeburg, and the duchies of Brunswick-Lüneburg and Holstein.
7. Upper Saxony, including Leipzig, Berlin, the duchy of West Pomerania, and the electorates of Saxony and Brandenburg.

Thomas Overbury in 1609, "it would be terrible to all the rest" of Europe.[12] Even for Germany it was in many ways a pleasant arrangement. It weakened her in political and military competition with unified states, but it gave her a local liberty, a religious and cultural variety that the Germans might reasonably prefer to such centralized and exhausting autocracies as those of Philip II in Spain and Louis XIV in France. Here was no tyrannical pullulating Paris sucking the lifeblood of a country, but a galaxy of famous cities each of which had its own character and vitality.

Despite this kaleidoscope of great towns and petty courts, Germany no longer enjoyed the economic ascendancy that she had held in northern Europe before Luther. The discovery of an all-water route from Western Europe to India, and the opening of the Atlantic to trade, had benefited first Portugal and Spain, then England and the Netherlands; they had injured Italy, which had formerly dominated trade with the East; and the German rivers and towns that had carried commerce from Italy to the north shared in the Italian decline. On the North Sea the ports of the Netherlands, on the Baltic those of Denmark and Poland, took most of the trade and the fees. The Hanseatic League had long since lost its old ascendancy. Lübeck was ruined in its long war with Sweden (1563–70). Only Frankfurt am Main retained its prosperity; its annual fair continued to be the best-attended in Europe, and made the city the center of Germany's domestic trade and international finance.

Money was as popular as ever. Edicts forbidding interest rates above 5 per cent were evaded everywhere. "The godless vice of usury," said a priest in 1585, "is practiced more zealously now by the Christians than formerly by the Jews." An "unchristian love of gold," complained a preacher in 1581, "has seized upon everybody and all classes. Whoever has anything to stake, instead of engaging in honest and strenuous work . . . thinks to grow rich . . . by all sorts of speculation, money dealing, and usurious contracts."[13] Hundreds of working people invested their savings with the Fuggers, the Welsers, or the Hochstetters, and were wiped out in repeated bankruptcies. In 1572 the banking firm of Loitz Brothers went bankrupt after gathering great sums from simple investors, who now lost their savings, even their homes.[14] The Fuggers were ruined by the bankruptcies of Philip II and Alva, whom they had helped to finance.[15] The Welsers failed in 1614, owing 586,000 gulden. Perhaps fear of inflation had driven people into such investments, for nearly every German prince stole from his people by debasing the currency, and counterfeiters and coin clippers abounded. By 1600 all German currencies were in a disgraceful chaos.

Population rose while production lagged, and misery verged on revolution. In all but Saxony and Bavaria the peasants were driven into

serfdom. In Pomerania, Brandenburg, Schleswig, Holstein, and Mecklenburg serfdom was established by law in or soon after 1616.[16] "In what
German land," asked a writer in 1598, "does the German peasant still
enjoy his old rights? Where does he have any use or profit of the common
fields, meadows, or forests? Where is there any limit to the number
of feudal services or dues? Where has the peasant his own tribunal? God
have pity on him!"[17] Many peasants went to work in the bowels of the
earth, but the profits and real wages of mining declined as American silver
entered Germany to compete with metal laboriously extracted from exhausted lodes. In the towns the old guild comradeship gave place to the
exploitation of journeymen (day laborers) by masters. In some industries
the working day began at 4 A.M. and ended at 7 P.M., with "breaks for
beer"; the braziers' guild exacted a ninety-two-hour week in 1573.[18] As
early as 1579 we hear of strikes against textile machinery in Germany.[19]
Only war was needed to make destitution unparalleled.

III. MORALS AND MANNERS

If we believe the moralists of this half century before the war, the
moral picture was as dark as the economic. Teachers complained that
the youngsters sent to them were not Christians but barbarians. "The
people bring up their children so badly," wrote Matthias Bredenbach in
1557, "that it becomes obvious to the poor schoolmasters . . . that they
have got to reckon . . . with wild animals."[20] "All discipline appears at an
end," said another in 1561; "the students are refractory and insolent in the
extreme."[21] In most university towns the citizens hesitated to go out at
night for fear of the students, who on some occasions attacked them with
open knives.[22] "A chief cause of the general depravity of the students,"
said Nathan Chytränsin in 1578, "is undoubtedly the decline in home training. . . . Now that we have slipped the yoke of ancient laws and statutes
from off our necks . . . it is no wonder that we find, among the larger part
of our young people, such unbridled licentiousness, such boorish ignorance,
such ungovernable insolence, such terrible godlessness."[23] Others thought
that "not the least among the causes why the young lapse into immorality
and lasciviousness are the comedies, spectacles, and plays."[24]

As for adults, the preachers described them as quarrelsome hypocrites,
gluttons, drunkards, and adulterers.[25] Pastor Johann Kuno complained in
1579, "Vice of all sorts is now so common that it is committed without
shame, nay, people even boast of it in sodomitish fashion; the coarsest, the
most indecent sins have become virtues. . . . Who regards common whore-
dom any longer as a sin?"[26] Pastor Bartholomäus Ringwalt thought in 1585
that those were "the last and worst times which have come upon the

world."[27] Profanity was almost universal among the men, regardless of creed.[28] Calumny had a festival. "My superintendent," wrote the Count of Oldenburg in 1594, "has complained to me of the manner in which Dr. Pezel, at Bremen, has abused and slandered him in one of his books, making out that he spent his days in gluttony, drunkenness and debauchery, that he . . . was a sheep-devouring wolf, a serpent, a he-goat, an abortion, . . . and that he must be gotten rid of either by hanging, drowning, or imprisonment, by the wheel or by the sword." The court preacher of the Elector of Saxony found that "almost throughout the length and breadth of Germany it has been falsely reported that I earn large gilded goblets in drinking matches, that . . . I so fill myself with wine that . . . I have to be propped up and laid on a wagon and carted off like a drunken calf or sow."[29]

Eating and drinking were major industries. Half the day of a well-to-do German was consumed in passing edibles from one end of his anatomy to the other. Burghers were proud of their appetites, which, like the dress of their women, served as heralds of their prosperity. A circus performer earned national fame by eating at one meal a pound of cheese, thirty eggs, and a large loaf of bread—after which stint he fell dead. Dinners lasting seven hours, with fourteen toasts, were not unusual. Weddings were in many cases riots of gourmandizing and intoxication. A jovial prince signed his letters "*Valete et inebriamini*" (Be well and get drunk). Elector Christian II of Saxony drank himself to death at the age of twenty-seven. A temperance society struggled against the evil, but its first president died of drink.[30] It was asserted that gluttony was shortening the tenure of life. Said Erasmus Winter in 1599: "Owing to immoderate eating and drinking there are now few old people, and we seldom see a man of thirty or forty who is not affected by some sort of disease, either stone, gout, cough, consumption, or what not."[31]

We must not take these contemporary complaints too seriously. Probably the majority of the people were hard-working, long-suffering, and literally God-fearing folk; but in history, as in journalism, virtue makes no news—which proves it usual. The wives of the burghers lived in a modest domestic privacy, absorbed in a hundred duties that left no time for greater sins than gossip; and many women of the upper classes, like Anna, wife of Elector Augustus I of Saxony, were models of conscientious devotion to their families. There were some pleasant aspects in that turbulent Germany: love of children and home, generous hospitality, gay dancing and good music, jolly games and festivals. The first Christmas tree in recorded history was part of a celebration in Germany in 1605; it was the Germans who surrounded the Feast of the Nativity with picturesque relics of their pagan past.

Dances and folk songs were begetting forms of instrumental music, and hymns were growing into massive chorales. Organs became monuments of architecture; harpsichords, lutes, and other instruments were themselves products of loving art; hymnbooks, especially in Bohemia, were sometimes gorgeously adorned. Protestant hymns were often didactic or polemical, sacrificing the tenderness of medieval sacred song, but the Protestant chorales were already pointing to Johann Sebastian Bach. Musical instruction was compulsory in the schools of all the creeds; the "cantor" —i.e., the professor of music—ranked only after the rector or principal in the scholastic hierarchy. Organists were as famous then as pianists now; Jakob Handl held high repute in Prague, and the Hassler brothers— Hans, Kaspar, and Jakob—thrilled congregations, often with their own compositions, in Dresden, Nuremberg, and Prague. Musical ability tended to run in families, not through any mystical heredity, but through the contagion of the home; so a veritable host of Schultzes took the name Praetorius. Michael Praetorius composed not only tomes of music, but also, in his *Syntagma musicum* (1615–20), a thorough and scholarly encyclopedia of musical history, instruments, and forms.

The great name in this age and field was Heinrich Schütz, unanimously honored as the father of modern German music. Born to a Saxon family in 1585, exactly a century before Bach and Handel, he established the musical forms and spirit that these men brought to perfection. At twenty-four he went to Venice, where he studied under Giovanni Gabrieli. Returning to Germany, he hesitated between music and law, but finally settled down as director of music at the Dresden court of John George, Elector of Saxony. From 1618 onward he poured forth choral compositions which, in their manipulation and contrast of choirs, solo voices, and instruments, fully prepared for the many Bachs. Now for the first time heavy German choral counterpoint was fused and lightened with the more melodious "concerted" style, which combined voices and instruments. To celebrate the marriage of the Elector's daughter (1627), Schütz composed the first German opera, *Dafne*, based upon Peri's opera of the same name performed in Florence thirty-three years before. A second trip to Italy influenced Schütz to give further prominence to solos and instruments in his *Symphoniae sacrae* (1629), setting to music Latin texts from the Psalms and the Song of Songs. In 1631 Saxony became an active theater of war, and Schütz wandered from court to court, even to Denmark, seeking choirs and bread; not till 1645 was he re-established in Dresden. In that year he created the style of German Passion music with an oratorio, *The Seven Words from the Cross*; here he set the example of giving the words of a single character to the same single voice, and of preceding or following the voice with the same strains in the instruments; Bach adopted this method in *The St. Matthew Passion*. Again opening up new paths,

Schütz published in 1657 *Deutsche Concerten*—cantatas that place him with Carissimi as joint founder of the dramatic oratorio. His *Christmas Oratorio* (1664) set another mark for Bach to aim at. A year later he reached his zenith with *The Passion and Death of Our Lord and Saviour Jesus Christ*, sternly scored for voices alone and unrelieved with arias. Soon thereafter he lost his hearing. He retired to the solitude of his home, and died at eighty-seven after putting to music a passage from the 119th Psalm: "Thy statutes have been my songs in the house of my pilgrimage."

IV. LETTERS AND ARTS

The outstanding literary productions of the Empire in this age were the translation of the Bible by the Bohemian Brethren (1588), and the Hungarian epic *Zrinyiasz* (1644), by Miklós Zrinyi. Germany, and particularly Frankfurt am Main, now (c. 1600) succeeded Italy as the busiest publisher of books. The Frankfurt book fair began in 1598 to issue semiannually a catalogue of publications. Literary societies encouraged poetry and drama, but literature was stifled by civil and ecclesiastical censorship. Lutheran, Calvinist, and Catholic leaders agreed that works considered injurious to the government, the official faith, or public morals should be forbidden; and, strange to say, the total number of books prohibited by Protestant authorities exceeded the total of those condemned by the Roman Church.[32]

Scholarship declined as controversy mangled truth. Matthias Flacius Illyricus and his aides compiled in thirteen folio volumes a history of the Christian church; but *The Magdeburg Centuries*, as their *Historia ecclesiae Christi* (1559–74) came to be called from its place of composition and its division by centuries, was as one-sided as the Catholic histories of that age, when every book was a weapon; so Gregory VII, to these centurions, was "the most monstrous of all monsters born," who had compassed the death of several popes before mounting the "Chair of Pestilence."[33] The finest German historiography of its time was Johannes Sleidanus' story of the Reformation, *De statu religionis et reipublicae Carolo V Caesare* (1555), so impartial that not even Melanchthon could forgive him.

Next to invective, the most popular literary form was the drama. Both Protestants and Catholics used the stage for propaganda; Protestant plays made much fun of the pope, and usually ended by conducting him to hell. The Catholic cantors of Switzerland produced Passion, Easter, and Last Judgment plays from 1549, in one case with 290 actors. The Passion Play of Oberammergau was first presented in 1634 as the fulfillment of a vow during the plague of 1633, and was repeated every tenth year, lasting from 8:30 A.M. to 6 P.M., with a two-hour intermission at midday. Italian actors entered Germany in 1568, and were followed by Dutch, French, and English. These troupes soon replaced private with professional performances, and they evoked many complaints by their remunerative obscenity.

Even more popular was the virile and versatile Alsatian satirist Johann Fischart. Falling gaily into the spirit of the age, he issued a series of anti-Catholic travesties so cleverly devastating that he was soon the most widely read writer in Germany. His *Bienenkorb des heiligen römischen Immensschwarms* (1579) attacked with passionate caricature the history, doctrine, ceremonies, and clergy of the Church; all Catholic convents were hothouses of debauchery and abortion; the Church had decreed that priests "might have free use of other people's wives"; six thousand infant heads had been found in a pond near a nunnery; and so on.[34] Another satire, *Jesuitenhütlein*, ridiculed the four-cornered hat of the Jesuits and denounced all their ways and ideas. In 1575, under a rollicking eight-line title, Fischart published a pretended translation, actually an imitation and proliferation, of Rabelais' *Gargantua*; here he derided all aspects of German life—the oppression of the poor, the maltreatment of pupils, the gluttony and drunkenness, the fornication and adultery—in a jumble of style and Alsatian dialect, seasoned with obscenity and wit. Fischart died at forty-three, having exhausted his vocabulary.

Almost as lively, and dying in the same year, 1590, at the same age, Nikodemus Frischlin ran through a dozen lives in one. At twenty he was professor of history and poetry at Tübingen; he wrote Latin verse with quasi-Horatian finesse, and scholarly commentaries on Virgil. At thirty-five he was dismissed for satirizing the nobility. Thereafter he lived with rollicking recklessness; he drank heavily, for wine, he said, was necessary to genius, and the verses of teetotalers were worthlessly watery; he was accused of ruining one girl and poisoning another; threatened with criminal prosecution for immorality, he fled from city to city; he dedicated a published lecture to eleven different notables, geographically distributed to provide him asylum anywhere; but he died from a fall when he had still not fully expressed his opinion of his enemies. They called him, in the manner of the time, "a stinking, mangy poet . . . a lying, roguish abortion of the Devil";[35] but he was the best poet that Germany could produce in that unhappy age.

Art suffered from the Protestant aversion to images, the decline of the Church as patron, the corruption of native styles by uncongenial Italian influence, the deterioration of taste by coarse morals and violent controversy, and, later, the consuming fire of war. The marvel of it is that despite these discouragements German craftsmanship produced, in the six decades before the war, several lordly palaces and stately town halls, a good painter, and some precious minor art. The collections of Emperor Rudolf II and Duke Albert V of Bavaria formed the nuclei of the famous Alte Pinakothek of Munich. Albert himself was a German Medici, making his court a haven for artists, beautifying his capital with architecture, and gathering sculpture into the imposing Antiquarium*—the first museum of ancient statuary north of the Alps.

In 1611–19 a Dutch architect built for Duke Maximilian I at Munich the Residenz,* which for centuries served as the home of Bavaria's dukes, electors, and kings. Gustavus Adolphus lamented that he could not remove to Stockholm this favorite example of the German late Renaissance. The Jesuits, in their own ornate version of baroque, raised fine churches at Coblenz and Dillingen, and the massive Hofkirche (St. Michael's)* in Munich. In a plainer and statelier style Santino Solari designed the Salzburg cathedral just a few years before the outbreak of the Thirty Years' War.

As the princes had appropriated most ecclesiastical wealth in Protestant Germany, architecture there ceased to be ecclesiastical and became civic, sometimes palatial. Immense castles were built: the Schloss Heiligenberg at Baden, famous for the ceiling of carved linden wood in its Rittersaal, or Hall of Knights; Aschaffenburg Castle* on the Main; Heidelberg Castle, still one of the major sights of Germany. A sumptuous *Rathaus*, or town hall, rose to house municipal administration in Lübeck,* Paderborn,* Bremen, Rothenburg, Augsburg,* Nuremberg,* Graz. The textile merchants of Augsburg engaged the city's leading architect, Elias Holl, to build their Zeughaus, or Cloth Hall. Bremen provided a Kornhaus and Frankfurt a Salzhaus for dealers in grain and salt respectively; but who would have expected vinegar to enshrine itself so tastefully as in Bremen's Essighaus?

Now, and in the next 150 years, palaces rose everywhere in Germany to shelter the triumphant princes in gay and curlicued baroque. The Margrave of Ansbach-Bayreuth spent 237,000 florins ($30,000,000?) on his Plassenburg Palace, in one of the poorest principalities in the Empire. In better taste was the electoral palace provided for the archbishops of Mainz. The domestic architecture of the period appears fascinatingly picturesque in tradition and illustration, but an angry physician described German houses in 1610 as composed of dark, smelly, filthy rooms seldom breathing fresh air.[36] Nevertheless the interior of the burgher's dwelling

---

* This and the other structures marked with an asterisk in this section were destroyed or severely damaged in the Second World War.

was the real home of Germany's minor arts, rich with adornments made by skilled handicraft: carved panels and ceilings, strong furniture carved and inlaid, railings of wrought iron, locks and bars cast in grandiose forms, figurines of ivory, goblets of silver or gold. The German burgher never had enough of decoration in his home.

Engraving, especially on copper, flourished in Germany even through the wars. Lukas Kilian and his brother Wolfgang began, about 1600, a remarkable dynasty of engravers which continued through the seventeenth century with Wolfgang's sons Philipp and Bartholomäus, and with Philipp's great-grandsons till 1781. German sculpture, however, suffered from attempts to imitate classic forms alien to the German mold and mood. When native carvers let themselves go they turned out first-class work, like the central and side altars cut in wood by Hans Degler for the Ulrichskirche in Augsburg, or the seventy figures carved by Michael Hönel for the cathedral of Gurk in Austria. A special feature of the age was the wonderful fountains, inspired by Italian exemplars: the Wittelsbacher Fountain before the Residenz at Munich, and the Tugendbrunnen, or Fountain of Virtue, before the Lorenzkirche in Nuremberg.

When Rubens heard that Adam Elsheimer had just died (1610) at thirty-two, he said, "Such a loss should plunge all our profession into deep mourning. It will not be easy to replace him, and in my opinion he can never be equaled in [painting] small figures, landscapes, and many other things."[37] Born in Frankfurt, Adam left for Italy at twenty and, after a stay in Venice, spent the rest of his life in Rome. Rubens prayed God "to pardon Adam his sin of laziness," but we do not know if it was laziness that made Elsheimer confine his work to small paintings on copper plates. It could hardly be laziness that made him give to his landscapes such minute finish as in *The Flight into Egypt*,[38] or such unique representations of light and air as made him, on his modest scale, a Rembrandt before Rembrandt. He seems to have been well paid for his work, but not sufficiently to meet his needs and tastes. He became bankrupt, was imprisoned for debt, and died shortly after his release.

Painting on glass was a favorite art in this age, first at Zurich and Basel, then in Munich, Augsburg, and Nuremberg; windows in convents and homes became as colorful as in a medieval church. The carving of glass appeared early in the seventeenth century in Nuremberg and Prague. The Hirschvogel family in Nuremberg was famous for artistic glass and pottery. Cologne and Siegburg warmed the German heart with stone jugs and mugs elegantly carved, and stoves were often housed in color-glazed earthenware. In the working of wood, ivory, iron, gems, and precious metals, the Germans were unsurpassed. Cabinetmakers were so highly esteemed that when one of them was condemned to be hanged for theft he was pardoned because he was so good an "art carpenter." The iron railing around the tomb of Emperor Maximilian I at Innsbruck is superb. Anton Eisenhut executed in 1588 liturgical vessels in such delicately designed and richly embellished silver that they still stand at the top of their kind. German goldsmiths were sought for everywhere, and their products readily found a European market. Drinking cups, goblets, and jugs of silver were made in a hundred humorous forms; Germans could drink themselves tipsy out of windmills, lanterns, apples, monkeys, horses, pigs, monks, and nuns. Even in their cups they waged the theological war.

V. THE HOSTILE CREEDS

The Diet of Augsburg (1555) had brought the religious strife to a geographical truce on the principle *Cuius regio eius religio*, "Whose region, his religion"—i.e., in each state the religion of the ruler was to be made the religion of his subjects; dissidents were to leave. The agreement represented a mite of progress, since it substituted emigration for execution; but it was restricted to Lutheranism and Catholicism, and the painful uprooting of many families added to the chaos and bitterness in Germany. When a ruler of one creed was succeeded by another of another, the population was expected to change its faith accordingly. Religion became the tool and victim of politics and war.

So divided in theology, Germany before the Thirty Years' War presented no simple religious map. By and large the north was Protestant, the south and the Rhineland were Catholic; but, as the Augsburg principle could not be thoroughly or hastily enforced, there were many Protestants in Catholic areas and many Catholics in Protestant lands. The Catholics had the advantages of tradition and unity; the Protestants enjoyed more liberty of belief, and they divided into Lutherans, Calvinists, Anabaptists, and Unitarians; even among the Lutherans there was a war of creeds between the followers and the opponents of the liberal Melanchthon. In 1577 the Lutherans formulated their faith in the Book of Concord, and thereafter Calvinists were expelled from Lutheran states. In the Palatinate, Elector Frederick III favored Calvinism and made the University of Heidelberg a seminary for Calvinist youth. There, in 1563, Calvinist theologians drew up the Heidelberg Catechism, which shocked both Catholics and Lutherans by rejecting the Real Presence of Christ in the wine and bread of the Eucharist. Catholics were tolerated in the Palatinate if they confined their worship to their homes; Unitarians were forcibly suppressed. In 1570 two men who questioned or limited the divinity of Christ were put to death at the insistence of Calvinist professors in the University of

Heidelberg. Frederick's son, Elector Lewis, preferred and enforced Lutheranism; Lewis' brother John Casimir, as regent (1583–92), preferred
and enforced Calvinism; and Elector Frederick IV (1592–1610) confirmed
that policy. His son Frederick V (1610–23) married Elizabeth Stuart
(daughter of James I of England), claimed the throne of Bohemia, and
precipitated the Thirty Years' War.

The struggle between Lutherans and Calvinists was as bitter as between
Protestants and Catholics, and it damaged Protestant co-operation during
the war, for each alternation of roles between persecutors and persecuted
left a heritage of hate. In 1585 Count Wolfgang of Isenburg-Ronneburg
removed all Lutheran functionaries in his territory and installed Calvinists
in their place; in 1598 his brother and successor, Count Henry, informed
the Calvinist preachers that they must leave within a few weeks, despite
wintry weather; in 1601 Count Wolfgang Ernest succeeded to the government, expelled the Lutheran preachers, and restored Calvinism. Similar
replacements of Lutherans with Calvinists occurred in Anhalt (1595),
Hanau (1596), and Lippe (1600). In East Prussia Johann Funck, accused
of Calvinist leanings, was put to death in the market place of Königsberg
amid popular rejoicing (1566).[39] Chancellor Nikolas Krell was beheaded
at Dresden (1601) for altering the Lutheran ritual in a Calvinist direction
and for supporting French Huguenots.[40] In 1604 Landgrave Maurice of
Hesse-Cassel adopted Calvinism; in 1605 he enforced it there and in Upper
Hesse; his troops beat back a resisting crowd of Lutherans and tore down
the religious images in the churches; preachers unwilling to change from
Lutheranism to Calvinism were banished.[41] In the Electorate of Brandenburg Lutherans and Calvinists disputed violently as to whether the consecrated Host was really Christ; finally the government decreed Calvinism
to be the true religion (1613f).[42]

Amid these fluctuations of truth what Melanchthon had called *rabies
theologorum* raged as seldom before or after in history. The Lutheran
pastor Nivander (1582) listed forty characteristics of wolves and showed
that these were precisely the distinctive marks of Calvinists. He described
the dreadful deaths of leading anti-Lutherans; Zwingli, he said, having
fallen in battle, "was cut into straps, and the soldiers used his fat—for he
was a corpulent man—to grease their boots and shoes."[43] Said a Lutheran
pamphlet of 1590: "If anybody wishes to be told, in a few words, concerning which articles of the faith we are fighting with the diabolical
Calvinistic brood of vipers, the answer is, all and every one of them . . .
for they are no Christians, but only baptized Jews and Mohammedans."[44]
At Frankfurt fair, wrote Stanislaus Rescius (1592), "we have noticed for
several years past that the books written by Protestants against Protestants
are three times as numerous as those of Protestants against Catholics."[45]

"These raging theologians," mourned a Protestant writer in 1610, "have so greatly aggravated and augmented the disastrous strife among the Christians who have seceded from the papacy, that there seems no hope of all this screaming, slandering, abusing, damning, anathematizing, etc., coming to an end before the advent of the Last Day."[46]

To understand this "theological rabies" we must remember that all parties to the dispute agreed that the Bible was the infallible word of God, and that life after death should be the main concern of life. And the picture must find room for the real piety that humbled and exalted many Lutherans, Calvinists, and Catholics behind the delirium of the faiths. The Pietists fled from the hustings of theology and sought in privacy some reassuring presence of divinity. Johann Arndt's *Paradisgärtlein* (*Little Garden of Paradise*) is still read in Protestant Germany as a manual of devout contemplation. Jakob Böhme carried the mood into a mystical union of the individual soul with a God conceived as the Universal Well and Ground of all things, containing all contradictions, all "evil" as well as "good." Böhme claimed to have seen the "Being of all Beings, the God, the Abyss, also the birth of the Holy Trinity."[47] A mind unsympathetic to mysticism will find only a whirlwind of absurdities in Böhme's *De signatura rerum* (*On the Signature of All Things*, 1621); it is consoling to discover that another mystic, John Wesley, described it as "sublime nonsense."[48] Better were the simple and sensuous hymns of the Jesuit Pietist Friedrich von Spee.

As everywhere in Europe, it was the Jesuits who led the Catholic crusade to recover lost terrain. They began by seeking to reform the Catholic clergy. "Pray God," wrote the Jesuit Peter Faber from Worms in 1540, "that in this city there are even two or three priests who have not formed illicit liaisons or are not living other known sins."[49] But the main strategy was to capture the young; so the Jesuits opened colleges at Cologne, Trier, Coblenz, Mainz, Speyer, Dillingen, Münster, Würzburg, Ingolstadt, Paderborn, Freiburg. Peter Canisius, head and soul of this Jesuit campaign, traversed nearly all Germany on foot, spawning colleges, directing Jesuit polemics, and explaining to German rulers the advantages of the old faith. He urged Duke Albert V to root out by force all Protestantism from Bavaria.[50] Through the Jesuits, the Capuchins, the reformation of the clergy, the zeal of bishops, and the diplomacy of popes and nuncios, half the ground won by German Protestantism in the first half of the sixteenth century was regained for the Church in the second half. Some forms of coercion were used here and there, but the movement was largely psychological and political: the masses were tired of uncertainty, controversy, and predestination; their rulers saw in a unified and traditional Catholicism a stronger support of government and social order than in a Protestantism chaotically divided and precariously new.

Realizing at last that their internal divisions were suicidal, the Protestants turned their pulpits and their pens against the Roman foe. A war of words and ink prepared for the war of guns and blood, and mutual vituperation mounted to an almost homicidal ecstasy. Words like *dung, offal, ass, swine, whore, murderer* entered the terminology of theology. The Catholic writer Johann Nas in 1565 accused the Lutherans of practicing "murder, robbery, lying, deceit, gluttony, drunkenness, incest, and villainy without fear, for faith alone, they say, justifies everything"; and he thought it likely that every Lutheran woman was a prostitute.[51] Catholics took the damnation of Protestants as an axiom of theology; but the Lutheran preacher Andreas Lang wrote (1576) with equal certainty, "Papists, like other Turks, Jews, and heathen, are outside the pale of God's grace, of forgiveness of sins, and of salvation; they are destined to howl, lament, and gnash their teeth everlastingly in the burning fire and brimstone of the flames of hell."[52] Writers on both sides told scandalous tales of each other, as we do now in the war of political creeds. The myth of the Popess Joanna was popular in Protestant literature. "People could see and know," wrote a clergyman in 1589, "what double-dyed knaves and villains the Jesuiwiders were [who] obstinately persisted in denying that the English whore Agnes had been popess at Rome and had given birth to a boy during a public procession."[53] The popes, said a sermon (1589), had always been, and still were, without a single exception, sodomites, necromancers, and magicians; many of them had been able to spit hellfire out of their mouths. "Satan often appeared visibly to the popes . . . and joined with them in cursing and trampling the cross of Christ underfoot, and held naked dances over it, which they called divine service."[54] Congregations drank in such intoxicants eagerly. "Children in the streets," said a Protestant clergyman in 1584, "have learned to curse and mark the Roman Antichrist and his damned crew."[55]

The Jesuits were favorite targets. In hundreds of caricatures, pamphlets, books, poems, they were accused of pederasty, adultery, and bestiality. A German woodcut of 1569 (still preserved in the Goethe collection at Weimar) showed the pope, in the form of a sow, giving birth to Jesuits in the form of little pigs. In 1593 the Lutheran theologian Polycarp Leiser published a Latin *Historia Jesuitici ordinis*, which described the Jesuits as practicing the most obscene vices with full license and pardon from the pope.[56] *Eine wahrhaftige neue Zeitung* (*A Truthful New Journal*, 1614) informed its readers that the Jesuit Cardinal Bellarmine had committed adultery 2,236 times with 1,642 women, and it went on to describe the agonizing death of the Cardinal, who was not yet dead by seven years.[57]

The Jesuits at first replied with restraint. Canisius advised temperate language; so did the Protestant pastor Johann Mathesius; but the public preferred vituperation to moderation. Protestant polemists accused the Jesuits of accepting the doctrine of the Jesuit Mariana defending tyrannicide; a German Jesuit replied that this was precisely the doctrine that ought to be applied to princes who forced Protestantism upon their subjects; but other Jesuits assured the Protestant rulers that they were considered legitimate princes, and that not a hair of their heads would be hurt.[58] The Jesuit Conrad Vetter published (1594-99) ten pamphlets in which he used the grossest terms of abuse, excusing himself on the ground that he was following the lead of Lutheran divines; these pamphlets were bought by the public as fast as they could be printed. The Jesuits of Cologne declared that "the stubborn heretics who spread dissension everywhere" in Catholic territory

> ought to be punished as thieves, robbers, and murderers are punished; indeed, more severely than such criminals, for the latter only injure the body, while the former plunge souls into everlasting perdition. ... If forty years ago Luther had been executed, or burned at the stake, or if certain persons had been put out of the world, we should not have been subjected to such abominable dissensions, or to those multitudes of sects who upset the whole world.[59]

In the same spirit the Calvinist David Parens, professor of theology at Heidelberg, summoned (1618) all Protestant princes to a crusade against the papacy; in this enterprise they should "stop at no kind of severity or punishment."[60] The barrage of pamphlets culminated with 1,800 publications in the one year 1618, the first year of the war.

As the power and the temper of the Catholics rose, a number of Protestant princes formed a Union of Evangelical Estates (1608), or Protestant Union, for mutual protection. The Elector of Saxony held aloof, but Henry IV of France seemed ready to help in any enterprise against the Hapsburg Emperor. In 1609 several Catholic rulers, led by Duke Maximilian I of Bavaria, formed a Catholic Union, which came to be known as the Catholic League; by August 1610 nearly all the Catholic states of the Empire had joined, and Spain offered military aid. The Protestant Union agreed (February 1610) to help Henry IV take possession of the duchy of Jülich-Cleves, but the assassination of the French King (May 14) left the Protestants shorn of their strongest ally. Fear ran through Protestant Germany, but the League was not ready for action. In January 1615 Landgrave Maurice of Hesse-Cassel warned the Protestant Union that "the Catholic League, protected by the pope, the king of Spain, the court of Brussels, and the emperor, . . . had ordered its munitions of war . . . with a view . . . to the extirpation of the evangelical religion."[61] Caspar Scioppius added to the excitement by warning the Catholics and the Lutherans (1616) that the Calvinists "intended to overthrow the Religious and Public Peace, and the whole of the Holy Roman Empire, and to eradicate the Augsburg Confession, as well as the Catholic faith, from the Empire";[62] perhaps this was an attempt to further divide the main Protestant bodies. Territorial conflicts between Austria and Bavaria weakened the Catholic League in 1616, and men again dreamed of peace.

But in Prague Count Heinrich von Thurn pleaded with the Protestant leaders to prevent the ardently Catholic Archduke Ferdinand from taking the throne of Bohemia. Emperor Matthias had left five deputy governors to administer the country during his absence. The governors overruled the Protestants in disputes about church building at Klostergrab, and sent the objectors to jail. On May 23, 1618, Thurn led a crowd of irate Protestants into Hradschin Castle, climbed to the rooms where two of the governors sat, and threw them out the window, along with a pleading secretary. All three fell fifty feet, but they landed in a heap of filth and escaped more soiled than injured. That famous "defenestration" was a dramatic challenge to the Emperor, to the Archduke, and to the Catholic League. Thurn expelled the Archbishop and the Jesuits and formed a revolutionary Directory. He could hardly have realized that he had let loose the dogs of war.

VI. THE THIRTY YEARS' WAR

1. The Bohemian Phase: 1618–23

Matthias sent to the Directory an offer of amnesty and negotiation; it was refused.[63] Archduke Ferdinand, ignoring the Emperor, dispatched two armies to invade Bohemia. Frederick V, Elector of the Palatinate, persuaded Charles Emmanuel, the anti-Hapsburg Duke of Savoy, to send to Bohemia's aid a force led by an able *condottiere*, Peter Ernst von Mansfeld; Mansfeld captured Pilsen, the stronghold of the Catholics in Bohemia; Ferdinand's armies retreated. Christian of Brunswick, Frederick's Chancellor, suggested to the directors that they would strengthen their defense and better exclude Ferdinand from the throne if they offered it to Frederick. On March 20, 1619, Matthias died, leaving Ferdinand the legal King of Bohemia and heir presumptive to the Imperial crown. On August 19 the Bohemian Diet declared Ferdinand deposed as its king; on the twenty-seventh it proclaimed Frederick of the Palatinate King of Bohemia; on the twenty-eighth the Imperial electors made the Archduke of Styria the Emperor Ferdinand II.

Frederick hesitated to accept his new honors. He knew that, as a leading Calvinist, he could not count on Lutheran support, while against him would be the Empire, the papacy, and Spain. He appealed to his father-in-law, James I of England, for an army; instead, the canny King sent him good advice—to reject the Bohemian throne. Frederick's gay and spirited wife, Elizabeth, did not urge him to accept, but she promised to share with good cheer whatever fate his choice should bring; and this promise she kept. Christian of Brunswick counseled acceptance. On October 31, 1619, the new King and Queen entered Prague and were enthusiastically welcomed by the Diet and the populace.

Frederick was still a youth of twenty, of fine character and chivalrous disposition, but too immature for statesmanship. One of his first actions after being installed in Prague was to order the removal of all altars and images from the national sanctuary, the Church of St. Vitus, and soon his followers similarly denuded other Bohemian shrines. The Catholic minority denounced the procedure, the Bohemian Lutherans frowned upon it; Lutheran Germany looked coldly on this enthusiastic Calvinist. On April 30, 1620, Ferdinand proclaimed Frederick a usurper and ordered him to leave the Empire by June 1; if he failed to do so he would be declared an outlaw and his property would be confiscated. The Emperor offered to guarantee the Protestant states of Germany freedom from attack if they would give the Catholic states a similar pledge; in the Treaty of Ulm (June 3, 1620) this offer was accepted. The Protestant princes argued that Frederick had endangered their liberties by defying Ferdinand. Elector John George of Saxony aligned his Lutheran state with the Catholic Emperor.

In August an Imperial army of 25,000 men crossed from Austria into Bohemia under Maximilian of Bavaria's general, Johan Tserclaes, Count of Tilly, who had learned his piety from the Jesuits and the art of war from the Duke of Parma. Near the White Mountain, west of Prague, this army met and routed the Bohemians (November 8). Frederick, Elizabeth, and their entourage fled to Silesia. Failing to raise an army there, the King and Queen dismissed their followers and sought refuge in Calvinist Brandenburg. On the day after the battle Maximilian of Bavaria occupied Prague. Soon Catholicism was restored; images were replaced in the churches; the Jesuits were called in; all education was put under Catholic control; no religion was to be allowed except Catholicism and Judaism. Communion in wine as well as bread was abolished; John Huss's Day, formerly a national festival, was made a day of mourning, with all churches closed. Thirty leading rebels were arrested; twenty-seven were executed; and for ten years twelve severed skulls grinned from the tower of the Charles Bridge over the Moldau.[64] All rebels were forbidden to emigrate. Their property was forfeited to King Ferdinand, who sold it at bargain prices to Catholics; a new Catholic nobility was established, on the basis of peasant serfdom. The middle and commercial classes almost disappeared.

While Maximilian of Bavaria was thus refuting Calvinism in Bohemia, Spinola, during the truce in the Netherlands, led a large force from Flanders to capture the Palatinate. Some minor Protestant princes raised a force to oppose him, and Frederick, leaving his wife in The Hague, joined their camp. When Spinola was recalled to the Netherlands by the renewal of the Dutch war with Spain, Tilly replaced him, defeated the Protestants (1622), and captured and pillaged Heidelberg. The great library of the university was packed into fifty wagons and transported to Rome as a gift from Maximilian of Bavaria to Gregory XV. Maximilian, returning in triumph from Bohemia, was given the Palatinate and its electoral privilege in return for his services to the Emperor. Catholic states now had a majority in the Electoral Diet.

The scope and thoroughness of the Catholic victory disturbed Catholic as well as Protestant potentates. The increased prestige and power of Ferdinand II threatened the "liberties" of the German princes; Maximilian was disturbed to find that he was permitted to hold the Palatinate and Bavaria only as dependencies of the Emperor. Pope Urban VIII sympathized with the French view that the Hapsburgs were becoming too strong for the good of France and the freedom of the papacy, and he winked at Richelieu's taxing of French Catholics to help German Protestants—and later a Swedish king—against a Catholic Emperor. In 1624 the amazing Cardinal suddenly transformed the political scene with a succession of diplomatic strokes. On June 10 he signed an alliance with the Protestant Dutch against Catholic Flanders and Spain; on June 15 he brought Protestant England into the bond; on July 9, Sweden and Denmark; on July 11 he persuaded Savoy and Venice to join him in an attempt to cut the Spanish-Austrian line of supplies and reinforcements through the Valtelline passes in the Italian-Swiss Alps. In 1625 Christian IV of Denmark brought 20,000 men to join Mansfeld's 4,000 in Lower Saxony. Alarmed, Maximilian urged the Emperor to send aid to Tilly, whose 18,000 troops had been reduced to 10,000 by weather, hunger, and disease. Ferdinand responded by summoning Wallenstein from Bohemia.

2. Wallenstein: 1623–30

His real name was Albrecht von Waldstein, and he regularly signed himself so.[65] His family was one of the oldest in the Bohemian nobility. Born in 1583, he was educated first by the Bohemian Brethren, then by the Jesuits; he married a rich widow, who soon died, leaving him her fortune. He multiplied it by buying, at prices made nominal by the depreciation of the Bohemian currency, sixty-eight estates confiscated by Ferdinand. He was an intelligent and progressive landlord; he improved agricultural methods and production, financed industry, organized schools, medical services, and poor relief, and laid up surpluses to feed his people in time of famine. He impressed his contemporaries not only by his military genius, but by his tall, thin figure, his pale, stern face, his nervous restlessness, his pride and arrogance, his hot commanding temper. His "immutable chastity"[66] made him seem superhuman. His confidence in astrology was more active than his faith in Christ.

He had endeared himself to Ferdinand by supporting him at every stage in the Archduke's rise to power; and from 1619 onward he lent the Emperor great sums that almost financed the throne—for example, 200,-000 gulden in 1621, 500,000 in 1623. He exacted no security for these loans; it was enough that he owned a fourth of Bohemia, could raise an army at will, and could lead it with superlative skill. When, in 1624, the Valtelline passes had fallen under French-Venetian control, and Spanish soldiers and supplies could no longer go from Italy to Austria, Wallenstein offered to mobilize 50,000 men and put them at the service of the Emperor. Ferdinand hesitated, knowing Wallenstein's love of power; but Tilly, in 1625, cried out for reinforcements. Ferdinand commissioned Wallenstein to mobilize 20,000 men. With startling speed this new army marched into Lower Saxony, well equipped, well disciplined, idolizing its commander, and feeding itself by ravaging the countryside.

Wallenstein repulsed Mansfeld at Dessau, and Tilly defeated Christian IV at Lutter (1626). Mansfeld died, and Christian found his diminishing army helpless and mutinous. The great alliance formed by Richelieu had fallen apart through Gustavus Adolphus' jealousy of Christian IV, through England's declaration of war upon France, and Buckingham's expedition to aid the Huguenots at La Rochelle; Richelieu had to withdraw his forces from the Valtelline passes, which were again open to Austria and Spain. Wallenstein, his army growing with each day, marched into Brandenburg and forced its Elector George William to declare for the Emperor. He pushed on into Christian's own duchy of Holstein, easily overcoming all resistance. By the end of 1627 all the mainland of Denmark was in his power.

The salt air of the Baltic inflated Wallenstein's plans. Now that nearly all the northern coast of Germany and most of Denmark were under the Emperor, why not build an Imperial navy, revive the Hanse, and, in alliance with Catholic Poland, establish Imperial control over the Baltic and North seas? Then the Dutch and the English could no longer bring lumber from Baltic ports through the Sound to build their fleets for control of the North Sea and its trade, or to close the Channel to Spain. Imperial possession of the Palatinate gave the Emperor control of the Rhine; so the Dutch would be blocked on river and sea; their power, their wealth, their obstinate revolution would collapse. Gustavus Adolphus would be shut up in the Scandinavian peninsula. Already in 1627 Wallenstein was styling himself Admiral of the Oceanic and Baltic Sea.

The German princes were not quite happy over his victories. They noted that whereas the army of the Catholic League, under Maximilian of Bavaria and the Count of Tilly, was now fallen to some 20,000 men, Wallenstein commanded 140,000 troops, and acknowledged responsibility only to the Emperor. So long as the Emperor had this army behind him, he could make short work of the princely "liberties." Indeed, Wallenstein was probably nursing the idea of ending feudal sovereignties and uniting all Germany into one powerful state, as Richelieu was doing in France and as Bismarck was to do in Germany 240 years later.

During the winter of 1627–28 the Imperial electors, meeting at Mülhausen, debated their hopes and fears. The Catholic electors were inclined to support Wallenstein, trusting that he would eradicate Protestantism from the land of its birth. But when Ferdinand deposed the Protestant Duke of Mecklenburg and transferred the duchy to Wallenstein (March 11, 1628), even the Catholic princes were alarmed by the Emperor's assumption of power to depose and appoint dukes by his sole will. The electors had one card to play against Ferdinand. He was about to ask them to name his son King of Rome—i.e., to guarantee the son's succession to the Imperial throne. On March 28 they notified the Emperor that while his armies continued under Wallenstein's command they would not guarantee the succession. And Maximilian of Bavaria warned him that the general's army and power, if not soon reduced, would dictate Imperial policy.

As if to point this warning, Wallenstein, apparently on his own authority, began secret negotiations with Christian IV, culminating in the Peace of Lübeck (May 22, 1629). To the surprise of Europe he restored to the Danish King Jutland, Schleswig, and the royal portion of Holstein, exacted no indemnity, but merely required the cession of Christian's German sees and military authority. What had motivated this generosity? Partly fear of a Western coalition against Imperial control of the Baltic and the straits; partly the belief that Gustavus Adolphus was planning to invade Germany. In the end, Wallenstein foresaw, the issue would be between himself and Gustavus, not Christian.

Ferdinand may have been disturbed by his general's assumption of diplomatic authority, but his rising suspicions and jealousy had to be concealed, for he was now planning the boldest move of his career, and would need the support of Wallenstein's troops at every stage of the perilous game. His Jesuit advisers had long been pleading with him to take advantage of his new power, and by Imperial edict to restore to the Catholic Church as much as possible of the property and revenues that had been taken from her since the outbreak of the Reformation, or at least since 1552. Ferdinand, strongly Catholic, saw some justice in the plea, but underestimated its practical difficulties. Since 1552 many properties originally belonging to the Church had been bought and paid for by their present possessors. To effect the restitution thousands of proprietors would have to be dispossessed, presumably by force, and the consequent chaos might throw all Germany into revolution. Maximilian of Bavaria had once favored the idea; now he was appalled by its scope and implications, and he urged the Emperor to defer it until a Diet could give it careful consideration. Ferdinand feared that the Diet would reject it. On March 6, 1629, he promulgated his Edict of Restitution. "There remains nothing for us," it said, "but to uphold the injured party, and to send forth our commissioners that they may demand from the present unauthorized possessors the restitution of all archbishoprics, bishoprics, prelacies, monasteries, and other ecclesiastical property confiscated since the Treaty of Passau" (1552). This was the Counter Reformation with a vengeance. It was also an assertion of absolute Imperial power, such as even Charles V might have hesitated to assume.

The edict was met with widespread and passionate protests, but it was enforced. Whenever resistance was attempted Wallenstein's soldiers were called in, and opposition collapsed everywhere except at Magdeburg, which successfully withstood Wallenstein's siege. Entire cities—Augsburg, Rothenburg, Dortmund—and thirty towns passed into Catholic hands; so did five bishoprics and a hundred monasteries. Hundreds of Catholic parishes were reconstituted. As the principle *Cuius regio eius religio* was applied by the new owners, requiring the subjects to accept the religion of the ruler, thousands of Protestants were compelled to apostatize or emigrate; from Augsburg alone eight thousand went into exile, including the Elias Holl who had just completed its stately town hall. Exiled Protestant pastors wandered about the country begging for bread; the Catholic priests who had replaced them petitioned the government to give them relief.[67] Only the coming of Gustavus Adolphus prevented the final success of the edict, and of the Counter Reformation in Germany.

Having used Wallenstein's army to enforce the edict, and finding no Protestant armies in the field, Ferdinand was no longer obstinate about retaining him. In May 1630 he asked the general to release 30,000 of his men for service in Italy. Wallenstein objected, urging that the King of Sweden was planning to invade the Empire; he was overruled, and the

30,000 men were taken. In July the electors again proposed the removal of Wallenstein. The Emperor agreed, and on September 13 he notified the officers of the army that their general had been replaced in supreme command by Maximilian of Bavaria. Wallenstein retired peacefully to his estates in Bohemia, knowing that Gustavus had landed on German soil and that the Empire would soon need a general again.

3. Gustavus' Saga: 1630–32

We must not picture the great King as a Galahad going forth to save the true religion from idolaters. His task was to preserve and strengthen Sweden in political independence and economic development; for these ends he fought against Catholic Poland, Orthodox Russia, Protestant Denmark; if now he dared to match his modest resources against Empire, papacy and Spain combined, it was not because these were Catholic, but because they threatened to make his country the vassal of alien and hostile potentates. He felt that the best defense against such a threat was to establish Swedish bastions on the mainland. Protestant Saxony hesitated, and Catholic France was led to ally itself with Gustavus, because they knew that the issue was no theorem in theology but a struggle for security through power. Nevertheless religion, though a minor motive among the leaders, was a passionate stimulus among the people, and its energy had to be added to patriotism to lift the populace to martial holocausts.

So Gustavus, disembarking his 13,000 troops in Pomerania, offered himself to the north-German states as the savior of Protestantism, and to France as a sword against the swelling Hapsburgs. He waited for reinforcements from Sweden, Scotland, Brandenburg, and Poland, till he had some 40,000 men, well disciplined, armed with the new-style flintlock (not the old matchlock) muskets, and trained to move swiftly with their light artillery. The commander was still young, only thirty-six, but despite his campaigns he had grown stout, and was a problem to his horses as well as to his enemies. Nevertheless he was too often in front of the fray, confidently following his golden beard to victory. His soldiers loved him not because he was lenient, but because he was just. While German armies were followed by flocks of prostitutes so numerous that special officers were appointed to keep them in order, Gustavus allowed no courtesan in his camp, though wives were allowed to serve their soldier husbands.[68] Every morning and evening each regiment attended prayer, and every Sunday it heard a sermon; here was the discipline of Cromwell's Ironsides a decade before Cromwell's wars. Like Cromwell, Gustavus forbade forcible conversions; wherever he conquered he left religion free.

He spent the remainder of 1630 in spreading his control through Pomerania and seeking allies. If he could associate in one crusade all the foes of the Hapsburgs, he might have an army of 100,000 men, fit to face Wallenstein's. On January 13, 1631, France and Sweden signed a bond by which the King would find the men, and the Cardinal would supply 400,-000 thalers ($4,000,000?) annually, for a five-year campaign; neither power was to make peace without the consent of the other, and Gustavus bound himself not to interfere with the exercise of the Catholic religion. Richelieu invited Maximilian to join this alliance; instead, the Duke-Elector sent Tilly to check the Swedish advance. Tilly took Neubrandenburg (March 19, 1631), and slaughtered the garrison of 3,000 men. Gustavus took Frankfurt an der Oder (April 13), and slaughtered the garrison of 2,000 men. While the King spent time in efforts to add John George of Saxony to his alliance, Tilly and Count zu Pappenheim besieged Magdeburg, which was still resisting the Edict of Restitution. On May 20, after holding out for six months, the city was taken; the victorious troops ran riot in four days of pillage; in the greatest shambles of the war 20,000 persons were slain—not only the garrison of 3,000 men, but 17,000 of the 36,000 inhabitants; and all of the city but the cathedral was burned to the ground. A contemporary writer described the scene:

> Then was there naught but beating and burning, plundering, torture, and murder. Most especially was everyone of the enemy bent on securing much booty. . . . What with blows and threats of shooting, stabbing, or hanging, the poor people were so terrified that if they had had anything left they would have brought it forth if it had been . . . hidden away in a thousand castles. In this frenzied rage the great and splendid city that had stood like a fair princess in the land was now . . . given over to the flames, and thousands of innocent men, women, and children, in the midst of a horrible din of heart-rending shrieks and cries, were tortured and put to death in so cruel and shameful a manner that no words would suffice to describe, nor tears to bewail it.[69]

Tilly, now an old man of seventy-one, did what he could to stop the massacre; he rightly predicted that the Protestant states would "without doubt be only strengthened in their hatred" by this destruction of one of their fairest cities.

On July 22, 1631, the Elector of Brandenburg placed all his resources at Gustavus' disposal; on April 30 John George allied Saxony with Sweden; and on September 17 the combined Swedish and Saxon armies overwhelmed the outnumbered forces of Tilly at Breitenfeld, near Leipzig. This was the first substantial Protestant victory in the war; it revived the spirit of the Protestant population; and the figure of the Swedish King, fighting without armor in the thick of that battle, covered with dust and sweat but guiding and leading his men fearlessly, became a heartening symbol to a people so recently divided, defenseless, and cowed by the army of Wallenstein. Mecklenburg was recaptured, and the deposed Duke was restored. One state after another entered the Swedish alliance; soon Gustavus controlled a line stretching across Germany from the Oder to the Rhine. He took up his headquarters at Mainz, in the heart of a region normally Catholic. In November John George marched his Saxon army, unresisted, into Prague, carefully sparing Wallenstein's estates on the way.

Ferdinand, left with no ally but impoverished Spain and no general except the aged Tilly, turned humbly to Wallenstein (December 1631), and asked him to raise an army for the rescue of Bohemia and the protection of Austria. The proud general agreed, but on extraordinary terms: he was to have supreme command of all Imperial forces; he was to have authority to negotiate and sign treaties, except with Adolphus; in lands conquered by him he was to have the right of confiscation and pardon. In April 1632 all these conditions were granted. Wallenstein collected an army and the funds to finance it, offered John George a separate peace, and recaptured Prague without a shot. The Saxon army retreated into Saxony.

Meanwhile Gustavus took the field and defeated Tilly at Rain (April 15); Tilly died a fortnight later of his wounds, and Gustavus occupied Munich. Wallenstein marched out of Bohemia and joined his army with Maximilian's. Gustavus was now greatly outnumbered in men; his allies, suspecting him of Imperial ambitions, were restless and unreliable; his troops, beginning to starve, were pillaging and alienating Protestants as well as Catholics. John George, in his cups, revealed his anxiety to rid himself of the Swedish King. Gustavus had hoped to capture Vienna, but now, fearing that John George would join Wallenstein, he turned north. At Nuremberg, conscious that the tide was running against him, he sent final instructions to Oxenstierna for carrying on the Swedish government and the war. At Erfurt he bade farewell to his wife. On November 16, 1632, at Lützen, near Leipzig, the two greatest generals of the age came at last face to face: Gustavus with 25,000, Wallenstein with 40,000 men. All day the armies fought and bled, wavered and re-formed. Wallenstein was forced to give way, but Pappenheim reversed that rout till, shot through the lung, he choked with blood and died. Gustavus, seeing his center retreat, put himself at the head of a regiment of cavalry and led a wild rally. A bullet struck his bridle arm, another his horse; he fell; a bullet entered his back; Imperial cuirassiers closed around him and asked who he was; he answered, "I am the King of Sweden, who do seal the religion and liberty of the German nation with my blood."[70] They drove their swords again and again into his body, and shouted out the news of his death. Bernhard, Duke of Saxe-Weimar, took over the command; and the Swedes, maddened by the loss of their King, carried everything before them, won the costly victory, and reclaimed Gustavus' body, riddled with shot and sword. That night the defeated rejoiced and the victors mourned, for the Lion of the North was dead.

4. Degradation: 1633–48

Thereafter greatness left the war. Richelieu took the leadership of the German Protestants, Oxenstierna carried on his dead master's will with wise diplomacy, Bernhard of Saxe-Weimar led the French, Banér and Torstensson the Swedes, to new victories; but the glory was departed and only the horror remained. The Protestant princes were half relieved at Gustavus' death; they grudged the heavy price he had been forced to take for rescuing them from Ferdinand; and in the process their fields had been ravaged by the rival armies, their cities had been destroyed, and a foreign King had led Germans against Germans to a hundred thousand deaths.

Wallenstein, having for the first time tasted defeat, seemed to lose his nerve. After Lützen he retired to Bohemia and slowly organized another army. But he too, now fifty, was tired of war, and he hoped for leisure to treat his gout. He negotiated independently with the Protestant leaders, even with Richelieu;[71] and Ferdinand must have known that Bohemian exiles, with Oxenstierna's approval, were plotting to place Wallenstein on the Bohemian throne.[72] When Bernhard of Saxe-Weimar led an army into Bavaria, Maximilian and Ferdinand begged Wallenstein to come to the rescue; Wallenstein replied that he could spare no men for such a move. He quartered his idle army on the Imperial estates in Bohemia; the Emperor asked him to lighten the contributions imposed upon these Imperial lands; Wallenstein refused.

On December 31, 1633, Ferdinand and his Council decided that their greatest general must be deposed. Rumors were disseminated through Wallenstein's army that he was plotting to make himself King of Bohemia, and Louis XIII King of the Romans. On February 18 Imperial orders were posted throughout his army, relieving him of his command. Four days later, taking a thousand men with him, he fled from Pilsen. At Eger, on the twenty-fifth, a few soldiers, hoping for reward, broke into his room, found him alone and unarmed, and pierced him through with their swords. "Presently," reported a contemporary, "they drew him out by the heels, his head knocking on every stair."[73] The assassins hurried to Vienna, where they received promotion, money, and land. The Emperor, who had spent days and nights in fear and prayer, thanked God for His co-operation.

The war dragged on fourteen years more. Ferdinand's twenty-six-year-old son and namesake replaced Wallenstein as commander in chief of the Imperial armies. He was a likable youth, educated, kindly, generous, loving philosophy, writing music, carving ivory, yet no fool on the battlefield. Helped by older generals, he overwhelmed Bernhard at Nördlingen in the most decisive Imperialist victory of the war. The Protestant forces neared collapse. Oxenstierna saved the situation by the Treaty of Compiègne (April 28, 1635), which committed Richelieu to fuller participation in the conflict; but the Protestant princes of Germany did not relish the prospect of a French cardinal determining their fate. One by one they followed John George of Saxony in making peace with the Emperor, who welcomed them because he saw himself faced with the armies, as well as the money, of France. By the Treaty of Prague (May 30, 1635) he agreed to suspend the Edict of Restitution for forty years, and in return most of the Protestant princes promised to help him and his allies to recover all territories lost by them since the coming of Adolphus. As these included Lorraine, the treaty was in effect aimed at France as well as Sweden; it was a reassertion of German unity against invaders. The religious question disappeared from the war. By the end of 1635 the army of Protestant Saxony was fighting the Protestant Swedes in northern Germany, where Banér and Torstensson, with a military genius worthy of Gustavus, struggled to hold some Continental possessions for Sweden's security.

In the west Bernhard stood off bravely the growing forces of the Empire. In 1638 France sent him funds and, better still, 2,000 troops under Turenne, who was already rising to fame as a general. So reinforced, Bernhard undertook a campaign memorable in military annals for tenacity of purpose and brilliance of strategy. He defeated the Imperialists at Wittenweier, and compelled the great fortress of Breisach to capitulate. Then, exhausted at thirty-four, he died (1639), and his army and his conquests, including Alsace, passed to France.

The old Emperor had left the scene in 1637, and Ferdinand III, inheriting an Empire of untaxable destitution, found it almost impossible to finance armies against a Richelieu who could still wring francs from impoverished France. In 1642 Torstensson carried the Swedish arms to within twenty-five miles of Vienna and won a major victory in the second battle of Breitenfeld, where the Imperialists lost 10,000 men. The defeated Archduke Leopold William, brother of the young Emperor, court-martialed his officers for cowardice, beheaded those of high rank, hanged those of less degree, and shot every tenth man in the ranks of the survivors.[74]

Every year seemed now to bring new blows to the new Emperor. In 1643 his ally Spain was broken by the victory of the Duke of Enghien at Rocroi; in 1644 Enghien and Turenne conquered the Rhineland as far north as Mainz; in 1645 Torstensson again swept down almost to the gates of Vienna, the French won a bloody battle at Allerheim, and a Swedish army under Count Hans Christoph von Königsmarck overran Saxony, took Leipzig, and forced John George out of the war. The Bavarian army had been driven out of the Palatinate in 1634; in 1646 Turenne invaded and devastated Bavaria itself, and the once proud Maximilian sued for peace and begged the Emperor to come to terms with France. Ferdinand III, not as somberly inflexible as his father, and hearing the cry of the prostrate Empire, sent his ablest negotiators to Westphalia to seek some compromise between the faiths and the dynasties.

He was too young to know that the carnage and the desolation were probably greater than men had ever wrought in one generation in any land before. There were not two armies but six—German, Danish, Swedish, Bohemian, Spanish, French; armies manned largely by mercenaries or foreigners having no attachment to the German people or soil or history, and led by military adventurers fighting for any faith for a fee; armies fed by appropriating the grains and fruits and cattle of the fields, quartered and wintering in the homes of the people, and recompensed with the right to plunder and the ecstasy of killing and rape. To massacre any garrison that had refused to surrender, after surrender had become inevitable, was a principle accepted by all combatants. Soldiers felt that civilians were legitimate prey; they shot at their feet in the streets, conscripted them as servants, kidnaped their children for ransom, fired their haystacks and burned their churches for fun. They cut off the hands and feet of a Protestant pastor who resisted the wrecking of his church; they tied priests under wagons, forcing them to crawl on all fours till they fainted with exhaustion.[75] The right of a soldier to rape was taken for granted; when a father asked for justice against a soldier who had raped and killed his daughter, he was informed by the commanding officer that if the girl had not been so stingy with her virginity she would still be alive.[76]

Despite the spreading promiscuity, the population of Germany rapidly declined during the war. The decline has been exaggerated and was temporary, but it was catastrophic. Moderate estimates reckon a fall, in Germany and Austria, from 21,000,000 to 13,500,000.[77] Count von Lützow calculated a reduction of population in Bohemia from 3,000,000 to 800,000.[78] Of 35,000 villages existing in Bohemia in 1618, some 29,000 were deserted during the conflict.[79] Throughout the Empire hundreds of villages were left without a single inhabitant. In some regions one might travel sixty miles without seeing a village or a house.[80] Of 1,717 houses standing in nineteen Thuringian villages in 1618 only 627 stood in 1649, and many of these were untenanted.[81]

Thousands of fertile acres were left untilled for lack of men, draft animals, or seed, or because peasants had no assurance that they could reap where they had sown. Crops were used to feed armies, and what remained was burned to prevent the feeding of foes. Peasants in many localities were reduced to eating hidden remnants or dogs, cats, rats, acorns, grass; some dead were found with grass in their mouths. Men and women competed with ravens and dogs for the flesh of dead horses. In Alsace hanged offenders were torn from the gallows to be eagerly devoured; in the Rhineland exhumed bodies were sold for food; at Zweibrücken a woman confessed to having eaten her child.[82] Transportation was too disrupted to let a local surplus feed a distant drought; roads were torn up with battle, or dangerous with brigands, or clogged with deserters and fugitives.

The towns suffered only less than the villages. Many of them were reduced to half their former population. Great cities were in ruins—Magdeburg, Heidelberg, Würzburg, Neustadt, Bayreuth. Industry declined for lack of producers, purchasers, and trade; commerce hid its head; once-wealthy merchants begged and robbed for bread. Communes, declaring themselves bankrupt, repudiated their debts. Financiers were loath to lend, fearing that loans would be gifts. Taxation impoverished everybody but generals, tax collectors, prelates, and kings. The air was poisonous with refuse and offal and carcasses rotting in the streets. Epidemics of typhus, typhoid, dysentery, and scurvy ran through the terrified population and from town to town. Spanish troops passing through Munich left a plague that in four months carried off 10,000 victims.[83] The arts and letters that had ennobled the cities withered in the heat of war.

Morals and morale alike collapsed. The fatalism of despair invited the cynicism of brutality. All the ideals of religion and patriotism disappeared after a generation of violence; simple men now fought for food or drink or hate, while their masters mobilized their passions in the competition for taxable lands and political power. Here and there some humane features showed: Jesuits gathering and feeding deserted children; preachers demanding of governments an end to bloodshed and destruction. "God send that there may be an end at last," wrote a peasant in his daybook. "God send that there may be peace again. God in heaven, send us peace."[84]

VII. THE PEACE OF WESTPHALIA

Ever since 1635 the rulers and their diplomats had been extending feelers for peace. In that year Pope Urban VIII proposed a congress to discuss terms of reconciliation; negotiators met at Cologne, to no result. At Hamburg in 1641 the representatives of France, Sweden, and the Empire drew up a preliminary agreement for a double conference to meet in Westphalia in 1642: at Münster France would treat with the Empire under the mediation of the papacy and Venice; at Osnabrück, thirty miles away, France and the Empire would treat with Sweden under the mediation of Christian IV of Denmark. This antiseptic segregation was made necessary by the unwillingness of the Swedish emissaries to confer under the presidency of a papal nuncio, and the refusal of the nuncio to sit in the same room with a "heretic."

Delays were caused by questions of safe-conducts and protocol. Torstensson's victory at Breitenfeld spurred the Emperor to promise that his deputies would arrive by July 11, 1643. Then the French delegates dallied while France arranged an alliance with the United Provinces against Spain. The Congress of Westphalia was formally opened December 4, 1644, with 135 members, including theologians and philosophers. Even then six months were consumed in deciding in what order of precedence the delegates were to enter rooms and be seated. The French ambassador would not negotiate unless he was given the title *Altesse*—Highness. When the Spanish ambassador arrived he shunned the French ambassador because neither would give precedence to the other; they communicated through a third person. France refused to recognize Philip IV's title as King of Portugal and Prince of Catalonia; Spain refused to accept Louis XIV's title as King of Navarre. The Swedish representatives quarreled and marked time until the resolute young Queen Christina peremptorily ordered them to make peace among themselves and with the enemy. Meanwhile men were going to their death in war.

As each party's armies were victorious or defeated, its envoys delayed or hurried negotiations; lawyers were kept busy inventing difficulties or compromises, tying or untying knots. France's generals were striking their stride; so she insisted on having all the German princes represented at the conference, though most of them had long since made peace with the Emperor; time was asked to stop till all the electors, princes, and Imperial cities had sent their diplomats. To weaken France, Spain signed (January 7, 1648) a separate peace with the United Provinces—which had just promised France to sign no separate peace; but the Dutch could not resist the chance to acquire, by a few strokes of the pen, what they had fought for through eighty years. France retaliated by refusing to make peace with Spain; their war went on till the Peace of the Pyrenees (1659).

The Congress might have adjourned without result had not the devastation of Bavaria by Turenne, and the attack of the Swedes upon Prague (July 1648), and the defeat of the Spanish at Lens (August 2) persuaded the Emperor to sign; while the outbreak of the Fronde in France (July) impelled Mazarin to concessions that would leave him free for war at home.

So, at last, the Treaty of Westphalia was concluded, at both Münster and Osnabrück, on October 24, 1648. Bloodshed went on for nine days more while the news traveled to the fronts. Humble and joyous Te Deums rose from a thousand villages and towns.

Let us admit that the negotiations had faced more complicated problems of adjustment than any peace conference before the twentieth century, and that they settled the conflicting claims as wisely as the prevailing hatreds, prides, and powers allowed. The terms of this Europe-remaking treaty must be summarized, for they condensed and produced much history.

1. Switzerland and the United Provinces won formal recognition of their independence.

2. Bavaria received the Upper (south) Palatinate, with its electoral vote.

3. The Lower (north) Palatinate, as an eighth electorate, was restored to Charles Louis, son of the dead Frederick.

4. Brandenburg acquired eastern Pomerania, the bishoprics of Minden, Halberstadt, and Cammin, and the succession to the bishopric of Magdeburg. France helped the rising dynasty of the Hohenzollerns to get these plums, with a view to raising another power against the Hapsburgs; France could not be expected to foresee that Brandenburg, become Prussia, would, under Frederick the Great, challenge France and, under Bismarck, would defeat her.

5. Sweden, chiefly through her victorious armies, but partly through French support at the congress, received the bishoprics of Bremen and Verden, the towns of Wismar and Stettin, and the territory at the mouth of the Oder. Since these were Imperial fiefs, Sweden had now a seat in the Imperial Diet; and as she already held Livonia, Esthonia, Ingria, Karelia, and Finland, she was now one of the Great Powers, mistress of the Baltic till Peter the Great.

6. The German principalities retained and confirmed their prewar liberties as against the emperors.

7. The Emperor had to be content with the acknowledgment of his royal rights in Bohemia and Hungary; so the Austro-Hungarian Empire took form as the actuality within the shell of the Holy Roman Empire. The economic back of the aging Empire was broken, partly by the reduction of population and the disruption of industry and trade through the war, but also by the passing of the great river outlets to foreign powers— of the Oder and the Elbe to Sweden and of the Rhine to the United Provinces.

8. The greatest gains went to France, whose money had financed the victorious Swedes and whose generals had forced the peace. Alsace was in effect yielded to her, with the bishoprics of Metz, Verdun, and Toul and

the fortress of Breisach on the German side of the Rhine; Louis XIV was now in a position to take Franche-Comté and Lorraine at his convenience. The aim of the now dead Richelieu had been achieved—to break the power of the Hapsburgs, to extend the frontiers of France, to improve French unity and defense, and to preserve in the Empire a chaos of principalities, a conflict between princes and emperor, and an opposition between the Protestant north and the Catholic south, that would protect France from the peril of a united Germany. France had replaced Spain— the Bourbons had replaced the Hapsburgs—as the dominant force in Europe; soon Louis XIV would be equated with the sun.

The hidden victim of the war was Christianity. The Roman Church had to abandon the Edict of Restitution, to return to the property situation of 1624, and to see the princes again determining the religion of their subjects; this, however, enabled the Church to banish Protestantism from Bohemia, the land of the Hussite Reformation. The Counter Reformation was checked; for example, it was out of the question that Poland should establish Catholicism in a Protestant Sweden twice as strong as before. The papal nuncio at Münster refused to sign the treaty; Pope Innocent X declared it "null and void, accursed, and without any influence or result for the past, the present, or the future" (November 20, 1648).[85] Europe ignored the protest. From that time the papacy ceased to be a major political power, and religion in Europe declined.

Some Protestants protested, too, especially those who had lost their homes in Bohemia and Austria. But all in all the treaty—fruit of a dead and a living cardinal—was a Protestant victory. Protestantism had been saved in Germany. It was weakened in the south and along the Rhine, but in the north it was stronger than before. The Reformed, or Calvinist, Church was officially recognized in the treaty. The lines of religious division established in 1648 remained essentially unchanged until, in the twentieth century, the differential birth rate began a gradual and peaceful extension of Catholicism.

But though the Reformation had been saved, it suffered, along with Catholicism, from a skepticism encouraged by the coarseness of religious polemics, the brutality of the war, and the cruelties of belief. During the holocaust thousands of "witches" were put to death. Men began to doubt creeds that preached Christ and practiced wholesale fratricide. They discovered the political and economic motives that hid under religious formulas, and they suspected their rulers of having no real faith but the lust for power—though Ferdinand II had repeatedly risked his power for the sake of his faith. Even in this darkest of modern ages an increasing number of men turned to science and philosophy for answers less incarnadined than those which the faiths had so violently sought to enforce. Galileo was dramatizing the Copernican revolution, Descartes was questioning all tradition and authority, Bruno was crying out to Europe from his agonies at the stake. The Peace of Westphalia ended the reign of theology over the European mind, and left the road obstructed but passable for the tentatives of reason.

BOOK III

THE TENTATIVES OF REASON

1558–1648

CHAPTER XXII

Science in the Age of Galileo

1558-1648

I. SUPERSTITION*

RELIGIONS are born and may die, but superstition is immortal. Only the fortunate can take life without mythology. Most of us suffer in body and soul, and Nature's subtlest anodyne is a dose of the supernatural. Even Kepler and Newton mingled their science with mythology: Kepler believed in witchcraft, and Newton wrote less on science than on the Apocalypse.

Popular superstitions were beyond number. Our ears burn when others speak of us. Marriages made in May will turn out unhappily. Wounds can be cured by anointing the weapon with which they were inflicted. A corpse resumes bleeding in the presence of the murderer. Fairies, elves, hobgoblins, ghosts, witches, demons lurk everywhere. Certain talismans (e.g., those found on Catherine de Médicis after her death) guarantee good fortune. Amulets can ward off wrinkles, impotence, the evil eye, the plague. A king's touch can cure scrofula. Numbers, minerals, plants, and animals have magic qualities and powers. Every event is a sign of God's pleasure or wrath, or of Satan's activity. Events can be foretold from the shape of the head or the lines of the hands. Health, strength, and sexual power vary with the waxing and waning of the moon. Moonshine can cause lunacy and cure warts. Comets presage disasters. The world is (every so often) coming to an end.[1]

Astrology, though increasingly repudiated by the literate, was still popular. In 1572 its teaching ceased in the University of Bologna; in 1582 the Spanish Inquisition denounced it; in 1586 Pope Sixtus V warned Catholics against it; but in the University of Salamanca it persisted, on and off, till 1770. The great majority of the people, and many in the upper classes, solicited horoscopes foretelling the future from the position of the stars. All babies of any consequence had their horoscopes cast soon after birth. An astrologer was hidden near the bedchamber of Anne of Austria at the birth of Louis XIV.[2] When Gustavus Adolphus was born his father, Charles IX, asked Tycho Brahe for a horoscope; the astronomer cautiously predicted that the boy would become king. Kepler doubted astrology, but

---

* For superstition, science, and philosophy in England in this period cf. Chapter VII.

buttered some bread with it, saying, "As every animal has been given by nature some means of getting a living, so the astronomer has been furnished with astrology in order to enable him to live."[3] Wallenstein paid for a favorable horoscope in 1609 and regularly took an astrologer with him on his travels,[4] perhaps to encourage his troops. Catherine de Médicis and her court repeatedly consulted astrologers.[5] John Dee enjoyed a high reputation as astrologer until he discovered that the position of the stars required that one of his pupils must exchange wives with him.[6]

The belief in magical arts was declining, with a bloody exception: this period was the heyday of judicial murders for witchcraft. Persecutors and persecuted alike believed in the possibility of securing supernatural aid by incantations or similar devices. If one could win the intercession of a saint by prayer, why not the help of a devil by courting him? A book published at Heidelberg in 1585, *Christlich Bedenken . . . von Zauberei* (*Christian Ideas on Magic*), laid it down as an axiom that "everywhere the whole universe, inward and outward, water and air, is full of devils, of wicked, invisible spirits."[7] It was a common belief that human beings could be "possessed" by devils entering them. In 1593 there was "a terrible panic in the little town of Friedeberg, for it was said that the Devil had taken bodily possession of more than sixty people . . . and had tortured them frightfully. . . . Even the pastor . . . had himself been seized . . . while preaching."[8] The story of the Gadarene swine (Matt., viii, 28–34) pictured Christ as driving demons from possessed persons; and had he not given to his followers the power to cast out devils in his name (Mark, xvi, 17)? Priests were called upon by their parishioners for a variety of exorcisms—to drive pests from the fields, to still storms at sea, to cleanse a building of evil spirits, to purify a desecrated church, etc.; Pope Paul V issued in 1604 a manual for such priestly services. Protestant writers condemned sacerdotal exorcism as magic, but the Church of England has recognized the value of exorcism as a healing rite.[9] Here, as in so many ceremonies, the psychological effect has been good.

Just as the people took the initiative in asking for exorcisms, so they were the prime movers in demanding the prosecution of "witches." Fear of the power of witches was widespread. Said a pamphlet of 1563: "To enter into relations with the Devil, to have him close at hand in rings or crystals, to conjure him, to enter into alliance with him, to carry on hundreds of magic arts with him, is more in vogue nowadays, among both high and low, learned and unlearned, than ever before." "Devil books" explaining how to get in touch with helpful demons were popular; one man sold 1,220 of them at two fairs in 1568.[10] In some cases the officers of the Roman Inquisition advised parish priests to "instruct the people in the fallacies of witchcraft," counseled disbelief in "the Witches' Sabbat," and recommended removal of a priest for listening too credulously to accusations of witchcraft.[11]

Pope Gregory XV (1623) required the death penalty for persons convicted of causing death by sorcery; but Urban VIII (1637) condemned Catholic Inquisitors "on account of their arbitrary and unjust prosecution of sorcerers, . . . extorting from the accused . . . confessions that were valueless, and abandoning them to the secular arm without sufficient cause."[12] Emperor Maximilian II decreed (1568) that those convicted of sorcery should have their confessions tested by challenges to perform magic in public; and the supreme penalty, after three convictions, was to be banishment. But the frightened populace demanded severity in examinations and haste in executions.

Civil and ecclesiastical authorities, sharing, or wishing to allay, this fear of witches, subjected the accused to rigorous trials, often using torture to elicit confessions. At Nördlingen the town council had a special set of torture instruments, which it lent to neighboring communities with the assurance that "by these means, and more especially by the thumbscrew, God has often been graciously pleased to reveal the truth, if not at first, at any rate at the last."[13] Torture by preventing sleep was one of the milder methods. Usually the desired admissions were obtained by torture, and the judges were only occasionally disturbed by the unreliability of such confessions.

The persecutions were least severe in Spain. In the province of Logroño the Inquisition convicted fifty-three persons of witchcraft and put eleven to death (1610); otherwise the accusations were usually dismissed as fanciful or vengeful, and executions for witchcraft were rare. In 1614 the Suprema of the Inquisition issued instructions to its officials to regard witchcraft confessions as neurotic delusions and to show lenience in punishments.[14]

An epidemic of witchcraft fears swept southeast France in 1609. Hundreds of persons believed themselves possessed by devils; some thought themselves changed into dogs, and barked. A commission of the Bordeaux Parlement was appointed to try suspects. A method was devised to discover the spots at which devils had entered the body of the accused: he was blindfolded, needles were stuck into his flesh, and any place where he failed to feel the injected point was judged to be the port of entry. Hoping to be pardoned, suspects accused one another. Eight were convicted, five escaped, three were burned; and spectators swore later that they had seen devils, in the form of toads, issuing from the heads of the victims.[15] In Lorraine 800 were burned for witchcraft in sixteen years; in Strasbourg 134 in four days (October 1582).[16] In Catholic Lucerne 62 were put to death between 1562 and 1572; in Protestant Bern, 300 in the last decade of the sixteenth century, 240 in the first decade of the seventeenth.[17]

In Germany Catholics and Protestants competed in sending witches to the stake. It is incredibly and yet reliably reported that the Archbishop of Trier had 120 persons burned at Pfalz in 1596 on the charge that they had made the cold weather last devilishly long.[18] A cattle plague in the Schongau district (1598) was ascribed to witches; the Bavarian Privy Council at Munich urged inquisitors to "show more earnestness and severity in your proceedings"; in consequence 63 witches were burned, and the relatives of the victims were required to pay the cost of the trials.[19] At Hainburg, in Austria, 80 were executed for sorcery in the two years 1617–18. In 1627–29 the Bishop of Würzburg is said to have put 900 witches to death.[20] In 1582 Protestant editors reissued, with their approval, the *Malleus maleficarum* (*Hammer of Witches*) which the Dominican Inquisitor Jakob Sprenger had published in 1487 to guide in the detection and prosecution of witches. Elector Augustus of Saxony decreed (1572) that witches were to be burned to death even if they had injured no one. In Ellingen 1,500 witches were burned in 1590, in Ellwangen 167 in 1612, in Westerstetten 300 in two years;[21] there were similar ecstasies in Osnabrück in 1588, in Nördlingen in 1590, in Württemberg in 1616; these latter statistics, however, are derived from contemporary newssheets notorious for inaccuracy. German scholars estimate a total of 100,000 executions for witchcraft in Germany in the seventeenth century.[22]

There were a few voices calling men to reason. We have noted elsewhere the protests of Johann Wier and Reginald Scot, and we have seen how Montaigne turned his skeptical humor upon the mania in the essay "Of the Lame or Crippled": "How much more natural and likely do I find it that two men should lie, than that one man in twelve hours should be carried by the winds from East to West, . . . [or] that one of us should be carried on a broom through . . . a chimney."[23] People who believe such things need medicine, not death. "When all is done, it is an overvaluing of one's conjectures, by them to cause a man to be burned alive."[24] Cornelius Loos, a Catholic professor at Mainz, attacked witch-hunting in his *Über die wahre und falsche Magie* (1592), but before he could publish it he was imprisoned and compelled to recant his errors.[25] Another Jesuit, the Pietist poet Friedrich von Spee, after serving as confessor to nearly 200 persons accused of witchcraft, denounced the persecution in a brave book, *Cautio criminalis* (1631): he admitted the existence of witches, but he deplored the arrests on baseless suspicion, the unfairness of the trials, the merciless tortures that would have forced the "doctors and bishops of the Church" to confess to anything.[26]

For every such opponent there were a dozen defenders of the oppression. Protestant theologians like Thomas Erastus, in 1572, and Catholic theologians like Bishop Peter Binsfeld, in 1589, agreed that witchcraft was real and that witches should be burned. The Bishop approved of torture, but recommended that repentant witches should be strangled before being burned.[27] The Catholic lawyer and philosopher Jean Bodin upheld the persecution in his *Demonomanie* (1580); a year later the Protestant poet Johann Fischart translated and expanded this book with gusto, and joined Bodin in urging a relentless severity.[28]

Nevertheless the mania waned. After 1632, when the Thirty Years' War became frankly political, religion ceased to hold so warm a place in men's hates. Printing was spreading, books were multiplying, schools were recovering, new universities were opening. Year after year patient plodders brought a stone to the rising pyramid of knowledge, and in a hundred cities curious men tested hypotheses with experiments. Slowly the area of the supernatural shrank, the sphere of the natural and secular grew. It is a dull, impersonal, fragmentary history, and the greatest drama of modern times.

II. THE TRANSMISSION OF KNOWLEDGE

The first heroes here are the printer-publishers who fed the inky stream on which knowledge flowed from mind to mind and from generation to generation. The great publishing house of the Estiennes was continued in Geneva by Henri Estienne II, and in Paris by Robert Estienne III. A similar dynasty was founded at Leiden (c. 1580) by Louis Elzevir; his five sons, his grandsons, and a great-grandson carried on his work and gave their name to a style of type. At Zurich Christopher Froschauer earned a place in the history of printing and scholarship by his careful editions of the Bible.

Libraries were providing new homes for old treasures. We have noted the Bodleian at Oxford, the library of the Escorial, the exquisite Biblioteca Ambrosiana at Milan (1606). Catherine de Médicis added many volumes and manuscripts to what is now the Bibliothèque Nationale. The new Vatican Library of Sixtus V (1588) seemed to Evelyn "the most nobly built, furnished, and beautiful of any in the world."[29]

Newspapers were sprouting. As far back as 1505 single-sheet *Zeitungen* (tidings) had been sporadically printed in Germany; by 1599 there were 877 such publications, all irregular. The oldest regular newssheet known to history was the weekly *Avisa Relation oder Zeitung* founded at Augsburg in 1609 and composed from reports of agents posted throughout Europe by merchants and financiers. The *Frankfurt Oberpostamzeitung*, founded in 1616, continued publication till 1866. Similar regular weeklies began in Vienna in 1610, in Basel in 1611. Soon Fischart was making fun of the "newspaper-believing" public and its credulous avidity for news. The inadequate and biased transmission of news, and the profitable dissemination of nonsense, barred the general public from any intelligent or concerted participation in politics, and made democracy impossible.

Censorship of publications was practically universal in Christendom, Catholic and Protestant, ecclesiastical and secular. The Church set up in 1571 the Congregation of the Index to guard the faithful against books considered injurious to Catholic belief. Protestant censorship was not as powerful and severe as the Catholic, but it was as sedulous; it flourished in England, Scotland, Scandinavia, Holland, Germany, and Switzerland.[30] The diversity of dogmas in different states allowed heretics in some measure to defeat the censorship by publishing their books abroad and importing copies clandestinely. Modern literature owes something of its wit and subtlety to censorship.

In divers translations, but always interpreted as the word of God, the Bible continued its career as the most popular of all books and the most influential in doctrine and language, even in conduct, for the worst brutalities of the time —wars and persecutions—quoted Scripture in self-justification. As the humanist Renaissance receded before the theological Reformation, the idolatry of the pagan classics was replaced by worship of the Bible. A commotion was caused when scholars discovered that the New Testament was written not in classical Greek but in the Koine of the populace; but the theologians explained that the Holy Ghost had used the common diction to be better understood by the people. Another heartache came when Louis Cappel, Protestant professor of Hebrew and theology at Saumur, concluded that the vowel points and accents in the canonically accepted Hebrew text of the Old Testament were additions made to older texts by the Masorete Jews of Tiberias in or after the fifth century B.C., and that the square characters of the accepted text were Aramaic substitutes for Hebrew letters. Johannes Buxtorf the Elder, the greatest Hebraist of the time, begged Cappel to withhold these views from the public as injurious to belief in the verbal inspiration of the Bible. Cappel published nevertheless (1624); Johannes Buxtorf the Younger tried to refute him, and argued that the points and the accents were also divinely inspired. The controversy continued through the century; orthodoxy finally yielded the points, and a modest step was taken toward appreciating the Bible as the majestic expression of a people.

Some of the most famous scholars in history belong to these years. Justus Lipsius, oscillating between Louvain and Leiden and between Catholicism and Protestantism, earned European fame by his corrective editions of Tacitus, Plautus, and Seneca, and surpassed all previous grammars with his *Aristarchus, sive De arte grammatica* (1635). He mourned the imminent death of European civilization, and warmed himself with "the sun of another new empire arising in the west"—the Americas.[31]

Joseph Justus Scaliger, "perhaps the most extraordinary master of general erudition that has ever lived,"[32] inherited from his famous father, Julius Caesar Scaliger, the throne of European scholarship. At Agen, in southwestern France, he served his father as amanuensis, and absorbed learning with every breath. He read Homer in three weeks and marched triumphantly through all the major Greek poets, historians, and orators. He learned Hebrew, Arabic, and eight other languages, ventured into mathematics, astronomy, and "philosophy" (which then included physics, chemistry, geology, and biology), and for three years studied law. His legal training may have helped to sharpen his critical teeth, for in the editions that he issued of Catullus, Tibullus, Propertius, and other classical authors he raised textual criticism from haphazard surmises to laws of procedure and interpretation. He had a wise respect for dates in the understanding of history; his greatest work, *De emendatione temporum* (*On the Correction of Dates*, 1583), for the first time collated the dates given by Greek and Latin historians with those given or indicated in the history, calendars, literature, and astronomy of Egypt, Babylonia, Judea, Persia, and Mexico. His *Thesaurus temporum* (1606) collected and arranged every chronological item in classical literature; and on this foundation he established the first scientific chronology of ancient history. It was he who suggested that Jesus was born in 4 B.C. When Justus Lipsius left Leiden in 1590, the university offered its chair of classical scholarship to Scaliger. After three years of hesitation he accepted; and thereafter, till his death in 1609, Leiden was the Olympus of savants.

Scaliger, like his father, was vain of their family's supposed descent from the della Scala princes of Verona, and he was acidly critical of fellow scholars; but in a forgetful moment he called Isaac Casaubon "the most learned of living men."[33] Casaubon's career explored the uses of adversity. He was born at Geneva because his Huguenot parents had fled from France. They returned to France when he was three, and for sixteen years he lived amid the alarms and terrors of persecution. His father was absent for long periods of service in Huguenot armies; his family often hid in the hills from fanatical bands of armed Catholics; he received his first Greek lessons in a cave in the mountains of Dauphiné. At nineteen he entered the Academy of Geneva; at twenty-two he became its professor of Greek; for fifteen years he held that post through poverty and siege. He could barely live on his salary, but he skimped on food to buy books, and he comforted his scholastic loneliness with kindly letters from the great Scaliger. He issued editions of Aristotle, Pliny the Younger, and Theophrastus, which captivated the learned world not merely by textual emendations but by illuminating notes on ancient ideas and ways. In 1596, when Henry IV had eased the theological strife, Casaubon was appointed to a professorship at Montpellier. Three years later he was invited to Paris, but the university had closed its doors to non-Catholics, and Henry had to take care of him as curator of the Bibliothèque Royale, at the comfortable salary of 1,200 livres per year. The economical Sully told the scholar, "You cost the King too much, sir: your pay exceeds that of two good captains, and you are of no use to your country."[34] When the great Henry died, Isaac thought it time to accept an invitation from England. James I welcomed him as a fellow scholar and gave him a pension of £300 a year. But the French Queen Regent refused to let his books follow him, the King pestered him with disquisitions, the London wits could not forgive him for not talking English. After four years in England he gave up the battle (1614) at the age of fifty-five, and was buried in Westminster Abbey.

In that age the title of scholar was honored above that of poet or historian, for the scholar was revered as one whose patient learning preserved and clarified the wisdom and beauty hiding in ancient literature and philosophy. Scaliger, entering Leiden, was hailed like a conquering prince. Claude de Saumaise, known to the world of scholarship as Salmasius, was desired of many nations; after Casaubon's death he was by common consent "the most learned of all who are now living" and, in general, "the miracle of the world."[35] What had he done? Born in Burgundy, educated—and converted to Calvinism —at Heidelberg, he shone forth, at the age of twenty, with a scholarly edition of two fourteenth-century writers on the controverted primacy of the popes, and, a year later, with an edition of Florus' *Epitome*. Work after work followed, thirty in all, marked by all-embracing erudition. He reached his peak with a tremendous folio of nine hundred double-column pages, *Exercitationes in . . . Solini Polyhistora* (1629). Solinus, a third-century grammarian, had brought together the history, geography, ethnology, economy, fauna, and flora of all the major countries of Europe in an encyclopedic work which a later editor christened *Polyhistor;* upon this text Salmasius hung notes covering with cosmic erudition the whole world of Imperial Rome. Choosing among a dozen invitations, he accepted a professorship at Leiden, where he was at once made head of a brilliant faculty. All went well until Charles II of England, then an exile in Holland, engaged him to write a condemnation of Cromwell for beheading Charles I. His *Defensio regia pro Carolo I* appeared (November 1649) only ten months after the execution. Cromwell did not enjoy it; he hired the greatest poet in England to answer it; we shall hear of it again. Salmasius wrote a reply to Milton, but died (1653) before completing it, and Milton took the credit for killing him.

With so much learning in a few, probably eighty per cent of the people in Western Europe were still illiterate. John Comenius spent forty years seeking to improve the educational systems of Europe. Born in Moravia (1592), rising to be a bishop of the Moravian Brethren, he never lost his faith in religion as the basis and end of education; there could be no wisdom without the fear of God. Though his life was made an odyssey of tribulation by the religious hatreds of his time, he remained true to the tolerant philosophy of the Unitas Fratrum:

> We are all citizens of one world, we are all of one blood. To hate a man because he was born in another country, because he speaks a different language, or because he takes a different view on this subject or that, is a great folly. Desist, I implore you, for we are all equally human. . . . Let us have but one end in view, the welfare of humanity; and let us put aside all selfishness in considerations of language, nationality, or religion.[36]

After writing half a hundred pedagogical texts, he summarized his principles in *Didactica magna* (1632), one of the landmarks in the history of education. First, education should be universal, regardless of sex or means: every village should have a school, every city a college, every province a university; advancement to higher education should be made possible for all who show themselves fit; the state must finance the discovery, training, and utilization of all the ability in its population. Second, education should be realistic: ideas should at every step be kept in touch with things; words in the vernacular or in a foreign language should be learned by seeing or touching or using the objects they represent; grammatical instruction should come later. Third, education should be physical as well as mental and moral; children should be trained in health and vigor through outdoor life and sports. Fourth, education should be practical: it should not stay in the prison of thought, but should be accompanied by action and practice and should prepare for the business of living. Fifth, more and more science should be taught with the advancing age of the student; schools of scientific research should be established in every city or province. Sixth, all education and knowledge should be directed to improving character and piety in the individual and order and happiness in the state.

Some progress was made. The German princes labored to establish an elementary school in every village. The principle of universal compulsory education was proclaimed by the Duke of Saxe-Weimar in 1619 for all boys and girls from six to twelve years of age,[37] with a month's vacation at harvest time, and by 1719 this system had been established throughout Germany. Secondary schools were still closed to women, but they multipled and improved. Twenty-two new universities were opened in this age.* Oxford was flourishing, as described by Casaubon in 1613; he was impressed by the remuneration and the social standing of the teachers there, as compared with their analogues on the Continent. Professors in Germany (1600) were so poorly paid that many of them sold beer and wine to eke out a living; at Jena the students caroused in taverns maintained by professors.[38] Spanish universities declined after Philip II, withering under the glare of the Inquisition; meanwhile several universities were founded in Spanish America—at Lima in 1551, at Mexico City in 1553, long before the establishment of Harvard College in 1636. The prospering Dutch organized six universities in this period. When Leiden successfully resisted Spanish siege (1574), the States-General of the United Provinces invited the citizens to name their reward; they asked for a university; it was so ordered. In Catholic and Calvinist countries education was controlled by ecclesiastics; in England and Lutheran lands it was largely administered by clergymen controlled by the state. In nearly all universities except Padua teachers and students were required to accept the official religion, and academic freedom was strictly limited by both the state and the Church. Religious differences put an end to the international character of the universities; Spanish students were confined to Spain, English students no longer entered the University of Paris, and Oxford continued till 1871 to exact from every candidate for a degree assent to the Thirty-nine Articles of the Established Church. Originative

---

* Jena (1558), Geneva (1559), Lille (1562), Strasbourg (1567), Leiden (1575), Helmstedt (1575), Wilno (1578), Würzburg (1582), Edinburgh (1583), Franeker (1585), Graz (1596), Dublin (1591), Lublin (1596), Harderwijk (1600), Giessen (1607), Groningen (1614), Amsterdam (1632), Dorpat (1632), Budapest (1635), Utrecht (1636), Turku (1640), Bamberg (1648).

thought tended to disappear from universities and to find refuge in private academies and noninstitutional studies.

So, in this age, private academies arose uncensored for study and research, especially in science. At Rome in 1603 Federigo Cesi, Marquis of Montebello, founded the Accademia dei Lincei (Academy of the Lynx-eyed), which Galileo joined in 1611. Its constitution defined its aim:

> The Lincean Academy desires as its members philosophers who are eager for real knowledge, and will give themselves to the study of nature, especially mathematics; at the same time it will not neglect the ornaments of elegant literature and philology, which, like graceful garnets, adorn the whole body of science. . . . It is not within the Lincean plan to find leisure for recitations and debates. . . . The Linceans will pass over in silence all political controversies and every kind of quarrels and wordy disputes.[39]

The academy was dissolved in 1630, but its purposes were carried on (1657) by the Accademia del Cimento (trial and proof). Soon similar societies were to be formed in England, France, and Germany, and the inspiring International of Science would lay the intellectual and technical foundations of the modern world.

III. THE TOOLS AND METHODS OF SCIENCE

First there had to be scientific instruments. The eyes could not see clearly enough, far enough, minutely enough; the flesh could not feel with requisite accuracy the pressure, warmth, and weight of things; the mind could not measure space, time, quantity, quality, density without mingling its personal equation with the facts. Microscopes were needed, telescopes, thermometers, barometers, hydrometers, better watches, finer scales. One by one they came.

In his *Magia naturalis* (1589) Giambattista della Porta wrote, "With a concave lens things appear smaller but plainer; with a convex lens you see them larger but less distinct; if, however, you know how to combine the two sorts properly, you will see near and far both large and clear."[40] Here was the principle of the microscope, the field glass, the opera glass, the telescope, a whole hatful of inventions, and all histology. The simple microscope, a single convex lens, had long been known. The invention that transformed biology was the compound microscope combining several converging lenses. The industry of grinding and polishing lenses was especially developed in the Netherlands—Spinoza lived and died by it. About 1590 Zacharias Janssen, a spectacle-maker of Middelburg, combined a double convex lens and a double concave lens to make the earliest known compound microscope. From that invention came modern biology and modern medicine.

A further application of these principles transformed astronomy. On October 2, 1608, another spectacle-maker of Middelburg, Hans Lippershey, presented to the States-General of the United Provinces (still at war with Spain) the description of an instrument for seeing objects at a distance. Lippershey had placed a double convex lens (the "object glass") at the farther end of a tube, and a double concave lens (the "eyepiece") at the nearer end. The legislators saw the military value of the invention and awarded Lippershey nine hundred florins. On October 17 another Dutchman, Jacobus Metius, stated that he had independently made a similar instrument. Hearing of these developments, Galileo made his own telescopes at Padua in 1609, which magnified to three diameters; these were the instruments with which he began to enlarge the world. In 1611 Kepler suggested that still better results could be obtained by reversing the Galilean position of the lenses, using the convex lens as the "eyepiece" and the concave lens as the object glass; and in 1613–17 the Jesuit Christoph Scheiner made an improved telescope on this plan.[41]

Meanwhile, on principles known to Hero of Alexandria in or before the third century A.D., Galileo had invented a thermometer (c. 1603). Into a vessel of water he placed the open end of a glass tube whose other end was an empty glass bulb, which he warmed by the touch of his hand; when he withdrew his hand the bulb cooled and water rose in the tube. Galileo's friend Giovanni Sagredo (1613) marked off the tube into a hundred degrees.

A pupil of Galileo, Evangelista Torricelli, closed a long glass tube at one end, filled it with mercury, and stood it with its open end submerged in a dish of mercury; the mercury in the tube did not flow down into the dish. Scholastic physics explained this as due to "Nature's abhorrence of a vacuum"; Torricelli explained it as due to the pressure of the surrounding atmosphere upon the mercury in the dish. He reasoned that this outside pressure would raise the mercury in the vessel into an empty tube freed from air; experiment proved him right. He showed that variations in the height of the mercury in the tube could be used as a measure of variations in atmospheric pressure. So in 1643 he constructed the first barometer— still the basic instrument of meteorology.

Armed with these new tools, the sciences called to mathematicians for improved methods of calculation, measurement, and notation. Napier and Bürgi, as we have seen, responded with logarithms, Oughtred with the slide rule; but a greater boon came with the decimal system. Tentative suggestions, as usual, had prepared the way. Al-Kashi of Samarkand (d. 1436) had expressed the ratio of the circumference of a circle to the diameter as

3 1415926535898 732, which is a decimal using a space instead of a point. Francesco Pellos of Nice in 1492 used a point. Simon Stevinus expounded the new system in an epochal treatise, *The Decimal* (1585), in which he offered to "teach with unheard-of ease how to perform all calculations . . . by whole numbers without fractions." The metric system in Continental Europe carried out his ideas in the measurement of lengths, volumes, and currencies; but the circle and the clock paid tribute to Babylonian mathematics by retaining a sexagesimal division.

Gérard Desargues published in 1639 a classic treatise on conic sections. François Viète of Paris revived the languishing study of algebra by using letters for known as well as unknown quantities, and he anticipated Descartes by applying algebra to geometry. Descartes established analytical geometry in a flash of inspiration when he proposed that numbers and equations can be represented by geometrical figures and vice versa (so the progressive depreciation of currency in a course of time can be shown as a statistical graph); and that from an algebraic equation representing a geometrical figure consequences can be algebraically drawn which will prove geometrically true; algebra could therefore be used to solve difficult geometrical problems. Descartes was so charmed with his discoveries that he thought his geometry as far superior to that of his predecessors as the eloquence of Cicero was above the A B C of children.[42] His analytical geometry, Cavalieri's theory of indivisibles (1629), Kepler's approximate squaring of the circle, and the squaring of the cycloid by Roberval, Torricelli, and Descartes all prepared Leibniz and Newton to discover calculus.

Mathematics was now the goal as well as the indispensable tool of all the sciences. Kepler observed that when the mind leaves the realm of quantity it wanders in darkness and doubt.[43] "Philosophy," said Galileo, meaning "natural philosophy," or science,

> is written in this grand book of the universe, which stands continually open to our gaze. But the book cannot be understood unless we first learn to comprehend the language and read the letters in which it is composed. It is written in the language of mathematics.[44]

Descartes and Spinoza longed to reduce metaphysics itself to mathematical form.

Science now began to liberate itself from the placenta of its mother, philosophy. It shrugged Aristotle from its back, turned its face from metaphysics to Nature, developed its own distinctive methods, and looked to improve the life of man on the earth. This movement belonged to the heart of the Age of Reason, but it did not put its faith in "pure reason"— reason independent of experience and experiment. Too often such reasoning had woven mythical webs. Reason, as well as tradition and authority, was now to be checked by the study and record of lowly facts; and whatever "logic" might say, science would aspire to accept only what could be quantitatively measured, mathematically expressed, and experimentally proved.

IV. SCIENCE AND MATTER

The sciences advanced in logical progression through modern history: mathematics and physics in the seventeenth century, chemistry in the eighteenth, biology in the nineteenth, psychology in the twentieth.

The great name in the physics of this period is Galileo, but many lesser heroes merit remembrance. Stevinus helped to determine the laws of the pulley and the lever; he made valuable studies in water pressure, the center of gravity, the parallelogram of forces, and the inclined plane; and at Delft, about 1690, he anticipated Galileo's alleged experiment at Pisa by showing, contrary to immemorial belief, that when two *like* objects of however different weight are let fall together from a height they reach the ground at the same time.[45] Descartes laid down quite clearly the law of inertia—that a body persists in its state of rest or in rectilinear motion unless affected by some external force. He and Gassendi anticipated the molecular theory of heat. He based his *Météores* (1637) on a cosmology no longer accepted, but the treatise did much to establish meteorology as a science. Torricelli (1642) extended his studies of atmospheric pressure to the mechanics of winds; these, he held, were the equalizing currents set up by local differences in the density of the air. Gassendi, that remarkable priest of all sciences, carried on experiments for measuring the speed of sound; his results gave 1,473 feet per second. His friar friend, Marin Mersenne, repeated the experiment and reported 1,380 feet, closer to the current figure of 1,087. Mersenne, in 1636, established the whole series of overtones produced by a sounding string.

Research in optics centered on the complex problems of reflection and refraction, especially as seen in the rainbow. About 1591 Marco Antonio de Dominis, Archbishop of Spalato, composed a treatise, *De radiis visus et lucis . . . et iride* (published 1611), in which he explained the formation of the primary rainbow (the only one generally visible) as due to two refractions and one reflection of light in drops of moisture in sky or spray, and that of the secondary rainbow (an arc of colors, in reversed order, sometimes faintly seen outside the primary bow) as due to two refractions and two reflections. In 1611 Kepler's *Dioptrice* studied the refraction of light by lenses; and ten years later Willebrord Snell of Leiden formulated the laws of refraction with a precision that made possible a more accurate computation of the action of lenses on light and the construction of better microscopes and telescopes. Descartes applied these laws to a mechanical calculation of radiation angles in the rainbow. Explanation of the color arrangement had to wait for Newton.

Gilbert's epochal discussion of terrestrial magnetism set off a train of theories and experiments. Famianus Strada, of the Society of Jesus, suggested telegraphy (1617) by proposing that two men might communicate through a distance by utilizing the sympathetic action of two magnetic needles made to point simultaneously to the same letter of the alphabet. Another Jesuit, Niccolo Cabeo (1629), gave the first known description of electrical repulsion. Still another, Athanasius Kircher, described in his *Magnes* (1641) a measurement of magnetism by suspending a magnet from one pan of a balance and counterpoising its influence by weights in the other. Descartes ascribed magnetism to the conflict of particles thrown off by the great vortex from which he believed the universe had evolved.

Alchemy was still popular, especially as a royal substitute for debasing the currency. Emperor Rudolf II, the electors of Saxony, Brandenburg, and the Palatinate, the Duke of Brunswick, the Landgrave of Hesse, all engaged alchemists to manufacture silver or gold.[46] From these experiments, from the needs of metallurgy and the dyeing industry, and from the emphasis of Paracelsus on chemical medicine, the science of chemistry was taking form. Andreas Libavius personified the transition. His *Defense of Transmutatory Alchemy* (1604) continued the old quest, but his *Alchymia* (1597) was the first systematic treatise on scientific chemistry. He discovered stannic chloride, was the first to make ammonium sulfate, was among the first to suggest blood transfusions as therapy. His laboratory at Coburg was one of the wonders of the city. Jan Baptista van Helmont, a wealthy nobleman who devoted himself to science and the medical service of the poor, placed his name among the founders of chemistry by distinguishing gases from air and analyzing their varieties and composition; he coined the word *gas* from the Greek *chaos*. He made many discoveries in his chosen field, ranging from the explosive gases of gunpowder to the inflammatory possibilities of human wind.[47] He suggested the use of alkalis to correct undue acidity in the digestive tract. Johann Glauber recommended crystalline sodium sulfate as "a splendid medicine for internal and external use," and "Glauber's salt" is still used as an aperient. Both he and Helmont dabbled in alchemy.

All these "natural sciences" shared in improving industrial production and martial slaughter. Technicians applied the new knowledge of movements and pressures in liquids and gases, the composition of forces, the laws of the pendulum, the course of projectiles, the refining of metals.

Gunpowder was used in mine blasting (1613). In 1612 Simon Sturtevant devised a method of producing coke—i.e., "coking" (cooking or heating) bituminous coal to rid it of volatile ingredients; this coke was valuable in metallurgy, as the impurities in coal affected iron; it replaced charcoal and saved forests. The making of glass was cheapened, hence windowpanes became common in this age. Mechanical inventions multiplied as industry grew, for they were due less frequently to the researches of scientists than to the skill of artisans anxious to save time. So we first hear of the screw lathe in 1578, the knitting frame in 1589, the revolving stage in 1597, the threshing machine and the fountain pen in 1636.

Engineers were accomplishing feats that even today would merit admiration. We have seen how Domenico Fontana aroused Rome by erecting an obelisk in St. Peter's Square. Stevinus, as engineer for Maurice of Nassau, developed a system of sluices to control the dykes—guardian of the Dutch Republic. Giant bellows ventilated mines; complicated pumps raised water into towers to give pressure for houses and fountains in cities like Augsburg, Paris, and London. Truss bridges were built on the simple geometrical principle that a triangle cannot be deformed without changing the length of a side. In 1624 a submarine traveled two miles under water in the Thames.[48] Jerome Cardan, Giambattista della Porta, and Salomon de Caus advanced the theory of the steam engine; Caus in 1615 described a machine for raising water by the expansive power of steam.[49]

Geology was still unborn, even as a word; the study of the earth was called mineralogy, and respect for the Biblical story of Creation checked all ventures in cosmogony. Bernard Palissy was denounced as a heretic for reviving the ancient view that fossils were the petrified remains of dead organisms. Descartes ventured to suggest that the planets, including the earth, had once been glowing masses, like the sun, and that as the planet cooled it formed a crust of liquids and solids over a central fire, whose exhalations produced geysers, volcanoes, and earthquakes.[50]

Geography progressed as missionaries, explorers, and merchants strove to extend their faith, their knowledge, or their sales. Spanish navigators (1567f) explored the South Seas and discovered Guadalcanal and others of the Solomon Islands—so named in the hope of finding there Solomon's mines. Pecho Paes, a Portuguese missionary, taken prisoner in Abyssinia (1588), visited the Blue Nile and solved an ancient riddle by showing that the periodic inundations of the Nile Valley were due to the rainy season in the Abyssinian highlands. Willem Janszoon was apparently the first European to touch Australia (1606), and Abel Tasman discovered Tasmania, New Zealand (1642), and the Fiji Islands (1643). Dutch traders entered Siam, Burma, and Indochina, but information about these countries and China came chiefly from Jesuit missionaries. Samuel Champlain, under orders of Henry IV of France, explored the coast of Nova Scotia and ascended the St. Lawrence River to the vicinity of Montreal. His followers founded Quebec and charted the lake that bears his name.

The mapmakers struggled to keep not too far behind the explorers. Gerardus Mercator (Gerhard Kremer) studied at Louvain and established there a shop for making maps, scientific instruments, and celestial globes. In 1544 he was arrested and prosecuted for heresy, but escaped serious consequences; however, he thought it prudent to accept an invitation to the University of Duisburg, where he became cartographer to the Duke of Jülich-Cleves (1559). In his life of eighty-two years he labored tirelessly to map Flanders, Lorraine, Europe, the earth. His famous *Nova et acuta terrae descriptio ad usum navigantium accomodata* (1568) introduced the "Mercator's projection" maps, which facilitated navigation by representing all meridians of longitude as parallel to one another, all parallels of latitude as straight lines, and both sets of lines at right angles to each other. In 1585 he began to issue his great *Atlas* (we owe this use of the word to him), containing fifty-one regional maps of unprecedented precision and accuracy, describing the whole earth as then known. His friend Abraham Oertel rivaled him with a comprehensive *Theatrum orbis terrarum* (Antwerp, 1570). Together these men freed geography from its millennial bondage to Ptolemy and established it in its modern form. Because of them the Dutch maintained almost a monopoly on mapmaking for a century.

V. SCIENCE AND LIFE

Biology had still to wait two centuries for its heyday. Botany grew leisurely through medical studies of curative herbs and the importation of exotic plants into Europe. Jesuit missionaries brought in Peruvian bark (quinine), vanilla, and rhubarb. About 1560 the potato was introduced from Peru to Spain whence it spread across the Continent. Prospero Alpini, professor of botany at Padua, described fifty foreign plants newly cultivated in Europe. From his studies of the date palm he deduced the doctrine of sexual reproduction in plants, which Theophrastus had expressed in the third century B.C. "The female date trees," said Alpini, "do not bear fruit unless the branches of the male and female plants are mixed together, or, as is generally done, unless the dust found in the male sheath or male flowers is sprinkled over the female flowers."[51] Linnaeus would later classify plants according to their mode of reproduction; but meanwhile (1583) Andrea Cesalpino of Florence offered the first systematic classification of plants—1,500 of them—on the basis of their different seeds and fruits. Gaspard Bauhin, of Basel, in his massive *Pinax theatri botanici* (1623), classified 6,000 plants, anticipating Linnaeus' binomial nomenclature by genus and species. Bauhin devoted forty years to preparing this *Table of the Botanic World*, and he died a year after its publication. It remained for three centuries a standard text.

The private herbariums of physicians were now evolving into botanical gardens maintained for the public by universities or governments. The earliest, established at Pisa in 1543, achieved renown under Cesalpino; Zurich had one in 1560, then Bologna, Cassel, Leiden, Leipzig, Breslau, Basel, Heidelberg, Oxford. Gui de La Brosse, physician to Louis XIII, organized the famous Jardin des Plantes Médicinales at Paris in 1635. Zoological gardens, as menageries for public amusement, had existed in China (1100 B.C.), ancient Rome, and Aztec Mexico (c. 1450); modern forms were opened at Dresden in 1554 and under Louis XIII at Versailles.

Zoology received less attention than botany, as it offered—except in mythical medicine—fewer cures. Ulisse Aldrovandi began in 1599 the publication of thirteen great tomes on "natural history"; he lived to see six through the press; the Senate of Bologna published the remaining seven from his manuscripts and at public cost; they were superseded only by the *Histoire naturelle* (1749-1804) of Buffon. The Jesuit polymath Athanasius Kircher began histology with his *Ars magna lucis et umbrae* (1646), in which he described the minute "worms" that his microscope had found in decaying substances. The belief in the spontaneous generation of tiny organisms out of rotten flesh—or even out of slime—was still almost universal, though Harvey was soon to reject it in his *De generatione animalium* (1651). Zoology was backward partly because only a few thinkers saw in animals the progenitors of men. But in 1632 Galileo wrote to the Grand Duke of Tuscany: "Though the differences between man and the other animals is enormous, one might say reasonably that it is little more than the difference among men themselves."[52] The modern mind was slowly climbing back to what the Greeks had known two thousand years before.

Anatomy was resting after its labors under Vesalius. Dissection of cadavers was still opposed—as by Hugo Grotius[53]—but the numerous "anatomy lessons" in Dutch art reflect a general acceptance of the procedure. The great name here, as well as in surgery, is Girolamo Fabrizio d'Acquapendente, pupil of Fallopio and teacher of Harvey. During his reign at the University of Padua the great anatomical theater was built there— the only such structure still completely preserved from that era. His discovery of the valves in the veins and his studies of the effect of ligatures led to Harvey's demonstration of the circulation of the blood. Knowledge of circulation of body fluids was advanced by Gasparo Aselli's discovery of the lacteals (1632), lymphatic vessels carrying milklike chyle from the small intestine. Indeed, Aselli, despite his name ("the little ass") described the circulation of the blood six years before Harvey *published* his theory. Andrea Cesalpino had expounded the essential theory in 1571, half a century before Harvey; he still clung to the old view that some blood passes through the septum of the heart, but he came closer than Harvey to explaining—by *capillamenta*—how the blood finds its way from the arteries to the veins. On a hundred fronts the noblest of all armies was advancing in the greatest of all wars.

VI. SCIENCE AND HEALTH

In that war for the conquest of knowledge the central battle is that of life against death—a battle which individually is always lost and collectively is regularly won. In fighting disease and pain the physicians and the hospitals had many human enemies: personal uncleanliness, public filth, noisome prisons, quacks with magical potions, "scientific" mystics, hernia setters, stone melters, cataract couchers, tooth drawers, amateur uroscopists. And new diseases ran a race with new cures.

Leprosy had disappeared, and protective devices had reduced syphilis; Fallopio had invented (1564) a linen sheath against such infection. (This soon came to be used as a contraceptive and was sold by barbers and bawds.[54]) But epidemics of typhus, typhoid fever, malaria, diphtheria, scurvy, influenza, smallpox, and dysentery appeared in several countries of Europe in this period, especially in Germany. Probably exaggerated figures report 4,000 deaths from a plague of boils in Basel in 1563–64; twenty-five per cent of the inhabitants of Freiburg-im-Breisgau carried off by plague in 1564; 9,000 in Rostock and 5,000 in Frankfurt an der Oder in 1565; 4,000 at Hanover and 6,000 at Brunswick in 1566.[55] Terrified citizens ascribed some plagues to deliberate poisoning; at Frankenstein, in Silesia, seventeen persons were burned to death on suspicion of "strewing poison."[56] In 1604 the bubonic plague was so severe in Frankfurt am Main that there were not enough people to bury the dead.[57] These are palpable exaggerations; but we are told, on good authority, that in a recurrence of the bubonic plague in Italy, 1629–31, Milan lost 86,000 and "no less than 500,000 died in the Venetian Republic. . . . Between 1630 and 1631 there were 1,000,000 victims of the plague in northern Italy alone."[58] The fertility of women barely kept up with the resourcefulness of death. Childbirth was made doubly painful by its frequent futility; two fifths of all children died before completing their second year.[59] Families were large, populations were small.

Public sanitation was improving, hospitals were multiplying. Medical education was taking a more rigorous form—though one could still practice medicine without a degree. Bologna, Padua, Basel, Leiden, Montpellier, Paris had famous medical schools drawing students from all Western Europe. We have a peculiar example of patient medical research in the thirty years of experiment by which Sanctorius tried to reduce physiological processes to quantitative measurement. He did much of his work while sitting at a table on a large scale; he recorded the changes in his weight from the intake and the outlet of solids and liquids, and he even weighed his sweat. He found that the human body gives off several pounds daily through normal perspiration, and concluded that this is a vital form of elimination. He invented a clinical thermometer (1612) and a pulsimeter as aids to diagnosis.

Therapy was graduating from toads to leeches. Some reputable physicians prescribed dried toads, sewn in a bag and hung on the breast, as a trap to catch and absorb the poisonous air that surrounded the body in plague areas.[60] Bloodletting by leeches or cupping was combined with plentiful drinking of water, on the theory that some of the intaken fluid would form fresh uninfected blood. Two schools of treatment contended for the victim: the iatromechanical, stemming from Descartes' teaching that all bodily processes are mechanical; and the iatrochemical, originating with Paracelsus, developed by Helmont, and interpreting all physiology as chemical. Hydrotherapy was popular. Curative waters were taken at England's Bath, the Netherlands' Spa, France's Plombières, and a dozen places along the Rhine and in Italy; we have seen Montaigne trying them and shedding stones on the way. New drugs like valerian (c. 1580), antimony (c. 1603), ipecac (1625), and quinine (1632) were introduced to Europe. The London pharmacopoeia of 1618 listed 1,960 drugs. Montaigne tells of special treats which a few doctors kept for patient patients:

> the left foot of a tortoise, the urine of a lizard, an elephant's dung, a mole's liver, blood drawn from the right wing of a white pigeon, and, for us who have the stone . . . the pulverized droppings of a rat; and such other tomfooleries that are more suggestive of magic and spells than of a serious science.[61]

Such delicacies were impressively expensive, and people in the seventeenth century moaned over druggists' charges more than over doctors' bills.[62]

Dentistry was left to barbers and consisted almost entirely of extractions. The "barber-surgeons" now included skilled practitioners like Ambroise Paré, François Rousset, who revived the Caesarean section, and Gasparo Tagliacozzi, specialist in the plastic reconstruction of ears, noses, and lips. He was condemned by moralists for interfering with the handiwork of

God; his corpse was exhumed from consecrated ground and was buried in unhallowed soil.[63] Wilhelm Fabry, "father of German surgery," was the first to recommend amputation of a limb above the diseased part; and Giovanni Colle of Padua gave the oldest known description of a blood transfusion (1628).

As in every age, the patients resented the doctor's fees; the comedians laughed at his long robe, red shoes, and bedside gravity. If we trust the satires of the comic dramatists, his social status was not much above that of the teacher; but when we note the history of Rembrandt's *Anatomy Lesson* we perceive a class of men holding a respected position in society and able to pay well for even a share in a great picture. And the most famous philosopher of the age, dreaming like all of us of a better future for mankind, thought of this as depending upon the improvement of human character, and of medical science as the likeliest agent of this basic revolution. "For even the mind," said Descartes, "depends so much on the temperament and disposition of the bodily organs that if it is possible to find some means by which men might commonly be made wiser and abler . . . I believe it is in medicine that it ought to be looked for."[64]

VII. FROM COPERNICUS TO KEPLER

We have left astronomy to the last, for its heroes come toward the end of this period and constitute its *pièces de résistance*.

The same Church that was to silence Galileo led the way in a major achievement of modern astronomy—the reform of the calendar. The revision that Sosigenes had made for Caesar about 46 B.C. had overestimated the year by eleven minutes and fourteen seconds; consequently, by 1577 the Julian calendar lagged behind the progress of the seasons by some twelve days, and ecclesiastical feasts had fallen out of the season for which they had been intended. Several attempts at calendar reform had been made—under Clement VI, Sixtus IV, and Leo X—but difficulties had been found in securing general agreement and requisite astronomical knowledge. In 1576 a revised calendar drawn up by Luigi Giglio was presented to Gregory XIII. The Pope submitted it to a commission of theologians, lawyers, and scientists, including the Bavarian Jesuit Christopher Clavius, famous in mathematics and astronomy; the final draft was apparently his work. Long negotiations were carried on with princes and prelates to secure their co-operation; many objections were made, and the effort to win the consent of the Eastern churches failed. On February 24, 1582, Gregory XIII signed the bull that established the Gregorian calendar in Roman-Catholic lands. To equate the old calendar with astronomic realities, ten days were to be omitted in October 1582, the fifth was to be accounted the fifteenth, and complicated allowances were to be made for the reckoning of interest and other commercial relations. To offset the error in the Julian calendar, only such century years as are divisible by 400 were to have a twenty-ninth day in February. Protestant nations resisted the change; in Frankfurt am Main and Bristol the populace rioted in the belief that the Pope wished to rob it of ten days; even Montaigne, avid of time, complained, "The eclipsing or abridging of ten days, which the Pope hath lately caused, hath taken me so low that I can hardly recover myself."[65] But slowly the new calendar—which would need no further correction for 3,333 years—won acceptance: by the German states in 1700, England in 1752, Sweden in 1753, Russia in 1918.*

A similar lag occurred in the acceptance of the Copernican astronomy. In Italy it might be studied and taught if presented as hypothesis rather than demonstrated fact;[66] Giordano Bruno defended it, and Campanella already wondered whether the inhabitants of other planets thought themselves, as earthlings do, the center and purpose of all things.[67] Generally, Protestant theologians vied with Catholic in denouncing the new system. Bacon and Bodin alike repudiated it.[68] More surprising was its rejection by the greatest astronomer of the half century that followed Copernicus' death (1543).

Tycho Brahe was born in 1546 in the then Danish province of Scania, now the southern extremity of Sweden. His father was a member of the Danish Council of State; his mother was mistress of the robes of the Queen. His rich Uncle Jorgen, disconsolately childless, abducted him, wheedled the parents into consent, and gave the boy every advantage of education. At thirteen Tycho entered the University of Copenhagen. According to Gassendi, he was drawn to astronomy when he heard a teacher discuss a forthcoming eclipse of the sun. He watched the eclipse come as predicted, and marveled at the science that had reached such prophetic power. He bought a copy of Ptolemy's *Almagest*, pored over it to the neglect of other studies, and never abandoned the geocentric view there presented in the second century of our era.

At sixteen he was transferred to the University of Leipzig, where he studied law by day and the stars by night. He was warned that this regimen would lead to physical and nervous breakdown. Tycho persisted, and he spent his allowance on astronomical instruments. In 1565 his uncle died, leaving him a large fortune. After settling his business affairs, Tycho hur-

---

* Ideally the calendar would have thirteen months, each of twenty-eight days, with a dateless holiday (or, in leap years, two) at the close of the year. Such a one-page calendar, with rotary devices to indicate the month and the year, could serve for every month indefinitely; each day of the week would fall on the same dates every month and every year; the business year would be evenly divisible into equal months and equal quarters. But, alas, this would confuse the saints.

ried to Wittenberg for more mathematics and astronomy; thence, driven by plague, to Rostock. There he fought a duel and had part of his nose cut off; he ordered a bright new nose of silver and gold and wore it the rest of his life. He dabbled in astrology and predicted the coming death of Suleiman the Magnificent, only to find that the Sultan had already died.[69] After much travel in Germany he returned to Denmark, busied himself with chemistry, and was brought back to astronomy by discovering a new star in the constellation Cassiopeia (1572). His carefree observations of this transitory star and his account of it in his first publication, *De nova stella*, gave him a European reputation, but shocked some great Danes, who considered authorship a form of exhibitionism incompatible with blue blood. Tycho confounded them by marrying a peasant girl. He seems to have felt that a simple housewife was the best mate for an absorbed astronomer and was the best match open to a man with a golden nose.

Dissatisfied with astronomical facilities in Copenhagen, he set out for Cassel, where Landgrave William IV had built (1561) the first observatory with a revolving roof, and Joost Bürgi had developed a pendulum clock which made possible an unprecedented accuracy in timing the observation and movements of stars. Fired with new zeal, Tycho went back to Copenhagen and interested Frederick II in projects for an observatory. The King gave him the island of Hveen (Venus) in the Sound, and a good pension. With this and his own means Tycho built there a castle and gardens which he called Uraniburg (Heavenly City), with living quarters, library, laboratory, several observatories, and a workshop to make his own instruments. He had no telescope; twenty-eight years were to pass before its invention; yet it was his observations that guided Kepler to epochal discoveries.

In twenty-one years at Hveen Tycho and his pupils gathered a body of data exceeding in extent and accuracy anything hitherto known. He took records of the sun's apparent motion every day for many years. He was one of the first astronomers to allow for the refraction of light and the fallibility of observers and instruments; so he repeated the same observation time and again. He discovered and reduced to law the variations in the motion of the moon. His meticulous tracing of a comet in 1577 led him to the now universally accepted belief that comets, instead of being generated in the earth's atmosphere, are true celestial bodies moving in fixed and regular courses. When Tycho published his catalogue of 777 stars, and marked them with loving care on the great celestial globe in his library, he had justified his life.

In 1588 Frederick II died. The new King was a boy of eleven; the regents who ruled him were not as patient with the pride, temper, and extravagance of Brahe as Frederick had been; soon the governmental grants ran low, and in 1597 they ceased. Tycho left Denmark and settled in Benatek Castle, near Prague, as the guest of Emperor Rudolf II, who looked to him for astrological predictions. Brahe imported his instruments and records from Hveen, and advertised for an assistant. Johann Kepler came (1600), and worked fitfully but devotedly for his difficult master. Just as Brahe was hoping to develop his massive accumulation of data into a reasoned theory of the heavens, he was struck down at table by a burst bladder. He lingered in pain for eleven days, and died (1601) mourning that he had not completed his work. The funeral orator said that he had "coveted nothing but time."[70]

VIII. KEPLER: 1571–1630

It turned out well for science that Tycho moved to Prague, for there Kepler inherited his observations, and deduced from them the planetary laws that prepared for Newton's theory of gravitation. From Brahe to Kepler to Newton and from Copernicus to Galileo to Newton are the basic and converging lines of modern astronomy.

Kepler was born at Weil, near Stuttgart, son of an army officer who repeatedly went off to war as preferable to domesticity. Returning at last, the father opened a tavern, in which Johann served as a waiter. The boy was sickly; smallpox crippled his hands and permanently impaired his vision. The Duke of Württemberg saw in him the possibility of a good preacher and paid for his education. At Tübingen Michael Maestlin, who as professor taught the Ptolemaic astronomy, privately converted Kepler to the Copernican theory, and the youth became so enthusiastic about the stars that he abandoned all thought of an ecclesiastical career.

After taking his degree he became a schoolmaster at Graz, in Styria, teaching Latin, rhetoric, and mathematics for 150 gulden a year, with free lodging, and adding twenty gulden by editing annually an astrological calendar. At twenty-five he married a woman of twenty-three who had buried one husband and divorced another; she brought him a dowry and a daughter; he added six children in due course. A year after his marriage he was forced as a Protestant to leave Graz (1597), for the new Archduke of Styria, Ferdinand, was a resolute Catholic who ordered all Protestant clergymen and teachers out of Styria. Kepler had given further offense by publishing *Mysterium cosmographicum* (1596), ardently advocating the Copernican system; hopefully he sent copies to Brahe and Galileo. After a year of despondent poverty he was saved by Tycho's invitation to Prague. But Tycho was hard to get along with; there were difficulties with religion and bread; the wife developed epilepsy. Then Tycho died, and Kepler was appointed his successor, at five hundred florins a year.

Brahe had bequeathed his records to him, but not his instruments. Unable to buy the best, Kepler found himself driven to study Brahe's observations rather than add to them. He could never have said with Newton, "I do not invent hypotheses"; on the contrary, his head hummed with them; "I have much store of fantasy."[71] His peculiar skill lay in testing hypotheses, and his wisdom lay in casting them aside when the consequences that he had mathematically deduced from them proved incompatible with the observed phenomena.[72] In seeking to plot the orbit of Mars he tried seventy hypotheses through four years.

Finally (1604) he reached his basic and epochal discovery—that the orbit of Mars around the sun is an ellipse, not a circle as astronomers from Plato to and including Copernicus had supposed; only an elliptical orbit harmonized with the repeated observations of Brahe and others. Kepler's agile mind leaped to the question, What if all the planetary orbits are elliptical? Rapidly he tested the idea with the recorded observations; it agreed with them almost completely. In a Latin treatise on the motions of Mars, *Astronomia nova de motibus stellae Martis* (1609), he published the first two of "Kepler's laws": first, each planet moves in an elliptical orbit, in which one focus is the sun; second, each planet moves more rapidly when near the sun than when farther from it, and a radius drawn from the sun to the planet covers, in its motion, equal areas in equal times. Kepler ascribed the differences in planetary speed to the greater emanation of solar energy felt by the planet as it neared the sun; in this connection he evolved from Gilbert an idea of magnetic attraction closely akin to Newton's theory of gravitation.

When Emperor Rudolf died (1612) Kepler moved to Linz, and again he lived by teaching school. His wife having passed away, he married a poor orphan girl. In providing his new home with wine he was fascinated by the difficulty of measuring the contents of a cask with curved sides; the essay that he published on the problem helped to prepare the discovery of infinitesimal calculus.

After puzzling for ten years over the relation between the speed of a planet and the size of its orbit, Kepler published, in his book *The Harmony of the World* (1619), his third law: the square of the time of revolution of a planet around the sun is proportioned to the cube root of its mean distance from the sun. (For example: Mars's time of revolution is demonstrably 1.88 times that of the earth; the square of this is 3.53; the cube root of this is 1.52; i.e., the mean distance of Mars from the sun will be 1.52 times that of the earth from the sun.) Kepler was so overjoyed by having reduced the behavior of the planets to such order and regularity that he

likened each orbital speed to a note on a musical scale, and concluded that
the combined motions make a "harmony of the spheres," which, however,
is audible only to the "soul" of the sun. Kepler mingled mysticism with his
science, illustrating again Goethe's generous saying that a man's defects
are the faults of his time, while his virtues are his own. We can forgive
the pride that wrote, in the preface to *The Harmony of the World:*

> What I promised my friends in the title of this book. . . . what,
> sixteen years ago, I urged as a thing to be sought—that for which
> I joined Tycho Brahe, . . . to which I have devoted the best part
> of my life—I have at length brought to light. . . . It is not eighteen
> months since the unveiled sun . . . burst upon me. Nothing holds me;
> I will indulge my sacred fury. . . . If you forgive me, I rejoice; if you
> are angry I can bear it. The die is cast, the book is written, to be read
> either now or by posterity, I care not which; it may well wait a cen-
> tury for a reader, as God has waited six thousand years for a dis-
> coverer![73]

In an *Epitome of the Copernican Astronomy* (1618–21) Kepler showed
how his laws supported, clarified, and amended the Copernican system.
"I have attested it as true in my inmost soul," he said, "and I contemplate
its beauty with incredible and ravishing delight."[74] The treatise was placed
on the Index of Prohibited Books because it argued that the Copernican
theory had been proved. Kepler, a pious Protestant, was not disturbed. For
a while he enjoyed prosperity and acclaim. His salary as Imperial astronomer was generally paid. From faraway Britain James I invited him (1620)
to come and adorn the English court, but Kepler refused, saying that he
would suffer from being cooped up in an island.[75]

He shared the prevailing belief in witchcraft. His mother was charged
with practicing it; witnesses alleged that their cattle, or they themselves,
had become ill because Frau Kepler had touched them; one witness swore
that her eight-year-old daughter had been made ill by Mother Kepler's
witchery, and she threatened to kill the "witch" if she did not at once
cure the girl. The accused woman denied all guilt, but she was arrested and
chained in a cell. Kepler fought for her at every stage of the proceedings.
The state's attorney proposed that a confession be drawn from her by torture. She was taken to the torture chamber and was shown the instruments
to be used upon her; she still asserted her innocence. After thirteen months'
imprisonment she was released, but she died soon afterward (1622).

This tragedy, and the impact of the spreading war, darkened Kepler's
final years. In 1620 Linz was occupied by Imperialist troops, and its inhabitants neared starvation. Through all the chaos he continued his labor
of formulating the observations of Brahe, others, and himself, in the Rudol-

phine tables (1627), which catalogued and charted 1,005 stars and remained standard for a century. In 1626 he moved to Ulm. His Imperial salary fell far in arrears, and he was hard pressed to feed his family. He applied to Wallenstein for employment as astrologer; he was engaged, and for some years he followed the general, casting horoscopes for him and publishing astrological almanacs. In 1630 he went to Regensburg to appeal to the Diet for the arrears of his salary. The effort consumed his last physical resources; he was seized with fever and died within a few days (November 15, 1630), in the fifty-ninth year of his age. All traces of his grave were swept away by the war.

His function in the history of astronomy was to mediate between Copernicus and Newton. He advanced beyond Copernicus by replacing circular with elliptical orbits, by abandoning eccentrics and epicycles, and by placing the sun not at the center of a circle but at one focus of an ellipse. By these changes he freed the Copernican system from many of the difficulties that had almost justified Tycho Brahe in rejecting it; through him the heliocentric view now won a rapidly widening acceptance. He transformed what had been a brilliant guess into a hypothesis worked out in impressive mathematical detail. He provided Newton with the planetary laws that led to the theory of gravitation. While keeping his religious faith fervent and undiminished, he revealed the universe as a structure of law, as a cosmos of order in which the same laws ruled the earth and the stars. "My wish," he said, "is that I may perceive the God whom I find everywhere in the external world in like manner within me."[76]

IX. GALILEO: 1564–1642

1. The Physicist

Galileo Galilei was born at Pisa on the day of Michelangelo's death (February 18, 1564), in the same year as Shakespeare. His father was a cultured Florentine, who shared in teaching him Greek, Latin, mathematics, and music. Not for nothing was Galileo an almost exact contemporary of Monteverdi (1567–1643); music was one of his perennial consolations, especially in his blind old age; he played the organ creditably and the lute well. He liked to draw and paint, and sometimes he regretted that he had not become an artist. In that wonderful Italy of his youth the flame of the Renaissance still burned, inspiring men to be complete. He mourned that he could not design a temple, carve a statue, paint a portrait, write poetry, compose music, guide a ship;[77] he longed to do all of these; and we feel, as we contemplate him, that he lacked only time. Such a man, under different accidents, could have been any kind of great man. Whether by nature or by circumstance, he turned in boyhood to making and playing with machines.

At seventeen he was sent to the University of Pisa to study medicine and philosophy. A year later he made his first scientific discovery—that the swings of a pendulum, regardless of their width, take equal times. By lengthening or shortening the arm of a pendulum he could retard or quicken the rate of oscillation until it synchronized with his pulse; by this "pulsilogia" he could accurately measure his heartbeat.

About this time he discovered Euclid. He overheard a tutor teaching geometry to the pages of the Grand Duke of Tuscany; the logic of mathematics seemed to him immeasurably superior to the Scholastic and Aristotelian philosophy that he had received in the classroom; clandestinely, with Euclid's *Elements* in his hand, he followed the lessons of the instructor to the pages. The tutor took an interest in him and taught him privately. In 1585 Galileo left the University of Pisa without taking a degree, moved to Florence, and, under the tutor's guidance, gave himself with passion to mathematics and mechanics. A year later he invented a hydrostatic balance to measure the relative weights of metals in an alloy, and won the praise of the Jesuit Clavius for an essay on the center of gravity in solid bodies. Meanwhile his father's means ran out, and Galileo faced the obligation to earn his own bread. He applied for teaching posts at Pisa, Florence, and Padua; he was rejected as too young. In 1589, as he and a friend were planning to seek their fortunes in Constantinople and the East, they heard that the chair of mathematics at Pisa had fallen vacant. Galileo applied for it in forlorn hope; he was still only twenty-five. He was given a three-year appointment, at sixty scudi per year. On this he could starve, but he could show his mettle.

He was mettlesome enough, for he began at once, from his professorial chair, a war on the physics of Aristotle. According to the Greek "the downward movement of a mass of gold or lead, or of any other body endowed with weight, is quicker in proportion to its size."[78] Lucretius[79] and Leonardo da Vinci[80] expressed the same view. Even in antiquity Hipparchus (c. 130 B.C.) had questioned the opinion of Aristotle "on bodies carried downward through weight"; and Joannes Philoponus (533 A.D.), commenting on Aristotle, thought that the difference in time of fall between two objects one of which is twice the weight of the other will be "either none at all or imperceptible."[81] Here we come upon a famous and disputed story. It appears first in an early biography of Galileo, written by his friend Vincenzo Viviani in 1654 (twelve years after Galileo's death), and claiming to be founded on Galileo's own verbal account:

To the dismay of all the philosophers, very many conclusions of Aristotle were by him [Galileo] proved false through experiments and solid demonstrations . . . as, among others, that the velocity of moving bodies of the same material, of unequal weight, moving through the same medium, did *not* mutually preserve the proportion of their weight as taught by Aristotle, but all moved at the same speed; demonstrating this with repeated experiments from the height of the Campanile of Pisa in the presence of the other teachers and philosophers, and the whole assembly of students. . . . He upheld the dignity of this professional chair with so great fame . . . that many philosophasters, his rivals, stirred with envy, were aroused against him.[82]

Galileo himself nowhere mentions the Pisa experiment in his extant writings; neither is it mentioned by two of his contemporaries who in 1612 and 1641 reported their own experiments in dropping objects of diverse weight from the top of the Leaning Tower.[83] Viviani's story has been rejected as a legend by some scholars in Germany and America.* Uncertain, too, is the tradition concerning the resentment of fellow professors at Pisa. He left that university in the summer of 1592, probably because he had been offered a loftier chair at a better fee. In September we find him installed at the University of Padua, teaching geometry, mechanics, and astronomy, and turning his home into a laboratory to which he invited his students and friends. He avoided marriage, but took a mistress, who gave him three children.

Now he made the researches and experiments that he gathered together only toward the end of his life in his *Dialogues Concerning Two New Sciences*—i.e., concerning statics and dynamics. He affirmed the indestructibility of matter. He formulated the principles of the lever and the pulley, and showed that the speed of freely falling bodies increases at a uniform rate. He made many experiments with inclined planes; he argued that an object rolling down one plane would rise on a similar plane to a height equal to its fall if it were not for frictional or other resistance; and he concluded to the law of inertia (Newton's first law of motion)—that a moving body will continue indefinitely in the same line and rate of motion unless interfered with by some external force.[84] He proved that a projectile propelled in a horizontal direction would fall to the earth in

---

* Aristotle's writings are often syncopated notes, which he probably amplified or modified in lecturing. The passage in *De Coelo* may have meant that in a resisting medium, including open air, objects of concentrated mass, like a coin, fall faster than articles great in size but small in weight, like a sheet of paper; this, of course, is true. But in a vacuum the coin and the paper—or a ball of lead and a feather—fall at the same speed; and even in the open air the paper, if crumpled into a compact mass, falls at nearly the same speed as the coin. If we note the modification in Viviani's statement—that the objects must be "of the same material . . . falling through the same medium"—the divergence between the Athenian philosopher and the Pisan scientist is much reduced.

a parabolic curve compounding the forces of impetus and gravity. He reduced musical tones to wave lengths of air, and showed that the pitch of a note depends upon the number of vibrations made by the struck string in a given time. Notes, he taught, are felt as consonant and harmonious when their vibrations strike the ear with rhythmic regularity.[85] Only those properties of matter belong to matter that can be dealt with mathematically —extension, position, motion, density; all other properties—sounds, tastes, odors, colors, and so on—"reside only in consciousness; if the living creature were removed, all these qualities would be wiped away and annihilated."[86] He hoped that in time these "secondary qualities" could be analyzed into primary physical qualities of matter and motion, mathematically measurable.[87]

These were basic and fruitful contributions. They were hampered by inadequacy of instruments; so, for example, Galileo underestimated the factor of air resistance in the fall of objects and projectiles. But no man since Archimedes had ever done so much for physics.

2. The Astronomer

Toward the end of his stay in Padua he gave more and more of his time to astronomy. In a letter (1596) to Kepler (seven years his junior), thanking him for the *Mysterium cosmographicum,* he wrote:

> I esteem myself happy to have as great an ally as you in my search for truth. . . . I will read your work . . . all the more willingly because I have for many years been a partisan of the Copernican view, and because it reveals to me the causes of many natural phenomena that are entirely incomprehensible in the light of the generally accepted hypotheses. To refute the latter I have collected many proofs, but I do not publish them, because I am deterred by the fate of our teacher Copernicus, who, though he had won immortal fame with a few, was ridiculed and condemned by countless people (for very great is the number of the stupid). I would dare to publish my speculations if there were more people like you.[88]

He professed his Copernican faith in a lecture at Pisa in 1604. In 1609 he made his first telescope, and on August 21 he demonstrated it to Venetian officials. Hear his account:

> Many of the nobles and senators, although of a great age, mounted more than once to the top of the highest church in Venice [St. Mark's], in order to see sails and shipping . . . so far off that it was

two hours before they were seen without my spyglass . . . , for the effect of my instrument is such that it makes an object fifty miles off appear as large as if it were only five miles away. . . . The Senate, knowing the way in which I had served it for seventeen years at Padua, . . . ordered my election to the professorship for life.[89]

He improved his telescope until it magnified objects a thousand times. Turning it to the sky, he was amazed to discover a new world of stars, ten times as many as had yet been catalogued. Constellations were now seen to contain a great number of stars invisible to the unaided eye; so the Pleiades were seen to be thirty-six instead of seven and Orion eighty instead of thirty-seven, and the Milky Way appeared not as a nebulous mass but as a forest of stars great or small. The moon was no longer a smooth surface, but a corrugation of mountains and valleys; and the vague illumination of its unsunned half could be explained as partly due to sunshine reflected from the earth. In January 1610 Galileo discovered four of the nine "moons" or satellites of Jupiter; "these new bodies," he wrote, "moved around another very great star, in the same way as Mercury and Venus, and peradventure the other known planets, move around the sun."[90] In July he discovered the ring of Saturn, which he mistook for three stars. Critics of Copernicus had argued that if Venus revolved around the sun it should, like the moon, show phases—changes in illumination and apparent shape; and they had held that there was no sign of such changes. But in December Galileo's telescope revealed such phases, and he believed that they could be explained only by the planet's revolution around the sun.

It seems unbelievable, but Galileo, in a letter to Kepler, affirmed that the professors at Padua refused to credit his discoveries, refused even to look at the skies through his telescopes.[91] Tiring of Padua, and hoping for a better intellectual climate in Florence (which was passing from art to science), Galileo named the satellites of Jupiter the Sidera Medicea after Cosimo II, Grand Duke of Tuscany. In March 1610 he dedicated to Cosimo a Latin treatise, Sidereus nuncius, summarizing his astronomical revelations. In May he wrote to the Duke's secretary a letter warm with the ardor and pride of Leonardo's appeal to the Duke of Milan in 1482. He listed the subjects that he was studying and the books in which he hoped to describe his results, and he wondered if he might secure from his master an appointment that would require less time for teaching and leave more for research. In June Cosimo named him "First Mathematician of the University of Pisa, and First Mathematician and Philosopher to the Grand Duke," with an annual salary of a thousand florins, and without obligation to teach. In September Galileo moved to Florence, without his concubine.

He had insisted on the title of philosopher as well as mathematician, for he wished to influence philosophy as well as science. He felt as Ramus, Bruno, Telesio, and others had done before him, as Bacon was urging in this same decade, that philosophy (which he understood as the study and interpretation of Nature in all its aspects) had gone to sleep in the lap of Aristotle, and that the time had come to escape from these forty Greek volumes and look at the world with loosened categories and open eyes and mind. Possibly he trusted too much to reason. "To demonstrate to my opponents the truth of my conclusions, I have been forced to prove them by a variety of experiments, though to satisfy myself alone I have never felt it necessary to make many."[92]

He had the pride and pugnacity of an innovator, though at times he spoke with a wise modesty—"I have never met a man so ignorant that I could not learn something from him."[93] He was an ardent controversialist, skilled to spear a foe on a phrase or roast him with burning indignation. In the margin of a book by the Jesuit Antonio Rocco defending the Ptolemaic astronomy, Galileo wrote, "Ignoramus, elephant, fool, dunce . . . eunuch."[94]

But that was after the Jesuits had joined in condemning him. Before his encounter with the Inquisition he had many friends in the Society of Jesus. Christopher Clavius confirmed Galileo's observations with his own; another Jesuit lauded Galileo as the greatest astronomer of the age; a commission of Jesuit scholars, appointed by Cardinal Bellarmine to examine Galileo's findings, reported favorably on all points.[95] When he went to Rome in 1611 the Jesuits entertained him at their Collegium Romanum. "I stayed with the Jesuit fathers," he wrote; "they had verified the actual existence of the new planets and had been constantly observing them for two months; we compared notes, and I found that their observations agreed exactly with my own."[96] He was welcomed by dignitaries of the Church, and Pope Paul V assured him of his unalterable good will.[97]

In April he showed to prelates and scientists in Rome the results of observations that revealed spots on the sun, which he interpreted as clouds. Apparently unknown to Galileo, Johannes Fabricius had already announced their discovery in De maculis solis (Wittenberg, 1611) and had anticipated Galileo's conclusion that the periodicity of the spots indicated the rotation of the sun. In 1615 Christoph Scheiner, Jesuit professor of mathematics at Ingolstadt, addressed to Markus Welser, chief magistrate of Augsburg, three letters in which he claimed to have discovered the spots in April 1611. Galileo, back in Florence, received from Welser a copy of Scheiner's communications. He discussed them in Three Letters on the Solar Spots, published at Rome by the Accademia dei Lincei in 1613. He claimed that he had observed the spots in 1610 and had shown them to friends in Padua. In the clash of claims to priority in discovering the spots, the friendship between Galileo and the Jesuits cooled.

Convinced that his findings could be explained only on the Copernican theory, Galileo began to talk of the theory as proved. The Jesuit astronomers had no objection to considering it as a hypothesis. Scheiner sent his objections to the Copernican view to Galileo, with a conciliatory letter. "If you wish to advance counterarguments," he wrote, "we shall in no way be offended by them, but will, on the contrary, gladly examine your arguments in the hope that all this will assist in the elucidation of the truth."[98] Many theologians felt that the Copernican astronomy was so clearly incompatible with the Bible that if it prevailed the Bible would lose authority and Christianity itself would suffer. What would happen to the fundamental Christian belief that God had chosen this earth as His human home—this earth now to be shorn of its primacy and dignity, to be set loose among planets so many times larger than itself, and among innumerable stars?

3. On Trial

Galileo met the problem uncompromisingly. "Inasmuch as the Bible," he wrote to Father Castelli (December 21, 1613), "calls for an interpretation differing from the immediate sense of the words" (as when it speaks of God's anger, hatred, remorse, hands, and feet), "it seems to me that as an authority in mathematical controversy it has very little standing. . . . I believe that natural processes which we either perceive by careful observation or deduce by cogent demonstration cannot be refuted by passages from the Bible."[99] Cardinal Bellarmine was alarmed. Through common friends he sent to Galileo a pointed admonition. "It seems to me," he wrote to the astronomer's pupil Foscarini, "that you and Galileo would be well advised to speak not in absolute terms [of the new astronomy as proved] but *ex suppositione*, as I am convinced that Copernicus himself did."[100]

On December 21, 1614, a Dominican preacher, Tommaso Caccini, began the attack, taking as his text an excellent pun, *Viri Galilei, quid statis aspicientes in coelum?*—"Ye men of Galilee, why stand ye gazing up into the heavens?" (Acts, i, 11)—and proceeding to show that the Copernican theory was in irresoluble conflict with the Bible. Other minor warriors sent complaints to the Inquisition; and on March 20, 1615, Cassini lodged a formal accusation against Galileo before the Congregation of the Holy Office (the Inquisition). Monsignor Dini wrote to Galileo that if he would insert into his publications a few sentences declaring the Copernican view to be *hypothesis*, he would not be disturbed,[101] but Galileo refused, as he put it, to "moderate" Copernicus. In a letter to the Grand Duchess of Tuscany, published in 1615, he wrote with bold clarity: "As to the arrangement of the parts of the universe, I hold the sun to be situated motionless in the center of the revolution of the celestial orbs,* while the earth rotates on its axis and revolves about the sun."[102] He went on to a broader heresy:

> Nature . . . is inexorable and immutable; she never transgresses the laws imposed upon her, or cares a whit whether her abstruse reasons and methods of operation are understandable to men. For that reason it appears that nothing physical which sense-experience sets before our eyes, or which necessary demonstrations prove to us, ought to be called in question (much less condemned) upon the testimony of Biblical passages which may have some different meaning beneath their words.

However, he promised submission to the Church:

> I declare (and my sincerity will make itself manifest) not only that I mean to submit myself freely and renounce any errors into which I may fall in this discourse through ignorance of matters pertaining to religion, but that I do not desire in these matters to engage in disputes with anyone. . . . My goal is this alone: that if, among errors that may abound in these considerations of a subject remote from my profession, there is anything that may be serviceable to the holy Church in making a decision concerning the Copernican system, it may be taken and utilized as seems best to the superiors. And if not, let my book be torn and burned, as I neither intend nor pretend to gain from it any fruit that is not pious and Catholic.[103]

But he added, "I do not feel obliged to believe that that same God who has endowed us with sense, reason, and intellect has intended us to forgo their use."[104]

On December 3, 1615, he went to Rome of his own accord, armed with friendly letters from the Grand Duke to influential prelates and the Florentine ambassador at the Vatican. In Rome he undertook to convert ecclesiastical officials individually; he upheld the Copernican system at every opportunity; soon "everybody" in Rome was discussing the stars.[105] On February 26, 1616, the Inquisition directed Cardinal Bellarmine to "summon before him the said Galileo and admonish him to abandon the said opinions, and in case of refusal . . . to intimate to him, before a notary and

---

* By the humor of history this is a proposition that no astronomer holds today. Perhaps all astronomy, like all history, should be taken as hypothesis. Of the beyond, as of yesterday, there is no certainty.

witnesses, a command to abstain altogether from teaching or defending the said opinions and even from discussing them. If he do not acquiesce therein he is to be imprisoned."[106] Galileo appeared before Cardinal Bellarmine on that day and declared his submission to the decree.[107] On March 5 the Holy Office published its historic edict:

> The view that the sun stands motionless at the center of the universe is foolish, philosophically false, and utterly heretical, because contrary to Holy Scripture. The view that the earth is not the center of the universe and even has a daily rotation is philosophically false, and at least an erroneous belief.[108]

The Congregation of the Index, on the same date, forbade the publication or reading of any book advocating the condemned doctrines; but in the case of Copernicus' *De revolutionibus orbium coelestium* (1543) it forbade the use of the book "until it is corrected"; and in 1620 it allowed Catholics to read editions from which nine sentences that represented the theory as a fact had been removed.

Galileo returned to Florence, lived in studious retirement in his villa, Bellosguardo, and kept out of controversy till 1622. In 1619 his disciple Mario Guiducci published an essay embodying Galileo's theory (now rejected) that comets are emanations of the earth's atmosphere, and vigorously criticizing the views of the Jesuit Orazio Grassi. The irate father, under a pseudonym, published an attack upon Galileo and his followers. In 1622 Galileo sent to Monsignor Cesarini in Rome the manuscript of *Il saggiatore* (*The Assayer*), answering Grassi, and rejecting, in science, all authority but observation, reason, and experiment. With the author's consent some members of the Accademia dei Lincei softened a few passages. In this form Urban VIII accepted its dedication and sanctioned its publication (October 1623). It is Galileo's most brilliant composition, a masterpiece of Italian prose and controversial skill. The Pope, we are told, enjoyed it; the Jesuits squirmed.

So encouraged, Galileo set out again for Rome (April 1, 1624), hoping to convert the new Pope to Copernican ideas. Urban received him cordially, gave him six long interviews and many gifts, listened to the Copernican arguments, but refused to lift the Inquisition's ban. Galileo went back to Florence consoled by Urban's declaration to the Grand Duke, "For a long time we have extended our fatherly love to this great man, whose fame shines in heaven and marches on earth."[109] In 1626 Galileo was heartened by the appointment of his pupil Benedetto Castelli to be mathematician to the Pope, and of another pupil, Father Niccolò Riccardi, as chief censor of the press. He hastened now to complete his chief work, an exposition of the Copernican and anti-Copernican systems. In May he took the manuscript to Rome, showed it to the Pope, and obtained the ecclesiastical imprimatur for its publication, on condition that the subject be treated as hypothesis. Back in Florence, Galileo revised the book and issued it (February 1632) under a long title: *Dialogo . . . dei due massimi sistemi del mundo—Dialogue of G. G., . . . Where, in Meetings of Four Days, Are Discussed the Two Chief Systems of the World, Ptolemaic and Copernican, Indeterminately Proposing the Philosophical and Natural Arguments, as Well on One Side as on the Other.*

The book might have brought Galileo less grief and renown had it not been for its beginning and its end. Said the preface "to the discerning reader":

> Several years ago there was published in Rome a salutary edict which, in order to obviate the dangerous tendencies of our present age, imposed a reasonable silence upon the Pythagorean opinion that the earth moves. There were those who impudently asserted that this decree had its origin not in judicious inquiry, but in passion none too well informed. Complaints were to be heard that advisers who were totally unskilled in astronomical observations ought not to clip the wings of reflective intellects by means of rash prohibitions.[110]

This was in effect to notify the reader that the dialogue form was a dodge to elude the Inquisition. In the dialogue two characters, Salviati and Sagredo —the names of two of Galileo's warmest friends—defend the Copernican system; a third character, Simplicio, rejects it, but with transparent sophistry. Near the end of the work Galileo put into Simplicio's mouth, almost verbatim, a statement that Urban VIII had insisted on being added: "God is all-powerful; all things are therefore possible to him; *ergo* the tides cannot be adduced as a necessary proof of the double motion of the earth without limiting God's omniscience." Upon which Salviati comments sarcastically, "An admirable and truly angelic argument."[111]

The Jesuits, several of whom were roughly handled in the *Dialogue* (Scheiner's ideas were called "vain and foolish"), pointed out to the Pope that his statement had been put into the mouth of a character who throughout the book had been represented as a simpleton. Urban appointed a commission to examine the work; it reported that Galileo had treated the Copernican system not as hypothesis but as fact, and that he had secured the imprimatur by clever misrepresentations. The Jesuits added, with foresight, that the doctrines of Copernicus and Galileo were more dangerous to the Church than all the heresies of Luther and Calvin. In August 1632 the Inquisition forbade further sale of the *Dialogue*, and ordered the confiscation of all remaining copies. On September 23 it summoned Galileo to appear before its commissioner in Rome. His friends pleaded his sixty-eight years and many infirmities, but to no avail. His daughter, now a fervent nun, sent him touching letters begging him to submit to the Church. The Grand Duke advised him to obey, provided him with the grand-ducal sedan chair, and arranged with the Florentine ambassador to house him in the embassy. Galileo reached Rome February 13, 1633.

Two months passed before the Inquisition called him to its palace (April 12). He was charged with having broken his promise to obey the decree of February 26, 1616, and was urged to confess his guilt. He refused, protesting that he had only presented the Copernican view as hypothesis. He was kept a prisoner in the palace of the Inquisition till April 30. There he fell sick. He was not put to torture, but may have been led to fear it. At a second appearance before the commission he humbly confessed that he had stated the case for Copernicus more strongly than against him, and offered to correct this in a supplementary dialogue. He was allowed to return to the house of the ambassador. On May 10 he was examined again; he offered to do penance and begged consideration for his age and ill health. At a fourth examination (June 21) he affirmed that after the decree of 1616 "every doubt vanished from my mind, and I held and still hold Ptolemy's opinion—that the earth is motionless and that the sun moves— as absolutely true and incontestable."[112] The Inquisition countered that Galileo's dialogues made quite clear his acceptance of Copernicus; Galileo insisted that he had been anti-Copernican since 1616. The Pope had kept in touch with the examination, but had not attended in person. Galileo hoped that Urban VIII would come to his aid, but the Pope refused to interfere. On June 22 the Inquisition pronounced him guilty of heresy and disobedience; it offered him absolution on condition of full abjuration; it sentenced him to "the prison of this Holy Office for a period determinable at our pleasure," and prescribed as penance the recitation of the seven penitential psalms daily for the next three years. He was made to kneel, repudiate the Copernican theory, and add:

> With a sincere heart and unfeigned faith I abjure, curse, and detest the said errors and heresies, and generally every other error and heresy contrary to the . . . Holy Church, and I swear that I will nevermore in future say or assert anything . . . which may give rise to a similar suspicion of me; and that if I shall know any heretic or anyone suspected of heresy, I will denounce him to this Holy Office. . . . So may God help me, and these His Holy Gospels which I touch with my own hands.[113]

The sentence was signed by seven cardinals, but did not receive papal ratification.[114] The story that on leaving the trial chamber Galileo muttered defiantly, *"Eppur si muove!"* (And yet it does move!), is a legend not traceable before 1761.[115] After three days in the prison of the Inquisition he was allowed, by order of the Pope, to go to the villa of the Grand Duke at Trinità dei Monti in Rome; a week later he was transferred to comfortable quarters in the palace of his former pupil, Archbishop Ascanio Piccolomini, at Siena. In December 1633 he was allowed to remove to his own villa at Arcetri, near Florence. Technically he was still a prisoner, and he was forbidden to wander outside his own grounds, but he was free to pursue his studies, teach pupils, write books, and receive visitors—here Milton came in 1638. His nun daughter came to live with him, and took upon herself the penalty of reciting the psalms.

4. The Patriarch

Apparently he was a broken man, defeated and humiliated by a Church that felt herself the guardian of the faith, hopes, and morals of mankind. His abjuration, after months of imprisonment and days of questioning that could have shattered the mind and will of a young warrior, was forgivable in an old man who remembered Bruno's burning thirty-three years before. But he was not really defeated. His book spread through Europe in a dozen translations, and his book did not recant.

He solaced his grief at Siena and Arcetri by summing up his physical researches in another major work, *Discorsi e dimostrazioni matematiche intorno a due nuove scienze (Dialogues . . . Concerning Two New Sciences)*. As the Italian press was closed to him by his condemnation, he negotiated secretly with foreign printers, and finally the Elzevir firm issued the book at Leiden in 1638. It was acclaimed throughout the learned world as raising the science of mechanics to a higher level than ever before. After its publication he continued to prepare additional dialogues, in which he studied the mechanics of percussion and adumbrated Newton's second law of motion. "In the last days of his life," says his first biographer, "and amid much physical suffering, his mind was constantly occupied with mechanical and mathematical problems."[116] In 1637, just before his eyesight began to fail, he announced his last astronomical discovery, the librations of the moon—the variations in that side of the moon which always faces the earth. And in 1641, a few months before his death, he explained to his son a plan for making a pendulum clock.

The portrait that Sustermans painted of him at Arcetri (now in the Pitti Gallery) is of genius incarnate: immense forehead, pugnacious lips, searching nose, penetrating eyes; this is one of the noblest faces in history. The eyes lost their sight in 1638, perhaps from too arduous gazing. He con-

soled himself with the thought that no man since Adam had seen so much
as he. "This universe," he said, "that I have extended a thousand times
. . . has now shrunk to the narrow confines of my own body. Thus God
likes it; so I too must like it."[117] In 1639, suffering from sleeplessness and a
hundred pains, he was allowed by the Inquisition to visit Florence, under
strict surveillance, to see a physician and hear Mass. Back in Arcetri he
dictated to Viviani and Torricelli and played the lute, till his hearing also
failed. On January 8, 1642, aged almost seventy-eight, he died in the arms
of his disciples.

Grotius called him "the greatest mind of all time."[118] He had, of course,
some limitations of intellect and character. His faults—pride, temper,
vanity—were literally the defects or price of his qualities: his persistence,
courage, and originality. He did not recognize the importance of Kepler's
calculations on the planetary orbits. He was slow to credit the work of
his contemporaries. He hardly realized how many of his discoveries in
mechanics had been made before him—some by another Florentine, Leonardo. The views for which he was punished are not precisely those that
astronomers hold today; like most martyrs, he suffered for the right to be
wrong. But he was not wrong in feeling that he had made dynamics a full-
fledged science and had widened the human mind and perspective by revealing, in greater measure than ever before, the frightful immensity of the
universe. He shared with Kepler the honor of winning acceptance for
Copernicus, and with Newton the distinction of showing that the heavens
declare the glory of law. And, like a good son of the Renaissance, he wrote
the best Italian prose of his time.

His influence pervaded Europe. His very condemnation raised the status
of science in northern lands, while lowering it for a while in Italy and
Spain. Not that the Inquisition destroyed Italian science: Torricelli, Cassini,
Borelli, Redi, Malpighi, Morgagni carried the torch on to Volta, Galvani,
and Marconi. But Italian scientists, remembering Galileo, avoided the philosophical implications of science. After the burning of Bruno and the
intimidation of Descartes by Galileo's fate, European philosophy became a
Protestant monopoly.

In 1835 the Church withdrew the works of Galileo from her Index of
Prohibited Books. The broken and defeated man had triumphed over the
most powerful institution in history.

CHAPTER XXIII

Philosophy Reborn

1564-1648

I. SKEPTICS

UNDER and amid the conflicts of national states, economic forces, political parties, and varieties of religious belief, the essential drama of modern European history was taking form: the fight for life of a great religion besieged and sapped by science, sectarianism, epicureanism, and philosophy. Is Christianity dying? Is the religion that gave morals, courage, and art to Western civilization suffering slow decay through the spread of knowledge, the widening of astronomic, geographical, and historical horizons, the realization of evil in history and the soul, the decline of faith in an afterlife and of trust in the benevolent guidance of the world? If this is so, it is the basic event of modern times, for the soul of a civilization is its religion, and it dies with its faith. To Bruno and Descartes, Hobbes and Spinoza, Pascal and Bayle, Holbach and Helvétius, Voltaire and Hume, Leibniz and Kant, it was no longer a question of Catholicism versus Protestantism, it was a question of Christianity itself, of doubts and denials rising about the dearest fundamentals of the ancient creed. The thinkers of Europe —the vanguard of the European mind—were no longer discussing the authority of the pope; they were debating the existence of God.

Many factors made for unbelief. The principle of private judgment, condemned by the Catholic Church as an invitation to doctrinal and moral chaos, had been proclaimed, established, and then condemned by nearly all the Protestant bodies; meanwhile it had undermined the citadel of belief. Multiplying sects fought one another like superabundant progeny, exposed one another's weaknesses, and left faith naked to rationalist winds. In their war they called both Scripture and reason to their support; the study of the Bible led to doubts of its meaning and infallibility, and the appeal to reason ended the Age of Faith. The Protestant Reformation achieved more than it desired. The assaults of Biblical criticism especially damaged a Protestantism that had recklessly based itself upon a divinely inspired Bible. Improvements in social order and human security softened terror and cruelty; men felt compelled to reconceive God in gentler terms than those of Paul and Augustine, Loyola and Calvin; hell and predestination became incredible, and the new morality shamed the old theology. The growth of wealth and pleasure made for an epicurean life, which sought a philosophy to justify it. Religion was a casualty in the wars of religion. The increasing knowledge of pagan morals and philosophies, of Asiatic cults and rituals, led to disturbing comparisons with Christianity; have we not heard Erasmus praying to "Saint Socrates," and seen Montaigne reduce religious creeds to the accidents of geography and the arbitrament of war? The growth of science revealed the operation of "natural law" in many cases—e.g., the path of comets—where faith had seen the hand of Providence. The educated classes found it harder to believe in miracles, even while the letterless gloried in them. And this earth which, in the fond mythology of the people, had felt the feet of God—was it, as Copernicus and Galileo implied, only a bubble and a moment in a universe immeasurably too vast for the jealous, vengeful deity of Genesis? Where had heaven gone, now that up and down changed places twice a day?

The mildest skeptics were the Unitarians, who in Italy, Switzerland, Poland, Holland, and England suggested doubts about the divinity of Christ. There were already a few deists, who professed belief in a God loosely identified with Nature, rejected the divinity of Christ, and wished to make Christianity an ethic rather than a creed; they were as yet sporadic and cautious, except when, like Edward Herbert of Cherbury, they had sufficient status to frighten the hangman; we shall find them more vocal after 1648. Bolder were the "Epicureans" of Germany, who laughed at the Last Judgment, which took so long in coming, and at hell, which was probably not so terrible after all, since all the jolliest company gathered there.[1] In France such men were called *esprits forts* (tough minds) or *libertins*, whose loose ways began to give its modern meaning to a word that had originally meant "freethinkers." In 1581 Philippe Duplessis-Mornay wrote a book of nine hundred pages, *De la Vérité de la religion chrétienne, contre les athées;* in 1623 the Jesuit François Garasse published a quarto of over a thousand pages, in which he denounced the *beaux esprits* who "believe in God only by way of form or as a maxim of state" and accept only Nature and destiny.[2] In that same year Marin Mersenne estimated the "atheists" of Paris at fifty thousand,[3] but that word was then so loosely used that he may have meant deists. In 1625 Gabriel Naudé explained that the divine revelations of laws to Numa Pompilius and Moses were fables invented to promote social order, and that the monks of the Thebaid had fabricated their stories of combats with the Devil to raise their reputation and milk the credulous mob.[4] François de La Mothe Le Vayer, secretary to Richelieu and tutor to the future Louis XIV, published in 1633 his *Dialogues of Orasius Tabero*, professing a general skepticism: "Our knowledge is asininity, our certainties are fictions, our whole world is . . . a perpetual comedy."[5] He was one of those whose faith faded before the multiplicity of infallible creeds. "Amongst that infinity of religions there is no man who does not believe that he possesses the true and condemns all the rest."[6] Despite his skepticism he married at seventy-eight and died in bed at eighty-four. Like a good skeptic, he had made his peace with the Church.

Much of this French skepticism was a negative echo of Montaigne. It became a positive and constructive force in Montaigne's friend Pierre Charron, a Bordeaux priest who gave him the last rites and inherited his library. Charron's *Traité de la sagesse* (1601), a three-volume description of wisdom, has been inadequately described as a systematization of Montaigne; it is, rather, an independent treatise, owing much to the *Essays*, but bearing the stamp of Charron's grave and courteous character. All knowledge, he says, is derived from the senses and is therefore subject to the many mistakes and limitations of the senses; truth is not for us. Fools argue that truth is proved by universal consent, and that *vox populi est vox Dei*; Charron believes rather that the voice of the people is the voice of ignorance, of opinions manufactured for them, and that one should be especially skeptical of what is widely believed.[7] The soul is a mysterious, restless, searching activity connected with the brain and apparently dying with the body.[8] Religion is composed of unprovable mysteries and many absurdities, and has been guilty of barbarous sacrifices and intolerant cruelties. If (as Voltaire would repeat) all men were philosophers, lovers and practicers of wisdom, religion would be unnecessary, and societies would live by a natural ethic independent of theology; "I would have a man virtuous without heaven and hell."[9] But considering the natural wickedness and ignorance of mankind, religion is a necessary means to morality and order.[10] Consequently Charron accepts all the fundamentals of Christianity, even to angels and miracles,[11] and he advises his sage to observe all the religious rites prescribed by the church to which, however accidentally, he belongs.[12] A true skeptic will never be a heretic.[13]

Despite these orthodox conclusions a contemporary Jesuit classed him with the most wicked and dangerous atheists,[14] and when Charron suddenly died, aged sixty-two, of an apoplectic stroke (1603), the pious called it God's judgment on his infidelities.[15] Shortly before his death he prepared a second edition, in which he softened his more reckless passages and assured his fellow clergymen that by Nature he meant God; his book was put on the Index nevertheless. For half a century it far surpassed Montaigne's *Essays* in popularity; *De la sagesse* had thirty-five editions in France between 1601 and 1672, and in the eighteenth century Charron was more influential than his master. But the same orderliness of exposition that attracted the classic seventeenth century seemed a dreary and scholastic didacticism in the nineteenth, and Charron was lost in the rediscovered brilliance and gaiety of Montaigne.

II. GIORDANO BRUNO: 1548–1600

Copernicus had enlarged the world. Who would now enlarge God, and reconceive deity in terms worthy of those numberless and imperturbable galaxies? Bruno tried.

He was born in Nola, sixteen miles east of Naples. Christened Filippo, he changed his name to Giordano when, aged seventeen, he entered the monastery of the Dominicans at Naples. There he found a good library, rich not only in theology but in the Greek and Latin classics, in Plato and Aristotle, even in Arabic and Hebrew authors who had been translated into Latin. His poetic nature took readily to the pagan mythology, which persisted in his thought long after the Christian theology had faded away. He was fascinated by the atomism of Democritus as continued by Epicurus and so majestically expounded by Lucretius. He read the Moslem thinkers Avicenna and Averroës, and the Jewish philosopher Avicebrón (Ibn Gabirol). Something of Hebrew mysticism entered into him and mingled with the ideas of Pseudo-Dionysius and Bernardino Telesio on the union of contraries in Nature and God; something, too, of the vision that Nicholas of Cusa had had of an infinite universe without center or circumference and animated by a single soul. He admired the rebellious medical mysticism of Paracelsus, the mystical symbolism and mnemonic devices of Raymond Lully, and the occult philosophy of Cornelius Agrippa. All these influences molded him, and inflamed him with hostility to Aristotle, to Scholasticism, to Thomas Aquinas. But he was in a Dominican monastery, and Aquinas was the intellectual hero of the Dominicans.

Inevitably the young monk troubled his superiors with objections, questions, and theories. Moreover, sex was simmering in his blood; he confessed later that not all the snows of the Caucasus could quench his fires; and there is some subtle connection between sexual and intellectual awakening. He took full priestly orders in 1572, but doubts continued to agitate him secretly. How could there be three persons in one God? How could a priest, with whatever formula, transform bread and wine into the body and blood of Jesus Christ? Twice, after his ordination, he was formally censured by his superiors. Suddenly, in 1576, after eleven years as a monk, he fled from the monastery, and for a while he hid himself in Rome. He discarded his monastic gown, resumed his baptismal name, and sought safety and privacy as a teacher of a school for boys in Noli, near Genoa.

So began sixteen years of wandering, in which the restlessness of his body kept pace with the vacillations of his mind. After four months in Noli he moved to Savona, then to Turin, to Venice, to Padua. To secure monastic hospitality he donned again the garb of a Dominican monk. Then on to

Brescia, to Bergamo, and over the Alps to Chambéry, where a Dominican monastery received and fed him. Then to Lyon. Then to Geneva. There, in the citadel of Calvinism, he again divested himself of his monastic robe. For two months he lived in uncongenial peace, earning his bread by correcting manuscripts and proofs. Among these was his own review of a lecture given at the University of Geneva by a Calvinist theologian. Bruno pointed out twenty errors in that lecture. The printer of his review was arrested and fined; Bruno himself was called to trial before the Consistory. He apologized and was excused. Disappointed to find that he had escaped one censorship to fall under another, he left Geneva, returned to Lyon, and passed on to Toulouse. There some measure of tolerance transiently appeared through the rivalry of Catholics and Huguenots and the influx of only slightly converted Jews from Spain and Portugal. Probably during Bruno's stay (1581) François Sanchez published at Toulouse his skeptical treatise *Of the Right Noble Knowledge . . . that Nothing Is Known (Quod nihil scitur)*. For eighteen months Bruno lectured on Aristotle's *De anima*. Then, for reasons unknown—perhaps desiring a more capital fame—he moved up to Paris.

He had acquired a reputation not only as a philosopher but as an expert in mnemonics. Henry III sent for him and solicited the magic secrets of a good memory. The King was pleased with Bruno's lessons and appointed him to a professorship in the Collège de France. For two years Bruno bore with peace. But in 1582 he published a comedy, *Candelaio (The Torchbearer)*, in which with verve and fury he satirized monks, professors, pedants, and—but let the Prologue speak:

> You will see, in mixed confusion, snatches of cutpurses, miles of cheats, enterprises of rogues; also delicious disgusts, bitter sweets, foolish decisions, mistaken faith and crippled hopes, niggard charities, . . . virile women, effeminate men . . . and everywhere the love of gold. Hence proceed quartan fevers, spiritual cancers, light thoughts, ruling follies, . . . advancing knowledge, fruitful action, purposive industry. In fine you will see, throughout, naught secure, . . . little beauty, and nothing of good.

He signed the play "Bruno the Nolan, Graduate of the Academy, Called the Nuisance."[16]

And so, in March 1583, he tried England. Henry III, "readier to recommend him to others than to retain his services,"[17] gave him letters of introduction to the French ambassador in London, Michel de Castelnau, Sieur de la Mauvissière. Now began Bruno's happiest interlude. For two years he lived and ate in the ambassador's mansion, free from economic necessities, writing some of his most important works, always finding refuge there from the storms precipitated by his character, and comforted in his controversies by a tolerant man of the world who knew better than to take metaphysics seriously. In that home Bruno met Sir Philip Sidney, the Earl of Leicester, John Florio, Edmund Spenser, Gabriel Harvey, and others of the finest minds in Elizabethan England. These conversations provided the basis of Bruno's symposium *La cena de le Ceneri*. He met the great Queen herself, and eulogized her in terms that were later held against him by the Inquisition.

In 1583 he requested of Oxford University the privilege of lecturing in its halls, and expounded his qualifications in terms that forever cleared him of any imputation of modesty.[18] Permission given, he spoke on the immortality of the soul and on "the fivefold sphere"—i.e., the planetary system of Copernicus. He was heckled by, among others, the rector of Lincoln College, as he tells us in his own way:

> Would you hear how they were able to reply to his [Bruno's] arguments? How fifteen times, by means of fifteen syllogisms, a poor doctor whom on this solemn occasion they had put forward as the very Corypheus of the Academy was left standing like a chick entangled in tow? Would you learn with what incivility and discourtesy that pig comported himself, and the patience and humanity of him who showed himself to be born a Neapolitan and nurtured under a more benign sky? Are you informed how they closed his public lectures?[19]

Later he called Oxford the "widow of sound learning" (*vedova de le buone lettere*), a "constellation of pedantic and most obstinate ignorance and presumption, mixed with rustic incivility that would exhaust the patience of Job."[20]

Our philosopher was no Job. He wrote brilliantly about the stars and found earthlings intolerably dull. He felt that his philosophical development of Copernican astronomy was a beneficent advance in understanding, and he was "a biting critic"[21] of all who rejected his views, though Florio found him, when appeased, "gentle and urbane."[22] His vanity was a trial to his friends as well as the wind in his sails. He gave himself the most magnificent titles—"doctor of the more developed theology, professor of purer and harmless wisdom."[23] He had the fervid imagination, the excitable eloquence, of a Neapolitan; wherever he went the sun of the south heated his blood. "For love of true wisdom," he said, "and zeal for true contemplation, I tire, torment, and crucify myself."[24]

Toward the end of 1585 he returned to Paris in the suite of the recalled ambassador. He lectured at the Sorbonne, exciting the hostility of the Aristotelians as usual. The war of the League against Henry III persuaded

Bruno to sample German universities. In July 1586 he registered at the University of Marburg; refused the right to lecture, he denounced the rector and went on to Wittenberg. For two years he lectured at Luther's university; departing, he voiced his gratitude in a soaring valedictory, but the theology of the reformers did not attract him. He sought the patronage of Rudolf II at Prague; the Emperor thought him fantastic, but gave him three hundred thalers and permission to teach at the University of Helm-stedt in Brunswick. For some months he was happy; then the head of the Lutheran Church there denounced and excommunicated him.[25] We do not know the upshot, but Bruno passed on to Frankfurt to Zurich to Frankfurt (1590–91), where he settled down to publish his Latin works.

By this time—one year before his imprisonment by the Inquisition—his philosophy was complete, though it never achieved clarity or coherent form. On looking into Bruno's chief writings we are struck by the titles, which are here given in abbreviated form.* Often they are poetic and obscure and warn us to expect rather reveries and ecstasies than a systematic or consistent philosophy. Hardly elsewhere, outside of Rabelais, shall we find such a gallimaufry of epithets, rhetoric, allegories, symbols, myths, "humours," conceits, bombast, trivia, exaltation, burlesque, and wit, piled one upon another in a nebulous confusion of dogmas, insights, and hypotheses. Bruno inherited the skill of the Italian dramatists, the scandalous hilarity of the macaronic poets, the slashing satire of Berni and Aretino. If philosophy means calm perspective, reasoned restraint, ability to see all sides, tolerance of difference, even sympathy for simpletons, Bruno was not a philosopher but a warrior, who put on blinders lest surrounding dangers should divert him from his goal—which was, two centuries before Voltaire, *écraser l'infâme*, to smash the infamy of obscurantism and persecution. There is something bitterer than Voltaire in the savage sarcasm wherewith he satirizes the theological idealization of unthinking faith:

> There is not, there is not, I say, a better mirror placed before human eyes than Asininity or the ass, or which demonstrates more clearly the duty of that man who . . . looks for the reward of the final judgment. . . . On the other hand, nothing is more effective to engulf us in the abyss of Tartarus [hell] than philosophical and rational specu-

---

* *La cena de le Ceneri* (1584) ("The Ash Wednesday Supper").
De la causa, principio, et uno (1584) ("Of Cause, Beginning, and the One").
De l'infinito universo et mundi (1584) ("Of the Infinite Universe and the Worlds").
Spaccio de la bestia trionfante (1584) ("Expulsion of the Triumphant Beast").
Degl' heroici furori (1585) ("Of the Heroic Frenzies").
Cabal del cavallo Pegaseo (1585) ("The Revelation of the Horse of Pegasus").
De magia (1590) ("Of Magic").
De rerum principiis et elementis et causis (1590).
De monade, numero, et figura (1591).
De innumerabilibus, immenso, et infigurabili.

lations which, born of the senses . . . , ripen in the developed human intellect. Try, try, therefore, to be asses, all ye who are men; and you who are already asses, study . . . to proceed from good to better, so that you may arrive at that end and dignity which is attained not by knowledge and effort, however great, but by faith, and which is lost not by ignorance and misdoing, however enormous, but by unbelief. If by this conduct you are found written in the book of life, you will obtain grace in the Church Militant and glory in the Church Triumphant, in which God lives and reigns through all ages. Amen.[26]

Bruno's vision of the universe is primarily aesthetic, a profound and wondering appreciation of an incandescent infinity; but it is also a philosophical attempt to adjust human thought to a cosmos in which our planet is an infinitesimal part of an unknowable immensity. The earth is not the center of the world, nor is the sun; beyond the world that we see (there were no telescopes when Bruno wrote) there are other worlds (as telescopes were soon to show), and beyond these other worlds are other worlds again (as better telescopes were to show), and so on endlessly; we cannot conceive an end, nor a beginning. And instead of the "fixed" stars being fixed, as Copernicus thought, they change their place constantly; even in the skies *panta rei*, all things flow. Space, time, and motion are relative; there is no center, no circumference, no up or down; the same motion differs when seen from different places or stars; and as time is the measure of motion, time too is relative. Probably many stars are inhabited by living, intelligent beings; did Christ die for them too? Yet in this endless immensity there is an invariable conservation of matter, an eternal and inviolable constancy of law.

Since the universe is infinite, and there cannot be two infinites, the infinite God and the infinite universe must be one (here is Spinoza's *Deus sive substantia sive Natura*—"God or substance or Nature"). There is no Prime Mover, as Aristotle supposed, there is motion or energy inherent in every part of the whole. "God is not an external intelligence . . . It is more worthy for him to be the internal principle of motion, which is his own nature, his own soul."[27] Nature is the outside the Divine Mind; however, this Mind is not in a "heaven above," but in every particle of reality.

The world is composed of minute monads, indivisible units of force, of life, of inchoate mind (here Bruno is a bridge between Lucretius and Leibniz). Each particle has its own individuality, has a mind of its own; and yet its freedom is not liberation from law but (as in Spinoza) behavior according to its own inherent law and character. There is a principle of progress and evolution in Nature in the sense that every part strives for development (Aristotle's *entelecheia*).

There are opposites in Nature, contrary forces, contradictions; but in the operation of the whole cosmos—in the "will of God"—all contraries coincide and disappear; so the diverse motions of the planets make the harmony of the spheres. Behind the bewildering, fascinating variety of Nature is the yet more marvelous unity, wherein all parts appear as organs of one organism. "It is Unity that enchants me. By her power I am free though thrall, happy in sorrow, rich in poverty, alive even in death."[28] (Though I am subject to law, I express my own nature; though I suffer, I find solace in recognizing that the "evil" of the part becomes meaningless in the perspective of the whole; though I die, the death of the part is the rejuvenating life of the whole.) Hence the knowledge of the supreme unity is the goal of science and philosophy, and the healing medicine of the mind (Spinoza's "intellectual love of God").

This crude summary of Bruno's philosophy leaves out all his spark and heroic frenzy, and implies in his thought a continuity and consistency quite alien to it, for it contains as many contradictions as asseverations, and a flux of moods agreeing only in cosmic inebriation. Another selection of his ideas could make him a magian mystic. He talked of the individual virtues of the several planets; he thought that persons born "under the influence" of Venus are disposed to love, rhetoric, and peace, those under Mars to strife and hate. He believed in the occult qualities of objects and numbers, and that diseases may be demons and may in some cases be cured by a king's touch or the spittle of a seventh son.[29]

His final delusion was his hope that if he returned to Italy and should be questioned by the Inquisition, he could (as well he might) quote enough orthodox passages from his works to deceive the Church into thinking him her loving son. Perhaps he hoped that Italy had not heard of the book he had published in England, *The Expulsion of the Triumphant Beast*, in which the beast to be expelled could be interpreted as Catholicism, or Christianity, or theological dogmas in general.[30] He must have longed for Italy, for how else shall we explain the eagerness with which he accepted the invitation of Giovanni Mocenigo to come to Venice as his teacher and guest? Mocenigo belonged to one of Venice's most illustrious families. He was a pious Catholic, but he was interested in occult powers, and had been told that Bruno was well informed on all branches of magic and had the secrets of a tenacious memory. The Inquisition had long since declared Bruno an outlaw to be arrested at the first opportunity, but Venice was famed for protecting such outlaws and defying the Inquisitors. So, in the fall of 1591, Bruno hurriedly left Frankfurt and made his way over the Alps to Italy.

Mocenigo gave him rooms and took lessons from him in mnemonics. The pupil's progress was slow, and he wondered whether his teacher was withholding from him some esoteric magical lore; meanwhile he trembled at the heresies which the loquacious and incautious philosopher expressed. Mocenigo asked his confessor if he should report Bruno to the Inquisition; the priest advised him to wait until he had drawn out his instructor more definitely. Mocenigo obeyed; but when Bruno announced his intention of returning to Frankfurt, Mocenigo notified the Inquisitors, and on May 23, 1592, Bruno found himself in the prison of the Holy Office in Venice. Mocenigo explained that he had acted "by the constraint of his conscience and by order of his confessor."[31] He informed the Inquisitors that Bruno was averse to all religions, though he liked Catholicism best; that he denied the Trinity, the Incarnation, and transubstantiation; that he charged Christ and the Apostles with having deceived the people through alleged miracles; Bruno had said that all friars were asses, defiling the earth by their hypocrisy, avarice, and evil life, that religion should be replaced by philosophy, that indulgence in "carnal pleasures" is not sinful, and that he, Bruno, had satisfied his passions to the extent of his opportunities;[32] Bruno had told him that "ladies pleased him well, though he had not yet reached Solomon's number."[33]

The Inquisition examined the prisoner at its leisure, from May to September 1592. Bruno pleaded that he had written as a philosopher and had availed himself of Pomponazzi's distinction between the "two truths"— that one might question, as a philosopher, doctrines that he accepted as a Catholic. He admitted his doubts as to the Trinity. He confessed that he had been guilty of many errors; he professed repentance and besought the tribunal, "knowing my infirmity, to embrace me to the breast of Mother Church, providing me with remedies suitable for my welfare, and using me with mercy."[34] The Inquisitors gave him no comfort, but returned him to his cell. On July 30 they examined him again, heard his confession and his plea for mercy, and again remanded him to his cell for another two months. In September the head of the Roman Inquisition instructed the Venetian Inquisitors to send their prisoner to Rome. The Venetian government objected, but the Inquisitors pointed out that Bruno was a citizen of Naples, not of Venice, and the Senate consented to his extradition. On February 27, 1593, Bruno was deported to Rome.

It was part of Inquisition procedure to let a prisoner brood in jail for long periods before, between, and after examinations. Almost a year passed before Bruno was brought before the Roman tribunal in December 1593. He was examined again—or tortured by questioning—in April, May, September, and December 1594. In January 1595 the Inquisitors met twice to study the record; in March 1595 and April 1596 Bruno, says the trial record, "was brought before the Lord Cardinals and was visited" in his cell "and was interrogated by them and heard concerning his necessities."[35] In December 1596 his complaints were heard "concerning food." In March

1597 he was brought before the examiners, who again "heard him concerning his necessities"; we are not told what these were, but the repeated pleas suggest nameless hardships, not including the long suspense aimed presumably to break down an ardent spirit into an edifying humility. Another year passed. In December 1597, another questioning; then another year in the cell. In December 1598 he was allowed paper and pen. On January 14, 1599, he was again summoned. Eight heretical propositions taken from his books were read to him, and he was asked to recant them. He defended his views, but agreed to accept the decision of the Pope as to the quoted passages. On February 4 Clement VIII and the Congregation of the Holy Office decided that the excerpts were plainly heretical. No mention of Bruno's Copernican views occurs in the record of the trial; the heresies related to the Incarnation and the Trinity. He was allowed forty days more to acknowledge his errors.

He was heard again on February 18 and in April, September, and November. On December 21 he declared that he would not retract. On January 20, 1600, he addressed a memorial to the Pope, claiming that the condemned propositions had been wrongly taken from their context, offering to defend them against any theologians, and again expressing willingness to accept the decision of the Pope. Thereupon, reads the record, "the most holy lord, Pope Clement VIII, decreed and commanded that the cause be carried to final measures, . . . sentence be pronounced, and the said Brother Jordanus be committed to the secular court." On February 8 the Inquisitors summoned Bruno, repeated the accusations, and told him that he had been allowed eight years in which to repent; that he had agreed to accept the decision of the Pope as to whether his propositions were heretical; that the Pope had so decided, and that the prisoner still persisted in his heresies, continuing "impenitent, obstinate, and pertinacious"; wherefore sentence was now passed upon him that he should be "delivered to the secular court, . . . to the Governor of Rome here present, that thou mayest be punished with the punishment deserved, though we earnestly pray that he will mitigate the rigor of the laws concerning the pains of thy person, that thou mayest not be in danger of death or of mutilation of thy members." The sentence was signed by nine cardinals, including Bellarmine. According to Caspar Scioppius, a German scholar recently converted to Catholicism and then residing in Rome, when the verdict was read to Bruno he said to his judges, "Perchance you who pronounce my sentence are in greater fear than I who receive it."[36]

He was at once transferred to a secular prison. On February 19, still impenitent, his body nude, his tongue tied, he was bound to an iron stake on a pyre in the Piazza Campo de' Fiori and was burned alive, in the presence of an edified multitude. He was fifty-two years old. On that same spot in 1889, a statue was erected to him by subscription from all quarters of the world.

III. VANINI AND CAMPANELLA

Nineteen years later a kindred spirit moved quickly to a like fate. Giulio Cesare Lucilio Vanini was born in southern Italy of an Italian father and a Spanish mother—powder mating with fire. After wandering over Europe like Bruno, sampling climates and theologies, and writing books whose occasional insights (as that man had once been a quadruped) hardly balanced the occult nonsense, he settled down in Toulouse (1617) and, again like Bruno, enjoyed there two years of peace. But an attendant at his lectures reported him as laughing at the Incarnation and questioning the existence of a personal God.[37] Another hearer, Sieur de Francon, gained Vanini's confidence, drew him out as Mocenigo had done with Bruno, and reported him to the municipal *parlement*. On August 2, 1618, he was arrested not by the Church but by order of the Procurator-General of the King. On the basis of his lectures he was accused of atheism and blasphemy, both of them crimes punishable by the state. Vanini affirmed his belief in God, but Francon alleged that the prisoner had more than once professed atheism, saying that Nature was the only God. The judges accepted the evidence, and despite Vanini's passionate protests and the piety that he showed in his cell, they condemned him—thirty-four years old—

> to be delivered into the hands of the executioner of justice, who shall draw him on a hurdle, in his shirt, with a halter about his neck, and bearing upon his shoulders a placard with the words ATHEIST AND BLASPHEMER OF THE NAME OF GOD; he shall thus conduct him before the principal entrance to the church of St. Stephen, and being there placed on his knees . . . he shall ask pardon from God, from the King, and from Justice for his said blasphemies. Afterward he shall bring him into the Place of Salin, bind him to a stake there erected, cut off his tongue and strangle him, and afterward his body shall be burned . . . and the ashes thrown to the wind.[38]

Tradition tells that as Vanini came from his cell to bear his agony (February 9, 1619), he exclaimed, "*Andiamo, andiamo allegramente a morire da filosofo*" (Let us go, let us go cheerfully to die like a philosopher).[39]

Tommaso Campanella too was born with Calabrian lava in his blood. He cooled it for a while in a Dominican monastery, studied Telesio and Empedocles, rejected Aristotle, ridiculed a papal excommunication, and was imprisoned for some months by the Inquisition at Naples (1591–92). Released, he took courses at Padua, and was indicted for unchastity. There he wrote his first significant work, *Prodromos philosophiae instaurendae* (1594), in which, like Francis Bacon eleven years later, he advised thinkers to study Nature rather than Aristotle, and outlined a program for the restoration of science and philosophy. Returning to Naples, he joined a conspiracy to free it from Spain; the plot was frustrated, and Campanella languished in state jails for twenty-seven years (1599–1626). Twelve times he was tortured, once for forty hours.[40] He allayed his suffering with philosophy, poetry, and visions of perfect states. His sonnet "The People" voices his resentment at the failure of the populace to support his revolt:

> The people is a beast of muddy brain
> That knows not its own force and therefore stands
> Loaded with wood and stone; the powerless hands
> Of a mere child guide it with bit and rein.
> One kick would be enough to break the chain;
> But the beast fears, and what the child demands
> It does, nor its own terror understands,
> Confused and stupefied by bugbears vain.
> Most wonderful, with its own hand it ties
> And gags itself—gives itself death and war
> For pence doled out by kings from its own store.
> Its own are all things between earth and heaven,
> But this it knows not; and if one arise
> To tell this truth, it kills him unforgiven.[41]

The most famous product of those weary years was his *Civitas solis*. Campanella imagined his City of the Sun as standing on a mountain in Ceylon. Its officials are chosen—and are removable—by a national assembly of all inhabitants over twenty years old. The magistrates so chosen choose the head of the government, a priest called Hoh. He and his aides rule in all matters, temporal or spiritual. They preside also over the union of the sexes, seeing to it "that men and women are so joined together that they bring forth the best offspring. Indeed, they laugh at us who exhibit a studious care for our breed of horses and dogs, but neglect the breeding of human beings."[42] Hence deformity is unknown. Women are communistically shared and sternly disciplined. They are required to take active exercise, which "gives them a clear complexion. . . . If any woman dyes her face or uses high-heeled boots . . . she is condemned to capital punishment."[43] Both the sexes are trained to war. Those who flee from battle are, when caught, put to death by being placed in a den of lions and bears.[44] Everyone is assigned to work, but only for four hours a day. Children are brought up in common and are psychologically prepared for a communistic sharing of goods. The religion of these people is a worship of the sun as the "face and living image of God." "They assert that the whole earth will come to live in accordance with their customs."[45]

This communist manifesto, echoing Plato, was written in jail about 1602 and was published in Frankfurt am Main in 1622. Perhaps it expressed the aspirations of the Neapolitan conspirators and may have contributed to Campanella's long incarceration. In time he made his peace with the Church and was released. He delighted Urban VIII by asserting the right of the popes to rule kings. In 1634 Urban sent him to Paris to save him from implication in another Neapolitan revolt. Richelieu protected him, and the tired rebel, recapturing his youth, died in a Dominican cell (1639). "I am the bell [*campanella*]," he said, "that announces the new dawn."[46]

IV. PHILOSOPHY AND POLITICS

1. Juan de Mariana: 1536–1624

The central feature of medieval politics was the unifying supremacy of the papacy over the kings; the outstanding aspect of modern political history is the conflict of national states freed from papal power; hence the first question that agitated political philosophy in the century after the Reformation was the demand of Catholic thinkers that papal supremacy be restored, and the demand of Protestant thinkers that papal authority be wholly destroyed. Papal polemists argued that absolute kings, claiming divine right and repudiating all restraints by religion, morals, and law, would tear Europe to pieces; the defenders of the Reformation replied that no supranational authority could be trusted to seek the good of mankind rather than its own power and profit; moreover, a supreme Church would stifle all freedom of life and thought.

The Scholastic philosophers of the Middle Ages, echoing Roman jurists, had derived all royal authority from the consent of the people rather than from God; consequently there was no divine right of kings, and a bad ruler might be justly dethroned. Calvinist thinkers, like Bèze, Buchanan, and the author of *Vindiciae contra tyrannos*, warmly seconded this view; but Lutheran and Anglican theologians supported the divine right of kings as a necessary offset to public violence and papal claims, and upheld the duty of obedience even to unjust kings.[47]

The defenders of popular sovereignty included many Jesuits, who saw in this view a means of weakening royal as against papal authority. If, argued Cardinal Bellarmine, the authority of kings is derived from, and therefore subject to, the people, it is obviously subordinate to the authority of the popes, which is derived from the establishment of the Church by Christ, and is therefore subject only to God. Luis Molina, a Spanish Jesuit, concluded that the people, as the source of secular authority, may justly—but by orderly procedure—depose an unjust king.[48] Francisco Suárez, "the finest theologian the Society of Jesus has produced,"[49] restated this view, with careful modifications, in countering the absolutist claims of James I, and upheld the right of popes to unseat kings. The Jesuit Juan de Mariana's defense of tyrannicide roused an international furor because it was alleged to have encouraged the assassination of Henry IV.

Mariana (whom we have already noted as the greatest historian of his generation) was in all ways a remarkable individual, renowned for learning, eloquence, and intellectual audacity. In 1599 he dedicated to Philip III, and published with the permission of the local Jesuit censor, the treatise *De rege et regis institutione (On the King and His Education)*. Anticipating Hobbes by half a century, he described a "state of nature" before the origin of society; men then lived like animals in the wild, free from all restraints but their physical limitations, recognizing no law and no private property, and following instinct in seeking food and mates. But there were inconveniences in this Rousseauian freedom; e.g., dangerous animals abounded. To protect themselves men formed social organization, the greatest of all tools yet invented and a necessary counter to the physiological organs of defense and offense given by nature to animals. By an explicit or implicit compact, the members of a group agreed to delegate their collective authority to a chief or king; but sovereignty remained in the people, and in almost all cases (as in the Cortes of Spain) a national assembly checked this delegated power, retained control of the purse, and formed a body of laws whose authority was superior to the king's.

Democracy, in Mariana's view, is made impossible by the unequal distribution of ability and intelligence among men. It would be ruinous to let policy be determined by plebiscites.[50] A limited, or constitutional, monarchy is the best form of government compatible with the nature of man and the survival of the state. It should be hereditary, for an elective monarchy is a periodic invitation to anarchy.

The king should be limited by laws, by religious and moral restraints, and by the right of the people to depose him if he becomes a tyrant. He must not change the laws or levy taxes without the people's consent. He "should determine nothing about religion,"[51] for the Church is superior to the state and must rule herself; nevertheless he must protect the national religion, for "if religion is neglected a state cannot stand firm."[52] The state should support religion in maintaining morality; it should condemn bullfights as encouraging brutality, and the stage as stimulating sexual license.[53] It should finance the care of the sick and the poor through a wide distribution of hospitals and charity; and the rich should give to the needy what they now spend on their luxuries and their dogs. Taxes should be high on superfluities, low on necessaries. The goods of the earth would suffice for all if they were rightly distributed.[54] A good prince will guard against the concentration of wealth. Private property replaced primitive communism because "greedy and furious avarice laid its hand upon the divine gifts and claimed everything for itself";[55] it is now a necessary institution, but in heaven communism will be restored.[56]

A tyrant may be deposed, he may rightly be killed, even, in some circumstances, by an individual.

> Who may justly be held a tyrant? . . . We do not leave this to the decision of any individual, or even to the judgment of many unless the voice of the people publicly takes part, and learned and serious men are associated in the deliberation. . . . [But] when a prince brings the country to ruin, abuses state property and the possessions of individuals, spurns public laws and holy religion, begins to assert himself arrogantly, insolently, and impiously, . . . [when] citizens have been deprived of the possibility of assembling for general deliberation, but are earnestly minded to put an end to the existing tyranny—and supposing this to be notorious and unendurable . . . if in such a case any individual comes forward who responds to the general desire and offers to put such a ruler to death, I for one shall not regard him as an evil-doer. . . . It is a salutary reflection that princes have been persuaded that if they oppress the state . . . they can be killed not only justly but with praise and glory.[57]

Mariana reminded his readers of historic tyrannicides—of Harmodius and Aristogeiton who killed Hipparchus, tyrant of Athens, and of Brutus who drove the tyrant Tarquinius from Rome; and he pointed out that Athens and Rome, indeed all literate Europe, honored their memory. But Mariana showed his hand and bias by half approving the recent (1589) assassination of Henry III by Clément:

> Henry III, King of France, lies dead, stabbed by a monk in the intestines with a poisoned knife, a detestable spectacle. . . . Jacques Clément . . . studied theology in the Dominican college of his order. He was told by the theologians whom he had consulted that a tyrant may be killed legally. . . . Clément died an eternal honor to France, as it has seemed to very many. . . . Many people consider he died worthy of immortality, while others, pre-eminent in wisdom and learning, think it blamable.[58]

Henry III, it will be recalled, had opposed the Catholic League and had ordered his aides to kill Henri, Duke of Guise, its leader. Philip II of Spain had supported and in part financed the League; he had agreed to the assassination of Elizabeth I and William of Orange. And Philip III had no objection to a doctrine that justified the killing of an enemy of Spain.

In 1599 Claudio Aquaviva, general of the Society of Jesus, ordered that Mariana's *De rege* should be "corrected." When Henry IV was murdered by Ravaillac (May 14, 1610), Aquaviva condemned Mariana's teaching on tyrannicide (July 8), and forbade its propagation in Jesuit instruction. Meanwhile Mariana had been arrested, not for praising tyrannicide but for arguing against Philip III's debasement of the coinage and warning him in a brilliant treatise, *De monetae mutatione* (1605), of the evils of inflation. Mariana suffered his confinement philosophically, survived it, and lived on till 1624, dying at the age of eighty-seven.

2. Jean Bodin: 1530–96

How different was Bodin! No theologian with his feet in the sky, no somber lover of the League, but a Politique after L'Hôpital's heart, a defender of toleration, a counselor and admirer of Henry IV. Born at Angers, probably of a Spanish-Jewish mother, he came to Paris in 1560, practiced law unprofitably, and lost himself eagerly in philosophy and history. He studied voraciously Hebrew, Greek, German, Italian, Livy, Tacitus, the Old Testament, Cicero, and the constitutions of all the West European states. He believed that the study of history is the beginning of political wisdom. His first venture into print was a *Methodus ad facilem historiarum cognitionem* (1566)—*Method for the Easy Understanding of History*. The student will find it jejune, rhetorical, verbose—the philosophic mind does not mature early. Bodin, at thirty-six, thought that history inspires us to virtue by showing the defeat of the wicked and the triumph of the good.[59] Nevertheless the book, after Machiavelli's *Discourses*, is the first significant work on the philosophy of history.

Here and in the later *De republica*, a century and a half before Vico and Montesquieu, is a systematic consideration of climate and race as factors in history. History is a function of geography—of temperature, rainfall, soil, topography. Geography determines character, and character determines history. Men differ in character and conduct according as they live on mountains, plains, or the sea. In the north they excel in physical strength and muscular energy, in the south in nervous sensitivity and subtlety of mind; men in the Temperate Zone, as in the Mediterranean nations and France, unite the qualities of north and south—more practical than in the south, more intellectual than in the north. The government of a people should be adapted to its geographically and racially determined character, which hardly changes in time. So the peoples of the north should be ruled by force, those of the south by religion.

In a minor work, *Réponse au paradoxe de M. Le Malestroict*, Bodin almost founded "political economy."[60] He analyzed the reasons why prices were rising so rapidly in Europe, discussed the evils of a debased currency, advocated freedom of trade in an age of natural and regional protectionism, and emphasized the relations between economic realities and governmental policies.

But his chef-d'œuvre—the most important contribution to political philosophy between Machiavelli and Hobbes—was *La République* (1576). Bodin used this word in its Roman sense, as meaning any state. He distinguished between the state and society: society is founded on the family, which has a natural basis in the relations of the sexes and the generations; the state is founded on artificial force. In its natural form the family was patriarchal—the father had absolute power over his wives, his children, and the family property; and perhaps civilization has dangerously reduced the patriarchal rights. Woman should always be subject to man, for she is mentally weaker; to raise her to equality would be a fatal disregard of Nature. The husband should always have the right of divorce at will, as in the Old Testament. The decline of paternal authority and family discipline (thought Bodin) was already sapping the natural foundations of social order. For the family, not the state, is the unit and source of order and morality, and when family unity and discipline decay, no number of laws can take their place.[61] Private property is indispensable to the structure and continuance of the family. Communism is impossible because all men are born unequal.[62]

Bodin is more realistic than Mariana and Rousseau in discussing the origin of the state; there is no nonsense here about a social compact or contract. Village communities might originate in such an agreement, but the state originated in the conquest of one group of families by another, and the leader of the victors became king.[63] The sanction behind the laws was not the will or "sovereignty" of the people, it was the organized force of the government. Consequently absolute monarchy is natural; it continues in the state the power of the father in the patriarchal family; no government is sovereign if it is subject to any laws but those of Nature and of God.[64] Just as Hobbes was to run to these conclusions in flight from the chaos caused by the English Civil War of 1642–49, so Bodin saw in an absolute government the only escape from the Religious Wars and the division of France; note that his book was published only four years after the Massacre of St. Bartholomew; it could have been written in the blood that ran in the streets of Paris. It seemed to Bodin that if the function of the state is to maintain order, it can do this only through absolute and inalienable sovereignty.

Hence the best form of government is unlimited and hereditary monarchy: it must be unlimited if it is not to end in chaos, and it must be hereditary to avoid wars of succession. Monarchy, like paternal authority, has prevailed over most of the earth and through the longest time; it has the sanction of history. Democracies have only briefly ruled states. They go to pieces on the fickleness of the people and the incompetence and venality of popularly elected officials.[65] "In every popular assembly the votes are counted without weighing them [for the quality of thought behind the vote]; and always the number of the foolish, the wicked and the ignorant is a thousand times greater than the number of men of worth." The salvation of democracy is that behind the pretense of equality only a small minority rules, and the balance of brains outweighs the count of heads.[66]

Bodin recognized that some escape would have to be found from absolutism if the monarch became a tyrant; therefore, perhaps illogically, he allowed the right of revolution and tyrannicide. He admitted that even his complete monarchies would in time decay and be overthrown by ineluctable change. Anticipating Hegel, he divided history into three periods, the first dominated by Oriental states, the second by Mediterranean nations, the third by north-European countries. Through this concatenation of rising and falling states Bodin thought he saw some progress. The Golden Age lies not in the mythical past but in a future that will reap the results of the greatest of all inventions—print.[67] And the sciences, he wrote (half a century before Bacon), "contain in themselves treasure that no future ages will ever be able to exhaust."[68]

Bodin was a freethinker with a wholesome regard for the Bible (or, rather, for the Old Testament—he almost ignores the New), and with strong convictions about the reality of witchcraft, angels, demons, astrology, and the necessity of building a state in accord with the mystic virtues of numbers. He called for the severest sentences against witches. He advised princes to maintain unity of religious belief as long as possible; but if a heresy should become powerful and widespread, it would be unwise to use force in its suppression; better rely on time to win the heretics to the official faith.

What that faith should be Bodin did not say. His own faith was dubious. In his strange *Heptoplomeres colloquium* (*Colloquy of Seven Men*), which he cleverly left unpublished (it was first printed in 1841), he pictured a Catholic, a Lutheran, a Calvinist, a Jew, a Mohammedan, an Epicurean, and a deist in disputation at Venice. Judaism comes off well, the Christian dogmas of original sin, the Trinity, and the Incarnation are more strongly attacked than defended; and only the belief in God emerges unharmed. Bodin's critics denounced him as a Jew, a Calvinist, and an atheist, and reported that he died without religion, "like a dog." But belief in the divine guidance of the world is vigorously expressed in *The Republic*, and atheism is put beyond the pale of toleration, as making nonsense of the universe.[69]

Bodin, like Hobbes, was a frightened man trying to reason his way to stability amid the flux of revolution and war. His greatest book was infected by his time; it was a philosophy for a disordered world longing for order and peace. It cannot compare with the urbane wisdom of the *Essais* of the less harassed Montaigne in those same years. And yet no one since Aristotle—except possibly Ibn Khaldun—had spread political philosophy over so wide a field, or defended his prejudices with so much learning and force. Not till Hobbes's *Leviathan* (1651) shall we find so resolute an effort to discover a logic in the ways of states.

3. Hugo Grotius: 1583–1645

If Huig de Groot is remembered when most of the pathfinders in his field of international law* are almost forgotten, it may be because he lived as well as wrote, and because he composed his classic in the interims of active diplomacy and perilous politics. Born in Delft, educated at Leiden in mathematics, philosophy, and jurisprudence, he won the praise of Scaliger for his Latin style, and at twenty-six earned the applause of his country for his *Mare liberum* (1604), which outlined maritime law, and argued for freedom of the seas for all nations—especially for the Dutch, who were challenging the Portuguese assumption of maritime monopoly in the Far East. Appointed historiographer for the United Provinces, he composed in almost classical Latin a spirited but accurate history of the great revolt. We have seen him fighting on the side of Arminian liberalism in the conflict between Oldenbarneveldt and Maurice of Nassau. Arrested, he confessed his errors,[70] and was let off with life imprisonment. His wife begged and was allowed to share his captivity. After nearly three years in jail he escaped, concealed by his wife in a chest of books, and fled to Paris (1621). Louis XIII gave him a small pension, and while Germany intensified its Thirty Years' War, Grotius, living in poverty, composed his *De iure belli et pacis* (*The Law of War and Peace*, 1625).

---

* Chiefly Francisco a Victoria, professor of theology at Salamanca, in *Relectiones* (*Lectures,* 1557); Alberico Gentili, professor of civil law at Oxford, whose *De iure belli* (*The Law of War*, 1588) anticipated Grotius' plea for freedom of the seas; and Francisco Suárez, whose massive *Tractatus de legibus* (1613) outlined a league of nations bound by international laws.

> I saw prevailing throughout the Christian world a license, in making war, of which even barbarous nations would have been ashamed, recourse being had to arms for slight reasons or no reason; and when arms were once taken up, all reverence for divine and human laws was thrown away, as if men were thenceforth authorized to commit all crimes without restraint.[71]

Machiavelli had argued that states cannot be preserved unless they are absolved from obeying the moral code laid upon their citizens; statesmen must be ready—usually by proxy—to lie, rob, and kill as amply as may seem to them desirable for the good of the state. For states, as yet, live in a jungle stage like that of families before states came; they know no law but that of self-preservation. Grotius admits that governments may be exempt from *lex*—i.e., "positive," man-made law; but he holds them bound to obey *ius naturale*. He defines this "natural right" or law as "the dictate of right reason showing the moral turpitude, or the moral necessity, of any act from its agreement or disagreement with a rational nature, and consequently [showing] that such an act is either forbidden or commanded by God, the author of nature."[72] Natural law, then, is that system of rights and duties which follows from the essential nature of man as a rational being living in a society. Whatever is necessary for his existence and his participation in society is his natural right, it is something due to his nature. The behavior of states should observe these rights.

Moreover (Grotius continues), it should be subject to *ius gentium*. Roman jurisprudence had used this term to mean the laws of peoples not included in Roman citizenship. When the western Roman Empire broke up, medieval jurists applied it to the relations of states with one another. In Grotius it becomes the vague accumulation of rules and restraints customarily accepted by the most developed nations in their mutual contacts. On these two bases—*ius naturale* and *ius gentium*—he builds his theoretical structure, the first modern formulation of desirable international law.

He by no means outlaws war in general. He knows that a group, like an animal, when it feels itself threatened in its dearest possessions or its life, will defend itself by any available means—if possible, by argument or law, and then, if these prove inadequate, by any force it can command.[73] Consequently, a state in like circumstances is justified in going to war to defend the lives and properties of its citizens. But war is unjust if it is waged for conquest, for plunder or land, or from the real or pretended desire to impose a beneficent government upon a people unwilling to receive it.[74] Preventive wars are unjust. "Some writers have advanced a doctrine which can never be admitted, that the law of nations authorizes one power to commence hostilities against another whose increasing greatness awakens her alarm. As a measure of expediency such a measure may be adopted, but the principles of justice can never be advanced in its favor."[75] Individuals are bound to refuse to serve in wars that they judge clearly unjust.[76]

Assuming, then, that a war can be just, every nation entering into it has certain rights. It may use deceit, make reprisals, capture spoils, take and use prisoners. But the nation has duties as well as rights. It should declare war before waging it. It should honor any treaty responsibly made for it, no matter with whom. In conquests women, children, and old men— indeed, all noncombatants—should be spared. Prisoners may be enslaved, but they should not be killed. Grotius welcomes one sign of progress: Christians and Mohammedans have ceased to enslave prisoners of their own faith.

It was a noble and moderate argument, despite its flaws. If natural law is a "dictate of right reason," who shall determine what reason is right? In a state this is determined by a government armed with force; ultimately a commandment of conduct is obeyed because the legislator can enforce it; might does not make right, but it makes law. International law waits for an international legislature buttressed by an international force; meanwhile it will consist chiefly of modest restraints and violable agreements accepted as convenient for the time being by the *powers* concerned. To define the "law of nations" as the customs of the most developed peoples again presupposes some authority competent to name the most developed; but where is he? In Europe? In China? In Islam? And can a government afford to let its citizens judge for themselves whether a war is just or not? It can if its machinery of indoctrination is adequate.

It was an illogical book, but a necessary one. A thousand unjust wars had been fought; it was good that someone should outline measures for mitigating incorporated homicide with mutually accepted restraints; good that wars of conquest or plunder should be condemned; good that a plea should be made for mercy to noncombatants and prisoners. The Thirty Years' War made a mockery of these distinctions and pleas; but when that madness abated, Grotius' book seemed all the more justified by the condition of Germany.

Richelieu, resolved to enter the Thirty Years' War, withdrew Grotius' pension, and the endangered author retired to Hamburg. In 1635 Oxenstierna sent him back to Paris as Sweden's ambassador. But, like most philosophers, Grotius was more at home with ideas than with men; he allowed his dislike of Richelieu, and then of Mazarin, to determine his diplomacy; and in 1645 he returned to the comfort of his books. Queen Christina invited him to stay at her court as a well-pensioned scholar, but he obtained her permission to retire to Germany. She arranged for his passage to Lübeck; the vessel was driven ashore by a storm; Grotius suffered from shock and exposure, and died at Rostock, August 29, 1645, aged sixty-two.

After 267 years Holland forgave him his liberalism and raised a statue to him (1886) in the city of his birth. In 1899 the delegates of the United States to the International Peace Conference at The Hague placed a silver wreath on his tomb in recognition that his book had for a time shared in mitigating the sport of kings.

V. THE EPICUREAN PRIEST

Shall we make a final pause on our way to Descartes and contemplate the mystery of a Catholic priest reviving the materialism of Epicurus? It was some measure of Europe's mental development that the Greek philosopher of pleasure, whose name had been for centuries a synonym for *atheist*, should now, in the spreading distaste for Aristotle, come into honor at the hands of a pious and irreproachable vegetarian who died from fasting too rigorously in Lent.

Pierre Gassendi began as a peasant's son near Digne in Provence. He showed so sharp and avid a mind that at the age of sixteen he was appointed teacher of "rhetoric" (literature), and at twenty-five professor of philosophy in the University of Aix. He took holy orders and became a canon and provost of the cathedral at Digne. By that time he had already begotten a passionate book of "paradoxical exercises" against Aristotle. Most of these he burned on the advice of friends, but the parts that he published in 1624 supported the Copernican astronomy, the atomism of Lucretius, and the moral philosophy of Epicurus. Here was a crying invitation to martyrdom, but Pierre was so amiable a youth, so modest in conduct, so regular in his religious duties, that nobody seems to have thought of burning him. Throughout his life he professed the doctrine of the "two truths" —that the conclusions apparently compelled by reason could be accepted in philosophy, while in religion one might still follow the orthodox faith and ritual as an obedient son of the Church. Gassendi ate his cake and had it.

At the invitation of Descartes' friend Mersenne he proposed some powerful objections to the Cartesian philosophy; let us defer them. In 1645 he took the chair of mathematics at the Collège Royal in Paris; but soon he fell sick with a lung ailment, and he returned to the sunnier climate of Digne. There he wrote his major works, all around Epicurus: *De vita, moribus, et doctrina Epicuri* (1647); *De vita, moribus, et placitis Epicuri* (1649); and a 1,600-page double-column *Syntagma philosophiae Epicuri* (1649).

While continuing to affirm his Catholic faith, Gassendi expounded to the Latin-reading world the philosophy of Epicurus and Lucretius—materialism, atomism, and the legitimacy of happiness. The "first cause" of all things is God; but after that initial push everything proceeded by its own inherent forces and laws. All knowledge comes from the senses and is of individual entities; "universals" or general ideas are useful tools of thought, but have no objective correlate. The soul is doubtless immaterial and immortal, but seems dependent upon the body, and memory is apparently a function of the brain. Sensual pleasure is not immoral if it is prudently moderate; but the least treacherous delights are those of the mind; mathematics, for example, can cause transports of joy. Gassendi himself, of course, was an Epicurean, not an epicurean; i.e., he accepted the philosophy of Epicurus, but he was not an addict of sensual pleasure; on the contrary, he led an extremely abstemious life. Attacked by fever after too long a fast, he was finished by his physicians through thirteen bloodlettings (1655).

Molière and Cyrano de Bergerac were among his disciples at Paris; Fontenelle, Saint-Évremond, and Ninon de Lenclos accepted his philosophy without his theology; Hobbes profited from talks with him; Locke may have taken from him some elements of sensationalist psychology through Gassendi's pupil and Locke's friend, François Bernier, who published an *Abrégé de la philosophie de Gassendi* in 1678. Newton preferred the atoms of Gassendi to the corpuscles of Descartes, and found in the Provençal priest an inkling of gravitation.[77] In the eighteenth century the latent materialism in Gassendi, and his emphasis on science and experience as against the logic of Aristotle or the metaphysics of Descartes, gave him a greater influence among the *philosophes* than any other French thinker but Descartes. What is it, then, that made Descartes for a century the fountainhead of an engulfing stream in modern philosophy?

VI. RENÉ DESCARTES: 1596–1650

First of all, he had a Jesuit education, which has been the starting point and whetstone of French heretics from Descartes through Voltaire to Renan and Anatole France; "In the Temple were forged the hammers which destroyed the Temple."[78]

He was born at La Haye in Touraine. His mother died of tuberculosis a few days later; he inherited the disease from her; as an infant he was so pale and weak and coughed so pitifully that the physician offered no hope of saving him. A nurse would not give him up as lost; she gave him the warmth and nourishment of her body. He came back to life, and perhaps for that reason he was called René—Renatus—reborn. His father was a prosperous lawyer, a councilor of the Parlement of Rennes, who at his death left his son an income of six thousand francs per year.

At the age of eight he was entered in the Jesuit College of La Flèche, which, says an ardent freethinker and famous mathematician, "seems to have given him a much better grounding in mathematics than he could have got at most universities at that time."[79] His teachers recognized his physical weakness and mental alertness. They allowed him to remain in bed beyond rising hours and noted that he used the time to devour one book after another. In all his metaphysical wanderings he never lost his admiration for the Jesuits, and in their turn they took his doubts with paternal indulgence.

At seventeen he went to Paris to sow wild oats; he found that he had none to sow, being as yet indifferent to women; but as a devoted mathematician he took to gambling, figuring that he could break the casino bank. He went on to the University of Poitiers, where he received degrees in civil and canon law. Having gained health and strength, he amazed his friends by enlisting in the army of Prince Maurice of Nassau (1618). When the Thirty Years' War gathered impetus, he joined the forces of Maximilian, Duke of Bavaria; an uncertain tradition pictures him as having taken part in the battle of the White Mountain.

Amid these campaigns, and especially in the long months when winter interrupted slaughter, Descartes continued his studies, especially of mathematics. One day (November 10, 1619), at Neuburg (near Ulm in Bavaria), he escaped the cold by shutting himself up in a "stove" (probably an especially heated room). There, he tells us, he had three visions or dreams, in which he saw flashes of light and heard thunder; it seemed to him that some divine spirit was revealing to him a new philosophy. When he emerged from that "stove" he had (he assures us) formulated analytical geometry, and had conceived the idea of applying the mathematical method to philosophy.[80]

He returned to France in 1622, arranged his finances, and set out again on travels. He spent almost a year in Italy: went (some say on foot) from Venice to Loreto, paid his tribute to the Virgin, saw Rome in the 1625 jubilee, passed through Florence, did not visit Galileo, and came back to Paris. There and in the countryside he pursued scientific studies. He accompanied the mathematician and military engineer Gérard Desargues to the siege of La Rochelle (1628). Later in that year he moved to Holland; and barring some visits to France for business purposes, he spent nearly all the remainder of his life in the United Provinces.

We do not know why he left France. Possibly, "having shown forth" his "reasons for doubting many things,"[81] he feared accusations of heresy;

and yet he had many ecclesiastical friends there, like Mersenne and Bérulle. Perhaps he sought to avoid friends as well as enemies, hoping to find in an alien land the social (but not intellectual) isolation in which he could give form to the philosophy that was seething within him. He disliked the bustle and prattle of Paris, but did not mind the busy traffic—soft-pedaled by canals—of Amsterdam; there, "in the crowded throng of a great and very active people," he says, he could "live as solitary and retired as in deserts the most remote."[82] It may have been to conceal himself still further that he changed his habitat twenty-four times in the next twenty years—from Franeker to Amsterdam to Deventer to Amsterdam to Utrecht to Leiden, but usually near a university or a library. His income allowed him to live comfortably in a small château, with several servants. He avoided marriage, but took a mistress (1634), who bore him a daughter. We are pleased to hear that when this daughter died at the age of five, Descartes wept humanly. We should err if we thought of him as coldly unconcerned with mundane affairs. We shall find him justifying many of the passions that moralists normally condemn. He had some himself, being subject to pride, anger, and vanity.[83]

It took a proud spirit to dare his scope. Consider what he undertook: mathematics, physics, astronomy, anatomy, physiology, psychology, metaphysics, epistemology, ethics, theology; who would venture today on such a circumnavigation? For this he coveted seclusion, made experiments, equations, diagrams, weighed his chances of escaping or appeasing the Inquisition, and sought to give mathematical method to his philosophy, and philosophical method to his life.

Where should he commence? In the epochal *Discours de la méthode*,* he announced a first principle that in itself could have brought the world of authority down upon his head; all the more so since the essay was written in readily intelligible French, and in an animated, captivating, first-person style; here were many revolutions! He would begin, he said, by rejecting all doctrines and dogmas, putting aside all authorities, especially of *ille philosophus, the* philosopher, Aristotle; he would start with a clean slate and doubt everything—*de omnibus dubitandum.* "The chief cause of our errors is to be found in the prejudices of our childhood[84] . . . principles of which I allowed myself in youth to be persuaded without having inquired into their truth."[85]

But if he doubted everything, how could he proceed? In love with mathematics, above all with geometry, which his own genius was transforming, he aspired to find, after his initial and universal doubt, some fact which would be admitted as generally and readily as the axioms of

---

* Written in 1629, published in 1637 in a volume containing also treatises on geometry, dioptrics, and meteors. *Meditationes de prima philosophia* followed in 1641, *Principia philosophiae* in 1644, *Traité des passions de l'âme* in 1650, *Traité de l'homme* in 1662.

Euclid. "Archimedes, in order that he might draw the terrestrial globe out of its place and transport it elsewhere, demanded that only one point should be fixed and immovable; in the same way I shall have the right to conceive high hopes if I am happy enough to discover one thing only which is certain and indisputable."[86] He hit upon it exultingly: *Je pense, donc je suis, Cogito ergo sum*, "I think, therefore I am"[87]—the most famous sentence in philosophy.* It was intended not as a syllogism but as an immediate and irrefragable experience, the clearest and most distinct idea that we can ever have. Other ideas should be considered "true" in proportion as they approach this primal intuition—this direct perception—in distinctness and clarity. Descartes' new "method" in philosophy, his *novum organum*, was to analyze complex conceptions into their constituents until the irreducible elements are simple, clear, distinct ideas, and to show that all such basic ideas can be derived from, or can depend upon, the primary consciousness of a being that it thinks. Conversely, we should try to deduce from this primary perception all the fundamental principles of philosophy.

It was again a revolution in philosophy that Descartes took as his starting point not external objects supposedly known but the conscious self. The Renaissance had rediscovered the individual; Descartes made him the hitching post of his philosophy. "I see clearly that there is nothing which is easier for me to know than my own mind."[89] If we begin with matter and rise through levels of organic life to man, we shall be tempted by the logic of continuity to interpret mind as material. But matter is known to us only through mind; only mind is known directly. Here begins modern idea-lism, not as ideal-ism in an ethical sense, but as a philosophy that starts with the immediate fact of ideas, rather than with things known through ideas. Descartes sets the epistemological theme of modern European philosophy: "No more useful inquiry can be proposed than that which seeks to determine the nature and scope of human knowledge."[90] Now for three centuries philosophy would wonder if the "external world" exists except as idea.

For just as it is difficult to pass from body to mind with any theory that does justice both to the apparently material source and agency of sensations and to the apparently immaterial nature of ideas, so Descartes, having begun with the self, finds it difficult to pass from mind to things. How does the mind know that the sensations that seem to attest an external world are anything more than its own states? How can it trust the senses, which so often deceive us, or the mental images that are just as vivid when "false" in sleep as when "true" in the day?

To escape from this "solipsistic" prison of the self, Descartes appeals

---

* St. Augustine had used the same starting point in seeking to refute the pagan skeptics, who professed to doubt everything. But who "doubts that he lives and thinks?" he asked. "For if he doubts, he lives."[88] Montaigne used the same argument against the Pyrrhonists in his "Apologie de Raimond Sebond." Descartes had read Montaigne.

to God, who surely would not make our whole sensory equipment a deception. But when did God come into this system that began so boldly by doubting all received beliefs? Descartes cannot prove the existence of God from evidences of design in the external world, for he has not yet shown the existence of that world. So Descartes evolves God out of the knowing self, very much as Anselm had done in the "ontological proof" six centuries before. I have, he says, a conception of a perfect being, omniscient, omnipotent, necessary, and eternal. But that which exists is more nearly perfect than that which does not; therefore a perfect being must include existence among his attributes. And who could have put that idea into me but God Himself? "It is not possible that . . . I should have in myself the idea of a God if God did not veritably exist."[91] For if God were a deceiver He would not be perfect. Therefore he does not deceive us when we have clear and distinct ideas, nor when He allows our senses to reveal to us an external world. "I do not see how He could be defended from the accusation of deceit if these ideas were produced by causes other than corporeal objects. Hence we must allow that corporeal things exist."[92] So the gap between mind and matter, subject and object, is marvelously closed, and Descartes, by the help of God, becomes a real-ist. Science itself—our confident belief in a logical, orderly, law-abiding, calculable universe—becomes possible only because God exists and cannot lie.

As we follow Descartes we see the infant Age of Reason recoiling in fear from the hazards of thought and seeking to re-enter the warm womb of faith. The *Meditationes* was reassuringly entitled *The Meditations of René Descartes on First Philosophy, in Which the Existence of God and the Immortality of the Soul Are Demonstrated;* and the book was dedicated to "the very sage and illustrious dean of the Sacred Faculty of Theology of Paris"—i.e., the Sorbonne. The dean accepted the dedication, but in 1662 the volume was placed on the Index of Prohibited Books "until it is corrected." It began on the same brave note as the *Discours:* "Today . . . since I have procured for myself an assured leisure in a peaceful retreat, I shall at last freely and seriously address myself to the general upheaval of all my former opinions."[93] He throws them out the window and then lets them in at the door. And not only the belief in a just and omnipotent God, but also in a human will free amid universal mechanism, and a soul immortal despite its apparent dependence upon mortal flesh. Yield as we must to the logic of an unbreakable chain of cause and effect in the world of matter and body, the freedom of our wills is one of those innate ideas which are so clear and distinct, so vivid and immediate, that no one ever doubts them in practice, however much he may play with them in abstract theory.[94]

The idea of God, of the self, of space, time, and motion, and the axioms of mathematics—all these are innate; that is, the soul derives them not from sensation or experience but from its own essence and rationality. (Here Locke would demur and Kant would applaud.) However, these innate ideas may remain unconscious until experience startles them into conscious form. The soul, then, is not a product of experience, but its active and originative partner in the production of thought. This "rational soul"—the ability to reason—is clearly immaterial; its ideas have no length, breadth, position, weight, or any other of the qualities that belong to matter.[95] "This 'me,' that is to say, the soul by which I am what I am, is essentially distinct from the body, and is even easier to know than the latter."[96] Therefore this immaterial mind or soul can, and surely does, survive the body.

Were these orthodox conclusions sincere, or were they protective coloration? Was Descartes so anxious to pursue his scientific studies in unpersecuted peace that he exuded metaphysics like some befuddling mist to hamper birds of prey? We cannot say. It is possible for a man to be a good scientist—at least in physics, chemistry, and astronomy, if not in biology—and at the same time accept the basic doctrines of Christianity. In one passage Descartes affirmed that reason "does not prevent us from believing matters that have been divinely revealed as being more certain than our surest knowledge."[97] His correspondence with Princess Palatine Elizabeth is eloquently pious and orthodox. Salmasius, visiting him at Leiden in 1637, described him as "a most zealous Catholic."[98]

And yet the last decade of his life was dedicated to science. He turned his rooms into a laboratory and made experiments in physics and physiology. When a visitor asked to see his library Descartes pointed to a quarter of veal that he was dissecting.[99] At times he spoke like Bacon of the great practical benefits that would accrue to mankind when science had made men "the masters and possessors of nature."[100] His subjective emphasis and his confidence in deduction often led him to dubious conclusions, but he worked creatively in several sciences. He insisted that science should replace the vague and qualitative abstractions of medieval physics with quantitative explanations in mathematical form. We have noted his development of analytical geometry and his adumbration of infinitesimal calculus. He solved the problems of doubling a cube and trisecting an angle. He established the use of the first letters of the alphabet to represent known, and of the last letters to represent unknown, quantities. He seems to have discovered the law of refraction independently of Snell. He studied fruitfully great forces exerted by small means, as by the pulley, the wedge, the lever, the vise, and the wheel, and he formulated laws of inertia, impact, and impetus. He may have suggested to Pascal that atmospheric pressure decreases with altitude,[101] though he was mistaken in declaring that a vacuum existed nowhere except in Pascal's head.[102] He suggested that every body is surrounded by vortices of particles whirling about it in spherical layers—a conception not unlike the present theory of magnetic fields. In optics he correctly calculated the angle of refraction; he analyzed the changes to which light is subjected by the crystalline lens of the eye; he solved the problem of correcting spherical aberration in telescopes, and designed lenses with elliptical or hyperbolic curvature free from such aberration.[103]

He dissected and anatomically described a foetus. He dissected (he tells us) "the heads of various animals in order to ascertain in what memory, imagination, etc., consist."[104] He made experiments in reflex action, and explained the mechanism by which the eye winks at the approach of a blow.[105] He developed a theory of the emotions resembling that of William James and Carl Lange: the external cause of the emotion (e.g., our sight of a dangerous animal) automatically and simultaneously generates a responsive action (flight) and the corresponding emotion (fear); the emotion is the accompaniment, not the cause, of the action. The passions are rooted in physiology and should be studied and explained as mechanical operations. They are not in themselves bad, for they are the wind in our sails; but when not moderated by reason they can enslave and ruin a personality.

The whole universe, except God and the rational soul, may be viewed as mechanical. Remembering Galileo and the Inquisition, Descartes is careful to present the idea as hypothetical: assuming that God has created matter and endowed it with motion, we can imagine the world evolving thereafter by the laws of mechanics, without interference. The natural movement of material particles, in a universe without a vacuum, would take a circular form, resulting in diverse vortices or whirlpools of motion. The sun, the planets, and the stars may have been formed by the concentration of particles at the centers of these vortices. Just as every body is surrounded by a whirl of fine atoms—which explains cohesion and attraction—so each planet is enclosed in a vortex of particles that holds its satellites in orbit. The sun is the center of a vast vortex in which the planets are swept around it in circles. It was an ingenious theory, but it fell apart when Kepler proved that the planetary orbits are elliptical.

Descartes proposed that if our knowledge were complete we should be able to reduce not only astronomy and physics and chemistry, but all the operations of life, except reason itself, to mechanical laws. Respiration, digestion, even sensation, are mechanical; see how beneficently this principle worked in Harvey's discovery of the circulation of the blood. Descartes confidently applied the mechanical conception to all the operations of animals, for he refused to credit them with the power of reasoning. He may have felt religiously compelled to do this injustice to animals; for he had based the immortality of the soul upon the immateriality of the rational mind, and if animals too had such minds they too would be immortal—which might be an inconvenience, if not to dog lovers, at least to theologians.

But if the human body is a material machine, how can the immaterial mind act upon it, or govern it by so unmechanical a power as free will? At this point Descartes lost his confidence; he answered desperately that God arranges the interaction of body and mind in mysterious ways, beyond our finite understanding. Perhaps, he suggested, the mind acts upon the body through the pineal gland, which is appropriately situated at the middle base of the brain.

The rashest act in Descartes' life was his request to Mersenne to send advance copies of the *Meditationes* to various thinkers with an invitation to submit criticisms. Gassendi, in reply, demolished Descartes' contentions with Gallic courtesy;[106] the priest was not convinced by the ontological argument for the existence of God. Hobbes objected that Descartes had not proved the mind's independence of matter and the brain. Privately (according to Aubrey) Hobbes "was wont to say that had Descartes kept himself wholly to geometry . . . he had been the best geometer in the world, but that his head did not lie for philosophy."[107] Huygens agreed with Hobbes, and thought that Descartes had woven a romance out of metaphysical webs.

It is simple now, profiting from three centuries of discussion, to point out weaknesses in this brave first modern "system" of philosophy. The idea of reducing philosophy to geometrical form condemned Descartes to a deductive method in which, despite his experiments, he relied too recklessly on his flair for reasoning. To make the clarity, distinctness, vividness, and immediacy of an idea the test of its truth was suicidal, for on that basis who would dare deny the revolution of the sun around the earth? To argue that God exists because we have a clear and distinct idea of a perfect and infinite being (do we?), and then to argue that clear and distinct ideas are trustworthy because God would not deceive us, is a form of reasoning as circular and dubious as Descartes' planetary orbits. This philosophy is dripping with the medieval Scholastic conceptions that it proposed to reject. Montaigne's doubt was more basic and lasting than that of Descartes, who merely removed traditional nonsense to make room for his own.

Even so there remained enough in his science, if not in his metaphysics, to make him fear persecution. His theory of universal mechanism left miracles and free will in a parlous state despite his professions of orthodox belief. When he heard of Galileo's condemnation (June 1633) he put aside the major work, *Le Monde*, in which he had planned to unite all his scientific work and results; and he wrote sadly to Mersenne:

This has so strongly affected me that I have almost resolved to burn all my ms., or at least to show it to no one. . . . If it [the motion of the earth] is false, all the principles of my philosophy [of world mechanism] are erroneous, since they mutually support one another. . . . But on no account will I publish anything that contains a word that might displease the Church.[108]

At his death only a few fragments of *Le Monde* could be found.

The attack came not (in his lifetime) from the Roman Church but from the Calvinist theologians in the universities of Utrecht and Leiden. They considered his defense of free will as a heresy dangerous to predestinarianism, and they saw in his mechanical cosmogony a descent to within a step of atheism. If the universe could get along with merely an initial impetus from God, it was only a matter of time till God would be absolved from that inaugural push. In 1641, when a Utrecht professor adopted the Cartesian system, the rector of the university, Gisbert Voetius, persuaded the city magistrates to ban the new philosophy. Descartes retorted with an attack upon Voetius, who answered bitterly and was rebutted by Descartes. The magistrates summoned the philosopher to appear before them (1643). He refused to come; judgment was passed against him, but his friends at The Hague intervened, and the magistrates contented themselves with a decree forbidding any further public argument either for or against Descartes' ideas.

He was consoled by the friendship of Princess Elizabeth, who with her mother, Electress Palatine Elizabeth, the dethroned Queen of Bohemia, was living at The Hague. The Princess was nineteen when the *Discours* appeared (1637); she read it with delighted surprise that philosophy could be so intelligible; and Descartes, meeting her, saw with delight that metaphysics could be beautiful. He dedicated to her the *Principia philosophiae* in terms of enraptured flattery. She ended as an abbess in Westphalia (1680).

Not quite so happy in Holland as before, Descartes now frequently visited France (1644, 1647, 1648). His patriotism was stirred by a pension from the new government of Louis XIV (1646). He angled for a post in the administration, but the approach of civil war—the Fronde—frightened him back to Holland. In February 1649 he received an invitation from Queen Christina of Sweden to come and teach her philosophy. He hesitated, but was attracted by her letters, which revealed in excellent French an eager mind already won to the "dear delight." She sent an admiral to coax him, then a warship to fetch him. He yielded, and in September he sailed from Amsterdam for Stockholm.

He was received with every honor, but was alarmed to find that the

Queen wished to be instructed three times a week, always at five o'clock in the morning; Descartes had long been accustomed to lie late in bed. For two months he conformed to the royal schedule, walking through the winter dawn and snow from his rooms to the Queen's library. On February 1, 1650, he caught a cold, which became pneumonia; on February 11 he died, after receiving the last rites of the Catholic Church.

He had taken as a motto *Bene vixit qui bene latuit*—"He has lived well who has hidden well"; but his fame had become international many years before his death. The universities rejected his philosophy, and the clergy sniffed heresy in his piety; but scientists applauded his mathematics and physics, and the fashionable world in Paris took up with pleasure the works that he had written in lucid and engaging French. Molière laughed at the *femmes savantes* who bandied vortices in salons but "could not endure a vacuum." The Jesuits had heretofore been tolerant of their brilliant pupil; they had silenced one of their number who had attacked him;[109] but after 1640 they withdrew their protection, and in 1663 they were instrumental in having his works placed on the Index. Bossuet and Fénelon welcomed Descartes' proofs of the basic Christian beliefs, but saw danger to faith in resting it on reason. Pascal denounced the reliance on reason as a reed shaken by the wind.

It was precisely this Cartesian trust in reason that stirred the mind of Europe. Fontenelle summed up the matter: "It is Descartes . . . who gave us a new method of reasoning, much more admirable than his philosophy itself, in which a large part is false or very doubtful according to the very rules that he has taught us."[110] The Cartesian doubt did for France—for the Continent in general—what Bacon had done for England: it freed philosophy from the barnacles of time and set it bravely sailing the open sea, even if, in Descartes, it soon returned to safe and familiar ports. Not that there was any immediate victory for reason; through France's most brilliant age, the *grand siècle* of Louis XIV, tradition and Scripture more than held their own; it was the epoch of Port-Royal, Pascal, and Bossuet rather than of Descartes' inheritors. But in Holland that same period was the age of Spinoza and Bayle, and in England it was the time of Hobbes and Locke. The seed was sprouting.

Descartes' work had some influence on French literature and art. His style was a refreshing innovation. Here was philosophy in the vernacular, dangerously open to all, and seldom had a philosopher spoken with such charming intimacy, recounting the adventures of reason as vividly as Froissart recounting an exploit in chivalry. That brief and digestible *Discours de la méthode* was not only a masterpiece of French prose; it set the tone, both in its language and in its ideas, for the classic age in France—for order, intelligence, and moderation in letters and arts, in manners and speech. Its emphasis on clear and distinct ideas suited the Gallic mind; its exaltation of reason became in Boileau the first principle of the classic style:

> *Aimez donc la raison; que toujours vos écrits*
> *Empruntent d'elle seule et leur lustre et leur prix.*

("Love reason, then; let your writings ever derive from it alone their luster and their worth.")[111] For two centuries the French drama became the rhetoric of reason competing with the turbulence of passion. Perhaps French poetry suffered from Descartes: his mood and his mechanisms left small scope for imagination or feeling. After him the ebullient chaos of Rabelais, the formless meandering of Montaigne, even the violent disorders of the Religious Wars, gave way to the rational arguments of Corneille, the rigid unities of Racine, the logical piety of Bossuet, the law and order, form and manners, of the monarchy and the court under Louis XIV. Unwittingly Descartes had shared in inaugurating a new style in French life as well as in philosophy.

His influence in philosophy was probably greater than that of any other modern thinker before Kant. Malebranche stemmed from him. Spinoza schooled himself in the Cartesian logic and found its weaknesses in expounding it. He imitated the *Discours* in his autobiographical fragment *On the Improvement of the Understanding;* he adopted the geometrical ideal of philosophy in his *Ethics;* he based his discussion of "human bondage" on Descartes' *Traité des passions.* The idealistic tradition in modern philosophy from Berkeley to Fichte started with the Cartesian emphasis on thought as the only reality directly known, just as the empirical tradition flowed from Hobbes to Spencer. But Descartes offered an antidote to idealism—the conception of an objective world completely mechanical. His attempt to understand organic as well as inorganic operations in mechanical terms gave a reckless but fruitful impetus to biology and physiology; and his mechanical analysis of sensation, imagination, memory, and volition became a major source of modern psychology. After the seventeenth century in France had buttressed orthodoxy with Descartes, the Enlightenment of the eighteenth century found rich roots in his methodical doubt, his trust in reason, his interpretation of all animal life in the same terms as physics and chemistry.[112] All the upholding pride of the expatriated Frenchman justified itself in his proliferating influence upon the mind of France.

The Great Debate between reason and faith was taking conscious form, but its modern history had only begun. Looking back over those ninety years from 1558 to 1648, from Elizabeth to Richelieu, from Shakespeare to Descartes, we perceive that the absorbing issues were still within the confines of Christianity, between competing varieties of religious faith based upon a Bible that all accepted as the word of God. Only in stray voices was there a suggestion that Christianity itself might be put on trial, and that philosophy might soon reject all forms of supernatural belief.

After these first steps in the conflict Catholicism remained supreme in Spain and Portugal, where the Inquisition still spread its terror and pall. In Italy the old religion had taken a humaner form, beautifying life with art and anointing mortality with hope. France compromised: Christianity survived vigorous and fruitful among the people, Catholic or Huguenot, while the upper classes frolicked with doubt, postponing piety to the eve of death. The Netherlands made a geographical compromise: the southern provinces kept Catholicism, while Calvinism triumphed in the north. In Germany Protestantism was saved by a French cardinal; but Bavaria and Austria were confirmed in their former allegiance, while Hungary and Bohemia were recaptured for the papacy. In Scandinavia Protestantism became the law of the land, but the Queen of Sweden preferred the ceremonies of Rome. In England Elizabeth proposed a gracious union of Roman ritual with national liberty, but English Protestantism, dividing into a swarm of sects, displayed its vitality and risked its life.

Amid this clash of armies and creeds the International of Science was laboring to lessen superstition and fear. It was inventing or improving the microscope, the telescope, the thermometer, and the barometer. It was devising the logarithmic and decimal systems, reforming the calendar, and developing analytical geometry; it was already dreaming of reducing all reality to an algebraic equation. Tycho Brahe had made the patiently repeated observations that enabled Kepler to formulate those laws of planetary motion which were to illuminate Newton's vision of one universal law. Galileo was revealing new and vaster worlds through his ever larger telescopes, and was dramatizing the conflict of science and theology in the halls of the Inquisition. In philosophy Giordano Bruno was letting himself be burned to death in the attempt to reconceive deity and the cosmos in terms worthy of Copernicus; Francis Bacon, summoning the wits to science, was mapping its tasks for centuries to come; and Descartes, with his universal doubt, was giving another cue to the Age of Reason. Morals and manners were molded by the vicissitudes of belief. Literature itself was touched by the conflict, and the ideas of philosophers echoed in the poetry of Marlowe, Shakespeare, and Donne. Soon all the wars and revolutions of the rival states would sink into minor significance compared with that mounting, spreading contest between faith and reason which was to agitate and transform the mind of Europe, perhaps of the world.

Bibliographical Guide

to editions referred to in the Notes

The letters C, P, J, and R after an author's name indicate
Catholic, Protestant, Jewish, and rationalist respectively.

ACKERMAN, PHYLLIS, Tapestry, the Mirror of Civilization, Oxford University Press, 1933.

ACTON, JOHN E., LORD (C), Lectures on Modern History, London, 1950.

ADAMS, BROOKS (P), Law of Civilization and Decay, New York, 1921.

ADDISON, JULIA, Arts and Crafts in the Middle Ages, Boston, 1908.

ALLEN, J. W. (P), English Political Thought, 1603 to 1660, London, 1938.

ALLEN, J. W. (P), History of Political Thought in the Sixteenth Century, London, 1951.

ALTAMIRA, RAFAEL, History of Spain, tr. Muna Lee, New York, 1955.

ALTAMIRA, RAFAEL, History of Spanish Civilization, tr. P. Volkov, London, 1930.

ARISTOTLE, Poetics, Loeb Classical Library, London, 1922.

ARMSTRONG, EDWARD (P), The Emperor Charles V, 2v., London, 1910.

ARNOLD, SIR THOMAS W., Painting in Islam, Oxford U. P., 1928.

ASCHAM, ROGER (P), The Scholemaster, London, 1863.

AUBREY's Brief Lives, ed. O. L. Dick, Ann Arbor, Mich., 1957.

BACON, FRANCIS, Philosophical Works, ed. J. M. Robertson, London, 1905.

BACON, FRANCIS, Works, ed. Spedding, Ellis, and Heath, 6v., London, 1870.

BAEDEKER, KARL, Belgique et Hollande, Paris, 1910.

BAIN, F. W. (P), Christina, Queen of Sweden, London, 1890.

BAKELESS, JOHN, The Tragicall History of Christopher Marlowe, Harvard University Press, 1942.

BARINE, ARVÈDE, La Grande Mademoiselle, tr. Helen Meyer, New York, 1902.

BASKERVILLE, HELTZEL, and NETHERCOT, Elizabethan and Stuart Plays, New York, 1950.

BATIFFOL, LOUIS, The Century of the Renaissance, New York, 1935.

BEARD, CHARLES, Towards Civilization, New York, 1930.

BEARD, MIRIAM, History of the Business Man, New York, 1938.

BELL, AUBREY, Cervantes, University of Oklahoma Press, 1947.

BELL, AUBREY, Portuguese Literature, Oxford U. P., 1922.

BELL, E. T., Men of Mathematics, New York, 1937.

BELLOC, HILAIRE (C), How the Reformation Happened, London, 1950.

BELLOC, HILAIRE (C), Paris, New York, 1907.

BELLOC, HILAIRE (C), Richelieu, New York, 1929.

BERNAL, J. D. (R), Science in History, London, 1957.

BERRY, ARTHUR, Short History of Astronomy, New York, 1909.

BISHOP, A. T., Renaissance Architecture of England, New York, 1938.

BLOK, P. J. (P), History of the People of the Netherlands, 3v., New York, 1898.

BLOMFIELD, SIR REGINALD, History of French Architecture from the Reign of Charles VIII till the Death of Mazarin, 2v., London, 1911.

BLOMFIELD, SIR REGINALD, Short History of Renaissance Architecture in England, 1500–1800, London, 1923.

BOAS, FREDERICK, Marlowe and His Circle, Oxford U. P., 1929.

BODIN, JEAN, Method for the Easy Comprehension of History, Columbia University Press, 1945.

BOULENGER, JACQUES, The Seventeenth Century, New York, 1920.

BOULTING, W., Tasso and His Times, London, 1907.

BOURNE, H. R. Fox, Sir Philip Sidney, New York, 1891.

BOWEN, CATHERINE DRINKER, The Lion and the Throne: The Life and Times of Sir Edward Coke, New York, 1956.

BRADBROOK, M. C., The School of Night: A Study in the Literary Relationships of Sir Walter Raleigh, Cambridge U. P., England, 1936.

BRANTÔME, SEIGNEUR DE, Book of the Ladies, Boston, 1902.

BRANTÔME, SEIGNEUR DE, Lives of Gallant Ladies, London, 1943.

BROCKELMANN, CARL, History of the Islamic Peoples, New York, 1947.

BROCKWAY, WALLACE, and WEINSTOCK, HERBERT, The Opera, New York, 1941.

BROCKWAY, WALLACE, and WINER, BART, Second Treasury of the World's Great Letters, New York, 1941.

BROWNE, EDWARD G., Literary History of Persia, 4v., Cambridge, 1929.

BROWNE, SIR THOMAS, Religio Medici, Everyman's Library, 1951.

BROWNE, SIR THOMAS, Works, 6v., London, 1928.

"BRUTUS, JUNIUS" (P), Vindiciae contra tyrannos, New York, n.d.

BUCHAN, JOHN, Oliver Cromwell, Boston, 1934.

BUCKLE, HENRY THOMAS (R), Introduction to the History of Civilization in England, 4v., New York, 1913.

BUPAL, PHILIPPE, Bernard Palissy, Paris, n.d.

BURCKHARDT, JACOB, Recollections of Rubens, Oxford U. P., 1950.

BURNEY, CHARLES, General History of Music, 2v., New York, 1957.

BURTON, ROBERT, Anatomy of Melancholy, New York, 1924.

BURY, J. B. (R), History of Freedom of Thought, Home University Library, New York, n.d.

BUTTERFIELD, H., The Origins of Modern Science, New York, 1951.

CAFFIN, C. H., The Story of Spanish Painting, New York, 1910.

CALVERT, ALBERT, The Escorial, London, 1907.

CALVERT, ALBERT, Royal Palaces of Spain, London, 1909.

CALVERT, ALBERT, Seville, London, 1907.

CALVERT, ALBERT, and HARTLEY, C. G., Velázquez, London, 1908.

Cambridge History of English Literature, 14v., New York, 1910.

Cambridge History of Poland, 2v., Cambridge U. P., 1950.

Cambridge Modern History, 12v., New York, 1907 f.

CAMÕES, LUIZ DE, The Lusiads, tr. Leonard Bacon, New York, 1950.

CAMPANELLA, TOMASO, The City of the Sun, in Ideal Commonwealths, New York, 1901.

CAMPBELL, THOMAS (C), The Jesuits, New York, 1921.

CARLYLE, R. W. (P), History of Medieval Political Theory in the West, 6v., Edinburgh, 1928.

CARLYLE, THOMAS (P), Oliver Cromwell's Letters and Speeches, 4v., New York, 1901.

CASSIRER, ERNST (P), The Philosophy of the Enlightenment, Princeton University Press, 1951.

CASTIGLIONI, ARTURO, History of Medicine, New York, 1941.

Catholic Encyclopedia, New York, 1912.

CERVANTES, MIGUEL DE, Don Quixote, 2v., Everyman's Library.

CERVANTES, Three Exemplary Novels, tr. Samuel Putnam, New York, 1950.

CHAMBERS, E. K., The Elizabethan Stage, 4v., Oxford U. P., 1951.

CHAMBERS, E. K., William Shakespeare, 2v., Oxford U. P., 1930.

CHARDIN, JEAN, Travels in Persia, London, 1927.

CHARRON, PIERRE, Of Wisdom, tr. George Stanhope, 3v., London, 1729.

CHENEY, SHELDON, A World History of Art, New York, 1937.

CHESTERFIELD, EARL OF, Letters to His Son, New York, 1901.

CHURCH, R. W., Spenser, New York, 1879.

CHURCHILL, WINSTON S., History of the English-Speaking Peoples, 3v., London, 1957.

CHUTE, MARCHETTE, Ben Jonson of Westminster, New York, 1953.

CHUTE, MARCHETTE, Shakespeare of London, New York, 1953.

CLARENDON, EARL OF, History of the Rebellion, 8v., Oxford, 1826.

CLARK, BARRETT H., Great Short Biographies of the World, New York, 1928.

CLARK, G. N., The Seventeenth Century, Oxford U. P., 1929.

COKER, F. W., Readings in Political Philosophy, New York, 1938.

COOPER, LANE, Aristotle, Galileo, and the Tower of Pisa, Ithaca, N. Y., 1935.

CORNEILLE, PIERRE, Théâtre, 2v., Paris, 1950.

COXE, WM. (P), History of the House of Austria, 3v., London, 1847.

CRAIG, HARDIN, The Enchanted Glass, Oxford, 1952.

CRAVEN, THOMAS, A Treasury of Art Masterpieces, New York, 1952.

CREIGHTON, MANDELL (P), Queen Elizabeth, London, 1927.

CROCE, BENEDETTO, Ariosto, Shakespeare, and Corneille, New York, 1920.

D'ALTON, REV. E. A., History of Ireland, 6v., Dublin, n.d.

DAMPIER, SIR WILLIAM CECIL, History of Science, Cambridge U. P., 1948.

DAVIES, GERALD S., Frans Hals, London, 1902.

DAVIES, R. TREVOR, The Golden Age of Spain, London, 1954.

DAY, CLIVE, History of Commerce, London, 1926.

DENOIRESTERRES, GUSTAV, Voltaire et la société francaise au xviiime siècle, 8v., Paris, 1871.

DESCARTES, RENÉ, Meditations, Chicago, 1925.

DESCARTES, Selections, New York, 1927.

DESJARDINS, PAUL, Poussin, Paris, n.d.

DIEULAFOY, MARCEL, Art in Spain and Portugal, New York, 1913.

DIMAND, M. S., Guide to an Exhibition of Islamic Miniature Painting, New York, 1933.

DISRAELI, ISAAC, Curiosities of Literature, 3v., London, n.d.

DONNE, JOHN, Poems, Everyman's Library.

DOWDEN, EDWARD (P), Michel de Montaigne, Philadelphia, 1906.

DU DEFFAND, MME., Lettres à Voltaire, Paris, 1922.

DUNNING, W. A., History of Political Theories from Luther to Montesquieu, New York, 1905.

EDDY, SHERWOOD, The Challenge of Europe, New York, 1933.

EINSTEIN, LEWIS, The Italian Renaissance in England, Columbia University Press, 1935.

ELLIS, HAVELOCK, The Soul of Spain, Boston, 1937.

Encyclopaedia Britannica, 14th ed.

EVELYN, JOHN, Diary, 2v., Everyman's Library.

FAGUET, EMILE, Dix-septième Siècle: Études et portraits littéraires, Paris, n.d.

FELLOWS, OTIS, and TORREY, NORMAN (R), The Age of Enlightenment, New York, 1942.

FIGGIS, J. N. (P), From Gerson to Grotius, Cambridge U. P., 1916.

FIRTH, SIR CHARLES, Oliver Cromwell and the Rule of the Puritans in England, Oxford U. P., 1953.

FISCHER, KUNO, Descartes and His School, London, 1887.

FITZMAURICE-KELLY, JAMES, History of Spanish Literature, New York, 1928.

FITZMAURICE-KELLY, JAMES, Some Masters of Spanish Verse, Oxford, 1928.

FLETCHER, C. R. L., Gustavus Adolphus, London, 1890.

FLORINSKY, MICHAEL T., Russia: A History and an Interpretation, 2v., New York, 1955.

FORD, J. D. M., Main Currents of Spanish Literature, New York, 1919.

FOSDICK, HARRY EMERSON (P), ed., Great Voices of the Reformation, New York, 1952.

FRAME, D. M., Montaigne in France, New York, 1940.

FRANCE, ANATOLE, The Elm-Tree on the Mall, New York, 1910.

FRANCE, ANATOLE, The Gods Are Athirst, New York, 1913.

FRENCH, ALLEN (P), Charles I and the Puritan Upheaval, Boston, 1955.

FRIEDELL, EGON (R), Cultural History of the Modern Age, New York, 1930.

FROUDE, J. A. (P), Reign of Elizabeth, 5v., Everyman's Library.

FROUDE, J. A. (P), Reign of Henry VIII, 3v., Everyman's Library.

FÜLOP-MILLER, RENÉ, The Power and Secret of the Jesuits, New York, 1930.

FUNK, F. X. (C), Manual of Church History, 2v., London, 1910.

GADE, J. A., Life and Times of Tycho Brahe, Princeton, 1947.

GALILEI, GALILEO, Dialogue concerning the Two Chief World Systems, tr. Stillman Drake, University of California Press, 1953.

GALILEI, GALILEO, Dialogues concerning Two New Sciences, tr. Henry Crew and Alfonso de Salvio, New York, 1914.

GALILEO, Discoveries and Opinions, tr. and ed. by Stillman Drake, Garden City, N. Y., 1957.

GARDINER, SAMUEL R. (P), History of England 1603–42, 10v., London, 1889–93.

GARNETT, RICHARD, History of Italian Literature, New York, 1898.

GARNETT, RICHARD, and GOSSE, EDMUND, English Literature, 4v., New York, 1908.

GARRISON, F., History of Medicine, Philadelphia, 1929.

GASQUET, FRANCIS (C), Henry VIII and the English Monasteries, 2v., London, 1888.

GEYL, P. (P), Revolt of the Netherlands, London, 1945.

GIBB, E. J. W., Ottoman Literature, New York, 1901.

GIDE, ANDRÉ, Living Thoughts of Montaigne, New York, 1931.

GOETHE, JOHANN WOLFGANG VON, Wilhelm Meister's Apprenticeship, tr. Thomas Carlyle, New York, 1901.

GOLDSCHEIDER, LUDWIG, El Greco, Phaidon ed., Oxford U. P., 1938.

GOOCH, G. P., English Democratic Ideas in the Seventeenth Century, Cambridge U. P., 1927.

GRACIAN, BALTASAR (C), The Art of Worldly Wisdom, tr. Martin Fischer, Springfield, Ill., 1942.

GRAVES, F. P., History of Education during the Middle Ages, New York, 1931.

GREEN, J. R. (P), Short History of the English People, 3v., London, 1898.

GROTIUS, HUGO, Rights of War and Peace, New York, 1901.

GROVE's Dictionary of Music and Musicians, 5v., New York, 1927.

GUARINI, BATTISTA, The Faithful Shepherd, London, 1736.

GUÉRARD, ALBERT, Life and Death of an Ideal: France in the Classical Age, New York, 1928.

GUINARD, PAUL, El Greco, Skira ed., New York, n.d.

GUINARD, P., and BATICLE, J., Histoire de la peinture espagnole, Paris, 1950.

GUIZOT, F. (P), Corneille and His Times, New York, 1852.

GUIZOT, F. (P), History of France, 8v., London, 1872.

HALLAM, HENRY (P), Constitutional History of England, 3v., New York, 1862.

HALLAM, HENRY (P), Introduction to the Literature of Europe in the Fifteenth, Sixteenth, and Seventeenth Centuries, 4v. in 2, New York, 1880.

HAMMERTON, J. A., Outline of Great Books, New York, 1937.

HAUSER, ARNOLD, The Social History of Art, 2v., New York, 1952.

HAYDN, HIRAM, The Counter-Renaissance, New York, 1950.

HAYDN, HIRAM, The Portable Elizabethan Reader, New York, 1946.

HAZLITT, W. C., The Venetian Republic, 2v., London, 1900.

HEARNSHAW, F. J. C., ed., Social and Political Ideas of Some Great Thinkers of the Renaissance and the Reformation, New York, 1929.

HEFELE, K. J. VON, Life and Times of Cardinal Ximenes, London, 1885.

HERRICK, ROBERT, Poems, Everyman's Library.

History Today, London.

HOGBEN, LAUNCELOT, Science for the Citizen, New York, 1938.

HOLZKNECHT, KARL, Backgrounds of Shakespeare's Plays, New York, 1950.

HONEY, W. B., European Ceramic Art, London, 1949.

HOOKER, RICHARD, Works, 3v., Oxford, 1888.

HORN, F. W., History of the Literature of the Scandinavian North, Chicago, 1895.

HUGHES, PHILIP (C), The Reformation in England, 2v., London, 1952f.

HUME, DAVID (R), Essays, Literary, Moral, and Political, London, n.d.

HUME, DAVID (R), History of England, 5v., Philadelphia, n.d.

HUME, MARTIN (P), The Court of Philip IV, London, 1907.

HUME, MARTIN (P), Spain: Its Greatness and Decay, Cambridge U. P., 1899.

HUME, MARTIN (P), The Spanish People, New York, 1911.

INGE, W. R. (P), Christian Mysticism, London, 1899.

JACKSON, CATHERINE C., Old Paris, London, n.d.
JAMES, B. B., Women of England, Philadelphia, 1908.
JANSSEN, JOHANNES (C), History of the German People at the Close of the Middle Ages, 16v., St. Louis, Mo., n.d.
JOHN, EVAN, King Charles I, London, 1952.
JOHNSON, SAMUEL, Lives of the English Poets, 2v., Everyman's Library.
JONSON, BEN, Plays, 3v., London, 1894.
JORDAN, G. J. (P), The Reunion of the Churches: A Study of G. W. Leibniz and His Great Attempt, London, 1927.
JUSTI, CARL, Diego Velázquez and His Times, London, 1889.

KELLOGG, J. H., The New Dietetics, Battle Creek, Mich., 1927.
KESTEN, HERMANN (R), Copernicus and His World, New York, 1945.
KIRBY, R. S., Engineering in History, New York, 1956.
KLUCHEVSKY, V. O., History of Russia, 3v., London, 1912.
KNACKFUSS, H., Van Dyck, tr. Campbell Dodgson, New York, 1899.
KNOX, JOHN (P), History of the Reformation in Scotland, 2v., New York, 1950.

LACROIX, PAUL, Arts of the Middle Ages, London, n.d.
LACROIX, PAUL, History of Prostitution, 2v., New York, 1931.
LACROIX, PAUL, Military and Religious Life in the Middle Ages, London, n.d.
LANDAU, R., Invitation to Morocco, London, 1952.
LANE-POOLE, STANLEY, Story of Turkey, New York, 1895.
LANG, ANDREW (R), History of Scotland, 4v., Edinburgh, 1902.
LANG, ANDREW (R), The Mystery of Mary Stuart, London, 1901.
LANG, P. H., Music in Western Civilization, New York, 1941.
LANGE, F. E. (P), History of Materialism, New York, 1925.
LASKI, HAROLD (R), Political Thought in England, Locke to Bentham, Oxford U. P., 1950.
LASSAIGNE, JACQUES, Spanish Painting from the Catalan Frescoes to El Greco, Skira ed., Geneva, 1952.
LA TOUR, P. IMBART DE (C), Les Origines de la Réforme, 4v., Paris, 1905f.
LEA, H. C. (P), History of the Inquisition of the Middle Ages, 3v., New York, 1888.
LEA, H. C. (P), History of the Inquisition in Spain, 4v., New York, 1906.
LEA, H. C. (P), Studies in Church History, Philadelphia, 1883.
LECKY, W. E. (R), History of European Morals, 2v., New York, 1926.
LECKY, W. E. (R), History of the Rise and Influence of the Spirit of Rationalism in Europe, 2v., London, 1910.
LEDNICKI, WACLAW, Life and Culture of Poland, New York, 1944.
LEE, SIDNEY, A Life of William Shakespeare, London, 1901.
LÉVY-BRUHL, LUCIEN, History of Modern Philosophy in France, Chicago, 1924.
LEWINSKI-CORWIN, E. H., Political History of Poland, New York, 1917.
LINGARD, JOHN (C), History of England, 9v., London, 1855.
LIPSON, E., Growth of English Society, London, 1949.

Livy, History of Rome, 6v., Everyman's Library.
Locke, John, Two Treatises on Government, New York, 1947.
Lodge, Richard, Richelieu, London, 1896.
Lovelace, Richard, Poems, Oxford, 1930.
Lowie, R. H., Are We Civilized?, New York, 1929.
Lützow, Count von (P), Bohemia, an Historical Sketch, Everyman's Library.
Lyly, John, Euphues: The Anatomy of Wit, London, 1928.

Macaulay, Thomas Babington (P), Critical and Historical Essays, 2v., Everyman's Library.
Macaulay, History of England, 4v., Everyman's Library.
Maclaurin, C., Mere Mortals, New York, 1925.
Madariaga, S. de, Spain, London, 1946.
Mâle, Émile, Religious Art from the Twelfth to the Eighteenth Century, New York, 1949.
Malherbe, Racan, Maynard, Poésies choisies, Paris, n.d.
Mantzius, Karl, History of Theatrical Art, 6v., London, 1903f.
Mariana, Juan de (C), General History of Spain, tr. John Stevens, London 1669.
Mariana, The King and The Education of the King, tr. J. A. Moore, Country Dollar Press, Chevy Chase, Md.
Markun, Leo, Mrs. Grundy: A History of Four Centuries of Morals, New York, 1930.
Marlowe, Christopher, Works, London, 1948.
Marx, Karl (J), Capital, 2v., Chicago, 1919.
Masson, David, Life of John Milton, 6v., New York, 1946.
Mather, F. J., Jr., Western European Painting of the Renaissance, New York, 1948.
Matthews, Brander, The Chief European Dramatists, Boston, 1916.
Maulde La Clavière, R. de, The Women of the Renaissance, New York, 1905.
Maverick, L. A., China a Model for Europe, San Antonio, Tex., 1946.
McCabe, Joseph (R), Candid History of the Jesuits, New York, 1913.
McKinney, H. D., and Anderson, W. R., Music in History, Cincinnati, 1940.
Meier-Graefe, Julius, The Spanish Journey, New York, n.d.
Mencken, H. L., New Dictionary of Quotations, New York, 1942.
Michel, Émile, Rembrandt, 2v., New York, 1894.
Michelet, Jules (P), Histoire de France, 5v., J. Hetzel et Cie., Paris, n.d.
Molmenti, Pompeo, Venice, 6v., London, 1906.
Monroe, Paul, Text-Book in the History of Education, New York, 1928.
Montaigne, Michel de, Diary of a Journey to Italy, tr. E. J. Trechtmann, New York, 1929.
Montaigne, Essays, 3v., Everyman's Library. References are to volume, essay, and page.
Morley, John (R), Oliver Cromwell, New York, 1902.
Motley, J. L. (P), Rise of the Dutch Republic, 2v., New York, n.d.
Motteville, Mme. de, Memoirs, tr. K. P. Wormeley, 3v., Boston, 1901.
Mousnier, Roland, Histoire générale des civilisations: Tome IV: Les xvime et xviime siècles, Paris, 1956.

Muir, Edwin, John Knox, London, 1920.
Muir, Kenneth, ed., Elizabethan and Jacobean Prose, Pelican Books, 1956.
Mumford, Lewis, The Condition of Man, New York, 1944.
Mumford, Lewis, Technics and Civilization, New York, 1934.
Murray, R. H., Erasmus and Luther, London, 1920.

Neale, J. E. (P), Queen Elizabeth, London, 1954.
Nichol, J., Francis Bacon, Edinburgh, 1907.
Nosek, Vladimir, The Spirit of Bohemia, New York, 1927.
Nussbaum, F. L., History of the Economic Institutions of Modern Europe, New York, 1937.

Ogg, David, Europe in the Seventeenth Century, London, 1956.
Ortega y Gasset, José, Toward a Philosophy of History, New York, 1941.
Owen, John (P), Skeptics of the French Renaissance, London, 1893.
Oxford History of Music, 7v., Oxford, 1929f.

Pascal, Blaise (C), Pensées, ed. Havet, 2v., Paris, 1887.
Pascal, Pensées, Everyman's Library.
Pascal, Provincial Letters, Boston, 1887.
Pastor, Ludwig (C), History of the Popes, 22v., St. Louis, 1898f.
Pater, Walter, Plato and Platonism, London, 1910.
Paulsen, Friedrich (P), German Education, New York, 1908.
Payne, E. A., The Anabaptists of the Sixteenth Century, London, 1949.
Penrose, Boies, Jr., Travel and Discovery in the Renaissance, Harvard University Press, 1952.
Peterson, Houston, ed., Treasury of the World's Great Speeches, New York, 1954.
Pliny, Natural History, 6v., London, 1855.
Pokrovsky, N. M., History of Russia, New York, 1931.
Pope, Arthur Upham, Catalogue of a Loan Exhibition of Early Oriental Carpets, Chicago, 1926.
Pope, Arthur Upham, Introduction to Persian Art, London, 1930.
Pope, Arthur Upham, Survey of Persian Art, 7v., Oxford U. P., 1938.
Powys, J. C., The Enjoyment of Literature, New York, 1938.
Prescott, H. F. M., Mary Tudor, New York, 1953.
Prescott, W. H. (P), History of the Reign of Philip II, 3v., London, 1878.
Prinzmetal, Myron, and Winter, William, Heart Attack, New York, 1958.
Putnam, G. H., Books and Their Makers during the Middle Ages, 2v., New York, 1898.
Putnam, G. H. (P), The Censorship of the Church of Rome, 2v., New York, 1906.

Quevedo, Francisco D., The Dog and the Fever, Hamden, Conn., 1954.

Raleigh, Sir Walter, Selections, Oxford, 1917.
Raleigh, Walter, Shakespeare, London, 1950.
Rambaud, Alfred, History of Russia, 3v., Boston, 1879.

RANKE, LEOPOLD (P), Civil Wars and Monarchy in France, 2v., London, 1852.
RANKE, LEOPOLD, History of the Popes, 3v., London, 1878.
READ, CONYERS (P), Mr. Secretary Cecil and Queen Elizabeth, London, 1955.
RÉAU, LOUIS, L'Art russe, 2v., Paris, 1921.
RÉGNIER, MATHURIN, Poésies choisies, Paris, n.d.
RENARD, G., and WEULERSEE, G., Life and Work in Modern Europe, London, 1926.
RETZ, CARDINAL DE, Memoirs, London, n.d.
RICHELIEU, CARDINAL, Oeuvres, ed. Jules Tallandier, Paris.
RICKARD, T. A., Man and Metals, 2v., New York, 1932.
ROBERTSON, J. M. (R), Short History of Freethought, 2v., London, 1914.
ROBINSON, J. H., Readings in European History, Boston, 1906.
ROEDER, RALPH (P), Catherine de' Medici and the Lost Revolution, New York, 1937.
ROGERS, J. E., Economic Interpretation of History, London, 1891.
ROGERS, J. E., Six Centuries of Work and Wages, New York, 1890.
ROOSES, MAX, Rubens, 2v., Philadelphia, 1904.
RUSKIN, JOHN, Modern Painters, 5v., Everyman's Library.
RUSSELL, BERTRAND (R), History of Western Philosophy, New York, 1945.

SAINTE-BEUVE, CHARLES A., Portraits of the Seventeenth Century, 2v., New York, 1904.
SAINTE-BEUVE, Port-Royal, 5v., Paris, 1867.
SAINTSBURY, GEORGE, History of Elizabethan Literature, London, 1893.
SANDERS, E. K., Bossuet, London, 1921.
SANDYS, SIR JOHN, Companion to Latin Studies, Cambridge, 1925.
SANGER, W. W., History of Prostitution, New York, 1910.
SARTON, GEORGE, Introduction to the History of Science, 5v., Baltimore, 1930f.
La Satyre Ménippée, Extraits, Paris, n.d.
SCHAFF, PHILIP (P), The German Reformation, 2v., Edinburgh, 1888.
SCHAFF, PHILIP (P), The Swiss Reformation, 2v., Edinburgh, 1893.
SCHEVILL, R., Cervantes, New York, 1919.
SCHOENHOF, J., History of Money and Prices, New York, 1896.
SCHUSTER, M. LINCOLN, ed., Treasury of the World's Great Letters, New York, 1940.
SEDGWICK, H. D., Henry of Navarre, Indianapolis, 1930.
SÉE, HENRI, Modern Capitalism, New York, 1928.
SELLERY, G. C., The Renaissance, University of Wisconsin Press, 1950.
SHAKESPEARE, Plays, ed. W. A. Wright, Garden City, N. Y., 1936.
Shakespeare's England, 2v., Oxford U. P., 1950.
SHAW, GEORGE BERNARD, Man and Superman, New York, 1914.
SHELLEY, PERCY BYSSHE, Works, ed. Dowden, London, 1891.
SICHEL, EDITH, Catherine de' Medici and the French Reformation, London, 1905.
SICHEL, EDITH, The Later Years of Catherine de' Medici, New York, 1908.
SICHEL, EDITH, Michel de Montaigne, New York, 1911.
SIDNEY, SIR PHILIP, Works, 4v., Cambridge U. P., 1939.
SIGERIST, H. E., The Great Doctors, New York, 1933.

SINGER, CHARLES, ed., Studies in the History and Method of Science, Vol. I, Oxford, 1917.

SINGER, D. W., Giordano Bruno, His Life and Thought, *with translation of* On the Infinite Universe and Worlds, New York, 1950.

SITWELL, SACHEVERELL, Southern Baroque Art, London, 1851.

SMITH, D. E., ed., Isaac Newton, Baltimore, 1928.

SMITH, PRESERVED (R), The Age of the Reformation, New York, 1920.

SMITH, PRESERVED (R), History of Modern Culture, 2v., New York, 1930.

SOMBART, WERNER, The Jews and Modern Capitalism, Glencoe, Ill., 1951.

SORIA, MARTIN, The Paintings of Zurbarán, Phaidon ed., 1953.

SPEDDING, J., Life and Times of Francis Bacon, 2v., London, 1878.

SPENCER, THEODORE, Shakespeare and the Nature of Man, New York, 1943.

SPENSER, EDMUND, Poetical Works, Oxford U. P., 1935.

STEPHENS, H. M., Story of Portugal, New York, 1913.

STIRLING-MAXWELL, SIR WILLIAM, Annals of the Artists of Spain, 4v., London, 1891.

STRACHEY, LYTTON, Elizabeth and Essex, New York, 1929.

STRANAHAN, C. H., History of French Painting, New York, 1907.

SULLY, DUKE OF, Memoirs, 4v., London, 1856.

SUTRO, ESTHER, Nicolas Poussin, Boston, 1923.

SYMONDS, J. A. (R), The Catholic Reaction, 2v., London, 1914.

SYMONDS, J. A. (R), Italian Literature, 2v., New York, 1883.

SYMONDS, J. A., Shakespeare's Predecessors in the English Drama, London, 1904.

TAINE, HIPPOLYTE, History of English Literature, tr. Henry Van Laun, New York, 1873.

TAINE, Italy: Rome and Naples, New York, 1889.

TAINE, Lectures on Art, New York, 1884.

TALLEMANT DES RÉAUX, G., Miniature Portraits, New York, n.d.

TASSO, TORQUATO, Gerusalemme liberata, Milan, 1942.

TAVERNIER, J. B., Six Voyages, London, 1678.

TAWNEY, R. H., Religion and the Rise of Capitalism, New York, 1926.

TEIXEIRA, PEDRO, Travels, London, 1902.

THIEME, HUGO, Women of Modern France, Philadelphia, 1908.

THOMPSON, J. W., Economic and Social History of Europe in the Later Middle Ages, New York, 1931.

THORNDIKE, LYNN, History of Magic and Experimental Science, 6v., New York, 1929f.

THORNTON, J. C., Table Talk, from Ben Jonson to Leigh Hunt, Everyman's Library.

TICKNOR, GEORGE, History of Spanish Literature, 3v., New York, 1854.

TILLEY, ARTHUR, Studies in the French Renaissance, Cambridge U. P., 1922.

TOYNBEE, ARNOLD J., JR., A Study of History, 10v., Oxford U. P., 1935f.

TRAILL, H. D., Social England, 6v., New York, 1902.

TREND, J. B., The Civilization of Spain, Oxford U. P., 1952.

TREVELYAN, G. M., English Social History, London, 1947.

TREVOR-ROPER, H. R., Historical Essays, London, 1957.

USHER, A. P., History of Mechanical Inventions, New York, 1929.

VACANDARD, E. (C), The Inquisition, New York, 1908.
VAN DOREN, MARK, ed., Anthology of World Poetry, New York, 1928.
VAN LAUN, HENRI, History of French Literature, 3v., London, 1876.
VARTANIAN, ARAM, Diderot and Descartes, Princeton U. P., 1953.
VERNADSKY, GEORGE, History of Russia, Yale U. P., 1929.
VOLTAIRE (R), Age of Louis XIV, Everyman's Library.
VOLTAIRE (R), Works, 22v., New York, 1927.

WALKER, WILLISTON (P), John Calvin, New York, 1906.
WALLACE, WILLARD, Sir Walter Raleigh, Princeton U. P., 1959.
WALSH, JAMES J. (C), The Popes and Science, New York, 1913.
WEBER, MAX, The Protestant Ethic and the Spirit of Capitalism, London, 1948.
WEBSTER AND FORD, Plays, Everyman's Library.
WEDGWOOD, C. V., The Thirty Years' War, Yale U. P., n.d.
WEISBACH, WERNER, Spanish Baroque Art, Cambridge U. P., 1941.
WERNER, SIGVART, Copenhagen, Copenhagen, 1947.
WHEWELL, WILLIAM, History of the Inductive Sciences, 2v., New York 1859.
WILENSKI, R. H., Dutch Painting, London, 1947.
WILLIAMS, CHARLES, James I, London, 1951.
WILLIAMS, F. B., Elizabethan England, Boston, 1939.
WINCKELMANN, JOHN, History of Ancient Art, 4v. in 2, Boston, 1880.
WINEGARTEN, RENÉE, French Lyric Poetry in the Age of Malherbe, Manchester, England, 1954.
WOLF, A., History of Science, Technology, and Philosophy in the Sixteenth and Seventeenth Centuries, New York, 1935.
WOLF, A., History of Science, Technology, and Philosophy in the Eighteenth Century, New York, 1939.
WRIGHT, THOMAS, History of Domestic Manners and Sentiments in England during the Middle Ages, London, 1862.
WRIGHT, THOMAS, Womankind in Western Europe, London, 1869.

ZWEIG, STEFAN, Mary Queen of Scots and the Isles, New York, 1935.

Notes

CHAPTER I

1. Froude, *Reign of Elizabeth*, I, 11.
2. Neale, *Queen Elizabeth*, 26.
3. Ibid., 37.
4. Froude, I, Introd., vii.
5. Read, C., *Mr. Secretary Cecil and Queen Elizabeth*, 32.
6. Ibid., 119.
7. Hughes, P., *The Reformation in England*, III, 46.
8. Froude, *Elizabeth*, III, 306.
9. Froude, I, 448.
10. Barnes, H. E., *Economic History of the Western World*, 205.
11. Hallam, *Constitutional History of England*, I, 245.
12. Lingard, J., *History of England*, VI, 324.
13. Christopher Hatton in *Shakespeare's England*, I, 80.
14. Neale, 61.
15. Ibid., 75-6.
16. *Shakespeare's England*, I, 5.
17. Neale, 386.
18. Froude, I, 120.
19. *Cambridge Modern History*, III, 289.
20. Froude, IV, 62.
21. Thornton, *Table Talk from Ben Jonson to Leigh Hunt*, 9.
22. Hallam, I, 133.
23. Neale, 80.
24. Read, 363.
25. Froude, II, 84.
26. *Camb. Mod. History*, II, 582.
27. Froude, I, 300.
28. Ibid., 103.
29. Ibid., 491.
30. Creighton, *Queen Elizabeth*, 254.
31. Church, R. W., *Spenser*, 116.
32. Lingard, VI, 321.
33. Aubrey, *Brief Lives*, 305.
34. Chute, *Shakespeare of London*, 145.
35. Bacon, Fr., *Philosophical Works*, 869; Apophthegm 55.
36. Froude, V, 206.
37. Sir John Hayward in Muir, K., *Elizabethan and Jacobean Prose*, 1.
38. Chute, *Ben Jonson*, 164.
39. Froude, I, 8, 14.
40. Ibid. and 145; II, 338; Allen, J. W., *History of Political Thought in the Sixteenth Century*, 199-200.
41. Ascham, *The Scholemaster*, 81.
42. Froude, III, 4.
43. Taine, *English Literature*, 160.
44. Smith, Preserved, *The Age of the Reformation*, 634.
45. Robertson, J. M., *Short History of Freethought*, II, 5, 6.
46. Bradbrook, *The School of Night*, 7; Boas, *Marlowe and His Circle*, 90; and the ed. of *Love's Labour's Lost* by A. T. Quiller Couch and J. Dover Wilson, London, 1923.
47. Bradbrook, 39.
48. Ibid., 12.
49. Robertson, *Freethought*, II, 10.
50. Green, J. R., *Short History of the English People*, ch. vii, sect. 3.
51. Froude, I, 183; IV, 65; V, 228.
52. Ibid., IV, 385-6.
53. *Camb. Mod. History*, II, 562.
54. Chute, *Ben Jonson*, 79.
55. Roeder, *Catherine de' Medici*, 492.
56. Froude, IV, 119; Neale, 215.
57. Payne, E. A., *The Anabaptists of the 16th Century*, 19; Lingard, VI, 170.
58. Pastor, *History of the Popes*, XVI, 250.
59. McCabe, *Candid History of the Jesuits*, 150.
60. Froude, I, 329.
61. Ibid., II, 345; Hughes, III, 159.
62. Macaulay, *Critical and Historical Essays*, I, 6; *Camb. Mod. History*, III, 349.
63. Lingard, VI, 122.
64. Hughes, III, 289.
65. Pastor, XIX, 441-2.
66. Ibid.
67. McCabe, *Candid History*, 148.
68. Ibid., 150.
69. Froude, IV, 284.
70. Ibid., 294-5.
71. Lngard, VI, 165; Froude, IV, 297.
72. Pastor, XIX, 458.
73. Hughes, III, 325-6.
74. Neale, 265.
75. Hughes, III, 363; Williams, F. B., *Elizabethan England*, 10.
76. Froude, V, 238.
77. Hughes, III, 380; Neale, 299.
78. Hallam, I, 169; Lingard, VI, 257.
79. Hughes, III, 392-6.
80. Allen, J. W., *History of Political Thought in the Sixteenth Century*, 216-7; Hallam, I, 190.
81. Hallam, I, 198.
82. Hughes, III, 408.
83. Lea, H. C., *Studies in Church History*, 508.
84. Neale, 178.
85. Hallam, I, 205.
86. *Camb. Mod. History*, III, 345.
87. Walton, Izaak, *Life of Richard Hooker*,

in Clark, B. H., *Great Short Biographies of the World*, 556.
88. Hooker, Richard, *Works: Laws of Ecclesiastical Polity*, I, x, 4, 8.
89. Ibid., VIII, vi, 11.
90. Ibid., I, i, 1.
91. Froude, IV, 237.
92. Ibid., 191.
93. D'Alton, E. A., *History of Ireland*, III, 199.
94. Froude, IV, 233, 236.
95. Ibid., 233.
96. Froude, II, 466.
97. *Encyclopaedia Britannica*, 14th ed., XV, 778b.
98. Froude, II, 211.
99. Nussbaum, F. L., *History of the Economic Institutions of Modern Europe*, 122; Froude, II, 468.
100. Barnes, *Economic History*, 265.
101. Acton, J. E., *Lectures on Modern History*, 152; Davies, E. Trevor, *The Golden Age of Spain*, 212; Froude, III, 309; V, 37.
102. Froude, V, 344.
103. Ibid., 400.
104. Michelet, Jules, *Histoire de France*, IV, 4.
105. Froude, V, 413.
106. Ibid., 430-1.
107. Spedding, J., *Life and Times of Francis Bacon*, I, 56.
108. Strachey, *Elizabeth and Essex*, 173.
109. In Eddy, Sherwood, *The Challenge of Europe*, 205n.
110. Strachey, *Elizabeth and Essex*, 6.
111. Clarendon, *Robert Devereux and George Villiers*, in Clark, *Great Short Biographies*, 603.
112. Spedding, I, 21.
113. Ibid., 179.
114. Ibid., 56.
115. Strachey, 65.
116. Spedding, I, 231.
117. Spedding, note to Rawley's *Life of Bacon*, in Bacon, *Philosophical Works*, 3.
118. Strachey, 172; Spedding, *Life of Bacon*, I, 227; Creighton, *Queen Elizabeth*, 279.
119. Holzknecht, *Backgrounds of Shakespeare's Plays*, 301; Chambers, E. K., *William Shakespeare*, I, 354; Strachey, 241.
120. Spedding, I, 343-8.
121. Strachey, 264-5.
122. Creighton, 295.
123. Strachey, 279.
124. In Muir, *Elizabethan and Jacobean Prose*, 39.
125. Ibid., 40.
126. *Hamlet*, III, iii, 15-23.
127. Bacon, *Advancement of Learning*, Preface to the King.
128. *Henry VIII*, V, v, 18.

CHAPTER II

1. A phrase of unknown origin, as old as 1300.—Mencken, H. L., *New Dictionary of Quotations*, 343.
2. Bernal, *Science in History*, 284; Wolf, A., *History of Science in the Eighteenth Century*, 630.
3. Trevelyan, *English Social History*, 191.
4. Rogers, *Economic Interpretation of History*, 38; Traill, *Social England*, III, 365; Froude, *Henry VIII*, I, 19; Lipson, *Growth of English Society*, 157f.
5. *Shakespeare's England*, I, 320.
6. Rogers, *Economic Interpretation*, 37; Rogers, *Six Centuries of Work and Wages*, 84, 88, 100.
7. Renard and Weulersee, *Life and Work in Modern Europe*, 94; *Shakespeare's England*, I, 331.
8. Creighton in Traill, III, 373.
9. Gasquet, *Henry VIII and the English Monasteries*, II, 515n.
10. Smith, P., *Age of the Reformation*, 476.
11. Beard, Chas., *Toward Civilization*, 227.
12. Trevelyan, *Social History*, 160-1.
13. Wolf, *History of Science in the Sixteenth and Seventeenth Centuries*, 614.
14. Thompson, J. W., *Economic and Social History of Europe in the Later Middle Ages*, 497.
15. Sée, H., *Modern Capitalism*, 55.
16. Trevelyan, *Social History*, 120.
17. Sarton, G., *Introduction to the History of Science*, IIIa, 324.
18. Addison, J. D., *Arts and Crafts in the Middle Ages*, 26.
19. Froude, *Elizabeth*, II, 88.
20. Chute, *Shakespeare of London*, 63.
21. Ascham, *Scholemaster*, 71-8 and end.
22. Einstein, Lewis, *Italian Renaissance in England*, 160.
23. Hughes, III, 137.
24. Goethe, *Faust*, Part II, lines 616-18, quoted in Haydn, H., *The Counter-Renaissance*, 362.
25. *Camb. Mod. History*, III, 362.
26. Chute, *Ben Jonson*, 41.
27. Trend, J. B., *Civilization of Spain*, 110.
28. Hughes, III, 144.
29. *Shakespeare's England*, I, 416.
30. Froude, *Elizabeth*, V, 462.
31. Trevelyan, *Social History*, 140.
32. Lingard, VI, 323.
33. *King Lear*, IV, vi.
34. Lingard, VI, 323.
35. Hallam, I, 35.

36. *Shakespeare's England*, I, 398.
37. Froude, *Elizabeth*, IV, 122-3; *Shakespeare's England*, I, 400.
38. Hallam, I, 234; Spenser, E., *Poetical Works*, Introd., xxiii.
39. Browne, Sir Thos., *Religio Medici*, Introd., x.
40. Garrison, *History of Medicine*, 819.
41. Bacon, Essay "Of Gardens," in *Philosophical Works*, 791.
42. *Merchant of Venice*, I, ii.
43. *Much Ado about Nothing*, III, iv.
44. Holzknecht, 44.
45. Philip Stubbs in James, B. B., *Women of England*, 250.
46. Wright, Thomas, *Womankind in Western Europe*, 334.
47. *Merchant of Venice*, III, ii, 89.
48. *Shakespeare's England*, II, 94.
49. Wright, Thomas, *History of Domestic Manners and Sentiments in England*, 456.
50. James I, *A Counterblast to Tobacco* (1604), in Muir, 89.
51. McKinney and Anderson, *Music in History*, 278.
52. *Oxford History of Music*, II, 221.
53. Ibid., 208.
54. Haydn, H., *The Portable Elizabethan Reader*, 666.
55. Burney, C., *General History of Music*, II, 306.
56. In the National Portrait Gallery, London.
57. Blomfield, R., *Short History of Renaissance Architecture in England*, 37.
58. Bishop, A. T., *Renaissance Architecture of England*, 34; Blomfield, 86.
59. Ibid.
60. Haydn, *Counter-Renaissance*, 13.

CHAPTER III

1. Burton, Robert, *Anatomy of Melancholy*, 7.
2. *Shakespeare's England*, II, 183.
3. Putnam, G. H., *Censorship of the Church of Rome*, II, 258.
4. *Shakespeare's England*, II, 217.
5. Cambridge *History of English Literature*, III, 369.
6. Garnett and Gosse, *English Literature*, II, 68.
7. Camb. *History of English Literature*, III, 372.
8. Ascham, *Scholemaster*, 17-23.
9. Haydn, *Portable Elizabethan Reader*, 183.
10. Lyly, *Euphues: The Anatomy of Wit*, 33.
11. Greene, Robert, *A Groats-worth of Wit Bought with a Million of Repentance*, in Taine, *English Literature*, 168.
12. In Muir, 28.
13. Symonds, J. A., *Shakespeare's Predecessors*, 435.
14. Saintsbury, *History of Elizabethan Literature*, 233.
15. Bourne, *Sir Philip Sidney*, 75.
16. Aubrey's *Brief Lives*, 278.
17. Bourne, 115.
18. Ibid., 27-30.
19. Ibid., 277.
20. Sidney, Philip, *Works: Defense of Poetry*, 9.
21. Sidney, *Works*, III, 14.
22. Ibid., I, 7.
23. Ibid., I, 16.
24. *Defense of Poetry*, 41.
25. Sidney, Sonnet xxxi.
26. Bourne, 326.
27. In Haydn, *Elizabethan Reader*, 394.
28. Bourne, 349.
29. Spenser, *Poetical Works*, 559.
30. Prefatory *Letter to Raleigh*, in *Poetical Works*, 407.
31. *Faerie Queene*, II, xii, 78.
32. Thornton, *Table Talk*, 1.
33. Van Doren, *Anthology of World Poetry*, 1026.
34. Aristotle, *Poetics*, 1449-50.
35. *Defense of Poetry*, 38.
36. Mantzius, *History of Theatrical Art*, III, 11.
37. *Shakespeare's England*, II, 241.
38. Chambers, E. K., *The Elizabethan Stage*, I, 255.
39. Holzknecht, 110.
40. Chambers, *Elizabethan Stage*, I, 258.
41. Shakespeare, *Twelfth Night*, II, iii.
42. *Pericles*, IV, ii.
43. Chambers, *Elizabethan Stage*, IV, 273-5.
44. *Henry V*, I, i, 13.
45. *Hamlet*, III, ii, 10.
46. Holzknecht, 153.
47. *Shakespeare's England*, II, 277.
48. *Hamlet*, II, ii, 354.
49. Mantzius, III, 228.
50. Marlowe, *Works*, Appendix, 428-30.
51. Bakeless, John, *Tragicall History of Christopher Marlowe*, 112.
52. Symonds, *Shakespeare's Predecessors*, 437.
53. Bakeless, 113.
54. Marlowe, *Tamburlane*, Part I, Act II, vii.
55. France, A., *The Gods Are Athirst*, 57.
56. *Ecclesiastes*, i, 18.
57. Marlowe, *Faustus*, I, i.
58. *The Jew of Malta*, II, iii.

59. Ibid., I, i.
60. Ibid., II, i.
61. *Tamburlane*, Part I, Act I, i.
62. Bakeless, 156; *Esquire Magazine*, December 1954.

CHAPTER IV

1. Chambers, *William Shakespeare*, II, 264.
2. Ibid., 257.
3. Lee, Sidney, *Life of William Shakespeare*, 22.
4. Chambers, *Shakespeare*, II, 188.
5. Ibid., 189.
6. Ibid., 259, 265.
7. Shakespeare, Sonnet xxix.
8. Sonnet cx.
9. Chute, *Shakespeare*, 269.
10. Sonnet clii.
11. Lee, 68.
12. Raleigh, W., *Shakespeare*, 150.
13. Chambers, *Shakespeare*, I, 434.
14. *As You Like It*, II, vii.
15. *King Lear*, IV, vi, 120.
16. *Timon of Athens*, IV, i, 35.
17. Ibid., IV, iii, 54.
18. Ibid., IV, iii, 151f.
19. *Troilus and Cressida*, II, ii, 166.
20. *Coriolanus*, I, iv, 57.
21. Thornton, *Table Talk*, 5.
22. *Encycl. Brit.*, III, 781b.
23. *Two Gentlemen of Verona*, I, i, 71.
24. *The Tempest*, I, ii, 129.
25. *Midsummer Night's Dream*, II, iii, 61.
26. *Hamlet*, II, ii, 310.
27. *Romeo and Juliet*, I, ii, 139
28. *Julius Caesar*, I, ii, 139.
29. *Tempest*, II, i, 47.
30. Hauser, A., *Social History of Art*, I, 422.
31. *Love's Labour's Lost*, I, i, 166.
32. *Richard III*, I, i, 1.
33. Ibid., I, i, 24.
34. *2 Henry IV*, IV, iv.
35. *1 Henry IV*, III, i.
36. *Much Ado about Nothing*, II, iii.
37. *2 Henry IV*, III, i.
38. *King John*, IV, ii.
39. *Troilus and Cressida*, III, iii.
40. *Midsummer Night's Dream*, I, iii.
41. *Merchant of Venice*, I, iii.
42. *Twelfth Night*, III, iv.
43. *Mid. Night's Dream*, I, i.
44. *Othello*, I, i.
45. *King Lear*, IV, vi.
46. *Hamlet*, I, iv.
47. Ibid., II, ii.
48. *Mid. Night's Dream*, II, i.
49. *Two Gentlemen of Verona*, IV, ii.
50. *Cymbeline*, II, iii.

51. *Measure for Measure*, IV, ii.
52. *Mid. Night's Dream*, V, i, 7.
53. Examples in Chambers, *Shakespeare*, 228-30.
54. *Comedy of Errors*, III, i, 76.
55. *Tempest*, IV, i, 199.
56. *As You Like It*, III, ii.
57. Shaw, Bernard, *Man and Superman*, Preface, xxviii.
58. *Hamlet*, I, v.
59. *Much Ado about Nothing*, V, i.
60. *Hamlet*, III, iv, 88.
61. Ibid., II, ii.
62. *Coriolanus*, IV, vii.
63. *Hamlet*, I, iv, 25.
64. *Richard III*, V, iii.
65. *Richard II*, III, iii.
66. *1 Henry IV*, III, i; cf. Haydn, *Counter-Renaissance*, 602f.
67. *Troilus and Cressida*, I, iii.
68. *King Lear*, V, ii, 9.
69. *Twelfth Night*, II, iii.
70. *King Lear*, IV, vi, 112f.
71. *Pericles*, II, i.
72. *Tempest*, II, i, 147-64.
73. *Hamlet*, IV, iv, 35.
74. Raleigh, *Shakespeare*, 61.
75. *King John*, III, i.
76. *Henry VIII*, II, ii; *Romeo and Juliet*, IV, ii.
77. *King Lear*, IV, i, 36.
78. Ibid., V, iii, 169.
79. V, ii, 10.
80. *King John*, III, iv, 108.
81. *Hamlet*, I, iii, 126-28.
82. *Macbeth*, V, v, 23.
83. *Merchant of Venice*, V, i.
84. *Measure for Measure*, III, i, 118.
85. *Hamlet*, I, iv, 67.
86. Chambers, *Shakespeare*, II, 194.
87. In Lee, *Shakespeare*, 179.
88. Jonson, *Timber*, in Chute, *Ben Jonson*, 340.
89. Lee, 177.
90. Ibid., 178.
91. Aubrey, 275.
92. Jonson, *Timber*, in Lee, 277.
93. Chambers, *Shakespeare*, I, 84.
94. Lee, 203.
95. Aubrey, 275.
96. Ibid., 85.
97. *Tempest*, I, ii, 5.
98. Ibid., IV, i, 148.
99. V, i, 48.
100. V, i, 181.
101. Chambers, *Shakespeare*, I, 89.
102. Holzknecht, 380-1.
103. Voltaire, Letter of July 19, 1776, in Denoiresterres, G., *Voltaire et la société française au xviiime siècle*, VIII, 108.

104. In Croce, B., *Ariosto, Shakespeare, and Corneille*, 284.
105. Voltaire, article on Dramatic Art, in Holzknecht, 387.
106. Goethe, *Wilhelm Meister*, Book II, chs. xiii-xvi.

CHAPTER V

1. Brantôme, *Book of the Ladies*, 92.
2. Ibid., 124.
3. Sainte-Beuve, *English Portraits*, 6.
4. Pastor, XVI, 283.
5. Lingard, VI, 12.
6. *Book of Discipline*, Heads I and III, in Knox, *History of the Reformation in Scotland*, II, 281-3.
7. Knox, *History*, II, 321-2.
8. In National Portrait Gallery, London, and in Uffizi Gallery, Florence.
9. Lang, Andrew, *Mystery of Mary Stuart*, 13, 61.
10. Knox, *History*, II, 10; Froude, *Elizabeth*, I, 255.
11. Knox, II, 8.
12. Ibid., 12.
13. Ibid., 13f.
14. Lang, *History of Scotland*, II, 107.
15. Ibid.
16. Muir, Edwin, *John Knox*, 240.
17. Knox, *History*, II, 29.
18. Lang, *History*, II, 110.
19. Fosdick, *Great Voices of the Reformation*, xxix.
20. Knox, *History*, II, 44-6.
21. Lang, *History*, II, 126.
22. Knox, II, 71-7; Lang, II, 127; Muir, *Knox*, 253.
23. Knox, II, 81.
24. Ibid., 83.
25. Ibid., 93.
26. Zweig, *Mary Queen of Scots*, 108.
27. Neale, *Queen Elizabeth*, 141.
28. Lang, *History*, II, 160.
29. Ibid.; Froude, *Elizabeth*, II, 50.
30. Lang, II, 162.
31. *Camb. Mod. History*, III, 272.
32. Lang, *Mystery*, 75.
33. Ibid., 108-11.
34. *Camb. Mod. History*, III, 273.
35. Lang, *History*, II, 171; Lingard, VI, 67.
36. Lang, II, 170-2.
37. Ibid.; Knox, *History*, lxxiii.
38. Zweig, 158.
39. Lang, *Mystery*, 236.
40. Acton, *Lectures*, 150-2; Lang, *Mystery*, 295, 353, 362.
41. Ibid., 133.
42. Lang, *History*, II, 188.
43. Neale, 161.
44. Lang, *Mystery*, 194.

45. Froude, *Elizabeth*, II, 307, 310.
46. Brockway and Winer, *Second Treasury of the World's Great Letters*, 112.
47. Hallam, I, 167.
48. Froude, *Elizabeth*, II, 407.
49. Ibid., 404; Lang, II, 200.
50. Lang, II, 203.
51. Lang, *Mystery*, 286.
52. Lingard, VI, 97.
53. Froude, III, 110.
54. Muir, *Knox*, 282.
55. Knox, *History*, I, vii.
56. Lingard, VI, 126.
57. Ibid., 128; Hughes, III, 278.
58. Roeder, *Catherine de' Medici*, 491.
59. Neale, 263.
60. Pastor, XIX, 450-2.
61. Lingard, VI, 187.
62. Ibid., 205-6; Pastor, XXI, 7-19.
63. Ibid., 25; Froude, V, 259-61.
64. Williams, Chas., *James I*, 76, 80-3; Froude, V, 294.
65. Zweig, 291.

CHAPTER VI

1. Fontenoy in Froude, V, 74.
2. Lang, *History*, 276, 294-6, 305, 395; Lingard, VI, 183.
3. Lea, *Studies in Church History*, 502-8.
4. Ibid., 500.
5. Lang, *History*, II, 243.
6. James I, *Basilikon Doron*, in Gooch, *English Democratic Ideas in the Seventeenth Century*, 41.
7. Lang, *History*, II, 278.
8. *History Today*, March 1956, 159.
9. Buckle, *History of Civilization*, IIa, 199.
10. Williams, *James I*, 132.
11. *Encycl. Brit.*, IV, 310.
12. Allen, J. W., *History of Political Thought*, 339-40; cf. Carlyle, R. W., *History of Medieval Political Theory*, 332f; Figgis, J. N., *From Gerson to Grotius*, 167-72.
13. Allen, op. cit., 342.
14. Quoted by Oliver Dick in Introduction to Aubrey's *Brief Lives*, xxx.
15. In Chute, *Ben Jonson*, 249.
16. Ibid., 268.
17. Ibid., 217.
18. Bowen, C. D., *The Lion and the Throne*, 315.
19. Aubrey, 67.
20. In Robinson, J. H., *Readings in European History*, 349; Allen, 254; Dunning, W. A., *History of Political Theories*, II, 217.
21. Allen, J. W., *English Political Thought*, 26.
22. Ibid., 124.

23. Lingard, VII, 17.
24. Allen, *English Political Thought*, 223.
25. Williams, *James I*, 192-3.
26. Lingard, VII, 19-22.
27. Ibid., 29.
28. Ibid., 40-3.
29. Ibid., 46-8.
30. Ibid., 50, 96.
31. McCabe, *Candid History of the Jesuits*, 198.
32. Lang, *History*, II, 508.
33. Aubrey, 21.
34. Hallam, H., *Literature of Europe*, III, 324.
35. Webster, *The White Devil*, in Webster and Ford, *Plays*, p. 91.
36. Webster, *Duchess of Malfy*, in Webster and Ford, p. 145.
37. Ibid., IV, ii.
38. Thornton, *Table Talk*, 15.
39. Thomas Fuller in Chute, *Ben Jonson*, 37.
40. Jonson, *Every Man out of His Humour*, Induction.
41. Thornton, 7.
42. Jonson, *Every Man out of His Humour*, Induction.
43. Thornton, 8.
44. Chute, *Ben Jonson*, 161.
45. Jonson, *The Alchemist*, II, i.
46. Baskerville, Read, etc., *Elizabethan and Stuart Plays*, 1077.
47. Herrick, *Poems*, 241.
48. Chute, *Ben Jonson*, 310.
49. Williams, *James I*, 189.
50. Introduction to Burton, *Anatomy of Melancholy*, p. x.
51. Ibid.
52. Burton, *Anatomy of Melancholy*, 8.
53. Ibid., 3.
54. Ibid., 79-80.
55. Donne, *Poems*, 83.
56. Ibid., 26.
57. Elegy XIII; Elegy II.
58. *Poems*, 182.
59. Ibid., 180.
60. Thornton, 4.
61. *Poems*, 253.
62. In Peterson, *Treasury of the World's Great Speeches*, 91.
63. Ibid., 92.
64. Walton, *Life of Dr. Donne*, in Peterson, 95.
65. Hallam, *Constitutional History*, I, 347; *Encycl. Brit.*, XVIII, 961b; Lingard, VII, 7.
66. Text in Schuster, M. L., *Treasury of the World's Great Letters*, 82-4.
67. Raleigh, Sir Walter, *Selections*, 61.
68. Ibid., 117.
69. Lingard, VII, 101.

70. Spedding, *Life of Fr. Bacon*, II, 288-9; Wallace, *Sir Walter Raleigh*, 261f.
71. Lingard, VII, 102.
72. *Encycl. Brit.*, XVIII, 961b.
73. Wallace, *Raleigh*, 315.
74. Raleigh, *Selections*, Introduction, 28.
75. Lingard, VII, 117.
76. Williams, *James I*, 258.
77. Hallam, *Constitutional History*, 109.
78. Ibid., 122.
79. MacLaurin, C., *Mere Mortals*, 137.

CHAPTER VII

1. Browne, Sir Thomas, *Pseudodoxia Epidemica*, in *Works*, Vols. II and III.
2. Thorndike, Lynn, *History of Magic and Experimental Science*, VI, 548-9.
3. Lecky, *Rationalism in Europe*, I, 38n; Williams, *James I*, 106-10.
4. Lang, *History*, II, 434.
5. Hughes, *Reformation*, II, 286n.
6. Ibid., 285.
7. Thorndike, VI, 550; Chute, *Ben Jonson*, 229.
8. Trevelyan, *English Social History*, 232.
9. Smith, Preserved, *History of Modern Culture*, I, 97.
10. Ibid., 95.
11. Robertson, *History of Freethought*, II, 13.
12. Huntington Library Bulletin, April 1934, p. 99.
13. Wolf, *History of Science*, I, 292.
14. Ibid., 426.
15. John, Evan, *King Charles I*, 153; Kellogg, *The New Dietetics*, 847.
16. Garrison, *History of Medicine*, 248.
17. Sigerist, *The Great Doctors*, 141.
18. Harvey, *Exercitatio anatomica de motu cordis et sanguinis*, in Hammerton, *Great Books*, 273.
19. Walsh, J. J., *The Popes and Science*, 396.
20. Aubrey, 131.
21. Prinzmetal, *Heart Attack*, 121-2.
22. Aubrey, 128.
23. Ibid., 130.
24. Ibid., 11.
25. Gardiner, S. R., in Garnett and Gosse, *English Literature*, II, 12.
26. Spedding, *Life of Bacon*, I, 542.
27. Aubrey, 9.
28. Macaulay, *Critical and Historical Essays*, II, 326-8.
29. Bowen, *The Lion and the Throne*, 428; *Camb. Mod. History*, III, 571.
30. Spedding, *Life*, II, 463.
31. Ibid., 633.
32. Ibid., I, 563.
33. Ibid., 569.

34. Bacon, *Philosophical Works*, 241.
35. Ibid.
36. Ibid., 244.
37. Ibid., 247.
38. Aubrey, 130.
39. Bacon, *Phil. Works*, 167.
40. Ibid., 76, 78; *De Augmentis scientiarum*, Preface.
41. *Philosophical Works*, 76.
42. *Advancement of Learning*, ch. 8.
43. Bacon, *Works*, ed. Spedding and Ellis, VII, 241.
44. *Novum organum*, i, 97.
45. Ibid., i, 82; and "Plan of the Work" in *Philosophical Works*, 250.
46. *Novum organum*, ii, 13, 17.
47. *Philosophical Works*, 144.
48. Ibid., 77.
49. Ibid., 50.
50. Spedding, *Life*, I, 111.
51. *Novum organum*, ii, 2.
52. Ibid., ii, 8.
53. Ibid.
54. *De Augmentis*, iv, 3.
55. *Novum organum*, i, 66.
56. *De Augmentis*, end.
57. Essay "Of Atheism."
58. Ibid.; *Advancement of Learning*, in *Philosophical Works*, 45; *De Augmentis*, iii, 2.
59. Essay "Of Atheism."
60. *Valerius Terminus*, ch. i, in *Philosophical Works*, 186.
61. Rawley's *Life*, in *Phil. Works*, 9.
62. *De Augmentis*, ix, 1.
63. Essay "Of Goodness."
64. Ibid.
65. "Of Marriage and Single Life."
66. Essays "Of Empire" and "Of the True Greatness of Kingdoms."
67. *De Augmentis*, viii, 3, in *Phil. Works*, 610-11.
68. "Of Vicissitude of Things."
69. "Of Seditions and Troubles."
70. *Phil. Works*, 727.
71. *History of Henry VII*, in *Works*, VI, 238-45.
72. In Nichol, J., *Fr. Bacon*, II, 4.
73. Pope's *Essay on Man*, line 282.
74. *Thema coeli*, in *Phil. Works*, 705; *Descriptio globi intellectualis*, ibid., 685.
75. In Friedell, *Cultural History of the Modern Age*, I, 335.
76. *The Advancement of Learning*, in *Phil. Works*, 167.
77. Wolf, *Science in the Sixteenth Century*, 640; Bernal, *Science in History*, 305.
78. Hallam, *Literature of Europe*, III, 72.
79. Nichol, J., II, 235.
80. *Novum organum*, i, 49.
81. Ibid., i, 26, 95.

CHAPTER VIII

1. Rogers, *Six Centuries of Work and Wages*, 103.
2. Ibid., table at p. 73.
3. John, *Charles I*, 167.
4. French, Allen, *Charles I and the Puritan Upheaval*, 100-2.
5. Robertson, J. M., *Freethought*, II, 24.
6. Ibid., 77.
7. Ibid., 76.
8. Ibid.
9. Aubrey, 135.
10. Belloc, H., *Richelieu*, 49.
11. McCabe, *Candid History*, 202.
12. Toynbee, A., *Study of History*, IX, 178.
13. Allen, *English Political Thought*, 237.
14. Ibid., 242.
15. Ibid.
16. Taine, *English Literature*, 259-62.
17. Hume, D., *History of England*, IV, 183.
18. Gardiner, S. R., *History of England 1603-42*, VII, 302.
19. French, *Charles I*, 281.
20. Lingard, VII, 181; Taine, *English Literature*, 265.
21. *Camb. Mod. History*, IV, 279.
22. Allen, *English Thought*, 194.
23. Carlyle, T., *Oliver Cromwell*, I, 93.
24. French, 306.
25. Schaff, *History of the Christian Church: The German Reformation*, I, 79.
26. Allen, *English Thought*, 283.
27. French, 281.
28. Markun, L., *Mrs. Grundy*, 114.
29. Weber, Max, *The Protestant Ethic*, 177.
30. Beard, Miriam, *History of the Business Man*, 387.
31. Allen, *English Thought*, 279f; Lingard, VIII, 190.
32. Ibid., 191n.
33. Thornton, *Table Talk*, 72, 106.
34. Browne, *Religio Medici*, 77.
35. Browne, *Works*, II, 226.
36. *Religio Medici*, 70, 34.
37. Singer, *Studies in the History of Science*, 222.
38. *Religio Medici*, 82.
39. Ibid., 1.
40. Ibid., 18.
41. Ibid., 25.
42. Ibid., 10.
43. Ibid., 179.
44. Ibid., 60.
45. Ibid., 92.
46. Herrick, *Poems*, 181.
47. Ibid., 178.
48. Ibid., 398.
49. Aubrey, 287.
50. Ibid., 289.
51. Ibid., 192.

52. Lovelace, *Poems*, 78.
53. Ibid., 18.
54. MacLaurin, *Mere Mortals*, 143-4; John, *Charles I*, 4; French, 16.
55. Bishop, *Renaissance Architecture*, 25.
56. John, *Charles I*, 65.
57. Ibid., 66.
58. Ibid., 133; Lingard, VII, 164.
59. Gardiner, S. R., *History of England 1603-42*, VII, 1.
60. Ibid., 41-3.
61. Tawney, *Religion and the Rise of Capitalism*, 173.
62. Ibid., 174; Allen, *English Thought*, 360.
63. Rickard, *Man and Metals*, II, 799.
64. Clarendon, *History of the Rebellion*, I, 323.
65. Ibid., 188f.
66. Carlyle, *Oliver Cromwell*, I, 94.
67. Lang, *History of Scotland*, III, 71.
68. John, *Charles I*, 207.
69. Morley, *Oliver Cromwell*, 72.
70. Clarendon, *passim*; Hume, D., *History of England*, IV, 174, 401.
71. Carlyle, *Oliver Cromwell*; Firth, *Oliver Cromwell*; Buchan, *Oliver Cromwell*.
72. Morley, *Cromwell*, 9.
73. Carlyle, *Cromwell*, I, 98.
74. Ibid., 108.
75. Clarendon, I, 300; Gardiner, *History of England*, IX, 230.
76. Thornton, *Table Talk*, 108.
77. Gardiner, IX, 251-2.
78. Allen, *English Thought*, 346f.
79. Morley, *Cromwell*, 91; Hallam, *Constitutional History*, II, 119; Allen, 354.
80. Clarendon, I, 452.
81. Ibid., 466.
82. Firth, *Cromwell*, 61.
83. Clarendon, II, 49 f.
84. Allen, *English Thought*, 313, 403-4.
85. Robinson, J. H., *Readings*, 356.
86. Schaff, *History of the Christian Church: The Swiss Reformation*, II, 565.
87. Firth, 149; Bury, J. B., *History of Freedom of Thought*, 86; Robertson, J. M., *Freethought*, II, 76.
88. *Camb. Mod. History*, IV, 312.
89. Firth, 147.
90. Ibid.
91. Macaulay, *History of England*, I, 100.
92. Gooch, *English Democratic Ideas*, 119, 179.
93. Ibid., 124.
94. Ibid., 128.
95. *Camb. Mod. History*, IV, 345.
96. Firth, 175.
97. Morley, *Cromwell*, 240.
98. Lingard, VIII, 110.
99. Morley, 267.
100. John, *Charles I*, 294.

101. Hume, *History*, IV, 485.
102. Churchill, W. S., *History of the English-Speaking Peoples*, II, 223.
103. Robinson, *Readings*, 359.

CHAPTER IX

1. Evelyn, *Diary*, I, 225.
2. Ibid., 87.
3. *Camb. Mod. History*, IV, 631.
4. Molmenti, *Venice*, Ib, 218.
5. Ranke, *History of the Popes*, II, 119.
6. Funk, *Manual of Church History*, II, 147.
7. Hazlitt, W. C., *The Venetian Republic*, II, 221; *Encycl. Brit.*, XIX, 1002.
8. Symonds, J. A., *The Catholic Reaction*, II, 105.
9. On the inaccuracies of both historians cf. Ranke, *Popes*, III, 106-38.
10. Montaigne, *Diary*, 93; *Shakespeare's England*, I, 216.
11. Byron, *Childe Harold's Pilgrimage*, Canto IV, line 2.
12. Molmenti, Ib, 181.
13. Winckelmann, *History of Ancient Art*, II, 316.
14. Taine, *Italy: Rome and Naples*, 232.
15. Symonds, *Catholic Reaction*, II, 231.
16. Ruskin, *Modern Painters*, II, i, 7, 13.
17. Evelyn, I, 160.
18. Ogg, *Europe in the Seventeenth Century*, 387.
19. Sitwell, *Southern Baroque Art*, 43.
20. Stirling-Maxwell, *Annals of the Artists of Spain*, III, 893.
21. Justi, *Velázquez*, 343.
22. Byron, *Don Juan*, xiv, 71.
23. Pastor, XVIII, 121, 125.
24. Ranke, *Popes*, I, 286.
25. Ibid., 273.
26. Pastor, XVII, 172.
27. Lea, H. C., *Inquisition in Spain*, II, 77.
28. Ranke, *Popes*, I, 322.
29. Montaigne, *Diary*, 125.
30. Bacon, Fr., Apophthegm 60, in *Phil. Works*, 869.
31. Sully, *Memoirs*, I, 218n.
32. Ranke, *Popes*, I, 341.
33. Pastor, XXI, 83.
34. Ranke, I, 342.
35. Lecky, *History of European Morals*, II, 97.
36. Sully, *Memoirs*, III, 29.
37. *Camb. Mod. History*, IV, 687.
38. Graves, F. P., *History of Education*, 219.
39. Monroe, Paul, *Text-Book in the History of Education*, 422.
40. Bacon, *De Augmentis*, vi, 4, in *Phil. Works*, 559.

41. Ranke, *Popes*, II, 90.
42. McCabe, *Candid History*, 97.
43. Symonds, *Catholic Reaction*, II, 121.
44. Campbell, Thos., *The Jesuits*, 394.
45. Filmer, *Patriarcha*, in Locke, *Two Treatises on Government*, 253.
46. Campbell, 271.
47. Symonds, *Catholic Reaction*, I, 218; McCabe, *Candid History*, 184.
48. McCabe, 191.
49. Fülop-Miller, *Power and Secret of the Jesuits*, 285.
50. Ibid., 290.
51. Ibid., 300-1.
52. McCabe, 299.
53. In Campbell, 445.
54. Montaigne, *Diary*, 141.
55. Ibid., 159.
56. Molmenti, *Venice*, IIb, 27.
57. Montaigne, *Diary*, 151.
58. Symonds, *Catholic Reaction*, I, 268-74. *The Cenci*, by F. D. Guerrazzi (Milan, 1872), is a novel.
59. Evelyn, I, 172.
60. Ibid., 161.
61. Ibid., Nov. 8, 1644.
62. Burney, *History of Music*, II, 510; Grove's *Dictionary of Music*, III, 591; Brockway and Weinstock, *The Opera*, 1-3.
63. McKinney and Anderson, *Music in History*, 321.
64. Ibid., 334.
65. Garnett, Richard, *Italian Literature*, 269.
66. Ranke, *Popes*, I, 369.
67. *Encycl. Brit.*, III, 132b.
68. Johnson, S., *Lives of the Poets*, I, 176.
69. Guarini, *The Faithful Shepherd*, p. 64.
70. Ibid., 177.
71. Hallam, *Literature*, II, 181.
72. Symonds, *Italian Literature*, II, 243.
73. Tr. by Leigh Hunt, in Van Doren, *Anthology*, 590.
74. Symonds, *Catholic Reaction*, I, 367.
75. Boulting, *Tasso*, 172-3.
76. Ibid., 183, 174.
77. Symonds, *Catholic Reaction*, II, 35; *Encycl. Brit.*, XXI, 831a.
78. Symonds, I, 369.
79. Boulting, 212.
80. Smith, *History of Culture*, I, 552.
81. Boulting, 259.
82. Tasso, *Gerusalemme liberata*, xx, 1087.
83. Galileo, *Opere, ed. nazionale*, IX, 69, in Smith, P., *History of Culture*, I, 552.
84. Disraeli, Isaac, *Curiosities of Literature*, II, 444.
85. Burckhardt, J., *Recollections of Rubens*, 8.
86. Pastor, XXII, 309.

87. Justi, *Velázquez*, 350.
88. Wittkower, *Gian Lorenzo Bernini*, 197.
89. Ibid., 2.

CHAPTER X

1. El Greco, Phaidon ed., 7.
2. Weisbach, *Spanish Baroque Art*, 35.
3. Robertson, *Freethought*, II, 38; Hume, M., *Spanish People*, 416.
4. Lea, *Inquisition in Spain*, III, 441.
5. Prescott, *Philip II*, II, 498.
6. Lea, *Inquisition*, IV, 253.
7. Cf. Cervantes, *Don Quixote*, Part I, ch. 28; Vol. I, 223.
8. Stirling-Maxwell, I, 45.
9. Lang, P. H., *Music in Western Civilization*, 267.
10. Calvert, A. F., *The Escorial*, 7.
11. Ibid., 65; Calvert, *Royal Palaces of Spain*, 4-6; El Greco, Phaidon ed., 11.
12. Stirling-Maxwell, I, 209.
13. Davies, *Golden Age of Spain*, 120.
14. Froude, *Elizabeth*, I, 375.
15. Motley, *Rise of the Dutch Republic*, I, 125.
16. *Encycl. Brit.*, XVII, 722c.
17. Motley, I, 125.
18. Hume, M., *The Spanish People*, 382; Motley, II, 12.
19. Trend, *The Civilization of Spain*, 128.
20. Motley, I, 125.
21. Voltaire, *Works*, XIVb, 278.
22. Mariana, *General History of Spain*, Supplement, p. 30.
23. Blok, *History of the People of the Netherlands*, II, 289, 119; cf. *En. Br.*, XVII, 722.
24. Cf. Robinson, *Readings*, 321; Armstrong, *Emperor Charles V*, II, 376; Hume, M., *Spain: Its Greatness and Decay*, 150.
25. Prescott, *Philip II*, II, 431.
26. Davies, *Golden Age of Spain*, 150.
27. Prescott, *Philip II*, II, 451.
28. Altamira, *History of Spain*, 384.
29. Madariaga, *Spain*, 36; Davies, *Golden Age*, 194.
30. Ibid., 198; *History Today*, June 1954, p. 427.
31. Ibid.; Lea, *Inquisition in Spain*, IV, 254-272.
32. Trevor-Roper, *Historical Essays*, 269; Altamira, *History of Spanish Civilization*, 133.
33. Davies, *Golden Age*, 121.
34. *En. Br.*, XXI, 132.
35. Prescott, *Philip II*, I, 68, 210; II, 26.
36. Ogg, 170.
37. Davies, 230.
38. Ibid., 233.

39. Hume, M., *Court of Philip IV*, 24; Spain, 211; *Camb. Mod. History*, III, 542.
40. *Don Quixote*, Part II, ch. 54.
41. Ximenes, Juan, *Life and Virtues of . . . Juan de Ribera*, in Buckle, *History of Civilization*, II, 46.
42. Lea, *Inquisition*, III, 397, 407-8; Ogg, 364; Hume, M., *Spain*, 212.
43. Lea, III, 410.
44. *Camb. Mod. History*, IV, 634.
45. Justi, *Velázquez*, 105.
46. Portrait in Hispanic Society of America, New York.
47. Rooses, *Rubens*, 486.
48. Stephens, H. M., *Story of Portugal*, 249.
49. Camões, *Lusiads*, Introd., xvii.
50. Penrose, *Travel and Discovery*, 72.
51. Camões, *Lusiads*, ix, 83.
52. Ibid., 89.
53. Bell, Aubrey, *Portuguese Literature*, 183.
54. Camões, Introd. xxix.

CHAPTER XI

1. Preface to *Galatea*.
2. Hallam, *Literature*, I, 53.
3. Schevill, R., *Cervantes*, 7.
4. Altamira, *History of Spanish Civilization*, 143.
5. Fitzmaurice-Kelly, *History of Spanish Literature*, 338.
6. Gracian, *Art of Worldly Wisdom*, 20.
7. Ibid., 29.
8. 32.
9. 36.
10. 49.
11. 71.
12. 144.
13. 150.
14. In Davies, *Golden Age*, 282.
15. Ticknor, *History of Spanish Literature*, III, 150; cf. Fitzmaurice-Kelly, *History*, 274.
16. In Smith, P., *History of Modern Culture*, I, 552.
17. Bell, Aubrey, *Cervantes*, 54; Ticknor, II, 58.
18. Ellis, H., *Soul of Spain*, 233.
19. Schevill, *Cervantes*, 134.
20. Lockhart, J. G., Introd. to Everyman's Library ed. of *Don Quixote*, p. xx.
21. *Don Quixote*, Part I, ch. xii.
22. I, xi.
23. I, xiii.
24. II, xxxii.
25. I, iv.
26. II, xxxii.
27. II, xix; I, xx; II, iv.
28. I, xxxix.
29. I, xxxvi.

30. Cervantes, *Exemplary Novels*, 5.
31. Ibid., 3.
32. *Don Quixote*, II, xlv.
33. Schevill, *Cervantes*, 353.
34. Powys, J. C., *Enjoyment of Literature*, 174.
35. Ticknor, II, 42.
36. *Don Quixote*, I, xxi; Bell, *Cervantes*, 27.
37. Tr. by E. Churton in Fitzmaurice-Kelly, *History of Spanish Literature*, 281.
38. Quevedo, *The Dog and the Fever*, 52.
39. Tr. by John Masefield in Van Doren, *Anthology*, 645.
40. Fitzmaurice-Kelly, *History*, 254.
41. Id., *Some Masters of Spanish Verse*, 98.
42. Id., *History*, 249-50.
43. Ford, J. D., *Main Currents of Spanish Literature*, 129.
44. Fitzmaurice-Kelly, *Some Masters*, 43.
45. Lope de Vega, *The Star of Seville*, in Matthews, B., *Chief European Dramatists*, 171.
46. Lewes, G. N., *Lope de Vega*, in Clark, *Great Short Biographies*, 596; Fitzmaurice-Kelly, *Some Masters*, 25.
47. Shelley, *Poetical Works*, 645.
48. Calderón, *Life Is a Dream*, II, ii, tr. D. F. McCarthy, in Matthews, 219.

CHAPTER XII

1. Stirling-Maxwell, *Annals of the Artists of Spain*, I, 349.
2. Dieulafoy, *Art in Spain and Portugal*, 243.
3. Mâle, Émile, *Religious Art from the Twelfth to the Eighteenth Century*, 170.
4. In the Escorial.
5. In Calvert, *Seville*, 108.
6. Lassaigne, J., *Spanish Painting from the Catalan Frescoes to El Greco*, 131.
7. *En. Br.*, XXII, 69.
8. Naples.
9. Lassaigne, 106; Guinard, *El Greco*, 54.
10. Goldscheider, *El Greco*, 10.
11. Caffin, C. H., *Story of Spanish Painting*, 72.
12. Guinard, 121.
13. Meier-Graefe, *The Spanish Journey*, 145.
14. Pacheco, in Guinard, 22.
15. Johnson in Prologue to Addison's *Cato*.
16. Soria, M. S., *The Paintings of Zurbarán*, 30.
17. In Justi, *Velázquez*, 83.
18. Duke of Wellington Collection, London.
19. Boston Museum of Fine Arts.
20. National Gallery, London.
21. Justi, 445.

22. Rouen.
23. New York; Frankfurt.
24. Dresden Gallery.
25. Modena.
26. Earl of Radnor Collection.
27. Stirling-Maxwell, III, 847.
28. Justi, 360.
29. Cheney, *World History of Art*, 619.
30. Vienna.
31. Washington.
32. Wallace Collection, London.
33. Vienna.
34. Calvert and Hartley, *Velázquez*, 176.
35. Ellis, H., *Soul of Spain*, 153.
36. Meier-Graefe, 151, 200-5.
37. Stirling-Maxwell, III, 946.
38. Guinard and Baticle, *Histoire de la peinture espagnole*, 170.
39. Louvre.
40. Dresden.
41. Pliny, *Natural History*, xxxv, 36.
42. Stirling-Maxwell, III, 1003.
43. Prado, Seville, Cádiz, Louvre, Leningrad.
44. Dulwich.
45. Rome, Galleria Nazionale.
46. Prado.
47. London.
48. Leningrad.
49. Altamira, *History of Spanish Civilization*, 137f.

CHAPTER XIII

1. Roeder, *Catherine de' Medici and the Lost Revolution*, 170.
2. Sée, *Modern Capitalism*, 49.
3. Roeder, 250.
4. Guizot, *History of France*, III, 319.
5. Acton, *Lectures*, 156.
6. Michelet, *Histoire de France*, III, 483.
7. Thieme, *Women of Modern France*, 38.
8. Roeder, 309.
9. La Tour, *Origines de la Réforme*, IV, 255f.
10. Hearnshaw, *Social and Political Ideas of . . . the Renaissance and the Reformation*, 29.
11. Walker, W., *John Calvin*, 381.
12. Guizot, *France*, III, 303.
13. Sichel, *Catherine de' Medici and the French Reformation*, 111.
14. Ibid., 24.
15. Brantôme, *Book of the Ladies*, 51.
16. Michelet, *Histoire*, III, 490.
17. Sichel, 10.
18. Brantôme, 59.
19. Sichel, *The Later Years of Catherine de' Medici*, 116.
20. Sainte-Beuve in Brantôme, 88.
21. Roeder, 361.

22. Ibid., 386.
23. Allen, *Political Thought*, 295.
24. Roeder, 254-6.
25. Ranke, *Civil Wars . . . in France*, I, 278-80.
26. Sichel, *Catherine de' Medici*, 119.
27. Pastor, *History of the Popes*, XVI, 179.
28. Batiffol, *The Century of the Renaissance*, 201.
29. Ibid., 198; Pastor, XVI, 167; *Camb. Mod. History*, II, 300.
30. Pastor, XVI, 179.
31. Ibid.
32. Ibid., 180-1.
33. Allen, *Political Thought*, 305.
34. Sichel, 191, 196-7.
35. Lea, *Studies in Church History*, 496.
36. Pastor, XVI, 172.
37. Michelet, IV, 418; Batiffol, 203.
38. Guizot, *History*, III, 334.
39. Ibid., 335.
40. Batiffol, 211; Sichel, 224.
41. Froude, *Elizabeth*, I, 346.
42. Ranke, *Civil Wars*, I, 336; Batiffol, 215; Roeder, 366-9; Sichel, *The Later Years*, 19; Pastor, XVI, 203.
43. Guizot, III, 328.
44. Ibid., 330; Pastor, XVIII, 116.
45. Guizot, III, 331.
46. Pastor, XVIII, 154.
47. Froude, *Elizabeth*, II, 446.
48. Sedgwick, H. D., *Henry of Navarre*, 34.
49. Ibid., 90.
50. Batiffol, 241; Belloc, *Richelieu*, 139n.
51. Pastor, XVI, 195-6.
52. Roeder, 428.
53. Guizot, III, 380.
54. Janssen, J., *History of the German People*, VIII, 114.
55. Ibid.
56. Guizot, III, 384.
57. Ibid.
58. *Camb. Mod. History*, III, 18.
59. Ibid., 19; Pastor, XIX, 485.
60. Michelet, III, 458.
61. Batiffol, 227.
62. Sichel, *The Later Years*, 160.
63. Michelet, III, 462.
64. Sichel, *The Later Years*, 162.
65. Ibid., 164.
66. Ibid., 161.
67. Ibid.; Roeder, 453.
68. Batiffol, 229; Sichel, *The Later Years*, 164.
69. Ibid., 167; Batiffol, 230.
70. Ibid.
71. De Thou in Robinson, *Readings*, 331; Sichel, *Later Years*, 180.
72. Michelet, III, 468; Roeder, 473.
73. Michelet, III, 476.

74. Ibid.
75. Acton, 160; Roeder, 463.
76. Ibid., 477.
77. Ibid., 479.
78. Ibid., 489.
79. Pastor, XIX, 488.
80. Michelet, III, 478.
81. Acton, 162; Pastor, XIX, 489.
82. Michelet, III, 483.
83. Pastor, XIX, 509.
84. Roeder, 464.
85. Batiffol, 236; Sichel, *The Later Years*, 194.
86. Pastor, XIX, 507; Froude, *Elizabeth*, III, 417.
87. Pastor, XIX, 500-12.
88. Froude, *Elizabeth*, III, 419.
89. Roeder, 506.
90. Sichel, *Later Years*, 205.
91. Guizot, III, 415.

CHAPTER XIV

1. Lacroix, *History of Prostitution*, I, 1170-1, 1276-91.
2. Sedgwick, *Henry of Navarre*, 83.
3. In Brantôme, *Book of the Ladies*, 212.
4. Brutus, Junius, *Vindiciae contra tyrannos*, 97, 109, 169; Carlyle, R. W., *History of Medieval Political Theory*, VI, 335; Coker, *Readings in Political Philosophy*, 351f; Allen, *Political Thought*, 331.
5. Ibid., 377.
6. Voltaire, *Age of Louis XIV*, 397.
7. Ranke, *Civil Wars*, I, 163.
8. Allen, *Political Thought*, 347-50; Figgis, *From Gerson to Grotius*, 180.
9. Notes to Sully, *Memoirs*, I, 207.
10. Michelet, IV, 41.
11. Ibid., 42.
12. Sedgwick, *Henry*, 223.
13. Michelet, IV, 60.
14. Maulde La Clavière, *Women of the Renaissance*, 469.
15. Sully, I, 299, 311-14; Michelet, III, 463; Guizot, III, 521.
16. Ibid., 522.
17. Michelet, IV, 60.
18. *Satyre Ménippée*, 59-73.
19. Guizot, III, 556; Campbell, *The Jesuits*, 217; Ranke, *Popes*, II, 55; Sully, I, 447; Fülop-Miller, *Jesuits*, 317.
20. Sully, I, 2.
21. Kirby, *Engineering in History*, 141.
22. Guérard, *Life and Death of an Ideal*, 119.
23. Schaff, *Swiss Reformation*, II, 699.
24. Laski, H., in Brutus, *Vindiciae contra tyrannos*, 9, 35.
25. Lowie, R. H., *Are We Civilized?*, 241.

26. Tallement des Réaux, *Miniature Fortraits*, 9.
27. Ibid., 5.
28. Sedgwick, 274.
29. Batiffol, 287.
30. Sully, IV, 128n.
31. Sully, III, 365; Michelet, IV, 86.
32. Sedgwick, 130-5.
33. Lacroix, *Prostitution*, II, 1306.
34. Ibid., 1300.
35. Sully, III, 31-2.
36. Sedgwick, 255.
37. Ackerman, Phyllis, *Tapestry*, 262.
38. Davis, *Golden Age*, 237.
39. Sully, II, 404-10.
40. *Camb. Mod. History*, III, 682, 684.
41. Janssen, *History of the German People*, X, 439n.
42. Sedgwick, 288-9.
43. Fülop-Miller, *Jesuits*, 127; Gooch, *English Democratic Ideas*, 23.
44. Sedgwick, 306.

CHAPTER XV

1. Barine, *La Grande Mademoiselle*, 279.
2. Ibid., 278.
3. Sanders, *Bossuet*, 54.
4. Michelet, IV, 197; Batiffol, 404.
5. Michelet, IV, 370.
6. *Catholic Encyclopedia*, XIV, 437.
7. Jackson, C. C., *Old Paris*, 45.
8. Belloc, *Paris*, 311.
9. Boulenger, *Seventeenth Century*, 49.
10. Michelet, IV, 200.
11. Acton, *Lectures*, 171.
12. Buckle, Ib, 399-406.
13. Ibid., 399.
14. 405.
15. 403.
16. Boulenger, 37; Barine, 15.
17. Jackson, 56.
18. Richelieu, *Oeuvres*, 18.
19. Michelet, IV, 156.
20. In Guizot, IV, 131.
21. Ibid., 46.
22. 63.
23. Richelieu, 173.
24. Guizot, IV, 79.
25. Michelet, IV, 295.
26. Schoenhof, *History of Money and Prices*, 186.
27. Nussbaum, *History of Economic Institutions*, 108.
28. In Acton, 179.
29. Michelet, IV, 327.
30. Guizot, IV, 173.
31. Richelieu, 152, 201.
32. Guérard, *Life and Death of an Ideal*, 123.
33. Tallement des Réaux, 63.

34. Belloc, *Richelieu*, 90.
35. Michelet, IV, 286; Boulenger, 35.
36. Retz, *Secret Memoirs*, 97.
37. Hefele, K. J., *Life and Times of Cardinal Ximenes*, 565.
38. Chesterfield, *Letters*, 28 (Oct. 16, 1747).
39. Lodge, *Richelieu*, 229.
40. Richelieu, *Memoirs*, 168.
41. Ibid., 125.
42. 181, 40.
43. 182.
44. 168.
45. 32.
46. 19.
47. 30.
48. 35.
49. Motteville, Mme. de, *Memoirs*, I, 67.
50. Tallement des Réaux, 27.

CHAPTER XVI

1. Charron, *De la Sagesse*, I, 24, in Haydn, *Counter-Renaissance*, 569.
2. Sichel, *Catherine de' Medici*, 6; Lacroix, *History of Prostitution*, II, 1159.
3. Sedgwick, *Henry of Navarre*, 55.
4. Brantôme, *Lives of Gallant Ladies*, 131-2.
5. Now in the museum of the Château d'Azay-le-Rideau.
6. Michelet, IV, 222.
7. Tallement, 132.
8. Sanger, Wm., *History of Prostitution*, 119.
9. Ibid.; Lacroix, *Prostitution*, II, 1350.
10. Montaigne, *Diary*, 6.
11. Sully, *Memoirs*, I, 482, 507.
12. Brantôme, *Book of the Ladies*, 79.
13. Wright, *Womankind in Western Europe*, 305.
14. Lacroix, *Arts of the Middle Ages*, 164.
15. Wright, *Womankind*, 302.
16. Montaigne, *Essays*, II, 12.
17. Lowie, *Are We Civilized?*, 34.
18. Burney, Charles, *General History of Music*, II, 217.
19. Ibid., 466.
20. Montaigne, *Essays*, III, 365.
21. Ibid., I, xxv, 185.
22. I, xxv.
23. III, xii, 300.
24. III, xii, 292.
25. I, xxxviii, 252.
26. I, xxv, 165.
27. Ibid., 163.
28. Ibid., 166, 172.
29. III, xiii, 324.
30. II, vi, 48.
31. Dowden, *Michel de Montaigne*, 45.
32. I, xxvii, 201.
33. Ibid.

34. Gide, A., *The Living Thoughts of Montaigne*, 14.
35. I, xxvii, 207.
36. III, x, 265.
37. III, v, 119.
38. Ibid., 105.
39. 73.
40. Cf. his paean to Paris in III, ix, 216.
41. III, v, 76.
42. II, viii, 71.
43. Gide, 12.
44. III, ix, 213.
45. III, iii, 49.
46. I, xxxviii, 253-6.
47. I, xxv, 149.
48. II, xxxii, 448.
49. Sellery, G. C., *The Renaissance*, 47.
50. Pater, *Plato and Platonism*, 174.
51. In Dowden, *Montaigne*, 240.
52. II, iii, 35.
53. II, xvii, 385.
54. III, v, 107.
55. III, ii, 24.
56. II, xxxvi, 523.
57. Ibid., 495.
58. III, xiii, 354.
59. Diary, 259.
60. II, xii, 256; Cicero, *De veritate*, 11.
61. III, xii, 291.
62. III, xiii, 379.
63. Sainte-Beuve, *Port-Royal*, II, 440.
64. II, xii, 306.
65. Ibid., 317.
66. In Spencer, Theodore, *Shakespeare and the Nature of Man*, 36.
67. II, xii, 237.
68. Ibid., 285-7.
69. 312.
70. 202.
71. 250.
72. 324.
73. 325.
74. Sichel, E., *Montaigne*, 54.
75. II, xvii, 371.
76. II, xii, 180.
77. I, xl, 269; *Camb. Mod. History*, II, 711.
78. II, v.
79. II, viii, 72.
80. I, xxx, 219.
81. II, xii, 198, 250.
82. I, xxx, 229.
83. In Dowden, *Montaigne*, 63.
84. III, vi, 144.
85. III, ix, 201; v, 105.
86. II, xii.
87. II, xii, 204.
88. Ibid., 251.
89. 225, 266.
90. I, xix, 90.
91. III, v, 78.
92. III, xi, 285.

93. II, xii, 130.
94. Ibid., 217.
95. 133.
96. Sainte-Beuve, *Port-Royal*, II, 428.
97. I, liv, 354; Tilley, A., *Studies in the French Renaissance*, 280.
98. II, xii, 225.
99. III, xi.
100. III, ix, 198.
101. III, viii, 173.
102. III, ix, 191.
103. III, xii, 301; ii, 26.
104. II, xi, 121.
105. III, x, 263.
106. *Diary*, 14.
107. Ibid., 17.
108. 49.
109. 107.
110. 150.
111. Cf. *Diary*, 166-9.
112. Ibid., 123.
113. *Essays*, III, iv, 59.
114. III, xiii, 368.
115. II, i, 8.
116. Jonson, *Volpone*, III, ii.
117. Mme. du Deffand, *Lettres à Voltaire*, 41; Jan. 28, 1759.
118. Malebranche, *De la Recherche de la vérité*, III, v; p. 264.
119. In Gide, 3.
120. Sainte-Beuve, *Port-Royal*, II, 379-453.
121. In Frame, *Montaigne*, 139.
122. Guizot, IV, 194.
123. Van Laun, *History of French Literature*, II, 181.
124. Disraeli, I., *Curiosities of Literature*, I, 451.
125. Malherbe, in Sainte-Beuve, *Portraits of the Seventeenth Century*, II, 47.
126. Boileau in Malherbe, Racan, Maynard, *Poésies choisies*, 9n.
127. Ibid., 24-7.
128. Winegarten, *French Lyric Poetry in the Age of Malherbe*, 8, 18.
129. Boulenger, *Seventeenth Century*, 122.
130. Faguet, *Literary History of France*, 341.
131. Régnier, De Viau, etc., *Poésies choisies*, 50.
132. Guizot, *Corneille and His Times*, 148.
133. Corneille, *Le Cid*, V, i.
134. Guizot, *Corneille*, 168.
135. Livy, T. L., *History of Rome*, i, 25.
136. Corneille, *Horace*, I, i.
137. Ibid., II, viii.
138. Sainte-Beuve, *Port-Royal*, I, 124.
139. Evelyn, *Diary*, I, 48.
140. Blomfield, *History of French Architecture*, II, 134.
141. Bupal, *Bernard Palissy*, 43.
142. In Sichel, *Catherine de' Medici*, 318; Michelet, *Histoire de France*, IV, 51.
143. Guizot, *Histoire*, IV, 571.
144. Sutro, E., *Nicolas Poussin*, 77.
145. Desjardins, *Poussin*, 71.
146. Mousnier, *Histoire générale des civilisations*, IV, 218.
147. Ruskin, *Modern Painters*, II, ii, 1.8.
148. Craven, *Treasury of Art Masterpieces*, 172; Stranahan, *History of French Painting*, 45.
149. Ruskin, *Modern Painters*, II, i, 7.5; IX, v.

CHAPTER XVII

1. Geyl, *Revolt of the Netherlands*, 16.
2. Sombart, *The Jews and Modern Capitalism*, 65; Sée, *Modern Capitalism*, 31.
3. Motley, *Rise of the Dutch Republic*, I, 217; Janssen, *History of the German People*, VIII, 13.
4. Motley, I, 217.
5. Janssen, VIII, 14f.
6. Voltaire, *Essai sur les moeurs*, ch. cxxxvi, in *Works*, XIVb.
7. Motley, I, 207.
8. Ibid., 206.
9. Blok, *History of the People of the Netherlands*, III, 11; Motley, I, 375f.
10. Ibid., 283.
11. Geyl, 78.
12. Ibid., 86.
13. Janssen, VIII, 19.
14. *Cambridge Modern History*, III, 200.
15. Acton, *Lectures*, 144.
16. Motley, I, 453-4.
17. Ibid., 465-8.
18. *Camb. Mod. History*, III, 207-8.
19. Motley, I, 478f.
20. Janssen, VIII, 23.
21. Motley, I, 526.
22. Janssen, VIII, 25.
23. Prescott, *Philip II*, II, 161.
24. Blok, III, 42.
25. Pastor, *History of the Popes*, XVIII, 97.
26. Blok, III, 51.
27. Pastor, XVIII, 101.
28. Motley, I, 628; Janssen, VIII, 123.
29. *Camb. Mod. History*, III, 232.
30. Motley, II, 72-4.
31. Geyl, 128; Lacroix, *Military and Religious Life in the Middle Ages*, 440.
32. Motley, II, 40.
33. Ibid., 101.
34. Voltaire, *Essai*, ch. cxxxvi; *Works*, p. 294; Hume, M., *The Spanish People*, 372.
35. Pastor, *Popes*, XX, 3.
36. Motley, II, 151.
37. Ibid., 169.
38. 515.

39. Geyl, 165.
40. Ibid., 130.
41. 128.
42. *Camb. Mod. History*, III, 250.
43. Blok, III, 121-3.
44. Geyl, 162; Pastor, XX, 9.
45. Motley, II, 646.
46. Robinson, J. H., *Readings in European History*, 325; Motley, II, 637.
47. Figgis, *From Gerson to Grotius*, 228.
48. *Camb. Mod. History*, III, 258.
49. Blok, III, 179.
50. Ibid., 239.
51. Geyl, 206, 215, 231; Ranke, *History of the Popes*, II, 221.
52. Blok, III, 415.
53. *Camb. Mod. History*, III, 646.
54. Blok, III, 413.

CHAPTER XVIII

1. Robinson, *Readings*, 556.
2. Prescott, H. F., *Mary Tudor*, 331.
3. Vienna.
4. Prado.
5. Brussels, Vienna, Louvre.
6. Brussels.
7. Rooses, *Rubens*, I, 9.
8. Pitti Gallery, Florence.
9. Uffizi Gallery, Florence.
10. Grenoble Museum.
11. Rooses, I, 638.
12. Burckhardt, *Recollections of Rubens*, 21.
13. Janssen, XI, 161.
14. Dresden.
15. Knackfuss, H., *Van Dyck*, 4.
16. Munich.
17. Lichtenstein Collection, Vienna.
18. Vienna.
19. Geneva.
20. Munich.
21. London.
22. Pitti Gallery.
23. Dresden.
24. Louvre.
25. Vienna.
26. Madrid.
27. Vienna, Madrid.
28. London.
29. Craven, *Treasury of Art Masterpieces*, 105.
30. Antwerp.
31. Fülop-Miller, *Power and Secret of the Jesuits*, 422.
32. Munich.
33. Hartford, Conn.
34. Antwerp.
35. Antwerp cathedral and Brussels Museum.
36. Vienna.
37. Vienna.

38. Sarasota, Fla.
39. Rooses, *Rubens*, I, 395.
40. Ibid., 417.
41. Pitti Gallery.
42. Boston.
43. Rooses, I, 414.
44. Munich.
45. Munich.
46. Hamburg.
47. Vienna.
48. Munich.
49. Munich.
50. Louvre.
51. Brussels.
52. The Hague.
53. Frick Collection, New York.
54. Windsor Castle.
55. Burckhardt, *Recollections*, 15.
56. Rooses, I, 600.
57. Louvre.
58. Vienna.
59. Knackfuss, 8.
60. Munich.
61. Frick Collection
62. Brussels.
63. Detroit.
64. Munich.
65. Vienna.
66. Antwerp.
67. Knackfuss, 9.
68. Pitti Gallery.
69. Wallace Collection, London.
70. Louvre.
71. Vienna.
72. Vienna.
73. Lichtenstein Gallery, Vienna.
74. Knackfuss, 76.
75. New York.
76. Ibid.
77. Frick Collection, New York.
78. Fitzwilliam Collection.
79. Dresden.
80. Munich.
81. Uffizi Gallery.
82. Blok, III, 333; Mousnier, 160.
83. Maverick, L. A., *China a Model for Europe*, 5.
84. Adams, Brooks, *Law of Civilization and Decay*, 107.
85. Nussbaum, *History of Economic Institutions*, 123.
86. Gooch, *Democratic Ideas*, 45.
87. Geyl, 211.
88. Ogg, *Europe in the Seventeenth Century*, 412.
89. Geyl, 238; Blok, III, 354.
90. Fischer, K., *Descartes and His School*, 212.
91. Taine, H., *Lectures on Art*, 322.
92. *En. Br.*, X, 498d.
93. In Taine, *Lectures*, 183.

94. Day, Clive, *History of Commerce*, 200.
95. Sée, *Modern Capitalism*, 32.
96. Wilenski, R. H., *Dutch Painting*, 132.
97. Baedeker, K., *Belgique et Hollande*, 383.
98. Chute, *Ben Jonson*, 301.
99. Geyl, 206.
100. Honey, W. B., *European Ceramic Art*, 31.
101. Wilenski, *Dutch Painting*, 10.
102. Taine, *Lectures*, 333.
103. Hauser, *Social History of Art*, I, 467.
104. Davies, G. S., *Frans Hals*, 19.
105. Amsterdam.
106. Haarlem.
107. Lord Northbrooke Collection.
108. Wallace Collection.
109. Devonshire House.
110. Haarlem.
111. Haarlem.
112. Haarlem.
113. Haarlem.
114. Amsterdam.
115. Antwerp.
116. Haarlem.
117. Berlin.
118. Louvre.
119. Cassel.
120. Mather, F. J., *Western European Painting of the Renaissance*, 461.
121. Chicago.
122. Berlin.
123. New York.
124. The Hague.
125. Michel, E., *Rembrandt*, I, 63.
126. Amsterdam.
127. The Hague.
128. The Hague.
129. The Hague.
130. Duke of Devonshire Collection.
131. Rothschild Collection.
132. Leningrad.
133. Louvre.
134. New York.
135. Brussels.
136. Amsterdam.
137. Michel, *Rembrandt*, II, 214.
138. Edinburgh.
139. Louvre.
140. Louvre.
141. London.
142. Berlin.
143. Cassel.
144. Berlin.
145. New York.
146. Washington.
147. Leningrad.
148. London.
149. Glasgow.
150. Cassel.
151. Still with the Six family in Amsterdam.
152. Berlin.
153. Frick Collection.
154. Wallace Collection.
155. Beard, Miriam, *History of the Business Man*, 316.
156. Marcus Kappel Collection, Berlin.
157. New York.
158. Louvre.
159. Amsterdam.
160. Leningrad.
161. Amsterdam.
162. Froment in Wilenski, *Dutch Painting*, 93.
163. Self-portrait in the Louvre.
164. New York.
165. I. de Brüyn Collection.
166. Rathenau Collection.
167. In Michel, *Rembrandt*, I, 259.
168. Wilenski, *Dutch Painting*, 93.
169. Ibid.
170. Meier-Graefe, *Spanish Journey*, 313.

CHAPTER XIX

1. Gade, *Tycho Brahe*, 150.
2. Werner, *Copenhagen*, 3.
3. Ranke, *Popes*, II, 150.
4. Fletcher, C. R., *Gustavus Adolphus*, 15.
5. Bain, F. W., *Christina, Queen of Sweden*, 8.
6. Fletcher, 43.
7. *Camb. Mod. History*, IV, 187.
8. Wedgwood, C. V., *Thirty Years' War*, 273.
9. Fletcher, 27.
10. Bain, 28.
11. Ibid., 10.
12. 42.
13. 162.
14. 96.
15. 97.
16. 95.
17. 166.
18. Pascal, *Provincial Letters*, introduction, 25.
19. Ranke, *Popes*, II, 355.
20. Ortega y Gasset, *Toward a Philosophy of History*, 18.
21. Horn, F. W., *Literature of the Scandinavian North*, 332.
22. Cf. Ranke, *Popes*, II, 353.
23. Bain, 358-61.
24. Ranke, II, 359; Bain, 180.
25. Voltaire, *Age of Louis XIV*, 60.
26. Gustafson in Bain, xvi.
27. Bain, 360.
28. Ogg, 446.
29. Bain, 224.
30. Ibid., 229.
31. Lewinski-Corwin, *Political History of*

Poland, 216-18; *Cambridge History of Poland,* I, 566.
32. Lednicki, W., *Life and Culture of Poland,* 125-6.
33. Ibid., 94.
34. *Camb. History of Poland,* I, 413; Robertson, J. M., *History of Freethought,* I, 426.
35. Lednicki, 102n.
36. Robertson, *Freethought,* II, 37.
37. *Camb. History of Poland,* I, 403-5, 410-11.
38. Ranke, II, 161.
39. Pokrovsky, M., *History of Russia,* 154.
40. Florinsky, M., *Russia: a History and an Interpretation,* I, 213.
41. Kluchevsky, V., *History of Russia,* II, ch. xiii; III, 21; Florinsky, I, 217.
42. Vernadsky, G., *History of Russia,* 65.
43. Réau, L., *L'Art russe,* I, 285.
44. Ranke, II, 155.
45. Florinsky, I, 226.
46. E.g., Pokrovsky, 169-70.
47. Ibid., 177; Kluchevsky, III, 20; Florinsky, I, 223.
48. Rambaud, A., *History of Russia,* I, 320.
49. *Camb. Mod. History,* V, 496.
50. Florinsky, I, 227; Pokrovsky, 182.
51. Kluchevsky, III, 31.
52. Rambaud, I, 341.

CHAPTER XX

1. Tavernier, *Six Voyages,* ii, 7.
2. Brockelmann, C., *History of the Islamic Peoples,* 316.
3. Pepys, *Diary,* Nov. 9, 1663.
4. Arnold, T., *The Preaching of Islam,* in Toynbee, A., *Study of History,* VIII, 165.
5. Finlay, G., *History of Greece,* V, 29, in Toynbee, ibid., 164.
6. Tavernier, i, 1.
7. Michelet, *Histoire de France,* IV, 444.
8. Brantôme, *Lives of Gallant Ladies,* 135; Landau, R., *Invitation to Morocco,* 64.
9. Gibb, E. J., *Ottoman Literature,* 3.
10. Ibid., 236.
11. Dimand, M. S., *Guide to Exhibition of Islamic Miniature Painting,* 4.
12. Pope, A. U., *Catalogue of a Loan Exhibition of Early Oriental Carpets,* 93-5.
13. Pastor, *Popes,* XVIII, 419.
14. Voltaire, *Essai sur les moeurs,* ch. cxxxi, in *Works,* XIBb, 270.
15. Preface to Part II of *Don Quixote.*
16. Motley, *Rise of the Dutch Republic,* II, 338.
17. Pastor, XVIII, 422.
18. Ibid., 427.
19. 436.

20. Lane-Poole, S., *Story of Turkey,* 218.
21. *En. Br.,* XV, 969a.
22. Teixeira, P., *Travels,* 62-6.
23. Pope, A. U., *Survey of Persian Art,* II, 1406.
24. Tavernier, *Six Voyages,* iv, 5.
25. Ibid.
26. Michelet, *Histoire de France,* V, 130.
27. *En. Br.,* XII, 705. The account follows the eloquent description in Arthur Upham Pope, *Survey of Persian Art,* II, 1185, and the notes of my visit to Isfahan in 1948.
28. Tavernier, v, 2.
29. Browne, E. G., *Literary History of Persia,* IV, 111.
30. Chardin, John, *Travels in Persia,* 134-6.
31. Ibid., 183, 167.
32. Teixeira, 114, 117.
33. Chardin, 143.
34. Ibid.
35. 146.
36. 279.
37. Tavernier, v, 14.
38. Arnold, Thomas, *Painting in Islam,* 89.
39. Chardin, 120.
40. Teixeira, 62.
41. Chardin, 187; Tavernier, v, 14.
42. Chardin, 191, 189.
43. Browne, E. G., *Literary History,* IV, 247.
44. Ibid., 287.
45. *En. Br.,* XII, 705b.
46. Sir Bernard Eckstein Collection.
47. Boston.
48. Pope, *Survey,* I, 7n.
49. Gulbenkian Collection. Pope, *Survey,* V, 978.
50. Boston.
51. Pope, *Survey,* V, 549.
52. Pope, A. U., *Introduction to Persian Art,* 162.
53. Chardin, *Travels,* 273.
54. New York.
55. In Pope, *Catalogue,* 17.
56. Pope, *Introduction,* 220.

CHAPTER XXI

1. Coxe, W., *History of the House of Austria,* II, 29.
2. Ibid., 67-72.
3. 130.
4. 94.
5. *Camb. Mod. History,* III, 719.
6. Tawney, R. H., *Religion and the Rise of Capitalism,* 122-4.
7. Janssen, *History of the German People,* VIII, 297-9.
8. Robertson, J. M., *Freethought,* I, 420.
9. Campbell, *The Jesuits,* 69.

10. Lützow, Count von, *Bohemia*, 217.
11. Acton, *Lectures*, 182.
12. Clark, G. N., *Seventeenth Century*, 136.
13. Janssen, XV, 32, 44.
14. Ibid., 29-31.
15. Thompson, J. W., *Economic and Social History of the Later Middle Ages*, 429; Rickard, *Man and Metals*, II, 565.
16. Janssen, XV, 148.
17. Ibid., 110.
18. 125.
19. Marx, Karl, *Capital*, I, 467.
20. Janssen, XIII, 147.
21. Ibid., 307.
22. 301.
23. 300.
24. Id., XII, 183.
25. X, 279.
26. XII, 96.
27. XI, 363.
28. Pastor in Janssen, XVI, 130.
29. Janssen, X, 277-8.
30. Wedgwood, *Thirty Years' War*, 46.
31. Janssen, XV, 421.
32. Putnam, G. H., *The Censorship of the Church of Rome*, I, 51.
33. Janssen, X, 11.
34. Ibid., 23, 45.
35. Id., XIII, 363f.
36. XIV, 12-14.
37. Wilenski, *Dutch Painting*, 61.
38. Vienna.
39. *Camb. Mod. History*, III, 153.
40. Schaff, *The German Reformation*, I, 64.
41. Janssen, X, 287f.
42. Ibid., 303-7.
43. 262.
44. 258.
45. 257.
46. 256.
47. Inge, W. R., *Christian Mysticism*, 277.
48. Ibid., 278.
49. Fülop-Miller, *Jesuits*, 346.
50. Janssen, X, 214.
51. Ibid., 103, 110.
52. 165.
53. 32.
54. 30.
55. 24.
56. 334-41.
57. 345.
58. 386-90.
59. 215.
60. 219.
61. 589.
62. 594.
63. Wedgwood, 81.
64. Nosek, V., *Spirit of Bohemia*, 99f.
65. Michelet, IV, 289n.

66. Wedgwood, 171.
67. Ibid., 255.
68. Fletcher, *Gustavus Adolphus*, 300.
69. Robinson, *Readings*, 345.
70. Fletcher, 283.
71. Guizot, *History*, IV, 160.
72. Wedgwood, 353.
73. Ibid., 360.
74. 450.
75. 207, 256-7, 410.
76. 475.
77. 516; *Camb. Mod. History*, IV, 418.
78. Lützow, 311; *Camb. Mod. History*, IV, 418.
79. Ibid., 417.
80. Renard and Weulersee, *Life and Work in Modern Europe*, 294.
81. Jordan, G. J., *The Reunion of Churches*, 15.
82. Wedgwood, 412; Ogg, *Europe in the Seventeenth Century*, 168.
83. Wedgwood, 413.
84. Ibid., 229.
85. *Camb. Mod. History*, IV, 688.

CHAPTER XXII

1. Thorndike, L., *History of Magic and Experimental Science*, VI, 160-5, 221, 239-40, 295; IV, 247; Garrison, F., *History of Medicine*, 37.
2. Voltaire, *Age of Louis XIV*, 18.
3. Smith, P., *History of Modern Culture*, I, 428.
4. Berry, A., *Short History of Astronomy*, 195.
5. Jackson, C., *Old Paris*, 25.
6. Smith, P., *Modern Culture*, I, 427.
7. Janssen, XII, 346.
8. Ibid., 329.
9. Los Angeles *Times*, July 2, 1958.
10. Janssen, XVI, 372-6, 495; XII, 325, 351.
11. Lea, *Inquisition in Spain*, IV, 243-4.
12. Vacandard, E., *The Inquisition*, 199.
13. Singer, Chas., *Studies in the History of Science*, I, 213.
14. Lea, IV, 235.
15. Michelet, IV, 183-6.
16. Janssen, XI, 388.
17. Id., XVI, 398, 478.
18. Lea, *History of the Inquisition of the Middle Ages*, III, 549.
19. Janssen, XVI, 416.
20. *Camb. Mod. History*, V, 758 (not 9,000, as in IV, 423).
21. Janssen, XVI, 512, 424.
22. Lea, *Inquisition in Spain*, IV, 246; cf. Janssen, XVI, 506.
23. Montaigne, *Essays*, III, xi, 285.
24. Ibid., 286.
25. Smith, *Culture*, I, 453.

26. Ibid., 454; Dampier, *History of Science*, 157.
27. Janssen, XVI, 390.
28. Janssen, XI, 379.
29. Evelyn, *Diary*, I, 139.
30. Putnam, *Censorship of the Church of Rome*, II, 237-69.
31. In Haydn, *Counter-Renaissance*, 531.
32. Hallam, *Literature*, II, 44.
33. Sandys, Sir John, *Companion to Latin Studies*, 855.
34. Putnam, G. H., *Books and Their Makers*, II, 96.
35. Masson, David, *Life of John Milton*, IV, 164.
36. Nosek, *Spirit of Bohemia*, 110.
37. Paulsen, F., *German Education*, 136.
38. Janssen, XIII, 277.
39. Galileo, *Discoveries and Opinions*, ed. Stillman Drake, 77.
40. Singer, *Studies*, 407.
41. Wolf, A., *History of Science, Technology, and Philosophy in the Sixteenth and Seventeenth Centuries*, 47; Singer, *Studies*, 412f.
42. Bell, E. T., *Men of Mathematics*, 55.
43. Butterfield, *Origins of Modern Science*, 67.
44. Galileo, *Il saggiatore*, in *Discoveries and Opinions*, 237.
45. Cooper, Lane, *Aristotle, Galileo, and the Tower of Pisa*, 14; Dampier, 143.
46. Janssen, XV, 281.
47. Wolf, 327.
48. Mumford, L., *Technics and Civilization*, 440.
49. Wolf, 544-5; Usher, A. P., *History of Mechanical Inventions*, 303.
50. Descartes, *Principia philosophiae*, Part IV, in Wolf, 351.
51. *En. Br.*, I, 689d.
52. Galileo, *Dialogue concerning the Two Chief World Systems*, Dedication, p. 3.
53. Michel, *Rembrandt*, I, 123.
54. Mumford, L., *The Condition of Man*, 213.
55. Janssen, XIV, 68.
56. Ibid., 83.
57. 80.
58. Castiglioni, *History of Medicine*, 561.
59. Garrison, 307.
60. Janssen, XIV, 81.
61. Montaigne, *Essays*, tr. E. J. Trechmann, II, 222, quoted in Craig, Hardin, *The Enchanted Glass*, 44.
62. Garrison, 291-2.
63. Ibid., 226.
64. Descartes, *Discours de la méthode*, Part VI, p. 62, in Vartanian, *Diderot and Descartes*, 18.
65. Montaigne, *Essays*, III, x, 262.
66. Putnam, *Censorship*, I, 128-9; Belloc, H., *How the Reformation Happened*, 281; Fülop-Miller, *Jesuits*, 399; Smith, P., *Culture*, I, 43.
67. Campanella, Letter to Galileo, Jan. 12, 1611, in Smith, *Culture*, I, 45.
68. Buckle, I, 101; Thorndike, VI, 42.
69. Gade, *Tycho Brahe*, 35.
70. Ibid., 187.
71. Kesten, H., *Copernicus and His World*, 346.
72. Whewell, *History of the Inductive Sciences*, I, 290-3.
73. Hogben, *Science for the Citizen*, 207; Kesten, 353.
74. Dampier, 139.
75. Berry, 194.
76. In Inge, *Christian Mysticism*, 298.
77. Galileo, *Dialogue concerning the Two Chief World Systems*, 105 (end of First Day).
78. Aristotle, *De coelo*, 4.2. 309, in Cooper, L., *Aristotle, Galileo, and the Tower of Pisa*, 64.
79. Lucretius, *De rerum natura*, II, 230-1.
80. Leonardo da Vinci, *Codex Atlanticus*, fol. 123ra, in Cooper, 69.
81. In Cooper, 47.
82. Viviani in Cooper, 26.
83. Ibid., 29-31.
84. Galileo, *Two Chief World Systems*, 147.
85. Galileo, *Dialogues concerning Two New Sciences*, 103.
86. Galileo, *Il saggiatore*, in *Discoveries and Opinions*, 274.
87. Ibid., 276-7.
88. Kesten, 348.
89. In Singer, *Studies*, 228.
90. Letter of Jan. 30, 1610, in Singer, 232.
91. Walsh, J. J., *The Popes and Science*, 393; Wolf, 29.
92. In Singer, 251.
93. Kesten, 396.
94. In Smith, *Culture*, I, 53.
95. Singer, 240.
96. Fülop-Miller, *Jesuits*, 397.
97. Singer, 240.
98. Fülop-Miller, 398.
99. Ibid.
100. Ibid.
101. Kesten, 371.
102. Galileo, *Discoveries and Opinions*, 177.
103. Ibid., 180.
104. 183.
105. Drake in Galileo, *Discoveries and Opinions*, 217.
106. Singer, 252.
107. Kesten, 375.
108. Wolf, 36.

109. Kesten, 379; Singer, 258.
110. Galileo, *Two Chief World Systems*, 5.
111. Ibid., 460.
112. Kesten, 388.
113. Singer, 269.
114. *En. Br.*, IX, 980b.
115. Ibid.; Wolf, 37.
116. Viviani in Singer, 279.
117. Kesten, 93.
118. Ibid., 395.

CHAPTER XXIII

1. Janssen, XVI, 132-4.
2. Robertson, *Freethought*, 483.
3. Ibid., 484.
4. Mousnier, *Histoire générale*, IV, 203.
5. Ibid., 201.
6. Owen, John, *Skeptics of the French Renaissance*, 676.
7. Ibid., 578-9.
8. Ibid.
9. 584.
10. 580.
11. Charron, Pierre, *Of Wisdom*, I, 61, 74, 79-80.
12. Owen, 598.
13. Cf. Charron, in Pascal, *Pensées*, ed. Havet, introd. xii.
14. Bury, *Freedom of Thought*, 75.
15. Owen, 570.
16. Singer, D. W., *Giordano Bruno*, 22.
17. Ibid., 24.
18. Owen, 274.
19. Bruno, *La cena de le ceneri*, Dialogue IV, in Singer, D. W., 33.
20. In Owen, 274.
21. Singer, *Bruno*, 137.
22. Ibid., 35.
23. Symonds, *Catholic Reaction*, II, 53-4.
24. Owen, 125.
25. Singer, *Bruno*, 146.
26. In Owen, 294.
27. Cassirer, *Philosophy of the Enlightenment*, 41.
28. Bruno, Dedication to *De la causa, preincipio et uno*, in Singer, *Bruno*, 103.
29. Thorndike, *Magic and Experimental Science*, IV, 425-7.
30. Owen, 290-3.
31. Singer, *Bruno*, 161.
32. Symonds, *Catholic Reaction*, II, 62.
33. Kesten, 323.
34. Singer, *Bruno*, 166.
35. Ibid., 172.
36. 179.
37. Owen, 390.
38. Ibid., 399.
39. 400.
40. Symonds, 128; Kesten, 328.

41. Tr. J. A. Symonds in Van Doren, *Anthology*, 599.
42. Campanella, *City of the Sun*, in *Ideal Commonwealths*, 147.
43. Ibid., 157.
44. 164.
45. 168.
46. Murray, R. H., *Erasmus and Luther*, 443.
47. Ranke, *Popes*, II, 13.
48. Carlyle, R. W., *Medieval Political Theory*, VI, 341.
49. Campbell, *The Jesuits*, 379.
50. Mariana, *The King and The Education of the King*, i, 2.
51. Ibid., i, 10.
52. Ibid., Preface, p. 108.
53. Ibid., iii, 15.
54. In Laski, *Political Thought in England, Locke to Bentham*, 85.
55. Mariana, *The King*, i, 1.
56. Ibid., iii, 2.
57. i, 6, pp. 144-9.
58. Ibid.
59. Bodin, *Method for the Easy Comprehension of History*, 11.
60. Allen, *Political Thought*, 395.
61. Bodin, *De republica*, i, 4, in Allen, 408-9.
62. Ibid., 410.
63. Bodin, *De republica*, i, 6.
64. Ibid., i, 9.
65. Ibid., vi, 4, in Dunning, *Political Theories from Luther to Montesquieu*, 107.
66. Ibid., in Allen, *Political Thought*, 436.
67. In Allen, 406.
68. Bodin, *Method for the Easy Comprehension of History*, in Allen, 399.
69. Allen, 400-1.
70. Blok, III, 463.
71. Grotius, Prolegomena, in Dunning, 161.
72. Grotius, *Rights of War and Peace*, I, i, 10, p. 21.
73. Ibid., I, ii, 1.
74. II, xxii.
75. I, xvii.
76. II, xxvi.
77. Lange, F. E., *History of Materialism*, I, 266.
78. France, A., *Elm Tree on the Mall*, 13.
79. Russell, B., *History of Western Philosophy*, 558.
80. Fischer, K., *Descartes*, 194f.
81. *Discours*, Part III, in Descartes, *Selections*, 27.
82. Ibid., p. 28.
83. Faguet, *Dix-septième siècle*, 6-7.
84. Descartes, *Principia philosophiae*, I, 71, in *Meditations and Principles of Philosophy*, 168.
85. *Discours*, Part II, in *Selections*, 12.

86. Descartes, *Meditations*, II, in *Selections*, 96.
87. *Discours*, Part IV, and *Meditations*, II, in *Selections*, 29, 99.
88. St. Augustine, *De Trinitate*, x, 10.
89. *Meditations*, II, in *Selections*, 106.
90. "Rules for the Direction of the Mind," VIII, in *Selections*, 69.
91. *Meditations*, III, in *Selections*, 125.
92. Ibid., 154.
93. Ibid., 89.
94. *Principia philosophiae*, I, xxxix.
95. *Meditations*, IV, in *Selections*, 127.
96. *Discours*, IV, in *Selections*, 30.
97. *En. Br.*, VII, 249d.
98. Ibid.
99. Lévy-Bruhl, *History of Modern Philosophy in France*, 29.
100. *Discours*, in Vartanian, *Diderot and Descartes*, 16.
101. Fischer, *Descartes*, 406.
102. In Smith, *Culture*, I, 194.
103. Smith, D. E., ed., *Isaac Newton*, 18.
104. Fischer, 229.
105. Garrison, *History of Medicine*, 258.
106. *Selections*, 222-47.
107. Aubrey, *Brief Lives*, 95.
108. Fischer, 231.
109. Fülop-Miller, *Jesuits*, 124.
110. Fontenelle, *Digression sur les anciens et les modernes*, in Fellows and Torrey, *Age of the Enlightenment*, 57.
111. Lévy-Bruhl, 33.
112. Vartanian, *Diderot and Descartes*, 205 and *passim*.

Index

Dates are of birth and death except for kings and popes, where they are of the reign. A single date indicates a *floruit*. A footnote is indicated by an asterisk. Italicized page numbers indicate principal treatment. All dates are A.D. unless otherwise indicated.

Abbas I, Shah of Persia (1587–1629), 525, *527-30*, 531-32, 534, 535
Abbas II, Shah of Persia (1642–67), 533, 534
Aberdeen, Scotland, 112; University, 113
Abrégé de la philosophie de Gassendi (Bernier), 636
absolutism, 7, 278, 280, 283-84, 323, 365, 375, 381, 383, 390, 401, 543; James I's divine-rights theory, 132, 133, 135-36, 138-39, 160, 178-79, 200, 204, 220, 627; vs. popular sovereignty, 246-47, 354-55, 367, 626-28
Académie Française, *see* French Academy
Academy of St. Luke (Rome), 268, 325
Accademia degli Incamminati (Bologna), 232-235
Accademia dei Lincei (Rome), 584, 605, 608
Accademia del Cimento (Rome), 584
Accademia della Crusca (Florence), 226
Accademia di Belle Arti (Bologna), 232
Accademia di Belle Arti (Milan), 226
Accoramboni, Vittoria (1557?-85), 145, 252
Accord (Netherlands, 1566), 444
Achaemenid Susa (fl. 400 B.C.), 535
Act of Abjuration (Netherlands, 1581), 455
Act of Pacification (Netherlands, 1576), 450
Act of Revocation (Scotland, 1625), 203
Act of Supremacy (England, 1559), 18
Act of Uniformity (England, 1559), 17-18
Acta Sanctorum, 417-18
Actes and Monuments (Foxe), 15
Actium, battle of (31 B.C.), 523*
Acton, John E., Baron, 121*, 346*
actors' companies, English, 42, 79-81, 89, 94, 147, 149
Adagia (Erasmus), 404
Admiral's company, 80
Adolphus, Duke of Holstein-Gottorp (fl. 1586), 499
Adone (Marini), 258, 432
Adone (Monteverdi), 256
Adrianople, Mosque of Selim, 521
Adriatic Sea, Venetian control of, 228, 522, 524
Advancement of Learning, The (Bacon), 172-174

Advertisement Touching the Controversies of the Church of England (Bacon), 40
Adwalton Moor, battle of, 213
Aegean Sea, Venetian ascendancy in, 522
Aeneid, The (Virgil), 264, 265, 293
Aerssens, Francis, 461
Afghanistan, 518, 530, 536
Africa, Spanish and Portuguese in, 274, 291-292
Agen, France, 340, 357
Agincourt, battle of (1415), 92
Aglaura (Suckling), 197
agnosticism, 409, 481
Agra, India, 159
Agreement of the People, An, 217-18
agriculture: England, 47, 184; France, scientific methods in, 366; Portugal, 290; Russia, 512; Spain, 274; United Provinces, 477; *see also* enclosures
Agrippa, Cornelius Heinrich (1486?-1535), 408, 616
Ahmadabad, India, 159
Ahmed I, Ottoman Sultan (1603–17), 431, 521, 525, 526
"Ainslee's band," 122
Aix-la-Chapelle (Aachen), capture of, 387; University of, 635
Akbar, Jellaladin Mohammed, Emperor of India (1556–1605), 247
Albania, 518
Albert, Cardinal, Archduke of the Spanish Netherlands (r. 1595–1621), 371, 458, 460, 467, 470, 471
Albert V, Duke of Bavaria (r. 1550–79), 549, 553
Albigensian heresy, 334
Albret, Jeanne d' (1528–72), Queen of Navarre, 334, 336, 345, 346, 348, 358, 393
Alcalá, University of, 281, 306
Alcalde de Zalamea, El (Calderón), 312
Alcázarquivir (Al-Kasr-al-Kabir), battle of (1578), 290
Alchemist, The (Jonson), 150
alchemy, 150, 539, 588
Alchymia (Libavius), 588

683

About the Authors

WILL DURANT was born in North Adams, Massachusetts, in 1885. He was educated in the Catholic parochial schools there and in Kearny, New Jersey, and thereafter in St. Peter's (Jesuit) College, Jersey City, New Jersey, and Columbia University, New York. For a summer he served as a cub reporter on the New York *Journal*, in 1907, but finding the work too strenuous for his temperament, he settled down at Seton Hall College, South Orange, New Jersey, to teach Latin, French, English, and geometry (1907–11). He entered the seminary at Seton Hall in 1909, but withdrew in 1911 for reasons which he has described in his book *Transition*. He passed from this quiet seminary to the most radical circles in New York, and became (1911–13) the teacher of the Ferrer Modern School, an experiment in libertarian education. In 1912 he toured Europe at the invitation and expense of Alden Freeman, who had befriended him and now undertook to broaden his borders.

Returning to the Ferrer School, he fell in love with one of his pupils, resigned his position, and married her (1913). For four years he took graduate work at Columbia University, specializing in biology under Morgan and Calkins and in philosophy under Woodbridge and Dewey. He received the doctorate in philosophy in 1917, and taught philosophy at Columbia University for one year. In 1914, in a Presbyterian church in New York, he began those lectures on history, literature, and philosophy which, continuing twice weekly for thirteen years, provided the initial material for his later works.

The unexpected success of *The Story of Philosophy* (1926) enabled him to retire from teaching in 1927. Thenceforth, except for some incidental essays, Mr. and Mrs. Durant gave nearly all their working hours (eight to fourteen daily) to *The Story of Civilization*. To better prepare themselves they toured Europe in 1927, went around the world in 1930 to study Egypt, the Near East, India, China, and Japan, and toured the globe again in 1932 to visit Japan, Manchuria, Siberia, Russia, and Poland. These travels provided the background for *Our Oriental Heritage* (1935) as the first volume in *The Story of Civilization*. Several further visits to Europe prepared for Volume II, *The Life of Greece* (1939) and Volume III, *Caesar and Christ* (1944). In 1948, six months in Turkey, Iraq, Iran, Egypt, and Europe provided perspective for Volume IV, *The Age of Faith* (1950). In 1951 Mr. and Mrs. Durant returned to Italy to add to a lifetime of gleanings for Volume V, *The Renaissance* (1953); and in 1954 further studies in Italy, Switzerland, Germany, France, and England opened new vistas for Volume VI, *The Reformation* (1957).

Mrs. Durant's share in the preparation of these volumes became more and more substantial with each year, until in the case of Volume VII, *The Age of Reason Begins* (1961), it was so pervasive that justice required the union of both names on the title page. The name Ariel was first applied to his wife by Mr. Durant in his novel *Transition* (1927) and in his *Mansions of Philosophy* (1929) —now reissued as *The Pleasures of Philosophy*.

The authors hope to present Volume IX in 1964 or 1965 as *The Age of Voltaire* (1715–56), and Volume X, the concluding work in the series, as *Rousseau and Revolution* (1756–89).